THE BRUCE TRILOGY

Book One
THE STEPS TO THE EMPTY THRONE

Robert the Bruce, both Norman lord and Celtic earl, is one of the great heroic figures of all time. But he was not always a hero – as he was not always a king. He grew towards both under the shadow of a still greater hero – William Wallace – in that terrible forcing-ground of heroism and treachery alike, the Wars of Independence which, from 1296 to 1314, hammered Scotland into the very dust until only the enduring idea of freedom remained to her.

Edward Longshanks, King of England, was the Hammer of the Scots, a great man gone wrong, a magnificent soldier flawed by consuming hatred and lust for power. These two fought out their desperate, appalling duel, with Scotland as prize – should any of Scotland survive.

But this tremendous story is not all blood and fire. Elizabeth de Burgh saw to that. Humour and laughter are here too, colour and beauty, faith and love. This enormous and ambitious theme of Bruce the hero king is no light challenge for a writer. Nigel Tranter has waited through nearly thirty years of novel-writing to tackle it. In this, the first of a trilogy, he ends that long apprenticeship and takes up the challenge.

THE BRUCE TRILOGY

Book Two
THE PATH OF THE HERO KING

A harried fugitive, guilt-ridden, excommunicated, Robert the Bruce, King of Scots in name and nothing more, faced a future that all but he – and perhaps Elizabeth de Burgh his wife – accepted as devoid of hope; his kingdom occupied by a powerful and ruthless invader; his army defeated; a large proportion of his supporters dead or prisoners; much of his people against him; and the rest so cowed and warsick as no longer to care. Only a man of transcendent courage would have continued the struggle, or seen it as worth continuing. But Bruce, whatever his many failings, was courageous above all. And with a driving love of freedom that gave him no rest. Robert the Bruce blazes the path of the hero king, in blood and violence and determination, in cunning and ruthlessness, yet, strangely, a preoccupation with mercy and chivalry, all the way from the ill-starred open-boat landing on the Ayrshire coast by night, from a spider-hung Galloway cave and near despair, to Bannockburn itself, where he faced the hundred-thousand-strong mightiest army in the world, and won.

THE BRUCE TRILOGY

Book Three
THE PRICE OF THE KING'S PEACE

Bannockburn was far from the end, for Robert Bruce and Scotland. There remained fourteen years of struggle, savagery, heroism and treachery before the English could be brought to sit at a peace-table with their proclaimed rebels, and so to acknowledge Bruce as a sovereign king. In these years of stress and fulfilment, Bruce's character burgeoned to its splendid flowering. The hero-king, moulded by sorrow, remorse and a grievous sickness, equally with triumph, became the foremost prince of Christendom – despite continuing Papal excommunication. That the fighting now was done mainly deep in England, over the sea in Ireland, and in the hearts of men, was none the less taxing for a sick man with the seeds of grim fate in his body, and the sin of murder on his conscience. But Elizabeth de Burgh was at his side again, after the long years of imprisonment, and a great love sustained them both.

Love, indeed, is the key to Robert the Bruce – his passionate love for his land and people, for his friends, his forgiveness for his enemies, and the love he engendered in others; for surely never did a king arouse such love and devotion in those around him, in his lieutenants, as did he.

Also by the same author,
and available from Coronet:

Black Douglas
Children of the Mist
Columba
Crusader
David the Prince
Druid Sacrifice
Flowers of Chivalry
Highness in Hiding

The House of Stewart Trilogy:
Lords of Misrule
A Folly of Princes
The Captive Crown

The James V Trilogy
Kenneth
Lion Let Loose
Lord of the Isles
Lord in Waiting
MacBeth the King

The MacGregor Trilogy:
MacGregor's Gathering
The Clansman
Gold for Prince Charlie

Mail Royal
Margaret the Queen
The Patriot
Price of a Princess
A Stake in the Kingdom
Tapestry of the Boar
True Thomas
Unicorn Rampant
The Wallace
The Wisest Fool

The Bruce Trilogy

The Steps to the Empty Throne
The Path of the Hero King
The Price of the King's Peace

Nigel Tranter

CORONET BOOKS
Hodder and Stoughton

First published as three separate volumes:

The Steps to the Empty Throne © 1969 by Nigel Tranter.
First published in Great Britain 1969 by
Hodder and Stoughton Ltd.
Coronet edition 1971.

The Path of the Hero King © 1970 by Nigel Tranter.
First published in Great Britain 1970 by
Hodder and Stoughton Ltd.
Coronet edition 1972.

The Price of the King's Peace © 1971 by Nigel Tranter.
First published in Great Britain 1971 by
Hodder and Stoughton Ltd.
Coronet edition 1972.

This Coronet paperback edition, 1996

20 19 18 17 16

British Library C.I.P.
Tranter, Nigel
The Bruce Trilogy
I. Title II. Tranter, Nigel. Steps to the empty throne
III. Tranter, Nigel. Path of the hero king
IV. Tranter, Nigel. Price of the king's peace
823'.912[F] PR6070.R34

ISBN 0 340 37186 2

Printed and bound in Great Britain by
Cox & Wyman Ltd, Reading, Berkshire

Hodder and Stoughton
A division of Hodder Headline PLC
338 Euston Road
London NW1 3BH

THE BRUCE TRILOGY

THE HOUSE OF BRUCE

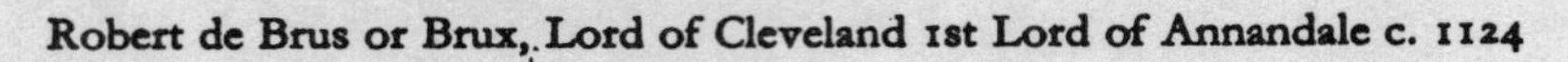

Robert de Brus or Brux, Lord of Cleveland 1st Lord of Annandale c. 1124

Robert 2nd Lord (fought at Battle of Standard 1138)

Robert 3rd Lord m. illeg. d. King William the Lion

Robert 4th Lord m. Isabel d. of David, Earl of Huntingdon, b. of William the Lion

Robert 5th Lord ("The Competitor") m. Isabel de Clare, d. Earl of Gloucester

Robert 6th Lord m. Marjory, Countess of Carrick

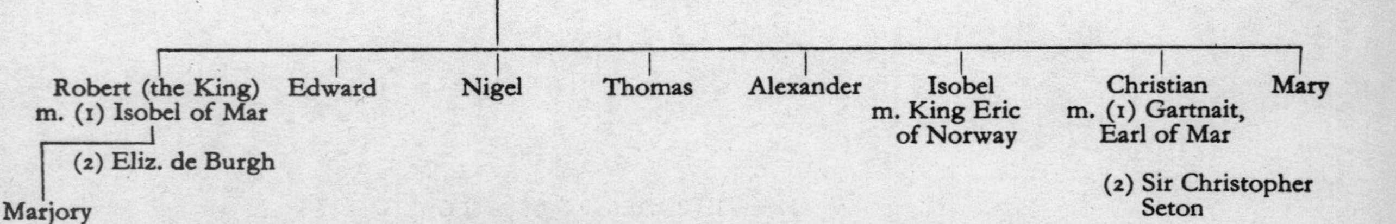

Robert (the King) m. (1) Isobel of Mar (2) Eliz. de Burgh — Marjory

Edward

Nigel

Thomas

Alexander

Isobel m. King Eric of Norway

Christian m. (1) Gartnait, Earl of Mar (2) Sir Christopher Seton

Mary

THE SCOTS SUCCESSION

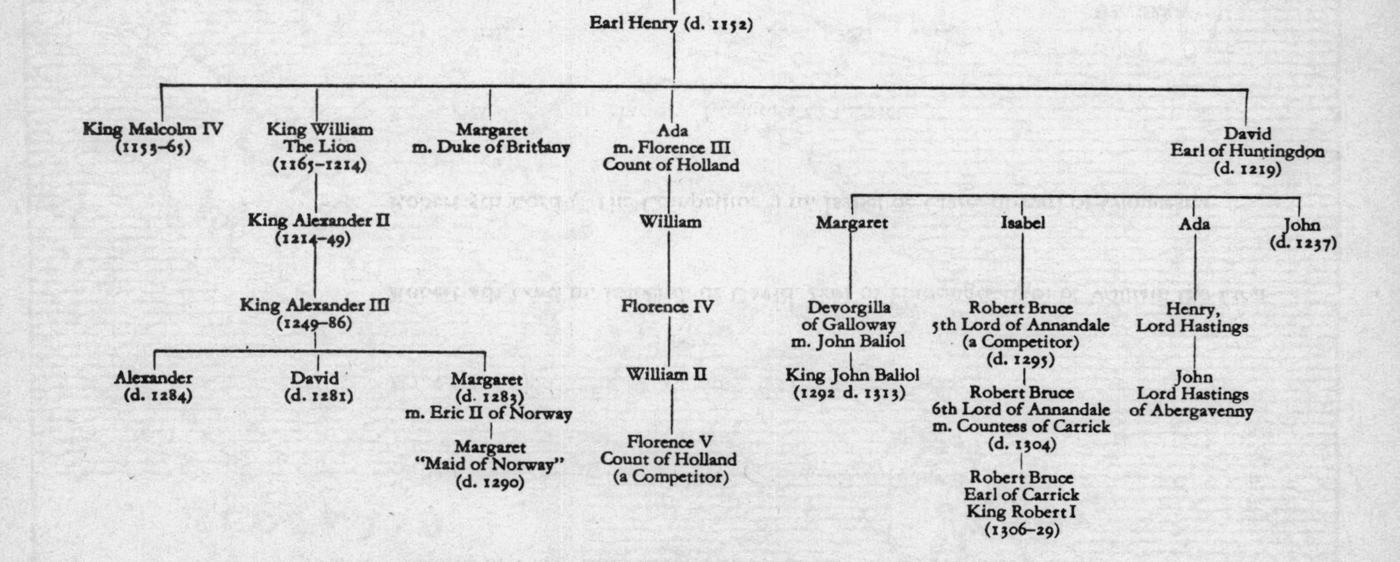

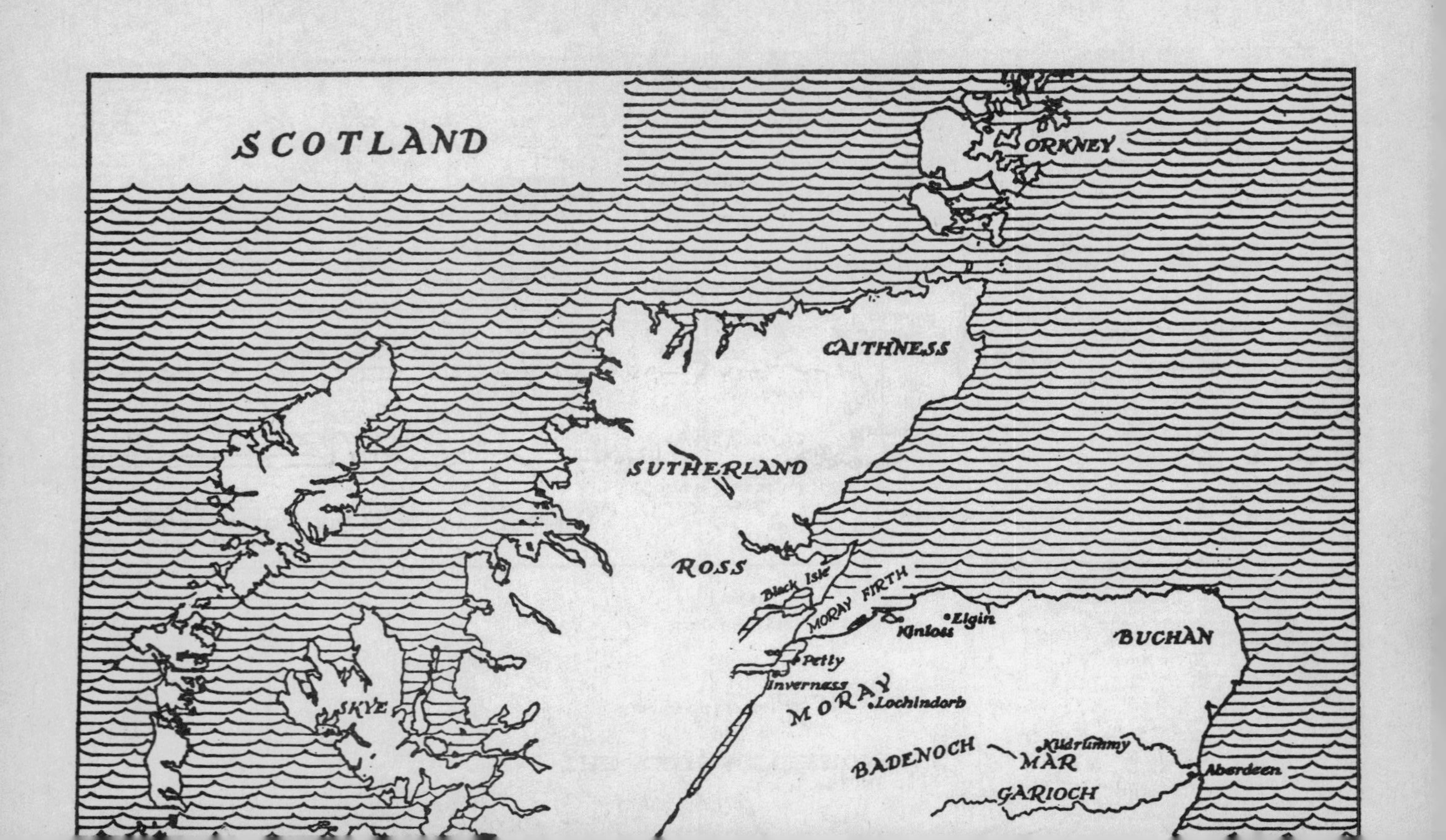
SCOTLAND
ORKNEY
CAITHNESS
SUTHERLAND
ROSS
Black Isle
MORAY FIRTH
Elgin
Kinloss
BUCHAN
Petty
Inverness
MORAY
Lochindorb
SKYE
BADENOCH
Kildrummy
MAR
Aberdeen
GARIOCH

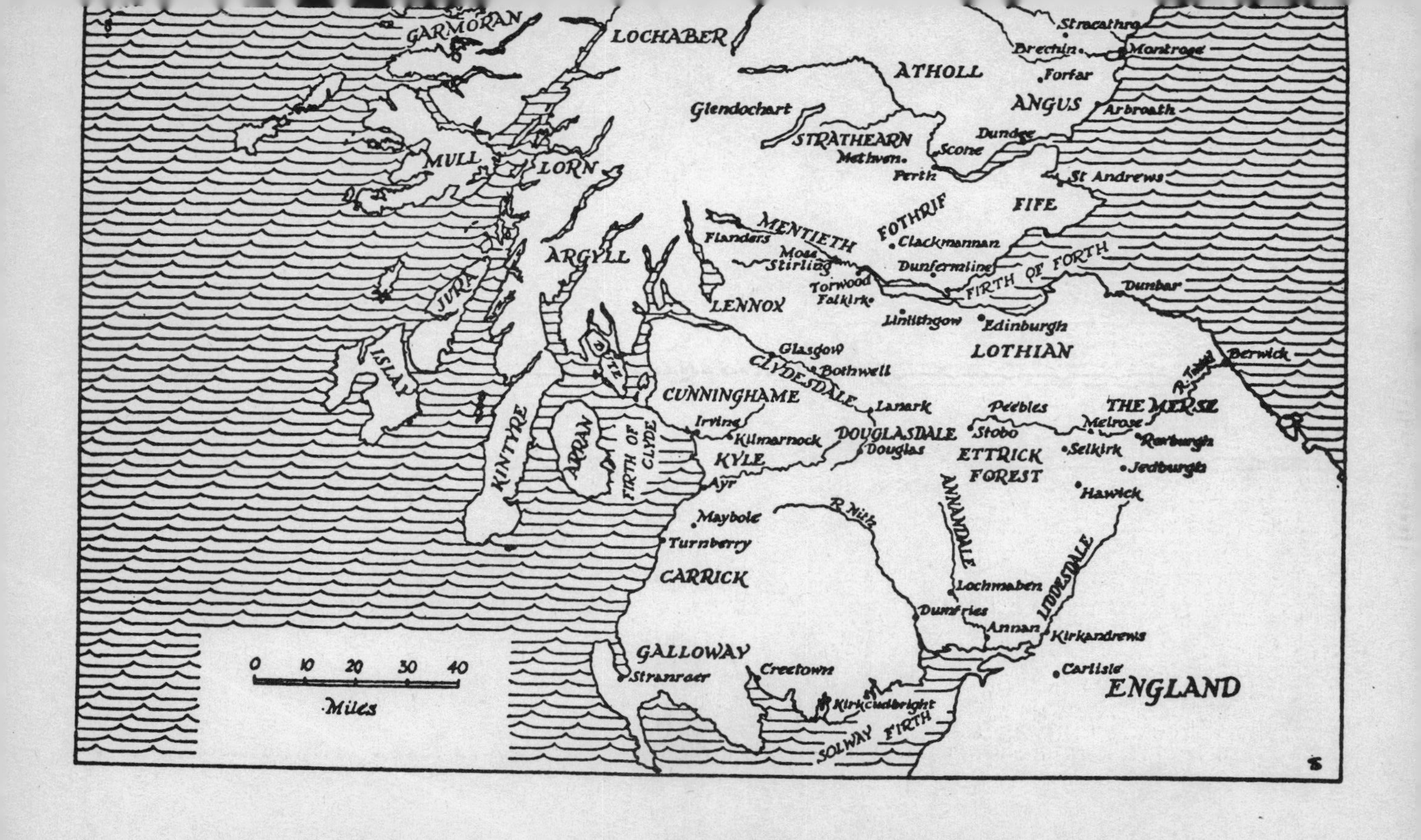
GARMORAN
LOCHABER
Stracathro
Brechin
Montrose
ATHOLL
Forfar
ANGUS
Arbroath
Glendochart
STRATHEARN
Dundee
Scone
Methven
Perth
St Andrews
MULL
LORN
FIFE
FOTHRIF
MENTIETH
Flanders
Clackmannan
Moss
Stirling
Dunfermline
FIRTH OF FORTH
ARGYLL
JURA
Torwood
Falkirk
Dunbar
LENNOX
Linlithgow
Edinburgh
ISLAY
Glasgow
LOTHIAN
Berwick
CLYDESDALE
Bothwell
CUNNINGHAME
Lanark
Peebles
THE MERSE
KINTYRE
ARRAN
FIRTH OF CLYDE
Irvine
Kilmarnock
DOUGLASDALE
Douglas
Stobo
Melrose
Roxburgh
KYLE
ETTRICK
FOREST
Selkirk
Jedburgh
Ayr
Hawick
R. Nith
ANNANDALE
Maybole
Turnberry
CARRICK
LIDDESDALE
Lochmaben
Dumfries
Annan
Kirkandrews
GALLOWAY
Creetown
Carlisle
0 10 20 30 40
Miles
Stranraer
ENGLAND
Kirkcudbright
SOLWAY FIRTH

Book One

THE STEPS TO THE EMPTY THRONE

Foreword

When, in 1286, the well-beloved Alexander the Third, King of Scots, fell over a Fife cliff to his untimely death, he left utter disaster behind him for his country. His only surviving heir was an infant grandchild, a girl—and a foreign girl at that, and sickly, Margaret the Maid of Norway, daughter of his own daughter who had married the King of Norway and died leaving only this baby. There could have been no less suitable monarch for turbulent Scotland—and almost immediately the dynastic feuding and designing began.

There were innumerable far-out claimants to the throne, mainly descendants of the three daughters of David, Earl of Huntingdon, younger brother of King William the Lion. Of all these, the two with undoubtedly the most valid claims to be next in line to the little Maid of Norway were Robert Bruce, 5th Lord of Annandale, and John Baliol. The former was the son of Earl David's daughter Isabel; the latter the grandson of her elder sister Margaret. Baliol's father was an English lord, his mother the famous Devorgilla, Lady of Galloway, founder of Baliol College, Oxford.

Robert Bruce lost no time in making his position clear. With his son, the sixth Robert, who had married the Celtic Countess of Carrick in her own right, another Galloway heiress, he invaded that wild and beautiful province of South-West Scotland against the Baliol interests now established there. And with success. In the civil war old Bruce—he was then seventy-six—won most of the province, including the royal castles of Wigtown and Dumfries (then considered part of Galloway) and the Baliol seat of Buittle, former headquarters of the ancient Lords of Galloway. He was now well placed to exert suitable influence on the child monarch when she should appear; and meantime to dominate Scotland.

Two events conspired to confound his plans. Edward the First, puissant warrior King of England, perceived a notable opportunity to take over Scotland as a vassal kingdom, by marrying his young son to the infant Maid—who was indeed his own grand-niece—and moved to that effect, at the Treaty of Birgham. Then, the same year, 1290, the said Maid died at Orkney, on her pathetic way to her new kingdom.

All was changed. Edward had placed himself in a position of political and military power, on the Border. Scotland was leaderless and disunited, the competitors for the empty throne balanced between civil war ind invasion.

Edward acted shrewdly. Dissimulating his own ambitions, he offered to preserve the peace by acting as honest broker. If the claimants to the Scots crown would submit their cases to him, he would act fair arbiter and so save strife.

It must be remembered that at this stage Scotland and England were good friends. The long centuries of warring had not yet started. Most of the Scots nobles owned lands in England, and *vice versa*—indeed they were nearly all equally Norman-French in origin. Edward was the foremost prince of Christendom, renowned, admired. His offer was accepted.

The Plantagenet, for his own purposes, in 1292 chose John Baliol as King of Scots. And, as an afterthought to the judgement, announced that he himself was Lord Paramount of Scotland.

Thereafter, for four inglorious years, the weak Baliol attempted to rule a restive Scotland whilst suffering Edward's dominance. This was no theoretical overlordship. Grimly, savagely, Edward rubbed his puppet's nose in the dirt. He summoned him to London to give accounts of his stewardship; even had him arraigned before the King's Bench of England for judgement, like any criminal. At length, in 1296, even Baliol revolted, and taking to arms, made a mutual support treaty with France, also suffering from Edward's oppression. The English invaded Scotland in overwhelming strength. The Bruces, and many like them, did not support Baliol – they never had done. The puppet-king fell, and Edward Longshanks was master of Scotland, at last.

Old Bruce, the Competitor, was now dead, and his son the sixth Lord of Annandale no warrior, though proud enough to have resigned his earldom of Carrick to his own eldest son, another Robert, aged twenty-two, rather than make fealty for it to Baliol.

The new Earl of Carrick was a very different character. Robert the Bruce is one of the great heroic figures of all time. But he was not always a hero—just as he was not always a king. He grew towards both, indeed, under the shadow of a still greater hero—William Wallace—in the terrible forcing-ground of heroism and treacher alike, the Wars of Independence which, thereafter until 1314, hammered and ground Scotland into the very dust, until only the faintest flicker of stubborn hope and the enduring idea of freedom remained to her. But hammered her into one equally enduring and undivided nation, nevertheless. Edward, King of England, was the Hammer of the Scots indeed, a great man gone wrong, a magnificent soldier flawed by a consuming hatred and a lust for power. Against this backcloth, young Robert Bruce and Edward Plantagenet, linked most strangely by a sort of mutual understanding and reluctant admiration, played out their desperate, appalling game, with Scotland as the prize—if there was to be any Scotland left at the end of it.

But not only these two. Almost as important was Sir John Comyn the Red, Lord of Badenoch, head of the most powerful house in Scotland and nephew of the fallen and discredited King John Baliol. To him Robert Bruce was as a spark to tinder—and well Edward knew it, and shrewdly blew on that spark until it should be a flame that should burn more fiercely than all the other fires he lit to turn Scotland to ashes; a dire conflagration that burned on in Bruce's heart long after the shocking day when blood soaked the high altar at Dumfries and a new Bruce was born.

But this tremendous story is not all blood and fire, battle and treachery. There is humour and laughter too, colour and beauty, faith and love—love of men and of women, beyond all telling. And pride—pride and a great ideal, when all else was gone.

PRINCIPAL CHARACTERS

In Order of Appearance

KING EDWARD THE FIRST: King of England; Hammer of the Scots.

ANTHONY BECK, BISHOP OF DURHAM: Capt. General of St. Cuthbert.

ROBERT BRUCE, EARL OF CARRICK: eldest son of Lord of Annandale.

JOHN BALIOL, KING OF SCOTS.

JOHN COMYN, EARL OF BUCHAN: High Constable of Scotland.

ROBERT BRUCE, LORD OF ANNANDALE AND CLEVELAND: son of the "Competitor".

LORD NIGEL BRUCE: third son of above

LADY ELIZABETH DE BURGH: daughter of the Earl of Ulster.

RICHARD DE BURGH, EARL OF ULSTER: friend and companion of Edward.

GARTNAIT, EARL OF MAR: brother-in-law of Bruce.

GILBERT DE CLARE, EARL OF GLOUCESTER: son-in-law of Edward and kinsman of Bruce.

SIR JOHN COMYN, LORD OF BADENOCH: head of the great Comyn family, and kinsman of Buchan.

SIR NICHOLAS SEGRAVE: an English knight and captain.

MASTER JOHN BENSTEAD: Clerk, and Keeper of King Edward's Pantry.

ELEANOR DE LOUVAIN, LADY DOUGLAS: second wife of Sir William Douglas.

JAMES DOUGLAS: heir of Sir William, later "The Good Sir James".

SIR WILLIAM DOUGLAS: 5th lord thereof.

LORD JAMES STEWART: High Steward of Scotland.

MASTER ROBERT WISHART, BISHOP OF GLASGOW: patriot.

SIR ALEXANDER LINDSAY, LORD OF CRAWFORD.

SIR JOHN DE GRAHAM OF DUNDAFF: one of the few noblemen who supported Wallace.

SIR ANDREW DE MORAY, LORD OF BOTHWELL: heir of Moravia.

WILLIAM WALLACE: second son of Sir Malcolm Wallace of Elderslie, a small laird and vassal of the Steward.

ALEXANDER SCRYMGEOUR: one of Wallace's band. Later Standard-Bearer.

SIR HENRY PERCY, LORD OF NORTHUMBERLAND: nephew of Surrey the English commander.

SIR ROBERT CLIFFORD, LORD OF BROUGHAM: an English baron.

LORD EDWARD BRUCE: second son of Annandale. Later King of Ireland.

MASTER WILLIAM COMYN: Provost of the Chapel-Royal. Brother of Buchan.

MASTER WILLIAM LAMBERTON: Chancellor of Glasgow Cathedral. Later Bishop of St. Andrews and Primate.

LADY MARJORY BRUCE: child daughter of Bruce.

LADY CHRISTIAN BRUCE, COUNTESS OF MAR: second daughter of Annandale. Later wife of Sir Christopher Seton.

MARGARET OF FRANCE, QUEEN: second wife of King Edward.

SIR JOHN DE BOTETOURT: bastard son of Edward. Warden of the West March.

JOHN OF BRITTANY, EARL OF RICHMOND: nephew of Edward and Lieutenant of Scotland.

SIR JOHN STEWART OF MENTEITH: second son of Earl of Menteith and Governor of Dumbarton Castle.

SIR CHRISTOPHER SETON: a Yorkshire knight married to Lady Christian Bruce.

SIR ROGER KIRKPATRICK OF CLOSEBURN: a Bruce vassal.

ABBOT HENRY OF SCONE: custodian of the Stone of Destiny.

ISABEL, COUNTESS OF BUCHAN: daughter of MacDuff, Earl of Fife, and wife of the High Constable.

AYMER DE VALENCE, EARL OF PEMBROKE: English commander.

THE DEWAR OF THE COIGREACH: hereditary custodian of St. Fillan's crozier, in Glendochart.

PART ONE

Chapter One

Even strong men, hard-bitten, grim-faced men winced as the horseman rode right into the church, iron-shod hooves striking sparks from the flagstones, their noisy clatter stilling all talk and reverberating hollowly under the hammer-beam roof. Stracathro was no mighty church, merely a prebend of the nearby Cathedral of Brechin, and horse and rider seemed enormous in its narrow echoing constriction.

Both mount and man were indeed large, the former a great and ponderous war-horse, massive of build, thick of leg, shaggy of fetlock, such as was necessary to carry the burly, weighty man with the extraordinary length of leg, clad in half a hundred-weight of steel armour richly engraved with gold. Right up to the altar steps, the length of the church, the horseman rode, with behind him other striding armoured figures led by one notably broad, squat, pugnacious of jaw, with a tonsured bullet head, who bore a mitre painted on his dented black steel breastplate. The waiting, watching men, as of one accord, drew further back against the bare stone walls of the little church.

Up the steps into the chancel itself the rider urged his cumbersome steed, there to pull it round in a lumbering half-circle, its great hooves scoring and slithering on the polished granite. Turned to face the nave and all the waiting throng the big man remained seated in the saddle, grinning. The thick-set individual with the underhung jaw took up his position at the other's right-hand stirrup, and the remainder, who had followed him up, ranged themselves on either side. The long shoulder-slung sword of one of them knocked over a tall brass candle-stick flanking the altar, with a crash, spattering hot wax. There was a curse. Somebody laughed loudly.

The man on the horse raised his hand. He was handsome, in a heavy-jowled, fleshy, empurpled way, in his late fifties but with strangely youthful-seeming hot blue eyes and a leonine head of greying hair, bare now, with the great crested war-helm banded with the gold circlet hanging at his saddle bow.

"Have him in, then," he cried. "God's blood—must I sit waiting here?" There was just the slightest impediment in the man's speech, but it lost nothing in forcefulness thereby.

As men at the door hurried out, a voice spoke up, old, quavering, but tense. "Highness—I do protest! To use God's house so! It is ill done . . ."

The speaker was a frail and elderly man, not in armour like most of those present but wearing the robes of an ecclesiastic, sorely stained and patched—William Comyn, Bishop of Brechin. This was one of his churches.

"Silence, knave!" A knight nearby raised a mailed gauntlet and struck the Bishop, a blow that sent the old man reeling. A second buffet was descending, when the steel-clad arm was grasped and held.

"Enough, Despenser! Let him be."

The English knight found himself staring into the grey eyes of a young man, richly dressed in only half-armour over velvet tunic and hose, worn with long soft doeskin thigh-boots and a short satin-lined heraldic riding-cloak slung from one shoulder. The velvet-clad arm that restrained the steel gauntlet was steady, strong, despite its soft covering.

"Curse you—unhand me! Unhand me, I say!" the Englishman shouted. "No man mishandles Despenser so. Even you, my lord Earl!"

"Then let Despenser not mishandle an old done man, see you. And a churchman, at that," the young man returned, though he released the other's arm.

"A traitorous clerk! Raising his voice . . . !"

"In this place, might he not have some right?"

The two stared at each other in very different kinds of anger, the one hot, the other cold. Sir Hugh le Despenser was a noted commander, veteran of much warfare; Robert de Bruce, twenty-two-year-old Earl of Carrick, was a scarcely-blooded warrior, his campaigning spurs still to win, a sprig of nobility, merely the son of his father—or more significantly, the grandson of his grandfather, the old Competitor, barely a year dead. All around men held their breaths, their glances more apt to dart up towards the figure that sat his saddle in front of the altar than towards either of the protagonists, or even old Bishop Comyn, who shaken, leaned against the wall.

The long-legged horseman was no longer grinning. His heavily good-looking features were dark, thunderous, a mailed hand tap-

tapping at that gold-circled helmet at his saddle-bow. Then abruptly he laughed, head thrown up, laughed heartily – and men breathed again. The hand rose, to point down the church.

"Whelps snapping!" he shouted, chuckling. "I'll not have it. Before the old dog! Enough, I say. If my friends must bicker, let them choose better cause than a broken-down old Scots clerk! A mouse squeaking in its barn! Shake hands, fools!"

The two down near the door eyed each other doubtfully; neither would be the first to reach out his hand.

"Robert, my young friend—your hand. Sir Hugh—yours." That was genial. Then, in one of the man's lightning changes of front, as hands only faltered, the big man roared. "Christ God! You hear me? Do as I command, or by the Mass, I'll have both your hands off at the wrist, here and now! I swear it!" And the speaker's own hand fell to the pommel of the great two-handed sword that hung at his side.

Hastily knight and earl gripped hands, bowing towards the altar.

As still the roof-timbers seemed to quiver with the sudden storm of fury, a clanking sound turned all eyes towards the door. The clanking was not all made by armour-clad men; some of it was made by chains.

Strangely, the new advent was brilliant, splendid, colourful, compared with all that was already in the church—where, apart from a few handsomely dressed individuals such as the young Earl of Carrick, most men were in the habiliments of war, not the vivid panoply of the tourney but the more sober and often battered practicalities of stern campaigning. Eight men came in. The first admittedly was an ordinary English knight, less well turned out indeed than many present, a mere captain of cavalry. But he carried one end of a rope. Behind him came a breathtaking figure, magnificently arrayed, a tall, slender man of middle years and great dignity, despite his hobbling gait, who walked with a slight stoop, head bent. Bareheaded, he wore no armour but clothes of cloth-of-gold and worked silver filigree with jewelled scintillating ornamentation, and over all a most gorgeous tabard or loose sleeveless tunic, heraldically embroidered in blazing colours, picked out in gold and rubies, depicting, back and front, the red Rampant Lion of Scotland on a tressured field of yellow, a coat of such striking pride, brilliance and vigour as to challenge the eye and seem to irradiate the somewhat sombre stone interior of the little church. In his hand he carried a flat velvet bonnet rimmed with pearls, to which was clasped with an enormous ruby, large as a pigeon's egg, a noble curling ostrich-feather that tinkled with seed pearls. On either side this splendid personage was flanked by an ordinary man-at-arms, each of whom kept a clenched hand on the bejewelled and bowed shoulders. The man was limping slightly, and being tall, had obvious difficulty in adjusting his stride to the short chain of the leg-irons which clamped his ankles. The rope from the knight in front was tied to his golden girdle.

Behind, between another couple of soldiers, came a burly man with a bandaged head, dressed in the finest armour in all that building, gleaming black and gold, but also with his legs shackled. He made a less careful business of the difficult walking, and in fact stumbled and tripped constantly, scowling and cursing, to the imminent danger of the handsome crimson cushion which he carried before him and on which precariously rested in sparkling, coruscating splendour the Crown of Scotland and the Sceptre of the Realm. A heavy portly figure, older-looking than his forty years, he kept his choleric head high and glowered all around him—John Comyn, Earl of Buchan, Constable of Scotland, the proudest and most powerful noble in a land whose nobles were proud above all else. Another rope was tied around his middle, and trailed behind to be held by the aproned grinning scullion from Montrose Castle's kitchens, who brought up the rear of the little procession, a white painted rod in his hand.

Some few of the watching throng bowed as the first chained man hobbled past, but most certainly did not. Many indeed laughed, some hooted, one spat. Robert Bruce of Carrick stared expressionless. Or nearly so, for his lip curled just a little; his was an expressive face, and it was schooled less perfectly than was intended.

The knight-led, scullion-finished group clanked and shuffled its way up to the chancel steps, and it was strange how, despite all the humiliation, the light seemed to go with it, drawn to and beamed forth by all the colour, the jewels and gems and gleaming gold. At the steps they were halted, with exaggerated abruptness, by the knight. At last the gorgeously-apparelled man looked up—and he had to raise his head high indeed to seek the face of him who sat the great war-horse that champed and sidled there.

"My lord King," he said, quietly, uncertainly. He had sensitive, finely-wrought features and deep, dark eyes under a lofty brow—but there was a slackness of the mouth and delicacy of the chin which spoke worlds.

The big man on the horse looked down at him, and in the silence of the moment all could hear that he was humming some tune to himself—and doing it flatly, for he had no music in him. He did not speak, or in any way acknowledge the other's greeting as the moments passed. Then he glanced up, to consider all in that church, unhurriedly, and yawned hugely, before his gaze returned to travel indifferently over the man waiting before him and to settle on the stocky, pugnacious-jawed individual with the tonsured head who stood at his stirrup.

"My lord Bishop of Durham—see you to it," he said shortly. "Do what is necessary." He snorted. "And in God's name be not long about it, Tony!"

Something like a corporate sigh went up from all who watched and waited and listened.

Anthony Beck, Prince-Bishop of Durham and captain-general of Saint Cuthbert's Host, perhaps the toughest unit of all Edward's army, stepped forward. "Sire," he said, bowing. "As you will." Then he turned to the shackled man, and thrust the round bullet-head forward, jaw leading. "John de Baliol, traitor!" he rasped. "Miscreant! Fool! Hear this. I charge you, in the name of the high and mighty Prince Edward, King of England and of France, of Wales and Ireland, Duke of Normandy and of Guyenne, and suzerain and Lord Paramount of this Scotland. I charge that you are forsworn and utterly condemned. You have shamefully renounced your allegiance to your liege lord Edward and risen against him in arms. You have betrayed your solemn vows. You have treated with His Majesty's enemies, and sought the aid and counsel of wicked men. You have in all things failed and rent your realm of Scotland. Have you any word to say why you should not forthwith be removed from being its king?"

The other drew a long quivering breath, straightening up, to gaze over the Bishop's head. He did not speak.

"You hear me? Have you nothing to say?"

"Nothing that I could say would serve now," the King of Scots muttered, low-voiced, husky.

"You will speak, nevertheless, I promise you!" Anthony Beck looked up at his master.

Edward Plantagenet did not so much as glance at either of them.

"What would you have me to say, Sire?" King John asked.

The other monarch patted his charger's neck.

Angrily Bishop Beck thrust out a thick forefinger at his victim. "You will speak. You will repeat these words. Before all. After me. By the King's royal command ..."

He was interrupted. "If His Grace will not speak, I will!" It was John Comyn, Earl of Buchan, from behind. "Neither you, sir, nor your king, have any authority so to command him. His Grace is King of Scots, duly crowned and consecrated. He owes allegiance to no man. Only to God Himself!"

Frowning, Edward flicked a hand at the Bishop, who strode forward, past the Scots monarch and the escort who still clasped his shoulders, and raising a mailed arm, smote Buchan viciously across the face. "Silence, fool!" he cried. "How dare you raise your voice in the presence of the King's Majesty!"

Blood running from his mouth, the bandaged Earl answered back "Base-born clerk! I am Constable of Scotland, and have fullest right to speak in this realm, in any man's presence."

A second and still more savage blow sent the older man reeling, and shackled as he was, he would have fallen had his guards not held him up. As it was, the crown and sceptre were flung from the cushion he held before him, and fell with a clatter to the floor.

Cursing, Beck was stooping to pick them up, difficult for a man in full armour. He thought better of it, and was ordering the guards to do so, when Edward Longshanks spoke.

"Let them lie," he said briefly. "His Grace of Scotland will pick them up!"

The unsteady Buchan made choking exclamation, and sought to bend down for the fallen regalia, but his guards jerked him back. King John turned to sign to him, with a shake of the head and a sigh. Stooping, he recovered the symbols of his kingship. He stood, holding the crown in his right hand, the sceptre in his left.

At a nod from Edward, Bishop Beck went on. "You will speak now, sirrah. Say after me these words. Before His Majesty, and all these witnesses. Say 'I, John de Baliol, King of Scots by the grace, permission and appointment of my liege lord Edward of England ...'"

For long moments there was silence broken only by the stirring of the horse. Then, head bent again, and in a voice that was scarcely to be heard, the other repeated.

"I, John de Baliol, King of Scots, by grace, permission, appointment of my liege lord Edward ..."

"Speak up, man! We'll have no craven mumbling. Say 'I do hereby and before all men, admit my grievous fault and my shameful treasons."

". . . admit my grievous fault. And . . . and my shameful treasons."

"'Do renounce and reject the treaty I made against my said Lord Edward, with his enemy the King of France.'"

". . . renounce and reject . . . the treaty with France."

"'And do renounce and reject, and yield again to my Lord Edward, my kingdom and crown.'"

A choking sob, and then the broken words, ". . . renounce my kingdom. My crown."

"'And do throw myself and my whole realm humbly at the feet of and upon the mercy of the said noble Prince Edward, King of England and Lord Paramount of Scotland.'"

"No! Never that!" a voice cried, from the back of the church. Other voices rose also, to be overwhelmed in the roars of anger and the clash of steel and the thuds of blows, as James Stewart, fifth High Steward of Scotland, and others near him, were rushed and bundled out of the building by ungentle men-at-arms.

Scowling, though King Edward appeared faintly amused, the Prince-Bishop waited until approximate quiet was restored. "More of such insolence, folly and disrespect, and heads will fall!" he shouted. "You have my oath on it!" He jerked that thick finger again at John Baliol. "I am waiting. My lord the King waits. Speak, man."

"Do not say it, Sire," Buchan burst out from behind him. "Not this. Of the realm. Not Lord Paramount. There is none such. Save you, Sire. It is a lie . . . !"

He got no further. This time the guards, even the scullion at his back, did not wait for Beck. With one accord they set upon the Earl and beat him down under a hail of blows. He fell to the stone floor, there at the chancel steps, and so lay.

High above, Edward Plantagenet watched from hooded eyes, a smile about his lips.

King John repeated the required words, falteringly.

The Bishop leaned forward, and snatched the Crown of Scotland from its owner's hand. "By His Majesty's royal command, you are no longer King of Scots," he cried. "The kingdom reverts to him who gave it to you. To do with as he will. You, John de Baliol, together with your son, heirs and all posterity, are hereby deprived of all office, rank, title, property and lands. You and yours are the King's prisoners; your lives, as traitors and felons, are his to take and do with as he will. In the name of Edward, King of England." He turned, and handed up the crown to his master.

Edward seemed almost as though he would reject it. Then, shrugging great shoulders, he took it, turned it this way and that in his hands, casually inspecting it. But he seemed little interested. Without warning, he tossed the glittering thing down to the knight in charge of the prisoners' escort—who only just managed to catch it. "Here—take it, Sir Piers," he said, with a laugh. "It is yours. Perhaps it will serve to pay your good fellows. The Jews may give you something for it!"

Something between a sob and a groan arose in that church—to be swiftly lost in a menacing growl.

The Bishop of Durham, when he had assured that King Edward did not intend to say more, resumed—not at first with words. Stepping close to the taller prisoner, he reached out and took hold of the splendid jewelled and embroidered tabard with the proud red Lion Rampant, grabbing it at the neck. With savage jerks of a short but powerful arm he wrenched and tore at it. To the sound of rending fabric, its wearer staggered, and as the glorious garment fell in ruin to the floor, something of the light and colour seemed to go out of that place.

The Bishop now took the sceptre away, and handed it to the scullion, who stood grinning astride the prostrate person of Buchan the Constable. He took in return the white rod of penitence and humiliation this man had carried, and thrust it at Baliol.

"This is yours, now," he said. "All you have, or will get! Save perhaps the rope! Now—down on your knees."

The other took the rod, head shaking. But he remained standing.

"Fool! Are you deaf? You heard me—kneel. Or do you not value your wretched life? Your traitor's skin?"

"I no longer value my life, my lord. Or I would not have come to submit to His Majesty. But how could I be traitor? How could the King of Scots be traitor to the King of England? I submit me—but I do not . . ."

John Baliol was too late by far with any such reasoning. Fierce and vehement hands forced him to his knees, beside the groaning figure of the Constable.

"Speak—for your life," the Bishop commanded. "You are now nothing, man. Not even a man. Dirt beneath His Majesty's feet, no more! He could, and should, take you out and hang you. Draw, quarter and disembowel you. As you deserve. And not only you. All your treacherous, beggarly Scots lords. Rebels against his peace. All should die. As the scurvy rebels of Berwick town died, who also spurned King Edward's peace." Only a month or so before, after the frontier town of Berwick-on-Tweed had resisted the English advance, Edward had ordered the slaughter of no fewer than 17,000 men, women and children in the streets, and the burning of every house, in this the richest town and seaport of Scotland. The Bishop's threats were scarcely idle, therefore.

Baliol sank his greying head. "So be it," he said. "I seek His Majesty's clemency. For the lives of all who have followed and supported me. Mistakenly. I humbly seek mercy."

"And for your own life also?"

The kneeling man looked up, from Bishop to King, and for a moment a sort of nobility showed strongly in the weak and unhappy features. "Very well," he acceded. "If that is necessary. If that is your requirement. I ask for your mercy on myself and mine, also." He paused. "That the cup be filled."

Beck looked a little put out. He frowned, then shrugged mail-clad shoulders. He turned to the Plantagenet. "Sire," he said. "All is done. In your royal hands is placed this felon's life. And the lives of all his people. Of his own will. To do with according to your mighty pleasure. There is no longer a King of Scots. Nor a realm of Scotland. All is yours." Bowing, he stepped back, duty done.

Edward even now seemed the bored and disinterested onlooker. He glanced round all the waiting company, as though, like them, he had been a mere spectator of a mildly distasteful scene. He appeared to shake himself out of a brown study.

"My lords," he said. "My noble friends. And . . . others. Have you had enough? I vow that I have. Let us be out of here. This place stinks in my nostrils. Come, Tony." And without so much as a look at the figure still kneeling there, he urged his heavy destrier forward.

Almost he rode down both Baliol and Buchan, even their escort; only the slow cumbersome movement of the war-horse permitted all to get out of the way of its great hooves. And everywhere the cream of two nations bowed low, as Edward of England passed on.

Or not perhaps quite the cream of two nations. For practically everyone in the church of Stracathro that July day of 1296, save some of the humble men-at-arms, was of one stock—Norman-French. Edward himself might be an Angevin, Baliol a Picard, Beck, or de Bec, and Comyn were Flemings and Bruce sprung from the Cotentin; but all were basically Normans. Of the true English stock there were none present, though there had of course been some intermarriage. Of the indigenous Celtic Scots, none likewise. Possibly the young Robert Bruce was the nearest to a Scot, for his mother had been the daughter and heiress of the last Celtic Earl of Carrick, of the old stock, whose earldom he had inherited. A Norman-French military aristocracy had for two centuries been taking over both kingdoms, indeed much of northern Europe—but only at the great land-owning and government level. Every word spoken in that church had been in French.

The cream of this aristocracy, therefore, both victors and vanquished, bowed as their master rode down towards the door—leaving a somewhat doubtful soldier-knight distinctly uncertain what to do with his utterly ignored and rejected prisoners. A round dozen earls were there, and more than a score of great lords—and some of those with Scots titles bowed lower than the English, not in abject vanquishment but in loyal fealty, for many of them, in unhappy and divided Scotland, considered that they had borne no allegiance to King John, looking on him as usurper, and worse, nonentity, not a few holding almost as large lands in England as here. For such men loyalty and patriotic duty were hypothetical and variable terms.

Edward was half way to the door when a man stepped forward, one of those not in armour. "Sire," he said. "A petition. Hear me, I pray you."

Across the church, the young Earl of Carrick, frowning suddenly, made as though to move, to speak, but thought better of it. His hand gestured towards the petitioner, however, eloquently. But ineffectually.

The King pulled up. "My lord of Annandale," he said, blank-faced. "I conceived you to be in Carlisle."

"You summoned all leal Scots to attend you here, Sire."

"Your lealty I do not doubt, man. But I appointed you governor of Carlisle. To keep the West Border. And Galloway. Here is a strange way of keeping it!"

The other bowed. He was a handsome man, of Edward's own age, quietly but tastefully dressed, with the long face of a scholar or pedant rather than that of a warrior, despite his governor's position. It might have been a noble face, the noblest in all that company, save for a certain petulant stubbornness.

"The West March is safe, Sire. I have three strong sons holding it secure for Your Majesty. With Galloway. I came to see this good day's work."

"Aye—you never loved Baliol, my lord! Nor loved *me* the more that I made him King of Scots, hey?" That was cracked out like a whip-lash. "So you came to see me eat my choice? To crow, Bruce? To crow!"

"Not so, Sire. I am your true man. And have proved it. From the first." That was true, at least. For this man, who bore the lesser title of Lord of Annandale, should have been the Earl of Carrick since he it was who had married the heiress-Countess; but he had deliberately resigned the earldom three years before, to his eldest son there across the church, rather than have to kneel and take the oath of homage for it to John Baliol as King. Robert Bruce, the father, was that sort of man. "I came to see Your Majesty's justice done on this empty vessel! A good day's work, as I said. But it could be bettered."

"You say so, my lord?" Edward looked at him, sharply.

"Aye, Sire. You have undone what you did three years ago. Unchosen your choice. You can make good now what was wrong done then. There was another choice. That you, in your wisdom rejected—for this! The Bruce claim. You can make *me* King of Scots, Sire. And complete your work."

Edward Plantagenet's florid face had been growing purple. Now he burst out. "Lord God in His Heaven! *You* tell me what I should do! Me, Edward. You! You came from Carlisle, a hundred leagues, to tell me this! Make you king? By the Blood of Christ—have I nothing else to do but win kingdoms for such as you! Out of my way, sirrah!"

Expressionless, Bruce inclined his grey head, as the furious monarch kicked huge jagged spurs into his charger's flanks.

But Edward reined up again in only a few yards, and turned in his saddle to look back over his heavy shoulder. "Mind this," he shouted, as everywhere men cringed. "You, Bruce. All of you. Scots curs. There is no King of Scots. Nor will be again. There is no kingdom of Scotland. It is now and henceforth part of my realm of England. A wretched, discredited province—but part! Your king I have deposed. Your Great Seal I have broken in four pieces. Your charters and records I have commanded to be sent from Edinburgh to London. Your Black Rood of St. Margaret is sent to my Archbishop. Your Stone of Scotland I shall take from Scone to Westminster. Your crown and sceptre are there—playthings for my men. There is nothing—nothing left for any man to play king over. And hereafter, all men shall take the oath of fealty to me, as King, for every inch of land in this Scotland. For every office. On bended knee. On pain of treason. Hear—and heed well."

He moved on.

But at the very door, again he drew up, and turned his head once more, this time over his other, his left shoulder—and his manner had undergone one of its drastic transformations. "Where is the whelp?" he demanded, almost jovially. "My friend the younger Robert? Ha, yes—there you are, my lordling of Carrick! See you, I counsel you, my young friend, to look to your father. If you would *remain* my friend! Look well. Your old grandsire, The Competitor, was trouble enough. He is well dead. I am a peaceable man, God knows—and want no more trouble. With Bruce. Or other. See you to it, boy—if you would have me to pay any more of your debts! Pay for all the fine velvet you are wearing! See that my lord of Annandale, your father, is escorted back to his charge at Carlisle—henceforth not to leave it lacking my express command. And you, then, join me at Berwick town, where we will consider your latest list of creditors!" Edward hooted a laugh. "Would I had had so lenient a liege lord!" He faced front again. "Come, my lords. Surrey—muster the guard."

Robert Bruce the younger stared across at Robert Bruce the elder, and his brow was black. Apart from that he offered no other recognition of his father, or indeed of anybody else, as he pushed out of the church. Few indeed now so much as glanced up towards the chancel steps, where the lawful King of Scots stood, forgotten as he was rejected.

Chapter Two

Impatiently the hard-riding little group pulled off the Tweedside roadway, splattered through the flooded water-meadows to the side, and the horses had to clamber, hooves slipping, up the raw red earth and outcrops of the broom-clad knowe beyond, to win back to the road again, in front of the slow-moving throng that blocked it. Young Robert Bruce cursed, in the lead. It was not that he was in any particular hurry; just that when he moved, he liked to move fast. And patience was not outstanding amongst his virtues. But it had been like this almost all the way from Galloway. All the world seemed to be heading for Berwick-on-Tweed—and all the world, on the move, tends to be a slow process. Seldom had Bruce made a more frustrating journey. It was as though everyone was on holiday, making for some great fair, important enough to pull them right across Scotland.

Not quite everyone, perhaps, and not quite in the fair-going spirit. It was the pride and circumstance, the substance of the land, that took its way by every road and highway, to Berwick, that August day, nobles, knights, lairds, landowners great and small, prelates and clerics, sheriffs, justices, officers of the higher degrees. And none looked in festive mood, or really anxious to reach their destination. Few, of course, by the very nature of things, were youthful, like the Earl of Carrick and his little troop of Annandale mosstroopers, who esteemed hurry for the sake of haste. For, in fact, Bruce himself was not especially eager to reach Berwick. His urgent mode of travel was merely habitual. Moreover, he had his nineteen-year-old brother at his side, and young brothers of that age needed to be left in no doubt as to what was what, and as to how to behave in a chivalric society.

Robert's snort of disgust was eloquent indeed as they spurred round the bend of the broomy knowe and there saw the road blocked once more, immediately ahead, and by a larger, slower and more ponderous company than heretofore.

"Save us—more of them!" he complained. "And crawling. Cumbering all the road. More fat clerks, for a wager—churchmen! Look at that horse-litter. Only some prideful, arrogant prelate would ride in such a thing. Filling all the highway . . ."

"Let us give him a fright, then!" his brother Nigel cried, laughing. "Shake up his holy litter and liver, in one! His bowels of compassion . . . !"

Nothing loth the other dug in his spurs, and neck and neck the two young men raced onwards, their grinning men-at-arms a solid pack close behind.

They were very obviously brothers, these two, and close friends. Robert had the stronger face—though the years might alter that—the slightly more rugged features. Nigel was the more nearly handsome. But both were of arresting looks, medium of height, slender but with good wide shoulders, fresh-complexioned, grey-eyed and with wavy auburn hair—the touch of red in it no doubt inherited from the Celtic mother. They had keen-cut almost bony features, vivid, mobile and expressionful, with something of their father's stubbornness of chin without the petulance of mouth. They looked a pair who would burst into laughter or sudden rage with equal readiness; yet there was a sensitiveness about their faces, especially Nigel's, which warred with the rest.

As they thundered down on the company ahead, the younger shouted. "A banner. Forward. See it? A bishop, at least!"

"Our own colours—red and gold! Can you see the device...?"

"A cross, I think. Not a saltire and a chief, like Bruce. A red cross on gold. We'll make it flap...!"

The other looked just a little doubtful now—but here was no occasion for hesitation. No man of spirit could pull up now, and have his followers cannoning into his rear while he mouthed excuses for a change of mind. A man must never look a fool before his men—especially if they were Border mosstroopers. Moreover, churchmen were all insufferably pompous and requiring of diminishing. They hurtled on.

Horsemen at the rear of the leisurely cavalcade were now looking back, at the urgent drumming of hooves. There was a certain amount of alarmed reining to this side or that. The riverside road was not only fairly narrow, but here, near Paxton, cut its way along a steep braeside of whins and bracken and thorn trees, with the ground rising sharply at one side and dropping steeply at the other. There was little room for manoeuvre—although if the company ahead had ridden less than four abreast, there would have been room for a single file to pass.

If there was some last-moment drawing aside towards the rear of the column, it did not extend to the middle, where an elaborate and richly-canopied litter in red and gold was slung between a pair of pacing white jennets, something between a hammock and a palanquin, curtained and upholstered. This swaying equipage, with its two horses, took up almost the full width of the track. Perhaps a score of men rode behind it, and another score in front.

With cheerful shouts of "Way for the Bruce! Way for the Bruce!" the laughing young men bore down on this dignified procession—and very quickly its dignity was dispersed in chaos as the tight-knit, hard-riding group drove in on it without slackening of pace. Like a spear-head the Bruces bored on and through the ruck of swearing, shouting men and rearing, plunging, stumbling horses. Low over their own beasts' necks the Bruces crouched, hands flailing at heaving flanks. Everywhere riders were forced off the track, mainly down the steep bank towards the river, in a bedlam of protest, malediction, neighings and mocking laughter.

The jennets with the litter were led on a golden cord by an elderly liveried horse-master on a substantial cob. He, like the escort, wore the red cross on gold on breast and back. At the uproar behind he turned and hurriedly raised a protesting hand. Quickly perceiving that nothing of the sort would halt or even slow down the oncoming group, he agitatedly sought to drag off some little way to the right, the river-side, the two litter-horses. But there was nothing effective that he could do, without the near-side beast going right over the lip of the bank, which would eventually have tipped up the litter and probably thrown out its occupant. Such conveyances, though an enormous aid to comfortable travel, were awkward indeed to handle in an emergency.

The Bruces came pounding on. There was obviously no space for them to pass the litter two abreast without headlong collision, and at the last moment Nigel, to the left, wrenched round his mount to force it up on the climbing bank a little way. Even so his brother's powerful stallion jostled and all but overthrew the gentle left-side jennet, causing it to stagger over, white legs sprawling wide. In its turn this pushed the other jennet over the edge, and the litter, slung between them, canted up at an alarming angle, leaning over to the right precariously, front high.

As he swept past, Robert Bruce's grin went from his face like sun behind a scudding storm-cloud. It was no proud priest who clutched the lurching sides of the curtained brancard but a young woman. And even in the hectic moment of passing, he recognised that she was a beauty.

Bruce seldom, by his very nature, did anything by half-measures. No sooner had the perception of error penetrated his consciousness than he was reining up in savage and utterly abrupt decision, with no least heed for the immediate consequences, his stallion neighing in shocked protest, rearing high on its hind-quarters, hooves slithering and scoring the dirt surface of the roadway in a cloud of dust and sparks, forelegs pawing the air. Almost it toppled over backwards, and only superb horsemanship kept its rider in the saddle.

Complete chaos ensued, as the following men-at-arms piled up in a pandemonium of agonised horseflesh, lashing hooves and flailing limbs. Fortunately all these mosstroopers were practically born to the saddle, and their mounts, unlike their masters' thoroughbreds, shaggy nimble-footed garrons bred to the hills and the hazards of the chase in roughest territory; otherwise there would have been disaster. As it was, two men were unhorsed, one garron went down—but struggled to its feet again—and the left-hand jennet was cannoned into again and knocked down on its knees.

Oddly enough, this last casualty had the effect of momentarily levelling the litter considerably, both sideways and fore and aft. Even as the cause of all this upheaval dragged his mount's head round to face the rear, with the brute still high on its hind legs, the young woman leapt nimbly out of her tossing equipage in a flurry of skirts and long silk-clad legs—no easy task from a reclining position and an unsteady base—to land directly in front of the rearing stallion and its appalled rider. She stood, apparently unconcerned at the danger from those wicked waving hooves, glaring up at the young man in proud and pale anger.

Mortified, Bruce sought to quieten his horse, bring its feet down clear of the girl and the other milling brutes, doff his velvet bonnet and stammer apologies, all at the same time. His code of chivalry, which could accept as no more than a mere understandable prank the riding down of an elderly churchman or a fat merchant, was outraged by any such insult to a young and attractive female—so long as she was a lady. Careless of all the commotion around him, save for this aspect of it, he shook his auburn head and sought for words of excuse, of explanation.

Words came rather more swiftly to the young woman. "Fool!" she cried. "Witless, mannerless dolt! How dare you, sirrah? How dare you?" Despite her choler and fright, her blazing blue eyes and quivering lips, she had a notably musical and softly accented voice, with cadences in it such as the Islesmen used.

Some part of Bruce's mind recognised and placed those cadences. But that was at the back of a mind at present fully occupied frontally.

"Pardon, lady!" he gasped. "I beseech you—pardon! My profound regrets. Of a mercy, forgive. I had no notion . . . a woman . . . a mistake, I promise you. We thought . . . we thought . . ."

"You thought to play the ape! The masterful ape, sirrah! By riding down peaceable folk. Driving them off your king's highway, in your arrogant folly. Using the weight of your prancing horseflesh in lieu of wits and manners! You need not ask pardon of me, sir." She raised her head the higher.

The girl had a high head anyway, on a notably long and graceful column of neck, a proud fair head held proudly on a tall and slender fair body. She was young for so much hauteur and authoritative vehemence, no more than eighteen probably, of a delicate yet vigorously-moulded beauty of feature. She had a wealth of heavy corn-coloured hair piled up high above lofty brows, from beneath which flashed those alive blue eyes. Despite her long slenderness she had handsome breasts, high and proud as the rest of her. She wore a travelling-gown of dark blue velvet, the swelling bodice patterned with silver and edged at neck and sleeves with fur.

"All day we have been held back by slow-moving folk, cumbering the road, lady." That was Nigel, rallying to his brother's aid.

"Quiet!" Robert's barked command was less than appreciative. "You have my regrets, madam. I will make any amends suitable." He said that stiffly. He would not grovel to any man, or woman either.

"Others have ridden all day. Without becoming boors!" she returned. "Your regrets are over-late. And your best amends, sir, will be to remove yourselves as quickly as you may."

"You are scarcely generous . . ." Bruce was protesting, when another voice broke in.

"What a fiend's name goes on? Elizabeth—what's to do?" A stern-looking thick-set man in early middle age, splendidly attired and clothed with most evident authority, had ridden back from the front of the ambling column. He would have been handsome had it not been for the great scar which disfigured his features from brow to chin.

"It is nothing, Father," the girl said. "You need not concern yourself. Travellers with more haste than manners—that is all. There is no hurt done."

"There had better not be, by God!" The newcomer glared around at all and sundry, as men and horses sorted themselves. "You were not upset? Outed? From your litter?"

"No. I . . . stepped down." The young woman raised an eyebrow at Bruce. "There is no profit in further talk. Nor in further delay of these so hasty young men."

"No? Yet you are in a rage, girl! I know that face on you!" the man declared. "If these have occasioned my daughter offence . . .!"

"Scarce that, my lord," she returned, with a flash of scorn. "Their offence will be if they linger further!"

Bruce cleared his throat. "I have apologised, sir," he said. "It was a mishap. We had no notion that there was a lady in it. I would not offer offence to any lady. Especially such as . . . such as . . ." His words tailed away—which, in that young man, was unusual.

"No doubt. You would needs be bold indeed to choose to offend Richard de Burgh's daughter!" the older man said grimly.

"De Burgh? You . . . *you* are de Burgh?"

"I am. Richard de Burgh, Earl of Ulster. And you, sir? Have you a name?"

The younger man drew himself up in his saddle. "Some, I think, would call it a name, my lord of Ulster, I am Carrick. Robert Bruce, Earl of Carrick."

"Ha! Bruce? A sprig of that tree! Carrick, eh? Then I went crusading with your father, my lord. And found your grandsire a sore man to agree with!"

"Many, I fear, so found!" Robert Bruce risked a smile. He actually bowed a little. "Myself he could see no good in. Nor my brother here, either."

The Lord Nigel grinned, and sketched a comprehensive flourish rather than a salute, less awed perhaps than he should have been. He knew the name, of course—who did not? Richard de Burgh, Lord of Connaught and Earl of Ulster, was the greatest Norman name in Ireland, one of the most noted warriors of the age—and, more important, King Edward of England's most trusted crony, adherent and companion-in-arms.

"It may be that the old devil had the makings of sense in him, then!" That comment was accompanied by a distinct twinkle of the eye, strange in so ravaged and stern a face. It was strange, too, how the Norman-French de Burgh voice had, in only three generations, acquired so liltingly Irish an intonation and character. "Your father, the Lord of Annandale—is he in health? And in the King's peace? Or out of it!"

"I scarce know, my lord. From day to day!" That was bold, in the circumstances.

The older man grimaced fierce appreciation of the fact. "Aye. No doubt. His Majesty's peace is not always easy to keep. But, as I mind it, your father was always a fool where his own good was concerned!"

"In that you have the rights of it," Bruce acknowledged. "I swear he . . ."

It was the Lady Elizabeth de Burgh's turn to clear her throat—

and she did it in no tentative or apologetic fashion. "These young lords travel in great haste, Father," she interrupted loftily. "That, they made all too clear! It is not for us to hold them back. Moreover, I would not choose this place and company to stand and talk!" Most evidently she disapproved of her righteous indignation being submerged under a masking tide of masculine camaraderie. She turned to her litter again.

Her father grinned, and nodded. He reined round his horse to ride back to his place at the head of his company.

The elderly horse-master, from gentling and soothing the jennets, was moving forward to aid his mistress into her equipage when he was roughly thrust aside. Young Nigel Bruce had leapt from the saddle, and in a stride or two was seeking to hoist up the Lady Elizabeth, with laughing gallantry. She did not reject his help, but, settling herself unhurriedly on to her couch, eyed him up and down coolly.

"What do I thank for this?" she asked. "My father's name? Or King Edward's?"

Abashed, the young man drew back. "I but . . . would serve you," he said. "A lady. And fair . . ."

"Was I not that when you tipped me out? A good day to you, sir."

The other returned to his horse, wordless, and with his brother, bowed, and rode on. It was no mean feat to have silenced the young Bruces. It was perhaps a pity that in their stiff constraint, however, they did not, could not, look back—or they might have perceived a notably different expression on the young woman's face.

They rode soberly now, in single file, past the remainder of the Ulster entourage, respectfully saluted de Burgh at the front, and then, once well past, spurred ahead, with one accord anxious to put distance between them and their humiliation.

"A hussy! A shrew! A very wild-cat!" Nigel exclaimed, as he drew up level with his brother. "Have you ever seen the like!"

"No. Nor wish to."

"So much to-do over so little a thing! Women are the devil! And yet . . . she is bonny!"

"So, perhaps, is the devil! Who knows?"

Their brooding over their wrongs did not last long—only as far as the outskirts of Berwick town. Thereafter where the broad silver river reached the azure plain of the sea, sparkling, clean, infinite, even the young Bruces, used as they were to the detritus of invasion and civil war, became increasingly preoccupied with other matters. Never had either of them seen the like of this. Here was offence of a different sort, on a different scale, offence to every sense—but especially, perhaps, to their noses. Everywhere they looked, in the narrow fire-blackened streets, were bodies—bodies in heaps and piles, bodies that hung and swung, bodies crucified, disembowelled, decapitated, mutilated and made mock of, bodies untidily asprawl or neatly laid out, bodies of all sizes, ages, and of both sexes, naked, clothed, half-burned. Every ruined house was full of them, every gaping window festooned, every street and alley lined with them, only sufficient of the causeways cleared to give meagre passage through the main thoroughfares. And all this vast dead populace of Berwick-on-Tweed was in an advanced state of putrefaction, for all had been slain weeks before. It was now August, high summer. The stench was utterly appalling, suffocating. The throbbing hum of the flies was like a constant moaning of this host of departed souls in their anguish, and the clouds of them like a black miasma over all.

Coughing, choking, next to vomiting with the stink of it, Nigel gasped. "What folly is this? Have they taken leave of their wits? The English. Letting all these lie? Should have been buried weeks ago."

"Left of a purpose. Edward overlooks nothing," his brother answered grimly. "This will be on his orders. A lesson. To all."

"But... to hold a parliament here! Amidst this."

"The more telling a lesson. The parliament's but a show, anyway. This, to point it!"

"God—it is not to be endured!"

"It will be endured. Because it must."

"It could raise revolt."

"More like to raise the plague!"

"Aye. In this heat. Is your King Edward mad?"

Even in the company of their own mosstroopers, Bruce glanced round and behind him quickly, frowning. "Watch your tongue!" he jerked, low-voiced. "I counsel you—save your breath!"

It was good advice. Seeking to breathe as little and as shallowly as they might, the brothers trotted through those terrible, silent streets of Scotland's greatest seaport and trading centre, the customs of which were said to have been worth a quarter of those of all England. They were climbing, by steep cobbled alleys and wynds still black with the blood that had cascaded down them to stain the very estuary, up from the wharves and piers and warehouses of the once-crowded lower town towards the lofty proud castle which crowned its soaring cliff-top promontory, high and serene above river and town and horror, the great banner of England streaming splendidly from its topmost tower. Up there, at least, the air would be pure.

Many travellers were climbing that long hill, and few there were whose faces were other than pale, eyes averted, lips tight. The Bruces pushed past none now. Haste was no longer valid, even to escape the smell.

At the gatehouse to the outer bailey of the castle they must perforce join a queue, inconceivable as this would have been in any other circumstances. All men-at-arms and retinues were being detached, irrespective of whose, and ordered peremptorily off to right and left, to wait and camp as best they might in the crowded tourney-ground and archery-butts which flanked the final steep and rocky knoll which the castle crowned. Only the quality travellers themselves, bearers of the royal summons, were being admitted over the drawbridge and into the castle precincts. But of these there was no lack, this August day; for never in Scotland's history had so many been required, commanded, to forgather in one place at one time. Patiently as they might, if less than humbly, and dismounted necessarily, the Bruce brothers took their places in the long shuffling column that only slowly worked its submissive way forward.

Over the hollow-sounding timbers of the bridge that spanned the dry ditch surrounding the towering ramparts, they reached, at length the arched stone pend that thrust beneath the gatehouse itself. Here a burly perspiring master-at-arms, supported by halberd-bearing minions in dented jacks and morions, scrutinised each arrival, and roughly separated sheep from goats, his rich Dorset voice hoarse with much shouting. As the Bruces drew close, awaiting their turn, Robert sought to occupy himself and his sorely-tried temper by considering the present state of the handsome flourish of heraldry carved above the archway. It represented the Douglas coat-of-arms, of a blue chief with stars on a silver field; but it was now hacked and defaced, spattered with dried thrown horse-dung, with hung over it a derisory bull's testicles and prickle, shrivelled in the sun. The veteran Sir William *le hardi* Douglas had commanded here, and had held out in this castle throughout the Sack of Berwick, surrendering to Edward only when water and food had run out. The surrender had been on honourable terms; but Douglas was said to be still in chains, and walking all the way to London Tower, like a performing bear, for his pains.

When they reached the master-at-arms, the fellow hardly so much as glanced at them.

"English? Or Scots?" he demanded unceremoniously.

Bruce threw up his head. "I am the Earl of Carrick," he said shortly.

"English or Scots, I said, man. Did you not hear?" That was weary but curt.

"Fool! Did *you* not hear?" Nigel cried. "Bruce! Earl of Carrick. We are Scots, yes—since our father should be King of Scots. But we have great English manors. In Durham, Yorkshire, Sussex and Essex. And our father is Keeper of Carlisle for King Edward . . ."

"I care not, cockerel, which dunghill your sire keeps! You are dirty Scots, curse you—so to the left you go, wi' the rest. Off wi' you. Next . . ."

When the Bruces would have protested, their arms were seized by the supporting guards, and they were ungently pushed and hurried through the pend.

Fiercely Robert broke free. "Hands off Bruce, cur!" he exclaimed, and at the sudden sheer blaze of fury in those steel-grey eyes, even the rough soldier blinked and released the arm, dropping his hand to his sword-hilt instead. Utterly ignoring him thereafter, the other stalked on, to turn left inside the outer bailey, his brother hurrying after him.

"Edward shall hear of this!" he grated—and then all but snapped off Nigel's head as he began to deliver himself of his own opinions.

It appeared after a few moments however, that King Edward might be some little time in hearing of the offence offered to his illustrious friends and supporters. For the Bruces found themselves joining another and still longer queue that wound its sluggish way round this side of the outer bailey, through a side postern door in the next tall parapeted rampart, and into the inner bailey, there to cross the cobbled courtyard to the kitchen entrance to the castle proper. This slow-moving column was strictly hemmed in and controlled by a double rank of armed guards, shoulder to shoulder—and when the Bruces perceived their lowly scullions' destination and tried to break away, in righteous wrath, they were savagely restrained and manhandled.

Nor were they permitted to turn back, as they would have done. Jabbing dirks and halberd-points left them little scope for argument or manoeuvre. Along with more amenable visitors, they were herded will-nilly along towards the kitchens.

It took a long time to reach that lowly doorway and the dark sweating-stone, food-smelling passages beyond, where the cream of Scotland's quality edged forward, pushed and jostled by cooks, servitors and menials carrying haunches of beef, trussed fowls, fish and the like. Climbing the narrow corkscrew stairways beyond, step by slow step, in the choking reek of pitch-pine torches, and making room for the impatient flunkeys and domestics with their trays and flagons, seemed to take an eternity—and even here the restricted space was much taken up with a lining of stationary scowling guards. It was the best part of an hour after reaching the outer gatehouse before the Bruce brothers stepped, by the service entrance, into the Great Hall of Berwick Castle, Robert at least seething with a cold rage such as he had never known, nor had cause to know, hitherto.

The Hall was a vast apartment, full of noise, colour and activity, heartening at first sight after all the weary trailing—although not all would confirm that impression after a second glance. Up one side of the great chamber were set long tables, groaning with good cheer, served by the busy menials, at which sat or lounged or sprawled drunk a gay and well-dressed company of laughing, talking or snoring men and women. At the head of the room was a raised dais, and on this was set a much smaller table, at one end of which sat King Edward in a throne-like chair, with Bishop Beck, the Earls of Surrey and Hereford, his commanders, and Master Hugh de Cressingham, a Justiciar of England. Nearby, and being used as an additional side-table for bottles, flagons and goblets, was a curious lump of red sandstone, flat and roughly oblong. High above, half way to the vaulted ceiling, in a little gallery, minstrels played soft music.

So much for the first glance. The second revealed a different aspect of the scene. The long queue of Scots notables still maintained its formation and patient shuffling progress. It was strictly confined to the other and right-hand side of the Hall, all but pressed against the stone walling indeed by drawn up ranks of guards—though all others ignored it. Right up to the steps of the dais area it went, to another table at which clerks sat, a table on which were no viands and which was placed directly behind the King's back, though at the lower level. And here, as each Scots landholder reached it, his name was called out, ticked off a list, and he was required to kneel on the floor and thus take an oath of homage to Edward of England for every inch of land he held. Here was no taking of the monarch's hand between his own, as homage was normally done, the oath not administered by any prelate; the monarch indeed never so much as glanced round from his eating and talk, and the clerks it was who demanded the oath, gabbling out its terms and ordering its repetition. Thereafter, homage done, the ignored suppliants were allowed to rise, bow low, and then sign their names or make their crosses on one of a great pile of sheepskins, each already lettered with the wording of the oath of fealty, sign or mark for each holding of land in each county or sheriffdom of Scotland, for each office or position held. Whereafter, the signatory was hustled away by men-at-arms to a side door, and out. They were being put through two at once, and as quickly as possible, but even so it took a deal of time. Hence the queue's lack of momentum.

"Dear God—see this!" Nigel Bruce cried. "See what they do! Look—there is Mar kneeling now. Gartnait, Earl of Mar, your own wife's brother. With that bishop. Save us—is it possible?"

His brother did not answer. Pale, set-faced, he was eyeing all that scene, noting all. He noted that it was only the English who sat at the long tables—all who ate and drank were Norman-English, or perhaps Norman-Irish or Norman-Welsh or Norman-French. He noted that none save the clerks at the signing table paid the least attention to the oath-taking, least of all those at the King's high table. He noted that none of the Scots, however illustrious, were being permitted to remain in the Hall after signing.

His wrath rose to choke him. Suddenly he strode out, bursting from the painful procession, pushing through the steel barrier of the guards.

"My lord King!" he shouted. "My liege lord Edward! I protest! It is I—Robert Bruce of Carrick. Majesty—I crave your heed."

There was much noise in that place, but even so his outcry must have been heard by most. Certain faces at the long table did turn towards him—but none up on the royal dais.

The guards were not slow to react. At first hesitating, in their surprise, they swiftly perceived that no sign came from the King, and a number hurled themselves upon the protester. He did not resist, knowing well that it could be accounted treason to brawl or engage in physical violence in the presence of the monarch. But he did raise his voice again. And this time it was directed not at Edward but at one of those who sat quite nearby at the long table.

"Cousin—my lord of Gloucester!" he called. "Your aid, I pray you." The guards were pushing him towards a door, not back to his place in the queue, as he said it.

A tall, thin, grave-faced man rose at the table—Gilbert de Clare, Earl of Gloucester, son-in-law of King Edward and cousin of the Bruces' father. He did not speak nor make any gesture towards his young relative, but after a moment, unhurriedly went stalking in stiff crane-like fashion up towards the dais table. At sight of this the guards halted in the pushing of their prisoner, and waited.

Gloucester bowed before the King, and said something low-voiced, turning to point back down the Hall. Edward glanced thitherwards, shrugged wide shoulders, and made a remark that ended in a hoot of laughter. He waved a careless hand. At the other end of the room, Bruce's pale face flushed scarlet. Gloucester came pacing back.

"Permit my lord of Carrick to return to his place in the file," he told the guards curtly, and without a word to his cousin, went back to his chair at the table.

Further humiliated, almost beyond all bearing, Robert Bruce was pushed back in the queue beside his brother. On the face of it no further attention was paid to him, any more than to the others. Nigel's muttered sympathy was received in stiff-lipped silence.

The Bruces' creeping progress towards the signing-table proceeded frozen-faced thereafter—until perhaps, half-way there, exclamation was in fact wrung from both brothers by the elaborate arrival of newcomers on the scene—not by any humble servitors' entrance these, but by the main Hall door. It was thrown open by a bowing chamberlain, and in strode Richard de Burgh, Earl of Ulster, followed by his daughter. A buzz of interest ran round the great chamber—to be lost in the louder noise of rising and pushing back of chairs, as Edward himself rose and turned to greet these honoured guests warmly, and perforce all others awake and sufficiently sober must rise also.

When they mounted the dais, the King slapped his old comrade on the back heartily, and raising the curtsying Lady Elizabeth, kissed her cheek with a smack, at the same time managing to nudge her father in the ribs in jocular fashion, obviously paying masculine tribute to her appearance. And admittedly she was very lovely, changed from her travelling dress into a magnificent shaped gown of pale blue satin, high-throated and edged with pearls, which highly effectively set off her fair beauty and splendid figure. She wore her plentiful ripe-corn-coloured hair looped with a simple circlet of blue cornflowers instead of the more usual elaborate headdress with net and horns. No large number of women were present, for the English were not apt to take their ladies campaigning with them, and the Scots summoned to the signing were all men; but such as there were shone but dully beside Elizabeth de Burgh, and by their expressions, knew it.

Little of admiration was reflected on the face of the Bruce brothers either. Indeed Robert's carefully maintained and haughty lack of expression was now cracked into something like a glower.

"A plague on them! This is beyond all!" Nigel growled. "Must we suffer this too? She will, she must see us here. Crawling like, like worms! Vanquished."

The man immediately before them in the column turned. "We *are* vanquished men, my lords," he said simply. It was Sir Richard Lundin, a middle-aged Fife knight known slightly to both.

"You may be. But we are not, sir," Bruce declared heatedly. "We ever fought on Edward's side. Opposed the usurper Baliol. And now—this!"

"My heart bleeds for you, my lords!" A young man looked back from further up the queue, speaking mockingly. "To have betrayed your own crowned liege lord and realm, and to have received *this* in reward!" That was Sir John Comyn, younger of Badenoch, nephew of King John Baliol and kinsman of the Constable, Buchan.

"Comyn! *You* to speak! You, who stole my lands. Bruce has never acknowledged any king save Edward, since Alexander died. Comyn swore fealty to Edward likewise. Can you deny it? And then turned rebel. Jackal to Baliol! For which treachery you were given *my* lands. And you talk of betrayal!" During John Baliol's three-year reign, he had forfeited the Bruces and divided their Carrick lands in Ayrshire amongst the Comyns, his sister's family.

"John Baliol was, and is, King of Scots. Nothing that you, or that tyrant there, can say or do can uncrown him. Crowned at Scone, on the Stone of Destiny. You it is, Bruce, that is rebel..."

"My lords, my young lords!" In between them the old Abbot of Melrose raised imploring hands. "Peace, peace, I pray you. This can serve no good. For any of us. Of a mercy, watch your words. Already they look at us . . ."

That was true. Despite the general noise and the evident policy of ignoring the Scots, the young men's upraised voices had attracted some attention, the fact that it was the Earl of Carrick again no doubt contributing. Edward himself had not glanced in their direction, but Surrey, his chief commander, now looked round and down. And sitting at the King's table now likewise, Elizabeth de Burgh was also considering them thoughtfully.

Perceiving the fact, Robert Bruce cursed below his breath, and looked determinedly elsewhere. Never had he felt so helpless, in so intolerable a position—he who should be Prince of Scotland if he had his rights. And to have that chit of a girl sitting there looking down on his ignominy . . . !

His brother was also looking carefully anywhere but at the dais table. To change the dangerous subject was as essential as was not meeting the young woman's interested gaze. He tapped Robert's arm.

"That piece of stone? With the flagons on it. What is it?" he asked. "How comes it here?"

His brother shook his head.

"They say that it is the Coronation Stone, my lord," Lundin informed. "The same that the young Lord of Badenoch spoke of—the Stone of Destiny. King Edward took it from Scone Abbey, and carries it south with him. To London. As symbol that there is no longer any king to be crowned in Scotland. So he misuses it thus—as stool for his viands . . ."

"God's curse on him!" somebody snarled, though low-voiced.

"I' faith—you say so?" Robert Bruce was interested now. "That ugly lump of red rock the famous Stone of Destiny? The Palladium of Scotland? Who would have thought it?"

"Only fools would think it!" That was Sir John Comyn again, scornfully. "This is not the Stone of Scone. It is some quarryman's block!"

"Then why is it here, at the King's side?"

"Edward Plantagenet says it is the Coronation Stone. And whatever else he is, he is no fool!"

"Nevertheless, that is not the true Stone, I tell you," Comyn insisted. "I know. I have seen it. At King John's coronation, at Scone. My kinsman Buchan placed him on the Stone, and put the crown on his head. I stood close by, holding the sword of state for him. Think you I would not know the Stone again if I saw it?"

"Hush, man—hush!" The Abbot of Melrose sounded agitated.

"Then what is this?" Lundin demanded.

"God knows! Some borestone for a standard, perhaps. But it looks to me new-quarried. Fresh. Sandstone. The true Stone is quite other. It is higher—to be sat upon. Dark, almost black. Harder stone. Polished. And carved. Carved with figures and designs. Erse designs. Not a dull lump of soft sandstone, like that . . ."

"Of a mercy, my lord—hold your tongue!" the old Abbot exclaimed, tugging at Comyn's sleeve. "They will hear . . ."

"What of it?" Comyn, known as the Red—although that was a family appellation and not descriptive of his colouring—was a fiery hawk-faced character, about Robert Bruce's own age, lean, vigorous, contentious. His father had been one of the Guardians of Scotland during the interregnum that ended with Baliol's enthronement, and had married Baliol's sister. The son, as heir of the Red branch of the most powerful family in all Scotland, a family that boasted three earls and no fewer than thirty-two knights, was a man whom few would wish to counter.

Nevertheless, even this proud and passionate individual must now bow the knee to English Edward—and bow it, mortifyingly to Edward's uncaring back—or be forfeited, dispossessed of his wide lands, and imprisoned as rebel. Owing to the fact that the three men in front of him were churchmen, and there appeared to be some dispute as to the lands they were to do homage for, Comyn was beckoned forward, there and then, and ordered to kneel. With ill grace and muttering, he obeyed.

The form of words, which all had heard *ad nauseam*, mumbled or chanted monotonously from the moment of entering that Hall, was once again read out. It committed the taker to fullest and sole obedience, worship and fealty to his liege lord Edward, by the grace of God King of England, Lord of Ireland and Duke of Guyenne, and to him only, his heirs and successors, to the swearer's life's end, on pain of death in this world and damnation in the next. It was noteworthy that Edward was not now calling himself sovereign of Scotland, Lord Paramount or other title which could imply that there was in fact any kingdom of Scotland at all. After the oath followed the list of lands, baronies and offices, in each county, for which the homage was being done, as feudal duty. In Comyn's case this extensive list, however rapidly gabbled through, took a deal longer than the oath itself to enunciate. Sir John, features twisted in sourest mockery, went through the required procedure, deliberately malforming the words from stiff lips. Then he rose, took the proffered quill, and signed the sheepskin with a contemptuous flourish, made the three required valedictory bows to the royal back at speed, and flung out of the chamber while his cleric neighbour was still on his knees.

Quickly it was Robert Bruce's turn. As he stepped to the table and one of the attendants demanded his name, rank and lands, he raised his voice loudly, addressing not the clerks but the dais-table.

"Here is error," he called. "I, Robert Bruce, Earl of Carrick, have already done homage to my liege lord Edward. At Wark, in England. In the month of March. His Majesty, that day, gave me this ring." He held up a hand on which a ruby gleamed warmly. "I call as witnesses to that homage Anthony Beck, Bishop of Durham; John de Warenne, Earl of Surrey; Humphrey de Bohun, Earl of Hereford. All here present, and at the King's table!"

There was a momentary hush in that room. Even Edward Plantagenet paused in his talk for a second or two. Then he resumed his converse with Richard de Burgh, without a glance round, as though nothing had happened, raising a goblet to his lips. A sigh seemed to ripple over the company. Bishop Beck gestured down peremptorily to the clerks.

"Kneel, my lord," the chief clerk said, agitatedly. "The oath. All must swear it. His Majesty's command."

"If my previous oath, willing, is considered of no worth, shall this, constrained, be the better?" Bruce cried hotly.

Furiously Beck rose at the dais-table. "Guard!" he roared. "Your duty, fools!"

Edward chatted on to Ulster—though that man looked less than comfortable. The Lady Elizabeth, at his side, was now considering not the line of Scots but her fingernails, head lowered.

Mail-clad guards stepped forward to grasp the Bruce's arms and shoulders. Perceiving that further resistance not only would avail nothing but would probably result in his Carrick lands not being restored to him but given to another, he dropped to the floor—but on one knee only. There he muttered the terms of the oath, after the clerk—and on this occasion this minion was so relieved that he did not issue the usual warnings to speak clear. Rising, Bruce took the quill, signed with barely a glance at the sheepskin, bowed briefly and only once, and stalked to the door. None sought to bring him back to complete the triple obeisance.

He was striding in black rage down the slantwise castle courtyard towards the outer bailey, to be off, when his brother caught up with him. And not only Nigel—an officer of the guard.

"My lord of Carrick," this individual said stiffly. "A command. A royal command. His Highness the King commands that you attend him at the banquet and entertainment he holds tonight. In this castle at eight of the clock. You understand, my lord? It is the King's pleasure and command that you attend tonight."

"God in His heaven!" Robert Bruce exploded. "Who is crazed —he or I?"

• • •

It was the same Great Hall, crowded still, and with minstrels playing—but with an atmosphere that could hardly have been more different. All now was colour and ease and laughter—King Edward's the heartiest of all. When the Bruces arrived, deliberately late, four dwarfs were entertaining the company with a tumbling act, aided by a tame bear, which seemed to amuse the warrior-king immoderately. Indeed he was pelting them with cates and sweetmeats from the tables, in high good humour, and even roared with mirth when the chief dwarf actually threw one back approximately in the royal direction. The brilliant company, taking its cue from its master, was in the best of spirits, with wine flowing freely. No least emanation from the dead, corpse-filled town below penetrated here.

Looking round on all that glittering and animated throng, the newcomers could see no other Scots. They knew a great many of those present, of course, for Robert in particular had been around the English Court, off and on, for years, holding almost as great lands in England as in his own country. But the constraint of the afternoon's proceedings was very much with them still—and obviously with others also, for such glances as came their way were all very quickly directed elsewhere, and none of the other guests came to speak to them. Not even Gloucester, or any other of their English kinsmen, came near their corner.

The dwarfs' act over, the King called for dancing. The floor was cleared and the musicians reinforced. Now the notable shortage of women was emphasised, and comparatively few of the men could take the floor for lack of partners. Edward headed up a lively *pas de deux*, with jovial gallantry choosing Elizabeth de Burgh as partner, her father following on with the Countess of Gloucester.

All others must press back to give the dancers space, so that the young Bruces, though hemmed in, were no longer lost behind a crowd. And when the heavily playful monarch and the graceful young woman glided past, both undoubtedly noticed the brothers standing there. Indeed Edward obviously made some comment, with a smile, to his partner. She did not smile, however. Nor did Robert Bruce.

The dance over, and a soulful lute-player taking over the entertainment while the guests refreshed themselves at the laden tables, a page brought a summons for the Earl of Carrick to attend on His Majesty. Set-faced, wary, Robert moved after the youth. Everywhere men and women watched, even though they pretended not to.

Edward was up at the dais end of the Hall again, selecting sweetmeats for Elizabeth de Burgh from dishes lying on the lump of red sandstone, which had not been moved since the afternoon. He turned, as Bruce came up and paused some distance off, bowing.

"Ha, Robert my friend!" he cried, in most genial welcome, holding out his hand. "Come, lad. Here is a lady to turn all hearts and heads! Even yours, I vow! The Lady Elizabeth of Ulster has made thrall of me quite. Let us see what she can do with you. Since someone must needs do so, it seems, on my behalf and service!"

Bruce inclined his head, but came only a little nearer that outstretched hand. "The Lady Elizabeth and I have met, Sire. This afternoon. Before . . . before what was done here," he said stiffly. "And her undoubted charms are not necessary. To win my loyal devotion to your service."

"No? Is he being ungallant, my dear? Or just plain Scots? For they are a stubborn and stiff-necked crew, God knows! What think you?"

She looked at the young man levelly, gravely. "I think that perhaps he conceives Your Majesty to have mistreated him. And sees not what any woman has to do with it!"

"Mistreated? I, Edward, mistreated him? No, no—the boot is on the other leg, I swear. Have I mistreated you, Robert?"

Bruce swallowed, but raised his head a degree higher. "I say so, Sire."

"Damme—you do?" The King looked incredulous, sorrowful and amused in one. "You, that I have nurtured! Lavished gifts upon. Paid your duns and creditors. By the Mass—here's ingratitude!"

"No, Sire. Not so. For what you have done for me, in the past, I am grateful. But, if I needed aid, debts paid, was it not because I had lost all in Your Majesty's service? My lands of Carrick, Cunninghame and Kyle, taken from me by Baliol for supporting your cause. I became a pauper, Sire..."

"Ha! A pauper, you say—for Edward! Behold the pauper!" The King gestured mockingly at Bruce's rich velvets, jewellery, gold earl's belt. "Would you say, my dear, that my lord of Carrick starves on Edward's bounty?"

The girl shook her head, wordless, obviously reluctant to be involved in this clash. Indeed, she was sketching an incipient curtsy, preparatory to moving away, when Edward reached out and held her arm.

"I humbly suggest that Your Majesty has had good value for the moneys you have disbursed on my behalf," the younger man declared carefully, picking his words. "You have had the use of a thousand Bruce swords and lances. Of our great castle of Lochmaben. We have kept Galloway in your peace..."

"All of which it was your simple duty to render, I'd mind you, Robert," the monarch interrupted. But he said it conversationally, almost sadly. "Else what for was your oath of fealty?"

"That I wondered, Sire. This afternoon! When you forced me to a second and shameful oath-taking. Abasing me before all, as though I were some defeated rebel!"

"Forced, boy? Needs must I *force* you to show your lealty to me?" Edward shook his leonine head, and turned to Elizabeth. "You see the stubborn pride of this young man? What am I to do with him? The signing of today's Roll, this Ragman's Roll, was too much for him. All others who hold land in Scotland must do new homage for it—as is only right and proper, since there is no longer any King of Scots. But not our Robert! I wonder why—on my soul I do? Could it be...? Could it be he has high tastes, the lad? In more than clothes and horses and the like—as my purse knows full well! Could it be that he sees himself, perhaps, as one day sitting in John Baliol's throne?" That was still directed at the young woman—indeed the King still held her arm. But the mock-sorrowful voice had suddenly gone steely. "His father, see you, had such notions. And his grandsire before him. How think you, my dear?"

"I do not know, Your Majesty. These are matters quite beyond my ken."

"But not beyond mine, Sire!" Bruce said, "And I say that you misjudge if you so think. No such notion is in my mind. My grandfather claimed the throne, yes. And Your Majesty chose Baliol rather than he. To the hurt of all, as it has transpired. But that is an old story. If my father still hankers after an empty crown, I do not."

"As well, lad—as well!" Sibilant, soft, there was nevertheless something almost terrifying in the older man's voice, despite the smile. "For that folly is done with. You hear? Done with. As Almighty God is my witness, there shall be no King of Scots again. No realm of Scotland. Mark it, Robert Bruce. Mark it, I say." He jerked his head. "Why, think you, that Stone lies there? On its way to Westminster. Why?"

"That I wondered," the girl said. "So strange and rude a thing. So, so lacking in any grace . . ."

"Graceless, aye! Like the people who cherished it. Rude and hard—but none so hard to break! I take it to London because, from time beyond mind, the ancients have declared that where that Stone lies, from there will Scotland be governed. Every petty king of this unhappy land has been crowned thereon. But none shall sit on it again. The Kings of England hereafter shall use it as their footstool! In token that the realm of Scotland is dissolved. Gone. For all time to come. I say mark it well, Robert."

"I mark it, Sire. I mark also that it is not as described by those who have seen the Stone of Scone! It is different. Not carven. Bare a foot high. Soft sandstone, rough-hewn. It is said that the true Coronation Stone is otherwise . . ."

"Dolt! Numskull! Insolent puppy!" Suddenly Edward Plantagenet was blazing-eyed, in quivering rage. "How dare you raise your ignorant voice in my presence! That is the Stone of Destiny. I, Edward, say it. I took it from Scone. I burned its abbey. I cast down its custodians. That it should be so ill-seeming a thing is but to be expected of this barbarous, damnable country! That is Scotland's uncouth talisman!" He leaned forward abruptly, snatched up a flagon, and smashed it down in fierce violence on the top of the sandstone block, with a crash. Wine and fragments splashed over all three of them. "And that is its worth and honour, by the Mass!"

At the noise the lutist faltered to a halt, and everywhere men and women fell silent gazing alarmed up towards the trio at the dais.

Edward raised a jabbing hand, to point at the musician. "Sing, fool! Did I command you to desist?" He glared round at all the company. "What ails you? What ails you, I say?"

Hastily all turned away, began urgently to talk with each other, to resume their eating and drinking.

Bruce wiped with his velvet sleeve some of the wine which had splashed up in his face. "Have I your permission to retire, Sire?" he asked.

"No, you have not!" The King swung on him, fierce eyes narrowed. "That Stone. Do you still, in your impertinence, say that it is not the Stone of Destiny?"

"No, Sire."

"As well!" He took a pace or two away, and then back. "Why in God's good name are you such a fool, Robert?" he demanded, but in a different voice. "Fools I cannot abide." He turned on the young woman—whose fine gown was now sadly stained with wine. "What think you? Is his folly beyond redemption? Could *you* redeem it, girl?"

She shook her head. "I myself am but a foolish woman, Your Majesty. If my lord of Carrick is indeed so foolish, then other than I must deal with him."

"Ha! Is that the way of it? You see—she does not want you, man! And I cannot say that I blame her."

The young man looked quickly from one to the other. "*I* cannot say that I understand you, Sire. In . . . in anything."

"Because you are a fool, as I say. You lack understanding. Let us hope that is all you lack! Think on that! I had plans for you. Other than just the payment of your debts. But I swear I must needs think again." Edward tapped Elizabeth's shoulder. "My dear, I fear the matter is beyond redemption. But see if a woman may instil a modicum of sense, if not wisdom, into that stubborn head. For I confess I have lost all patience with it."

Without a further glance at either of them, majesty stalked off, beckoning to the ever-watchful Bishop of Durham.

Mystified, Bruce stared at the young woman. "Of a mercy—what means all that?" he demanded. "Has he taken leave of his wits? Or is he drunken? What does he mean? What has he conceived against me? And how come *you* into it?"

Troubled, she bit her lip. "He is strange, yes. But you know him better than do I. Before today, I had not seen him since I was a child."

"I thought that I knew him passing well. Always he was passionate. Changeable. A man of moods. But he has ever seemed to esteem me well enough. To trust me. What have I done that he should treat me like this?"

"I do not know. But from what he has said, I think that he questions your loyalty. You have come from Galloway, have you not? Perhaps what you were doing in Galloway aroused his suspicions?"

"I was in Galloway, yes, when he summoned me here. Baliol was Lord of Galloway, before Edward named him king. Owned great lands there, heired from his mother, Devorgilla of the old race. Bruce also held Galloway lands, which Baliol took when we clove to Edward. Since Baliol's fall, I have been visiting these . . ."

"And the former King's lands also?"

"I could scarce help pass through some. And why not? He seized all my Carrick lands, and gave them to Comyn . . ."

"No doubt, my lord. But perhaps tales have reached King Edward. From Galloway. Perhaps he believes that, now that King John Baliol is gone, *you* are seeking his great Galloway lands. And more than his lands. My father says that Galloway, properly mustered, could raise ten thousand men. Perhaps, my lord, His Majesty would prefer that the son of the man who now claims that he should be King of Scots should not control those thousands?"

He frowned at her. Chit of a girl as she was, she talked now like Richard de Burgh's daughter.

"There is no truth in that," he said. "I have no thought to raise men. Against Edward. I have ever been loyal. I have raised men *for* him . . ."

"Loyal, my lord? Loyal to Edward of England? But not to Scotland, it seems. There are loyalties and loyalties!"

He stared at her. "What do you mean? Baliol was ever the enemy of our house. When he became King, we fought against him. What else? Would you have had us lick his boots?"

"You put Bruce before your Scotland?"

"Would you not put de Burgh before Ireland?"

"No. *I* would not."

He shrugged. "What is Scotland? A rabble of hungry, quarrelling lords. A land rent in pieces. A pawn in this game of kings."

"Then is not here, perhaps, your answer, sir? If Bruce will put Bruce before Scotland, may he not put Bruce before Edward also? And when his father claims the Scots throne, Edward must needs look at Bruce with new eyes. And listen to the tales that men tell."

"You think that is it? But there is no truth in it, I tell you. My father is something of a fool. Weak. But stiff-necked. Perhaps he is, indeed, what Edward calls *me*! He will talk, but not act. He is a man of books and parchments, not the sword. Edward need not fear him."

"It is you he fears, I swear—not your father. And thinks to change his plans for you . . ."

"Aye—plans. What plans? What was he talking of, that he needs now to think again?"

"You do not know?"

"No. How should I know? He has told me nothing. Summoned me here, and then insulted me! Told me nothing, save that I am a fool. And, perhaps, traitor . . . !"

Elizabeth de Burgh looked away. "You had a wife, my lord?"

He nodded. "Aye. Isobel. Daughter to the Earl of Mar. We were wed young. She died. Two years ago. Giving birth to our daughter Marjory."

"I am sorry." She drew a deep breath. "I have learned, since I came to Berwick, *why* my father brought me from Ireland. To this Scotland. It was King Edward's command. He thought to marry me. To you!"

"Lord God!"

She raised her head, in a quick gesture. "Well may you say so, my lord! Such match would have been as unwelcome to me as to yourself, I assure you. More so. So, I give thanks for the King's change of mind!"

"But . . . but this is crazy-mad. Why? Why should he have had us to wed? Unknown to each other. How would such a match serve Edward?"

"That he did not reveal to me. But he is my god-sire. My father has long been his close companion. Perhaps he thought to bind you closer to him, thus. Make you more his man . . ."

"I' faith—by foisting a wife on me! My father chose my first wife—a mere child. My next I shall choose for myself..."

"And welcome, sir—so long as you do not choose Elizabeth de Burgh!"

"H'rr'mm. I am sorry. I but mean that..."

"Your meaning is very clear, my lord. But no clearer than mine, I hope. Let us both thank God for His Majesty's doubts! It has saved me the distress of refusing him. And you! I bid you a good night, sir." With the merest nod she turned and swept away, making for a door.

It did not take long for Robert Bruce to seek escape also, though by a different door. Nigel could look after himself.

But, as in the afternoon, King Edward proved that he had keen eyes. A messenger again came hurrying after the truant.

"His Majesty regrets that you saw fit to leave without his express permission, my lord," he was told, expressionlessly. "His Highness, however, will overlook the omission. But he commands that you attend the parliament he holds here at noon tomorrow. On pain of treason. You have it, my lord of Carrick...?"

• • •

Scotland, in 1296, was not notably advanced in parliamentary procedure; but the parliament held at Berwick that 28th of August was by any standard the most extraordinary the ancient kingdom had ever seen. For one thing, although it was held on Scottish soil and to deal with the affairs of Scotland, it was purely an English occasion; only English commissioners had power to vote, although the summoned Scots representatives were there, under threat of treason, in greater numbers than ever before. No Scot might even speak, unless he was specifically invited to do so. Even the Englishmen, indeed, did little speaking, save for Bishop Beck, who stage-managed all. And his clerks. It was, in fact, no parliament at all, but a great public meeting for the announcement of the details by which Edward Plantagenet's dominion over conquered Scotland would be implemented. Although the King left most of the actual talking to Beck and his henchmen, his opening remarks made very clear what was required of the assembly, and what would result from any failure to achieve it, or the least questioning of the programme—as witness to which he there and then announced orders for the arrest and imprisonment of any who had failed to obey the summons to attend, including even an illustrious prelate, the Bishop of Sodor and Man. Thereafter, Edward's interventions were infrequent, but as telling as they were brief.

The main business was to announce the machinery by which Scotland would hereafter be governed. John de Warenne, Earl of Surrey, would be Viceroy; William de Amersham, Chancellor; Hugo de Cressingham, Treasurer; William de Ormesby, Justiciar. The clerks Henry of Rye and Peter of Dunwich were appointed Escheators, officials with general supervision over all revenues north and south of Forth respectively. Another clerk, William Dru, would be Bishop of St. Andrews, and therefore Primate, since Bishop Fraser had fled; and would administer also the earldom of Fife and the customs of Dundee. The royal servants John Droxford, wardrobe-keeper, Philip Willoughby, cofferer and Ralph Manton, tailor, with others, would have oversight over all other earldoms and baronies as King's Procurators. Every Scots stone castle would be garrisoned by English soldiers, and every wooden one burned, without exception. All Scots official records were to be sent to London. Heavy taxation was necessary to pay for the recent campaign, the administration, and the army of occupation; this would be enforced on all classes, and the Church in especial, with the utmost rigour. And so on.

In the quite prominent position to which he had been conducted, Robert Bruce listened to all this, features controlled, and wondering why he had been required to attend. It was not until late in the proceedings that he learned. The clerk at Beck's left hand, reading out a list of minor enactments and edicts, found another paper passed to him. He read it out in the same monotonous gabble.

"It is hereby commanded that the Lord Robert Bruce, sometime Earl of Carrick, shall forthwith proceed to the lands of Annandale formerly held by his father, and there receive into the King's peace, with all necessary persuasion, all occupiers of land, all arms-bearing men, and all lieges fit of body and mind. These he shall cause to take oath of allegiance to King Edward, all under the supervision of Master John Benstead, clerk of the King's pantry. Thereafter the said Lord Robert shall muster these said men of Annandale in arms and proceed to the contiguous lands of the traitor William, Lord of Douglas, formerly keeper of this castle, where the wife of the same, who has already incurred the King's displeasure, is wickedly and treasonably holding out against the King's peace in the Castle of Douglas. There he shall destroy the said castle, waste the said lands, and bring captive the said Lady of Douglas to the King's appointed officers here at Berwick for due trial and punishment. All this the said Lord Robert shall perform, and such else as may be directed by the said Master Benstead of His Majesty's pantry, it being expressly forbidden that he proceed into the lands and territory of Galloway. By the King's royal command."

As the clerk continued with the next edict, Bruce sat as though turned to stone, though the knuckles of his clenched fists gleamed white. A man, he knew, could accept only so much and remain a man. Edward was testing him, but beyond acceptance. On Edward Plantagenet's head be it, then . . .

Chapter Three

Another Great Hall in another castle, another oath-taking and roll-signing—though few here could do more than make their rude marks against their names and holdings, and fewer still knew what they were signing for before their lord's son and the Englishmen. The farmers, shepherds, drovers, horse-dealers, millers, smiths, packmen and the like, of Annandale, one hundred and fifty square miles of the best land on the West March of the Border, were not knowledgeable or greatly interested in the political situation or in who occupied thrones or made laws. They followed their lord, paid their rents, gave of their service—and hoped, this done, to be left in approximate peace to lead their own lives. If their lord—or, at least, their lord's son, young Robert—summoned them to the Castle of Lochmaben in their hundreds, and required them to utter some rigmarole of words, and scratch crosses and marks on papers, they were perfectly willing to humour him, however much of a waste of time it might be. If, thereafter, they were to go riding, armed, in the tail of the same Lord Robert, as was rumoured, then few would find this any great trial, since such ploys usually resulted in sundry pleasurable excitements and sports, cattle and plenishings cheaply won, new women to be sampled. The Annandale men had had little enough of this sort of thing these last years, with the Bruces dispossessed temporarily, and the absentee Comyn Earl of Buchan getting the rents; and latterly the English captain and small garrison established in the castle, though arrogant and objectionable, had not greatly troubled the local folk. Some little friction there had been earlier on, mainly over their attitude to the women, but the independent, hard-riding Border mosstrooping population was not one to offend lightly, and the Englishmen numbered no more than four score, a mere token garrison. So a sort of mutual live-and-let-live had developed. But now, with the Bruces back, more than this could be looked for.

Robert Bruce lounged in a high chair at the dais end of the Hall, looking bored and restless; but at least he did not turn his back on the queue of oath-takers, nor eat and drink while they made their patient way through the prescribed procedure.

Indeed, sometimes he nodded, raised a hand, or called a greeting to this man or that, whom he recognised, and even occasionally came down to speak with old acquaintances amongst the tenantry—for here it was that he had spent much of his childhood, although Turnberry, up in Ayrshire, was the principal seat of the Carrick earldom.

Nearby, also on the dais, another man sat throughout the prolonged business, though he gave no appearance of boredom or restlessness; he was in fact sound asleep—Sir Nicholas Segrave, captain of the castle's garrison, a grizzled veteran of the wars, grey-headed, inclining to stoutness, still a good man in a fight but grown appreciative also of the benefits of quiet inaction.

But if these two on the dais seemed to lack interest in the proceedings, there was one who could not be so accused. The man who sat behind the signing table, with the Lochmaben steward and his minions, watched all with a keen and careful glance. He was a small, misshapen man, almost an incipient hunchback, discreetly dressed all in black, thin, with a darting beady eye, and lank black hair that fell over his chalk-white face. Efficient, industrious, shrewd, Master John Benstead, clerk to the royal pantry, was a man of swift wits, sarcastic tongue and some learning—indeed an unfrocked priest it was said, and always knew just what he was doing. In these last winter months he had lived closer to Robert Bruce than any of his brothers—and that young man had come to loathe the very sight of him. He was now snapping questions of Dod Johnstone, the steward, about almost every man who came up to the table, and taking quick notes of his own on a sheaf of papers—for what reason, none could tell. But if none liked it, since it made all uncomfortable, none questioned it either—even Bruce himself, who had not been long in recognising that though *he* was the earl and men took this oath of allegiance to Edward through him as feudal superior, it was this deformed clerk who was, in all that counted, the master. One was the all-powerful King of England's trusted servant, with unspecified but comprehensive authority; and the other, whatever else, was not. Even Sir Nicholas, up there on the dais, though he got on passing well with the young lord, now took his orders from this base-born clerk, however reluctantly.

The interminable process at the table—which was clearly much more concerned with the new and damnable notion of tax-assessment than with the ostensible allegiance-giving—was nearing an end for this grey March day, and Benstead was closely cross-questioning an impassive upland farmer as to his stocks of wool—for by a new edict all Scots wool was to be confiscated and sent to the nearest port for shipment to London for the King's use—when there was an interruption. A booted and spurred courier came hurrying in. It was noticeable that though the man bowed perfunctorily towards the pair on the dais, it was to Master Benstead that he made his way, to speak low-voiced, urgently.

Sir Nicholas, with an old campaigner's ability to waken at need and completely, bestirred himself and stumped down to see what was to do. After a moment or two, Bruce swallowed his pride and did the same.

The messenger, an Englishman, had come from Lanark, from Edward's newly-created Earl of Clydesdale and Sheriff of Lanark and Ayr, William de Hazelrig. His tidings were dramatic. Sir William Douglas had escaped from his bonds in the south, and was believed to be heading for Scotland again, if he was not already over the Border. Moreover, open revolt had broken out in Galloway, where James Stewart, the High Steward of Scotland, and Bishop Robert Wishart of Glasgow, had risen in arms against the English garrisons. It was thought that Douglas would make for Galloway to join these traitors, since he had married the Steward's sister. But before that he might well seek to collect a force of men on his own estates in Douglasdale. The Earl of Carrick, at Lochmaben, had been charged with the duty of dealing suitably with the Douglas lands. He must see to it without delay that this renegade gained no men there, that he was apprehended if he came thither, and that the territory of Douglasdale was left in no condition ever again to be a danger to the King's peace.

"You hear, my good young lord?" Benstead asked, pointing a

long, ink-stained finger at Bruce. He infuriated the latter in innumerable ways, but in none more effectively than this deplorable habit of referring to him as his good young lord. "Your delays stand revealed. Indicted. If this Douglas reaches his lands before you do, and gathers men there to aid these rebels in Galloway, then *you* will be held responsible. I have told you."

"And I have told you, sir, that in winter months there can be no campaigning in these hills. You are not in your Lincolnshire now! To take a large force over into Douglas Water means the covering of forty miles of savage hills, choked passes, flooded valleys, rivers in spate, no bridges. It could not be done, these past months. But nor was there any danger from there, since no more could the Douglases have moved in force. Sir Nicholas knows that, if you do not, Master Pantler!" To term the man this was Bruce's retort to the good young lord phrase.

"I know that you could have raided Douglasdale before the winter closed in—and did not, my lord. Despite my advice. I know likewise, even though I *am* no soldier, that it is no longer winter, and men determined in the King's service might have been amove ere this! As have these rebels in your Galloway, it seems! Perhaps it is as well that His Majesty forbade that you go into Galloway, when he did!"

"What do you mean by that? I do not take you, sir. Perhaps you will explain?"

The other looked quickly from Bruce to Sir Nicholas Segrave and the courier, and shrugged his twisted shoulders. "I would not wish to see a loyal and noble servant of the King's Highness endangered amongst rebels, that is all," he answered smoothly.

Sir Nicholas intervened. "This rising? In Galloway. How large a matter? You say the High Steward, and one of their bishops . . .?"

"It is serious, I fear. Now that King Edward has gone campaigning in Flanders, these treacherous Scots think that they may safely rebel. They must be taught otherwise. Eh, my good lord? There have been a number of petty revolts, all easily put down. But this is more dangerous. The Steward, despite his strange title, is an important lord. And the rascal Bishop of Glasgow, this Wishart, is the most potent of their prelates. I would have thought that the man Baliol's fate would have taught them their lesson!"

"Galloway was Baliol's country, and these have risen in Baliol's name," the courier amplified. "They declare that he is still their king, the fools. But neither the Steward nor the Bishop are soldiers—whereas this Douglas is. Therefore my lord of Clydesdale says that it is of the utmost importance that he does not join them. He says that my lord of Carrick must act without delay. In the King's name."

"As he shall. Eh, my lord?"

Bruce inclined his head. He had put off the unsavoury business of harrying his neighbour's lands for as long as he could. Not that he had too nice a stomach for raiding and feud, in the time-honoured fashion; but Douglas was an old friend of his father's, distantly related indeed, and it went against the grain to attack his wife and family during his absence in captivity. It seemed, however, that he could procrastinate no longer. Better that he should do it, perhaps, than Hazelrig from Lanark, a man renowned as a butcher.

"It will take a little time to muster sufficient men," he said.

"Two days, no more," Benstead asserted. "We have planned it all, times without number these last months. You agree, Sir Nicholas? Two days." He turned to the courier. "My salutations to your lord, at Lanark. Tell him that my lord of Carrick will be hammering at the gates of Douglas Castle three days from now. And that every effort will be made to lay hands on its master. But once we have his lady and children, we shall have the means to halt his treasons, heh? Through them we will bring the cur to heel very promptly—or my name is not John Benstead! Tell my lord of Clydesdale that it is as good as done."

Bruce turned away and left them there, the clerk's mocking laughter following him.

• • •

So, a few days later, a mounted host of some six hundred men wound its way through the green Lowther Hills, forded the waters of Daer, Potrail, Elvan and Snar, feeders of Clyde, crossed the high peat-pocked moors beyond, and over the lonely pass of Glentaggart where the snow still lingered in the north-facing corries, rode down the Glespin Burn into the fair wide valley of the Douglas Water. Bruce and Sir Nicholas Segrave led, with a contingent of half the English garrison; the rest were all Annandale men, irregulars, tenantry rendering their feudal service. Their stocky, short-legged shaggy garrons, used to the hills, made a notably better job of the difficult terrain than did the English regulars' cavalry horses. To the satisfaction of all concerned, Master Benstead had elected to remain behind, allegedly on account of pressure of paper work, but, Bruce was pretty sure, actually to conduct a great search for hidden wool, while most of the able-bodied men and heads of households were away with their lord.

But there was some cause for dissatisfaction also. Hitherto, ostensibly in the interests of secrecy, so that they might descend upon the Douglases unawares, there had been none of the looked-for and prescribed harrying and laying waste of the land. These barren uplands, of course, were scant of people and houses, and admittedly this was not the best time to encumber themselves with flocks and herds. But it made dull riding for so puissant a force.

In the early afternoon of the second day, with the richer broad bottomlands of Douglasdale opening before them, the temptations became much greater. There were still some four miles of populous country to cover before Douglas Castle, when Bruce halted his force and ordered all to gather round and attend well to what he said. Clad in a handsome suit of chain-mail under a heraldic surcoat of red and gold, girdled with a golden earl's belt, a plumed helmet on his head, he caused his horse to mount a little knoll, and spoke from that.

"My friends—we are here, not for our own advantage but to bring this Douglasdale into the King's peace. Remember it. There may well be pickings for one or two, when our work is done. But not until then, I say. You hear me? Our task is to reach Douglas Castle quickly, before the Lady of Douglas and her folk have time or opportunity to put it in state of readiness against us. For we are not prepared or equipped for a seige, as you must know. It is a strong house, and we have no engines to reduce it. So we hasten. It is understood?"

Men murmured or growled, but made no more specific protest at such a poor programme for Border mosstroopers.

"I do not think to see much fighting," Bruce went on. "Even if they are warned of our approach, they cannot have had time to assemble any strength. We shall surround the castle and hope to rush the gates, demanding surrender in King Edward's name. Only if they hold against us need there be bloodshed. Have you anything to add, Sir Nicholas?"

The veteran nodded. "If a woman commands here, we may save ourselves much trouble," he said. "We will take two or three children. Bring them before the castle with ropes round their necks. Threaten to hang them if the castle is not yielded. Hang one, if needs be, as example. No woman will hold out then, I wager."

Bruce frowned. "I do not make war on women and children, sir," he declared, shortly.

"No? It is a woman and her cubs we have to oust from this house, is it not? If they resist, many will die. Which is better—one child or many grown men? And likely other children thereafter? This is war, not a tourney, my lord!"

"Nevertheless, we shall do this *my* way," Bruce said levelly. He did not want to quarrel with the Englishman—was not sure indeed who was truly in command of this expedition. The mass of the men were his, and in theory he was the leader—but he knew that in fact he was little more than a puppet of the English, and Benstead would support this gruff and experienced soldier against him to the hilt. And Benstead, unhappily, stood for Edward Plantagenet in this.

So, when they rode on, the younger man went out of his way to be civil to the knight, to avoid any rupture. They had got on well enough together hitherto—largely thanks to a mutual reaction towards clerks in authority, though essentially they had little in common. Segrave would make a dangerous enemy, Bruce well realised.

Scouts sent ahead reported that Castleton of Douglas, the township clustered round the fine church of St. Bride near the castle demesne, was strangely quiet, with nobody stirring—though no visible sign of alarm.

"It could mean that they have gone. Learned of our coming, and fled," Bruce commented, sounding more hopeful than he knew.

"Or moved into the castle. To hold it against us," the knight countered. "As like the one as the other."

His companion had his own reasons for thinking otherwise, but did not say so. He was the more disappointed then, when, after clattering through the seemingly deserted village—and sending pickets round the back lanes to ensure that no armed men lurked there—they came to Douglas Castle on its mound above the bends and water-meadows of the river, to find the drawbridge raised, all gates closed, and the Douglas banner streaming proudly from its keep.

"I thought as much," Sir Nicholas said grimly. "This lady requires to be taught a lesson."

"Not by hanging bairns, at least," his companion returned.

Douglas Castle, though not so large as Lochmaben, and no fortress like Berwick, was an imposing place, and because of the riverside cliff and the swampy nature of the approach, difficult to reach save by the narrow causeway which led to the drawbridge and gatehouse of the outer bailey. It was a typical stone castle of enceinte, consisting of a lofty stone keep, four-square and massive, having five storeys beneath a battlemented parapet, surrounded by twenty foot high curtain-walls to form a square, with circular flanking-towers at each corner. There were the usual lean-to subsidiary buildings within the curtain-walls, but these scarcely showed from without. Now, men could be seen pacing the parapets that surmounted curtains and towers.

With a trumpeter sounding an imperious summons, Bruce rode forward, Segrave at his side. At the gap of the deep, wide, water-filled ditch, where the drawbridge should have reached, they perforce halted. They were well within arrow-shot of the gatehouse here. The younger man raised his voice.

"I am Robert Bruce, Earl of Carrick, come in the King's name. I request that this bridge be lowered and that I be admitted to speak with whoever holds this castle," he cried.

After a little delay a voice answered from a barred gatehouse window. "This is Douglas's house, and Douglas holds it. Bruce of Carrick is known. But in what king's name does he speak?"

"There is but one king now. King Edward."

"Douglas does not recognise King Edward of England as having any authority in this realm of Scotland, save what he holds with a sword," came back the careful reply. "Does Bruce bring Edward's sword to Douglas Castle?"

The other knew a strange reluctance to admit that he did. "I bring Edward's peace," he said. "And would speak with the Lady of Douglas."

There was something like a hoot from the gatehouse. "We all know of Edward of England's peace! Death's peace is kinder! And does Bruce require half a thousand men, to speak with the Lady Douglas?"

Segrave raised his voice. "Have done," he shouted shortly. "Douglas is traitor and outlaw. Has broken custody. His house and lands are forfeit. Must be yielded to the King. Yield, then. Or suffer!"

"Ha—there speaks an honest voice, at least! Edward Plantagenet's true voice. The Lady of Douglas speaks with none such."

"Then the worse for her, fool...!"

Sir Nicholas bit off the rest of that. With a vicious hissing whine, three arrows came flying past the right ear of each horseman, close enough to fan their cheeks—and to cause each to duck involuntarily, and their beasts to rear and sidle in alarm. Such carefully-placed shots obviously bespoke expert bowmen, and could equally well have been each three inches to the left and in the eye-sockets of the trio.

Segrave, cursing explosively, wheeled his heavy mount around, and went spurring back to the host, shouting that they would hereafter do things *his* way, the trumpeter crouching low in the saddle and nowise behindhand. But Bruce, seeking to quieten his horse, held his ground at the bridgehead. He raised a gauntleted hand—and hoped that any quivering would not be seen from the gatehouse.

"That was Sir Nicholas Segrave, who captains it at Lochmaben," he called urgently. "Hear *me*. Robert Bruce."

There was a pause, short enough no doubt but seeming an eternity to the man who sat there as target for a second flight of arrows. Helmeted and armoured in chain-mail he might be, but these marksmen could wing their bolts to his unprotected face; besides, at that range, a shaft, even if it failed to pierce the mail, could drive the same bodily into a man's heart or lungs.

No arrows hissed meantime, but a woman's voice, high, thin but clear, sounded. "My lord—Eleanor de Louvain, wife to Douglas, speaks. Your father I knew. And his father before him. Edward's men both. What has the son to say to *me*, who would spit in Edward's false face?"

Bruce let his breath go in a sigh of relief—although he was unprepared for the venom in that. This woman was herself English, a widowed heiress that Douglas had carried off without Edward's permission, on the death of his first wife some years before; it appeared that he had made a good Scot of her. "I say that I wish you no ill, lady. You or yours. This house must be yielded to the King—as, by his command, must every stone castle in Scotland. But there need be no bloodshed. Your people may come forth unharmed. Go where they will."

"My people, sir? And my children? And myself?"

Bruce hesitated, as well he might. And as he did so, from behind him sounded the drumming of hooves. Turning, he saw that perhaps a score of riders had detached themselves from the host, and were cantering back towards the village, three quarters of a mile away. One glance sufficed to establish that they were all

English men-at-arms of the Lochmaben garrison. The young man had no least doubt as to their mission.

He turned back, face set. "If you yield the house, no hurt shall befall you, lady. On my knightly word," he cried.

"Why should I trust your word, when you come in Edward's name, my lord?" The high voice was less firm and certain now. "That tyrant cares naught for promises. Have you forgot that my husband was Governor of Berwick?"

"It is *my* word—not Edward's . . ." Bruce was returning, when, like the hissing of a pitful of snakes, a flight of many arrows sliced the air above him. Flinging himself low over his mount's neck, he nevertheless saw three men throw up their arms on the parapet of the gatehouse tower, and one to topple headlong and fall with a splash into the moat.

Uproar followed. Swearingly savagely, amidst angry shouts from both front and rear, the lone horseman dragged his charger's head round, and rode furiously back the two hundred yards or so to his own people.

Segrave's bowmen, dismounted and kneeling, were already fitting second arrows to their strings.

"Hold! Stop, fools!" he yelled. "I commanded no bloodshed . . ."

Segrave gestured with a scornful forward wave of his hand. The second volley of long feathered shafts sped towards the castle.

"I said *no*, man! How dare you . . . !"

"You may command these cattle-thieves and shepherds," the knight said, as Bruce came up, and threw himself down from his saddle, "But even so, only by the King's permission. These *I* command, my lord. And to better effect!"

"Better? You have ruined all, man. They will hold out against us now. Have no faith in our word. And you have soiled my name."

"Then your name is easily soiled! Have I not told you—this is war? We are not here concerned with the honour of high-born lordlings! I have my duty to do . . ."

"You call slaying during a parley duty?"

"Parley! Talk! You win no wars with talk, young man. I know my duty, if you do not." He turned away, ordering his archers to raise their aim to the parapet of the keep itself, targets having all disappeared from closer at hand.

In wrath and frustration Bruce watched—and even in his ire could not withhold his admiration for the magnificent shooting of the English bowmen. That keep's topmost parapet was more than three hundred yards away, yet straight and true the arrows flew to it, zipping between the gaps and crenellations. As he gazed, a scream came thinly to them from that lofty exposed platform. Arrows were shot back at them from the castle, to be sure, but they all fell far short. Archery had never been highly developed or favoured in Scotland. The English long bow, high as a man and shooting a yard-long arrow, made of yew, a tree unknown in Scotland, had fully double the range of the Scots short bows or arbalests. It was also infinitely more accurate. Here, only the odd spent shaft from the castle came anywhere near them.

Quickly the Douglases perceived how ineffectual was their fire. Their shooting ceased, and no more men showed themselves at parapet or loophole. Sir Nicholas called a cease-fire. Bruce left him without another word, and mounting his horse again, rode off in a rageful silence.

He made a circuit of the castle—no easy task amongst the knowes, bogland and river-channels. He noted how thinly spread even six hundred men looked, when extended round a wide perimeter. From a strategic height he surveyed the scene and its possibilities, and thereafter set about regrouping his force. Instead of trying to maintain any unbroken ring, he concentrated his mosstroopers, in parties of fifty or so, where they might best command a comprehensive view of the castle and surroundings. Night-time patrols were going to be difficult.

This took time. When he returned to the main gatehouse front, it was to find Segrave's men hacking and hammering now, erecting a crossbar supported on two uprights, out of the timbers of a nearby cowshed. The bar stretched about ten feet above the ground. Men were being sent in search of ropes.

"Segrave," Bruce announced tensely, at sight of all this, "I tell you, I will not permit the hanging of innocent hostages. Nor even the pretence at it. I have not forgotten my knightly vows, if you have!"

"Permit, my lord? Permit, you say? How think you to permit, or not to permit, what I do? I am King Edward's captain here. What are you?"

"I am the Earl of Carrick, and commander of this host."

"For so long as *I* permit it! You are a name only, man. You no more command here than you command at Lochmaben Castle. King Edward has more trusted servants than you, sir. And needs them, by God!"

"There will be no hanging, Segrave."
"I have my orders."
"From that clerk? From Benstead? I congratulate you!"
Sir Nicholas looked grim but said nothing.
"Very well. We shall see." Bruce rode away again.
Back he went, to the first of the groups of fifty mosstroopers. "Half your men to come with me," he told their leader, and proceeded on round the perimeter.
When he had made the circuit of Douglas Castle for the third time, he had some two hundred rough horsemen at his tail.
As this company rode back towards the causeway area, Bruce could see that there was now some major activity going on beside the completed gallows, with men clustered around in a close circle. Exclaiming, he dug in his spurs.
Faces turned as the newcomers pounded up—including three notably white faces in the midst of it all. Three children, two boys of eight or ten, and a girl somewhat older, were being held on the backs of three horses, their hands tied behind their backs, rough gags in their mouths. Already a rope was around the girl's neck and slung over the cross-bar above her. The same was being done for the boys. The youngsters' terrified eyes made eloquent appeal.
"Sir Nicholas Segrave—cut those children free and let them go," Bruce shouted hoarsely.
There was no response. The English men-at-arms went on with their grim work.
"You heard me, Segrave? I will not have it." Bruce drove his horse forward, into the crowd of watching men, hand on sword-hilt.
"Fool! Young swollen-headed fool!" the knight cried. "Have I not told you? These need suffer no hurt. Unless the Douglas woman is a deal less chicken-hearted than you are! If they hang, it is of her will. Leave men's work to men, if you are so nice of stomach, my lord!"
"I said set them free . . . Englishman!" Deliberately Bruce added that last word.
Segrave did not fail to grasp the significance of it. He glanced around him quickly. "*Your* way, many men will die. Many children will be fatherless. Your own people's children. And these of Douglas likewise. Remember that. My way costs a deal less! Cannot you see it, man?"
"I see shame! Shame that will not be done in my presence. Set them free."

"No."

Bruce's answer was swift, in the thin skirl of steel, as his long two-handed sword was drawn from its sheath. "You have but forty," he jerked. "I have six hundred. You will do as I say."

"You . . . you would not dare! Draw steel against the King's own men? This is rebellion! Treason!"

"Not so—since I command here. Release those bairns."

"No, I say! These men—they are not yours. They are the King's men. All of them. They have sworn allegiance to him. They will do as *I* say, his officer. Not you, fool . . . !"

"Think you so? They are Bruce's men. Bruce of Annandale. We shall see who they obey!" He swung round in his saddle. "Swords, I say!"

Like the screaming of the damned, the savage sound of two hundred blades being wrenched from their scabbards sounded high and shrill above the snarling, menacing growl of angry men.

Sir Nicholas Segrave had not survived decades of warfare by being any sort of a fool. He recognised actualities when he saw them. Narrow-eyed he glared, then shrugged. He turned to his men. "Set them down," he ordered shortly. He strode over to where his horse stood, and mounted.

"You are wise in this, at least," Bruce said evenly.

"And you are not! For this you shall pay. Dearly!" The knight gestured to his trumpeter. "Sound to horse," he commanded.

The man blew a few short blasts, and everywhere the English soldiery turned and made for their mounts.

"What do you intend?" Bruce demanded.

"I leave you. To your treason. Your folly. I go. But I shall be back, my lord. Never fear! With sufficient men to teach you and your treacherous rabble a lesson. You will learn what it costs to set at naught King Edward's authority, I promise you!"

"How may that be? When *I* command. In King Edward's name . . . ?"

Segrave's snort of contempt was converted into a shouted order to his men to follow him, as he reined round and urged his horse to a trot. The men-at-arms fell in behind him, in column, and without a backward glance at the silent ranks of the Scots, rode off south by west.

Robert Bruce stared after them, biting at his lip.

Chapter Four

His men, save for a few retained with him, back at their positions around Douglas Castle, Bruce paced the turf beside the empty gibbet, cudgelling his brains, and more than his brains. He was under no misapprehensions as to the seriousness of the predicament into which he had got himself. Segrave had been only too accurate when he declared that this would be looked upon as rebellion. Treason might be stretching it to far, but rebellion it would be named. By Edward's administration in Scotland—the Englishmen, Benstead; this Hazelrig, so-called Earl of Clydesdale; Cressingham, the Treasurer, who now was the real ruler of Scotland; Surrey, the viceroy—these would see it as the revolt of a hated and despised Scots lord against the King's authority. So it would be blazoned forth by Benstead and Segrave, and so it would be accepted. As rebellion, Edward himself would hear of it, eventually.

But long before Edward, in Flanders, heard, there would be violent reactions here in Scotland; nothing was more sure. The English would act swiftly; they always did, instead of arguing interminably with each other as was the Scots way. Benstead himself could not find many more men for Segrave than the rest of the Lochmaben garrison, but he would apply to Lanark for them, where the governance of this south-west corner of Scotland was centred. Lanark was no more than ten miles north of Douglas, as the crow flew—and it was strange that Hazelrig himself had not set about the reduction of its castle instead of leaving it to Bruce, from Lochmaben. Except that that had been King Edward's specific instructions. Segrave might even go direct to Lanark from here. Although he was more likely to report to Benstead first, and pick up the rest of his garrison. In two days, or three, then, there would be an English force here at Douglasdale, a heavily-armed, veteran host against which his Annandale men, however gallant, would be like chaff in the wind.

What to do? If he could quickly reduce this castle, of course, and have it occupied and its chatelaine prisoner before such punitive force arrived, he might redeem his reputation with Edward's men. That was possible, but by no means certain. Segrave and Benstead would consider themselves insulted—and the insulted Englishman was not readily appeased. They would insist on humbling him, demand reparation, reprisals—and none in Scotland in the year 1297 had any doubts as to the style of English reprisals. Edward's example at Berwick was to be a model as well as a warning. Undoubtedly an angry punitive force would do much more than hang two or three children. His gesture here, then, would be nullified, wasted, thrown away. And his reputation, in another sense, with it.

What alternative was there, then? He could bolt. Run. Gather his men and take themselves off, into the empty hills, before the English arrived. Scarcely a noble course, but perhaps wise. Or was it? He would have become a fugitive. For what? Outside Edward's peace, and with nothing to buy himself back into it. Moreover, would these men of his be prepared to turn fugitive with him? Abandon their homes, holdings, womenfolk, to the English ire? For nothing.

But, suppose he could take the Lady of Douglas with him? Persuade the castle to yield, and instead of waiting for the English, take her and her family with him. Into the hills. The great Forest of Ettrick was less than a score of miles to the east. No English would follow them there. Then he would have something to bargain with. Burn the castle and capture its lady—had not these been his orders? If he had achieved them, could Edward's men claim he was in rebellion? The Lady Douglas would make a valuable hostage for him; something to chaffer with. Again less than knightly perhaps—but could he afford knightly sentiments in this pass?

There was always a last resort, of course. He could throw in his lot with the true rebels. With the High Steward and the Bishop of Galloway and their like. Make for Galloway. Accept the man Segrave's charge of revolt, and become a rebel indeed. There were times without number, these last grim months, when he had been brought to the contemplation of it, had toyed with the notion. As would any man of spirit deliberately and consistently humiliated. Even that Elizabeth de Burgh had all but suggested it. What was it she said? That he was loyal to Edward but should be loyal to Scotland. And he had asked her what Scotland was? And rightly so. But . . . these English could go too far. Yet, outright rebellion? It would mean war to the knife, for him. With Edward. The King would never forgive him. And Edward, unforgiving, was a dire thought. It would mean the life of an outlaw, hunted day and night. The forfeiture of all the great Bruce lands. Not only in Scotland but in England. And what hope had these rebels, in fact? Against the power and might of England and the fury of the Plantagenet?

So Robert Bruce paced and harried his wits and his heart and his conscience—and came to no conclusion. Save only this, that it was growing towards dusk and something must be decided before darkness fell—for it would be difficult indeed to ensure that there was no break-out from the castle under cover of night. If his quarry were to steal away in the dark, he would be left without even a bargaining-counter, however poor.

His mind made up thus far at least, Bruce stripped off his handsome heraldic surcoat of linen, and tying it to a lancepoint, like a banner, gave it to one of his men to carry by his side. Hoping this would serve as a flag of truce, he and an extremely doubtful companion paced slowly, on foot, towards the castle ditch once more.

It made an unpleasant walk. But no arrows came at them, no reaction of any sort was evident, no challenging shout was raised.

At the drawbridge-end, Bruce halted and lifted up his voice. "Hear me. Hear me, I say. The Earl of Carrick would speak again with the Lady of Douglas."

He was answered at once. "You are a bold man, Lord of Carrick. Whatever else! Wait you. I send for my lady."

Bruce nodded and waited, seeking to collect his thoughts.

It was some time before the woman's high voice sounded, from a small gatehouse window. "I am here, my Lord Robert. What kindness would your King Edward do me now?"

The young man shrugged. "I speak not for Edward Plantagenet now, lady. But for myself," he said. "I regret what was done. Before. The shooting of arrows. While we talked. It was against my commands. Segrave's Englishry . . ."

"No doubt, sir. It was ill done. But what we might have looked for, from Edward's men. As what they sought to do later. With the children."

"You saw?"

"We saw, yes. They are gone?"

"Aye, gone."

"Your Segrave would have slain those children? Hanged them, before our eyes!"

'I do not know. In the end. Perhaps he would not. Only the threat. To cozen you. I do not know."

"But *I* know. His kind have done the like before. Many times.

If I had still refused him, he would have hanged them. And you? You would not have it?"

"No. I would not. Could not."

"I fear you are too tenderhearted to be Edward's man, my lord."

"Sir Nicholas Segrave, I mind, said the same!" Bruce gave back. This shouting was difficult. "I . . . I would speak with you, lady. Not thus. But decently. As becomes our quality."

"I am content to judge your quality from here, my lord! What have you to say?"

Bruce sighed. "Just this. Now that the English are gone, you would do well to open to me. You may trust me, Bruce. You have naught to fear from me."

"Then, my lord, why sit you round Douglas Castle? Go back whence you came. If I have naught to fear from you, I will do very well here!"

"No. Do you not see?" Exasperated, finding this long-range discussion trying in the extreme, he shook his head. "The English will be back. They *must* come back. It is Edward's command. They will come in strength. They will have you. And in ill mood. You must see it? Yield your house to me, now, and I will make a show of spoiling it. Then I will take you away. And your children. Before they come . . ."

"Where? Take me where, my lord?" Clearly he was interrupted.

"To a safe place . . ." There was another interruption, more shouting, but from behind him this time. And Bruce was almost thankful for it, at his wits' end as he was for what he might say to convince and reassure the woman. Some of his men were waving to him, urgently, and pointing. Beside them was a helmeted and leather-jerkined newcomer, obviously an English man-at-arms, and a steaming horse.

"A messenger, lord," the cry came. "Frae Lochmaben. Wi' tidings. Instant tidings, he says . . ."

Bruce hesitated, concerned with how this would look from the castle. Then he called back "Send him to me." Towards the gatehouse he added, "Your pardon, lady."

The courier came forward, far from eagerly, escorted by none. He was clearly as tired as he was doubtful.

"Well, man? You are from Sir Nicholas Segrave? What is your message?"

"Not so, lord. It is Sir Nicholas that I seek. First. To him I was sent. By Master Benstead . . ."

"Eh? Then . . . then you have not seen him? Segrave? Met with him?" Bruce stared. "How came you here?"

"By a great weariness of hills, lord. By Moffat town, see you. And Abington. And Roberton Water." This was a sing-song voiced Welshman, not English, and of some intelligence.

"So! You missed them, then. They would go back as we came—by Lowther. Sir Nicholas returns to Lochmaben. For . . . for more men."

"And is like to need them! But will not find them there, lord. Master Benstead's tidings are of rebellion. War!"

"You mean this Galloway revolt?"

'That, and a deal more. They have broken out of Galloway and marched north, these rebels. They are none so far off, look you—nearing Ayr . . ."

"Ayr, you say?" That was making north, with a vengeance! Nearly fifty miles north of the Galloway border. No more than thirty miles west of this Douglas, indeed. "Then none are opposing them?"

"So it looks, lord. All the country rises to join them. But that is not the worst. The Lord Earl of Clydesdale is dead. Slain."

"Hazelrig? Dead? You mean, in battle? He sought to halt them . . .?"

"No, lord. Not these. Another. He was murdered. Slain in his own town of Lanark. By one Wallace. Some brigand, leading broken men, outlaws. Lanark is now in their hands."

"By the Rude! Lanark fallen? Then these are no broken men! Think you such could take the Sheriff's town of Lanark, and Hazelrig's castle? Stuffed full with Edward's soldiery . . . !"

"Scarce that, lord. It was cunningly, shrewdly done. Most of the Sheriff's force had been sent towards Ayr. To stem the rebels from Galloway. This man Wallace—they say he is the son of some small Renfrew knight, a vassal of the Steward's—struck by night. He is not as the other rebels, led by lords and bishops. A man of no account, a brigand hiding in the hills and forests. By some trick he gained entry to Lanark Castle, and slew the Earl. They say in vengeance for his wife's death. Then turned on the town. The townsfolk aided him. By daylight Lanark was his."

"But, man—this is scarce believable! What were Hazelrig's captains doing? It is the garrison town of the South-West."

"One, Sir Robert Thorn, hangs from the castle's keep, in place of King Edward's banner, they say! The other it was came to Lochmaben with these tidings, looking for men. Sir Hugh le

Despenser. Wounded. Finding no men there, he rode on for Dumfries."

'So-o-o! The South-West is aflame? Edward's iron grip prised loose!"

"Meantime, Lord—meantime, only! But only the South-West. Master Benstead says that there are revolts in the North also. In Ross, wherever that may be. And Argyll, or some such place. But these are afar off. Here is the danger. These sheriffdoms of Lanark, Ayr, Carrick and Galloway—the command of these is vital to the King, Master Benstead says."

"Aye. No doubt he is right. And who *does* command here now, with Hazelrig dead? And Despenser wounded and gone? Who commands in Edward's name, now?"

The courier raised an eloquent hand. "Saving your lordship's presence," he said, diffidently, "*you* do! That was what I was to tell Sir Nicholas, look you. That now he must act in the name of the Earl of Carrick. Meantime. There is none other of earl's rank. My lord Earl of Surrey is at York, they say. Until he appoints other, you command, lord. With . . . with the advice and direction of Master Benstead and Sir Nicholas Segrave, to be sure. I was to say that, mind you . . ."

Robert Bruce's bark of laughter drowned the rest. "*I* command? God save us—*I*! The Earl of Carrick commands now, for King Edward, in the South-West! Here's a jest, by all that's holy!"

"In name, lord. Under direction. Master Benstead was strong on that. You are to gain this castle of Douglas with all speed, and then march for Lanark. Guided by Sir Nicholas. Seek to join with the Lanark force that went to Ayr, to hold the rebels. Threaten Lanark together, but await further orders from Master Benstead . . ."

"*Orders?* To Edward's commander?"

The Welshman coughed. "Instructions, lord. Guidance. Counsel—call it what you will. I am a rough man, lord. No doubt I word it ill. But I was sent, in truth, to Sir Nicholas. He it was was to speak with you . . ."

"You speak full clearly, my friend! And to the point. Never fear. And I thank you for it. Is . . . is that all?"

'Yes, lord. Have I your permission to go? I must still seek Sir Nicholas."

"He will be back at Lochmaben before you are. A shorter road than you came. But go if you will. Tell Master Benstead that I have his message. And his . . . guidance! Now, I must speak with this woman . . .'

As the courier went back towards the others. Bruce, his head in a whirl, faced the gatehouse. Somehow, he must have time to think. All was now changed. In the light of it all, so much called for decision. Instant decision. He must have a little time . . .

"Lady," he called. "My regrets that I have kept you waiting. I have important tidings. Of the utmost importance. To us all. You likewise. But not such as I may shout out to all the world! I must speak with you. Privily. It is essential."

"Very well, my lord," she answered. "Have I your word, as an earl of Scotland, that you will *only* speak? Will make no move to take or harm me?"

"You have. On my oath."

"Then the drawbridge will be lowered. Part-lowered. So that I may walk out on it. None of your people to come near, my lord. Only you. It is understood? And you must wait a little."

He nodded. The longer he might wait, the better. Had ever a man so much to decide in so short a time? Here was a crossroads in his life. Which road he took now might determine all his future.

Sending back his impromptu standard-bearer, Robert Bruce commenced to pace up and down the bank of the moat.

He scarcely heard, presently, the clanking of the portcullis chains or the creaking of the timbering as the massive drawbridge began to come down. His mind, his judgement, his emotions, his whole character and personality, were involved in a turmoil of debate, of contradiction, of conjecture, as never before. And yet, somehow, behind it all, the decision was already made.

With the bridge lowered to within some ten feet of its base, so that it formed only a moderate incline, armed men appeared from the gatehouse arch. And out from among them walked two persons—a woman and a boy.

The Lady of Douglas was younger than Bruce had expected; in her early thirties probably, slightly built but most evidently pregnant, not handsome but not ill favoured, with a proud and confident look. The boy was no more than twelve years old, well-built, sturdy, dark, almost swarthy indeed. He held the woman's hand, and held his head high as they paced out on the echoing timbers.

They came to the lip of the bridge, and so stood, looking down at Bruce. "Well, my lord—what have you to say?" Lady Douglas asked. And, as an afterthought, "This is James Douglas, my husband's heir."

"My sorrow, lady, that we should meet in such case." Bruce was frowning blackly, not at her or the boy but in concentration—however it might seem to them. "Do you know where Sir William Douglas is?"

"If I did, think you I would tell you, sir?"

"I think he may be none so far away. If I agreed to take you to him, would you come with me, madam?"

"Take me . . .? To him?" She stared down at him. "Do you think to mock me now, young man . . .?"

"Not so. Why should I mock you? I do not know for sure, but I think that Sir William may be with the other rebels. Who were in Galloway. His former good-brother, James the Steward, and the Bishop of Galloway."

"Rebels, sir? These are no rebels. How may they be rebels, who rise, in their own land and in the name of their own king, against a foreign tyrant?"

"Aye—it may be so. At any rate, these, I have just learned, are now near to Ayr. Thirty miles, no more. Will you come with me to Ayr, lady?"

"With you? *You?* To Ayr? But . . . but . . ."

"My lord," the boy said tensely but strongly. "if you jest with us now, you are no true knight! This, this lady is in no state for that. For any true knight to make fool of. Did King Edward of England send you to her for that?"

It was bravely said. This boy could not be the Lady Eleanor's son. He must be the child of the first marriage. He was, therefore, nephew of James the Steward—named after him, no doubt.

Bruce inclined his head. "King Edward sent me here to take this lady, and you, to his officers," he told the boy carefully. "But now, I find, *I* am his chiefest officer in these parts! And I have come to think that it might be best to take you to Ayr."

"Why?" the woman demanded. "Or do you seek to trick us? Use us as hostages? Before my husband . . . !"

"No. Give you into your husband's keeping, rather."

"I do not understand. You are Edward's man. My husband is Edward's enemy. What mean you . . .?"

"I am my own man, lady—not Edward's. Bruce supported Edward against the usurper Baliol, yes. But Baliol is no longer here. Nor indeed is Edward! Both across the sea. And Bruce is no puppet to be jerked this way and that . . ."

"You mean, my lord, that you change sides?"

He frowned. "Say that I must choose, in this pass, to do what is best. Wisest. For all. The South-West is aflame, it seems. And Ross and Argyll too, they say. How much else, God knows. Hazelrig is dead, at Lanark. All is changed. From when I was sent to take you . . ."

"Then why not go away, sir? Leave us in peace?" the young James Douglas broke in.

"You would not long thank me for that! Segrave and more English will be back, you may be sure. Douglas Castle would have but a brief respite. And then you would be in more unhappy state. You saw the style of Segrave!"

"So you would go to my husband, and these others, at Ayr? Taking us as, as . . . as sureties? Not hostages but tokens? Tokens, my lord. That they may accept you as honest!" Eleanor Douglas was considering him shrewdly. "I think that I perceive it. They are more like to trust you, if you do not come empty-handed! Bruce, who was Edward's man!"

"You are less than gracious, madam." That was stiff.

"Perhaps." There was a few seconds' pause. She shook her head, in a welter of indecision. "Can *I* trust you, then?"

"Would you rather that I handed you to the English? Or left you to withstand their fury here?"

She sighed. "No. Since I cannot long hold this house against a host. I will come with you. Your reasons for taking me to my husband may be ignoble, sir—but it may best serve my need meantime. I will come with you."

Bruce had flushed a little and knew it, but hoped that it might not be apparent in the half-light. "I do not acclaim your niceness of feeling, madam," he said shortly. "But at least your choice is wise. Will you go, then, and make ready? To ride. Send your folk away, to their own places. Disperse them. That there be no bloodshed when the English come. They may ill-use your house somewhat—but that is small price to pay for lives and freedom. Do not delay, for we ride as soon as we may."

"Ride? Tonight? It is near dark . . . !"

"Yes, tonight. I wish to have you away from here, out of Douglasdale and into my own country of Carrick, by daylight. To delay here now would be folly. And in your state we may not ride overfast." He glanced at her swollen belly. "So, haste you, lady."

She shrugged. "Very well. If so it must be. Come, Jamie . . ."

Bruce turned, blank-faced, and strode back in the gloaming light to his waiting men. Curtly, there, he issued orders that all his host was to be brought back forthwith, abandoning the positions around the castle. All were to assemble.

When his six hundred were gathered before him in the gloom, Bruce had a horn blown for silence, and addressed them.

"My friends," he said, "hear me. This realm is in sore straits, as you all know well. Men know not which way to turn. There has been revolt against the English who lord it here. Lanark is fallen. The High Steward, and a host, is at Ayr. I . . . I have decided to join them."

In the pause there was an absolute silence save for the wary calling of curlews bewailing the night.

"It is that, or marching against Lanark, to seek to recapture it. For the English. Which do you prefer?"

There was a muttering, quickly stilled.

"I think King Edward's cause may no longer be Bruce's cause! And I would not do battle against those who revolt. So I go to Ayr. Who comes with me?"

Again the murmuring arose, this time to continue, to grow loud and prolonged, as men discussed and argued.

After a while, Bruce had the horn blown again. "I could command that you come with me," he said. "But you are my father's vassals. Not my own. He is Lord of Annandale, not I. And my father is King Edward's Governor of Carlisle. If you join me in this, who knows, you may suffer for it. Your homes, your wives and bairns. So I give you choice. It is *my* decision. You make yours."

There was more talk, some of it heated. One voice rose above others, presently.

"Lord—do we fight for this Edward? Or against him? We do not know rightly. You had us to swear an oath. To Edward. Did you no'?"

Bruce drew a deep breath. "An oath, yes. But a commanded oath. An oath given under duress. It is not binding, as is a true oath. So teaches Holy Church. It may be annulled. I, similarly, swore allegiance to Edward. Under duress. But I did not swear to make war against my own people. Not to slay my own folk. No man, I say, holds his own flesh and blood in hatred. I am Earl of Carrick. My own folk of Carrick live yonder." He pointed to the west. "The English would have me lead you, to fight. For them. Against Scots, I cannot, will not, do it. I must join my own people of Carrick. And the nation into which I was born."

He had stopped, at his own last words. He had not known that he was going to say these things. They had come out of him of their own volition, to his surprise. He stood, biting his lip.

Some of his ranked listeners cheered. Some murmured. More stood silent.

Bruce shook his head. "A man must choose his own course," he said slowly, as though to himself. "Aye, a man must choose. Choose *you*, then. You are free to do so. My father's men, not mine. Those who would may turn now. Ride back to Annandale. To their homes. Those who would come with me to Carrick, I welcome. Let each man choose freely." He turned abruptly, and walked away from them.

It was almost an hour later, and quite dark, before the castle drawbridge clanked down again, and, lit by pitch-pine torches, a small party came riding out. Bruce rode to meet them, Lady Douglas, wrapped in a voluminous travelling-cloak, had another child with her now, riding pillion behind young James, a little boy of four or five—Hugh Douglas, her own son. There were also a couple of tiring-women and a few armed servitors.

The Annandale host was now drawn up in two companies—and one was many times larger than the other. Of something under six hundred, only about seventy had elected to go with Bruce into this doubtful adventure—and these were mainly young men, unattached, lacking responsibilities. The rest were for home, discretion and the daily round. Their lord's son was the last to blame them.

There was no further discussion or farewells. Without ceremony, the two groups parted company, the smaller trotting off south by west up the Douglas Water, the larger turning away eastwards towards the Castleton and the unseen welter of hills beyond.

Behind them, other folk were slipping out of Douglas Castle also now, quietly, singly and in little groups, and disappearing into the night.

. . .

Picking their careful way by bridle-paths and cattle-tracks, Bruce's party followed the Douglas Water hour after hour through the spring night, slowly making height as the river shrank and lifted towards its genesis on the lofty flank of mighty Cairntable, where ran the Ayrshire border amongst the long heather hills.

Long before Douglas Water could lead them to its remote birthplace, they had struck off almost due westwards by a drove-road over the high, bleak watershed moorlands where the head-streams of the River Ayr were mothered, and the wastes of Airds Moss stretched in peat-hag and scrub. By dawn they were slanting down out of the wild uplands between Sorn and Ochiltree, almost twenty weary miles behind them and only a dozen to go to the town of Ayr, and the sea.

Not that it was Ayr, in fact, for which Bruce was making. He was on the edge, now, of his own ancient earldom of Carrick, comprising the nine parishes of South Ayrshire, with Turnberry Castle, sixteen miles south of Ayr town, its principal seat—and his own birthplace. Turnberry was not for him meantime, however, for its castle had been garrisoned by the English, like Lochmaben, since Comyn had been driven out of it. But Maybole, the largest burgh of Carrick, lay somewhat nearer, and might well supply him with sufficient men to serve his purpose. The English force from Lanark were unlikely to have gone as far south as Maybole.

Tired and travel-worn, they came to the little town in its enclosed green valley, in the early forenoon—to find it in a bustle and stir of excitement. The High Steward's host had passed through it, going north, two days before, and had demanded the adherence of a contingent of the town's menfolk, for the revolt. These had been assembling, with varying degrees of enthusiasm, and were now almost ready to march. The Steward and the Bishop were not at Ayr, but a few miles further north of it, at Irvine. They had passed Ayr by, for there the English contingent from Lanark, said to number about five hundred, had installed themselves; with the place's own garrison, they were considered too strong to assault meantime.

Bruce was well enough pleased with this situation. He had intended to raise a token force, since these were his own vassals, to accompany him to the rebel base. Now they were already assembled for him. As Earl of Carrick, he ordered more to be mustered and to come on later. After rest and refreshment, with an augmented company of about three hundred, he and the

Douglases set out once more, northwards, towards Irvine. The Lady Eleanor was bearing up notably well, even if she remained less than friendly.

They made a wide half-circuit round Ayr, fording Doon and Ayr's own river about three miles inland from the sea. Thereafter, with only occasional glimpses of the town, on their left, they rode through the rolling and populous territory of Kyle until, in late afternoon, they saw the huddle of roofs that was Irvine's royal burgh, dominated by its monastery and Seagate Castle, at the blue sea's edge, with the smoke of an army's cooking-fires rising like a screen around it. Bruce sent forward three emissaries, one of them a magistrate of Maybole brought along for this purpose, to make known his approach and identity.

Presently, while still perhaps half a mile from the town, a fairly large mounted party could be seen coming out towards them. Well out of bowshot-range this company halted, and sent forward two horsemen, one of knightly appearance.

These came cantering up, and Bruce saw that the knight was the same Sir Richard Lundin who had stood before him in the sorry queue to sign the Ragman's Roll at Berwick those months ago. He raised hand in salutation.

"My lord—here is a strange meeting," Lundin called. "I greet you. But my Lord James, the Steward, commands that you leave your company here and come on alone to speak with him."

"As Earl of Carrick, I obey no commands, here in Ayrshire, from the Steward or other, Sir Richard," Bruce returned, but not harshly. "I will, however, come with you of my own goodwill. And gladly. Go you and tell the Lord James so."

Nodding, the knight turned and cantered back whence he had come.

Bruce told his people to wait where they were. But the Lady of Douglas declared that she would come with him.

"Not so, madam," he returned. "You remain here with the others, if you please. Until we see what my reception is."

"So! It is as I thought! You use me as a hostage, sir. You bargain with me. To your shame!"

"Say that I look well to your safety, lady. Until I learn what is to befall. But I will take the lad James. To greet his uncle."

So the young man and the dark boy rode on alone towards the waiting party.

They were within a hundred yards or so when, with a cry, a big burly man, in rusted but once handsome armour, burst out from the Irvine group and came spurring towards them. "Jamie!" he shouted, as he came, "Jamie!"

"Father!" The boy went plunging to meet him.

Bruce watched their reunion, a touching scene, the more unexpected in that Sir William, Lord of Douglas, was known to be a fierce, temperamental and wayward character, as unpredictable as he was ungovernable. Bruce had not met the man but his reputation was known to all. Now he was embracing his son like any more gentle father.

Others rode forward now, foremost amongst them a tall, elderly, cadaverous man, armoured all in black without the usual colourful heraldic surcoat. Tight-lipped, rattrap-jawed, thoughtful of mien, his sour and gloomy features were redeemed by great soulful brown eyes, wildly improbable in such a face—James Stewart, fifth High Steward of Scotland. Bruce knew him, of course; he had been one of the Bruce supporters in his grandfather's claim to the throne.

"My lord of Carrick," this apparition announced in a lisping voice—for his tongue was loose and on the large side for his tight mouth, and he dribbled somewhat, "I had not looked to see *you* here. Do we greet you as friend, or foe? What is your purpose here?"

"The same as is yours, my lord Steward, I would say," Bruce replied. "To help raise the banner of freedom."

"*You* say that? Edward's man!"

"My own man, sir."

"And your father's son!"

"My father will choose for himself. *I* have chosen to come here. Would you have had me choose otherwise?"

"No-o-o." The older man rode closer. "You change sides, then?"

"Sides, my lord? Say that I do not take arms against my own flesh and blood. While that was not required of me, I preferred Edward's train to the man Baliol's. As, I think, did you! Today, all is changed. The sides, not I."

Doubtfully the other was considering that when Douglas came thrusting from his son's side, voice raised.

"My wife, Bruce?" he cried. "You hold her? You dare to lay hands on Douglas's wife! Meddle with me and mine . . . !"

"I brought the Lady of Douglas to you, my lord. For her well-being and safety. She awaits you, there. Unharmed. As is your son . . ."

"Aye, Father," the boy called eagerly. "He is good. The Lord Robert has treated us kindly. Saved us from the English . . ."

Without a word, Sir William wheeled his horse around and set off into a gallop towards the Maybole contingent. After a moment's uncertainty, the boy went hot-foot after him.

The Steward looked from them back to Bruce. "You surprise me, my lord. But the support of Bruce is welcome—so be it is true, sure, honest. Those are men you have brought to our cause?"

"Some seventy from Annandale, two hundred from Maybole. More are to come."

"And we can do with all such. At Ayr—did you have sight of the English?"

"I kept my distance. Saw nothing stirring."

"Aye. Well, come you. We shall go see Wishart, my lord Bishop. Like myself, he stood your grandsire's friend. When Edward Plantagenet chose the wrong king for Scotland . . ."

Chapter Five

That night, in the hall of Eglinton's Seagate Castle at Irvine, Bruce sat at ease, as he had not done for many a day. With him, at the long table, lounged a goodly company—better than he had known or anticipated. As well as the deceptively gentle-seeming and almost diffident Robert Wishart, Bishop of Glasgow, the Steward, and Douglas, were the Steward's brother, Sir John Stewart of Bonkill; Sir Alexander Lindsay, Lord of Crawford; Andrew Moray, Lord of Bothwell, heir of the great de Moravia family of the North; Sir John the Graham, of Dundaff; Sir Robert Boyd of Cunninghame; Thomas Dalton, Bishop of Galloway; and Sir Richard Lundin, as well as other knights and barons of less renown. This revolt, it seemed, was no flicker of a candle-end. The new recruit was comforted, the more so as, after an initial hesitation, almost all had accepted him warmly enough. As the only earl present, of course, though the youngest save for the Graham, he outranked all.

The discussion of future strategy inevitably dominated the evening's talk. Bishop Wishart was for moving on Glasgow, from which bishop's burgh he could assure them of much support; the Steward, whose lands of Renfrew and Bute were in that direction, inclining to agree. Moray of Bothwell, however, declared that this would be a waste of time and strength, at this stage. They should make for the North. All Scotland north of Forth and Clyde could be theirs, with but little effort. That was where the English were weakest. His own uncle had risen, in Ross and Aberdeenshire. And the Comyns, the most powerful house in all Scotland, were there—and hated Edward. They must link up. Graham, whose lands were in Perthshire, supported him; but Douglas declared that they must hold the West March of the Border, above all, and so prevent Edward reinforcing in the west. Then attack across country to Berwick itself, the headquarters of the English dominance. Cut that trunk, and the branches would wither away.

Back and forth went the argument. With the two senior leaders advocating Glasgow, of course, there was most weight in that direction; but on the other hand, Sir William Douglas was the most experienced soldier present, and his views, forcefully given, carried conviction—at least to Bruce, though he could not like the man. Moray's scheme won least backing. It seemed to Bruce a longer-term project—and any talk of linking with his family's enemies, the Comyns, raised his hackles.

He had listened, hitherto, silent save for a brief question or two. Now, he spoke. "You each near convince me that all are right, all best, my lords," he said, with what he hoped would sound like diffidence. "I am young, and little experienced in war. But I would think that our first concern is not Glasgow or the North. Even the Border, though that should take precedence, I think. It is here, on our own doorstep. Ayr. Here we sit, with an English garrison but a dozen miles away. Should we not deal with these, before all else?"

It was Wishart, in his mildly hesitant voice, who answered that. "We have not failed to consider this, and the like questions, my son. But we have decided that the taking of strong castles is not our first task. We must seek to contain such as come in our way, yes. But to use up our strength and precious time on the slow business of besieging such holds would be unwise. We could waste all our forces, sitting outside a few such castles."

"Aye, my lord Bishop." Having just come from sitting outside Douglas castle, Bruce scarcely required this to be pointed out. "But Ayr is no great fortress. Its old castle was small—one of my mother's father's houses. The English have built a new castle there, I am told. But it is not yet finished and not large. The garrison can be no more than a couple of score. The five hundred men they say are at Ayr are the force from Lanark. Hazelrig's men. They cannot all be cooped up in the castle."

"They built a great barn. A barracks," their host, de Eglinton, told them. "To house the men while the new castle was building. And to hold the Sheriff's stores. The Lanark men lodge in this."

"Is the castle finished?"

"Yes, this month past."

"Nevertheless, they will not crowd five hundred men into it, I wager."

"You know not what you say, Bruce." That was Douglas, harshly. "They do not have to be *in* the castle to defy us, hold us off. Under its walls and within its baileys, five hundred men could laugh at a great army. If it lacks siegery engines. Their archers, close packed along the castle walls, could keep us at a distance—their damned English archers! If *you* do not know them, I do! With longbows on their parapet-walls, we could not get near them."

"By night . . .?"

"By night, man! Think you these English are fools?" Douglas, who gloried in being no respecter of persons, undoubtedly had his reservations about the service Bruce had done him. "They will have beacons blazing on every tower and wallhead. Turning night into day. Had you fought English veterans, you would know better than to talk such havers!"

Frowning darkly, Bruce clenched his fists. "The man Wallace, whoever he is, would seem to think differently from you, sir!" he gave back warmly. "Or he would not have won Lanark!"

At mention of the name, silence fell on that room, sudden, noticeable. Bruce looked round at all the different faces and saw reserve, stiffness, now masking them all.

After a pause, it was the Bishop who spoke. "Your spirit, my lord of Carrick, is praiseworthy. We all welcome it, I am sure. But we must be guided by the voices of experience. Fervour is not sufficient. My lord of Douglas is right. We must not squander our resources. These English at Ayr, though too many to assail, under the protection of their castle, are not of numbers large enough to menace our rear. We shall leave them."

"Aye, by God—but I am right in the other also!" Douglas cried, banging the table with his fist. "That we should turn south. To the Border. Leave your Glasgow and north of Forth. They will wait. Make the West March secure, and then turn on Berwick, I say. That is where we may hit the English where it hurts them most . . ."

"My lord of Douglas has large lands in the West Borders!" Moray interrupted tersely.

"What of it, man? From those lands we shall win many men."

"Sir William would avenge his defeat at Berwick, I swear!" the Graham put in. "But we have more to do than restore his honour! We have all Scotland to win."

"You know not what you say, sir . . . !"

Still they argued, loudly, acrimoniously, with the Bishop and the Steward seeking to calm, soothe and guide. Here were divided counsels, with a vengeance.

Douglas was still holding forth, seeking to carry the day by main force, when the door was thrown open and three newcomers entered. And, strangely, even Douglas's forceful eloquence died on his lips.

Perhaps it was not so strange, for the visitors presented no ordinary sight; or, at least, one of them did not. Quite the largest man that Bruce had ever set eyes upon stood there, a young giant of nearer seven than six feet, of a width of shoulder and length of arm that would have been gross deformity in anyone less tall. Bareheaded, with a wealth of curling auburn hair and a bushy beard, this extraordinary individual had a smiling open face, high complexion and intensely bright blue eyes. He wore a sort of long tunic of rusty and battered ring-mail, with boiled leather guards bound on both arms and legs, making these enormous limbs look even larger. A huge two-handed sword, quite the mightiest weapon Bruce had ever seen, was sheathed down his back so that its great hilt stuck up behind the man's head. He was probably four or five years older than Bruce himself—certainly under thirty. His companions scarcely merited a glance in comparison. One was a ragged priest, half in armour; the other little more than a youth, though armed to the teeth.

"I greet you all, my lords and gentles," the giant said, deep voiced but genial. "It is a fine night. To be up and doing!"

Sir John the Graham alone of the company got to his feet and strode to welcome the newcomers. Douglas raised his voice.

"Who . . . who, a God's name is this?"

"Wallace. Wallace of Elderslie," somebody told him.

Exclamation, comment, remark rose from the company as Wallace clasped the Graham to him affectionately—and beside him that well-built young knight looked a stunted stripling. Bruce turned to his nearest neighbour, the Lord of Crawford, though his eyes remained fixed on the newcomer.

"This man? This Wallace. Who is he?" he asked.

"You do not know, my lord? You have not heard of the Wallace?" Lindsay said, surprised. "When all Scotland rings with his deeds." He corrected himself. "All Scotland of the baser sort, that is!"

"I have heard of Wallace of Riccarton. A small knight, nearby here somewhere. Vassal of my grandsire."

"This is nephew to him. His father, Sir Malcolm, younger brother to Riccarton, got Elderslie, at Renfrew. A mean enough place, of the Steward's. This is the second son. His brother will laird it there now, since their father was slain by the English at Loudoun Hill."

"Ha—slain? And did I not hear that this man's wife was slain, also? At Lanark. For which he slew Hazelrig?"

"Aye. So you are not entirely ignorant of the Wallace, then, my lord!"

"I heard his name only yesterday. For the first time. As an outlaw, a brigand."

"Aye, that is the style of him. A man of no breeding. Of the old native stock. Little better than the Irish." De Lindsay, of good Norman blood, coughed a little, recollecting that Bruce's own mother, and his Carrick earldom, were of the same Celtic origin, however respectable was his father's line. "He impudently belabours the English. They say that he has slain a round hundred of them himself, with that ox-shaft of a sword!"

"He is a skilled warrior, then? A champion?"

"Skilled no! He fights, they say, like a brute-beast. Without regard to the knightly code."

"But you say he is the son and nephew of knights . . .?"

The object of this dialogue had stalked across the hall, to bow briefly in front of the Steward, whose vassal he was. Now he interrupted all talk with his deep rumbling voice.

"My friends, I am new come from the Forest. From Ettrick. With news. From the East March. From Berwick. The English are on the move. Surrey, they tell me, has dispatched an army north, from Newcastle. A great army. Forty thousand foot, no less. Though bare a thousand horse. Under command of Surrey's grandson, Henry Percy. To deal with your rising, my lords."

"Forty thousand . . .!" Bishop Wishart could not keep the quaver out of his voice.

Men stared at each other, appalled.

"Aye. So it is time to be up and doing, is it not, my friends? Not sitting here, at table!" Wallace laughed as he said it, however, and reached out a huge hand to grasp and tear off a foreleg of mutton from a roasted carcase on the table. He bit into it, there and then, standing there.

"Forty thousand foot will move but slowly," Douglas declared heavily. "Ten miles a day, no more. No need to spoil our dinner!"

"Sir Robert de Clifford has three thousand at Berwick. Half cavalry. They will be on their way now. In advance of the greater host."

"You are well-informed, fellow!"

"I make it my business to be, my lord. Since my life could depend on it. Captured, lords are ransomed. *I* would hang!"

"That is true, at least!"

"Certainly these tidings force us to a swift decision," the Steward intervened. "And since this great host comes from the south, it would be folly, with our small numbers, to go meet it. We must move north, then. Seek to raise more men in the North."

"I shall rest happier behind the walls of Glasgow town . . ."

"Rest, my lord Bishop?" Wallace took him up, chuckling. "Rest, I swear, is no word for use this night. With much to do."

"Tonight, man? You would have us go tonight? It is not possible. Such haste would be unseemly. Besides, most of the men will be asleep . . ."

"So, I think, may be the English."

"English? What English? What mean you?"

"The English in Ayr, my lord. But a few miles away. We must smite them. Before it is too late."

"Attack Ayr? Tonight?"

"What folly is this?"

"Is the man mad?"

Everywhere voices were raised in protest.

"That is why I came to Irvine, my friends," the big man asserted, when he could make himself heard. "To take Ayr."

"The more fool you, then!" Douglas cried. "Away with you, and take it, then! If you can. Me, I shall finish my dinner. Douglas does not skulk by night, like some thief or cutpurse!"

"Aye—enough of this. Have done with such talk."

"You will not take a strong castle by night, man." That was Lindsay speaking. "Think you its walls will be unmanned, its bridge down, its gates open? These English are not as they were at Lanark—unawares. These know we are here, and will be on their guard. You will not take another castle by surprise."

"No? That is my lord of Crawford, is it not? Then hear this, Sir Alexander. Last night, from Ettrick, I came by Tweedsmuir and over into upper Clydesdale. By Crawford, indeed. And took your Tower Lindsay, in the by-going! Around midnight. Thirty Englishmen now hang from its parapets. That is all its garrison today. It is your house again, my lord—cleansed of the English who held it. You may possess yourself of it, at will. As I did, last night!"

Not only Lindsay stared at the giant now, speechless.

"So, my lords, let us to Ayr," Wallace said smiling.

Men eyed each other, ill at ease.

"This . . . this was a notable feat, Wallace," the Steward got out, sucking his spittle." And Tower Lindsay is a fine house. But Ayr is quite other. A town. With a great garrison. Five hundred men."

"Nor do we go skulking and creeping in darkness. Like broken men and outlaws," somebody said significantly.

The Bishop coughed. "Besides, my son, it is against our policy. To waste our precious strength on reducing fortresses and castles. These can wait. When the land itself is ours, they will drop off like over-ripe fruit."

"You think so? Then you will give me no men, my lords? For this attempt, I have but fifty of my own band," Wallace said, quietly now.

"Fifty or five hundred—it would make no difference," Douglas snorted.

Bruce was moved to speak. "My lords, I think that we should consider this more. I believe that Ayr should not be left behind us, untouched. It could endanger us. Moreover, its fall, after Lanark, would be great cheer, encouragement, for all Scotland. I do not know about attacking it by night. Here I have no experience. But assault there should be."

The big man was looking at him keenly. "Who speaks so, my friends?" he asked. "I do not know this lord, I think."

"It is the Earl of Carrick, man," the Steward said shortly.

"Carrick! Bruce? The young Lord Robert? Edward's lordling—here?"

There were gasps, murmurs, a snigger or two. Bruce set his jaw but did not answer.

"My lord of Carrick has joined us," Wishart explained. "With three hundred men."

Wallace had not taken his eyes off the younger man. "Scotland's case must be better than I had known, then!" he commented carefully. "But ..." He shrugged great shoulders. "King Edward, it seems, is a good teacher. In war. *He* would not leave Ayr unassailed. The Lord of Carrick is right in this ..."

"No!" Douglas roared. "Failure at Ayr would not only tie us down. It would spell the end of this rising. Until we have mustered a great force, we must keep moving ..."

"Is not that what I urge on you, my lords? To move! Now!" Wallace demanded. "*I* shall move, at least. Here and now. For that I came. Alone if need be. I go to Ayr. Who comes with me?"

Only Graham, who was already standing, nodded his head. There was some shuffling of feet under the table, but no man rose.

"Very well. A good night to you, my lords. God be with you—and God help this poor Scotland!" Wallace threw down the gnawed leg of lamb and strode for the door, his two companions almost running at his heels. Sir John the Graham looked round the company, shrugged, and went after the trio.

After a moment or two, Robert Bruce pushed back his chair. "You will bear with me if I take my leave," he said, to them all. "I think that there may be something to see, tonight. Fifty men against five hundred should show some sport, at the least! I go watch it."

In silence he left the hall. At the door, he found Andrew Moray of Bothwell at his side.

• • •

Out in the Seagate of Irvine, by a slender sliver of horned moon they found Wallace's men already mounting their shaggy garrons—and a ruffianly crew they seemed, though heavily armed. At sight of the two noblemen, Wallace, not yet mounted, paused.

"Who is this?" he demanded, peering. "Ha—my lord of Bothwell. And, yes—it is the Bruce! What would you, sirs?"

"I would come with you. To see what fifty men may do,"

Bruce jerked stiffly. "If you will so much trust Edward's lordling!"

"Trust? I trust my eye, my arm and sword, and God's good mercy my lord. Little else. But come if you will."

Bruce and Moray went for their mounts. The horse-lines of the host were down at the main encampment, between the comparatively small Seagate Castle and the river. By the time they got back, Wallace and his band had gone, but left Sir John the Graham behind to bring them on. Wallace was making for Ayr by the coast, he told them. They would have to hurry to catch up —for that one never daundered, however indifferent the quality of his horseflesh.

The three young noblemen—for Moray, the eldest, was no more than twenty-five—skirted the town to the south-west and rode fast, southwards, by the rolling sandy links of Fullarton and Gailes, with the long Atlantic tide sighing along the glimmering strand of Irvine Bay, on their right. It made easy, unobstructed riding, for night-time, with the moon giving just sufficient light to warn them of the few obstacles of the open bents. Nevertheless, better mounted as they were, it was long before, almost at the squat salmon-fishers' huts of Barassie, they perceived the dark mass of the main body ahead of them. They were one-third of the way to Ayr.

Riding hard, talk was difficult. But Bruce did ask of the Graham if he knew why the man Wallace was so set on an attack on Ayr?

"He has debts to pay. At Ayr," the other threw back, in snatches. "His mother's brother, Sir Ronald Crawfurd of Crosbie, was Sheriff of Ayr. Edward made Percy—Henry Percy of Northumberland—Sheriff. In his place. Percy appointed as deputy one Arnulf. Of Southampton. This Arnulf, an evil man. Called a justice-ayres there. Called Sir Ronald. And others. Sir Bryce Blair. Sir Hugh Montgomerie. Others. To advise him, he said. He slew them, when they came. Out of hand. A trap. Hanged them. From the beams of the new barracks. Wallace has sworn vengeance."

"And that we do tonight?"

"We shall see."

With the narrow curving headland of Troon reaching out into the bay, on their right, they at last caught up with Wallace.

After crossing the further links of Monkton and Prestwick, Wallace turned inland, to skirt Ayr town to the east. They forded the river at The Holm, and then circled round through a terrain of knolls and broken pastureland, back towards the sea, south of the town. They climbed a long low ridge of whins and outcrops, startling sleeping cattle, and drew up on its grassy summit.

Sir William Douglas had been right about English precautions at the Castle of Ayr. Down there, flanking the estuary of the river, the town lay spread before them, dark, sleeping. But, a little way apart, nearer, on a mound to this south-east side, the new castle was not dark and gave no aspect of slumber. No fewer than eight bright beacons blazed from its high walls, making the place almost seem to be afire, and casting a red and flickering glow over all the surrounding area. From this ridge it was too far to see men, but there could be little doubt that watchers patrolled those battlements.

"English Arnulf does not sleep without watch-dogs!" Graham commented.

"Even watch-dogs may blink. Or be chained," Wallace returned easily.

Leaving the three nobles, he gathered his band around him, and splitting them up, gave them instructions, pointing this way and that. Bruce could not make much of the snatches he heard, save that somebody called Scrymgeour was to take charge of the castle. It seemed a large order.

In two groups the men rode off downhill, westwards, and were lost in the shadows. Wallace returned with only half a dozen, including the slim youth, whose name was Boyd, and the priest, Master John Blair.

"Come with us, my lords," he called. "If creeping and skulking is not too much for your stomachs!" In the field, he sounded rather less respectful of noble blood than he had done in Seagate Castle.

After a bare half-mile further, nearer the sea, they were directed to dismount and leave their horses, tied up, in a leafy hollow. Then they went forward quietly. Bruce perceived, from the beacons, that they were heading away from the castle vicinity, half-left, towards the coast. A halt was called presently, and Wallace went on alone. When Bruce and Moray exchanged a few wondering words, the priest curtly ordered them to be silent.

Wallace came back after quite an interval, and beckoned them on. Quietly they followed him past a pair of cot-houses, where the smell of smoored peat-fires was strong, and across some tilled land, where they cast long shadows to the left, in the glow of the castle fires, quarter of a mile off. There was rising ground beyond, of no great height, dotted with black shadows—some of which proved to be bullocks, but most whin and broom bushes. At the knobbly crown of this, where there was ample cover amongst the prickly bushes, Wallace, crouching low himself, waved them down on their knees.

"As far as you may come," he said softly. "Wait you here. Do not move from it, see you, if you value your lives. For any man, not of my band, who moves out there tonight, dies!"

"What do you do?" Bruce demanded. "Why bring us here?"

"You will see, my lord—never fear. Just wait."

"Is there nothing that *we* can do, man?" Graham demanded.

"No work for high-born knights!" the other returned, grimly. "But, if I have not come for you before two hours from now, you may do as you will, my lords. For William Wallace will be no more!"

With no further directions for them, the big man slipped away, extraordinarily quiet and agile for so vast a person. The three rejected nobles found that the rest of the party had disappeared also, and they were alone on their whinny knowe.

"He thinks as little of us as he trusts us!" Bruce said, frowning.

"Perhaps he has reason," Graham gave back.

"What mean you by that?"

"He knows us not—and there are many false, these days. Myself he knows a little—I fought with him at the Corheid. A small fray. But that was nothing. And you—you, my lord, yesterday were Edward's man. By repute. Were you not?"

Bruce shrugged. "If I seemed so, it was because I was not *Baliol's* man. I am no more Edward's man than are the many whom he forced to take the oath. The Steward. Your father, Moray. Lindsay. Bishop Dalton. All these swore fealty." He paused, and smiled a little, in the dark, if twistedly. "Although, to be sure, I learned but yesterday that I am now Edward's chiefest commander in the South-West! Now that Hazelrig is dead. In name. Because I am earl. And here I crouch, this night!"

His companions had no comment to make on that.

They seemed to wait a long time, so that they grew stiff and chilled. Once they thought that they heard a suddenly choked-off cry from somewhere fairly near at hand—but it might have been only a night bird. There were unseen rustlings amongst the whin bushes below them, though these again could have been caused by bullocks. Otherwise, the environs of Ayr, that night, might have been as quietly peaceful as was usual and suitable. Time passed heavily for high-spirited young men of high degree.

Then, and this time there was no doubt about it, a high thin scream rang out from no great distance in front of them, its mortal agony raising the hair at the back of the listeners' necks. And quickly thereafter a blaze of flame leapt up, seemingly only about two hundred yards ahead. It grew in size and brightness and was followed by another nearby. Then another. And still another. The crackle of fire sounded, and then muffled clamour, yelling.

Swiftly the fires increased, fanned by the sea breeze. And by their ruddy light, the watchers at last perceived something of what was happening. In front of them, across a dip, was a great building on a low parallel ridge, simple in design but long, bulky, two-storeyed, gabled and obviously timber-constructed. At a guess it might be two hundred feet long and forty wide. And against its many doors and windows, at ground floor level, fires were blazing up—evidently gorse and broom and straw had been piled high at every opening and set alight. Sparking, spluttering, flaring like great torches, this tinderlike and resinous stuff roared devouringly—and dark figures could be seen piling on more and more of the fuel that grew so profusely all around. Already the wooden walls of the place were beginning to burn.

"The Barns!" Graham cried, need for whispering past. "The English barracks. God's Blood—look at that! Wood—it is all of wood. It will burn to ashes."

"It is . . . it is full? Of men . . . ?" Bruce's voice faltered.

"Full, yes. You heard Eglinton. The English, from Lanark, were quartered there. No room in the castle for hundreds. They will be . . . inside there!"

"Saints of Christ—this is a hellish thing!" Moray groaned.

"Aye." Sombrely Bruce nodded. "But did you see Berwick town?"

The muffled shrieks and cries and cursing from within the building were terrible now, rising high above the throbbing roar of the flames. They saw a door crash down, in a great fountain of sparks, and dark frantic figures came rushing out—to be met by slashing, stabbing steel that flashed red in the firelight. A huge leaping shape could be distinguished, silhouetted against the glow, great sword high.

Soon the walls of the barracks were well alight and there was no need for further fuel. The number of waiting figures around increased. Men were jumping, now, from upper windows, in a frenzy, many with hair and clothes ablaze. None could fail to be seen in that lurid fatal light, and none who escaped hot fire escaped cold steel. The sounds that came across the shadow-filled dip from the Barns of Ayr were now blood-curdling, indescribable.

The shrill neighing of a trumpet, from the direction of the castle, drew the three watchers' eyes momentarily. They could not see what went on at that distance, nearly quarter of a mile away —but they could guess.

"They will come out. Lower the drawbridge and sally out. To aid these. And Sandy Scrymgeour and his men will have them," Graham declared excitedly. "They cannot sit within, and watch this!"

"The man is a devil! Wallace! To plan such savagery. Godless! It is unchristian, heathenish!" Moray said. "True men do not fight so."

"Maybe so. But I will tell you one man who would not blink an eye at what is done here tonight," Bruce returned grimly. "Edward Plantagenet! Nor Bishop Anthony Beck, either."

"Aye. It may be that Scotland needs such as this William Wallace, in this pass," Graham nodded. "But . . . it takes a deal of stomaching."

The roof of the barracks was ablaze now, the entire long building a flaming pyre.

Fewer men seemed to be waiting around the doomed barracks, with no sign of Wallace's gigantic figure. No doubt the main scene of operations was shifting to the castle vicinity. The roar of the fire drowned any noises that might be emanating from there.

Restlessly and with very mixed feelings, the trio waited amongst the whins. Their every instinct and urge was to move out, to be active, involved—but Wallace's warning as to possible consequences had been as convincing as it was grim. And nothing that they had since seen inclined them towards disobedience. Though they would not, could not, call it that, of course; obedience was not an attitude that fell to be contemplated by such as these.

They waited where they were, then, in major frustration and impatience, pacing about amongst the bushes to keep warm, since there seemed no further need to hide themselves.

A most unpleasant smell was now reaching them on the sea wind, from the burning building. It was a considerable time since they had seen any men jumping from the upper windows; indeed, no upper windows were now visible, in the unbroken wall of flame.

A scattering of lights showed in the town.

Eventually the priest, Blair, materialised, face streaked with soot, dark eyes glittering in the ruddy light.

"Wallace requires your presence, my lords," he said shortly. "Come with me."

It was eloquent of the effect of the night's experiences on the three that they none of them took active exception to the summons or the ragged cleric's abrupt delivery thereof, but followed him without comment or question.

Turning their backs on the blazing Barns of Ayr, they made for the castle, finding themselves on a roadway between the two buildings.

Soon they were aware of people. Over on their left, a crowd was standing, silent, townsfolk obviously. Dimly seen in the light of the flames, they stood in their hundreds, unmoving, huddled there seemingly rooted, watching, only watching, strangely noncommittal. The priest ignored them entirely.

The walkers came across the first bodies lying sprawled about a hundred yards from the castle's dry ditch. They lay scattered, as though cut down individually, in flight perhaps. Bruce stooped to peer at one or two—for the beacons on the castle ramparts were fading now, untended. These were men-at-arms, all similarly clad, in jacks and small pointed helmets with nose-guards—English obviously. There were perhaps a dozen of them, dotted along the roadway. Then, near the draw-bridge-end, was a dark heap, almost a mound. Here men had died fighting, not running, back to back probably, assailed and surrounded as they issued from the castle. How many there might be there was no knowing. None moved, at any rate. The priest, his hitched-up robe flapping about leather-bound legs, led on without pause or remark—though once he muttered as he slipped on blood, and recovered his balance with difficulty.

Four ruffianly characters, swords in hand, greeted them less than respectfully at the bridge-end, but let them pass. Men were leading out horses from the castle, fine beasts, laden with miscellaneous gear.

They crossed the inner bailey, where more bodies lay. Somewhere a woman was screeching hysterically, and there were groans from nearer at hand.

The castle's interior still smelt of mortar and new wood,

though overlaid now by the smells of blood and burning. Master Blair conducted his charges up the wide turnpike stairway to the hall. There many torches flared, to reveal a dramatic scene. William Wallace stood up on the dais, at the far end, towering over all, with the man Scrymgeour, head bound with a cloth, young Boyd, and one or two others, nearby. Half-way to the door a group of older men stood, white-faced, in some disarray of dress, none armoured, their agitation very evident. Above all, three men hung on ropes from the beams of the high roof, one in armour, one part-clothed, the one in the centre wholly naked. This last was middle-aged, heavily gross, paunchy, his body lardlike and quite hairless, obscene in its nudity. He twitched slightly.

"Ha, my lords!" Wallace called, at sight of the newcomers. "Come, you. Here are the provost and magistrates of this good burgh of Ayr. Some of them. And there," he pointed upwards, "is one Arnulf, who called himself Deputy Sheriff. Also the captain of this castle's garrison, and his lieutenant." To the townsmen he added, "You see before you the Earl of Carrick, the Lord of Bothwell and Sir John the Graham. I ask these lords to receive this town and castle, in the name of John, King of Scots."

Moray looked doubtful, Graham glanced at Bruce, and that young man raised his voice. "*I* will not, sir," he said loudly, clearly. "There is no King of Scots, today. John Baliol was a usurper, and failed the realm. He has vacated the throne. He is now in France. I, for one, can accept nothing in his name."

His companions did not speak.

Wallace looked thoughtfully at them, tugging his beard—which was noticeably singed on one side. "So that is the way of it!" he said. "All men may not hold as you do, my lord."

"That may be so. But I so hold. And state."

"Who, then, may speak in the realm's name? This burgh and castle is taken. In whose name?"

Bruce saw that Wallace was concerned to live down the name of brigand and outlaw that had been pinned upon him, that he sought an aspect of legality for what he did. That was why they had been brought here.

"Who better than the High Steward of Scotland?" he said. "I shall receive Ayr in his name, if so required."

"Aye. Very well. My lord Earl of Carrick, heir of the House of Bruce, receives Ayr burgh and castle, cleansed of the English invader, in the name of James, Lord High Steward of Scotland," the big man intoned impressively. "Is it agreed?"

No one being in any position to say otherwise, the thing was accepted, with nods and shuffles.

Eyeing them all, Wallace smiled thinly. "So be it. My lords, no doubt you will now ride to acquaint the Steward of this matter. Sir John—you could aid me here, if you will. You, my friends of Ayr—get you back to your town. I want every house searched. For Englishmen. Some there may be yet, in hiding. A great grave to be dug. The streets and wynds cleared of folk. All to return to their homes. You have it?" Briskly he issued these orders, and stepped down from the dais. "Now—I have work to do . . ."

Bruce and Moray, finding themselves dismissed as well as redundant, were not long in making their way back to their horses, a little aggrieved perhaps that Graham should have been singled out for employment, and had left them so promptly. They did not go near to the burning barracks. The roof had fallen in now, and some of the walling collapsed.

In thoughtful frame of mind the two young men rode for Irvine again. Some distance on their way, after crossing the Holm ford, they looked back. New fire was rising at Ayr, from the castle now—and it was not the wall beacons rekindled. The keep itself was ablaze.

"I' faith—that man does nothing by the half!" Moray said. "He has ungentle ways. Fears neither God nor man, I swear. But . . . with a few more Wallaces this Scotland would soon be clear of the English, I say."

"You think so? I do not." Bruce shook his head. "Your father, I believe, would not say so. He is hostage in an English prison, is he not? Like I have, he has seen Edward's might. His armies in battle array. His chivalry by the thousand. His archers, longbowmen, by the ten thousand. It is these must be defeated before Scotland is free of Edward Plantagenet. This Wallace can surprise a garrison, capture a castle, slay a few scores, even hundreds. But against the English massed power what could he do? Or a score like him?"

"Then . . . then you believe this vain? Of no avail? Yet you joined us. Left Edward's side for ours."

"Aye. But not to play outlaw. Not to war with dagger and torch and rope! This may serve its turn, give the common folk cause for hope. Rally doubters. But, if Scotland is to gain her freedom, it is not the Wallaces who will win it, I say. It is ourselves, man. Those who can command and lead thousands, not fifties. Mark it—it is not those we have left behind in Ayr who can save Scotland, in the end. But those we ride to Irvine, to tell. And their like."

"And these—these bicker and dispute. And hold their hands!"

"Aye. There you have it. These cannot agree. There is no leader. I know Edward and the English. Divided counsels, pin-pricks, gestures, will not defeat them. Only armed might. And a firm and ruthless hand directing it."

"Wallace has such a hand, at least . . . !"

"Wallace! Think you the lords of Scotland will follow such as Wallace, man?"

The other was silent.

Chapter Six

The sun was warm, the scent of the yellow gorse flowers was strong, the larks trilled in the blue above, and men relaxed, sat, sprawled, strolled or slept all along the Irvine waterside. For hours they had waited there, at first drawn up in serried ranks, foot in front, cavalry behind, bowmen in knots—pitifully few, these last. But now, in the early afternoon, the ranks were broken, the groups scattered, and men relaxed, all the urgency gone out of the host and the day. Which was no state for any army to be in. Its leaders might have maintained some more suitable spirit—but by and large the leaders were not there, nor had been most of the long day.

The Scots insurgent force had moved out of Irvine, south by east, early in the morning, on word of the English approach. Wallace had sent that word, that Clifford was now no further off than Kilmarnock, a mere six miles away, with Percy coming up from Lochmaben. Even then, the Steward, the Bishop and others, had been for a prompt withdrawal northwards, while there was yet time, making for Glasgow; and only Douglas, this time reinforced by Bruce, Moray and Lindsay, had managed to carry the day in favour of resistance. They had marched out to take up strong defensive positions along the line of the River Irvine and its tributary the Annick Water, facing south and east across what was largely swampland, water-meadows and even a small loch, to slow down any English attack. It was an excellent position—although rather strung-out for their numbers, which still reached only about four thousand. The position was almost too strong in fact, since it produced too great a feeling of security, too defensive an atmosphere altogether.

Bruce and Moray paced a grassy bank above their own lines, ill at ease and short of temper. Since the affair at Ayr, they had drawn together. Andrew Moray's quiet and thoughtful nature making an excellent counter-balance to Bruce's impetuosity. But today even Moray was disgruntled and impatient. They had marshalled their men together, the Annandale and Maybole contingents—the latter now much reinforced—and the Bothwell company from Lanarkshire, totalling in all almost a thousand. They had selected a good position at the right of the long line, not more than a mile from the sea, and holding the Warrix ford. But as the day wore on, and Wallace's scouts were sent back with word that the English were still at Kilmarnock, obviously awaiting the arrival of Percy's force from Lochmaben—where Wallace had in fact boldly attacked them two nights before with indecisve results—Bruce had urged action, a sally. It was crazy, he declared, to let the two English hosts join up, when they might prevent it. A flanking movement with their cavalry could cut off Kilmarnock, north and south. The foot could march the six miles in two hours. Kilmarnock was no strong-point, no citadel or walled town—and the townsfolk would turn against the invaders' rear when they saw the opportunity. Wallace and his men could go in, to rally them.

But there was no convincing the majority of the other lords. It would be folly to desert the strong position here, most said. Others, the most senior, were still advising a retiral northwards. Even Douglas was not for attack meantime.

So it had gone on all day. Wallace himself had sent Sir John the Graham—who was now frequently in his company—to urge the lords to move over to the attack, more or less as Bruce advised. But without avail.

It was in a thwarted and discouraged frame of mind, therefore, that the two young noblemen heard some shouting and commotion from further up the riverside, and, for want of better employment, walked in that direction to see what went on. They discovered Lindsays and Montgomeries, their neighbours in the line, in some consternation and excitement.

"Lundin has ridden off. Deserted to the English!" one of them told the newcomers. "Sir Richard Lundin. He rode off, through our left, there. Over that bit ford. Towards Kilmarnock. With his esquire and three men . . ."

"They say he has had enough. Of folk who dinna ken their ain minds!" another supplemented. "The English aye ken that, at least!"

"This is nonsense!" Bruce declared. "You talk like fools."

"It's true. We saw him, my lord . . ."

"Perhaps he rides as messenger? Courier?" Moray suggested.

"To the English?"

"Who else? They would not send him to Wallace. Such as he!"

"Courier for what, then? What have they to say to the English?" Bruce frowned. " 'Fore God—we shall look into this!" He turned, to hurry back for his horse. They rode hastily back to the Mill of Fullarton, where the insurgent leaders were gathered. They heard upraised voices even before they entered the musty-smelling place.

It took some time for them to gather what was in debate—that it was not now whether to attack or not, but in fact whether to stand fast, retire, or make terms. Shocked, the young men demanded what this meant.

Many of the others seemed actually to welcome their arrival, as opportunity to expound their views and seek support. Out of the declamation and persuasion, they learned that a new situation had arisen.

Clifford had sent an envoy from Kilmarnock, a Scot, one Sir Archibald Livingstone. He had brought two messages. One, that the main body of the English foot, allegedly now fifty thousand strong, was less than thirty miles away, having already won through the Mennock Pass. And secondly, that he, Clifford, well understood that what had prompted this revolt of the Scots lords was the command, issued from London, that all Scots nobles, like their English counterparts, should forthwith muster men and, under heads of families or their heirs, bring them to join and assist King Edward in his war against the French. This, the Earl of Surrey, Viceroy for Scotland, recognised to be not only unpopular, but mistaken policy, and bound to provoke serious misgivings in Scotland, the French war being scarcely more popular in England. He, Clifford, therefore, and Sir Henry Percy, Sheriff of Ayr, had the Viceroy's authority to declare that those Scots lords and knights who had assembled in arms in protest against this policy, if they yielded now, dispersed their forces, and gave certain assurances for their future good and loyal behaviour, would be received back into the King's peace without further penalty. Moreover, the Earl of Surrey undertook to try to persuade King Edward that such commands for Scots levies for the French war should be withdrawn.

All this took some time to be enunciated, by many mouths, with much interpolation, question and refutation.

Douglas's strong voice prevailed over all, eventually. "It is a trick, I tell you!" he cried. "A ruse, to have us yield. Without fighting. This, of going to war in France. Have you heard of it? Have any? He would cozen us."

"Why should he? With his force. With fifty thousand and more, need he trick us?"

"The English, it may be, want no revolt in Scotland, while Edward and his main might is in France," Lindsay declared, "Clifford and Percy have men enough to beat us, to destroy us here. But they would rather have peace. Not have to fight."

"Aye—we cannot win. Not against fifty thousand. I say they are right," Sir John Stewart of Bonkill said.

"It is madness to fight!"

"Better to make for Glasgow, while there is yet time."

"If they would treat with us, we are fools to reject it..."

Douglas managed to shout them all down. "Fools, aye! If we yield! We have a strong position. They are not over-eager to attack. The people of the land are for us. Would you surrender without a blow? Could you raise your heads after, if you did?"

"Not only our heads, yes—but our arms, my lord," the Steward intervened thickly. "Do you not see it? At this present we cannot prevail. We may hold off Clifford and Percy, with their horse. But when the fifty thousand foot come up, we are lost. I had been of the opinion that we should hasten northwards, with our force intact. But now, I think we might be better to accept these terms. And fight another day. They are easy terms, are they not?"

"So say I," Lindsay concurred. "These are easy terms, yes. Why they should make them so easy, I know not..."

"A trick, I say!" Douglas insisted.

"It may be so. But what are we disadvantaged? They make this excuse for us—this of us rebelling because we do not wish to take our men to France. Which none of us had so much as heard of, by the Mass! This must mean that they do not want a clash. I say we should take advantage of this. Rise again, as the Steward says, when they and their great host are gone south again..."

"No!" That was young Andrew Moray, in a burst of hot anger, "This is betrayal! Did we raise the banner of freedom for this? To yield without a blow struck? I, for one, will not do so. My lord of Carrick—will you?"

Bruce cleared his throat. "My Lord Steward," he said, not looking at Moray. "This of hostages? Assurances. What is meant by that? What hostages do they want?"

"That is not certain. So Sir Richard Lundin has gone to Clifford. To discover their mind on this. When we hear..."

"What matters it?" Moray interrupted, his normal quietness gone. "Our position, our duty, is clear. We have taken up arms against the invader of our land. We have not been beaten. We stand in our own land, amongst our own folk. I say we cannot yield thus, whatever their terms. I was for attacking, before Percy joined up with Clifford. I was against making any move to the north. Now, I say, better that than this shameful submission."

"Aye! Aye!"

"No! The Steward is right."

"We still would have to face the fifty thousand. At Glasgow. The weaker for moving."

"Fools... !"

There was uproar in that mill. In it, Moray turned on his companion, urgently.

"Bruce! Why did you not speak out? You who wanted to attack? Why ask about hostages? You came here to have them fight. Not surrender. Why have you kept silent, man?"

"Because I am using my head, Andrew," the other said. "As others would be wise to do. This needs thinking on. Why do the English act so? It is not like them. I know them better than do you. This is a strange thing—in especial when they have a great army nearby. This finding excuse for us. But... Edward himself is far away. And Surrey is a very different man..."

"Dear God you would not submit, man? Surrender?"

"Submit! Surrender? These are but words, I tell you. There are times to fight. And times to talk. If the English wish to talk, I say, let us talk. And fight another day, when we are in better case. It may be the Steward and Lindsay are right. Today, I fear, we cannot win. So let us talk."

"This is strange talk," Moray insisted. "From you. Less than honest, I think! There is something in all this, more than you say. You see more in this than these others?"

Bruce took his time to answer. "It could mean so much. Something new. Something that could transform all Scotland's state. Clifford, Percy, Surrey, would not dare to send such message about this of the French war being unpopular unless it was indeed so. Unless they knew that Edward had indeed made a great mistake. Unless, I think, there was near to revolt in England itself. Edward has been long at war. All his reign he has been making war. Against Ireland, Wales, Scotland. Now France. It may be that his own people at last have had enough of their blood shed, their treasure spent. If they are turning, at last—then all could be changed, for Scotland. Do you not see it? We should not fight the English, then—but rather aid them."

Moray shook his head, bewildered. "This is beyond my understanding . . ."

There was more talk, continuing argument, and no decision. Then there was an interruption. Wallace and Graham arrived—and immediately the scene was changed. Decisions crystallised, hardened. Wallace was like that. No half-measures or uncertainties survived his presence.

"My lords, my lords!" he cried, stilling all other voices. "What is this I hear? I spoke with Lundin. On his way to Clifford. Not only will you not attack, he says. But you talk of submission. I cannot believe this is true. Tell me that he has taken leave of his wits, my good lords!"

There was a profound silence—the first Fullarton Mill had known that day. Men glanced at each other, rather than at the clenched-fist giant. Douglas, who normally filled any vacuum with his strong voice and views, would not demean himself to submit answers to such as William Wallace. Others either felt similarly, or dared not meet their inquisitor's hot eye.

Save Bruce, that is. After a few moments, he spoke. "Sir—a new situation has arisen. Did Sir Richard not tell you? Of this matter of a muster for France. And the English offer. This may change all."

"How may it change our struggle for freedom, my lord?"

"It may foreshadow revolt in England. Or, if revolt is too great a word, discontent, resistance. I do not believe they would make such offer to us, this excuse for us, otherwise. If it is so, Surrey may wish to have his fifty thousand back in England!"

"Is that not the more reason to fight? If they are of two minds. Looking back over their shoulders?"

"I say probably not. I say that if the English would indeed

bring their arrogant king to heel, we should aid them in it. Not fight them."

"What the English do with their king is *their* concern, not ours. Or, not mine. Though, to be sure, it may be yours, my lord! I have feared as much."

"What do you mean, sir?"

"I mean that your conversion to our cause was something sudden, my lord of Carrick! You have large lands in England. All knew you one of Edward's men. It may be that you are still more concerned with Edward's case than Scotland's!"

There was a shocked murmur, as Bruce raised a pointing hand. "You doubt my honesty? *You!*"

"I doubt your interests. Your judgement. Where your heart lies. I doubt the judgement of any man who even for a moment considers submission to the English, my lords!" And Wallace stared deliberately round at them all, head high, in reproach and accusation both.

"Curse you . . . !"

"This is not to be borne!"

"How dare the man speak so? To us . . . !"

"My lords—friends," Bishop Wishart cried. "This talk will serve us nothing. Wallace is a man of fierce action. He has wrought mighty deeds. But we must needs take the long view, here. Consider well our course. For the best . . ." The old man's words quavered away.

Wallace obviously took a major grip of himself. "I regret, my lord Bishop, if I spoke ill. But—what does the Earl of Carrick propose? Surrender all our force? Accept this English offer? Make our peace with Edward? If this is so, I say—not Wallace! Never Wallace!"

"Nor Graham either!" the younger man at his side declared.

Bruce was also mastering his hot temper. "I say, since we cannot fight fifty thousand, let us talk with them. Talk at length. Learn what we can. Gain time. And while we talk, send messengers privily to raise the country further. It may be that we will find the English glad to wait. If trouble is brewing in England. I say, let us talk, dissemble, prevaricate, make time."

"We shall make time better, my lord, by remaining free men," Wallace declared, almost contemptuously. "The realm will be freed by war, not talk. Better the sword than the tongue, I say!"

"For *your* sort of war, may be. The surprising of a garrison, here and there. The burning of this castle, or that. The raid by night. This is all we may do with our present support and numbers. It is good—but not good enough, my lords." Bruce was speaking now, earnestly, to them all. "We will not free Scotland of the English so. They are notable fighters, with many times our numbers. They have their bowmen, their chivalry, their hundreds of thousands. Think you we can counter these by night raids, fires and hangings?"

"Is this why you left Edward's camp to join us, my lord of Carrick?" demanded the Graham bitterly. "To tell us that we could not win? To sap our wills and courage?"

"I did not! I came because I must. Because I saw that I must needs choose between Scotland and England. Not John Baliol's Scotland—*my* Scotland! I'd mind you all, my father should be King of Scots today! Let none forget it."

There was silence in that mill, again. Not even Wallace spoke.

"I chose Scotland then. But not to beat with my bare fists against castle walls! More than that is required. Wits, my friends—in this, we must use our wits. We need them, by the saints! Wallace, here, can do the beating at the walls. He does it well. Moreover, I would mind you, *he* cannot talk with the English. They would hang him out of hand! As outlaw and brigand! He knows it." Bruce jabbed a pointing finger at the giant. "We all know it. But it is not so with *us*, my lords. They offer to treat with us. I say treat, then, in this situation. I know Surrey. I know Percy, his nephew. I know Clifford, of Brougham. These are not of Edward's wits, or Edward's ruthlessness. I would not say treat with Edward Plantagenet, God knows! But these are different. Treat. Talk. Discover what is in their minds. What worries them. Something does, I swear. Gain time. This, I counsel you, my lords. And let Wallace go fight his own war. With our blessing!"

An extraordinary change had come over the arguing company. Without warning, as it were, young Robert Bruce had established himself as a leader—not merely the highest in actual rank there, but a man who had come to know his own mind. He had not convinced them all, by any means. It is doubtful, indeed, if many fully understood or accepted what he said. But suddenly he had grown in stature before all. It was as though a new voice had spoken in unhappy Scotland. And more important even than the voice was the manner.

"There is much in what the Earl of Carrick declares," Bishop Wishart said, into the hush. "I believe he has the rights of it."

"I, too," the Steward nodded. "There is wisdom in this. I agree."

"And I do not!" Wallace cried. "I agree with my lord only in this—that the English will hang me if they can! For the rest, I say that you deceive yourselves. Myself, I waste no more time, my lords. There is much to be done. If *you* will not do it, I will. I give you good day—and naught else!"

"I am sorry for that . . ." Bruce began, and paused. The big man, turning on his heel, had halted as the priest, Blair, came hurrying in, to speak a few words in his ear.

Wallace looked back. "You have company it seems! Company *I* would not care to meet. They approach under a flag of truce. I do not congratulate you, my lords. I have no stomach for supping with the devil! I am off."

"And I with you," Sir John the Graham cried.

Moray of Bothwell took a single step as though to follow them, but thought better of it.

There was a stir of excited talk at the word of the English approach. The debate was not now whether to receive them, but who should do so, and on what terms. There was no more agreement on this than on anything else. In the end, the entire company trooped out of the mill—to find the Englishmen, with Sir Richard Lundin of that Ilk, to the number of about thirty, assembled in the yard outside.

The two groups stared at each other, for a little, grimly wordless.

Then a tall, willowy young man, who sat his horse under the proud blue and gold banner of Northumberland, held just slightly higher than the white sheet of truce, dismounted, his magnificent armour agleam in the afternoon sun. Thin-faced, pale of hair and complexion, almost foxy of feature, he scanned the assembled Scots, his manner nervous-seeming. At sight of Bruce his glance flickered. At his back, another man got down, slightly older, dark, solidly-built, heavy-jawed, tough-looking. The rest of the English remained in their saddles. Lundin came round to stand amongst his compatriots.

"I am Percy," the willowy young man said, in a voice as high and reedy as himself. "I come in the name of my uncle, John de Warenne, Earl of Surrey, Viceroy of this Scotland."

None answered him.

"I am Clifford," the darker man declared harshly. "Warden of the West March."

"The *English* West March!" That was Douglas, who himself had been the Scots Warden of that March.

"The West March," the other repeated, flatly.

Sir Henry Percy, Lord of Northumberland, looked quickly away from Douglas. His glance was of the darting sort. Now, insofar as it was directed at any, it flickered around Bruce.

"My Lord Robert," he said, "I regret to see you here." And added, with a little cough, "Kinsman."

Bruce smiled briefly. Their relationship was of the most distant sort, and had not been stressed hitherto. He took it that this mention implied some need felt by the Percy.

"I am nearer to my earldom of Carrick, here, my lord, than you are to your Northumberland!" he returned.

"I am the Sheriff of Ayr," the other said.

"Edward of England's sheriff!" Douglas countered.

"The King's Sheriff. As *I* am the King's Warden!" Clifford jerked.

"England's king. Not Scotland's."

Percy and Bruce both cleared their throats at the same time, and caught each other's eye. Clearly there was as much difference of temperament and approach between the two Englishmen as between Douglas and Bruce. Clifford, son of Isabel de Vieuxpont, of Brougham, one of the greatest heiresses in the North of England, was another plain soldier nevertheless, who spoke his mind. Percy had not come to speak his mind, it seemed. And he took precedence in rank, and as representing Surrey. It was perhaps not Bruce's place to speak, for although he was the only earl amongst the Scots, the Steward was one of the great officers of state, as well as an initiator of this revolt, and the Bishop of Glasgow was senior in years. But neither Steward nor Bishop raised their voices, and much might depend on what was said now. Also how it was said.

"You ride under a flag of truce, my lords," he observed. "I think that you did not bring that to Irvine to discuss offices and positions?"

"No. That is true." Percy nodded, with apparent relief. "We have come to discuss terms. To, to offer you an . . . accommodation."

"Terms? Accommodation? We are not suitors for such, my lord."

"Then the bigger fools are you!" Clifford barked.

"We learn from Sir Richard Lundin that you would know more fully what we propose." Percy went on.

"And what do you propose?"

"That you, who are rebels, surrender on terms. Generous terms, I say." Clifford was making his position very clear.

"Surrender, sir? Without a blow struck? In our own land? To an invader?" Bruce kept his voice almost conversational. "Surely you misjudge, my lords."

"By God, we do not! We could crush you rebellious dogs like that!" Clifford snapped his steel-gauntleted fist shut eloquently.

"But have not yet attempted the feat, sirrah! I would think that the time to talk terms or surrender is when one or other is prostrate in defeat?"

Percy waved a hand. "Sir Robert—*I* will speak. In the name of the Viceroy. If you please." He coughed again. "If we do battle, my lords, *we* must win. We know your numbers. We have many times as many. You are brave men, no doubt, and would fight well. But the end could not be in doubt. Do you wish to die? Is there need for so much bloodshed? Amongst fellow-subjects of King Edward?"

There was a muttered growl at that. Douglas hooted.

"You all have sworn allegiance to Edward," Percy reminded. "Even my lord of Douglas!"

"Under duress, man! How much do you value such swearing, Englishman?"

"Forsworn traitors!" Clifford cried. "What use talking with such? Their word is valueless. They will break faith whenever our backs are turned."

No one attempted to deny it.

But Percy was made of different metal, no less sharp perhaps for being more pliable. "You are all Edward's subjects," he pointed out, and raised his hand, as the murmurs began again. "Hear me, my lords. You are Edward's men all. But free men. Not serfs. In feudal duty, yes. But with your baron's rights. As have I and Sir Robert, here. We are all Edward's men. But we have our rights. And in England, at least, we cherish our rights not a little! We accept that you should do so likewise."

There was quiet now, as all searched that uneasy-eyed, foxy face. Clifford kicked at the earth with his armoured foot.

Percy went on. "We know why you have taken arms against your liege lord. It was foolish—but to be understood. You did this in order that you should not be constrained to fight in the King's foreign wars. You had been better, my friends, to come talk with us. With your fellow-barons. In England. Rather than put hands to your swords."

The Scots eyed each other doubtfully, since none had so much as heard of this obligatory foreign service before that day. Douglas was obviously about to say as much—but Bruce spoke quickly.

"And what would our fellow-barons of England have said?"

Percy licked thin lips. "They would have said, belike, that they were no more eager for the French war than were you, my lords. And that it behoved all His Highness's loyal liegemen, of both realms . . ." The other amended that. ". . . of both nations, to apprise him that this French war was unwise and against the will and judgement of both peoples."

He paused, and this time not even Douglas was for interjection. All the Scots had cause furiously to think—Bruce none the less because he had anticipated something of this.

"So . . . England mislikes Edward's French war?" he said, at length.

"That is so. The land has been overlong at war. We are taxed too dear. This new war is too much . . ."

"Do not tell me that the English have lost their stomach for war!" Douglas interrupted. "That I shall not credit. Here is a trick . . ."

"We are none the less warriors—as you will discover, my lord, soon enough! If you do not listen to reason. But . . . to start a new and long war overseas is folly. We have had twenty years of war, and more. Our coffers are empty. Our fields untilled. Our people weary of it."

"Yet you come against us. In Scotland. With fifty thousand men!" The Steward had found his difficult tongue at last.

"You are in revolt. Rebellion must be put down. We are loyal to our King. It is foreign war that we resist. Make no mistake, my lords—here is no charter for rebels!" Percy's superficial thin hesitancy did not cloak the real man beneath it, there.

"But you would have us, the Scots, with you? In this resistance," Bruce pressed him.

"Yes."

"But . . . does not our revolt serve you well enough, then? Is not revolt in Scotland more apt to bring King Edward home than Scotland in submission?"

"Not so. You know Edward. Revolt will but stiffen his neck. He lives for war, for conflict, for conquest. Revolt will not prevail with him."

"What will, then?"

"A parliament. A united parliament. Of all his lords and barons. Not only of England, but of Scotland also. And Wales. Aye, of Ireland. A parliament that speaks with one voice against these wars."

Bruce drew a long breath. So that was it! At last. The English lords would bring their warlike monarch to heel. It had come to that. No revolt, but a rising of a sort, nevertheless. And if such was contemplated, it was not surprising that Percy and Surrey should be in the forefront. For the grandsire of one and the father-in-law of the other, Richard Percy of Northumberland, had been one of the great barons of England most prominent in forcing the Magna Carta on King John. By the same means. A united display by the nobles. And for such a display, now, not only would the Scots nobles be valuable—for Edward had declared that there was hereafter only one realm and one parliament; but the English nobles must have their men readily available—for their own protection. Edward would listen to their voice only if it was backed by the power he understood. So they wanted no revolt, and no armies of occupation, in Scotland.

Bishop Wishart was speaking. "We may wish you well, my lord. But why should Scotland aid you in this? Edward fighting in France would serve us better than Edward home, and angry!"

"Aye! Aye!"

"Not so. The yoke would be greatly eased for you. Side with us, in this, and we swear you shall gain by it. In earnest of which, my uncle, the Viceroy, will already ease many of your burdens. If you accept his terms."

He had their interest and concern now. Men talked with their neighbours, low-voiced. Douglas was still declaring that it was all a trick, however.

"I say Douglas is right," Andrew Moray asserted, in Bruce's ear. "I do not trust this Percy a yard! And even if it is not a trick, why should the Scots aid the English lords? It is all to their advantage . . ."

"Ours also—if we play it right, Andrew. Besides, nothing is changed in our case, here. We still cannot fight fifty thousand, and win. Here is occasion for talk. Much talk."

"Too much talk! Wallace had the rights of it."

The Steward raised his voice. "These terms, my lord of Northumberland, that you spoke of? What are your terms?"

"The terms are the Viceroy's, my lord. They are light, I think. Such as you can surely accept. To return to the King's peace, only this is necessary. That you disperse your men-at-arms. That you deliver up the murderer Wallace. And that you commit to us certain hostages, as assurance for your continuing loyalty. That is all."

That did not fail to produce animated debate. Looked at from one aspect, these were indeed light terms. Of course the men must disperse—but they could be reassembled, if need be, in a matter of days. As for Wallace, he could look to himself. But what was meant by hostages? That was the question on every lip.

Half a dozen voices asked it, aloud.

Percy's glance flickered like lightning—and this time notably avoided Bruce's. "The hostages need not be many," he said. "But they must be of worth. Substance. Of notable consequence. They must come from the greatest among you. From the Earl of Carrick. From my lord of Douglas. From my Lord Steward. And my lord Bishop of Glasgow. These."

There were caught breaths. Also, undoubtedly, some sighs of relief from the unnamed.

"These you name?" the Steward asked, thickly. "What hostages?"

A cough. "From you, my lord—your son and heir, Walter Stewart. From Douglas, his heir. From the Earl of Carrick, his infant daughter. From the Bishop, all precious relics from the cathedral of Glasgow."

Out of the exclamations, Bruce's voice rasped. "You make war on children and babes, then, my lord!"

"Not so. These hostages will suffer nothing. Indeed they will do very well, better than here in Scotland, I vow! They will lodge with kinsmen, in England. Secure. Honoured guests. Your own daughter, my lord, shall lodge in my own house of Alnwick. Where also now lodges the Lady Elizabeth de Burgh, my cousin—whom you know of! The Steward's son, Walter, may also lodge there—since his mother is likewise a de Burgh. Is it not so, my lord? Sir William of Douglas's wife is the lady Eleanor de Louvain, from Groby, in Northumberland. She may return there, with her children. In the state of Scotland today, will they not all be better so disposed?"

It was specious, but clever. In one respect, all the Percy had said was true. The families of men in revolt were always in danger. If those required to yield the hostages were in fact honest in their acceptance of the terms, the said hostages would indeed be as safe, as well off, so disposed, as at large in unhappy Scotland meantime. And for the four named to refuse this gesture was to reject the whole terms, to deny and fail their colleagues. None failed to see it.

"My daughter is far from here," Bruce jerked. "I cannot yield her to you. She is in my sister's care. At Kildrummy. In Mar. Hundreds of miles north of this."

"You can send for her, my lord. And meantime, these others—the Steward, the Bishop, and, perhaps, my lord of Crawford—will stand surety for her delivery?" Percy almost smiled.

"How now?" Moray murmured, at Bruce's ear. "Are you still for talk with the Englishmen? For terms, man?"

The Steward spoke, with an accession of dignity. "This of the hostages is grievous. We will have to consider your terms. And inform you. But we cannot yield Wallace. He is gone."

"You can bring him back."

"You do not know William Wallace, if you say that! He is his own master. He will come for none here. We can no more deliver up Wallace than fly in the air, sir! You must needs take him for yourself."

"Very well. We shall do so. You wish time to consider these terms?"

"Yes. There is much to consider."

Percy looked at Bruce. "You also, kinsman?"

Set-faced he inclined his head.

The Englishman did likewise. "Then we shall go. And return tomorrow. A good day to you, my lords. And . . . consider well." Nodding to Clifford, he turned for his horse.

"One word, Percy." That was Bruce suddenly. "In all this we have but your word. How do we know that you do not deceive us? As my lord of Douglas feared? That other than yourself would resist Edward."

"Percy's word is sufficient, is it not?" the other returned. "But if you require proof—ask these." He gestured towards those behind him. "They will tell you that two of the greatest earls in England, Norfolk and Hereford, have refused Edward's commands to cross the Channel, with their armies. As contrary to the terms of Magna Carta. Others follow their lead. Is it enough? Or must I name more names?"

"It is enough, yes."

When the Englishmen were gone and the debating began again, it was clear that the great majority of the Scots were for accepting the terms. Even Douglas appeared to be convinced that it was no trick—the news of the resistance of the mighty Earls of Norfolk and Hereford, the Bigods and Bohuns, had stilled even his doubts. He was against the surrender of young James Douglas as hostage, naturally—but otherwise agreed that to challenge the English to battle, at this stage, was not politic. Only Andrew Moray remained obdurate.

"I will not submit. To these terms, or any," he declared, to Bruce. "My people up in Moray and the North are in revolt. I cannot fail them, here. I will go to them. And you, Bruce? You can stand there and consider the yielding up of your own child?"

"They have not got my Marjory yet!" the other returned grimly. "I said to talk, did I not? Talk, rather than fight and be beaten. I still say talk. At length. While the English settle their quarrel with their king."

"Why bide here for it, man? Why not slip away? Go north. Come with me. All Scotland lies open..."

"Not *all* Scotland, Andrew. See you—you and Graham and others may slip away so. Your lands all lie to the north. Even Bothwell is not yet touched. You can raise men and means, from them. But most here, like myself, have their lands in this South-West. Most already overrun by the English. Our sole power comes from our lands and our men. You know that. If we run for it, northwards, we are becoming little more than landless men, outlaws, swords for sale! Is that how we, her great lords, can best fight for Scotland? Resist Edward? I think not. Douglas, the Steward, Crawford, and the rest—they are in the same position. I say talk, then. These terms will keep us talking for long. Go you, if you will..."

• • •

Bruce's strategy of talk, and more talk, was more successful, almost crazily so, than he, or anyone, could have hoped. A month later, no less, they were still talking at Irvine.

It was not all merely effective delaying tactics, of course, though that played its part. Events and conditions far from Ayrshire had the greater effect. And the fact that no one really wanted to fight was highly relevant—for Clifford the fire-eater was despatched on the more congenial and active duty of chasing Wallace. Indeed, if

Bruce was the initial designer of what became known, and chuckled over, as the Capitulation of Irvine, the most long-drawn capitulation in Scotland's story, Wallace was the true protractor of it. With Edward Plantagenet's help.

Wallace disappeared from Irvine into the fastnesses of the Ettrick Forest, his favourite refuge and a notorious haunt of broken men. From there, in an extraordinary short time, he emerged again with a tough and highly-mobile cut-throat band of perhaps two hundred. Avoiding embroilment with English garrisons in Lanarkshire, he made a lightning descent upon the town of Glasgow, where Bishop Anthony Beck had gone to collect the cathedral relics and to initiate a campaign for English hegemony over the Scots Church. Taken completely by surprise, the English in Glasgow were overwhelmed, and Beck was forced to flee, a salutary experience for that exponent of the Church Militant.

Wallace well knew that this kind of warfare depended for its success on continual movement and surprise. He did not stay at Glasgow but, reinforced considerably, moved north into the Lennox where the earl aided and abetted him, being no Norman but of the old Celtic stock. Clifford was now tailing him, but far behind. Wallace made a swift and unexpected dash right across Scotland, to Perth, and at Scone managed to surprise Edward's Justiciar of Scotland, William Ormsby, holding harsh courts, who escaped with his life but left behind much valuable booty. Then, by tremendous forced marches across the mountains Wallace descended upon the English-held towns of Brechin, Forfar and Montrose, to wipe out what Edward had done there to John Baliol. All fell. He linked up here with Andrew Moray, who had hastened north to lead his father's people of Moray and the Black Isle, and could now claim the enemy-held castles of Inverness, Urquhart, Elgin and Banff. Together they turned south for Dundee.

This was a brilliant campaign for the summer of 1297. But it was, of course, superficial. Nothing was consolidated behind this guerilla fighting, and it could not be claimed that the so-called rebels held the territory they so vigorously swept through. But it all had an enormous effect, nevertheless, on the Scots people. The name of William Wallace was on every lip. Their lords had failed them, but the common folk saw Wallace as their saviour. Young men flocked to him from far and near, from highlands and lowlands from east and west and north—many of them against the wishes of their own feudal superiors. He had an army now, even though a rag-tag one. And some barons were supporting him, other than Graham and Moray—for word had gone out from the talkers at Irvine, privily, to rouse the land. With this host, Wallace attempted what he had not hitherto risked, the siege of a major fortress and garrison town—Dundee, where he had been educated, and whence came Scrymgeour and many of his band.

If all this had its inevitable effect on Percy's negotiating position, affairs in England had almost more. Edward, with his ally Guy, Count of Flanders, was attacking Philip the Fair, of France, with doubtful success—and at the same time fighting something like a rearguard action with his own recalcitrant barons at home. Many others had joined Norfolk and Hereford in refusing foreign service, some of them of lofty rank indeed. The King could do little against them without coming home, but what he could he did. Many were dismissed their offices by hasty decree—including Surrey, who was demoted from being Viceroy of Scotland, and one Brian Fitz-Alan appointed in his stead. But even royal decrees have their limitations, unless backed by force on the spot, and Surrey was still commander of the northern armies, since they were largely composed of the Northumbrian and Cumbrian levies of the Percies and other North-Country lords. Fitz-Alan, then, required Surrey's co-operation—and got but little.

This bore notably on the spun-out negotiations at Irvine—which, indeed, neither side was now in any hurry to bring to a conclusion. One defeat for Edward in France, and the entire dynastic situation in England would change, and the Scottish position with it. All balanced on a knife's-edge, and men marked time, waiting—save for William Wallace, that is. Percy restored Ayr Castle—which had been only superficially burned—and lodged there, contenting himself with only occasional meetings with the Scots lords at Irvine. Or some of them—for Douglas had soon tired of this, and slipping off to his Nithsdale estates, had gathered together some men and surprised and taken Sanquhar Castle. He had not yielded young James Douglas as hostage, either—and so was now proclaimed outwith the King's peace, outlaw. Bishop Wishart, too, after Wallace's raid on Glasgow and Beck's discomfiture, was declared responsible for his see, and surrendered into English custody at Roxburgh Castle, as a sort of personal hostage for Glasgow. But Bruce, the Steward, Crawford and others continued with the play-acting of negotiation, their men in the main dispersed, looking over their shoulders to north and south. All had English estates as well as Scottish. The fifty thousand foot turned and marched homewards, as far as Berwick.

So passed an extraordinary summer. Bruce's two-year-old daughter Marjory remained safely at Kildrummy Castle, in the care of his sister, Christian, Countess of Mar. And his father, the Lord of Annandale, was dismissed from his position as Governor of Carlisle—by express command from France.

Everywhere men waited.

Bruce received a letter—delivered by Percy himself, no less. It was in feminine writing, and was sealed with the arms of Ulster and de Burgh. It read:

My lord,

What are you? A loyal man, I understand. A rebel I understand. But what is a man who sits and talks? A clerk? King Edward thought to wed us. Should I thank God for my escape?

Elizabeth de Burgh.

Bruce, in hot anger, crushed the offending paper into a ball, and threw it from him. Later, he retrieved it and spread it smooth again—and once more crumpled it up. He almost burned it, but did not.

Chapter Seven

As is so often the case, the most carefully thought-out courses, the most masterly inaction and most delicately-balanced fence-sitting, can all be brought to naught in a chaos of violence and unprofitable turmoil - and often by the merest accident or conjunction of otherwise unimportant events. It was so in late August of 1297. Two unconnected incidents, neither in themselves significant, brought about the collapse of so much that had been patiently contrived. And the men who used their wits were overwhelmed in the consequent conflagration just as surely as were the strong-arm realists and fire-eaters.

Edward Plantagenet won a small and insignificant engagement in the north of France, which became magnified by rumour, in England, into a major victory; and an English knight escaped from beleaguered Dundee, by sea to Berwick, with the word that the great fortress-town would have to capitulate to Wallace within a couple of weeks, for lack of provisions.

It so happened that the Earl of Surrey was at Berwick Castle when both tidings arrived, in the process of handing over the civilian duties of Viceroy to Fitz-Alan, Lord of Bedale, in the company of Master Hugo Cressingham, Treasurer and real administrator of Scotland, who made his headquarters at Berwick. It was a humiliating situation for the great Earl of Surrey; moreover he and Cressingham, whom he despised as an upjumped cleric, were on bad terms. Out of this, the entire situation for Scotland suddenly changed. Fitz-Alan, the new broom, wished to prove himself as Viceroy; Cressingham demanded immediate action for the relief of Dundee; and Surrey, with the word from the south that a great victory in France secured, Edward would now come home to set his English house in order, panicked. He had a name and reputation to save. He was still commander-in-chief in the North; and fifty thousand men still lay encamped near Berwick.

So action, crude and vigorous, took the place of dialectics. Blood would flow, not words.

The first indication of this dramatic change reached Ayrshire by urgent courier to Sir Henry Percy, in peremptory terms. The High Steward, Crawford and certain other Scots lords, with the main body of the English forces at Ayr, were to be sent to join Surrey's army forthwith, on its advance on Dundee by Edinburgh and Stirling. But Percy himself was to proceed at once in the other direction, south to Carlisle, taking the Earl of Carrick with him, there to assemble as large a reinforcement army as he could in short time, for the aid of his uncle. Bruce's father, though replaced as Governor of Carlisle by the Bishop thereof, was still detained at that castle. His great lands of Annandale teemed with men, the richest territory in South-West Scotland. The Bruces must provide their thousands from Annandale – on pain of treason.

The velvet gloves were discarded now, with a vengeance.

Percy's cavalry descended upon the unsuspecting Scots, who found themselves under what amounted to arrest, at Irvine. There was no argument or debate now. The Steward and the rest were taken off northwards. Percy and Bruce rode south. The Capitulation of Irvine was over, and the Leopards of England showed their spots again, dark, clear and unchanged.

In the circumstances, Bruce's reunion with his father at Carlisle was less than happy. They had never got on well together, the father finding the son headstrong, independent, and, in especial, extravagant; the younger saw his parent as indecisive, interfering, ineffective, and mean. The son's expensive ways, as compared with his sire's parsimony, had been a stumbling-block between them for long. This was why, as much as because he could not bring himself to make an earl's fealty to his rival John Baliol, the elder Bruce had handed over the old and impoverished Celtic earldom of Carrick, which he had gained by marriage, to his son, and thereafter washed his hands of him—retaining, of course, for himself, the infinitely richer if less lofty-sounding Lordship of Annandale. There was seldom love lost when these two met.

Bruce found his father practically a prisoner in Carlisle Castle—though he did not admit the fact—with the Bishop in command. Percy did not delay in making known his uncle's demands for a large contingent of armed and mounted men from Annandale, his hesitancy of manner now scant cloak for brusque authority – and left father and son to their own company.

"How dare he! How dare that insolent puppy speak me so!" the elder Robert Bruce cried, trembling with outrage. "I, who should be King of Scots!"

"Yet you will bear it, Father—since you must. As must I. For you are *not* King of Scots. And, like me, you are Percy's prisoner in all but name.'

"I am no prisoner, boy! By envy and malice and Edward's spleen. I have been superseded as Governor here—that is all. As though I care for that! If Edward Plantagenet does not know his friends, and trusts instead such as Percy and Surrey, the more fool he! I shall not give them one man from Annandale. They may whistle for their men!"

"Brave words! You did not speak them to Percy!"

"I shall. *You* may lick the boots of such as he. I do not."

"I lick no boots. Nor ever shall. But I recognise facts. Power. The reality of power."

"You! Power? You recognise fine clothes. Jewels. Blood-horses. Women. You recognise those who will pay for your debts! You licked Edward's boots for gold, did you not? *He* paid your debts. Is it Percy, now?"

With a great effort Bruce held in his hot temper. "I lick no man's boots, I tell you," he repeated heavily. And changed the subject, stiffly. "How do you propose, my lord, to assert yourself? Against these commands."

"I shall go. Leave. I do not remain here, in Carlisle, to be insulted and mistreated, by God!"

"Where shall you go? If they let you. Your lands in England, in Essex and Huntingdon, will scarce offer you protection against Edward! And Annandale, of all the dales of Scotland, lies most open to the English. Its mouth, wide and open to the Border, cannot be defended. Only at its head amongst the hills. And there the English hold Lochmaben."

"I shall not go to Annandale. Nor into England. I go to Norway. To Isabel. I shall seek King Eric's aid. To put me on my throne of Scotland. I shall return with a Norse army."

His son stared, almost unbelievingly. Although, knowing his father, he perhaps should not have been so surprised. Bruce the elder had ever lacked any conspicuous sense of the practical.

"But . . . but this is folly!" he exclaimed. "Eric will not aid you. Not with men, an army. He has his own troubles. Nearer home . . ."

"He is my good-son. To have me King of Scots would greatly strengthen his hand. In his own wars."

The Lord of Annandale had been potent, if not practical, and his countess-wife fertile. They had had five sons and four daughters. And the eldest child, Isabel, had married four years earlier King Eric the Second of Norway, as his second wife. The family had not seen her since—but she was indeed Queen of Norway.

Her brother knew the uselessness of argument with his sire. "They will not let you go," he said. "The English."

"Why should they stop me? I am a free man. I have been put down as Governor—but that is not my doing. It is *your* fault. For your folly, at Irvine. Of turning rebel, at the wrong time! Always you were a fool, Robert! And have cost me dear."

The young man turned away, and strode to the window to gaze out, while he mastered himself. It was a small and undistinguished tower chamber, very different from the fine Governor's apartment which the Bishop now occupied. Without facing his father, he spoke, level-voiced.

"They will not let you go. Unless you seem to aid them. I know these English—if you do not. Though you should, 'fore God! They are merchants. They bargain, always. If they have power, they give nothing for nothing. You can bargain for your freedom with your Annandale men."

"Men! *You* say that? You, the untimely rebel! You would give the English our Annandale men—to fight against our own folk?"

"To fight, no. To assemble and ride, yes."

"What do you mean?"

"I mean that these are your vassals. Bruce's vassals. By the thousand. The English wish them assembled, in arms. Very well. Let them assemble. It is a thing we dared not have done, ourselves. But on Surrey's orders . . . ! Then, when we ride north, we shall speak with a different voice! Who, think you, these Bruce levies will obey? Percy? Or Bruce?"

"You mean . . . you mean that you would take them . . . and then change sides? Turn your coat, man?"

"My coat is already turned, is it not? Whatever side I must needs seem to wear! In my need, I cannot afford the luxury of wearing only one side of my coat, my lord!"

"But . . . what of your honour, man? Have you none?"

"Honour? I have been learning what honour means! If Scotland is ever to be free, if Scotland is ever to have its own king again, Bruce or other, we will have to think again on what means honour. Does Edward know the word, I wonder? But . . . enough of this. These men of Annandale, my lord, are your vassals—not mine. Yet. But with your permission, and Percy's aid, I shall make them into an army. To use against our enemies. Your enemies. Those who have so despitefully used you."

The older man chewed at his long upper lip in indecision. "You have your own men. Of Carrick. Use them," he jerked.

"I cannot. Think you Percy would allow that? Carrick, all Ayrshire, is watched, garrisoned, held. Thick with English. A few men I might raise—were I free to do so. But I am not. Here it is different. We would be acting on Surrey's orders. Do you not see it? And do you not see that you have here much to bargain with? Say to Percy that you wish to retire in peace. That your sixty years weigh heavy on you. That you will give me authority to raise your vassals of Annandale. But that you must be allowed to go, in peace. From here. Where you will. Do not say to Norway, I counsel you!"

"Aye." The other had started pacing the floor. "Aye—and when I return from Norway. In the spring. You will have an army waiting for us? To gain my throne?"

His son lifted wide shoulders. "God willing," he said cryptically.

So, for once, father and son were agreed, or seemed to be. Percy, when told, appeared well content. He requested Bruce to proceed forthwith to Annandale—with Sir Harry Beaumont and a contingent of two hundred cavalry to aid and escort him. Other recruiting-agents were sent through Cumberland, Westmorland and Northumberland. Percy himself departed across country eastwards, for a brief visit to his own Alnwick, to raise more men there. One week, and all must be back at Carlisle.

In Annandale, Bruce found all his brothers, in Annan Castle itself, on its mote dominating the straggling red-stone town amongst the green tree-dotted meadows of the deep-running river. Edward, two years younger than Robert, was acting as his father's deputy in this great lordship, a dark, smouldering-eyed, intense young man, despite his name, all Celt; Thomas, just twenty, quiet, slow of speech, but giving the impression of a coiled spring; Nigel, cheerful, irrepressible, wooing half the girls of the town; Alexander, only sixteen, but clever, studious, more diffident than the others. They made a contrasting group, with only a hot temper uniform to them all. Their unmarried sister Mary, a laughing tomboy of a girl of seventeen, acted chatelaine to an undisciplined and lively household in the great gloomy castle.

When Bruce could win free of Sir Henry Beaumont, who clung closer to him than any brother—and whom the Lady Mary was eventually deputed to distract—he took the others into his confidence, and was not long in winning their whole-hearted enthusiasm, Nigel's in especial. All agreed to co-operate in the raising of the men, and all clamoured to accompany the eventual contingent northwards. That would have been folly, but it was agreed that Edward and Nigel should come campaigning.

Thereafter the Bruces rode far and wide through Annandale and lower Eskdale and Nithsdale, which all formed part of the lordship, summoning to the standard the young men of the rich and populous Solway lands. Armed service with their lord was, of course, together with rent in kind, the basis of all land tenure, and able-bodied men between sixteen and sixty could not refuse, from lairds and substantial farmers down to shepherds, foresters and herd-boys. The Lordship of Annandale was particularly highly rated in this respect, being a crown fief of no fewer than twenty-five knights' fees—that is as a condition of the original royal grant to the first Robert de Bruis seven generations before, it had been required to produce, on the king's demand, the equivalent in men, arms and horses, of the followings of twenty-five knightly lairds at, say, fifty men each. Much more than that could be raised now, at a major mobilisation. Bruce reckoned that Annandale could muster three thousand, at a pinch, even in a week; but such was not his intention now, whatever Percy might say. There was no point in denuding and impoverishing the land, in present circumstances. Half that number would be enough.

Five days of recruiting and selecting and mustering saw just over fifteen hundred men assembled at Annan, few enthusiastc, for the presence of Sir Henry's two hundred English horse, in whose close and unremitting escort the Earl of Carrick was very clearly little better than a captive, left few doubts as to which side they would be fighting for. Not that the Annandale men were aggressively Scottish; with their territory wide open to the English border, and great hill masses cutting them off from the rest of Scotland, for generations they had been under southern rather than northern influence. But fighting against their fellow-Scots was another matter—though they had no option, if their lord so commanded.

The sixth day they rode back to Carlisle—rode, for Annandale was a notable place for the breeding of horseflesh, the sturdy, stocky, long-maned garrons which the English mockingly described as ponies but which were in fact full-grown sure-footed horses, though short in the leg. Every man was mounted. This, of course, was one of Surrey's requirements, being short of cavalry. On ahead, Edward and Nigel Bruce flanked their brother, within a tight cohort of Beaumont's men, who were taking no risks with a prisoner who now commanded seven times their own number.

Carlisle was like an ant-hill disturbed, with thousands of the levies of North Country English lords milling around. But the vast majority of these were footmen, it was to be noted—and Bruce sent Nigel back to warn his Annandale host, at the encampment they were allotted beside the Eden, to watch over their horses. There would be many envious glances cast in their direction, that was certain; and Scots might well be looked on as fair game. They should keep out of the town, therefore, or there might be trouble.

A surprise awaited the Bruces at the citadel. Percy was already returned from the east, and he had brought Elizabeth de Burgh with him, for some reason. Unwarned, the young men came face to face with her in the Great Hall—to their distinct unease. She was entirely self-possessed—but betrayed no delight at the meeting. Going on for his interview with Percy, after a somewhat abrupt greeting, Bruce at least was in a turmoil of mixed resentment and speculation.

Percy received the brothers civilly enough, even congratulating them on the numbers of men raised—although he had hoped for perhaps five hundred more, he indicated. He appeared to accept the adherence of the two younger Bruces as no more than appropriate. They would ride north the next day. He mentioned, as an afterthought, that his kinswoman, the Lady Elizabeth de Burgh, had accompanied him to Carlisle, with his wife. His visitors made no comment.

Bruce did not fail to seek a reason for this move. He did not flatter himself that his own presence at Carlisle had itself attracted the young woman across the country. Moreover, the assembling of an army, in a hurry, was no occasion for feminine jaunting. Therefore Percy, who was a cold-blooded fish if ever there was one, and did nothing without a cause, must have brought her for a purpose. She was Edward's god-daughter, the child of the monarch's closest friend—and no doubt it was widely known that the King had once contemplated marrying her to Bruce. Presumably as a precaution, to bind him closer. That could scarcely apply now. But Percy might believe that there was still something between them. He must hope, in some way, to use her to bring pressure to bear. But how? And why?

Bruce, at any rate, did not propose to assist him in whatever was his project. He would avoid the girl. Not that he had any difficulty in this, at first, for Elizabeth appeared to be no more anxious than he for any association. The citadel was swarming with people. The Bruces kept themselves to themselves.

That night, however, the Bishop of Carlisle held a banquet for the leaders of the new army, and the Bruces were summoned. Precedence, for seating, presented an obvious problem, but the Bishop got over the difficulty by providing a special table for the Scots, at the back of the dais. And to Bruce's side here, presently, the prelate brought and seated Elizabeth de Burgh, before all the company, a gesture calculated to attract the maximum of notice, with so few women present and this one the most high-born as well as far and away the most beautiful.

Bruce, although not normally lacking in the powers of speech, on this occasion was practically wordless. Without herself being forthcoming, the young woman was at least civil, but she obtained little response from her right hand neighbour. Fortunately at her other side, the Lord of Annandale saw no reason for either resentment or embarrassment, and finding a courteous listener, launched into anecdotes of the Crusade on which he and Richard de Burgh had accompanied King Edward, in their youth.

Wine, however, had the effect of making Bruce the Elder sleepy, and as the repast proceeded, his talk grew thick and disconnected, and presently died away in puffs and little snores. Elizabeth, although she could not be unaware of the admiring glances cast on her by many, and especially Edward Bruce on his father's left, chose to turn to her heavily silent neighbour on the right.

"So, my lord, you now neither talk nor rebel!" she said, pleasantly.

He frowned. "I keep my own counsel," he jerked, in reply.

"So I perceive. And unpleasing counsel it must be, I think."

"Why think you so?"

"From your face, if naught else! You look uncommon sour, sir! And since the counsel you keep to yourself can scarcely be to your own congratulation."

He began to speak, but thought better of it, and closed his lips tightly.

"You are Edward's man again," she went on, conversationally. "How happy His Majesty!" And when he still did not reply, "You found rebellion unprofitable, did you?"

He answered her questions with another, and abruptly. "Why are you here?" he demanded.

She took a moment or two to answer. "Because I was brought. With the Lady Percy, my cousin."

"Brought, aye. You are not sitting beside the Lady Percy!"

"No doubt she sees sufficient of me. I am living with her, while my father fights with the King in France. Moreover, has she not Sir Robert Clifford to entertain her?"

"So I see. And she is welcome to him! Why were you brought here, then?"

She looked at him thoughtfully. "I do not know," she said. "*You* did not ask Sir Henry to bring me?"

"I did not!" That was vehement.

She smiled faintly. "At least, I see, you are honest in some things, my lord!"

"Are you saying that I am *dis*honest in others, madam?"

"It may be that I used the wrong word, sir. Should I have said frank? Open? Single-minded?"

"You have no very high opinion of me!"

"I do not deny it. Have I reason for it? Am I mistaken about you, my lord? I sent you a letter."

"Aye. I received it. Scarce a letter, it was. An insult, rather!"

"I asked a question then, too. That I might, perhaps, think the better of you. And you did not answer."

"How could I answer such a thing? You asked if I was a man! Or a clerk? And should you thank God to have escaped me!"

"So at least you read my letter."

"More than once. To see if there was any kindness hidden in it. But I found none."

"Kindness? You looked for kindness, then? From me?"

"Women can be kind, can they not? Understanding. There was no understanding, there."

"What did I fail to understand? You could have told me, in answer."

He drew a long breath. It was on the tip of his tongue to speak, to explain something of his position, what he was seeking to do. But he could not, dare not. He shook his head.

"It is of no matter," he said curtly. "What *is* of matter is why you are here. What made Percy bring you? It is concerned with me, for sure. What does he want?"

She sighed a little. "I told you, I do not know. Is it important?"

"It could be. Did he not tell you. Give you some reason? Some task? Perhaps to question me?"

"Think you I am Henry Percy's spy, sir? His informer?"

"You could be. Without intending it. Why bring you? Or his wife? It is a strange time and place to bring women. And to set you here, by me."

"It was the Bishop who did that. But I can leave you, sir, and gladly, if you please?"

He ignored that. "Either he would have you to learn something from me. Or else to sway me. Why?"

"That I should sway *you*, my lord! If he thinks so, he knows little of either of us! And what should I learn from you that he cannot ask himself? That I would tell him?"

"If I knew, I would not be asking. It seems, however, that he does not trust me."

"And is that so strange? Men who change sides so quickly are seldom trusted."

He bit his lip. "Can you not conceive that I may have reasons? That I may be more honest than you think? You, who sit secure in English halls. In Edward's goodwill. When a kingdom is at stake, woman!"

She eyed him closely at that, and said nothing.

Fearing that he had blurted out too much, he frowned, and changed his tack. "Percy himself is perhaps unsure of Edward's goodwill. With reason. If Edward returns quickly from France, heads may fall. You are close to Edward. Could it be that he would use you to gain Edward's favour?"

"I cannot think that King Edward looks on me so warmly. I believe I may have disappointed him."

He weighed that. "But you *are* his god-daughter."

"Is that important? In this matter? Might it not be more important that I am James the Steward's niece? By marriage."

"Ha!" Bruce sat up. "I had forgot. His wife is Egidia de Burgh."

"My father's sister. And, now I think on it, Henry Percy has mentioned the fact to me, of late. More than once."

"This makes more sense. The Steward led this late revolt. I have been close with him. He is now being taken to join Surrey's array, making for Dundee. Where we are going. Now that there is no king in Scotland, and Buchan the Constable lies low in the North, the Steward is the greatest officer of the realm."

"And is he not this William Wallace's lord? Wallace his vassal?"

"So—you know of that also! Aye, Wallace's small lands are held of the Steward."

"Henry Percy said as much."

"I think, then, that we get down to the roots of it now. On how the Steward and myself may make common cause with Surrey, much depends in Scotland. And Surrey's and Percy's reputations with it. And you, my lady, it is thought might weigh heavily with us both."

She shook her corn-coloured head. "It is a weighty edifice to build out of so little!"

"Perhaps. But let us make some test of it. Tomorrow, if we leave you behind here at Carlisle, I will accept that I may have misjudged. But if you are carried with us northwards, into Scotland, then I am like to be right."

"We shall see. But I tell you, my lord, that Elizabeth de Burgh will be pawn in no man's game—Edward's, Percy's . . . or yours! Mind it well!"

Thereafter, for such time as the banquet continued, they got on rather better, able to talk together at least without striking sparks.

The following morning when, amidst much blowing of trumpets and shouting of commands, the various component parts of an army of over eight thousand mustered and moved off over Eden, northwards into Scotland, the Ladies Percy and Elizabeth de Burgh, to the surprise of many, rode with them.

• • •

They marched by Esk to Canonbie, and then up Liddesdale, the horse making no attempt to hold back to the pace of the foot; but even so it was a fairly slow progress. It took the three thousand cavalry two days to cross over the Note o' the Gate pass, to Hawick in Teviotdale. The day following, the leaders were at Selkirk, on the edge of the great Ettrick Forest, when a messenger reached them from Surrey's army, now nearing Stirling, the first crossing of the long Forth estuary which so nearly, with that of the Clyde, cut Scotland in two. The courier came not from Surrey himself, however, but from Cressingham, the Treasurer, in the name of the Viceroy, Fitz-Alan. Percy had sent word ahead, by fast rider, to inform of his coming, his numbers and his route. The reply astonished and incensed him. Cressingham, as Treasurer and cost-conscious, declared that they already had quite sufficient men in arms to deal with such as the scoundrel Wallace and his riff-raff, and consequently the reinforcement army would not be required. It was the Viceroy's wish that Sir Henry returned whence he had come, and disbanded his force.

The thin-lipped, hesitant-seeming Percy's fury was a sight to behold, on receipt of this extraordinary message. He trembled, shivered, looked almost as though he would swoon with rage. He knew well, of course, of the bad blood between Cressingham and his uncle, Surrey. Clearly this was done out of spite, the wretched Treasurer—who indeed had made himself the most hated man in Scotland—prevailing on the new Viceroy to over-ride the authority of the commander-in-chief. But out of a stuttering torrent of white wrath, it became clear that Percy had no intention of obeying. He was a soldier, in arms, and he took his orders from the military commander, not from such a low-born clerk as Master Cressingham. Or even Fitz-Alan. Until detailed commands arrived from Surrey himself, they pressed on.

In this he was supported vigorously by Sir Robert Clifford and most other leaders—indeed by Robert Bruce likewise, whose plans would have been put in much disarray by any turning back now.

Three days later, on the evening of 11th of September, emerging from the Pentland Hills into the West Lothian plain, with the foot now left far behind, the army was again halted by information from the north. But this time it was no mere courier who came to them, but two dishevelled knights, Sir Ralph Basset and Sir John Lutton, with a straggling party of men, some wounded. And their tidings were of disaster.

There had been a great battle, they declared. At Stirling Bridge, over the Forth, twenty-five miles to the north. They had been tricked, betrayed, scattered and ill-led. Surrey's army. It was no more. The man Wallace and an unnumbered great host of rascally Scots had lain in wait for them there. At this bridge. Amongst tidelands and marshes. It had been no fair fight. The work of mean men. Half of the English array across the bridge and on the mile-long causeway beyond. Wallace had attacked, through swamp and bogs. No room to fight. No room to turn. Horses hamstrung, or sinking in the mire. Arrows, spears, knives—no honest chivalry. All in confusion. The Welsh cravens fleeing back, casting away arms and armour. The bridge taken and held behind them. Hundreds drowned trying to swim back. Others still trying to swim across to their aid. Then treachery in the rear, south of the bridge. The damned Scots with Surrey, betraying them. That Steward. The Earl of Lennox. Crawford. Lundin. All turned coat. Attacked the rear. Roused the people of Stirling. To slay and murder. It was a massacre . . .

Appalled, Percy and his companions fired questions at the exhausted men, sought to piece together the picture, to learn the present position. Wallace had been besieging Dundee, fifty miles to the north-east, had he not? Surrey had between fifty and sixty thousand men . . .?

Not any longer! God alone knew how many still lived. Cressingham was dead. The Scots were said to have flayed him, and cut up the skin to send round the country. A hundred and more knights were slain—most without having opportunity to fight as knights should . . .

"And Surrey? And Fitz-Alan?"

Surrey was in full flight for Berwick. Fitz-Alan—none knew where he was. Everywhere men were fleeing, as best they could. Wallace's hordes pursuing, cutting down. And everywhere the common Scots folk were waylaying, slaughtering, from every wood and copse, devils behind every bush. Men and women both. The whole plain of Forth was a shambles. And there was Edinburgh to get through. Before the Border and Berwick. That was why they had come this way, hoping to win through to the West. Before news of the victory turned every hand against them. All over this accursed land the people would be rising.

Hurriedly, distractedly, the leaders of Percy's force conferred. Once their five thousand foot came up, they were a strong force. If they had been but a day or two earlier, they might have saved all. Or, perhaps, been swept away with the rest! If sixty thousand could be so broken, would an extra eight thousand have made the difference? How many, in God's name, had this Wallace managed to muster?

But their foot would take days to catch up with them. They were probably not at Selkirk yet. And had they days to spare? To wait? All Scotland would be rising around them, drunk with the smell of victory, thirsting for bloody vengeance. Wallace would have time to gather together his forces again. It would be sheerest folly to wait. Even Clifford conceded it.

What, then? Would three thousand cavalry, tight-knit and driving forward, turn the tables? While the Scots were yet disorganised? Rallying what was left of Surrey's host. Men eyed each other, and eyed the Bruces, and read doubt in each other's eyes—and knew without saying it that there would be no such thing.

Retire, then? Back, whence they had come? Or to Berwick, to join Surrey? Or west, to Ayr, to hold the South-West, for which Percy was responsible as Sheriff and Governor?

There was some argument about this, complicated by the fact that their foot contingent would still be back amongst the Borderland hills. Eventually it was decided to rejoin the infantry, and then to head east through the hills for Berwick.

Robert Bruce took no part in this discussion, having ample to think about on his own, since the news changed all. Presently he had a few brief words with his brothers, who were hiding their excitement less than successfully. As he was doing so, his glance caught that of Elizabeth de Burgh, who, with Lady Percy, sat her horse a little way apart. It was an eloquent and significant glance.

During these past long days of riding, and nights spent in remote English-held castles, Bruce and the girl had inevitably seen a lot of each other. They had come to a sort of acceptance, a tolerance, of each other's attitude, which could not be called an understanding but which at least enabled them to maintain civility. Awareness had been pronounced between them from the first, however unsympathetic in its outward reactions; now there was a mutual playing down of the friction which seemed to generate spontaneously.

When the hasty and disjointed conference around Percy and the two newcomers had reached a conclusion, and an about-turn was announced, Bruce raised his voice.

"My lord of Northumberland," he said, stiffly formal. "You and yours may make for Berwick. I, and mine, do not."

There was a sudden silence from the leaders' group.

"What do you mean?" Percy asked tensely, after a moment or wo.

"I mean that I have not come so far into my own land, to turn back now."

"We have decided otherwise. That King Edward's cause will best be served by turning back to Berwick, for this time."

"It may be so. But I go on. And my host with me."

"Go where, sir? And for what purpose?"

"For good and sufficient purpose."

"There speaks a forsworn traitor and rogue!" Clifford cried. "Have I not always said as much? That he could not be trusted a lance's length?"

"Sir Robert Clifford," Bruce declared quietly, "for these words you shall answer, one day. At lance's length! But . . . here and now, I think, is not the time."

"No," Percy agreed coldly. "More is at stake now. More is required than such barren talk. My lord of Carrick—your men are mustered in King Edward's name. You are here in his service. And under *my* command. I'd mind you of it."

"And may I mind *you* of something, my English friends? You are deep in this Scotland. Part of a beaten, broken army. With a long way to go before you may rest your heads secure. Moreover, half of these men behind you are my father's. Scots. Who, think you, will they obey, in this? Do you wish to put it to the test?"

So it was out, at last, gloves off, the mask down. With a jerk of his head Bruce sent his two brothers spurring back to the main body, their errand clear, obvious.

Even Percy had no words now.

Clifford had. "He came with this intention. To desert us. The treacherous turn-coat! He planned it all. Back in Carlisle. I said we should leave him. Should bring his men, but not Bruce himself. They are all the same, these Scots. I'd trust an adder before any of them! This is treason, by God! Bruce is traitor, for all to see!"

"These are hard words, sir. Perhaps I spoke too soon? That this was not the time to break that lance!" Bruce raised a hand to point at Clifford. "Perhaps Sir Robert had better answer for his words now. After all. Honour demands it..."

"Honour! *Your* honour! In flagrant treason, you talk of honour?"

"Has it not entered your head, man, that what would be treason to the English is not treason to the Scots? That we cannot commit treason against a conqueror, a usurper? If the Scots commit treason, it must be against their own realm and king. Only an unthinking fool would say other. And that I name you, Sir Robert—an unthinking fool! Is that sufficient for *your* honour? So—shall we form our respective hosts into lists, my lords? Make a tourney-ground? While Sir Robert and I fight it out, *à l'outrance*. It will be my pleasure..."

"No, I say!" Percy intervened, in pale-faced anger. "I forbid any such childish folly! This is war—not tourney-ground posturing. Enough of this."

"If you prefer war to jousting, my lord—let us have it. We are not unevenly matched. We shall have our own battle, here on this hillside, if you will? Scots against English. What could be fairer? Put all to the test. Of war..."

"No, by the Mass! It shall not be." Percy's thin voice rose alarmingly. "Think you I do not know what you are at? To keep us here. To delay our retiral. In hope that our presence is discovered. That Wallace's hordes come up with us..." His words were lost in the murmuring and muttering of his companions, the two knights from Stirling's debacle loud amongst them. All eyes were turning northwards, as something of the fear of these communicated itself to the others.

"Very well," Bruce said, and had to repeat it, loudly. "Then here we part company, my lord."

"You shall pay dearly for this—that I swear, Bruce!" Clifford shouted, in frustrated fury, and was the first to rein round and ride back towards the host.

As the others followed suit, Bruce waved his hand to his brothers. As they gave their orders for the Annandale men to draw apart and ride on, he urged his mount over to where the two women sat their horses, silent spectators of the scene. He did not speak, but searched Elizabeth's face.

"So you change sides once more, my lord!" she said.

He knew that was what she must say—but had hoped, somehow, that she would not.

"You think it? You think that is what it is?" he demanded.

"What else? That, or you have been acting a lie for long."

He spread his hands. "A lie? What is the lie, and what is the truth? I have not changed in my own mind. I have done what I must. In a storm, a man does not speak of lies and truth, but seeks to keep his bark afloat! To reach its haven."

"And you have a haven in mind?"

"Aye. I have a haven in mind."

Percy had ridden up, frowning. "Come," he commanded the women brusquely.

His wife, a tired-faced and anxious woman with fine eyes, sighed. "This is men's business, my dear," she said. "Leave it to them. Since we can effect nothing." She reached out a hand to the girl's wrist. "Come, yes."

Something of the way she had said that caused Bruce to look keenly from her to Elizabeth, wondering.

The younger woman seemed to ignore them all. "You intended this?" she put to Bruce. "From the beginning? To use this march, these men, for your own ends? Before ever there was the word of this victory. When we talked, at Carlisle that night. Even then, you had conceived it all? And let me name you . . . what I did!"

Wordless at her sudden intensity, he nodded.

"You did not trust *me,* then?" She seemed to be unaware of the Percies at her side.

Still he did not speak.

"If Wallace had not won his victory—what then?" she persisted. "What would you have done?"

He glanced at Percy. "This. The same. Though with bloodshed, perhaps. If we had been withstood."

She let out a long sigh. "Then I am glad," she said simply, and the intensity seemed to go out with her breath.

Percy was looking angry, apprehensive and bewildered, in one. He grasped Elizabeth's bridle, and pulled her beast round after his own.

She did not resist him now. But she turned in her saddle. "Tell my uncle, the Steward, that I wish him well. He and his. And . . . and may God go with you."

Biting his lip, Bruce watched her ride away.

And so the host divided, there on Torphichen heights, in silence, without blows or any other leave-taking. The Scots sat their horses and watched as the English turned and trotted off, file upon file, whence they had come, southwards for the Pentland Hills and the long secret road to the Border.

PART TWO

Chapter Eight

Scotland rejoiced. Abbey and church bells rang day after day, bonfires blazed on the heights for nights on end, folk danced in the streets of towns and on village greens. The English were gone—all save the garrisons of a few impregnable but isolated fortresses, Lochmaben, Roxburgh, Edinburgh and Stirling itself, where the gallant Sir Marmaduke Tweng, who almost alone on the English side had come out of the disaster with untarnished reputation, still held out. But these could achieve nothing, and did little to dampen the enthusiasm, relief and joy of the people. The name of William Wallace was on every lip, prayed for in every kirk, honoured in every burgh and village and hamlet. The Scots, never hero-worshippers until now, acknowledged their saviour, and delighted the more in that he was one of themselves, of the old race, a knight's son admittedly, but of the people. Everywhere the acclaim rang out.

Or, not quite everywhere perhaps. In many a castle and manor of the land there were reservations—even in not a few whose owners had won them back, out of English occupation, thanks to Wallace. The nobles saw a little further than the common folk. They saw the established order endangered. Their men, their own vassals, were everywhere flooding to join this Wallace, quite ignoring their feudal duties and service to their lords, the system on which the entire community was built. Land, enduring, indestructible, viable, calculable land, was the unit on which a realm must be based; not persons, who were ephemeral, unreliable, removable, and who could and did pass away. The land did not die, and the great families who managed the land were not going to pass away either. Yet Wallace held only a miserable few acres of this land, and claimed the people as all-important. And he was not even a Norman, his mother-tongue not French but the Erse gibberish.

Few, of course, even of the most proud, lofty and influential of the lords, denigrated the scale, brilliance or the effect of Wallace's

Stirling Bridge victory. Moreover, although only in a minor capacity and in the later stages, he had been supported in his victory by some of the great ones—the Steward himself, Lennox, Crawford, Macduff, son of the Earl of Fife; and, of course, the Graham. Sir Andrew Moray of Bothwell had been his principal lieutenant, and had indeed fallen, mortally wounded it was said. So Wallace could no longer be called outlaw, brigand, claimed as something like a Highland cateran and guerilla fighter. Even men with legitimate doubts had to recognise realities.

Robert Bruce was one of the doubters, of course, although his concern was rather different from the others—not so much for the land, nor yet the people, but for the kingdom. Wallace's blow had been struck for the people; but it was a blow for the kingdom also, and so must be acclaimed, supported. But Wallace himself did not represent the kingdom's cause; Wallace might indeed endanger the kingdom. He had fought in John Baliol's name.

Bruce, that vital September, did not in fact encounter Wallace. When he arrived at battle-torn Stirling, with his Annandale men, it was to find the Steward and many of the lords assembled there, but Wallace himself gone, pursuing the fleeing English with all his mounted strength. All was falling before him, and he was maintaining the impetus to such an extent that he was said to be actually making for Berwick itself. There was even a suggestion that he intended to drive on, down into England.

This would be folly, all the Scots lords agreed, Bruce included. They sent couriers after Wallace, advising him strongly against any such course. Nothing would be more likely, Bruce pointed out, to reunite the English, at present at sixes and sevens, than an actual invasion of their land.

There was much to do at Stirling, with a whole land, suddenly freed from a fierce and authoritative grip, to be brought under control. The lords and bishops applied themselves to this, under the frowning regard of Stirling's great fortress, still English-held, but impotent, not really besieged even yet, but contained. Buchan, the Constable, had come south with his cousin, John Comyn, Lord of Badenoch; so that there were two great officers of state to represent the highest authority in the land and take charge of the attempts at administration. Again, in the name of King John Baliol.

Bruce protested about this, declaring that Baliol had abdicated and renounced the throne. His deposition and humiliation by

Edward could be overlooked perhaps; but not his renunciation and fleeing the country. He was no longer King, in any sense. To act, here, in his name, was not only wrong but folly.

The matter was complicated. In the past, when the Kingdom of Scotland had been without an effective monarch, for one reason or another, a Guardian had always been appointed to act on behalf of the Crown and bear the supreme authority. Obviously such a Guardian should be appointed now. But who should be the Guardian? Normally it would be one of the great nobles, who should also be a military leader, with powerful forces at his back—since he had to wield the sword of state. The Steward would have been suitable, as to rank and position, but he was no military leader, no leader of any sort, in fact, and his slobbering speech no aid to high dignity. The Earl of Buchan, High Constable, as an earl, could claim seniority in rank, and was indeed a veteran soldier, with large following; but he had played an equivocal part in this rising, had indeed, at Surrey's command, taken the field against Moray's rebels in the north, though half-heartedly and ineffectually. His reputation had suffered, and the common folk of Stirling booed him in the streets, the more so as Moray himself lay dying.

There was another candidate for Guardian, however, Buchan's cousin, the same Sir John Comyn the Red, Lord of Badenoch, who with Bruce had formed part of that unhappy queue to sign the Ragman's Roll at Berwick a year before. He was ambitious, vigorous and an effective soldier—and the Comyns were undoubtedly the most powerful family in the land. Moreover, his mother was John Baliol's sister.

Bruce might have claimed the Guardianship for himself—and undoubtedly would have done had he been less of a realist. For he recognised that he was little more popular with the Scots people than was Buchan. Everyone knew that he had been Edward's man. The Red Comyn even referred to him as Bruce the Englishman. He had taken no actual part in the recent fighting; all had been over when he arrived at Stirling with his little host. His youth was no insuperable difficulty—but he could not claim to be a military leader; though he had been knighted, he had won his spurs at joustings in the tilt-yard. He could not command the confidence necessary for a Guardian, he knew.

But of one thing he was determined—the Red Comyn should not be Guardian. It was not only that he hated the man's arrogant mocking style. John Comyn said openly that if John Baliol had indeed vacated the throne by leaving the country, and taking his young son Edward with him, then he, as his nephew, was next in line to be King.

A more immediate and practical problem than the Guardianship and civil administration, however, quickly made itself evident to the assembled lords—simply that of food. Food for man and beast. The harvest had not been ingathered over much of the land—indeed, because of the English occupation and its harshness, and the removal of wool and grain to England, there had been but little sown, little to reap. Everywhere barns, stackyards and storehouses were empty, and the grim shadow of famine began to grow in war-torn Scotland. No doubt in the more remote parts there was still a sufficiency; but in the areas over which the armies had operated, hunger was growing as the days shortened. By the nature of things, Stirling district was worst hit. The lords could no longer feed their men-at-arms. A general break-up became inevitable.

Bruce's fifteen hundred was the largest single contingent there, and consequently required most food and forage. He was faced with the choice of sending them home to Annandale, to disband; leading them south to join Wallace, who had taken Berwick and was now besieging Roxburgh Castle; or going over to the West with them, to his own area of Carrick, where there was no famine as yet. This last appealed most strongly. A body of fifteen hundred men-in-arms was too useful an asset in the present state of Scotland to disband and throw away, however much of a problem it presented logistically. Wallace was still talking about invading England—now, not only for military and vengeance reasons, but for food; and Bruce had no desire to be involved in any such ill-advsised adventure which would only expedite reprisals.

In mid-October, then, the Bruces left Stirling for Ayrshire, glad to be away. Already there had been clashes with the Comyns in the streets of the town. Andrew Moray had died two days earlier, a good man gone.

It was strange to ride through the countryside, Lanarkshire and Ayrshire, and find the English gone—for here in especial their rule had been most complete, all-embracing, with every town and castle garrisoned. Now, like snow in the smile of the sun, they had quietly withdrawn, disappeared—and in their place many of the tollbooths had small portions of Cressingham's skin nailed to the English gibbets. Bruce was now able to ride, for the first time for years, to his own birthplace, the principal seat of his earldom, Turnberry-in-Carrick, home of his Celtic ancestors for generations. Typically, the English had left it in good order, not burned or destroyed—for they would soon be back, they declared.

But the Bruce brothers had barely disposed themselves in Turnberry Castle, and commenced the process of stocking up with winter fodder for man and beast, than they were rudely jolted. An exhausted messenger came from Annan, via Stirling, from Thomas and Alex Bruce. Annandale was in smoking ruin, sacked, devastated. Sir Robert Clifford had come north, with a great host of Cumberland men, and laid all the Bruce lands waste. Ten townships were destroyed, hundreds slain, Annan itself sacked—though the castle had held out—the harvest all burned and the cattle driven off or slaughtered. Clifford had left again, with his booty—but the lordship was in dire distress.

So Turnberry was abandoned again, and the Bruces spurred southwards in wrath. But some of the wrath, the brothers well knew, was now directed against themselves, as their men contemplated broken homes, ravished women, and widespread ruin to return to—done while they had been held by their young lords kicking their heels in the north. Defiant gestures were all very well for lordlings; but Annandale had ever been too vulnerable to English attack to hazard. The old lord had known that well. But the old lord was gone, apparently, none knew where. And his sons had failed Annandale . . .

Bruce himself was not unaffected by a sense of guilt. He would be the seventh Bruce lord of Annandale, and the first to allow it to be cruelly ravaged. As he rode furiously through the devastated land and saw the burned homesteads, desecrated churches, the corpses of men, women and children choking wells and ditches, hanging from trees, crucified on gates, a great weight of responsibility settled upon him—allied to a cold hatred. It was on his account that these people had suffered. But woe to those who had caused the suffering.

At the douce red-stone town of Annan, blackened and charred now, below the castle that still stood intact on its mote, they learned the full grim details from Thomas, Alex and Mary. Clifford had come raging from Carlisle with thousands, mainly foot—although they had returned to England mounted. It had not been any military campaign but purely a savage punitive onslaught. Indeed Clifford's orders to his men had been every man for himself, no quarter to be given, no prisoners taken, all booty and plunder to remain the property of whoever could take it. The Bishop-Governor of Carlisle had lent him troops for the outrage, offended by Bruce the Elder having bargained Annandale men for his own freedom and then seen them change sides. As a consequence, hell had been let loose on Annandale.

Robert Bruce had now more than enough to keep him busy, without concerning himself overmuch with affairs of state. It was a notably hard winter, setting in early with snow and ice and gales, and folk in no state to cope. The needs of his own people took up all his wrathful energies. He set himself to organise the transfer of grain and cattle from Carrick to Annandale, rehousing and rehabilitation of refugees and homeless, rebuilding and repairing whole townships and villages. He had never applied himself like this in his life, and was glad enough to tire himself out day after day. This he could do, must do. The rest could wait.

Thoughts of Elizabeth de Burgh came to him not infrequently, but she seemed to occupy a different world to his.

Occasionally word of the doings of men outside this South-West reached them. William Wallace had indeed invaded the North of England, and a bitter and harsh retaliatory campaign he appeared to have waged, giving the Northumbrians and Cumbrians precisely the same sort of treatment that had been meted out to the Scots. Tales of savagery, violence and slaughter percolated through to Annandale—and though, in his present mood, Bruce was not inclined to feel squeamish towards the English, part of his mind told him that this must result in a hardening of the enemy's determination, a uniting of fronts, and ultimate fury of attempted reprisals. There were ten times as many English as Scots, and this simple truth was something that they had to live with, to ever take into account. Their every effort, therefore, should be to divide and disunite, not to unify. This campaign, however justified, would have that effect, for certain.

Great convoys of grain and cattle and sheep were said to have been sent back to Scotland. This at least was satisfactory. But the cruel weather triumphed over cruel warfare, and the now distinctly undisciplined Scots army was forced back across the Border before Christmas. Wallace, it was said, had retired to his favourite refuge in Ettrick Forest, and his mixed host had largely dispersed to their homes all over the land.

Then came the first and inevitable counter-attack. Surrey drove north again, on the east side, and retook Berwick and Roxburgh. But the weather was too much for the English likewise. The advance could not penetrate the snow-blocked passes of the hills which guarded most of Scotland's southern counties, and ground to a halt. It was stalemate, meantime, in the worst winter of living memory.

It was late February before the icy grip began to relax—and with it came word from the south that King Edward, from France, had commanded that there be no major invasion of Scotland until he came in person to lead it—ominous tidings. When that would be was not revealed, but rumour said in the late spring. Perhaps spurred by this grim warning, movement stirred again in Scotland. Wallace sallied forth from the Forest, to besiege Roxburgh Castle, and his emissaries were once again going through the land calling men to his standard. None came to Annandale. But in early March a courier arrived from James the Steward, to announce a great assembly of the magnates and community of the realm to be held in Ettrick Forest, at Selkirk, in the middle of the month, and requested the Earl of Carrick's presence thereat.

Bruce considered well. He recognised that important decisions could not be put off for much longer. If Edward was coming, then the ranks had to be closed and vehement steps taken. He himself could not hide away here in Annandale indefinitely. And he might usefully influence the steps that might be taken. The fact that the assembly was being held in the Forest, in Wallace's own chosen haunt, not in Stirling or Edinburgh or at Scone, was surely significant. It meant in large measure an acceptance of Wallace as leader. The lords were to come to him, not he to the lords. Bruce decided that Annandale might now be left to his brothers' care. He would go to Selkirk.

• • •

It was hills and passes for every mile of the fifty that stretched between Annan and Selkirk, and the snows and floods still blocked much of the way, impeding and delaying Bruce and his small escort more seriously than he had anticipated. He was hours later than intended in reaching the venue of the assembly, in that fair hub of green valleys where Ettrick, Yarrow and Tweed all joined, amongst the oak, ash and pine glades of the greatest forest south of the Highlands. The gathering was being held in the ruins of what had once been the Abbey of Selkirk, a Tyronensian foundation of David the First's, which 170 years before, had been removed twenty miles further down the Tweed, to Kelso, for convenience. The remains, though abandoned, were extensive and picturesque, providing a certain amount of shelter, but more of dignity, for a large-scale conclave. As Bruce rode down through the haughs of Yarrow towards it, he saw the entire wide valley-floor filled with encampments and horselines the silken pavilions of lords and knights, banners and standards everywhere, the blue smokes of a hundred cooking-fires rising over all.

It seemed that the actual conference and council was already started, being held partly in the open, in a sort of amphitheatre formed by the broken-down former choir of the abbey, backed by the square of the cloisters and opening on to the neglected sunken gardens and pleasance. Here a great crowd of folk were assembled, of all sorts and conditions, gazing up to where, in the paved approaches to the gaping chancel, the quality and landed men and churchmen stood, or sat on the flanking cloister benches. Up in what was left of the choir stalls certain great ones were seated, in the centre of which was the Steward, who appeared to be presiding. A cleric was holding forth.

". . . all kinds and conditions of men, their treasure, their toil, their very lives," he was declaring, in a richly sonorous voice. "This being so, it is necessary, essential, that due and proper direction be given them. With authority. The Church can do this, in the name of God and His kingdom. But who may speak, with full authority, in the name of this earthly kingdom of Scotland? My Lord Steward—you occupy high office and bear a proud name, of excellent repute. But you cannot speak in the name of the King's realm. My Lord Constable—nor can you. You are one of the great Seven Earls of Scotland, and have authority to raise the realm in the King's cause. But you cannot speak in the realm's name, so that all men must obey. I say that it is entirely necessary for the governance and saving of this kingdom that one be appointed, here and now, lacking the King's royal presence—appointed by the magnates of the realm here assembled, who may take fullest command in all matters, and speak for this ancient people. I do declare that this assembly is entitled to name itself a parliament of the estates of Scotland, and that it should hereby appoint one to be Guardian of the realm."

In the applause and acclaim Bruce, peering over the heads of spectators, asked of a black-robed Dominican friar who it was who spoke.

"That is a great man, Master William Comyn, brother to the Earl of Buchan, sir. They say he will soon be bishop. He is Provost of the Chapel-Royal."

"A Comyn! Then we know what will be coming next!" Bruce began to edge forward through the throng.

The speaker continued. "The Guardian must be strong, else he is useless, my friends. He must dispose of great forces. He must be renowned as a warrior, a man of great repute. Also he must be strong in support of Holy Church. I say to you that such a man stands here amongst us. He is indeed the head of the family of which I am the humblest member. A family which none will deny is the strongest, the greatest, in this land. Which boasts three earls, three bishops, and no less than thirty-three knights. I say to you that none is more fit to be Guardian of Scotland than Sir John Comyn, Lord of Badenoch."

There was considerable acclamation for this nomination, but Bruce noted that it was confined to the quality. Few of the watching throng raised voice—but there was a ground-swell of muttering. Although they were powerful indeed in the North, in the South here the Comyns were not popular. They were too closely identified with the despised Baliol.

Bruce, in his edging forward, had reached a point where he became aware that, behind a massive broken pillar of the former transept, William Wallace stood, towering hugely over a group of his lieutenants—these no longer a ragamuffin crew but now all clad in excellent armour and broadcloth, no doubt captured. Only Wallace himself was dressed exactly as previously in rusty chain-mail and leather guards—perhaps because he could find none amongst his defeated enemies of size sufficient to supply him. He stood listening to the proceedings, hidden from most in his retired position, expressionless.

The Constable was now adding his support to his brother's nomination. It may have cost him dear to do so, for there was said to be little love lost between the two John Comyns, Buchan and Badenoch; but though an older man, more experienced, and out-ranking his distant cousin, he could not but concede that the other was chief of the name. Their mutual Norman great-great-grand-father had married as his second wife the heiress of the ancient Celtic mormaership and earldom of Buchan; Badenoch was the heir of the first family, himself of the second. And in public, the Comyns always put up a united front.

Earl Malise of Strathearn spoke next. He proposed, as somebody must, in decency, that James, High Steward of Scotland, be appointed Guardian. He was formal, brief.

Men stirred uncomfortably. The Steward was well enough respected as an honest man and a patriot. But as mouthpiece of the nation . . . !

From his presiding seat in the choir, James Stewart raised a thin open hand and waved it back and forth. "I decline. I decline such nomination," he said thickly. "I am old. Of insufficient strength. A younger man is required. I decline." At least, that is probably what he said, though his difficult tongue and slobbers muffled it. But the gesture of his hand was sufficiently clear.

The Abbot of Dunfermline suggested that a bishop of Holy Church might well prove the wise choice, uniting all classes and divisions of the people. He would have proposed their beloved Robert Wishart, Bishop of Glasgow, who had once acted Guardian previously, he said—but unhappily he was a prisoner of the English. The Primate, Bishop Fraser of St. Andrews, had just died, exiled in France. Bishop Crambeth of Dunkeld was also in France, ambassador to the French king. He therefore named Thomas of Dundee, Bishop of Ross.

There was now some applause amongst the commoner folk, for Bishop Thomas was one of Wallace's supporters. But there was no like enthusiasm visible amongst the ranks of the nobility; nor indeed amongst much of the clergy, where Ross was considered to be too junior a see to be thus exalted.

A new voice broke in, musical, with lilting Highland intonation. "My lords and friends," a slight, delicate-seeming but winsomely good-looking youngish man said, "hear me, Gartnait of Mar. I say that if there is one man who should be Guardian of Scotland, it is Robert Bruce of Annandale, who should rightfully be our King. But since he is not within the realm at this present, I say to you that his son should be appointed—the Lord Robert, Earl of Carrick. He is not here, but is expected . . ."

Bruce cursed beneath his breath. His brother-in-law, the Earl of Mar, meant well, no doubt; but this was not the time to advance *his* name. Gartnait, although amiable, had always lacked practicality. He was much troubled by his neighbours, the Comyns, of course, and no doubt was as much concerned to counter their ambitions as to aid Bruce's.

"Bruce *is* here, my lords!" he cried aloud, interrupting Mar, and pushing strongly forward now, through the press, to break out into the open flagged space which had once been the abbey's nave. "I come late—but not too late, I say!"

There was a great stir and exclamation now, on all sides—by no means all of it enthusiastically welcoming, as he strode up to where the Earl of Mar stood, clapped his sister's husband and first wife's brother on the shoulder, and bowed to the Steward.

"You give me leave to speak, my lord?" he said strongly.

James Stewart nodded.

"I have heard what is proposed, my friends," he said. "Not only as regards myself, but others. And I too say that a Guardian of the realm should be appointed. Now. But not myself, who have fought no battles, earned no plaudits, am but untried amongst you. My father, were he here, would himself be no candidate for Guardian—that I swear. If he were to present himself to you, I say, it would be as your rightful King, not Guardian . . . !"

A wave of reaction, cheers and dissent mixed, comment and question, greeted that, a new vigour and excitement manifested itself throughout the great gathering.

Bruce held up his hand. "But my father is *not* here. I have heard the names suggested as Guardian, and I say that, good and sound men as these are, they do not, cannot, meet the case, my friends. Only one man can fill Scotland's need today. Only one man will the people follow. Only one man, at this juncture, can speak with the voice that not only the folk but England, Edward Plantagenet, will hear and heed. That man is William Wallace of Elderslie. I name you Wallace as Guardian!"

It was as though a dam had burst, and the emotions of men surged free in clamour. The very surrounding hills seemed to shake to the shout that arose and maintained. Not all of the vociferation was favourable, of course, but the vast mass of it was wildly so. Almost to a man the common folk, the men-at-arms, the lesser lairds and small land-holders, even the bulk of the clergy, roared their approval, hands high or beating each other's shoulders, feet stamping. It was amongst the nobles, needless to say, that the opposition was expressed, but compared with the mighty explosion of applause, it was a small thing that faded where the other went on and on.

It was some time before Bruce could make himself heard again. "I commend . . . I say, I commend your judgement!" he shouted. "This man has done what no other could do. He has rid us of the English . . ."

Again the uproar.

"Hear me—hear me, my friends. He has rid us of the English, I said. Aye—once! But they will be back. Nothing on God's earth is more sure! They will be back. And so he must needs do it again. I know Edward. Aye, some blame me, they say, that I know him over well! But this I say, that when Edward himself comes chapping at our door again, then we shall need a united realm to withstand him. And more than that, a leader whom all the people will obey and follow. Therefore, I say, William Wallace it must be. None other . . ."

He was interrupted. "And I say this is folly!" It was Sir John Comyn, the Red, himself. "Here is confusion. It is a Guardian of the realm we seek to appoint—not the commander of a host. Wallace has shown that he can do battle, yes. But he is no man for the council-table, no meet representative . . ."

His words were drowned in outcry and protest, angry this time, with an ominous underlying growl. Fists were shaken, even swords were drawn and waved. Everywhere the nobles looked apprehensively around them, at the gesticulating crowds.

The Steward was trying to speak, but Bruce prevailed. He had young and excellent lungs, and no impediments to speech.

"There are sufficient and more for the council-table!" he declared. "Many to advise Wallace. All too many! But the Guardian must carry the people, not just the Council. If Scotland is to withstand Edward of England in his might and wrath. Here is the heart of it. Only the nation in arms will save us, then. And only one man, I declare, can raise this nation in arms, lacking its King . . ."

When the noise again slackened, it was not the Lord of Badenoch but another Comyn, who took up the issue, Master William the churchman.

"What my lord of Carrick says is not in dispute," he claimed, with the careful moderation and reasoned appeal of the practised orator. "None question William Wallace's notable deeds, or his ability to rouse the people. That he must do. But more than this is required of the Guardian. There are decisions of state and policy to make. He must unite more than the common folk—he must unite the lords of this realm. Will Wallace do that? You say, my lord, that he must withstand King Edward. But he must speak with him also, treat, negotiate. Will the proud Plantagenet speak with such as William Wallace . . . ?'

"I say that he will. Edward is proud, yes. But he is a man of deeds, not of words. Because Wallace is of the same kidney, he will respect him where he would not you, sir. Or myself, indeed. Think you he cares for any Scots lord? But the man who defeated Surrey in open battle is altogether different."

The Comyns were not quieted yet. "I know Edward also—to

my cost!" That was Buchan, the Constable. "He does not eat his words. He has named Wallace outlaw, cut-throat, promised to hang him. Think you he will swallow that, and deal with him? Never! Moreover, the Guardian of Scotland speaks in the name of the absent King of Scots. How can this man do that? He is not even a knight! You, my lord, of all men, should know better. The Kingdom cannot be represented by one who is not of the *noblesse*, the men of honour. How shall knights and lords follow and yield their voices to one who is not even of their order . . .?"

"By the Rude—is that what concerns you, my lord?" Bruce cried. "Then we shall see to it!" He swung on his heel, and strode across the moss-grown flagstones, spurs clanking, to where Wallace had stood quietly amongst his own group throughout, a grimly silent spectator of the scene. In front of the giant he halted, and with a screech of steel drew his sword, the short travelling sword that hung from his golden earl's belt. "William Wallace," he declared, voice ringing, "I, Robert Bruce, knight, earl of this realm, do hereby dub you knight. In the name of God and St. Andrew." He brought down the flat of his blade on one great shoulder, then on the other—where it clashed against the long upthrusting handle of the other's own famous and enormous two-handed brand that was said even to sleep with the man. "Earned on the field of battle, if ever knighthood was. Be you faithful, fortunate and bold! Stand, Sir William Wallace!"

There were moments of utter silence, surprise, elation, even consternation. Then, in that green ruin-strewn hollow of the hills, pandemonium broke out, to make feeble and pedestrian even the tumult that had succeeded Bruce's previous proposal of Guardian. In wild emotion, men went all but crazy with jubilation, approbation and a sort of unholy glee. The thing was done, suddenly, dramatically, totally unexpectedly, there before them all—and could nowise be undone. Sir William Wallace!

While undoubtedly there were not a few present who questioned the wisdom, the propriety, even the taste of what Bruce had done, none could doubt his right so to do. In theory, any duly dubbed knight could himself dub another, provided that he had proved his prowess on the field of battle or in single combat, and was accepted as a man of renown; but in practice, only kings, princes, commanders of armies, and very great nobles ever did so, the last but seldom and in special circumstances. Nevertheless, as the holder of one of the ancient Celtic earldoms of Scotland—and knighted most royally by no less than King Edward himself

—none could contest the validity of Bruce's action, even without his claim to being second heir to the throne.

Even the Comyns, therefore, stood dumbfounded, impotent, silenced by their own cherished code. Everywhere the nobility and chivalry of Scotland were in like case.

The Earl of Mar was the first to move. As the din continued, he walked over to Wallace and clapped him on the shoulder, wordless. Words could not have been heard, anyway. The Earl of Lennox came to do the same. These were the only earls present, apart from Carrick, Strathearn and Buchan. Then the Steward stood, and came from his seat to congratulate the new knight. Crawford followed suit, and others, some others, likewise.

As for Wallace himself, for once he seemed quite overcome by events. He stood there, his open features working, his great hands gripped together in front of him, knuckles showing white. He did not speak, had not spoken throughout, appeared all but dazed by his abrupt transition. The last man to be called a respecter of persons, or impressed by mere forms and ceremonies and titles, he was nevertheless very much a man of his age, and only too well aware of what this unlooked-for metamorphosis could do for him. By one brief and simple rite, in that chivalric age, he had been made respectable, transferred to the ranks of the men of honour, given a status that none could take away from him. Knighthood, in 1298, was no empty honour. Much that had been almost inconceivable only a few moments before was now possible. William Wallace was no fool, and however reluctant to be beholden to young Bruce, or any other lord, he would not have rejected this accolade, even if he could.

Bruce was not finished yet. Into the gradually ensuing hush, he spoke. "As Earl of Carrick, and therefore member of the high council of this kingdom, I do now request of that council to declare and appoint Sir William Wallace of Elderslie, Knight, to be Guardian of Scotland, as from this present." He looked first at the Steward, and then nodded to his brother-in-law, Mar.

It was a shrewd thrust, addressing his nomination to the high or privy council. Such body undoubtedly existed, but it had not met formally for long. More important, for his present requirements, it had had no new members appointed to it for years. Therefore, save for one or two elderly men, only those who automatically belonged to it by virtue of their high office or position, could at the moment claim to be members. These were the great officers of state, the senior bishops, and the earls. At one blow,

Bruce had silenced much of the opposition. The Red Comyn, for instance, undoubtedly would have been a privy councillor if that body had been properly appointed; but lacking King or Guardian, no recent additions had been made.

Mar was about to speak, when Lennox forestalled him. As another of the old Celtic nobility, he had no love for the Normans in general and the Comyns in particular.

"I, Malcolm of Lennox, agree," he said. "I say Sir William Wallace for Guardian."

"Aye. As do I," Mar added.

"No!" That was Buchan, gazing round him anxiously. As well he might. Apart from the Earl of Strathearn, and the Steward himself, there was only one other certain privy councillor present, the Bishop of Galloway—and coming from that airt, he was almost bound to be a Bruce supporter. He was.

"I also say for Wallace," the Bishop announced briefly.

"As do I," Malise of Strathearn nodded.

There was a brief pause, and the Steward, licking his lips, spoke. "Does any other . . . of the council . . . say otherwise, my lords?"

"I protest!" Sir John Comyn cried hotly. "At this, of the council. It is a trick, a ruse. Who knows who is of the council? It has not met. These three years and more. Bruce would trick us all. I say all lords and knights may speak. And vote."

There were cries of agreement from not a few, but Bruce shouted through them.

"I declare that the voices of individual lords and knights, however puissant, have no authority in this. Only a parliament duly summoned, or else the council, can appoint a Guardian. This assembly cannot be a parliament—since who had authority to call one? Therefore, the council only may speak for the realm. And there are councillors enough here."

"So . . . so I hold and sustain," the Steward nodded, though obviously uncomfortably. "Can you deny it, my lord Constable?"

Unhappily Buchan eyed his cousin. "In other circumstances . . ." he began, and waved a helpless hand.

"I call the vote," Lennox said.

"Aye." James Stewart acceded. Does any other member of the council speak?"

There was none other to speak.

"I see no need to vote, then. The issue is clear. Five have

spoken for—no, six. One against. If I myself were to vote, nothing would be altered. My lord Constable—will you withdraw your opposition, that all may be more decently done?"

Buchan sighed, and nodded, in one.

"So be it. I declare Sir William Wallace, Knight, to be Guardian of this Scotland—in the name of the famous prince, the Lord John, by God's grace King of Scots."

Strangely, there was comparatively little acclaim and demonstration now. Men seemed to be sobered suddenly by what was done, what the implications were, what this dramatic action foreshadowed. It was as though an irrevocable step had been taken, an assured order all but overturned. All were for the moment abashed. Even Bruce, who should have protested about this being done in the name of Baliol, did not do so.

All looked at Wallace.

That giant appeared to come out of a trance. Almost like a dog shaking itself, he heaved his huge shoulders and raised his auburn head. He gazed round on them all, out of those vivid blue eyes, unspeaking still, a tremendous, vital figure, the very personification of innate strength, vigour and resolve. Then slowly, waving his supporters back, he began to pace forward from his transept.

Not a sound was heard as he stalked up the choir steps and came to stand before the Steward. That man rose, and after a moment, bowed deeply before the other. Then he moved slightly aside, and gestured to Wallace to take the seat he had vacated, the simplest of tokens, but fraught with significance.

Something like a corporate moan rose from the great company.

Wallace inclined his head, and moved into the Steward's place. But he did not sit. He turned, to face them all, and raised a hand.

"My friends," he said, and his deep voice shook with emotion. "I thank you. I thank you, with all my heart. For your trust. I swear before Almighty God that it will not be betrayed. God and His saints aiding me, I shall not fail you. Much is needed. I shall demand much of you. But, for myself. I shall give all. This I vow—and you are my witnesses."

The murmur that swept the crowd as like the distant surge and draw of the tide on a long strand.

"And now, my friends, to work." With a flick of his hand Wallace seemed to thrust all that had transpired behind him. Emotion, by-play, ceremony, had had their moment. Typical of the man, all was now decision. "There is much to do, I told you. Most can and must be done hereafter. But it is right that some shall be done here, before you all—and be seen to be done. The council, for one. I know but little of these things—but it is clearly in need of renewing, of enlarging, as my lord of Badenoch says. My first duty, therefore, as Guardian, is to see to this. I now ask Sir John Comyn, Lord of Badenoch, to join it. Also Sir Alexander Lindsay, Lord of Crawford; Sir Alexander Comyn, Lord of Lumphanan; Sir Alexander de Baliol, Lord of Cavers; Sir William Murray, Lord of Tullibardine; and Master William Comyn, Provost of the Chapel-Royal."

Even Bruce gasped at this swift recital, rapped out like the cracking of a whip. At first, like others, he had thought it unsuitable lacking in fitness, for Wallace to plunge so immediately into the exercise of his new authority. But now he saw, as all men of any understanding must see, how astute a move this was. Wallace had been appointed in the face of Comyn opposition; and since they were the most powerful family in the land, he would have them as a burden on his back. But, by this sudden move, he had changed the situation dramatically, and put the Comyns, especially Sir John, into a position of acute difficulty. He had singled out three of them for advancement, in this his first official act. The Red Comyn had himself indicated that the council was in need of new blood. Now, to refuse to sit on it, especially in the company present, was almost unthinkable. Yet it meant that the mighty Comyns were thereby accepting favour at Wallace's hands, the very first to do so, demonstrating to all their acknowledgement of his authority. He had them in a cleft stick.

Bruce almost laughed aloud as, after an agonising moment or two, Sir John inclined his arrogant head, unspeaking. The other surprised nominees murmured varied acceptance.

Apparently satisfied, Wallace went on, "Two other matters. This realm had an ancient alliance with France. The French are now attacked by the same foe as are we—Edward of England. We must see to it that both realms act in common against him. Make a treaty of aid, one with the other. If Edward, as is said, does return from France to lead attack against us again, then the French should attack England in the south. It is our blows, here in Scotland, and into England, that will have brought him back. This must be our enduring policy. King John saw this three years ago, but was forced by Edward to denounce his treaty. We must renew it. I say that we should send envoys at once to King Philip, new envoys. It is in my mind to send Master John Morel, Abbot of Jedburgh. And Sir John Wishart of the Carse, brother to the imprisoned Bishop of Glasgow."

Men stared at each other. The proposal was a sound one, and the envoys named no doubt suitable enough. But none could fail to be astonished at this naming of names. That Wallace should already not only have his road mapped out, but have men in his mind to carry out his designs, could only mean that he had been prepared beforehand for some such eventuality. But his knighting and appointment to the Guardianship had been wholly at Bruce's sudden instigation. How then . . . ?

Bruce himself, listening, came to the conclusion that he had underestimated and misjudged his man. He had thought that, by these actions of his, he had hoisted him into the Guardian's seat; it looked now very much as though Wallace had been prepared to assume it, on his own.

Distinctly chagrined, if not humbled, Bruce listened to a further demonstration of the big man's forethought and sheer ability. He, the former outlaw and small laird, had the effrontery there and then to create a new Bishop of St. Andrews and Primate of all Scotland—or, at least, to take the essential steps therefor. He did it, first by adding Master William Comyn's name as a third envoy to France; then by announcing the senior bishop present, Galloway, as Chancellor of the realm, or first minister of state; and finally proposing one William Lamberton, Wishart's chancellor of Glasgow Cathedral, as Bishop of St. Andrews, in the room of the late Bishop Fraser—adding that, on his necessary visit to Rome to be consecrated, he should also present to the Pope the Scottish realm's entire and leal duty to His Holiness and its request that the Holy See declared its disapproval of Edward of England's invasions and savageries, and threaten him with outlawry from Christendom, anathema and excommunication if he persisted in such wicked warfare.

Quite overwhelmed, the company listened. Never had anyone present heard the like of this, such vehement forcing of the pace, such high-sounding a programme, such confidence of delivery—and all done before a great gathering of the people, not behind the closed doors of the council-chamber.

The Comyns were silenced—for Master William had undoubtedly been hoping for St. Andrews for himself, as a senior member of the chapter and brother of the Constable; Galloway bought off, who might have claimed the Primacy, Wishart being a captive and Crambeth of Dunkeld overseas; and all muffled up and confused by this ambitious bringing in of the Pope as possible ally in the struggle.

—For what? Amongst Wallace's group of immediate supporters, a tall, strong-faced, keen-eyed churchman stood beside the Benedictine friar, John Blair. By the way the others were looking at him, it was evident that this man must be Master William Lamberton. A long sword-hilt peeped from beneath this individual's black robe. Another Benedictine, and a fighting one, apparently. So Wallace was making a bid to control the Church, as well as the state. One of his own band Primate and Galloway Chancellor. And Pope Boniface was a Benedictine also, it was said.

There were murmurs, growls, alarmed looks, amongst the nobility and some of the churchmen, but no vocal or affirmed opposition. That this was not the place, nor the time, any man of discernment would understand. This was Wallace's day, and any who openly opposed him would go down.

Grimly the giant considered them all, waiting. Waiting for the outcry that did not materialise. Then he nodded, and turned.

"My lord Steward," he said, "it is enough. I thank you for your patience, your courtesy. I thank all. Let a feast, a great feeding, be prepared. For many are hungry. There is much food here in the Forest—the famine has not touched it. Many wild cattle, many deer. Sufficient beasts are already slain. All shall eat and drink tonight." And, the King's representative having given his orders to the King's Steward, he bowed briefly and, waving to his own close group to follow, strode by the vestry door out of the ruined chancel.

Later, with the camp-fires lighting up the March evening, and the rich smells of roasting beef and venison filling the night air, a very thoughtful Bruce, in company with the Earl of Mar, pacing the shadowy, broken cloisters of the abbey, was startled by a deep voice speaking close behind them. They swung round, to find Wallace there, with the man Lamberton. Like so many big men, he seemed to have the ability to tread very softly.

"So, my lords," he said, "you commune closely! As well you might! For in this Scotland, I think, the very stones listen and whisper. And there will be much whispering tonight. How long, think you, before word of this days doings reaches Surrey? And Edward?"

The two earls, who had indeed been discussing Wallace, looked a little uncomfortable.

"What mean you, Sir William? By that!" Bruce asked tensely.

"That wise men do well to look over their shoulders—that is all," the other answered lightly. "This is a notable realm for traitors, is it not?"

Was this, could it possibly be, some sort of warning? "I do not take you, sir," Bruce said.

"Then you are less shrewd than I esteemed you, my lord! The House of Comyn may not love Edward Plantagenet. But they may prefer him to William Wallace! Or even Robert Bruce!"

"So-o-o! You fear the Comyns will not accept what is done?"

"Only if they must, I think. And they are very strong. I ask you, my lords, as men of the same noble rank and station as these—should I feel secure, when Edward strikes, with the Comyns in arms at my back?"

Bruce glanced at Mar, and cleared his throat. "I do not know!"

"Nor do I! Master Lamberton, here, believes that I should not."

The tall priest spoke in a crisp voice that smacked of the field rather than the chancel. "I do not name them traitors," he declared. "But I hold that they believe themselves better suited to rule Scotland than is Sir William Wallace! And will not hesitate to stab him in the back, if by so doing they may take over that rule. And esteem themselves to have done Scotland service! To do so, they must be most fully assembled in arms. As they can, in answer to the Guardian's summons to the nation. The Comyns could raise ten thousand men. A sore host to have at your back, in battle!"

"True. But how may this be countered?" Mar demanded. "You cannot keep the Comyns from mustering their men. Nor deny them the right to fight for the realm."

The cleric lowered his voice. "My lord—you control the vast earldom of Mar, a mighty heritage in the North. My lord of Carrick, yours is the Lordship of the Garioch, nearby in Aberdeenshire—half a province. Moreover, Sir Andrew Moray is dead, woe is me—but his brothers are sound for Wallace, and hold the great Moray lordships of Petty, Innes and Duffus. All these abut the Comyn lands. If you, my lords, were to go north and, with the Morays, muster the men of these lordships—as all will be called upon to do by the Guardian—then you have a force assembled on the Comyns' doorstep, do you not? Men so mustered in arms are ever . . . restless. However firm you hold them in, there will be some small spulzie and pillage. Reiving, as we say in the East March of the Border, whence I come. On neighbours' lands. Comyn lands. I swear, so long as they are there, no Comyn host will come south!"

Bruce almost whistled beneath his breath. Here was a crafty, nimble-witted clerk. Could it be that this was where the advice came that was turning Wallace from mere warrior into statesman?

"You would play the realm's nobles one against the other, Sir Priest?" he challenged.

"They need but little encouragement in that, my lord! I but urge that, since all the land must be mustered in arms, it is only wise that sound men muster alongside those who might be led otherwise. I wish for no bloodshed, no fighting. But a due balancing of forces."

"And Bruce *is* sound, in our cause, to be sure!" Wallace put in, smiling into his curling auburn beard. "Since he it was who made me Guardian! With my lord of Mar's aid."

If there was derision in that, it was fairly well covered over. Bruce saw very well that Wallace trusted none of the lords, himself included. He was for sending him north, away from his own great reservoirs of manpower, Carrick and Annandale, to far Garioch, his sister's portion when she married Mar. There to distract Comyn, the Red Comyn in especial, who was his rival in so much.

"How do you know that I will not make common cause with the Comyns?" he demanded.

Wallace actually laughed, apparently having followed the younger man's train of thought accurately. "Because John Comyn is Baliol's man," he said simply. "And you are . . . yourself!"

The acuteness of that silenced Bruce for the moment. Mar spoke.

"If our hosts are up in Moray and Mar, facing Comyn, then we cannot be aiding you here against the English."

"A commander needs more hosts than one, my lord. It is wise not to pit all at one throw. He needs a reserve. Your combined hosts, in the north, will well serve as that."

In other words, Wallace was well content to fight Edward with his own common folk, the masses assembled direct from the nation, holding the great lords' levies at a distance. Bruce saw it, if Mar did not.

"Beware, sir, that you do not estimate Edward Plantagenet too lightly!" he said.

"That I do not," the big man assured. "By God, I do not! But all shall not be won, or lost, in one battle."

There was a mutual silence for a little, as the four men considered each other. Then Bruce shrugged.

"You are Guardian of Scotland," he said.

"Aye. Thanks to you, as I say."

"I wonder!"

"You doubt my thanks, my lord? That is foolish. You did for me, then, what no other could, or would, have done. The knighting. I will not forget it. For that, at least, I do most surely thank you. Your reasons for doing it I do not know. But the deed was good. Of much value. For this, I am in your debt."

"It was merited," Bruce said shortly. "Never was knighthood more so."

"Not all would agree with you! But ... that is no matter. What matters now is the future. How long do you give Scotland? You who know Edward. Before he comes hammering at our gates?"

"Three months. A month to return from France. A month to set his own house in order—to bring the English nobles to heel. A month to raise the men to march north. I give Scotland until June."

"Aye. You have the rights of it, I think. Three months—and so much to be done! So much!"

"You can do it," Lamberton said, in his crisp voice. "You only. For the folk are with you."

"We shall see, my friend. So you, my lords, go north..."

Chapter Nine

Strangely enough, that spring and early summer of 1298 was one of the happiest periods of Robert Bruce's life—for which he had to thank William Wallace. He was, in fact, essentially a fairly cheerful and light-hearted character—had he not a reputation for extravagance and display?— and the last two years of stress and deep involvement in national tumults had superimposed a gravity and tenseness on his nature which was not normal. Now there was an intermission, a period of enforced detachment—or so he was able to convince himself. His prolonged periods of sham negotiation at Irvine and hard unremitting restoration work in Annandale, had prepared him to embrace the satisfactions of Kildrummy as it were with open arms.

He had not made his way there in unseemly servile haste, of course. He had his dignity to consider. He informed Wallace that he would take over the duties of governor of the South-West, with headquarters at Ayr—and Wallace had acceded with good grace, since it would have been impracticable to appoint anyone else in opposition to him. He had returned from Selkirk to Annan, set affairs there in order, specifically commanding that there was to be no general muster of the Annandale men, save for the lordship's own defence, whatever instructions might come from the Guardian. Then, taking Edward and Nigel with him, he had ridden north to Ayr, where he installed Edward as deputy, to raise the area in arms, including his earldom of Carrick, refortify the castle and keep an eye on Lochmaben—which, being to all intents impregnable, was still in English hands, like Stirling; possibly the insufferable Master Benstead was still there. Then he and Nigel, his favourite brother, had set out on the two hundred mile journey to Aberdeenshire.

Kildrummy Castle, principal seat of the age-old Mar earldom, was a handsome establishment set amongst the uplands of the Don, and guarding the mountain passes to the north-east. A remote secure place, centred in a world of its own, with the most magnificent hunting country for hundreds of square miles around, it was little wonder that its lord seldom chose to leave its fair attractions. Bruce found it much to his taste.

There was more than the place itself to hold him. Here his little daughter Marjory had been brought, when her mother, Mar's sister, died. She was now a laughing, chubby brown-eyed girl of three, and Bruce, who had accepted fatherhood as he had accepted marriage merely as one more normal development in a man's progress, now discovered delight, wonder, pride. This roguish, impulsive, affectionate child was his, all his, in a way that nothing else was his—and he had not realised or appreciated it before. On Isabella's death, at seventeen, soon after the baby was born, he had been anxious only to deposit the unfortunate infant with his sister Christian, take himself off, and forget the whole sorry business, a loveless marriage arranged by his father, an ailing, delicate young woman who cared nothing for the world outside Kildrummy, and then left him at nineteen with a puling, bawling girl-child. But now, here was Marjory Bruce, a poppet.

Christian Bruce, Countess of Mar, was herself good company, the gayest of the family, all vigour, energy and laughter, and twice as much a man as her gentle, slightly melancholy husband. Though womanly enough in all conscience, so that young men were ever round her like a honey-pot; Gartnait of Mar was probably wise enough not to leave home too frequently. She welcomed her brothers with enthusiasm, and proceeded to ensure that time did not hang heavily for them. Nigel himself was a happy-natured, carefree soul, and an excellent companion to take the mind off affairs of state.

Not that all was hunting and jollity, of course. The business of mustering a host went on, with wapinschaws, archery contests, trials of strength, games and races, to keep the men engaged and in training. No doubt the Comyns were doing the same, not so relatively far away—but in this land of vast distances, high mountain ranges, and little sense of involvement with the rest of Scotland, no ominous signs of it disturbed them. Bruce did pay one or two visits to the Bruce lordship of the Garioch, consisting of fifteen parishes, to the east, the rents of which had been Christian's marriage portion. Here he arranged for eight hundred men to assemble at the somewhat tumbledown old castle of Inverurie, and to train for service—Nigel would command these, in due course.

April passed into May, with the snow gone from all but the north-facing corries of the surrounding mountains, whins blazing and cuckoos calling endlessly in all the endless green valleys around Kildrummy. Word percolated through from the outside world occasionally, but seemed to lack urgency up here. Edward had returned from France, and had apparently made a great show of coming to terms with the nobles. He consented to ratify and confirm the terms of Magna Carta and the Charter of Forests, and agreed that the new taxes and tallage should only be levied with the acceptance of the nobility, prelates and knights, and withdrew the edict about compulsory foreign service. But, having done this, he had set up his headquarters at York, even moving the exchequer and law-courts there, as a sign of his displeasure with the south and as convenient for his campaign against Scotland. There was also news that Lamberton had gone to Rome, and that Philip of France had accepted a treaty of mutual aid with Scotland. Wallace had been disciplining his army, hanging not a few who had been pillaging and running wild. The burghs were all raising armed bands, the various crafts vying with each other. Roxburgh and Stirling castles still held out. A Comyn host, said to number six thousand, was assembled in the Laigh of Moray

This last did cast some small shadow at Kildrummy, and Bruce rode north by devious hill passes, further north than he had ever been, to Petty, on the coast east of Inverness, headquarters of the great de Moravia family, of whom Sir Andrew Moray had been the heir—the lord thereof still being Edward's prisoner. Here he found Andrew's two brothers, Alan of Culbin and William of Drumsagard, had already raised fifteen hundred men, while their uncle, Master David, a priest, had gone still further north to raise Avoch and the Black Isle of Cromarty. He also learned that Andrew's widow had given birth to a posthumous son, another Andrew to carry on the line. Giving Wallace's authority, he took the fifteen hundred, with young Alan of Culbin to command them, and rode back to Mar with them, doing a little harmless spoliation and fodder-gathering in outlying Comyn lands *en route*, as per instructions.

Back at Kildrummy, in early June, the news was more grave. Edward had assembled a mighty army at York, and was moving north. He was said to have no fewer than four hundred knights and gentlemen of chivalry, under the Earl Marshal, the Great Constable of England and the Earls of Gloucester, Lincoln, Arundel, Surrey and Warwick, besides the Scottish Earls of Angus and Dunbar. There was also the ominous Bishop Beck, 2,000 heavy cavalry, 2,000 light cavalry and no fewer than 100,000 foot and archers. These figures were almost certainly exaggerated, but clearly Edward was in deadly and determined mood.

There was another piece of news which indicated that however busy Wallace must be in preparing to resist invasion, he was not failing to use his wits in other directions. King Philip of France's signature of the treaty of aid was all very well, but he had not sought to use Edward's return home to implement the bargain by any renewed attack on the English, either on the Flanders borders or by massing for invasion of southern England. So Wallace had sent a new delegation to Paris, to urge military action upon him—and this was headed by John de Strathbogie, Earl of Atholl, and none other than Sir John Comyn, the Red. To have got Comyn out of the way at this juncture was a shrewd move, and might well make the Comyn forces mustered in Moray less dangerous—for the Earl of Buchan was less of a firebrand than his young kinsman.

These tidings were not rumour or hearsay, at any rate, for they had been brought to Kildrummy by the daughters of the Earl of Atholl himself. Strathbogie was the adjoining lordship to Mar on the north-west, and Atholl had married Mar's other sister. Christian Bruce, always a romantic, and a born matchmaker, had invited the Ladies Isabel and Mary de Strathbogie to Kildrummy, clearly for the delectation of her brothers. They were pleasant, amiable, uninhibited girls, not beauties but comely enough and high spirited. Nigel was appreciative at least, and was getting on excellently with Isabel. Bruce, however, found some disinclination to live up to his reputation, with Mary—although he was by no means offended by her company, of which his sister saw to it that he had plenty.

A week or so after his return from Petty, riding back from heron-hawking up the Don, Bruce, momentarily alone, was joined by Christian.

"You look thoughtful, Rob," she said, eyeing him keenly. "Indeed, you are much in thought these days. Not as I mind of you. I wonder why?"

"We live in thought-making days, Tina," he returned easily.

"We always did. You are but twenty-four—early to become a greybeard! You used to be otherwise, brother—uncommonly so! Something of a rakehell, even. And a notable wencher! Does that sport no longer rouse you, Rob?"

He shrugged. "Say that I have other matters on my mind, lass."

"I think you have!" She looked at him quickly, and away. "But it is possible to . . . to allow some small distraction, on occasion, is it not? I would not have you turn into another Gartnait!"

It was his turn to look. "Gartnait . . . he does not satisfy you, Tina?"

"No," she admitted, simply.

"I am sorry. He is an honest, kindly man—if scarce a hero! Generous—and not disapproving, I think?"

"True. All true. But it is of *you* we speak, brother—not me! What do you think of Mary Strathbogie?"

He smiled. "She is well enough. Good company. And sits a horse well."

"She might sit a man well, too, Rob!"

"No doubt. Who is eager? She—or you?"

"Not you, it seems!"

"Should I be so?"

"You are still Robert Bruce, are you not? And Mary would make warm trysting. Or better, a good wife. Your Marjory needs a mother. And Mary dotes on the child."

"Insufficient recommendation for a wife, Tina!"

"She has more than that to commend her. She is kind, strong—not like Isabella Mar, a weakling. And she is taken with you, I can see. And mind, Rob—there are not so many women the Earl of Carrick might wed. You could not wed less than an earl's daughter—and there is no routh of such to choose from."

"Even so, I shall wait awhile, lass. My wife, see you, should I marry again, might need even greater qualities than you give Mary Strathbogie."

"You mean . . . you mean . . .? Nigel thinks that you might one day try for the throne. Is that so, Rob?"

"Has any greater right? After our father?"

"Right, no. But is that what matters, Rob? What good would the uneasy crown of Scotland do you? Even if Edward of England let you, or any, have it. You would have to fight long and hard to gain it. And fight as hard to keep it. Does that tempt you? A lifetime of fighting. For what? The empty, barren name of King!"

"Need it be so empty? Barren? Does not this realm require a king? Grievously."

"Need that unfortunate be Robert Bruce?"

He shrugged.

"So . . . you look for a queen, as well as a wife?"

"Did I say I looked for any woman?"

"No. But you are sure that Mary will not serve, it seems. So you have thought of it." Christian leaned forward to scratch her mare between the ears. "Nigel thinks that you are . . . concerned with another. An Irishwoman. The Lady Elizabeth de Burgh. Is it so, Rob?"

"It seems that Nigel thinks too much. Talks too much!"

"So it is true? There is something in this?"

"Nothing," he said shortly.

"Yet you have seen much of this Ulsterwoman? Found her to your taste?"

"Edward once thought to have me wed her. To bind me closer to him, no doubt. But she liked the notion as little as did I!"

"Yet you still see her?"

"Not by our own seeking. She lodged with Percy, while her father was with Edward, in France. Percy sought to use her, to work on me. Not knowing."

"Not knowing what?"

"That we battle together as soon as we see each other. That there is only strife between us."

She considered him thoughtfully. "Strife? Battle? It is thus between you? Then, Nigel has cause for his fears, perhaps!"

"Damn Nigel! He has no more cause to fear than he has to talk. What has he got to fear?"

"An entanglement with one so close to Edward . . .?"

"She approves of rebellion—that is how close to Edward she is! But what of it? I am not like to see her again."

"I wonder! Since you both esteem each other so ill, I think that you will!" Christian smiled a little. "This Elizabeth de Burgh—what is the style of her?"

"She is proud. And lovely. And believes me two-faced," he jerked. "That is all. Enough of this, of a mercy! Where is Nigel?"

"Where do you think? He makes excuse to fall behind. With Isabel. She nothing loth. But *you* leave Mary with Gartnait! You could be more the man than that!"

"Very well. I will go to her. But . . . let her not hope for too much."

Bruce was spared any prolonged skirmishing with the friendly Lady Mary. Two days later the messenger arrived from Wallace. He requested that the Earl of Carrick hasten south, with all the force at his command and at all speed. Edward was moving fast, was in great strength, had already taken Berwick, burned the abbeys of Kelso, Dryburgh and Melrose, and was marching on Edinburgh up Lauderdale. Wallace would require all the help he could muster, to halt him, preferably at Stirling. Once the English were beyond Forth, there would be no holding them, in their present numbers. This message was not to go on to the Comyn host, in Moray. They would hear, no doubt—but, it was hoped, not in time to affect the issue.

The intermission was at an end.

• • •

Bruce, Nigel and young Alan de Moray of Culbin—Mar stayed at home—led their combined host of about 3,500 southwards as fast as they could. But Mar and Moray were not Annandale, a great horse-breeding area, and the vast mass of their men were not mounted. They had 170 miles and more, to reach Stirling, and though the men were in the main tough, wiry hillmen, their very numbers, and the need to forage for food, precluded any phenomenal rate of travel. Twelve miles a day, over mainly mountain country, was quite as much as they could manage.

Two more of Wallace's messengers reached them during the journey southwards, urging haste. Edward had surprised all by circling Edinburgh, not waiting to take it as expected, contenting himself with taking its port of Leith, as a haven for his anxiously awaited supply ships. Wallace had been falling back before him, deliberately devastating the land in the English path, a land already all but famine-sticken, ordering the folk away with their remaining cattle and destroying all grain, hay and fodder that might remain. Edward's invaders were said to be starving, and his ships delayed, so that there were troubles, the Welsh archers mutinying and eighty had been slain, it was said. Wallace's tactics were to lure the enemy back and back, over devastated land, right to Stirling and the Forth crossing, the most strategic point in all Scotland to hold a great army; but, perceiving it, Edward was pressing after the Scots at whatever the cost, before Wallace could properly clear the land in front. It had become a race for the narrows of the Forth.

Bruce's host had just left Dunblane, between Perth and Stirling, in the early morning of 23rd of July, when Wallace's next courier came up with grim tidings. The Guardian's army could not reach Stirling in time—that was clear. The huge majority of his force was infantry, the common people; and Edward's cavalry, in their vast numbers, were pressing them hard. He would try to hold them somewhere in the Falkirk vicinity, a dozen miles south of Stirling. And though cavalry was what Wallace most required, he had been only doubtful in his welcome to an unlooked for reinforcement which had just arrived, even though led by the High Constable of Scotland. The Earl of Buchan had put in an appearance with some hundreds of Comyn horse; he had evidently heard the news, up in the Laigh of Moray, and leaving behind his great array of foot, had raced south with his horsemen, by the coast route, while Bruce had been so much more slowly marching his combined host through the mountains. Buchan was allegedly hastening to Wallace's rescue; but the latter was uneasy and urged Bruce to do likewise, to leave his foot behind and ride with all haste for Falkirk.

It was about twenty miles from Dunblane, by Stirling Bridge, to Falkirk. Bruce did not delay. He had nearly 700 horse, mounted hillmen on short-legged Highland shelts, in the main. Leaving Alan Moray to bring on the thousands of foot, he and Nigel spurred ahead with this company, unhampered.

At Stirling Bridge they found Wallace's advance party preparing to hold it, if need be. They urged on the northerners anxiously. The English were in greater numbers than anything known before, they said; the plain of Lothian was black with them. Wallace was standing at Callendar Wood, just east of Falkirk—but it was no site to compare with this Stirling. These men were clearly in a state of alarm.

It was afternoon before they rode out from the dark glades of the great Tor Wood above Falkirk, to look down over the swiftly dropping land eastwards towards Lothian, with the grey town nestling below, at the west end of the wooded spine of Callendar Hill. At the other end of that long spine, no doubt, was the battle. But none of the newcomers tested their eyes or wits seeking for signs of it there. They did not have to. For below them, on the wide spread of green braesides between the town and this Tor Wood, was sufficient to take their attention. Scattered all over it were parties of horsemen, in small groups and large, all riding fast and all riding westwards, away from the battle area. Of foot there was no sign—save for the stream of refugees beginning to leave Falkirk, with their pathetic baggage, making uphill, like the cavalry, for the deep recesses of the Tor Wood.

There could be little doubt what it all meant.

Grimly Bruce jutted his jaw. "We are too late, I fear," he said to his brother. "Too late. Cavalry was Wallace's need—and there is his cavalry! Fleeing . . . !"

They hurried on downhill. The first batch of horsemen they came up with, about a dozen, wore the colours of Lennox. Bruce halted them, demanding news.

"All is by wi'," their leader called, scarcely reining in, obviously reluctant to stop. "They were ower many. Armoured knights. A sea of them. And arrows. Like hailstanes! It's all by wi' . . ."

"The battle? All lost? What of Wallace?"

"God kens! He was wi' the foot."

"And they?"

The man shrugged. None of his colleagues, anxious to be elsewhere, amplified. Already they were urging their spume-flecked horses onwards.

"Stay, you!" Bruce cried authoritatively. He pointed. "I see no blood. No single wound amongst you. What sort of battle was this?"

Scowls greeted that, and angry words. Men pointed backwards, in protest, outrage. But they were edging onwards.

"You are Lennox's men, are you not? Where is your lord?" Some shook their heads. Some pointed on, up the hill, some back. Clearly none knew.

Unhappily the Bruces rode on, the seven hundred doubtful behind them.

The next group they encountered wore the blue-and-gold of Stewart, led by a knight in armour.

"You are Stewarts," Bruce challenged him. "Who are you? And where is the Steward?"

"We are of Menteith. I am Sir John Stewart of Cardross. I know not where the Steward is. Or my lord of Menteith. All the lords have gone . . ."

"Gone where, man? Is all over? The battle?"

"God knows! There may be fighting still. The foot. Wallace's rabble. In their schiltroms of spears. Since they cannot flee. But all else is finished."

"You . . . you deserted Wallace and the foot?"

"Deserted! Who are you to talk of deserting? You were not there. They hurled all their strength at us. Between the schiltroms. Their cavalry and bowmen both. Thousands on thousands of them. The Constable's array broke first. In the centre. Then they were in amongst us. Behind us. We had no choice . . ."

"The Constable, you say? The Comyns—they gave way first? But there were no great number of them . . .?"

"The Constable took command of the centre cavalry. As was his right. The English threw all their strength at him . . ."

"Aye. Enough . . ." Without waiting to hear more, Bruce waved on his company.

The long but fairly low and gentle hog's-back of open woodland that was Callendar Hill sank at its east end to the valley of the Westquarter Burn. Where a tributary stream joined this below the south-east face of the hill was an area of marshland surrounding a small reedy loch. On the open slopes above this, Wallace had drawn up his army to make its stand. It was a reasonably good defensive position, the best that the Falkirk vicinity had to offer probably; but it was all on a comparatively small scale, and the water barrier only a minor one. The loch and marsh itself would not take cavalry, but the burn that flowed at either end of it could be splashed through. As an impediment to a vast army, therefore, it was inadequate. And worst of all, the relatively short distances involved meant that the long-range English and Welsh archers could remain drawn up on the east side of the loch and still pour their arrows into the Scots ranks beyond.

Bruce and his people, their formation somewhat broken up by negotiating the woodland and the streams of fleeing wounded, reached the last of the trees. They saw the land across the valley as literally black with men and horses and all the paraphernalia of war, stretching almost as far as eye could see, a dire sight. Though this enormous concourse was not in fact engaged, too great to be marshalled and brought to bear on Wallace's chosen ground. Only the cavalry and the archers were involved, as yet—to the Scots' downfall.

For, of course, it was in these two arms that Wallace was weak. His great mass of spearmen and sworders, however nimble and tough, were of little avail against these. The Guardian had drawn up his host in four great schiltroms, square phalanxes of spearmen, densely packed, facing out in all directions, bristling hedgehogs of pikes and lances and halberds, on which an enemy would throw himself with but little effect. Between these he had set his comparatively few bowmen, backed by the cavalry of the lords. And thus awaited the onslaught.

But unhappily all was within range of the massed thousands of Edward's long-bowmen, who with a methodical, disciplined expertise poured in a continuous stream, a flood, of their deadly yard-long shafts. Against these the Scots were helpless, their own few archers hopelessly outranged, and indeed the first to fall, as primary targets of the enemy. Thereafter the hissing murderous hail had been raised to fall mainly upon the cavalry behind. Here the execution was less lethal, because of breastplates, helmets, chainmail and toughened leather; but even so there was much havoc, especially amongst the horses.

Under cover of this fatal deluge, Edward's pride, his heavy chivalry had swept round the loch and crossed the burns in two horns; the left under Roger de Bigod, Earl of Norfolk, and Humphrey de Bohun, Earl of Hereford; the right under Bishop Beck of Durham and no less than thirty-six senior captains. These both drove uphill, and as the bowmen ceased to shoot at a given signal, bore in in five great prongs of perhaps a thousand each, ignoring the squares of spearmen and concentrating all on the lines of cavalry ranked between the schiltroms. It was then that High Constable Buchan signalled in turn, and at it the Scots nobility broke and turned back. The command was to reform in one mass up the hill, to put in a powerful counter-attack downhill; but this never materialised. The protective shelter of the wood was too great a temptation, and the Comyns' example infectious. The Scots chivalry rode off the field of Falkirk, to fight, perhaps, another day.

This had left Wallace and his foot in four isolated groups, round which Edward's armoured horse eddied and circled unhindered. Not all of the Scots nobility and gentry had bolted with the cavalry of course. Many had gone to join Wallace, on foot. But these found themselves on the outside of the bristling walls of spears, with the grim-visaged angry spearmen in no mood to open and break their tight ranks to let them in. Mostly they died there under the trampling hooves of the English destriers.

By the time that Bruce and his seven hundred arrived on the scene of carnage, all this was a thing of the past. There were only the two schiltroms now, the debris of the others making a trampled bloody chaos of the long slope. These two that were left had lost much of their shape and were tending to coalesce; but they were still fighting, doggedly, their perimeter dead being swiftly and steadily replaced by men from within the squares, to die in their turn as the massed horsemen raged round and round, driving in with lance and sword, battle-axe and heavy mace.

Many of Edward's proud chivalry littered the slopes of Callendar Hill, also, the horses in particular skewered, hamstrung and disembowelled by those deadly spears. The heaps and piles of slain, of both sides, grew thicker and thicker towards the foot of the slope—for this was the way that the battle moved, not uphill towards the wood and escape. The English cavalry were exploiting the advantage of site that should have belonged to their Scots counterparts; downhill. They were thundering in charges time and again down the slope, to overwhelm the schiltroms by sheer weight and impetus, in a trampling, screaming avalanche of horseflesh and armoured humanity. Already the lowermost Scottish spearmen were up to their knees in the mire and water of the valley-floor. Perhaps Wallace was deliberately allowing this to happen, for in the soft ground the heavy cavalry would be unable to come in at them. But then, there was still the serried ranks of the waiting archers, not to mention the vast mass of the so-far uncommitted English foot.

For desperate moments Bruce sat his mount, eyeing that scene. What could he do? Nothing that he might attempt could possibly turn the tide of battle now. To stand still was inglorious, useless. To turn and flee like the others was unthinkable. His men were not armoured. He himself, like Nigel, was in travelling clothes, not full mail. Most of them bestrode Highland shelts. They were the lightest of light horse. Against some of the best heavy chivalry in all Christendom, battle-trained veterans—and outnumbered six or eight to one.

There was only the one condition in their favour, and one thing that they might attempt. The element of surprise would be theirs—for none of the English would look for a return of the Scots horse now. And Wallace himself might yet be saved. They could all see him, unmistakable, in the upper front rank of one of the schiltroms, towering over all, his great brand whirling and slicing. Fighting like a hero, yes—but not like a general.

Bruce made up his mind. He turned to his men of Mar, Garioch and Moray. "My friends—you see it! See it all. We can save Wallace. That is all. Drive down after me. In a wedge. A spearhead. No halting. No fighting. Straight through. If I fall, or my brother, keep on. Drive down through all. To Wallace. Scotland depends on Wallace. Mount him, and as many as you may. Behind you. Then round and back for these woods. Do not wait. Our beasts are lighter, more swift, sure-footed. Come. And shout slogans." He whipped out his sword. "On, then! A Bruce! A Bruce!"

Scarcely enthusiastic as his North-countrymen could have been, they followed, without demur or hesitation.

The Bruce brothers side by side at the apex, they gradually worked themselves into a great arrowhead formation as they thundered down the braeside, yelling. It was not perhaps the most exactly disciplined manoeuvre, but they made a dramatic, effective and fast-moving entry on the scene—and one that it would be very hard to stop.

They had perhaps five hundred yards to cover, the last third strewn with bodies and slippery with mud and blood. The English cavalry down there were in milling, circling thousands, though with many standing back, looking on, unable to push their way in at the surrounded spearmen, ploutering in the deep mire, or just licking their wounds. But many as there were, expecting nothing of this sort, they were not marshalled to resist and break up such an attack, however many times their numbers. Nor, at this stage of the battle, were they under any unified control. Trumpets began to neigh within moments of the attack becoming apparent. But more than that was required to organise and present a coherent front; and the very diversity of trumpet calls bespoke too many commanders. There was no over-all general of the chivalry, on the spot; Edward himself had been kicked by a horse the previous night, while he slept on the ground like any soldier, and was sufficiently incapacitated to be directing this battle from a distance.

Time, here, was all-important. Bruce, at the front of the V, saw that they would, in fact, bore through to the battling Scots almost inevitably, and probably without great difficulty or casualties. It was the turning and getting away again that would be a problem. But he also perceived another inevitability; they could hardly help but ride down the upper front ranks of the Scots themselves, for they dared not rein back and lose their impetus too soon. It made grim recognition.

But it was the littered debris of the fighting that demanded their major attention in this crazy, furious descent, as they drove down through the dead, the dying and the wounded, amongst screaming men and fallen, hoof-lashing horses. Their hill-ponies, the most sure-footed mounts there were, nevertheless had not been trained to battle and blood, and savagely firm mastering was necessary to hold them on through the hell of it, to keep the wedge in shape and straight on course.

A hundred yards or so from the first of the beleaguered Scots, a hastily turned and jostling group of English cavalry barred the way. As he hurtled down on them, Bruce waved his sword round and round above his head, redoubling his shouting, the men behind doing the same, a fearsome sight. It was asking more of flesh and blood than it could take for stationary horsemen to stand there unflinching in the face of such furious downhill onslaught, however armoured. Well before the impact, the Englishmen were reining aside. Some bold spirits actually spurred on to meet the crash in movement at least; but most pushed to one side or the other, turning back, breaking away.

Bruce drove for the point of greatest confusion. Nigel was laughing almost hysterically just half a length on his left.

A red-faced knight in rich armour was suddenly before them, eyes round, mouth open. Bruce, flinging himself aside in his saddle to avoid the wild swinging blow of a gleaming battle-axe, all but cannoned into his brother. Jerking his beast's head back, as he swept by the knight, he felt their legs scrape together. His own sword slashed back-handedly right across the knight's surprised face in red horror. Then he was past.

There was another man directly in front—but he had his back to them, bolting out of the way, as well he might. But he was not nearly quick enough. His blade straight before him, stiff-armed, like a lance, Bruce drove the point in right below the back of the fellow's helmet. The victim pitched forward over his mount's neck, dragging the struck sword right out of its owner's hand. The man's careering mount carried him away to the side, falling.

There were two more in front—but these were decidedly getting out of the way. Swordless, Bruce was shaking a clenched fist at them, when he realised that he was in fact through the press. There were still mounted men between him and the Scots spears, but these were not drawn up, not standing, not going to challenge that mass of yelling riders.

And now, this other problem. How to draw up, not only himself but the close-packed ranks behind him, so as not to crash too terribly into the waiting ranks of spearmen? Those spears in themselves! Would men, seeing themselves about to be ridden down, not be apt almost involuntarily to seek to save themselves? By using their spears? On the riders-down? *He* would.

Dragging desperately at his beast's head with his right hand he raised his left, to make urgent circling signals, half-right, praying that the men behind would in their frenzy perceive what he meant and the need for it. Savagely he dragged and jerked at his horse, and stumbling, its legs sprawling at the suddenness of the change of direction, the brute did manage to swing right. Bruce heard a crash immediately behind him as somebody went down, unable to take the turn. He hoped it was not Nigel.

Still he bore right, so that now he was plunging along the wavering edge of spears, their blood-red tips before his eyes. Some were raised, to allow him passage, but others remained thrust out still, menacing. There were screams at his back now, where some of his Northerners had been unable to bring their beasts round in time and had crashed into their fellow-countrymen. Bruce did not glance round.

His eyes were on Wallace. He stood just behind the kneeling front row of spearmen, a little way along to the south, leaning now on his great sword, head bowed. He had lost his helmet and appeared to be wounded, blood running down his face and into his red bushy beard—though with so much blood splashed everywhere, it need not be his own. Stooping, he nevertheless stood above the press of those around him like a forest tree amongst bushes.

Bruce was seeking to draw up now, with the pressure behind slackened by the turn. He waved and shouted to Wallace.

"Quickly!" he cried. "Come. A chance. To win free. To me, man."

The giant raised his head to stare, but made no other move. He did not answer. He looked dizzy.

"Hurry, I say! Do not stand there," Bruce yelled. "We cannot wait, or all is lost. They will rally. Come."

Wallace shook his head, and gave a single dismissive wave of a huge bloodstained hand.

"Fool!" Bruce was close to him now, shouting and gesticulating over the heads of kneeling men, horse sidling nervously. "Do you not see? You must break out. While you may. Or you are a dead man."

"You . . . you would have me leave these? Abandon my folk? Away with you, Bruce." That was thickly, unevenly cried out. The man was obviously far from clear-headed.

"You can do no good here now. Come away. And fight again . . ."

"No! Run from my friends? Never!"

Others were pleading with him now, arguing, pointing—Scrymgeour his standard-bearer, Blair the priest, Boyd. Bruce saw behind them the drawn and anxious face of James the Steward. And Crawford. All the nobles had not deserted the Guardian.

Desperately Bruce remonstrated, his voice breaking as he heard the battle joining behind him, the English recovering from their surprise and beginning to hurl themselves against the light Scots horse.

"Wallace!" he yelled. "You are the Guardian. Of Scotland. All Scotland. Not just these. If you fall now, Scotland falls. Mind who you are—the Guardian . . ."

Nigel was shouting now, at his side. "These others can break. Into the marsh, and away. Where horse cannot follow. Many will escape. If *you* stay, all will die."

"Aye! Aye!" All around men saw the sense of that, and cried

it. Hands were pushing and pulling Wallace forward, towards the Bruces.

The 700, or what was left of them, now formed a chaotic barrier between the Bruces and the enemy, those towards the rear turned to face outwards and taking the brunt of a so-far disorganised English attack. Others were mounting fellow-Scots behind them.

"Get the Steward," Bruce ordered his brother. He waved to others. "Crawford. Lennox. Scrymgeour. I take Wallace..."

A Mar-man pushed up with a riderless horse. "Here—for Wallace."

"Aye..."

Eager, desperate hands were propelling the reluctant giant forward, all but lifting him on to the head-tossing, wild-eyed garron. He seemed to be no longer actually resisting.

Hardly waiting for the big man to be astride, Bruce grabbed the other's reins. A swift glance round had shown him that the only possible route of escape was southwards, up the Westquarter Burn. There were English there, yes—but not in the numbers that were behind them, massing everywhere.

"Come!" he commanded. "After me. A wedge again. Keep close." He dug in his spurs.

It was a ragged and much smaller wedge that began to form again behind him, to pound away southwards, along the front of spears. Many of his men had fallen, not a few chose their own route of escape, the rear ranks were too closely engaged to break away with the others. But perhaps two hundred could and did obey his call, and made up a formidable enough phalanx for any but an organised English squadron of cavalry to seek to halt.

They were burdened now, of course, with two men to most horses. They had no longer the advantage of a downward slope. And they were in softer, boggier ground. But this last militated more against the heavier enemy horse than themselves. It was no headlong gallop, but at best a canter. But a determined canter, before which the scattered enemy swerved away, even if thereafter they closed in on the flanks and rear. Indeed, from all sides the English gave chase rather than sought to intercept, but even double-burdened, the nimble hill-ponies were swifter, lighter, than chargers.

Wallace, swaying about alarmingly in the saddle, his long legs positively trailing the ground, was pounding along between Bruce and Nigel, who now had the Steward clinging behind him, heavily-armoured and a great weight. Bruce heard trumpets braying a new and distinctive call, from across the valley. He guessed what that meant, and his heart sank.

The arrows began to come at them in a matter of moments thereafter. They were nearing extreme range, and a moving target —but the bowmen needed only to loose off into the brown mass.

Havoc quickly followed. Nigel's horse was one of the first to fall, pierced through the neck, and throwing both riders. They were all but ridden down immediately. Bruce, reining round violently to the right, more uphill, to increase the range and change of direction of flight, yelled for his brother and the Steward to be picked up—but did not himself slacken pace or leave grip of Wallace's reins. Somehow the pack behind him swung after him, their formation much broken. And still the arrows hissed down on them, amid the screams of men and horses.

Bruce was surprised to find his right ankle gripped, and glanced down to see Nigel leaping along beside him, mud-covered, bare-headed and lacking his sword now also, but apparently unhurt. Bruce reached down a hand and somehow his brother, after three or four attempts, managed to haul himself up behind him, lying stomach down over the beast's broad and heaving rump.

"Steward safe . . . safe," he gasped in Bruce's ear, as he got himself upright.

"Many down?"

"Aye. Curse the bowmen!"

"Not long now. Range. Too far . . ."

The hail of arrows had at least one advantage; they effectively inhibited over-eagerness on the part of the English pursuers. These advisedly left a very clear field for their archer colleagues.

Bruce was now leading almost directly uphill towards the wood but perhaps quarter of a mile further south than where they had come down. This meant, of course, that it was the rear ranks of his party which had to take the main punishment from the bowmen, with only the odd spent shaft falling forward amongst the leaders. Only a heroic dolt would have had it otherwise—and Robert Bruce was not that.

At last, in the blessed shelter of the trees, Bruce pulled up his spume-covered, panting, almost foundered horse. All around him others did likewise. Wallace gripped his saddle-bow and stared blindly ahead of him, wordless. The Steward came up, spitting blood, on a garron from which the owner had fallen. Scrymgeour and Blair came running to Wallace's side.

Bruce looked back, downhill, on chaos and confusion. There was no longer any pattern to the scene, only a hopeless medley of men and horses, heaving and surging this way and that, darting, circling, eddying—or not moving at all. The schiltroms had finally broken up, and most of the spearmen appeared to be seeking escape through the marshland, where the cavalry could not follow, or even in the loch itself, splashing through the shallows, or swimming in deeper water. Some were fleeing uphill towards these woods. Many would escape—but more would die.

Bruce was looking for more than the fleeing foot. Scattered all over the littered slopes, the remnants of his own seven hundred were striving to make their way up here, in ones and twos and small groups, avoiding contests and heroics. Most seemed to be likely to succeed, with the enemy perhaps lacking in enthusiasm for any difficult chase and the battle won; after all, Edward's host was said to be next to starving, horses' fodder as scarce as men's. Bruce was thankful to see that many of his Northerners were winning clear—for no more than one hundred and fifty had managed to follow immediately at his back.

He turned to Wallace. "You are wounded, Sir William? Can you go on? Sit that beast? Or . . . shall we make a litter?"

The big man stared downwards. "I . . . am . . . very well," he said.

"That you are not! But can you ride . . .?"

"I am very well," he repeated, heavily. "But others . . . are not. Those who looked to me . . ."

"Here is folly, man! A battle lost, aye—but others to be fought. And won! What good repining . . .?"

"So many dead. Fallen. Pate Boyd. Sim Fraser. Rob Keith. Sir John the Graham. Young MacDuff of Fife, the Earl's son. Sir John Stewart . . ."

"Aye, my brother," the Steward broke in thickly. "I saw him shot down. An arrow. And my son . . .? Where is Walter?"

"I saw him. Taken up on a horse," someone called. "Riding to the north . . ."

"Quiet!" Bruce burst out, cutting the air with his hand. "Here is no time for this talk. Men have fallen, yes. Fighting. They came to fight. And fall, if need be. Time enough for talk, after. But what now? What to do? *Edward* will not wait and talk."

"Aye." Obviously with a great effort, the dazed Wallace pulled himself together. "You are right, my lord. And I thank you. We fight on. But not here. We cannot stand south of the Forth. Even at Stirling. Not now. We must rally again in the hills to the north. And burn the land behind us. Burn Stirling. Burn Dunblane. Burn Perth, if need be. Starve them. Starve England's war host. That is his weakness, now. No more battles, backed by nobles that I cannot trust! I was a fool, to think that I could out-fight Edward Plantagenet, his way. No more! I fight my own way, now. Wallace the outlaw! The brigand . . .!"

"You are still Guardian of this land, man."

"Aye—and I shall fight Edward with the land. What he can ride over but never defeat. Would God I had used my own wits, instead of listening to others. But it is not too late. While Scotland lives, it is never too late! And Scotland will not, cannot, die." The man's great voice shook with a mighty emotion.

Bruce scarcely shared it. "So it is Stirling now?" he demanded impatiently. "Stirling, and beyond. The North?"

"Yes. Take me to Stirling, my lord. But not the North, for you. The lurking in the hills. The raids by night. The burning. The ambuscade. The knife in the back. This is no work for great lords! So back to your West, Bruce—to your own country. And mine. You claimed to be Governor of the South-West, did you not? Go there, then. Hold the South-West. Harry the English West March, if you can. While we starve Edward. Raid into England. Nothing will harass hungry men more than the word that their homes are threatened, endangered. Go west from Stirling, my lord—and such other lords as are not fled! I shall require the West at your hands."

Bruce eyed him levelly for a moment, and then nodded. "Very well, Sir Guardian. Now—Stirling . . ."

Chapter Ten

In the selfsame hall of the castle of Ayr where Wallace had hanged Percy's deputy sheriff, Arnulf, and where Percy himself resided during the long farcical negotiations of Irvine, Bruce paced the stone-flagged floor, three weeks after the battle of Falkirk. Only one other man shared the great shadowy apartment with him, its walls still blackened by Wallace's burning, the August evening light slanting in on them through the small high windows. This man sat at the great table, eating and drinking—and doing so in the determined fashion of one hungry, though tired, even if his mind was hardly on what he ate. He was dressed in travel-stained and undistinguished clothing—non-clerical clothing, too, and with dagger still at hip, and a sword laid along the table nearby, strange garb for the Primate of all Scotland. For this was William Lamberton, now duly consecrated and confirmed by the Pope as Bishop of St. Andrews and leader of the Church. A good-looking, strong-featured grave man, youthful-seeming for so high an office, at thirty-five, he nevertheless looked older than his years tonight, weary, stern. But he watched Bruce at his pacing, keen-eyed, nevertheless.

"It would not serve," the younger man declared, shaking his head. "Not with him, of all men. I could not do it. Besides, Wallace is wrong in this. Mistaken. He should not give up the Guardianship. You must persuade him against it, my lord Bishop."

"You do not know William Wallace, if you think that I could! Once he has determined a matter in his mind, nothing will shake him. He is now so decided. He deems himself to have failed the realm, at Falkirk fight. To have forfeited the trust of the people . . ."

"That is folly. The folk all but worship the man! As they do no other."

"Think you that I have not told him so? New back from Rome as I am, I have seen and tested the will of many in this. But he will not hear me. He says that though they still may trust him, he is not fit to be Guardian. That the Guardian must have the support of *all* the realm. And that he has not. The nobles will have none of him . . ."

"*Some*, no. But who will? Show me any man who will receive the support of all!"

"It is not enough. For Wallace. After Falkirk. Fifteen thousand died on that field, and he takes the blame to himself."

"Fifteen thousand . . .? So many?"

"Aye. In a battle which he now says should never have been fought. He takes all the blame—however much others blame the lords who rode off. Says that he should have known better than to front Edward so. Or to trust these others."

"The man must be ill. In his mind. A defeat, by the largest most powerful army ever to invade Scotland, is no disgrace. All commanders must accept defeats. And fight on . . ."

"Wallace will fight on, never fear, my lord. But not as Guardian. Especially as the Comyns threaten to impeach him."

"What! Impeach? The Comyns...?"

"Aye. Buchan and the others claim that he mishandled all. Did not send for them. Indeed of intention would have kept them away. From the battle. They claim that he has divided the land..."

"God forgive them! This is beyond all. And you would have me to work with these?"

"Wallace would. And, since he will by no means remain Guardian, I deem him right in this, at least. Many other lords and knights follow the Comyns. Would even make Red John the King." Lamberton looked at Bruce shrewdly, there. "John Baliol's nephew. There is only one way to unite the realm, in face of Edward, Wallace says. A joint Guardianship. You, and John Comyn of Badenoch."

"I say it is madness. We can scarce exchange a civil word! How could we rule together?"

"It would be difficult. But not impossible. What is *not* difficult, today? You are not bairns, my lord. So much is at stake. If Bruce and Comyn would agree, the nobility would be united. And Wallace working with you, carrying the common people with him, for he has learned his lesson, he says. And myself, speaking for the Church. The three estates of the realm. As one, for the first time..."

"Comyn would never serve with me. He hates me. Besides, he is in France."

"Wallace has sent for him. To come home. With this offer. If you do not accept, I swear Comyn will! And who else is to control him, as joint Guardian? The Steward? Buchan, his own kinsman, another Comyn? Mar? Atholl? Menteith...?"

Helplessly Bruce shook his head again. "No—none of these. But... John Comyn! Even Buchan himself would be less ill to deal with..."

"Buchan led the flight at Falkirk. That will not be forgotten by the people. They would never accept *him* as Guardian. But the Lord of Badenoch was not there. And whatever else, he is a fighter. None doubts *his* courage."

Bruce halted in his pacing, to stare at his visitor. "How many of the Scots folk accept *me*? I am told that they think of me as Edward's man."

"They did, yes. But no longer. You did not fail at Falkirk. You saved Wallace."

There was silence for a little. Then Bruce shrugged. "If I say that I will consider the matter, it must not be taken that I agree," he said, heavily. "That I promise anything. Better to convince Wallace to continue as Guardian."

"He will not. That I promise *you.*"

"Where is he now?"

"At Scone. Above Perth. Assembling men. That is where I have come from."

"And Edward? They tell me that he is moving into the West?"

"That is true. He hoped to find food. The English are hungry, my lord. Are not we all? But they are scarce used to it! Edward has heard that the famine has not hit the West so badly. Moreover, he has work to do here! And the West is not yet burned in his face. Wallace burned all before him, right up to Perth. Perth itself. After Falkirk, Edward went to Stirling. There he found all burned black. Save the Dominican Priory. He lay there fifteen days, a sick man. Kicked by a horse they say. But his armies did not lie. He sent them north and east and west. To Perth and Gowrie. To Menteith and Strathearn. To Fothrif and Fife. Seeking food. And harrying, slaying, devastating the country. 'Use all cruelty,' he ordered—Edward Plantagenet! How many thousands they have slain, God knows. Far, far more than on the Falkirk field. Women and children. Especially on the lands of those who supported Wallace—the old Earl of Fife's lands. Menteith's. Strathearn's. Murray of Tullibardine's. And the Church's. Mine. My St. Andrews is now a smoking desert. He spares neither kirk nor monastery, monk nor nun. Dunfermline. Balmerino. Lindores. Dunblane. Inchaffray. All these abbeys and their towns. And many another. No mercy. All to be destroyed. And now he has turned west. To punish Lennox, the Steward, Crawford. And yourself, my lord!"

"Aye." That came out on a long sigh. "Edward, at least, will no longer think me his man! He comes here, you think?"

"He has sworn to punish all whom he says rebelled against his peace! Will he spare Bruce, whom once he held close? But who now holds the South-West against him. *You* should know, if any!"

"He will not. But . . . I cannot hold the South-West against him. Not against this great host. You know that."

"I know it. But you can do what Wallace has done. Deny him food, drink, comfort. Burn the land before him, my lord. Leave him nothing. Burn this castle and town. For, God knows, what you do not burn, *he* will! Alas for this poor Scotland! But only so shall we save her freedom."

"Freedom, yes. And freedom . . .? Is it worth this, my lord Bishop? This cost?"

"Freedom is worth this and more, my friend. Freedom is worth the last breath we draw. Freedom is life. And the life after life. Is there aught greater? Faith, worship, charity, peace—what are these, without freedom to exercise them? Freedom is the soul of the nation. What profit all else if we lose it?"

Long Bruce gazed at the wary man's stern face, deeply moved by his vibrant words. He inclined his head. "Very well. Tell Wallace that I burn the South-West. For freedom. As my brothers even now are burning over the Border. The Lord Nigel I sent to Annandale, then to Galloway, to raid over the West March. But . . . dear God—it is easier to burn other men's lands than your own!"

"I know it, friend. How many men have you assembled here?"

"Four thousand. So few against Edward's hordes."

"Four thousand men can do a deal of burning . . . !"

• • •

So Edward Plantagenet, leaving a blackened smoking desert behind him at Glasgow and the lower Clyde, marched south, up Clyde with his legions—and found only smoking desert before him. Rutherglen, Bothwell, Lanark, he found empty, black, smouldering, and all the land around and ahead billowing unending smoke-clouds in the hazy autumn sunshine. Like an army of Goths and Vandals, grim-faced, their eyes red-rimmed from more than their own smoke, Bruce's men of Carrick, Cunninghame and Kyle, with volunteers from far and near, efficiently, methodically, destroyed the land, their own land, herding the people with roughest kindliness into the hills. Towns and villages were emptied, the thatches pulled off the roofs to burn in the streets, with all stored food and fodder that could not be carted away. Churches and monasteries were denuded of all that made them places of worship, and left vacant shells. Castles and manors were cast down, where possible, rendered untenable, undefendable, and left open, deserted. Farm lands were wasted and despoiled, hay and grain fired, standing corn trampled flat, all beasts and poultry that could not be driven off into the hills slaughtered and tossed on to the blazing barns and byres and cot-houses. Mills, markets, fisheries, harbours, hutments—all were cast down and devastated, in a twenty-mile belt from the sea to the burgeoning purple heather of the wild uplands—now fuller of folk than they had ever been before. From Clydesdale right down into Galloway the pattern was repeated, and the smoke rose over a once-fair land, by day a black rolling pall that darkened the sun, by night a murky red and ominous barrier stretching from horizon to horizon. The folk co-operated, in the main, even did their own burning. There was short shrift for those who objected.

The English, in fuming rage, sought other adversary than fire and smoke, and found none—save odd and pathetic hiders in woods and deans and caves, whom they outraged, tortured and hanged. Day after day they marched south, a blackened snarling host, the fine colourful display of their chivalry dimmed and soiled now, angry, ravenous men; and each day their march grew longer, as their empty bellies forced them on, hoping, hoping for some area undestroyed, some green oasis in the black desert overlooked. But there was none, save in the high fastnesses of the flanking hills, Scotland's ultimate refuge, where Edward dared not let his mutinous men stray—for such as did seldom returned. A great deal of food is necessary to feed over 100,000 men. The leadership was losing control. Great bodies of troops were running amok, fighting with each other, falling sick by the thousand, doing unmentionable things in their terrible hunger. Shaking his fist at the gaunt ruins of the burned-out castle of Ayr, reached on the 27th day of August, Edward, in impotent fury, after giving orders that Bruce must be pursued deep into his Carrick hills, right to the Mull of Galloway if need be, countermanded it all, and ordained the swiftest possible withdrawal to the Border, to English soil. It was as near flight as anything the Plantagenet had ever faced. He left a woeful trail of the weak, the sick and the weary behind him, of men and horses and equipment. And out from the wilderness lairs the folk of the charred land crept by night, knives in hand.

The King, with the view of fair England at last, on 6th September, and much in sight reeking, as black as what lay behind them, turned in terrible, savage wrath on Annandale, the last of the Scottish dales, which the younger Bruces had largely spared, after all their building-up from Clifford's raid. Now even that expert, in Edward's train, had to confess himself mastered. If a land can be crucified, the lordship of Annandale was, that September of 1298. When, in the remote tower of Loch Doon, amongst the great heather hills where Carrick and Galloway meet, Nigel brought word of it, Robert Bruce would have wept if he could. Tears were a luxury few Scots could rise to that autumn.

Edward himself was near to tears, at Carlisle, where he halted at last, too tough a nut for the Bruce brothers to have cracked. But they were tears of sheerest choler. For not only had he to bear the humiliations of his undignified scramble back to his own soil, and the frustrations of a campaign abandoned in mid-course, with the benefits of a great victory squandered, and the outrage of mutinous soldiery—now his own lords turned mutineer. And not merely a few disgruntled nonentities, but the greatest of all —Norfolk, the Constable; Hereford; Lincoln; Northumberland. These, and lesser barons, when they heard that Edward was intent only on garnering vast food supplies, re-equipping and disciplining his army, and then marching back into Scotland to complete his task, refused flatly to co-operate. They claimed that this was not only profitless but contrary to the promises that the King had made on his return from France, that he would rule henceforth with the acceptance of his nobility and parliament. In fury the monarch named them treasonable, seditious dogs—and though, on second thoughts, he hastily convened a council, there at Carlisle, and named it a parliament, it was too late. Norfolk, Hereford, and those likeminded, marched off with their followings for the south, leaving an angry sovereign and a make-believe parliament to pass edicts for further ambitious mobilisation, the large-scale provisioning necessary, and the equipping of a great fleet of vessels which would proceed round the Scottish coastline, keeping pace with the armies, and supplying them without fail. This, and the wholesale forfeiture of the lands of all Scots nobles, not only those who had supported Wallace but those who had failed actively to support Edward; and the apportioning of these immense properties to the English lords and knights who remained with the King at Carlisle—though the new owners were faced with the problem of how to take possession. The greatest of these, Guy de Beauchamp, Earl of Warwick, got the Bruce lands, and others, to retain his support.

Then, after a fortnight, Edward marched his somewhat refreshed if still grumbling host north into Scotland once more, but only as a token thrust this time, an indication of what would happen in the spring when campaigning was once again feasible. He moved up Liddesdale, spreading desolation, to Jedburgh, which he sacked and levelled with the ground, wreaking especial vengeance on its great abbey. Contenting himself with this gesture and foretaste, he turned south for Newcastle, Durham, and his winter quarters at York.

Scotland's sigh of relief was grim as it was faint.

• • •

Another sort of relief it was to ride through the green-golden valleys and quiet glades of Ettrick Forest, and see hamlets unburned, churches and shrines intact and cattle grazing peacefully in clearings and water-meadows. To eyes become accustomed to the charred wilderness that was most of Southern Scotland that autumn, this was a bitter-sweet solace. Bruce and his brothers trotted through it all in the mellow October sunshine, in answer to the Guardian's summons, allegedly the last such that would come from Sir William Wallace.

They found Selkirk and its ruined abbey in an even greater stir than on the previous occasion, when Wallace had been knighted and proclaimed Guardian; for this time, more of the nobility and clergy had come, aware of the drama and importance of the proceedings. Their encampments, pavilions and banners were everywhere in the spreading haughlands of the Ettrick, their men-at-arms too many and truculent for peace and comfort. Churchmen were almost as numerous as barons, with their retinues, with no fewer than ten bishops, and abbots, priors and other clerics unnumbered. Lamberton was making his authority felt.

The Bruces found Wallace installed in the old royal castle of Selkirk, a ramshackle, sprawling place built as a hunting lodge for David the First. With him was the Steward, his son Walter, Crawford, Menteith, Lennox and the old Earl of Fife; also, of course, Lamberton and his galaxy of prelates. The Primate was undoubtedly something of a showman, stern though he appeared to be, and there was considerable attempts at dignity and display, including a throne-like chair at the head of the great hall table, for the Guardian, with a huge tressured Rampant Lion standard hung on the wall behind it. The herald King of Arms was present with his minions, and busy establishing precedences and places, superintending the setting up of banners, fussing over details. In view of the appalling devastation that surrounded this green sanctuary of Ettrick Forest, the unburied multitudes, the famine and want and despair, it all seemed as pointless as it was unreal, even ridiculous.

Wallace himself certainly gave the impression that he thought it so, standing about ill at ease and unhappy. Seldom can a man have looked less at one with the surroundings of which he was the central figure. He had changed not a little since Falkirk. He was thinner, more gaunt, older-seeming altogether, and though of course still enormous, of less commanding presence than heretofore, despite the finery which seemed to sit so uncomfortably on his huge frame. His great hands were seldom still, groping about him as though seeking the sword, the dirk, the battle-axe, which were almost extensions of himself, but today were absent. He looked a man at odds with his fate.

He came great-strided to greet Bruce, at least, with an access of animation. "My lord, my lord—you have come! I thank God for it." He gripped the younger man's hand and shoulder. "It is good to see you—for much depends on you hereafter."

Bruce looked doubtful at that, his glance searching past the other for Comyn.

Wallace perceived it. "The Lord of Badenoch is not yet arrived," he said. "But he comes, he comes."

"His coming here, like mine, is the least of it, Sir Guardian! We shall never agree—that I swear."

"Do not say so. If sufficient depends on it, any two men can seem to agree, however ill-matched. Even I have learned that lesson! Think you I have loved all that I have had to deal with, work with, this past year and more? And enough depends, here, on my soul! The future of this realm, no less."

"Scarce so much as that, I think..."

"Yes. So much as that. See you, my lord—the magnates of this Scotland are divided. By many things, many feuds, much jealousy, warring interests. But, in the end, all depend on the Crown for their lands and titles. You know that. And the Crown is vacant—or nearly so. I act in the name of King John Baliol, since the Crown must be vested in some name. *De jure*, he is still King. *De facto*, he is not, and the throne empty. One day, if Scotland survives, she will have a king again. That king will be either a Baliol, a Comyn or a Bruce. You know it. John Baliol has a son, Edward—a child. Held, like his father, hostage by the King of England. King John has renounced the throne, for himself and his son, at the demand of King Edward. Renounced and abandoned. Therefore, it is scarce likely that John or his son shall ever reign. So the king shall be your father, the Bruce. Or John Comyn, Baliol's nephew."

Bruce made an impatient gesture, at this rehearsal of facts only too well known to him.

"Aye—you know it. All men know it, my lord. Therefore, since the nobles hold all they have of the Crown, they must take sides. For Comyn or Bruce. In order that they may retain their lands from the winner in this contest. Divided, as I say. And Scotland cannot afford a divided nobility, today, see you, when she fights for her life. So, your father being none knows where, only you, and Comyn, can heal the division. By acting together. Joint Guardians. Nothing else, and no other, will serve."

That was a long speech for Wallace, who was not notably a man of words.

Bruce could not refute the validity of any of it. But it was personality, not validity, that was his trouble.

"John Comyn will not work with me," he said flatly. "We have never agreed on any matter. Nor are like to!"

"But when the matter is the saving of the realm? For whoever may eventually sit on its throne? Can you not, at least, *seem* to agree, my lord? Since neither of you, I vow, would wish the other to be Guardian alone!"

That left the younger man silent.

Lamberton had joined them. "The Comyns have been sighted, my friends," he said. "They are riding down from Tweed. A great company of them. The Constable's banner alongside that of Badenoch, they say. They have come far. From Spey. I do not think that they have come for nothing! John Comyn intends to be Guardian, I swear—whoever else may be!"

Bruce did not fail to take the point.

The Comyns arrived with a deal more circumstance than had the Bruce brothers, in splendid clothing and array, confident, assured, and with an indefinable appearance of prosperity and lack of tension, which contrasted notably with the demeanour of most of those assembled—for, of course, they came from the North, untouched by famine or war. The drawn, guarded, battered look which had become so much part of the others showed in them not at all. They had brought a train of over a score of knights, their own clerics, standard-bearers, pursuivants, trumpeters, entertainers, even a group of Erse-speaking, barbarously-clad West Highland chiefs. There was no doubt that they had come prepared to take over the rule in Scotland.

It was their complete assurance, their unspoken but unmistakable assumption of authority, which almost automatically forced Robert Bruce into a position from which there was no drawing back. At no specific moment did he make his decision. The thing was obvious, no longer to be debated.

John Comyn of Badenoch and he did not actually speak to each other for quite some time, after the arrival, eyeing each other warily, like a pair of stiff-legged dogs considering the same bone, by mutual consent keeping their distance—a metaphysical distance, not an actual one, for inevitably amongst the small circle of the high magnates of the realm, they could not avoid being in the same group frequently. Bruce was apt to find the Red Comyn's brilliant, fleering eyes fixed on him—and realised that his own were drawn equally to the other. But neither went the length of words.

As closely as they watched each other, undoubtedly Wallace watched them both. Lamberton also. All there did, indeed; but these two in especial, and did more than watch. They manoeuvred, they guided, they tempered. And skilfully, their policy to ensure that Bruce and Comyn, or their supporters, did not come into any sort of clash before the thing could be brought to a conclusion. Wallace was less proficient at it than was the Bishop, perhaps.

As soon as it might be done with decency, the King of Arms had them all to sit down to a repast—and all his fussing about precedence was now seen in a new light. As far as the great ones were concerned, everything had been thought out. Normally, in any castle-hall, the dais-table stretched sideways across the head of the chamber, while the main table ran lengthwise down one side of the great apartment, leaving the rest free for the servitors, entertainers and the like. Now, since practically everyone present in Selkirk's castle would have been entitled to sit at the dais-table, this had been brought down to add to the length of the other. Moreover at its head, where the Guardian's great chair was flanked by two others, two further small tables had been placed at right angles, with a couple of seats only at each. At that to the right was placed Buchan the Constable, with Lamberton the Primate at his side; on the left was seated James the Steward, with the herald King. There was no certainty as to which great office of state was senior; but Buchan was an earl and the Steward was not. In the same way, at the main table-head, Bruce was placed on Wallace's immediate right, and Comyn on his left; again there could be no quarrel, since Carrick was an earldom and Badenoch only a lordship. Other nobles found themselves equally heedfully disposed. There were no solid groups of pro-Comyn or pro-Bruce supporters. And everywhere Lamberton's clerics were set between, to act as both catalysts and buffers. The Scots lords, used to jockeying for the best places by initiative or sheer weight, were taken by surprise, and strategically seated where they could cause least trouble.

Bruce and Comyn thus were sitting in isolated prominence—but the mighty figure of Wallace was between them. Moreover, Bruce had Buchan sitting at the little table, next on his right, while Comyn had the Steward to contend with, on his left. Seldom can there have been less general converse at so illustriously attended a meal.

Wallace spoke to each of his immediate companions, and sometimes to them both, seeking to involve them in mutual talk which he might control. But they were a mettlesome pair to drive tandem, and it was a somewhat abortive exercise. The Guardianship issue was not actually mentioned.

"How long have we, think you, before Edward attacks once more?" Wallace asked, presently—a safe subject, surely. "How serious are his troubles with his lords?"

"Do not ask me, Sir Guardian," Comyn returned quickly. "*I* have no dealings with the English. Ask Bruce. He knows Edward passing well. Or his friend Percy may have told him!"

Bruce drew a swift breath. Then he let it out again, slowly and raised his wine goblet to his lips.

"My lord of Carrick has put himself more in Edward's disfavour than has any other in Scotland," Wallace said heavily. "He burned the South-West in Edward's face, forcing him to call off his campaign. Much of the land burned Bruce's own. As for Lord Percy, I think he is scarce likely to call my lord his friend, now!"

"Yet the woman Bruce is like to marry is Percy's kinswoman. And bides with him, at Alnwick, does she not? While her father fights for Edward in France. Against our French allies!"

"Curse you, Comyn! I am not like to marry Elizabeth de Burgh. Edward would have had it once—but now would not, you may be sure!"

"Yet she is a comely wench. And well dowered, I swear! Edward's god-child—a useful go-between..."

"I'll thank you to spare the Lady Elizabeth the soiling of your tongue!" Bruce exclaimed, leaning forward to glare round Wallace.

"My lords! My lords—of a mercy!" the big man cried. "Moderate your words, I beg you. Here is no way to speak to each other."

"Have I said aught against the lady? Save that she is Edward's god-daughter. Bruce has a guilty conscience, I think, to be so thin of skin!"

"What knows a Comyn of conscience!"

"My lords—at *my* table, no guest of mine will be insulted. By whomsoever. I ask you to remember it." Wallace brought down his vast fist on the board with a crash to make the platters, flagons and goblets jump—and not a few of the company also. Then pushing back his chair abruptly he rose to his full commanding height. All eyes upon him, he raised his tremendous vibrant voice.

"My lords and friends, fellow subjects of this realm, I, William Wallace, Guardian of Scotland, crave your close heed. I took up that duty and style seven sore months ago. Now the time has come to lay it on other shoulders than mine. They have been ill months for our land. We have survived them only at great cost. But there are as bad, and worse, to come. Let none doubt it. The man, Edward Plantagenet, is set on this. He will make Scotland part of his crown. A lowly servile part. If he can. While breath remains in him. That is sure. And he has ten men for every man of us."

He paused, and though all present were aware of all this, men hung on his careful words.

"I say to you that I know now what I should have known before—that *I* cannot fight Edward the King. I can fight his underlings and minions. I can, I have done, and I will. But not Edward himself. Only Edward's own kind can fight Edward—I see that now. And I am . . . otherwise. Scotland's own king it should be who fights him. But since that is not possible now, it falls to the Guardian. Therefore, I cannot remain Guardian. Falkirk proved that. The Guardianship must be in the hands of Edward's own kind." Deliberately he looked round on them all. "In this realm today there are two men who could, and should, be Guardian. Two men whom all must heed, respect, obey. For what they are, and who they are. They are here at my side. Sir Robert Bruce, Earl of Carrick, grandson of Bruce the Competitor;

and Sir John Comyn, Lord of Badenoch, nephew to the King. King John. On these two, who are both of Edward's kind, I lay my burden. Jointly and together. These two can, and must, unite this realm against the English usurper. These two I charge, in the name of God and of Scotland—fight Edward! Save our land." He pointed. "My lord Bishop of Galloway—the seals."

As men exclaimed, from further down the table, the Chancellor rose, to bring up the two silver caskets that were his charge, and set them before Wallace, opening them to display the Great Seal of Scotland, and the Privy Seal.

The first the big man took out, and raised up—and it required both hands to do it. Not because it was so heavy, but because its bronze was in two parts, two exact halves. He held them high.

"My friends," he cried, "Here is the Great Seal of this realm and nation. I broke it. This day I broke it. For the good of all. Now, before anything may be established and made law, bearing the Seal of Scotland, these two parts must be brought together and set side by side. One, in the name of the Crown, the magnates and the community of this ancient realm, I give to Sir Robert the Bruce, Earl of Carrick. The other to Sir John the Comyn, of Badenoch. I do now declare them both and together to be Joint Guardians of Scotland. To them I hereby pass the rule and governance. Declaring that I, William Wallace, will from now onward be their leal and assured servant. God save them both, I say."

As all men stared, the giant thrust his chair far back, and bowing to Bruce first, then Comyn, turned and strode down the length of that great table, right to its foot, where he gently pushed aside his own standard-bearer, Scrymgeour, modestly seated there, and sat himself down in his place.

Something like uproar filled the hall.

Each holding his half of the Great Seal, Bruce and Comyn gazed at one another before all, wordless.

Gradually the noise abated, and men fell silent, all eyes upon the pair at the head of the table, clutching their half-moons of bronze. All knew that these two hated each other. All knew that they represented mutually antagonistic claims to the throne. Moreover, there could be few indeed who could have accepted Wallace's dramatic gesture in itself as any kind of valid appointment. It was not for the outgoing Guardian to appoint a successor; that was for the barons of the realm to choose, their choice to be confirmed by a parliament. What Wallace had done in itself carried no real authority. Yet, if these two indeed elected to accept it as such, none there were in a position to contravert it, even if they so desired.

The hush was broken by the scrape of Bruce's chair on the rush-strewn flagstones, as he rose. "My lords," he said thickly. "Here is a great matter. Here is the need for decision. I, for myself, do not want this duty, this burden, that Sir William Wallace has laid upon me. I am young, with no experience of the rule of a realm. I have much to see to, without that. My lands are devastated, great numbers of my people homeless, hungry, living in caves and under tree-roots. Winter is coming upon us—a winter that will test us hard. And in the spring, Edward will return. But . . . all this, if it is true for Carrick and Annandale and Galloway, is true also for much of Scotland. Save, perhaps, the North." He glanced down at Comyn. "The land faces trial. Destiny. All the land. The people. The need is great. And in this need, unity is all-important. Only unity can save us from Edward of England. None shall say that Bruce withstood that unity. If you, my lords, will have it so, I accept the office of Guardian. With . . . whomsoever." He sat down abruptly.

There was acclaim. But it was tense, almost breathless, and brief. Every glance was on John Comyn.

That man sat still, toying with the segment of bronze. He seemed to be under no strain, no sense of embarrassment that all waited for him. His sardonically handsome features even bore a twisted smile, as he examined the broken seal in his hand. The seconds passed.

When a voice was raised, it was Bruce's. "Well, man?" he demanded.

"This of the seal was cunning," the other said, almost admiringly amused. He looked up, but not at Bruce. "How think you, my lord Constable?" he asked his fellow-Comyn conversationally.

Buchan huffed and puffed, looking towards his brother, Master William, the cleric, some way down the table. Almost imperceptibly that smooth-faced man nodded.

"Aye. So be it," the earl grunted. "In a storm a man may not always choose the haven he would."

"Ha—neatly put, kinsman!" John Comyn acceded. "No doubt you are right. So there we have it. Joint Guardian—heh? With Bruce! God save us all!"

It was moments before it sank in. That this was acceptance. That Comyn was in fact going to say no more. That, smiling and still lounging in his chair, he was reaching for his goblet, to drink. And that he had pocketed his half of the seal. The thing was done.

As the recognition of this dawned, the company broke forth in excited chatter, comment, speculation. There was no longer any semblance of order. Men rose from their places and went to their friends and fellow-clansmen. Chiefs and lords beckoned their knightly supporters, prelates put their heads together and rubbed their hands. Down at the foot of the table, Wallace sat expressionless.

But after a while, as the noise maintained, the big man signed to the Bishop of Galloway. That cleric raise his hand, called out, and when he could make no impression, banged a flagon on the table for silence.

"My lords—this matter is well resolved. But it falls to be confirmed. To be accepted and duly made lawful. By a parliament, I, therefore, as Chancellor of this realm, for and on behalf of the Guardianship, do call such meeting of parliament tomorrow, at noon, in the former abbey here. To be attended by all and sundry of the three estates of this kingdom. At noon, my lords, gentles and clerks. So be it. God give you a good night."

Bruce rose, and looked down at Comyn. "This means . . . no little . . . accommodation, my lord," he said slowly. "It will tax our patience, I think, ere we are done."

"You think so? Patience is for clerks, and such folk. It is not a quality I aspire to, Bruce!"

"Nevertheless, you will require it, if I am not mistaken! As shall I!"

"If you esteem it so high, then I shall leave it to you! Myself, I see the case calling for quite different virtues. Valour. Daring. Resolution. Spirit. These, and the like."

"Such as the Comyns showed at Falkirk field?" That erupted out of Robert Bruce.

The other was on his feet in an instant, fists clenched. "By the Rude—you dare speak so! To me! You—Edward's . . . lackey!"

"For that, Comyn . . . you shall . . . suffer! As God is my witness!"

For moments they stared eye to eye. Then John Comyn swung about, and stormed from the hall. Few there failed to note it.

There was a deep sigh at Bruce's back, from William Lamberton.

• • •

Next day, in the ruined abbey, a tense and anxious company assembled, anticipating trouble naked and undisguised. And they were surprised, relieved, or disappointed, according to their varying dispositions. A night's sleeping on it, second and third thoughts, and the earnest representations of sundry busy mediators—mainly churchmen, and Master William Comyn in especial—had produced a distinct change of atmosphere. Nothing would make Bruce and Comyn love each other, or trust each other; but it was just conceivable that they might sufficiently tolerate each other to work, if not together, at least not openly in opposition.

At any rate, John Comyn arrived at the abbey, with his supporters, apparently in a different frame of mind. He favoured Bruce, even, with a distinct inclination of the head, did not address him directly, but appeared to be prepared to co-operate in some measure with Wallace, Lamberton and the Chancellor. Presently he allowed himself to be escorted to the Guardian's seat by the Steward, while Buchan, stiffly, silently, did the same for Bruce. They sat down, a foot or two apart, not looking at each other but not fighting either. The Primate said a brief prayer over their deliberations, and the Bishop of Galloway, as Chancellor, opened the proceedings by asking if it was the Guardians' will and pleasure to declare this parliament in sitting—even though lacking.required 40 days' notice.

Two nods from the chairs established the matter.

There was much routine business to get through, administrative detail which had piled up during Wallace's regime and which required ratification by parliament, most of it of minor importance or uncontentious. There was, in especial, the new French treaty and its ramifications to discuss. John Comyn, who had been sent to take a leading part at its negotiation, now sat silent, allowing his able kinsman, Master William, of the Chapel-Royal, to speak of this—which he did clearly and persuasively. The King of France's promises regarding armed help and intervention were noted and approved—and queries as to how much they were worth were kept to a minimum. Lamberton then gave some account of his negotiations with the Pope, at Rome, on Scotland's behalf, with assurances of Papal sanctions against Edward. Indeed, he had to announce that this, plus France's representations, had already resulted, they had just heard, in Edward releasing King John Baliol and his son from strict ward; they were now more or less free, in the custody of the Pope, at Malmaison in Cambrai.

No cheers greeted this news. Indeed a pregnant silence fell, as men looked at Bruce to see how he took it. He sat motionless, expressionless. In a parliament it was normal for the King to preside, but not to intervene in the actual discussions unless to make some vital and authoritative pronouncement. The Guardians were there as representing the King. Bruce could scarcely express forebodings about John Baliol's limited release.

Then there were a number of appointments recently made by Wallace, which fell to be confirmed, few of any prominence. But one raised eyebrows. Alexander Scrymgeour, of Dundee, his own standard-bearer in all their affrays, had been appointed Standard-Bearer of the Realm, and Constable of Dundee—the former a new office of state.

Buchan was on his feet to question it immediately. "My lord Chancellor," he said, "here is a strange matter. A new office. Is this the time to create new offices of state? Such should be by the King's own appointment. And . . . and if Standard-Bearer there must be, it should be one of the King's nobility. I move against."

There were a number of ayes from the assembly—but some growls also; the first sign of a clash.

"Do you contest the right of the Guardian to create such office, my lord?" the Chancellor asked mildly.

The Constable hesitated. "No," he admitted, after a moment. "But it requires confirmation by this parliament. And by the new Guardians. I move that confirmation be withheld."

"Noted." Galloway looked round. "Does any other wish to speak on this matter?"

"Aye, my lord Chancellor—I do." Wallace, standing in a lowly position but tending to dominate by his very presence, spoke up. "With great respect to my lord Earl, I would say that the creation of this office is no whim or caprice. Nor the filling of it by Alexander Scrymgeour. In this our realm's warfare, none I swear will question who suffers most. The common people. Few will deny who has achieved most in it, as yet. The common people. Even you, my lord Constable, will not gainsay that if the people of Scotland lose heart, or fail in their full support, then the realm is lost. The common folk, then, must see that they are considered. Represented. Given their due place. I say, who are more fitted to bear the Royal Standard of Scotland than one of themselves? And of them, who more fitted than Alexander Scrymgeour, who has fought in every conflict against the English, fought with valour—and stood his ground! I crave, my lords temporal and spiritual, barons of Scotland and gentles all—confirm the office and appointment both."

There was a curious sucking noise as the Steward, rising, sought to control his saliva. "I so move," he got out, and sat down.

This was it, then. So soon. The moment of decision. All eyes were fixed on the two new Guardians who sat side by side looking straight ahead of them, rather than on the Chancellor, Wallace or Buchan.

Galloway, tapping fingers on the stone recumbent effigy of a former abbot, which served him as desk, looked in the same direction as all others. "Before putting this to the vote, I think, the minds of the two Lords Guardian should be known," he said, and for once his confident sonorous voice was uneven.

Promptly Bruce spoke. "I accept the office, and accept and agree to confirm Alexander Scrymgeour as Royal Standard-Bearer of Scotland."

Seconds passed as all waited. Then John Comyn smiled suddenly, that brilliant flashing smile of his which not all found an occasion for joy. "Why, then, we are in happy accord, my friends," he declared easily. "For I too accept and accede. Let the excellent Scrymgeour bear his standard . . . so long as he can!"

The sigh of relief that arose was like a wind sweeping over the Forest outside. Men scarcely noticed the Chancellor's declaration that he thought there was no need for a vote, or Buchan's snorting offence and the angry look he cast at his kinsman. Everywhere the thing was seen as much more than just Scrymgeour's appointment; it was the sought-for sign that these high-born rivals might yet sink their personal preferences for the common good.

But even as the Chancellor, like others, relaxed a little, he was suddenly alert once more. John Comyn was speaking again.

"Since appointments are before us," he said crisply, sitting a little forward in his chair, "here are some that I require. For the better governance of this kingdom. My lord of Buchan to be Justiciar of the North. Sir Alexander Comyn, his brother, to be Sheriff of Aberdeen and keeper of its castle. Sir Walter Comyn to be Sheriff of Banff, and keeper. Sir William Mowat to be Sheriff of Cromarty, and keeper thereof. Sir Robert Comyn to be Sheriff of Inverness. Sir William Baliol to be Sheriff of Forfar. And Master William Comyn, of the Chapel-Royal, to be Lord Privy Seal and elect to the next bishopric to become vacant. All that due rule and governance may be established in the land."

Bruce all but choked, as all around men gasped and exclaimed. Never before had a parliament been presented with such demands from the throne, such an ultimatum. For clearly that is what it was. This, then, was Comyn's price for superficial co-operation. He had come prepared. Already the Comyns possessed enormous power in the North; with these key positions in their hands, they would be in complete control of all the upper half of the kingdom, not only theoretical but actual control.

Bruce bit his lip, as the startled Chancellor groped for words, looking in agitation for guidance, first at Bruce, then at Wallace and Lamberton. Agog, the assembly waited.

Bruce had only brief moments for decision, a decision there was no avoiding. Either he accepted, or refused agreement—and was thereupon branded as the man who broke up the Joint Guardianship, refused to make it work, out of enmity to Comyn. After Comyn had made his gesture of acceptance. The fact that that was on a tiny matter, a mere empty title, while this was a wholesale grab for effective power and dominance, would not help him. That Comyn had chosen to cast down the gauntlet now, before all, had obviously come prepared to do so, was evidence that if he, Bruce, countered him, the Joint Guardianship was finished before it had begun. Nothing was more sure.

Yet, how could it possibly continue, or succeed, on these terms? As good as a knife at his throat. Was there any point in going on with the farce?

There was only one faint glimmer of light that presented itself to Robert Bruce in those agonising moments. All the appointments Comyn had so blatantly demanded were in the North. Apart from the question of the Privy Seal and bishopric, he was at the moment confining his hegemony to the North. Always Scotland had tended to divide into two; the land south of the Forth, and north, echo of the old kingdoms of the Northern and Southern Picts, and their Celtic successors. It might be that Comyn was more or less proposing, not joint guardianship but divided guardianship, one to rule north of Forth, the other south. If this was so, it could change the entire situation. The South was smaller in territory but infinitely more rich and populous. Or had been, before it had burned itself. And it was the South that must bear the brunt of Edward's ire . . .

Lamberton was speaking—and clearly he had been thinking along the same lines as Bruce. ". . . since such appointments undoubtedly would strengthen the rule of the Joint Guardians. In the North. To the internal peace and security of the realm. A similar list of nominations; made by the Earl of Carrick, for the South, would be to the advantage of all. A . . . a balanced responsibility. Of the Joint Guardians. On such joint security the kingdom might rest firm. In this pass." He was looking hard at Bruce —as indeed were all others.

That young man took a deep breath. "Very well," he said, shortly. "I accept these appointments. And shall produce my own, in due course. Proceed."

In the buzz of talk that followed, John Comyn turned in his seat to stare at his companion long and levelly.

After that there was little more than formalities. The main confrontation and decisions had been made, and all knew it. In effect, Scotland would be partitioned into two mighty provinces, North and South. It was the natural, age-old division, and in line with the two great houses' spheres of influence—for though the Comyns held lands in Galloway, and the Bruces in Garioch and Angus, these were very marginal to their main power.

There was, of course, an unspoken corollary, which few failed to perceive. When Edward struck, the South would have to face him first. And it would be wise, then, for Bruce to look back over his shoulder. And if Edward over-ran the South, and could be held again at Stirling, as before, then the North would become all there was of Scotland. In which case, there might well be a new king in the land.

The parliament in the Forest broke up. It was agreed that the Guardians should meet again at Stirling, where North and South joined, in a month's time, to confer, and sign and seal edicts, charters and the like, with their two halves of the Great Seal.

Robert Bruce, with his brothers, rode south again for Annandale, ruler, in name at least, of Scotland south of the Forth.

Chapter Eleven

So commenced months of trial and frustration as difficult as any Bruce had experienced, with problems multiplying, patience taxed to the limits, and his hatred and distrust of John Comyn gnawing like a canker within him. He felt himself to be hamstrung, almost helpless, ruler in little more than name, able to achieve as little for himself and the Bruce cause as for the country as a whole, a land burned out and a people in dire straits, living in makeshift shelters and ruins, and on the verge of starvation. It was a wet and dismal winter, with little snow but floods making travel difficult—and Bruce seemed to spend his time in wet and uncomfortable travel, constantly on the move, though having little to show for his journeyings. He had nothing that he could feel was home, no real base or headquarters even—for Annandale was too far south for practical use, and his castles of Turnberry and Ayr, like all others, were but burned and blackened shells, and Lochmaben, the all-but-impregnable, was back in English hands. He went to Stirling monthly, for his formal meetings with Comyn—grim and profitless episodes which he loathed—and which only were made bearable by the patient ministrations and devices of the churchmen, especially Lamberton and William Comyn—the last proving himself to be able, shrewd and co-operative, however clearly ambitious. Without these two the Joint Guardianship would not have survived even the first acrimonious encounters.

Lamberton was in fact Bruce's mainstay and prop, without whom he would have thrown up the whole sorry business. More than that, he became a friend as well as guide, a strong, constant, clear-headed man, less stern than he seemed, with a faculty for quiet understanding and even a wintry humour. He was, indeed, if anyone was in these grievous months, the real ruler of Scotland, tireless link between the undamaged North and the devastated South. If Bruce travelled endless uncomfortable miles, then the Primate did double and treble, since not only did he move between the Guardians but he kept in touch with Wallace, who had made Dundee his headquarters for the recruiting of a new people's army—not to mention seeing to the rule of the Church from his own St. Andrews.

Nigel Bruce, too, was a major comfort to his harassed brother, his close companion throughout, a consistently cheerful, extrovert influence and link with happier, carefree days. But Nigel was of little help where guidance and good advice were required, seeing everything in simple blacks and whites.

Bruce's problems, during this period, fell mainly under three heads; to prepare for invasion; to alleviate something of the distress of the people; and to try to get at least the elementary machinery of government working again. All were almost equally difficult, in the prevailing state of the country. He could appoint his nominees to the key sheriffdoms of Lanark, Ayr,

Dumfries, Galloway and the like—his brother Edward in this last position—but these were little more effective than he felt himself to be. Of revenue there was none, so that the sheriffs had only their own pockets, and those of their friends, to call upon, to pay for their efforts—and friends do not long remain so in such circumstances. Had it not been for the whole-hearted support of the Church, little or nothing would have been achieved. The ecclesiastics still had some of the garnered riches of generations hidden away, and now expended them liberally. Moreover, they had great local influence over the minds of the common folk, and could rally and persuade where commands and threats from higher authority were meaningless.

Lamberton gave good reports of Wallace's force, growing in Angus and Fife. But to some extent, this was of little comfort to Bruce. For Wallace made it clear that this was very much a people's army, destined and trained for guerilla warfare, not to be hurled headlong against the English chivalry. Which left Bruce with the task of mustering an anti-invasion army from, as ever, the levies and tenantry of the lords. And since these were needed for the widespread local rehabilitation works, and moreover he had not the wherewithal to feed them, *en masse*, this had to remain very much a paper force, problematical indeed as to numbers and availability.

And all the time, the shadow of the Comyn thousands, and how they would be used, hung over all. Lamberton brought word that John Comyn was assembling great numbers in the North—employing them meantime admittedly to further his sway over the wild Highlands—as perhaps was his right and duty. But their presence, a hundred or so miles to the north of him, was no aid to Bruce's sleep, of a night.

Then, with the long wet winter over at last, and the campaigning season drawing near, a messenger found his way to Bruce at Tor Wood Castle, between Falkirk and Stirling, where he was awaiting Comyn for the April meeting—Stirling Castle still being held by the English, which made the town below its walls unsuitable for the Guardians' conclaves. This was a wandering Dominican friar, who spoke with an English accent. From his leather satchel he brought out a letter, its folds somewhat creased and grubby, but sealed resplendently with the arms of de Burgh of Ulster. The recipient waited carefully until he was alone, even from Nigel's presence, before he broke that seal and read the strong, flowing writing.

My Lord Robert,

I greet you fair and wish you very well. It is long since I spoke with any who has seen you in your person. But I hear of you and of some of your doings from time to time. Although as to how truly, I do not know. For you are scarcely well loved, here at York.

This all men are agreed upon, however, that the Earl of Carrick is now in the rule, with another, of the Scots kingdom. A matter which greatly displeases His Majesty, as you will guess. I must believe it true, and do much wonder at your so high elevation. Not that I deem you unfit, but that I would have doubted your will for it. But if it is so, you have the goodwill of one, at least, in this England.

I cannot conceive that your high office will bring you much of joy, so heavy is Edward's hand against your realm. But this I believe may be to your comfort. The King, although he still makes pretence of marching against Scotland shortly, will not do so. Not for this year. Of this I am assured, and so would have you to know it. For he now does hate the Scots so sorely that he will have no invasion but that he leads himself. He will not so lead, this year. For not only does he have much trouble with his lords, of which you know, the Earls of Norfolk, Hereford and Northumberland in especial, who do say that he has forsworn himself over the Great Charter and the forest laws. But he is to marry again. This same summer. He is to wed the Princess Margaret, sister to King Philip of France, with whom he has lately been at war, in order to make stronger his hold on that country. The lady is said to be even now on her way from France. Edward will make a pilgrimage to St. Albans for blessing for this union, and will marry at Canterbury thereafter. Few know of this as yet, but he told me of it himself yesterday. My father is to go with the King, to St. Albans, and I go to meet the Princess, as one of her ladies. So I hasten to send you word, hoping that the tidings will perhaps something lighten your burden for this year.

I think of you often, my lord. And sorrow that our paths be so wide apart. Although, God knows, we do scarce agree so well when we are close. But I am of a shrewish and haughty disposition. Or so my father and brothers assure me. So that it may be that you are the better off at a distance. Do you not agree? You also are of an awkward mind, as I know. And stubborn. Unlike your brothers, whom I could bend between any two of my fingers, I think. No doubt we shall suit each other best by writing letters. So will you write to me, my lord?

I grieve for Scotland, and the folly and hatred of men. In your fight I wish you God-speed, and confide you to the watchful protection of His saints.

I send my remembrances to your foolish brothers. And, to the ruler of Scotland, all I have of deference.

ELIZABETH DE BURGH, *written from the house of one Uhtred, a clothier, of York.*

ADDENDUM: *The King would now have me to wed Guy de Beauchamp, Earl of Warwick, but I mislike the smell of his breath.*

Bruce rose up, to pace the floor of the little bedchamber which was all that the minor castle of Tor Wood could provide for him. Then he stopped, to read the letter through once more. He was much affected—and oddly enough, even more immediately by that last addendum than by the important news of Edward's forthcoming marriage and consequent postponement of invasion. It was on this, and on the paragraph where the young woman spoke of his brothers, that he concentrated his re-reading.

He was still at it, frowning, when the clatter of hooves and jingle of harness and arms below drew him to the window. Comyn had arrived, with a great company, all resplendent. The man always rode the country as though he were king! Bruce's blood all but boiled at the sight of him, so confident and assured, darkly handsome features twisted in that mocking smile. Lamberton was with him, at least. Lamberton was always present at their meetings now, determined that they should not be alone together. William Comyn, also, smooth as an egg.

Bruce remained in his room, perusing his letter. And even when Nigel came running up the narrow turnpike stair to tell him that Comyn waited below, he curtly dismissed him. He would be damned if he would go hastening to meet the fellow.

Lamberton mounted the stairs, after a while. He looked weary, older, but greeted Bruce with a sort of rueful affection. He glanced quickly at the letter in the younger man's hand, but asked no questions. He contented himself, after the normal civilities, with mentioning that there were a great number of papers for the Guardians' signature and sealing, and that the Lord of Badenoch was in vehement mood, and spoiling for a gesture against the English, claiming to have 20,000 men under arms and ready for a move.

That brought Bruce back to realities, and he went downstairs with the older man in more sober frame of mind.

The hall at Torwood was no more than a moderately-sized room and was already overcrowded with Comyn's entourage. Bruce would have had them all out, for it seemed to him no way to conduct the business of state before all this crew; but he had had this out with Comyn before, and an unseemly argument it had been—worse probably than putting up with the crowd's presence, since this was the way the other wanted it. There were larger measures at issue.

Comyn himself lounged at the table, and did not pause in his eating, although the others all bowed at his co-Guardian's entry.

"Ha, Earl of Carrick," he cried, from a full mouth, "where have you been hiding yourself in this rat's hole? I' faith, I feared I would have to send for you!"

"*Send*, my lord?"

"To apprise you of my presence. And that I have come a long way. And have no desire to spend the night in this rickle o' stanes!"

Their host, Sir John le Forester, Hereditary Keeper of the Forest of the Tor Wood, clenched his fists, but kept silence.

"No doubt Sir John will be relieved to hear it," Bruce returned shortly. "Since we already must bear grievously on his household."

"He will be paid." Comyn shrugged. "I say that it is unsuitable that we should continue to meet in such a place. Like furtive felons. Well enough for Wallace and the like. But not for Comyn. We represent King John, and should meet in King John's palace of Stirling."

"I cannot believe that it has escaped your lordship's notice that Stirling Castle is still in the hands of Englishmen!"

"Aye. After all these months. And not only Stirling. But Edinburgh. Both in Scotland south of the Forth. Not to mention Roxburgh. And your Lochmaben. A poor state of affairs."

"Meaning, sir?"

"Meaning, sir, that *you* are lord of the South. That these strongholds are all in your territory. And that no attempt has been made, I think, to expel Edward's lackeys from any of them."

Bruce strove to keep his voice steady. "My lord, you know very well that these are four of the greatest fortresses in the land. In determined hands, all can withstand siege for months, for years if may be. Well provisioned, and with their own deep wells, they are impregnable. Without great siege engines—of which I have none. Moreover, with a territory in ruins, I have more to do than waste men in idle siegery. Isolated, these fortresses can do us little harm."

"I say there speaks folly. While Edward holds these castles, and denies us the use of our own land, we are still in his occupation. Not free men. They are a reproach and a scorn. I say we cannot make pretence to lead this Scotland while these remain held against us. Stirling and Edinburgh, in especial."

"Then, sir—you reduce them! If you can. You have the men assembled, I hear. Your North is not devastated. And you do not have to watch a hundred miles of Border."

"Will Bruce have Comyn free his castle of Lochmaben for him!"

"Reduce Stirling first, and we shall see!"

"Very well. I shall move against Stirling, forthwith. And when Edward marches, we are the nearer at hand."

Bruce narrowed his eyes, almost spoke, but did not.

"My lords," Lamberton said, "is it wise to waste your strength on these castles? When King Edward crosses the Border it will be in mighty force. We shall not be battling for castles, but for our very lives. Using the land against him again, tiring him, starving him, wearing him down. I see little virtue in seeking to take these castles, which he may be able to retake in but a few months time."

"There speaks a clerk, beat before he so much as draws sword!" Comyn scoffed. "You do not talk of war, my lord Bishop, but of brigandage. Think you I have mustered 20,000 men—and will muster more—to skulk and hide, to pick and peck? We shall face Edward like men—but choosing *our* battlefield, not his. As Wallace did at Falkirk, a mis-fought field if ever there was one. Let Bruce here slink and stab if he will. Comyn will fight to win, not to weary."

"Brave words, my lord," Bruce grated. "And where do you think to hold Edward thus? Where do you choose your battlefield?"

The other grinned. "Why, at Stirling belike! The best place, is it not? In all the land. Even Wallace could win, there. Aye, I shall hold the English again at Stirling. And meantime take Stirling's castle."

"Abandoning all the South to Edward!"

Comyn shrugged. "That is *your* responsibility, is it not? If you would have my counsel, it is that you should retire behind Forth yourself. The Bishop here has admitted that *you* cannot hold Edward in open battle. South of Forth it may be true. Only harass and impede. That is not sufficient. I say give him the South to starve in, then fight at Stirling. Fight to win."

There was a murmur of agreement from his supporters.

"No! Only a man lacking heart would say that. The best of Scotland is in the South. The richest, fairest land. The greatest number of the people . . ."

"And the Bruce lands!"

"You would abandon all this to the invader? I say no."

"How many men have you assembled? To face Edward?"

Bruce cleared his throat. "I do not keep many so assembled. There is over-much for men to do in this stricken land. But in a week I can muster 7,000. In two weeks, four times that."

"Can? *Hope* that you can! Will Edward give you two weeks? I prefer my army as men, not as promises! With *my* men, then, I shall assail Stirling Castle. With your promises, my lord, do what you will!" Comyn rose to his feet, as though he had granted an interview and it was now over. "My Lord Privy Seal—where are the papers to sign? These plaguey papers . . . !"

Bruce was actually trembling with suppressed rage and the effort to restrain his hot temper, the fists gripping his golden earl's sword-belt clenching and unclenching. Lamberton, watching them both closely, intervened.

"It is probably well decided, my lords. One policy to support the other. But not only my Lord of Badenoch will be at Stirling. Holy Church has made shift to muster men from its own lands. No mighty host, but sufficient to achieve much. A balance, shall we say? Four thousand of them, 1,500 horsed. And Wallace has lent us Scrymgeour, the Standard-Bearer, to lead. With Wallace's own host—now 15,000, I am told—my lord of Carrick's rear should be secure."

Both lords looked at the Primate quickly, at that—and Comyn went on looking. Neither commented, though a little of the tension eased out of Bruce.

"The papers for signature, my lords Guardian," Master William Comyn said, setting down a sheaf of documents before them on the table. "The lead for the sealing is heating below . . ."

Later, with the Northerners gone, Bruce, in his own small chamber again, turned to Lamberton.

"It is good to hear of your Church host. A comfort." Bruce took a pace or two about the room. "Wallace . . .?" he said. "You return to St. Andrews, my lord Bishop? Just across Tay from Wallace at Dundee. You will see him? Soon? Good. Then, will you tell him, from me, secretly, that we need not look for Edward's invasion. Not this spring."

"Not . . .? No invasion . . .?"

"No. Not this year, I think. Edward will be otherwise employed. He weds again."

"Dear God! Edward will wed? Soon?"

"Aye. He goes on a pilgrimage to St. Albans. In preparation. Weds at Canterbury. This summer. To the Princess Margaret of France. I fear we risk losing our French allies!"

"Saints cherish us—this is news indeed! You are sure of it? No idle tale?"

"I have it . . . from one I trust. Close to Edward's person."

"So! Then . . . then we have time. We have been given time, precious time. Thank God, I say!" The Bishop paused. "But, my lord—you did not tell him. My lord of Badenoch. You said naught of it . . . !"

"I said naught," the younger man agreed heavily. "Better that he does not know, I think."

"Is that right, my lord? He is your fellow-Guardian."

"Right? I do not know if it is right. But I deem it *wise*. Let Comyn learn it in his own time. Tell Wallace. But others need not know. Yet. I require the time more than does Comyn."

When Lamberton left him, Bruce asked him to have sent up to him paper, a quill and ink. Also a lamp, for the window was small and the light beginning to fade.

It was dark long before the young man finished. Letter-writing did not come easily to him, and in his vehemence he had to send for three more quills before he was finished. He wrote:

My lady,

I do greatly thank you. Your letter came to me this tenth day of April, at the Torwood of Stirling, and I received it with much favour. Your God-speed and goodwill I do treasure. And, I think, do much require. For I am in sorry state here. But the better for your heed for me.

I counsel you to beware of Guy de Beauchamp. He is a man of ill living. Do not consider him. Beware, I say, of any whom Edward would have you to wed. He would but use you, as he uses all, for his own purposes.

The word of his marriage is of great moment and does much aid to my mind's ease. For this I do thank you. Even Edward is scarce like to come warring to Scotland quickly after his wedding.

The more surely in that his wife will be sister to King Philip, with whom we are in treaty of mutual aid. I have no doubt that treaty will be brought to nothing hereafter. But meantime it stands. This gives us time, in Scotland. But God knows, not I, whether I can achieve what is required, in time.

You say well when you conceive that my present state will not bring me joy. Being Joint Guardian of Scotland with this man John Comyn is so ill a fate as to drive me all but from my wits. I think that you know of him, a masterful man of ill tongue, respecting none. But strong, in his own parts, as well as heading the powerfullest house in this realm. We have never agreed, nor ever shall. To act with him in amity is not possible. To bear with him is beyond all supporting. Yet I needs must, on the face of it, if the kingdom is not to fall apart before Edward. Only Comyn and Bruce, it seems to be, can so unite the lords and barons of the land into one, and so oppose England. But the good God alone knows if it is possible, for I do not.

Comyn will be king, if he may. Nothing is more sure. That would be an ill day for Scotland, and I would die first. For it would be the end of Bruce, I think. Anything better than that.

I do not believe that you are a shrew, my lady. Haughty it may be.

I would have news of my father. We are not close, but I am sufficient his son to wish to know how he fares. And he is true heir to Scotland. I fear that Edward may wreak wrath on him because of me. Where he is I do not know. He spoke of proceeding to Norway, to my sister, but I do not think it. He is like to be living on one of his English manors, which you know of, if Edward has not warded him. If you can learn aught and will write it to me, I shall be the more indebted. I think much of you, Lady Elizabeth. I do not believe that we are better thus far parted. I believe I am less stubborn than I was.

The salutations and esteem of ROBERT BRUCE OF CARRICK, GUARDIAN OF SCOTLAND.

Those last three words he scored out, and wrote beneath;

Here is folly, for I am guardian of nothing, scarce even of my own pride and honour. I pray God that He keep you. Also that He holds off Edward until our sown corn may be grown, and reaped, so that we may fight him at least with full bellies.

Chapter Twelve

The land was fair again, green—better even, turning golden under the August sun, the rigs of corn already yellowing on every valleyside, beasts looking sleek and fat again on the braes. It was a wonder, a transformation, and men rejoiced with an elementary rejoicing at the recurrent bounty of the seasons, a thing which they had not had occasion to consider, in Southern Scotland, for long. Another month. Give them another month, and honest weather, and the harvest would be in. One more month.

But there were ominous signs if not in the landscape. The English, who had withheld all these spring and summer months, were becoming active again. They had reinforced Edinburgh, Dunbar and Roxburgh Castles, and were sending out probing sallies from the latter and Berwick into the East March of the Borderland, even into Ettrick Forest. Why? They would not restart this without orders. King Edward was gone south to his wedding, yes—but he had issued commands for public prayers to be made in all parts of his kingdom for the success of his arms against the rebellious Scots. He had not forgotten, in his newfound felicity—and as a bridegroom of exactly sixty summers, he might well be content with only brief honeymooning. But they would have another month, surely...

Even Robert Bruce, who these days had developed something of a hunch to his wide shoulders, and a sombre, brooding aspect to his expressionful rugged features, felt the lift and release of it all, of what he saw. The land was no longer black. He had prayed for this, these months, and had been granted them. Nigel sang cheerfully at his side, as they rode, and he almost joined in more than once—unsuitable as this might be for Scotland's Guardian.

Eastwards from Lanark, where Bruce had been conducting an assize of justice, they climbed into the hills out of Clydesdale, by Biggar and Broughton, moving into the unburned land of Ettrick Forest.

This time, Bruce rode at the head of a great company of lords, knights and men-at-arms. He had learned this lesson, at least; that dealing with his fellow-Guardian called for display as well as patience. Moreover, this was not just to be another meeting or council, but with action contemplated. So he had, riding close behind him and his brothers, as well as James the Steward and his son Walter; Gartnait, Earl of Mar; John de Strathbogie, Earl of Atholl; Lindsay, Lord of Crawford; old Robert Wishart, Bishop of Glasgow, out of English hands again; Sir John de Soulis of Liddesdale; and Sir Ingram de Umfraville, brother to the Earl of Angus. As well as many other notables. A thousand and more horsed and armed retainers jingled behind, on long column of march, through the winding valleys.

They made not for Selkirk this time, but for Bishop Lamberton's rich manor of Stobo, on the upper Tweed west of Peebles. This was because of the English raids from Roxburgh, one of which had recently penetrated sufficiently deep into the Forest to burn Selkirk and part of the lower Ettrick and Yarrow valleys, as warning and foretaste. It was as reprisal for this, and in answer to Comyn's taunts regarding military inactivity, that Bruce now rode eastwards.

They came to the wide haugh of Tweed, at Stobo, in the late afternoon, to find its meadows and pastures a great armed camp, out of which the church on its knowe, the Bishop's manor-house and the Dean's little tower, rose like islands. Comyn had arrived first, from his prolonged siege of Stirling Castle, and clearly he had come well supported, as the colourful host of banners flying down there indicated.

It turned out, ominously, that the other Guardian had brought, as well as Buchan, Alexander, Earl of Menteith; William, Earl of Sutherland; Malise, Earl of Strathearn, Alexander MacDougall, Lord of Lorn, his brother-in-law; Sir Robert Keith, the Marischal; Sir David Graham, Lord of Dundaff; and others of similar prominence. It looked as though this was to be a trial of strength with more than the English.

Lamberton, more than aware of all the stresses and strains, was taking his own precautions. Churchmen were everywhere, with all the trappings of religion, relics and the like. Also heralds, with the King of Arms busy with formal pomp and circumstance. Massed trumpets signalised the appearance of Bruce's contingent, and re-echoed from all the round green hills. The Primate was seeking to smother animosities in formality.

The two sides mingled in the wide haughland with a sort of grim wariness, watched over and fussed around by the droves of clerics. There was no clear cut distinction between North and South, for there were Comyn supporters in the South and Bruce supporters in the North; but by and large the division was fairly clear, and none the less because external danger threatened.

John Comyn himself did not come to greet the newcomers, and there was no association until the leaders forgathered in the Bishop's dining-chamber for the evening meal; no real association even then, for Lamberton placed one Guardian at each end of the long table with himself in the middle. The hospitality was lavish, and music, minstrelsy and entertainment went on throughout and continuously, so that there was little opportunity for either co-operation or clash. Wine flowed freely, and it was clear that there would be no serious talking that night with all tired after long riding. A great council was arranged for the following forenoon. It could not be called a parliament, for such required a summons of forty days; but with most of the Privy Council present, it would carry sufficient authority for practical purposes.

The Guardians had not exchanged a single word, directly, by the time that the company broke up to retire to bed, Comyn in the Dean's tower, Bruce in the manor-house itself. The latter and Lamberton, however, talked late into the night.

In the event, it was driving rain in the morning, shrouding the hills, and no conditions for holding a large meeting in the open, as had been intended. The largest room of the Bishop's manor-house was much too small, as was the church. The nearest large chamber was the Hospitium of St. Leonard's, at Peebles, a few miles to the east. There was a castle there also, actually a royal hunting-lodge, but it was a small place.

So to the town of Peebles a great company rode, through the rain, by a Tweed already grown brown and drumly with the hill burns' swift spates. Men forgot their dynastic and clan rivalries for the moment, to look anxiously up at the lowering clouds, and to hope that the good weather was not broken for long and the harvest put in jeopardy.

But in the refectory of the Hospitium at Peebles, even as the Prior welcomed his numerous distinguished guests, all the churchmen's efforts at peace-keeping were abruptly brought to naught. Upraised voices in angry altercation drowned the Prior's. All eyes turned.

"... jumped-up scum! Those lands are mine, I say. And I'll have them back, Wallace or no Wallace!"

The speaker—or shouter, rather—was the Lord of Dundaff, Sir David Graham, younger brother of Wallace's friend, Sir John, who had died heroically on Falkirk field. But brother of a different kidney, a vociferous supporter of Baliol and Comyn. Now he was shaking his fist up in the face of a tall and rather gangling man, largely built but giving the appearance of being but loosely put together, who flinched somewhat at the truculence of the smaller man's outburst.

"The lands are not yours, sir. Never were," this other protested. "They but neighbour yours. And you may covet them. But they were granted to my brother, granted by my lord Guardian . . ."

"Unlawfully granted! Those lands of Strathmartine are ours. Graham's. Always we have claimed them. No upstart bonnet-laird from the West shall have them, I say. The Earl of Carrick had no right to grant them. Any more than he should have knighted such as you . . . !"

"Sirrah!" Bruce rapped out, sharply. "Watch your words."

"It is truth. Strathmartine is Graham land. And you gave it to . . . a felon!"

"Knave!" Stung to fury, the big shambling man dropped his hand to the hilt of his dirk. He was Sir Malcolm, Wallace's brother, recently knighted by Bruce out of respect for his brother's fame. A very different man from the giant Sir William, he was like a blurred, indeterminate and somehow bungled version of the other.

Still more swiftly the Graham's hand dropped, and his dagger was whipped out.

"Fool! Put that away. Are you mad?" Bruce cried.

"This . . . mountebank called me knave! Me, Graham!"

"Sir David! Drawn steel, in the presence of the realm's Guardians, is treason!" That was Lamberton, in his sternest voice. He pushed forward towards the irate knights. "Sheath your dirk, man. I command you. Sir Malcolm—stand back."

"Treason!" Graham cried, beside himself. "*You*, Wallace's creature, to say that! And what of Wallace's own treason? He is bolted. Gone. Fled the country. In time of our need. Without the permission of the Guardians! Here is treason, if ever there was. And you say treason to *me*!"

"You babble, sir. Bairns' havers!" the Primate declared coldly. "Sir William has gone overseas. On a mission to the rulers of nations. To the King of Norway, the Pope, and the King of France. To seek bind them together against Edward of England. How dare you raise your voice against the man who saved this realm! The man your own brother died for!"

"You would have us believe such tales? Is this the time to desert the nation? To go journeying round Christendom? With Edward Plantagenet hammering at our doors! Expected to invade us any day . . ."

"Edward is marrying. In the south. All know it. We had a space for breath. Sir William Wallace was our best ambassador. A man whose name will open all doors . . ."

"I gave no authority for Wallace to leave the country." All faces turned, as this new cold voice intervened, the Red Comyn's voice. If men had been keyed up before, they were more so now.

"You were informed, my lord," the Bishop said.

"I gave no permission, as Guardian."

"*I* gave permission," Bruce declared. "We waited for yours. Requested it, and waited. Time was short. When you sent no answer, my lord, either way, I gave the required permission. As Guardian."

"We are *Joint* Guardians, sir. What Comyn withholds, Bruce cannot grant."

"What the realm's need demands, and when one will not act, the other must needs do so!"

"Ha, you say so? Here is a convenient policy for knavery!"

"I request that you choose your words, my lord. And recollect that Wallace left from Leith, from *my* jurisdiction."

"My lords, my lords!" The Primate, concerned by the broadening of the conflict to include the two Guardians, held up an imploring hand. "Here is no cause for disagreement. Sir William went first to Norway, where my lord of Carrick's sister is Queen. Then to the Pope, at Rome, on a mission from myself as head of Holy Church in this land . . ."

"He went, I say, in the face of the enemy!" That was Graham again, hotly. "He, the warrior! The hero! Who is supposed to lead the people. Edward beat him once—so he scuttles before the Plantagenet comes to finish his work! A craven, as well as a traitor and an upstart! I ask *his* lands, of the Guardians—not that he take mine!"

"As God's my witness—this I'll not stand!" Sir Malcolm cried, and with the rasp of metal his own dagger came out.

"No! No, I say! Put back your steel. Both of you. In the name of Almighty God, in this holy place, I command it!" Lamberton strode forward, hand outstretched.

"Stand back, Sir Priest! Or your wordy wind-bag may be punctured!" the Graham snarled, flickering his dirk in a lightning gesture at the Bishop. "Leave this overgrown mummer to a better man!"

"By God's Blood, this is too much!" Bruce burst out, and flung himself towards the others.

In almost the same instant Comyn and Buchan leapt into action.

Chaos reigned in that normally quiet refectory for the sick and aged.

The Comyns were slightly nearer to the Graham than was Bruce—for he was of their party. Buchan the Constable, a pace or two ahead of his kinsman, reached the angry group first just as Lamberton was stretching out an authoritative and fearless hand to be yielded Graham's weaving steel. Furiously the Earl buffeted the Bishop aside, sending him staggering against Bruce, who came up on the other side.

"How . . . dare . . . you! Comyn!" Bruce shouted, above the hub-bub. "By the Rude—you shall pay . . ."

"Comyn dares more than that!" It was Sir John the Red who answered thus, and coming up, struck Robert Bruce with the back of his hand full across the face.

It was as though a curtain of silence fell suddenly and completely over the raftered hall. With an uncanny abruptness the shouting and noise died away, as all stood appalled, rooted to the spot in horror at what was done, at what that blow stood for. The only sound, in a matter of seconds, was the heavy breathing of the two richly-clad Guardians of Scotland, standing only a foot or so apart, proud flashing eye to eye. Even the Primate and the High Constable were forgotten for the moment.

Bruce, trembling all over almost uncontrollably with the fierceness of his battle with utterly destructive rage, was stark white save for the scarlet hand-mark on his left cheek and jaw. He swayed, as though drunken, in the extremity of his emotion. Comyn himself for once was not smiling. He stood motionless, almost frozen, wary, as though perhaps himself shocked by what he had done; but resiling nothing, giving no hint of regret, of weakening.

It was Nigel Bruce who moved. With an oath, he grabbed at his jewelled dirk, to raise it high. "Dastard!" he whispered. "You . . . struck . . . him!"

Even as the weapon drove down, Bruce seemed to be released

from the straitjacket of his emotion. Like an uncoiling spring he hurled himself against his brother, beating aside the dagger. Comyn had not stirred, even flinched.

"No!" he cried. "No! *My* quarry! Mine. Mine only." Panting, still with one hand on his brother's wrist, he pointed with the other. "Comyn—I should kill you. For that. Now. Before all. But . . . but it is not the time. Or the place. Not yet. One day, I will pay that debt. I promise you. As all these, and God and His saints, will be my witness! Till then—wait, you! Wait, and regret!"

"Thank God, my lord—thank God!" Lamberton exclaimed. "For your lenity. Your forbearance. Fortitude." He swung on Comyn. "And you, my lord—shame on you! Here was infamy. Unworthy. Unworthy of any noble knight . . ."

"Quiet, priest!" the Red Comyn jerked, from stiff lips. "Enough." He looked at Bruce. "At any time, my lord of Carrick, should you wish to take this matter further, I am at your service. And shall cherish the day!"

"Do so. For it will be your last!" the other said levelly.

Master William Comyn, of the Chapel Royal, laid a hand on the arm of his brother Buchan, who was about to speak, and raised his own mellifluously soothing voice. "My lords and gentles all—we have come here for urgent business. A council. Not for profitless wrangling. Much is at stake. I pray that we may move to that business. If the Lords Guardian will take their seats. At the Prior's table . . ."

"Sit!" Bruce swung on him, eyes wide. "Think you that I will sit at any table? With *him*? Now? Do you, man?"

"Here's a mercy, at any rate! I am to be spared that!" Comyn found his smile again.

"My lords, my lords—think! Consider. You are both Guardians and governors of this realm, still." Lamberton supported his fellow-cleric. "The realm's affairs must go forward."

"This joint guardianship is over," Bruce declared shortly.

"On this at least we are agreed." The other bowed elaborately.

"Scotland deserves fairer than that, I think," the Primate said slowly, authoritatively, and with great dignity, looking from one to the other sternly. "Those who take up the realm's direction may not so toss it away, without loss to their honour. I beg your lordships to perceive it. And for your good names' sake recollect your duty."

Those were hard words for such as these. But William Comyn reinforced them, although in his own more suave fashion. "I am sure that my lord of Badenoch, at least, will know his duty. And will well serve the realm, now as always." He eyed his kinsman meaningly.

There was a pause, and then Bruce shrugged. "To business, then," he said. "We will consider this of the guardianship at another time. But—I will not sit there. With that man!"

Comyn was about to speak when Lamberton forestalled him. "Very well," he acceded. "The form of it matters little. Let us proceed, here standing." He pointed. "The clerks may use the table." Without pause he went on. "The matter of Sir William Wallace's mission to the rulers has been dealt with and, I submit, is not profitable for further discussion here and now." And before any might plunge again into those troubled waters, added, "The besiegement of Stirling Castle proceeds. My lord of Badenoch may wish to speak to it?"

Thus invoked, Comyn could scarcely refuse to participate, in his own project. "It goes but slowly," he said, seemingly casual. "My people have assailed it for ten weeks. With little gain, as yet. Save that we constrain the English closely, and have driven them into the inner citadel. But it is strong. The strongest place in Scotland. We shall have it, in time, never fear. And investing it demonstrates to the whole land that at least *some* will draw sword against the invader!" He tossed a glance at Bruce.

"I commend my lord of Badenoch's assault on Stirling," that man commented shortly. "Even if barren of result!"

"The Earl of Carrick might have better fortune were *he* to take up arms against one or other of the less powerful holds the English enjoy in his territories! His own house of Lochmaben, in especial."

None failed to see significance in that; but not all probably perceived the fuller implication. The main object behind holding this meeting here in the Forest was in order, thereafter, to lead a united assault on the great English-held base of Roxburgh, which lay some thirty miles down Tweed, near Kelso and the actual borderline. Bruce, ever chary of becoming bogged down in siege-warfare, had only been persuaded to this by Comyn's threats that he would do it alone, if need be. Such a move undoubtedly would look as though the other Guardian was dragging his feet, in the popular view. Hence the great array of magnates and nobles, of both factions, here assembled. Yet now Comyn was talking about Lochmaben and not mentioning Roxburgh.

"I have not the same itch to take castles as has this lord," Bruce declared, slowly. "Even my own. Which is very strong also. As Sir John Comyn knows—since he assumed possession of it during the short reign of King John Baliol . . . !"

"Whom God save and protect!" Comyn rapped out.

In duty bound, many requested the Deity to save the King.

"No doubt," Bruce went on dryly. "But, despite its strength, the English in Lochmaben can do us little harm. They cannot be reinforced without a major invasion."

"I have heard it said," Comyn observed, looking round him, with his hard grin, "that Bruce may be well content to leave the English in Lochmaben. That, should Edward triumph, he may find it a convenient stepping-stone back into the Plantagenet's good graces! Idle havers, no doubt . . ."

"Damnation! This is a malicious lie . . . !"

"Idle havers, no doubt, as I say!" the other repeated loudly. "But a warning of how men's minds may go. Is it not?"

"My lords," Lamberton intervened again, with a sort of weary urgency, "Lochmaben is of less importance in the realm than are the others. Roxburgh is otherwise . . ."

"Aye," the Earl of Mar broke in, "Roxburgh is only a mile or two from the Border. It can be supplied and reinforced with ease by the English . . ."

"Which means, my lord, does it not, that it is scarce worth our troubling with?" Comyn asked. "Since, even if we succeed in taking it, as soon as we are gone, the English can retake it. With ease, as you say. If worse does not befall."

"But . . . but . . . ?"

"They are raiding from there. Becoming devilish bold!" Mar's other brother-in-law, Atholl, supported him. "Did we not come this far to teach them a lesson? At Roxburgh?"

"My information is that they are much reinforced. Their raiding is no more than a ruse to draw us there. Into a trap, with large English strength waiting on their own side of Tweed." Comyn spoke in jerking, unusual fashion, clearly ill at ease on this. But it was equally clear that, whatever the reason for this change of front, his mind was made up. "It would be folly to advance on Roxburgh, in the circumstances."

All men stared at him now, Bruce included. He at least had no doubts as to what this meant. It was highly unlikely that Comyn could have any new information regarding Roxburgh, or that there could be any large English force approached so near without word being brought to Bruce himself. Therefore it was merely an excuse. Comyn, now, would not proceed on any joint action. It was as simple as that. There was to be not even a token co-operation between the Guardians.

Even Buchan was taken by surprise, obviously. He peered at his cousin, and coughed. "A simple blow, John. A show of strength," he suggested. "We need not make a siege of it, if the signs are contrary. But a raid, at least. Into England. Since we are here in force . . ."

"No!" the other snapped. "It would be folly. I march only with my rear secure!"

There was no question what he meant by that. The guardianship was irrevocably, blatantly, split.

As all there contemplated the ruin of it, and perceived the dread shadow of internecine civil war to add to bloody invasion, Lamberton, flat-voiced, sought once more to ease the tension, to salvage something from the wreck, to make time for calmer thinking.

"The Lords Guardian have rejected the suggested raid on Roxburgh, then," he said. "But there is more business. Appointments. First, the Wardenship of the West March. Sir William Douglas, in English hands, has been Warden. While prisoner, his deputy has been Sir Christopher Seton, here present. There are now tidings that the Lord of Douglas has died in the Tower of London. May God rest his soul. Whether he died of Edward's malice, or of bodily ill, we know not. But, my lords, a new Warden is required."

It was skilfully done. The fiery Douglas had been popular, something of a hero, if an awkward one. The announcement of his death, as a prisoner, made a major impact, and set up an angry clamour against the enemy—a healthier demonstration than heretofore. In the stir, it was agreed almost without discussion that Sir Christopher Seton, the deputy, should be raised to full wardenship. He was a sound Bruce supporter.

One or two other appointments were quickly disposed of thereafter, following as far as possible the non-controversial line of Comyn nominees for those in the North, Bruce for the South. Lamberton steered them deftly through that strange, standing assembly, with the curt nods or complete silence of the two hostile Guardians accepted as the ultimate authority of the kingdom. Men stirred, shuffled and fidgeted as the formalities were hurried through.

Undoubtedly all now were anxious for the uncomfortable proceedings to be over. Yet men dreaded what might follow, once the two factions were released from the Primate's dexterous handling and patient but firm authority. That these two men, Comyn and Bruce, could go on ruling Scotland conjointly, for the kingdom's well-being, or their own, was manifestly impossible. But neither was going to resign and leave the other in supreme power. And even if both were to resign, who could effectively replace them? They represented the two great power-divisions of the country, and any other successors would in fact be nothing more than the nominees and puppets of these two. For a land which so desperately needed unity, Scotland was in a sorry state.

As the half-desired, half-dreaded moment arrived, when the proceedings were being closed by William Comyn, the Lord Privy Seal, announcing that the necessary papers and charters were there on the table for the Guardians' signature and sealing, it was a much less smooth and assured clerical voice which at this last moment galvanised the company. Old Robert Wishart, Bishop of Glasgow, had aged noticeably from his spell in an English dungeon. He quavered painfully.

"My lords—we cannot break up so. The government of the realm, in this disarray. It is our bounden duty, before God and the people of Scotland, to take further steps for the better rule of the land. My Lords Guardian, you must see it?"

"I see it." Bruce acceded briefly, but shrugged helplessly.

Comyn showed no reaction.

"The Crown rests in two hands," the old prelate went on, panting a little, "Those two hands may be strong, but they . . . they are scarce in harmony. Why should there not be three hands? If there is joint guardianship, there could likewise be triple guardianship. I commend such to you. I commend to you all my lord Bishop of St. Andrews, Primate and spokesman of Holy Church in this land, as Joint Guardian with the Earl of Carrick and the Lord of Badenoch."

Into the hum of excited comment, James the Steward, Wishart's old colleague, managed to make thick interjection.

"I agree. I say, I agree."

Bruce was about to announce hearty and thankful approval, when Lamberton himself caught his eye and almost imperceptibly shook his head, before looking expectantly at Comyn. Bruce held back, in belated recognition that what he signified approval of, his rival would almost automatically oppose.

Comyn, narrow-eyed, kept them waiting, while he weighed

and calculated. It was his kinsman, the Lord Privy Seal, who spoke.

"Here is a notable proposal. Which could well serve the realm, I think." Whatever was his reason, Master William was being very co-operative this day.

Ignoring Bruce entirely, Comyn turned to Buchan. "How think you, Cousin? Shall we have the priest?"

Lamberton actually raised a hand involuntarily to restrain the hot flood that rose to Bruce's lips.

The Constable had the grace to flush. "The rule of the realm must go on," he muttered.

"Very well. So be it." The Red Comyn turned away, with a half-shrug, towards the table. "Now—these papers . . . ?"

"My lord . . . !" Robert Wishart gasped. "My lord—the Earl of Carrick! Do *you* agree?"

Strangle-voiced, Bruce got it out. "Aye."

"God be praised!" The old man's voice broke. "Then . . . I declare . . . he is . . . I declare the Bishop of St. Andrews is Guardian of the realm. My lord, my good lord . . . !"

The assembly at last broke up in disorder. But the thing was done. There were now three Guardians in Scotland. And one, men acknowledged with relief, was strong enough and supple enough perhaps for the unenviable task of holding the balance between the other two.

After the signing and sealing there was no pretence at further co-operation between the two great factions. It was clear that despite the rain, Comyn was for heading north again at once. He was going, he declared loudly, back to real work, after his bellyful of clerks, idlers, poltroons and their talk, back to the siege of Stirling. Others could go where they would—to hell, if need be!

Watching the Comyns and their following ride off, Bruce pale-faced, fists clenched, found his shoulder gripped by William Lamberton.

"My son, my very good friend—may God reward you for your restraint this day," the Bishop-Guardian said. "It cost you dear, I know. But—it saved the kingdom. Not once, but many times. I thank you, my lord, from the bottom of my heart."

"I feel soiled. Besmirched. The name of Bruce spat upon. Trampled by that . . . that devil! That braggart!"

"I know, I know. But do not fear—no men think Bruce reduced by this day's work. Quite otherwise. You have added to your stature, my good lord. That is certain. But . . . do not name

Comyn braggart, I pray you. Do not delude yourself. Whatever else he is, he is not that. It will pay us to remember it."

"Perhaps. But, whatever he is, he will suffer for today. On that I give you my oath! Before Almighty God!"

The older man sighed, and shook his head. "Perhaps God will save you from that oath—who knows? But—what do you now? Roxburgh?"

"No. I am none so keen on castle-baiting. Time can be better used. There is much else for me to do."

"Nevertheless, I think it would be well to heed one matter that Comyn said, my friend. Lochmaben. You were wise to lay siege to Lochmaben. What he said, of men's talk, could be true. At least make the gesture of investing your castle."

"You think . . . ? Men do talk so of me? It is not just Comyn's spleen? That I reserve Lochmaben, for Edward's favour?"

"Men are foolish. And uncharitable. I have heard the like talk. Better that you should proclaim it false, by your deeds."

Bruce looked away and away, beyond the rain-shrouded Peebles hills.

Chapter Thirteen

Fires blazed redly against the October blue night sky, on every rounded height that flanked the seven lochs of Lochmaben and were reflected in the prevailing blue-black waters, scores of conflagrations that burned brightly and were being replenished, flames that would be seen from great distances, from all Annandale and Nithsdale and the plain of Solway, even from far Carlisle and the English Cumberland fells behind. And for once they were not burning homes and farmsteads and churches, not even balefires of warning; but bonfires of joy and celebration. For Lochmaben's great castle was in its own people's hands again, after long enemy occupation, the captured garrison imprisoned in the dungeons which had held and seen the last of so many Annandale folk these past years. Now there was no single English-held enclave in all the South-West. Moreover, the harvest was safely in at last, and the weather held. There was cause for rejoicing and bonfires.

Robert Bruce, pacing the timber bretasche, or overhanging parapet-walk of the main central tower of Lochmaben high on the great motehill of earth, and looking out at it all over the surrounding waters, recognised that he had cause for gratification. He it was who had given permission for those beacons to be lit. A success was welcome indeed, after all the months of labour and frustration. The sheer military action itself, the overcome challenge, had been welcome—and the acceptance of Sir Nicholas Segrave's surrender a notable satisfaction—even though the deplorable pantryman, Master Benstead, it seemed, had been withdrawn to England almost a year before. But satisfaction was not really in the man's mind, that night, nevertheless.

None knew better than he how superficial, how temporary, was this celebration. Lochmaben might be his again, meantime—but for how long? *This* harvest was gathered and secured—but would there be another? The basic situation was unchanged. The monstrous shadow of Edward Plantagenet loomed over all divided Scotland still, behind those joyous bonfires, and there was little reason to believe that the future would be any brighter than the past.

Indeed Bruce at least knew the reverse to be likely. He had come up here, to the battlements, to be alone, and to be able to read again the letter which crackled inside his doublet—for beacons blazed here on the topmost parapet also, and would give him light to read, unattended, as was impossible in the crowded castle below. That letter which was itself secret satisfaction and disquiet both. But he was not alone. His brothers Nigel and Edward, and his brother-in-law Gartnait of Mar, had followed him up; and while the former pair knew their brother sufficiently well to perceive the signs that he would be glad of their absence, and had withdrawn round to the other side of the keep's high walk, the latter, an amiable but somewhat stupid man, took no such hint and clung close, talking, talking.

The fact was that the Earl of Mar, who tended to hide himself in his northern fastnesses, was in process of building up the capture of Lochmaben Castle into the adventurous highlight of a not very exciting life. He had committed himself for the first time, against the English, and the venture had been successful. Not that only, but it had been a spectacular and dramatic business, two nights ago, and he had taken an active if minor part. It looked as though the fall of Lochmaben was going to be Gartnait of Mar's theme of conversation for a long time to come.

Admittedly, it had been no ordinary and prolonged siege, than which no military activity could be more dull. It had been Bruce's own conception, for, though he had been born at Turnberry, he had spent a large part of his boyhood here, at his paternal grandfather's favourite castle. It was an old-fashioned place, not one of the new stone castles at all, but a mote-and-bailey stronghold of the sort that had been general for three centuries, built of timber and covered over with hardened clay. If any imagined this to be a frail construction for such a place, they would be mistaken. The artificial mote-hill rose to about fifty feet, and the soil which went to its heightening had been dug from all round in the form of deep encircling ditches, up to thirty feet wide. There were four of these ditches at Lochmaben, each defended by a high wooden palisade, with inner shelf-like parapet-walk and drawbridges. The inner one enclosed a ring-shaped court, around the central mound, in which were the kitchens and domestic quarters, the men-at-arms' barracks, the storehouses and the stables. Also the castle well. Up on the summit of the mote-hill was the great square keep itself, its massive timbers covered in many feet of baked clay plastering, so that it could not be fired from without. Well-provisioned, such a place was well-nigh unconquerable.

But Bruce, sitting down with his host outside it, had had childhood memories which stood him in good stead. That well, in the inner bailey, which permitted prolonged resistance, was nevertheless the place's weakness—though few probably knew it. Deep down it connected not with a spring, which was usual, but with a running underground stream of fair size. A stream that flowed into the Castle Loch some two hundred yards to the south by an inconspicuous exit amongst piled rocks and elder scrub. Bruce had found that exit, playing as a boy, and explored the stream's winding tunnel-like course underground as a boy will, until he had found himself at the foot of the stone-faced well-shaft, with the glimmer of daylight high above. He had never forgotten.

So, on a suitably dark night of cloud and drizzle, he had mounted a sham attack on the outer defences, under Edward, to keep the garrison occupied, and set burning great quantities of cut reeds and brushwood to westwards, to form a blowing smoke-screen to blind the defenders. Then he himself had led three boatloads of men, with muffled oars, from the nearby town, under Nigel and Mar, to the hidden mouth of the stream. The underground course had seemed infinitely smaller, more cramping and alarming than his boyhood recollection; but at length, bruised and coughing with the smoke from the pitch-pine torches, they had reached the well-foot. Its rope and bucket was up at the surface, but the agile Nigel had worked his way up the long shaft, back hard against one side, feet walking up the other, and thereafter quietly let down the rope for the others to follow. The inner bailey had been deserted.

Thereafter a score of desperate men had crept up the steep mote-hill to the central keep, screened by the drifting smoke, to find it standing open and practically empty, all the garrison manning the perimeter palisades, gatehouses and outer defences. Securing the citadel, they had then attacked the bewildered and scattered defenders from the rear, one bailey at a time. Sir Nicholas Segrave, still the castle's Captain, had surrendered his sword at the main gatehouse, like a man betrayed.

Gartnait of Mar had scarcely ceased to talk of it since.

A commotion down in the same inner bailey, over a hundred feet below their lofty stance, with horsemen arriving and torches waving, gave Bruce the excuse he sought. Not every belted earl would run errands, even at the behest of another of the same, but Mar was essentially a modest and gentle man—as his spirited wife complained. His brother-in-law sent him down to find out what was to do.

Alone, Bruce drew out the letter—which he had only had opportunity to skim hitherto—and moved closer to the nearest beacon, for light. It read:

My lord Robert,

I take up my pen again with much concern for you. And some little for myself, should I be discovered thus writing. For King Edward has little mercy on those who counter him, as you do know, even though they be women. Certain ladies here have discovered it to their cost, of late. For this marriage seems to have shortened his temper. So that I fear that I may write but little tonight, for I am much constrained and seldom alone. The Queen is at chapel, for the King has become mighty religious and I have craved excuse over a woman's pains. But she and the others will be back.

Foolish that I am, my lord, to waste precious time and words so. I write from York again, where we are recently returned from London. But not from the house of Uhtred the clothier. I am very grand now, in the Lord Archbishop's palace no less. For I am chief of the Queen's ladies. But we are cramped here mighty tight, nevertheless, and I had more of private space amongst the cloths and wool.

But we do not stay at York. In two days we go north to Newcastle where the King assembles another great force against Scotland. He is very wroth about the assault on Stirling and promises dire punishments against his rebellious Scots. He is wroth too with his lords, for many do say that it is too late now in the year for invading Scotland. And that he goes back on his promises to them, in this continuing warfare. God knows they are right. It is a kind of madness with him. He has forbade, by public proclamation, all joustings, tournaments and plays of arms, saying that every knight, esquire and soldier must rather come to do duty against the Scots. I fear then, that by your receipt of this writing, the King will be riding against you, to Stirling.

Your letter did find me at Canterbury and I much esteem it. I am sorry for your state and pray that it may be lightened. The Lord John Comyn I remember and did not like. We did not agree. But nor did I agree with the Lord Robert of Carrick. Is it not so? Even though you do not believe me shrew. Or say that you do not. Perhaps you cozen me. But may the Devil roast John Comyn.

I have heard tidings of your father. He dwells quietly and peaceably on his manor of Hatfield Broadoak in Essex. It is said he has been sickly. The King does not speak of him. He speaks of you, I fear, but less than kindly.

Guy de Beauchamp, of Warwick, is not now in the King's favour, and so I am spared. But he would have me to wed instead Humphrey de Bohun, the new young Earl of Hereford. Do you esteem him the more acceptable, my lord?

From Newcastle when the King marches into Scotland we women are to be left at the Percy's castle of Alnwick where I was beforetime. Near to you in your Border hills although I cannot conceive that we should meet. I do much fear for you and yours, in Edward's wrath. Keep you out of his way my lord Robert.

I hear the Queen returned below.

I know not whom I may obtain to bring this letter to you. Another wandering friar will be safest, it may be. God be with you. I am in haste.

From York, in the night of sixth October, by ELIZABETH DE BURGH.

Humphrey de Bohun, of Hereford! That puppy! Bruce frowned fiercely on the firelit night. A dandified young fool. And shamefully rich. He could no more manage Elizabeth de Burgh than he could fly in the air!

The reader forced his thoughts to the more immediately vital matter of the date. The letter had taken three weeks to come from York, via the Bishop of Galloway—for it was now the end of October. Edward, then, might well have left Newcastle, by now, on his murderous way. Stirling, she said. Making for Stirling, to relieve the siege. Lamberton must be warned. And Comyn, of course. And Wallace was not yet home from across the seas...

Mar, panting with the climb, arrived back at the parapet-walk with a young esquire, a stranger, who looked as though he had fallen into more than the one bog on his way to Lochmaben.

"Courier from Seton. Warden of the March," he burst out. "Edward is at Berwick! God save us—Edward is at Berwick, Robert! This... here is the Earl of Carrick."

"My lord—my master, Sir Christopher Seton, salutes you," the youth said, his voice declaring his fatigue. "He sends this message. The King of England is at Berwick with a great host. But Sir Christopher learns that he has trouble. His greatest lords have refused to advance into Scotland. Thus late in the year. His first aim was to relieve Stirling Castle. But they will by no means accompany him. There is great upset in the English camp. But... Sir Christopher hears that the King comes here. Instead of Stirling..."

"Here! You mean—Lochmaben?"

"So says Sir Christopher, my lord. He has spies in the English camp: The word is that the King's wrath is beyond all telling. But his earls are solid against this venture. He has heard of your siege of this castle. Belike he does not know that it is fallen. He swears that he will teach the Earl of Carrick a lesson, at the least. He rides tomorrow for Lochmaben."

"The fiend take him! And these earls? Will they follow him to Lochmaben? But not to Stirling?"

"No, my lord. They and their levies—the main host—move not out of England. But the King has men enough of his own, and hired Welsh archers, with the Cumberland levies of Sir Robert Clifford, to serve for this."

"How many?"

"Sir Christopher says near to ten thousand. Half of them Welsh longbowmen."

"Dear God! And I have less than a third of that. And not two hundred of them archers!"

"Robert! Can you get more? In time?" Mar demanded, in agitation.

"No. Not enough, by half. Not men to face Edward—the greatest soldier in Christendom! Not archers. Or armoured chivalry."

"Then . . . then what? What will you do?"

"Do what I must," Bruce answered grimly. "Go. Retire before him. Give up Lochmaben again. Play the craven! Give Comyn cause for glee! I can do no other. I cannot hold this castle against Edward—even if I would. I cannot fight him in the field, with hope of success. Even survival. So I retire. It is simple as that."

"Where? To Ayr? Lanark? Turnberry?"

"No. Edward could follow to any of these. But we think that he will not go so far as Stirling. There is the best battle-ground of all Scotland. So to Stirling we shall go. Lamberton keeps his Church host watching Stirling. Scrymgeour, with Wallace's people, will come there. Comyn is there. Bruce must needs go also. If a stand is to be made, it should be there. We retire to Stirling."

"Aye. That is best. And quickly."

"Tomorrow. At first light. No sleep for us this night. Nor for the townsfolk. For they must go. Flee again into the hills or Edward will visit his wrath on them. But—by God, we will play Edward's own game, this time! Sir Nicholas Segrave and his captured men go with us. And I leave a letter for the Plantagenet. Any slaughter of my people of Annandale, and Segrave hangs. With his garrison. Every one. Come—we have work to do . . ."

• • •

The driving late-November rain blattered against the small half-shuttered windows of Torwood Castle, on the high ground above the plain of Forth, and the wind shook the doors and lifted the reeds and rushes strewn on the stone flooring of the draughty hall. Comyn had not so much as thrown off his soaking cloak, and drips from it fell on to the parchment, to the distress of the clerks, as scornfully he added the flourish of his signature to the document.

"Here's a waste of ink and paper!" he declared. "What worth in it? Think you Edward of England will pay heed to such as this? I say he will throw it on his fire!"

"Yet it will have been worth the sending, my lord—even if he does so," Lamberton insisted, stooping to append his own signature. "For it will strengthen our hands with the Holy See, and with the states of Christendom. To have said that we have made the offer of truce. See you, Edward's claim is that we are rebels. *His* lieges in rebellion. This letter makes it clear to all men that we write as the Guardians of an independent realm. After receiving this, though he may spurn it, yet he cannot say that we have accepted his overlordship—we, who act for the King of Scots."

"Bah! Clerkly havers, Sir Bishop! Words written on paper, however fine, will no more affect Edward than a fly on his sleeve. The sword, and a strong arm behind it, alone does he recognise..."

"He recognises the wrath of Almighty God, sir, with the power of Holy Church to display it!" the Primate said sternly. "He recognises His Holiness of Rome, and his spiritual powers. He is much at his devotions these days, my lord of Carrick has heard. And this offer of truce is, in fact, written as much for Pope Boniface as for Edward Plantagenet. The copy which goes to Rome may achieve more than that which goes to England. I work for the threat of excommunication."

Bruce, who had already signed the impressive parchment, spoke—but carefully addressed his words to Lamberton only. "Moreover, my lord Bishop, although Edward would wish to reject this, he may find it convenient. He is much at odds with his lords. He cannot proceed further against us meantime, without their aid. He has already returned to Berwick from Lochmaben. A truce might serve him well enough. Give him the time he needs to come to terms with his earls..."

"Aught that serves Edward well can only serve us ill," Comyn interrupted. "We are not all so concerned to please him!"

Wooden-faced, evenly Bruce went on, still looking only at the Primate. "If he *accepts* this letter, this truce, and acts on it, even to his own advantage, it is more to ours. Not only giving us time also. But it commits him to dealing with us as a sovereign kingdom, not as rebels. Here is its importance. Before all men. We loudly make it known to all Christendom. Copies to all rulers. If Edward accepts the truce, he accepts our right to make it. Yet if he does not, he will *seem* to do so. For he cannot invade us again, with any hope of success, until next spring. And until he has won round his lords. So we have him, by this. Lochmaben was but a gesture. Brief, unimportant, to save his face..."

"Is *Bruce's* face the fairer for that gesture?" Comyn barked.

"To have yielded his own castle, without a blow! To the man who paid his debts . . .!"

"God's mercy—can you see no further than your nose, man? At least I did win my siege of Lochmaben. While you sit still around Stirling!"

"My lords! Such talk is unprofitable and ill becomes you." Now that he was Guardian himself, Lamberton could and did speak with a greater authority. He picked up the parchment. "My lord of Carrick is right. This is carefully worded. Edward would be wise to read it as carefully, before he throws it in his fire!" As device to cool the suddenly risen temperature, he commenced to read the preamble:

To the Lord Edward, by God's grace king of England, by the Guardians and community of the realm of Scotland—greeting. William by divine mercy bishop of St. Andrews, Robert Bruce earl of Carrick and John Comyn the younger, Guardians of the kingdom of Scotland in the name of the famous prince the lord John, by God's grace illustrious King of Scotland, appointed by the community of that realm, together with the community of the realm itself . . .

"A spate of words! Vain puffing words!" Comyn scoffed. "Sound and repetition. To bring me from Stirling, for this!"

"Words, in affairs of state, may speak as loud as a drawn sword, my lord. We declare hereafter that King Philip of France's truce with Edward, signed at the Peace of Paris, required that all prelates, barons, knights, towns, communities and inhabitants of Scotland should be included in the truce, and all hostages given up. We declare that this clause has been broken. We therefore request King Edward to comply with these terms forthwith. To retire from Lochmaben and from Scottish soil. And to enter into a collateral truce with this realm. If he does so we are willing to desist from all aggression of England during the period stipulated." The Primate waved the parchment. "We know that he has, in fact, already withdrawn from Lochmaben Castle, though leaving an English garrison. So now he will seem to have carried out this demand. He is no longer on Scottish soil, nor like to be for six months at least. He has now wed the King of France's sister. Therefore he cannot declare the Peace of Paris void. I say that he may burn this letter—but in the eyes of the world he will seem to have heeded it. Is this not sufficient merit to bring a Guardian of Scotland eight miles from Stirling, my lord?"

Comyn shrugged, for once at a loss. But only for moments. "That is as may be," he jerked. "We shall see how tender is Edward to empty words. But . . . you have your paper and my signature. Let us have it sealed and be done. For I have more important business. At Stirling."

"What do you do at Stirling, these long months?" Bruce asked, as though interested. "Is it not something tedious? Sitting there?"

"Sitting! Who sits? Stirling is not some defenceless, decrepit hold! It is the greatest fortress in Scotland. Or England. A-top a rock four hundred feet high. But . . . I have it in my grasp now. It will not be long. Now that Edward has turned back, they will not survive. No food has reached them for five months. I promise you they will yield before the year's end. Our next meeting, I say, will be held where it ought to be. Not in this rat's-hole but in the palace of Stirling."

Without further leave-taking than that, the Lord of Badenoch stormed out of Tor Wood's hall.

His fellow-Guardians eyed each other.

"I cannot longer bear with this," Bruce said slowly. "You will have to find another Guardian for Scotland, my friend."

"And leave Comyn in power? Over you?"

"I cannot bear with him longer. You must find a way out, my lord Bishop. And quickly. Before one of us slays the other . . . !"

• • •

The corporate sigh that swept over the crowded Great Kirk of Rutherglen that sunny May morning of 1300 was eloquent, however disparate were the elements of which it was composed—regret, satisfaction, alarm, I-told-you-so. Men had long seen this coming, in one form or another; indeed had come to this parliament expecting no less. But the significant and ominous implications for Scotland could be lost on none.

The Earl of Carrick, standing in front of the right hand of the three Guardians' chairs set facing the nave, at the chancel steps, raised his hand for quiet. "Therefore, I say that I can no longer, in honest and good faith, serve this kingdom as Guardian. I do hereby lay down that burden and duty, to this parliament. For the better rule and governance of the realm." Turning, he bowed stiffly to Bishop Lamberton beside him, and stepped a little way apart.

The Red Comyn smiled thinly, and played with his jewelled dirk-hilt.

Heavily the Primate spoke, from the central chair. "This decision is to Scotland's loss. My lord's mind is made up, and we must needs accept it. But . . . since the Earl of Carrick remains what he is, head of the greatest house south of Forth, and an aspirant to the throne when it shall become vacant, it is, I say, inconceivable that he should be esteemed of lesser rank than the Guardians. The South-West cannot be governed lacking Bruce's aid and participation. Accordingly I move that my lord retains the style and title of a Guardian, while not actively sustaining the office. This for the benefit of all."

There was no lack of reaction to that, acclaim from the Bruce supporters and the churchmen, dissent and scowls from the opposing faction. Comyn himself did not scowl, but he did look very keenly, thoughtfully, from Lamberton to Bruce, and then flicked a hand.

"Here we are in strange case," he said. "Bruce, it seems, desires to retain the benefits of office, without the cares and responsibilities."

"What benefits?" Bruce jerked.

"Not so," Lamberton declared." It is a matter of seemliness. The Guardianship represents the throne. It is seemly that the Earl of Carrick should remain in name therein. To the greater authority of the office as a whole."

"Words again! Forms! Styles! When what the realm needs are swords. And deeds!"

"Your own party have a new nomination for such form and style, have they not, my lord?"

"Ha!" Comyn said slowly. "You would deal and chaffer, my lord Bishop! Is that it? You offer substance for this shadow? Very well. Accept Sir Ingram de Umfraville as third Joint Guardian, in Bruce's place. And my lord of Carrick may keep such style and title as pleases him!"

"I desire no such empty style," Bruce ground out. "I retire from the Guardianship. And do commend to this parliament Sir John de Soulis, Warden of the Middle March, in my place."

"Wait! Wait, I beg of you," Lamberton said, though his tone held authority rather than begging. "Here is cause for closer consideration than this. We esteem Sir John and Sir Ingram. But the status of the Guardianship is here involved. The name of an earl of Scotland should grace the office still . . ."

"It did not when Wallace was Guardian," somebody pointed out.

"Wallace was sole Guardian. And had to give it up because he lacked sufficient authority."

"My cousin of Buchan is earl, as well as Constable. And would serve suitably," Comyn observed lightly.

"No! Not that," the Lord of Crawford cried. "Two Comyns we can never accept."

There was uproar in the church.

Comyn stood up, to quell it, "I say then," he shouted, glaring menacingly around, "appoint Sir Ingram de Umfraville third Guardian, and allow the Earl of Carrick the style but not the power. And then, a God's name, have done with it! There is more important matter to decide. And to do. Edward has rejected our truce, and musters again at York. Galloway has risen in civil war. And the Earl of Carrick has done little to quell it. There is man's work to be done—not clerkly bickering over titles! Have done, I say." He sat down.

It was cleverly done, the vigorous lead of a practical soldier. Many cheered it. Yet it gave Comyn what he desired, while seeming to go along with Lamberton's suggestion. De Umfraville was a valiant and influential knight, cousin to the Earl of Angus and a kinsman of both Baliol and Comyn. He was firmly of the Comyn faction. Bruce, having word that Umfraville's name was to be put forward, had nominated Sir John de Soulis, an equally renowned warrior, Lord of Liddesdale and one of his own supporters. On a vote, with the churchmen supporting Bruce, de Soulis might have won. Now, in order to have Bruce merely retain the name of Guardian, Lamberton was seemingly bartering away the effective power. Bruce doubted the wisdom of it—although he was only too well aware of the advantages to himself of keeping equal rank with Comyn.

The thing was accepted, since most were prepared to trust Lamberton's judgement. Sir Ingram de Umfraville was appointed Guardian, and came up to the chancel to sit in Bruce's vacated chair. The other remained standing, a little way off.

Comyn was not long in showing his hand. After some formal business, he announced that the internal strife in Galloway must be put down, since it endangered the security of the realm and invited English aggression there. Stirling Castle being now in his hands, and his forces freed from that important task, he would now personally lead a campaign of pacification in Galloway. With de Umfraville, of course. And added, as a cynical afterthought.

". . . where my lord Constable has already preceded me, on a reconnaissance."

That explained the absence of the Earl of Buchan from the parliament.

Bruce stood silent. Comyn intended to take over the South-West, that was clear. Galloway had always been in the Bruce sphere of influence—although Buchan did own land there, the barony of Cruggleton. The man was utterly unscrupulous, ruthless, unrelenting. And cunning. It was not beyond him to have engineered the Galloway disturbances himself, for this very purpose. He implied that Bruce should have put down the trouble himself—when he knew only too well that Bruce's forces were spread right along the eighty miles of the borderline, watching England. And had been for six weeks.

William Lamberton looked understandingly, sympathetically, over towards the younger man, but shook a warning head.

How much could a man take?

The parliament broke up. Men had come to it fearing civil war. That it had not come to this, as yet, was to Bruce's credit. But Comyn was in the ascendant now, for all to see.

Sick at heart Bruce rode south again to rejoin his brothers commanding the long slender line that watched the Border.

Chapter Fourteen

The campaign of 1300 was all fought in Galloway and the South-West. That it reached no further was the measure of the Scots success; but it left that great area in ruins once more. The English invaded from Carlisle, on Midsummer's Day, after a delay which almost certainly was partly accounted for by the Pope's remonstrances on the rejection of the Scots truce offer, reinforced by Wallace's representations at Rome. But Edward's fears of excommunication were at length overborne by his consuming hatred of the Scots, and when he marched, he did so with a magnificent army of over 60,000. Bruce had 8,000, but they were strung along the borderline; Comyn had 15,000 in Galloway, where he had been hanging men by the score, mostly Bruce's adherents; and

Scrymgeour had the absent Wallace's people's army of some 12,000 more waiting in reserve on the north side of Forth.

Edward stormed through lower Annandale for Dumfries. Once again that fair vale became a blackened wilderness, while Bruce dared do no more than harass the English flanks and rear. Then with the early fall of Dumfries and Caerlaverock Castles, the Plantagenet turned west across Nith and entered Galloway. It seemed that he was intent on defeating the Scots in the field rather than on merely gaining territory.

In the past Comyn had talked boldly about the need to confront Edward with the chivalry of Scotland, to gain any lasting success; just as he had talked slightingly of Wallace's guerilla warfare and Bruce's caution about pitched battle, and his scorched earth strategy. But now, faced with four times his own numbers, and the huge preponderance of bowmen, he pursued similar tactics himself, and played them skilfully. He fell back deeper and deeper into Galloway, a difficult country for campaigning, cut up with great estuaries, rivers and hill ranges, extending Edward's lines of communication even further without committing himself to battle. These lines of communication Bruce made it his business to assail.

Once again the strategy paid off, although at terrible cost to the countryside involved. The proud Plantagenet, with his vast and splendid array of armoured and bannered chivalry, and corps of archers unequalled in all the world, found all food and forage burned before him, and his supply lines constantly cut behind him. He ground to a halt at Kirkcudbright. He had, out of past experience, arranged for a shadowing supply fleet to keep his army serviced from the sea; but he had not understood how shelving and shallow were the estuaries of the wide Solway Firth, and at how few points might shipping approach land.

That Edward actually agreed to parley with Comyn and Buchan, at this stage, was indication of his supply embarrassments. But the Scots proposals—the restoration of King John to his throne, a mutual non-aggression treaty, and the right of the Scots-Norman nobles to redeem their English estates from those to whom Edward had granted them—the Plantagenet brusquely brushed aside. He promised mercy, but demanded unconditional surrender.

Comyn, Buchan and Umfraville withdrew, angrily, and against the advice of many, decided to make a stand at the River Cree, near Creetown. Disaster followed, in the first pitched battle since

Falkirk. Although Comyn had chosen the mud-flats of the Cree estuary as battlefield, where Edward's heavy cavalry were at a disadvantage—indeed most knights fought on foot—the terrible host of longbowmen decimated the Scots from afar before ever a single blow was struck. It was the clothyard-shaft once more which won the day, rather than the knightly lance and sword. Themselves horseless, the Scots leaders fled across the quaking tidelands, to escape into the hills—such as did not remain lying in Cree mud.

Edward turned back to deal with Bruce. It was mid-August.

Bruce had no intention of emulating Comyn's recent folly. He drew in his harassing forces and retired before the returning English, laying waste the land as he went—very soon his own land, again. Northwards he turned, from Dumfries, up Nithsdale and through the hill passes to Carrick and the plain of Ayr, Edward pressing hard after him—a most trying retreat, but keeping at arm's length from the enemy advance-guard, burning rather than fighting. And though, at length, Edward's ships were able to supply him at the port of Irvine, it was now late in September and the English army was in a state bordering on mutiny, magnificent no longer. The road back to England lay a smoking menace behind it. Moreover, Scrymgeour had now brought a large guerilla contingent to aid Bruce, and the Church army was standing at Stirling, with Comyn, to hold the vital waist of Scotland.

Edward made a virtue of a necessity. He sent offer to Bruce of a six months' truce. This to enable him to withdraw unmolested over the burned-out terrain to England again, without serious loss from guerilla attack. Lamberton advised acceptance. It had little practical value to the Scots; but it did concede to them the status of combatants with whom the King could deal, instead of the rebels he named them. By the end of October his forces were back in their own land, save for the garrisons in such castles as Lochmaben and Roxburgh. But he swore a great oath, as he crossed the Border, that he would return and lay waste the whole of Scotland from sea to sea, and force its rebellious people into submission or death.

If Edward had little cause for satisfaction from it all, no more had the Scots. The South-West was again devastated. The only real battle fought had been a bad, almost shameful, defeat, and Comyn's military reputation had suffered seriously. If Bruce's had not, he was nevertheless becoming known as a leader who could only burn and destroy his own territories. This situation could not go on and on. And the truce, whatever status it might give them, was only until the next campaigning season.

Morale in Scotland sank low, that winter. If only Wallace would return, men sighed. If only Comyn and Bruce would cut each other's throats, others muttered. If only Lamberton was allowed to run the country unhindered, the churchmen prayed. But none of these things happened.

Lamberton was now an unhappy man, indeed. He obtained no co-operation from the other two Guardians, and most of his proposals were automatically outvoted two to one. Comyn was in his vilest frame of mind, soured by his debacle on the Cree, and for once aware of his unpopularity amongst the people. Umfraville proved to be no statesman, and completely under the younger man's influence. The government of the land sank to new low levels.

It was an open winter, fortunately. The Primate-Guardian besought the Earl of Carrick to come to his manor of Stobo, in the Forest, there to pass Yuletide with him. Bruce was concerned at the appearance of his friend, when he reached Stobo from Turnberry. He had aged grievously in these last months, and there was a strain, tension and brittleness about him unknown previously.

"This cannot continue," he told the younger man, when they were alone before a fire in the Bishop's private sanctum. "To all intents the ship of state is rudderless, drifting helpless. I can do little or nothing. The Comyns would have me out of the Guardianship—and I would thank God to be free of it! But if I go, John Comyn reigns supreme. Now. As he hopes to reign from the throne, one day. I say this would be disaster for Scotland. But ... we can no longer make pretence to work together."

Bruce nodded. "And if *you* cannot, no man can."

The other sighed. "As to that, I do not know. But *this* I know. I cannot longer continue. And even if I could, it would avail nothing. The realm drifts to ruin, calamity. And Edward waits."

"You will not relinquish the Guardianship? To Comyn!"

"I do not know. God help me—I do not know! I do not see which way to turn."

It distressed Bruce to see this man, on whom he had relied so surely, thus broken, at a loss. "The realm needs you. Desperately. There is none other. Of your stature. And Comyn alone as Guardian—for Umfraville is the merest puppet—would be disaster. No man's life would be safe. Is there no way that he may be unseated?"

"I have thought of it, day and night. But he is too powerful. Already he all but controls Scotland. I may seek to steer the ship of state, but Comyn captains it. Because he holds the sword. You should not have resigned, my friend. You must see it, now?"

"I reached my limit, with Comyn. As you now have done, it seems," Bruce said sombrely. "He wears men down as water wears a stone."

"What to do, then? In mercy's name, what to do? He is like a savage animal now. But cunning, too. Smarting from the wounds his pride received at the Cree. Judging men to hate him—as they do. But the more determined. For spirit he does not lack."

"See you—this of the Cree fight. Of his guilt, for that. Of men hating him. This may we not use? A parliament may not only appoint a Guardian—it may unseat one. Could we not so sway a parliament that it would vote Comyn down?"

Lamberton did not answer, gazing deep into the fire.

"My party is sure, in its vote. The Church will vote, in the main, as you direct. The burghs will vote as Scrymgeour, Wallace's lieutenant, says—and he hates Comyn. The Comyn faction is large, yes—but I believe, in this pass, with other men as sour as he is, it could be outvoted."

"And think you Comyn would meekly accept dismissal? Demit office and walk away? When he controls the power of the realm. Without civil war? Which God forbid! And Edward at our doors."

Bruce had risen, to pace the floor. "Not a parliament's vote then—but the *threat* of it! You say he is sore at his unpopularity. He who acts the practised soldier. He would not enjoy a parliament that called for his resignation, named him bungler, at fault at the Cree. Even craven. I say he would sooner resign than face that."

The Bishop looked up at him. "You think it? It may be so. Yes, it could be. But . . . he would ensure that Umfraville and another held the Guardianship. Another puppet. With himself behind them. He would never leave me as master. For he mislikes me now, as he mislikes you."

"Scarcely so, my lord, I think—scarcely! But . . . if you offered to resign also? On condition that he did. And with the threat of a vote of parliament against him. A bargain. And Umfraville too. All Guardians resign. Because of the defeat. A new man appointed. One man. Might he not accept that?"

"Aye. But who? Who would be that man? Who would serve any better?"

"De Soulis. Sir John de Soulis. Of Liddesdale. Do you not see it? He is wed to Buchan's sister, and is therefore a kinsman of Comyn's. But he is a true man. Honest, as all do know. He was one of my grandfather's auditors, when he claimed the throne. Is sound in the Bruce cause. Comyn, I think, would accept de Soulis. And I would trust him. Moreover, he is a good soldier. And coming from Liddesdale, has been fighting the English all his days."

"You think he would do it? Accept the task? As sole Guardian. Knowing the ill will, the back-stabbing, the thanklessness of it all?"

"He was prepared to do it, in May, at Rutherglen. If we both besought him . . ."

Lamberton rose. "My friend—you have at least given me hope again. It is possible. Pray God de Soulis will aid us . . ."

• • •

By early spring John de Soulis was sole active Guardian of Scotland—but with the Guardianship now in scant repute and men looking for power elsewhere. Comyn, like Bruce, and for the same reasons, retained the style and title of Guardian. Lamberton and Umfraville did not.

Comyn, no doubt, believed that he could control de Soulis, a kinsman. But he, and the realm, found the new Guardian, an ageing, stocky, silent man, tougher than seemed probable. He refused to be bullied or frightened. Bruce gave him full support. As did Lamberton and the Church. Wallace's people also. But the Comyn's power was still the major factor in the land. They controlled all Scotland north of the Forth, save the West Highlands and the Isles, which no man could control; and increasingly demonstrated their dominance in the South also—for Comyn's last act as Guardian had been to push through the appointments of his own nominees to most of the southern sheriffdoms. Everywhere unattached and doubtful lords and barons decided that it was wise to side with Comyn. The man was behaving like commander-in-chief, almost like a king, riding the land, holding musters of arms, sitting in at sheriffs' assizes, declaring the size of levies required from each baron and knight, demanding moneys and aid from abbeys and priories. De Soulis might sit in Stirling Castle as nominal and conscientious ruler, refusing to be controlled by Comyn; but he on the other hand could by no means control Comyn, nor attempted to.

Chaos mounted in the land—the land which awaited Edward.

Bruce watched it all with a sort of sullen hopelessness. He had no 8,000 men this year, to string along the Border. His lands of Annandale and Carrick had been so devastated again that his people, as well as being as sullen and demoralised as he was himself, were scattered, huddling where they could, scratching a living for themselves, and with sickness rampant—in no state for military service, willing or unwilling. He had some hundreds under arms, mainly vassals' men from undamaged areas; but these he kept in secret places in Ettrick Forest and the Borderland hills. He had promises of contingents from his supporters, of course, lords like the Steward, Crawford, Mar and Atholl, when invasion actually was imminent. But meantime he could only watch—northwards more sharply, even, than southwards.

Even de Soulis, honest man, worried Bruce in one respect. He did all in the name of King John. The Guardians, hitherto, had issued their edicts and processes of government in their own names, although they claimed nominally to be acting on behalf of the throne. De Soulis seemed to see the position differently. He did all merely as Baliol's deputy, always using a style that gave King John himself the authority, all being signed by the Guardian only in his absence. "These letters patent be valid at our will, this ninth year of our reign, by John de Soulis, knight, Guardian of our kingdom." The new Great Seal was struck, bearing the name and title of King John on the obverse, de Soulis only on the reverse. And Wallace, it was reported from Rome, had succeeded in winning the Pope's full support for a reinstatement of Baliol as ruling monarch.

The Bruce star was far from in the ascendant.

The truce with England expired on the 21st of May—and it was known that all winter Edward had been preparing the new campaign, despite his prolonged correspondence and assurances to the Pope. He marched promptly the day afterwards, and this time brought his son north with him, Edward, Prince of Wales. The English army split into two, in Northumberland, the King heading the main drive to Berwick and the east, while his son and Surrey made for Carlisle and the west. This time the Scots were to fight on two fronts.

Bruce swiftly found himself in trouble, for Edward, after a feint northwards from Berwick, which sent a Scots force hastening to the Lammermuir passes to harry him therein, quickly turned north-westwards up Tweed. Never before had any major invasion taken this mid-country route through the Forest and the hills of the central uplands, where small numbers could so easily hold up large. But nothing could long hold up Edward's scores of thousands, and though Bruce's people contested almost every pass, river-crossing and ambush-site, they were only dealing with the English advance-guard. Edward took his time, pressing inexorably onward. Kelso, Dryburgh and Melrose Abbeys went up in flames, Selkirk fell, and then Peebles. Bruce was driven back and back into the high barren wildernesses of Tweedsmuir, where Clyde and Annan were born as well as Tweed. Then Edward paused and circled skilfully to seal off all the valley-mouths and passes out of that lofty area, turning it from a citadel into something like a vast prison. Individuals could get in and out of it, by lonely hillsides and secret burn-channels; but not large bodies of men.

It was clear that Edward, well served with spies, had set his main strategy, at this stage, against Bruce. And now Bruce, as a fighting force, was largely immobilised.

Meanwhile, the Prince of Wales and Surrey turned into Galloway, with Comyn retiring before them, risking no more pitched battles. De Soulis himself, after deciding the real lines of the English thrusts, positioned himself, with the Church army and Wallace's guerillas, between Lanark and the sea, to deny if he could the Clydesdale access to the north.

Edward seemed to be in no hurry, this time. He consolidated as he went, and once out of the Tweedsmuir hills, struck westwards, to reach the sea at Ayr and Irvine, where his fleet was standing off, with supplies. He had successfully isolated the three Scots forces, Bruce to the east, Comyn to the south and de Soulis to the north. Moreover, this time he had food and forage, arms and siege-equipment readily available from shipping.

He turned north, to besiege Bothwell Castle, the strongest hold in Clydesdale, de Soulis falling back before him. This was a new kind of campaigning for Edward. But as to its effectiveness there could be no question.

That there was something else new about it began to dawn on the Scots as the summer passed into autumn. Despite all the Plantagenet's fierce vows of vengeance earlier, there was little of mass savagery, burnings and sackings. It seemed as though he was seeking, this year, to separate the Scots leadership from the people, trying to antagonise the countryside as little as possible. Moreover, his ships were still unloading supplies in late September, when Bothwell fell, with no signs of a retiral to England. It looked very much as though Edward intended to winter in Scotland.

A new variety of apprehension settled on the land.

Bruce, in his Border hills fretted like a caged eagle. He was not idle, picking away at the English flanks, sallying here and there. But he was held and confined, almost insultingly, and kept out of touch with what went on elsewhere.

When specific news did reach the remote Blackhouse Tower, a Douglas hunting-place deep in Yarrow, which Bruce had made his headquarters, it could hardly have come with more authority—since it came, unexpectedly, by the mouth of the Primate himself. William Lamberton arrived, with only two companions, at dusk of an evening of early October, tired and raggedly-clad as a wandering friar, yet nevertheless looking a good deal less worn and haggard than when last Bruce had seen him. Apparently he found war less of a strain than dealing with John Comyn. Though his information was none the less dire, for that.

"Edward has gone to winter at Linlithgow," he told the younger man. "Aye—he bides in Scotland, to our sorrow. But he is cunning. There have been no burnings, pillagings. He is indeed *paying* for the meat, the grain and the hay he requires! So the land has not risen against him, as before. The folk are weary, helpless, hopeless, to be sure. So, with his armies holding all in check—you here, de Soulis in lower Clydesdale, Umfraville in Galloway, and Lothian and the Merse his own, he sits secure enough in Linlithgow, his ships serving him in the Forth. And in this state he now offers us truce! Of nine months, no less! Edward, magnanimous, offers Scotland truce!"

"By all the saints—truce! He invades, occupies the land, sits down, his feet on our necks—and offers truce?"

"Aye—the Plantagenet tries new tactics. It may be, with more hope of success. The truce is aimed at the Pope, and our doubtful ally the King of France, I swear. It is a gesture. But he loses nothing by it. He is well placed indeed—and this will allow him to remain so, without trouble, through the winter and spring."

"But will de Soulis accept it?"

"What else can he do? He does not know of it yet. It is noteworthy that Edward sent the proposal to *me*. At St. Andrews. As Primate. It is beneath his dignity to treat with a mere knight. He would drive wedges between us, with more than his armies!

This year of our Lord, 1301, the Englishman is being clever! I brought the word straight to you, my friend. To talk of it. Before I tell de Soulis."

"What can I do?" Penned here..."

"You can advise me. For, God knows, I do greatly need advice." The Bishop sighed. "De Soulis, I think, will do as I say."

"Perhaps. But Comyn? What will Comyn do? What *does* Comyn? You have not so much as named him."

"Aye—Comyn. There is the rub. Comyn, as ever, plays his own game." Lamberton glanced sidelong at his companion. "Have you heard? What he does?"

"I hear nothing here. Or little that I may trust. He is in Galloway, is he not? Fencing with Edward's son."

"He was. But is no longer. He has left Umfraville to command in Galloway, and with Buchan has slipped north, by unfrequented ways and little-known passes. He is now safe in Stirling Castle, and massing new forces north of Forth."

"Then he is doing more good than I am!"

The other stroked his chin. "That is as may be. But, on his way north, he made pause. To attack Lochmaben. He took much risk, for the Prince of Wales was not far away..."

"Attack Lochmaben? Comyn? Besiege the castle...?"

"No siege. He burned the town."

"He burned... my town!" That was a whisper. "Dear God!" The other laid a hand on Bruce's arm. "He is a man consumed with hatred."

"So... am... I!"

"No. Do not say it. Hate, of all man's failings, is the least profitable. Leave hate to Comyn. It will serve him but ill."

"I shall be avenged. For Lochmaben. Nevertheless..."

"I think that you have more potent matters to consider than vengeance, my friend. Dealing with Comyn, as we have learned, demands not only patience but a clear head. Burning Lochmaben may have been the spleen of the man. But he threatens your interests more deeply than that."

"What do you mean? He threatens my interests with every breath he draws!"

"Aye. But now in a way we had not thought on. You know how de Soulis has been doing all in the name of King John. Acting as though Baliol still reigned and was only absent. De Soulis has done so as giving him, and the realm, the greater authority against Edward. A king against a king. This I could not contest. But now I have learned that Comyn is behind it. More than that, I have learned *why*. He seeks to have Baliol established as king again, before all. And then for him to abdicate, nominating and securing John Comyn as his successor."

This time the hissing intake of breath was all Bruce produced for reaction, although it was eloquent enough.

"Baliol is now at his family's ancient home, at Bailleul-en-Vimeu, in Picardy. In the care of Philip of France. Comyn has sent to Philip, urging that King John be sent back to Scotland. And with a French army. Forthwith."

"Philip will never do it. Edward is now his brother-in-law."

"Philip may. Wallace has been to him and much affected him. Moreover the Pope is in favour of this. And offers inducements. Wallace has convinced them both that King John should return. Wallace is honest in this. He knows naught of Comyn's plot."

Bruce was striding the small, draughty room now. "This—this then, could be the end of the Bruce claim! To the throne. The end of the Bruces themselves! For Comyn, as king, would not rest while there was one of us left alive to challenge him. This would be utter disaster."

"Disaster for more than Bruce," the Primate agreed sombrely. "Disaster for Scotland. John Comyn on the throne would be the end of more than Bruce."

"What can I do? I would seek him out and slay him with my own hands. But he will be well guarded. He is no fool..."

"That is not the way, no." Lamberton leaned forward. "Your father? The Lord of Annandale. He could be the answer. He is the true heir to the throne. *His* father should have been king, not Baliol. If he now would return to Scotland. Proclaim himself king. Before Baliol could come from France. If your father returned, and made such proclamation, Comyn's plot would go agley. Even though he did no more than that. Then it would be for parliament to discuss and decide. Where the Church is strong..."

"My father...! He is but a broken reed. I do not believe he would do this."

"If you went to him? Explained. He is proud of his claim. He challenged Edward with it, at Stracathro..."

"How could I go to him? Held here. He is in Essex. A sick man. Done. Always he was weak, feckless. We never agreed. Think you, at this ill hour, he would heed me? Bring down Edward's wrath on his grey hairs, by claiming the throne Edward says is his!"

The older man spoke slowly. "Edward will be near as anxious as Bruce to keep Comyn from grasping the Scots throne."

His companion paused in his pacing to look at him. "What do you mean?"

"I believe that Edward, were he to hear of this plot, would be forced to think deeply. He might prefer to have your father *claiming* the throne than Comyn being given it by Baliol. See it as another way of splitting Scotland, of giving him time. He would never admit that the throne was not his own. But he might well make it possible for your father to return and make his claim. Edward would reject it forthwith—but it would keep Baliol, and his nephew Comyn, from any easy victory by such device."

Bruce stared into the flickering fire, biting his lip.

"I could see that Edward learned of it. In these truce negotiations."

"I do not know. I do not know. This is . . . too much . . . for me. To decide. I must consider."

"As must we all. For Scotland's fate is at stake. One way or the other."

"It would mean . . . working with Edward. Against Comyn."

"Put it otherwise. Say *using* Edward to save Scotland. And Bruce. From Comyn."

"You believe it is possible?"

"Who knows? But possible, yes. Perhaps more than possible. And, my good friend—how else can you stop Comyn taking the throne? Bruce's throne?"

The younger man was silent.

"Think of it, then. While I go to de Soulis. With this of the truce. Consider it well, in this hawk's nest of yours. There is a little time. Baliol and the French will not sail in winter's weather. If they sail. But—there would be much to be done before the spring . . ."

Chapter Fifteen

It was, of course, a farce of a truce—all knew it. Little more than a springboard poised for the English to resume their campaign, with maximum advantage, when weather and the state of the land were propitious. But it did offer certain advantages to the

Scots also. Preparations could be made on their side likewise; and although the English armies largely maintained their strategic positions, and sensible men gave them wide berth, people could move fairly freely about the land again.

Bruce was released from his confinement in the high Tweedsmuir section of the Forest at last, and was able not only to go and consider the strategic situation that now ruled, but the state of his properties and lands. It made a sorry prospect. All the lordship of Annandale, the earldom of Carrick and the large Bruce lands in Galloway, had been so fought over, burned and destroyed, by one side or the other, that they made little better than a wilderness. His castles of Turnberry, Annan, Loch Doon and Tibbers were largely demolished, and their towns in ruins; and all the lesser castles and towers likewise cast down. Lochmaben was still garrisoned by the English, and its town, which would have survived, as of use to the invaders, had been burned by Comyn. Bruce found that he had not a single house left fit for his habitation, in all his great domains; and his tenants and vassals were fled, scattered or dead. As a force in the land, he was all but spent.

North of the Forth, Comyn's lands were vast and untouched. He was assembling new and unwearied thousands.

Because, indeed, he had little choice of domicile for his few hundred remaining men-at-arms, Bruce continued to keep them in the Forest; though meantime he made himself a little more comfortable, at the Bishop of St. Andrews' manor of Stobo, than he could do at the remote and windy Blackhouse Tower; even though a large English force lay at Peebles, six miles away. Lamberton himself was not there. After concluding the truce, he had gone straight to France, to try to persuade King Philip not to support Comyn's plot for sending Baliol back to Scotland.

It was from the direction of Peebles that, one grey day in mid-January 1302, with Tweed running thick and brown from melting snows, Bruce's watchers brough him word that a small English party was approaching Stobo; some great man, with esquires, clerks and a score of armed guards, riding with quiet confidence.

The visitor proved to be none other than Sir John de St. John, newly appointed English Warden of Annandale and Galloway, and one of Edward's closest aides. A dignified, handsome, courteous man of middle years, richly dressed, he was almost necessarily soldier as well as courtier, a veteran of the French wars and the man sent by Edward to deputise for the Earl of Fife, whose right it had been to seat John Baliol on the Stone of Destiny at his crowning at Scone, nine years before. Bruce knew him, and liked him better than most of the Plantagenet's entourage—even though he came as usurping master of Bruce's own territories.

St. John made it clear that, for this visit, he would prefer that his nominal position *vis-à-vis* Annandale, Carrick and Galloway, should be ignored.

"I have come, my lord, directly and secretly, from His Majesty," he declared when they were alone. "King Edward sends you greetings and goodwill. Notable goodwill, considering all that has transpired, I may say!"

"Indeed?" his host observed, grimly. "That I will believe when I hear what else you bring, Sir John!"

The other smiled thinly. "You are sceptical. But my master can be generous and far-seeing. I believe that he is being both, in this. He has always esteemed you, as you know well. Even though he has had to move against you, on occasion. And not without cause, you will concede."

"I concede nothing, Sir John. Save that your master is a hard and crafty tyrant, a cruel invader and usurper, who has devastated this land time and again. And *my* lands. Left me nothing but my name. And a modicum of wits. What does he want now?"

"These words are extreme and foolish, my lord. I had hoped, as had the King, that you might have learned to use those wits to guard your tongue. However, as far as I am concerned, they have not been spoken. You have suffered greatly, yes, in a mistaken cause. You have been cheated and cozened and used, yes—but not by His Majesty. The King believes that it is time that you returned to his peace."

"Ha! Edward's peace! Say Edward's maw, his slavery, rather. Is this his generosity?"

St. John was patient. "The King was your friend once. He believes that he could be your friend again. Better, a deal better, than many with whom you have been working. Trusting. The Lord of Badenoch, for instance."

"M'mmm. I have not trusted the Lord of Badenoch for some time!"

"As well! He does not love you. He aspires to the Scots throne. And is willing to do anything to gain it. *Anything*, I say. He cannot do so, of course, since that throne is now united with that of England. But he will try. And since he sees you as an obstacle, you will suffer, my lord."

"You are tender for my interests, sir."
"I am not. But the King is."
"Why?"
"He has not lost all his love for the Earl of Carrick. And he has never loved John Comyn."
"So he would use me to bring down the other? And so preserve for him the stolen throne of Scotland!"
"I say that you judge harshly. And foolishly. Since you have not heard what the King proposes."
"Then tell me."
"The King offers you a return to his peace. With all offences absolved and forgotten. He promises to consider well your advice on all Scottish problems. Indeed to set you over much of his realm here, if so you would have it. He offers compensation for your lands destroyed in war. Maintenance from his privy purse while your fortunes recover. Freedom from disinheritance of any lands which my lord your father may leave you in England. Permission to visit your father ..."
"Ha! Now why should Edward, in his goodness, offer me that?"
"Your father is ailing. An old and sick man. You would wish to see him. Possibly to bring him back to Scotland. To be under your closer regard."
"Aye. No doubt. His Majesty is ... thoughtful."
"He offers that if any rights of yours, or your father's be brought in dispute by the Lord of Badenoch, or others, you shall have justice in His Majesty's own courts."
Bruce looked up sharply. "Rights? Which rights, Sir John?"
"The King did not specify which. His words were 'any rights'."
"I would remind you that my father claims rights—indeed sole rights—in the Scots crown!"
"Claims, yes. That fact is known to the King. After all, he judged against your grandsire's claims, nine years past."
"I see. So that is the sort of justice we would get in His Majesty's courts!"
"Justice is justice. A hearing you would receive. Any rights, His Majesty said. And you have others that may be threatened, have you not? Your very earldom of Carrick? The lordship of Annandale? John Comyn would deprive you of these, if he could."
"Perhaps. But might find it difficult!" The younger man

shrugged. "But why does King Edward send you to offer all this. So long a list of graciousness! He must greatly desire me in his peace. Why?"

"I am his servant, my lord—not his confessor. He does not open all of his mind to me. But this is his will. And he thinks kindly of you still."

"I take leave to doubt it . . ."

"Before you do so, here is token of it. He would have you to wed the daughter of his closest friend. The Lady Elizabeth de Burgh."

"God in His heaven! Again?"

"Yes, my lord. And the fair lady herself sends you warm greetings. And hopes that she may see you. Soon."

"See . . . ? She is here? In Scotland?"

"The Queen is come to join the King, at Linlithgow. And the Lady Elizabeth with her."

Bruce turned away, too disturbed to risk speech.

St. John tactfully went to warm his hands at the fire. Over his shoulder, he went on. "One last token of the King's goodwill. He would grant you the wardship and marriage of the young Earl of Mar."

"Eh? Wardship? What do you mean?" Surprised out of his emotion, Bruce looked round. "You have mistaken, sir. Mar is my sister's husband. And is older than I am."

It was the Englishman's turn to show surprise. "*Is*, my lord? Do not tell me that you did not know? Gartnait, Earl of Mar, is dead. Slain in a tussle with Comyns. In his own country."

"By the Mass! Gartnait dead? Slain? And by the Comyns . . . !"

"We believed that you would know of it." St. John coughed. "It is . . . regrettable. But—by granting you the wardship of your nephew, the Earl Donald, my lord, the King gives you in effect another earldom. Mar as well as Carrick. Until the lad is of age. And an earldom in the North. Adjoining Comyn's country! You have a lordship up there, do you not? The Garioch. Mar could serve you notably well."

Bruce required no such reminders. Mar was a great and ancient earldom which Gartnait, gentle man, had never exploited. The wardship of its heir, so long as Edward dominated Scotland, was a potentially powerful weapon.

"Edward must require my services greatly!" he said slowly.

"A mistaken view, my lord. His Majesty can achieve all, master Comyn, and Scotland, without Bruce. But can Bruce now achieve *anything* without King Edward? I urge that you consider it. Consider it well. I return to Peebles. And shall come again tomorrow. For your decision. I hope, my lord, that it will be to conduct you to Linlithgow." St. John paused, clearing his throat. "The Lady Elizabeth said to give you this last word. A wise rebel, she said, knows what to rebel against. That is all. She believed that you would understand. And that she would see you at Linlithgow."

• • •

Two days later Robert Bruce, with Sir John de St. John, rode down into the West Lothian plain of the Forth, to the vast armed camp surrounding the red-brown castle on its green hill above the wide loch. He scarcely recognised the place. A whole new wooden city had been erected in regimented lanes and streets to house an army and its followers and horses, through a Scots winter. Great lumber-trains were in constant passage to and from the same Tor Wood, above Falkirk, where Bruce had rescued William Wallace three years before.

St. John had sent word ahead, of their coming, and King Edward had evidently decided to make the most of the occasion. He sent the Scots Earl of March and Dunbar, who all along had sided with the English, along with the Earl of Ulster and Bishop Anthony Beck of Durham, to meet the newcomers and conduct them through the drawn-up lines of much of the army, from which a succession of fanfares of trumpets greeted them. A resplendent corridor of over 200 mounted knights in full armour and heraldic surcoats flanked their climb up the castle-hill; and before the arched courtyard entrance Edward Longshanks himself, despite the inclement weather and threatening rain, stood awaiting them, a massive and magnificent figure, backed by much of his Court. It was a welcome fit for a king.

Edward did not actually open his arms to Bruce, but his greeting was otherwise as for the prodigal son. He hailed him genially, gripped his hand and patted his shoulder.

"Robert, my young friend!" he cried. "Here is a happy day, which has been too long in dawning. I rejoice to see you. To welcome you back into my peace."

The other did not trust himself to speak. He bowed stiffly, and less low than he might have done. The King did not let him withdraw his hand.

"These years I have missed you, boy," Edward declared jovially. "Hard years, and you have suffered. But you have grown a man, I think. Learned your lesson in a hard school. But that is all done with, now."

"I am glad to hear you say it, Sire. Since you were the teacher!"

"Ha! And you will thank me for that teaching. You will see. Sir John—I thank you for your good offices. The Earl of Carrick will have cause to thank you also. Come, now—the Queen would meet you . . ."

Linking arms with the younger man, Edward led him slowly through the bowing ranks of the gaily-dressed crowd, pausing here and there to exchange an affable word with earl, bishop or lord. Bruce went uncomfortably—and not only for the difficulty of matching his pace to that of the extraordinarily long legs of the monarch; his suspicion and wariness was like an armour about him. This was not the Edward Plantagenet he knew.

Linlithgow Castle was a palace rather than a fortress, and now it was thronged as never before. In a lesser hall where two great log fires blazed, Queen Margaret sat with her ladies, at needlework, while a minstrel sang softly to the languid pluckings of a lute, from a deep window-embrasure. Fine tapestries and hangings covered stone walls which undoubtedly had been bare until recently, and the floor was thickly strewn with skins.

Bruce, his arm still in the royal grasp, bowed; but his glance was only momentarily on the Queen's narrow, keen features, before sliding off round the room. He found Elizabeth by a far door, and their eyes met, and held, for seconds. Then, almost imperceptibly, she shook her head and looked towards the Queen. He nodded, as briefly, and bowed again.

"Your Majesty," he said

"So here is the Lord Robert, of whom all speak," Margaret of France exclaimed. "Come to grace our Court at last. You have been long in coming, my lord."

Philip the Fair's sister was less beauteous than her brother, but she was almost certainly a stronger character. A pale, thin, almost gaunt woman in her mid-thirties, over-dressed, she had fine eyes, though darting, shrewd. Edward Plantagenet, in his late years, might have acquired a tartar.

"Had I known of your fair presence, Majesty, I might have come the sooner." It was a long time since Robert Bruce had made that sort of remark.

"La—a flatterer! They did not tell me that you were that. Come, and let me judge if that is all you are!" She held out a slender hand for him to kiss.

"Robert once was one of the gayest of my train, my love," Edward said. "He has a sober look to him, these days. Perhaps we will cure him of it, eh?"

"I scarce think *you* will, Sire. But I may. With a little help . . . from others!" The Queen raised her voice. "Elizabeth! Where are you hiding, girl?"

The idea of Elizabeth de Burgh hiding anywhere was sufficiently bizarre to bring smiles to most faces. She came forward unhurriedly, head held high, a striking, proud beauty, aware of her own potency. Her blue eyes looked directly at none of them.

"You two are old friends, are you not?" the Queen said.

"I have met my lord," Elizabeth acceded, coolly.

The King chuckled. "They were near affianced once. And might be again!"

"In Your Majesty's mind," the girl gave back evenly. "And to other lords, likewise."

Edward's smile faded for a moment, and then returned. "Say that my Majesty's mind is ever heedful for your welfare, lass," he said. "Eh, Dickon?"

Richard, Earl of Ulster, who had followed them in, inclined his handsome head, but did not otherwise commit himself—though he eyed his daughter sidelong.

Queen Margaret's quick eyes were busy all around. "You, my lord?" she said to Bruce. "How goes your flattery now?"

"I flatter none. Your Majesty, or other," he answered, taking his cue from the girl. "I admire the Lady Elizabeth. Who would not? But I would not presume to claim close friendship."

"You are cautious, sir. I am disappointed. I mislike cautious men!"

"I have need to be cautious, Madam. My first meeting with this lady, I tipped her out of her litter. She named me witless dolt. And . . . and masterful ape! I think she has not forgotten. Nor, i' faith, have I!"

"So!" Intrigued, the Queen was all eagerness, looking from one to the other. Bruce perceived that he had probably overdone it. "You did not tell me, Elizabeth. Shame on you! Here is a notable tale! Tipped you from a litter? How long ago? It is years since you have seen him, is it not? And you have thought of it still? And he . . . !"

Bruce had not anticipated being grateful to Edward Plantagenet; but that paladin did not enjoy being in less than the centre of the stage for long, and intervened now.

"You must have mercy on the Lord Robert, my dear. He has ridden far. Sir John will conduct him to his chamber, and refreshment. That he may the better grace our table. We eat, lad, within the hour . . ." The royal gesture to St. John was not to be mistaken.

At the banquet which followed, Bruce was given the place of honour—which did little to calm the turmoil of his mind. He sat between Edward and his son—which at least meant that he was spared close inquisition by the Queen, who sat on the monarch's left. Edward of Carnarvon, Prince of Wales, had grown from boy into young man since last Bruce had seen him and proved to be a secret-faced, diffident youth of eighteen, who all the time kept a wary eye on his father—as well he might. Bruce found little to say to him. He had had no opportunity for a private word with Elizabeth—and now she was seated at some distance, with so many great lords and prelates requiring precedence. Her father was on the Prince's left hand, and Lancaster, holder of five earldoms, on the Queen's right.

Edward remained amiable, almost alarmingly so, pressing food and drink on his guest. So far there had been no hint of reproach, much less condemnation. Nor was there any hint of what was behind this change of front, what the Plantagenet required from him. That it did not all proceed from the essential kindness of his heart, Bruce had little doubt.

At length, when the meal had progressed to the stage of picking, toying and drinking, with entertainment from tumblers, jesters and musicians, the younger man was driven to direct questioning. "Sire," he said "you have brought me here for good purpose, I have no doubt. What do you require of me?"

The other looked at him as though astonished. "Why, Robert—your good company and presence. Your love and leal esteem. What else? Is that so strange?"

"You have been fighting me, hunting me, burning my lands, taking my castles. I see little of love and esteem in that. Why have you changed?"

"Because circumstances have changed, boy. Then we were at war, and you chose to go against me, to my sorrow. Now there is truce. I hold this land, South Scotland, in my hand. And shall soon hold the North. All is changed. You have lost much. No longer is your insurrection any threat to my peace. I may allow my natural affection for you to prevail. Did not Sir John tell you all this? Is it not proven by my tokens of goodwill offered?"

"I conceived there to be something more, Sire. Your Majesty is namely for hard bargaining!"

"You say so? But, that is when I am fighting. When I have won, it is otherwise. Think you I cannot be magnanimous?"

"You believe that you have won, then?"

"Should I not? I sit here in Linlithgow's hall, secure. My armies straddle the land."

"There is a deal of Scotland north of Forth."

"No doubt. But I have conquered it before. And can do again, if need be. It is my hope that I shall not have to."

"The North will not yield tamely. If that is what you hope."

"You think not? But . . . *you* have yielded, have you not?"

"No, Sire. I have not yielded."

"No?" Edward turned in his great chair, to eye the younger man wonderingly. "Do my eyes, my wits, fail me?"

"I came under the safe conduct of an honourable man, Sire. Sir John de St. John. Who vowed, in your royal name, that I could turn and go again, freely, should so I decide. I came, in time of signed truce, to discover your mind. Further to what St. John told me. Is that yielding?"

The King toyed with his goblet, narrow-eyed. "But you came, my young friend—you came!" he said softly.

"I came, yes. But I did not bring my brothers, Sire! If by mischance I am prevented from returning to them, there are four of them still to head the Bruce power!"

"What Bruce power?"

The other took a quick breath, but was silent, biting his lip.

"Let us not misjudge, my young friend," Edward said, then. "Between power and love. Esteem. You have no power. None left. But my esteem and love can raise you again. High. High as you must needs be if you are to counter John Comyn." He paused. "Let us look reality in the face, Robert. It has ever been my custom."

"I have, perhaps, more power left than you believe."

"I think not. I have made shift to discover. Your earldom of Carrick lies shattered and occupied by my forces. Your father's lordship of Annandale is a blackened waste. As are the Bruce lands in Galloway. You have less than three hundred men, hiding like outlaws in Ettrick Forest. That is your strength and power, Robert. A notable heritage squandered."

"Squandered . . . ! You are well informed, Sire. But have you forgot? I have friends, allies, kinsmen. As well as brothers."

"Most in little better state than you are! How many would give what they have left to aid one so weak as the Earl of Carrick? Weak, that is, today. Tomorrow you could be strong again. For you have a better friend than any of these, lad. You have Edward of England for friend."

Bruce said nothing.

"This matter of the earldom of Mar. The late lord was your brother-in-law twice over, was he not? Your sister's husband, and your wife's brother? Control of the heir and his inheritance, until he is of age, could greatly aid you."

"And will. I am my nephew's closest kinsman."

"If I grant you that control. The wardship of all earls who are minors is in the gift of the Crown."

That was true only if Edward was King of Scots. But this was no time to debate that assumption.

The Plantagenet did not give opportunity, anyway. "There are three great royal properties, hunting-forests, bordering on the Mar earldom. Each with strong castles. Kintore, Darnaway and Longmorn. At present keeperless. The man who held those, with Mar and the Garioch, would be a force in the North, indeed. Comyn's country."

Bruce still made no comment.

"I make a progress up to those parts in a few months, sword sheathed or sword drawn. When the weather opens. Think on it, Robert. Think on it." Abruptly the monarch pushed back his great chair, and rose. All men hastily rose after him. "My dear," he said to the Queen, "we retire. You will be tired. Come." He held out his arm. Edward of England had had enough of being pleasant for one evening.

Bruce looked ruefully after the hastening ladies. Elizabeth de Burgh was the only one who was not tripping and scurrying. But even she had had time for only a single significant glance at him, in passing.

• • •

It was fully two hours later, with Bruce preparing for bed in the small tower room which he had been allocated—eloquent of his present prestige, as sole occupant, in the overcrowded palace where great men were sharing rooms—when a tapping at the door announced a slender, pale and pimply youth, a walking clothes-horse of magnificence, who introduced himself as Harry Percy, a page of Her Majesty, and son of Northumberland. He came from the Lady Elizabeth de Burgh, he declared in a dramatic whisper. Would the lord Earl accompany him? But discreetly, very discreetly. And to wear a cloak.

While declining actually to tip-toe after this chinless apparition who was the Lord Henry Percy's son and heir, Bruce did follow him, intrigued. He was led down a winding back stairway, across a cluttered yard where wine-barrels were stacked, through a range of stabling to the outer-bailey, and then by a postern gate, where an armed guard looked the other way, stamping his feet with the cold. Thereafter, down a grassy hillside path of a pleasance garden, they came to the shore of Linlithgow Loch. Here a skiff lay, dipping to the babble of the black water. Harry Percy pointed.

"The island, my lord," he breathed. "You can just see it." And with elaborate caution, like a stealthy crane, he paced back whence he had come.

Bruce seated himself in the boat, and took up the light oars.

The island was nearer and smaller than it had seemed in the darkness, a mere couple of hundred yards from the shore. It was probably no more than an acre in extent, grown with ornamental trees and bushes. There was a little jetty, with rustic steps and rail. Here a dark cloaked figure stood.

"Come, my lord. And haste you. For it is plaguey cold!" Elizabeth greeted him. She held out a hand to aid him ashore.

He said nothing, was in no state for eloquence. But he hung on to that hand.

"This way," she directed, leading him along a narrow path through dripping bushes. "You were sufficiently discreet, I hope?"

"Discreet . . . !" he croaked. "*You* speak of discretion!"

Her tinkle of laughter sounded amused, at least.

A more solid blackness loomed before them, a building of some sort. She drew him inside, and closed the door.

"It is a bower. A summer bower, fashioned like a grotto," she explained. "More comfortable in summer than now, I fear. But at least here we may speak alone. We are safe." She disengaged her hand.

It was Bruce's turn to jerk a short laugh. "I can think of few women who would bring a man to such a place, in the night, and then declare that they were safe!"

"Why, sir—am I mistaken in you?" She did not sound really alarmed.

"That I do not know. But . . . I am a man, you'll mind, Elizabeth!"

"But a cautious man. Did not the Queen say so?"

He sensed the smile behind the words, though he could not see it. He could see only the vague cloaked shape of her—but he was very conscious of her woman's presence, her nearness, in that confined space.

"I would not say that caution has been my guide in life, till this," he told her, a little breathlessly. "Any more than yours, I think."

"I have been sufficiently cautious where *you* have been concerned, at least. Have I not? Until now, perhaps."

"Elizabeth—you have been kind, most kind. Your letters—I do not know how I would have done lacking them. They saved my reason, I think. Apart from the word of Edward's plans, which so greatly aided me. For that, I thank you. But the letters . . . their words, their warm, kind words. I have read them and read them. I carry them always. Indeed I have them here, in my doublet now . . ."

"Then that is very foolish of you, sir! I believed you to have burned them. For my name is on them. If they fell into wrong hands, were shown to the King . . . ! Besides, I would not have thought it of you. Of Bruce, Lord of Carrick, who was Guardian of Scotland. A warrior, a man above such soft toyings. No callow youth—indeed, a married man, with a daughter . . ."

"A man who needs a woman the more, then."

"Ha! A woman? But Bruce can have any woman. Almost! Can he not? Can have many women. Lord of great possessions. Of men—and of women! He needs not to cherish poor paper and ink to his bosom."

"No," he said. His hands reached out to grasp her arms, through the cloak. "No. Not now."

She did not draw away from him; but nor did she come closer. "You have not forgot that I named you witless dolt. And masterful ape!"

"No," he agreed. "Nor ever shall." He pulled her to him, his lips seeking her face in the hooded cloak.

The young woman turned her face away a little, so that his lips met only the damp fur-trimmed broadcloth. "My Lord Robert," she objected, "if a woman you so greatly need, perhaps I might even find one for you. There are many at this Court who would serve you willingly, even hotly, I swear! For myself, I am . . . otherwise."

"What do you mean? Otherwise?"

"I am no . . . serving-woman, sir. I am Elizabeth de Burgh."

"You think I do not know it, woman? Think you I would be thus with any other? It is Elizabeth de Burgh I want, have ached and pined for, have dreamed of, sought and awaited. Aye, and prayed for. All these years. You—your beauty and proud spirit. Your adorable person and comeliness." He had pushed aside her hood now, and was gasping this into her hair and against her ear, her soft turned cheek.

"So it is *my* body you want, my Lord Robert? Not just any woman's. Here is advance . . . !"

"Aye, your body, girl. But your love, also. Your love, your heart . . ."

"Ah, but love is a different matter." She turned to face him again, but held her head well back, almost pushing from him, as though she would search his face there in the darkness. "Love is not just hot desire. Such as I can feel in you. As I have felt in other men. The heart is more than the body . . ."

"Do I not know it! My heart has beat for you, and only you, for long grievous years. My body longed for yours, yes. But the body that holds your heart, my love. I want, desire, need both. My love for you has been eating me up. These many, many months. When I despaired ever to see you again. Yet still loved and hoped. And now—to have you, hold you, here! It is more than flesh and blood can stand . . ."

"Ah, Robert—so it *is* love! Then, my dear, I yield. Sweet God, I yield me!" Suddenly, fiercely, she was pressing forward, against him. "And, save us—I conceive your flesh and blood to be standing very well, my heart . . . !" she got out, before his mouth closed on hers, and their lips and tongues found greater eloquence than in forming foolish words.

The man's hands were almost as busy as his mouth—nor were the girl's totally inactive, either. He shrugged his own cloak to the floor, and hers quickly followed it. Then he was tugging at her gown, while still he all but devoured her with his kissing. Her defter touch came to aid him, and the taffeta fell away from her shoulders. The pale glimmer of her white body was all that he could see, but his urgent fingers groped and stroked and kneaded the smooth, warm, rounded flesh of her, serving him almost better than his eyes, her nobly full, firm breasts filling the ecstatic cups of his hands to overflowing, as they overflowed the cup of his delight.

Suddenly he was down, kneeling, his lips leaving hers to seek those proud, thrusting breasts, the exultant nipples reacting with their own life and vigour. She bent over him, crooning into his hair, her strong arms clasping him to her, rocking.

But their need was a living, growing thing, a progression, and quickly even this bliss was insufficient. He drew her down to him, pulling at the gown's folds which a golden girdle held around her waist; and willingly she came, loosening it. The spread cloaks on the floor received them, and with swift, sure co-operation she disposed herself, guiding his clamant manhood and receiving him into her vital generosity.

The man fought with himself to control the hot tide of his passion, to give her time. Blessedly she required but little, and together their rapturous ardour mounted and soared to the high, unbearable apex of fulfilment. With blinding, blazing release, and a woman's cry of sheer triumph, they yielded themselves in simultaneous surrender into the basic, elemental oneness, a profundity of satisfaction hitherto unknown to either.

So they lay there in the darkness, in blessed quiet and joyful exhaustion.

Presently Elizabeth spoke, murmurously, stroking the man's sweat-damp hair. "To think . . . that I . . . was cold!"

"Cold? You!" His speech was a little slurred. "My adored and adorable. My heart and soul. My joy. My, my woman!"

"Your woman, yes. And my man. *Mine*, Robert Bruce!"

"Aye. Yours. It had to be. From the first. Elizabeth." He turned her name over from slack lips, savouring it. "Elizabeth, my Elizabeth. You gave yourself as you do all else, my Elizabeth. With all your heart. And person. No laggard, sluggard lover!"

"You think me bold? Shameless? Unwomanly?"

"Bold, yes. Shameless, yes. For where is cause for shame? And were you not bold, brave, strong, a woman of your own mind, you would not be Elizabeth de Burgh of Ulster. But unwomanly . . . I' faith, my dear, could there be anything more womanly than this, in all creation? I swear not." And he ran strong, possessive, enquiring hands over all her rich voluptuousness, lingering, pressing, probing. "Woman!" he sighed, burying his face between her breasts.

"This body, yes. Oh, yes—that is woman. But I at times wonder whether I am sufficiently woman in my spirit. My father declares me more man than my brother! Perhaps I think too like a man. Have a man's passions . . ."

He chuckled. "As you have just shown me?"

"Even so, it may be. In that I *joyed* in it, so! Is that not the man's part? Is not the woman said to be the giver? The man the taker? I . . . I take, I fear. As much as I give!"

"Aye, you took me into yourself with a right goodwill, lass, I'll not dispute!" He grinned, kissing and fondling, "As woman. All woman. Taking me, and giving yourself, in most female fashion, by all the powers!"

"There is a difference. Between taking and giving. In this. I cannot take without giving. But—I cannot give without taking. Some women can, must. I cannot. I am taking you, my heart, my man. Mine! I warn you—mine! Elizabeth de Burgh shares with none."

"Jealous, is it? A jealous woman?"

"Aye. Jealous. In some things, I fear. In this. In you."

"So! I must not look at another woman? I am bound hereafter by these fair chains?" He twisted a coil of her yellow hair round his fingers.

"Since you are a man, you will look, yes. Well I know it. You may look. Touch. Play with. Who knows, even lie with. This I could bear. Even laugh at, I think. But—should you ever give your *heart* to another. Take it from me. Then I would not forgive. Or accept. I would leave you. I might . . . I might kill you! So beware, Robert de Bruce! Think well."

"How can I think well, woman? With your nakedness filling my arms! Think any way? You bludgeon my poor wits. These—how may a man think with such as these stirring, pushing, belabouring him?"

"Shall I cover them, then? It grows cold, perhaps. It must be cold, though I feel it not . . ."

"No. Of a mercy—no covering! Not yet. Not yet a long while. The night is young. And we have waited long. So long. At least, I have. You—can it be that you have loved me also? Wished for me? These years?"

"Witless one, indeed! Think you I would be here now, otherwise? Think you I write such letters to *any* man in need? Why think you I resisted all the King's schemes to marry me to others? Worked on my father to oppose him in this . . .?"

"And I did not know it! I believed that you might think a little kindly of me, yes. When you wrote so. And when last we met, and parted. But never this . . ."

"You would not have had me to declare my love, sirrah? Before you did? Bold I maybe, but scarce so brazen. Though, mercy on us, few might agree! If they could see me lying bare as the day I was born, in a man's arms. On this island. Waiting. Waiting for . . ."

"Aye, waiting. For the man to become a man again! As he will, my love—I promise you! You aiding him! You know men, I think? How it is with men. That is clear . . ."

"You mean that I am no shy virgin? Does it trouble you?"

"No. Not so . . ."

"Few girls grow to womanhood in war-rent Ireland and remain virgin. Even de Burgh's daughter. In especial, de Burgh's daughter, it may be! For I was not of the shrinking sort, I fear. And I have managed my father's household since I was fifteen, played the countess since my mother died. But, if I am less than chaste, Robert, I am no harlot. Many men would have me. But I have known none since I saw you that day on the road to Berwick. When you unseated me. Overturned me, in more than my litter . . .!"

"My dear—you shame me. For *I* have been less, less constant. Lacking you. Scarce believing that I should ever have you. I am not so enamoured of virginity. In woman or man. Any mouse, any craven, can be a virgin. You, I would not expect to be. Nor wish. Although, see you, once you are my wife . . .!"

"Wife? Then you would wed me, my lord?" That came a little more quickly than what had gone before.

"What else, woman? Elizabeth de Burgh lies thus, and asks?"

"Elizabeth de Burgh loves. And gives. And takes. But . . . marriage. That is other. That is what King Edward desires. Now. You may not wish to seem to humour him?"

"Aye. Edward would use us, no doubt. We must see that he does not. Or only insofar as it serve *us*."

"That is why I was cool to you. Before the Queen. I would not have you *forced* into marrying me! I have that much pride . . ."

"And a little more, I think. But forced into marrying me you will be! By myself! By you. None other. If you will have me?

For not only do I greatly love you, Elizabeth, my heart. But I need you by my side. Always. Will you wed the ruined Earl of Carrick, Ulster's daughter?"

She ran her fingers lightly over his face. "Perhaps I might. Indeed, I feel wed to you now. This, it may be, is our true marriage. Yes, Elizabeth de Burgh will wed Robert de Bruce. And hold him fast. Till death do them part." She shivered.

He made to draw the cloaks and clothing closer about them.

"It was not cold," she said. "It was a sort of joy."

"Joy?" Suddenly he was sombre, lying there. "I fear that being wife to Robert Bruce will not be all joy. I am scarce the sort of husband to offer you peace and comfort, lass. I was born to trouble, I think. I have lived with it for long. And see scant signs of betterment ahead. Whatever Edward promises . . ."

"Am I one to shirk trouble, think you? Ulster's daughter?"

"No. No, I think not."

"And Ulster's daughter can bring the Earl of Carrick more than her heart and body. My father is the greatest lord in Ireland. He can field more gallowglasses than any man in all Scotland. He is rich, with a score of castles, and manors by the hundred. My dowry will not be scanty. And, allied to Ulster, Bruce will not be weakened."

"Aye. This I have not failed to think on. But . . . Edward must have thought of it also. And your father is his closest friend."

"Close, but not servile. He has opposed the King many times. Is indeed well placed to do so. He is no man's puppet."

"Yet I swear that Edward believes this match to *his* benefit."

"He can make mistakes. He has made many. He misjudges your coming to Linlithgow, does he not?"

"That is my hope. But—who knows? Edward is . . . Edward. He is no fool. I am at a loss to know what he plans for me. Not only in this of the marriage. It is strange. He gets me here, offering great things. Many things. To my advantage. And when I am at my lowest. Least danger to him. Apparently forgiving all my rebellion. Why? It is not like him. He would use me against Comyn, of course . . ."

"Yes. I think that he sees you as the best way of dividing Scotland. So my father believes. If he is to keep Scotland down, without each year having to come campaigning in war, he must keep the Scots divided against themselves . . ."

"Always we are that, by the Rude! Without Edward's aid!"

"Perhaps. But that means that one side must not *win* in this struggle. For if it does, the land will be united behind the winner. At this present, your enemy Comyn grows too strong. Matters have gone his way, while you have suffered and lost ground. So Edward would build you up again. Lest all men flock to Comyn. Who, it is said, would try for the throne. This above all must be stopped. The King would even make you Governor of Scotland, I think. *His* governor. Or so says the Queen. But, get you too strong, in turn; let Comyn be brought low—and he will bring *you* down. It is simple. He has come to know the Scots. How you ever fight amongst yourselves. So he uses you."

"Aye. It could be that. But, offering so much? You, in marriage. Why so much?"

"He is a strange man. I believe that he has a true fondness for you. Of a sort. He would bind you to him if he could. If you would play his game, he would cherish you, I think. But you would wholly have to accept his rule of Scotland."

"That I will never do. I am Bruce."

"He still must believe that he can win you, bribe you, frighten you, hold you. He will work on you, seek to mould you, as a potter moulds his clay. Use you and mould you."

"I am no clay to be moulded. I will watch him always. Like a hawk. And seek to use *him*. Make him win Scotland for me! With your help, my dear."

"So you stay? Here, with Edward. In what he calls his peace?"

"So long as I may. With profit. And you, my wife. Is that not what you would wish? Why you sent the message that I should come? By St. John."

"It is, yes. But—there are dangers in it. For you. Let the King once suspect that you are but waiting to turn against him, and he will be ruthless. Without mercy. However fond he may seem."

"I know it. And you? What of you? If you are my wife?"

"I shall be Elizabeth de Bruce," she said simply.

"Aye, bless you. But it could be to your grievous hurt. What would *you* have me to do?"

"I would have you to be what you are. To do what you must. I do not like puppets. That dance to any man's strings. Or woman's!"

"Or woman's . . .? I think, my love . . . that I am prepared . . . to dance! Now. To your string, again . . .!" His voice had gone thick, husky.

She gurgled willing laughter. Affairs of state and dynastics went down before the assault of still more elemental forces.

• • •

They were wed within the month, in the handsome Church of St. Michael, which shared the green hill with Linlithgow Castle, in ceremonial and magnificence seldom seen in Scotland—all at the King's own planning and expense. Edward himself aiding her father to lead the bride to the altar. Old Bishop Wishart of Glasgow officiated, assisted, of all men, by Bishop Beck of Durham—Bruce acceding with a sort of grim forbearance which he was coming to wear like a garment. He would have wished his friend William Lamberton to have married them, but the Primate was still in France; anyway, Edward might not have permitted it in a protégé of Wallace. For, whatever else he might be prepared to wink at meantime, he would not countenance the man Wallace as other than a low-born outlaw. No fewer than fifteen earls attended, and the King may have rubbed his hands that four of them were Scots who had fought against him—Atholl, Lennox, Menteith and Strathearn—this not counting the child Earl of Mar who acted page to his uncle. James the Steward was there, with his lady, Egidia de Burgh, sister of Ulster. Also many of the sore-battered lords of Bruce's party. Of the other faction, needless to say, none came or were invited. It was noticeable that few Scots churchmen graced the occasion; less so that none of Wallace's people came.

Seldom can there have been a marriage so politically contrived, where bride and groom co-operated so satisfactorily.

PART THREE

Chapter Sixteen

Spring came a deal earlier and more kindly to Southern England than it ever did to Scotland, Bruce noted. Already, in March, there was a lightness in the air, a stirring in the woodlands and copses, and a trilling of larks above the rich Essex plain, such as would not be seen in Scotland for a month yet. It was the first spring that he had ever spent in the fair, fat English countryside, despite the presence of Bruce properties here, and he savoured all with a sort of rueful appreciation, all the signs of peace and security, of wealth and ease and genial living that he saw around him. Rueful, for settled and assured as it was, it was all ephemeral, hardly real, for him. This was but an interlude; and though something in his nature responded to it all, he knew that it was not for him, in fact ever, suitably as he and his might appear to blend with the goodly scene, there and then.

For it was not only the rich landscape and air of well-being which affected him, but his own present seeming identity with it all. Surely the condition of few men could have been so radically transformed in one short war? He rode to London, from his father's great manor of Hatfield Broadoak, like any prince, summoned to celebrate the Shrove-tide carnivals with the King. Dressed with a richness to which he had never hitherto aspired even in his most extravagant youth, with his wife as splendid on his right, he rode, magnificently mounted, his brother Nigel brilliant as a peacock at his other side with their cousin Gloucester, married to Edward's daughter. Horsed musicians made melody for them as they went, and half a hundred lords and knights and their ladies trotted behind him, glad to do so. For none was higher in King Edward's apparent regard than the Earl of Carrick, none more smiled upon, more liberally favoured. Where the unpredictable monarch heaped gifts and privileges, much could overflow to others conveniently nearby.

At least there was no danger of all this prosperity going to Bruce's head. Indeed, Elizabeth not infrequently chid him with being unnecessarily wary and foreboding about it. His contention that Edward could, and would, as easily take it all away again, she admitted—but pointed out that by no means all of it was the King's to give or take back. Her own handsome dowry of £10,000 for instance, and the ten manors that went with it. The revenues of the Bruce English estates, which were much larger than either of them had realised, and more wealthy, having an accumulation of receipts scarcely touched for years—with Robert Bruce senior now an ailing shadow of his former self, all but a bed-ridden recluse, spending nothing. Moreover, although the King could remove him from the wardship of the far-away earldom of Mar, in theory, the amassed products of it, thriftily garnered by the careful Gartnait, were already at Bruce's disposal.

He was prepared to concede that all this might be so. But experience had made him chary of good fortune. Though meantime he agreed that it might be wise to spend lavishly—since it all might not be his to spend for much longer. And there was such a thing as making friends with the mammon of unrighteousness while you had it.

The laughing, resounding company made gay progress through London's narrow streets—even though the smells caught at their breaths—but at the Palace of Westminster there was a different atmosphere, decorated for carnival but with no heralds or emissaries sent to greet them, or even welcoming smiles. Sober-faced guards and courtiers indicated that Majesty was in wrathful mood. There was bad news from Scotland.

They found the Great Hall, hung with evergreens and coloured lanterns, and set for feasting, thronged with anxious-looking men and women, who stood in groups and spoke low-voiced. While many turned to bow to Lancaster and Gloucester, it was noticeable that most looked askance at Bruce. They were motioned onwards to the throne-room, where the King was holding a hurriedly-called Council.

A pursuivant slipped in ahead, to inform of their arrival—but it was ominous how long it was, despite the illustriousness of the waiters, before he returned to beckon forward the leaders of the Essex party. Moreover, he signed to the Gloucester Herald not to trumpet the entrance of his lord. Royal Gilbert of Gloucester, Edward's son-in-law as well as Bruce's cousin, looked distinctly chilly at such treatment.

But when they entered the throne-room, Elizabeth holding back a little reluctantly with the other ladies, any petty irritation was quickly lost in sheerest apprehension and alarm. There was absolute silence, save for the sound of heavy breathing from the throne at the far end of the chamber. Right down the long central table men sat stiffly, looking as though they would have risen to their feet, but dared not.

Edward Plantagenet, angry, was a fearsome sight—and worse, emanated a terrifying aura, like a baited bull about to charge. But a cunning, killer-bull that would charge with shrewd deadliness rather than blind fury. He sat hunched forward, purple of face, great head out-thrust, jaw working slowly, rhythmically.

The newcomers bowed—and received no acknowledgement. Gloucester coughed. "My lord Edward—greetings, sire. Had you sent word to us of this Council, we would have attended earlier."

The King ignored him. He was staring at Bruce.

That young man, requiring all his hardihood, held his head high and stared back.

"Perfidious . . . rebellious . . . dogs!" Edward said, at length, enunciating each word as though savouring it. "Base . . . treacherous . . . dastards! Scots!"

Bruce held his tongue if not his peace.

"After my royal patience! My clemency. My forbearance. All wasted. Spurned. Spat upon! By graceless rogues and low-born scum! But, by God's precious blood, they shall suffer! I swear it!"

Bruce did not feel it incumbent upon him to argue.

"Speak, then—curse you!" the King roared suddenly, jabbing a finger towards Bruce, all men jumping. "Speak, man. You—Bruce! These are your friends, your precious countrymen. You are all alike—murderous rebels!"

The other gestured with his hand. "How may I speak, Sire, until Your Majesty informs me what's to do? I know nothing of this."

"Aye—you would say that! Why should I believe you? Are you more to be trusted than the rest? Working against me, despite all I have done for you? There has been bloody rebellion in Scotland. Widespread attack. The slaughter of my servants. It is the ruffian Wallace—I swear it! Behind all. Returned, and spurring on lesser rogues and knaves to murder and treason. It is not to be borne! You knew Wallace had returned, I vow?"

"I had heard so, Sire. But I have been in England with you, since before the truce expired in November. If hostilities have now been resumed . . ."

"Hostilities resumed . . .!" Edward all but choked. "Traitorous revolt and shameful massacre—and you name it hostilities!" The King, crouching, part rose from his throne as though he would launch himself down the chamber at Bruce. But, drawing a deep gulping breath, he swung round instead, to point at a cleric who sat at a side table. "You," he commanded, "tell him."

It was the same Master John Benstead, former royal pantryman who had once lorded it at Lochmaben. Bruce had not noticed him. He stood, a hunched crow of a man, bowing deeply.

"Your gracious Majesty—where do I begin? I do not know how much the Earl of Carrick, and these other lords, may know."

"Begin at the beginning, fool! But be quick about it."

"Yes, Sire. To be sure, Sire." The Pantler turned his chalk-white face in the direction of Bruce. "Since the truce ended there have been small risings all over South Scotland. Attacks on castles, on the King's garrisons. Ambuscades. The work of the man Wallace and his brigands, no doubt. Sir John Lord Segrave, His Highness's Governor, made protest to him they call the Guardian, the Lord of Badenoch, who followed on Sir John de Soulis. You know of this . . .?"

Bruce nodded. De Soulis had relinquished the guardianship in order to go in person to France, with Buchan and de Umfraville, on the return of Wallace and Lamberton, with new proposals about Baliol; and John Comyn had had himself appointed sole Guardian in his place, with the Bruce faction for the time being out of the running.

"The Lord of Badenoch made insolent reply. So His Majesty commanded Governor Segrave—brother to Sir Nicholas, whom you had occasion to know, my lord, at Lochmaben!—to march north from Berwick. With 20,000 men. To punish Wallace's outlaws, who were in the Tor Wood of Stirling. He reached Roslin, in Lothian, in the valley of the Esk, his army in three divisions. And encamped for the night..."

"The fool! The thrice-accursed dolt!" Majesty interrupted. "To encamp, apart. In three arrays. In such close valley as the Esk."

"Yes, my lord King. The Scots, under the Lord of Badenoch himself, fell upon Sir John's array, while yet it slept. With great slaughter. In unfair fight. A shameful thing, unworthy of Christian men! Many were slain, some fled, but most were taken prisoner. Sir John himself, and his son. Also Sir Nicholas, his brother. And my own self. Then came the word that our second array was warned, and advancing to our aid, under Master Ralph

Manton, Cofferer to Your Majesty's Wardrobe. The Scots were then beyond all in villainy. Before facing Manton, they slew all the captives. In wanton slaughter. Without mercy. Sir John and Sir Nicholas with the rest. Sixteen other knights, and all their men. Myself and one or two others they spared. Because we were priests. But all others were butchered . . ."

"Wallace's work, Satan roast him, for a surety!" the monarch cried. "The man is no more than a savage beast."

"I think not, Sire," Bruce intervened, greatly daring. "Sir William Wallace fights hard. But he would not slay defenceless prisoners. This I warrant. I know him. The night attack, while they slept—this could be his work. But not the slaying."

"Aye, you know him, my lord. All too well! You had the presumption to dub him knight—this oaf, this savage! A mockery of knighthood. But all men know that he is no true knight."

"If he is not knight, Sire, then nor am I, who knighted him. And *you* knighted me!" Bruce swung on the cleric. "You, Master Benstead—did you see it? With your own eyes, did you see Wallace slay a single captive? Or hear him order it done?"

"Not . . . not of myself, no."

"Who gave the orders, then?"

"The Lord of Badenoch himself, Sir John Comyn."

"Aye. That I can believe! But Wallace—where was he . . .?"

"This is not a court of law, and Bruce the judge!" Edward thundered. "Keep silent, sirrah. Proceed, Clerk."

"Yes, Sire. Ralph the Cofferer's army was ill led. His people fought stoutly, but Comyn had 8,000 horse. They were forced to yield . . ."

"Forced—bah! What forced them to yield? A craven spirit? A clerk leading!"

"Not so, Majesty. I myself saw Master Ralph cut down three before he yielded. But he had ridden into a trap. He tried to retire, in the narrow valley, but could not. He was captured, with much booty—payment for Your Majesty's garrisons." At the monarch's fight for breath, Benstead hurriedly went on. "Scarce was the fighting over when the third division, under Sir Robert de Neville, came up. And again, to free themselves of the prisoners, the Scots slew all. Even Master Ralph himself. I heard him pleading for his life, to Sir Simon Fraser who had captured him, claiming his priestly immunity. But the dastard Scot pointed to his armour and said lewdly that he trusted to this rather than to God's protection, and that the sword he had yielded up was bloody. Then this blasphemer, Fraser, drew his own sword and struck off first the Cofferer's left hand, then his right, and finally, with a single great blow, his head—God's curse on him everlastingly! This I saw."

"Sim Fraser! That renegade, whom once I cherished!" Edward exclaimed. "You see, my lord of Carrick, how much faith is to be placed in the Scots?"

"I see, Sire, men at war, fighting for their lives and land. As Your Majesty has done times amany. May I ask Master Benstead how fared Sir Robert Neville?"

The cleric shrugged. "What chance had he? Unawares he rode to his death. He and his fought well, and long, but without avail. This time there was no quarter, no prisoners taken. Save for a few who escaped by flight, all died."

"Out of 20,000 who left Berwick, how many survived, man? Other than a handful of frocked priests!"

"A few hundreds, perhaps, Highness. No more. I was exchanged. For three Scots knights, held at Berwick . . ."

"Aye—and scarce a good bargain! Enough of this, then. Sit down, man." The King pointed at Bruce. "Now, my Scots lord—what have you to say?"

The younger man looked about him, at the others, and spread his hands. "What is there for me to say? I have accepted Your Majesty's peace. Am I to be responsible for those who have not? I condemn this slaying of prisoners. What else can I say?"

"You can admit that the Scots are of all men the most perfidious and vile! Ingrates. Liars. Assassins. Brute-beasts to be stamped underfoot as I would stamp on an adder! Admit that, sirrah!"

Bruce remained silent, tight-lipped.

"So! You will not? You disobey my royal command—preferring your animal countrymen! So you are one with them. And deserving equally of my righteous retribution. That, if you will not admit, you cannot deny."

"I do deny it, Sire. Since returning to your peace I have kept your peace. What more would you have me to do? By coming to you, I have forfeited any sway that I had in Scotland . . ."

"I will tell you what I would have you do. What you *will* do, Robert. You will end this soft and idle living which I have allowed you here. You will come back to Scotland with me. And aid me in what I should have done long ere this. Aid me in the destruction of that evil land! Hitherto I have been merciful. I will be merciful no longer. And you will be as my right hand, Robert Bruce! You hear?"

The other bowed stiffly, wordless.

Edward sat back. "Here then is my decision. From this day, the armies will assemble. The greatest force that England has fielded. No excuse for service will be accepted from any lord, baron, knight or prelate in all my realms. This Shrove-tide carnival, and all such fancies, are cancelled. The whole nation will march with me. And with the Earl of Carrick! And when we return, Scotland will be but an ill memory. This is my command. My lords—see you to it." The King heaved himself to his feet.

Speechless, men rose, to bow.

As an afterthought, Edward jerked. "The Earl of Carrick to be escorted to his quarters, forthwith. And there guarded. Well guarded."

. . .

The assembly, set for York, took months. It was not only the gathering in of hundreds of thousands of men and horses and equipment from all over England and Wales, even from the English provinces of France; it was the collection of a fleet of ships, in the Tyne and Tees estuaries, and the loading of supplies sufficient to maintain such vast numbers of men in a devastated land for many months. It was early May before the mighty host began to move northwards.

Inevitably it moved slowly. But there was no hurry. Nothing could possibly withstand so enormous a concourse of armed men, nothing even delay it—save only its own ponderous size and weight. Some said that there were 250,000 men; but who could tell, or try to count so many? By its very size and complexity there was little of the atmosphere of war and fighting about the expedition—the more so in that Edward had brought along his Queen and she her ladies. Many of the great lords did the same.

Elizabeth de Burgh, although no longer the Queen's principal lady-in-waiting, was still one of her entourage, and as such accompanied her husband. Bruce was not exactly a prisoner, as had almost been his position in the South; indeed superficially he might have seemed an honoured member of Edward's Court—save that other men now were chary indeed of any association with him. But he was well aware how closely the King watched him, how iron-firm was the hand which gripped as well as sometimes patted his shoulder. For Edward, after his first rage, had behaved with a bewildering inconsistency towards the younger man, affectionate one moment, mocking and spiteful the next, but ever keeping him close as a son—closer indeed than he kept Edward of Carnarvon, Prince of Wales, a young man for whom his father appeared to have little regard. This inconsistency was, however, a surface thing. Bruce, like Scotland, was to be humbled, all men knew.

After a final inspection of shipping at Newcastle, the expeditionary force moving only a few miles a day, came to Morpeth on the 9th of May, there to split up. The Prince of Wales, with Lancaster and Surrey to aid and advise him, was given 100,000 men and sent to chastise Scotland's West. He took, more or less as hostages, Nigel, Edward and Alexander Bruce—the latter two having been for most of the last year at Cambridge University with him, where King Edward, in his gracious period, had sent them at his own expense, ostensibly out of kindness but more practically to keep them out of Scotland. Edward Bruce and the Prince had become friendly at university—but few believed that the association would have scope to ripen.

The monarch, with the main body, held to the east side of the country, crossing the Border and reaching Roxburgh in early June.

As was to be expected, there was no fighting. In fact, they saw Scotland smoking long before they reached it. Wallace's guerillas had had plenty of notice. Methodically they destroyed before the advancing English. There was little for Edward to do—although his outriders ranged far and wide, seeking any unburned territory, any unravaged land or village, savaging, hanging, crucifying any refugees or wretched hiders that they came across. Only the abbeys, monasteries and churches had been left intact—a pointless scruple, since they were more worth harrying than almost any other property. The destruction of arable land was difficult—but river-banks could be broken down, for flooding; dykes, ditches and mill-lades levelled; cornfields systematically trampled; orchards hacked down; wells poisoned. All that would burn was burned. Again there was no hurry; all could be done thoroughly.

At this rate it took the force a full fortnight to reach Edinburgh. Here the fortress had never been relinquished by the English, and the townsfolk, under its shadow, had perforce remained quiet, never rising in revolt. But if they expected therefore to escape Edward's heavy hand, they were much mistaken. With judicial impartiality he hanged one-tenth of the magistracy and leading citizenry, slew one-tenth of the populace by speedier methods, and burned one-tenth of the town—although, owing to the uprising of a summer wind, rather more than the due proportion of the mainly timber buildings happened to catch fire. All this he forced Bruce to watch, even to seem to preside over, with himself, making jocular remarks about John Baliol, or any who thought to be his heirs, scarcely being likely to consider that there was any kingdom left to plot over.

The Plantagenet's treatment of Scotland's notoriously non-rebellious city might give the others something to think about.

While this went on, the majority of the invasion forces were carefully laying waste Lothian and the plain of Forth, again despite its record of acquiescence, driving Wallace's men ever westwards but never actually coming to grips with them. There were signs of Comyn's chivalry being reported, now, but no battles developed. The Guardian was undoubtedly retiring on Stirling Bridge, there to contest the crossing of Forth in the classic fashion.

But Edward had thought of this. He had his shipwrights build three mighty pontoon bridges, at King's Lynn, and these had been towed up by sea. Now he had them placed across the river at a narrowing, five miles downstream from Stirling, and had his light horse swarming across before the Scots knew what was happening. Comyn had hastily to abandon his prepared positions, before he was cut off from the rear, and retired at speed northwards. Wallace and his people were trapped on the wrong side of Forth, and had to take refuge in the far recesses of the Tor Wood where it stretched into the lonely morasses of the Flanders Moss.

And now, as it were on virgin territory, Edward could demonstrate that he had meant what he had sworn in his throne-room at Westminster. Nobody had had time to scorch the good earth of Fife and Fothrif, nor had most of the folk opportunity to flee. The King's peace, therefore, fell to be established in fullest measure.

It was on a late June evening, at Clackmannan, a few miles north of Forth, at the foot of the steep Ochil Hills, that Robert Bruce lay on his couch in the glowing light of his handsome tented pavilion, sprawled but not relaxed. Elizabeth was pressing wine on him, seeking to soothe and ease the tension that now almost permanently had him in its thrall, and that was etching hard lines deep in his rugged features. They were alone, as they so seldom were on this ghastly, endless, death-filled progress, no watchful lords, guards, esquires or servants actually in the tent with them. It had been a long and harrowing day.

"Come—wash the taste of it away with this, my dear," Elizabeth urged. She was strong, understanding, patient, and because of her position and wealth, able to help much. What he would have done without her, these months, he did not know.

He pushed away the proffered goblet. "No. It would make me sick, I swear. My stomach is turned, I tell you! It is too much. I cannot bear with more of this, Elizabeth. That devil has me beaten, destroyed, damned—as much as he has this wretched land! All day and every day he grinds me into the dust of his hatred, even as he smiles and strokes, mocking me. My belly is galled with his insults, poisoned by his spleen. I tell you, many a time I have been near to drawing my dirk and plunging it into his black heart . . . !"

"Hush you, hush you, Robert!" That girl was not easily scared, but she lowered her voice, glancing anxiously around at the golden-glowing silken hangings of the tent, refulgent with the evening sunlight. "These walls are thin. Watch your words, of a mercy!"

"I watch my words the livelong day! While Edward slays me with his! My life is not worth the living. My head rings with words I dare not speak. My nostrils reek with the stench of fire, of burned flesh. My eyes see only savagery decked in smiles and laughter, dead men's eyes reproaching me—aye, and live men's fingers pointing! Pointing at Bruce, as traitor, as turncoat . . . !"

"Not so, my heart. Do not say it. You mistake. It is not at you that men point . . ."

"I say it is. Do you think I do not know? All this day I have been with him at Dollar. Doleur, they say the name once was—and God knows it is meet today! Receiving the submissions and homage of barons and landed men from all this Fothrif. Led in, some at horses' tails, some bound or in chains, some lashed with whips—receiving them in a nunnery with all its orchards and pleasances hung with corpses. Forced to sit beside him, while men were brought to their knees before him. Think you I did not see what their eyes said, whatever their lips muttered? They could not look in Edward's eye—but they could look in *mine*! Sitting there, his hand on my arm . . ."

"It is evil, yes. Grievous. A shameful thing. But you *must* bear it, my love. You must harden your heart. He will break your pride, your spirit. You must not give him the victory."

"There is half of Scotland before me, yet. To see stricken. Crushed. Weeks, months of this venom . . ."

Bruce's voice died away as there was a commotion at the tent door, the armed guard clanking weapons. The entrance-curtain was thrust aside unceremoniously, and two men strode inside unannounced, stooping because both were tall. Both were Plantagenets, though one did not bear the name.

"Ha, Robert! You rest, lad? Plied with refreshment by fair hands, heh? Would I were in your shoes! *My* lady prefers to eat sweetmeats and stitch fool threads!" Edward bowed gallantly to Elizabeth. "But no rest for the King. Despite his years!" At sixty-four, he was heavy, purple of face, but his basic vigour little diminished.

Bruce was slow to rise, striving to school his features. He bowed briefly, unspeaking. Elizabeth had curtsied more promptly.

"News, Robert—tidings," the King went on. "Good, and less good. From France. And from the West. John, here, brings it. From the West. Of folly and knavery. *My* son's folly. And *your* people's knavery! Eh, John?"

The massively tall and sombre-eyed young man with him, so uncannily like the other in build and face, inclined his dark head. Travel stained but richly armoured, he was Sir John de Botetourt, Edward's own bastard, and now Warden of the West March. A man of few words but strong hand, he let his sire do the talking.

"My son—my *other* son—Edward of Carnarvon, lacks much. But wits, most of all! Nor has your friend Lancaster greatly aided him it seems! They have mired themselves in your Galloway and Carrick bogs, a plague on them! A mighty host wasted, in chasing scum! *Your* scum, Robert! Your wretched savages of the West are resisting everywhere. In their accursed hills. It is shameful—not to be borne. My commands, my splendid host, being thwarted by this beggarly rabble. Who act in your name, by the Mass! *Yours*!"

Bruce moistened his lips, but said nothing.

"So you will leave me, Robert, meantime. I must bear to lose your joyous presence! For a space. As must you, my dear. You will go back with John, here, to the West, my friend. You will go and tell your treacherous people to lay down their arms. You will take order with them, hang the leaders, teach them what it means to defy the King of England. You will do more than that. You will muster them to *my* arms! To fight against their rebellious countrymen, not their liege lord. I want a Bruce host in the field, Robert. Fighting by my side. By *our* side! You understand?" Edward was eyeing his victim levelly.

"That I can by no means do, Sire," the younger man declared flatly. "I have no authority in the West, since I have yielded to your peace. My earldom is taken over by others. I have no power and jurisdiction now."

"There you underestimate, Robert. Underestimate my love for you. For you have *my* power. More potent than any earldom of Carrick. To use, lad—to use. Moreover, you shall have authority over more than your former vassals. I want men from more than Carrick, Galloway and Annandale. So you shall be Sheriff of Ayr and Lanark. For the present. Here is sufficient authority to act—even for Robert Bruce!"

The other blinked. "I . . . I do not wish this appointment, Sire."

"But I do, my friend! And it shall be. From this moment, you are Sheriff of Ayr and Lanark, with all the duties thereto belonging! Sir John here, your deputy and companion. Close companion! In token of which I require from your sheriffdom, within the month, 1,000 picked footmen, duly armed. Also a further thousand, half horsed, from your own lands of Carrick and Galloway. These, the first token. Within the month. More to follow. It is clear?"

"But, Sire—you have hundreds of thousands of men! What want you with these? Unwilling . . . !"

"Each one will be worth many of my own, wisely used, lad. You would not begrudge me them? In your loyalty?"

Bruce looked at his wife, helplessly. She nodded, almost imperceptibly.

"I shall go with my lord, to aid him, Sire," she said. "You would not part husband and wife?"

"Alas, my dear—I fear it is necessary. The Queen requires your presence. She greatly leans on you. And this is men's work—mustering forces and hanging rebels. Not such as you may aid in. Moreover, lass—you will but bring Robert back the quicker, will you not? To win back to your side I swear *I* would do all in notable haste! It will be so with him, I vow."

There was silence in that tent for a space.

Then Edward laughed. "But, save us—I have almost forgot the *good* tidings! Eh, John? From France. As you know, my uncouth allies the Flemings surprised and defeated my good brother-in-law of France at Courtrai. Last July. His fortunes have scarce mended since. The foolish fellow has come to blows with His Holiness of Rome! So I have had to act to save him from himself—as kinsman should! Now, at last, he has signed a peace. No truce, but a final peace. After all these years, England and France are at peace. The Holy See also. Is this not excellent?"

Bruce drew a deep breath. "And . . . the terms?"

"Terms? Why, scarce any, Robert. Merely some . . . adjustments. To our mutual advantage. One which will rejoice your heart, I have little doubt. The man Baliol to be held secure in his own house at Bailleul-en-Vimeu. Henceforth. He and his son. Never to return to Scotland. Does this not please you?"

The other knowing Edward Plantagenet, did not commit himself.

"One or two other small matters. We have, as it were, exchanged our allies! Problems, as they were. I relinquish all interest in Flanders and the Flemings—a small loss! And Philip *le Bel* relinquishes all interest in Scotland and the Scots. As is only proper. So an ages-old stumbling block is removed. Is it not satisfactory?"

Hoarsely Bruce spoke. "And the Pope?"

"Why, Pope Boniface also joins in this goodwill. He declares Scotland and Flanders, both, in wicked rebellion. And all who bear arms against me, or Philip, their lawful sovereigns, in danger of hellfire! Were you not wise, my good Robert, to submit to my peace when you did?"

Wordless, Elizabeth moved over, to put her arm in Bruce's, a simple but eloquent gesture which drew a quick frown from the King.

"You seem less joyful than you should, my lord," he grated, suddenly harsh, accusing.

"Should I rejoice, Sire, to see my country utterly betrayed and abandoned? By all. By its most ancient ally. Even by Holy Church?"

"Betrayed, sirrah! *You* to say that? Robert Bruce speaks of betrayal!"

When the younger man answered nothing but looked steadily, directly into the other's choleric eyes, the King thrust out a jabbing, pointing hand.

"We shall see. None betrays Edward, and does not suffer. And Edward is Scotland. Now. Forget it at your peril—you, or any. You will leave at once. Tonight. Ride with Sir John. For Ayr. See you to it." Without any other leave-taking, he turned abruptly and strode from the tent, de Botetourt silent at his heels.

Husband and wife turned to gaze at each other. After a moment, Elizabeth flung herself into the man's arms.

• • •

It was many months before Bruce saw his wife again, appalling months for Scotland and grievous for Robert Bruce; months in which Edward stormed his brutally determined way northwards, by Perth and Coupar and Arbroath and Brechin, over the mouth to Aberdeen, and onwards to Banff and Elgin and Kinloss, within sight of the blue mountains of Ross; further than he or any other invader had ever gone, leaving utter desolation behind him in a blackened swathe from the sea to the Highland hills. One by one the Comyn's northern strongholds had fallen until the last remote strength of Lochindorb, on its island in deepest Strathspey, was brought low, and no major strength in all the land, save only Stirling Castle, remained opposed to the conqueror. That is, except for the eyries of Highland chiefs who were interested in neither the one side nor the other.

During those months Bruce in fact sent no thousands of West-countrymen to increase the King's mighty northern host. It had not been easy to avoid doing so—but after long battling with Edward personally, he found his bastard son de Botetourt rather less hard to get round. Not that Sir John was a lenient guard or mild of temperament—quite the reverse; but he lacked his sire's shrewdness and experience, and Bruce was able to deceive him where he could not have done the King. He managed time and again to put off the required transfer of men, mainly on the grounds that they were more urgently needed there in the West than by the so victorious monarch. He ensured that this was so by secretly fomenting strategically-sited and timed revolts and uprisings in various parts of his domains and sheriffdoms—not too difficult to do here in his own earldom. His newly-mustered vassals and levies were kept busy dashing hither and thither in Galloway and Carrick, ostensibly keeping King Edward's peace. Edward himself would have seen through it and clamped down sternly. De Botetourt may have suspected, but he could prove nothing, and was somewhat beyond his depth in dealing with

Bruce. Moreover he could not deny the need to put down all armed rising in the rear of the Prince of Wales' army, and was much aware of the threat of a link-up with Wallace, who was still active in the central forests and marshes between Clyde and Forth—a danger which Bruce never failed to stress. The Prince, too, was unhappy in his Galloway adventure, finding that vast province a most awkward place to campaign in, as others had done before him. He sent conflicting demands to Botetourt and the Sheriff of Ayr—and Bruce was glad on more than one occasion to despatch south to him parties of men who should have gone north to Edward.

But it was a dire and sorry business, for all that, however great a relief it was to be quit of the monarch's personal presence. His bastard made a sullen and unattractive companion, and Bruce had also to put up with quite a lot of his old foe Clifford, whom the Prince had installed as a sort of governor of Annandale and keeper of Lochmaben. Oddly enough, Clifford had as lieutenants two men who Bruce had thought to be dead—the Lord Segrave, demoted and disgraced but still alive; and Sir Robert Neville, also alleged to have been slain at Roslin. Apparently Master Benstead had not been entirely to be trusted as informant and courier.

It was with mixed feelings, then, that in early October, Bruce received a peremptory summons from Edward, sent from the castle of his own nephew and ward, at Kildrummy in Aberdeenshire, to come north forthwith, still in de Botetourt's care. Presumably the King had come to accept the fact that the West experiment had failed, and that Bruce would be of more value in the North where, for his own interests, he might be expected to desire to keep down any resurgence of the Comyn power. Edward had cancelled his appointments as Sheriff of Ayr and Lanark, making him instead Sheriff of Moray, Nairn and Inverness, and reminding him that he was keeper of the royal forests of Kintore, Darnaway and Longmorn, as well as controller of the earldom of Mar. In name, at any rate. Edward himself was returning south, to winter at Dunfermline in Fife; Bruce was to hold the North, in his name, against any attempt of Comyn. But he would not be left to hold it alone; he would have ample help. Which meant that he still would be a well-guarded prisoner.

So, with the shortening days, Bruce and de Botetourt rode northwards through a ravaged, shattered land. Only the hope that he might find Elizabeth at the end of his journey gave the former any satisfaction.

In this, at least, he was not disappointed. Edward had left behind at Kildrummy, as well as some few thousand Englishmen, both Elizabeth and her father, Richard de Burgh, to ensure Bruce's good behaviour and co-operation in the North.

• • •

Kildrummy was good for Robert Bruce. As on the previous visit, he was able partly to relax, here amongst the skirts of the great Highland mountains. The air, the people, the entire tempo and tenor of life was different, easier, more genial. The stresses and strains of war and dynastic manoeuvre seemed far away, and even Edward's heavy hand had made but little impression on this mighty land of vast horizons. He had burned a few towns in Aberdeenshire and Moray, yes; but the people hereabouts did not live in towns and villages, being a pastoral folk wide-scattered over a thousand hills and valleys. It was strange that this should be the fierce Comyn's land, for it seemed out of sympathy with all he stood for. Or so mused Bruce that Yuletide, as 1303 gave way to 1304.

He had not, in fact, come to blows with John Comyn as yet, that man having kept his distance. Word of him came intermittently from places wide apart, mainly in the West—Galloway, the Lennox, Argyll, and as near as Lochaber. He was still free, still resisting after a fashion, still sole Guardian of Scotland; but he could effect little, fugitive rather than commander or ruler, and for some reason he avoided the North-East, where Bruce, in name at least, now governed—and where he and Buchan and the other Comyns might between them have raised many thousands more men. Bruce often wondered why—but he was thankful.

Such thoughts were always at the back of his mind—even as he stood this Yuletide night in the hall of Kildrummy, eyeing the pleasantly domestic scene. By the light of two great log fires and many candles, a children's game was in progress, involving Donald, the boy Earl of Mar, Marjory Bruce, and young John de Strathbogie, heir to the Atholl earldom. Assisting were Elizabeth, Christian, Countess of Mar who was taking her widowhood philosophically, and, crawling about on hands and knees, none other than Richard, Earl of Ulster. The last, with a few drinks to aid him, made an excellent charger for Donald, replacing

Bruce, exhausted and sore of knee. The ladies undoubtedly had the best of this game, requiring only to look gracious, curtsy occasionally, and commend the noisy activities of the children. Elizabeth and Christian were already close friends, although so different in temperament. The former was taking her new stepmotherly duties seriously.

Bruce was laughing heartily and heartlessly at his father-in-law, an excellent thing, when a servant came unobtrusively up to him.

"My lord, a friar has come seeking you. A ragged, wandering friar, but asking for your lordship's self. Secretly. He says you will see him if I say he comes from Stowburgh or some such."

"Stowburgh . . .? Ha—Stobo! Stobo, is it?" Bruce glanced over at the others quickly, caught his sister's eye, and shook his head briefly. Then he slipped out, with the servitor.

It was Lamberton, as he had guessed, a weary and dishevelled figure to be Primate of Scotland. This device of dressing as a begging friar might enable him to move about the land with some freedom, but only on foot and with the minimum comfort. The Bishop looked almost an old man, although he was little more than forty. Last time Bruce had seen his friend, he had been disguised thus. It was two years ago.

Stiffly formal until they could be alone in a private room, the two men then gripped each other with some emotion.

"God be praised for the sight of you!" Lamberton said unsteadily. "It is long, long. I have feared if ever I would see you again. Feared that I was a done and broken man. Priest of a done and broken land. And you lost to both of us . . ."

"Not that, my friend—not that. I am not lost. Yet! Although at times I know not where I go. Which way. Whether indeed there is anywhere to go. Save into the Plantagenet's bloody arms! Where most men think me already, I swear!"

They looked at each other.

"Were we wrong, then? In error?" the Bishop asked. "In what we put our hands to?"

"God knows. But we have achieved little. Or, *I* have. Save sorrow and affliction, the land destroyed. Everywhere, save in Galloway, Edward supreme. Myself a watched puppet, forced to dance to this tune. You, head of the Holy Church, a furtive skulker, forced to creep and crawl, hungry . . .!"

"The land is not destroyed. Not yet. Nor, pray God, ever will be. Sore stricken, yes. But not beat, not destroyed." He paused for a moment. "And something is achieved, at least. What I came chiefly to tell you. Comyn will yield. He is seeking terms from Edward."

"So-o-o! Comyn! *He* is beat, then?"

"Aye. Or, shall we say, forced to a new course. There has been great talking, great debate, great wrath. John Comyn sees no hope of success in this warfare. He will yield if Edward accepts him to what he calls his peace. And restores him to these his Comyn lands."

"His lands! Aye, his lands. Now that the North, his lands, are in Edward's hands, the man is less bold a campaigner! While it was the South, it mattered not! His lands are his price, then!"

"Part of it. And I think that Edward knew it, always. He is shrewd, cunning. That is why *you* are here, my friend. Edward knew that you, sitting supreme in the Comyns' lands, was more than the man could stomach. If it had been just the English, he might have lain low, left them and hoped for better days. But Bruce . . . ! So he yields to Edward. On terms. And your removal from the North, his sheriffdoms back again—these are his terms. As Edward foresaw from the first, I do swear!"

"Dear God! Plantagenet . . . and Comyn! Curse them both—they are the bane of my life! They stand between me and all that is worth having . . ."

Lamberton looked at him steadily. "At least the throne is safe from him, now. Him and Baliol both. This of France and the Pope. Ill as it is, it means Baliol will never return to Scotland. So . . . the throne stands vacant. As never before."

Bruce drew a long quivering breath. Then abruptly he changed the subject. "Comyn would yield, then. But what of the others? There is more than John Comyn opposing Edward."

"All see it as Comyn does—save one. All will yield. Save William Wallace."

"Ha—Wallace! Aye, Wallace will not yield. Ever. And who supports Wallace?"

"None. Save his own band. And William Lamberton!"

"Save us—so it has come to that? We are back to where we started!"

"Not quite, friend. Not quite. There is an evil here you may not have thought on. When Comyn yields, it will be as Guardian of Scotland. This Edward requires, and this Comyn will agree. So he yields Scotland, not just John Comyn. And yielding Scotland to Edward's peace, leaves Wallace, who will not yield, an undoubted and disavowed rebel and outlaw. And those who aid him."

"But that would be betrayal! Throwing him to the wolves!"

"Will Comyn care for that? He has ever hated and despised the man. Though, see you, we must give Comyn his due. He has fought bravely and ably. Moreover, there is more to the terms he seeks than just his own weal. In surrendering Scotland he asks that our laws and liberties be protected. And that there should be no disinheritance of other lords' lands as well as his own. But he will not speak for Wallace."

"What are we to do, then? What *can* we do?"

"Nothing, I fear. I tried to sway Comyn, but to no avail. Wallace will have to look to himself. Edward will never treat with *him*. But the people will aid him. He has their love . . ."

"Aye. And what guidance do you have for *me*? In my present state?" Bruce asked.

"That you endure, Robert—that is all. Endure. Seem to go along with Edward, where you may with any honour. Your time, if it comes, will only come out of patient endurance. As will Scotland's."

Bruce's sigh of acceptance of that was almost a groan.

Lamberton would not, dare not, stay at Kildrummy, tired as he was. At any time someone might recognise the Primate. Given food and money for his further journeying, he was not long in taking leave of his friend, commending him to God's care, and then slipping out into the cold and windy dark, quietly as he had come. He was going to Wallace, somewhere in the Tor Wood, a hundred miles to the south.

• • •

A month later, in early February, the anticipated summons had come from Dunfermline. The Earl of Carrick, no longer it seemed Sheriff of Moray, Nairn and Inverness, was to be brought south without delay, by order of the King's Majesty. As bald and unvarnished as that.

The Kildrummy party found a changed atmosphere prevailing when they reached the ancient grey town on the north side of Forth, from which Malcolm Canmore had ruled Scotland. The smoke of war had dispersed, superseded by the smell of triumph. The Scots had finally surrendered—or all of them that were worth acknowledging. Comyn, the so-called Guardian, was due to yield himself two days hence, at Strathord near Perth, and

Edward was in expansive mood. He welcomed them all affably, publicly commended Bruce for his alleged notable aid in bringing the rebels to heel in the North, and announced more or less unlimited wassail and celebration to mark the establishment of peace, Edward's final and distinctive brand of peace. A parliament would be held to formalise matters—an English parliament, of course, but with some suitable Scots taking their places. Bygones would be bygones.

The first large-scale demonstration of the new genial dispensation was not the parliament but an elaborate reception, at Dunfermline, of the surrendered Scots leadership. Edward had a fondness for defeated opponents in clanking chains, wearing sackcloth and ashes, and otherwise emphasising the evident; but on this occasion it was to be different. The victor would be magnanimous, and the vanquished made aware of how mistaken and foolish, as well as wicked, they had been.

The ceremony was held in the Abbey itself, since the English earlier had burned down the Great Hall of the palace, one of the finest buildings in the land. It was packed, for the occasion, with half the nobility of England, and all foreign ambassadors.

Bruce found himself very much part of the proceedings, to his discomfiture. The King and Queen had thrones set up within the chancel, with the Prince of Wales seated a little to one side. Bruce was commanded to come and stand directly at Edward's left hand, with Ulster at the right, Elizabeth being required to take up a similar position beside the Queen, with her aunt, the Steward's wife, at the right. Not only so, but the Bruce brothers, with the exception of Alexander, who was still at Cambridge, had been summoned to Dunfermline also, and were now placed behind the thrones. None looked any more happy than their elder brother; but there was no doubt that the impression given was that the Bruce family was the principal support of the King as far as Scotland was concerned.

When all was in readiness, a fanfare of trumpets sounded, and the great church doors were thrown open. Then, as musicians played a funereal dirge, the Scots filed in.

Edward evidently had been concerned to make this a very different affair from the somewhat similar occasion eight years before, at Stracathro parish church, when John Baliol had made his submission. Now the iron fist was to be hidden in the velvet glove. There was no armour, little steel, and certainly no warhorses in sight. The King and his whole Court were in a glittering splendour of gold, silver and jewellery, velvets, satins and silks. The Scots had also been told to eschew all armour and warlike garb—and a sorry, ragged, threadbare crew they looked in consequence, patched and out-at-elbows. For these were men surrendered only after long and unsuccessful campaigning in the field, living rough and in the saddle. Their armour, however rusty and battered, would have had some dignity; but denied it they had come to court little better than a band of scarecrows. They held their heads the higher therefore, of course—but it was difficult to maintain any martial carriage shuffling forward to the slow strains of a dirge.

Three gorgeously-apparelled English heralds led, setting the desperately slow pace. Then, alone, paced John Comyn, the Guardian. Bruce, watching, was almost sorry for his enemy. Not that the man looked humbled, or other than a proud fighter forced to take part in folly; but unkempt, unshaven, shabbily-clad and obviously weary, he represented defeat, a grievous state for the Lord of Badenoch. He did not hang his head, however, but, avoiding looking at the King, stared levelly at Bruce as he walked.

Behind him came Lamberton, the Steward, Buchan the Constable and the Earls of Lennox and Strathearn. The Steward was better dressed than the others; perhaps his wife had managed to smuggle clothing to him. The Primate was not in his wandering friar's rags, but not a great deal finer. Buchan was limping from a leg wound. Lamberton exchanged a quick glance with Bruce, and then gazed straight ahead.

There followed the main body of the Scots lords, temporal and spiritual, led by de Umfraville, the former Guardian, the Lord of Crawford, the Bishops of Glasgow and Galloway, Master William Comyn. De Soulis was still in France, Wallace's enormous figure notably absent.

The sight of them all stirred a great wave of emotion in Bruce. These grim years he had sought to steel himself against emotion, a weakness he could not afford. But in the face of his former associates and comrades in arms, thin, war-ravaged, humiliated, he groaned a little—though he did not know it. He saw himself as they must see him, and swallowed.

Edward, smiling genially and tossing comments and identities to his wife loudly, waited until no more of the surrendered Scots could be crammed into the great church. Even after a trumpet had stilled the mournful music and a herald demanded silence for the King's Majesty, he chatted on, apparently casual, to the Queen, to Ulster, to Bruce—however unforthcoming the latter. Then, as the ranks before him fidgeted, stirred, he gestured to them.

"Welcome, friends, to my peace," he exclaimed. "You come belatedly to my Court and presence. But now here, you are welcome."

None attempted answer to that.

"So many faces well known to me," the King went on, jovially. "Some less ruddy, it may be, than when last I saw them! So many who swore fealty to me at Berwick, that day—eh, Robert my friend? You were there assisting!"

"Scarce assisting, Sire. Then. Any more than today." That was level, almost expressionless, from stiff lips.

Edward ignored it. "Friends of yours. Friends of my own—or so they swore! Absent friends—so long absent. Now wisely returned to my peace. But . . . less wise than you, Robert. Better that they had followed your lead the sooner?"

Biting his lip, Bruce forced himself to meet Comyn's baleful stare.

Edward actually turned in his throne, to grin at the younger man. "You are silent, lad? Does the sight of these your friends distress you? On my oath, it should not! For you greatly aided in bringing them here, did you not?"

"You credit me with too much, Sire," Bruce got out. "I have done nothing. Towards this."

"Ha—you were not always so modest, Robert! How say you, my lord of Badenoch? Are not you—is not all this Scotland—beholden to my lord of Carrick for leading the way into my peace? And then labouring valiantly to establish it."

Comyn bowed, wordless.

"Another modest man!" Edward's smile was wearing thin. "Yet you both set yourselves up to rule this realm of mine. In *my* place. And that is treason is it not, my lords?"

Into the quivering quiet which greeted the enunciation of that dread word, it was William Lamberton who spoke. "My lord King," he said clearly, firmly, "the Lord of Badenoch, as Guardian of Scotland, has surrendered on terms. We with him. To which terms Your Majesty has assented. We are here to claim those terms. There was not, and could not be, treason. From Scots, to the King of England. But even had there been, you annulled it. By treating. This is established usage, known by all. Which none can contest."

"God's eyes—you are bold, Sir Priest! You will be the clerk, Lamberton? Whom the outlaw Wallace raised up."

"I am William Lamberton, appointed to the see of St. Andrews by the Guardian and Council of Scotland, and consecrated Bishop thereof by His Holiness of Rome."

"The Crown appoints to bishoprics, sirrah! And *I* am the Crown!" Edward thundered. "Hereafter keep silent. No man speaks in my presence save by my invitation."

Bruce flashed a glance of acknowledgement at his friend, who had so evidently sought to divert the Plantagenet from his strategy of seeming to establish Bruce as largely responsible for the downfall of his fellow-countrymen, and so still more deeply dividing Scotland.

Edward turned back to Comyn. "You, my lord—if you still have a tongue in your head! Did you or did you not swear fealty to me at Berwick, eight years ago? Do you deny your signature on that Ragman's Roll?"

"I do not, Sire," the other admitted. "But an oath taken under duress is not binding."

"So that is how you keep your word! Why, then, should you expect me to keep mine now? As to these so-called terms."

"Your Majesty assented to the terms under no duress. You could have rejected them. *We* could not have rejected your oath, at Berwick, and saved our heads."

"You have a nice sense of honour, sirrah! As well for you that Edward of England is otherwise. For, by the Mass, the heads of every one of you should fall this day! As forsworn rebels and traitors. But . . . I honour my word. Even to such as you. The terms stand. Your lives are spared, your lands are not forfeit. And the laws, customs and liberties of this part of my realm shall remain unchanged. Some of you I shall require to go into exile furth of Scotland, at my pleasure. For the better peace of this my realm. In exchange for these mercies, I accept your fullest surrender. Yours, and that of all who have risen in arms against me. Save one—the base murderer Wallace! Him I will nowise accept to my peace. Now or ever. It is understood?"

Lamberton seemed about to speak again, despite the King's warning, but Bruce's quick head-shaking halted him.

Edward leaned forward, pointing that imperious finger at Comyn. "My lord, where is he? I do not see the man Wallace.

Yet I commanded that you bring him with you. To me. Bound. Where is he?"

"Wallace is not a man easily bound. Or brought. Or found. Of this Your Majesty is well aware. Your servants have sought him often enough . . ."

"Where is he, man? Do not bandy words with me!"

"I do not know, Sire. Wallace . . . is Wallace. A man apart. He heeds no man's voice . . ."

"He shall heed mine, by God's wounds! And you also. All of you. See you, Comyn—I want Wallace and shall have him. I give you command to find him. To deliver him. And I do not give you overlong. Wallace was at that devilish massacre at Roslin. When you slew, as prisoners, better men than yourselves. You commanded there, my lord of Badenoch. With Sir Simon Fraser, Sir Alexander Lindsay of Crawford and Sir David Graham of Dundaff. I require Wallace of you all. I will do most favour to whosoever shall capture him, in expiation of that vile deed. And let the others beware!"

"Sire—this was no part of the terms . . ."

"Silence! You have heard me. See you to it." As so often happened, Edward Plantagenet tired suddenly of the scene he had himself prepared. Without warning he stood up. "It is enough. This audience is over. Away with them." He reached over and almost lifted the Queen out of her chair, and turning his back on the entire alarmed assembly, strode with her up the chancel, to the vestry-door, and out.

Belatedly the trumpeters grabbed their instruments and blew a notably ragged and uneven fanfare.

The eyes of Bruce and Comyn met in a long hard glare, before the heralds pushed the latter round and hustled him off.

Few there contemplated the festivities to follow with any delight.

Chapter Seventeen

Heavily, even tripping a little with weariness on the worn stone steps, Robert Bruce climbed the narrow turnpike stair of the Sea Tower of St. Andrews Castle—well named, with the spray from the surging waves below actually coming in at him through the arrow slit windows as he mounted, and the chill March wind off the North Sea flapping his long mud-stained travelling-cloak. The single smoking pitch-pine torch-flame, flickering and waving wildly in the draughts, did little to light his footsteps. He cursed as he stumbled for the third time, sword clanking, spurs scraping —but his cursing was spiritless, automatic, and not only with physical weariness. It seemed a long time since he had even cursed with spirit and enthusiasm.

The door on the third-floor landing was thrown open before even he reached it, and Elizabeth held out welcoming hands to him. "My dear," she said, "I prayed that it might be you. Thank God that you are back!"

He took her in his arms, and she clung to him, wet as he was. "Bless you, lass! You are the first sight to gladden my eyes in three weeks." He kissed her hungrily, and then held her away at arm's-length. "Dear God—you are bonny! Fairer, more beautiful, than ever, I swear! You are the saving of me, and that is plain truth."

"Has it been so bad, Robert?"

"Bad? Worse than bad. I have been mocked and trodden under by these English like any condemned felon. Day in, day out. To send me to hunt Wallace was ill enough. But to place me under Clifford, who has ever hated me, and who lords it over my Annandale! And Segrave, a man soured with disgrace. And that bastard Botetourt. This was beyond all bearing. Yet, God forgive me, I had to bear it! A round score of days and nights of it. Of Clifford's and Segrave's spleen. Safe to bait me as they would. By Edward's permission!"

"One day you will repay them, my heart. But . . . Wallace? Did you catch him?"

"No. For that, thank all the saints! A fine dance he led us. All over the Forest, in foulest weather. But never once were we within reach of him. Fraser we almost caught, twice. At Peebles and at Tweedsmuir. But Wallace, never. He was always an hour gone from every hiding-place we flushed—though we quartered Ettrick Forest for him. More than once, mind, I was able to lead those devils the wrong road—for none of them knew the Forest as I did . . ."

"Oh, I am glad! Glad." Elizabeth was aiding him off with his soaking and mud-stained outer wear, before the blazing fire in the little tower chamber which was all that even Lamberton could provide for the Bruces in his over-crowded Castle of St. Andrews, where Edward was holding his parliament.

"Aye. Had we indeed captured Wallace, I scarce know how I would have done. That Edward should send *me* on such errand, and in such company . . . ! But he will be beside himself now. Beyond all in fury. For if he hates me, tramples me, it is as nothing to his hatred of Wallace."

"He has, I think, more to dwell on tonight than your failure to bring him Wallace," the young woman interrupted. "The King is ill, Robert."

"Ill? Edward ill? Sick?"

"Yes. It was at today's parliament. He was speaking. Very angry that Stirling Castle still holds out against him. When he was seized. A great choking and gasping, that felled him. I was with the Queen, watching. His face was blue, like to burst with blood! Always he has had too much blood. We feared him dead . . ."

"Feared! By the Rude—why fear?" Bruce cried, eyes alight as they had not been for long. "Edward dead might mean life for many. For us. For this Scotland. But . . . he is not dead? Only ill, you say."

"Ill, yes. And making recovery, they say. I am not long back from the Queen's chamber. She is much upset. They are bleeding him. The fever abates. But it is a warning. To be heeded . . ."

"Heeded, yes. Pray God he does *not* heed it!"

She shook her fair head. "Do not say it, Robert. He can be hard, cruel. But he can be kind, too. I have known much kindness from him. He is my father's friend. He is a king, and kings are not to be judged as other men."

"They need not become monsters! As he has done. I esteemed Edward once. But he has forfeited all esteem."

"And yet, he still has esteem for *you*. In some measure. Today, before the parliament broke up, he appointed you, with Wishart, Bishop of Glasgow, and Sir John de Moubray, to take rule in Scotland. Until his nephew, the Lord John of Brittany, can come to be Governor . . ."

"A trap, I vow! Another trick. An empty title, with his underlings firm in control. Have you forgot that he made me Sheriff of Ayr and Lanark? Aye, then Moray. With no more power than a babe at the breast! Wishart is an old done man. And Moubray is a creature of the Comyn's. So much for Edward's esteem! He would but use me again."

"It may be so. But at least he *seems* to honour you. And more. You three are empowered to work out a new policy for Scotland. The new Scotland as he names it. What he called a constitution.

To be presented before a great parliament at Westminster in the autumn of the year . . ."

"What is this? A constitution? A new constitution for a new Scotland! For a beaten, humbled vassal Scotland, in thrall to the Plantagenet. A province of England, ruled from Westminster. This he would have me to make up—Robert Bruce!"

"It might give you opportunity to serve Scotland well," she pointed out. "Better that you make up such a constitution than some others, is it not?"

"I' faith, no! Think you Edward will accept anything that does not give him all he wants? And then can use my name, and Wishart's to take the blame for it, when the bite hurts. Bruce, the traitor, contrived this! Do you not know Edward yet, my dear?"

"You cannot concede him any good, Robert? Anything?"

"The only good thing I will concede to Edward Longshanks is that he desired me to marry *you*, my dearest! For that, and that only, I am his debtor."

She smiled. "You still believe yourself favoured in that? Still find me to your taste?"

"To my taste? Save us, girl—I'll show you how much to my taste you are! Here is simple proving. As I have been desiring to prove since I entered this room! Why waste we time talking!" And he advanced on her, weariness apparently quite forgotten.

"No, no!" Laughing, she backed away. "That is not what I asked. You rise too fast, my lord! I but questioned whether you still find me a good and dutiful wife . . . ?"

"And that is what you yourself will prove, young woman. Here and now!" he declared. It was not a large apartment, and her backing away soon was halted.

"Foolish fool! Here's no time. Besides . . . you will be hungry. I have food and drink . . ."

"Hungry, yes! Well you may say it. But they have not starved me of *food*, see you!" He had her now, urgent, knowledgeable hands pressing, moulding, caressing. Her protests were vocal only, and easily stopped with kisses; and her person made no resistance—indeed her hands were soon aiding his with her gown. In glorious disorder he picked her up bodily in his arms and, no light weight as she was, strode with her to the couch.

Elizabeth de Burgh was all woman, and no passive partner in love-making. In mutual fervour and uninhibited passion they took and received each other, mounting swiftly, joyfully, to tremendous cataclysmic fulfilment.

As well they were so swift. Scarcely were they lying back, in murmurous relaxation, than they heard footsteps on the stairway, and voices. They waited, for there were two more storeys above; but when a knocking sounded at their door, Bruce sat up, cursing again—although this time the spirit and vigour had returned.

"Wait you," he called, out of it.

In haste they drew on and rearranged their clothing—though even so there was a quiet calm and dignity about that young woman's movements that seemed to be part of her very nature.

They were only approximately restored to respectability when Elizabeth went to open the door. Bishop Lamberton stood there, with another man who louted low respectfully. If the Primate noted anything amiss, in heightened colour and dishevelment, he did not remark on it.

"Your pardon, my friends, for this intrusion," he said. "I would not trouble you, with my lord so newly returned. But I believed that you would wish to hear this man's tidings, without delay. He comes from England. From Essex, Robert."

"My lord, I come from Hatfield Broadoak. Sent by the steward of the manor. Your father, my lord—he is dead. I have ridden day and night to bring you word."

Bruce drew a long breath.

"I am sorry," Lamberton said. "But he had retired from this world for long, Robert. He would not be loth to go, I think."

Elizabeth turned to her husband. "A father is a father," she said.

"Aye. God rest his soul." Bruce nodded. "I was no good son for him. We never agreed, all my days. I do not weep for him, in death—when I scarce thought of him in life. That would be folly. But at least I acknowledge that, as son, I failed him."

There was silence in that little fire-lit room. Then Bruce asked the courier for details. He rewarded him generously, and dismissed him to find food and rest. Lamberton remained.

"So we have a new situation, Robert," the Bishop said, when they were alone. "You are now Scotland's heir. Rightful king of this unhappy realm. Its only hope."

"Hope!" Bruce barked the word. "What hope am I? What hope is there in me, or for me? Or for Scotland? I have long ceased to hope, my friend. Or . . . or had. Until . . . until . . ."

"Until you heard of Edward's sickness? Aye, there could be hope there. We must not wish his death. But if he is stricken in body, the man might think more of his latter end and less of imposing his will on Scotland. For this we may lawfully pray.

Though, they tell me that he is already much bettered. So that he may not yet heed God's warning."

"I do not think he will. Edward is too old to change now. His hatred the strongest part of him! My hope is not that he will change, but . . . !" He left the rest unsaid.

"You have reason for bitterness, my friend. Who in Scotland has not?" the Primate commented. "But if Scotland is to survive, *you* must survive. To be its king. You are no longer your own man, my lord. Nor even this lady's. You are Scotland's man now. And Scotland never more greatly needed a man, strong, wise, constant, patient . . ."

"God help me—I am none of these!"

"I think that you are. Or can be. *Must* be. Great things are demanded of Robert Bruce, now. But a great reward, a great heritage awaits you. In all true men's eyes you are now the only possible aspirant to the throne. You, or one of your young brothers after you. Comyn based his claim on being Baliol's nephew. Baliol, a wrong choice from the first, is now totally discredited and debarred, his name a hindrance and no aid. Moreover, Comyn, in surrendering not only himself but the whole kingdom to Edward, has forfeited any personal support. . . ."

"I also yielded, you will mind! On your advice."

"But not in the same degree. Or on the same conditions. It was Comyn's misfortune to surrender as Guardian and commander. He has thrown away any claim to the throne."

"But what can I do? The throne of Scotland! What is it? Even if I could reach it."

"It is the symbol and surety of the continuance of this ancient realm and people. Lacking it, we are nothing. Supporting it and supported by it, we are a kingdom, a community of men, small, poor perhaps, but proud, independent, masters under God of our land and destiny. It is our grievous weakness that we are so prone to disunity. To this end, if no other, we need a king, an undoubted monarch, to rule and unite us. That monarch should be, must be, Robert Bruce."

"Should be, perhaps. But what is possible? While Edward lives?" That was Elizabeth.

"Only patient waiting. Readiness. Quiet preparation. Resolution. Only these are possible meantime. And notable caution. For when Edward hears of the Lord of Annandale's death, he will the more closely watch his son. Knowing that he holds the throne which should be that son's."

"He could watch me no closer than he does!"

"He might seek to hold you in ward. A prisoner, in truth."

"Would that be any worse than what he does? Shame me? Mock me? Send me to capture Wallace . . . ?"

"Ah yes, Robert—yes!" the young woman cried. "To be held. Shut up. Lodged in a cell. Taken from me . . . !"

"It would be more grievous, friend. Assuredly. And you did not, indeed, catch Wallace. I did not think you would!"

"It was grievous enough. If Wallace had been taken, and *I* had had hand in it . . . !"

"That would have been bad. For more than Wallace. But I believe he will never be taken. Unless he is betrayed. But he has the love of the people. Could any man sell Wallace?"

"I do not know. I do not know. Even Comyn would not do that. But some lost, damned soul, eaten with gall, there might be."

"Pray that you are wrong. And pray that none betray him and bring him before *you*, as one of Edward's three governors. You have heard of this? That with Moubray and my lord of Glasgow, you are appointed to the rule. Until John of Brittany comes."

"I shall refuse to rule Edward's Scotland."

"Are you sure, Robert? Think you. It is *your* Scotland—not Edward's. You might do much to soften the worst of an English harshness. And, one day, when you are King, your people will know that you are also their friend."

"When I am King." The younger man shook his head, looking away and away.

Elizabeth came to slip her arm in his.

Chapter Eighteen

The stink of fire and stale burning still clung to the Great Hall of Stirling Castle—really the parliament-hall of the kingdom, and the most splendid apartment in Scotland—emanating from the charred timbers of the fine lofty hammerbeam roofing, set alight by Edward's own ballistas and siege-engines, with their flaming missiles, a year before. The place was draughty too, that early November afternoon, from the gaps in the masonry made by the English mangonels, trebuchets and battering rams in the long siege, and as yet inadequately patched. It was not, in fact, a suitable venue for such a meeting, and the group of a dozen or so who sat at one end of the vast table built to seat hundreds, looked somewhat lost and uncomfortable in all this decayed and battered magnificence. But John of Brittany, Earl of Richmond, King's Lieutenant of Scotland, was a stiffly formal, dignified man, an upholder of ceremonial and etiquette, markedly unlike his puissant uncle, and he insisted on holding his council-meeting herein.

The assembled councillors were uncomfortable in more than their surroundings. Added to their normal resentment at having thus to obey the summons of an alien governor, and their mutual suspicions and hostilities, but little healed by general adversity, they were more sorely divided today than usual. Wallace had been captured three weeks before; and this, the successor of the Privy Council of Scotland, was split into three over the business—those who were sadly depressed thereby, those who were not, and those who cared little for the fact of it but reserved the right to cast disapproving glances at the man whose lot it had been to deliver up the national hero to English Edward.

Sir John Stewart of Menteith was only too well aware of his unhappy position, and showed it. He sat a little way apart from all others, a young man, dark, almost swarthy, with tight secretive features and a slight, tense body. Younger son of Walter, the late Earl of Menteith, and uncle of the present young Earl, although he had fought well against the English, he had recently caught the eye of Edward and been appointed Sheriff of Dumbarton and Keeper of its great castle. It was as holder of that position that he was present at this council.

There was a diversion as an English herald threw open a door and announced the entry of the three advisers of His Majesty's Lieutenant and Governor. These were old Bishop Wishart, Sir John de Moubray and Robert Bruce—now that John of Brittany was here in person, demoted from ruling triumvirate to special advisers. Those already assembled greeted them variously, nodding or scowling according to taste.

As the newcomers moved to take their seats near the head of the vast table, John Comyn of Badenoch spoke.

"Come, come, Menteith," he called loudly. "Give place. The Earl of Carrick, friend of Wallace, will not wish to sit beside the man who gave Wallace over to the English! Even though he is such good friend to King Edward also!"

Men drew quick breaths. Comyn was the more embittered since the general surrender, and none expected his attitude to Bruce to mellow; but this casting down of the gauntlet immediately on his enemy's appearance was hardly anticipated. This was the first meeting of the newly-constituted Lieutenant's Council.

As Bruce paused on his way to his chair, Menteith jumped to his feet, flushing hotly.

"My lord of Badenoch is again Sheriff of Moray," he declared. "Had the man Wallace been found and captured in *his* sheriffdom, would he have done other than I did? As I *had* to do?"

"The question scarce arises, sir. Being a modest man, I would have seen to it that whoever gained the glory of taking this notable outlaw, it would not have been me! I would have conceived my duty to lie . . . elsewhere! At the time. Besides, my lord of Carrick would not wish to sit beside me, in any case. Nor I him!"

"My lords! My lords!" Robert Wishart's frail voice quavered. "Peace, I pray you."

But Menteith, who had been simmering in frustrated silence for too long, was determined to exculpate himself, caring nothing for the quarrel between Bruce and Comyn.

"I did neither more nor less than my duty," he cried. "Ralph de Haliburton came to me at Dumbarton. Said that he believed Wallace to be hiding at Robroyston. He demanded that I apprehend him. Declared that he had been sent by King Edward, from England, for this very purpose. In the train of this Sir John de Moubray." And Menteith pointed a finger at Bruce's and Wishart's companion.

Moubray, a kinsman of Comyn's, shrugged. "Haliburton came north with my company, yes. From Westminster. I knew naught of the business. He had been a prisoner. Had fought bravely. One of the defenders of this castle of Stirling. When it fell, he was carried captive to England. He had gained his release—how I knew not—and joined my train, to return home. That is all I knew of him."

"We know now, then, how he bought his release!" Crawford growled. "The dastard!"

"But how did *he* know?" That was James the Steward, looking now but a shadow of his former self. "Know where Wallace was? How to come to him. For years others have sought Wallace, and failed to find him. How did this man do it?"

"He had a brother in Wallace's band. He is brother to Sir Henry de Haliburton," Menteith told them. "He must have made shift to find his brother. And so found Wallace. They would not suspect him, for those one hundred and twenty, at Stirling, had held all Edward's might at bay for many months. Heroes. None would doubt one of that company."

"And you? You played this felon's game, sir? And yielded up Wallace!" Bruce said.

"What else could I do, my lord? *You* went seeking Wallace yourself one time, did you not? In duty, since you could do no other. Haliburton asked servants from me. To seek him. Then brought him to me, bound. As sheriff. How he laid hands on the man, I know not. But having him, I could not let him go. I had no choice but to hand him over to the King's Lieutenant."

"Some might have used their wits to find another course, man."

"Is this Edward's friend that speaks? Or Wallace's?" Comyn asked, grinning wickedly. "The Lieutenant's adviser!"

Bruce sought to ignore him. He sat down, even though it was beside Menteith. Lamberton came to sit at his other side. But Comyn was not to be silenced thus.

"My lord says that some might better have used their wits, to get round Edward's commands," he went on. "As, it may be, did Bruce himself when Edward asked for his siege-engines to aid batter down this Stirling!"

"Not mine. His own siege-engines," Bruce gave back. "Left in my castles of Lochmaben and Turnberry."

"But he thanked you for them, nevertheless. Most graciously, if I mind aright!"

"Aye. And for the same reason that *you* speak of the matter now! For the further dividing of this realm against itself! Let us have no doubts as to that, my lords. While blame is being laid."

There was a murmur of agreement from not a few of those present. Lamberton spoke up.

"My lord of Carrick has the rights of it. This endless fighting amongst ourselves but aids our English masters. We are here for Scotland's good, not its ill. Soon this Richmond will come. A stiff and difficult man, but honest, I think. Something lacking in wits, himself, it may be—but with cunning hard minions, as we have reason to know. De Bevercotes and de Sandale are men who will guide him towards harshness, to the hurt of this realm. It must be our task to counter them, to move this nephew of Edward to gentler, better rule. It will demand all *our* wits. All our wisdom and patience."

The Steward, and one or two others, applauded.

"What will they be wanting from us?" the Earl of Atholl asked. "What will be the main business they put before us?"

"We understand it to be the carrying out of certain provisions passed by the Westminster parliament," Bruce answered. "Certain have already been implemented. Others have not. These others, it seems, are difficult. Grievous it may be. It seems that the English require our assistance in carrying them forward. Whether we can give it remains to be decided. But some here may tell us more. Before the English come. As you know we were required to send ten Commissioners to the Westminster parliament. Under the new constitution. Four of them are here present. If they would inform us further . . ."

He was interrupted by a stamping, clanking bodyguard of English men-at-arms, and the herald announcing, in noticeably more deferential tones, the arrival of the most noble and puissant Earl of Richmond, Lieutenant of Scotland of the high and mighty King Edward of England, whom God preserve. All men to stand.

Most of the Scots made but a poor business of getting to their feet, some barely raising their posteriors from their seats.

John of Brittany paced slowly in, flanked by two richly-dressed older men, and followed by a cohort of clerks and officers. For a man only a year or two senior to Bruce himself, Richmond seemed almost elderly. Tall, thin, sombre-featured, prematurely grey, he gave a notable impression of years, gloom, disillusionment, and possibly indigestion, with little of the Plantagenet about him. With his stiff gait, balding head and down-turned mouth, he seemed as unlikely a ruler of turbulent Scotland as nephew of Edward Longshanks.

His two companions redressed the balance somewhat. Both had the hard-bitten look of experienced administrators, self-made and ruthless, although one was a plump cleric and the other a square, stocky soldier. Master William de Bevercotes was Edward's Chancellor in Scotland, and Sir John de Sandale, Chamberlain.

When these three had seated themselves, amidst much fussing of clerks and arranging of papers, Richmond looked gravely, heavily, down the ranks of his Scots councillors, scrutinising each face and seeming almost to count them as he did so. It was a slow process, and the Breton evidently in no hurry. At last he broke the uncomfortable silence.

"Seventeen," he said, almost querulously. "Seventeen. I named twenty-two for my Council."

Comyn snorted eloquently, others coughed, and Lamberton spoke.

"Yes, my lord Lieutenant. All were apprised. The Earl of Dunbar and March is still with King Edward in London. The Bishop of Moray is indisposed. The young Earl of Menteith is represented by his uncle, Sir John Stewart of Menteith. As to the others, I know not."

Richmond took his time to digest that. Almost he chewed on it, underhung jaw working—and did not look as though he liked the taste.

"Fullest attendance is required," Master Bevercotes said, thinly for such a well-fleshed man. "Obligatory."

The Scots looked at each other. Bruce spoke, evenly.

"My lord, you have here seventeen of the greatest lords in Scotland, spiritual and temporal. Enough, surely, to advise you?"

The Lieutenant eyed him thoughtfully, but did not commit himself. Then he seemed to begin a recount, just to make sure.

John Comyn was not the man to accept much of this treatment. "I have come a long and hard road to attend this Council," he said. "I move to business."

De Sandale rapped out an oath. "Insolent!" he said.

"Sir!"

"My lord Lieutenant," Lamberton intervened hurriedly. "We are very ready to lend such aid and counsel as you may require. All here are men of weight and responsibility. Four indeed have been Guardians of this realm . . ."

"This *former* realm!" Richmond corrected. He could think and speak quickly enough when he so desired, apparently.

None commented on his amendment.

"Do you desire me to proceed, my lord?" the Chancellor asked.

That required consideration also. At length, Richmond answered. "First to the matter of Wallace."

"Yes, my lord. Exactly, my lord." Bevercotes beamed approval. "The man Wallace, by all means." He shuffled his papers. "My lord Lieutenant has word this day. From His Majesty in London. The man Wallace is dead."

Consternation greeted his statement.

"Taken, examined, tried, condemned and executed. For treason. On . . . where is it? Yes—on the 23rd day of the month of October. Ten days past this day."

"Treason . . . !" Bruce got out. "Treason against whom?"

"Treason, sir, against his liege lord. And yours! King Edward of this realm."

"But . . ." A jolt to his knee beneath the table, from Lamberton, gave Bruce pause.

"May we hear more of this trial? If your lordship pleases," the Primate said.

Richmond nodded, and the Chancellor read from his paper.

"The prisoner Wallace, after being lodged within the house of one William de Leyre, alderman, in Fenchurch Street, was brought by the mayor, aldermen and magistrates of the said city of London, to trial at Westminster Hall. By order of His Majesty. Before the King's Justice, Sir Peter Mallorie. The outlaw Wallace was thereupon impeached as traitor to the King's royal person and authority, in that he did notoriously and shamefully slay the King's lieges, burn his abbeys, towns and villages, storm his castles, imprudently call parliaments in that part of the King's realm called Scotland, and set at naught the royal commands. In especial that he did slay and murder the duly appointed Sheriff of Lanark and many other officers, in particular at the King's castle of Ayr. After burning many to the death . . ."

"That was war, not treason!" Bruce protested. "The two realms were in a state of war. How could it be treason?"

"My lord of Carrick—may I remind you of my presence!" Richmond said sternly.

"The prisoner admitted all," the Chancellor read on. "He but made claim that since he had not sworn fealty to the King's name and person, he was no subject of King Edward, and so his acts were not treasonable. Justice Mallorie made observation that if only those who had sworn the oath of fealty could be guilty of treason, then most of the King's subjects could turn traitor with impunity . . ."

"My lord," Bishop Wishart broke in, frail voice cracking. "Does King Edward distinguish nothing between his English subjects and the Scots?"

"Nothing, my lord of Glasgow. As *you* should know right well. Scotland is part of the realm of England, and its people subjects of His Majesty."

"So says Edward now. But it was not so when Sir William Wallace so acted," Bruce countered. "He was in lawful arms against invaders."

"He was a rebel!" de Sandale declared harshly. "As were you all. All rebels. Worthy of death. But His Majesty was merciful. Too merciful, it seems! He took you back into his peace. But when surrender was made, Wallace refused the King's peace,

Wilfully. With war over, he remained at war. An outlaw. He had no rights, therefore. No call on mercy."

"No call on mercy!" Lamberton repeated heavily. "He was a brave man. If he should have received mercy, he did not plead for it—that I swear!"

"He received his deserts, my lord Bishop," Master Bevercotes declared primly. He consulted his papers. "Found guilty by the Court, the traitor Wallace was tied, naked and in chains, at the tails of horses, and dragged four miles through the streets of the city, to the much acclamation of the loyal populace. At Smithfield, he was part-hanged in his chains, and cut down while yet alive. Thereupon he was disembowelled, and his entrails burned before his eyes." The Chancellor moistened his lips, and raised his voice to overspeak the snarling growl which was arising round that table. "Thereafter the prisoner's head was cut from his body. Then the limbs. The said head was affixed to a pole to be set on London Bridge. And the said limbs thus distributed—the right arm sent to Newcastle-upon-the-Tyne; the left arm to Berwick-upon-the-Tweed; the right leg to St. John's Town of Perth; and the left leg to Aberdeen. By order of the King's Majesty."

The tension in that draughty hall was tight as a bow-string, as men sat, scarcely breathing. Yet John of Brittany appeared to be completely impervious to it, or unaware of it. He was rustling amongst other papers.

"Yes," he said, after an unbearable moment or two. "Thank you, Master Chancellor. That is the matter of Wallace. For your information, my lords. Now we proceed to more urgent business. I think, first, this of the failure of much of the Church in this land to pay its share of the costs of the late war. My lord of St. Andrews . . . ?"

The crash of Bruce's chair falling over backwards as he thrust it from him, rising to his feet, brought Richmond to a sudden stop.

"My lord Lieutenant," he said, thick-voiced. "I pray to be excused from further attendance at this Council."

Outraged, the other stared up at him. "My lord—do I hear you aright? Excused . . . ? Or are you taken sick . . . ?"

"Aye, sick! Well you say it. Sick at the evil that has been done. I, for one, will have no further part in working with such monstrous rule and governance. You are Edward of England's Lieutenant and representative. I can no longer act on your Council."

"Robert! My lord . . . !" Lamberton's warning, beseeching hand came up to grasp Bruce's arm—and was roughly shaken off.

"Sir—this is beyond all!" Richmond declared. "Have you lost your wits? Sit down, my lord . . ."

"No. I leave the loss of wits to you and yours! To your master and kinsman, in especial! To have turned ravening savage and brute-beast . . . !"

"Silence, sir!" De Sandale the Chamberlain was on his feet now, pointing. "To so asperse His Majesty's name! And in the presence of His Majesty's Lieutenant! How dare you . . . !"

Bruce did not so much as glance at him. "Wallace was a noble man. Not noble as we here are noble, perhaps—but nobler than any here by his deeds! A man all here should have been proud to call friend. And did not, to our shame! In him was the true spirit of this Scotland. And Edward Plantagenet dealt with him as he would not a dog!" Furiously he shouted down the protesting English. "Wallace was no traitor. How could he be? To an English king, when he fought only for the Crown of Scotland? Which Crown . . . which Crown . . ." He faltered, as well he might, even wincing at the vice-like urgency of the Primate's grip on his arm. But he went on, a little differently. "A traitor is traitor only to his country, or his friends, or to those that trust in him. Was Wallace ever traitor to his country? Was Edward ever his friend? Did Edward ever trust him? Some here might, by others, be named traitor. *I* have been! But not Wallace. And yet, he is treated worse than any murdering scullion!"

"You have run mad, my lord of Carrick!" Richmond said, as Bruce paused for breath. "What you say is stark treason."

"Mad? The madness is not mine, but Edward's. Madness indeed. Do you not see it? The folly of it, as well as the sin? The people of Scotland loved William Wallace. Better than any man who ever lived in this kingdom. As they do not love any here. Edward, by this evil, will set every heart in Scotland ablaze against him. As all his burnings and slayings and conquests have not done. They are a strong, hard people, as Edward has learned. This will turn them to steel. Against himself. Against his rule. The blood shamefully shed at your Smithfield is but the first of a flood, I tell you! It will make ill ruling of this land, my lord of Richmond, that is certain. And I—I will not aid you to do it." He made a final gesture with his hand. "I have asked your permission to withdraw, my lord. Now I go."

"Aye, go! Go, Earl of Carrick. Before I have my officers take you. As I ought. Throw you into close ward . . . !"

Bruce did not answer, being already on his way to the door,

with uncertain officers and clerks hesitating. It was John Comyn who interrupted.

"You must needs take Comyn also, then, my friend!" he said, rising. "For once, Robert Bruce has the rights of it! I never conceived this Council of worth. I will no more serve on it, now, than he. I, nor mine." He looked down at the Earl of Buchan. The Constable, puffing and grunting, rose to his feet.

Despite Richmond's protests, amidst a great scraping of chairs, the Council broke up in disorder.

Bruce found Comyn at his shoulder, in the passage outside. "I did not think it was in you to do it!" the latter said. "Edward will not like it."

"I do not do only what Edward likes."

"You do *much* that Edward likes!"

Bruce swung on the man. "You think so? Why then does Edward hate me? Tell me that, Comyn. He hates me almost as much as he hated Wallace. Why, if I do his will?"

The other looked at him searchingly. "And you? You hate Edward?"

"Aye. I hate Edward. And all that he stands for."

Lamberton was there, now. "My lord—less loud! Those words could be a rope round your neck! If another such was needed! I advise that you put distance between yourself and this Stirling. And as swiftly as you may."

"Aye—do that, Bruce." Comyn laughed. "Hide, you! And if your South will not sufficiently hide you from Edward Plantagenet, come North! Come to Badenoch! Can I offer you fairer ... ?"

• • •

But despite all the good advice, Bruce was still in Stirling town that night—and, oddly enough, at Lamberton's urging. Indeed the Primate was his sole companion as they hurried through the dark, narrow streets, heads down against the smirr of chill November rain.

Comyn was lodged in the Blackfriars' Monastery, where one of his clan was Prior. Lamberton summoned the Prior to his own door, and required a private room and the Lord of Badenoch privily informed.

Comyn came presently. Although not actually the worse for liquor, clearly he had been drinking. He stood with his back to the door of the small sparsely-furnished chamber, eyeing his visitors curiously in the mellow lamplight.

"So soon!" he commented. "Bruce takes refuge with Comyn already? From Edward's wrath!"

"We have come for a word in your private ear, my lord," the Bishop said. "Believing that you will heed. And come to some agreement with us."

That was not strictly true. Lamberton may have believed it, but Bruce was highly doubtful. He had come only at his friend's strong persuasion and almost against his own better judgement. The Primate had argued that, for the first time, Comyn had that day acted, if not in co-operation with Bruce, at least in parallel. Had even commended Bruce's step before all. Here was opportunity not to be missed, therefore.

"Agreement?" Comyn repeated. "You grow ambitious, my lords!"

"Perhaps. For Scotland. It is time, I think, that we grew ambitious for this unhappy realm. All of us. For her freedom. For her very survival."

"Scotland's? Or your own? Bruce's? Which?" The words were a little slurred, but the challenge was swift enough.

"The survival of us all. As other than slaves. Wallace's fate may be our last warning. His dying cries our final awakening. Then, at least, he will not have suffered in vain."

"Fine words, Sir Bishop. But what do they mean?"

"They mean, Comyn," Bruce interposed bluntly, "that if Scotland is to be saved, then first and foremost you and I must come to agreement. The realm cannot afford your faction fighting mine. Either we come to terms, or the Kingdom of Scotland can be forgotten. Become but a memory. And Wallace has given his life for nothing."

"Terms?" the other said. "And what are Bruce's terms? To Comyn."

"Scotland needs a king. Only an acknowledged monarch will now rally her. To take up arms against the conqueror. Baliol's arrow is shot. None will fight for him now. Not even you, I think. He does not desire the crown. I say the crown should be mine. You say otherwise . . ."

"An old story, Bruce. These terms?"

"One of us must be the King of Scots. Mine is the direct claim. Through the old line of our kings. Yours only through the discredited Baliol. But . . . I offer terms, that this impasse may be resolved. Withdraw your claim and support mine, and I will hand over to you all the Bruce lands in Scotland—save only some small properties for my brothers. Or . . ." He took a deep breath. ". . . or hand over to me all the Comyn lands, and I will stand down in your favour as King."

The other stared, moving a step or two forward from the door. "You *are* in your right mind, man?" he demanded.

"I am." Bruce jerked his head. "My lord Bishop will confirm what I say."

"That I do," Lamberton nodded. "My lord of Carrick's offer is a true one. Made on my own advising. For the sake of the realm. His the crown and yours the lands. Or yours the crown and his the lands. If the Scots people will accept you as King. Which would you?"

"But . . . this is scarce believable! To offer up the Bruce lands. The greatest in Scotland . . . !"

The other two exchanged quick glances. It was significant that it was the broad acres that Comyn thought of first, rather than the empty crown.

Swiftly the Primate took him up. "Aye, the greatest in Scotland. A notable offer, such as never has been made before. Especially since *your* claim to the throne is now weakened. This would make you a greater lord and earl than ever Scotland has known."

"And, if my claim is so weak, why make this offer?"

"Because, weak or no, there can be no true decision as to the kingdom while you hold to it. Without dividing the land. Internal strife. If we are to unite against the English, at last, one of us must stand down. So I offer all that I have to offer." That was Robert Bruce.

It was not often that John Comyn appeared at a loss. In fact never had Bruce seen him irresolute, before this night. He paced the small chamber, biting his lip. He stopped, presently.

"If this is a trick . . . !" he said.

"No trick," Lamberton assured. "In the name of Saint Andrew of Scotland. I swear it. And will do, before any company you name."

"Save that it must be kept secret," Bruce put in. "This, coming to Edward's ears, would be my death-warrant!"

Comyn looked at him, long and hard.

"Which do you choose, my lord?" Bruce challenged him.

"It . . . it would require to be written. And sealed," the other declared. "I would so require."

"So would we!" Lamberton agreed grimly. He reached inside his damp travelling-cloak and brought out a leather satchel, from which he took four folded papers, a pen, a horn of ink, and a block of wax. Also flint and tinder. "All is in readiness, my lord. Four indentures. Two promising the throne to my lord of Carrick, and his lands to you; and two the other way. Sign which you will. My lord here will sign its neighbour. And the other two we shall burn. Each will keep a copy. Secretly. Yours is the choice. For the realm's fair sake."

Only Comyn's heavy breathing sounded as he took the papers closer to the lamp, reading closely. He took an unconscionable time about it, seeming to weigh each word of all four indentures. But, at length, he laid them down on the table.

"The pen," he said.

Wordless, Lamberton handed over the quill and opened ink-horn.

John Comyn looked up into Bruce's eyes for a long moment, then stooped and dashed off his bold signature, quill spluttering. It was on one of the papers that conceded the crown to Bruce, and the Bruce lands to himself.

His rival emitted a long sigh, and picked up the pen Comyn had thrown down. Without comment he signed the companion document.

"I sign as witness to both," Lamberton declared. "Have you your seals to hand, my lords?"

And so the thing was done. As the heated wax, with the two seals impressed thereon, cooled, and the last black fragments of burned paper fluttered to the floor, the three men looked at each other.

"When do I get your lands?" Comyn asked.

"On the day I am crowned King."

"Will that day ever dawn?"

"We must see that it does. Between us."

"With the aid of Holy Church," Lamberton added.

"Why should you . . . why should *we* be able to achieve now what we could not do before?"

"Because we are fighting, in the main, one man. Edward. And Edward is not the man he was. Edward's sickness could be Scotland's saving."

"He recovered well."

"Aye. But once the heart gives such warning, no man is ever the same. The finger of God is on him," Lamberton said. "And we have heard that since he returned to London he has had another slight seizure. A sign to him. And to us. To be ready."

"It could be years, even so."

"It could be, yes. But at least we can be prepared. To move. Not to await his death. To act when Edward himself cannot lead his hosts northwards. For that day we wait." Bruce spoke urgently. "So secrecy is all-important. You will see it. I charge you, Comyn, tell no man of this night's work. If it got to Edward's ears, all would be lost. My life not worth a snap of the fingers!"

"And my lord of Badenoch's life also, I would point out!" the Bishop added, significantly. "Edward would feel little more kindly to the one than the other. Both would be taking from him the Scots crown which he usurps." He picked up the two sealed papers, assured that the wax was firm, and handed each man that with the other's signature.

Almost reluctantly now they took the fateful documents, wordless. Abruptly Comyn turned to open the door, and held it wide for his visitors.

They parted no better friends than heretofore.

Chapter Nineteen

With much trepidation, however much he tried to hide it, Robert Bruce waited amongst the gaily-dressed and glittering throng, his wife at his side. He had been against bringing her, first to England at all, and then to this Palace of Westminster. But she had insisted on both, declaring that she would not let him come without her. Not that he himself had been anxious to come; very much the reverse. But what could he do? Edward's summons, although courteous, even friendly, had been a command not a request, for the attendance of his well-loved Lord Robert at the celebration of the royal birthday, his sixty-seventh. To have refused would have been a declaration of war, premature and foolhardy; yet this acceptance was putting his head into the lion's mouth, with a vengeance. It was Elizabeth's belief that her presence with her husband could do no harm, and might possibly do good.

The pair from Scotland were interested, and to some extent encouraged, by the attitude and bearing of the courtiers who thronged around them, waiting for the royal entrance to this great reception and entertainment. All were respectful, attentive, and at least as friendly as they were ever likely to be. Which presumably meant that if Edward had sent for Bruce to rend him, he had let no hint of it escape to those close to him—for nothing was more certain than that if he had, it would have been reflected in the quality of the Bruces' reception by his Court. Not only this night but in the four days they had been in London. That the King had not sent for them for personal audience during that time, admittedly could be interpreted either way; but at least it implied that the Plantagenet was not in any fury of haste to explode his anger on them. Edward was unpredictable, of course.

The new Gloucester, Ralph de Monthermer, who had succeeded Bruce's late cousin Gilbert de Clare, as husband to King Edward's daughter—and bore the title by courtesy while the child was a minor—stood beside them with his somewhat horse-faced countess. Gloucester gave no impression of wrath to come. A friendly, modest man, he could not keep his eyes off Elizabeth—who was tonight looking at her loveliest.

"The King's health?" Bruce asked—by no means the first such enquiry he had made since coming south. He hoped always to hear some inkling, some clue as to the true condition of the royal heart.

"Eh? Ah, yes. The King." With difficulty Ralph of Gloucester partially withdrew from contemplation of more pleasing subjects. "His health, yes. It is improved. Indubitably much improved."

"Excellent," Bruce commented heavily. "After that last small seizure. In the autumn, was it? Nothing more?"

"Nothing. He is himself again. For which God be praised. For Edward of Carnarvon is little fit for the throne. Not yet."

"He lacks his father's fire, yes."

"More than that. He chooses ill friends. Prefers the company of singers, mummers and mimers, players. Priests of the baser sort. He does not play the man."

"I would have thought that England might have had enough of warrior kings!"

"We would esteem a few years of peace, yes. But now that Scotland is subdued; Wales and Ireland also; and we are in treaty with France and the Pope, peace there is. It must be preserved, you will agree, Cousin. And a weak king, you must admit, is a sure road to war and rebellion."

"Edward has never been a man of peace. Think you he will be content with peace now? Or is this sickness like to affect him? Prevent him from leading more campaigns? In person?"

"Who knows? Queen Margaret will keep him from that. If she may . . ."

A fanfare cut short this exchange. Everyone bowed as a herald announced the resounding titles of Edward, by God's grace King of England, Lord of Scotland, Ireland and Wales, Duke of Normandy and Aquitaine.

It was not only the reference to Scotland which made Bruce's brow darken as he bowed with the rest, but the manner of the King's arrival. He positively swept into the great chamber, no more like an ailing man than Bruce was, smiling, jovial, dragging his pregnant wife along by the hand, high-coloured and heavy but as full of energy as of goodwill. It was a sore disappointment.

But disappointment was quickly overlaid by a more urgent emotion—apprehension. The royal summons to Bruce had been for no mere social celebration—that was not in Edward's character. Richmond, or more likely Bevercotes, would have sent a full account of the proceedings at Stirling in November last. There had been no repercussions in the meantime. Bruce had been left alone to manage his own affairs, on his estates, and had taken no further part in the rule of Scotland. Now he must look for a reckoning. Elizabeth came close, and slipped her hand within his arm.

To the soft strains of the musicians, the King made unhurried progress towards the twin thrones at the head of the hall, having a gracious word with lords and ladies in passing. Quite quickly Queen Margaret espied Elizabeth, and began to draw her husband towards her former favourite lady-in-waiting.

"A good sign," Elizabeth murmured. "The Queen at least suspects no clash, I think."

"Edward may not have revealed his mind. Even to her. He is a law unto himself."

The King did not allow his consort to hurry him unduly, certainly. The royal progress was agonisingly slow for the pair from Scotland.

At last the two couples were face to face, with the Queen reaching out to embrace the curtsying Elizabeth, and Bruce bowing again.

"Ha, Robert—do I see you well?" Edward demanded genially. "I vow I can scarce discern you, so dazzled are my old eyes by your lady's beauty!" And he in turn bowed gallantly.

"I am well, Sire, yes. And you?"

"Never better, lad. Never better. You will rejoice to hear!" And the older man eyed him directly.

Bruce swallowed. "All Your Majesty's subjects must rejoice at that," he said.

"They should, lad—they should!" Edward agreed. "As you will see, my wife has no reason to complain of my . . . inadequacy!—Yours has less to thank you for, by the looks of her!"

The other inclined his head slightly. "There is time and to spare, I hope."

Edward's smile faded for a moment. "Who knows!" he gave back, shortly. He turned to Elizabeth. "My dear, you gladden as well as dazzle our eyes," he said. "We have missed you."

"Ah, yes," the Queen agreed. "So much. So very much. There is none like my Elizabeth."

"Your Majesties are too kind."

"This lord of yours," the King said. "He tells me that he is well. Yet he has been hiding himself away. In Annandale and Galloway, I am told. Neglecting the rule of my Scotland."

"There has been much to do, Sire, in the Bruce lands. Much to put to rights. After these past years. And you have servants in plenty to rule Scotland," Elizabeth pointed out.

"None so many when my Scots lords withdraw their aid and duty!"

"My lord of Richmond is well able to govern Scotland, Sire," Bruce claimed. "He has . . ."

"My lord of Richmond is a fool! But I am not, Robert—I am not!"

"Yet Richmond's troubles in Scotland stem from the slaying of Wallace here in London. And the manner of the slaying," Bruce said, through tight lips.

"To be sure. Your notions on Wallace were reported to me!" That was coldly enunciated. "Do you wish to add to them now?"

"No, Sire. That would be to no purpose. I but remark that your nephew's present difficulties arise from the people's anger at Wallace's cruel death."

"And you will not aid him in those difficulties? At my command?"

"Your Majesty's command I must obey," the younger man said woodenly. "If my lord of Richmond seeks my aid, in your name, then I must needs give it."

"I am glad that you perceive that fact, Robert."

"Edward—my legs!" the Queen broke in. "I am weary of standing. With this great belly of mine! Let us sit, of a mercy!"

"To be sure, my love. Come. Elizabeth—you also." He glanced back at Bruce. "We shall talk of this later, my lord." With curt dismissal, the King moved on.

Elizabeth looked unhappily at her husband, but could not refuse to obey the royal command, especially when the Queen's hand was on her arm. Bruce was left standing alone.

And he remained alone. For now the watchful courtiers, practised in discerning favour and disfavour, perceived the difference of treatment as between man and wife, and shunned him. Even Gloucester, though he did not ignore him entirely, tended to keep his distance.

A programme of music, dancing, miming, tumbling and the like followed, during all of which the Scot remained isolated, separated from Elizabeth and avoided by almost all the company. Too proud to approach those who looked away, Bruce fumed what seemed endless hours away in ill-suppressed rage. He could not take himself off, as he would have wished, and leave Elizabeth behind; moreover, Edward had cunningly said that they would talk more later—which was as good as a command to stay.

Once, while meats and drink were being brought in by a host of servants, Elizabeth did manage to slip away, temporarily, from the Queen's side, for a word with her husband.

"I am sorry, my heart," she murmured. "This is hard to bear. But . . . it is perhaps less ill than might have been. The King is teaching you one of his lessons."

"And I must needs stand here and suffer it! Before all. Like a corrected child! I cannot come up to you, at the thrones, without being invited. I cannot leave. And all these know I am now frowned on, and frown in turn . . ."

"I grieve for you. But we did fear worse, Robert. After what you said and did at Stirling. At least this chastening hurts only your pride. And he cannot intend more dire punishment, or he would not act thus. With the hour growing late . . ."

"With Edward, who can tell? The devil could be hatching greater evil!"

"Not at this hour. Not tonight. And the Queen grows very weary. The child is heavy in her. She will soon seek to retire. Then we should see an end to this . . ."

The Queen's weariness, however, took a long time to affect her husband's enjoyment of the evening. And when Edward did finally rise, to escort her out, amidst genuflection from all present, he in fact led her down the opposite side of the room from Bruce's position, and without a glance thitherward. The younger man did not know whether to be relieved or further infuriated—although Elizabeth, released and rejoining him, was in no doubts.

They were too soon in debating the issue. A court official came hurrying back through the throng to the Bruces.

"My lord, His Majesty requires your attendance. At once. Follow me," he said briefly.

Exchanging glances, they moved after him, though without haste.

The King was talking to Gloucester just outside in the vestibule, the Queen looking very pale and near to tears. He broke off.

"My lord," he said, as the Bruces came up, unsmiling now, "I had intended to speak you further. On another matter of grave import. But Her Majesty is fatigued. The matter must keep. But not for long. You will attend on me, at my privy quarters in this house, tomorrow. At noon. You understand?"

"At noon. Yes, Sire. As you command."

"Aye, as I command. And see you, my friend—come well versed in explanation! As to your . . . ambitions! You may have a queen for sister, Robert—but that is as near the royal estate as you will ever win! Noon, tomorrow. Come, my dear."

Monarchy moved off.

Eyeing the Plantagenet's massive back, Bruce murmured, set-faced. "So now we come to it! Tomorrow noon I will hear the real reason for my summons to London!"

• • •

Back at their lodging they were still discussing the King's intentions, fearing that he might have heard some rumour of the bond with Comyn, when knocking sounded at the street door. Elizabeth's alarm was immediate, and out of character; but Bruce pointed out that the knocking was discreet rather than peremptory. He had lived long enough on the edge of danger to sense the difference.

One of his servants brought in a cloaked figure wearing no insignia, colours or livery. This man waited silent until the servitor had gone. Then, assuring himself that nobody listened outside the door, he brought out from beneath his cloak a pair of spurs. In the other hand he held out a silver shilling.

"From my lord of Gloucester," he said quietly, cryptically.

Bruce looked from the man to Elizabeth. "Aye," he said heavily. He took both the spurs and the coin.

The visitor reached out, wordless, and turned over the shilling, so that the likeness of King Edward's head was uppermost.

Bruce nodded. "I perceive the message," he said. "You will

thank your lord. Here—take this." He handed him back the silver coin.

"I thank *you*, my lord." The man bowed briefly to the wide-eyed Elizabeth, and turned away.

"My friend," Bruce said to his back, "I do not wish further to endanger you. But, as a citizen of this London, can you tell me if all the city gates are kept locked of a night?"

"All," the other nodded. "But I have heard it said that the watch will open any, if commanded in the King's name."

"I see. For this also I thank you."

Without another word the visitor departed.

Two hours later the small Bruce party, of no more than a dozen men-at-arms and servitors, with Elizabeth muffled and cloaked to look like a youthful page, rode quietly through the narrow sleeping streets of the February night, to Eastgate. At the walls and gatehouse there Bruce reluctantly, and with a deal more confidence of voice than he felt, shouted authoritatively.

"Watch! Watch, I say! Waken, fools! Dolts—awake! Open, in the King's name."

There was some small delay, nerve-racking but inevitable. No argument, however, or enquiry. Bruce's imperious second demand, with some realistic cursing, was followed by the rattle of chains and the creaking of the great double doors, as they swung wide.

The Scots clattered through the cobbled pend, and took the dark Essex road beyond, and heard the gates clang to behind.

A mile or so on, they turned due north, something under four hundred miles of hard riding before them. It was nearly 3 a.m. They could probably reckon on a start of anything from five to nine hours. As well that Elizabeth was strong and an excellent horse-woman.

• • •

It was a desperately tired and bedraggled company—though three short, two servants and a man-at-arms having fallen out—which, four days and three nights later avoiding Carlisle, crossed the Border near Kirkandrews. Whether they had been pursued they did not know. After fording the Esk, they came within a mile or so to the lesser Glenzier Water, which they must also cross before turning westwards through the low green hills for Annandale.

It was as they were approaching this second ford that they perceived two horsemen already splashing across, but from the other direction. There was little for comment in this, perhaps—save that anyone taking this route could only be making to cross the Border, and by the inconspicuous road that avoided the English garrison-town of Carlisle. But Bruce, however weary, may have been hypersensitive to certain colours. He reined up, pointing.

"Do my eyes deceive me, or are those men wearing the Comyn colours of blue and gold?" he demanded.

Elizabeth narrowed heavy, red-rimmed eyes. "Yes," she nodded. "Blue and gold. Is it of any matter?"

"They are a long way from home, for Comyns. And heading south."

"John Comyn has lands in Dumfriesshire, has he not? And Galloway?"

"Yes. But these are riding away from them. For England. And avoiding Carlisle. As we have done. Why?" With a toss of his shoulders, he seemed to shake off his fatigue. "Come."

He reined his all-but foundered horse around—the fourth he had ridden since leaving London—and led his silently protesting party back the way they had come for a little distance, to a thicket of scrub oak and thorn in a marshy hollow, which they had passed through a minute or two before. Into this he turned his people, right and left, to hide amongst the trees.

The two horsemen appeared presently, trotting unconcernedly. One was young, well-dressed, an esquire presumably; the other a bearded man-at-arms riding slightly behind. Bruce allowed them to come nearly up to his hiding-place, then spurred forward into their path.

"Wait you, friend," he called. "One moment. How come you to ride this road to England, this day?"

The young man had drawn up, startled, hand dropping to sword-hilt. Behind, the soldier was quicker, his whinger whipped out with a scrape of metal. Looking round, the former was in time to see four of Bruce's own men-at-arms emerging from the thickets at the other side of the road.

"What is this, sirrah?" he demanded hotly. "How dare you!"

"I but asked your business, sir. The Border is but a mile away, and no place between. It concerns me who crosses that Border."

"Why should it? I am on lord's business. A great lord, Comyn, Lord of Badenoch's business. Do you dare, sir, to question?"

"I do," Bruce answered, mildly enough. "And with cause. For I am Sheriff of Dumfries. And was Scots Warden of this March . . . when Scots wardens meant anything."

"Sheriff . . . !" the other repeated falteringly. He looked round again, and saw that he and his man were now quite surrounded. "Who are you, sir?"

"The name is Bruce. You may have heard of it? You are a long way from Comyn country, friend."

"Bruce? The . . . the earl!"

"The same. You do not look, friend, as though you had ridden from Badenoch and the Spey?"

"No, my lord. Only from Dalswinton. From my lord's house near to Dumfries . . ."

"Comyn is there? At Dalswinton?"

"Yes. The Justiciary Court meets this week at Dumfries. My lord attends."

"And you? Your business, sir?"

"My lord's business. Not mine. Nor yours, my lord!"

"Mine, yes. If you are for crossing this Border. And on this road you can be going nowhere other. But . . . see you, your lord and I are in bond to each other. You have naught to fear."

The other was silent.

"I am waiting, sir. And tired! Your business in England?"

"I am not at liberty to tell, my lord."

"You will not long be at liberty to refuse!" Bruce commented grimly. "Do you carry letters?"

Nibbling his lip, the younger man shook his head.

"I think that you do. Tell me who they are for, and if you know their purpose. If you do, I may not require to do more than look at the superscription and seal."

"I will not, cannot, do it."

"Fool! Who knows, the letter may be for me! I have been in England. Comyn could well be writing to me. A warning, perhaps."

"The letter is not for you, Earl of Carrick."

"Then, a God's name, who is it? You have admitted you have a letter. As Sheriff of this shire I require you to let me see."

The unhappy courier shook his head stubbornly. Bruce jerked a brief command to his men. They kneed their mounts close. One drew sword, to point at the esquire's throat. Two pinioned each an arm. Two more engaged the guard behind, who only put up token resistance. A sixth reached out to fumble in the victim's bulging saddle-bags.

It took a little while, amidst some shouting and protest, for the horses sidled and pranced. But at length this last man brought out a sealed paper package. He handed it over to Bruce.

Apart from the seal, which showed the Comyn arms of three golden wheatsheafs on a blue ground, the package was entirely plain, without superscription. Unhesitantly Bruce opened it. Inside was another sealed package. But this one had a superscription. It read:

TO HIS HIENES EDWARD KING OF INGLAND, AT WESTMINSTER

"Ha!" Bruce leaned over, to show this to Elizabeth. "See where John Comyn's letter goes!" He swung back to the courier. "You knew this. You were taking this to King Edward, in London. You must have known. But—do you know what is in it?"

White-faced now, the other shook his head.

"Tell me. Or I shall open it."

"I do not know. My lord said that it was most secret. That . . . that I guard it with my life!" The young man's voice broke.

"Aye." With a swift gesture Bruce broke open the second seal, and unfolded the stiff paper.

The inner side was written upon. But enclosed in it was another folded paper. And this bore another seal. But not Comyn's. This was Bruce's own. With his signature likewise. Witnessed by William Lamberton.

"Christ . . . in . . . His . . . heaven!" he whispered.

"Robert! What is it?"

"What is it?" he got out, thickly. "It is death! It is my neck! My head—sent to Edward! For execution! By the living God—our bond! I did not believe . . . that any man . . . could sink so low! My death-warrant. And Lamberton's. Here is infamy beyond all telling!"

She reached over and took Comyn's copy of the crown-and-lands agreement, which Bruce had signed that November night in the Blackfriars Monastery at Stirling.

With fingers that trembled now with emotion her husband smoothed out the folds of the enclosing letter. It was notably brief:

Hienes,

Since you require proof of the matter wch I wrote to you before. Here is proof. I desire to receive it back by bearer. Also that yr Hienes seems not to have seen it. For it is mch value and dangerous. Bruce has the other like, wth my name and seal. If yr Hienes takes him you will win it for yr proof and purpose.

I remain yr Hienes servant,

JNO COMYN OF BADENOCH

"The forsworn dastard! For this John Comyn shall die! I swear it, by all the saints!"

Anxiously, Elizabeth looked at her husband. She had never seen him like this, so black of brow, so savage of expression.

"It is vile treachery, yes. Thank God that we won out of London when we did! This was what Edward was meaning. He knew of this, all the time."

"Aye. Comyn had written him, betraying all. Edward demanded proof. For my trial! Had we not bolted when we did, I would never have left London alive. Gloucester saved my head!"

"What will you do, Robert? Now?"

"Do? I will do what needs to be done. What I should have done long since. Make a reckoning with John Comyn! I will . . ." He paused, looking at the anxious courier. "Here is not the time and place to talk of that. Nor are these two the men to hear it. They must remain silenced. Close warded. Until the matter is resolved. We will take them with us, to Lochmaben."

"My lord—here is no fault of mine . . ." the esquire faltered.

"None. Save to own a dastard lord! You will suffer nothing, so long as you cause no further trouble. Do as you are bidden. But I cannot let you go free, until I have come to a conclusion with your master. That is certain."

They rode on northwards for Lochmaben, and the shadow of evil was like a threatening cloud about them.

Chapter Twenty

The red-stone town of Dumfries was busy that frosty February morning, with Edward's English justices in session at the castle, and half the lords and lairds of the South-West summoned to be present, either to speak to complaints, seek redress, support charged feudal vassals, or give account for their heritable jurisdictions. Soldiers and men-at-arms were everywhere, English and Scots. The citizenry, well aware of the potential explosiveness of this mixture, tended to keep indoors and out of sight.

Bruce had been heedful about the numbers of his own men he brought into town from Lochmaben. Too many would arouse comment, might seem like a challenge, and provoke trouble with the English. On the other hand, that he might well require a substantial force of men went without saying. On the principle that a great lord was entitled, in most circumstances, to a train of from fifty to a hundred, just to maintain his dignity, he had brought about seventy-five selected horsemen. But, as well, he had arranged that certain of his more important local vassals and supporters should make independent entry to the town, with their own smaller followings. With these, he reckoned that he could call upon a couple of hundred men, at short notice, if the need arose.

His information that Comyn would be in town today was quickly confirmed. He learned that his enemy, who was much involved in this bout of litigation, had installed himself at the small monastery of the Franciscan or Grey Friars, founded by the Lady Devorgilla, Baliol's mother, in the Castle Wynd, conveniently close to the castle itself. Here Bruce sought him—to learn that his quarry was at present attending the court nearby, but would be back. Bruce declared grimly that he would wait.

He had with him his brothers Nigel and Thomas, and his new brother-in-law Sir Christopher Seton, whom Christian of Mar had recently married. As Bruce anticipated, the news that he was back in Scotland and in fact here in Dumfries, very speedily was conveyed to Comyn in the castle, who promptly found his business there insufficiently vital to detain him from coming to verify the matter.

With a party of relatives and supporters he arrived at the monastery, and even though warned, the sight of Bruce sitting waiting for him before the fire of the refectory undoubtedly perturbed him. He stared.

"I had not looked to see you, my lord. Back. Here in Scotland," he jerked. "So soon."

"No? I warrant you did not! But I am here. Safe and in order." Bruce's voice may have sounded steady enough, but only iron control hid the quivering tension that had been part of the man since the fact of Comyn's treachery had struck him four days before.

"You come from London? From Edward?"

"From Edward, yes. That surprises you?"

"Only that you are not long gone. To return so soon . . ." Comyn shrugged. "You saw the King? Spoke with him?"

"I did."

The other obviously was nonplussed. "He treated you . . . kindly?"

"Not kindly, no. Edward is seldom kind to Scots."

"Did he speak . . . of me?"

"What he said is for your privy ear, my lord."

"Ah, yes. To be sure." Comyn looked around him at all the interested throng of his own supporters and Bruce's, filling the small refectory. He beckoned to the Prior, who fussed about, in a flutter with all this splendid company. "Where may I speak alone with my lord of Carrick?" he demanded.

"My poor house is full, my good lord. With all this of the assize. I can clear a chamber for your lordships, if you will. But . . . if you would but talk together, for a short time, the chapel is nigh. And empty."

"The chapel, yes. That will serve. Take us there."

The Prior led them out of a side-door and down a cloister-walk. At a short distance behind them Bruce's brothers and Sir Christopher Seton followed on, as did Comyn's uncle, Sir Robert, and his kinsman Master William.

Their guide opened another door at the end of the cloister, which proved to be the vestry entrance to the little church, leading directly into the choir.

Gesturing to the others to stay at the door, Comyn beckoned Bruce forward to just before the altar itself. "We may speak safely here," he said.

"A strange place for what falls to pass between you and me!" the other commented.

"As well as another. What have you to tell me, Bruce?"

"Sufficient to prove you a viler scoundrel than I knew defiled the face of this Scotland!"

"Christ God! You dare to speak so!"

"Aye, and more! And speak with good cause. Dastard! Judas!"

Comyn's hand dropped to the jewelled hilt of his dirk. "You will unsay that, Bruce!" he whispered. "No man speaks so to John Comyn, and lives!"

"Unsay it? I will prove it!"

The other's dagger was half-out of its sheath before he realised that Bruce's hand was reaching into a pocket, not for his own dirk.

"What say you to this?" Bruce held out his signed bond, and the enclosing letter to Edward.

Comyn's swiftly indrawn breath was as eloquent as any words. He stared at the out-thrust offering.

"I am waiting?"

His opponent moistened his lips. "Where . . . did you . . . get that?" he got out.

"What matters it? Since I have it now."

"I have been betrayed, then..."

"Betrayed! *You* to speak of betrayal! You, who made this compact with me. To be your King! And then betrayed me to Edward—to a certain death! Lamberton also—since he signed witness."

"Faugh! To betray traitors is no fault!"

"Traitors! You name me traitor? Is it possible . . . that this forsworn wretch . . . should so name Bruce?" And his hand rose, to point a quivering finger at the other.

Swift as thought Comyn smashed down the accusing hand with his own clenched fist—his left, since his right was still clutching the dagger-haft.

"Aye—traitor, as I have ever known you! Sold to Edward, always. Sold, for his favour. And his Ulsterwoman, de Burgh...!"

Whether at the snarling mention of Elizabeth's name, or at the physical blow to his arm, the second such that Comyn had struck him, something snapped in Bruce's overwrought brain as surely as a breaking bowstring, releasing a scalding red tide which rose swiftly to engulf him. The tingling downstruck hand went straight to his dagger. Scarcely knowing what he did, certainly not hearing the cries from the doorway, he whipped out the weapon and, beating aside the still upraised hand that had struck him, drove the steel deep into John Comyn's breast.

With a choking, bubbling groan, the other collapsed sideways against the altar, handsome features contorted, limbs writhing, and slid to the stone floor.

Dazed, unseeing, Robert Bruce stood, panting for breath.

The horrified shouting of the watchers by the door changed to action. Sir Robert Comyn, nearest, came running forward, drawing his sword. Nigel Bruce sprang after him, but the two clerics threw themselves in his way; while young Thomas stood appalled, paralysed. Not so Seton. A veteran soldier, he knocked Master William to the ground with a single blow, and leaping over him, raced after Sir Robert.

Comyn's uncle, cursing in fury, rushed on Bruce, who stood unmoving, as though stunned by what he had done. He did not attempt to parry or even dodge the blow which the older man aimed at him.

The other's sword-thrust was rageful rather than shrewd. And Bruce, unlike his fallen enemy, had anticipated that this might be a day in which armour would be a wise precaution, and was clad in a jerkin of light chain-mail. The slashing angry swipe drove him staggering backwards against the altar, in turn, but the steel did not penetrate the mail.

With a great roar, Seton hurled himself upon Sir Robert, his own blade high. Down it crashed, not in any wild swiping but in sheerest expert killing, on the unprotected neck of the older man. Head all but severed by that one stroke, Robert Comyn fell, spouting fountains of blood, over the body of his nephew.

Nigel came running to his brother now. "Robert!" he cried. "You are hurt? Stricken? Curse him! Robert speak! God's mercy—are you sore hurt?"

Bruce did not answer, did not so much as shake his head.

"Rob—answer me!" Nigel was running over his brother's steel-girt torso with urgent hands.

"He is but dazed, man," Seton panted. "His harness would save him . . ."

"Quick!" Thomas Bruce exclaimed, hurrying to them, and pointing backwards. "They have gone. The churchmen. To tell the others. The Comyns. They will be back. Seeking blood! Let us away from here."

"Aye," Seton agreed grimly. "That is sense, at least. Come. Take his arm. An arm each. He will be well enough. The other door. To the street. Haste you!"

So, without a glance at the fallen Comyns, a brother supporting him on either side, the silent, glazed-eyed Bruce was led, hustled indeed, down the nave to the little church's main door, Sir Christopher striding ahead, reddened sword still in his hand.

They emerged into the cold, frost-gleaming Castle Wynd. The alleys and entries of the climbing street were filled with chilled, waiting Bruce supporters. Nigel yelled for horses.

Men came starting out, at sight of their lord's party and the bloody sword. Shouts filled the crisp air.

Two knights came running, drawing their own swords—Sir Roger Kirkpatrick of Closeburn, nearby, and Sir John Lindsay, a kinsman of Crawford's. Nigel was still demanding horses, but Kirkpatrick came right up to his feudal master.

"What's to do?" he demanded. "My lord—are you hurt? What is this?"

Bruce shook his head.

"Get our men assembled," Seton cried. "There will be trouble."

"They are near. On the green. And on the castle hill. And

behind yonder church. A trumpet blast will summon them. But . . . what's to do? That blood? Whose is it?" Kirkpatrick, a big, rough, fierce man, was not to be put off.

At last Bruce spoke. "I doubt . . . I have slain . . . the Comyn," he said, slowly, distinctly.

"God's eyes! Comyn? Himself? Where?"

"God pity me—at the altar. In the church." That came out as a groan.

"In the church? Praises be—where better? For that snake! And you doubt it? Doubt he's slain? Then, by the Mass—I'll make sure of it!" Kirkpatrick thrust past them, on the word, and into the church doorway, followed by Sir John Lindsay, Sir Robert Fleming and a few other men.

"Watch you!" Nigel shouted after them. "They will be there. The rest of them. By now. Take heed, man!"

Neither Kirkpatrick nor any of the others so much as looked back.

Rapping out an oath, Seton turned and hurried after them.

Whether with the cold, or just the passage of time, Bruce's trance-like shock was beginning to wear off. He was still shaken and not himself, but he became increasingly aware at least of the dangers inherent in the situation. He shook off his brothers' hands.

"My trumpeter," he jerked. "Get him. Quickly. To me. Up at the castle-yard. You, Tom. Nigel—gather some men. Find and take the Comyn horses. Away with them. Then join me up at the castle. See to it."

"You are well enough . . .?"

"Yes. Go. Quickly. There is no time to lose."

Left alone for the moment, Bruce stared bleakly, unseeing, before him. Then he looked down at his hand. It was splashed with blood. Hastily he sought to wipe it away, his breath catching. Then he desisted. No amount of rubbing would wipe away this day's work. He might as well accept that. The deed was done, and there could be no turning back. What lay ahead he could not tell—save that nothing would ever be the same again for him. He had slain a man. Not in honest battle, but in blind anger. Committed murder. Done the unforgivable thing. Taken another man's life with his own hand. And in God's house, before His very altar. The unholy upon the unforgivable . . .

Even that was not all. He had murdered the most powerful man in Scotland. With a following great enough to turn the land upside-down. Moreover he was completely lost with King Edward. Nothing could repair that break now. Suddenly all his ropes were cut. He was a bark adrift in a rising storm.

Or not quite adrift, perhaps. Alone, yes. For ever alone now. Anchors and warps gone. Sore beset. But still he had a rudder. And a purpose. Made simpler now. Wholly simplified indeed, since it was now all or nothing. There was nothing left to him now but to fight. Fight to the death. Fight to win, or to lose. No alternative course, any more.

To the fight, then! With a new enemy to face, instead of John Comyn. His own conscience.

He set off, heavy-strided, up the cobbled climbing street.

• • •

The shrilling trumpet brought men streaming up on to the grassy hillock on which Dumfries Castle was built—no major fortress this but rather an administrative centre in a provincial walled town. All sorts of men came to that imperious summons, by no means all Bruce levies; many were, if not neutral, at least little involved, some were Comyn supporters, and not a few were English men-at-arms. But Bruce's people were there as a disciplined body, under the personal command of their lord. Moreover they all were mounted. They displayed all the difference between men of purpose and authority, and mere onlookers.

Nigel was one of the last to join his brother on the seething castle hill, where an air of strange and heady excitement prevailed, with rumours flying thick and fast.

"The Comyn horses are driven off," he reported. "The leaders' beasts, that is. And many others. Little trouble."

"Yes. And Christopher? Kirkpatrick?"

"I have not seen them. Do you think . . .?"

"I think if any can look to themselves, these can."

"What do you do now?"

"Take Dumfries. I have no choice."

"What . . .?" Astounded, Nigel stared at him.

"I have crossed my river, now," his brother said evenly, almost sternly. "There is no turning back. I can only go forward. Whatever the cost. But that is for myself. You—you need not go where I go. You, or any. For it will be a sore road. There is time, still, to turn back. For you. If you will."

Nigel looked across at his younger brother, brows raised. "You are not wandering? In the head? That blow . . ."

"Look," Thomas pointed. "Christopher. And the others."

Seton, Kirkpatrick and Lindsay, with some small following, were hastening up the rise towards them. They had the look of victorious men. Others made way for them automatically.

"Well?" Bruce, the new Bruce, barked the single word.

"You were right, my lord," Kirkpatrick shouted back, grinning. "A botched blow! He was still alive. I finished your work. The Red Comyn is dead. And others with him. Not a few! And this world the sweeter!"

A long shuddering sigh broke from the listening crowd.

Bruce looked at the newcomers long and levelly. Then he spoke, tonelessly. "Very well. I thank you for completing my work." He took a deep breath, and turned. "And now, there is more work to do, my friends. Much more. This castle, for a start." He pointed upwards, to where the Leopards of England flew above the highest tower. "That banner. I'll have it down, see you."

There was a corporate gasp from the company, a gasp that developed and changed into a rumbling roar as men perceived something of the significance of this declaration. Englishmen in the crowd began suddenly to look alarmed.

There were a number of men-at-arms at the castle gateway, but these were a ceremonial guard for the justices rather than any sort of garrison. Already, from the sitting in the hall, the chief magistrate, Sir John Kingston, had sent officers to enquire the reason for the trumpeting and noise outside, and to demand respectful quiet. As Bruce led his mounted cohort directly for the gateway, these turned and hurried away.

If the captain of the guard-house was of heroic stuff he wisely decided, in the face of a force ten times the size of his own, that this was not the occasion to demonstrate it. He and his men exchanged eloquent glances and promptly took themselves off after the officers.

There was no moat and drawbridge here, and Bruce led his men through the gatehouse pend and into the courtyard, without hindrance. There he halted, sitting his horse, while he gave his lieutenants orders to secure all gates and strongpoints, to man the parapets, and to bring him that banner. To Nigel he gave special instructions.

"My compliments to King Edward's justices," he said, "Inform them that their duties here are now over. And that I will provide them with safe-conduct over the Border. Forthwith."

His brother laughed aloud, and without dismounting, he or his men, rode indoors.

Soon he was back. "They have locked themselves into the hall," he reported. "I shouted your commands. But they said they will have no dealings with rebels. And that you are to disperse your force at once. Or all will be arraigned for treason."

"For judges, they much lack judgement!" Bruce declared grimly. "Have woodwork chopped down. And brushwood from outside. Those whins on the braeside will burn well. Pile all against doors and windows, and set alight. See how they judge *that*!"

Nigel's chuckling was stilled by the steely expression on his brother's face. He hurried off to do as he was told.

A warning shout from high above was followed by a muffled clatter that set Bruce's horse sidling. The Leopard standard of Plantagenet, wrapped round an English guard's helmet, and cast down from the parapet aloft, lay there on the flagstones.

A hoarse cheer rose from all who saw. Bruce had the thing handed up to him.

It was not long before, without the incendiaries waiting for brushwood, smoke was billowing along the corridors and vaulted passages of Dumfries Castle. And swiftly if belatedly the judicial qualities of those within asserted themselves. A messenger emerged from the smoke-enshrouded hall to request passage for His Majesty's judges.

Bruce ordered the pile of burning woodwork at the main hall-door to be cleared a little to one side—but only a little. The justices, clerks, officers, litigants, prisoners and soldiers alike, in consequence, had to hop and skip nimbly through as they emerged.

Sir John Kingston would have made suitable and dignified protest, out in the courtyard, but Bruce curtly cut him short.

"Enough, sir. Spare us this. We in Scotland have seen enough of English justice. More than enough to have any respect for its practitioners. Have you forgot the justice Sir William Wallace received?"

The angry growling from the onlookers was enough to convince Sir John that the moment was inopportune.

"You will be escorted to the Border, at Carlisle. You will be roped together, until then." And when shocked heads were raised, Bruce added, "And you may praise God that the ropes are not used to hang you!"

Without further exchange, Edward's representatives were

marched off, under guard, the summons-bell rope of the castle, used symbolically, a loop round each neck, to link them together. The roar of derision and unholy joy from the waiting throng outside, as these feared and hated dignitaries passed out from the gatehouse, could have been heard all over Dumfries.

So was struck the first blow of the second War of Independence suddenly, without warning, almost by accident.

When Bruce himself rode out from the castle, it was to find the crowd vastly increased, the citizenry now obviously present in large numbers. Bruce's appearance was greeted with loud and prolonged cheering. If there were not a few nominal Comyn vassals and supporters there, they did not proclaim the fact. Confused and leaderless, yet caught up in the vital sense of occasion and excitement, for the moment they went with the tide.

With his people marshalled into a great semi-circle behind him, Bruce faced the throng, and had his trumpeter blow for silence.

He spoke slowly, almost broodingly, with nothing of triumph and drama, however dramatic might be his actual words. "My friends—this day, the tenth of February, of our Lord the thirteenth hundred and sixth year, we commence to cleanse our land. We have commenced here at Dumfries. Sir John Comyn, Lord of Badenoch, turned traitor and is dead."

There was an uneasy stirring amongst the crowd, but no outcry.

"Cleansed, yes," Bruce went on steadily. "We have also cleansed this castle. The English are gone from it, with scarce a blow struck." He picked up the Leopard standard from his saddlebow, and shook out its handsome folds. "Here is the usurper's banner, from the tower." He crumpled it up in his fist, and tossed it to the ground, contemptuously. "It will serve for a shroud for Comyn. He has well earned it!"

There was reaction now, but no shouting, no clamour. Something in the manner, voice and expression of the young man who sat his horse and spoke so sombrely, precluded that. Men whispered, shuffled, stared at each other. And waited.

Bruce held up his hand. "This castle is but the first of many which we must take and cleanse. Till all the land is cleared. And that will take long. Long. Let none doubt it. Edward of England will come for his banner—nothing more sure. We shall have to fight. Fight as we have never fought before. But not for so long, I think. For Edward is grown old. And sick. This is in our favour." He paused, and looked round. "Sir Roger Kirkpatrick, you will be captain of this Castle of Dumfries. To hold it secure. You will hoist another and better banner on that tower. And see that it flies there, against all comers."

"To be sure, my lord," Kirkpatrick cried, loudly. "Trust me for that. Bruce's banner will not fall like that rag, there!"

"Who said Bruce's banner?" Very slightly Bruce raised his voice. "Find you our royal standard of Scotland, my friend. The tressured Lion Rampant, red on gold. And raise that, see you. For all to see. In my name. For this day, I, Robert, do claim, take and assume my rightful and true heritage, the throne of Scotland. I stand before you now as your liege lord, Robert, King of Scots!"

For endless breathless moments there was complete and astonished silence. Men and women questioned their own ears. Only the slow ringing of the Greyfriars Monastery bell, tolling for the dead, broke the hush.

It was the Yorkshireman, Sir Christopher Seton, who first recovered himself. Wrenching out his sword for the second time that day, he held it high. "God save King Robert!" he cried. "God save the King! The King!"

It was as though a damned-up flood had been abruptly released. Pandemonium broke loose. The entire company went almost crazy in a frenzy of excitement and emotion. Men shouted, laughed, capered, threw their bonnets in the air, shook hands, even embraced each other. Women skirled, sang, wept, fell on their knees and prayed. Hardened knights and veterans of the wars kissed the cross-hilts of their swords and blinked away weak tears. The least demonstrative just grinned foolishly.

Nigel and Thomas Bruce, as amazed and dumbfounded as anybody else, were too overwhelmed to do more than gabble and stammer and stroke their brother's arms.

Of all that great gathering only the central figure himself remained apparently unaffected. Bruce sat unmoved and unmoving amongst the wild tumult, stiff and upright in his saddle as though carved there in stone. Never had he looked less pleased, less jubilant or exultant. And never more determined.

Out of the joyous confusion a pattern developed. Again it was the Englishman, Seton, who initiated it. He jumped down from his horse, casting away his sword with a clang. He came to Bruce's side. Half-bending on one armoured knee, he held up two hands, open and a little apart.

"Majesty," he exclaimed hoarsely, "I would be first to swear my oath of fealty. Give me your royal hand."

"Not Majesty, friend," Bruce told him. "In this Scotland we leave majesty to such as Edward Plantagenet! Grace, we say. By God's grace. Majesty I do not aspire to. But if ever a man required God's grace, I do!" He gave his brother-in-law his hand nevertheless.

"Aye, Sire." Taking the hand flat between his own two palms, Seton kissed it, then so holding it, said, "I, Christopher Seton, swear before Almighty God and all His saints, to be Your Grace's true man, in fealty and homage, in life and in death. I hereby declare Robert, King of Scots, to be my liege lord, and no other. Amen!"

This brought every other mounted man of gentle blood off his horse and into a clamorous queue, Kirkpatrick foremost. It was Seton himself who held them off, belatedly insisting that the King's brothers must have precedence. So Nigel and Thomas each took Robert's hand within their own, stumbling and stuttering in their near-distraction—yet even so somehow looking askance at their brother's set, stern features.

Before the rest of the eager columns of aspirants took the oath, Bruce raised the much-kissed hand for quiet.

"My friends all," he said. "I warn you. My service will be a hard one. It cannot be otherwise. English Edward will not smile on those who kiss this hand, this day. Think well before you do so. For me there can be no turning back now. I win this realm of Scotland's freedom, or die. But for you the die is not yet cast. Think well, I say."

Whatever brief stouns at the heart those ominous words may have aroused amongst his hearers, not one of the queue left place. Indeed more urgent was the clamour to reach his hand.

Bruce suffered the long oath-taking ceremonial with a grim patience. But as soon as it was finished, he commanded silence again.

"I cherish your loyalty, value your trust," he declared. "But now we have work to do. Only one castle, one town, and a few hundred of men, at this moment acknowledge the King of Scots. All must be brought to do so, willingly or unwillingly. I go back to Lochmaben, and command that all leal men rally to my standard there. But on the way I must take Dalswinton Castle, Comyn's house—for we can afford to let no enemies hold it. Likewise we must take Tibbers, which, though mine, is English-held. It commands the Nith pass into Ayrshire. Sir Christopher—I charge you to take it. And hold it. I give it to you. Sir John Lindsay—Caerlaverock must be secured. In these Solway marshes. The passage from Carlisle. See you to it. Surprise will be our most potent weapon. To strike before any look for war. This will serve us. Go now—enough of talk. And if I could, I would say God go with you! To work."

"God save the King's Grace!" somebody shouted. "God bless King Robert!" Immediately the cry was taken up by the entire gathering in a ringing and repeated chant, amidst cheers. To its resounding echoes, Robert Bruce rode downhill from Dumfries Castle, into the town, making for the north gate.

. . .

Elizabeth and Christian Bruce were sitting before the fire in the February dusk, stitching tapestries and watching the children play, when the brothers got back to Lochmaben. Bruce stood in the doorway eyeing this pleasantly domestic scene almost guiltily, before venturing in.

Elizabeth looked up, a little anxiously for her. She was well aware, of course, that her husband had gone to Dumfries that day specifically to confront Comyn with his treachery. However cosy the scene seemed now, she had been on edge all day. But she did not question him, waiting for the man to speak.

Not so Christian of Mar, now the Lady Seton. She seldom waited for anyone to speak first. "So, my brave brothers," she greeted them, "are you struck dumb by our beauty? Or has that reptile Comyn escaped you?"

"No," Bruce said briefly.

"No? What does no mean? Have you settled with the man?"

"I have, yes."

"Then I vow you are precious dull about it, Robert! And what have you done with my great ox of a husband? Do not tell me you let Comyn master *him*!"

"No. Christopher is well enough. He is gone on an errand for me. To Tibbers."

"Tibbers? And why, a mercy's sake? Why go to Tibbers? The English hold it, do they not?"

"It is my hope that they will not, for much longer."

"So! You send my foolish Yorkshireman to ask his fellow-Englishmen to give you back your Tibbers! You are become mighty bold, my Lord Robert, of a truth . . .!"

Elizabeth raised a hand to quell her irrepressible sister-in-law. "Let him tell it at his own pace," she urged.

But Nigel could contain himself no longer. "Quiet, you, by all the saints, Christie!" he burst out. "Your tongue is like a bell in the wind! And show something more of respect, I charge you. Call your brother Grace, now—not Lord!"

"Grace...? What folly is this?"

Elizabeth did not speak, but her hand went up to the white column of her throat.

"He is the King!" Thomas exclaimed excitedly. "He has taken the kingdom."

Bruce looked at his wife, not his sister. "Scarce that!" he said. "The kingdom will require a deal of taking, I fear!"

"Robert, You... you... what have you done?"

"Well may you ask, my dear. What can I say...?"

"*I'll* tell you what he has done," Nigel declared. "He has slain the Comyn and assumed the crown. Here is Robert, King of Scots!"

The two women stared, even Christian silenced. They both rose to their feet.

Bruce, still in his armour, strode forward to take his wife's hand. "My heart," he said, "What can I say to you? I have done what is beyond telling, this day. I come to you with hands stained with blood. I slew Comyn, yes. But not in fair fight. I dirked him, with this hand. And in church. Before God's altar! I come to you, a murderer...!"

"No!" Nigel insisted. "It is not so. He struck him down, yes. But not to the death. Kirkpatrick it was that killed him. Later."

"Besides, Comyn called him traitor! And struck him with his hand. I saw it, heard it." Thomas told them, voice breaking with emotion.

"I murdered him," Bruce repeated evenly. "Whoever finished my work. Drew on him, when his hands were empty..."

"In a church, you say?" Elizabeth faltered. "An altar...?"

"Aye—God pity me! He fell... against the altar."

"So long as he fell!" Christian commented briefly. "That man is better dead."

Elizabeth bit her lip. "I am sorry, Robert."

"Yes. It was ill done. I lost my wits. A kind of madness. I scarce knew what I had done. Until too late..."

"God in His heaven!" Nigel cried exasperatedly. "All this talk of what is of no matter anyway! The death of a proven traitor—who had to die. And naught said of what matters everything! That now you are King of Scots. And you, Elizabeth, are Queen." He ran forward, to half-bend one knee, as far as his armour would let him, and took her hand. "Highness!" he said, kissing it. "Your most faithful subject and servant." His younger brother hastened to follow suit.

Elizabeth shook her head. "It is less simple than that, I fear," she said sadly.

"Aye. Nigel speaks in innocence," Bruce agreed grimly. "Would that innocence were mine! Apart from the guilt on me, do you not see what this must cost? I am no true King until my coronation. And for that I require the aid of Holy Church. Think you Holy Church will smile on a murderer?"

"Why must you call it murder ...?"

"Because that is what it was. Moreover, it is what my enemies will call it."

"But the chief churchmen are your friends, not your enemies. Lamberton, Wishart, and the rest."

"Not all. Cheyne, of Aberdeen. Andrew, of Argyll. Both Comyn men. And have you forgot Master William, cleverer than any? Who saw the deed done. The Comyns have many churchmen. The Pope is now no friend to Scotland. These will petition him for my excommunication—nothing surer. And if they do not, Edward will! And an excommunicated man could not be anointed King!"

There was silence for a little. Then Christian spoke. "It is a long way to Rome," she observed.

"Aye. There lies my one hope. A swift coronation, before my enemies' emissaries can reach the Pope and bring back his edict. Without the Pope's authority, only the Primate could excommunicate, I believe. And Lamberton will not do that, I think. All, then, depends on haste."

"All ...?" Elizabeth echoed. "You do not fear the excommunication itself?"

"I fear the righteous wrath of God," he told her levelly. "I know well that I have grievously incurred it. In itself, I have no reason to fear any man's lesser condemnation." Bruce took her hand. "My heart—what I have done was a great sin. But that done, the rest had to follow. You will see it? The kingship. I had to act. Forthwith. There could be no delay. All then fell to be won, or lost. You understand?"

"I understand *that*, yes."

"I endanger you, by it. Endanger all here. I know it well. I have told these two. I tell you. The decision was mine. Others need not suffer for it. *You*—you are free to choose."

"I am your wife."

"To be sure. But this is a desperate venture. A new life that, short or long, will never again be the same. And liker to be short than long, I fear!"

"I married Robert Bruce for better or for worse. I knew when we were wed that this day might dawn. Would almost certainly dawn. I did not think to see it happen this way, Robert—but what of that? I am your wedded wife—whatever you have done. And now, it seems, your queen."

"That, see you, Edward will never forgive."

"Edward is no longer my king. You are, my dear."

He raised the hand he held to his lips. "I thank you, lass."

"So what now?" the impatient Christian asked.

"Now I send letters. I inform Edward—as one monarch to another." Almost he smiled. "Who knows—the news might even serve our cause enough to stop his heart! More urgent, to William Lamberton. This very night. Nigel—you had best go. He is at Berwick still, I think—summoned there by Richmond, as adviser. He must be told all, with nothing hidden. I will ask him to arrange an immediate coronation. If he will..."

"Lamberton will do it," Nigel asserted. "He has been your friend always. You have a bond with him, have you not?"

"A bond cannot tie a man's conscience. In especial, a churchman's. I can only hope. And you—you can pray!"

Elizabeth looked at him long and searchingly. "My love," she said gently, "I think that you should come with me. A little quiet refreshment. Write your letters later."

He drew a hand over his brow. "Later. Later, yes."

"When last did you eat?" she asked.

"Eat? I... I do not know."

"I thought as much. And even kings must eat! Come... Sire!"

Chapter Twenty-one

HURRIEDLY assembled though it was, the train that set out northwards from Lochmaben that bright and breezy March morning was a splendid one—the King of Scots on his way to Scone for his coronation. Whatever the dark uncertainties of the future, and all the thronging problems of the present and the guilt of the past, Bruce had sought to lay all aside for this great and significant event. His coffers had been drastically raided, scraped indeed, his feudal vassals summoned from far and near, his womenfolk charged to prepare a magnificence of raiment and gaiety of colour and spectacle not seen in Scotland for half a century. Five hundred rode on this leisurely, seemingly joyful, 100-mile pilgrimage, a third of that number ladies, with scarcely a suit of armour or shirt of mail in sight—although, not in sight but far out on either flank, powerful armed contingents rode a parallel course, to ensure against any surprise attack from Richmond's occupying forces, Comyn sympathisers, or other enemies. A company of mounted instrumentalists and minstrels led the procession, dispensing sweet music; banners fluttered by the score; gorgeously-caparisoned horses, heraldically-emblazoned litters, silks, satins, velvets and jewellery, dazzled the eye. Bruce himself wore a cloth-of-gold tabard, with the Lion of Scotland embroidered in red front and rear, picked out in rubies; and his queen was in royal purple velvet, tight of bodice and long flowing of skirt, high-standing collar and cuffs trimmed with seed pearls. Marjory, now a delicately lovely child of eleven, and making her first public appearance, was dressed wholly in white taffeta. Christian, with her sisters Mary and young Matilda, the baby of the family, her son Donald of Mar, and the four Bruce brothers, were little less fine.

But perhaps Bruce's greatest satisfaction, in all this display, was in what was immediately in front of him and behind the musicians, where rode three churchmen—the Dean of Glasgow, the Abbot of Inchaffray and the Vicar of Dumfries. They carried a gold and jewelled pectoral cross, a great banner with the arms of the See of Glasgow, and a precious relic, allegedly a bone of Saint Kentigern. But more important than what they carried was what they represented—the support and blessing of Holy Church, proved by a parchment in Bruce's own possession, signed by Robert Wishart, Bishop of Glasgow, the diocese in which the deed was committed, granting him full absolution for the death of John Comyn, on grounds of personal and national necessity. Bruce's conscience may have been little the lighter for this document, but his wits indeed were.

And, despite all this brilliance of circumstance and colour, he required every scrap of encouragement which he could muster. For, although it was nearly six weeks since the day when he had stabbed Comyn and proclaimed himself King, the fact was that so far no large proportion of the nation had rallied to his standard. Here in the South-West, his own domains, the response had been good; but elsewhere it had been patchy indeed. He had issued a twenty-four hour warning for mobilisation, to the whole realm—but what response there might be to it, who could tell? The common people, who had followed Wallace, had greeted the claiming of the crown with enthusiasm, in the main. But these had little to lose, and at this stage not a great deal to contribute. It was the landed men, the nobles, lairds and knights, whom he must have, able to provide armed men, horses, money. And these held back. They were scarcely to be blamed, perhaps—even Bruce did not condemn them too fiercely. The land was in English occupation, and though Richmond's forces were limited, anyone coming out in Bruce's support was a marked man for the inevitable day when Edward sent his legions north again to wipe out this affront. By then, that Bruce would be in any position to withstand, or to protect his supporters, was highly questionable. Ten years of bitter warfare had borne too heavily on such as these to leave many starry-eyed enthusiasts.

It was, therefore, with roused feelings that, riding down towards the grey town of Lanark, Bruce saw a tight and strong well-mounted company of about a hundred come spurring over a grassy ridge from the east, to meet the royal cavalcade at a tangent, lances glinting under a large blue-and-white banner. There were not a few Scots families which flew blue-and-white colours—but here in Lanarkshire the chances were that it was Douglas.

A young man, slender, swarthy, dark-eyed, graceful of carriage, led this squadron on a magnificent stallion. He drew rein a little way in front and to the side of the advancing column, and leapt down, to stand, waiting.

Bruce had his trumpeter sound the halt, and sitting his horse, beckoned the young man forward.

"Who are you, my friend?" he asked. "And would you ride with me to Scone, this day?"

The other bowed deeply. "I would ride with you farther than to Scone, my lord King," he said impulsively, clear-voiced. "I am James Douglas. Whom once you took out of Douglas Castle. To Irvine, and my father."

"Ha! James Douglas? Sir William's son. To be sure. I mind you now. Save us—you make me feel old! A boy then, a man now."

"Your man, Sire." He took the outstretched hand between his own. "Four days ago, only, I was of age. For long years I have waited for this. To come to you. Even when you were not King.

With my strength. As Lord of Douglas. Before, I could not. Others held me back. Now they can do so no more. And now I am come. In time for your Grace's crowning! God be praised!" All this was jerked out with a breathless urgency.

Bruce looked down into the eager dark eyes, and found an unaccountable lump in his throat. "Aye, lad," he said. "And I am glad. But . . . why? What did I ever do for you? Save escort you and your step-mother to your father? Whose soul rest in peace. All those years ago."

"Nine years, Sire. I have well counted them. Five of them in France. Think you I could forget what you did that day? Outside the walls of Douglas. How you saved the children from hanging. By Segrave. How you defied King Edward's commands. How you came to us in courtesy, offered us rescue, conducted us to safety. Then threw in your lot with the rebels. You, who were named Edward's chief commander in the South-West! I vowed then that when I was a man, I would seek to be a man like the Earl of Carrick!" James Douglas paused, and swallowed. "Your Grace's pardon. I . . . I forgot myself!"

"Would God more in this realm would forget themselves, my lord of Douglas!" Suddenly Bruce rose in his stirrups, and dismounted. Hastily everywhere men jumped down, not to remain seated when the monarch stood. "Give me that sword, lad," he said.

Wonderingly the younger man drew, and handed over the handsome weapon.

"Now, kneel." He tapped each bent shoulder with the flat of the blade. "I dub thee knight. Be thou a good and faithful knight until thy life's end. Arise, Sir James!"

Quite stunned with the suddenness and proportions of the honour done him, Douglas stood at a loss.

Leaning a little in her saddle, Elizabeth, who had watched and listened interestedly, held out her hand, well aware of what this all meant to her husband. "My felicities, Sir James. For the first knight of my lord's creating."

"Not the first," Bruce said sombrely. "I knighted Wallace. May you, sir, be more fortunate than he!"

"That is in God's hands, Sire. But if I can strive to be one half so true a knight, I shall rejoice. I thank you, with all my heart, Your Grace." Douglas took the Queen's hand. "Highness, I am yours, and the King's, to command. Always. To the death."

"This is too joyous a day to talk of death," she told him. "*Live* for us." And she smiled down on the lively, eager, almost worshipping face.

"That too, Madam . . ."

"Aye, my friend—so be it," Bruce said. "This day we ride my realm without swords and lances and armour. For once! So take you these fine Douglas blades of yours, and find Sir Christopher Seton. He rides some way to the west, holding our flank secure. Leave them with him. He will use them well. Then come back to our side, my lord of Douglas. You shall be our good augury and fortune, on the way to Scone . . ."

• • •

The Abbey of Scone, a few miles North of Perth, above the cattle-dotted meadows of the silver Tay, was a fair place in a lovely setting. Admittedly it was not so fair as once it had been, for Edward had been here in 1296, and part-destroyed the Abbey when he took away its precious Stone, the symbol of Scotland's sovereignty. And sent another punitive raid two years later. But there had been considerable rebuilding since then, much renewing of burned woodlands and a ravaged countryside in this the ancient Pictish capital and most hallowed spot in Scotland, where rose the Moot-hill that had been the centre of rule and the coronation-place of the most ancient kingdom of all Christendom. For this day, at least, all traces of ruin and devastation were covered up and hidden. All was colour, flourish and acclaim.

A tented city had been set up, on the flats by the river, below the twelve acres of abbey buildings and the Moot-hill, furnished with the gorgeous silken pavilions of lords and bishops, the bowers of ladies, the lodges of lesser men, the canopied shrines of religious orders and holy relics, the booths of merchants and craftsmen, the enclosures for entertainers, tumblers, musicians and the like, the tourney-grounds, race-courses and playing-fields, stretching to the vast horse-lines and cattle-pens. Every sort of standard, flag, banner and pennon flew, ecclesiastical, heraldic, burghal, guild and purely decorative. Late March, it was scarcely the time of the year for such outdoor activities; but the weather was kind, and though a stiff breeze blew, the sun shone.

Robert Bruce had reason for some satisfaction. It was no feeble or humiliating affair, such as might have been. None could point the finger of scorn and claim that this was only a shameful pretence at a coronation. There were three earls present—four if young Donald of Mar was counted; John de Strathbogie, of

Atholl; Malcolm of Lennox; and Alan of Menteith—although he had been more or less dragooned, and his uncle, Sir John Stewart of Menteith not only was not present but had refused to yield up Dumbarton Castle to Bruce. There were three bishops—the Primate, Glasgow and Moray—with a number of mitred abbots and priors. Of lords, apart from Douglas, there were Hay of Erroll and his brother; Lindsay of Crawford; Somerville of Carnwath; Campbell of Lochawe; and Fleming of Cumbernauld. James the Steward, aged and sick, had sent his surviving son Walter. And there were a great many barons, knights and lairds, the most prominent of whom were Sir Hugh, brother of the heroic Sir Simon Fraser of Oliver; Sir John Lindsay; Sir Robert Boyd, who had just captured Rothesay and Dunaverty Castles for Bruce; Sir David de Inchmartin and Sir Alexander Menzies. Alexander Scrymgeour, Wallace's lieutenant, the Standard-Bearer, was there. The Bruce family itself made an impressive phalanx, with Seton and Sir Thomas Randolph, a nephew.

But, though all this was well enough, it was scarcely possible not to reflect on who was *not* present. Two-thirds of the earls and bishops and three-quarters of the lords had found it necessary or expedient to be elsewhere—although all had been summoned. There was no overlooking this fact. Most significant, perhaps, for a coronation, was the absence of the young MacDuff, Earl of Fife, whose duty and privilege it was to place the new monarch on the fabled Stone of Destiny and to crown him thereafter. Some whispered indeed, with head-shakings, that without the magic symbol of the Stone, and lacking the MacDuff presence, it could be no true crowning.

William Lamberton arrived at Scone within hours of the royal party's coming, and it was Bruce who quickly thereafter sought the Bishop, in the Abbot's quarters, not *vice versa*.

"My lord King!" the older man protested, as the other was shown into his chamber. "This should not be! You should have let me seek audience. I was but preparing myself first, after my journeying . . ."

"Tush, man! Seek audience—you?" Bruce interrupted. "Has it come to this, between us?"

"Conditions have changed, Sire," the Primate said. "Notably."

"Changed, yes. But how much? Between us, my old friend? That is what I came to discover. And at once."

"They cannot be the same ever again, Sire, I fear. Since we are now master and subject."

"Master and subject! That is for the ruck. Say what you mean, man."

"Mean, Your Grace? I do not understand . . .?"

"Have done, my lord Bishop! You know well what is between us. Blood! Murder! Say it."

"If it is John Comyn you speak of, his blood does not lie between you and me. You have absolution, have you not?"

"Absolution, yes. And why granted? Because you so ordained? That I might not be debarred the throne? Before the Pope in Rome excommunicates me!"

"In part true, Sire. But only in part. Your slaying of Comyn was a sin, yes. The manner of it. I do not gainsay it. But a sin meet for absolution. Given repentance. Since the man was evil. Had plotted your own death. And would have done so again. It was Comyn, or Bruce! If ever a man ensured his own death, that man was John Comyn."

"So . . . you are still my friend?"

"If Your Grace will still consent to name me so."

"Thank God! This, I think, I feared most of all." Bruce reached out to take the other's hand. "The excommunication I could have tholed. God's judgement hereafter I must await. But *your* estrangement would have been beyond all bearing."

Much moved, the Bishop for once could find no words. He gripped the younger man's hand for long moments before he raised it to his lips.

"This of the kingship," Bruce went on, after a while. "Having defied and fled from Edward, and slain Comyn, I had to move. To take the throne, without delay. Before Edward could have the Pope excommunicate me. From a coronation. It was over-soon, for our plans, for Scotland. But my hand was forced."

"Think you I do not know it? It had to be. Over-soon, yes. But better that than over-late. Now, we must set the crown on your brow, for all to see, in fashion that none can question. And to that end, Sire, I would have you speak with the Abbot here. Abbot Henry."

"I have already met the good Abbot."

"Yes. But he asks for this further audience. He says that he has something to show to Your Grace . . ."

"A mercy, friend! While we are alone, must you so grace and sire me? I was Robert before. And to you, would be Robert still."

"Very well, Robert my friend—if it is your royal wish . . ."

"It is. Now—what would this abbot show me?"

"That he must declare himself. So he assured me . . ."

So King and Primate went in search of the Abbot of Scone, and presently found that busy man superintending the decoration of the great semi-ruined church for the next day's ceremonies. Master Henry was an old man, but bore his years and trials lightly. Small, grizzled, eager, he was almost monkey-like, the negation of the pompous cleric, quick and agile, but shrewd. He chuckled and laughed and rubbed his hands much of the time, and would abide no doleful monks in his establishment, declaring that there was more amusement and hearty joy to be won from religion than from any other subject, that God was the prime humorist and that the major sin against the Holy Ghost was a sour and gloomy piety.

When Lamberton beckoned him to the King, he came grinning, and making a most sketchy obeisance, led them aside, to announce, in a stage whisper, that he had something to disclose. Then almost on tip-toe, he conducted them through a side-door and down a winding stair. On the ledge of the last slit-window was a lantern, which he lit with a flint, and led on downwards into the dark honeycomb of crypts beneath the main church.

"Save us—is it a corpse you have for us, man?" Bruce asked.

"Wait you," the little man advised.

Amongst the damp and dripping vaults, stone and lead coffins and rusted iron yetts of that shadowy, chill place, the Abbot selected one massive door, and opened it with one of the keys hanging from his girdle. Stepping inside a small vaulted cell, he held the lantern high.

The two visitors stared. The place was empty save for a solid block of stone that gleamed black and polished in the lamplight.

"By all the Saints!" Lamberton murmured. "The Stone! The true Stone . . ."

"The Stone . . .?" Bruce demanded. "You cannot mean the Stone of Destiny? The Stone of Scone? Itself!"

Master Henry skirled laughter that echoed in all the vaults. "I do that, my lord King. None other." He rubbed his hands. "Yon's the right Stone. Your Coronation Stone, *My* Stone."

"So-o-o! I heard that Edward took a false Stone to London. Or so some said. But . . . how did you do it, man?"

"Did you expect me to let the accursed Southron have Scotland's most precious talisman?" the little man demanded. "I am

Abbot of Scone. Custodian of Scotland's Stone. It belongs here at Scone. And there it is."

"But how, man? How?"

Lamberton was kneeling beside the thing, running his hands over it. The block was about twenty-four inches high and twenty-eight long by twenty wide, a heavy, shiny black cube, its top dipped slightly in a hollow, the whole curiously wrought and carved with Celtic designs. It had two great rolls, or volutes, like handles, sculptured on either side, to carry it by—but when the Bishop sought to raise it, he could not do so much as move it an inch.

"Aye—this is it. The true Stone," he exclaimed. "I saw it. At Baliol's coronation. This . . . this is next to a miracle!"

"No miracle," the Abbot chuckled. "Just cozening. I cozened Edward Longshanks—that is all."

"Out with it," Bruce commanded, impatiently.

"Och, well—see you, it was not that difficult, Sire. King Edward had sworn, yon time, to destroy Scotland. To bring down its throne, to burn this abbey, to take away its Stone. Sworn before all. The Stone was in my care. Was I to allow that? I could scarce prevent him from burning my abbey. But I could try to save the Stone. He had warned me. Three days warning I had. So I had it taken from its place hard by the altar. By night. Secretly. Eight stark men bore it, in a covered litter. They bore it down Tay, four miles. To Boat of Moncrieffe. And ferried it across. Then they carried it up Moncrieffe Hill, and hid it in the cave where Wallace sheltered one time, Sir John Moncrieffe of that Ilk aiding them." The old man licked grinning lips. "And myself, I had the masons cut a great skelb of stone out of the quarry here. A rude block enough, but stout and heavy. And this I set before the altar. For Edward of England!"

"And . . . he took it. Your lump from the quarry. Knowing no better? It is scarce believable."

"As to that, Sire—who knows? Yon Edward is a man with the pride of Lucifer. He had sworn he would carry Scotland's Stone back to London. He may have jaloused that this was false. But there was none other—and a stone he must take. It would serve as well as the other, for most! It *has* served, has it no'?"

"By the Rude—here is a wonder!" Bruce cried. "Perhaps that is why he was so angry, that time at Berwick? Knowing it false. Man—I have never heard the like!" He stepped forward to touch

Scotland's famed talisman with reverent hand. "The Stone of Destiny. For my crowning. Here is good augury, indeed."

"Here is the work of a leal and stout-hearted man," Lamberton said, deep-voiced.

"You are right. My lord Abbot—for this I owe you more than I can say. All Scotland is hereby in your debt. I thank you. The Stone could scarce have had a better custodian."

"My simple duty, Your Grace. And my pleasure." The little man performed almost a skip of glee. "Nights I lie awake, and think of Edward Plantagenet with his lump of Scone sandstone! It is my prayer that he was not deceived. That he knows it false. I think it so. For, two years after he took it, he sent an ill band of Englishry back here, to wreak their fury on this place again. They came only here, from Stirling. They smashed and raged and defaced, in fury. They broke down everything that had been left and that we had set up again—the doors of this church, the refectory, dormitories, cloisters. Laid axes to every cupboard, chest, casket and plenishing. It was hate, naught else. I think Edward knows well that he was cozened—and does not like it. But dares not confess it, lest all men conceive him fooled! So the English are saddled with their stolen false Stone, and can scarce come back for this one. Is it not a joy?"

Shaking their heads, the other two considered the diminutive cleric—and Bruce found a smile, even if Lamberton did not.

Next day, therefore, the King of Scots at least was enthroned on the Stone of Destiny, even if there was no MacDuff to place him thereon. To the deafening clamour of trumpet fanfares the new monarch strode alone up through the crowded church to the high altar, and there seated himself upon the ancient Stone, which legend claimed to have been Jacob's pillow in the wilderness, brought to Ireland by Scota, Pharaoh's daughter, from whom the Scots took their name; but which was more likely to have been the portable altar of a travelling saint, possibly Columba himself, fashioned out of a meteorite. There Bruce sat while Abbot Henry brought up his Queen to sit on a throne opposite him, and the Primate, leading the Bishops Wishart and David of Moray, paced out of the vestry, themselves gorgeously attired, bearing magnificent robes of purple and gold in which to deck the King. These were canonicals, saved and hidden by Wishart at the sack of Glasgow, and now produced for this momentous occasion. The trumpets silenced, a great choir of singing boys chanted sweet music, while the bishops and abbot robed Robert Bruce ceremonially, and acolytes filled the air with the fragrance of their swinging censers.

The service that followed was impressive, if inevitably lengthy, conducted by the Abbot and the Primate, the sonorous Latinities of the Mass rolling richly, the anthems resounding, the silent pauses dramatic. Then to the high, pure liquid notes of a single singer reciting the *Gloria in Excelsis*, William Lamberton took the ampulla, and consecrating it at the altar, turned to anoint the King with oil.

Bruce, stern-faced as Lamberton himself, gazed across the chancel, hearing and seeing little, aware more vividly of that other high altar and the blood-stained figure collapsing against it, a picture which would haunt him until his dying day.

While the people still shivered to the aching beauty of that lone singing, conjoined with the dread significance of the holy anointing, they were rudely roused, to the extent of almost gasping with fright, by the sudden, unheralded, furious clashing of cymbals, that went on and on, as old Robert Wishart hobbled to the altar to take up the crown. It was in fact no true crown—Edward had seen to that—being but a simple gold circlet, taken from some saint's image; but no more valid diadem survived in all Scotland, and this must serve. To the shattering clangour of the cymbals, the aged prelate placed the slender symbol over the Bruce's brow.

"God save the King! God save the King! God save the King!" Drowning even the clashing brass, the great cry arose and continued, every man and woman in the crowded church on their feet and shouting—save only Bruce himself and Elizabeth. On and on went the refrain, like an ocean's tide crashing on a shingle beach, as all gave rein to their pent-up emotions. Looking across at her husband, the Queen perceived his lips to be moving, in turn.

"God save me! God save me, indeed!" he was whispering.

She would have run to him then, if she might.

At length the trumpets triumphed, and to their imperious ululation the Bishop of Moray brought Bruce the sceptre for his right hand, from the altar, while Abbot Henry brought him the Book of the Laws. Then, from the front of the nave, the Earl of Atholl came forward with the great two-handed sword of state. He knelt before Bruce and proffered it for the monarch to touch. Then, holding it up before him, he took his stance behind the Stone.

The Earls of Lennox and Menteith brought up the spurs and the ring, respectively, and Scrymgeour the Standard-Bearer stalked forward with the great Lion Rampart banner of the King, dipped it over Bruce's head, and then laid it on the altar.

The main coronation procedure completed, Lamberton stepped across, to bow before the Queen and place another golden circlet over her corn-coloured hair. Kissing her hand, he raised her, and led her across the chancel to the King's side, where she curtsied low, and took her husband's hand between both her own, the first to do him homage. Her throne carried over by acolytes, she seated herself at his right hand.

There remained but the ceremony of homage-giving, when all landed men and prelates might come up to take the King's hand and swear fealty, their names and styles called out by the King of Arms, a lengthy process but not to be scamped.

At last it was all over, and the royal couple could go outside to show themselves to the common folk who had gathered in their thousands to acclaim them.

The remainder of the day, and the day following, were given over to feasting, jousting, games and entertainments for all classes and tastes, with music and dancing late into the night. Bruce made a number of celebratory appointments to his household and to offices of state, granted charters and decrees, and created knights. There was only one flaw in the colourful tapestry. A courier arrived from the South-West, to inform the King that Sir Aymer de Valence, Earl of Pembroke, had been appointed commander in Scotland, to succeed the somewhat feeble John of Brittany, and had arrived at Carlisle to assemble a great army. De Valence was no puppet, but a fierce and able soldier, a second cousin of Edward's and, significantly, brother-in-law to the dead Comyn. Moreover Edward had sent the Prince of Wales on after Pembroke, gathering a second army; and he himself was preparing to come north.

It had had to come to this, sooner or later.

Two forenoons later, when Bruce was in conference with his lords, he was brought new and more surprising tidings. There was a latecomer to the coronation scene—none other than Isabel, Countess of Buchan. It was perhaps strange that the King should immediately interrupt his Council and go in person to greet this lady, the young wife of one of his most consistent enemies. But Isabel of Buchan had been Isabel MacDuff before her marriage, sister of the Earl of Fife.

He found the Countess with Elizabeth and Christian, little more than a girl, but a sonsy, high-coloured, laughing girl, strange wife for the dour, elderly High Constable of Scotland. She sank low before him.

"My lord King," she said, "I am desolated. That I am come too late. I have ridden for twelve days. Four hundred miles. Ever since I heard. For Your Grace's coronation. And come too late by two days. It is a sore sorrow."

"Why, lady—here's a woeful mischance," Bruce said, raising her. "Had we but known. To come so far. You must, then, have been in England?"

"At my lord's manor of Fishwick, in Leicestershire. He has made his peace with Edward. Since . . . since . . ."

"Aye—I understand. And you left my lord behind?"

"Yes, Sire. He . . . he knew not that I came."

"So! A leal subject, indeed—if less leal a wife!"

"I am, first, MacDuff of Fife's daughter! When I learned, to my sorrow, that my brother, the Earl Duncan, preferred to bide at Edward's Court in London than play his rightful part in the crowning of his King, I made haste to come myself. That there should be a MacDuff, if only a woman, to place the crown on your head. Lacking the Stone of Scone, this at least I could do. I took my husband's best horses. And now—now it is all too late . . . !" Her eager voice broke.

Bruce thrust out a hand to clasp her bent shoulder. "Not so, lass—not so. Would you had been here two days ago, yes. But today is also a day. I do greatly esteem the presence of a MacDuff—especially so fair a one! In order that you should do what only MacDuff can rightfully do. You shall crown me again, forthwith. And seat me on the true Stone of Destiny also. For it is here, despite all. The Stone of Scone. The Abbot Henry saved it. Edward has a false boulder, a worthless lump of building-stone, to cherish at his Westminster! We shall have a second crowning. And none shall say that Robert Bruce is not truly King of Scots!"

The girl burst into tears, there and then.

So, that afternoon, in another brief but joyful ceremony, the Countess of Buchan led her sovereign to the Stone, and there placed the gold circlet over his brow, to the lusty cheers of the concourse. And, as lustily, Bruce kissed her for her services, declaring that he felt a King indeed.

Chapter Twenty-two

Although Bruce ordained that the festivities continue at Scone for some days longer, the very next morning he himself, with Elizabeth and a small Court—including the Countess of Buchan whom the Queen appointed her principal lady-in-waiting—set off on a progress through the land. Admittedly it was partly a recruiting drive, with Aymer de Valence's invasion threat bearing heavily on his mind—but it was advisable, necessary, that the King should show himself to as large a number of his people as was possible.

Meanwhile emissaries, including his brothers Thomas and Alexander, and the Bishops of Glasgow and Moray, rode south, east and west, to raise troops and rouse the country—especially south-west, where lay the greatest opportunity to harry and distract Pembroke.

The King chose to travel northwards, for it was there that the Comyn influence was strongest and must be countered. His progress was not entirely formal and processional, for he took the English-held royal castles of Forfar and Kincardine on the way. But most of the time was spent visiting towns and abbeys and communities, receiving tokens of loyalty, dispensing largesse and requiring the fealties of local barons—including the reluctant Malise, Earl of Strathearn, whom he more or less kidnapped. All the while, however, he had, as it were, one eye turned backwards, one ear listening for tidings of Pembroke and the English.

The royal company had left Aberdeen for Inverness, and were in fact at the Mar castle of Kildrummy when the vital word reached them. Pembroke had moved—and in no uncertain fashion. Presumably perceiving that every day's delay was likely to strengthen Bruce's hand, he had left his main body of foot at Carlisle, to await the arrival of the Prince of Wales, who had now reached Lancaster with another large army, and had spurred onwards with some three thousand picked horse. Refusing to be distracted either right or left after crossing the Border, he was driving due north at an impressive pace, avoiding all entanglements and leaving any opposition to be looked after by the slower-moving main body. Fairly clearly Edward's particular orders were to close with Bruce at all costs and bring him to immediate battle.

His general orders to all ranks were, however, to slay, burn and raise dragon—that is, to show the dreaded dragon banner which proclaimed that no mercy was to be granted.

In the Council that followed the King was offered varied advice, but most urged that he withdrew promptly into the deeper fastnesses of the Highlands, where the English could not follow, leaving Pembroke to his own devices, and living to fight another day when he had suitable forces assembled. Bruce himself was the principal objector to this superficially wise and reasonable course. It was not that he was rash, unthinking or over-sanguine. But he was the new-crowned monarch, he pointed out. To start his reign by disappearing into the safety of the trackless mountains, abandoning his people to the unchecked fury of the baulked invaders, was not to be considered. If he was to maintain any credit with his subjects, he must challenge Pembroke somehow, and be seen to do so. He might fail the first test, but he must not seem to shirk it.

Somewhat reluctantly those of most experience conceded that.

Bruce's reasoning and judgement might be sound, but how to implement it was another matter. There was not more than 600 fighting-men with the King at this juncture, and though many more could be raised, from comparatively near at hand, within a day or so, and thousands in a week or two, Pembroke's swift advance denied them the time they required.

Lamberton, whom Bruce had appointed Chancellor meantime, seizing on this need for time, declared that they must use cunning. Valour for all to see was all very well for the monarch, but his ministers could afford to be more devious. He proposed that while the King was ready to meet Pembroke in the field, he himself should hasten south and seek a parley with the English civil authorities, make moves towards entering into negotiations. As Chancellor. This might blunt the edge of Pembroke's drive and effect a delay—especially as it was requested that such negotiations should await King Edward's own arrival. Doubt and delay—those could be valuable weapons in the circumstances, and every weapon must be used.

Bruce demurred. Hints at such early surrender, even though they had no base in fact, were repugnant. Also it would put Lamberton himself in a position of extreme danger, when the deceit was discovered—as in due course it must be. If the Chancellor was available for negotiations, he would equally be available for capture.

The other shook his head. It was a risk that fell to be taken. They all were adventuring all. Danger was their lot, every one, from henceforth until the kingdom was won and secure.

So it was accepted, and thereafter the royal party turned its face south again, the King calling on all leal men to rally to his standard. But Lamberton hastened ahead, making for Edinburgh where the English civil administration had its base. None doubted that he was putting his head into the lion's mouth.

By mid-June Bruce was at the Abbey of Coupar, at the west end of Strathmore, with 4,000 men, a quarter of them cavalry, when he learned that Pembroke was at Stirling and had halted. Whether this was on account of Lamberton's gesture at opening negotiations, they could not tell. But it gave the King a little more time to wait for his hoped-for reinforcements.

Only a few had come in, a day or two later, when the next courier arrived from the south. Pembroke had not been wasting his time. He had been sending out detachments to take loyalist castles, and amongst others had captured old Bishop Wishart at Cuper Castle in Fife. Worse, the Earl of Buchan had come north from England, and had called to arms the whole force of Comyn against Bruce. Now he was marching to join Pembroke, who was on his way to Perth.

Grimly Bruce abandoned his waiting game. Time, it seemed, was no longer in his favour. He gave the word to break camp and march. Elizabeth and the ladies he left behind in the care of his brother Nigel.

On the 18th of June the King of Scots approached the walled city of Perth, so close to Scone where three months earlier he had been enthroned. In the city, Aymer de Valence, Earl of Pembroke, lay, with reputedly 6,000 chivalry, 1,500 more than Bruce's total force, and with Sir Henry Percy and Sir Robert Clifford as lieutenants. Taking up a position with the wide Tay on his left hand and the marshes of the incoming Almond on his right, the King sent forward a colourful party of heralds and trumpeters, under the King of Arms, to declare that the King of Scots wished to know the business of the Earl of Pembroke in his city of Perth. Let him come forth and give an account of himself.

De Valence announced in reply that he could not have dealings with traitors to his King Edward. And he was very comfortable where he was.

Bruce had to weigh the pros and cons of this. Pembroke was a proved and veteran fighter and no craven; moreover he had the larger force. And it was against his honour and reputation to hold back thus in the face of the enemy. He must have good reason for waiting, therefore. Was he expecting reinforcements? Or was this the result of Lamberton's activities? Had he been ordered to hold his hand while the Primate's peace feelers were investigated?

Would delay benefit Bruce more than the invaders? The Prince of Wales was held up in Galloway, fulfilling his father's injunctions anent savagery. Edward himself, by his physicians' orders, was having to travel very slowly, and was said to be no further north than York. Bruce himself was hoping for adherents from all over his kingdom. He would wait, therefore—and seek to cut off the English supply routes into Perth. The word of their new King already besieging the English invaders ought to be a fillip to the morale of the Scots people.

But before adopting such programme, Bruce sent a further and more explicit challenge to de Valence, that all should be plainly established for the folk to see. He urged Pembroke, or Percy, or Clifford, to come out and put their differences to the test in knightly fashion, by single combat with himself, by chosen champions, by set battle, or in whatever fashion they would. To which Pembroke answered that he should be patient; the day was too far spent—but he might fight with him next day.

So Bruce, shrugging, sent out detachments to control all the roads leading to Perth, and foraging parties to collect supplies for his host—which had been on the march long enough to have a very depleted commissariat. And, as evening fell, moved his main force some three miles westwards, to set up camp on the long, low, tree-dotted ridge of Methven that flanked the River Almond to the south, a reasonably strong position, with the land falling away to north and south, yet with opportunity for retiral and escape, by wooded lands to the west, towards the Highland hills. They would see if Pembroke had intention, or stomach, for fight the next day—the Feast of St. Gervase.

There was some talk of the King spending the night in the small castle of Methven. But Bruce preferred to camp with his men. Besides, the laird, Sir Roger de Moubray, had been a Baliol supporter, and might well still be pro-Comyn.

It was the first night that Bruce had been parted from Elizabeth since the coronation. It was chilly, with intermittent showers, and he slept fully clad beneath his cloak, amongst a grove of hawthorns.

As well that he did. In the early hours of the morning he, and all others, were aroused by the urgent shouts of sentinels. The enemy was upon them, the cries rang out. To arms! To arms!

It is never actually dark in Scotland, of a June night, but the cloud and overcast greatly hindered vision, especially amongst the scattered woodlands of Methven ridge. Starting up and staring around, Bruce could make out nothing distinct or detailed, save only the sleepy confusion of his own men. Dragging on his jerkin of chain-mail, he shouted for Sir Neil Campbell, who was acting guard-commander. But of that stout fighter there was no sign. Young Sir James Douglas, who was never now far from the King, declared that men said that Campbell had ridden off eastwards just before the first shouted alarm had rung out.

Bruce ordered his trumpeters to sound the rally, as precaution.

Barely had the high neighing notes died away than they were answered, and from no great distance to the eastwards. A somewhat ragged and breathless rendering it was—but there was no doubting its tenor and significance. It was the advance, English version.

Shouting for his own mount, Bruce ordered to horse to be sounded. Even as he cried it, he heard, felt indeed beneath his feet, the thunder of drumming hooves, thousands of hooves.

There was no time for any thinking out of tactics. Commanding that three main groups be formed, under his brother Edward on the right, the Earl of Lennox on the left and himself in the centre, and indicating that they so face the foe, there was no opportunity for even this limited manoeuvre to be completed before the dark mass of charging cavalry loomed out of the shadowy gloom before them, seeming to spread right across the ridge in solid menace.

To stand and wait, stationary, for such a charge, was as good as to seek annihilation. Bruce was ordering the advance, when diagonally across their front a single rider spurred, from the north-east. It was Sir Neil Campbell of Lochawe, guard-commander.

"Sire!" he yelled, "they attack from the north. Two assaults. They circle to the north. Out of the valley. To take us in rear. A large force. Rode down my few guards. Shouting A Comyn! A Comyn!"

Cursing, the King directed Lennox and the left to swing off, to seek to deal with this threat, and waved on his main body.

It was hopeless of course. Taken by surprise, short in numbers—for the foragers were still absent, as were the detachments to close the Perth roads—scattered, bemused and lacking the impetus successfully to meet a massive charge, the royal force was beaten before ever it met the enemy. It was not so much a defeat as a rout. Valour, leadership, experience—these might affect the issue for individuals and small groups, but on the outcome of the day they were irrelevant. Pembroke and his disciplined English cohorts smashed through and overwhelmed the Scots in a single furious onslaught, hardly slackening the pace of their charge. In a few brief moments the King's force was reduced to no more than chaos, and a number of desperately struggling groups of individuals.

In the forefront, Bruce himself was unhorsed and thrown to the ground in the first headlong clash. Only James Douglas, first, and then Sir Gilbert Hay, leaping down and flailing their swords above the fallen monarch, saved him from being trampled to death. Others sought to make a ring round them, with Alexander Scrymgeour and the royal standard proclaiming the King's position.

It proclaimed it to the English likewise, of course, and swiftly the greater pressure was swung on Bruce. In the mêlée of a cavalry fight no great degree of coherence is possible; but Pembroke was an experienced commander and was swift in seeking to control his force. He was already swinging round his flanks, right and left, to ensure that the Scots had no opportunity to rally and reform.

A riderless horse was found for the staggering Bruce—there were all too many of them to choose from—and he was aided into the saddle. Seton spurred close.

"We must cut our way out, Sire," he cried. "Onwards. East. Quickly. Behind them."

The King peered around him, dazedly. "The others . . .?"

"Not possible. All is lost here. Cut up. No rallying . . ."

"He is right, Sire," Hay agreed, "All we can save is you! And must!"

"Edward . . .? Over on the right . . .?"

"God knows!"

"That way, then . . ."

In a tight phalanx the little group drew even closer around the King and drove forward, others joining themselves to it. But quickly the opposition solidified. A large body of knights materialised against them, and with shouts that here was the Bruce, made furious onslaught.

The King, recovering from his shake, dealt effectively enough with the first assailant to reach him. Swerving in the saddle to avoid a jabbing sword-point at the throat, like a lance-thrust, and standing in his stirrups he thereafter swung round his own great two-handed blade in a sideways swipe that struck the knight on the back of his neck and pitched him forward over his mount's head helmet spinning. But there were another two attackers immediately at his back, and the King was their chosen target. Part unbalanced by his own slashing stroke he was the more vulnerable to the double assault.

The man on the right wielded a windmilling sword, but he on the left bore an upraised mace. In the instant of decision Bruce chose the latter—for though the sword was menace enough, one blow from a heavy mace could end all there and then. Ducking low, he dragged his horse round, to drive it straight at the mace-wielder, and thrust up his lion-painted shield to take the smashing blow. It beat down and numbed his left arm, all but jerking it out of its socket. But the attacker was left, for the moment thereafter, almost defenceless. Hay was on the King's left side, and having disarmed his previous assailant, now swung on the maceman, and felled him with a single blow.

But Bruce paid the price of his swift decision. He flung himself round to face the swordsman on his right too late by seconds. The great blade struck him a downward hacking buffet on the shoulder and, sideways in the saddle as he was, toppled him headlong. The chain-mail turned the edge of it, but the pain was stouning. He crashed to the ground, only part-conscious.

Once again the ring formed around the fallen monarch, and men died there to save him. Eager hands raised him, while steel clashed on every side.

"God's curse on him—the dastard traitor!" Hay gasped. "Did you see who struck him down? Moubray! Philip Moubray."

"What? Roger of Methven's son?"

"Aye. The felon! He has brought them down on us..."

"Quick—hold him up. He swoons again. His horse..."

Somehow they got Bruce hoisted into the saddle again, where he slumped, swaying. But before Hay and Douglas could themselves remount, the Scots ring was broken by a new assault, again aimed determinedly at the King. Bruce, his sword lost, his head swimming, was in no state to defend himself. His previous assailant, young Sir Philip Moubray, led again. He drove right up alongside the reeling monarch, and seeing him disarmed, grabbed his shoulder.

"I have him!" he yelled. "I have the Bruce! Yield, Earl of Carrick!"

That cry of triumph and the fierce pain of the damaged shoulder, convulsed Bruce. Cringing, and seeking to strike out blindly at the same time, he jerked round—and the movement and agony was too much for his precarious equilibrium. He overbalanced quite, and fell to the ground for the third time that grim midsummer morning.

Almost crazed that he might lose a prize which King Edward would reward surely with an earldom at least, Moubray leapt down to straddle his fallen victim, shouting to his colleagues to close in around him. But before they could do so, Sir Christopher Seton, with a roar of fury, thrust in, completely overturning one horse and rider in the excess of his rage, and, reaching Moubray first, towering above him, felled him with a mighty blow.

Then the big Yorkshireman performed a feat which was to be forever afterwards remembered of him. Leaping down and tossing away his sword, he picked up his half-stunned brother-in-law almost as though he had been a child, and lifted him high on to his own horse in an access of next to superhuman strength. Then, as the others spurred to protect him, he clambered up behind the King.

Without any more delay, searching for Edward Bruce or anyone else, the tight knot of the King's closest friends set about the business of beating their way, swords flailing right and left rhythmically, monotonously, out of that shambles, eastwards. In the face of their savagely dedicated determination few remained long in their path.

So, ingloriously, the new King of Scots left his first battlefield, only semi-conscious.

His escort won through the rear of the English array, and swinging away southwards in a wide arc through the marshlands of Methven Moss, were able to turn back westwards. The Highland hills, a black barrier ahead, beckoned like a blessed haven in a storm.

Chapter Twenty-three

The larks trilled joyously high in the blue, the cuckoos called hauntingly from the lower birch-woods, and the myriad bees hummed lazy contentment from the rich purple carpet of the bell heather and the blazing gold of the whins which crackled in the early July sunshine; while the tumbling, spouting, peat-stained Dochart shouted its laughter up from its rocky bed, all in praise of as fine a noontide as that lovely land of the mountains could proffer. But the man who sat alone on the heathery knoll, chin cupped in hand, elbow on knee, and stared eastwards towards Ben Lawers and Loch Tay, heard and saw and felt none of it. His brow was dark, his jaw set, his thoughts bitter. And it was not the pain of a broken shoulder that troubled him; he scarcely felt that in his present state.

He sat alone only because he would have it so; for down in the camp by the riverside there were friends enough who felt for him, who often gazed up towards him, most of whom indeed had already shed blood for him. But the King, in his deep hurt, wanted none of them. He was sick, sick not so much of pain and the body but of the heart, the mind, the spirit; and was by no means to be comforted.

None denied that he had cause for bitterness, for hurt; but few accepted his self-censure, his burning sense of personal blame—which can be the sorest burden a man can carry.

Robert Bruce was not unduly introspective, self-centred or guilt-conscious as a rule. As a youth and younger man he had not been noted for a sense of responsibility indeed. But he had undoubtedly changed, of late. His brothers, and those closest to him, averred that the change dated substantially from the murder of Comyn. Guilt was now seldom far from his mind. And the fact that the Pope had indeed now pronounced the dread sentence of excommunication upon him, however much it might be politic to make light of it, was like a leaden weight on his soul. He felt that the hand of God was against him—and deservedly so. Moreover, equally daunting was his awareness that so many others must pay the price for his fault.

This last assumption was hard to gainsay, at least. It was two weeks since Methven, two weeks of flight, of skulking and hiding in the mountains of Strathyre and Breadalbane, while survivors, refugees and broken men joined him, singly and in little parties, bringing with them the grim details necessary to build up a true picture of what that shameful debacle had cost. A glance at the camp below, by the Dochart, revealed the broad outline. Barely 500 men were there—all that was left of the King's army. His brother Edward was there; and Christopher Seton. But Thomas Randolph, his nephew, was captured. The tight group which had carried him off the field—and whom he now blamed for that very thing—James Douglas, Gilbert Hay, Robert Boyd and Robert Fleming, were present, though nearly all wounded to a greater or lesser degree. Also the Earl of Atholl, the Bishop of Moray and Sir Neil Campbell. But that was all.

The long list of the dead was like a knell tolling in the King's mind; for the vast majority of those surprised at Methven were now dead. Fortunate indeed were those who had fallen cleanly in the heat of battle for, true to his master's orders, Pembroke had carried the dragon flag, and the wounded and captured had been slain out of hand. Only a few of the highest ranks had been taken prisoner. And these, with the exception of Thomas Randolph—saved not out of mercy, but that he might be used against his uncle—had all been summarily hanged, drawn and quartered; Sir Alexander Fraser, Sir Simon's brother; Sir Hugh Hay, brother to Gilbert of Erroll; Sir John Somerville, Lord of Carnwath; Sir David Barclay of Cairns; Sir David de Inchmartin; and Alexander Scrymgeour, the Standard-Bearer, dying the same death as his master Wallace. All had paid the price for supporting Bruce. The Earl of Lennox was wounded and missing, the Earl of Mentieth captured and none knew whether alive or dead. Even the Earl of Strathearn, forced almost at the sword-point to the coronation at Scone, and not present at Methven, was taken and sent south in chains.

Nor was that all. Lamberton himself, the King had just heard, had been apprehended at his cathedral of St. Andrews, and with Bishop Wishart, in irons both, sent with every indignity to London.

As for the people, the common people, *his* subjects, they died in their thousands, in a reign of terror that was going to leave little for Edward himself to do when eventually he reached unhappy Scotland.

So Robert Bruce sat and called himself accursed, a man who brought death, destruction and horror upon all. He was not far from breaking-point.

It was almost with dread, then, that he presently glimpsed the flash of sunlight on steel, and the colours of banners and gaily-canopied litters, approaching from the direction of Killin and Loch Tay—which he had come up here to look for. He had sent a message to Blair-in-Atholl, where Nigel had been guarding the Queen's party, to join them here, a two-days' march westwards. Now he wondered how he could face Elizabeth.

That he did not go down to meet her was the measure of his depression and despair.

Eventually Nigel brought her up the hillock, but at a sign from her, left Elizabeth some little way from his brother's position. The Queen came on alone.

"Robert!" she said, going to him, hands out. "At last. Together again. I have prayed for this. How I have prayed!"

"Prayed? For *this*?"

Three words could scarcely have been more eloquent. Closely, concernedly, she eyed him, reaching to take one of his hands. Her splendid fairness was heart-breaking, this fine noonday. He looked steadily away from her.

"Prayed, my dear. That I might at least see you again. See you, touch you, hold you—and alive! Was it so ill a prayer? At least it has been granted."

He did not answer.

"But you are hurt. Your shoulder..."

"*I* am hurt? Who talks such folly, when all is lost and better men die by the hundred, the thousand!"

"Such better men are not my husband," she answered simply. "Let me see it. Your shoulder, Robert."

"Leave it," he jerked. "It is less than nothing."

"My dear," she said quietly, sitting down beside him. "Tell me."

"Tell! What is there to tell? Save evil. God's hand turned against a lost and condemned sinner. Punishment. Retribution. Poured out. Not on the sinner, but on those who aided and supported him. His friends. Hugh Hay. Alexander Fraser. Somerville. Barclay. Inchmartin. Scrymgeour. And others by the score. Dead—all dead. Tortured and shamefully slain. Thomas Randolph a prisoner. Lamberton in chains. And Wishart..."

It all poured out, the pent-up pain and remorse and sorrow, in a searing, passionate flood, all the disappointment, the frustration, the disillusionment, the desperation.

She listened quietly, with no word spoken.

At length the spate wore itself out. Elizabeth touched his sweating brow.

"It is grievous, my heart. All grievous. I am sorry," she said. "But why torture yourself with it? The fault is not yours."

"Not mine? Then whose is it, before God?" he demanded. "Did other than I slay Comyn? Did other than I declare himself King? All stems from that."

"Comyn deserved to die. More, he *had* to die. Had you not slain him, another must. And this your kingdom requires a king."

"Not a king who leads to disaster."

"Any king can lose a battle."

"It was not a battle. It was a massacre. We were taken unawares. Asleep. Because of my fault. I had challenged Pembroke to fight, that afternoon. Twice. He refused, and said that he might fight the next day. Like a fool, I took him at his word. It did not cross my mind that he would steal out on me by night, six miles, to Methven. Betrayed by Philip Moubray. We were taken by surprise. But the fault was mine."

"In any fight, Robert, *one* must lose . . ."

"But I—I was carried off the field. To safety. While others, thousands, fell. Or, lacking leader, yielded. And were then slaughtered like dumb cattle!"

"That shame was not yours, but Edward's. And it was right that you should be saved. Necessary. You are the King. The King lost, and all is lost."

"Scotland, I swear, were better without this King! For he is lost, even so. Lost and damned!"

"No! No, I say!" Suddenly Elizabeth de Burgh changed. She sat up straight, her eyes blazing, and turning to him gripped his undamaged arm—but not tenderly. "You speak like a child. A child sorrowing for itself! This is not the Robert Bruce I wed. I married a man—not a brooding, puling bairn!"

He recoiled from her, almost as though she had struck him. "Woman—you do not know what you say . . . !"

"I know full well. Hear *me* speak—since you, Robert speak folly! I would liefer have the man for husband who slew Comyn and defied all Edward's fury, than . . . than this weakling!"

He groaned. "You say this? You, also? God pity me . . . !" That was a whisper.

"Aye, God pity you, Robert Bruce! And me, wed to you! And this land, with a faint-heart for King! A broken sceptre, indeed!"

He stiffened. "You are finished?" he asked.

"No, I am not. You *took* that sceptre. None thrust it upon you. You *are* the King, now. Crowned and anointed. There is no undoing it, no turning back. So—if you are the King, for God's good sake *be* the King! A weak king is the greatest curse upon a nation."

He stared at her, biting his lip.

"What was it that we did at Scone?" she demanded, her beauty only heightened by her passion. "Was it only a show? Play-acting? Or was it the truth? God's work? Did Abbot Henry save the Stone for nothing? That oil on your brow—what was it? A priest's mummery? Or the blessed anointing of God's Holy Spirit upon you? *You*, only. Which? For if it was truth, then it gave you authority. Above all men. Whatever you have done, you are now God's Anointed. Take that authority. Use it. Wield your sword of state. You have many loyal men still. A whole people still looks to you, in hope. Fight on. Avenge Methven. Be Robert the King!" Abruptly her voice broke, and her fiercely upright carriage seemed to crumble. "Oh, Robert, Robert—be Elizabeth de Burgh's man!"

Slowly he rose to his feet, looking from her down to the camp, and then away and away.

"Say that you will do it, my dear," she pleaded now.

"For you . . . I think . . . I would do anything. Anything!"

"Thank God! Do it for me, then. If for naught else . . ."

There was an interruption. A strange-looking figure was climbing the knowe towards them, one or two of the King's people trailing rather doubtfully behind. The man was elderly, enormous but frail and stooping, bearded to the waist, and clad apparently and wholly in a great tartan plaid, stained and torn, draped about his person in voluminous folds and peculiar fashion, and belted, oddly, with a girdle of pure gold links, in a Celtic design of entwined snakes. He was aiding himself up the hill with a long staff having a hook-shaped head, like a shepherd's crook.

Nigel Bruce had waited, some way back from the royal couple. Now he stepped forward to halt this apparition. But the old man waved him aside peremptorily—and when this had no effect, raised his staff on high and shook it threateningly, screeching a flood of Gaelic invective of such vehemence and power as to give even Nigel pause in some alarm.

The ancient gold-girdled ragbag came trudging on, right up to the monarch. He said something less fierce, in the Gaelic.

Bruce, whose mother had been a Celtic countess in her own right, knew something of the ancient tongue; but not sufficient to understand this swift flow, liquid and hurrying as a Highland river, and strangely musical to be coming from so uncouth a character.

"I am sorry, friend," he said, when there was a pause. "I do not know what you say."

The other looked him up and down disapprovingly, then shrugged the bent tartan-draped shoulders. "You are Robert son of Mariot, daughter of Niall, son of Duncan, son of Gilbert, son of Fergus, son of Fergus?" he demanded, and added, "*Ard Righ*," almost grudgingly.

Bruce at least knew those last two words, which meant High King. He nodded. "I am he."

"And I—I am the Dewar of the Coigreach," the other said dramatically and waved his staff.

Bruce dredged in his bemused mind for what this might signify. And then recollected. The *Coigreach*, of course. It was the lengendary pastoral staff of Saint Fillan, one of the most celebrated of all the ancient Celtic saints, a prince of the royal Dalriadic house, out of which the united kingdom of the Picts and Scots had come, and Abbot of the long defunct Culdee Abbey of Glendochart—and a leper, it was said. A precious relic since the eighth century, this crozier was handed down in a long line of hereditary custodians, known as Dewars or Diors, who were venerated all over the Celtic Highlands and islands as holy men.

"I greet you, Dewar of the Coigreach," he acknowledged. "How can I serve you?"

The other snorted. "*I* came to serve you!" he corrected. "I have come to bless you. Who is this woman?"

"She is the Queen. My wife."

The Dewar sniffed, and shrugged. But he raised the crozier, with its curious, elaborately-wrought bronze head, and extending it over the royal couple, launched into a stream, a flood, of Gaelic. When he at length lowered the staff, he added factually, "You are now blessed with the Blessing of Saint Fillan."

"I thank you," Bruce said, level-voiced. "But I would remind you that I have been excommunicated by the Pope. His Holiness of Rome."

"The Pope? Who is the Pope?" the Dewar asked haughtily. "And where is Rome? It is not in Ireland, the Cradle of the Church. Do you question the authority of Saint Fillan?"

"No." Bruce swallowed. "No, I do not."

"As well." The ancient scratched amongst his rags, eyed Elizabeth balefully, and then, without any leave-taking, even so much as a nod, turned and went stumping off down the hill, as independent as he had come.

Bruce, from looking after him, stared at his wife.

Elizabeth's eyes were shining. "Robert! Robert!" she cried. "It is a miracle! God be praised! See you, the Old Church has come to the rescue of its prince. The Romish Church may excommunicate you—but this is a Church older than Rome. And it blesses you! Takes you for its own." Her laughter was high-pitched, tinged almost with hysteria, but with its own joy. "Here is a lesson, as well as a blessing. For the King. To remember whence he came. It was a Celtic kingdom, not a Norman one. And you are half a Celt. I am less so—but I have some Celtic blood. And, and I do come from Ireland! The Cradle of the Church, no less! It is a sign, my dear. Come most timely."

"A sign, yes." He nodded, a new light in his eye. "I believe that it is. A sign. Perhaps I have been *led* to Saint Fillan's land. To this Glen Dochart where his abbey was. He was, you might say, a forebear. In some degree. Since King Malcolm Canmore, my ancestor, was of his line." He raised one shoulder. "And Malcolm's Romish wife, Margaret, it was who brought down the Celtic Church! An old story. Another Queen stronger than her husband . . . !" He looked at her.

"I am not that." Elizabeth shook her head. "In much I am weak, foolish. But in my love for you, Robert, I am strong. Strong with *your* strength. It was your strength that first drew me to you. You are strong still—only weary. In pain. Mourning your friends. And alone. As only a king may be alone. But now I am with you again. To restore part of your strength. That I had borrowed—in exchange for my heart!"

He drew her to him, there on the hillock in sight of all. "Quiet, you," he said gently. "You have said enough. Done enough. Done it all. I will be strong, yes. Strong, now. Until one day I give you a whole realm to cherish. Instead of one stumbling man, Elizabeth de Burgh."

"To that I will hold you, Robert Bruce," she agreed, glad-eyed. "I . . . and Saint Fillan!"

Hand in hand they turned, to face downhill.

Book Two

THE PATH OF THE HERO KING

PRINCIPAL CHARACTERS

In Order of Appearance

DAVID DE MORAY, BISHOP OF MORAY: Uncle of patriot Andrew Moray.

DEWAR OF THE COIGREACH: Hereditary Keeper of St. Fillan's staff.

DEWAR OF THE MAIN: Hereditary Keeper of St. Fillan's left arm-bone.

LADY ELIZABETH DE BURGH, the QUEEN: Wife of Robert the First and daughter of Earl of Ulster.

LADY MARJORY BRUCE: Eleven-year-old only child of the King.

ROBERT BRUCE, KING OF SCOTS: Fugitive, a few months after coronation.

SIR EDWARD BRUCE, EARL OF CARRICK: Eldest brother of above.

SIR NIGEL BRUCE: Next and favourite brother.

SIR CHRISTOPHER SETON: English knight and friend of Bruce. Second husband of Lady Christian, Countess of Mar, Bruce's sister.

LADY ISOBEL, COUNTESS OF BUCHAN: Sister to Earl of Fife. Wife of Buchan, who fought for English.

SIR JAMES DOUGLAS: "The Good Sir James" Lord of Douglas. Friend of Bruce.

SIR GILBERT HAY: Another old friend, Lord of Erroll.

SIR NEIL CAMPBELL: Chief of Clan Campbell and Lord of Lochawe.

JOHN DE STRATHBOGIE, EARL OF ATHOLL; Brother-in-law of Bruce's first wife.

SIR ALEXANDER LINDSAY: Lord of Crawford, a Bruce supporter.

SIR ROBERT FLEMING: Lord of Biggar, a Bruce supporter.

SIR ROBERT BOYD OF NODDSDALE: A Bruce supporter.

MALCOLM MACGREGOR OF GLENORCHY: Chief of Clan Alpine.

MALCOLM, EARL OF LENNOX: A great Celtic noble, friend of Bruce.

ANGUS OG MACDONALD: Self-styled Prince and Lord of the Isles. Second son of Angus Mor, Lord of Islay.

CHRISTINA MACRUARIE, LADY OF GARMORAN: Chieftainess of branch of Clan Donald; widow of brother of late Earl of Mar.

Sir Robert Clifford, Lord of Brougham: English commander.
Master Nicholas Balmyle: Official of St. Andrews: former Chancellor of Scotland.
Sir Aymer de Valence, Earl of Pembroke: English commander-in-chief in Scotland.
Master Bernard de Linton: Vicar of Mordington. Secretary.
William de Irvine: Armour-Bearer to the King.
John Comyn, Earl of Buchan: Lord High Constable of Scotland. Siding with the English.
Sir Thomas Randolph, Lord of Nithsdale: Son of a step-sister of Bruce.
Sir Alexander Comyn: Brother of Buchan, Sheriff of Inverness and Keeper of Urquhart Castle.
Sir Hugh Ross: Eldest son of the Earl of Ross.
Sir James Stewart: 5th Hereditary High Steward of Scotland.
Walter Stewart: Son of above.
William, Earl of Ross: Great Celtic noble.
Alexander MacDonald of Argyll: Chief of clan. Enemy of Bruce.
Sir Robert Keith: Hereditary Knight Marischal of Scotland.
Lady Matilda Bruce: Youngest sister of the King.
Lady Isabella de Strathbogie: Sister of Earl of Atholl.
William Lamberton, Bishop of St. Andrews: Primate. Friend of Bruce.
Master Thomas Fenwick: Prior of Hexham-on-Tyne.
Sir Henry de Bohun: Nephew of Earl of Hereford.
Gilbert de Clare, Earl of Gloucester: Nephew of Edward the Second.
Ralph de Monthermer: Step-father of above. Second husband of Edward the First's daughter.
Sir Marmaduke Tweng: Veteran English knight. Former keeper of Stirling Castle.
Sir Philip Moubray: Scots knight. Keeper of Stirling Castle for the English.
Henry, Earl of Hereford: Lord High Constable of England.

BANNOCKBURN

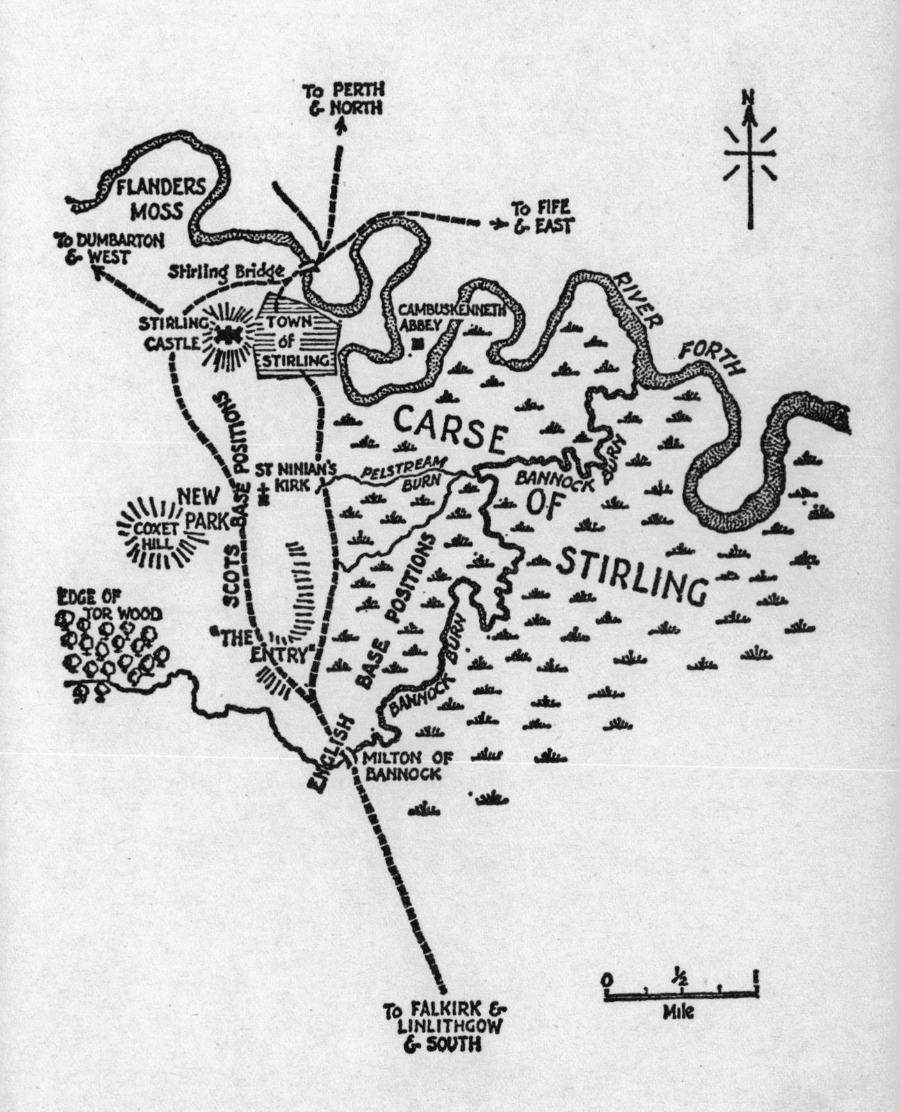

PART ONE

Chapter One

The Abbey of Glendochart was a ruin, of course. Had been for centuries. But there was a little shrine there still, amongst the grassy mounds and moss-grown stones that nestled under the high heather hills. It could not be called a church or chapel, either from its appearance or its intrinsic character — indeed Holy Church itself would have been the first to deny it any such title, just as she would sternly condemn any suggestion that the mounds and heaps of masonry, of which this was the last remaining entity, had ever been a true monastic limb of the Body of Christ. Holy Church was, as ever, very strong about such matters, however much she might bend to the winds of expediency in others. And the ancient Celtic Church of the Culdees, long put down, God be praised, was still anathema.

That was why David de Moray, Bishop of Moray, though a cheerful and anything but pompously clerical exponent of the Church Militant, sat outside and a little way off, his back turned to the low, squat and entirely plain little building, more like a croft-house than a sanctuary, and contemplated instead the magnificent soaring skyline of Ben More and Stobinian, 3,000 feet above them, where the cloud-shadows sailed serenely across the quartz-shot stone and the purple July bell-heather, and the desperations of men seemed remote indeed. The Bishop, however, did not wholly idle away this rather deplorable interval; he honed the edge of his great two-handed sword with a most rhythmic and methodical stroke.

At a little distance, on the grassy haughlands of the River Fillan, the men lay at ease, some 500 of them, mainly Lowland men-at-arms but with some clansmen from the Southern Highlands, Campbells, MacGregors, MacLarens and the like, eyeing each other with no love lost, but glad enough to laze for a little in the smile of the July sun. They anticipated little lazing hereafter, for some time to come. Some of them took the opportunity to wash soiled and bloodstained bandaging in the clear sparkling water of the Fillan.

Inside the small low-browed building it was dark, by contrast, and not a little stuffy; indeed a blunt man might have called it smelly, despite the illustrious quality of the folk who crowded it — for unchanged clothing, untreated wounds and horse-sweat added to the human variety, can make a potent admixture, even without the smoke from the two guttering wicks that burned in beaten iron bowls at either end of the rough stone altar at the east end of the cabin. There were perhaps forty people crammed into that confined space, some kneeling or squatting but most standing, happy when they could lean against the walling, about ten of them women. Some bowed their heads reverently, some yawned, some frankly slept, with one or two emitting quite unknightly snores — though more than that, obviously, was required to halt the flow of liquid, musical-sounding Gaelic, quite unintelligible to almost all of them, that went on and on. Two men, up at the altar, produced this — and when one faltered for lack of breath, the other took over without pause.

If the Bishop outside did not look particularly priestly, in chain-mail and sword-belt, at least he had a cross and a mitre painted on his ragged surcoat. These two had not a single sacerdotal emblem or vestment between them. One was a young man, of stocky but good physique, red-haired, dressed in a short kilt of faded saffron stuff, with an open and sleeveless calfskin waistcoat, black and white, and nothing else. The other was an elderly stooping ruin of a man, of once mighty build, wrapped in a voluminous ragged tartan plaid, and grey-bearded right down to the massive gold belt of snake-links that winked in the flickering lamplight and kept his tatters approximately in place. They made strange ministrants for the singsong liturgical chanting which they gabbled endlessly. Yet none, north of the Highland Line at least, would have questioned their authority. They were two of the hereditary Dewars of Saint Fillan, custodians of the sacred relics of that royal saint of the ancient Celtic Church; the old man, the Dewar of the Coigreach, Fillan's bronze-headed pastoral staff of six centuries before, which now lay along the altar-slab; and the young, Dewar of the Main, the saint's left arm-bone encased in a silver reliquary, which lay beside the staff. The other three Dewars, custodians of less important relics, were not present, being unfortunately under the thumb of Macnab, *Mac-an-abb*, chiefly descendant of the hereditary Abbots of Glendochart, a supporter of the unlamented and abdicated King John Baliol and of his Comyn kinsmen. But these two were the principal Dewars, and if anyone could convey the blessings of Saint Fillan and of the strange former Culdee Church, these could.

Crowded as the place was, a little space was left in, as it were, the first row before the altar, for three persons who knelt — a man, a woman and a child. The man, in mail, auburn head bare, was in his thirty-second year, medium-tall of build, wide-shouldered, strong-featured with a rough-hewn sort of good looks, but strained-seeming, drawn, and bearing one shoulder slightly lower than the other as though in pain. The woman was tall, well-made, and of a proud and generous beauty, five years younger, her heavy corn-coloured hair bound with a golden fillet, richly dressed in travelling clothes somewhat crumpled and stained. The child, a girl of eleven, slight, dark and great-eyed, daughter of the man and step-child of the woman, stared about her in the half-dark and coughed with the lamp-smoke. She at least made no gesture at prayerful reverence.

Strangely enough it was her father, not normally a prayerful or very religious-minded man, who seemed most impressed by the proceedings, most anxious to take part, to be identified. Occasionally his lips moved. His wife eyed him sidelong almost as often as she looked at the altar and the two strange figures before it. She was attentive, concerned — but her concern was not really with what went on but with its effect on the man at her side. None knew so well as she did how important this curious interlude was for the King.

Almost, indeed, it represented a sort of salvation for a man sunk in guilt, the guilt of both murder and sacrilege, excommunicated by the Pope of Rome — whatever his own Scots bishops might say — beaten in battle within weeks of his coronation, a fugitive in his own country. This blessing and acceptance, by even this attenuated remnant of the former Church of the land, put down by the Romish order for over two centuries but persisting in these mountains in some degree still, was of vital moment. And not only to his bruised and harried spirit. The two extraordinary figures before him, lay Dewars though they were, nevertheless were accepted as holy men of major importance all over the Celtic Highlands and Islands. And since all the Lowlands, south, east and north, were barred to Robert Bruce, occupied by the English invaders, or his enemies the Comyns and their supporters, his future, in the meantime, must lie in these Highlands and Islands. This day's proceedings, therefore, represented hope.

Not all his followers, huddled in the ruins of Glendochart Abbey in Strathfillan, understood how vital all this was to the King, or looked on it as more than a passing madness on the part of a man tried to the limits. Catholics all, good, indifferent or only nominal, they looked askance at this outlandish performance by a couple of heathenish Highland caterans, in what was little better than a cattle-shed — and the only praying they did was that it would soon be over. Only those closest to Bruce — his brothers Edward and Nigel; his sisters Mary and Christian, with the latter's husband, Sir Christopher Seton; the Countess of Buchan who had placed the crown on his head those weeks before; and one or two of his surviving nearest friends, like Sir James Douglas and Sir Gilbert Hay, had any idea how much their cause might be affected by this weird ceremony.

How long it might have gone on had they not been rudely interrupted, there was no knowing. A messenger came hurrying in and pushed his way to the front, stumbling in the dark and cursing audibly. He reached and spoke to Edward Bruce, who rose, but gestured him on to the kneeling King.

"My lord King," the man whispered hoarsely. "Sir Robert Boyd sends me. From your rearward. The Earl of Buchan comes up Dochartside. In force. From the Loch of Tay. Two thousand horse, Sir Robert says. English with him, under Percy."

"A curse on it! They have found us, then . . ."

"Aye, we are betrayed again," Edward Bruce declared, from behind, not troubling to lower his voice.

"Buchan, you say? The Comyns?" The King glanced over his shoulder, shrinking with the pain of it, to where the Countess of Buchan knelt behind his sisters, his wife's principal lady-in-waiting and wife of the Constable of Scotland who was thus pursuing him even into these mountains. He sighed, and rose to his feet, lifting a hand to the Dewar of the Main, the young man, who was presently holding forth.

"My friend," he called, "I am sorry. Your pardon — but we must go. The enemy approaches. In strength. We must ride. I thank you . . .'

Had it been the old man, he probably would have paid no heed and continued haughtily with the ritual. But the other faltered into silence and became suddenly just a young and somewhat embarrassed Highlandman. His companion glared, tugging his long beard, and grabbed his staff off the altar in protest.

"I am sorry," the King repeated. "Your blessing I much value. Your faith and order I will seek to cherish. But now we must go. Remembering kindly Glendochart." He took the Queen's arm and nodded to the Princess Marjory. "Come."

Out in the sunshine the Bishop was waiting for him, leaning on his sword. "Trouble, Sire?" he asked. "Not the English? In these hills . . . !"

"The Comyns. Buchan leads them. With Percy." Bruce turned to the messenger. "How near are they?"

"They were past Luib when I rode, Sire. Sir Robert retiring before them. To the loch-foot . . ."

"Then we have but little time. Two thousand, you say? Too many for us, by far, as we are. We can but run for it."

"Where? Encumbered as we are with wounded. And women." Sir Edward Bruce, the eldest of the King's four brothers, was dark, thin, wiry and of tense-nerved disposition. "I say that we should fight. Seek a place to ambush them. Use this land against them . . ."

Sir Nigel, a little younger, handsomely dashing, laughter-loving and the King's favourite, agreed. "To be sure. Even though they are four to one. We have skulked and hidden enough, by God! Here, in this boggy valley, with the river and the hills, is no place for their chivalry. Hemmed in. We can bring them to battle on our terms . . ."

There were cries for and against amongst the circle of lords and knights that clustered round the King, fairly evenly divided.

Bruce shook his auburn head. "Use your wits," he requested his brothers. "Think you I would not stand and fight, if I might with any hope of success? But if the Comyns are riding up Glendochart, it is because they have been led here. No host would venture into these trackless mountains by chance. They must be guided to us. Which means that we have been betrayed. And the only folk who could betray us hereabouts are the Macnabs. When Patrick Macnab came not to greet us, in his own country, I deemed him no friend. Now, I see why he did not come! He has hastened to bring our enemies down upon us. And if they are so led, then think you we could ambush them? Take them by surprise? In daylight? This is *their* land. They will know every inch of it. And we have no time to wait for darkness. They would be on us in an hour. No — we have no choice, my friends. We must ride. And westwards. We must make for Sir Neil's country on Loch Awe. With all speed that we may. Forthwith. Sir Neil Campbell — you will lead . . ."

The Campbell chief, a dark, swarthy, youngish man of sombre looks but a notable fighter, was nothing loth. He had been anxious not to linger in this area of Breadalbane and Mamlorn, Saint Fillan's land or no, these last five days; it was too close and linked to the domains of his hereditary enemies, the MacDougalls of Argyll and Lorn. And the Lord of Lorn was wed to a sister of the late, murdered Sir John Comyn the Red, Lord of Badenoch.

Despite the complaint that they were encumbered with women, and wounded from the disastrous battle of Methven nearly three weeks previously, the King's small host was not slow about moving off. They had a sufficiency of practice. Campbell, with an advance party of four score, went first. Half an hour after the arrival of Boyd's courier, the haughland of the Fillan was empty save for the two Dewars and some of the local folk. With the enemy only about six miles behind, this was not too soon.

They rode up Strathfillan, the upper portion of Glendochart, making for Tyndrum, where the routes forked, one to go west by south, by Glen Lochy and Glen Orchy to the foot of Loch Awe; the other north over the mouth of Mamlorn and across the desert wastes of the vast Moor of Rannoch, to Lochaber and North Atholl. There was no other choice. The great mountain barriers hemmed them in.

The Queen and Marjory rode beside Bruce. It was nothing new for Elizabeth de Burgh, daughter of English King Edward's greatest friend, the Earl of Ulster, to be hunted, a fugitive. Since she threw in her lot with Bruce four years before, she had known little of peace and security in a savaged and war-torn land. But for young Marjory this was her first taste of campaigning. She had been reared in care and seclusion at her dead mother's old home, the remote, strong castle of Kildrummy in Mar, seat of that earldom, by her aunt and uncle twice over — for the late Earl of Mar had married Bruce's sister Christian, now Lady Seton, and Bruce's first wife had been the Lady Isabel of Mar. She had been brought south only to attend her father's hurried coronation. Marjory saw all as adventure and pleasurable excitement.

They had gone a bare two miles, and reached a stretch where the valley narrowed in and its floor was scored by quite a deep gorge through which the river rushed and spilled in foaming rapids, when an uproar in front halted them. The lie of the land and a thrusting shoulder of the braeside hid what went on — but there was most evidently a clash of arms.

Swiftly Bruce reacted. He pointed Sir James, the Lord of Douglas, forward. "Find me what's to do, Jamie," he commanded. "Campbell sounds to have run into trouble. Discover how much." He turned to Hay. "Gibbie — back, to halt and alert all the column."

Nigel spurred close. "If Campbell is beset, let us to his aid," he exclaimed, his sword already in hand.

"Wait, you," his brother said. He looked about him keenly. "An ill place for fighting."

It was. A steep bank of heather and scree rose directly on their right, to the north, curving back out of sight. Only a dozen yards or so to the other side what amounted to a cliff dropped to the river in its gorge. A place with less scope for manoeuvre would be hard to imagine.

Even as they looked, clamour and tumult broke out well to the rear, more violent than that in front.

"By the Rude — it is a trap!" the King cried. "An ambush! They have us." Quick as thought he jerked his horse's head round to face the steep slope, signing to his wife and daughter and the other women to do likewise.

All down the strung-out line there was confusion.

"Nigel — forward, and tell Douglas. And Campbell. We must up. Break out of this trap, this valley." He pointed higher. "Edward — back. To Hay. Get our people up out of this kennel. Then word back to Boyd and the rearward. Off with you." The rest, those near him, he waved onwards, upwards.

It was a steep climb for the horses, nearly 200 feet of rough going, demanding a zigzag ascent. They were perhaps half-way up this, in a long ragged line, perhaps 300 men, with the King and his immediate group, including the women; well in front, when the long ululant winding of a horn sounded from above, echoing amongst the enclosing hills. This was succeeded by a wild and savage shouting from hundreds, thousands of hoarse throats. And over the skyline appeared wave after wave of yelling, gesticulating men.

Bruce reined up in momentary indecision — although, in almost automatic reaction, he was tugging free the long two-handed sword sheathed at his back. He had suffered a grievous surprise at Methven, but never had he been so unready for battle as this.

The women, of course, were his first anxiety. Urgently he turned in the saddle. "Back!" he shouted to Elizabeth. "Down again. Get them back."

The Queen, daughter of a long line of warriors, neither panicked nor hesitated. Grabbing her step-daughter's bridle, she dragged both horses round, calling to the other ladies to follow her downhill. Bruce blessed her, even as he commanded his trumpeter to sound the rally.

There was no time for any positioning, any marshalling. The attackers had not much more than 200 yards to cover from their hidden waiting-place behind the rise. They were afoot, bare-shanked Highlanders to a man, but leaping, bounding in their charge almost as fast as cavalry, brandishing their Lochaber-axes and claymores, and yelling their slogans, a terrifying sight. Few wore more than the short kilt, to fight in, and many had cast away even these and were completely naked save for their rawhide brogans. On the face of it, mounted men in armour should have been vastly superior as fighting-men to these unprotected howling savages. But Bruce knew better than that. For one thing they had an enormous advantage in numbers; and they were on their own ground. Also they had the benefit of surprise, with the horsemen scattered. But most serious of all, the Highlanders were charging and the mounted men were not only stationary but were so on a steep and slippery downwards slope.

The Earl of Atholl, the Bishop, Sir Alexander Lindsay, Sir Robert Fleming and one or two others had spurred forward to the King's side, past the hurrying women. All along the hillside the knights and men-at-arms were seeking to draw together, to consolidate for mutual aid and protection.

There was insufficient time for this. Like an angry flood the Highlanders were upon them. Bruce, still in front, found half a dozen attackers leaping at him, each with a claymore in one hand and a dirk in the other.

His damaged shoulder, relic of the Methven fight, was a grievous handicap in wielding the great five-foot-long two-handed sword. Nevertheless, standing in his stirrups and aided by this elevation, he cut down three of his assailants with his first tremendous right-and-left slashes, before the residual wrench of his swing so tore his shoulder as to leave him gasping and it numb and useless. His efforts thereafter to lay about him with the one hand were less than successful. When only his chain-mail saved him from two crippling thrusts, he tossed his sword at one of the bounding men, and drew his battle-axe instead.

All around was chaos, complete and desperate. There was no line, no certainty — save that the mounted chivalry was getting the worst of it. Each horseman was an island in a sea of milling, smiting clansmen. And the island were steadily growing fewer. For the Highlanders were attacking in especial the horses, darting in and ducking beneath them, to slash open the bellies with their dirks. Everywhere the screaming, rearing brutes were falling, their armoured riders crashing.

Bruce, with a swift glance around, perceived that there was only one end to this, and that would not be long delayed unless something was done at once. Bending low over his mount's neck, he slashed furiously with his axe in a figure-of-eight motion, to drive back the two men who were at the moment assailing him, at the same time seeking to knee the horse round. It was the rearing beast's pawing hooves rather than the battle-axe which knocked over one of the men; but the other, a gigantic figure, claymore gone, hurled himself bodily upwards, hands clawing, in a crazy attempt to clutch the King and drag him from the saddle. Bruce managed to twist aside, kicking spurs into his horse's flanks. The giant failed to grasp the monarch's person, but one hand closed on the fine cloth-of-gold heraldic cloak that Bruce wore instead of the usual surcoat, embroidered with the red Lion Rampant of Scotland worked with the Queen's own hands. Tearing it away at the magnificent jewelled brooch that clasped it in place, the Highlander fell back clutching not the King but this trophy.

Bruce's trumpeter had disappeared, and his master had to shout, as he spurred downhill, lashing out at those who tried to stop him, with that wicked red-gleaming axe.

"A Bruce! A Bruce!" he yelled. "To me! To me A Bruce!"

That was a slogan for charge and victory, not for retreat and defeat. But something had to be done to break off this dire and fatal struggle, and to try to save the women.

Gathering blessed momentum the King plunged downhill, his brute sliding and almost sitting on its haunches. Momentum — that was what was required against these caterans, mounted momentum.

Sadly few of his company were in any position to perceive their sovereign's manoeuvre, or successfully to break away to join him. Close pressed and confined, most could by no means win free. By the time that Bruce was through the mêlée and could glance back and about him, no more than fifty or sixty out of the original three hundred appeared to be even mounted.

He did not slacken the speed of his descent, but plunged on down to the shelf above the gorge, where Elizabeth had the women clustered in an anxious, great-eyed knot, ten or eleven of them. Fortunately all were fairly young and good horsewomen — or they would not have been in this fugitive company in the first place.

The King had no pride in what he did. To be leading the flight from a stricken field was gall and wormwood for the Bruce. But it was necessary, if any were to survive — and no one else was doing it.

Down to them he came, his mount's slithering hooves scoring great red weals in the braeside. He pointed.

"Westwards!" he shouted. "On. Only way." Most of the women were in fact facing in the other direction.

"Robert! You are hurt?" the Queen cried. "Your shoulder . . .?"

"Nothing," the King threw back. "Wrenched, that is all." He looked back. Atholl and Lindsay were close behind, Bishop Moray and Fleming and a few others followed after, two horses bearing double burdens.

They dared not wait. Putting himself at the head of the little group of women, Bruce led on along the track above the river, westwards, at a canter. The foremost survivors caught up with them, to form a sort of cordon, while others trailed along at varying distances. It made a sorry scene.

After only a few moments, rounding the bend in the glen-floor, they met Nigel Bruce, Douglas and Campbell with the residue of the advance guard, fleeing in the opposite direction. It was a pathetic remnant of not more than a score out of the eighty, with again some horses carrying two men.

Bruce only reined in, did not halt, and wasted no words on inessentials. "How many? In front?" he demanded, waving to the newcomers to turn round again.

"Two hundred. Three," Campbell panted. "Took us by surprise. Rocks rolled down. Arrows. Houghed the horses . . ."

The King cut him short with a chopping motion. "They follow? Pursue you?"

"Yes. If you continue thus you will run into them . . ."

"Better that than back. Thousands behind! More in rear. A trap. Come — form a wedge. Quickly. We must cut through . . ."

He did not have to explain. The wedge, or arrowhead cavalry attack, was a classic formation, given bold or desperate men and trained horses. Plus fierce momentum. Pressed close in a tight inverted V behind a purposeful and unflinching leader, each man keeping exactly his position, there was practically nothing, in flesh and blood at least, that could stop or withstand such a charge — even when, as often happened, the said leader, the tip of the arrowhead, and his immediate flanking men, who bore the brunt of the impact, were carried along dead or dying by the necessary momentum, borne up by the close press of the rest. All knew it. But not with a core of women and a bairn for the arrowhead!

They worked themselves into formation, nevertheless, a company of about forty now, hedging the women in, with stragglers adding themselves all the time. It was not so well-shaped and tight a wedge as many would have wished, but at least it made a solid and determined body, driving on at a fast canter once more.

Round a further bend of the trough, they suddenly were face to face with the enemy. Running along the shelf and some way up the bank to the north came a horde of Highlanders, in wild spirits and no sort of order or discipline, a bloodthirsty crowd elated with victory, chasing a defeated foe. Undoubtedly their shock was great at abruptly being confronted, instead, by a charge of cavalry however modest in numbers. The check in their racing advance was obvious and eloquent. But still they came on, though with less confidence.

The King, at the apex of his formation, did not hesitate. Instead he shouted, "Faster! Faster!" and raising his battle-axe on high, yelled, "A Bruce! A Bruce and Scotland!"

His companions took up the cry bravely, even some of the women skirling their shrill contribution.

Somewhere at the rear of the Highland party one of their war-horns began to wind, leadership tardily asserting itself. But it was too late, whatever the signal represented; indeed, probably it only increased the confusion, as some held back or faltered while the majority pressed on.

The horsemen crashed into the flood of wild-eyed, shouting men with enormous impact. No amount of valour or fighting skill could withstand it. Bowled over like ninepins, the Highlanders went down in swathes, more felled by the impetus and the lashing hooves than by the flailing weapons of the riders. As he was swept on through the throng of bodies, in fact, Bruce's own battle-axe never once made contact with a foe. His useless shoulder greatly hampered him, of course; but even so he was borne up and carried forward so closely by the press of his companions that there was little that he could do to affect the issue, other than to retain his position and shout his Bruce slogan.

It was not a matter of piercing a front, for the Highlanders were merely a mob streaming along a terrace of the hillside. It was like cleaving the current of a rushing torrent, rather, with loss of momentum the direst danger. So the riders spurred their foaming, frightened mounts even more than they wielded their swords; and spectacular as was the downfall of the foe, probably no great numbers failed to rise again thereafter. Not one of the horsemen was brought low, at any rate, and the women within the shield of steel and horseflesh scarcely saw their enemies.

At last they were through the main crowd. But the King spurred on as hard as ever, well aware that the clansmen would rally behind them and that all could yet be lost. On up the glen he led the hard-riding company, on to where Campbell's advance party had been ambushed, marked all too clearly by the litter of dead and dying men and horses. Here some dismounted and slightly-wounded survivors emerged from hiding-places to join them — but the King had to steel his heart against any waiting for these, meantime. Some few got pulled up, pillion, behind riders, but to most Bruce gestured upwards, shouting that they should climb out of that fatal gut of the valley, north by west into the empty hills. He drove on.

He was making for a levelling of the trough which they could see some way to the west, where it looked as though horses would be able to get out without the dangers of steep, slow climbing. Beyond, half-right, there appeared to be a jumble of small, low hillocks with open woodland — the sort of cover they required.

They saw no more of the enemy and were able, presently, to set their beasts' heads to the lessened slope on the right and at last to win out of that grim valley. Half a mile more and they were amongst the knowes and scattered birches that spread over a wide area to the north of Tyndrum, the outskirts of the Forest of Mamlorn. Here, surely, they would be secure, for the moment. Thankfully Bruce drew rein, and turned to his wife and daughter.

"God be praised at least you are safe here!" he gasped.

Marjory, who had kept up throughout as well as any, now burst into tears of reaction. Elizabeth leaned over to put an arm around her.

"Hush you, hush you," she murmured. "It is by with, now. Remember — you are a king's daughter!"

"You have done well, lass," her father said. "Very well. All of you." He looked at the women. "Would that I could say as much for myself!" Sheathing his axe, he reached a hand out to his wife. "My dear — you ill chose a man to wed!" he said.

"*I* chose well enough. It is the others who chose ill!" The Queen shook her head. "There are over many traitors in your realm, my lord King!"

"Do not name them traitors. Not yet. I am too newly their king. I need time to win them . . ."

"An eternity will not win you MacDougall!" his brother Nigel broke in. "That was he. The Lord of Lorn and his clan. Come out of the west. Seeking you. He is wed to Comyn's sister . . ."

"MacDougall! So great a man! Then . . . Lorn is closed against us. Argyll. A whole province."

"I could have foretold it, Sire," Sir Neil Campbell declared sourly. "Not the ambush, but MacDougall's hatred. As Comyn's kin. He has been brought here by Macnab. They are close."

"Macnab, then, has cost me dear this day! Called both Buchan and MacDougall down on us, from east and west. To trap us in his Glen Dochart. What have I ever done against Macnab . . .?"

"While his creatures, those Dewars, kept you constrained, bethralled, with their heathenish mummery! Bait to his trap!" That was John de Strathbogie, Earl of Atholl, married to a sister of Bruce's first wife, and bleeding from two slight wounds.

"No! That I will not believe," the King cried, "The Dewars would not do that. Not so misuse what they hold most sacred on earth. The old man, I swear, was honest. His blessing true."

None might flatly contradict the monarch — but only one was prepared to agree with him; his wife.

"True, yes," she said. "These you may trust. The blessing was sure." Whether she believed it or no, Elizabeth de Burgh knew what that blessing meant to her husband.

"You were caught from the rear?" Nigel asked. "The main body? Where is Edward? Hay? The others . . .?"

"God knows! They came on us from above. In their thousands. We had to cut our way out. For the others, we can but wait. And pray . . .!"

* * *

Their waiting, at least, was not quite unproductive, whatever the result of their praying. In a couple of hours the King's party, hidden in the woodlands, had almost doubled itself, fugitives finding their way thither in ones and twos, exhausted, dazed, wounded or just dispirited, but none on horseback. Edward Bruce and Sir Gilbert Hay were amongst the last to arrive, the former still unsteady from being unhorsed and all but stunned by his own armour. The tail of the column had been as badly cut up as the rest, they reported, being overwhelmed before either of them could reach it. They had seen nothing of Boyd's rearguard, and feared the worst.

A long silence had now settled on the weary and dejected company. So far, the MacDougall host had not come seeking them here. But all knew that it was only a question of time. They would be reorganising, and possibly waiting for darkness. For if Bruce's own survivors could pick out this wooded hillocks area as an obvious refuge, then undoubtedly the Highlanders could do the same.

The King had been pacing, alone, a patch of green turf amongst the heather between two knolls, with the twisted gait of a man in physical pain, and the twisted expression of equal mental pain. Abruptly he halted, and it was his brother he looked at, not his wife and daughter.

"There is nothing for it," he said harshly. "We must part company. We cannot go on, thus. We are but playing our enemies' game. Here is no country for knights and chivalry. Or for women! Yet, out of these mountains, if I survive, I can raise thousands. Moreover, all else is closed to me. If I am to win back my strength, as your king, to challenge Edward of England, and the Comyns again, I must have time. As it were to lick my wounds, as might a lion. A sorry lion! And only in these Highland hills may I do it. But not as proud leader of a knightly host. As a cateran against caterans, rather. That way only lies survival."

It was a strange speech for the Bruce, for any monarch. They all gazed at him, unspeaking, waiting.

"So, Nigel — you will take the Queen and the ladies. With strong escort. Take them far north and east. To Kildrummy, in Mar. Out of this west country. To safety . . ."

"No, Robert — no! Not that . . .!" Elizabeth cried.

"Yes, my heart. It must be. I say yes. Indeed, it is my royal command. Here is no life for women. You would not tie our hands? Nigel will take you to Kildrummy. You will take all the horses that are left us — for you will need them, and they will serve us nothing who remain here. We shall do better afoot. We shall make for Sir Neil's country of Loch Awe in Argyll. And come to you again, when we may."

The Queen could not dispute openly, of course. But she looked unconvinced.

"And what if Edward Plantagenet comes for us at Kildrummy?" Nigel asked.

"Then you will go north. Even further. Ever north. Beyond the great firths. As far as you must, to gain these ladies' safety. Where Edward cannot follow. Even to the North Isles, if need be. They will receive you kindly, for our sister's sake who is their queen in Norway. These who I hold most dear, I trust into your hand. The married men, and the wounded, will go with you. My lord of Atholl. Sir Christopher Seton. Sir Alexander Lindsay. Sir Alan Durward. Sir John de Cambo. My lord Bishop of Moray. The rest will turn cateran, here. With Robert Bruce!"

The buzz of excited exclamation and comment that followed was interrupted by the arrival, mounted, of Sir Robert Boyd and about a dozen of his rearguard, weary and battle-scarred. Boyd was lifted down from his horse, sorely wounded in the leg. He gasped out his report. They had been caught between the two enemy forces, and had had no option but to fight their way out, towards their main body, with appalling losses. Boyd, who had been one of William Wallace's closest lieutenants, was a doughty veteran, though but thirty, and his survival of major importance; but the loss of almost nine out of ten of his rearguard was dire news. It meant that out of a total force of some five hundred, Bruce had now not one fifth remaining.

Boyd's leg-wound was also a blow. It meant that he would be unable to remain with the King's dismounted party — and he was the most experienced guerilla leader they had. But at least he was strongly in favour of the King's plan, and would be a source of strength to Nigel's party. He declared that the sooner they split forces the better. His own flight hither undoubtedly would have been observed, and it would be guessed that the royal survivors were assembling here. He urged that the Queen's company should make off immediately due northwards through the Mamlorn passes before these could be cut. The rest could then filter off through this open forestland in small groups, on foot, to come together again at a chosen rendezvous. In Glen Lochy perhaps. Campbell would know...

That was accepted. Bruce drew Elizabeth aside a little way.

"My dear," he said, "I am sorry. But... better this way."

"Better for whom? Not for me."

"For you, yes, also. In the end. Would you relish being a hunted fugitive?"

"So long as I was with you."

He shook his head. "I would not have my wife harried like a run deer. Nor can I have our men having ever to think of women's safety. You must see it, my love. But, by the Rude, I am going to miss you! The thought of it is like lead at my heart."

"Miss, yes. For me, life will be no more than an emptiness. And it may be long, long."

"Not a day, not an hour, longer than needs must. That I promise you."

"Must? Must? Robert — must indeed you do this? Must you go on with a hopeless struggle? You have tried and tried again. Why continue? Why not come north also? North indeed. Let us go to the North Isles. Together. To the Orcades. In your sister's husband's realm. Where none will assail us. Where we may live together in peace, you and I. Until a better day dawns. Edward of England is an old man, and sick. He will not live for very long. We are young, and can wait..." Her voice tailed away in a manner strange indeed for that strong-minded young woman.

The Bruce stared at her, closely. Never had he heard Elizabeth speak like this, the woman who had been his strength and stay. "Dear God," he whispered. "*You* ask that?"

Slowly she raised a troubled downcast gaze to meet his. And then her chin rose also, suddenly proud again. "No!" she said. "No. That was not I who spoke. Not Elizabeth de Burgh. Not your wife. Not the Queen. Forget that it was said. Said by a tired and foolish woman, in sorrow for herself. Heed it not, Robert — but go and do your duty."

He all but broke, then, more affected by her self-rebuke than by her pleas. "My love, my sweet, my very own," he said. "It may be that you have the rights of it. Who knows? But... I took the crown, for better or for worse. I swore to free and save this realm, if it is within my power to do so. As yet, I have proved but a sore king for Scotland. Two battles, and both shamefully lost..."

"Neither were battles. Both traps set by traitors, rather." That was more like Elizabeth.

"Perhaps. But in both I was taken by surprise. And should not have been. I thought that I had learned my lesson, at Methven. But no. Many have died for my error. I set up advance and rearguards, yes — but forgot that in these mountains that is not how war is fought. I must redeem myself, Elizabeth — not flee to safety."

"Yes, I know it. Forgive me. But I hoped that, though the other women, and Marjory, went . . . that I might stay with you. For I am strong of body, and care nothing for discomforts of camp and field. But . . . I see that it cannot be. I will go to Kildrummy, with your daughter. Or if need be, to the Isles. And await you there. There to assail the ears of all the saints in heaven continually, to watch over and preserve you, and bring you back to me!"

"Amen to that," he said. "Now — Marjory . . ."

So the leave-taking was got over, with haste and not a little foreboding — for none there required to have spelled out to them the chances against any swift or happy reunion. To Nigel the King spoke at greater length — for though he was his favourite brother, and trustworthy to the end, he was of a carefree and happy-go-lucky disposition, and Bruce was entrusting to him not only his wife but the heiress to his throne. He urged him, privily, to be guided by Boyd rather than by Atholl or Lindsay, more lofty in rank as these might be.

Elizabeth was the Queen again, calm in control of her women and herself. She bade her husband farewell with steadfast dignity and restraint, even though her lip quivered in the process. Mounting, they were gone, leaving about thirty men amongst the evening shadows of the trees.

They gazed after the departing riders, all young men, the King in fact the second oldest there, some ten knights and esquires, with a score of personal attendants and men-at-arms, all horseless for perhaps the first time in their lives. Whatever they said, whatever had been implied, they could not but feel themselves as lost, naked and abandoned — all perhaps save Sir Neil Campbell, the only Highlandman present. A month before, these had been amongst the very flower of Scotland's chivalry; today they were little better than broken men, hunted outlaws.

Bruce himself, after a few moments, deliberately set the pattern of it. Twisting round, and grimacing at the pain of his shoulder, he called, "To me, Jamie. Aid me out of this shirt of mail. Such wear is not for us, my friends. Hereafter. Off with your armour and helmets. Put away two-handed swords, battle-axes, maces and the like. Henceforth we use dirks and daggers. Tonight, after dark, we go down again to the field of battle. They will scarce look for us there. To rob the slain. The MacDougall slain. We want plaids and tartans and sheepskins. Brogans for our feet. Broadswords. Targes. From now onward we forget that we are knights and lords. Food we shall require, likewise — and must win it where we may."

The young Lord of Douglas, but newly of age, aiding his hero out of the chain-mail, tender for a damaged shoulder, protested. "Your Grace cannot turn cateran. Like any low-born bareshanked Erse bogtrotter . . .!"

"My Grace can, and will. Indeed must. Since only so will any of us survive. And I intend to survive, my friends. Do not doubt it. Come — we have work to do . . ."

Chapter Two

Survival is a very compelling preoccupation, taking undoubted precedence over all others, in the last resort. Moreover, it carries its own built-in mental and emotional security system, excluding all other influences and anxieties which might endanger the individual's physical preservation. Long-term, hypothetical, even ethical problems tend not only to become largely irrelevant but fade altogether from the mind, in the said last resort. Concentration on survival of necessity becomes basic.

So it was with Robert Bruce and certain of his comrades in the month that followed. Certain only, because, in the test, some inevitably fell by the wayside, one way or another. Some were not of the stuff of survival, mentally or physically; some were unfortunate; some came to conceive that anything would be better than a continuation of these conditions, and opted out; some, quite simply, died. Four weeks after the Glendochart debacle, ten men only remained with the King — his brother Edward, the lords Douglas, Hay and Campbell, an obscure knight named Sir William Bellenden, and five common soldiers.

Not that there was now any observable difference between the men; indeed, if there was any ranking amongst the ten, leadership was frequently taken by a squat and uncouth Annandale moss-trooper named Wat Jardine, whose sheer powers of survival and self-help exceeded all others. All were equally filthy, unshaven, lean, brown and weather-beaten, half-naked in ragged tartans. Not once in those weeks had they slept under a roof. They had eaten raw meat more often than cooked, from stolen cattle and hunted deer and wild-fowl — even raw fish, although it turned their stomachs — but more often had to fill the said stomachs with blaeberries, fungus and wild honey. They had been hunted like brute beasts — and like beasts they had rounded and rended and slain, when they might. They had come to look on all men as their enemies, and the empty wilderness their only friend, night and storm their occasional allies.

They had never reached Argyll. The Campbell's territories which stretched from Loch Awe to the Western Sea, were hemmed in unfortunately from the east by part of Lorn, Mamlorn and Nether Lorn, as well as the lands of the Macfarlanes, MacNaughtons and MacLachlans, chiefs allied to MacDougall. In consequence every glen and pass and access they found held against them, with the whole country roused. Each shift and attempt they made ended in failure — and the diminution of their numbers. Moreover, Neil Campbell now feared that even if they reached his lands, they would there be invaded by forces too great for him to withstand.

So they had at length turned back. Malcolm Earl of Lennox was believed to have escaped after Methven, and now represented the only major noble free, and committed to the King's cause. South towards the Lennox they had turned, therefore, avoiding all the main glens and making their indirect and secret way around the lofty shoulders of the great mountains. Ben Lui, Ben Oss and Ben Vorlich, and many lesser peaks.

Now they were on the dark edge of long Loch Lomond, near the north end. It was a mid-August night, and for two days they had been in hiding in Glen Falloch to the north, resting up by day and prospecting the possibilities of escape by night. For they were still in Macfarlane country, enemy territory, and their presence in the area known. They were being sorely hunted. Just across the loch was MacGregor land, where they would expect to be comparatively safe — for though MacGregor was not necessarily a King's man, at least he was at permanent feud with Macfarlane, Macnab, and to a lesser degree with the MacDougalls. The Campbells also, as it happened — but that probably would not seriously affect the issue. Moreover, south of the MacGregor lands lay the great country of Lennox, the first of the West Lowlands. Somehow the fugitives must get across the mile-wide and twenty-five-mile-long loch — for the valley-floor to the north, in Glen Falloch, was watched for every yard of the way by the Lord of Lorn's minions, as they knew to their cost. Search parties were scouring the area for them, and Falloch had become too hot to hold them.

Unhappily, Macfarlane had obviously decreed that all the many boats of the small lochside communities should be put beyond the reach of the refugees. Bruce and six of his companions now sat silent, in a cranny amongst the rocks above the black lapping waters, having each pair covered their allotted search-area, at great risk, even as far as half a mile inland, but without the least success. All boats on the west side of Loch Lomond, that night, were evidently securely hidden or under lock and key.

The silence was grim rather than dispirited or despairing. These men were long past that. They were now fined down to surviving from hour to hour. Disappointments, failures, losses, reverses, were but incidental, to be accepted and absorbed into the pattern of survival. Any who indeed survived this prolonged ordeal would emerge very different men, men of steel, tried, tested, tempered. And ruthless.

James Douglas and Dod Pringle, one of the men-at-arms, emerged like silent shadows out of the gloom, and squatted down beside the others.

"Nothing," the young lord said briefly, flatly.

"No," the King acknowledged.

"A raft. Of driftwood. Tied with ropes of twisted bracken," Campbell suggested.

"For ten? To sail a mile?"

"Two can swim. They can draw it."

"It will be dawn in two hours. No time. We would be seen."

"Tomorrow night, then."

"If we live."

"Some will. *You* must."

The use of titles and honorifics had long since been given up.

Edward Bruce, always highly strung, a man like a coiled spring, had become almost half-crazed these last weeks, in glittering-eyed tension, his hand seldom far from his dirk-hilt. One of their number he had already slain, in a sudden fit of rage. He was a killer now, and even in that fierce company men eyed him warily and kept their distance. He spoke now.

"Back there. A mile. There are two cot-houses. At the lochside. Women in them. I heard them. A boat they will have. Somewhere. I will make them talk."

"No," his brother said. "Not women."

"I say yes. Cross this loch we must. Squeamish folly will serve nothing."

"I do not make war on women. I have enough on my mind." That was final.

There were mutterings for and against — for no man's word was law in this company now.

They were interrupted. Another little group emerged from the shadows of the alder thickets on the left, the remaining pair, Sir William Bellenden and the Annandale mosstrooper, Jardine. But there was a third figure, whom Jardine had gripped in a savage, arm-twisted hold, and bent forward almost double. At first Bruce thought the prisoner was an old woman, hung about with rags. Then he perceived the long grey beard.

"Found him by the lochside," the mosstrooper jerked. "Spying on us, for a wager! Jabbers nothing but his heathenish Irish."

The King, leaning closer to peer, distinguished even in the darkness the dull sheen of gold at approximately the waist, the entwining serpents of a magnificent belt.

"Fools!" he cried. "This is the Dewar! The Dewar of the Coigreach. Unhand him. He is a friend."

"Then why does he lurk here? At this hour?" Bellenden asked.

The old man launched into a flood of Gaelic, furious, vituperative, outraged, however unintelligible. Jardine would have silenced him with a buffet, but the King caught his arm.

"Say on, Master Dewar," he directed. "But in the tongue we may understand, of a mercy!"

The other obliged, and eloquently. "Spawn of the devil! Offspring of Beelzebub!" he declared, with a sibilant vehemence that lacked nothing in venom for all the Highland softness of intonation. "To lay their foul hands on the Dewar! To defile Saint Fillan! May they roast on the hottest hob of hell everlastingly! May the cries of their torture ascend eternally!"

"To be sure. To be sure," Bruce agreed. "Their offence will receive due punishment, undoubtedly. But — what brings you here, my friend? To Loch Lomondside?"

"You do. Who else? You, Sir King. I came seeking you." Evidently Bruce's totally unkinglike appearance did not confuse the Dewar.

"Here? In the dark? How knew you to look for me here?"

"Much is known to the Dewar."

"It is? Then, not only *you* will know we are here?"

"To be sure. All the Highlands know that you are on the wrong side of Loch Lomond. But only I know how you may win away from here."

"Ha! You do?"

"I have brought you a boat, see you."

They all stared at him, and then at each other.

"How can you have brought a boat?" Edward Bruce demanded.

The other did not trouble to reply.

The King rubbed his unshaven chin. "My friend — I am grateful," he said. "But the lochshore is watched. All Glen Falloch is watched. We fear that all boats will be denied us. Even yours."

"You know not what you say," the Dewar replied scornfully. "Come — I will take you up to it. But quietly."

"This could be a trap," Bruce's brother jerked. "Leading us into our enemies' arms."

"Aye. Belike they sent the old man to cozen us," Bellenden agreed. "To betray us. Once more."

"I think not," the King said. "This Dewar of the Coigreach gave me Saint Fillan's blessing. He would not betray me now."

"I would not trust him. I would not trust any of these Highland savages," Edward asserted, hand feeling for dirk.

"You would not?" Sir Neil Campbell, Highlander himself, asked thinly.

"Enough!" the King snapped. "The decision is mine — and I trust the Dewar. Sir — we will follow you, and gladly. But — where is your boat?"

"You shall see. So be these fools go quietly! Come."

The old man, despite his stooping shuffle, could move surprisingly quickly. Turning, he led them away from the lochside, through the shadowy junipers and scattered birches, up and down amongst the knolls and hummocks, muttering to himself in seemingly disgusted fashion, but nimble — and not so much as glancing behind to ensure that they all followed. He twisted and turned, and sometimes actually doubled back on his tracks, so that his mutterings were echoed by some of those behind. And once or twice he stopped still, and waited, almost as though sniffing the air, before moving on at a tangent. In the dark, and without landmarks, it was difficult to say what general direction they were taking; but Bruce had the impression that they were going southwards and roughly parallel with the loch.

For perhaps twenty minutes he led them on this roundabout progress, without word or indeed glance at his companions; but however irritating and mystifying a process this was, at least he led them to avoid contact with others, their enemies or the cot-houses of local clansfolk — though once they heard voices at no great distance.

At length they emerged at the waterside again — and after the constriction of the trees and knowes, visibility seemed to be enhanced. At least they could see that they were opposite a small tree-clad offshore island. It was difficult to say, in the gloom, how far off it was — possibly only two or three hundred yards.

From out of the lochshore boulders at their very feet a figure rose — to the hasty indrawn breaths of the fugitives and reaching for dirks. But the old man threw a brief word at him, and was as briefly answered; and Bruce, peering, perceived that this was in fact the younger Dewar, the custodian of the saint's arm-bone.

Almost without pause the old man waded straight into the loch, not so much as troubling to hitch up his trailing rags. He did not beckon them, though the younger Dewar gestured them on.

Bruce, following fairly close behind their guide, was surprised to find the water rising no higher than his knees, as he waded out. Nevertheless, in a few moments, there was a smothered yelp and some splashing behind him, and he turned to find one of his colleagues in the loch almost up to his neck. He could have sworn that, amongst the objurgations and exclamations behind, he heard the old Dewar sniggering in front.

Their guide had not, in fact, seemed to be heading directly towards the island, but slightly to one side. Then he suddenly changed direction, turning almost at right angles, as it were back on course. Bruce realised that they must be on one of the hidden under-water causeways, of which he had heard, dog-legged or zigzag, allowing access to certain islands by those who knew the secret. He turned to James Douglas, immediately behind, to warn the others to keep close and to turn exactly where he did.

They reached the island safely, and the old Dewar consented to explain. This had been a former sanctuary of Saint Fillan, where he retired for contemplation, and there were still remains of a cell and altar amongst the undergrowth. It was the Dewars' duty to tend this, and other shrines, and for this they sometimes required to use a boat. This they kept here.

He showed them the craft, in a little creek at the far side of the islet, with some pride. But it was tiny, little more than a coracle, only large enough to hold two, or at a pinch, three.

"By the Mass—is that all!" Edward cried. "That cockle-shell!"

"It is a boat!" Bruce declared. "Which is the great matter."

"It will carry the King across the water," the old man said. "For the others of you, I care not!"

"I am the King's brother, fool!"

"So much the worse for the King!"

Bruce intervened. "Peace, my friends. Here is much to be thankful for. It but means that we must cross two at a time. So that we have not long to spare. Before dawn. Let us waste none of it."

It seemed that the younger Dewar was to act boatman. He declared that a patrol of Macfarlanes had passed along the shore shortly before their arrival, heading north. He thought that there would be no more, for some time at least; though there might also be patrols in boats beating up and down the loch.

Though Bruce would have drawn lots for it, all others agreed that he must go across first — moreover the elder Dewar all but had apoplexy at any other suggestion. The King elected to take Sir James Douglas with him.

They climbed cautiously in — for it was quite the smallest craft either of them had ever been in, and moreover gave the impression of being half-rotten in its frail timbering. The water slopping about in the bottom could have been caused by rain, of course. The King expressed his thanks to the old man, as the younger inserted himself beside them — but their saviour maintained his peculiarly mocking and ungracious attitude to the end, even though the valedictory flood of Gaelic he sent after them might conceivably have been an addendum to the Blessing of Saint Fillan.

It made an alarming voyage. The coracle was grossly overladen, with three aboard, and Loch Lomond made itself all too evident. Indeed quickly it became clear that too much of the loch was coming inside with them, and the two passengers were soon as busy as the paddler, scooping the water out with their cupped hands, since bailer there was none. The possibility of enemy boats out here watching for them was never far from their minds.

The actual crossing was probably less than a mile — but it seemed to take an unconscionable time, with the craft heavy and sluggish to a degree and, whether from its construction, inexpert paddling or overloading, seeming to sidle and move crabwise rather than straight forward. But at last the far shore loomed in sight, dark and apparently thickly-wooded. Their escort deposited them on a shingly beach and, surprisingly, considering the course followed, seemed to know exactly where he was. He told them that a little way to the right and up the steep hillside, beside a waterfall of the first burn they came to, was a cave where they could hide. He advised that they hide there all the next day and only move south by night — for though this was now MacGregor country, it was only sparsely populated, and the MacDougalls, Macfarlanes and the rest would not hesitate to come raiding across if they suspected that their quarry had won over.

Bruce was anxious about the boat on the return journey, with the Dewar unable to paddle and bail at the same time; but the other assured that with only the one in the craft, the intake of water would not be nearly so great. He launched away again with the minimum of delay.

Leaving Douglas at the waterside, the King went in search of the cave. Once he had found the burn flowing into the loch over an apron of whitened pebbles, it was not difficult, entailing only hard climbing for some 300 feet up a steep braeface of scrub-covered rock and scree. The waterfall splashed in a drop of about thirty feet near by. It was a fair-sized cavern — although ten would tax its accommodation — formed out of a deep crevice over which a great flat rock had fallen. It was dry and secure, and better than many of their recent refuges.

Back at the shore, Bruce found that the second boatload had not yet arrived. Indeed they had to wait for some time before Edward Bruce and one of the men-at-arms were delivered. At this rate it would be dawn long before the ferrying was done.

In the event, dawn broke with only six of the party across. Fortunately it was a still morning, and the mists that rose everywhere on the surface of the water might serve to hide the little boat. When, after what seemed an endless wait, the watchers on the east shore did spot it again, certainly the craft was quite close inshore before it emerged from the vapours. Moreover it looked so low in the water, so lump-like, that it could almost have been a floating log. This impression was caused, it turned out, not only by the fact that the coracle was at least half-full of water, and that the three passengers were leaning forward almost flat and paddling that way with their hands; but that Wat Jardine, one of the two who could swim, was actually in the loch behind, clinging on with his hands and kicking out with his feet. This was the entire company, for since the boat did not have to be returned after this trip, the young Dewar had remained behind and would come for his property on some other occasion.

He and his elderly colleague had sent a message, however, by Gilbert Hay. The King and his party should not move from the cave; not until nightfall. Not until a guide had been brought, to lead them southwards.

"The fools! They think that we must be led like bairns!" Edward exclaimed. "That we cannot find our own way here. As we have done before."

Campbell nodded. "Our own guides we will be."

"We owe these Dewars much," Bruce demurred. "This at least we can do."

"To what purpose? We are our own best guides. And if MacGregor is indeed loyal, what need . . .?"

"I have said what we shall do, my lord," the King observed evenly. "Saint Fillan's blessing I will honour."

"As you will, Sire." That was the first sire, or my lord either, to have been heard in that company for days.

Emptying the waterlogged boat, and hiding it amongst the loch-side alders, they climbed to the cave.

All day they lay hidden up there on the stony face of Creag an Fhithich, the Raven's Crag, and though they slept, two were always awake, on watch. And, intermittently, there was much to watch. A mere mile away, on the far shore of the loch and on the hillsides beyond, frequently activity was evident, by groups large and small. In the afternoon, boats appeared on the loch, searching shore and islets. And later, a strong company actually came down their own side of the water, only a few hundred feet below them. That they were not MacGregors seemed evident by their wary and heedful attitude; they were watching as much as searching. Fortunately they were not concerned with the steep stony braeface directly above.

All the King's party were awakened for this — and few felt disposed to sleep again thereafter.

By dusk all were fretting to be off, but Bruce insisted that they wait. Besides, to move before it was fully dark would be folly. But it was long past dark, and tempers strained, before a watcher reported movement up the burn-channel. The fugitives crept out of the cave, to crouch and hide amongst the rocks around. They were not going to be caught in any trap.

Two men materialised out of the shadows, panting heavily. One was recognisable as the stocky person of the Dewar of the Main; the other was much larger in every way, a tall and massive figure, gasping the more in consequence.

"Sir King," the younger man said hoarsely, "is it yourself?"

"I am here, yes. We were fearing that you were not coming. It is late, man."

"Late, yes. We dare not come sooner. To be seen . . ."

"*Dare* not? Watch your words, man!" That was his large companion.

"Lest we be seen. To come here . . ."

"You have brought us a guide?" Bruce said. "To lead us south to Lennox."

"In a way of speaking." The younger man gestured. "MacGregor."

The big man inclined his head. "MacGregor," he repeated.

"Yes. That is well. Think you there will be enemies — MacDougalls and Macfarlanes — on this side of the loch? Still? Some passed below us early!"

"It may be so," the Dewar nodded. "They may well now fear that you have crossed. Your boat, therefore, should hold well to mid-loch, see you . . ."

"Boat! No more boats, by God!" That was Edward. "We had enough of your boats, last night."

"By boat, yes," the MacGregor guide said shortly. "It is my decision."

"*Your* decision, by the saints! We make our own decisions, fellow!"

"Quiet, Edward . . .!"

"On MacGregor land, *I* make the decision, whatever. Mind it, Southron! I am Malcolm, son of Gregor, son of Hugh."

"I care not whose son you are! I am the King's brother, now Earl of Carrick . . ."

"Fool! Think you such new kingship is of any moment to a son of Alpin?"

"Alpin!" Bruce exclaimed. "Malcolm, you said? Son of Gregor, was it? Son of Hugh. You are not . . . MacGregor himself? Of Glenorchy? The chief . . .?"

"I am MacGregor, yes. Himself. And my race is royal. None so royal."

"MacGregor is come to take you to the great Earl, Sir King," the Dewar explained. "The Earl of Lennox. His friend . . ."

Bruce scarcely heeded. That this, one of the proudest men in all the Highlands, in all Scotland indeed, should have come in person to act their guide, was significant, whatever way it might be considered. The MacGregors were not one of the greater clans, as far as numbers went, but they had an importance far beyond their size. They claimed to be descended from Gregor, brother of King Kenneth MacAlpine, and if so, were the most direct representatives of the original Scots royal line, a dynasty lost in the mists of antiquity. Their main territories were Glen Orchy and Glen Strae, at the head of Loch Awe, but there the Campbells had been encroaching and there was bad blood between the two clans. This area on the east side of Loch Lomond comprising Glen Gyle and Inversnaid was of minor importance, and the chief's presence here was a surprise. Was it for good or ill? This could mean a welcome accession of support — or, equally, it could mean more treachery.

Bruce glanced quickly at the Campbell chief. In these Highlands, clan feuds mattered a deal more than national wars. Sir Neil, never a diplomatic or forthcoming individual, could precipitate immediate trouble. But would he do it on MacGregor territory?

Apparently not. "I am Neil, son of Colin Mor, of Lochawe, of the line of O'Duin," he said briefly.

"I had heard that you were of this King's company," the MacGregor returned, equally cryptic.

"We are honoured, much honoured, MacGregor, to have *your* company," Bruce said hurriedly. "We had not looked for so notable an escort."

"You are on my lands," the other returned simply.

Bruce was afraid that his brother might blurt out that, in theory at least, all the land in this realm was the King's; it was the sort of thing that Edward would do, in his present frame of mind. Fortunately, he forbore.

"The Earl of Carrick has made himself known to you. Here now is Sir James, Lord of Douglas. Sir Gilbert, Lord of Erroll. Sir William Bellenden. And other friends . . ."

"Let us be done with this talk," Edward jerked. "This of the boat? Do we hazard this?"

All knew what he meant. MacGregor could be leading them into a trap.

"I have the blessing of Saint Fillan," Bruce said slowly, carefully.

There was silence, while men considered that.

"None could be more potent, at all," the Dewar observed. "MacGregor will agree."

"That is truth," the chief nodded. "That saint is patron to my name and line. At his call I am here. For this, and because you are the friend of my friend."

If the King thought that MacGregor should rather have come out of loyalty to his liege lord, he did not say so, content that these other loyalties should ensure his good faith.

"That is well," he acceded. "My friend, and yours? Do you mean the Earl of Lennox?"

"The same. Malcolm, son of Malcolm, son of Maldwyn, son of Aluin, son of Aluin, of the Levenach. To him I can take you. And only I."

"Only . . .? Why so?"

"Because he is in hiding."

"Hiding? The Earl? In his own Lennox?"

"Even so. His castles are all occupied by *your* enemies. He pays dear for supporting King Robert Bruce!"

"Aye. Nor Lennox only." Sombrely Bruce nodded. "We are in your hands, then, MacGregor. Take us to Lennox. If you will."

They left the cave, not to clamber down to the waterside again, but to climb upwards by a steep and difficult ascent amongst the rocks and slippery screes — this apparently because just a little farther to the south, almost sheer cliff overhung the lochshore, which would have forced anybody travelling down it to traverse a very narrow strip between water and cliff, providing a perfect site for an ambush. If their enemies suspected that the fugitives were on this side of the loch, that corridor would be closely watched.

At length they reached a long ridge, about 600 feet above the water. It seemed much lighter up here, and the sense of constriction which had oppressed them for days lifted somewhat. Along this bare ridge they moved, for about two miles, before they began to slant down half-left over smoother grassy slopes into a parallel valley formed by the Snaid Burn. Here cattle grazed, and it was a strange sensation for the fugitives to pass close to cot-houses without skulking and creeping. Presently they came down to Inversnaid, where a sizeable township clustered round the seat of one of the MacGregor chieftains. Men were astir here, and quiet salutes greeted the chief; but no attention was paid to the others, King or no King.

Turning west again, on a well-trodden track down the steep ravine of the Snaid, here practically a prolonged waterfall, they emerged once more at the loch. But it was a very different beach. Here were more houses, and from them a stone jetty thrust out into the dark waters. Not a few boats were moored or drawn up thereabouts; but tied to the jetty was one the like of which the visitors had never seen — save only Campbell. It was long and narrow, high of prow and stern, with a single central mast on which hung a great boom with furled sail. At bows and stern were raised platforms and double-banked along each side were the black ports for many oars.

"A galley!" Bruce exclaimed. "A chief's galley! Yours, MacGregor?"

"Mine."

"But how, a God's name, comes a galley on Loch Lomond? A sea craft. On an inland water?"

"Where MacGregor goes, there goes his galley."

"But how, man? You come from Glenorchy, in the north, do you not? Above Lorn."

"My galleys ride on Loch Etive, of the Western Sea," he said. "When I would come to these southern lands of Clan Alpine, I sail out into that sea, and down through the isles, to Tarbert at the head of Kintyre. There my Gregorach draw my galley out, set it on round tree-trunks, and pull it across the low neck of land one mile to Loch Fyne. I sail down that loch, to Bute Kyle, and then up Loch Long. Only two miles divide the head of Long from this Lomond. Again my oarsmen draw the galley across the land. On this Lomond, then, my galley is supreme."

"I' faith — here's a wonder . . .!"

"You learned that trick from the Northmen's king," Neil Campbell observed sourly. "Magnus, Hakon's goodson, did the same, before Largs fight. When he burned the Lennox."

"You mistake, Wry-mouth," the other gave back. "Hakon learned it from MacGregor. Clan Alpine has been so doing since before there was ever a Campbell to defile Argyll!"

"God's patience . . .!"

"And we sail in your galley?" the King intervened.

"What else? When you sail with MacGregor."

Now there were men all round them, fierce-looking—but no fiercer than themselves—bristling with arms. To one, MacGregor gave a command. He blew loud and long on a great curling cattle-horn, the whooping, moaning ululations echoing and re-echoing amongst all the enclosing hills. Bruce and his companions, after weeks of hiding, could scarcely forbear to demand quiet, secrecy, abashed at this blatant drawing of attention to themselves. But clearly they were now in the company of no skulkers. MacGregor of MacGregor, on his own heather, was not the man on whom to urge discretion.

The horn had been the signal for the galley to be manned. Men poured aboard in surprising numbers, equipped with their great rawhide and studded targes, circular shields, which they proceeded to hang over the sides of the vessel, forming a sort of armour-plating thereon.

"Where were all these when we needed them?" Edward Bruce growled. "These past days, when we were hunted like beasts, just across this loch! The MacGregor is something tardy in his duty, I say!"

"Better tardy than never. Or against us," the King murmured, lower-voiced. "Indeed, I think he is not here for *my* sake, even now. He is doing this because the Dewars besought him. And for his friend Lennox's sake. Let us be grateful for such mercies as come our way, brother."

The chief ushered his visitors aboard, the lesser men to the bow platform, the greater, with himself, to the stern. Bruce was surprised to see how many oars the vessel used, twenty on each side, in two banks, long powerful sweeps, each worked by two men seated on cross thwarts. With a relay of swordsmen standing by to take their turn at the sweeps. MacGregor must have had nearly 200 men aboard.

They cast off immediately and efficiently, and the huge square sail was unfurled—with all that oar-power, and since there was little wind, Bruce imagined more to display the MacGregor arms of crossed oak-tree and sword, painted hugely thereon, than for propulsion. With surprisingly little splash and fuss for so multiple a motive-power, they moved out into the night-bound waters, and swung southwards, down-loch.

It made a very strange sensation for Bruce and his party to be sailing openly, indeed dramatically, on the great sheet of water which had for so long been their bugbear. Especially when, presently, the helmsman began to chant a lilting haunting melody, rhythmic and repetitive, in time with the beat of the oars, which the rowers took up in deep pulsing power — one of the many boat-songs of the West. To the surge and thrust and ache of this they thrashed down Loch Lomond, sweeps flashing, spray flying, at a speed which none of the Lowlanders had believed possible on water. Greyhounds of the sea they knew these galleys to be called, but this headlong progress was beyond all their imagining, exhilarating, challenging.

This aspect of challenge preoccupied the fugitives. MacGregor might be puissant and redoubtable, but the MacDougall Lord of Argyll and Lorn was still more powerful. This shouting aloud of their presence might be magnificent, but it was surely foolhardy.

But when Bruce indicated as much to their host, he was met with scorn. "Who will question MacGregor's galley?" he asked simply. "Besides, there is no other on the loch."

"At least they will know where we go."

"Where MacGregor goes," the other amended. "Why should they believe King Bruce with him?"

Loch Lomond broadens out to the south, and at its foot it is almost five miles wide, and dotted with islands. Ten or so miles down towards this the galley drove. Whether or not the chief was right and none dared to interfere with MacGregor's galley, they saw no other boats throughout — although their passage must have been entirely evident to any who watched.

After perhaps an hour, with the widening of the loch, the looming black shadows of the great mountains drew back and dwindled as they sailed out of the Highlands and into Lennox. Bruce had quite expected that they would be conducted to one of the many islands. These, after all, would in the main belong to the Earl of Lennox, and might provide refuges. But, no. The galley drove on through the island area without diminution of speed, MacGregor himself directing the helmsman. The regular splash of forty blades meeting the water in unison, the creaking of oars, and the gasping pant of the men, dominated the night with purpose. The smell of sweat was like a miasma that travelled with the ship.

The foot of Lomond spreads out into flat level country, ranged only distantly by low hills. The galley, in fact, was making for the very south-east corner, where the River Endrick flowed in through farflung marshland. Now MacGregor slowed his rowers drastically, peering ahead keenly. Soon a leadsman in the bows was shouting soundings, as the water shoaled.

The chief pointed suddenly, and the helmsman nodded. Posts could be distinguished rising out of the water. Three of them were visible, obviously in a line.

"The mouth of the Endrick," MacGregor mentioned. "Deep water channel."

They eased in towards the posts, and soon it was apparent that there was a long line of them. The galley was edging along very slowly now, following the posts closely. It was not long before there was a low black belt at either side of them, darker than the water — reed-beds. The channel, twisting now, was narrowing notably.

At length the chief called a halt and, oars raised upright, they nosed forward to one of the posts. The helmsman used a steering-oar to manoeuvre the craft round, across the channel. Two men jumped down into the reeds and shallows. The water came barely to their middles.

MacGregor nodded. "Sir King," he said, "Come you." And with no more ceremony than if he were dismounting from the saddle, leapt down into the water.

Bruce could not but follow, and his colleagues after him, with but a word of farewell and thanks to the young Dewar — who apparently was coming no further. The water was not cold, but the muddy bottom was unpleasant.

MacGregor was already wading strongly in an easterly direction, parting the tall reeds and rushes before him as he went. In a stumbling, slaistering, cursing line, the others trailed after.

How far, in actual distance, they went, it was difficult to compute. It seemed a long way in the blanketing, featureless reed-sea, so difficult of passage, with wild-fowl exploding into alarmed flight continually, and somewhat heavier creatures, roe-deer perhaps or even cattle, splashing away into deeper fastnesses. Possibly they covered no more than a mile, however indirect their route — and how the MacGregor knew where he was going was a mystery. But he seemed never at a loss — and none had sufficient breath to question him.

At length a new sound, from the splashing and splatter, the quacking of ducks and the whistle of pinions, rose from the marshes — the sudden baying of hounds, and from no great distance ahead. Their guide halted, and responded promptly with great hallooing cries of "Gregalach! Gregalach!"

The dogs continued to bark, and the chief ploughed on directly towards the sound.

Soon the water began to shallow, and the dark mass of scrub or woodland loomed ahead. Then they were climbing out on to firm grass-grown ground — but now armed men, restraining snarling wolfhounds, were milling around them. MacGregor demanded to be taken to their lord.

They appeared to be on a fair-sized island in the marshes, a hidden place of scrub and bushes and open turf, many acres in extent. There were tents here, camouflaged with fronds and branches, forming quite a large secret encampment.

A man of middle years, slightly built, of narrow head and fine features, was standing before the largest tent, staring. Him MacGregor approached, shaking water off him like a dog.

"I disturbed your sleep, friend?" he cried. "But you will forgive me. See you whom I have brought you."

"I heard your Gregalach. Have you brought me news . . .?" The other was scanning the newcomers in turn, in the gloom of near dawn. He showed no sign of recognition — and little wonder.

"Malcolm!" the King exclaimed. "My lord!"

"I am Malcolm of Lennox, yes. Who speaks me so?"

"Save us — do you not know me?"

"My lord — is this your greeting to the King's Grace?" young Sir James Douglas reproached.

"Grace? The . . . the King?" the Earl faltered, peering. "What mean you? The King is dead . . ."

"Not yet, Malcolm my friend — not yet!" Bruce said, and went to him.

Lennox, a curiously sensitive man to be a military leader — though he was that by birth rather than by inclination — was quite overwhelmed. He could find no words; indeed he wept on Bruce's shoulder — to the embarrassment of most there. Not of the King himself, however. Bruce had learned to despise no man's emotions, confronted with the stresses of his own.

"My good lord," he said.

"I believed . . . you slain . . . at Methven," the other got out. "I have mourned you. Wept for you. Since. Aye, and mourned this Scotland with you!"

"I was wounded. As I heard were you. Led off the field . . ."

"Thank the good God for it! This night I shall for ever praise! The night my liege lord returned to me. And my hope. Returned. For I had lost all hope. Here, in this desolation of waters . . ."

"Aye, my friend — I also. Almost I lost all hope likewise. Until it, and I, was saved. Saved by my Elizabeth. And the Dewars of

Saint Fillan. Now, I think, I shall not again lose my hope. While life is in me. And if I, excommunicate, who spilled blood on God's altar, can have hope — why then, I say, hope should be lost for none!"

To make amends for this display of emotion, Lennox offered his guests food and drink. Despite the remote and primitive nature of his refuge, he appeared to be well supplied, and the fugitives ate well, hugely indeed, for the first time for weeks, wolfing cold meats and fish, oatcakes and heather honey, washing it down with wine and the potent spirits of the country.

Their own spirits rose in consequence, their host's with them.

It was obvious that Lennox had been very depressed, deeming all his cause lost and himself a broken man, a mere fugitive on his own broad lands. Not that his state had compared in any way with that of the royal party, for though a refugee on this strange secret island in the reeds, he was in the midst of his own people and vassals, and lacked for little. But his castles and houses were denied him, occupied by supporters of the Comyns or the English. Assuming Bruce dead and further resistance useless, and living thus in winter out of the question, he had apparently decided on betaking himself off, first to the Hebrides and thence to Ireland, where he had links, there to await better days.

Bruce took him up on this, over meats. How had he intended to reach the Isles? Or Ireland? For if this had been a suitable progress for Lennox, it was the more so for himself, and urgently so, with his enemies only a jump or two behind him.

The Earl, clearly alarmed at this intimation of imminent pursuit, said that he had made no arrangements as yet — but that his notion had been to sail by small boat from the Clyde to the Isle of Bute, where the High Steward, he hoped, would provide him with a sea-going vessel to reach the Hebrides. They were only a dozen miles from the Clyde coast, at Dumbarton.

The King found no fault with that — except that the Governor of Dumbarton Castle was still the same Sir John Stewart of Menteith who had delivered up William Wallace to the English — and Dumbarton dominated all the upper Clyde estuary. He might well seek to repeat the process with Bruce.

That gave them pause, until Sir Neil Campbell announced that he had a younger brother, Donald, who had married a Lamont heiress and gained a rich property at Ardincaple, farther down the coast from Dumbarton. If they could reach Sir Donald at Ardincaple, he could provide boats for Bute.

"We must cross Macfarlane and Colquhoun country to get there," Lennox pointed out.

"Where lie Colquhoun's sympathies?"

"Humphrey de Colquhoun is a vassal of my own," Lennox said. "But he was wounded at Methven, and like me, lurks in hiding . . ."

"I will get you to Ardincaple, through any beggarly Macfarlanes or Colquhouns whatever!" MacGregor interrupted briefly, disdainfully. "So be it you may trust the Campbell when you get there!"

"I have a higher opinion of my friends than have you, sir," the King declared, before Sir Neil could rise in wrath. "But I thank you for your promise — and trust MacGregor to perform it."

"Tomorrow night? It must be done by night."

"Tomorrow, yes." Bruce looked at Lennox.

"I will be ready," the Earl said. "To come with you. Tomorrow night."

The King eyed him keenly. "My lord — no need for you to come. We are hunted men. Dispossessed of our lands. Knowing not where we will next lay our heads. Not so yourself. You have still great possessions. Lord of a whole province. Your castles may be occupied, but you need not become a hunted man. Thousands would take you into their houses . . ."

"And think you, Sire, that I could sleep of a night in any house, mine own or other, knowing my liege lord homeless, hunted? No, Your Grace — where Bruce goes hereafter, there goes Lennox, God willing!"

Much affected, Bruce gripped the other's hand, wordless. The earl might shed easy tears, but he lacked nothing in manly resolution.

So it was decided, MacGregor would leave for his galley forthwith, and return early after dark the next night. Meanwhile Campbell would slip off alone, like any cateran, with a Lennox guide, to reach his brother at Ardincaple, so that boats could be assembled for the voyage to Bute.

The MacGregor and the Campbell left almost simultaneously — but not together.

Chapter Three

All in that little ship, heaving on the long Atlantic swell, were used to seeing impressive castles. Bruce himself owned a round dozen of them, at least, as Earl of Carrick and Lord of Annandale and Galloway and Garioch — even though all were now in English hands and of no use to him. Lennox had almost as many. But none of the vessel's passengers had ever seen the like of this, as, rounding the jutting headland a bare half-mile out from that wicked shore, they stared upwards.

To call the place an eagle's nest, a sea-eagle's nest, was the feeblest inadequacy. The headland of Dunaverty itself soared sheerly hundreds of feet above the crashing waves, and the thrusting narrow bastion or stack, linked to the main cliff by the merest neck, rose higher, a dizzy pinnacle of rock. And on the very apex of this, a mere extension of the beetling stack, the castle was perched, clinging unbelievably to the uneven summit and precipitous sides, itself tall, narrow, almost incredible, an arrogant challenge not to man but to sea and sky. A great banner flew proudly from the topmost tower, and though this was dwarfed by height and distance, it could be seen to bear a simple device of a single black galley on white, undifferenced, the emblem of the Isles.

But impressive as it might be, it was not the castle nor this fluttering galley which held the watchers' gaze, in the end. Farther west than the castle-rock another headland reached out, considerably lower but farther into the sea than the other, to curve round southwards in a crook and to act as a mighty breakwater. And in the sheltered anchorage thus formed, protected from the ocean rollers and the prevailing winds, was a sight as strange as the cliff-top castle. Row upon row of true, long, low, lean galleys lay there, their masts and great slantwise spars a forest — but a disciplined forest — their white sails furled like a flock of sea-birds' folded wings, their tall carved prows upthrust like the heads of a host of sea-monsters. Someone counted twenty-seven of these killer-wolves of the Western Sea, another thirty. Lying tethered there, motionless but menacing, they made a startling impact.

"I' faith — Angus Og himself must be at Dunaverty this day!" Bruce exclaimed. "None other could have that pack of hounds in leash! And, unless I mistake, that is the undifferenced Galley of the Isles flying above yon hold."

"Does it bode good? Or ill?" Edward Bruce demanded.

"God knows! But Angus Og MacDonald hates Alexander MacDougall of Lorn!"

"The Steward sent word of your coming here, to the captain of this castle, Sire," Campbell said. James the High Steward of Scotland, from Bute, had provided this ship. "So they know that we come."

"And this MacDonald has come in person to receive us!" the King's brother snarled. "I'd sooner lack him! I trust none of these Highland savages."

Sir Neil Campbell, although he himself had no love for the MacDonalds, stiffened. One day there would have to be a reckoning.

"My Highland subjects are no more savage, neither better nor worse than most of those nearer home, Edward," the King reproved. "And, it seems, we are in their hands now. Do not forget it."

Nevertheless, Bruce drummed fingers on the hilt of his great sword. What they were seeing undoubtedly represented a complication, and a drastic one. Dunaverty Castle, at the very tip of the great peninsula of Kintyre which thrust out towards Ireland, was in fact, save for the Isle of Man, the southernmost outpost of the former kingdom of the Isles, and most strategically situated to dominate the sea-lanes between the Hebridean north and Ireland, Man and England. On his assumption of the crown, Bruce had sent Sir Robert Boyd here, to make sure of Dunaverty, one of his first acts. And Boyd had, somehow, taken the castle, and left it in the care of a captain. Now, it seemed, Angus Og of the Isles had taken it, in turn. What did this imply? Were they running their heads into a noose, here? Not that they could turn back now.

And even if the self-styled Lord of the Isles had decided that Dunaverty should be his, why was he here in person? Impressive as this outpost was, it was nevertheless a very unimportant corner of the vast and farflung territory of the Isles, which included not only the Inner and Outer Hebrides, but great portions of the West Highland mainland, not excepting this seventy-mile-long peninsula of Kintyre. That Angus Og, its lord — or prince, as he still called himself — should happen to be at Dunaverty this day, was highly significant, whether by chance or otherwise.

"Those galleys are not long in from the sea," the experienced chief of Clan Campbell pointed out. "See — men work on them, wash down decks, coil ropes. I would say that they were not here last night." He did not sound overjoyed.

None commented.

Turning into the bay, the King's ship made for necessarily humble and inferior moorings at the tail-end of the tethered fleet.

Campbell and Edward Bruce were for once in agreement that it would be wise to send an emissary to the castle, first, to test the climate of welcome; but the King would have none of it. No skulking and standing off could avail them anything here. Their vessel, however stout, could neither outsail nor better in fight even one of these leashed greyhounds. They had come to Dunaverty as the nearest secure hold which their enemies would be unlikely to challenge. For better or for worse, here they were. There was nowhere they might flee from the Lord of the Isles.

Bruce himself led the way ashore — perforce across the decks of three or four galleys, where tough, bare-torsoed and kilted clansmen eyed them grimly, and pointedly returned no greetings. On dry land, staggering slightly after the rolling and pitching of the notoriously hazardous sea passage round the Mull of Kintyre from the sheltered waters of the Firth of Clyde estuary, the royal party proceeded round the bay beside the crashing lace-white combers, to where a long, zigzag flight of steps was cut sheerly in the naked face of the cliff, a dizzy ascent but apparently the only access from shore to castle.

The climb, on worn and uneven steps, without so much as rope as guard or handrail, was not for the light-headed. There was not a little pressing against the inner rock wall and keeping of eyes steadily averted from the outer drop. In the dark, or in a storm of wind or rain, the thing would have been nothing short of suicidal. Fortunately the King had a good head for heights — and where he led, none could decently refuse to follow.

At the cliff-top these stairs evidently led to a tiny postern-gate in the soaring castle walls, the start of whose masonry was barely distinguishable from the living rock. But since the steps were on the cliff proper, and the castle crowned the almost detached stack, it was necessary to bridge the gap. This was achieved by a lengthy, sloping and removable gangway which reached across the yawning abyss at a somewhat acute angle, some forty feet long by not much more than three feet wide, this again without handrail. A less enticing approach to a house would be hard to imagine.

The landward access appeared to be by drawbridges over three deep water-filled ditches across a narrow neck of ground. But the outer of these bridges was up, and men were clearly waiting for the visitors at the narrow postern across the ghastly gangplank.

Bruce did not hesitate. Without even a backward glance at his companions, he stepped out on to the sloping spidery planking, and strode up. It was at least ribbed with cross-bars for the feet to grip — though equally these could cause the feet to trip. He did not once look down but kept his gaze firmly on the group who watched and waited beyond. Nevertheless he was far from unaware of the appalling drop so close on either side. Was this typical of Dunaverty's reception of guests?

Certainly the appearance of the men so silently awaiting them was fierce enough, off-putting. Half a dozen of them stood in or beside the narrow doorway in the beetling wall, big men made bigger by the tall pointed helmets they wore, mostly furnished with flanking pinions of sea-eagles, or curling bulls' horns, in the antique Norse style. These did not wear the stained and ragged tartans, but saffron tunics, belted with gold, some with chain-mail jerkins and some with piebald calfskin waistcoats, great swords slung from every shoulder, dirks at hip, and hung about with massive silverware and barbaric jewellery. None were bearded, but all save one had long and heavy down-turning moustaches which hid their mouths and produced a distinctly menacing impression.

The man who lacked the moustache was different from the rest in other ways also. He was younger for one thing, in only his mid-twenties, very dark, almost swarthy, and though not short — indeed well-built — the least tall of the group. He wore no helmet or mail, only the plain kilted saffron tunic, and carried no sword but only a ceremonial dagger. It may have been in contrast to those fiercely down-turning moustaches, but his lips, visible where the others were not, seemed almost to smile. He stood in the centre of the party, and there was no doubting the authority with which he held himself, however careless.

"Wait you!" a voice rang out, while Bruce was still only two-thirds across that alarming planking. It was not the young man who spoke. "Who comes unbidden to Dunaverty? Is it Robert Bruce, who calls himself King of Scots?"

Bruce halted — although it demanded all his hardihood on that grievous perch, and he knew that those behind him must be equally preoccupied. "I am Robert, King of Scots, yes," he answered, "Come seeking the love, protection and hospitality of Angus, Lord of the Isles. Do I find it at Dunaverty?"

"I am Angus of the Isles," the young man agreed. "How can I serve Robert Bruce?" His predecessors had been careful never to admit specifically allegiance to the Crown of Scotland, even when Alexander the Third had bought the alleged suzerainty of the Isles from Hakon of Norway.

"By holding out the hand of friendship, my lord. And . . . and by letting me off this accursed tree! I vow I grow giddy!"

Angus Og laughed aloud at that frank avowal. "Well said, Sir King!" he cried. "Come, then. Myself, I near grow ill but looking at you all!" And he held out his hand.

Bruce's sigh of relief was drowned in those from behind him. He waited for no further invitation.

Angus Og's hand-grip was that of an equal and no vassal, but Bruce did not find fault with it. Sufficient that it was strong and frank.

"Well met, my friend," he said. "Your fame is known."

"As is yours. *And* your misfortunes."

"Those, yes. But they will pass. Here is good fortune, at least — to find *you* at Dunaverty."

Introductions followed, in the crowded narrow court within the postern, the King's party impressive only in their names and titles — for though Lennox and the Steward both had sought to rig them out in better clothing, the fugitives still were less than well and appropriately clad, the King himself little better than the rest. Their martial-looking opposite numbers turned out to be the chiefs of Jura, Gigha, Ardnamurchan and others of the great Isles confederation. By and large they were civil, but no more than that.

It seemed that Angus Og MacDonald's presence here was indeed something in the nature of a coincidence. He had called in Dunaverty some days previously, on his way to a meeting on Rathlin Island with one Malcolm MacQuillan of Antrim, an Irish kinglet who had in fact been occupying Dunaverty when Boyd had taken it for Bruce just before the coronation. MacQuillan was now demanding back the castle, and Angus, who had sent his minions to eject Boyd's captain, had had a look at it before meeting MacQuillan. When the Steward's courier, therefore, had come to Dunaverty two or three days before, he had been sent straight on to Rathlin which, although off the coast of Antrim, was only fourteen miles from Dunaverty. Angus had interrupted his conference with MacQuillan, and come back to receive Robert Bruce — for good or ill.

The implied question was clear. What did Bruce want with the Prince of the Isles?

The King was frank. "Two things I seek of you, my lord," he said. "First, refuge. Shelter for me and mine, who have been hunted men for too long. While we rest. Regain our strength. Plan our course. None may give us this better than yourself. And second, your support. In arms."

"Against whom, Sir King?"

"Against those who occupy my kingdom. Against Edward of England. And against the Comyns and their friends, who support him. Such as MacDougall of Lorn and Argyll!"

The younger man looked at him from under down-drawn brows. "You have many enemies. And Comyn, I think, has many friends. Are these all yours?" And he gestured towards the little group with the King.

Bruce drew a deep breath. "These represent thousands. Many thousands. My lord of Lennox can field six thousand. My lord of Douglas four thousand. Campbell of Lochawe as many — more, it may be. My lord of Erroll, a thousand. The High Steward two thousand. My own lands of Carrick, Annandale and Galloway . . ."

"*Can* field, Sir King! Can. But do not!"

"My lord — all these *have* fielded their men. And will do so again. For eight years we have been fighting the might of Edward . . ."

"And losing!"

"And losing, yes. Though not always. When we fought aright. And in unity. Pitched battles we do not win. Against many times our numbers. Edward's chivalry, and the English bowmen. But a different kind of war we can win. Wallace taught us that. Small actions. Castle by castle. Using the land against him. Burning all before him. Starving him and his hosts. Edward may win the battles. But he grows old. Sick. Tired. *I*, God willing, will win the war!"

"With . . . help!"

"With help, yes. Yours, I hope, my lord. With others. Since I thought to count you my friend."

"Some friendships may cost a man dear."

"Well I know it. And I have nothing to offer. Meantime. One day, I hope . . ."

"The friendship of Angus of the Isles is not to be bought."

"I know it. But a King, his kingdom won, can and should reward his friends and helpers."

For moments they eyed each other. Then the Islesman nodded.

"It may be so. We shall see. For the first, for refuge, shelter, you shall have it. In my islands. For the other, for men and swords and ships, I must needs think. And consult with *my* friends. We shall see, King Robert Bruce. Meantime, my house is yours. For as long as you will . . ."

With that they had to be content.

* * *

The windy, lofty house of Dunaverty was not Bruce's for long, despite its present lord's assurance. The very next day a visitor arrived, having come hot-foot across Kintyre after sailing from Arran — Sir Robert Boyd of Noddsdale, no less; the same who had taken this castle, for Bruce, six months before, and whom the King had last seen after the rout in Strathfillan, wounded, and leaving to escort the Queen's party northwards to Kildrummy. Boyd, of course, was taken to Angus Og before he saw the King — but that young man was not long in bringing him.

"Trouble," he said briefly, gesturing.

The veteran Sir Robert sank on his knee before Bruce, and took his hand to kiss it. He brought startling tidings. An expedition was assembling at Dumbarton, under Sir John Stewart of Menteith, the governor thereof, and Sir John de Botetourt, Edward of England's bastard son. It was known already, somehow, that Bruce had sailed for Dunaverty, and sea-going ships were being requisitioned all up and down the Clyde to carry this expedition in pursuit. The Steward had heard that de Botetourt alone had 3,000 men. They might have sailed from Dumbarton by this.

Angus of the Isles looked as thoughtful as did Robert Bruce, at these tidings.

It seemed as though they had been betrayed again. Treachery haunted Bruce. It had never occurred to the King, even though his enemies discovered where he was, that they would pursue him into these island fastnesses. Edward Plantagenet must be very determined indeed to have him — and very angry. This was grievous, in more than just the renewal of pressure on hunted men; it meant that Angus Og would be forced to come to some sort of decision about his attitude before he was ready. Bruce had hoped to be able to work on the man. This could hardly fail to be to his disadvantage.

It did not take the Lord of the Isles long to make up his mind as to immediate tactics, at least. Eyeing his fierce-looking chiefs, he turned back to Bruce.

"Sir King," he said, "I fear that you cannot remain at Dunaverty. My sorrow that it is so — but your Englishry leave me little choice. Either you must go, or I must fight them. And I do not know that I am prepared to go to war with Edward of England!"

"I understand," Bruce nodded. "This I feared."

"Do not mistake me," the younger man went on. "It is not that I am afraid to fight Menteith and this Botetourt. They have many more men than I have here present — but my galleys, I swear, would tear their ships apart, like eagles amongst lambs! But that would be to challenge Edward. War. This I may do. One day. But then it will be *my* war. Not another man's."

As men drew breath, the King bowed stiffly, silent.

Angus Og shrugged. "I speak plainly, friend — for I am a man of plain speech. But what I say I mean. And I have named you friend. My friend you are. I will not leave you to be taken by your enemies. We sail with tomorrow's dawn. I return to Rathlin, where I have business to finish. I promised you refuge. You shall sail with me to Rathlin. And from there go whither you please. All my isles are open to you. Or you could go to Antrim. Ireland. The Irish coast is but four miles from Rathlin. *I* go thither, to Antrim. Yours is the choice. A galley of mine shall carry the King of Scots where he will." A long speech for Angus Og.

Bruce raised his head. "For that I thank you, my lord. If I

cannot be your suzerain, I can and do at least accept your friendship!"

Their eyes met, and each smiled slightly. These two at least understood each other, however their respective supporters might glower.

When the Islemen had withdrawn from the King's apartment, Boyd, grave-faced, asked that he might speak to Bruce privily. They moved together out on to a parapet-walk that hung vertiginously above the wrinkled sea.

"Your Grace — forgive me," the knight said, "but I have more grievous tidings for your ear than these you have heard. My sorrow that it is I must bear them."

"Grievous? What, man? Out with it."

"Sire — your brother. The Lord Nigel. He is dead. And not only he. Your good-brother, Sir Christopher Seton. And his brother John . . ."

"No! Dear God — no! I'll not believe it . . .!"

"It is true, Sire, God's truth. Kildrummy Castle fell. We reached Kildrummy, with her Grace and the ladies. In time. But de Valence, Earl of Pembroke, knew it and was there within a day or two. Besieged us. And the castle was betrayed. Set fire to, from within . . ."

"Betrayed again! Will it never end?" Suddenly Bruce gripped the other's wrist. "Elizabeth? My wife. The Queen. She is . . .?"

"The Queen, Sire, is escaped. And your daughter. Won safe away. When the Lord Nigel learned that Pembroke approached, he sent them away hastily, secretly. With the Earl of Atholl. For the North Isles . . ."

"Thank Christ-God! That Nigel would do. But . . . Nigel! My brother — my dear brother? He died? At Kildrummy?"

"No. Not at Kildrummy. He was captured. Wounded. With the others. As was I. In the burning castle. Traitors set afire the stores of food and grain in the great hall. And then, in the smoke and confusion, opened the postern to the English. We were all captured. But I escaped, on the way south. I and Lindsay. All were taken south to Edward. At Berwick. And there they were slain. As Wallace was slain. Hanged. Cut down while still alive. Disembowelled. And their entrails burned before their eyes . . ."

"Ah, no! No!" A sobbing groan escaped from the King's lips. Abruptly he turned away, to stride some way along that dizzy walk and stare out over the isle-dotted vastness of the Western Sea, gripping the stonework of the parapet, knuckles gleaming white. Of his four brothers. Nigel had always been the favourite. "Nigel!

Nigel!" he moaned. "What did I do to you? What did I do to you when I grasped this accursed crown?"

Boyd stood where he was, silent, waiting, askance.

At length the King turned back, his features set. "Forgive me, friend," he said. "You say . . . Christopher Seton also? My friend. My sister's husband . . ."

"Aye, Sire. Drawn, hanged, and beheaded. At Dumfries. With his brother, Sir John."

"He . . . he was the first to swear me fealty! And here is how I rewarded him!"

"The others also. All who were captured at Kildrummy. Sir John de Cambo. Alexander the Scrymgeour. Sir Alan Durward . . ."

Bruce raised his hands, almost beseechingly. "Have mercy! Have mercy on me! It is more than I can bear. All my brave, true, leal friends . . ."

"Leal, Sire — but King Edward hanged and beheaded them as traitors! And the Steward said to mind you — he will do the same to yourself, King or none. And to all with you. His young son — the Steward's only remaining son, Walter — is with you here. He urges Sire, that you send him home. Then flee the country. Not to Ireland — for Edward's arm is long. But to the North Isles. Orkney. Where my lord of Atholl takes the Queen. And thence to Norway, where Your Grace's sister is queen. This I was to urge on you. The Steward prays you. His prayer and his advice."

"And yours, my friend?"

The veteran knight looked down. "Who am I to advise the King?"

"Robert Boyd has more knowledge of war than ever had James the Steward, I think. He is a good man, but no soldier."

The other nodded. "Myself, then, I say — do what is in your own mind, Sire. *Mind* — not heart! For you have a King's head on your shoulders, I swear. And never did Scotland need it more!"

For a long moment Bruce searched the man's rugged features. Then he drew himself up. "It may be that you are right. God's will be done, then — for I am God's anointed, for this Scotland. But God's will, I say — not Edward Plantagenet's! I will tell the Steward that . . ."

* * *

Bruce did not, in fact, go to the North Isles, nor yet to Norway, great as was the temptation. That he had the means, in one of Angus Og's galleys, and might be with his wife and daughter within a few days, all but overbore him. But he steeled himself with almost the last words Elizabeth had spoken to him. "Go, and do your duty." And whatever his heart said, his mind knew where lay his duty.

So, at Rathlin Island, where Angus of the Isles took him, and they looked across the narrows to the shores of Ulster, Bruce decided that, as King of Scots, however ineffectual, his place was in his own realm of Scotland. He would not even go to Ireland with Angus Og — for it transpired that the real reason for the Lord of the Isles' presence on Rathlin with almost 2,000 men, was to co-ordinate, with Malcolm MacQuillan of the Glens of Antrim, a great joint raid on the territory of the Bissets, an Anglo-Norman family whom Edward of England had made lords of much of Antrim — and indeed of this Rathlin, also — over the heads of its native chiefs. Such raiding was typical of Isleman employment — but of no interest or use to Bruce. So he would take Angus Og at his word, borrow a galley, and sail northwards through the Isles and along the West Highland seaboard. Who could tell, he might find support up there, as well as refuge. The Earl of Ross, that far-away potentate, was as yet uncommitted in the struggle for Scotland. He might be convinced that the advantage lay with Bruce and independence, in the long run.

This was a shrewd blow at Angus himself, for the Earl of Ross was in fact the Lord of the Isles' rival for almost complete hegemony in the North. But the younger man did not rise to the fly, apparently content to tackle one project at a time. He stood by his promise, however, and allotted the King and his party a twenty-six-oar galley under the command of one MacDonald of Kiloran, and wished them well. If the Bruce was still in his territories when he got back from the Irish expedition, they would forgather again.

On the 20th of September, therefore, one of the great fleet of galleys turned its back on Rathlin Island and the Ulster coast, and set off northwards into the Sea of the Hebrides. It was significant, however, that the banner which flew at its masthead, like that painted on the great square sail, was the black Galley of the Isles, not the red Lion Rampant of Scotland.

Chapter Four

The slanting golden afternoon sun of early October, playing on the isle-dotted, skerry-strewn sea, brought out a depth of colour, of light and shade, of sheer breathtaking beauty, such as Bruce, for one, had never before contemplated. In the weeks that he had spent in the Isles, beauty had become commonplace, part of his life. But this of the level rich autumn sun in its flooding of the Sound of Eigg, was beyond all telling. The sea, blue and green and amethyst, picked out with the sparkling white of breakers on the multi-hued, weed-hung skerries, was no more than a setting for the jewelled islands that rose in aching loveliness all around, the turning heather of their flanks stained crimson, their cliffs slashed with violet shadows, their cockle-shell sands dazzling silver against the refulgent gold. Without ever having been greatly concerned with natural beauty, the King's trials, disappointments and sorrows had made him receptive to many influences which once he would have failed to perceive. And beauty such as this might put even his troubles into perspective.

But shouts came from near by, as he leaned on the poop rail in contemplation. They were sailing northwards towards the majestic purple peaks of the Isle of Rhum, with Eigg and Muck on their starboard bow, so that he had been gazing half-right. But others had been looking in the opposite direction, half-astern to port, into the dazzle of the westering sun. And now MacDonald of Kiloran, up in the bows and shading his eyes into the golden glare, was calling back to the helmsman, near whom the King, Douglas and Lennox stood. His shouts were in the Gaelic, but the pointing hand drew all eyes.

In all the glitter and eye-hurting brilliance of the westerly prospect, it was difficult at first to discern anything to account for the shouting. But presently, with many gesticulating, it became evident that there were solid shapes amongst all that dazzlement, even though these themselves seemed to be gleaming.

Kiloran came long-strided down the narrow catwalk between the rowers. "Three galleys, two and one," he informed. "And, if I mistake not, the two fly the red and gold of Ross."

"Ross?" Bruce echoed. "And that concerns you?"

"When they chase a birlinn flying the Galley of the Isles — yes!" the other replied shortly. Then he was shouting again to the rowers and helmsman.

Immediately that galley was transformed. From voyaging quietly northwards on its colour-stained way from Coll to Lochalsh in the narrows of Skye, with the oarsmen pulling almost idly at their long sweeps, to the gentle chanting of a haunting melody, it became of a sudden a ship of war again, braced, tense, determined. Round in a great foaming half-circle it swung, the sail-boom creaking, the canvas shivering and flapping, the rowers straining fiercely, the blades churning the blue water white.

Kiloran soon was seen to be steering an intercepting course. The relief crew of oarsmen were as obviously arming themselves.

"What do you intend?" Bruce asked of the MacDonald.

"To teach Ross whose seas these are."

The other might have pointed out that, since this was still Scotland, these were the King's seas. Also that Angus Og had lent him this galley for *his* purposes, not for challenging all comers. A few months ago he would undoubtedly have said so. But Robert Bruce had been learning in a hard school. He held his peace.

His eyes were now able to cope with the glare and glister, and he could make out, perhaps two miles away, the three craft, the two larger most evidently pursuing the smaller, and overhauling it fast. They were heading in an almost due easterly direction, towards the mainland, just north of the great peninsula of Ardnamurchan. How Kiloran could declare that they bore this colour or that device, Bruce did not know.

What quickly became clear, as they themselves swept across the sea at a speed unprecedented as far as the Lowlanders were concerned, was that the hunters, from the earldom of Ross or elsewhere, were not going to be diverted by the intervention of a third party; and also that they would have closed with their quarry before the would-be rescuers could reach the scene, fast as the latter were moving.

"It is another of your lord's galleys? Angus Og's?" Bruce asked, of Kiloran. "The Earl's ships are far south, are they not? I would not have thought they would have dared such piracy against the Lord of the Isles."

"Not one of Angus's, no. See you, there is a fish below the Galley. On sail and banner. That is for Garmoran. MacRuarie. Christina, of Garmoran. But of our Isles federation. Of the kin of Somerled. The Rossmen would scarce have dared attack one of Angus of Islay's own. So we go teach them!"

They were still almost a mile away when they distinctly heard, across the water, the crash and clash and yells as contact was made, and the two larger vessels bore in close on either side of the smaller, shearing off oars and skewering oarsmen in bloody chaos. Grappling-irons thrown in to hold the three craft together, men poured over into the birlinn from port and starboard, drawn swords flashing in the sun.

The rowers in the King's galley were now driving their sweeps in what almost amounted to a frenzy, the chanting, not to waste precious breath, superseded by the beating of time by sword on shield, in a rhythmic clanging which grew ever faster, punctuated by a sort of barking cough which was indrawn gasping breathing of fifty-two oarsmen — a curiously savage and menacing sound. The galley tore on in a cloud of spray.

Now, with the other vessels almost stationary, they overhauled them at speed. The devices on the flapping sails were clear — the black galley above a long black fish; and three red lions on gold.

"You intend to attack?" Bruce demanded.

"What else? I shall run in at the stern."

"You will be outnumbered. These are larger galleys than yours."

"What of it? Do you count heads, Sir King, before you draw your sword?"

"I do — if I may, yes!"

"So does not fight MacDonald! Bide you and yours in safety here, then, Leave this to MacDonald."

"I think you mistake me, sir," the King said quietly.

They drove in towards the sterns of the three ships. Hand-to-hand fighting was in progress in the well and after-parts of the birlinn, bodies dropping or being tossed over the side all around.

"What do we do, Sire?" Sir James Douglas demanded. "Join in? Or hold back?"

"This is no quarrel of ours," Lennox said. "It is foolhardy . . ."

"Perhaps. But these MacDonalds are our hosts," Bruce pointed out. "We live on their bounty. Let every man make his own choice. I, for my part, will pay the debts of hospitality."

"Sire — is it wise?" Lennox persisted, low-voiced. "If these are the Earl of Ross's ships. Ross is one of your earls. A most powerful lord. Needlessly to offend him, for the sake of this Angus of the Isles! Who does not even acknowledge your suzerainty . . ."

"Malcolm, my friend — apart from the sacred laws of hospitality, these waters are most certainly within the Lordship of the Isles. If these are Ross's galleys, then he is engaging in piracy. My duty, as sovereign lord of them both, is surely to uphold he who has the right of law . . ."

The laws of piracy or hospitality notwithstanding, Lennox — who in fact merely hated fighting — was the only protester; indeed the remainder of the King's company were all preparing themselves for the fray. Warriors all, they would have been grievously disappointed and resentful had their liege lord's choice been otherwise — as well Bruce knew. After months of skulking and frustration, all were in fact itching for a fight, their master not the least.

Their approach and run in did not go unnoticed, needless to say. Clearly a certain amount of disengagement was going on in the birlinn, with some warriors jumping back into the two attacking ships.

Kiloran's tactics were uncomplicated to a degree. He merely drove his craft straight for the assailed birlinn — and therefore in between the sterns of the two galleys which closely flanked it. As they ran in, the forward oarsmen raised their sweeps high, to avoid impact, and even before the crash of collision, lessened by the rear oarsmen backing water with the expertise of long practice, grapnels were being hurled into the enemy vessels and lines tightened. Yelling MacDonald slogans, the first boarders were leaping over, left and right, seconds later.

In the absence of any guidance from Kiloran, or anyone else, the King's party acted as each thought fit. They had all congregated at their own galley's high poop and they could not be amongst the first wave of boarders. They had to jump down, and press forward along the narrow gangway between the rowing-benches, where they were jostled and pushed aside by oarsmen shipping their sweeps and rushing to join the attack. Some flung themselves over into one or other galley as best they could, but most remained in a tight knot behind the King himself.

Bruce in fact followed Kiloran, who he guessed would make for the enemy leaders. He had clambered up over their own bow-platform and on to the raised stern of the birlinn. It was there that the most intensive fighting seemed to be taking place.

Bruce, like most of his Lowland colleagues, had chosen the short battle-axe as the most practical weapon for such close fighting, where the long two-handed swords would be at something of a disadvantage. Most of the Islemen were wielding claymores, but even these were on the long side for crowded decks. Some had already abandoned them for the handier and deadly dirk.

The King leapt down from the prow of his own craft to the poop of the birlinn, a drop of about five feet across a gap of six — and almost ended his personal engagement there and then. For only a tiny portion of the crowded deck was available for leaping on, and this was already slippery with blood. Bruce slithered on landing, and fell headlong. Only a desperate effort saved him from tumbling over into the sea — an effort which was not aided by the crash of a writhing body across his own and its struggles thereafter to avoid the dirk-jabs of a third contestant, jabs which in the circumstances were just as likely to end up in Bruce as in the selected target. What might have eventuated had not James Douglas and Gilbert Hay jumped down, to all intents on top of the sprawling trio, there is no knowing. They despatched the dirker, and pushed his wounded victim off, with scant courtesy, in some uncertainty as to which side either belonged to.

There was no opportunity for niceties, even towards the fallen monarch. Before Bruce was fully upright again, the three of them were engaged by about half a dozen of the Rossmen, who left off their assault of a group at the head of the poop steps to attend to the newcomers. Bruce, aware of a red-dripping claymore blade slashing down on him, ducked and jerked aside urgently, cannoning into Hay, and almost overbalancing again on the heaving, slippery deck. But he had clung on to his battle-axe throughout, and now brought it up in an underhand swipe, more instinctive than shrewd — which however did make contact with the attacker sufficiently to knock him back against one of his colleagues — thus saving Douglas from a vicious thrust.

But now the superiority of the short-shafted axe over the long sword-blade was quickly demonstrated, for in-fighting. Moreover, Bruce was something of an expert with this clumsy-looking weapon. Unwieldy as it seemed, it could do major damage in minimum time, not requiring anything like the precision of sword strokes, the swinging circle, or the point-versus-edge decision — for, in fact, wherever it struck or at whatever angle, it was effective, whether it hacked, slashed, shattered or merely numbed.

Steadied back to back with Hay, with half a dozen short smashing blows Bruce had cleared a space before him, one man crashing to the deck, head opened, one disarmed and cringing a pulverised shoulder, and a third backing away, only grazed but suitably alarmed.

But this very clearance held its dangers, for it gave room for swords to swing and thrust. The axeman had to keep close or be outranged. And he had to remember his back. Hay, a seasoned fighter, would look to that last; and Douglas, though younger and less experienced, was trained to the tourney in France, and would support both.

So Bruce leapt forward, smiting hugely, while these strange tactics still confused the Highland sworders — than whom, indeed, there were few better. Some wore helmets, but more did not; and there was no armour, other than toughened leather jerkins and arm and leg paddings, save for a little chain-mail amongst the leaders,

Most indeed were bare to the waist, with only tartans and saffron and targes — small round shields — as protection. Plus their own agility, swiftness and great oarsmen's muscles.

Hay and Douglas, perceiving that Bruce had got into his stride, contented themselves with protecting his rear and flanks, backing up behind him while the King formed the driving apex of the triangle, lashing, thrashing forward with tremendous vigour and controlled accuracy. Robert Bruce, at his best, in action, was of a calibre few could rival, and few indeed would wish to challenge. He had not forced his way into the empty throne merely because he was his father's son and of the blood of the ancient kings . . .

How many went down before that deadly weaving axe he did not know, for apart from the disciplined determination of this close-set trio, there was great confusion aboard the birlinn — valour, yes, but little coherence or direction. The reason for this was probably the fact that MacDonald of Kiloran, having singled out the chieftain of the Rosses, had cut his way straight to him, to engage him in mortal combat — from which lesser men respectfully drew back. He had brought the other down, too, a thick gorilla of a man of middle-years and fiery red hair, with a claymore through the gullet. But he was himself thereafter slain, almost casually, by one of the onlookers, with a dirk in the back — this leaving both sides without effective leadership.

Bruce became aware of something of this when, tripping over a body and down on one knee, momentarily endangered, he perceived that it was Kiloran.

Recovered, thanks to his friends, he perceived something else hitherto unnoticed — that the group at the head of the poop steps, towards which he was driving, was in fact centred round a woman. This was sufficiently unexpected to disconcert him somewhat, slightly to put him off his stroke. But when a sword-tip ripped open his doublet sleeve, scoring a shallow flesh wound along his forearm — the first actual blood he had shed in this encounter — he very quickly retrieved his due concentration. The more fiercely vehement on account of his lapse — and of the stinging pain — he leapt in under the swordman's dropped guard, and cut him down from shoulder to breastbone.

The fight, although it continued with unabated fury, was subtly changing its character. It was, in fact, becoming more coherent and meaningful, as lack of leadership was replaced by a more positive urge — at least amongst the Rossman. As though by some sort of telepathy, these began to accept that they had probably bitten off more than they could conveniently chew, and that a return to their own galleys would be the reaction of reasonable men. As yet there was no breaking off, no acknowledgement of defeat — for undoubtedly the attackers still outnumbered the others; but the climate of battle had altered. Possibly it was the advent of the Lowlanders, with their strange weapons and unexpected tactics, that disconcerted the raiders.

At any rate, the birlinn's poop quite quickly became a deal less crowded — even though there was not so very much more room to stand because of all the sprawling bodies on the deck. For the first time since jumping aboard, Bruce, gasping for breath, had opportunity to glance around him. The scene was confused, but only moments were required to establish the basic situation. Robert Boyd waved to him from the prow platform, giving the thumbs-up sign. Nodding, the King turned back.

The woman, four men with reddened swords and dirks close-guarding her, stood watching him, braced against some of the mast cordage. She was fairly young, he saw now, and darkly striking, with great eyes, long raven hair that blew in the breeze, and skin of an alabaster whiteness that gave the impression of transparency. But not for a moment did Bruce imagine that her whiteness had anything to do with fear or alarm. Every line of her bearing proclaimed a proud unconcern for danger or indeed bloodshed. There was blood on one forearm, raised to shield her eyes against the blaze of the sinking sun — but it was almost certainly not her own. She appeared to be concerned only with an inspection of himself.

In the circumstances, Bruce could do no other than adopt a similar attitude, leaving the final stages of the battle to others. Secure in his reliance upon the two stalwart knights immediately behind, he bowed, panting. Axe-wielding is breath-taking work.

"Who are you, sir?" the lady called, clearly above the din. "I am Christina MacRuarie of Garmoran. Whom do I have to thank for this deliverance?"

So it was Christina herself. A notable character, and in a sort of way, a kinswoman of his own. "You have to thank . . . our fallen friend, there. MacDonald of Kiloran," he told her, pointing down at the deck. "Myself, I am Robert of Scotland. The Bruce. I greet you warmly. And rejoice to name you cousin." He flattered himself that that was not bad for a man who had been laying about him with a battle-axe moments before, shortage of breath notwithstanding.

She was not really his cousin — no blood relation whatever, Christina of the Isles, as she still signed herself, was the only child and heiress of the late Alan MacRuarie, Lord of Garmoran. This Garmoran, which included the great mainland tracts of Knoydart,

Moidart, Morar and Arisaig, and the islands of Rhum, Eigg and Gigha of the Inner Hebrides, and Uist and Barra of the Outer, was one of the principal divisions of the Isles confederacy. Christina therefore was the great-great-granddaughter of the mighty Somerled, just as Angus Og was the great-great-grandson, their grandfathers brothers. The link with Bruce was only by marriage, for she had wed Duncan, younger son of Donald, Earl of Mar. Duncan had been Bruce's first wife's brother. He was now dead, and here was his young widow, married at fifteen and now ten years older.

"Bruce! The King! Himself!" she cried. "*Dia*—here is a wonder! Can it be true?"

"True, yes. Think you any but himself would covet Bruce's name and style, this day?" the King said wryly.

She pushed forward, between her wary guards. "Your Grace!" she exclaimed. "How come you here I know not. But you are welcome to my territories. And for more than this service you do me." She took his hand, dripping blood as it was. But she did not curtsy, nor raise it to her lips. Instead she leaned over and kissed him on the cheek. She was a tall, lissome creature, only an inch or so shorter than Bruce himself.

"You are kind," he jerked, a little taken aback, both at this gesture and her ability apparently to divorce herself entirely from the battle and carnage which still raged elsewhere than on this poop-deck. He himself was less detached, gazing round him and catching the eyes of Douglas and Hay.

"The day—it goes well, I think. They have had enough. They go back. These Rosses. If that is what they are. Back to their own galleys..."

"To be sure. They know what is good for them. Let them go. But ... Your Grace's arm? You are wounded."

"A nothing. The merest scratch."

"Let me see..."

"Better that you look to Kiloran."

But she insisted on herself examining and ministering to his hurt, gesturing to others to look to the fallen MacDonald—who indeed proved to be dead.

Edward Bruce, Neil Campbell and Robert Boyd had taken charge elsewhere, and the situation was rapidly coming under control. Already one of the attacking galleys was sheering off, and the remaining Rossmen were fighting their way back to the other. The issue obviously settled, few contestants were now anxious any more to risk their lives on either side, and the final exchanges were more or less formalities. Some badly placed boarders jumped or were pushed into the sea, but by and large the retiral was effected with minimal opposition, the grapnel-ropes cut, and the second vessel pulled away. Cheers and jeers from the birlinn and the MacDonald galley proclaimed the end of the engagement.

None of the King's party had been killed, and of the few wounds none were serious. Undoubtedly the bloodiest part of the fray had been before they arrived. Nevertheless, Bruce and his colleagues found themselves deriving the greatest credit from the affair and, by Christina downwards, were acclaimed as the victors and rescuers — which was a little embarrassing, being scarcely true. Nothing would do but that they should all accompany the chieftainess to her house of Castle Tioram in Moidart — to which she had been making, from South Uist, when attacked. With Kiloran dead and his second-in-command wounded, it seemed a reasonable programme. Moidart, on the mainland just north of the great Ardnamurchan peninsula, was apparently little more than an hour's sail away. And Christina MacRuarie was obviously a determined and autocratic young woman.

* * *

Castle Tioram, which they came to in the blue October dusk, sat impressively on an abrupt rocky half-tide island almost stopping up the narrow mouth of the sea-loch of Moidart, whose heavily wooded shores rose high and dark on either side, shadowy in the twilight. The castle, though less spectacularly sited than Dunaverty, was larger, and clearly of considerable strength, built on the antique plan of a lofty perimeter wall of enceinte, some thirty feet high, that followed the irregular outline of the rock, topped by a parapet and wall-walk, with embryo flanking towers at sundry corners and no central keep. Within this embattled perimeter indeed, when their hostess had led her visitors in at the narrow and portcullised sea-gate above the galley-pier, it was not like a castle at all; but rather a village, consisting of a long low hall-house with thatched roof, a chapel, cot-houses, storehouses, stables, byres and the like, all scattered within the curtain-wall — more like a walled town in miniature. Resinous pine torches, lit by the score for their welcome, bathed all in a ruddy flickering glow broken by inky shadows, and the smell of wood-smoke, animals and roasting meats was highly acceptable to hungry voyagers.

The hall-house, however undefendable in itself, was infinitely more commodious and comfortable than any castle. Christina was obviously used to dispensing hospitality in a large way, and found room for Bruce's people with seeming ease. The King was given a large room which, he suspected, was the lady's own, and had certainly no complaints to make.

If any of the Lowlanders had had a notion that they would have to endure semi-barbarous conditions, they were speedily disillusioned. The feast that followed, considering the speed with which it had been conjured up, was on a scale and of a quality worthy of any great noble's establishment in the south, and the wines better than most could offer. Fully a score of Garmoran chieftains sat down with the visitors, in a sort of court — although Christina herself was the only woman present — their wolfhounds making up for their lack of womenfolk. But the behaviour of these was civil and orderly — indeed more so than many a hallful of belted knights and lords. If most were loud in their assertions as to what they would have done had they known of their lady's danger at the hands of the dastardly Rossmen, that was only natural. Taking their tune from her, they were all notably respectful towards the Lowland King, for Highlandmen.

Only the entertainment which accompanied the meal was somewhat strange to the visitors. Instead of minstrels, tumblers, clowning dwarfs or even dancing bears and the like, here were men, not all ancient by any means, who told endless stories about fabulous heroes and quite unbelievable deeds, interspersed with lengthy genealogies which seemed to be an integral part of the performance — and which were listened to, surprisingly, with evidently rapt attention. Since all this, however, was in the Erse, or Gaelic, which few of the newcomers understood — the Bruces did, since they had had a Celtic mother — and since it was not the southern custom to pay any close heed to mere background entertainment during a banquet, the King's people by and large tended to talk through it all — which clearly did not commend itself to their hosts, though there were no overt reproaches. Bruce, on Christina's right, grew uncomfortable; but his brother Edward, on her other side, was not affected, himself being fairly completely preoccupied by the lady's charms — and making it very clear. Edward was ever interested in the opposite sex.

Christina MacRuarie, who looked quite capable of telling guests at her table, or anybody else for that matter, to be quiet if she so desired, did not do so. She appeared to listen to Edward with one ear, while at the same time she did not neglect the King on her right, keeping his platters and goblets filled — yet managing also to seem to attend to the storytellers.

But presently, with a venerable, white-bearded seannachie bowing himself out, to unaccountable applause, and the youngest tale-teller of all stepping forward from halfway down the great table to take his place, the atmosphere began to change. Even Edward Bruce sat forward to watch and listen.

For this young man, although he had his head bandaged and one arm hung limply at his side, was an orator of a different order. Full of energy and fire, his words came out in rushes and spurts and flourishes, with dramatic pauses, and gesturings of his sound arm — and although the words themselves were still in the Gaelic, something of their import and urgency reached even to those who could not understand them.

Bruce listened keenly, especially when he heard his own name coming into it all — not as a king but as a renowned warrior travelled from a far country. The oration was in fact an extempore, vivid and highly stylised and elaborated version of the afternoon's galley-fight, with everything dramatised and turned into heroics, all noblest valour, fairest beauty, blackest treachery and haunting romance — a sort of instant saga. Thus, evidently, were the famed Celtic epics born. Bruce perceived that he was very much this one's hero, as his hostess was the noble heroine whom he had come so far to rescue. Somewhat embarrassing as this might be, he was not blind to the advantages it might have for his cause in these latitudes, amongst people at once so warlike, extravagant and histrionic as these.

All but exhausted, the young man finished on a telling note of the victorious Robert of Alba, the noble blood of his wounds being staunched by the beauteous Christina of the Isles, who then conducted him and his noble band to her ancestral halls amongst the fairest prospects of all the Hebrides. He was summoned to the head of the table to receive his lady's congratulations and thanks amidst the plaudits of all. Bruce did some swift thinking. The orator was introduced to him as Ranald MacRuarie of Smearisary, son of Christina's natural half-brother Roderick. He had, in fact, though young, been captain of the attacked birlinn. He was, therefore, of some consequence in the Garmoran polity. The King stood up.

"That sword?" he said, pointing to a huge two-handed brand which hung on the wall near by, beneath a tattered banner. "Whose is it?"

"That is the sword of my ancestor, Somerled the King," Christina told him.

"So much the better," he said. "I crave your permission?"

Assuming the said permission, he strode over and took the weapon down. Returning, he raised it high — with difficulty, on account of its weight and the stiffness of his now bandaged arm.

"Come, friend," he said to the young man. "I, Robert of Scotland, salute you. In your words and in your deeds." He brought down the great blade, more heavily than he intended, on one of the somewhat alarmed orator's shoulders. He should have tapped the other shoulder also, but feared in his stiffness that he was more likely to strike the already bandaged head in between, and contented himself, letting the weighty weapon sink to the floor. "I dub thee knight. Be thou a good and true knight until thy life's end. Stand, Sir Ranald MacRuarie MacDonald!"

There was a few moments of silence, and then exclamation and outcry from all over the hall. There was wonder, acclaim and criticism in it — the last from some of his own people, his brother included, shocked at this debasement of knighthood on little better than a young savage.

Bruce was not perturbed by the note of disapprobation, especially when it was so clearly overborn by the acclaim and even glee. He himself had no doubts that his impulse had been a sound one. He had, with a single stroke of a sword — and Somerled's sword at that — not only made a notable impression on these people and given a unique impetus to a new-forming legend which might well prove extremely useful to his cause, but had established the fact of his kingship and royal prerogative before them all, doing something that no other could or would do. Moreover he had established a precedent, made a Highlander a knight — and if this was accepted, as it looked like being, it implied also the acceptance, here at least, of his suzerainty.

If the young man himself seemed quite dumbfounded, Christina at least was obviously delighted. She actually clapped her hands. "A King indeed?" she cried. "Here is a royal chivalry, honour. I thank you, Sire — on my heart I do!"

"This young man is your substitute and deputy, lady," he returned, bowing. "Might knighthood be bestowed on a woman, on your fair shoulders would fall this blade. In salutation."

"Your Grace is kind — and I am grateful. But perhaps there may be . . . other salute? More meet for a woman!" And she met his eye frankly.

Bruce inclined his head, but found this a good moment to make a display of handing over the sword to the new knight. They seated themselves again, and the banquet continued.

It was already late and Bruce, smothering yawns, was debating how he might, without offence to his hostess — who certainly gave no impression of weariness — intimate that his couch called, when an elderly man whom he had seen before, frail and stooping, came to whisper in Christina's ear. She raised her brows, and turned to the King.

"Sire — this Murdo Léigh is the physician who looked to your wounds, you will recollect. He now attends to others. Amongst whom is one of the prisoners from the Ross galleys. A man of some substance, it seems. He talks of your affairs. Murdo fears that he is dying, but does not believe him deranged. He believes that you should see this man. For he speaks of your wife. The Queen."

Bruce rose at once, frowning.

Together they followed the old man out and across the courtyard and into a reed-thatched lengthy bunkhouse, but dimly lit by a few flickering torches. Here many men lay on sheepskin litters, some groaning. They were brought to one, huddled very still beneath a ragged plaid, grey of face, eyes closed. They feared that he was already dead.

But presently the eyelids flickered, and the old physician kneeled, to speak in his ear.

"I have brought the King. The Bruce. The Sasunnach King. He is here, man. Tell him what it is. What troubles you. Tell him."

The dying man stared up at Bruce. His lips moved, but no sound issued.

"Speak up, man ..."

Bruce knelt on the rush-strewn floor beside the sufferer. "You have word for me? Of my wife?" he demanded. "What do you know?"

The other's eyes rolled up, and his lids closed. But after a moment he opened them again, and whispered. "The sanctuary. I ... I swore ... ill would ... come of it. The sanctuary ... violated."

"Sanctuary? What sanctuary? What do you mean? Tell me, man."

"Duthac," the other muttered. "The saint. It was ... ill done."

"Of a mercy! What is this of saints? What was ill done?" Bruce gripped the man's arm.

The old Murdo signed to the King to wait. He spoke more gently in the other's ear. "Friend — heed you. Here is opportunity. To unburden your soul. You go to be with God. Soon. You said that your soul was heavy. A weight of guilt. I have no priest — but here is the King. You said it was God's judgement — that you should be cut down by the Sasunnach King. Here he is. Speak while you may."

In a fever of anxiety Bruce looked up at the woman. She touched his shoulder and shook her head.

The Rossman stared past them all, up at the shadowy, smoke-wreathed roof, unwinking. Then he spoke again, more clearly though no more strongly. "My lord commanded it. He cared nothing ... for the sanctuary. We took the women ... out of it.

This Queen. And the child. Slew their men . . . there at the altar. My lord commanded it . . ."

"Dear God — what are you saying? The Queen? And the child? My Marjory? Speak plain, man — for sweet Christ's sake! What lord? What sanctuary?"

"Saint Duthac's. At Tain. My lord of Ross. Chief of our Clan Aindreas. William, the Earl. The other earl — Atholl. He was fleeing, with the women. North. To the Orcades, they said. The English king's men after them. Fleeing through my lord's territories. My lord sought to take them. They took refuge in the chapel. Of Saint Duthac. At Tain. A noted sanctuary. We caught them there . . ."

"You caught them! Took them? You took the Queen? And my daughter? You slew . . . slew . . .?"

"Only the men. Who would have stayed us, lord. At the altar. God forgive me! Not the women. Atholl, the other earl, wounded. My lord William handed him over. To the English. With the women. It was ill done . . ."

"God! When? When was this?"

But the other seemed to be seized with a bout of agonising pain. Only groans came from him.

"Answer me, wretch!" Bruce cried, almost beside himself. "When was this infamy?" He shook the moaning man.

There was no answer, no further meaningful words, just the grievous sounds of a man in his extremity. With a fierce effort Bruce sought to take a grip upon himself, rising to his feet.

"So — Edward!" he panted. "Edward Plantagenet — he has my Elizabeth! And Marjory. By the damnable treachery of William of Ross. God Almighty's curse upon him!" On a gasping intake of breath he paused, eyes widening. He was staring at Christina MacRuarie, but he did not see her. "No — God's curse on *me*! Myself — it is myself that is accursed! Myself, I tell you. You heard? At the altar. Taken at the altar. At this Tain. As I took John Comyn's life at the altar. At Dumfries. Jesu God! It is *I* who did this. *I* who betrayed my wife and daughter . . ."

"Sire! My lord Robert — do not say so. You cannot blame yourself for this. For the villainy of Ross. Do not scourge yourself . . ."

Blindly he turned away, making for the door.

In the courtyard she caught up with him, reaching for his sound arm. "See — come with me," she urged. "We will speak of this quietly, privately."

He removed his arm, though not roughly. "I thank you. But I would be alone. I go to my room. I thank you — but this is for myself, apart. Go back to your guests. Say that I am wearied. That my wound pains me. Goodnight. And . . . and say a prayer, lady, for Robert Bruce! Of your mercy . . ."

Chapter Five

The days that followed were as grievous as any that Robert Bruce had had to bear, despite the comforts of his present refuge, the goodwill of his hostess, the sympathy of his friends and the beauty of his surroundings. He had thought that he was armoured now, hardened, against further fierce hurt and sorrow, that he had plumbed the depths of suffering; in ten years of war and destruction and Edward Plantagenet's malice and Comyn's hatred, in the ruin of his fortunes, the frustration of his hopes, the living with treachery and defeat; in the terrible deaths of his brother Nigel, his brother-in-law Christopher Seton and so many of his supporters and friends; in the torture of a whole people. But it was not so. His despair over Elizabeth was beyond all that had gone before, his agony of dread almost enough to send him out of his mind, his utter helplessness a crucifixion. Worst of all, perhaps, his sense of guilt, that never left him, day or night, the general background of guilt in that all surely stemmed from his murder of John Comyn before the altar at Dumfries; and the more immediate and personal guilt in that he had refused Elizabeth's pleas to let her remain with him, had sent her away — to this. While he himself remained safe, secure.

His heart ached also, of course, for his daughter Marjory, so young, at twelve, to be suffering for her father's sins, failures and ambitions. And for his sisters Christian and Mary, Isabel Countess of Buchan who had crowned him, and the rest of his womenfolk. What English Edward would do to them all, God alone knew — but chivalry and mercy played no part in either his warfare or his statecraft. Bruce had only one faint gleam of hope — in that Elizabeth was the daughter of Richard de Burgh, Earl of Ulster, Edward's closest friend and companion-in-arms. For de Burgh's sake he might conceivably stay his hand from the worst, from the most unthinkable atrocities. But, knowing the King of England, he did not delude himself with false optimism.

Bruce did not spend those days sitting in idle brooding, of course. He forced himself to activities in which he had neither satisfaction nor interest, grateful only when these tired him out sufficiently to dull the pain and fears that haunted him. Which was, indeed, quite frequently, for this was the season of the stags roaring on all the mountain-sides around Castle Tioram, when the deer-hunting was at its best — and Christina MacRuarie determined that nothing which she might do to distract and entertain her guests should remain undone. There was great hunting almost every day, of wolves and boars and even seals, as well as deer; salmon-spearing in the river narrows; hawking for the multitudinous wild-fowl, and especially the long skeins of geese that ribboned the sky at dawn and dusk. There was feasting, music, story-telling, and the vigorous Highland dancing, until far into the night, evening after evening. Love-making too, for those so inclined — although Edward Bruce appeared to achieve no real success in his frank pursuit of their hostess herself. The King sought to act his part in all this, and not play the skeleton at the feast — though none were deceived.

Not that any there looked upon this sojourn in Moidart as any sort of holiday. It was only a breathing-space, wherein time fell to be filled in. This Hebridean interlude, though forced upon the King and his friends by sheer necessity, as the only area of Scotland where he could be safe from his enemies, and respite from being hunted fugitives essential, nevertheless had a positive and never-forgotten objective — the obtaining and marshalling of men, once more to prosecute the war. How these men were to be won, whether cajoled, bargained for or merely hired, was less than clear — but these Highlands and Isles were in fact teeming with men trained to arms, whose main delight indeed was to fight. Somehow, some proportion of them must be harnessed to the King's cause. That they were in theory all his own subjects was something of a grim joke. But any success in such harnessing depended upon information, tidings, knowledge in some measure of what went on elsewhere — otherwise, for Bruce to be isolated in these remote fastnesses spelt defeat indeed. So Christina of Garmoran was prevailed upon to send out messengers, enquirers, spies, north and south, by sea and mountain-track — and while her visitors waited for results, this entertainment.

In all this, Christina's attitude to Bruce himself was of a warm understanding, a care and concern that was noteworthy in so vehement and proud, not to say imperious, a young woman. It would be fair to say that she cherished him, who was scarcely of the cherishing kind. He sought nothing of the sort, of course, and, in his preoccupation with his anxieties and guilt, may have seemed less than appreciative. But he was well aware, too, that this woman might well be brought to play an important part in his eventual strategy, both as a supplier of men and as a link with other chiefs, even to work on Angus of the Isles himself. So he by no means wholly rejected her attentions. Besides, she was a woman, and handsome — and he not unimpressionable, even in these circumstances.

It was ten days after the arrival in Moidart, and the night of the return of the first of the Garmoran couriers, that Bruce, far from cheered by this man's tidings, made excuse to retire early from the feasting and entertainment, and went to his room. He did not immediately repair to his couch however, for unless very weary indeed, sleep did not come easily these nights — and it had been a wet and chill day, with no hunting. Part-undressed and wearing a bed-robe of the late Alan MacRuarie's, he paced the skin-littered floor of his chamber.

The messenger had come from the Comyn lordship of Lochaber and the MacDougall lordship of Lorn — useful listening-posts for spies, in that they were very much in the enemy camp. He had brought back word which no interpretation would make other than depressing. In Aymer de Valence, Earl of Pembroke, King Edward had obviously found a Governor of Scotland after his own heart. Terror stalked all the Lowlands. Not only in the south, below Forth and Clyde, where these past years terror had been more or less endemic; but in the north and east, or such parts as were not Comyn-dominated. Angus and Mar and Moray in especial were suffering — for in these great provinces Bruce had much support — and Pembroke was now wreaking his master's will on Inverness. His, it appeared, was an effective and methodical terror, not weakened by blind hatred, and he left little in his tracks to resurrect. With the Earl of Ross now committed to Edward's cause, the farther north was equally enemy territory, and Bruce's adherents being rooted out ruthlessly. The only hint of consolation was that the Bishop of Moray, loyalest of the loyal, was said to have eluded the enemy net and was thought to be making for Orkney, with some few stalwarts.

As to the Queen, the only word was that she had been taken, with her companions, straight to King Edward, who was settling down to winter at Lanercost Abbey, near Carlisle. There he had promptly hanged Atholl — and to protests that no earl had been hanged, in England or Scotland, within the memory of man, had answered by prescribing a higher gallows and a longer rope for Earl John de Strathbogie. What he intended to do with the women, none knew — but the rumours were many and dire.

That Edward had chosen to set up permanent headquarters at Lanercost, remaining on the Border and not returning to London or even York, for the winter, was as grim news as any. It implied that though Scotland was to all intents crushed, and Pembroke's campaign now no more than a mopping-up, the Plantagenet was determined to go further, and personally to superintend the process. Which could only mean that this time Scotland was to be ground into the very dust, and that the hunt for Bruce himself was to be continued, probably intensified.

That man, pacing his floor, was going over all this, when a knock at the door revealed Christina MacRuarie herself. She was dressed in a furred bed-robe not unlike his own, her long dark hair hanging free.

"Your Grace," she said, "My lord Robert — I heard you walking and walking. This will not serve. Not in my house. Not for the hero who came to the rescue of Christina of the Isles. Who shed blood for her." That was spoken as though rehearsed. She came in and shut the door behind her.

It could have been true that she had heard him, for this was a timber-built house within the castle walls, and her room was next to his — indeed this obviously had been her own bedchamber, and she was presently occupying its ante-room. She must have left the hall very early, however — soon after himself, presumably — for the noise of pipe-music and dancing still sounded.

He inclined his head, waiting.

"Sire — it is not good. For a man to fret and gloom so. Not right. Your burdens are sore, heavy — but they are not such as to unman Robert Bruce." She spoke a little breathlessly now, for her. "You hold too much to yourself, my friend."

"Perhaps," he acceded. "But that is part of my burden. Being a king is lonely work."

"Need it be so lonely? I think not. For a king is a man first, with a man's needs, a man's temper and person. You do not renounce your manhood in your kingship, do you?"

"You think that I do?"

"I think it, yes. In part. That is why I have come. I have sought to bring the man out, from behind the king — on the hill, in the hunt, the fast, the dance. With little success. Now I come to your bed-chamber, Robert. For I believe that you need a woman. Yet you have looked towards none that I have offered. So now . . ." She paused. "So now I have brought myself!" And she threw open the furred robe.

She was completely naked beneath it.

He stared, wordless, moistening suddenly dry lips.

The whiteness of her was startling, an alabaster white even in the mellow lamplight, only emphasised by the jet-black triangle at the crotch and the large dark circles which tipped her breasts. Compared with this woman Elizabeth was honey-coloured, almost golden, more rounded, more generous of hip and thigh and bosom. Not that the man was conscious of any comparison between his wife and this who was offering herself to him. But the distinction was there, unbidden, inevitable, the contrast of two proud and beautiful women.

For Christina MacRuarie had her own beauty, however different, of form as of feature. And that she was very desirable no whole man could have gainsaid.

She stood so, for a little, eying him directly, only her visibly heightened breathing hinting that perhaps she was less bold and sure of herself than she appeared. She held out one hand.

"Do I please you, Robert?" she asked.

He swallowed. "Aye. Yes, indeed. You . . . you are very fair. Well-fashioned," he said thickly, hoarsely. He kept his own hands to his sides.

"And . . . and do I stir your kingship's manhood?"

He further moistened those lips. "You could scarcely . . . do otherwise! But, but . . ."

"Yet you stand abashed like any callow youth! Or less than a proper man. I vow your brother Edward would not be so backward!"

"Edward has not a wife. Whom he has brought to ruin. To dire danger, and sorrow. Would you have me further to betray my wife?"

She let the drawn-back folds of her robe fall together again, and shook her head. "Betray, no. Christina of the Isles is no betrayer of men, or women. Nor would lead others to betrayal. This is . . . other."

"What, then?" he demanded, more harshly than he knew.

Holding her robe closed before her, she came forward to him. "Robert—how long since last you lay with a woman?" she asked.

Blinking, he ran a hand through his hair. "God knows! Two months. Three. I cannot mind . . ."

"Yet you are of a lusty habit, they say. No half-man."

He did not speak.

She seated herself carefully on the edge of his bed, her own bed. "Why think you that I have come here, this night? To your chamber?" She added, as an afterthought and almost tartly, "Sire!"

"You tell *me*, lady," he said.

"Very well. I have not come because I am panting for you! Neither for your manhood nor yet your king's Grace! Nor is this my habit. Nor even have I come out of my gratitude, that you saved me and mine from the Rossmen. I came because I believed that you needed a woman. A woman's body, and a woman's comfort and tenderness. And since, it seems, you will not of yourself take a woman, I provide one. And since you are the King, and my guest, only *I* will serve. Christina. No other, I swear, would be sitting here, on your bed, putting all into words for you!"

"That at least is true!" he agreed, less stiffly. "What makes you think that I so greatly need a woman?"

"Because *I* am a woman, and have watched you. The signs are not lacking. Because a lusty man, and married, with time on his hands, is less than himself when deprived. And when the King is less than himself, many may suffer. More than those many should. Moreover, because in your fretting waiting in my house, you make but ill company. For me, and for your friends."

"You say so? For that I am sorry," he told her, stiff again.

"So are all who love you."

He stared down at her, frowning. What she said was true, of course — almost every word. He knew it, had long known it, without acknowledging it. Was he a fool, then . . .?

He flushed, as he realised that his man's eyes were busy, however sluggish his wits — for, leaning a little towards him, the woman's robe gaped open, so that both breasts were entirely evident, one exposed to the nipple. Her breasts were not large, but strangely pointed, firm, hard-seeming for a woman who had borne a child, as she had done. She had not fed the boy herself, it seemed. But if the breasts were not themselves large, the aureoles were larger and darker than any he had seen, and notably rousing admittedly. Moreover, the furred folds had fallen aside from one leg, and the white thigh and bent rounded knee were only a little less stimulating than the bosom. Indeed, sitting there, half-covered, she was altogether more tellingly desirable than when she had stood opposite him, wholly displaying her nakedness. More than his face flushed.

Probably she perceived something of these reactions, for she drew the robe back over her leg, though not very effectively, but raised her other hand to his sound arm.

"Come, sit, Robert," she said. "Tell me of your Queen. Your Ulsterwoman. Is she very beautiful? I have heard that she is."

He sat, since standing he was the more distracted. But to sit and discuss Elizabeth with this all-but-naked Isleswoman was less than suitable.

"She is, yes," he agreed shortly. "Beautiful, and leal."

"And she would have you monk, during this long parting?"

"Would not any wife?"

'Not any, no. Some, yes. *I* would not. With months, possibly years, between. My man's heart I would have cleave to me. His manhood, his body, denied me, I would not deny *him*."

For a moment that bedchamber of Castle Tioram in Moidart gave place to another room, darker, smaller and no bedchamber, whatever had taken place therein — the little rustic garden-house on the island in Linlithgow Loch where, four years before, Elizabeth de Burgh had yielded herself to him in passion and love. After that joyful, cataclysmic union, she had spoken to him very much as this Christina spoke now. What was it she had said? That she would be a jealous wife. That if she married him she would require him to be faithful. In his heart. That he might amuse himself with other women, even lie with them. But if he gave his heart to another, she would turn from him and never forgive him. Even might kill him, she had said. Those may not have been her words, but that was the gist of it.

And now, this.

"Your Queen and I, then, are of a different sort," she went on. "So be it."

"Different, yes. In much. But not . . . but not . . ." Absurdly, he felt that he had to be fair to Elizabeth in this.

Speculatively she eyed him. But she rose, pulling the robe close again. "I will go, then — since I cannot serve your need. Remember hereafter, Robert, that it was *your* need that brought me. Only that."

He looked up at her, biting his lip. They said that there was no hatred to rival that of a woman rejected. This woman's aid, co-operation, influence, he greatly required. And she was indeed beautiful . . .

"Do not go," he said.

Their eyes met, and held.

"Do you not know your own mind, Sire?" she asked. "Or is it your body you do not know?"

"As to my body, there is no doubt, woman!" he told her. "Nor indeed in my mind, I think. It was my heart that gave me pause."

"We are not concerned here with your heart," she declared levelly. But she looked away.

He had a flash of insight there, that perhaps she lied. But he put the thought from him.

"Then give me . . . what you came to offer. And find me . . . grateful."

"Grateful?"

"Aye, grateful." He stood up, and stepped forward to her. "And more than that. Desirous. Demanding. Needful. Hungry." He reached out an ungentle hand to wrench back her bed-robe from her white loveliness.

"So — you are a man, after all!"

"Let me prove it, Christina of the Isles!"

"You have all night to do that, Sir King!" She flung the robe away. "Let us see if there is a saga to be made of this also!"

* * *

If thereafter Robert Bruce suffered twinges of a new sort of guilt, at least he made better company, and for more than just his hostess. None failed to perceive the change in the King — and few failed to find a reason for it.

It was a strange development, manifesting itself not in any new zestfulness, triumphant masculinity or obvious satisfaction; rather in a relaxation of manner and temper, a greater friendliness towards his companions, a kind of lowering of guards. Clearly he felt less cut off from his fellow men and women, more in need of what others had to offer in sympathy and personal support. Indeed, although humility was not a word that was ever likely to be associated with the Bruce, a sort of modesty grew on him. He had never been arrogant or overbearing but there had been perhaps a certain unapproachability, a reserve. Always there would be something of this, but now there was a distinct easement.

He even spoke frequently, to others, of the Queen and her perilous situation, as of his own helplessness, something that he had not done before. That she was much on his mind, whatever his current recreations, was evident to all.

Of course the affair with Christina did not limit itself to a single engagement. Living in such close proximity, occupying adjoining rooms, that would have been almost impossible. And there was no question as to their mutual physical satisfaction; neither had cause to complain of the other's adequacy or accomplishment. No coy teasings or lovers' tiffs were there to punctuate their association. Vehement characters both, once decision was taken, there were no half-measures.

Nevertheless, as time passed, Bruce recognised danger signals. He realised that he was becoming dependent on this woman, that not only was her physical presence becoming necessary to him but that her strong and vivid character was of growing influence upon him, upon his plans and his thinking. He was able to tell himself this way lay not only betrayal of Elizabeth but folly, the endangering of his cause. He accepted that it was not Christina's fault, or deliberately caused — at least, he thought not. But the conviction grew upon him that he trod on thin ice. It was time for him to break loose. Despite the onset of November gales, and the implicit assumption that the winter was upon them, when men drew up their ships and laid by their swords until the campaigning season returned, Bruce decided to make a move.

The couriers and spies had meantime been reporting back to Moidart, from many parts — although some there were who never returned. From their news the King was able to piece together a picture of the national situation as a whole. Basically all of Scotland was prostrated under the heavy heels of the English and the Comyn faction, plus those agile men who always looked to the winning side. But this was only a superficial impression. The enemy grip was tighter in some areas than others, just as the underlying Bruce support was stronger, manifesting itself in small revolts, rioting and civil commotion, ambushes of parties of occupying troops, night assaults on isolated garrisons, and the dumb non-co-operation of the people. The South-West, from Glasgow down to Galloway, centring round Bruce's own earldom of Carrick, was the most restive, aided by many small guerilla bands, relics of Wallace's great force, operating from the upland wildernesses of Ettrick, Merrick and Kells. Fife, where the Church influence was predominant, despite the Primate Lamberton's imprisonment in England, also was in a constant turmoil; as was South Angus, and Dundee said to be a hot-bed of revolt. There was significant word, too, from more than one source, of rifts between the Comyns and their English overlords, with actual fighting in Badenoch. The Bishop of Moray was reported to be recruiting men and ships in the Orkneys. The picture, overall, was of a nation defeated and held down but not subdued, seething with unrest — no satisfactory prospect for King Edward. A small surge of hope was renewed within the Bruce.

There was no further news, as yet, about the Queen or Marjory or of the other women in Edward's grasp.

While all this was encouraging in some measure, there was no blinking the one great ominous shadow — the Plantagenet's continued presence at the Border. Rumour had it that he was sick again — but still refusing to go south to the comforts of home life in London. Which could only mean his utter determination to destroy Scotland once and for all, and Bruce with it, in the coming season, once the days were long enough for effective warfare, the hill passes open for his heavy chivalry, and the coastal seas calm enough for his supply fleets. In 1303 he had let loose quarter of a million troops on Scotland. His present prolonged preparations probably meant an onslaught on a similar scale — and this time upon a prostrate foe and undefended land.

Anything Bruce could do, therefore, it became evident, must be attempted before the spring, while he still had men who might rise for him throughout the country — for nothing seemed more certain than that afterwards there would be no more such alive. Which surely meant that he should not be lying in idle dalliance at Castle Tioram, winter or no winter. Could he even make winter fight for him?

One maddening aspect of the situation was to be surrounded by fighting-men, in these Highlands and Isles, who would not fight for him. Or, at least, who would not unless their chiefs told them to. And what had he, Bruce, to offer the said chiefs — who looked on the Lowland Scots much as they looked on the English, and certainly accepted no sort of allegiance, or duty to support them. Offers of position and privilege, as reward, in the freed Scotland, should it ever be free again, would have little relevance. Yet these great numbers of fierce fighters were available. Angus Og indeed, like lesser chiefs, built much of the Isles economy on the hiring out his broadswords by the thousand, mainly to the ever-warring Irish princelings — as he was doing, and leading them in person, at this present. Bruce undoubtedly could hire them likewise — had he the wherewithal. But today, he had not two gold pieces to rub together.

Yet, apart from the empty Scots treasury, altogether, he was, in theory, one of the richest lords in Scotland, owner of vast lands and estates, whole towns, almost provinces. Carrick was his, and rich Annandale; much of Galloway; the lordship of the Garioch, in Aberdeenshire, and many other lesser estates. Moreover he controlled the great earldom of Mar, as guardian of his nephew. Riches indeed. And it was nearly the Martinmas Term, when the rents of all those lands were due to be paid to him. If indeed, most, or many, of his people and tenants and vassals remained loyal to him, even as lord, much less king, and if they would probably rise and shed their blood for him — as they had done in the past — might they not still pay their rents to him? Even in today's circumstances, and though almost certainly the English invaders would be mulcting them as well? It was worth a trial. He could send out rent-collectors, at least.

Then there was the position of his two remaining younger brothers to consider, Thomas and Alexander. Apparently the enemy had not managed to lay hands on them, and the rumour was that they were in hiding somewhere in Galloway, instigating much of the insurrection there. Alex was now a priest, in name at least

Dean of Glasgow, though barely twenty-five. Thomas, a year older, and long-headed, had been the stay-at-home of the family, content to manage the great Annandale estates. They should be found, and brought here to the Isles.

So Bruce borrowed a small galley from Christina, and sent his brother Edward, and with Sir Robert Boyd and Sir Robert Fleming, a Galloway man, to aid and also possibly to restrain him. They were to sail secretly to Galloway, seek out Thomas and Alex, then try to collect as much of the Annandale and Carrick rents as they might, and return to Moidart. He would meet them here again, God willing, for Yuletide.

For he himself was for the sea again, also. In Angus Og's lent galley, he would continue on his northwards travels, interview the northern chiefs, seeking men and support, avoiding the Ross lands. And on round the top of Scotland to the Orkney Isles, to link up with the good Bishop David of Moray, there to draw up mutual plans. He hoped that when he returned to Castle Tioram, at Yuletide if possible, it would be in shape to take the first steps towards regaining his throne.

None knew better than he how many, how weary and how long-continued those steps must be. But at least a start would be made.

Chapter Six

After the spacious timber halls, the snug comforts, and much Yuletide feasting of Christina's hospitable house — to say nothing of her person's liberality — the small stone chambers of Kildonan's keep were bare, cramped and draughty, with the chill February wind finding its way in through a host of cracks and crevices. The crash of waves from far below was a muted thunder, as background for the whistle of the wind and the rattle of the timber shuttering of the small windows — ominous indication of the seas running in even these comparatively sheltered waters of the Firth of Clyde, and scarcely propitious sailing weather. But Robert Bruce and his friends were used to storms and high seas, these days, seasoned mariners. After the Sea of the Hebrides, the Minches in midwinter, and rounding Cape Wrath into and out from the dreaded Pentland Firth between Scotland and Orkney, these Arran waters held little terror.

It was chillier, draughtier, less comfortable, in that tower-room than even was normal of a February night however; for the shutters of the lower unglazed half of one window were wide open, so that the night came in in blasts and buffets setting the lamps flickering wildly and gouts of choking wood-smoke billowing out from fireplace and chimney. The glass of the upper part was too thick to give any prospect, letting in only light and no view even by day.

Despite the chill, the King himself sat near the open window, a plaid round his shoulders; he and his colleagues had taken to the Highland custom of wearing plaids at most times, finding them the most effective protection by day and night, on shipboard, in the heather, as surcoat or as blanket. Indeed Bruce, now weather-beaten, curly-bearded and long of hair, looked entirely the Highlander, and a tough and fierce one — so much so that the captured English captain of this hold, whom Douglas had seized, still refused to believe that this was indeed the King of Scots.

Bruce's glance, though he listened to the talk of his friends, kept turning to that open window, as it had been doing since darkness fell. The others, James Douglas in especial, had offered many times to relieve his self-imposed, chill vigil and exchange a seat nearer the fire; but the King had shaken his head. So much of his hopes and plans could depend on what he saw from that window.

For, due south-east of this southernmost tip of the Isle of Arran, where Kildonan perched on a cliff above a tiny harbour, lay the Ayrshire coast of mainland Scotland. More than that, it was the King's own coast of Carrick. Only fifteen miles away from where he sat, his great castle of Turnberry, principal seat of the earldom, stood above these same heaving waters, his birthplace, now occupied by Englishmen. What was Scots in his blood, as distinct from Norman-French, stemmed from just over there, where his Celtic ancestors had ruled the South-West. These days, Robert Bruce was turning to the Celt in him, in more than his clothing. The ancient blood stirred.

But it was not just Celtic blood and wishful thinking that stirred the King tonight. He was looking for a sign, a signal. Sir Robert Boyd and Sir Robert Fleming were, if God was kind, over there now, spying out the land, secretly visiting key vassals, carrying the royal message. They had been gone for five days now. If conditions were not impossible for a landing, they were to light a balefire of driftwood in a place he had told them of, a corner of beach under small screening cliffs about a mile north of Turnberry, known as Maidens. Here the fire, facing into the north-west, would not be apt to be seen from landwards but should gleam clear across the firth to Arran. To be lit either this night, or the next — the timing was important.

So Bruce peered into the stormy dark till his eyes ached, scarcely aware of the cold, and listened to his friends' idle talk with only one ear. There were not many of them to chat, in that upper room — apart from Edward, only the Earl of Lennox, James Douglas, Gilbert Hay and Neil Campbell. The others of his company were far scattered — though he hoped, and would have prayed if he had dared, that his younger brothers were not so very far away at that moment.

Edward Bruce had been successful in his mission in November, duly finding their two brothers, Thomas and Alex, in Galloway; and thereafter managing to collect a sizeable sum in rents. Most rental was paid in kind, of course — in grain, beasts, labour and armed service; but many of the larger vassals elected to pay at least some proportion in money, and the Bruce brothers had brought back to Moidart gold and silver, little enough for a great earldom's rent-roll, but a large sum indeed in the Hebridean economy, where a gold piece was a rare sight. After their reunion at Yule, then, the three brothers had been despatched to Ireland with most of the money, to seek out Angus Og — who with his mercenaries was wintering in comparative comfort in Antrim, as seemed to be his preferred custom — there to hire as many gallowglasses, Highland or Irish, as the money would buy. Thereafter they were to bring their new host to Rathlin Island, where Sir Reginald Crawford, a kinsman of the late Wallace, from Galloway, would meet them and guide them to a planned invasion of the mainland, in Galloway itself, where insurgent support was awaiting a lead. This to coincide with Bruce's own projected landing at Carrick.

All this had gone more or less as planned, and ten days ago Edward Bruce had brought word from Rathlin that Thomas and Alex were there, with 800 men, had met Crawford, and intended to descend on the Galloway coast on the night of the 9th of February, in the neighbourhood of Loch Ryan — tomorrow night.

The final member of the King's former close company, Sir William Bellenden, had been left at Orkney with Bishop David, to aid in an invasion of the North, to coincide with these two attempts.

Bruce waited there at the window until after midnight, reluctant to concede that there would be no signal that night. At length, with Edward and Lennox already retired, and the other three dozing by the dying fire, he sighed, and stood up, stretching stiffly.

"There is still another night," he said. "And Robert Boyd will not fail me. If the thing is possible. And if he is safe. If he has not been taken . . ."

"Sir Robert is cautious and wise, Sire. He will be safe," Douglas said, rising hurriedly. "And if there is no sign, we can still go to Galloway. Join the others."

"Aye. But much would be lost. All would be the more difficult.

The English, once warned, could seal off Galloway. The Carrick landing could prevent this. By linking up with those who fight from the mountains, from Ettrick and Merrick. Pray you for Boyd's signal, then. A good night to you . . ."

Bruce had barely seemed to lay his head on his pillow in the small mural chamber that was all this stark hold offered him, when he was awakened by Douglas shaking his shoulder.

"The signal, Sire! It burns! It burns!" the younger man cried. "The watch saw it, from the parapet-walk. It still burns clear."

"Eh . . .? What hour is it, Jamie?"

"Near to four. Four of the clock."

"It is late. Late. To be sending the word . . ." But Bruce rose, and wrapped his plaid around him again.

Up at the tower-room window, there was no need for Douglas to point. In the windy dark, apart from the line of phosphorescence from the breaking waves on the beach far below, the only thing to be seen was the bright point of light, reddish-yellow, that grew and contracted, waxed and waned in brilliance, away to the south-east, as they watched. Obviously a fire.

"It is the right airt?" Douglas asked.

"Yes. That is just north of Turnberry Head. So be it. Boyd's signal, yes. But . . . so late. Why has he delayed?"

"He could have been prevented, Sire. From reaching the place. Forced to a long detour. Hunted by the English. In enemy-held territory, anything may constrain . . ."

"Think you I do not know it, man! Have I not spent weeks, months, in enemy-held territory?" That flash of irritation was unusual in the King, who kept a close watch on his tongue. "Boyd is an experienced soldier. He knows that it is too late, now, for us to embark our men, win across the firth, and land in Carrick in darkness. Four o'clock. It is but four hours to dawn. It will take two hours to cross, in this wind and sea. If not more. Not the galleys, but the small craft."

Hay and Campbell had joined them at the open window. "And we must have time, over there, for our dispositions," the latter pointed out. "Further darkness."

"May not Sir Robert have thought of that, Your Grace," Douglas suggested. "And thus be giving us plenty of warning for tomorrow night. Giving us all day to prepare. If he had waited until a safe time after dark tomorrow, it would have cut into that night. And if he had lit his fire earlier, we would have made the crossing *tonight*. This way he gives us time."

"It may be so, Jamie,' the King acceded. "We can well use that time, whatever else. To make our preparations. To eat well and sleep well. We sail tomorrow evening, then, at first dark, and shall have a long night of it. Meantime we can sleep again. It may be we shall need it all . . .!"

* * *

The wind and seas had abated a little, but it was still an unpleasant crossing, the following night, especially for the smaller boats. Bruce had 300 men, 200 of Christina's Moidartach, granted free and for love, and 100 sent by Mackenzie of Kintail, not so much for love as for hatred — hatred of the Earl of Ross, Mackenzie's unfriendly neighbour. Christina had provided an extra galley too — indeed she had had to be dissuaded from accompanying the expedition herself; but even so, further transport was necessary, and the smaller, slower craft were scarcely adequate for the winter seas — especially as the incoming tide was racing up the firth from the ocean, south-westerly, the same direction as the prevailing wind, while the flotilla was proceeding on a course at almost right angles, south by east, with consequent rolling beam seas. Fortunately the men were Hebrideans and used to the sea, or they might have made but a doubtful fighting force at the end of it.

There had been some speculation that Boyd might have lit his beacon again tonight, to guide them in; but as yet there was no sign of it. The night was dull and cold, with occasional slight sleet showers, inclement for sailing in open boats but suitable enough for the activities ashore.

There were no stars to navigate by, but three-quarters of the way across Bruce decided that a cluster of lights that showed faintly must be from Turnberry Castle itself. In which case they were too far to the south. He shouted an order to the helmsman, in his leading galley.

Presently they could hear the thunder of the breakers on the shore, an ominous sound; and after some minutes of anxious peering into the mirk, Bruce thought that he could distinguish the long belt of white that would be the seas disintegrating on the savage reef of skerries that half closed Maidenhead Bay from the south. Another half-mile and they ought to be able to turn in, around the north end of the reef, and run into the comparatively sheltered corner of bay behind, the rendezvous where the balefire had blazed.

Soon they swung in, tossing violently as they passed the tail-end of the skerries, and thereafter quickly felt the sea's motion to abate. The re-entrant of the bay ahead was dark, under low cliff, giving no sign of life. The King remembered two salmon-fishers' cothouses there, where he had played as a lad.

Cautiously, sail furled, Bruce's galley nosed forward, the sweeps dipping gently. There was no jetty or landing-stage, but an easy boat-strand of sand and pebbles, where three fishing cobles were already drawn up.

Skilfully manoeuvred, the vessel's forefoot crunched into the shelving shingle with a minimum of shock, amongst only small waves. Had the wind been northerly, or the landing unprotected from the south, it would have been a very different matter. Bruce himself was one of the first to jump down, caring nothing for the cold splashy shallows, and more affected by this stealthy return to the mainland of his kingdom than he would have been prepared to admit.

There was no one there to greet them. No movement showed on the dark shore.

Edward's galley moved in now, with the smaller craft, like a brood of ducklings, close behind. His brother came striding over the pebbles.

"Where is Boyd?" he demanded. "And Fleming. They should be here."

"I had looked for them, yes. Perhaps they do not expect us so early. Have not seen our arrival. They may be waiting in one of those cabins."

The King led a group up over the shingle and the sea-grass to where the dark low bulk of the cot-houses loomed. With sword-hilts they beat on the closed doors, demanding to open in the name of King Robert.

Only alarmed fishermen opened to them.

When these men's immediate fears were allayed, they declared that only themselves were in the hovels, no lords or great men. Sir Robert the Boyd had been here, yes — but that was four days back. He had sworn them to secrecy and had bade them gather drift-wood for a great fire. On the beach. Not to be lit until he returned. But he had not returned.

"Not returned, man?" the King burst in. "What do you mean? You lit the fire, lacking him?"

"No, lord. The fire is not lit. We await Sir Robert. As he said . . ."

"But — by the Rude! The fire *was* lit. That is why we are here. It was a signal."

"No, lord. Saving your lordship's presence. The fire is not yet lit. The wood still there. Down below the cliff . . ."

"Dear God! Then the fire we saw last night . . .?"

"Not here, sir. That would be the alehouse up at Shanter. Some drunken English soldier set it afire. Last night. Two of them died in it, they say. And Mother MacWhannel herself. God rest her soul! A great blaze..."

"Christ's mercy! We have come then on a wild-goose chase!" Edward cried. "A burning alehouse!"

Appalled, they stared at each other in the darkness.

"Thank God we have learned it in time, at least!" Lennox said. "We can return to Arran, and little harm done."

"Oh, no...!" That was young James Douglas.

"There speaks a lily-liver. A craven!' Edward accused. "We have not come all this way to turn back now."

"My lord...!"

"My friends — peace!" Bruce intervened. "Here is matter for better debate than this. My lord of Lennox may be wise. We have made a grave mistake, it seems..."

"You would not turn tail?" his brother demanded, incredulously. "We have successfully landed. Unopposed. Is that not the great thing...?"

"It is important. But there are greater things. Robert Boyd is the most experienced campaigner we have. And an Ayr man. That is why I sent him. He was to light his fire if he deemed conditions at all possible for our invasion. It seems that he has not done so. Therefore must we not believe that he deems the venture impossible? Or too dangerous?"

"He may be captured, Sire. Or dead," Hay put in.

"It may be. Does that aid our decision?"

"Save us — we cannot turn back now!" Edward insisted. "Without so much as a sight of the enemy. That will not win back your kingdom for you!"

"I have so far shown the Scots people only defeat and disaster. My first attempt in this new campaign must be successful. Or at least no defeat. Or my cause is the worse served, greatly the worse."

"Yet, if we go back to Arran now, Sire, with no blow struck, is not your case equally hurt? When it becomes known." That was Neil Campbell.

"I would not turn back to Arran. Not now. I would sail south. To Loch Ryan. To join my brothers in Galloway. But..." The King paused. He turned to the fishermen. "Have you any notion as to how many is the English garrison at Turnberry?"

"Many, lord. Many."

"Aye, man — but *how* many? Are they in scores? Or hundreds? Or many hundreds? Only a mile away. Surely you have some notion."

"Hundreds, sir. Many hundreds. I do not know. Four, five hundred, it may be. So many they cannot mostly lodge in the castle. They fill every house in the Castleton. As in the Kirkton. In the kirk itself. And the mills and farm-touns around. So many."

"They are scattered, then? Lodged separate? In groups. Apart."

"Aye, lord. They needs must."

"And their masters? The knights and captains? Where are they?"

"Where but in the castle, sir. Where lords and knights would bide. With the great lord, the Percy . . ."

"Percy!" Bruce actually gripped the speaker's arm. "Percy, you say, man? Do you mean Henry Percy? The Lord of Northumberland?"

"The same, yes. He commands here now. As Governor and Sheriff."

"Lord save us!" The King swung on the others. "You hear? Henry Percy it is, who sits in my house. Rules my earldom! That smooth snake!"

Bruce was not the only one roused at the mention of the Northumbrian's name. They had scores to settle with the Percy.

"And his men are scattered!" Edward cried. "His captains with him in the castle. If this dolt speaks truth."

"As why should he not? Fearing no surprise assault, it is what they *would* do. And . . . the Castleton of Turnberry is a quarter-mile from the castle, no less!"

Suddenly there was no more talk of turning back. Percy's hated name, and the thought of his men dispersed, had changed all that, as far as Bruce was concerned.

"Henry Percy keeps but poor discipline, I think. If his men, drunken, are burning down alehouses at four of a morning!" he said. "It may be we could teach him a lesson."

"That is better talking, by the Mass!" Edward agreed. "How do we go about it? Isolate the castle, first?"

Bruce turned to the fishermen's spokesman, Cuthbert, by name, it appeared. "Friend — these English soldiers? Can you tell us where they are lodged? Besides the Castleton and the Kirkton. Each mill and farm-toun and place. All that you know."

There were six men in all, and between them they worked out a list of some eight separate locations where Percy's troops were billeted around Turnberry, some as much as a mile away from the castle — one indeed only a comparatively short distance inland from this bay, at Maidens Mill, where there was a troop of perhaps thirty horse and some archers. Practically all the locations the King and Edward knew, so that they could visualise the terrain and lay-out.

Bruce led his group back to their 300 Highlanders, who were now all disembarked and waiting on the shingle. He called for quiet, and spoke to them in their own tongue, his own mother's tongue.

"I have work for you, after your own hearts," he told them. "Quiet, deadly work. Not open battle, you understand, but quiet effective killing. Surprise. There are more of these Englishmen than there are of us, but they are lodged in small numbers, fifty here, seventy there. I need not tell you, surprise, quiet, speed — this is the heart of the matter. None must give warning to other. None must escape to raise any general alarm. Above all, no hint of it must reach the castle, where trumpets could sound to rouse the whole country. So, no fires. Is it understood?"

A fierce elated murmur rose from the Islesmen's ranks.

"Our first is a mill, quite near, where fifty or so sleep. We will surround it, closely, that none may break out. Then the killers will move in."

"Prisoners, Sir King?" somebody asked.

"We can afford no men to guard prisoners," Bruce answered evenly.

There was a sort of rumble from deep throats.

"After that, we divide into three companies. Under myself, the Earl of Carrick, and the Earl of Lennox. One will watch the castle. The others will find the rest of the soldiers' lodgings, and deal with them. If we lack success, if the alarm is given, we all come together at the Kirkton. The church stands on a grass mound midway to the point and the castle, and is easy found. Is all understood? Good. Come, then — and quietly."

With one or two guards left on the boats, Bruce and his brother led the way inland. They followed the course of a stream in its ravine, the Maidens Burn, almost up a waterfall at first, and then, away from the shore, through a winding tree-grown dean, where they must go single file, frequently leaping or splashing through the water. At length, they came to a widening of the little dell. And here, beside a dark mill-pond and swirling lade, were grouped four buildings — Maidens Mill itself, a tall granary, the miller's house and a double cottage with range of stabling. Silently Bruce motioned his followers to encircle all this.

There was no light or sign of guard or sentry. A faint stirring of horseflesh came from granary and stabling.

The 300 started to close in. Bruce had feared barking dogs, but none such sounded. The miller undoubtedly would have kept dogs in such a lonely place; therefore, either the soldiers had got rid of them, or the miller was no longer here.

When the ring was sufficiently tight, Bruce passed the whispered word round to halt, and the assault parties to move in. And to remember that the miller and his people were to be spared, if at all possible. About one third of the force soundlessly detached itself, forming four groups, two larger parties for the mill and the granary, two smaller for the millhouse and the cottages. At a given signal, they all advanced on their objectives together.

Bruce and his companions waited outside with the main body. By common consent this was accepted as no work for kings or those of knightly quality — and admittedly they would be less efficient at it than the Highland caterans. Tensely they stood, and the King, for one, had to steel himself to an acceptance of what he had ordained.

In fact, as a horror, it was less harrowing than anticipated, for gently-born watchers. The Islesmen were indeed experts. There was remarkably little fuss and noise. Only one actual scream rang out, high-pitched — and it was swiftly choked off. There was a certain amount of groaning, gasping, bubbling, some thuds and scuffling, the clatter of steel on stone flags, and a succession of bumps which was almost certainly a body falling down the granary stairs. Otherwise, apart from the sidlings and whinnyings of frightened horses smelling blood, there was little or nothing to intimate massacre to uninitiated watchers. No single refugee burst out from any of the buildings. In a remarkably short space of time, the shadowy Highlanders began to emerge, wiping their dirks and murmuring chuckled pleasantries to one another.

They left a strange sort of muffled and jerky stirring behind them, nevertheless, more seemingly evident of life than heretofore. Dead men lie less quiet, for a while, than do mere sleepers.

The Islesmen's leaders reported all done thoroughly, decently and in order. There had been no sign of anybody that had looked like a miller or member of his household — certainly no women; all appeared to be just Southron soldiery. There would be considerable pickings?

Bruce said that they must wait for that until the night's work was done. He did not question whether all were dead within, nor did he venture inside to see.

Forming up, they moved on up the burnside, with a new and feral menace about the Hebrideans that somehow communicated itself to the others, a sort of lip-licking anticipation and relish. Even the King felt it, and tried to put it from him.

Upon the grassy rabbit-cropped links, amongst the shadowy

gorse-bushes, they came to their next objective, a small farmery. Considerably before they reached it they perceived that this would be a less simple proposition. For here lights burned, and as they drew stealthily closer, the sound of uncouth singing, and a thumping beating of time thereto, reached them. It was not yet midnight, of course.

Bruce called a halt, while he considered. Caution suggested that they should perhaps leave this lively billet until later, in the hope that the Englishmen would quieten down and retire to sleep shortly, as was suitable. On the other hand, it would delay the programme to come back here, and this farm of Auchenduin lay between the Kirkton and the sea, so that its people, if roused, would be in a position to interfere with any enforced retiral on the boats. Moreover, the singing sounded distinctly slurred, and punctuated with raucous shouts, which seemed to indicate a fair degree of intoxication. Bruce decided to risk an assault. After all, making all that noise anyway, a few more shouts and screams would not be apt to be noticeable.

There was some low-voiced bickering amongst the Highlanders. It seemed that the previous killing party were assuming that they would continue with the good work, whereas the others wanted to share in the proceedings. Almost they were coming to blows on the matter. The King had sternly to order peace, and commanded that a new selection of dirkmen be given their chance.

The farmhouse itself was small and mean, little better than a cabin; but the associated buildings were quite extensive, barns, stables and byres, for formerly much cattle had grazed on these grassy links — Bruce's cattle. It was from these outbuildings that the singing emanated, where the troops were presumably quartered. The King's own party drew their swords this time, and moved close in with the rest of the encirclers, in case this proved to be a less tidy exercise.

It did — although the knightly swords were not in fact required. None of the enemy ever actually emerged from the buildings, but the process of elimination was clearly a much lengthier and noisier one, with shouting and yelling, the clash of steel and the crash and tumble of fitments and bodies. This went on at some length, so that Bruce was constrained to detach another couple of score of eager participants from the surrounding cordon, to send them in to aid and speed the work. He kept glancing over his shoulder, southwards towards the Kirkton, less than half a mile away. Admittedly all was dark in that direction, and the blustery wind was from the south-west; but an unholy noise was undoubtedly arising from Auchenduin steading.

At last the racket began to abate, and the Islesmen to emerge from the buildings. Some few were wounded now, and presently one was carried out dead. But there was no depression, most evidently. It seemed to have been a thoroughly enjoyable affair for the Moidartach, really more satisfactory than at Maidens Mill; these were of course professional sea-raiders and killers, however addicted to poetry, the sagas, music and dancing. They claimed that there had been all of four-score Englishry in there. None would trouble Scotland again.

This experience convinced Bruce that he was wise to leave the Kirkton and the Castleton until later. These were villages, or at least hamlets, with a number of houses, and the danger of noise, disturbance and resistance would be the greater, especially with the local people there to complicate matters. Much better to pick off the outlying billets first — and according to the fishermen there were still four more of these to account for.

So again ordaining that there was to be no plundering meantime, and that the horses were to be left in their stables, the King divided the company there and then into three parties of approximately a hundred each. Edward, with his overbearing and impetuous nature, did not get on well with others — with men, that is; he did well enough with women usually — was given Gilbert Hay as lieutenant, Hay being a quiet, level-headed but effective man. They were to deal with another smaller farm-steading to the north, and a second mill on the Morriston Burn. Ninety minutes was all the time they could be spared for this, and they would have the longest distance to travel — so haste was essential. Lennox was sent to watch the castle exits, with Neil Campbell, a hardened fighter, to stiffen him. Their task meantime was to avoid conflict if possible, avoid detection, but to ensure that the English leadership was prevented, if roused, from issuing forth to take charge of the situation. Bruce himself, with James Douglas, would tackle the castle brewery and the main kennels and falcon-yard. These being both close to the castle walls would demand extra care and quiet. They would all meet again at the Kirkton in about ninety minutes, for a joint attack.

Douglas, who had remained very silent until now, voiced his views to his monarch and hero as they moved off, southwards, with their hundred men.

"This is ill employment for a King, as for noblemen, Your Grace," he declared. "I never thought to see the day when I would skulk and steal and slay sleeping men, like any thief in the night!"

"It is not pretty work," Bruce agreed. "But necessary. How would *you* order it, Jamie?"

"I do not know," the other admitted frankly. "I have had but little experience of war." Sir James was just twenty-one, and had spent six years as a refugee in France, with Norman relatives. Tournaments and jousting had been all his military education. "But surely other than this."

"Aye," the King said heavily. "But if you are going to serve me and my cause, lad, you will have to be prepared to soil those white hands of yours. Oh, yes — you have done well as a fugitive in the heather, Jamie. Taken your part and complained nothing. I have watched you. But when ill work fell to be done, anything that went less than well with your honour, it was not James Douglas who did it. That I noted also!"

The younger man bit his lip and said nothing.

"See you — once I thought as you do. But I have learned in a hard school. Eleven years I have been a-learning. I have learned that a nation that fights for its very existence cannot always afford the luxury of honour. I have had two stark teachers, Edward of England and William Wallace. For long, the lords of Scotland prevailed nothing against Edward, who cares no whit for honour or chivalry or anything such. Only Wallace knew how to fight Edward. Against the overwhelming might and utter ruthlessness of the Englishman, Wallace alone made headway. He fought no pitched battles, made no knightly sallies, accepted no challenges. He slew by night, surprised, ambushed, outwitted. He burned a small castle here, took a village there, harried the flanks of armies, cut their supplies, wasted the land before them. And only Wallace did Edward fear. This, Jamie, is Wallace's kind of warfare. And it is the only kind Bruce can afford to wage today."

"Since needs must, some must do it, yes," Douglas conceded. "But . . . must the King?"

"The King? What is the King, man, but the representative and leader of his people? I have thought much of kings and kingship since that coronation-day at Scone. Would you have your King to stand back, not to soil his hands with what he would have others do on his behalf? That is not as I see the King's part, Sir James. Nor yet Douglas's part. Remember who you fight. Remember that day when first we met. Ten years ago, at Douglas Castle. Remember how the English then were prepared to fight, to win your castle. By hanging children before your eyes, so that the Lady Douglas's tender woman's heart would be wrung into yielding her house rather than see it done. Mind you that!"

"And yet, Sire, it was because *you* were so otherwise, because you threw aside all your position and safety, your credit with King Edward, to save those same children, that I saw Robert the Bruce as worshipful. Then, and have continued so to do. All those years ago I swore that, one day, I would be the man of this noble knight."

It was Bruce's turn to be silent. He could by no means refute what his friend had said. And at the back of his mind he was well aware that what he had been enunciating was as much to convince himself as Douglas.

They were nearing the Kirkton now, and must by-pass it to reach the brewery. There was no opportunity for further debate. The King frowned as he strode forward.

The castle's former brewery was situated beside another small stream, and with its maltings, brewhouse and stores formed a sizeable establishment. No lights showed here, however, and it was unlikely that there would be dogs present. A couple of scouts, sent forward, came back to report that there were men in the maltings and storehouse, but not in the brewhouse. There appeared to be no horses — evidently these were footmen, archers perhaps, quartered closer to the castle than were the cavalry.

Bruce divided his party seventy–thirty this time. With only a third of the former manpower, he could not afford any close-knit outer cordon. Instead, the outside thirty were set to watch windows and doors for possible escapers. The seventy should be sufficient for what was required within.

"Your permission, Sire, to lead the killers," Douglas requested formally.

"Not so, Sir James. This is my part. You will command out here." The stiffness went out of Bruce's voice. "Though, God knows, I but go in with them — do not lead them. Since they know the task better than I do."

Accordingly the King did not announce his heading of the pursuit, but merely slipped in amongst the last of the party of thirty or so entering the maltings, drawing his dirk like the rest. He did not know whether or not to wish for some return of the former animal elation that had swept the company after the first bloodletting.

Inside the building it was very dark, making even the outside mirk seem light. At first Bruce could distinguish nothing. But the Moidartach appeared to have cats' eyes, and moved with entire confidence. Before he began to achieve any real vision, however, he became aware that the Highlandmen were all in fact hurrying past and up a stairway, unseen but sensed, ahead. Making after them, he blundered into a stand of tall yew bows, which he saved from falling with a clatter only by a desperate effort. Evidently this was indeed an archers' billet, and they used the basement only for their equipment.

A choking, gurgling noise from above indicated that the slaughter had begun. It was followed by a scream quickly muffled. Thereafter the sounds were more like those of many dogs worrying rats. The Islesmen used their plaids to smother their victims at the same time as they stabbed and slashed. Reluctantly the King forced himself to climb those stairs.

He was only part way up when the sort of general scuffling above was punctuated by a sudden scrambling and slipping, involved with bitten-off Gaelic cursing. Swift movement, the padding of bare feet, heralded a running man at the stairhead. The merest hint of light came from a window up there, and against it Bruce was able to make out a figure, evidently dressed only in a shirt. This came hurtling down upon him in panting panic.

The King acted without hesitation, almost without thought. Throwing himself in the path of the escaper, he grabbed the man with an encircling left arm — the formerly damaged arm, now healed — and in the same movement raised the drawn dirk and plunged it deep into the other's breast. As the shocked gasp began to rise to a shriek, he released his grip on the dagger and raised the hand to clamp it over the open mouth. He was vaguely aware of teeth sinking into his flesh as the man slid down within his grasp and thereafter to the steps. He wrenched his hand free, and his victim rolled away bumping down the stairs.

A little unsteadily Bruce went after him. It was only the second time in his life that he had used a dirk on a man, many as had been his sword-thrusts — and that other had been John Comyn at the Dumfries altar, the deed that came between him and his sleep. The Englishman was twitching and making strange snoring noises, and the King knew that he ought to cut the throat, as his minions above were doing, but jibbed at it. He waited there, instead, retrieving his dirk, for other possible attempts at escape.

None developed. The first Highlandman down the stairs made short work of the King's victim, without any request. The brewery was won, without casualty to the attackers.

Bruce remained lacking in elation, as they pressed on towards the kennels and falcon-yard, a little way south of the castle walls and ditches.

He had been concerned about this last assault, leaving it late, for here had been kept his pack of hunting-hounds, and a great hullabaloo and outcry was possible. But not so much as a single sounded as they approached, and it looked as though Percy had dispensed with the brutes, or at least kept them elsewhere. This time, the King allowed Douglas to go in with the attackers to the silent, unlighted square of low buildings, without demur.

It was soon over, here, with the smallest number of sleepers so far, mainly cooks, grooms and servants apparently. James Douglas looked stiff and, somehow, even in the darkness, gave the impression of being very pale, as he came out. He made no comment to Bruce — who indeed sought none.

The programme now called for a return to the Kirkton, and a united assault upon it, with time in hand. But well before the King's party reached the hamlet they heard noise therefrom, which grew to uproar.

"A plague on it — they are roused! That is an attack," Bruce exclaimed. "Whose folly is this . . .?"

He had no need to ask that, of course. Lennox was not the sort to initiate assaults, out of turn or otherwise. This would be Edward Bruce demonstrating his independence.

At the run now, the King led his men on, with the din ahead continuing. One of the Islesmen's leaders presently tugged at the royal sleeve, to point away to the left, where he declared two figures had shown briefly, fleeing in the other direction. Even as he spoke, someone else called out that he had seen a man running off on their right.

"Damnation!" Bruce cried. "Escapers. These will warn the Castleton. The castle itself. Edward is a headstrong fool!" He ordered some of the Moidartach to race after the fleeing men from the Kirkton, to try to prevent them giving the alarm elsewhere.

At least, it meant presumably that Edward's people were winning in their premature attack. The noise was gradually lessening.

This reading of the situation was confirmed as they came to the Kirkton. There was a certain amount of moaning, and screaming of women, with many dark shapes lying around, but the fighting appeared to be over. The houses clustered round a grassy mound, on the summit of which the church stood, a notable landmark. It was up there that any remaining activity seemed to be concentrated.

Hurrying up the hill, Bruce found his brother inside the church itself — which apparently had been used as one more barracks. All seemed to be over here too, though the number of bodies lying scattered amongst the gravestones indicated that it had been a fight, not a massacre of slumberers.

"My lord of Carrick — a word with you," the King called sternly. "Over here."

"Ha — is that you, Rob? You came too late. It is all by with. Hot while it lasted. But more sport than knifing sleepers!"

"We are not here for sport," the other snapped. He jerked his head. "Those women skirling? More sport?"

"You would not grudge our caterans a little play, man . . .?"

"By the Rude, I would! Any women here are villagers. Our own people. Moreover, they are my subjects. Mine. I have come to free them, not to savage them. Jamie — see you to it. With your sword, if need be. Quickly." He turned back to his brother. "As for you, Edward, you are a fool. Witless! And worse. You have disobeyed my commands. I told you to await me here. For a joint attack. I told you plainly . . ."

"Save us, Rob — what's to do? We finished these other two billets quickly. They were no trouble. Arrived here early. Why wait, when I could take the place? Save time?"

"Because I *said* to wait."

"God in Heaven — I am not a child! Think you I need your guidance, Rob, for all I do . . .?"

"Enough, my lord! It is the King who speaks — not Rob Bruce! When I give my royal command you, as all others, will obey. Mind it, hereafter. You have like as not made ruin of this night's work. You had not sufficient men to surround all this village. You have taken it, yes. But some escaped. To warn others. We saw them. They will warn the Castleton. Percy himself, in the castle, it may be. Percy still has men enough to destroy us, probably. Armour Horsed knights. Men-at-arms. You may have won me this Kirkton, but you are like to have lost me the night!"

His brother said nothing.

"Enough, then. Get your men assembled. And quickly. We move at once. For the Castleton. With all speed."

The Castleton of Turnberry, the main village which had grown up to serve the principal seat of the Carrick earls, lay less close to the castle itself than was usual — this because of the cliff-top position of the fortalice, with no sheltered or convenient area near by. More than a quarter-mile south-east, and as far from the Kirkton, its village nestled amongst the trees of a shallow valley.

The Bruce brothers' united company of 200 was left in no doubts but that the Castleton had been warned. Lights were glowing and shouts sounding, as they approached; even a trumpet neighed shrilly on the night. That trumpet would be heard in the castle, without any doubt likewise.

Despite Bruce's lecture to James Douglas, what followed was a much more acceptable instalment of the night's work than what had gone before, though undeniably more expensive and less efficient. Men emerged from all the houses of the Castleton. Indubitably many were more intent on flight than fight, while not a few were still bemused by sleep or drink, but none had left their arms behind them. Two hundred attackers were insufficient to employ any surrounding tactics, and the resultant battle, without any real line or focus, was incoherent in the extreme, no more than a confusion of individual tussels and duels in the darkness, running fights with leadership and direction almost impossible on either side. What advantage there might be was with the attackers, with surprise and the night tending to fight for them; but on the other hand, the assailed were fighting for their lives, and moreover had the feeling of the great castle's support near by to sustain them. Neither side knew how many might be arrayed against them.

Bruce suddenly found himself alone, and engaging two men simultaneously, one armed with a halberd and the other with a short cavalry sword. His own longer blade dealt with the halberd effectively, shearing through the wood staff with a single great slash, and then cutting down the bereft wielder with a swift backhanded stroke. But this left him open to the other man's stabbing rush, and he had to jump backwards and sideways urgently, blindly, to avoid the vicious thrust. There was an unevenness in the ground, only a group of tussocks but enough to send him sprawling — and with the recoil from his own swinging blow, he overbalanced and fell his length.

Possibly that fall saved him, for a stabbing thrust can be quickly extended and realigned. He fell away just in time from that darting point — and his opponent thereupon tripped headlong over the same obstacle and crashed to the ground likewise. Bruce was able to rise first, and though his sword had been jerked from his hand, he was able to whip out his more useful dirk. Still only on his knees, before the other got that far, the King drove his dagger between the bent shoulders.

This was his only contribution to the engagement, though, retrieving his blade, he went in search of further involvement. The fight was so scattered and fluid that he could find nobody he could usefully engage. And he was distracted by coming upon James Douglas standing leaning on his sword, dizzy from a knock on the head received from some sort of club — whose late owner lay near by. By the time that Bruce had ascertained that his young friend was not grievously injured, the battle was, if not over, at least in its final stages, with Highlandmen everywhere pursuing their fleeing foes.

Concerned lest his force become so scattered as to be out of his control, the King sounded the recall, on the fine curling horn of a Moidart bull which Christina had presented to him — even though this must be heard in the castle. It was that castle's probable reactions that worried him now. Lights were showing from many of its slit windows, but no fighting or uproar was as yet apparent, from that direction.

When at least the majority of his force was re-assembled — though with quite a number missing, either casualties or still chasing the fugitives — the King hurried them on towards the cliff-top castle itself. Half-way there they were met by one of Lennox's men, sent to discover progress and to report that the castle was roused, but that so far its occupants had not attempted to sally forth.

Bruce pressed on, with the sea-wind, laced with sleet, in his face now. Presently he reached the narrows of a promontory crowned by the great soaring fortress which had been his birthplace. The cliffs here were not high, but the castle walls rose tall and sheer, occupying every inch of the mound's summit. The only landward access was by the narrow neck of the promontory, across which the usual deep and wide ditch had been cut. Massed across this neck of land, just out of arrow-shot from the gatehouse tower, Lennox and Campbell waited, shivering, with their hundred men.

"Here's a devilish cold vigil, Sire," Lennox complained. "They have made no move, no attempt to issue out, as yet. The draw-bridge is part-lowered, in readiness. We can hear their horses' hooves ringing in the courtyard. So they could ride out swiftly and are prepared. But all they have done is shoot a few arrows at us..."

"Percy will not know, in the dark, how many we are," Campbell put in. "He is a cautious man."

"Have you men down on the shore?" the King demanded. "There is a small jetty there. Boats. And a postern gate, with stair-way down." At the others' silence, he frowned. "You have not? Damnation — then they may have already sent out men. By boat. To gain information. To seek help."

"I am sorry, Sire. We did not know..."

"The fault is mine, friends. I should have told you. It may be too late now..."

He directed a picket to make its way down to the beach, never-theless. And presently a man came hurrying back, with the word that they had been just in time to glimpse a boat pulling away from the little landing-stage under the cliff. Too late to halt it.

"A curse! So we *are* too late! Percy may be cautious, but he is no fool. He has got his messengers away."

"What matters it?" Edward demanded. "They will but learn, for him, that he has lost his men. All of them furth of the castle. Little joy in that, I say."

"And *I* say that is the least of it. Think you that is all Percy will have ordered? He will have sent for aid. Ayr is but a dozen miles, with its garrison. Irvine and Cumnock have garrisons likewise. Even Maybole, five miles away. And there are a dozen castles, English-held, no farther. He could have a thousand men here soon after daylight — mounted, armoured men. What use our caterans and their dirks, then?"

None offered an answer to that.

"I fear our shaft is shot. For this night," Bruce decided. "We cannot take this strength. And if I know Percy, he will not come out. He will wait there, secure, for reinforcement. And for daylight. To see our strength. And that we can by no means afford."

"We go, then?"

"Yes, we go. It must serve. We have struck a blow that all Scotland will hear of. My folk will know that their King is back!"

"We retire on the galleys, Sire?" Lennox asked. "Back to Arran . . .?"

"Of a mercy — not that!" Edward protested. "Not after this. When we have made our landing, and struck the first blow."

"No, not back to Arran," his brother agreed. "Or, not myself, nor most of you. You, my lord of Lennox, will take the boats, and a small company, to Arran. There to assemble and send on to me the more men that Angus Og and the Lady Christina will provide. The rest of us will make for our Ayrshire hills, around Loch Doon. Base ourselves there, near to Galloway. Make contact with my brothers. Raid from there. And build up our strength."

"Thank God for that, at least!" Edward commented. "Let us be on our way, then."

"First, a word or two might not be wasted, here," Bruce said. He nodded towards the castle. He handed his horn to Hay. "Blow it loud and long, Gilbert," he directed, and strode forward, near to the ditch's edge.

When the curious moaning notes of the horn died away, the King raised his voice. "Ho — the castle!" he shouted. "Do all sleep sound in Turnberry this night?"

A voice answered him from the gatehouse parapet promptly enough. "Who is there? Who dares come knocking at my lord of Northumberland's door, at this hour?"

"One who has a better right to that door than Henry Percy! Get him, man. I would speak with him."

"Fool! Watch your words. Do you not know that this is the seat of His Majesty's Governor here? Sheriff of Ayr?"

"You have your Majesties awry, fellow! Tell your lord that Robert Bruce, King of Scots, whose territory he defiles, whose castle he usurps, demands his ear. And quickly."

There was silence from the gatehouse. But quite soon another and thinner voice spoke — proof that the Percy had been in fact standing by. "Henry Percy speaks, my lord of Carrick," it said. "What folly is this? Where have you come from?"

"Costly folly for you and your like, Percy. As you will find out. And the Earl of Carrick is now my brother, here. Mind it. Also, *he* is Sheriff of Ayr. I require your surrender of my castle of Turnberry forthwith. Yield it, and you shall go unharmed. Carrying my message to your master at Lanercost. That I require my kingdom at his bloodstained hands. And my wife also! Before every Englishman in Scotland dies the death of yours!"

They could almost hear Percy choking. "Are you out of your wits, Bruce?" he demanded, with difficulty. "Have your hurts, your defeats, turned your head? By morning, my men will have you cut to pieces . . ."

"Your men are all dead, Percy. Every one. They will not come to your aid. At the Castleton. The Kirkton. The stables. The brewery. Maidens Mill. And the rest. All dead. Cleansed. As all Scotland will be, one day. That message you will take to Edward Plantagenet."

There was no response from the castle now.

"Will you yield, then? And save your life?"

"No." Though that was hoarse, it was definite enough.

"Very well. You will regret it. I will find another messenger for Edward. Hide you there in my castle, Percy. I do not choose to destroy my own house, where I was born. But . . . your days are numbered. If I were you, my lord — which God forbid! — I would slip out of that postern, to the beach, while the dark is still kind to you. And take boat across Solway to your English shore. For they say you are a cautious man."

No word answered that.

Ordering Hay to sound a derisory blast on the horn to indicate that the King of Scots had spoken the last word, Bruce turned to Lennox.

"Keep your men here, in view from the castle, until I send for them. Then take forty, and back to the boats. Sail for Arran. Meantime, we go collect our booty. Horses. Food. Armour. Dead men's weapons. An hour should be sufficient. Then we head for the hills of Doon and Minnoch." He grasped the earl's hand. "Bring me more Islesmen and Irish, Malcolm, so soon as you may. I shall need every one. And God go with you."

"And with Your Grace . . ."

Chapter Seven

Robert Bruce surveyed this his handiwork, at least, with some satisfaction — however otherwise his general frame of mind. The stag was a noble one, of ten points, and for the end of a long winter, moderately plump — which was not unimportant, with a score of men waiting to feed on it. And they were unlikely to get another that day. His arrow had taken it through the throat — even though he had aimed for the heart; but then, he was unused to these English long-bows and their cloth-yard shafts, purloined from the brewery at Turnberry. The Scots used much shorter and handier bows, if with correspondingly shorter range and less hitting-power. Still, none need know that he had aimed at the heart and hit a good eight inches to the left, since the stag was as dead one way as the other. At least he had done better than Gibbie Hay, who had missed his mark altogether.

Kneeling, he drew his dirk to blood the beast by cutting the jugular vein. They would have to cut it all up, as well as gralloch it, for the brute would weigh fourteen or fifteen stone at least, he calculated, requiring three men to carry it the couple of miles back to their cave. He might as well play the butcher now, while he waited for the others to come up.

Bruce had killed, eventually, in the narrows of a small side glen at the foot of Loch Doon, in the wild mountain country where Ayrshire rose to the Galloway border, under mighty Merrick, where they had spent the two weeks since Turnberry. Using his remaining score of Islesmen almost as hounds, he and Gilbert Hay had managed to have the three deer they had spied manoeuvred through the close country of steep hillsides, waterfalls, bogs and hanging woods, towards this trap of a narrow glen, the caterans spread out in a great semi-circle to windward, closing in to give the beasts just enough of their scent to make them uneasy and moving in the other direction, without alarming them so that they bolted off at speed. This was a tactic which Bruce had learned in Christina's Moidart, and very different from the traditional southern method of hunting deer on horseback. The two marksmen had waited in the throat of the glen for the stags to drift within bowshot. The two younger beasts had in fact bolted off at a tangent, uphill, long before they were in range; but this heavier animal had come on, by fits and starts, into the trap, disdaining to be flushed and flurried. Bruce had seen Hay, from a somewhat higher position than his own, across the glen, shoot and obviously miss. His own shaft, of a minute later, at fully ninety paces, was, all things considered, commendable enough.

He was bending over to make the first belly cut of the gralloch when, out of the corner of his eye, he glimpsed movement. Across the glen, and up. It was Hay, standing and waving. And not the congratulatory waving of one hunter to another; an urgent beckoning, rather.

The King straightened up. Hay was no excitable enthusiast, to gesture to his monarch like that, without due cause. As the other continued to beckon, Bruce wiped his red blade on the stag's shaggy mane, sheathed it, and rose.

"Company, Sire," Hay called softly, at his approach, and pointed.

From this position it was possible to see down the main valley of the Doon below the loch-foot. And coming up the riverside track, less than a mile away, was a mounted party of about forty, arms and armour gleaming in the last rays of the sinking wintry sun.

Bruce rubbed his bearded chin. "Men-at-arms," he said. "I cannot think that they come to this remote wilderness looking for other than ourselves. Yet too small a company to be English sent to take us, surely. I believe they must be our first supporters, Gibbie!"

"And not before time, Sire!" Hay observed grimly.

That was hardly an unfair comment. Despite the stirring activities of the night at Turnberry two weeks before, no upsurge of support had materialised for the King of Scots, whatever might be the glee at Percy's discomfiture. No rallying to Bruce's standard had developed, even amongst his own feudal vassals of Carrick and Kyle. After waiting for ten days in these hills, he had been forced to the recognition that more positive recruiting was necessary, and had sent out his lieutenants, each with about four-score Islesmen, to try to raise fighting men. Edward had gone south, to the great Bruce lordship of Annandale; Campbell south-west into Galloway, to try to link up with the other two Bruce brothers; Douglas north-east to Douglasdale and the Moray lordship of Bothwell. This temporary dispersal of force was accepted only reluctantly; but apart from the urgent need for reinforcements, the food situation for even 300 men, in these empty fastnesses, had rapidly become a major problem, and the booty from Turnberry fast consumed. Hence the daily hunting on the part of the score who remained.

Bruce and Hay slipped discreetly down through the woodland thickets, making for a point where the newcomers must pass close and could be surveyed secretly. The Islesmen could be trusted to remain out of evidence until called for.

Unobserved they reached their vantage-point only a little while before the mounted party came jingling up. And quickly they perceived that there was in fact no need for secrecy. Riding at the head of the visitors' column was a youngish woman, and at her side Sir Robert Boyd.

The King stepped out into the track before them, holding up a hand. "Welcome, my friends," he cried. "Chris — you make a fair sight! Sir Robert — we feared you dead. Or at the least, captured."

There was a great to-do of exclamation, greeting, dismounting and hand-kissing. The woman was a cousin of Bruce's own, the Lady Christian of Carrick, of the old Celtic line; and the forty well-equipped men-at-arms her own contribution to his force. It seemed that it was on the women of Scotland that its monarch must rely.

Bruce embraced his kinswoman, with some emotion. "God bless you, Chris!" he said. "You are the first. The first of all the Lowlands to rally to my cause."

"Aye — we are become a race of mice, not men!" she declared vehemently, clasping him to her and bestowing great smacking kisses. "Fearful of every English shadow! Time indeed that you returned and shamed us into valiant deeds again. Would I could have brought you more than two-score, Robert my liege lord — but as you know, I have but small lands."

"You have brought me more than just two-score fine fellows, woman — you have brought me hope and faith again. When I needed them."

Boyd coughed. "Your Grace will need all the faith and hope you may muster, I fear," he said significantly.

"Aye. No doubt, Sir Robert. The more I have to thank the Lady Christian, then. But, man — where have you been? And how knew you that I was here? At Loch Doon?"

"I heard that you had landed, that night. At Turnberry. All the land has heard that! Despite that I had sent no signal. Deeming conditions to be unpropitious for a landing. In Carrick, at least. But I did not learn your whereabouts. Until I encountered Douglas, two days past, on his way to his own country. He gave me the news of Your Grace. And the error of the fire. Knowing that the Lady Christian had these men for you — she alone of all I approached — I went to her. So we have come here, secretly."

"Aye. That was right. There is little fervour for my cause, then?"

The other shook his head. "Men are leal enough. I think. And the common folk would rise for you. But the quality, the lords and lairds and knights, are sore afraid to move. They have suffered too much in ten long years of war, lost too much. Lost heart, most of all, I fear, Sire, that you have a sore hill to climb, ahead of you."

"Have I not always known it, man!" The King spoke shortly. "But, come—here is no way to treat a lady, who has journeyed long miles to see me. We are camped at a cave behind those crags. Up that small side glen. A mile. But you will have to walk your horses, to reach it..."

As they picked their way by deer-paths and difficult climbing tracks, leading the horses, Boyd contrived to draw a little way ahead, alone with the King. Picking his words, he spoke slowly.

"Back there, I said that Your Grace would have need of all the faith and hope you might muster. To my sorrow I did not say that lightly."

Bruce looked at him quickly. "You have more news for me than you have told?"

"I have, Sire—God forgive me! Grievous news. Once before, I brought you the like. The Galloway venture has failed. It is disaster. All there is lost."

"Christ's mercy—no! Not ... not ...?"

"Aye, Sire—the worst. Sir Dugald MacDouall and the MacCanns, Comyn vassals, fell on them the day after the landing at Loch Ryan. Unawares, it seems. How it was done I have not heard. Whose the blame. But it was a rout. And thereafter, massacre."

Fiercely Bruce gripped the other's arm. "My brothers?" he demanded.

Boyd moistened his lips. "MacDouall took them, alive. With Sir Reginald Crawford. And Malcolm MacQuillan, of Antrim, who led the Irish gallowglasses. Him he slew. But your brothers, and Crawford, he sent to King Edward, at Lanercost. Edward ... Edward hanged and then beheaded them all."

For long moments there were no words, no sounds other than their passage through the dead brackens. Then a moan of sheerest desolation broke from the King's tight lips.

"Alex!" he whispered. "Tom! Oh, God—it is more than I can bear! First Nigel. Now Alex, Tom! Paying the price, all paying the price of *my* sin. The price of John Comyn's blood!"

"The price of Edward Plantagenet's savage hate, *I* say! The man is no better than a ravening brute-beast."

"Edward is ... Edward. But I—I am accursed! Lost. Excommunicate, indeed! Forsaken of God and man..."

"Scarce that, Sire. You still have leal friends. Leal to their last breaths . . ."

"Aye — to die for me also! And so to add to my guilt."

The other was silent. He looked sidelong at his stricken liege lord as they went. "Sire," he said at length, his normally strong voice uncertain. "I have still more news."

Bruce strode on, set-faced. He might not have heard.

"It concerns your ladies. The Queen. The Princess. Your sisters . . ."

The suddenly indrawn quivering breath was more eloquent than any words. The King stopped in his tracks.

"They are not . . . not slain," Boyd went on hurriedly, almost gabbling for so slow and deliberate a speaker. "The Queen is sent, a prisoner, to a house in Holderness on the Humber. To be held close. Alone. The child taken from her . . ."

"Edward does that! To Elizabeth. His own god-daughter, whom he claims to love?"

"Yet that is the best of it, Sire. Hear me. Marjory, the child — she is sent to London. Alone. To the Tower. Not to be spoken to by anyone. There to be hung in a cage. On the outer walls of the Tower. For all to gaze at. Like an animal. In the open. A cage, of timber and iron."

"What . . .!" That was a strangled cry.

"The Lady Mary, your sister, also. She to be hung in a similar cage. On the walls of Roxburgh Castle. Day and night. In cold and heat. The Countess of Buchan likewise, who crowned you — she on the walls of Berwick . . ." The knight's voice tailed away.

Bruce was staring at the other unseeing, his features working strangely. Then he turned to stride on, at something near a run; and when Boyd would have hurried with him, flung round and pushed him away, violently. He stalked on alone up that twisting climbing path, not a word spoken.

"The Lady Christian, Countess of Mar," Sir Robert called after him desperately, as though he must at all costs be quit of the last of his terrible news. "Your other sister. To be confined to a nunnery, for ever . . ."

There was no sign from the King. Boyd turned and held the others back, duty done. At least he could gain him solitude for his agony.

But presently they caught up with Bruce, at the edge of the boisterous burn whose glen this was. It was near the foot of the tall crags of naked rock which had been pointed out from a mile away, with the valley now very narrow and steep, almost a ravine. Oddly enough the burn was actually wider here than it had been throughout; but here was the only place where it might be crossed, at a brief stretch of comparative shallows, perhaps thirty feet across, with a spray-spouting waterfall just above and foaming cataracts below.

Expressionless the King turned to Boyd, Hay and the lady, as they came up. "Cousin — let me carry you across," he said levelly. "The rest, follow exactly where I tread. A foot wrong, and you will be swept away. Lead each horse with great care. It is like a causeway, smooth rock, and slippery. And it is not straight." That sounded almost like a child's learned lesson repeated.

He picked up the woman in his arms, and now she found nothing to say to him, in the face of that granite-like sternness of expression. He stepped into the swirling water with her, and waded across with steady deliberate pacing, counting the steps until making a dog's-leg bend two-thirds of the way over. Setting his burden down, wordless, at the far bank, he paused, to watch the progress of the others. Gilbert Hay, eyeing him, thought that he had never seen a face so abruptly and direly changed. It was as though the living flesh had been overlaid and cast in hard, unyielding bronze, the lively eyes hooded and dull-glazed. No man sought to catch those eyes.

When all were across the hazard of the torrent, Bruce led on slantwise uphill, away from the water, to skirt the foot of the crags, amongst the rock-falls and screes. For perhaps a quarter-mile more they climbed, until they came to a single Highland sentinel beside a great boulder. Beyond was a sort of re-entrant in the cliffs, with a scooped dip before it and at the foot, the yawning mouth of a cave.

There was no room here for the horses, and Hay took them, and the men-at-arms, down to a hidden green hollow near by, amongst gorse-bushes and scattered hawthorns, where the few beasts left from Turnberry were hobbled. Bruce ushered his principal guests into the cave. Behind the lady, he paused, turning to Boyd.

"Cages, you said? In the open air? On walls? In winter? For a child! And women!" He spoke as though he used a foreign language, carefully, without intonation. "I did not mis-hear?"

"Cages, Sire. High on the outer walls of London Tower, Roxburgh and Berwick Castles." Boyd raised his eyes to his monarch's face, and quickly dropped them again.

They went inside.

* * *

Later, with Boyd and two men sent to escort his cousin through the night-bound hills back to her small property of Newton, south of Maybole, Bruce crouched at the back of the cave, where it bent and lowered to form almost a separate little chamber, hidden from the rest. A log as seat, he sat hunched, staring with unseeing eyes at the spluttering, smoking makeshift lamp, contrived from melted fat and a wick of cord in, strangely, a handsome silver quaich or drinking-vessel, one of the spoils of Turnberry though with the Bruce arms engraved thereon.

Alone he had sat there, for how long he knew not, facing the beetling dark walls and the hell of his own lot. He had been low before, all but crushed by the hammer-blows of fate, of treachery, of Edward Plantagenet. But he had never been so low as this. Before his tortured mind's eye had passed the long appalling procession of his friends and kin and supporters, those whom he or his cause had brought to ruin, shame, agony and death. Wallace, barbarously butchered. Andrew Moray, slain. The Graham, slain. Gartnait of Mar, his brother-in-law, assassinated. Simon Fraser, tortured and hanged—like his brother Alexander, like Hay's brother Hugh. Somerville of Carnwath, Barclay of Cairns, David de Inchmartin, Scrymgeour the Standard-Bearer dying the death of Wallace. William Lamberton, his closest friend and ally, chained a prisoner. As was old Bishop Wishart of Glasgow. Nigel, laughing, lively Nigel, hanged, drawn and quartered. And now Alex and Tom hideously executed also. Christopher Seton the same. His Elizabeth in solitary confinement. His little daughter like a caged beast for all to mock at. One sister and Isabel of Buchan likewise. Another, gay, lightsome Christian, walled in a convent. Randolph, his nephew, in prison. Others, countless others, suffering or past suffering. Because he had presumed to defy the usurper and put on the fatal crown. Or because he had stabbed John Comyn at God's own altar . . .

He had been King a year. And what of his kingdom did he hold? This cave, in his own lost earldom of Carrick. His strength? One remaining brother, the least loved, and a small handful of knightly friends. Less than 400 men. Nearly all wild Highlandmen, with him not for him or his cause but for love of their chieftainess. His lieges, the folk of his realm? They turned from him, stayed at home—as who would blame them! The invader was everywhere supreme, buttressed by unlimited power and numbers, sustained by traitors, egged on to consistent atrocity by the burning hatred of their lord, Edward. Edward, who would never relent, never for a moment relax the pressure. Edward the scourge of God on Scotland and on Robert Bruce.

There it was, the scourge of God! God had raised His hand against the presumptuous man who, a murderer, had dared to claim the holy anointing. Robert Bruce, the Lord's Anointed! Heaven help Scotland, with such for monarch! A King whom Holy Church had put forth, as anathema. To whom no priest dare offer the sacraments. The Bruce, outcast of God and man. Today a hunted, haunted fugitive. Tomorrow . . .?

Tomorrow — what betterment could be looked for tomorrow, in the name of truth? None. No least likelihood of improvement. The reverse, indeed. For after Turnberry, every English nerve and sinew would strain to punish and revenge, Edward's fury beyond all bounds. If forty men was all the response of Scotland to the night of Turnberry and her King's return — and these the gift of a kinswoman who had ever foolishly doted upon him — what hope of the future? A fool, he had said that she gave him hope and faith. Boyd and she, then, had taken such back with them again. For there was no hope, no faintest gleam of hope, in all the grim scene, in fact. And faith was not for such as Robert Bruce.

What, then? What remained for him? He was not yet old — though he felt ages old. He was but thirty-three. He was unlikely to die yet awhile, save by violence. He could seek that violent end, and find it no doubt, with little difficulty, many aiding. But would that not almost certainly involve the end of these last few who still trusted in him, his handful of leal friends? Douglas, Hay, Campbell, Boyd. And Edward, his headstrong brother? Would he have *their* blood also on his soul? Not that. Lead them back to Arran, then? Secretly. Thence to the Isles, where they could sell their swords to Angus Og for his Irish wars. A sad descent for such as these — but it would save them from the Plantagenet. He himself go on, alone, and lose himself in the greater world, beyond. Put all behind him, and go. Go where? Was there anywhere for him in all that world? Would he not be better to end it all, quietly, in the empty sea? The king without a kingdom, the earl without an earldom, the knight without honour, the friend whose friendship spelt death.

The knight without honour? He had vowed those vows of knighthood once — madness that it was Edward Plantagenet himself who had conferred that knighthood, heard those vows! Edward! Those vows he had taken before another altar. Amongst them, to take up his sword in the cause of the true faith, against the Infidel. Not to rest while the savage Unbeliever occupied Christ's holy places. His father and grandfather before him had both fulfilled that knightly vow — Edward, even — and gone on a Crusade. Was that at least not left to him? Was that not a better way to die? A single, simple knight again, to throw himself against the Saracen, and so make an end. Might there not just possibly, conceivably, be some small, faint glimmer of credit for him there? One drop of remission in the ocean of his guilt?

Thus far the man had got, in that dark hole beneath the crags of Doon, and thereafter lapsed into a state of almost mindless depression and stupor, when, out of it, he perceived that though his wits had sunk into dull vacancy, his eyes had not. He had, in fact, been heavily watching a spider which was striving assiduously to attach its slender thread to a point on the sheer rock wall of the cave. He realised that he had watched as four times it went through the difficult and involved process, without success. Its thread hung from the cave roof some three feet above Bruce's head, and the point on the vertical wall to which the creature wished to link its web was roughly the same distance lower and two feet to the left. The spider's method was to race down its line, from the ceiling, at such speed as to generate a strong pendulum swing, in the hope that this would carry it sufficiently far to the left to reach the lateral wall. In this it was successful twice out of the four attempts; but each time the contact with the comparatively smooth surface was too brief to gain a footing. Thereafter the spider had to swing back to the perpendicular again and then scramble up its long thread once more all the way to the roof, to repeat the process.

The man's lethargic watching grew to interest and a sort of actual concern, as the fifth attempt again ended in failure, and after a momentary hold on the wall the creature was dragged back once more, again to recommence its laborious upward climbing.

The sixth effort showed intelligence as well as determination. This time the spider swung itself at a slightly different angle, to reach a spot a couple of inches to one side and fractionally higher. It looked as though this might work, possibly giving a slightly better foothold—but no, gravity was again too great, and once more thread and spider fell backwards, frustrated.

"It is of no avail," the King muttered, shaking his head. "Can you not see it? Too stark..."

But the animalcule would not admit defeat. Undeterred, before even its line stopped swinging it was clawing up again to the roof, to launch itself downwards with unabated resolve. And this time, when its pendulum swing brought it to the wall, it managed to hang on. Almost breathlessly the man watched it, willing the creature success.

It remained on the vertical rock, its thread pulsing gently in the smoky, flickering lamplight.

"Now, by the saints—here is a wonder!" Bruce exclaimed aloud. "A sign, if ever there was one! If this creeping mite in a hole in the earth can so set its will to conquer, can Robert Bruce, crowned King of this realm, do less? Six defeats did not deter it. Shall I despair more easily?" He stood up, stooping since he must in that place. "Here is my lesson — from heaven or from hell! I shall not give in yet awhile. Nor yet awhile to seek my death amongst the Saracens! That can wait. Yet, I do swear to God, if He will hear me this once, out of this pit, that, my battle here in Scotland won, I *will* go to His holy places, and draw sword for His name. By all that is holy! But . . . first, this my realm's freedom!"

Filled now with a sudden access of restless strength and the need for action, or at least movement, Bruce strode out past the sleeping ranks of his men in the outer cave, out into the starlit night. A half-moon was rising to the south-east, washing the crowding hillsides in wan pewter and inky shadow. With a brief word to the two watchful sentinels, the King paced away along the track they had made at the foot of the crags.

It was not long before he realised that he was being followed, at a distance. He turned.

"Who is that? I would be alone," he jerked.

"It is but Hay, Sire," the Lord of Erroll called. "In case you need aught."

"Aye, Gibbie. Do not heed me. Go back and sleep."

He moved on until he came to the burnside, where earlier he had brought the others across. And there, with the moonlight glittering quicksilver on the dancing waters, he sat himself on a boulder, to stare out into the night, unseeing. But now his mind dwelt no longer on the past, on his sorrows, even on his wife and daughter in their extremity. He counted and assessed and planned.

Galloway, partly his own Bruce sphere of influence, had stabbed him in the back, yes. Because the MacDoualls, who claimed anciently to have been princes thereof, had seen opportunity to strike a savage, grudging blow for their long lost hegemony. That might be forgiven — but not the sending of Tom and Alex, wounded and bound, to Edward of England. That must be avenged. But, more important than any vengeance, a gesture must be made to show all Galloway, all Scotland indeed, that the royal cause was still potent, not to be flouted. That the King *would* avenge his own and strike down traitors. The English could wait awhile — if they would! This was between him and his own subjects.

Galloway was a great and wide province, and ill to conquer — as even Edward Plantagenet had found to his cost. No country for a handful of men to assail. But its mountainous north was different, fierce, empty, cut off by high passes, where a few, knowledgeable and desperate, could make the land fight for them. Not far from these Carrick hills — indeed, the one ran into the other. And he knew them well.

A limited campaign in North Galloway, then. Entice his enemies therein, to ambuscade, skirmish, attrition, raiding. Wallace's warfare again. Even these sixty men in such territory could, skilfully deployed and led, engage hundreds. Where, then? The Glenkens? The Rhinns of Kells? Merrick? Glen Trool?

Bruce was going over in his mind the North Galloway geography, visualising each stretch of that far-flung, lofty terrain, and the low-lying areas which might be successfully raided from each, when he started up, suddenly alert. Above the steady noise of the water, he had heard a different sound. It had seemed like the baying of a hound.

Tense, he listened. But the sound was not repeated. Could it have been only the call of some night-bird? Or a wolf? There were still wolves in these hills, though seldom seen now. Yet it was hound that his innermost mind had said, immediately — a hound baying in the night. And so far as he knew, there would be no hound within a dozen miles, with Loch Doon Castle in ruins.

After a while Bruce sat again, and sought to return to his possible strategies and tactics. But now he was listening all the time, his mind less wholly concentrated.

It was not a hound that he heard, presently, but the bounding clatter of a stone rolling down a steep hillside. From across the burn, some way to the left he thought, nearer to the main valley.

He cursed the noise of the waterfall above and the rapids below, which drowned all but higher and intrusive sounds. Rising, he climbed higher up the bank, in an attempt to rise above the rushing, splashing interference.

Suddenly movement close at hand made him jump like a nervous horse. But it was only Gilbert Hay again, coming down the track.

"Somebody comes, Sire," the other whispered. "I heard a hound, back there, I swear. As I sat."

This was no occasion for berating Gibbie for disobeying a royal command. "I heard," Bruce nodded.

"Could it be Boyd, back already?"

"Too soon, by far. But it might be some of our friends. Returning with aid."

They waited, staring towards the shadowy wooded hillside. Presently they thought that they caught the chink of metal against stone.

"If we can hear that, they are very near . . ."

"And come mighty quietly. Secretly! Would any of ours come so? I think not . . ."

"There, Sire! Movement." Hay pointed.

The hawthorns and scrub ended perhaps thirty yards from the water's edge, across there. Now there were darker shapes, and stirring, amongst the shadows of the trees. Peer as they would, the watchers could distinguish no details.

Then something about one of the foremost figures became plain. It was the strained backward-leaning gait of a man who restrained a dog from too hurried a pace. This, and two other figures, moved out from the denser shadows into the moonlight, cautiously. Obviously many more remained behind, hidden.

"So-o-o!" Bruce breathed out. "No friends would so come. Led by a bloodhound! They must have followed Boyd's and my cousin's tracks, back here."

"Quickly, Sire — back to the cave. While we are still unseen."

"No. They have to cross this burn. And it is not easy. Here is the place to hold them. Go you back for our people, Gibbie."

"You go, Sire. Allow that I wait here . . ."

"Do as I say, man. But, Gibbie — give me your sword." Bruce, for his preoccupied moonlight walk, had come away unarmed save for the dagger which never left his hip. Hay had been more circumspect.

Reluctantly the other yielded up his blade. He slipped away.

Sword in hand the King watched. The three men and the bloodhound were crossing the open belt of dead bracken to the waterside. One of the trio was very tall and massive, armour glinting. He clearly held the third man by the shoulder — and that man kept his hands behind his back in unnatural fashion, probably tied there. He could be seen to be wearing the short philabeg of the Highlands. Some others of the newcomers have moved a little way out from the trees. Bruce could distinguish only one horse. And no helmets gleamed in the moonlight.

The watcher deduced much from what he saw — and recognised more immediate danger than he had anticipated. These were no English soldiers. Probably Galloway men, under a tall chief. And they had a captive Highlander, which meant probably that they had ambushed Boyd's little party and taken at least this one prisoner. And here was the menace of it — this man would know the secret of this ford.

At the waterside it was obvious that the captive was indeed demonstrating the route across — no doubt it was the price of the poor devil's life. The newcomers would be all across the ford long before Bruce's people could arrive. How many they might be he could not tell. But they must be delayed, if at all possible. Nowhere else was there such an advantageous place to hold up an enemy.

The King raised hand to mouth. "Ho, there!" he shouted. "Stand you! Who comes? Like robbers in the night?"

There was a startled pause. Then a voice answered. "I am Roland MacDouall of Logan. Brother to Sir Dugald MacDouall. Who challenges MacDouall in these hills?"

A wave of cold fury came over Robert Bruce at the mention of that hated name. Here was the brother of the man who had delivered up Tom and Alex to shameful death. Come seeking *him*, now!

"Robert Bruce challenges you, traitor!" he called back, voice quivering. "The King of Scots. You have come to judgement!"

Again there was a pause, no doubt of surprise — as well there might be, at that answer. The Gallovidians would not, could not, know that he was alone, of course; but they could probably see that no large party awaited them.

No words replied, at any rate. For answer the big man turned with his prisoner and hurried back to the others. There, after a few words to his followers. he mounted the horse, and with two others now gripping the Islesman prisoner, led the way down to the ford, sword drawn. A great surge of men streamed after them, on foot — more than the watcher had anticipated.

The most elementary discretion decreed that Bruce retire hastily after Hay. But he was in no mood for discretion. Long-strided, he went down the bank to the burn again.

"Come, MacDouall!" he cried. "Come pay for my brothers' blood!"

King and horseman reached the water's edge at the same moment, ten yards apart. Bruce had tossed away his plaid, to free his arms. Even in that twilight he could have looked little the monarch.

MacDouall, with the hound-leader to guide him to the exact crossing-place, rode straight in. Bruce, a little downstream because of the dog's-leg bend in the underwater rock formation, went to meet him. A yard or so short of the actual bend, he halted, the cold water swirling about his knees.

The other was no fool, and the seeming confidence of the single royal defender would give him pause. He had undoubtedly been told of the narrowness of the causeway, and the fierceness of the torrent was obvious. In swordery the mounted man should have the advantage; but if he had no room to manoeuvre and so must make a direct frontal attack, his advantage was much reduced. And no horse is at its best in rushing water.

The chieftain made a hasty reappraisal. He pulled up, switched the sword to his left hand, whipped the short lance that flew his pennon from its socket at the back of his saddle, and almost in the same swift movement hurled it at his opponent.

Bruce, the moment he saw that transfer of the sword, guessed what was coming. He both dodged and ducked, but he had little more room for any change of stance than had the horseman. He all but overbalanced, his left foot actually slipping off the rocky platform. Staggering, he remained approximately upright only by a fierce effort and the use of his sword dug down as support. The spear-like lance-tip ripped along his right arm, tearing open his doublet sleeve, its pennon actually flicking across his face. With a yell, MacDouall spurred forward.

Bruce had only moments. Though still teetering unsteadily, he twisted round and, following the other's example, grasped his sword-hilt with his left hand. The lance had plunged into the water, and the current had swung its shaft round against his right leg. Quick as thought he stooped to grab it up and, raising it high, hurled it back—although the effort nearly overturned him again.

He would have had less excuse, even so, for missing his mark than had MacDouall; for it was at the horse that he aimed, and the beast was no more than eight or ten feet from him. The lance-point took the creature in the neck, full in the soft of the gullet, and drove in deep.

With a gasping, bubbling whinny, the brute rose high on its hind legs, spouting blood, forefeet beating the air. Side-stepping away to its left, it toppled over the edge of the causeway into deep water, in thrashing ruin.

MacDouall just managed to throw himself out of the saddle in time. But because of the way his mount collapsed, his leap to clear himself from those lashing hooves brought him down just beyond the causeway, at the other, downstream, side. Desperately he clutched down at the slippery rock for a grip, in the rushing torrent, weapon relinquished.

Bruce did not hesitate in any chivalric gesture. Sword back in his right hand, he brought it down with all his force on his attacker, where neck joined trunk. MacDouall's scream choked away to swift silence as his head went under, and the dark current swept him away.

The mass of the enemy had held back at the burnside, while their mounted leader opened the attack. Now, with yells of rage, they came on, struggling with each other as to who should be first, unaware of the full hazards of the crossing, its slippery narrowness.

Quickly they became better informed, as, right and left, men fell or toppled or were pushed into deep water. There was an interval of complete chaos before the situation became clear, with Bruce, in mocking shouted invitation, urging them on.

Somebody did take charge, ordering all back, and to advance again only two at a time, shoulder to shoulder. So they came on in a long line, not a broad front, feeling their way with their brogans' toes, out towards the defiant lonely figure in midstream.

There a situation had developed calculated both to aid and to hinder them. The horse in its death throes had got itself held across the causeway, its heavy saddle presumably having caught against the upstream edge of the rock. So that there it lay stranded, mostly under water, flailing and churning the stream in foam and spray. It made it fairly obvious just where the bend in the passage lay; but on the other hand it constituted a distinct barrier for men to advance past.

Bruce did not fail to perceive this last, and moved up as close as he dared to the obstacle.

The first pair reached the other side of the animal, yelling their hate. It is possible that they might have preferred a more wary approach, but they were pressed on by those behind. The leader sought to engage the King with his sword, over the horse's body, while his colleague scrambled past. Bruce acquiesced in this long-arm sword-play — but when the climber was almost over, drew swiftly back, and turning, ran the man through with the greatest of ease, heaving his sprawling person off downstream, before returning to the sparring.

Another man quickly took the casualty's place; and now, with the horse's struggles dying away, the first swordsman and self-appointed leader pressed closer, to give the climber better support. But not good enough yet, for no man could effectively get himself over a largely submerged horse in a swift-running torrent and engage someone standing behind it with his sword at the same time. The moment when he must ease himself down, to find a foothold again on the slippery stone beneath, was vital — or fatal. Bruce let this individual get exactly so far, them stepped back, and with a back-hand slash sent him sprawling after his predecessor.

The leader could not but perceive the insufficiency of this tactic, and tried an improvement. He himself, and another, plunged forward to clamber over the carcase at the same time, whilst a third moved up close behind and above them, sword swinging. Bruce crouched low, to be under the sweep of the blade, which could not be depressed for fear of flaying the others, and from this position jabbed a vicious thrust that took the first man over in the groin. The other got further, but while still floundering for a foothold and raising his blade, the King's swiftly disengaged steel swung sideways and upwards and knocked him staggering, a buffet rather than a sword-stroke, but one which, on that precarious stance, drove its victim over the edge into deep water. As despairingly he sought to gain a grip on stone, to save himself, Bruce had ample time to aim down a shrewd lunge that finished the matter off, and then to turn and put out of his misery the screaming agonised companion.

Two more were already struggling to take the places of this pair, and getting in each other's way in the process. These were the easiest victims yet. Panting, the King jabbed and hacked down on them. They fell away without contributing the least advantage to their cause other than the tiring of the defender's arm.

That was six disposed of — seven counting MacDouall himself. Bruce began to laugh aloud, although something gaspingly.

Now, the second leader gone, the attackers suffered a period of major confusion. They could be no means flee in the face of this one swordsman, even though he might be the King of Scots; but nor could they see a way to overcome him. Moreover more and more of their people were pressing on along the narrow causeway behind, unable to see what went on, in danger of pushing the foremost off into the river. Bruce's laughter, jeers and challenges scarcely helped.

As so often is the case in such a situation, all this frustration and lack of direction boiled up in a sudden, furious and disorganised rush forward — which, in other circumstances, by sheer anger and weight of numbers, might well have succeeded in its object; but on that cramped and unsure stance only precipitated further disaster. Yelling men crowded, jostled and impeded each other, were pushed this way and that, especially from behind and still were unable to get at their quarry, whose flickering, darting steel kept them at the far side of the horseflesh barrier — save for three who fell, pierced, across the horse, two remaining caught there and actually heightening the said barrier. The third was swept away in the current.

Somebody threw a sword, javelin-like. Bruce saw it coming and eluded it with ease, for such weapons make but unwieldy missiles. But others saw this as a preferable alternative to close-range death, and projectiles began to fly, clubs and daggers as well as swords. Few were effectively aimed, for of course on such a narrow front the men ahead got in the way. But Bruce was much preoccupied in dodging the hurled objects, and more than once all but lost his footing in the process. Once indeed he was struck, but only a glancing blow that did no damage.

He perceived that this development could change all, and urgently decided to risk a ruse. As another dirk spun past his ear, he produced a high yelp, as of pain, and went down on one knee in the water, steadying himself thus with difficulty against the pull of the river, and leaning forward on his sword as though stricken.

The effect was immediate. There was a great shout of triumph, and the long narrow column surged forward again to the barrier. Bruce waited until two men were almost across it, and at their most vulnerable, and then leapt up, sword flailing. Unready for this, the pair were disposed of in four slashing strokes. He was able to run through a third, behind them, before the others flung themselves back against the pushing tide of their fellows. One tripped as he did so, probably over a leg of horse or man, and the King managed to disengage his blade and make a wild, weary hack at the floundering man which, more by luck than skill, struck him on the side of the head and knocked him off the causeway on the downstream side where it was deepest. He disappeared.

Gulping for air and dizzy from fatigue, Bruce reckoned that was fourteen slain, or at least put out of action.

His pounding heart sank as more dirks now came whirling through the air at him — for this was the greatest threat, and it was surely only a question of time until one found its mark. And then, above the angry baffled yells in front, he heard other and more distant shouting behind, higher up the hill. Gibbie seemed to have been a long time about bringing aid — though probably that was only an illusion.

The enemy heard the shouting also — and possibly even on the whole welcomed it. They were by no means poltroons, but leaderless, out-manoeuvred, and perceiving no way out of their punishing predicament, they now had the excuse to turn tail and extricate themselves from a thoroughly unprofitable engagement — which they could scarcely have done in the face of just one man. At any rate, as with one accord, those on the causeway turned the other way and began to stream back to dry land again.

Hay and the Islesmen came scrambling down the bank, crying their slogans, with the Carrick men-at-arms a little way behind. Distinctly unsteady on his legs, Bruce waded back to meet them.

"After them, Gibbie," he panted, as his friend came up. "Before they can reform. No leaders now. Keep them running and they will not stop. For long."

"How many of them, Sire?"

"About 200. Less ... less fourteen! See — there is a horse to get over ..."

Somewhat light-headed, the King sat himself down heavily on the same boulder that he had used earlier, while his men surged past. He realised that there was a long score down his right forearm, dripping blood, but fortunately not deep. In something of a daze he heard the noise of conflict receding, across the burn, the wild eldritch whoops of the Islesmen sounding more like a hunt than a battle. The Gallovidians would, presumably, know that there were only some sixty to oppose them — since their prisoner would have told them — but failure is a progressive business, and lack of direction notably bad for morale. None evidently any longer were preoccupied with victory.

Presently Sir Gilbert returned, with most of the Carrick men and some few prisoners.

"They flee, Your Grace — they flee," he announced. "They make no stand. You, Sire? You are well?" He perceived the blood on the bare arm. "You are wounded? Dear God — Your Grace is hurt?"

"Nothing, Gibbie. The merest scratch. Of a lance-point. Thank heaven no others had lances, but their leader. And this small blood he paid for! One MacDouall. From Galloway."

"MacDouall? Not Sir Dugald ...?"

"His brother. A start is made in the payment of treachery also."

"The saints be praised for that! And that you are yourself again...

"The saints — and a spider, Gibbie. A spider, I say!"

Chapter Eight

It was not everyone who loved Sir Neil Campbell of Lochawe, a dark, unsmiling, secret man, unforthcoming, alone. But Bruce, in these last testing months, had conceived a fondness for him, an appreciation of his unflinching quiet loyalty, as well as his dependability and courage. After all, he of them all was making the most immediate sacrifice in remaining with this small company round the King, the only Highland chief amongst them. His territories in far Argyll were in little danger from the English invaders. He could go home and live in security and at ease at any time.

Bruce embraced him now, heartily, when Campbell dismounted,

despite the mere score of men he had brought back, as a result of his long absence, to this beautiful wooded basin of Glen Trool amongst the mighty glooming Galloway mountains, however mocking Edward Bruce might look, and disappointed as were the others.

"It is good to see you back safe, Neil my friend," he said. "I feared that you might have come to ill in this Galloway. No place for a friend of mine, these days!"

"No," the other agreed. "Your Grace's cause scarce flourishes amongst these traitors. You . . . you have heard the evil tidings? Of your brothers?"

"I have heard," the King returned briefly.

"I am sorry. What may a man say?"

"Nothing. It is time for doing, not saying. And we have made a start."

"Aye — so I heard. Even in Galloway your doings are spoken of. The blows you have struck against the invaders and their minions. I had little difficult in learning that you were in these mountains. But finding you was none so easy. We have been in every valley of this land, I think, seeking you!"

"We have been on the move, yes. Seldom two nights in one place. Struck swift blows, and then moved away as swiftly. But . . . these are small blows. Pin-pricks, no more. Sufficient only to show our people that their King is active. Insufficient to serve our cause effectively. We must do a deal more than this — and soon."

"You have done sufficient to bring Pembroke here. Into Galloway. That at least. You have heard?"

"Yes. We know that he had been called to Carlisle, to suffer a tongue-lashing from King Edward. And now he has come back here. Up to the Cree. That he sits astride the Cree at Minnigaff. But fifteen miles away. And sends probing companies up these valleys. But he will not adventure his strength into the mountains. And we, with only 300, dare not challenge his thousands in the plains. We had hoped that you might have been able to bring us more than these, friend." Bruce glanced over at the score or so of mounted men Campbell had led in.

"I scarce thought I could gain even such few," the other said. "These are Bruce vassals of your own. From the Urr. It is hard to convince men that Your Grace's cause can succeed."

"Aye." That came on a sort of grim sigh. His brother Edward had brought back barely 200 from the great Bruce lands of Annandale — which a year or two before had raised 5,000. Boyd, who had been ambushed by the MacDouall party that day three weeks ago, on the Doon, and only escaped, with the Lady Christian, because they were fleetly mounted had managed to return in due course with Sir Robert Fleming and another two score — that was all. And Douglas was not yet back from Lanarkshire. There was still no surge to the King's standard.

"Until we strike a resounding blow against the English power itself, our folks will not flock to us," Edward broke in. "If they will not come to us — the English — we must go to them! Not against Pembroke — he has too many. But there are others. Clifford. Botetourt. St. John Percy himself — they say that he is now at Caerlaverock. Dumfries. We must choose one of these. Select the weakest, and strike."

"Clifford has now joined up with Pembroke," Campbell informed. "Or so it is said. King Edward's bastard, de Botetourt, is at Sanquhar. St. John holds Ayr and Irvine. They encircle you . . ."

"Three hundred lightly armed can do little or nothing against thousands of armoured chivalry. In open battle," the King insisted. "Our only hope is to make the country, the land itself, fight for us. So, by some means, we must coax these English out of *their* plains into our hills. There must be a way . . ."

"They are not fools," Boyd asserted. "They will not budge from Minnigaff and the Cree. Why should they? They can wait . . ."

"Some have already budged," Campbell interrupted him. "A company of them are none so far away. We had to make shift to avoid them, on our way here. Light horse, cantoned at Low Minniwick, in the Water of Trool."

"English horse! So near?" Bruce exclaimed. "We knew nothing of this. They must be new come. How many?"

"About 200, I would say. Sent out to probe for you, I have no doubt. By Pembroke."

"Yet camped . . .? In daytime?"

"I' faith — we could have these, at least!" Edward declared.

All round there was a stir of excitement, of anticipation, now.

"You say that they are cantoned, Neil? At Low Minniwick, down Trool? Settled, at least for this night."

"Yes. We were warned of them by the miller at Bargrennan. So we took to the hills. And looked down on them from the ridge of High Minniwick. They were camped — cooking-fires, horse-lines, pickets. Two squadrons, I'd say. They did not see us."

"Then why wait?" Edward demanded. "Why wait till this to tell us, man? We should be on our way — while it is yet light. Minniwick is but five or six miles away. Here is too good a chance to miss."

"Wait you, brother," the King said quietly. "Time enough. Let us use our wits before we do our swords. I have a notion that here may be the chance we have looked for. Not just to slay 200 Englishmen. But to draw Pembroke." He turned to Campbell. "If these are new come — as they must be, for they were not there yesterday, when we rode by — then they have been sent up from the main army. Yet only eight miles, into these foothills, from Minnigaff. And already camped. They must be making this Minniwick a centre, to send out patrols. Into all the side valleys, seeking us. Not to attack us — to *find* us. Some will be up here, at Loch Trool, by tomorrow, for a wager. Tomorrow, then, we must aid the English to find us! But not just a patrol — a host!"

They all gazed at him now, tensely, there by the lovely water of lone Lock Trool, under the frown of the Merrick mountains. It was the last day of March 1307, Passion Sunday.

By dark the entire party, mounted and on foot, was on the move down Trool Water in its winding wooded glen. Four miles they went, by the riverside track, then struck off half-right, to ford the incoming Water of Minnoch, and then start to climb, over slowly rising scrub-covered slopes. It was empty foothill country here, with the valley floors narrow and tending to be waterlogged. There were no villages or even houses, other than the occasional summertime shieling for herdsmen.

The company moved fast, for in that terrain the tough and agile Highlanders could cover the ground fully as swiftly as the horsed men-at-arms, and a deal more silently. In less than two hours they were fairly high on a long gentle whaleback of ridge that ran approximately north and south, flanking the Minnoch valley on the west, which valley, an extension of the Trool, had now widened out somewhat. The woodlands had dwindled away, and only the odd hawthorn dotted the ridge. There were cattle grazing on these rolling upland grasslands, shadowy shapes that plunged off into the gloom in brief alarm at the approach of the purposeful party. Presently, below them a little way, a dog barked its own alarm from the small farmery of High Minniwick, unseen below the crest of the ridge.

Islesmen scouts went ahead, in case the English had posted sentinels on this high ground; but no warnings came back to the main body. Campbell accompanied Bruce in the lead, and at length brought him to a sort of escarpment on the east side of the ridge, where the ground dropped away rather more steeply, in a long consistent grass slope, down to the riverside flats. The dull red glow of a number of scattered and dying fires punctured the darkness down there.

"Low Minniwick and the English encampment," Campbell said shortly. "Half a mile."

Bruce gathered his leaders round him. "This is not just Turnberry again," he told them. "There will be sentinels here. Possibly pickets patrolling round the camp. And we do not want a complete massacre, see you. Sir Neil says there may be 200. I want fifty alive, at the least. But held. So see to it that your men understand. All must be under tight rein. This will be done exactly as I say." And he looked towards his brother significantly.

Men murmured acknowledgement.

"The Islesmen will go down first. Quietly. Take up positions around the camp. Their leaders will prospect the closer approach, for our cavalry. The lie of the ground. To inform us, when we get down. The horse will move down slowly, as silent as may be. To near the camp. Only when I give the word will you charge. If there is an alarm, we will attack only when I blow my horn."

These orders were transmitted to the men. In a few minutes the Islesmen melted away into the darkness.

They gave them perhaps seven minutes' start, and then the horsed men-at-arms, dismounted, with the two Bruces and the four knights, led their beasts slowly downhill, quietly picking their way, seeking to avoid the chink of hoof on stone, the rattle of harness and the clank of arms. They were by no means entirely successful in this — but they hoped that the fitful night wind and the rush of the headlong river would blanket the noise.

No alarm rang out, at any rate. Indeed it was hard to believe that a large encampment of soldiers lay so close ahead.

Bruce was becoming anxious that they were drawing altogether too close, in view of those fires, one or two of which were to be seen as more than just embers, when two figures rose up out of the shadows in front. They were Islesmen, and reported, in whispers, that all was well. There were about a dozen sentries, but they were clustered around two fires at either end of the camp, one at the bottom, near the horse-lines; the other, that looked brightest from here, up near this top end. While the Highlanders had been waiting, two of the guard had strolled round the perimeter of the cantonment, and then back to their companions. They had not made any probes into the darkness beyond the faint firelight.

Bruce nodded. "Half of your men to the horse-lines," he directed. "Cut the tethers. As quiet as you can. As many cut before the beasts stir, as may be. Their stir will bring the guard to see what troubles them. We will hear when that happens. I will sound my horn. You will drive all the horses you can in amongst the sleeping men. The rest of the Moidartach to attack from the left. We, here, will charge mounted. How is the ground, for a charge?"

"Fair," he was told. "A burn-channel to the left, with broken banks. Avoid that. Some wet, in front — but nothing that will hold you back."

"It is well. Off with you." Bruce passed the word for his own people to mount.

They waited for what seemed too long a time, thankful only for the noise of the river to drown the chinking bits and bridles and the stamping, scuffling hooves. They heard in fact no stirring from the enemy horse-lines. But presently men could be seen to rise from the dark huddle round the farthest-away fire, and start to move away, towards where the tethered beasts must be. But they did not hurry or sound any alarm.

Then there was a sudden shout, quickly bitten off. Then more cries. Bruce's horn was at his lips at the first yell, and the wailing hooting ululation of it rang out, even as he kicked in his spurs.

In two lines, on a broad front, the 200 horsemen drove on, downhill, straight into a canter, then a gallop — though they had scarcely time for that before they were into the enemy lines. The beat of their hooves shook the slope, and the thunder of it was pierced by the cries of "A Bruce! A Bruce!" and the high yelling of Gaelic slogans from left and right, as the Islesmen raced in, swords and dirks raised.

In the event, it was all over in a ridiculously brief period. Most of the sleepers had little opportunity to do more than stagger to their feet before the fierce tide of slashing horsemen crashed down on them, and through, their confusion increased by the stampede of their own mounts careering in panic through their lines transversely, driven by yelling Highlanders. Bruce found himself beyond the last line of sleeping men and stacked arms, reining up his rearing mount at the very riverside, with only one effective sword-thrust delivered.

He had intended to turn his squadron directly round and plunge straight back for a second charge; but he perceived that in the chaos of frantic riderless horses, reeling sleep-dazed men and bounding cut-throat Highlanders, any such move would be folly, as likely to ride down their own people as the bewildered enemy. Instead, he shouted for some of his horsemen to divide and make sweeps round on either side, encircling the encampment, to spread terror and prevent escapes. He and his knights, with the rest, sat their restive mounts, waiting.

They were not required. It was entirely evident, before long, that the English were wholly demoralised and overcome, that there was no organised resistance and could not be. The Islesmen were in their savage element, and presently the King was blowing loudly on his horn again, to end the carnage, and leading his colleagues in, to enforce his will.

Fresh wood heaped on the fires revealed a ghastly blood-drenched scene of ruin and confusion. It seemed scarcely credible that such havoc could have been created in so few minutes.

Creating order out of the bedlam took a deal longer. A slightly wounded but wholly unnerved youngish man, in rich but bedraggled clothing, was brought before the King by Fleming.

"Here is their commander, Sire. He calls himself Sir Alan de Scrope. Do we burden ourselves with prisoners?"

"What say you to that, Englishman?" Bruce asked, sternly. "You, who sleep so sound on Scots soil! *Your* King only takes prisoners to hang and disembowel them, does he not?"

The other answered nothing.

With a semblance of order restored, Bruce called his leaders apart. They had almost 100 prisoners, in fact, and undoubtedly others had escaped in the turmoil and darkness. But this was as planned.

"Now," he said, "we set our lure. This English knight, with most of his people, we are going to send up Glen Trool. On foot. We shall cry this aloud. Say that we shall give them trial there, tomorrow, and hang them on trees at the loch-head. Make much talk of that sort. Naming Loch Trool. But a smaller number of the prisoners, perhaps a score, we will hold here, after the others are sent off. For a time. Then allow them to escape, with their news!"

Though Edward frowned, Hay chuckled. "To Pembroke! You think it will bring him?"

"De Valence is cunning as a fox," Boyd reminded. "Will he rise to our lure?"

"He cannot do nothing. And de Scrope, see you, is a notable name. You may not know it, but Sir Geoffrey de Scrope is Chief Justice of the King's Bench, in London. This puppy will be a son or nephew. I think Pembroke must attempt a rescue. When he hears that we intend to hang him. He must so hear, therefore. We have captured good supplies and wine and ale with these English — they do not stint themselves. We shall seem to make merry on it — and grow careless of our prisoners. And our talk. Insecurely guarded, and near some of their own horses. We will allow an escape. I swear they will not be backward! They will scurry down Minnoch, to Pembroke at Minnigaff. They will have him out of his bed before daybreak, I warrant."

"And we wait for him, here?" Edward showed more interest.

"Not here. We must coax him up the glen. Round the head of

the loch. There is a place there, I have seen, most apt for ambush. Of a large force. Pembroke may not come himself, but surely a large force he must send. He must think he has the King of Scots bottled up, penned in Glen Trool. His people careless, drunken — or near so. We must coax . . ."

Smiling now, they put their heads together.

So, by dawn, Low Minniwick was deserted — save for a ravaged farm-steading and a few Englishmen tied to trees, naked, heads shaven, and with scurrilous things daubed in blood on their white skins, including the names — Valence, Clifford, Botetourt, Percy. But they were alive — and would not die of cold yet awhile. If a punitive force came this far, these would give it information — and send it after the perpetrators, hot-foot.

Bruce's small host was now much split up and dispersed. Some few were up on the high ground again, watching, to signal any English approach. Some were no great distance up the riverside track to the loch, moving slowly, trailing their wings as it were, should there be any early pursuit, decoys. Boyd, with the main body of men-at-arms, held the mass of the prisoners up near Loch Troolhead. While the King himself, with the Islesmen, climbed a steep mountainside above the far, east side of the loch, with the first of the slanting April sunlight just beginning to blind them with its early dazzle.

This east side of upper Glen Trool was very different from the west. Where the other was thickly wooded and rose in great steps and terraces towards lesser heights first, and then to high frowning Merrick itself, on this side the land rose steep, stony and bare in an almost unbroken sweep to the towering summit of Muldonach, more than 1,500 feet higher than the loch. A single thread of narrow track crossed the face of this naked braeside, rising and falling, now near the water's edge, now many scores of feet above it. This track, the only one to lead southwards on that side, Bruce and his party had left, to climb steeply upwards, panting breath-clouds in the sharp morning air.

There was one sizeable break, or shelf, on the face of that long hill, a rough terrace about half a mile long some 300 feet above the water. This was their objective.

When they reached it, breathless, it was to find it deeper than the King had anticipated from a distance, more broken. But this was immaterial. It averaged perhaps 200 yards in width, was far from consistently flat, and was pitted with heather-grown hollows and aprons of trapped water and emerald-green moss. But mainly it was bare, backed by screes, and as well as surface-water it had trapped a great variety of stones and boulders, tumbled from higher. Bruce was well satisfied. The whole hillside was stony, of course; but this trap would save them much work and time. And from the low ground they could remain hidden save on the very lip of the shelf. And the view down the valley was not to be bettered, right down to the Cree, indeed across the Wigtown peninsula itself, to Luce Bay and the Solway.

He set his Highlanders to the collection, rolling and positioning of great stones and boulders, by the hundred.

With still no sign of movement from down the valley, and assured of progress here, leaving the Islesmen at work, and a look-out to signal any approach from the south, the King went long-strided downhill again, concerned to correctly position his few cavalry. In an operation of the scale he visualised, 200 was pitifully few. And a percentage of that had to be left to guard and accompany the prisoners.

He gave the impatient Edward the command of seventy-five, and sent them off along the narrow track above the lochshore, to the farthest-away position about a mile to the south-east, where a fair-sized stream coming down the mountain had carved a deep, steep ravine, which must serve to give them cover. At all costs they must remain hidden therein until signalled, especially from across the loch. Campbell was to take another seventy-five up the right-hand of the two narrowing glens into which the main valley split at the head of the loch, to hide around the first bend. Boyd and Fleming would retain approximately fifty mounted men, with the prisoners, waiting by the shore at the start of the east track, ready to show themselves and to move off south by east. Bruce detailed the signals, for each group, stressing the need for the most exact timing. More he could not do. Taking Hay for lieutenant, he set off once again to climb the hill to his Islesmen.

So commenced the trying, testing waiting, the enforced idleness. It was well enough for the men; they were all weary with the night's exertions and lack of sleep — though most of the Islesmen continued to add to their vast supply of boulders and rocks, now marshalled for a quarter-mile along the lip of the shelf. But Bruce himself could not rest, even though look-outs were posted to give ample warning of eventualities. He sat there in the heather, staring down the long fair valley, flooded now with sunlight, while the larks shouted above him, straining tired eyes for the first hint of movement, glint of steel.

An hour he sat, fretting, and half another, a prey to fears that he had misjudged, that Pembroke was not to be lured, provoked, coaxed. That, or else he was coming in great force, and taking an unconscionable time to effect it.

It was neither movement nor the gleam of armour which brought an end to his fretting, but a thin column of smoke rising above and behind the ridge of High Minniwick, almost three miles to the south, where he had posted a picket. That meant that the English were indeed coming, and were visible from there at least.

There was no need to strain the eyes, presently. Like a dark river alongside the silvery one, but flowing the wrong way, a dense column of men began to appear from round one of the far bends of the lower valley. It could not be a broad column, because of the constriction of the terrain; but that it was long became ever more evident. On and on came the ranks, emerging into view, seeming endless, too far away as yet for details, but by the pace, all mounted. There were brief breaks in the purposeful procession, but only between divisions and cohorts. New sections followed on monotonously.

"It is an army!" Hay cried. "He has sent a host, no mere striking force. I have counted twelve already — twelve divisions. And still they come. We cannot challenge such numbers, Sire!"

The King said nothing.

At last there seemed to be an end. At a conservative estimate that column was well over a mile long. Before the tail was much past the confluence of Minnoch and Trool, the head was reaching the foot of the loch.

"Fifteen, I counted," Hay declared. "What can we do, Sire? Fifteen divisions of the best soldiers in Christiandom. And we have 300. Mosstroopers and caterans!"

"We fight on our chosen field," Bruce pointed out. "That means much. Besides, what means fifteen divisions? Are they in scores or hundreds or five-hundreds, How many abreast do they ride? They can scarce ride more than three on that ground. Three files of three, mounted, would take up a dozen yards and more. That is . . . let me count it . . . say, 1,200 to a mile, no more. None so vast a host."

It was Hay's turn to remain silent, however eloquent he looked.

Loch Trool was more than two miles long but less than a quarter of that in width. By the time that the head of the English column was half-way up the west side, Bruce, from his elevation, could distinguish considerable detail, not much more than a mile away across the water. He reckoned that they did indeed ride in threes, a goodly array in the forenoon sun, standards, banners, pennons flying, the steam of horses, and everywhere the gleam of armour.

"I cannot think that there are more than a hundred to each

division, Gibbie," he decided. "Fifteen hundred in all, perhaps . . ."

"Five times our numbers!"

"Aye — but in bad country for cavalry. The standards at their head — can you make them out? The colours? The Leopards of England fly at this side, yes — but what of the other? Beyond. Not the azure and gules of Pembroke, I think."

"It is chequered, is it not? Blue and gold?"

"The azure and, or, checky, of Clifford of Brougham! By the Rude, he has sent Clifford!" Bruce's eyes had narrowed, in more than the glare of slanting sunlight. "Clifford, of all men, I would bring low! Once I challenged Robert Clifford to personal combat. After Stirling Bridge. He refused me. I swore that one day I would repay his insults. Pray God and all His saints for me, Gibbie, that this may be the day!"

The other mumbled something indistinct.

"He is worse than Percy. A black-hearted savage! For the challenge I made him, he crucified all Annandale. Slew 2,000 of my people. Burned Annan and a score of villages. Tortured, raped, trampled. And now he rides there!"

"Sire — he is an evil man. But a notable commander. If you will not retire, at least give the signal to move!"

"I said that I would let them come level with the Maiden Isle. They are not there yet. All depends on timing, man . . ."

At length the glittering head of the colourful array reached the vicinity of the islet, two-thirds of the way up the loch. Bruce turned and waved to the first of a hidden chain of caterans.

Reaction was not long in manifesting itself. From the woodland at the head of the loch, about a mile in front of the English, Boyd's party streamed out, in flight, heading south by east for the loch-shore track, a mixed company of some fifty mounted men herding about eighty dismounted prisoners.

Even at that distance, across the water, the watchers could hear the shouts of Clifford's men as they saw their quarry. Equally evident was the sudden increase of pace, as the leaders spurred to the chase. Bruce nodded grimly.

Now they must wait again, a tenser and even more taxing waiting, while they watched the drama unfold. Timing was indeed of the essence, yet so much was unpredictable and might go wrong. It demanded an iron resolution to sit there and do nothing, to withhold the next signal until the precise moment — which might well never come.

It was all a matter of pace and distance and ground; the contrasting paces of a fast-riding pursuit and a slow-moving huddle of dismounted prisoners; of a gap between, short enough to lure on the former beyond all hesitation, yet long enough to allow the latter to be kept ahead until the next stage of the programme; and this situation affected, complicated, by the fact that, in the woods which Boyd's party had just left, was the hidden barrier of the lock's main feeder-river to be got over bridgeless, and the marshlands of the loch-head beyond, difficult for horsemen.

So that, although the English van made up on the Scots at a great rate, reaching the loch-head trees while Boyd and Fleming were still ploutering with their charges through the bogs less than half a mile ahead, it was a little longer before Clifford and his knights emerged from the trees again, into view. And meanwhile there occurred behind them a great pile-up of the long English train, and not a little confusion.

The marshland forced Clifford to a walking pace and to practically single-file progress. Even so, he was into its emerald-green uncertainty before Boyd's party was out at the other side, no more than 500 yards separating them now.

But thereafter the going improved, as the Scots and their unhappy captives gained the firm though narrow lochside track. Driving the prisoners like a flock of unwilling sheep, shouting and beating them with the flats of their swords, the Annanadale moss-troopers hurried them along, while behind them the trumpets shrilled, neighing cavalry orders.

Sir Gilbert Hay could not keep still, in his alarm and concern, biting his nails and declaring that disaster was inevitable unless there was a miracle, that the English *must* catch up far too soon for their project to work. The King should blow his horn now, and let Boyd and his men save themselves at least and leave the damned prisoners. Clifford would still pursue . . .

Bruce did not so much as glance at him.

Clifford was no fool. When he and his nearest won out of the marsh and on to the start of the track, he was little more than a quarter-mile from his quarry. But behind him only a sparse, attenuated thread of men were picking their way through the quaking water-meadows as yet, most of his host still hidden by the woods, some even still in sight beyond, held up in the queue to cross the river. The watchers could almost see him fuming there, a splendid figure in colourful heraldic surcoat over shining armour, magnificently mounted, the blue-and-gold plumes of his helmet tossing, while his numbers so slowly grew.

Bruce and Hay could see, now, that the enemy was not so stupid as to make a wholly blind and headlong advance through this obviously dangerous country. A fair-sized column had detached itself, and now emerged from the trees to the northwards following the river up to where it split into the two tributary glens — obviously to stop any flank attack from that quarter. Clifford would well know that the fifty or so herding the prisoners was not all Bruce's force. Campbell was up there in the right-hand glen. But Campbell had his instructions — and at least he had hillmen as his little force, Annandale mosstroopers, not low-country heavy cavalry.

Boyd was now almost directly below Bruce and his waiting Islesmen. A few of the prisoners had fallen by the way, jumped or been pushed down to the shore or into the water, and had been left. But the great majority were still being herded along southwards.

Clifford was displaying exemplary patience. He could see, of course, the entire empty flank of Muldonach Hill ahead of him and of his quarry, and would reckon time to be very much on his side. Slowly his following was catching up with him.

When, at length, a trumpet announced the resumption of the advance, he still did not hurry off at a canter. The narrowness of the track meant that they could not ride more than two abreast, sometimes not even that. Any rush along it would mean only a few reaching the Scots unsupported. A slow trot would serve them well enough.

Hay, in his efforts to report exactly how far both Boyd and the enemy had got, down below, was in danger of showing himself, and was sharply rebuked by the otherwise silent monarch.

"But they are within bowshot of Boyd now," he exclaimed. "Clifford is almost directly below. Almost upon them. Another minute or so and it will be all over!"

"Not so. Clifford and his knights do not use bows and arrows! Boyd knew his task — a sound veteran. He will draw them along until the last moment. Minutes yet. Even then he will put the prisoners between him and Clifford — a hold-up on that path." Bruce had drawn himself forward in the heather, to peer over and down. "Wait you, Gibbie. How much of a commander's task is but waiting!"

No more than 200 yards now separated the tail of one party from the head of the other. Boyd was stretching it manfully. The climax could not be long delayed now; but every second counted, with more and more English committed to that hillside path.

Boyd made his move. Abandoning the captives at last, he pulled out his men, past and through them, and trotted on beyond — but even now not at top speed.

The prisoners promptly turned to face the other way. But if they expected any rapturous welcome from the rescuers, they were disappointed. Clifford's shouts to them to get off the track and out of the way could be heard right up at the high terrace.

They did not do so with any alactrity, perhaps understandably, and there was a certain amount of delay and disorder as the pursuit reached them. More men went rolling down the steep bank, amidst curses and shrill cries of protest. Then Clifford was through, his pace increased to a canter, after the fleeing Scots.

Bruce was almost counting the yards now. Boyd was nearing the ravine where Edward was hidden. He was to ride straight on, over the burn and past. But the English could hardly fail to notice the hoof-marks of Edward's company turning off. Then would be the moment of truth.

Clifford was out of sight of Bruce's position now, his long tail of men stretched across the wide skirts of the hill. How to tell the precise moment? Whether he would in fact turn in, on Edward, go on after Boyd — or take fright, and send back warning, so that full surprise would be lost?

Thinly, the noise of distant shouting came from in front.

Bruce waited no longer. Rising, he stepped back, and raised his hand, to wave. Right and left he turned, waving.

All along the lip of that hillside shelf the Islesmen sprang into furious action. Within a few seconds of the signal, scores of boulders, great and small, had been tipped over the edge of the terrace, to begin their headlong bounding descent.

The King turned to Hay, at last, and threw the Highland hunting-horn to him. "Now, Gibbie!" he cried. "Sound! Blow you, loud and long!"

High and hollow, its winding, hooting belling never to be confused with the brassy blare of trumpet or bugle, the horn's message wailed and echoed amongst the thronging hillsides, far and near. Before it died away, the screams of men and horses were ringing out from directly below.

The first rocks were smashing down upon the English line, hurtling indiscriminately but in such numbers as to be utterly, comprehensively disastrous. There could be no taking action to avoid the bounding, crushing, erratic hail of them. The horsemen were totally without protection on that naked braeface, beasts and riders flung like skittles, in utter ruin.

On and on the fusillade of grey granite continued, each stone, even the smallest, a projectile of fierce velocity by the time it had plunged down the hundreds of yards of steep slope. The enemy cavalry was spread two abreast along that narrow track for well over a mile, and within a few brief seconds, practically all its central files, for almost half a mile, were swept clean away in mangled bloody chaos, down in flailing hooves and limbs to the water.

There was no need for all the collected rocks to be launched away, in fact. Indeed, Bruce, himself all but appalled by the scene of blind havoc he had conjured up, was in two minds whether to order the downhill charge planned, to complete the immediate debacle below. It was scarcely necessary, and the Islesmen's eager broadswords could be needed elsewhere.

"Gibbie!" he yelled. "Take a few. Two score. Down there. To finish the task. Then along, to aid Boyd and Edward. You have it?"

"Aye, Sire. And you?"

"I take most. Right. Campbell has the heavy end of this. And fewest men. Though not Clifford. Give me the horn . . ."

So, desisting in the rock-rolling, the Highlanders divided into two unequal companies, both surging over the edge, to go bounding downhill, shouting their slogans, broadswords out. The lesser number went straight down, though spread along quite a wide front, to finish off the broken horror of a column which now largely littered the loch-shore; the greater went racing slantwise, right-handed, northwards, down towards where the stone fusillade had tailed off, Bruce leaping at their head, thankful indeed for action.

Down there confusion enough reigned already. Utter disaster ahead, and cut off from their main leadership, the long files of horsemen were most obviously in doubt whether to press on to the aid of their fellows, and meet possibly a similar fate, or to turn back and get off this devilish constricting track and exposed hillside. The sight of Bruce's horde of charging caterans bearing down on them seemed to convince the majority, at least. Not without difficulty and delay, the truncated column turned on itself and began to hurry back whence it had come.

But now the noise of clash ahead became evident to them. Campbell had not led his seventy-five straight down out of the eastern-most side glen, which would have brought him into the soft marsh-land, but slightly uphill to the south, over the base of a shoulder of Muldonach. Now, in extended order, they flung themselves down at the vital hinge of the enemy line, where it left the solid ground of the track-head for the quaking water-meadows. His move, of course, would have been entirely evident to the detached English flanking party sent up to stop the mouths of the two glens; but these were on the wrong side of a rushing mountain torrent, and helpless to do more than hasten down again to the ford in the woodland, half a mile below.

Campbell's charge, with all the benefits of impetus and purpose, as well as surprise, swept another sizeable section of the enemy column into irretrievable disorder. There were still many hundreds of the English array disengaged, but they were strung out over a great area and on hopeless ground for cavalry. Pockets of resistance and discipline developed, but by and large panic took its fatal grip.

The sight and sound of Bruce's yelling Islesmen clinched the matter as far as the enemy south of the marsh was concerned. None who could get away awaited their impact. Some, rather than queue to take the winding marsh-path, plunged into the loch itself; but most risked the quagmires of the water-meadows.

Many got away, of course. But large numbers did not. For those green levels were treachery indeed for horsemen. And hunting the floundering cavalry like baying hounds came the leaping Islesmen, agile and light-footed. Great was the slaughter in that bog.

Bruce left the caterans to it. Campbell's mosstroopers, on the lighter garrons of the Annandale hills, were chasing what was left of the fleeing column, by the single marsh-track. It seemed obvious that there would be no English stand this side of the river — and possibly not beyond it. The King grabbed a riderless horse, and set off back along the hillside track.

He reached the area of shambles where the stones had done their fell work, to find only dead and dying there. Hay and his men had already completed their task, and hurried on towards the ravine. Bruce spurred his heavy English charger in their slippery, blood-soaked tracks.

He had not gone far when a single horseman rode to meet him. It was Sir Robert Fleming, a sallow, thin-faced youngish man with great brown eyes almost like a woman's.

"All is by with, Your Grace," he called out, excitedly. "They are fled. When the Lord Edward came out on them, from the rear, and we turned back on them, from the front. They were caught. In no formation. They fought for a while, as best they could. But . . ."

"Clifford, man?" the King interrupted. "What of Clifford?"

"He fought his way through us, Sire. We could not hold them. There were more of them than there were of us, even so. We in front could not do more. They cut through us, and on southwards. Fleeing . . ."

"You mean Clifford has escaped? A curse on it — I have lost him!"

"What could we do, Sire? When it came to close combat, they were better armed, armoured and horsed than we. Clifford and his knights. We went down before them. We lost not a few. Boyd is wounded . . ."

"Aye. I am sorry, Sir Robert. It is but that I sought him. Wanted Clifford for myself. A . . . debt of honour. A selfish whim!"

"At least, the Lord Edward pursues him hot-foot. I think he will not stop until he reaches Cree."

"Perhaps. Aye, perhaps, friend. Who knows, it may be as bitter a notion for Clifford to have to live with than if I had worsted him here in Glen Trool. But . . . that man will seek vengeance. And take it, as he has done before, on innocent folk, I fear." The King shrugged. "Another time, perhaps." He straightened in the saddle. "Go you back, Sir Robert. My compliments to Boyd. You have done well. I hope he is not sore hurt. And tell Gilbert Hay to send his fleetest rider after my brother. With my royal command that he is to turn back forthwith. Not to continue the chase. It is profitless, dangerous. Back with him. And Hay to bring on all able men to the ford at the loch-head. Quickly. We may need every man, yet. You have it?"

The two men parted, each to hurry whence he had come.

But back at the ford in the wood, nearly two miles away, Bruce found no battle either. Sir Neil Campbell, mud-covered from a fall from his horse in the bog, revealed that it was all over here too. The English flanking party, on meeting the refugees of the main body fleeing across the ford, had evidently decided that only fools threw good money after bad. They had not even waited to oppose the Scots themselves taking the ford, as they might have done successfully, but set off southwards, down the west side of the loch, at speed, still a disciplined if unblooded force amongst their broken and unhappy compatriots. Campbell had a picket trailing them — but he reckoned that they had seen the last of that squadron of wise men.

The King drew a long quivering breath. "So the day is ours, Neil — all ours! I thank God — and you all — for it. We needed it, i' faith! But . . . that is today. Tomorrow — what of tomorrow? Pembroke is not yet committed, did not come himself. And he has a mighty force. Tomorrow they will be aswarm in these valleys like a wasps' nest disturbed."

"Enough for today that we have won this battle, at least," the other grunted.

"It was no battle — only a skirmish. But we shall call it a battle, yes. Make much of it — for our own purposes. So long as we do not deceive ourselves. The battle of Glen Trool, no less — the first battle we Scots have won against the English in the field since Stirling Brig! So let the word go out, that men may take heart. All over the land. But *we* know better, Neil . . ." The King reined round. "Now — to work. I want to be far from here before nightfall."

Chapter Nine

It was well over a year, not indeed since his coronation, that the King had sat at ease, or at all, under a roof of his own. That he should be able to do so now, even though the roof was a small and unimportant one, was perhaps a sign, an encouragement, however modest. That it should be back within a few miles of the point where he had made his February landing on the Carrick shore of the mainland, nearly three months before, could be another satisfaction — although it could also be the reverse, depending on which way the thing was viewed. Progress, or the lack of it. At any rate, Bruce did stretch before a hearth that he could call his own, that early May evening, and was moderately thankful — that is, for so long as he carefully kept his mind on the immediate situation and did not contemplate the appalling dimensions of the task before him.

Tired, after a long day in the saddle, he sat in the little hall of the Tower of Kilkerran, house of one of his Celtic vassals, Fergus son of Fergus, amongst the green foothills of the pleasant Water of Girvan, four miles south of Maybole, capital of his own Carrick, and only eight miles inland from Turnberry. Turnberry Castle itself was still held against him, and must remain so for the foreseeable future; he had neither the siege equipment nor the time for reducing powerful fortresses. But it was *only* the great castles which were held against him in Ayrshire now. Elsewhere he and his could ride at large, a month after Glen Trool.

Pembroke had been unexpectedly inactive since that affair. Not to be wondered at, perhaps, if it was true, as rumoured, that he had been summoned once more peremptorily to Lanercost in Cumberland to give an account of himself before the angry Edward Plantagenet. Bruce admittedly would not have enjoyed being in de Valence's shoes, in that respect; but by the same token, it could be assumed that it would not be long before he was back again, greatly reinforced and spurred on to mighty endeavours against the hated Scots — he or another.

But meantime the King's cause could be said to prosper, even though not spectacularly. With the main English army still at the Cree, holding that vital hinge between the Borders and Galloway, Bruce had moved north into Ayrshire. Daily men came to join him from Carrick, Kyle and Cunninghame, not in their thousands admittedly, not great lords and barons, but lesser men — a few knights, many lairds, and common folk. More important, perhaps, even than those who actually joined him, was the climate of opinion, the acceptance, at least in these parts, that the royal cause was no longer hopeless and to be shunned at all costs. Turnberry, Loch Doon, and Glen Trool had had their effect. Scots in more than Ayrshire held their heads a little higher.

None knew better than Robert Bruce, of course, how small-scale and ephemeral was such success. But at least it was a change from failure, from disaster and near despair. Even though that very day he had heard that Sir Philip Moubray, one of the Comyn faction — the same who had unhorsed him and nearly captured him at Methven eleven months before — was heading south from Stirling with 1,000 men, to try to drive him back into the arms of the English on the Cree. Bruce's commanders were summoned here to Kilkerran for a council on this, tomorrow, when his scouts should have reports for him.

It was not one of the commanders however who presently was announced as seeking audience with the King, but a very different sort of visitor.

"Master Nicholas Balmyle, Official of St. Andrews, craves word with Your Grace," Gilbert Hay informed, at the door. "Will you see him?"

"Balmyle?" Bruce sat up. "By the Rude — yes, I will see Master Nicholas!"

The man who was ushered in was small, neat, compact, richly-dressed in clerical garb, self-possessed and still-faced. He bowed slightly, but made no move to hurry forward to kiss the royal hand.

Bruce eyed him keenly, as well he might. Here, reputedly, was one of the cleverest men in Scotland, and one not hitherto notable for wearing his heart on his sleeve. He had indeed been Chancellor of Scotland for two years, under de Soulis' Guardianship — which made him the last Chancellor, or chief minister, the realm had had, before all Scots government was swept away. The two pairs of eyes met and held — Bruce's sterner than he knew, the cleric's level, emotionless but shrewd.

"Here is surprise, Master Nicholas," the King said carefully. "It has not been my pleasure to see you, for long. Even at my coronation!" The former Chancellor, Official of St. Andrews and Canon of Dunblane, had been one of the many notable absentees from that ceremony.

"That was an occasion for the great, Highness," the other returned composedly. "Not for lowly servants of Holy Church, such as myself."

"Lowly?" the King jerked. "You?"

"Aye, Sire. Younger son of a small Fife laird. A mere canon, an official in holy orders. And my good father-in-God's humble messenger and steward."

"Ha!" Bruce's somewhat suspicious glance widened. "You mean . . .?"

"That I have brought Your Grace a letter from my master. From the Lord Bishop of St. Andrews, Primate of this realm."

"From William Lamberton! From my friend!" That was eager.

"Yes." Balmyle drew out from within his dark cloak an unaddressed folded paper, battered and crushed but still sealed closely. "This reached me only days ago. By devious means. Within another, instructing me to convey it to Your Grace forthwith. And in person."

"From England?" Bruce took the letter.

"A friar in the train of Bishop Beck of Durham brought it. Secretly. My lord Bishop is held at Barnard Castle, on the Tees.

Opening the seals, the King strode to the window, to read. But he turned, and gestured to the table. "Meats. Drink, Master Nicholas . . ."

The folded paper contained another within it, this addressed to the High and Mighty Prince, Robert King of Scots, wherever he might be found. This opened, read:

My liege lord and good dear friend.
I have learned that there is occasion that this writing may be conveyed to Scotland in secrecy. I hasten to advantage myself, and pray God that it may in due course reach Your Grace.

My hope is that it finds you in good health. I think that this must be so for the word reaches this Durham, where I am held, of the works of no ailing man, of shrewd blows struck against the invader and those of your own subjects who betray their king. That you may prosper in these efforts is my constant prayer. And that I, held close here, may not aid you in your struggle is my as constant sorrow.

It may be that I can offer some small guidance even so, confined as I am, my lord Robert. I gain certain informations here from a source that you might not look to. That source is the Prince Edward of Carnarvon, styled as of Wales. His father the King loves him not, as you will know. I find this prince a very different man from his sire. He is much here at this castle, for King Edward mislikes to have him overmuch at Lanercost, preferring his bastard Botetourt. Yet the prince must be near for councils, since in name he commands part of the English host. He speaks much with me, being a man greatly confused and in need of spiritual guidance, yet wilful and petulant. And gets little guidance from Anthony Beck who the King makes all but his keeper.

But to the nub of it, Sire. King Edward is more ill in health than is told. His son believes that he will not see another winter, for he fails fast. His hatred for you and for Scotland fails nothing nevertheless, and he is mustering another great army of invasion for the summer. But he cannot himself lead it, that is certain.

When God takes Edward Plantagenet to Himself and England has a new king, it may be that I may be of some small service to you, my friend. For he esteems me in some measure, that I know. He will be beset around by hard and strong men, his father's men, and he loves not Scotland. But he lacks his sire's resolution and on that I may be able to play. So that I pray that this my captivity may not be all loss.

Of other tidings. I learn that your lady-wife the Queen is at Burstwick Manor, in Holderness in Yorkshire, no great distance from here. If I may I shall seek to get word to her. I have heard that King Edward has reduced his shameful command that your daughter the Lady Marjory should be hung in a cage on the walls of London Tower. His own Queen is said to have besought him for the child. She is to be held in the Tower, alone, but not caged, God be praised. Ill as that is. Others are less fortunate, at Berwick and Roxburgh, it is said. But of this wickedness you may know better than I.

If this writing reaches you, it will be by the hand of Nicholas Balmyle, my Official of St. Andrews. I commend him to Your Grace as an able and reliable servant whom you may use in my place, in my absence. Through him I seek still to guide Holy Church in Scotland, in some measure. I have asked him to bring you the tokens of that Church's support. You may trust Balmyle.

And now may God Almighty guard, keep and strengthen you, and His peace rest upon you, my son. I pray for you daily, and weary for the sight of your face.

I subscribe myself your father-in-God, true friend, and most leal subject.

WILLIAMW ✠ Episcopo Sancti Andrea.

Written in bonds at the Castle of Bernard Baliol in the County of Durham, this 12th day of April from our Lord's birth 1307 years.

Much moved, the King stared out of the window over the fair

green prospect bathed in the mellow light of the setting sun, before turning back to his visitor.

"Master Balmyle," he said, "I owe you much for bringing me this letter. From one who is close to my heart. It is of great value to me. And comfort. I thank you."

The other, from sipping wine, laid down his goblet. "I rejoice Sire, if I have been the means of bringing you solace. It may be that I may have brought you even more. Of other sort."

"You say so? My friend, I have learned the folly of pride. All your comfort and solace I will esteem. I am a glutton for it!"

The other nodded. "Below, in one saddle-bag, my servant guards gold to the value of 5,000 merks. From the treasury of the Diocese of St. Andrews, for Your Grace's needs."

"Five thousand merks! Of a mercy — here is generosity! Princely generosity to a penniless prince! Solace indeed, Master Balmyle."

"My lord Bishop's instructions."

"I scarce thought so much gold remained in this Scotland! That the English had not stolen."

"Holy Church makes shift, Sire, to protect her own. So that she may cherish her own, in need."

"Aye. But I had not thought to hear the name of Robert Bruce on that roll!"

The little cleric made no change of expression. "The Church is fallible and can make mistakes. But she recognises her own sheep. Even when at times they stray. So long as they are repentant."

"What do you mean?"

"I mean, Sire, that in my other saddle-bag below is different solace. More costly than any gold. Priceless. The wafer and the wine. That can be the Sacrament of our Lord."

"What . . . what are you saying, man?" That was little more than a whisper. "The Sacrament! Holy Communion! For me? You must know that I am excommunicate. From Rome . . ."

"We believe that the Holy Father was misinformed. Ill advised. In this matter. My lord Bishop believes that if he was free to visit His Holiness, or even to send an envoy, he could have the excommunication lifted. He is convinced of your penitence for the slaying of Sir John Comyn. Therefore, he would not have the misfortune of *his* imprisonment to limit the mercy of God towards you. By his command I am to dispense the Holy Sacrament to you. If so you will. After preparation."

"The mercy of God . . .!" The King stared at him. "The mercy of God indeed! Dear Jesu — I had not looked for God's angel in the person of Nicholas Balmyle!"

The other permitted himself a small smile.

"When?" Bruce demanded. "You speak of preparation . . .?"

"Your Grace lives amongst alarums and perils. Later tonight, if you will. An hour of prayer, perhaps . . ."

His alarums and perils must have seemed altogether too apt, for the sudden sounding of a trumpet, the drumming of hooves and the shouts of men halted the cleric in his speech. Bruce moved back to the window.

A large company of mounted men, some hundreds strong, was approaching at a canter from the north, with a stirring aspect of dash and élan, well-horsed and armoured. And at their head fluttered a large silken banner, white with an azure chief on which three silver stars stood out.

"Douglas!" the King exclaimed. "Jamie Douglas!" Swinging about, he brushed past his surprised visitor, out from the hall, and went down the winding turnpike stairway three steps at a time, in scarcely regal fashion.

Douglas came clattering into the tower's little courtyard just as Bruce reached it, and drawing up his splendid charger to a slithering, caracoling halt, with sparks striking from the cobblestones, flung himself down and strode, spurs jingling, the few paces to the King, and dropped on one knee. He reached for the royal hand.

"My liege lord Robert!" he panted. "God be praised! For the sight of you again."

The King smiled. "Sakes, Jamie — am I so fine a sight? I'd not have thought it. You, now — that is a handsome mount you have there. You have me envious, I vow! And your fine armour — gold-inlaid, no less! Whom have you been robbing, lad?"

"The armour is my dead father's. And something big for me! And the stallion was Cliffords's. Yours now, Sire."

"Clifford's? You also have been crossing swords with that miscreant?"

"Not in person, to my sorrow. Although I heard that *you* had, Sire. But I have dented his shield, at least! He had been given my castle of Douglas."

"Ha! And now he is the poorer, eh?"

"Yes. He will not sit in my hall again!" Douglas's rather delicate nostrils flared a little as, narrow-eyed, he looked away.

Bruce searched his young friend's face keenly. There was something different about James Douglas. He had been away only some six weeks, but he seemed older by a deal more than that. Somehow, somewhere, those boyishly good-looking features had hardened, set, matured. He held himself differently too, with an assurance and command not formerly evident, to give balance to his eagerness.

"I perceive that you have much to tell me, Jamie," he said, taking the other's arm. "Come you inside. See, we have a roof above us! A table to sit at. Even wine to drink. Not only my Lord of Douglas is fine, this day! Come — tell me this of your castle. And where you got all those stout fellows . . ."

"That I shall, Your Grace. But there is other news that you should hear first, I think. More urgent. You have heard this of Philip Moubray? The dastard who struck you at Methven field. He is now keeper of Stirling Castle, for his treachery."

"I heard. He is moving south, with a sizeable force — 1,000, they say — to drive me into Pembroke's arms. If he can!"

"He was, Sire — he was. No longer is."

Bruce paused in the ascent of the stairway.

"By this, Sire, he may well be back at Stirling — since, to my sorrow I could not win at him, slay him. But he has few of his thousand with him, that I promise you!"

"You clashed with them, Jamie? *You* did?"

"If you, with 300, could rout 3,000 at Glen Trool — then I, with the same number, was not to shy from 1,000, on my own Douglas moors?"

"Not 3,000. Half that." The other stroked his chin. "Go on."

"It was last night. We were on our way here, by the Douglas Rig pass over Cairntable, when herds of mine brought us word that Moubray had come up from Bothwell and was camped in Kennox Water, making for the Shire Stone pass over to Cummock — only a few miles east of our route. It seems that he did not know that Douglas was back in Douglasdale! I waited for full darkness, then crossed the heather of Dryrigs and Kennoxhead, and attacked him from two sides, in his valley, without warning. While still he slept. As . . . as Your Grace taught me!"

"Aye." Grimly the King inclined his head. "That is the style of us, this year of grace! And you had them?"

"We had them. Some escaped, with Moubray. But not many."

Bruce touched the younger man's arm. "God forgive me that I must teach my friends in such school as this," he said. "I, who knighted you!"

Douglas raised a laugh, if a harsh one. "I did better than that at Douglas Castle!" he said.

"You did?" The King glanced back at Gilbert Hay and Neil Campbell, who, listening, were following them up the stairs. "Perhaps you should tell us here, Jamie. I have a visitor in the hall. A priest. Is your tale one for priestly ears? I would not have this one esteem us too ill!"

"Does any whey-faced clerk's esteem concern us, in this pass?" Campbell asked.

"I think it might do, yes. This once."

So, there in the narrow, dark stairway, Douglas told them stiffly, jerkily.

"When I left you that day, I came secretly to Douglasdale, by night. To find evil. Beyond telling. King Edward had given my lands and house to Clifford. My people were ground down. Harried, slaughtered, raped. What he and his creatures had done to fair Douglasdale! I counted thirty bodies, women and bairns amongst them, hanging in one wood. *My* people."

None spoke, as he paused.

"I understood then, Sire, what you had meant. When you spoke me that night at Turnberry. I saw how much honour meant, and the knightly code! In war. I vowed vengeance. For my poor folk. And took it."

The King gazed down at his feet. "It is need, sheer necessity, and expediency, that I preach, Jamie—not vengeance," he said.

The other might not have heard him. "Despite their savagery, these English were godly men, it seemed! Of a Sunday, they filled the Kirk of Saint Bride, at Douglas, it was said. Two days after I reached Douglas it was Palm Sunday. Tom Dickson, my steward, said he would attend Mass that day. With others. If there was room for them, with all the English. I said that I was less nice, and would wait outside. The garrison marched out, from the castle—a notable sight. A few of us watched them, from hiding. In the midst of the service, Dickson and his good fellows rose, and drew their steel, hidden till then. We rushed the door from without. We... we let none escape. Of the English. Save only their priest."

Bruce nodded. "I had a notion that this might not suit priestly ears!"

"Dickson died there. And others," Douglas went on, flat-voiced. "We went back to the castle. They had left it but little guarded. Even the drawbridge was down. With loads of hay for their beasts, we gained entrance, none suspecting. Said the captain had commanded it. Then we turned on them. It was easy enough. They had left a feast preparing. For Palm Sunday. For all the garrison. Such of my folk as were left in Douglas were near to starvation. I summoned all to the castle. To partake, with us. Before they left. For all must go. None could remain in Douglasdale after that. I took them away, into the Lowther Hills, to distant villages and shielings. They would have had me stay, to be sure. To hold the castle. But my place is with you, Sire, I told them. Aye, and I told them that

I had rather hear the lark sing than the mouse squeak. This you had taught me also — that holding castles is not for us."

"So you left your house again, Jamie? That must have hurt sorely. Even in your father's best armour!"

"I left my house, yes. My people took all they might carry that would not delay them. Then all else we took and piled high. In the Great Hall and the Lesser Hall, in the Armoury, the kitchens, in every room. In the gatehouse and every tower and watch-chamber. In the inner and outer baileys. The English had stocked Douglas well — stolen from better men. We took it all, meat and meal, fish and fowl, fodder and bedding. Every stick and stitch of plenishing and furnishing. Every beast that the folk might not take, in their haste, we slew and piled atop — cattle, sheep, swine, even some horses. And atop of these we put the Englishmen, Clifford's captain highest, with his cook. And fired all. Oil and fat there was in plenty, to aid the flames. Douglas burned well. For three hours we could see the smoke of my house, as we led the folk eastwards into the hills. Douglas's larder, they named it!"

For long moments after he had finished, none found words.

"Am I not, Sire, your most apt pupil?" the youngest of them grated at length.

The King reached out to grip his steel-clad shoulder, and then turned to renew the ascent of those stairs.

James Douglas did not avail himself of the Holy Sacrament, after his monarch, that night.

* * *

Bruce sat his horse, fretting — the same fine stallion which had been Clifford's and which Douglas had insisted his liege lord must use, along with the magnificent armour from Douglas Castle. He had schooled himself to patience and waiting, in his long struggle; but hitherto it had been waiting for battle to commence, then action. But this May morning it was a greater, sorer test — to sit, inactive, watching, while battle actually raged, battle on a scale unseen in Scotland since Methven, or Falkirk.

That was the point. This was battle, not raid, skirmish, ambush and the like. And he playing general today, not swordsman, warrior, even captain. As he had planned this, his place was here, on the high ground of Loudoun Hill, watching, a spectator. Not even directing — for it was past that stage. There might be work for him, and the small body of men who sat their horses behind him and Hay, some four-score mosstroopers as fretful as himself; but not now.

It was foolish to compare this with Falkirk in especial, where

King Edward had had so many scores of thousands that he could not bring them all to bear. Here there were only some 5,000 men involved altogether — for it was but the van of Pembroke's great army that was engaged, admittedly the cream of English chivalry, but no more than 3,000 in number, it was thought. And 800 or so flanking infantry, running at either side — MacDougall of Lorn's Highlanders, sent south in haste. His own force, though the greatest he had commanded since Methven, was but 1,200 all told.

Nevertheless, this was set battle, something that Bruce had set his face against, until now. And still would have avoided. But Pembroke, galled and frustrated by pin-prick defeats and his master's wrath, had issued a public challenge. He challenged the so-called King of Scots to stand, to act the man, the soldier, the knight, not the cut-throat brigand, to meet him in fair fight, and see how puissant he was then. All over the land this challenge had been trumpeted. Bruce was fighting a battle for his people's minds, as well as this physical warfare of flesh and steel. For that long-term and more abstract advantage, he felt that he must accept this English gesture, for once at least. And had chosen this Loudoun Hill, carefully, for his battle-ground, where Pembroke must pass.

All night they had worked, busy indeed, digging, cutting, carrying, the King labouring with the others. So that now, with battle joined, he could sit there, high above it all, with the morning sun streaming at his back, playing general, the King — and hating it.

Not that the battle was quite joined yet. Pembroke, the sun in his eyes, and riding slightly uphill at that, had formed his 3,000 into two great lines, with MacDougall's Lornmen racing along on the flanks. The van, with de Valence's own banner, blue and white with red martlets, flying beside the Leopards of England in the centre, charging forward shoulder to shoulder, at an earth-shaking canter, the fastest pace such heavily-armoured cavalry could achieve, in a blaze of colour and brilliance. Behind them, a quarter-mile back, the second line followed, meantime at a quiet trot, below Percy's standard. Gloucester, with the main English infantry, should have been behind that again — but Bruce, by a series of feints and stratagems, had delayed the great body of foot coming through the hill passes, and they were still miles off.

Facing Pembroke's charging threat, below in the level grassy ground that flanked the road — the main road, by the Irvine's valley, from Ayr to the east and north — 600 Ayrshire spearmen were drawn up, waiting in three schiltroms, or boxes, their friezes of pikes projecting like hedgehogs' quills. However sure and disciplined they appeared, their inadequacy in numbers was direly apparent. Jamie's silken Douglas banner flew over the central formation. Boyd and Fleming commanded on either side of him. The rest of Bruce's people, apart from his own group standing there on the hill, were disposed in no such tidy or military formations on the two flanks. They looked something of a rabble indeed, all foot — for these flanks were no place for horses, even moss-troopers' garrons. Edward commanded on the right with 300; Campbell with 200 on the left, the cateran Islesmen amongst them. Their ragged ranks seethed and were never still — for the best of reasons. Few of them stood on ground firm enough to hold them up for more than a few seconds.

Bruce, an Ayrshire man himself, had selected this battlefield after much thought. Pembroke, from Ayr Castle, had challenged the Scots to meet him, if they dared, at or on his way to Bothwell, in Lanarkshire, where he was to hold a conference of English local governors and sheriffs — no doubt to deal with the rising loyalist tide. The vale of the River Irvine, through which his route threaded, tailed out into the side of this Loudoun Hill, and thereafter the road climbed to cross high open barren moorland for many miles. Heedfully he had chosen. The ground below him was flat for some distance, open, and covered with fine sheep-cropped turf, ideal for cavalry. And broad, fully 800 yards of it, from the western approach on either side of the road. But this pleasing stretch was set between two peat-bogs of black and green treachery and great extent, plain for all to see. What was not so plain, at least from the lower ground, the west, was that the firm ground in fact narrowed, not dramatically but steadily eastwards; so that, where the three schiltroms were sited, there was not 800 but barely 500 yards between the quaking margins. And there was still more to the site than that — blistered hands and aching backs testified to it, that morning. Stretching from side to side across it, at hundred-yard intervals, deep and wide trenches had been dug — and then covered over lightly with scrub and branches thatched with turf. At a distance of more than a few yards these were practically indiscernible.

That front line of charging knightly might was a sight both to stir and strike terror.

Its ruin and disintegration was a shocking thing to watch, even for those it menaced. At first, only the keenest and most experienced eye could have perceived that something was amiss, as the extreme ends of the long line began to be forced inwards. In a charge of heavy cavalry, already close-packed, any major constriction can swiftly lead to trouble. The fine level front began to buckle and bend. At that pace and impetus it was not easy for the tight-knit ranks to give, to find room for their colleagues being pressed in on them. As a result, many on the flanks could neither draw up nor in, and were forced to hurtle on into the soft peat-moss—with immediate disaster. And along the line generally the enforced huddling together at speed began to tell, and there was some collision, horses and riders overthrown, with others crashing over them. And steadily the firm ground narrowed.

De Valence of course did not fail to see the danger, and the remedy. His trumpets sounded and his captains waved back the flanks desperately, to turn the advance from a straight line into a wide wedge, a great spear-head. At a thundering charge this, though simple in theory, was no easy manoeuvre to accomplish, with 1,500 men involved; but these were superbly trained and disciplined cavalry, perhaps the finest in Christendom, and the difficult adjustment began to take shape, although not without losses.

It was just as this transformation was taking place that the centre of the line reached the first of the covered trenches. Perhaps Pembroke and his leaders, had they been less preoccupied with changing their formation, might have perceived the slightly artificial appearance of the ground immediately ahead, carefully as the Scots had sought to camouflage it. As it was, they crashed into the trap headlong, and into utter chaos. The ground gave way beneath the heavy chargers' hooves, and down in hurtling ruin the flower of English chivalry fell, in a storm of flailing and breaking limbs, clashing armour and the screams of men and beasts.

Those ditches were a score of feet wide and a dozen feet deep. There was no jumping them or avoiding them, and with the impetus of the advance and the weight behind, no drawing back. Had it not been for the bodies piling in and filling up the gap, thus forming bridges, few would have got across.

As it was, probably more than half the van did win over that grim obstacle, in some fashion and in dire disorder. But it was the major leadership that had taken the brunt of it, and so lay lowest. Only the lesser knights and captains found themselves left to take command. That they led the survivors in only slightly abated attack, said much for their nerve and spirit. But it was a ragged charge now.

In only a hundred yards, of course, and in inevitable impairment as a fighting force, they hit the second trench. Complete confusion reigned, and all forward movement ceased.

Throughout, MacDougall's Highlanders had been leaping and bounding, light-footed, amongst the bogs and mosses on either side, Edward's and Campbell's motley companies awaiting them. At sight of the ruin befalling their main host, they faltered somewhat.

But they were fearless fighters, and pressed on, if with less assurance. In the slaistering mire of green slime and black peat-broth, they clashed with their own fellow-countrymen in fierce hand-to-hand fighting.

"Now, Sire — now!" Gilbert Hay cried, at Bruce's side. "Down on them now, and we shall have them before their rear comes up."

"No," the King said shortly. "Our horses would be of no more avail down there than are their own. Amongst the trenches or the bogs. Wait. The others know their tasks."

It was evident that none of the van was in fact going to get as far as the third trench, and therefore the schiltroms. For now, between the ditches, Edward's and Campbell's men were breaking off their contests with the MacDougalls and streaming in amongst the milling and disorganised cavalry and dismounted riders. James Douglas was breaking up the central schiltrom and sending its 200 men off round the flanks to assist in dealing with the MacDougalls. They cast away their pikes in favour of swords and dirks as they ran. The other two formations stood unmoving meantime, like their monarch above.

Possibly that steady waiting contributed something to the battle, nevertheless. The sight of it may have been the last straw, the final influence to convince the enemy, the van at least, that the day was without profit. At any rate, the tide turned — and once turned became a flood. In only a few moments, all who could escape were surging back. Many were unable to cross the horror of that first ditch, and fell to the Scots swords there. But the majority went streaming westwards.

And because the bogs restricted them to the firm ground, the horde of fleeing men and beasts could not do other than come into headlong confusion with the still advancing second line, under the Lord Percy. Perhaps with another leader the day might yet have been saved — for this reserve host still outnumbered the Scots. But Henry Percy was a cautious man, more of a schemer and administrator than a soldier. The sight of the disaster ahead, the still unblooded Scots schiltroms beyond those ghastly trenches, and the panic effect of the fleeing men on his own ranks and consequent disorder, decided him. His trumpets sounded the retiral.

After that it was devil take the hindmost. The Lornmen on the flanks saw themselves deserted, and broke away, to escape if they might through the morass. There was only the fighting of individuals, selling their lives dearly. Flight and pursuit were the order of the day. Bruce and his four-score remained unemployed, unnecessary.

"God's mercy — a victory, Sire! A victory!" Hay exclaimed. "Of a sort!" He sounded less than elated. "And we have not struck a blow!"

The King drew a great breath. "A victory, yes. A victory, not of arms and skill and courage, but of low cunning. Another brigand's victory, Gibbie. My answer to Pembroke's challenge. But ... I thank God for it, nevertheless. One day, perhaps, we will fight these English in the field, man to man, and beat them fairly. But that day is not yet — not for long. Come — we will go down and see if we can find de Valence. At least I have wiped out the shame of Methven. When he struck *us* by night ..."

They did not find the earl amongst the slain. Someone said that he had been seen clambering out of that first trench, known by the blue-and-white of his handsome surcoat and helmet plumes, limp in his heavy armour to find a riderless horse, and ride back and away. Some notable men were amongst the dead, and more would be deep under the bodies in that ditch. None appeared to be amongst those with whom Bruce had personal accounts to settle. A report did spoil the muted triumph of the victory — the fact that more than one had seen his own nephew, Sir Thomas Randolph, his mother's grandson by her first husband, prominent in the English van, easily identified by his great height, as well as his arms and colours. He had been taken prisoner at Methven, and ransomed, one of the very few spared by King Edward. Now it was to be seen why.

Bruce gave orders to stop all pursuit of the fleeing enemy. The Earl of Gloucester, with the main body of English infantry from Galloway, was not far away. They were not finished yet. If these could be kept from joining Percy ...

The hunting-horn sounded the recall, and reassembly.

Edward Bruce was, as ever, one of the last in. "We have them running!" he cried. "Running like whipped curs! Now they know who is master in Scotland!"

"Master, brother?" the King asked. "I am not yet master of this my own Ayrshire! And Ayrshire is but one county of Scotland. We have met the English in one field, and prevailed. By our wits. That is all. And Edward Plantagenet sits at Carlisle and musters his hundreds of thousands. Let us never forget that man — for he will not forget us!"

"He is dying ..."

"I should still fear Edward, even were he dead! Such hatred will survive even the grave, I do believe ..."

Chapter Ten

Almost against his better judgement Bruce was besieging the town and castle of Ayr — after a fashion. It was rather ridiculous in fact, with the numbers of properly armed and disciplined men he had at his disposal, and with no sort of siege equipment. But both the English themselves and his own subjects seemed to expect it, and he was in something of a quandary as to what to do next, anyway. So he made pretence of encircling Ayr — and was ready to be up and away at short notice.

After Loudoun Hill he had managed to trap his cousin's husband Ralph de Monthermer, Earl of Gloucester, and the mass of English infantry — the same who had timeously sent him the spurs and the shilling that night in London a year and more before, and so undoubtedly saved his life from Comyn's betrayal and Edward's vengeance. There, in the hills behind Cumnock, there had been a great slaughter, by night, when the English and Welsh archers could not see to draw on their foes. The darkness had aided escape also, of course, and Gloucester himself, with large numbers of his force, had fled here to Ayr, to join Percy therein. Pembroke had apparently fled from Loudoun Hill in the other direction, for Bothwell. But Clifford, somewhat in disgrace no doubt, had been bringing up the English rear and baggage, from Minnigaff and the Cree, and getting word of Gloucester's disaster, had avoided all engagement and likewise made hurriedly for Ayr. So that there was now a large if somewhat demoralised force in the town, many thousands strong, including two of Bruce's chiefest foes.

But there was more than these in Ayr. There were some thousands of townsfolk, as well as men thronging there from all Carrick, Kyle and Cunninghame. Their King's victories, small as they were, at last were beginning to rouse the people, to give them hope, to stir up young men to join their liege lord in arms. The hostility of these, with the citizenry, undoubtedly preoccupied the invaders, and added to the siege-like atmosphere.

Indeed daily the numbers of Bruce's force increased hearteningly. Few great men as yet committed themselves — although with so many of these dead, prisoners or in exile, this was scarcely to be wondered at; while many had always been in the Comyn camp. But the sons of this laird or that, with a dozen or a score of men, variously armed, came riding in every day, as well as great crowds of masterless common folk. Feeding, marshalling and controlling these was an ever-growing problem, and took up much of the time of Bruce and his little band of lieutenants. That this could better be achieved in the fertile and populous lowlands surrounding Ayr, than in the wilderness where he would have preferred to be, was another reason why the King lingered, though warily, in his sham siege — while he kept his rear free for quick retiral into the hills.

He had taken up his residence, meantime, in his cousin Christian of Carrick's house of Newton-upon-Ayr, Turnberry still being held strongly against him, and was able to live in more comfort than he had known for long. It was pleasant, of an evening, to dine well here, and to contemplate Clifford and Percy, only a mile or two away, tightening their belts — for food was known to be getting very scarce in Ayr's citadel these June days — although undoubtedly those two would be the last to starve.

It was in such frame of mind that Bruce and his companions, after a long day trying to lick into shape the heterogeneous collection of volunteers, lounged in the Lady Christian's apple-orchard, when the look-out from the tower's parapet shouted that ships were appearing from around the Heads of Ayr, to the south, many ships. Cursing, all lethargy banished in an instant, the King was up and running for the tower-door. This had been one of his fears — that King Edward might send up relief and reinforcements by sea to his beleaguered minions at Aye. His bastard, Sir John de Botetourt, it was said, had developed a taste for seafaring, these days, and had earlier been savaging the Clyde ports and havens in a campaign of sheer piracy and plunder — a truer son of his father than was Edward, Prince of Wales.

When Bruce reached the high parapet, however, with the watch shouting that it was a great fleet, it was to know something of relief, at any rate.

"Those are galleys, man!" he cried. "Highland galleys — not English ships."

The watch, who had not said that they were English, wisely held his peace.

The King's relief was only partial. There were fully twenty large galleys out there, their hundreds of oars flashing with rhythmic motion as they caught the light of the sinking sun. Whose they were was not apparent. Not many Highland chiefs could muster such a fleet — but two who could were MacDougall of Lorn and the Earl of Ross.

Then, as the leading vessels turned directly into the bay, and their great square sails bellied to the westerly breeze, the vivid emblem of the Black Galley of the Isles stood out clear on each, undifferenced, unmistakable.

"Angus Og!" Bruce exclaimed. "Thank God it is he! Whatever may bring him here. Jamie! Neil! Down to the boat-strand with you. To wave them in. In case they make for the harbour. Take my banner." The English still held Ayr's harbour, dominated by the castle. "If it is Angus Og himself, pay him all respect. And bid him here, to me."

So presently, heralded by the shrill music of strutting, blowing pipers, a colourful company came up the north side of the River Ayr, across the water from the town proper, kenspeckle in saffrons and tartans, horned helmets and eagles' feathers, piebald calfskins and gleaming Celtic jewellery. Bruce awaited them before his cousin's gatehouse.

Angus Og, in full war panoply, and flanked by an almost overwhelming phalanx of chieftains in barbaric splendour, stalked in front — and he at least was smiling.

As they came up, James Douglas at his side, raised hand and voice. "Sire — here is the noble Angus Og MacDonald, Lord of the Isles . . ."

His words were drowned in the blast of a horn, and a much more powerful voice followed it, to shout "Angus, son of Angus son of Ranald, son of Somerled the Great, of Islay, King of the Isles and Lord of Kintyre. To Robert, King of Scots, greeting!"

Bruce swallowed. So they were back to that, again! But he smiled also — and when Robert Bruce smiled, the stern graven lines, in which his features had set these days, were transformed quite. He stepped forward, hands out.

"My lord and good friend Angus!" he said. "I rejoice to see you."

The other came to meet him, and they gripped hands and clasped shoulders, as equals and comrades-in-arms rather than as monarch and subject.

"I salute you, King Robert," he returned. "Here is a day to remember. Seannachies will sing of it."

"You say so?" Bruce blinked. "Then I am glad. You have brought news?"

"I have brought myself, and mine." That was simply said. "News enough, I would think."

"M'mm. Yes. To be sure. And you are welcome, my lord. All of you."

Angus Og did not actually frown, but his open boyish though swarthy face stiffened. "I am glad that I am welcome, sir. I had not expected otherwise, with one thousand broadswords!"

"I' faith — you mean . . .?"

"I mean, Sir Robert, that I am come to make cause with you. Against our enemies. With a score of galleys, two score chieftains and a thousand men. Straight from Ireland I have come."

"By the Rude — do I hear aright?" The King did not attempt to hide his surprise. "You have come to fight? Angus of the Isles joins my host . . .?"

"He comes to *aid* your host, shall we say?"

The other was not concerned to split hairs over the definition, there and then. He gripped the Highlander's arm. "Here is a great, notable day indeed. You have changed your mind, my friend, since that day at Rathlin Island?"

"You have changed it for me, Sir King. At Rathlin, I said that I would war with Edward of England for my own hand and in my own time. *Your* cause was scarcely hopeful. You have made it otherwise, these last months. The Glens of Antrim are not so far away that I have not heard of your doings. I have come to make your war mine. I have matters to settle with the English and their friends, over that sorry business at Stranraer. When your brothers were defeated. Many of the men slain then were mine, hired to you. Murdered, after the battle. And my friend, Malcolm MacQuillan, Prince of Antrim, beheaded. We can settle these scores together, you and I."

"So-o-o! Here then is the most sure sign of belief in my final victory, I swear! Of any I have received. That Angus Og should deem it prudent, worth his while to support me!"

If the Islesman sensed criticism in that, he did not say so. "Even so, it could be that I erred. Deemed wrongly," he said. "You are going to need my support sooner than I thought. As we came up the firth we spied and ran down an English craft, making for Wigtown Bay and the Cree. It bore couriers. Edward the King marches. Edward is on his way."

"What!"

"We took his messengers. With orders for Pembroke, Botetourt and the rest. Edward has risen from his sick-bed. He has given his travelling-litter to the cathedral at Carlisle, as a thank-offering for recovery, and mounted his war-horse again. He leads a host of 200,000, for the Border. To wipe Robert Bruce off the face of this Scotland!"

Stricken to silence, the King looked at him.

"I near thought again, as to joining you, then," Angus Og added, grimly. "But here I am."

"He is on his way? Now? He could be in Scotland by this?"

"Scarce so fast. It was at noon today we took his vessel. It had sailed from the port of Silloth only at first light. Edward was then making for the fords of Solway."

"Then we have a little time. To get away from Ayr. Into the high hills. It is back to the mountains with us. But tomorrow's dawn will serve. I will give orders for all to be ready to move with daylight. To a place where Edward cannot reach us. God's curse on the man — his spleen is as good as life to him! Will I never be free from his malice?"

The other shrugged. "He will die one day."

"His body, yes. But will his hate? Such all-consuming bitterness . . .?" Bruce drew himself up. "But, my sorrow that I should hold you standing here, my lord. You and yours. Come — this is my cousin's house. But she keeps a good table. Tonight we can still take our ease. And tomorrow, march. What will you do with your galleys, friend?"

"Send them across to the Isle of Bute. To the old Steward, at Rothesay. They can await my summons there . . ."

* * *

It was two weeks later, in the lofty lonely hills around Loch Doon again, on the Galloway border, before Bruce gained sure news of Edward, news that he could trust. Every spy and scout reported tales and rumours, not only his own but his various commanders' scouts — for the Scots host was now split up, inevitably, since none of these high narrow valleys could contain and support large numbers, and the royal force now totalled nearly 4,000. The tales said that King Edward was here, or there, making for the East March, or Edinburgh, or Galloway, or even returned to Carlisle. Pembroke, it was known, had come back to Ayr, with a Comyn army plus more MacDougalls; while Botetourt was lying off the coast, with shipping.

It was, as so often was the case, a friar who brought firm tidings — for, because of their cloth, these could move about the country more freely than other men, and their Orders were international. This one, a Benedictine, came to Bruce in his cave above Loch Doon — the same in which he had watched and taken heart from the spider — where he and Angus Og, Neil Campbell and one or two others who were not off with detached commands, sat round a crackling log fire and grilled venison steaks on spikes. He announced that he came from the Abbey of Melrose, across the Forest of Ettrick, sent by Master Nicholas Balmyle.

"The King of England is dead, Sire," he declared. "Edward is no more!"

Bruce laid down his steak carefully, features schooled, expressionless, and slowly rose to his feet. All around him men held their breaths. "Say that again, Master Friar," he got out, thickly. "And speak truth, if you value your soul!"

"It is verily so, Your Grace. Master Nicholas had the word direct from Carlisle. Sent by a canon there, who is kin to him. King Edward the First is dead. And his son proclaimed King Edward the Second."

Bruce's face worked strangely. Then abruptly he turned and stalked away, out of the cave-mouth. A babble of excited talk rose behind him.

It was a minute or two before he returned. "Your pardon, Sir Friar," he said. "Your news affected me. Have they offered you meat, drink, after your journey? Sit at ease, while you tell me all that you know."

"He died, Sire, at Burgh-on-Sands, but eight miles north of Carlisle. Still on English soil, making for the fords across the Solway sands, with his mighty host. He breathed his last, they say, facing Scotland. And cursing it."

Silent, the King nodded.

"His bile was stronger than his body," Angus Og said. "His black heart could not carry the weight of him, in armour and a-horse, after his sickness. He had too much blood, all men knew!"

"Yes, lord. But, as we were told, it was the news of Loudoun Hill, of King Robert's victory, that struck him down, rather than the journeying. He was stricken with an apoplexy."

A sort of choking groan came from Bruce. "So . . . so *I* killed Edward! In the end, I killed him."

None remarked on that.

"He recovered his wits before the end," the friar went on, eyeing the King doubtfully. "The Prince of Wales was summoned to his side. As was the Bishop of Carlisle — who told it to this canon. King Edward charged his son straitly. He caused him to swear an oath, to God and all His saints, in the presence of his lords and barons. That he would continue the fight to the death against the Scots. That he should not rest until he had brought down Robert Bruce to the dust, to die a felon's death. As had his brothers and the man Wallace."

Only the crackle and hiss of the fire made comment.

The speaker, a dark, youngish man, moistened his lips, his glance darting around uneasily. But he forced himself to go on.

"Further, the King required the Prince to promise that so soon as the breath was departed from his body, he would take that body and boil it in a great cauldron. Boil it until the flesh was separate quite from the bones. The flesh could be buried, where mattered not. But not the bones. These his son was to carry with him against Scotland, then and thereafter. To remain with him, night and day. And as so often as the Scots might in insolence rise in rebellion against England, he should assemble his fullest strength, and carry the bones against them. Not to be buried or laid to rest until that contumacious nation was totally subdued." The friar swallowed. "Only then did Edward Plantagenet yield up the ghost."

A long quivering sigh escaped from Robert Bruce's lips. It was many seconds before he spoke, none venturing to precede him. "Edward!" he said, almost whispering. "Edward — who once loved me as a son, he said! God pity him. God pity me, also! His mercy on that tortured soul — as on my own. I see it all. The knife turned in his heart. Satan laid his dark hands on each of us! Damnation — before the Day of Judgement!"

"Do not say it, Sire." That was Neil Campbell, harshly. "Edward is dead. The manner of his going matters nothing. We should be rejoicing, not glooming dark thoughts."

"He is right," Angus Og agreed. "No profit in such. Your chiefest enemy is no more. Thank God for it, and be done!"

Bruce eyed them, almost as though they had been strangers. "Little you know," he said. Then he shrugged. "Very well, my friends. Edward is dead. But Edward's might and his armies remain, his commands and his commanders. And his son. What of Edward the Second?"

"The word from Carlisle, Sire, is that the new King has a mind of his own. He has not obeyed his father over the boiling and the bones, oath or none. He is sending the old King's body back to Westminster for due and decent burial."

"Ha — he is? So that is the style of him! I' faith — he has long lacked love for his father. But never dared to show it, until now!"

"He has summoned all his barons and lords spiritual and temporal to come pay him fealty, at Carlisle, forthwith. Already he has made new appointments . . ."

"Aye, no doubt. But what of Scotland? What does he say of Scotland?"

"He has likewise summoned all Scots lords and landed men to come and do him homage. At Dumfries. Before this month is out. On pain of forfeiture."

"So! In this at least he is his father's son! What of his army?"

"Some of it he has already sent across Solway, it is said. They are marshalled on Your Grace's lands of Annon."

"Aye! They would be! The war, then, goes on, Edward living or Edward dead! To be sure, the son would have little choice in that.

All England is set to bring down Scotland. His lords will force him to go on with it, even should he lack the will."

"As to will or no, already he has appointed a new commander and Viceroy. In place of the Earl of Pembroke. The Lord John of Brittany, Earl of Richmond, his own cousin."

"You say so? John of Brittany again — that sour pedant! Aye, they were ever friends. So Pembroke is disgraced?"

"You have hit him hard, Sire," Campbell put in. "Caused him many defeats. Made him look a fool."

"Yet he is no fool. And a better soldier than ever John of Brittany will be — who indeed is no soldier at all. Which we must seek to turn to our advantage. All this will require much thought. Have you any other news for us, Master Friar?"

"Master Balmyle said to tell Your Grace that the King, the new King, has already put the Prince Bishop of Durham, Anthony Beck, from his Court. And is very close with John Stratford Bishop of Winchester — who is an old friend of the Bishop of St. Andrews."

"Good! Good — that may bring some easement to my friend Lamberton. You will thank Master Balmyle for all these tidings. I shall not forget his good offices. He will have heard that the old Bishop of Dunblane has died. Tell him it will be my endeavour to see that he is elected in his place. And you also, my friend, I shall not forget. You have earned my gratitude. Your name . . .?"

"Bernard, Sire. Bernard de Linton. From Mordington, in the Merse."

"Then I thank you, Brother Bernard. One day I shall need able and trustworthy clerks . . ."

The friar withdrawn, Angus Og spoke. "Fair tidings in the main, Sir King. What do you do now?"

"Nothing, friend. We wait. For Edward of Carnarvon. To see what *he* will do. He has still 200,000 men in arms. Not fifty miles away. To our 4,000. Besides many nearer still. In that respect little has changed. The English are still the English. Only now they are led by a weak man, not a strong."

"It may be so. But I did not come here to wait, to sit idly in these hills," the Lord of the Isles pointed out. "My broadswords like nothing less than rusting in their sheaths! My galleys are not for gathering barnacles in creeks of Bute. I came to fight. And I have debts to pay."

"You shall have your fighting, my lord, never fear! Your bellyful! But not yet. I do not wish to force the new Edward's hand. He is no warrior — but he commands many of the finest warriors in Christendom. We shall await to see what he does with them. He is concerned now with homage-taking, not fighting, it seems. Let him have it, then. That will do us no hurt. And we shall see how many Scots lords hurry to kiss his hand at Dumfries. That will interest me, see you!"

"If few do, Sire — then he must needs march north," Campbell declared. "He cannot sit idle, after summoning them on pain of treason and forfeiture."

Bruce nodded. "That is as I see it. We will wait till then. Meantime gathering our strength . . ."

"In my country, one does not gather strength by waiting but by smiting!" the Islesman asserted strongly. "*I* do not wait patiently, to pay my debts."

"These debts, my lord . . .?"

"In Galloway. The MacDoualls. Five hundred of my men died shamefully at their hands. Time they were avenged."

This was obviously a large part of Angus Og's reason for aligning himself with them. "Aye. But I too have debts to pay in Galloway. Two brothers sent to Edward, to die! Think you I have forgotten, man? But I choose *my* time when to pay my debts. See you, Angus my friend, if we go raiding into Galloway now, not only do we provoke the English into action, but we cut ourselves off from the rest of Scotland. They could box us up in Galloway."

"My galleys could lift us out, by sea."

"Not 4,000 and more. When I punish Galloway, I shall do it in force. So that the MacDoualls will not forget. It will be no hurried raid. But . . . I will make you a promise. Hold your hand until the English show what they will do. And then, if we can be free of them for a space, I will come with you to Galloway. I want your thousand men close to my hand."

Angus Og shrugged.

PART TWO

CHAPTER ELEVEN

ROBERT BRUCE lay on his back and gazed up at the cobweb-hung rafters of the roof. It was a poor way to pass Yuletide, and a poor place — even though, in a fashion, the house was his own. Did that make it easier? He was long past caring greatly where he laid his head, or how lowly his couch — but this Mill of Urie was cold, draughty and moreover bug-infested. He was all too well aware of all three imperfections.

He lay still, however, motionless — apart from the frequent uncontrollable shivering, that is — not even allowing himself to scratch at the bug-bites. Though these were a minor irritation, compared with the other sores and grievous itching. He forced himself to forbear, not so much because the friar had advised it — he was not the man to set store by the instructions of any mumbling physician, however holy — but partly as a discipline for himself, and partly because he found that the least movement, the rubbing of the plaids that covered him, on his sores set them itching beyond all bearing. There were so many of them, his entire skin a red and angry patchwork, dry and flaking.

It required no little effort to hold himself still, not only on account of the itch and the cold, but because of the febrile restlessness that possessed every muscle of his body, urging him to toss and twist and jerk; but he did not cease to tell himself that if he could master his unruly spirit and errant emotions, and hoped to master a kingdom, then he could surely hold his body still. So he lay, as he had lain for seemingly endless days and nights.

No doubt he had been foolish. The sickness had first struck him some weeks before, when he had first reached Aberdeenshire. All of course, including the plaguey old monk, with the undoubtedly wholly unjustified local reputation for healing powers and piety both, that Gibbie had found for him, had urged him to take to his bed there and then. But he had not come all this way into the North to lie in bed and shiver. He had come to show the Comyns, and their allies, who was King in Scotland, up here in their own territory. So he had refused to halt in his Comyn-devastated lordship of the Garioch, to become an invalid, insisting on pressing on, up towards Buchan, to get to grips with John Comyn, Earl thereof, who still called himself High Constable of Scotland, and still was prepared to accept Edward of Carnarvon as Lord Paramount of Scotland rather than recognise Bruce as King — even with his own young wife hanging in a cage on the walls of Berwick Castle. Fevers and foolish weaknesses of the body could and must give place to the imperatives of rule and war. For over two weeks, then, in winter Aberdeenshire, in the great rolling lands of Mar, Cromar, Midmar and Formartin, he had hunted and harried the Comyns, in their enormous outlying domains, latterly carried in a litter. He had done great damage, burned many houses, hanged many men, but fought no battles — for Buchan himself lay infuriatingly low, allegedly in his great and remote castle of Dundarg on the far North Buchan coast, assembling his strength. At length, with no decision achieved, and his own weakness ever growing, shamefully, inexorably, until he was too limp to make more than feeble protest, his brother Edward ever taking more the command, they had brought him back here in his litter to this wretched Mill of Urie beside the burned-out ravaged shell of his castle of Inverurie, messuage-place of the once-great lordship of Garioch, how many days ago he could not tell.

A knock at the rough plank door brought a frown to the man's already set features, but only that. A second knock, and a third, went equally unanswered. He wanted no company, no chattering, fussing, pitying attentions, no gawping witnesses of his helplessness, however sympathetic. But the door opened nevertheless, and Gilbert Hay came in. And for as long as it was possible for that loyal uncomplicated young man to look apologetic, he did.

"Your Grace — the monk is here. Brother Mark," he said. "To attend you. Anoint you and salve your sores . . .'

"No!" the King said.

"But it is time, Sire. Past time, he says. Four times each day, the friar says, it is necessary . . ."

"No!" That was a bark, the voice strong if nothing else was. "Begone!"

Hay retired.

Bruce lay, muttering. It was hard enough to lie still, to master every itching, agonising, shuddering inch of him, without having to put up with fools and hypocrites.

He tried, for the thousandth time, to concentrate his mind on the military situation and its threats. He was direly short of men again, having had to leave James Douglas and fully two-thirds of his total force, to hold the South-West and watch the Border. It had been taking an enormous risk to dare this northern expedition at all, of course — but the Comyn threat had to be met before any progress could be made in Scotland. After spending weeks at Carlisle and Dumfries, holding fealty ceremonies and a parliament, the new King Edward had, in September, made a purely token advance into Scotland, with most of his vast host, perhaps 150,000 men. It had been a triumphant procession rather than any campaign for, since opposition would have been pointless, Bruce had made none, remaining deep in the Loch Doon mountains and restraining his brother Edward and Angus Og both, with difficulty. Moving only a few miles a day, the English had taken weeks even to reach Cumnock in Ayrshire. And there King Edward had halted, held court, made sundry proclamations to the effect that he was satisfied that his realm of Scotland was securely in his peace, knew its master and would hereafter be more kindly governed; and then turned his army round to face the south again, and deserting it, with most of his high nobles, hurried off ahead to far-away London for his coronation, leaving John of Brittany to rule Scotland. In these circumstances, after a brief punitive expedition into Galloway, to fulfil his promise to Angus Og — though it had scarcely satisfied that warrior — Bruce had turned to the North, to show his face and flag to more of his waiting, watching kingdom.

But he had gathered fewer troops on the way than he had hoped for. The English grip on the centre of the land was strong, with all the great fortresses in their control, with large garrisons at Edinburgh, Glasgow, Stirling, Dunfermline and Dundee. It was no part of the King's present intention to fight his way northwards county by county, and he and his small mixed force had had to go by devious ways, holding to the high ground, the marshes and empty areas and avoiding centres of population. This had produced very disappointing recruiting, and with a wet summer, very late harvest and winter approaching, the countrymen had shown little enthusiasm for military adventuring. The Lord of the Isles, disgusted, had been sent off on a parallel northerly course up the West Highland side of the land, to prevent any link-up between the forces of Buchan and MacDougall of Lorn, if possible. So, with only small contingents of men joining him in Perthshire and Angus, Bruce had come across Dee, to the Garioch and the start of the true Comyn country, with no more than 700 men — to find his lordship devastated and almost devoid of the manpower he had hoped to raise there. Few English were up here, but many Comyn bands. Fortunately, here Sir Alexander Fraser of Touch, and his brother had joined the royal array with 300 men; but even so it was a tiny force with which to face the Comyn country. But David, Bishop of Moray, had come south from the Black Isle of Ross to his own diocese of Moray, with a force of Orkneymen. It had been to link up with him that Bruce had pushed on and on, northwards, ill as he was. With Buchan himself keeping his distance at this stage, and Angus Og still not come over from the difficult mountainous terrain he had to traverse in the West, it had been only tip-and-run warfare hitherto, infuriatingly small-scale, time-wasting, with Edward Bruce making most of the running.

Of Bruce's band of close companions, only Gilbert Hay remained here with him at Inverurie, captaining a mere 200 men. Edward, fretting with impatience, had gone with the Frasers to show the King's banner in the coastal areas of Formartin, north of Aberdeen, as much to try to coax Buchan out of his strongholds as anything else. Neil Campbell had left them weeks ago, at Perth, with Angus Og, to slip home to Argyll, to see what the MacDougalls might have done to his patrimony there, and to try to return with a force of Campbells — although he was scarcely hopeful in this, for a Highland chief who deserted his clan territories for a long period, as he had done, could seldom count on much loyal support. Boyd was away recruiting in West Garioch, and Robert Fleming sent ahead northwards to make contact with Bishop David.

How to deal with Buchan himself, of course, was the problem which most agitated Bruce's fevered and at present ineffective mind. John Comyn, Earl of Buchan, in his person, his position and his influence represented the major Scottish threat to the King. That other John Comyn, Lord of Badenoch, had left a young son, and his kinsman, the High Constable, had assumed guardianship, and with it leadership of the greatest family in the land, a family which could field thirty knights and some 10,000 men, without calling on all the many and powerful allies and connections, such as MacDougalls of Lorn, the Earl of Ross and all the many Baliol branches. He had co-operated with the English, even while hating Edward Longshanks who had so shamefully humiliated him at Stracathro years before; how much more so might he be expected to aid Edward of Carnarvon, of whom he was said to approve?

The King had made little headway in his bed-bound strategy, when there was a further knocking at the door. Once more Gilbert Hay stood there.

"Sire," he said, "visitors."

"No."

"But these Your Grace will wish to see. I swear it."

"Be off, man! Think you I do not know my own mind?"

Hay was pushed aside, and Neil Campbell entered the cold and shabby room.

"Lord, Sire — here's a sorry business! I never thought to see you abed at this hour."

The King eyed him sourly, and offered no welcome.

"This sickness — how bad is it? Your stomach is it?" the other demanded. "Nothing that a flagon of *uisge-beatha* will not cure, I vow! Our good Highland spirits. Drive out these vapours, and make you a man again in short time. I have brought many flagons."

"Fool!" Bruce snarled. "Spare me your witless chatter, if that's the style of it! I hope you have brought me more than liquor from Argyll, since you are come? How many men?"

"Four hundred. The most I could raise, in the time. More will follow. MacDougall has borne sorely on my lands, curse him! But I have brought you more than men and *uisge-beatha*, Sire. From the West . . ."

The invalid was no longer listening to him, nor even looking at him. He was gazing past the man's shoulder. Christina MacRuarie stood there, behind, smiling at him.

All his resolutions about non-movement and bodily control were forgotten, as he raised himself on an elbow, to stare.

"Christina!" he panted. "You! How come you here?"

"With Sir Neil, as he says, my lord Robert. Grieving to see you so. I was in Lochaber, where I have lands, when I heard that Sir Neil was back on Lochaweside. I hastened there to gain news of Your Grace, learned that he was returning to your side, and prevailed on him to bring me with him."

Bruce bit his lip. "This is no place for a woman," he muttered.

She looked around her, mouth turning down. "Nor for a man! Any man, least of all a King! More meet for cattle." She came forward to the bedside. "You are not displeased to see me, Robert?"

He gave a jerk to his head, a gesture which might have been variously interpreted, but did not speak.

"I am sorry indeed to find you in this state," the woman went on. "As well that I came, I think. It looks as though I am needed here!"

"I will be well enough. Shortly."

'That we must ensure. But lying in this cold kennel will not help." Christina turned to Hay. "Is this the best you can do for him, Sir Gilbert?"

"He . . . His Grace would have it so," that unfortunate asserted. "The castle is but a burned shell. The steward's house likewise. This mill is the only roofed house left in Inverurie . . ."

"The more reason for making better of it, sir. Not so much as a fire . . .!"

"Let him be," Bruce intervened. "*I* chose this place."

"Then you must have lost your wits as well as your health!" she returned spiritedly. "Any hovel of a cot-house, with a fire and a woman's care, would be better than this. Are you grown men, or bairns?"

The King sank back on his couch, and turned his head away. "I would be alone," he said.

"Yes — leave us alone," the Isleswoman agreed promptly, "My lords — or your mercy, begone!"

The groan of protest from the bed was wasted on all. The two knightly cravens seized the opportunity to escape without delay.

The woman came round to the other side of the bed, to sit on it. "What is your trouble, Robert?" she asked in a different voice. "What has stricken you so? This is not the Robert Bruce I know."

"How can I tell? Some fever. It struck me some weeks back. Soon after Campbell left me. A weakening sickness. I am weak as a child. My joints ache. My skin burns. Yet I am cold, cold."

She put her hand to his clammy brow. "A fever, yes. How strange is your skin! Angry, broken."

"Is it so all over. Chafing, scaling. It near drives me mad!"

"I have never seen the like. Poor Robert — it is a grievous thing. But, 'fore God, this is not the way to mend it! Lying untended in this chill barrack."

"Not untended — the saints pity me! There is an old monk, a friar. One Mark, of Kintore. Reputed hereabouts as a physician. He would dose me every hour with his noxious stews, daub me with stinking brews made from the offal of toads and the like! The man's a pious hypocrite, forby . . ."

"Then we will be quit of him. I will be your physician now. A *cailleach*, my old nurse, taught me much of the art. It is time you were rescued, from monkish and knightly fools both! And from yourself, I think! Let me but restore myself, from my journey, and we shall make a start."

"No need . . ." the King began — but he might as well have spoken to the wind.

Christina MacRuarie was as good as her word, and better. It was not long before she had the invalid out of that millhouse altogether and into a nearby cottage whose occupants presumably got short shrift. Admittedly this was small, little better than a cabin, with earthen floor, turf roof, and walls of smoke-blackened clay; but somehow she had got the place cleaned up, arranged a more comfortable bed, and brought in some simple furnishings from heaven knew where. Moreover it was warm, with a well-doing fire of holly and ash logs.

Bruce, of course, did not admit that this was any great improvement; indeed he complained that the heat made his itch the worse. But that was an error of tactics, for Christina promptly declared that that would soon be put right. He discovered that she intended to wash him down with some salve of her own concocting. No amount of outraged protest had any effect on her — and the deplorable Gibbie Hay, not to mention Neil Campbell who had brought her, not only had deserted him quite but were completely in the woman's pocket.

The sufferer's resistance to this feminine assault on his integrity was vehement, but more vocal than physical. The strength just wasn't there, he discovered — and this was a young woman as vigorous as she was determined and unscrupulous. Neither royal commands nor appeals to her better nature were of any use. Taking shameless advantage of the situation, she stripped him naked and began to wash off the friar's medications from his shrinking body with warm water.

"*Dia* — but you are thin, Robert!" she declared, ignoring all that he was saying. "You are worn down to the bone! This is the work of no sudden sickness. What has happened to you?"

Bruce well knew himself to be in poor shape. Long months of privation, poor feeding, and sleeping out in all weathers had taken their toll. He recognised that his present illness was more probably a result of a general physical run-down, than the other way round.

"I have had little time for growing fat," he told her briefly.

"I know what you have been doing, and how you have been living. Sir Neil has told me much. And the word of your fightings and warfare has not failed to reach even Moidart. But this — this wretchedness of the body speaks of more than hard living. And this of the skin. So dry and red. It is grievous to see . . ."

"Then, of a mercy, cover me up, woman!" he exclaimed. He was acutely embarrassed by this open inspection of his shuddering cringing body. Even though he had lain with her not a few times and they were no strangers to each other's nakedness, to have Christina, or any woman, peering and poking and dabbing at him, was highly distressing, highly unsuitable — and not a little humiliating in the all too obvious feebleness of his shrunken masculinity.

Paying no attention to his requests, she went on with her ministrations. But perhaps she gave him her own comment. "We must make a man of you again," she said. "I swear this is not what I rode all the way from the West to see! Turn over, Robert — turn over."

Her washings and anointings, however to be deplored, at least produced some easing of his itch. Not that he admitted it. And he had to concede that she kept Brother Mark away, indeed kept everybody away. Moreover the food which she brought him presently was incomparably better than any he had been offered for long — not that he had any appetite for it. The fact that she sat by his bed and more or less forced it into him, of course, was cause for legitimate complaint.

In the midst of all this feminine attention, the Earl of Lennox arrived unheralded from the South, with 200 men. Even Christina MacRuarie could not prevent a belted earl from having audience with his monarch, and Bruce was enabled to pour a flood of his troubles into his old friend's ear. Unfortunately Malcolm of Lennox was altogether too much of a gentleman successfully to resist the Isleswoman's methods, and before long found himself on the wrong side of that cot-house door. The King more or less resigned himself to the inevitable.

Nevertheless that night Christina alarmed him in a new and major fashion; first by producing a pile of sheepskins and plaids over and above his own; and then by authoritatively allowing Lennox, Campbell and Hay, and one or two others, to come and say a very brief goodnight before shooing them out again like a henwife with poultry, and shutting the door behind them in remarkably final style. By the light of the flickering log-fire she laid out the sheepskins, one on top of another, on the floor at the side of his bed, and arranged the plaids on top, thereafter proceeding calmly to undress herself. The King eyed all this with mixed feelings; but even so he was quite unprepared when, standing in unabashed, complete and lovely nakedness, she threw back the covers of his own bed, and urged him to move over somewhat as she was coming in beside him meantime. The sick man's protest that he was in no state for haughmagandy or anything of the sort, met with no least response.

Settling in alongside him, she took him in her arms, not fiercely or passionately, but gently, comfortingly, her soft firm shapeliness enfolding him. He held his limbs stiffly — but that was all his reaction.

"You needed a woman once before, Robert," she murmured. "I think you need one again — only differently. The other will come, in time. But now you require some cherishing, some kindliness."

"I am not a child, a babe!" he mumbled, seeking to turn away.

But she held him strongly. And because she lay slightly higher in the bed than he, and her breasts warmly and caressingly encompassed his face, he found it scarcely feasible either to move or complain satisfactorily. Here was a struggle which apparently he did not sufficiently wish to win.

So he lay, and presently even began to relax. Sensing it, she gathered him a little closer, not to smother or constrain him but to soothe and cradle him. Gradually the warmth and smooth strength of her had its way with him, and he felt more at rest than he had done for long.

"Why do you do this?" he asked presently, not very clearly, from the hollow of her bosom.

"Because some woman should. And because of my love for you. One day, perhaps, your Queen will thank me for it!"

At that the man stiffened momentarily, but she calmed and quelled him with hand and voice, almost as a mother might.

"Hush you, hush you," she said. "Your Elizabeth will look for a man, will she not? When she comes back to you? Not a shrivelled gelding. Nor yet a corpse! *She* cannot cherish you. So I shall."

He did not argue the point.

"Have you had news of her? Of her state? Of late."

"Aye. Bishop Lamberton makes shift to send me word when he may. He is warded not far from her, has contrived to visit her. At Burstwick Manor, in Yorkshire. She is held secure, but less hardly than in Edward's days — the old Edward. She is well enough. But . . ." He left the rest unsaid.

"You did not give her a child?"

"Think you our state was such that she would have thanked me for making her pregnant? We have been on the move, hunted or homeless, almost since we were wed."

"She might have thanked you for it now, nevertheless! And your daughter? How is it with her?"

"I do not know. She was held, alone, cut off from all, in London Tower. But Lamberton, though prisoner himself, has some small credit with the new King. He said that he would seek his mercy on the child. I pray God for her, daily. For them both . . ."

"Yes, yes." Again the soothings. "This other Edward is not the mad tyrant that his father was. He will be kinder to a child. Your Marjory will be none the worse — for children throw off these hurts more readily than we fear. It is not good — but all might be worse, see you. One day the sun will shine again for them. And for you." She settled herself more comfortably, stroking the back of his head. "But now, rest you. Sleep. Is the itch troubling you?"

"Aye. But not as it was. I can thole that. It is the itch in my mind that irks me most. So much to be done, while I lie here helpless . . ."

"Never fear but we will put that to rights. We have made a start to it. You are not shuddering and trembling now, at least. You are no longer cold, Robert?"

"*I* am not. But I cannot forget those who are. My sister Mary. And Isobel of Buchan. In their cages on Berwick and Roxburgh walls. In this winter cold. For my fault. I dream of them, hanging there. Weak women . . ."

"Women, I vow, will survive the like better than most men," she asserted. "We are none so fragile a tribe! But think no more of it now. Be at peace. Sleep."

But he had to get it out, now that he had someone to tell, someone with whom he did not have to maintain a pose of royal reserve and confidence. He poured it out, all the bottled-up agitation and concern which had been racking his mind as he lay helpless. He told her of the nagging guilt of his brothers' deaths; his fears of his surviving brother Edward's headstrong violence, excellent cavalry commander as he was; his disappointment that still no great men and no really large numbers were rallying to his banner — even the powerful Lennox had only been able to gather his paltry 200. He had money to purchase support, thanks to the Church — but still men held back. He told her of his fears that young James Douglas, in whose care he had left the South-West, would not be experienced enough, or strong enough, to hold it. He told of his own recurring doubts and near despair — but thereafter was moved to speak of the spider in the Galloway cave, his desperate resolve, his vow one day to go on a Crusade if only victory was granted him.

The woman listened without further chiding, perceiving his need. And presently something of the urgency went out of his voice, and pauses developed that grew more frequent and longer. At length he slept.

And after a while Christina of Garmoran gently eased herself away from the man's side and slipped from the bed. She covered him again heedfully, and for a few moments stood there, warmly naked in the dying firelight, considering him, before betaking herself to the couch she had made near by.

* * *

There was no doubt that Christina's arrival and ministrations were good for Bruce. In two days, indeed, she was having to change her attitude and urge care, restraint, when he sought to be on his feet again. Admittedly, while she was out of the cottage and he did venture over the side, it was to find himself a deal weaker than he had realised, light-headed and unsteady on his legs; so that he was safely back between the plaids when Christina returned. But even so this was a major advance, of the spirit more than of the body — though the itch was undoubtedly much lessened by the bathings, the red patches less angry, the shivering gone.

Oddly enough it was his brother Edward who was responsible for effecting the major cure. He came clattering into the Milton of Urie two afternoons after Christina's arrival, all shouts and clashing steel, demanding were they *all* asleep here, *all* sick men abed? Buchan was upon them, in force. Had it not been for him, Edward of Carrick, they would all be dead men, not sleeping, by now. Etcetera.

This brought Bruce out of his bed and reaching for his clothing, demanding details. "What do you mean? Have you clashed with Buchan? The earl himself? Hereabouts? In what force? Where is he now?" All weakness was for the moment forgotten.

"Not Buchan himself, no. It was Brechin. Our nephew Sir David de Brechin, one of his captains. But Buchan himself is not far off. At Oldmeldrum, they say . . ."

"They say! They say! Who says? Fact, man — I want fact!" The King was transformed, vehement, commanding again, with so little of the invalid about him that even Christina was astonished. "Oldmeldrum is but five miles away. Where is David de Brechin? Talk sense, my lord!"

Edward seemed about to expostulate, but a look at his brother's face changed his mind. "Brechin is now running. Back to Oldmeldrum no doubt. Like a whipped cur. I taught him his lesson — but not before he had wiped out your picket to the east, on the Bourtie heights. Making here from Udny, I found our dead near yon cairn on the Bourtie ridge. They had been surprised and cut down to a man. De Brechin, with about 200 men, was in the low ground making for the Souterford and here, when I reached him. He has not half 200 now!"

"The enemy so near? Dear God! Sir Gilbert — what of your sentinels? What means this, sir?"

Hay flushed. "I am sorry, Sire. I have heard nothing of it. No word has been sent to me. Of enemy approach. I have sentinels posted, scouts out, all around. But . . ."

"Aye! I have lain too long, by the Rude! When my foes can ride within a mile of me, and I know naught of it!"

The Lord of Erroll bit his lip, but said nothing.

Bruce whipped back to his brother. "Speak on," he jerked. "And tell it as it happened. But shortly."

Edward explained. He had been returning from his harrying of the low coastlands of Formartin, on the edge of Comyn territory, with his 350 men, when his scouts learned that the Earl of Buchan himself, with a large force, was marching south-by-west from the heartlands of Buchan towards Inverurie. The scouts could not tell numbers, but it was thousands rather than hundreds — too many for him to challenge. So he had made all haste here, but sent back men to find the enemy host, and report. Then, only an hour or so ago, he had come on the slain Bourtie outpost, and then on the advancing de Brechin — his banner and arms clear. He had managed to trap him against a bluff and a curve of the river. Brechin had managed to cut his own way out, with some few of his people, but left most behind him. He, Edward, had taken no prisoners — but before they died, one or two of the Comyns had said that Buchan was positioned on the south face of Barra Hill, just south of Oldmeldrum, with many men, one said 2,000, another 3,000.

"So! Buchan would cross swords with me. In person! Perhaps he had word that I was sick. Well, I shall not disappoint the High Constable of this my kingdom!" Bruce produced a smile, grim but the first for long enough. "You have done well, Edward. I thank you. But whoever commands our sentinels on that east flank hangs tonight — if he is still alive then! Gibbie — you will see to it. But not now. You have much to do, first. We all have. Out, and sound the assembly. Christina — aid me on with my harness."

"Robert — my lord King!" the Islewoman protested. "This is not for you. A sick man, you cannot go riding to battle . . ."

"I am no longer a sick man — thanks to you, woman! Besides, this has made me hale and sound. No medicine could have cured me as this news has done! I have four great enemies in Scotland, apart from the English invaders, four men who have earned my wrath more than all others — Buchan, the Earl of Ross, MacDougall of Lorn, and MacDouall of Galloway. One of them is now near, come seeking me. Think you I will fail him — or myself?"

She spread her hands helplessly, recognising the finality of his voice.

"Now, quickly. No more of talk. My lords — to your duty. Christina — that shirt of mail . . ."

So, within the hour, the royal army of just over 1,500 men marched out of Inverurie, northwards, the King of Scots at its head under his own great red-and-gold Lion Rampant standard carried by his armour-bearer, William de Irvine — even though the said esquire had also to prop up his royal master in the saddle. Only half a head behind rode Christina of Garmoran, no royal commands having been effective in holding her back at the Milton.

They crossed the Burgh-muir and thereafter splashed across the Urie at the same Souterford where the litter of dead bodies, men and horses, testified the accuracy of Edward Bruce's claims. The road to Oldmeldrum followed the far east bank of the river for a couple of miles before swinging away due northwards up the long gentle slopes of a flank of Barra Hill. This was a foothills land of green rolling hogbacks and smooth grassy ridges, almost devoid of trees, with wide waterlogged troughs between. Oldmeldrum lay, a grey village on the lip of one of these lesser ridges ahead, with a clear prospect in this direction — and obviously not to be attacked directly from the low ground in front. Bruce sent the Earl of Lennox off, with some 200 horse, to make a diversion to the left, to the west, skirting the boggy Loch of Barra, for the higher ground of Lethenty and Harlaw, from which he could circle round on firm ground towards Oldmeldrum and menace Buchan's flank. He himself swung the main body, the majority on foot, sharply right-handed, off the line of the road, to follow the Bourtie valley round the back of Barra Hill itself. At this stage they were still out of sight of Buchan's position.

Barra Hill was no mountain, rising to little more than 600 feet, but it was the bulkiest and most prominent height in the area. Buchan almost certainly would have look-outs placed along its crest, and both his own and Lennox's progress would be only too evident from the heights. There could be no surprise, therefore — but they might hope for some confusion.

Up the gentle green Bourtie valley, only a shallow depression in the grassy hills really, they advanced steadily north by east with protective screens of outriders right and left. Bruce could have sent parties out to clear the ridge above them, but deliberately did not do so. Now and then they caught glimpses of movement up there, and were satisfied.

The King, though distinctly light-headed and scarcely in full control of his limbs, nevertheless felt more like himself than he had done for long. Possibly Campbell's Highland water-of-life was indeed helping — though he insisted that it was that which made him dizzy. Christina watched him from just behind like a hen with one chick.

On and on up those sheep-dotted valleys they pressed, with the long bulk of Barra Hill hiding all to the left, and the land gradually shelving and opening to the north-east. In time, they had gone well past the line of Buchan's position, even past Oldmeldrum itself, and the intervening hill was beginning to tail away into broken moorland. If some of Bruce's entourage, Edward included, began to fear that his sickness had affected his wits, they had perhaps some excuse; but the King's stern and jaw-clenched expression did not invite questioning.

At length, with the lie of the land forcing them ever eastwards into a wilderness of moorland hummocks, Bruce called a halt to this deliberate, almost leisurely progress. And now all was changed. As though he had suddenly wakened from some sort of trance, he had his whole force swing directly round on itself and head back whence it had come — but now at the utmost speed of foot and horse both. Back and up to the crest of Barra Hill, he commanded, with all haste. The foot he sent running and leaping across the soft ground, directly towards the whaleback ridge; the cavalry had to take the longer round-about route, for firmer going, before they could swing off right-handed to face the fairly steep ascent of the hill itself.

It was a ragged, scattered and breathless rabble that eventually reached the summit ridge of Barra Hill that late afternoon of Christmas Eve of 1307, as the light was beginning to fade from the overcast sky, Bruce himself reeling in his saddle, with Gilbert Hay positively holding him up at one side, and Irvine at the other. There was visibility enough left to discern the situation, however. And none on the ridge any longer doubted the sick monarch's wits.

The country was spread out before them, clear and open within a five-mile radius. And half-right, only about a mile away, a great host was streaming northwards, back through Oldmeldrum, in full retiral and some obvious confusion. From here it was evident that it had been drawn up in a strong position on the terraced south-facing shoulder of the hill below the village, overlooking the low ground, the loch and the road from Inverurie, its flanks well secured. But such position would have been of no avail in any attack from the rear, the north, from behind Oldmeldrum. Bruce's ruse had worked. Buchan's scouts, spaced along this dominant ridge, and now fleeing after their main body, had sent word that the royal force was making a great pincers-move to the north-east. Lennox's manoeuvre, plain to view on the other side, would give the same impression. The Comyn, concerned not to be trapped from the higher ground to the north, had abandoned his position and turned his whole army round, to make for a new defensive site further back. The King did not wait until all his array was drawn up on the hill-top He ordered his trumpets to blare the advance, the charge, and leaving Hay and Fraser to bring on the foot with all speed, plunged headlong downhill, in the forefront of his line, dizziness apparently gone. Edward led the cavalry on the right and Campbell on the left. Only a little way in the rear, Christina

MacRuarie maintained her position, black hair streaming like a banner in the wind.

Buchan did not fail to perceive the threat of this unexpected assault, and made swift dispositions to meet it — or tried to. But to turn a host of horse and foot round on itself, in any sort of order, is not a thing to be rushed. When the host is already strung out and scattered in some confusion by a previous sudden about-turn, and on the move to find a new position in the rear, the manoeuvre becomes little short of the impossible. Chaos developed on the northern flank of Barra Hill, as the royal array thundered down from the main ridge, trumpets braying, hooves drumming, armour clanking, with everywhere men yelling "A Bruce! A Bruce!"

Buchan was no poltroon, and he had stout and able lieutenants, notably Sir Walter Comyn of Kinedar, Sir William Comyn of Slains, Sir Alexander Baliol of Cavers, Sir David de Brechin — who arrogated to himself the title of The Flower of Chivalry — and the veteran Sir John de Moubray. They managed to rally much of their cavalry, but had less of a grip on the infantry. Indeed quickly the latter got completely out of hand, milling this way and that in disorder and in panic, so that soon their own horse were riding them down, led by the knights, in their desperate efforts to turn back and create a front of sorts against the enemy.

From the start of the charge the Comyns had only some five or six minutes to turn, reform and take up a defensive position, before the King's cavalry was upon them. It was not possible. While still the leaders were seeking to bring up and marshal their scattered men, the foremost ranks of the royal horse surged up in a yelling smiting tide. As might be expected, it was the right wing under the fiery Edward Bruce which reached them first.

Even so, Buchan's knights and chivalry put up a good fight, less than prominent as was their master in the business. But against the impetus of that charge, the lack of central direction, the utter chaos behind with the foot useless and fleeing, they were beaten before they started — especially when Lennox's squadron put in an appearance along their right flank. Moreover, almost certainly the fact that the King himself was seen to be leading the assault in person under his renowned royal standard, had a notable effect, not least on his High Constable. Bruce's reputation as a strategist had swept the country in these last ten months — and Buchan for one had thought him safely prostrate on his sick-bed.

At any rate, the Comyn line broke well before the loyalist foot reached the scene of battle — and once broken, Buchan himself was one of the first to be off. With Edward Bruce most evidently trying to hack his way through the press to him directly, he disengaged, leapt down from his heavy charger, grabbed a fleeter riderless mount, and clambered into the saddle with remarkable agility for a man of his years and bulk, in massive armour. He galloped off northwards. Many perceived it, and followed him — though Brechin and Moubray, scorning such behaviour, continued the fight.

But with the arrival of Hay and Fraser with the infantry, obviously it was all over. Most of the remaining armoured knights managed to draw together into a small, compact and fiercely effective phalanx, and so cut their way out and back. Had Bruce himself been in any state for serious fighting, it is probable that none would have escaped. But he was not, keeping upright in his saddle being his main preoccupation now; and Edward was of course in hot pursuit of the fleeing Buchan, despite the swiftly falling darkness.

Enough was enough, the King decided — especially with Christina MacRuarie at his elbow vigorously proclaiming the fact. The day was won, and with minimum loss. It was becoming too dark for effective tactics anyway, or any major pursuit. He ordered Irvine to sound the recall. Edward would pay no heed even if he heard it.

So leaving Hay, Campbell and the Fraser brothers to deal with the wounded, the prisoners and the battlefield generally, the King, with Christina and Lennox, not unthankfully returned to ride the few miles back to Inverurie, his couch drawing him now, in reaction, like a magnet.

It was late evening before Edward of Carrick returned, having pursued Buchan all the way to Fyvie, almost ten miles to the north, where there was a strong castle held by the English. He was hot that the victory had not been properly followed up — and since he could scarcely blame the King, he blamed Lennox and Campbell instead, the former in especial, who, he pointed out, had been fresh and with scarcely opportunity to draw sword.

His brother, sighing, called him over to his couch. "Edward," he said, low-voiced, for in that small chamber all might have heard. "You lack nothing in courage. And you are a good commander of light cavalry — few better. But let us pray God that my life is spared to me! For as King of Scots in my place you would not survive a month! Of a mercy, use your wits, man! Command, leadership, rule, demand more than throwing yourself at the nearest enemy like a bull, and berating all others for not doing likewise! You must have friends as well as defeated foes. Remember it, I charge you — for *I* need friends if you do not!"

That night Bruce was not content to be cherished and mothered in his cot-house bed. Later, after the man was asleep, Christina, beside him, lay and gazed up at the smoke-blackened but firelit roofing, and she frowned as often as she smiled.

Chapter Twelve

"Men," declared Christina MacRuarie, "are all fools! Greater or lesser in degree, but all fools. Even kings, it seems! And never so great fools as where women are concerned."

Robert Bruce kept his back turned, and wisely forbore to answer.

"You are the great ones. Under heaven, you rule all! All save your own silly wits. How think you would manage *without* women?"

"More quietly, at the least," the King said, and sighed.

He was gazing out of the window of his bedchamber, which was in fact the sub-Prior's room of the Blackfriars' Priory of Aberdeen, looking pensively northwards towards the Castlehill and the towering walls of Aberdeen's fortress, still held by a strong though beleaguered garrison of Englishmen. He was not really thinking, at the moment, about that symbol of the enemy's unrelenting grip upon his kingdom — although it, and so many others like it, was a constant preoccupation, a challenge, which one day would have to be faced and dealt with; but not yet; he was not ready for the expensive and time-consuming business of reducing major fortresses. His mind was more immediately concerned with the projected programme for that very afternoon of early April — if only the woman would be quiet and let him think.

But Christina was in no mood for quiet contemplation. She had a grievance. And a woman with a grievance is no aid to cerebration — especially one so masterful as the Lady of Garmoran.

"Am I not just as entitled to sit at your Council as any man?" she demanded, not for the first time. "I have supplied you with men and aid and shelter. I know as much of affairs in these parts as do any of your lords. I have given you better advice than most. I have even been at your side in battle. What do I lack for a seat at this Council-table? Tell me, Robert — what do I lack? Other than proud and arrogant manhood. And . . . and its dangling equipment!"

He smoothed hand over mouth, at that, lest she saw the grin reflected in the window-glass. "Nothing," he admitted. "That only. Manhood. And you have other equipment that more than compensates, my dear! But, see you — that is the nub of it, as I have told you. Because you are a woman the others would resent your presence. At a Privy Council. Never, I think, has any woman attended such — even a queen. I know their minds on this. They like you well, admire you. Edward indeed would bed you if he might, as you know! But a Council is men's business . . ."

"A Council is for counsel. And I can give better counsel than who will sit there. Than witlings like Gilbert Hay. Clerks like the Bishop of Moray. Nice fumblers like Lennox. Or fat lowborn burghers like this Provost of Aberdeen — a fellmonger, a tanner of hides!"

"Then give your counsel here, Christina. In my own ear. Always you have my privy ear. You can reach me when and where the others can not . . ."

"That is naught to the point, and you know it. This Council is for debate. Discussion. Hearing the word and advice of others, and to make comment, support, or discover error. For that I must be there. You are to discuss Angus of the Isles' plan to invade Lorn and Argyll. My lands flank Lorn to the north. Think you I do not know more of this matter than your Southrons? You will talk of a campaign against Ross. I and my clan have been fighting Ross for many years . . ."

"Christina — all that is true. And your guidance I shall value. As I have done hereto. But a woman at my first true Privy Council I cannot have. I know my fellow-men. This Council is all-important. Aberdeen is the first city in all my realm to fall into my hands — even though its castle still holds out. All the kingdom will hear what is done and said today. I have taken much thought to the style of it . . ."

"The more reason that a woman's voice should be heard. And be known to be heard. Abroad. Are not half your subjects women?"

A discreet knock sounded at the door — for which Bruce was decidedly grateful. He strode to open it, to find there young William Irvine, son of the Annandale laird of Bonshaw, who had joined him as esquire and armour-bearer after Glen Trool, relieving Gibbie Hay of certain such duties.

"Your Grace — my lord Bishop of Dunblane is new come. And seeks audience. He is below, in the chapter-house."

"Ha! Nicholas Balmyle? Here, in Aberdeen! Yes, he shall have audience. I will be down to the chapter-house forthwith."

Bruce turned back, to complete his dressing, belting the cloth-of-gold tunic with the splendid embroidered scarlet Lion Rampant of Scotland, and donning the purple cloak trimmed with fur, which was the gift of the citizens of Aberdeen. He was to be very fine today, part of the stage-managing of this his first real Privy Council, wherein he planned to act the monarch rather than just the soldier. Much would depend on this afternoon, and he was at least concerned to look the part. He had once, it seemed in another life, been something of a dandy in his dress, little as more recent appearances would have suggested it.

"You look a very picture of elegance," the woman observed sourly — which was strange, for partly this dressing-up had been her idea, the handsome thigh-length tunic made under her supervision.

"I thank you," he returned, smiling. "I am glad that I please you in this, at least!" And he escaped.

Downstairs he found the calmly self-contained person of Nicholas Balmyle, newly appointed Bishop of Dunblane. And with him the dark Benedictine friar Bernard de Linton, the same who had brought Bruce the news of the late King Edward's death, at Loch Doon. They bowed, the King greeting them warmly.

"Sire," Balmyle said, "we rejoice to see you afoot and all but yourself again, after your grievous sickness. We thank God and His saints for your delivery."

"Aye, my lord Bishop — do that. But also thank you the Earl of Buchan. Who contrived to effect my final cure, after his own fashion! At Barra Hill."

Balmyle looked mystified. "You say so? But two days before we came north from St. Andrews seeking Your Grace, I heard from a source you know of that my lord of Buchan has fled Scotland and is now in Yorkshire. To the displeasure of King Edward, who it seems had newly appointed him warden of Annandale, Carrick and Galloway."

"Buchan in England? I' faith — here is good news. After two small defeats, and with still a round dozen of his strong castles in his Comyns' hands, he flees the country? I had scarcely hoped for this. It should make my task the less sore. But . . . you had the word of it from my friend? From Bishop Lamberton? Have you also a letter for me? Is that why you have come here, my lord?"

"In part, Sire. Here is a letter. It was enclosed within one from the Primate to myself."

Bruce took the folded paper, bulkier than that he had received before, and still sealed. He did not open it, as Balmyle went on.

"I have come on other account also, Sire. Another letter has reached me. From Rome. His Holiness has approved of my appointment to the See of Dunblane. And summons me to the Vatican for consecration."

"Then here also is excellent news, my lord. For the Pope does not love me, or my cause, and I feared that he might refuse to confirm you bishop. To your loss, and mine. For you have proved my friend. And I need the support of lords spiritual as well as temporal. And few of either are prepared to give that support, I fear."

"They will, Sire — they will. In time. But while the English remain in possession of most of the land, is it to be wondered at? With death by hanging and disembowelling the penalty. Not all have Your Grace's strong courage . . ."

"But *you* have, my lord. And our friend, here." He looked at the friar. "To venture all this way, through enemy-held land, with this letter and your news."

The younger man, de Linton, inclined his head. He was sensitive-looking, gaunt, stringy and tall, with prominent bones. "My courage is but weak, Your Grace. But my conscience is the stronger."

"Aye. Well said, Master Bernard."

"I had to come to seek your royal permission, Sire, to leave the country," the Bishop went on. "To journey to Rome for my consecration. And while in Rome to seek to have the Primate's revocation of Your Grace's excommunication confirmed by the Pontiff."

"Aye. Though whether you succeed in that is more in doubt. My enemies will do much to prevent it. All the English and French bishops — aye, and some of the Scots! Yours will be a lone voice, my friend. But, yes — you must go. To Rome. And God-speed. Though I shall be the poorer for your absence."

"I thank you. And shall hasten my return. Meantime I have brought you Master Bernard. To remain with you, if so you will have it. To be a link between you and Holy Church. With myself, and with Bishop Lamberton, my father-in-God. That letters may still pass. As well, he is an able scribe, well versed, and I have found him both wise and true. He will serve you in many ways."

"That is well thought of. I' faith, I need a secretary. A King needs pen as well as sword. You will be my secretary, Master Bernard. And, by the Rude, you could not have come more aptly. For today, within the hour, I hold a high council. You shall act secretary thereat. And you, my lord Bishop, shall attend it, as of right. With Bishop David of Moray, who is here. It falls out most aptly, does it not?"

"Sire, I thank you," the Bishop acknowledged. "But may I trespass on your time a little longer? I have brought more than my news to Aberdeen. Two items. Another thousand merks in silver, for one . . ."

"Save us, friend — here's generosity indeed! Another thousand! You put me greatly in your debt. But I can use it, I'll not deny. Your last provision is near done — spent in the main in feeding and arming men. I thank you, from my heart."

"Thank not me. Thank my lord Primate. It is on his orders, and from the revenues of his See of St. Andrews, that the money comes. I still administer it for him, as best I may."

"Then thank God for William Lamberton and Nicholas Balmyle both, say I!"

"The other matter I am less sure of Your Grace's gratitude," the little cleric said, in his slightly pedantic, composed style. "I but serve my lord of Douglas in this. He sends loyal greetings — and a prisoner."

"Jamie? You have seen James Douglas, my lord? How goes it with him? Is all well?"

"Well enough, Sire. He is in health, but kept direly busy. He is a scourge to every Englishman not shut up safe within castle walls! He has become a notably fierce young man — as he must needs be, to be sure. But with something of innocence also. He seldom sleeps two nights in one bed, ranging the Lowlands from one end to the other, his sword never out of his hand."

"Aye. I laid a heavy burden on his shoulders, in leaving the South in his care. But of my close lieutenants him I could best trust with the task. And as lord of Douglasdale, and his famed father's son, he bears a name and style that men must respect. But my service has borne hard on him."

"As to that he makes no complaint, I think. But he has captured this notable prisoner, and sends him to you, by my hand. He waits without. Have I Your Grace's permission to bring him in?"

The King nodded. "I have not a few sins on my soul, other than the death of John Comyn," he said slowly. "You speak of James Douglas's innocence yet. But it is the rape of his innocence that bears sorely on my conscience. I taught him to hate. And to slay without qualm, without mercy. That sword you spoke of, I put into his hand. He was young, and good, and his heart gentle, and I made him killer . . ."

Bruce's grieving words faded as Friar Bernard ushered a fourth man into the room, a tall, darkly handsome, well-built young man, with a flashing proud eye and a noble brow, possibly the most handsome man that Scotland could produce in that age. He stared.

"Thomas. . .!" he whispered.

His own nephew, Sir Thomas Randolph, Lord of Nithsdale, bowed stiffly and remained silent.

"My lord of Douglas captured Sir Thomas in a fray in Ettrick Forest. Along with Sir Alexander Stewart of Bonkyl—who I understand also used to be Your Grace's friend. Their troops were English, however. Stewart was wounded. But this being Your Grace's own kinsman, my lord asked me to bring to you. For . . . for disposal!"

"Yes. To be sure. I thank you, my lord Bishop." The King, still eyeing Randolph, was frowning darkly in perplexity. He had liked this young man, spirited and talented as he was good-looking, and hitherto namely for being upright to a degree, his half-sister's son. Bruce's own mother, Marjory, Countess of Carrick in her own right, before she wed his father had been married to one Adam, Lord of Kilconquhar, of the ancient lofty line of MacDuff, Earls of Fife. A child of that marriage, a daughter, had wed Sir Thomas Ranulf of Nithsdale, another Celtic lord who had Normanised his name to Randolph. Here before him was the fruit of that union, a sprig of the most purely Celtic nobility, allegedly the soul of honour and the mirror of chivalry, whom Bruce himself had delighted to honour with knighthood at his coronation, Scot of the Scots, with no taint of Norman blood in him. Yet there he stood, a traitor caught in his treachery, a man who had, it seemed, bought his life at the expense of his honour. He had fought for Bruce at Methven, been captured, and almost alone of the long list of noble prisoners, escaped shameful execution, to fight thereafter for Edward Plantagenet.

"I have not seen you since Methven fight, nephew," the King said, controlling his voice. "Though I have heard of your doings. I believe you were at Loudoun Hill. At Pembroke's side!"

"I was," the younger man agreed, as carefully. "To my sorrow."

"Your sorrow? You regret it, then?"

"My sorrow is for this Scotland. And for you, my lord. That so sorry a travesty of battle should have been fought in the name of this realm. My regret for myself only that I had no opportunity to use my sword against your person."

The Bishop coughed, and seemed about to rebuke the young man, but Bruce held up his hand.

"You would have fought me, slain me, then? At Loudoun Hill? If you had been able?"

"I would have fought you there. Or otherwhere. In fair and knightly combat. To redeem, if I might, the honour of my mother's house!"

"Fair and knightly combat! Yet it was I who knighted you, man. At Scone. Four years ago. Have you forgot?"

"I have not forgot—and judge it my greatest shame, my lord."

Bruce drew a long breath. "You do not mince your words, nephew. It seems that you do not like me. Yet we used to be friends, as well as kinsmen."

"I used to deem you honourable, sir."

Again Bruce restrained Balmyle. "I see that you name me sir, not Sire. Lord not Grace. Yet you helped make me King, at my coronation, Thomas."

"You have besmirched that anointing and coronation. You have dragged the royal dignity in the mire of murder and brigandage. You have tramped the code of chivalry underfoot. I no longer recognise you as my King. And would God I need not admit you as kin!" The young man's pleasantly-modulated voice quivered a little, there.

As Bishop and friar stirred with disquiet, appalled indeed, Bruce's patience was heavy, iron-bound.

"So you took Edward Longshanks for King? Edward who disembowelled knights. Who hanged three of your own uncles and your aunt's husband. Who hung another aunt and your kinswoman Isobel of Buchan in cages on castle walls. You preferred his kingship to mine?"

"The old King's misdeeds do not wash out yours, sir. And in the field he fought fairly, honestly, at least. The greatest warrior in Christendom. But you—you slay by night, like any thief. You ambush, you trick, you deceive. You have become no better than the man Wallace. You have not once battled in fair fight since your flight to Ireland."

"Ireland . . .? What is this of Ireland?"

"After Methven, when I was captured, you fled your realm. Leaving others to bear the English yoke. That is what I mean. And then returned with a horde of hired Irish cut-throats, foreign savages, to gain by terror and murder what you could not gain by honest means . . ."

"So that is what they told you!" Bruce eyed the other with dawning comprehension. "You have been cozened, Thomas. Fed with lies and half-truths. Led by cleverer men than you are, so that you might be used as a stick for my back, a dagger under my armour. My own nephew! Do you not see it? I was never in Ireland. I never left my own realm. I was in the Highlands and the Hebrides. The men I landed with again at Turnberry, from Arran, and those my brothers led into Galloway, were my own subjects. Islesmen—when none in the Lowlands would rise for me!"

The other looked momentarily nonplussed. "They said . . . they said . . ."

"Aye, they said! And you believed. Did James Douglas tell you no better?"

"Douglas! He is no better than yourself! Trained in your school. His knightly vows forgotten. I would have no truck with him — though once I judged him honest."

The King sighed. He could have shaken this good-looking, headstrong son of his sister. Shaken him for the ignorant, self-righteous puppy he was. Yet, at the back of his mind, he knew a sort of relief, too. Relief that at least his blood, his mother's Celtic blood, had not after all apparently curdled to dastardly treachery as he had feared. Not in vile, craven self-seeking, at least. Whatever else he was, this young man before him was no craven. For if he believed that he, Bruce, was as he said, then his present defiant words and attitude could only lead to the rope or cold steel. It had been one of the hurts that nagged at him in many a sleepless night, that young Randolph should have changed sides, sold his King and his kinsman, in cowardice. Now he was at least beginning to understand.

After all, only a few years ago, even though it seemed in another life, when he was Randolph's age, he had thought much as this one did, filled with fine chivalric ideals, judging all by the knightly code, seeing war as only an extension of the tournament. Thus they had been brought up, to look on Edward Plantagenet, for instance, as the epitome of romance, Christendom's model, the crusading prince, the Norman-French influence all-important — even though Randolph was in fact pure Celt. Even James Douglas had been of this mind — until rudely taught otherwise. This other still lacked the teaching, that was all.

"Thomas," he said, with a major attempt at reasonableness, "you berate me for not waging fair fight, as you name it. For ambushing and tricking my enemies. Winning my battles by my wits rather than the strength of my right arm. You conceive this not to be knightly, or the kingly way. I agree with you that it is not knightly. But a king has more than chivalry to think on! But, at Methven — was that a knightly fray? When Pembroke, with whom you seem proud to fight, stole upon us by night, forced us to battle scarce awake. Did you conceive *that* knightly, that night?"

When the other made no answer, the elder went on.

"Pembroke so acted because this was war, not jousting. Not the lists and the tourney-ground. We are fighting now, not for honour, or glory; but for freedom, our very lives. And the continuing existence of Scotland. So I fight to win, lad, as best I may, using what weapons I have . . ."

"*You* fight for a throne! A kingdom, for yourself. And would plunge all that kingdom in blood to gain it! Is that freedom?"

"Would you have the English to rule Scotland?"

"Once *you* did not find that so ill! When Baliol would fill the throne, not Bruce. Is Plantagenet any worse a king for Scotland than Bruce? Or Baliol? Or Comyn? When Plantagenet would spare the land the everlasting bloodshed, the fire and famine and devastation?"

They stared at each other for long moments, two strong men more like each other than they knew.

At length Bruce shrugged. "I have not time to deal with you now," he said. "You have drawn sword against your liege lord. You swore me fealty at my coronation. So you broke your oath and committed treason, both. For that, you know the penalty?"

"I do. I seek no mercy at your soiled hands, my lord."

"Yet I would show mercy if I might. For you are of my own blood. Nephew — let us start afresh." He extended a hand, open, palm upward. "We will talk of it more fully later. But meantime be reconciled. You have for a while forgotten your allegiance. Now, let us be reconciled."

"No, sir. I have been guilty of nothing to my shame. You arraign my conduct. It is yourself who ought to be arraigned. Since you have chosen to defy the King of England — to whom *you* more than once took oath of fealty — why do you not debate the matter like a true knight, in a pitched field? If you dare! Until you do that, I am no man of yours — whatever my blood."

"That may come hereafter, nephew. Who knows how long hereafter? *I* shall choose that day, not the invaders." His voice changed and he made a gesture of finality. "Meantime, since you are so rude of speech, it would be fitting that your proud words should meet their due punishment. But . . . for the sake of my sister's memory, I shall hold my hand. You will be put close in ward until you know better *my* right and *your* duty. Master Bernard — summon the guard . . ."

* * *

At the long refectory table of Aberdeen's Blackfriars Priory, the first Council of the reign sat in session. Bruce was at the head and his brother at the foot, and between them at either side were about a score of men, the King's close companions with an assortment of others, carefully chosen; Angus of the Isles, who had come from containing MacDougall in the West; the Bishop of Moray, ridden south especially for the occasion, leaving his force to watch the Comyns in the North; their host, the Prior of this establishment;

and the Provost of the Burgh of Aberdeen, a man much overawed by the company he was keeping. A notable absentee was Bishop Cheyne of Aberdeen, a Comyn nominee and supporter. The new Bishop of Dunblane sat near the King, and on his other side, at a small table of his own, Master Bernard sat with ink-horn, quills and paper.

Edward Bruce was holding forth, urgently, thumping the table in no council-chamber manner. "... And so first things first, I say! Let the Lord of Argyll and his MacDougalls wait, I say. We will deal with them in due time. They will do but little harm in the West, meantime. With Campbell to the south of them, the Lady of Garmoran to the north, and my lord of the Isles to the west, surely they do not threaten us unduly?" He glanced fleetingly at Angus Og. "Whereas, I tell you, the Comyns do! Still they do. Their defeat at Barra was not properly followed up. It hit their pride but left them but little diminished. My later defeat of Buchan at Aiky Brae, to the north, was more complete, with more men slain. But it was still only the remnants from Barra. The Comyn power is still scarce touched. And it is the greatest power in Scotland today, even yet. Their castles of Dundarg, Slains, Kinedar, Rattray, Kelly and Ellon — and these are only the great ones — control the country. The English, I say, are less menace than the Comyns, since they are more scattered and have to hold down the countryside. The Comyns have their force here concentrated, in Buchan and Moray and Badenoch. They must be dealt with first, and at once."

There was a murmur of agreement from the majority of those present.

"I support my lord of Carrick, Sire," Bishop David of Moray said, an unlikely-looking cleric, the church-militant indeed. "You say that you have word that the Earl of Buchan has fled into England. That may be good — or not so good. He is no longer young and they say he is ailing. A disappointed man. He has not led the Comyns with the fire and thrust of the late Lord of Badenoch, his kinsman. Now, if he is gone, another may take his place. In the leadership of the Comyns. He has a brother, Sir Alexander — he who holds the castles of Urquhart and Tarradale. And many cousins, fiercer even than he. I know them. I have lived my life amongst them. They are smarting now, from Your Grace's blows. But they are far from defeated. They could raise 8,000 against you, Sire. Perhaps 10,000, given opportunity. And they will, if you let them. We must strike them before they think to act without Buchan's palsied hand."

"The Bishop fears for his own fat Moray lands, I think!" Angus

Og declared. "These Comyns are licking their wounds. They may be all these lords say. But they have been twice beat, and will not seek another beating meantime, for a wager. But MacDougall has not been beaten. The old man, Alexander, son of Ewan, son of Duncan, son of Dougall, is also ailing, like this Buchan. But his son is not. I know John Bacach of Lorn — after all, we are kin. His mother was a Comyn, Badenoch's sister. He loves you less than does his father, Sir King. And he is strong. Strong as a man, and strong in men. These talk of 10,000 Comyns. I shall believe that number when I see them! But John of Lorn can field 5,000 broadswords at a snap of his fingers! And you learned their quality at Strathfillan, did you not? I have been fencing with them these past months, keeping your left flank. I believe John Bacach MacDougall is finished with fencing. That is why I am here. I say you must deal with him before all else."

"I agree with my lord of the Isles," Neil Campbell put in. "The Comyns may still prove a threat. But John of Lorn is a threat *now!*"

"I think that true, Sire," Lennox nodded. "The MacDougalls have allies right down the West — as you learned to your cost. Macnabs, Macfarlanes, MacLarens, MacMillans, MacAlisters. I know John of Lorn also. He is a different man from his father — and it is he we have to deal with now. If my lord of the Isles believes him set on battle, he could set all the West on fire, right down to the Clyde. And then the South-West lies open before him. With only young Douglas holding it . . ."

"The West! The West!" Edward interrupted scornfully. "These lords are all from the Highland West, brother. MacDougall is a rogue and a traitor, and must be taught his lesson, yes. But his thousands are but Highland sworders. Good at a tulzie, yes. I ask none better in an ambush or a night's raiding. But the Comyn's main might is in armoured horse. Cavalry. Such as win wars, not tulzies!"

The King opened his mouth to speak, then closed it again. This was a Council and he was here to be advised. He would let them have their say. He nodded encouragement to Aberdeen's portly, red-faced Provost, sitting on the edge of his chair and evidently eager to speak but diffident in the presence of all these great nobles and bishops.

"Your royal Grace," he began hoarsely, and faltered, looking round the table. "If it may please Your Highness, I . . . I would say a word."

"You have our ear, friend. Say on."

"Aye, weel. This toun o' Aberdeen. It has welcomed Your Highness right kindly, has it no? Right kindly. The folk favour you. But you havena' taken the castle. It's stuffit full o' Englishry yet. It's ower strong to be taken. And it can be supplied frae the sea. We canna stop that, for it glowers ower the harbour. And the English hae ships at Dundee. So, Highness, by your leave, I'd say dinna go stravaiging through to the West after thae wild Hielantmen and leave us to the mercy o' the Comyns and the English baith! Or it'll be the end o' us. Buchan is no' that far awa' — but twenty miles. If you dinna put doon the Comyns first, they'll be doon here chapping at our doors afore you're across the Mounth! And the English frae the castle in our backyards And Your Highness will hae lost Abderdeen. And we . . . we'll hae lost mair'n that!"

"Well said, Sir Provost. Your point is taken. I shall not forget Aberdeen and its good folk, never fear. Do any others wish to speak further to this matter?"

"Sir King," Angus Og said, "Malcolm of Lennox spoke of John MacDougall threatening the South-West. I say that he is more like to turn north. I have the word that he has been sending messengers to William of Ross. They were ever unfriends, until this. But since neither love you . . ."

"The Earl of Ross!" Bruce's voice actually quivered, with the fierce effort of suppressing the flood of emotion that name aroused in him — the man who had taken his wife and daughter from the sanctuary at Tain, to hand over to the English. "He . . . he . . . MacDougall joins hands with Ross?"

"So goes the word in the West. Any day now the high passes will be open, the snows gone and the floods subsided. Then, I think, John of Lorn will turn north-east, not south-west, to join up with Ross. And then, Sir King, you will be faced with trouble enough for any man!"

A shaken silence greeted his words. He did not have to underline the size of the threat for any man there. The Earl of Ross was second only to the Lord of the Isles himself in power in the North-West. The third most powerful man was MacDougall of Lorn. Ally these two in a joint campaign, throwing in their whole might, and there was nothing north of the Highland Line that could withstand them. Even Edward Bruce, for once, made no comment.

His brother drummed finger-tips on the table. "My lords," he said at length, "if this is indeed so, then the danger is great and we must take steps to meet it, somehow. Yet my lord of Carrick is right also, about the Comyns. As is the good Provost of this Aberdeen about the danger to his city. And *I* have scores to settle with the Earl of Ross!" He paused. "See you, in this letter I spoke of, sent me by my lord Bishop of St. Andrews, he says that the King of

England has betrothed himself. To the twelve-year-old Isabella of France. He is even now gone to France for the nuptials — you might think in some haste considering the years of his bride! He has planned a great coronation for the new Queen, when he returns. In May. He is much fond of such celebrations, is this Edward of Carnarvon. Moreover, he has much offended his lords by raising up his pretty favourite, the Gascon named Piers Gaveston, and creating him Earl of Cornwall. Now he has left all England in his charge, while he is abroad, a puppet of no stature, hated by all the nobility of his realm. So there will be trouble, my friends — that I warrant. What with Edward's absence in France, the coronation when he returns, and the offence of his lords. Bishop Lamberton believes, and I agree with him, that there is like to be no large invasion of Scotland this summer. So, at the least, we need not be ever looking over our shoulders to the south."

Satisfaction was voiced by all at this news.

"So now, my lords — here is my proposal. My brother, the Earl of Carrick, will take our main force and proceed forthwith to deal with the Comyns. Wait you — wait! I myself, with the Lord of the Isles, the Earl of Lennox and Sir Neil Campbell of Lochawe with a lesser force, will cross to the West, to join the Islesmen already there, collecting what more we may from the Lennox, the Campbells and other leal chiefs. We will be there, not to come to grips with MacDougall, but only to threaten him, at this juncture — since we have not the might to challenge him and the Comyns both. But if we do this, and I am there in person. I do not believe that MacDougall will risk marching north to join up with Ross, leaving me on his border. Moreover, I will seek to prevail on the Lady Christina of Garmoran to have her people make a similar sally along the eastern shores of Ross, to distract the Earl. And my lord of Moray, *your* men to feint at Easter Ross and the Black Isle. Then, my friends, when the Earl of Carrick has harried the Comyn country into submission, we will march north to meet him at Inverness — in three months' time, may be. To face Ross united again. And when we are finished with Ross, turn back to deal with MacDougall in earnest! How say you? We must use this campaigning season to bring all the North to heel, if we can, whilst the English are otherwise occupied."

There was a great storm of acclaim and approval, round that table, men almost unanimous in their enthusiasm and their recognition of the breadth and sweep of this comprehensive programme, this proposed solution of the deadlock. Even Angus Og was impressed; and Edward was of course highly delighted. His abilities were being recognised, at last.

Bruce let the exclamation and comment continue for a little, and then brought the Council to order again. "This is no light task," he said. "Let us make no mistake about what this course will demand of us. Of us all. Patience, discretion, the holding of our hands. For any major defeat, at either side of the country, would spell disaster for both. We must all fully recognise what are our objectives, and hold to them strictly. Going no step further, to endanger all. In the West we are there only as a gesture. We will fight no great battles. And this is equally so with you, my lord of Carrick. Your business is not to hazard my main force in battle — mind it! Your task is to subdue the Comyn country so that never again will that house threaten mine. Heed not their castles, unless they are easy. It is their lands, these vast lands from which they draw their men, the great masses of their men — these are your objective. So long as the Comyn threat, of mighty armed intervention, remains, the English have us by the throat. My throne remains insecure. And many in this realm, God knows, take their lead from Comyn. So — an example must be made. For the good of the kingdom. The whole province of Buchan must be taught its lesson, who is King in Scotland. You understand, Edward?" That was rapped out, Bruce's features graven grim, his eyes hard. "Your task is to harry Buchan, not to fight battles. For that purpose and that only, you shall have my main host. And with it the Bishop of Moray, Sir Robert Boyd, Sir Robert Fleming and Sir Alexander Fraser, to aid and advise you. I shall expect them all, and the host no less in numbers, at Inverness in three months' time. And Buchan laid low so that no Comyn shall raise voice or sword against me, ever again! You have it? All of you — you have it? Answer me!"

It was not often that Robert Bruce played the imperious autocrat. He did so now advisedly, deliberately, and with good reason. No man failed to be affected, and Edward Bruce for once was positively subdued.

There was some little remaining business, mainly concerned with the containing of the English in Aberdeen Castle, and defensive works to prevent any invasion by sea. Also the implications of Lamberton's letter that he had been now given a sort of limited freedom, on the payment to King Edward of 6,000 merks fine, and on the strict injunction that he did not return to Scotland, Edward indeed apparently believing that he could use him to help bring the Scots to heel. The Council agreed that, in the circumstances, Lamberton should seem to go along with the English in this, and at the same time, if possible, both serve as spy and encourage that King in his follies.

But the pressure had gone out of the conference, and all were eager to be away from the table, and at ease to talk, discuss and argue freely. The King drew the proceedings to a close, therefore — and rising, beckoned Gilbert Hay to his side.

"Gibbie," he said quietly, "you did not hear your name spoken in all that. Because I have an especial task for you. I think you used to be friendly with Thomas Randolph, my nephew?"

"Used to be, Sire — but not since he turned traitor!"

"There are traitors and traitors, Gibbie."

"This one the greater, in that he is your own kin. All should be dead! I heard that he had been brought here. What is Your Grace's will for him?"

"What would *you* do with Thomas Randolph, once your friend?"

"I would hang him. As *his* friends have hanged so many of us."

"If I was to hang all those who take part against me, I fear I would be hanging half of my subjects! No — I still have hopes for my sister's son. He conceives himself to be a man of honour — and myself otherwise! I want you to take him in hand, Gibbie. He is in close ward, yes. But we will take him with us, into the West. Get his parole — and, an honourable man, he will keep it! He will be in your charge. Entreat him kindly, but firmly. Work on him — as the English have already done. He is surprisingly innocent, I am convinced. He has much to learn. You are the best man to show him his error. Show him that I am not the brigand he takes me for. Show him that the knightly code will not win a war against ten times our numbers. Show him how the English really fight, behind their glitter of chivalry."

"If so you command, Sire. But I think you are too nice, too soft of heart. I'd take rope to him, and be done!"

"It is my head, not my heart, that commands in this, my lord of Erroll! Any fool can hang his prisoners. But there may be many who think like Randolph, many of my subjects. I may serve my cause a deal better by showing mercy and persuading that young man to be my living friend than my dead enemy! He is a man of parts, with great lands. And of the old race. I have not so many of these that I should hang them, when I might convert them. And Thomas Randolph converted would sound loud in Scotland. See you to it, my friend."

Less than convinced, Hay bowed.

At last, that evening, the feast given by the Guilds of Aberdeen for the monarch and Council over, Robert Bruce had privacy to draw from his doublet the unopened letter which had been contained within the other sent by William Lamberton. Even the sight of the strong and somewhat carelessly formed handwriting set his heart stirring. Feasting, drinking and dancing still went on below, and would for hours yet, if he knew his brother Edward; but he had managed to slip away, he hoped scarcely noticed, leaving the same Edward cavorting with a Christina who was at some small pains to show her liege lord a certain coolness. That suited the King well enough this night. He was as fond of gaiety as any — he had been accounted too gay, once — and had been starved of it, like the others, for too long; but that crushed unopened letter had lain over his heart for long hours, setting up its own vibrations within him. Now, in his own bedchamber, he broke the seals.

He read:

My loved lord and dear husband.

I have written you many letters these weary months, for my own heart's ease only, knowing they could not come to you. And so burned them in the fire, that in their very smoke some small waft of their love and aching might sail on an air kinder than men north and north over the long leagues to Scotland and my dear. Foolish woman that I am.

But now, I write in sudden gladness, so that I can scarce hold this quill from trembling, and you may scarce be able to read these feeble words for splutters of ink and tear-drops — I who am no weeper, as you know. Fool, indeed. But these are tears of joy, my sweet, in that at last I may write in the hope that you may read. For Bishop Lamberton is come to me, the first friend's face I have seen in more than a year. Who says that he has means to carry a letter to you secretly. I thank God for it.

I thank God also, Robert, for the tidings the Bishop gives me of you. Hereto they have told me only that you are a hunted outlaw, a murderer, a slayer of the innocent, harried and driven. Or else that you are fled the country, gone beyond the seas, in Ireland or Norway. Yet since you cannot be both, in truth, I have taken heart from their lies. And know at least that you were alive, and a trouble to these my captors.

Now, the saints be praised, I learn that you are indeed still your own true man, and mine, a scourge to your enemies, winning victories and waging war for your kingdom. So prayers are answered after all, and I rejoice.

I am held close prisoner here, but you must not deem me ill-used or woeful. I see no friendly faces, and live the plainest. But I have a garden to walk in and dwell, I swear, a deal more comfortably than does my lord. None treat me as Queen, but at least I am the Earl of Ulster's daughter. When I hear of what is done to the other women of our company, and to your poor daughter Marjory, I could hate my own betterment. But Robert, how I do long for you. Estate, and bodily wellbeing, these matter less than nothing when I have not you in company. Would that you had heeded me in Strathfillan, and allowed that I remain with you. No privations and wanderings and dangers, at your side, could have matched the sorrows of this long separation.

I heard, my dear, what King Edward, the old Edward, did to your brothers. To the gallant Nigel, and to Thomas and Alex. As to Christopher Seton. My heart bleeds for you. I pray nightly for the souls of them, as for the damnation in hell of he who did these monstrous things. It is almost beyond belief that a man could be so vile. Yet I thought not ill of my God-sire once. I believe that only a sickness of the mind could have served for this.

Who knows how the new King will deal with us. He is much other to his father and a lesser man in most things, I am sure. But I do not believe that he will relent in any degree towards Scotland or to yourself. And therefore to me. So I do not deceive myself that he will let me return to you, save you make him. And God knows how that is to be done, for I do not. Although I pray for it unceasingly. The Bishop, it is clear, thinks as I do, and he knows this King better than do we. Robert, my good Robert — how in Christ's sweet name are we to come together again?

Ah, forgive me, my brave lord, that I should write so. It is no wife's part to assail your eyes and ears with my woman's wails. Indeed, the fact that I can be no wife to you is the worst of me. For my body, as my mind and heart, does long for you. And you know that I am near as lusty of temper as you are. You wed no modest, gentle milk-white Queen, my lord King, no meek sufferer, so that sometimes I do fear for my reason . . .

These last sentences had been scored through with a spluttering pen, but were readable enough. And eloquent.

Heed me not, Robert. This is not my true self that writes so. I am but carried away by this so unexpected link with you. Somehow you have of a sudden seemed to come very close, so that I feel I must needs grasp out at you, to hold you, keep you, lest you go from me again. When indeed all there is, out there, is a patient Bishop waiting for this foolish paper. But it is too late to write another, better letter now. I have kept your friend waiting too long already.

Here is the truth of it, Robert. I need you. I miss you beyond all telling. But I can wait. Oh yes, I can wait, never fear. One day,

God willing, I will be wife to you again. But meantime, my love, I know your man's need. I know you to be a hot man. Meet your need for women as best you may, Robert. I wed you knowing that need. But of a mercy do not tell me of it. I am foolish. You have my understanding in this. But scarce my blessing. Take who you will my, Robert — but oh my heart, love only

your
ELIZABETH

That last line and signature was scarcely decipherable, a straggling scrawl, blotted and tailing away. The reading of it brought quick tears to the man's own eyes.

Long Bruce sat, on the sub-Prior's bed, with that letter in clenched hand, motionless, though sometimes his lips moved, and once or twice he groaned a little. From below, the sound of music and revelry rose faintly — strange sounds from a monastery.

Then he stiffened as another sound came close. There was a brief knock at the door, and Christina MacRuarie opened it. She stood there slightly flushed but looking very handsome.

The King looked at her, but scarcely saw her.

"You read your letter again, rather than dance? Or even sleep?" she demanded. "Are bishops' letters so much to your taste?"

"It is from my wife," he said slowly. "Elizabeth."

"Oh," She stared, biting her red lip. "Your pardon. She . . . the Queen? She is well?"

He inclined his head.

"Then, Sire, I think . . . that you will not be requiring me? This night?"

"I thank you — no," he said. "A . . . a goodnight to you, Christina."

She shook her head, and in those darkly vivid eyes was a strange expression, compounded of pain and pity, regret and a deep understanding. And something more. Without a word she turned and left him there.

Chapter Thirteen

The singer's voice rose strong, clear, tuneful, yet with a haunting sadness, to pause on a rising, questioning note that was at once and strangely both plaintive and challenging, a note that was allowed to die away into the blue hush of the night and merge with the lap-lap of the wavelets on the lochshore and the sigh of air in the scattered Scots pines whose sturdy gnarled trunks redly reflected the glow of the camp-fires. Quivering, the composite liquid sound seemed to soar away over heather and water, for long breathless moments before the tremendous, fiercely positive refrain crashed out again from a thousand throats, yet in perfect unison and unbroken melody. Robert Bruce shivered, though not with cold, as his mother's Celtic blood responded to the ancient magic of it, even though he understood only a little of the distinctively West Highland Gaelic of the saga's wording. Words are by no means essential to emotion, especially of a summer's night amongst the endless mountains that throng long Loch Ness.

It was a young giant who sang, clad in saffron tunic, piebald calfskin jerkin and gem-studded harness, with strongly mobile features and shoulder-length tawny hair which, like the great ox-horned helmet he had laid by, spoke of the Norse influence which for centuries had permeated the Gaelic Hebrides. Only in the Celtic civilisation, with its emphasis on the arts of living, in music and song and poetry, design and beauty would a young man who sang thus, before all, not be considered effeminate; this singer need fear no such imputation, at any rate, for he was a renowned warrior, Seumas son of Donald, son of Ranald, of Oronsay, one of Angus Og's chieftains.

As the rich, vibrant tenor commenced yet another verse of the ballad — the tenth, or perhaps the twelfth — the King, asprawl on a springy couch of pine-twigs and bracken, gazed round at the scene with some measure of real satisfaction. For here, surely, was something that he had achieved, and only he. Never before, since the realm of Scotland became a unity, had a King of Scots been able to do what he was doing. Here was a wholly Highland host, only the Earl of Lennox — who was a sort of tamed Highlander himself — sitting at his right, and Gibbie Hay, with his charge Thomas Randolph, were Southrons, the former frankly asleep, the latter looking stiffly bored. All the rest, chiefs and chieftains, from Angus of the Isles and Neil Campbell of Lochawe, down to the running gillies and horse-boys, were clansmen, Highlanders to a man — Islesmen of the MacDonald and MacRuarie confederation; Campbells from South Argyll; MacGregors whom they had collected at Glen Strae and Glen Orchy, under their intimidating chief Malcolm himself; Macleans of Morvern; and most interest- of all, Macphersons, Cattanachs, Shaws and Mackintoshes from Badenoch, Comyn lands which they had passed through on their move north from Lorn — but which, unlike the true Lowland Comyn country of Buchan, had only been gained in conquest by its Norman lords, not married into, so that its Highland population showed no enmity to Bruce, and following the example of the West Highland chiefs contributed their quota to the royal advancing army. Hitherto no King of Scots would, or could, have entrusted himself to a Highland army, since the Lowlanders looked upon these people as barbarians, little better than vermin, not to be associated with nor trusted. Yet here he lay, secure and accepted, within a company of 4,000 and more of these Highlanders, on the southern shore of Loch Ness, hundreds of miles deep within their mountain fastnesses. Moreover, using them to counter another Highland army, just across the water.

The King turned his glance, as he had done frequently that early August night, away from the dramatic scene of blazing fires and flaring pitch-pine torches and the thronged colourful ranks of fierce-looking clansmen, lit by the glow of the flames, against the twisted silhouettes of the trees and the black outlines of the crouching mountains — turned to the north. Loch Ness, although all of twenty-three miles long, was little more than a mile wide here, between Dores and Inverfarigaig: and across that mile more fires gleamed red against black hills.

For what seemed leagues those points of light glowed and flickered, left and right, marking the north shore of the loch, though they were less bright to the right, the north, where Urquhart Bay curved deeply back at the mouth of Glen Urquhart. The sky was overcast and dark for an August night, so that the host of fires showed the brighter, where the Earl of Ross's army awaited them, had awaited them for days; indeed, from all accounts, for weeks, on the borders of his great territory. For all Scotland to the north of where they camped here was in the grip of William of Ross, since it consisted of but the two mighty earldoms, and Sutherland happened to be heired by a minor, whom Ross dominated. Caithness was a no-man's-land, disputed between the crowns of Scotland and Norway, but in fact its unruly clans were also under the thumb of Ross. How many men lay encamped across Loch Ness none knew for certain — though there were tales of tens of thousands. That was undoubtedly an exaggeration — but there was enough to give Bruce pause, at any rate.

His glance, as had happened before, tended to dwell upon a certain point over there, some way east of directly across the dark waters. Here the pattern of lights was different, the gleams smaller and feebler and clustered close together, some indeed one above another. And it was noticeable that none of the larger lights looked close to these, on either side. For these indeed were not fires at all, but lights from windows, candle lamp or torch — the lights of Urquhart Castle on its rocky thrusting peninsula to the south of Urquhart Bay. That was Crown property, a royal castle, strong and strategically placed at the mouth of Glen Urquhart, guarding the only road to lead into the north-east between Inverness and the Western Sea. And presently held by Sir Alexander Comyn, brother of the Earl of Buchan.

The King rubbed his chin, eyes narrowed.

The singing was succeeded by Highland dancing, seemingly wild but essentially disciplined nevertheless, with the wailing, shrilling, groaning music of the bagpipes bubbling and skirling to hills and sky, when Bruce suddenly came to a decision and rose to his feet.

Angus Og, from near by, looked up. "You join the dancing, Sir King?" he asked, brows raised.

"Not tonight. I think that I will make a call. Across the loch. The night being dark."

"Now? By night? You mean — in force?"

"No. A secret call. Private, very. Come you with me, my lord?"

The other hesitated. "If so you wish. And believe it worth the doing."

"I believe it worth the trial, at least, yes. There are more weapons than swords in a King's armoury, friend."

Though all there who could hear looked uncertain, many wished to accompany the monarch nevertheless. But Bruce declared that two small boats were all that should go, the second only as a precaution in case of trouble. For days the Highlanders had been collecting boats from all up and down the lochside for many miles, assembling them hereabouts; also felling trees for rafts, for the boats to tow over. The shoreline was a mass of craft therefore, for 4,000 men would take a deal of ferrying across that mile of water, should it ever come to that.

Ordering the dancing to continue, the King led a little group out of the circle of the firelight and down to the shingly beach. Angus Og, Hay and Randolph — who was religiously taken everywhere that Hay went — joined Bruce, with two gillies for the oars, in one boat; Lennox, Campbell and the young man whom Bruce had knighted with Somerled's sword at Castle Tioram, Sir Ranald MacRuarie of Smearisary, went in the second boat. Christina MacRuarie had returned to Moidart, meantime, during the recent Lorn campaign, but had sent her nephew, Sir Ranald, with 400 men, as her link with the King. A popular young man with the Highlanders, because of his story-telling abilities, he now rejoiced in the somewhat empty title of royal cup-bearer. At the last moment a long lean dark figure came scuttling down to the strand, and came clambering aboard the King's craft, all flapping black robes, much to the scorn of Angus of the Isles — Master Bernard de Linton, the secretary. Shrugging, Bruce let him stay.

The oarsmen were set to row half-right, north by east, and at their quietest.

Presently, above the creak of rowlocks and splash of blades, Bruce heard sounds at their backs, and stared astern.

"There are craft behind us," he jerked. "Following."

"More than one," the Lord of the Isles agreed grimly. "Think you I would allow the whole leadership of this host to risk capture over there? Without a sufficiency of broadswords at our backs to ensure our safety."

The King frowned. "I said two small boats," he snapped. Then he waved a hand, assenting. "So be they keep out of sight. And quiet, I told you, it is not swords I am concerned with, this night."

With their own fires become mere points of light, in turn, strung along the southern shore, and some of the enemy's seeming alarmingly near now, the oarsmen, pulling very gently, drew in towards the dark and lofty bulk of Urquhart Castle on its bluff of headland. From this water-level its high walls, battlements, flanking-towers and soaring central keep looked impressive indeed, daunting. It was after midnight now, and few windows showed a light.

About fifty yards from the rocks, Bruce ordered the oarsmen to be still, and raised his voice. He did not shout, but called.

"Ho, the watch! Hear me. Does any keep watch in Urquhart Castle of a night?" Only on an overcast night at this time of year could they have won thus close, unspotted.

Swiftly he had reply. "Hey — fit's that? Fa's there?" a broad Aberdeenshire voice gave back, from one of the flanking-towers' parapets. "Guidsakes, is't a boat?"

"It is your King, man. Fetch you Sir Alexander Comyn, who captains this my castle of Urquhart."

"Eh . . .? Guidsakes — the King? Bruce . . .?"

"Fat's to do, Tosh?" somebody shouted, from another tower. "I can see twa boats. Sma' yins . . ."

'Quickly, fool!" Bruce commanded. "Tell Sir Alexander that King Robert requires speech with him. And no outcry, or you will suffer for it."

"Ooh, aye. Aye. Wait you . . ."

It was nerve-racking for them all to sit there, swaying on the water, so close to their toes — for Ross's patrols assuredly would be on the watch along all that waterfront, save just immediately in the vicinity of the castle's promontory. Bruce was torn between thankfulness, after all, for the presence of Angus Og's supporting craft somewhere behind, and the fear that these larger boats would loom visible from the main shore.

It seemed a long time before another voice sounded from the castle — not from any flanking-tower this time but evidently from a window of the great keep, though there was no light.

"Who claims to be the Bruce?" it demanded, in very different tones. "At this hour?"

"I do, Alexander Comyn. Your liege lord, whose castle you now occupy. You know my voice, as I know yours. In whose name do you hold the castle of Urquhart against me, sir?"

There was a pause, as well there might be. For Comyn to admit that he held it by right of conquest was to put himself in the wrong, since there was no question but that Urquhart was a royal castle. To say that he held it in the name of King Edward would be something of a humiliation for the proud Comyn, who undoubtedly considered himself an ally of the English King rather than a vassal.

"I hold it in the name of King John," he replied, at length. "King John Baliol."

"Then you are the only man in Christendom, Sir Alexander, who still calls John Baliol monarch!"

The other made no comment.

"I have come for my castle," Bruce went on. "Yield it to me, Sir Alexander, as is your duty and right, and you may remain its keeper."

The gasps of those beside him in the boat drowned any reaction that Comyn might have made.

"You hear me, sir? Do your duty. Yield me Urquhart, and I will forget the past. I will confirm you as keeper."

Still there was no perceptible reaction from the castle. Bruce cleared his throat. This calling across seventy or so yards of water was trying on the vocal cords.

"I have always considered you a man of some understanding, Comyn. No hot-headed fool, to throw away life and fortune on a lost cause. You have too much to lose, for that. And your Comyn cause is lost, whatever happens here. You know that. You have heard what is done in Buchan?"

"I have heard of savagery and shame. Of destruction. A fair land made a desert. A whole province harried without mercy. Do you boast of that?"

"I am not here to boast, sirrah. I am here to offer you terms. Or to destroy you. Destroy you as Buchan is destroyed. That Comyn shall never again threaten Bruce. The choice is yours.

Make your peace with me, your liege lord. Or fall—not to rise again."

"I am not like to fall, my lord. This castle is strong. And my nephew, the Earl of Ross, has a greater host than yours, encamped around Urquhart. You will not easily win across Loch Ness to come at me."

"Ross and his host are not here to save *you*, Comyn! They are here only to prevent me crossing the loch and entering their country. If they are outflanked, as they will be, they will leave you, like a stranded fish! They love you not, a Southron." Bruce took a chance. "I warrant the Earl of Ross, nephew though he may be, is not with you in my castle, Sir Alexander! Nephews are not always strong in their duty." And the King glanced over at Thomas Randolph.

Silence from the castle. Ross's mother was indeed Sir Alexander's sister, who had married the second Mac-an-Tagart Earl; but the Rosses remained purely Highland in outlook, with little interest in the Lowland Comyns.

Summoning reluctant lungs to the task, Bruce proceeded. "My brother, the Earl of Carrick, has finished laying Buchan low. He has done it thoroughly, and on my command. Not a single castle or place of strength, not a single slated house, or town or village remains to Comyn therein. Now he marches to meet me here. He is not far off, Sir Alexander. To the east. It is for him I wait, for he has my main host. But I have sent the word for him to come by the *north* shore of this loch, not the south! He will cross the river at Inverness. That town will not, cannot, withstand him. I expect him here tomorrow, Comyn. How long, think you, will Ross linger round Urquhart Castle when my brother appears on his flank? And with Lachlan MacRuarie, of whom you will have heard, marching from the North-West. He will retire up Glen Urquhart, to seek a stronger line in Strath Glass, where he may not be outflanked. You know it."

The continuing lack of response from the dark building was very eloquent.

"I offer you better terms than you deserve, sir." Bruce's voice growing hoarse and tired, now. "But I have a realm to win and to govern, and require the services of strong and able men, whether they love me or no. I would have Comyn, if not my friend, at least not my enemy. Your brother, the Earl of Buchan, is a broken man, and ill. Now in disgrace in England, it is said. The Comyn power is broken quite. You are the last to hold out against me. Let there be an end to this folly, Sir Alexander. Why should more men die? *My* subjects. Yield me this castle, and Tarradale on the Black Isle, also a royal house but held by you. Come into my peace. Then, I say the past is past. You shall remain keeper here, and your lands shall not be forfeit. How say you?"

"I . . . I must think on it. I require time to consider. To consider well . . ."

"Then you are a fool as well as a traitor, Comyn!" That was Angus Og, who could restrain himself no longer. "This King is over-kind, I say. He offers you a deal more than would I. It is Angus of the Isles who speaks. Most of the men yonder are mine. I have taken and burned many a stouter hold than this. Myself, I would have no parleying. And *you* would hang on your own dule-tree tomorrow!"

Bruce smiled to himself, at that.

From the other boat, only a couple of lengths away, someone else spoke up. "This is Malcolm of Lennox. You know me, Alexander Comyn. Do as His Grace asks, I pray you. We have had enough of killing and hatred. The King is right. And he is a true man. He keeps his word. What gain to you now by withstanding him? This our country, our kingdom, needs to be built up — 'fore God it does! Not torn apart. King Robert is the man to do it. You were ever the best of the Comyns. Will you not aid him in it?"

"Well said, Malcolm," Bruce murmured.

"Would you have me betray my own kin?" the voice from the castle came back. "The Earl of Ross?"

Bruce answered. "I ask no man to betray other. There has been too much betrayal in this Scotland. I say that you will serve Ross well. He cannot win against the rest of Scotland. None come to his aid. He hoped for aid from John of Lorn. But *we* have just come from Lorn. MacDougall licks his wounds. He has not come north, nor will do. And yesterday we captured a courier from Ross. To King Edward of England. Beseeching aid. Saying that he was sore pressed. That he had insufficient men to protect all the North. That unless he received English aid soon he must retire into a closer country. Knew you of this letter?"

That elicited no reply.

"Edward will not aid him, Comyn. *You* know that. Has he aided Comyn? This Edward is not as his father. Ross will win aid from none. The sooner he perceives it, the better. I do not wish to fight him. Even he, who delivered up my wife and daughter, I will receive into my peace. Tell him so. He is my subject. And by yielding me this castle, open his eyes, man."

"I must consider it. Give me time to think on it . . . Sire."

Bruce caught his breath in his hoarse throat. That one reluctant word, from Comyn's lips! Sire! It might serve — the thing might serve!

"Very well, Sir Alexander," he called. "Think you. Think well. I give you until tomorrow's noon." Edward had sent word that he would arrive the next forenoon. "This is a royal castle. Somewhere in it will be its royal standard, the Lion Banner of Scotland. Tomorrow, fly that standard above this castle, and pull down your Comyn colours — and I accept you into my peace. Keep your own banner flying — and I destroy you. Is it understood?"

"It is understood."

"Very well. I bid you a good night, sir. And may tomorrow's sun shine kindly for Scotland! For us all!"

Thankfully the rowers dipped their oars, to pull away.

"You are a strange man, Robert Bruce." Angus Og declared, as they headed back into the south-west. "Both cunning and trusting. Fierce enough, yet too kind of heart. You truly would forgive the Comyn all?"

Bruce was staring at the dark shapes of fully half a dozen larger boats which now loomed out of the night ahead of them. "It is not my heart that is so kind, I fear, Angus, my friend," he said slowly. "My head, rather. I am cursed, or blessed, with a head that speaks different from my heart, in many matters. Or perhaps it is that a king must have two hearts? One his own, and one for his kingdom, his people. And the first must needs give way to the second — or his coronation vows are worthless. I do not say that I forgive Comyn — yet. One day, perhaps. But I will keep my promise to him. If he submits."

"Oh, he will submit," Hay said. "You heard that Sire? There spoke the decision he will make, I swear."

Out of the quiet that followed, another voice made itself heard, one that seldom spoke. "My lord," Sir Thomas Randolph said, "was it truth that you said? That you would accept even William of Ross to your peace? The Earl? He who betrayed your lady?"

"God helping me, yes. Even he. For the sake of this realm."

"This, I say, is too much!" Campbell put in, vehemently. "I say Your Grace will turn mercy into weakness. And as such, men will see it."

"Not mercy, Neil. Nor yet weakness, I think. It is policy. God knows I find no mercy in my heart for William of Ross. But if I am to rid Scotland of the English invaders, I cannot afford a single enemy at home that I may win over or disarm, by word or deed. And Ross has thousands, who would take much beating, in the field."

Randolph spoke again, stiffly, formally — and sounding very

young. "Then, my lord — if tomorrow Sir Alexander Comyn yields, and comes into your peace, I too will do likewise. He is an honourable knight. I can do no less."

"Did I hear a puppy bark?" the Lord of the Isles snorted.

"You heard a man with a notable conscience, my lord. An inconvenience which is not laid upon us all!" Bruce kept his voice grave. "Well said, nephew. We shall see."

"I fear there will soon be more traitors in Your Grace's company than true men . . ." Campbell was beginning, when the King interrupted, abruptly changing the subject.

"My lord of the Isles — you would hear me tell Comyn that Lachlan MacRuarie approaches from the north-west, to threaten Ross's right flank. He does — but we know that he cannot be nearer than Kintail, and so near three days' march. Scarce so near as I made him sound! I think we must . . . dissemble a little, tomorrow. Despite all our noble words and conscience! If my nephew will overlook it, this once! The MacRuarie host is too far away for my purpose — but young Sir Ranald here has 400 men — and a MacRuarie banner! If you gave him some men of yours, say 600, to a fair showing, and sent him round this loch, to approach from the west, he might well be mistaken for his bastard uncle!"

"Ha!"

"How long would it take, think you, for your swift Highlandmen to get to the head of this Loch Ness, across the Oich River, into the hills to the north, and so up this far again?"

"It is sixteen miles and more to the fords at Bunoich. Six to Invermoriston on the north shore. Then up into the hills of Balmacaan, behind Mealfuarvonie, another eight — a hard eight. Thirty heather miles in all. In eight or nine hours, if need be, my people could be where you would have them."

"I would not have believed that men could cover rough country at that pace — had I not already seen your Highlandmen doing as much! Good — then we shall have them away forthwith, this night. And see if young Sir Ranald commands men so well as he tells tales of it! You will lend him your hundreds, Angus?"

"You command this host, Sir King — not I. But . . . is this thrust for fighting? Or only to make your fair showing? For if there is to be battle over there, I shall want some of my own tried captains in command, and no stripling fireside knight!"

"They will fight only if they must. But send whom you will . . ."

Next morning, after early rain, the great camp by the lochside was astir with activity. Scores of boats, and as many rafts, were assembled, manned and marshalled into flotillas, and embarkation and disembarkation practised, with raft-towing exercises out as far as mid-loch. Bruce sighed with relief when the last of the rain lifted off the hilltops, and the first watery sunbeams lit up the Great Glen of Scotland, giving crystal-clear rainwashed visibility — for visibility was all-important today. He sent trumpeters and hornblowers off to sundry eminences and viewpoints up and down the loch, to sound their calls and assemblies intermittently, and ordered all troops not engaged in the boat and beach-landing exercises to march and counter-march over a wide area of the shoreline, with all banners flying and pipes playing — but only in places where they would be seen and heard from across the mile-wide waters. Some of the Highland chieftains grumbled and snarled at this folly of play-acting; but the King was adamant. The air of excitement generated, however artificial, grew none the less.

Then in mid-forenoon, Gilbert Hay called to the King, and pointed almost due west, across the loch. High on the long purple ride that ran north-eastwards parallel with the shore, from the fine peak of Mealfuarvonie, a dark crest had appeared, almost like a forest of young trees grown suddenly there. But the flash of steel in the sun told a different story, and by straining the eyes it was just possible to distinguish the square black-and-white banner that rose above its approximate centre.

"So, Angus," Bruce exclaimed, "Your Islesmen have not failed us! Eight hours, no more. Show me any other fighting-men who could cover thirty roadless mountain miles in such time! What will my lord of Ross say to that, think you?"

'He will have heard, hours back, that they approach, for he is no fool and will have had his scouts well placed."

"That alters nothing. So long as he does not know that they came from this side of the loch. Believes them Lachlan MacRuarie's host."

"It is good that we can see them so clearly," Hay pointed out. "For if we can see MacRuarie up there, a mile and more back from the loch, then we need not fear that Ross cannot see our busyness here."

"As you say. How think you Comyn feels this morning?"

They looked towards Urquhart Castle, where the blue-and-gold Comyn flag still could be seen fluttering above the keep.

"I vow he bites his nails, and scans all that he can see from his topmost tower! If he has not already made his decision."

As the royal forces kept up there almost feverish activities, the leaders' eyes kept turning ever more and more to the north-east. Edward Bruce, the triumphant harrier of Buchan, had sent word that he would join his brother that morning, from Inverness a dozen miles away, and the King's urgent orders were that he should advance along the north shore of Loch Ness until he made first contact with Ross's left flank outliers. At first light that morning another mounted courier had been sent hot-foot to Edward, who was meantime laying tentative siege to English-held Inverness Castle, as to the importance of the arrangement, and its timing They could see for miles towards the loch-foot at Dochfour, from the knoll directly behind the main camp. He should have been in sight before this. Could the hot-head already have taken action against Ross, somewhere to the north, while he still had command of Bruce's main army? By the Bunchrew or Moniack valleys, perhaps, thinking to take Ross in the rear? It was the sort of thing Edward might do . . .

As time went on and the sun rose towards the meridian, the King grew agitated, pacing the turf of the knoll. He should not have relied on Edward in so ticklish an issue as this.

When at last a shout went up, the fingers pointed, it was not towards Dochfour and the foot of the loch that eyes turned, but along the wooded shore road on their own side of the water. Less than a mile away, towards Dores, there was a sizeable gap in trees, and there a mounted cavalcade could be seen, the red-and-gold Bruce banner at its head.

"God's curse on all witless headstrong dolts!" the King cried. "Why am I plagued with such a brother! My orders were clear. Clear enough for a babe. But not for Edward . . .!"

As the mounted party drew near, appearing and disappearing amongst the woodland at a round canter, it could be seen that it was a gallant company indeed, all splendid armour, new-painted heraldic shields, silken surcoats, tossing plumes, flowing horse-trappings, waving pennons — and all superbly mounted. But it was not an army. There were not more than some fifty men, though most of them appeared to be of knightly rank.

The King eyed their brilliance from under down-drawn brows.

They came jingling up, Edward at their head, more magnificent than any had ever seen him. He wore black polished plate armour, engraved with gold, and even his chain-mail was threaded with gold wire; his black chased helmet bore scarlet and yellow ostrich plumes, his sword-belt and even his spurs were of gold. He raised a gauntleted hand in flourished salutation, as he pulled up a notable stallion richly caparisoned.

"Well met, brother," he called heartily. "I greet you right royally! Here's a good day for our cause. I hope, though, that I see you well? You look thin, Robert, thin."

The King moistened his lips. He looked by comparison shabby, in peat-stained clothing and rusty mail. He was always at his worst with this brother of his, and knew it. Nigel had been hot-headed too, and probably less able in some ways than Edward; but at him had not always felt the need to rail and contend.

"I am well enough," he said evenly, dredging for patience. "I scarce need ask how you are! I rejoice to see you so fine! But I had not looked to see you *here,* this morning!"

"I was so near, it were folly not to come. To bring you my good news in person. And to show you how we may best deal with this traitor Ross."

Bruce bit back hot words. He looked from his brother to the ranks of glittering chivalry at his back, not a man of which was not the picture of knightly pride and circumstance. He saw Sir Alexander Fraser and his brother Sir Simon, Sir Robert Fleming, Sir John Stirling, Sir William Wiseman, Sheriff of Elgin, Sir David Barclay and his brother Sir Walter, Sir John de Fenton and Sir William Hay, a kinsman of Gibbie's. It was as good as a court Edward had to ride with him. It was very evident that these had been conducting a very different kind of war to his own, and a profitable one.

"Where is my host, my lord?" he asked, carefully. "My main army?"

His brother waved from the saddle approximately north-easterly. "Back yonder. North of the river. Ten miles. Boyd has it . . ."

"North of the *river*? The River Ness? I said the loch. North of the *loch*, man!"

"What matters it? A mile or so more or less? So long as they are across the river. That Ross may not hold it against us. See you, brother — this notion you have of crossing the loch in boats is folly. You will lose most of your men. Even though they are only Highlandmen! Ross can defend the far shore with ease. Throw you back into the water. Have you counted the cost? I have a better plan, by far. Beyond Inverness to the north is a narrow plain, by the side of the firth. Off it open two valleys, the waters of Bunchrew and Moniack. These lead into the mountains of The Aird, behind Ross's position. Up these, and we can take him in the rear. I told Boyd to halt my host at the place called Dochgarroch. By the river. From there I can send the foot up a small side valley, and so through the hills to the greater one of Bunchrew. The horse will have to take the longer way round, by the Dunain. When they see a smoke signal from me, on some hill-top here. Your Highlanders would best go round the head of the loch and make a sally from the west."

The King, who had been holding himself in with difficulty, spoke curtly. "My lord — do I understand that you have taken upon yourself to countermand my express orders? That you have told Sir Robert Boyd to take my host — *mine*, not yours, Edward — no further than this Dochgarroch? When I commanded that you bring it along the loch until you made contact with Ross's left flank?"

At his brother's flinty sternness, the other lost a little of his fine assurance. "I told you — this way we can confound Ross. Save many lives . . ."

"Dizzard! Think you Ross does not know Bunchrew and Moniack Waters? In his own territory? Think you *I* did not consider them? But . . ." He cut his hand down sharply in a chopping motion. ". . . Whether you thought or did not think, is of no consequence. I commanded, and you disobeyed. How dare you, sir!"

For long moments the two brothers stared into each other's eyes, there before all. None thought to intervene.

Edward put as bold a face on it as he might. "I did what I believed for the best. For your cause . . . Sire."

"In this kingdom none countermands the King's commands — none, I say! You hear? All hear?" Robert Bruce's voice quivered, but only with his attempt to keep under control the hot ire that boiled up within him. "I heed and take advice from all. I let my mind be altered, in debate. I do not claim all wisdom. But . . . my orders are royal commands. And any who choose to disobey them are guilty of treason. Treason! Do you hear?" He paused, and swung his wrathful gaze on all who listened, before returning to his brother. "Any — be they the highest in the land or the lowest. Remember, all of you — if you value your heads!"

There was a complete silence from all near by, broken only by the jingle of bits and bridles, and the stamping of hooves. From further afield a trumpet brayed to the surrounding hill, its echoes a bedlam.

As though accepting that as a sign, an assent, the King drew a long slow breath, and changed his tone. "This Dochgarrach? I know the place. It is too far to be seen from Castle Urquhart, is it not? Eight miles? Does any here know the castle well? It stands high, on a rock out into the loch. But not to view as far as Dochgarroch, I fear."

"I know it, Sir King," Angus MacFarquherd Mackintosh, Captain of Clan Chattan, said from behind. "It is too far. Not to be seen. There is higher land between."

"Aye." That was almost a sigh. "Then, my lord of Carrick, you have destroyed *my* stratagem. I never thought to throw men's lives away by attacking Ross across the loch, in these boats. I am less fond than are you of killing. Even Ross and his thousands are my subjects — and a king does not slay his subjects unless he must. What I may gain by any other means than the sword, I will. I let you loose on Buchan for a purpose, as example. Today, I had no intention of fighting. And my main host, visible there at the foot of the loch, was part of my design. You have brought it to naught."

Edward shook his head, helplessly. "I did not know. You did not tell me . . ."

"No — I did not tell you. I *commanded* you!" The King turned roughly away. "Now I must think anew . . ."

"But, Robert — Sire! My news! You have not heard my news. Hear me. Last night, the English in Inverness Castle asked for a truce. They are willing to surrender the castle, if we will spare them their lives, let them sail away. They have not failed to hear of my doings in Buchan, I swear! They sweat for their skins! They must be short of provision, to offer this. So I sent their messengers back, with their tails between their legs — like whipped curs should have! They will surrender without terms, I told them. And they will, you see. Any day. So that there will be only Banff Castle in all the North, held by Englishmen — for it can only be taken by sea. Aberdeen has fallen. That Provost and his citizens have won into it — how I know not. *I* have taken Fyvie, Elgin, Forres and Nairn from the English, and Kinedar, Slains, Rattray, Cairnbulg, Dundarg and Inverallochy from the Comyns. The Bishop of Moray now threatens Tarradale in the Black Isle. If we but take our courage in our hands and beat Ross now, all the North is yours! Do you not see it?"

"I see, brother, that there is a tide flowing our way, here in the North. And I rejoice in it. And give thanks for what you have achieved, with my host. But I also see, across this loch, some ten thousand, it may be, of fierce clansmen, ready to fight to the death. On their own territory, where they fight best. And know best. In mountains, where our chivalry is at disadvantage. Here is no attacking small bands, castles, villages and townships. This is battle, on a great scale. It may be that in time we should beat them. At much cost, which I can ill afford. And MacDougall of Lorn remains in the West, undefeated. I do not fight battles until I have tried other methods."

Edward began to speak, but the King held up his hand.

"You talk of courage. I have never doubted yours, brother. Perhaps you have more of the quality than have I! It is your wits, your judgement, I doubt. Even in this of Inverness Castle. I say the English offer of surrender must be accepted. On terms. Ross will hear of it, and be the less assured. The sight of the Englishry marching of their own will out of Inverness and sailing south will do my cause more good than any prolonged siegery. Then we shall pull down the castle, like all the others, that it never again be held against me. I hope that you razed all these other yielded strengths as I ordered?"

As the other cleared his throat and sought for a judicious answer, someone else spoke.

"Sire — you have said wisely, generously. Like a true king. In all this. And none can doubt your courage."

"Ah, nephew — I thank you!" Bruce turned to bow, in only lightly disguised mockery.

"Our traitorous kinsman still with you, I see!" Edward said, thankful to change the subject.

Randolph ignored him. "More than castles may yield, Sire — when the time is come. Will Your Grace now accept me as your leal man? Your subject. Receive my hand and sword, as your true knight?" That was awkwardly, jerkily said, from stiff lips. "I submit me — as I promised."

The King eyed the young man's tensely handsome features, and then, as the significance of those last words dawned upon him, swung on his heel to stare elsewhere, much farther away.

There, across the water, Urquhart Castle glowed warm red-brown in the sun, against the blue loch and the purpling hills. And clear to see above its lofty keep floated a different banner now to the blue-and-gold of Comyn — the Lion Rampant of Scotland.

"God be praised!" Bruce breathed. "So it served. After all."

In the exclamations and chatter that followed, Gilbert Hay touched the King's elbow, and pointed farther away still, towards the loch-foot. He did not speak.

It was sun on steel again, glinting and flashing though far away, the tiny gleams reflecting over a wide area.

"Ha — by the Rude! So there we have it!" the King cried. "Praises be! Comyn saw that sooner than did we. Robert Boyd knows his duty, if others do not! My true veteran warrior! Brother — see you there. Sir Robert Boyd knows whose host he leads. He did not halt at your Dochgarroch, but brought them on right to the loch. As I commanded you. Mark it well. As Sir Alexander Comyn, in Urquhart, marked it. And has signified his capitulation to me by that Lion Standard. For this I planned. Here is more burden on the Earl of Ross than any blood-soaked attack." He jabbed a finger in the other direction, due westwards. "There, on the ridge of Mealfuarvonie, MacRuarie and a thousand clansmen stand. Here we marshal a host of boats. There Boyd threatens and Comyn yields. Ross will retire, *must* retire, northwards. Up Glen Urquhart. Abandoning this line of Loch Ness and the Great Glen. He cannot make stand again until Strath Glass or Strath Farrar. So we gain a victory of sorts, and much country. Without a man slain!"

There was a great clamour of acclaim, with everywhere men surging forward to hail the King. The knights behind Edward, as with one accord, dismounted and came to make belated obeisance. But Bruce had turned away, towards Randolph again, who still stood with Hay, a pace or two behind. He held out his hand.

"Sir Thomas," he said, "you have keen eyes. A keen judgement in some matters. And a keen notion of honour. May they serve me and my cause well hereafter. This is an auspicious day. I receive you into my peace, and gladly. You are a free man, nephew. And all that is yours shall be restored to you."

Randolph sank down on knee before his uncle, and took that lean hand between both of his. "My liege lord," he said, thickly. "I thank you. From my heart. I pray your royal forgiveness, for past deeds done and past words spoken. Hereafter, none shall serve you more faithfully."

"So be it, lad." The King looked down, and felt — indeed looked — very old compared with the unlined and nobly handsome face upturned to his, despite his own mere thirty-four years. "But I warn you, my service may try you hard. As it does others."

He turned to receive the homage of the now thronging knights.

Presently he looked over their heads to Edward, who still sat his fine horse, set-faced. "Come, brother — enough of bickering and hard words. Perhaps I am too sore on you. You in particular — since I am sore on all, I fear. This is too good a day to spoil. Come, you."

The other's face lightened, and he leapt down, his magnificent mail clanking, and strode to grasp the outstretched hand, wordless.

"You are mighty fine, Edward. Whose spoil is that you wear?" Bruce demanded, thumping the other's armoured shoulder.

"My lord of Buchan's. The spoil of Dundarg. And I have brought better for you. A whole train of it! The spoil of a province. And of the proudest, richest house in all Scotland."

"Aye. You will tell me of all your campaign presently. I have heard something of it, even in the West. All the land talks of the Harrying of Buchan. But meantime we make more play with these boats. Marshal them differently, farther down the loch a little, opposite Urquhart. With much show. As though we had changed our plans, and will pour all our forces in through the castle, now that it has declared for us. Instead of assailing the beaches. Ross could not halt our ingress to the castle, from the loch. So he will hasten his withdrawal, I think . . ."

Some time later, the cry went up that a small boat was coming sailing across the loch towards this position. Presently it was seen that what had looked like a sail was in fact a large white flag.

"So Sir Alexander Comyn comes to make his peace with me," the King commented. "Bringing the keys of his castle. We must receive him suitably. In some style."

"I *hanged* my Comyns," Edward mentioned briefly.

But in a little, the sharp-eyed Hay was calling that it was not Comyn in the boat. There were four occupants, two rowers and two others, both young and in Highland dress. Interested, the party round Bruce watched and waited.

As the craft beached on the shingle, and the two young men jumped out, one holding aloft the white flag, Angus Og drew a quick breath.

"Hugh!" he exclaimed. "Hugh Ross, himself. Son of the chief, Eldest son. He of the red hair."

"Ha-a-a! You say so? Ross would talk, then!"

The red-headed newcomer was an open-faced, freckled, pleasant-looking man in his early twenties, well-built and richly clothed. He and his companion came pacing self-consciously up the beach towards the silently watchful and impressive group.

"I am Sir Hugh de Ross, son of the Earl," the redhead declared, in a rush. It was of passing interest to Bruce that this Highlander chose to Normanise his name thus. "This is a cousin, Ross of Cadboll. We have a mission from my father. To Sir Robert the Bruce, formerly Earl of Carrick." He was addressing himself to Edward, not Robert, perhaps not unnaturally in view of the difference in their appearance.

"I am King Robert. I greet the son of the Earl of Ross. And his kinsman. But how is it that you style yourself knight, sir?"

"King Edward of England knighted me. The old king."

"Ah. So we have at least that in common, sir. For he knighted me also! You would seem to have served him better than I did!"

The young man looked a little disconcerted. "I obey my father's commands, my lord."

"To be sure. A dutiful son — if less dutiful subject! Were you at Saint Duthac's chapel, at Tain? When your father violated that sanctuary, and tore my wife and daughter from before its altar, to hand over to your English Edward?"

"No, sir. I was crossing swords with Angus of the Isles — whom I see now at your shoulder. In the Western Sea. I do not make war on women and children. My father must answer for himself. He was seven years Edward's prisoner in the Tower of London. After capture at Dunbar fight. And released only on terms, four years ago. I think that he did not relish another spell in an English prison!"

"So he sent my women there instead!"

The other did not answer, and Bruce beat down the hot anger within him which was always so liable to rise and choke him when he most needed to be calm and clear-headed.

"So the Earl of Ross sends you as his messenger, sir?"

"Yes. He sends you offer of truce."

The gasps with which this bald statement was received came not only from the King. Nearly everyone who heard gasped. A truce! Offered, not sought, even. The gesture of a monarch to an equal. Even Angus Og, who might have adopted the same line himself, was outraged that the Earl of Ross should do so.

"Here's an insolent dog!" Edward exclaimed. "A truce, says he! That, from an accursed rebel! And a Highlandman, at that!"

"What mean you by that, sir?" Angus snapped.

"I mean here's a treacherous rogue acting the prince. Expecting us to treat with him. A truce, he says. He *offers* it, by the Mass!"

"Sir — I do not know your name. But none speaks of my father in my presence, and thinks to escape my steel! White flag or none." The red-head took a pace forward, hand on sword-hilt.

"Peace, peace!" the King intervened. "In *my* presence, none quarrel and bandy words! This is the Earl of Carrick, Sir Hugh — my brother. He should not have spoken of your father as he did. I declare it as unsaid. But — this of a truce. Subjects do not make truces with their monarch, sir."

"My father does not accept you as his monarch."

With a hand raised, Bruce quelled the snarl of wrath that rose around him. "Whom *does* my lord of Ross accept as his liege lord, then? Edward of England? Son of he who imprisoned him?"

"No, sir. John Baliol. Who abdicated only under duress, and still lives."

"How could he be King of Scots, when he lives the life of a recluse, in France? Has not set foot in Scotland for a dozen years?" Bruce caught himself up. "But I am not here to debate my kingship with you, sirrah. I was duly and properly crowned king two years ago. And am so accepted by all save a few stiff-necked rebels, as your father. And the Comyns. The Comyns I have dealt with. Now it is your turn."

"No parliament has yet accepted you as King, sir," the young man persisted. "Until it does, no man can be proclaimed rebel who holds to King John."

"Dear God — this is too much!" Edward cried. "You will stand and listen to such impudence, Sire? For if you will, *I* will not!"

"Patience, brother — as I seek patience. Here is a young man of courage, at least. Who takes his stand on forms and ordinances. We must humour him with the forms he respects. You would have a parliament approve my kingship, sir? So would I. But it must be a true and free parliament. And while the English invaders remain in Scotland, none such is possible. You would not deny that?"

"A parliament can and should confirm the power of a new monarch." That was the Earl of Lennox, speaking with authority. "But it does not make the monarch. Nor can unmake him. Once duly crowned."

"And I was duly crowned. At Scone. By its abbot. On the true Stone. The Bishop of St. Andrews anointing. The crown placed on my brow by one of the line of MacDuff. Your father was summoned thereto, sir. He did not come. He could have come, and made objection. He, one of the seven great earls of Scotland. Indeed it was his duty, if he believed me usurper."

"Did the Lord of the Isles, here, attend your coronation? Or any other from the Highlands — save only the Campbell?"

"Have done with this folly of words!" Angus Og broke in. "Words and more words! The sword speaks truer." And he gripped his own. "Sir King — send this puppy whence he came, I say."

"Aye — so say I!" It was not often that Edward Bruce and the Islesman agreed. Indeed, now, led by Neil Campbell, most of the notables there raised their voices to like effect.

"Wait, my friends," the King insisted. "If we accept the sword as the truest speaker, then the strongest rules all, and the weaker must fall. Like right and justice. This Sir Hugh Ross has invoked forms and allegiances. So be it. We will show him that in these we are stronger also. For this is a realm I seek to rule, not a tournament, nor a bear-pit! You, sir — you say that your father denies recognition of my kingship, and accepts John Baliol's. You deny John Baliol's abdication. Who forced that abdication? The King of England. Therefore the King of England is John Baliol's enemy. And therefore your father's. Is he not?"

Wary, the other inclined his head slightly.

"Yet, I have here a letter from your father. To the King of England. Captured, two days back." Bruce turned. "Master Bernard — you have the letter? Aye — give it to me. This, Sir Hugh, is your father's signature and seal? He writes to the King of England asking for soldiers, money, aid, to fight against his own fellow-subjects in Scotland. This letter then, by your own showing, by every form and observance, is treasonable. The work of a traitor. To me — or to John Baliol! Deny it!"

The young man bit his lip, eyes darting, silent.

"So! Now — this your mission here? What does the Earl of Ross say to the King of Scots?"

Sir Hugh cleared his throat, obviously much put out. "He offers ... he suggests a truce, my lord. In any fighting between you. For a time. Three months. Six months — as you will. Each side to swear no advance on present positions, or any armed conflict. Each side to yield hostage to that effect. As pledge."

"Why?" That was barked out.

"Why — in the name of God?" Angus Og burst out. "Need you ask why? Because he is outflanked and outwitted! Because he would hold Ness-side and not have to retire up Glen Urquhart to Strath Glass. Because he would give himself time to gather more men. To await the coming of winter, when the passes are closed against you and you cannot attack him. Save by sea. We can all see why!"

"You mistake me, my lord," Bruce answered coolly. "I asked not why there should or should not be a truce. But why he would have me yield a pledge. A hostage. Me, the King."

The young man blinked. "It was my father's word," he said.

"And your father's word requires such support, sir? It does not stand of itself? So — what pledge does the Earl of Ross offer me, to reinforce his promise?"

"Me," the other answered simply. "Myself."

"I' faith — you! You, as hostage?"

"Yes, sir. His eldest son. Heir. To remain with you. In token of his honest intentions that there shall be no breaking of the truce."

"I see." Bruce paused, and actually smiled slightly. "You have made something of a strange entry to my Court and company, Sir Hugh Ross! But — who knows, you may come to adorn it well! Like, I hope, Sir Thomas Randolph. You two should agree well together! But, see you — this may be my lord of Ross's pledge and surety. Mine is otherwise. My simple royal word. The word of the King of Scots. I give no other surety to any subject, or any man. So send you your cousin here to tell your father so. It is all the surety he will get — or require. You understand?"

The red-head bowed.

It was some moments before it dawned on the company what was here involved. The King was accepting the truce. Uproar broke out.

Bruce allowed his friends their head for a little, and then rapped out a stern "Silence!" Even so, the required quiet took some time to settle.

"This truce I will uphold," he declared strongly. "It may serve the Earl of Ross. It also serves me. We shall come to a conclusion another day. A three months' truce, Sir Hugh. As from this day. It is agreed."

"Yes, sir. Three months. That means until early November. Until then, each side holds its hand."

"So be it. And you, sir? I am prepared to accept your father's word in this. You may return to him."

The young man hesitated, and then jutted his chin. "No, my lord. I still obey my father's commands. To remain with you, as his hostage. That he ordained, that I will do."

Bruce eyed him directly, thoughtfully, for a few seconds, seeking to assess the reasons behind this. He conceived this young man to be honourable — which was more than he did of his sire. Was that it, then? Hugh Ross himself did not trust William Ross, and was seeking to ensure his father's good faith thus? It could be.

"Very well," he said briefly. "Send your cousin back with this word. Then put yourself in charge of Sir Thomas Randolph, my nephew. You will have much in common! That is all."

The Rosses bowed, and went back to the boat.

The King slowly searched the faces of those around him. "I see you doubt my judgement. All of you," he said. "I am sorry for that But the decision is mine, and I have made it. Rightly or wrongly."

"It cannot be right, Robert," Edward exclaimed. "To come to terms with the man who betrayed your wife and Marjory. And my sisters. I cannot understand how you could stomach it, 'fore God!"

"It is the King who stomachs it — not the husband and father and brother!" Bruce grated.

"Even so . . ."

"The King to accept an offer of truce from a rebel!" Campbell said, dark head shaking. "This I could not have believed, Sire."

"When you have Ross forced to retire!" Angus Og weighed in. "Of all times *not* to hold your hand! We are fighting-men, are we not? We came here to fight Ross. And now, when your stratagems have succeeded, and he sees that he is in trouble, you treat with him. If *he* needs this truce, you do not."

"I say that His Grace is right," Thomas Randolph put in, greatly daring, as all stared at him in surprise and offence. "This way much bloodshed will be spared. Time gained and no harm done. Ross holding the North behind this line will not hurt the rest of the kingdom, or His Grace's cause. For three months or six. So the King may turn his attention elsewhere."

"Thank you, nephew," Bruce nodded. "I see that you have more in that handsome head than mere notions of chivalry and honour!" He turned to the others. "See you — Ross needs this truce, as my Lord of the Isles says. He says *I* do not. But I can *use* it. Ross sent that letter to King Edward. He hopes for help from England. *We* know, thanks to Lamberton, that he will not get it. Even though he writes other letters which we do not intercept. Edward of Carnarvon is otherwise occupied. Ross no doubt still hopes for aid from MacDougall of Lorn. This we must see that he does not obtain. But — be sure that he wants help! That is what matters. If we ensure that he gets none, then three months will not save him. Nor harm us. And meantime, we can go back and deal with MacDougall! With all our power, this time — no gesture. When he least expects us!"

When no one found anything they could controvert in that, he went on.

"This truce allows me to come to grips with Lorn this year. Still time, before the winter sets in. Here is a great matter. If we can bring down MacDougall and the West before this truce expires, I cannot see Ross in haste to seek battle with us thereafter. This could save me a year of campaigning — as well as the much war and bloodshed Randolph speaks of."

Lennox nodded. "Here is good sense, true judgement. Thank God for your quick wits, Sire."

Angus Og, who much preferred to fight on the coasts rather than inland, so that he could use his great fleet of galleys, shrugged acquiescence.

"What do we now, then?" Edward demanded. "Between our two hosts, we have 8,000 men. And not to strike a blow!"

Bruce smiled, relaxing. "Never fear, brother — there will be blows aplenty for you. And before long. We march to Inverness forthwith. Receive the surrender of that castle, and demolish it — allowing the English to sail away. Leave the Bishop of Moray to hold that town and watch this line. We shall turn south-west. For Argyll and Lorn again. I would be knocking at MacDougall's door before he hears of this truce, if that may be! From now on, we move fast."

Even Edward could not complain of that programme.

"Master Bernard — before we march, prepare me a paper to send to Sir Alexander Comyn yonder. Appointing him my Sheriff of Inverness. To work with Bishop David. He is an able man. We must use him, keep him content in our service . . ."

Chapter Fourteen

Drawing rein, Robert Bruce pointed, laughing heartily, easily, in more frank and honest mirth than his colleagues had heard from him for long. Bruce had been a mirthful young man once, too light-hearted for his father, seeing life through amused eyes wherever possible; if twelve years of war, sorrow, treachery and disaster had overlaid his high spirits, not with gloom so much as with a habit of sternness, of grim wariness, of self-protective constraint, it was all only an armour. The true man underneath was still sanguine, light-some, laughter-loving — if scarcely, any more, young of heart.

The occasion of mirth now was, as so often, the mild misfortune of another. Gilbert Hay's horse had stumbled in one of the in-numerable black peat-hags of the vast desolation of the moor, all but pitching its rider over its left shoulder. Gibbie, who had been dozing in his saddle in the warm afternoon sunshine of high August, had saved himself only by a major effort — but had over-done his sudden backwards and sideways jerking to such extent as to topple over the other side of the brute and into a little pool whose brilliant emerald-green coverlet was only a mossy scum to hide the thick black peat-broth beneath. Floundering in this gluti-nous mire, the unfortunate Lord of Erroll had covered himself more comprehensively in mud the more he struggled.

"Peace, Gibbie — peace!" the King besought. "Still, you. Float on it — do not swallow it!"

Similar unkind advice and comment came from all around, few failing to find amusement in the situation in that still fewer there had not been in something of the same predicament in these past days of mighty journeying across the rugged face of Highland Scot-land.

"A curse . . . on you all!" the bemired Gilbert spluttered. "This God-forsaken country!" He hurled a handful of the filth in the general direction of his monarch. "You are welcome . . . to your . . stinking realm!"

"Lese-majestie!" Bruce declared severely. And, as Thomas Ran-dolph jumped down to go to the aid of his friend, added, "Put him under, Thomas — under! Lese-majestie is a grievous sin. And to throw mud at the Lord's Anointed worse! Sir Hugh alone may do that — eh, my friend? Since you alone do not recognise me as King!"

Young Ross's grin faded, with his uncertainty as to how to take that. He made a cheerful hostage, and mixed well with the others — better than the more reserved Randolph ever had done; but he was always uneasy at the King's mild mockery and teasing. He in fact paid Bruce just as much respect as any of the company, while yet refusing resolutely to accord him the royal style and address. He got over his present difficulty by dismounting and aiding Randolph to extricate Hay.

While this was proceeding, Bruce turned in his saddle to look back, northwards, over the fantastic scene. In all Scotland there is nowhere quite so savagely and remorselessly desolate, so enormous in its waterlogged, rock-ribbed, peat-pocketed emptiness, as the Moor of Rannoch, so awe-inspiring in the sheer sullen immensity of its seventy square miles of brooding moon-landscape, and all only intensified and thrust into starker relief by the loveliness of its frame of distant blue mountains — Buchaille Etive and all the Glen Coe giants to the north the Black Mount massif to the west, the peaks of Rannoch and Glen Lyon to the east, and all the complex of Mamlorn to the south. Here is scenery, sheer territory, on a stupendous, daunting scale, and man the merest irrelevance.

Yet it was the men, the thousands of men, that Bruce considered, strewn over the face of the land behind him like ants on a forest floor. There were, of course, scouts ahead; but he, in the lead, had paused perhaps five miles out into the waste from the towering jaws of Glen Coe, Behind him, almost all the way back to those fierce mountain portals, his army straggled and spread. It seemed absurd even to think of it as an army, in the circumstances. After the long constrictions of the glens, where their 8,000 had perforce made a narrow column six miles and more in length, now men and animals spilled out and scattered far and wide, to pick a way for themselves across the wilderness of lochs and lochans, pools, runnels, burns, bogs and peat-mosses, as best they could, more like a plague of voles in migration than a royal and military force. The Highlanders took it all in their stride, of course; but the Lowland troops and cavalry were making heavy going, and the progress was slow indeed. If they were to be attacked now, on the verge of Lorn as they were, they would be helpless as a vast flock of stupid sheep. Except that no one *could* attack them effectively here, on any large scale, for the same conditions would apply to them. Bruce was not fretting, therefore, at their vulnerability, as he would have been almost anywhere else; nor even at the delay — though it did make nonsense out of his declaration that this descent upon Lorn should be swift and unheralded. MacDougall, in fact, could hardly have failed to be informed of their return, days ago. Although he could not be sure, of course, as yet, that they intended to turn due west and attack him; they could be on the way south, by Strathfillan and Loch Lomond, to Lennox and the Lowlands.

Something of all this was in the King's mind, when men's attention was diverted from Gilbert Hay. Two of the forward scouts were coming hurrying back, Highlanders mounted on sturdy broad-hooved garrons that coped with the treacherous ground as born to it. They were nearing Campbell country here, and the scouts were drawn from that clan. As usual with the Highlanders, ignoring the King, they carried their news directly to their chief.

"A company approaching, Sire," Sir Neil called. "Some two miles ahead yet. A small company, mounted. But armoured."

Armour never failed to reveal itself, even at great distances, in sunlight.

"How small?"

"No more than two score."

"They may be scouts of a larger force. Take a party forward, Sir Neil, to investigate."

When, a little later, the King's entourage topped one of the innumerable basalt ridges which ribbed that expanse, to view even more extensive barrenness ahead, it was also to perceive that Campbell had had no difficulty with the newcomers. He was quite close at hand, indeed, riding back with a little group of knights, handsomely equipped and mounted Lowlanders. And over these fluttered a silken banner showing a blue chief above a white field.

"Douglas!" Bruce cried, and dug in his spurs.

They met at no very salubrious spot, amongst reeds, tussocks and standing water; but careless of royal status or dignity, the King leapt down at the same moment as did the other, and strode to embrace the younger man heartily.

"Jamie, lad — here's joy! My good Sir James!" he exclaimed. "What brings you here I know not. But you are welcome, by the Rude! Welcome indeed. For I have missed you, Jamie."

"Your Grace ... my liege ... Sir Robert!" Douglas could not find words, shaking his head. "It has been long ..."

"Aye, long. But our joining again the sweeter. Let me look at you." He held the other at arm's length. "Aye — James Douglas as ever was!"

"Why should I change, Sire? But you — you are changed, to my sorrow! You are thin, wasted. I heard that you had been sick. You are not well, yet ...?"

"Well, yes — well again, lad. That is past."

"You drive yourself too hard, Sire. Too much campaigning, scouring the face of the land, hard living. You were not bred to this ..."

"Bred to it? No. I was not bred to it. Were you? Were any of us, save these Highland chieftains? Yet it is my blood and birth and breeding that has put me in the middle of Rannoch Moor this day, that set my hand to this plough. But . . . what brings *you* to Rannoch, Jamie? You, whom I left my lieutenant in the South?"

Douglas looked down. "No doubt, Sire, I should not be here. Should not have come, myself. Should have sent couriers, letters. But the news is urgent. And . . . and I hungered to see Your Grace's face again. It is a year and more . . ."

The King shook the other's shoulder, and his own head—but understandingly, not censoriously. "Aye, Jamie—we are flesh and blood, God knows! And God be thanked! Men, not graven images of duty and obedience and form. But . . . your urgent news?"

"Galloway has broken out in revolt again. Major revolt. MacDouall, once more. But with English aid. Too great a task for me. He had Umfraville aiding him also—Sir Ingram. And an English force under Sir John de St. John. I had not the men to face them—have not sufficient, in truth, to hold what I have."

"Galloway again! In Heaven's name—am I never to be free of Galloway's spleen? And not just Galloway. Umfraville—who was Guardian of the Realm, once! Still hating me. I' faith—hate dies slow in this Scotland . . .!"

"The English still hold all the line of castles from Lochmaben to Caerlaverock—Tibbers, Dalswinton, Dumfries. Cutting off Galloway. And Buittle in Galloway itself—a strong place. I dared not move against them, leaving the rest of the South bare. So I left Sir Alexander Lindsay and Sir Walter de Bickerton in charge, at Selkirk in the Forest which I have made my base, and hastened north. I believed you to be assailing the Earl of Ross, in Moray and the Great Glen. But I learned in Atholl that you had come to terms with him—which I could scarcely believe—and had turned south, by Lochaber, for the West. So I came hot-foot, by Tummel and Rannoch."

Bruce's expression had returned to normal—grim, guarded, narrow-eyed, calculating, the brief interlude of naturalness, of being himself over.

"So-o-o!" he breathed. "The Scots remain . . . the Scots! Preferring far to fight each other than the enemy! What curse is there on this people, what devil's seed sown in us, that we must ever stab our brother's back rather than our foe's?" He swung round to face the semi-circle of his leaders. "My friends—have you heard? My lord of Douglas brings ill tidings. Galloway is in open revolt again. With aid both Scots and English. Umfraville, no less. With the Comyn fall, he will now lead the Baliol faction. I had hoped him either tamed or tired! And Sir John de St. John — he who led me to Edward Longshanks at Linlithgow, and my wedding! One of the ablest of the English. This is no small MacDouall insurrection."

"Christ God's curse upon them all!" the Lord of the Isles exclaimed. "I told you! I call all to witness — I told you! At Loch Doon. That we should lay Galloway low. Not any petty ride around the place, waving a flag and hanging a few scoundrels, as we did. But with our fullest power, and no quarter. Fire and sword, to the whole accursed province! As you have done with Buchan. But you would have none of it. I had 500 Islesmen to avenge in Galloway!"

The King held in his own temper. Only Angus Og would have addressed him so. But Angus was Angus, and this no time to stress style and courtly manners.

"My lord, you did so advise," he admitted. "But it was not vengeance that was my great concern. It was the new King Edward's plans. Which we did not know. I had to think of all my kingdom, not just Galloway. I conceived that a light lesson would serve. I was wrong. It has not done so. And now we must pay for my error, and do what should have been done a year ago."

"It will be but the harder."

"True. But *we* are the stronger."

The Islesman looked bleak indeed. "I will take my galleys to Galloway!" he said, almost whispering. "They shall learn what it means to have insulted MacDonald!"

Eyeing him a little askance, the King said, "We shall see. This must be well considered . . ."

Edward Bruce had come up from a visit to Lennox in the rear, during the Douglas greeting. Now he broke in.

"We now abandon one savage for another? MacDougall for MacDouall! Leave Lorn and fall on Galloway."

"No!" Campbell cried. "That would be folly. Lorn is at hand, Galloway far . . ."

"And MacDougall a menace to your Campbell lands in Argyll! Have you thought of Carrick? Annandale? Which MacDouall and the English harass?"

"My lords — we are not fighting for lands or properties. Any more than for vengeance," Bruce intervened. "We fight for the freedom of a whole people, the saving of a kingdom. If *you* forget it, I do not. Let me hear no more of such talk. Win the kingdom, and all the lands therein shall be yours. But win the kingdom first!"

Sir Thomas Randolph spoke up. "Sire — my lands of Nithsdale are near to Galloway, and so menaced. But I say to strike at this Lorn first."

"You are uncommon noble, nephew!" his uncle mocked, as Douglas looked up, interested in his late prisoner's new role. "But then, we can well understand that you would rather fight MacDougall's Highlandmen than your late friends the English!"

Randolph flushed hotly, caught the King's eye, and swallowed.

"You have other reason for urging that we hold to Lorn, Sir Thomas?"

"I have, Sire. Galloway stands alone. Even in successful revolt, it would not bring down all the South. But allow Lorn and Ross to join forces, and you could lose all the North again, truce or none."

"You have it, nephew! That is as I myself see it. MacDougall is still the greater danger. I proceed to Lorn, therefore, as planned. But Galloway — that wound must be staunched before it bleeds us white. I will think on this . . ."

So the great sprawling array straggled on across the Moor of Rannoch. And now the King fretted again, at the slow rate of progress.

They won out of that terrible wilderness, and down towards the wooded shores of lovely Loch Tulla, as evening fell, with the mountains closing in again and the going becoming firmer, surer. Bruce decided to camp here, where there was shelter and fuel, and the possibility of deer in the woods for skilled hunters to kill — for the feeding of so large a host in empty country was an ever-present headache. He had been preoccupied, thoughtful, since Douglas's appearance. Now he called his lords together, round him.

"I halt the main host here, early, although we have covered but little ground this day," he told them. "For tomorrow we shall be into Lorn, and it is best that the men be well rested and fed, in fighting trim. If may be. Out of this Loch Tulla flows the River Orchy, down to Loch Awe and the Western Sea. We follow it, tomorrow. Here then, we part. Most to camp for this night. But some to push on swiftly."

"Who?" Edward jerked.

"You, brother, for one. I have considered this thing well. In the campaign against MacDougall, the heavier Lowland cavalry will be of scant use. I fear. Wasted, in mountain warfare. I would have you take most of it — say 600 men — and ride hard for the South. By the mounth of Marlorn, Strathfillan, Loch Lomond, across Clyde, and so down to the Forest of Ettrick. And thence to Galloway."

"Ha!" Edward breathed. "So you have come to sense, Robert!"

"I have come to decision, my lord! You are strong for harrying and slaying! Here then is a task after your own heart. Collect what men Lindsay and Bickerton can spare you from Douglas's force in the Forest. Gain as many as you may from our own lands of Carrick and Annandale. You have my royal authority to call for all support wherever you may. Then descend upon Galloway with all speed. Waste no time on the English-held castles. Avoid set battles, if you may. But deal with Galloway!"

His borhter was grinning, fiercely. They were very different men. "It shall be so, by the Mass!" he declared. "Galloway shall pay the price, this time. I shall deal with Galloway as I dealt with Buchan."

"No," the King said. "Not quite that, Edward, I charge you. This war, not punishment. And glutted men fight but slackly. The English will always be at your elbow. This will not be Buchan again. But, see you — win me Galloway, and you shall be Lord of Galloway. *Your* province, brother."

There were moments of silence, as the significance of this sank in. It was a notable promise, of an enormous heritage, a princedom indeed — the first such kingly bestowal of the reign. It would spur on Edward, or any man. But also, of course, if Galloway was to be his own thereafter, Edward would not wish to destroy and harry it any more than he must. None there failed to see the meaning of this.

"I thank you, Sire," the other said, carefully.

"Aye. Sir Robert Boyd will be with you, as lieutenant. Heed his counsel. You shall have most of my knights. And hereafter, if I can spare more of my main host, I shall send it."

"Does Douglas come with me?" Edward undoubtedly was jealous of James Douglas's position in the King's esteem.

"No. Not yet. My lord of Douglas remains with me here." He turned. "My lord of the Isles — you also, if you will, to move swiftly tonight. Ahead, to the sea. Secretly. Your galleys lie off Kerrera isle, still? In the Firth of Lorn, threatening MacDougall? Yes — then will you make shift to reach them, and bring them to my aid? MacDougall lies in Dunstaffnage Castle, at the mouth of Etive. There I shall seek him. He will try to halt me before that, to be sure. But Dunstaffnage is my target. Will you menace it by sea? And bring your galleys up Loch Etive, to support my advance"

"I would sooner sail south. To strike at Galloway."

"No doubt. And so you shall. Aid me at Dunstaffnage and Etive, and then sail for Galloway. Your galleys will travel more swiftly than men and horses." He took Angus Og's agreement for granted. "How soon can you have your ships in Loch Etive?"

"If they are still in the anchorage of Kerrera, as I commanded, I can have them sailing up Etive in two or three hours. But I must get to Kerrera first. Through MacDougall country. Or skirting it. Forty miles. To Gallanach. Then a boat across to Kerrera island."

"Starting now, my lord? How long?"

"Riding through the night, I could be down Glen Orchy and crossed Loch Awe by sunrise. Through the Glen Nant and Glen Lonan hills to the Sound of Kerrera in daylight, Campbell country. I could be at the sea by nightfall. At this hour tomorrow I could be with my galleys."

"God willing," the King commented. "Good. Then the day following, can I look for you in Loch Etive?"

"Yes. When, depends on the tide. The mouth of that loch shoals badly. Only at high tide could we win through."

"Very well. Tomorrow this host will move down Glen Orchy, and along Aweside. Then through the Pass of Brander the next day, to Etive . . ."

"That pass will be held against you. It is the key to Lorn. A sore place to win through."

"Well I know it. But I cannot ferry thousands across Loch Awe, as you will go. So Brander it needs must be. There is no other route, is there? For an army. We must win through Brander, then. Your galleys threatening MacDougall's rear, in Etive, should aid us."

"It will be hard task, Sire," Campbell put in. "Remember Clifford in Glen Trool. Brander is ten times worse. It is like to the gates of hell!"

"It is Glen Trool that I *am* remembering, Neil. We must reverse Glen Trool."

Angus Og, like others, looked doubtful. But he shrugged. "So be it, Sir King — I ride for Gallanach and Kerrera. Tomorrow's morn I will have my galleys under Cruachan, at the far side of Brander. Wherever *you* may be! Let us eat . . ."

So, less than a couple of hours later, the two very different companies set out from the new camp by Loch Tulla, from the ruddy glow of fires into the wan shadows of the August late evening; Angus, with perhaps a score of his captains, on shaggy Highland garrons, to head south by west down Orchy; and Edward and his glittering knightly throng to lead his 600 jingling men-at-arms south,eastwards by the main drove road across the mounth of Mamlorn, for the Lowlands. There was no question but that Edward at least, went in high spirits.

Watching them go, with his much reduced little band of close companions, Bruce sighed. "Much Scots blood will be shed before we all forgather again, I fear. My sorrow that it must be I who ordains it."

"Do not blame yourself, Sire," Douglas said.

"Who shall I blame?"

"The dead Edward. Edward of England," Lennox averred. "On him alone lies the blame for all. One man's hatred and lust for power. All those years ago. A great man, a great king, turned sour!"

"Aye — so great a man consumed! By a worm at his heart. Why, Malcolm — why? I honoured Edward once. Esteemed, almost worshipped him. Loved him better than my own father. He was the greatest prince in Christendom, the finest knight, the best soldier, the ablest ruler. Edward Plantagenet. And yet — this! Destroyed and destroying. For what? For a notion, a false notion. Laced with spleen."

"He thought to play God," Campbell put in briefly. "And we all suffer."

"Aye. All men suffer when a king errs," Bruce nodded sombrely. "And the greater the king the greater the suffering. Here is a lesson for me, at least — however small a king! If ever I think to play God! Watch it, my friends — and save me from myself."

"With the Scots to rule, there is little risk of that, I think!" Thomas Randolph said — and for once brought smiles.

* * *

Another camp by another loch, a loch as great as Loch Ness, this one, one of the largest and longest in Scotland. Lying north-east and south-west, Loch Awe's club-foot thrust off a long toe north-westwards, into the narrows of the fierce defile of Brander, down which it poured its outflow, the brief but major River Awe, four miles, no more, to the arm of the sea called Etive. In the other direction the loch presented a mile-wide barrier for twenty-three miles, almost to the sea again at Craignish, a mighty moat guarding the country of Lorn. Trackless impassable mountains, in a vast semi-circle, sealed off the north.

It was early morning, and the lately risen sun was streaming rays slantwise down the valley of Glen Orchy at their backs, into the wide green upland amphitheatre which cradled the foot of the loch. Bruce was standing on a birch-crowned knoll above the shore, and staring due westwards to where the water altered all its character, exchanged all its blue-and-gold loveliness, mirrored amongst green and purple hills, for a narrowing smooth dark torrent that swept dramatically into the grim portals of a mighty gorge, there to disappear in sombre shadow. Brander.

The daunting place dominated all this north end of the loch, below the tremendous multi-peaked mass of Cruachan. It was unlike any pass the majority even of the Highlanders had ever seen, a huge, flooded, steep-sided gullet of the mountains, vast in scale, a barren rock-lined funnel with unbroken sides soaring from 800 to 1,200 feet before easing off into the normal hill-flanks above. All the floor of that long defile was deep dark green, deceitfully smooth but swift-flowing water, with no banks or shores. And there were three miles of it.

All night Bruce's scouts had been bringing in reports, and the King had scarcely closed his eyes throughout. The pass was held in great strength by the enemy. There was a single slender track along its north side, the only road, at wildly varying heights above the water, clinging like ivy to the rock-face. How consistently the length of this was held could not be ascertained, because scouts could not get past the first block. This was at a point about a mile along where, at a wooded cleft, a fairly strong party was stationed, guarding timber barricades. But high above, on the side of Cruachan itself, where the steepest walls of the defile levelled off somewhat, were large numbers of MacDougall clansmen, ranked all along the hillside. No doubt, beyond, at the far end of the pass, there would be more waiting.

Shades of Glen Trool indeed — save that here everything was magnified many times.

All the royal camp had been active since dawn, but for the last hour or so the King had stood alone, silent, apparently fascinated by that yawning chasm to the west, preoccupied to a degree, staring just staring. His leaders brought him reports, from scouts, of the readiness of the various companies, and he accepted these with mere nods, scarcely seeming to hear. Men eyed him almost as much askance as they eyed what Campbell had called the jaws of hell.

James Douglas came to speak, at length. "All is ready, Sire. Fourteen hundred of the youngest, noblest Highlanders, in four companies — under the MacGregor, the Mackintosh, MacDonald of Lochalsh and Sir Ranald MacRuarie. With 200 light bowmen. All stripped to the lightest. Waiting."

Bruce looked up towards the mountain-tops, still shrouded in the white night-caps of fleecy mist, tinged golden now with the early sun. "How long before those mists clear, Neil?"

"Two hours yet. At this season."

"And the wind? It will freshen?"

Campbell, whose castle of Innischonell was less than a dozen miles to the south, shrugged. "About the same time. I cannot give you any certain hour, Sire. But, with this weather, the mounting sun draws the wind off the sea and up the hillsides. It is a thing we have to beware when we stalk the deer. It is partly this wind which blows away the thinning mists from the tops..."

"So the wind first?" Not a breath of wind now stirred the quiet morning.

"Yes. Or so is usual."

"Then let us pray this is such a day! So be it. Off with you both. You have only two hours — and this must be timed most closely." The King held out his hand. "The day depends on you both. Yours is the most dangerous part, Neil my friend. With no knightly glory! But all rely on it. Your people have all the flints and tinder? Jamie — your greatest task will be to hold back the rash. After your great climbing. Watch for it. Go, then — and God be with you..."

So back eastwards along the lochside the four companies marched off, into the dazzle of the sun; and any MacDougall scouts and look-outs posted in vantage positions to the west could not but assume retiral, or possibly some regrouping to attempt a crossing of the loch by boat farther south.

But, round a thrusting shoulder of the mountain, out of sight from the west, the Falls of Cruachan came crashing down in foaming white water, in a series of great steps and stairs, from the lofty and vast corrie cradled amongst the topmost peaks of the mountain. Through the centuries this cataract had worn a deep and steep ravine for itself. Up into this the eager bands of Highlanders turned, and began their tremendous climbing.

Bruce waited, anxiously watching the clinging mists that wrapped the summits above some 2,000 feet. If that cover were to lift too soon...

He gave them a trying, uneasy ninety minutes; and then, with the mists most evidently thinning and retreating, he marshalled his residual forces and gave the order to advance westwards, towards the pass, remaining armour at the front. They did not hurry.

The increasing narrowness of the track elongated the column grievously, inevitably. Gradually the towering jaws of the defile closed in on them. Word came back from forward scouts that small enemy pickets were retiring by stages before them. They would draw the invaders on, to the timber barricade a mile deep in the pass, as Bruce had drawn Clifford at Glen Trool.

The first stirrings of air reached them as they entered the gorge. In a little while there was a distinct breeze from the west, in their faces. With a sigh of relief the King halted his long column about half a mile in.

Men's noses caught the tang of burning before ever their eyes perceived the thin blue film of smoke ahead. Quickly that film darkened, however, and soon it was not blue but murky brown, until great billowing clouds of it, growing ever thicker, swept up the pass on the westerly wind. Neil Campbell and his company had played their part. Having climbed most of Cruachan, and descended beyond, they had fired all the heather and bracken hillside at the western entrance of Brander, and the pass was now acting as a vast funnel or flue.

Streaming-eyed, blinded and choking in the acrid flood, Bruce's force still waited. Now it was their ears' turn. All listened.

It was not easy to hear, for sound does not carry downhill so readily as up, and the sullen roar of the river was close at hand. But presently, high and thin, those keenest of hearing could discern the yells and shouts and clash of battle, far up above them. Douglas and his three companies had hurled themselves down from the very mountain-tops, out of the mists upon the waiting MacDougalls half-way up the hillside. Campbell would now be moving back to aid them. And Angus Og might well be making his presence felt farther west still.

The King again ordered the advance, slowly, into the smoke.

Soon they overran their scouts, who warned that the barricade was just ahead, around a bluff. Warily the armoured men moved in.

However bewildered by the smoke, and the obvious trouble above, the enemy here had not deserted their post. They had no warning of the invaders' approach however, with the smoke, and the first of the royal troops were clambering over the timber obstructions, swords and battle-axes poised, before the alarm was shouted.

Wild and bloody fighting followed, incoherent, unsophisticated to a degree. Tight-lunged, stinging-eyed men hacked and slashed and battered blindly, Bruce himself in the forefront, wielding a mace for this hit-or-miss warfare. But the defenders were massively outnumbered, and in only a few minutes the position was won.

The King's men pressed on along the pass, the smoke thick as ever.

One or two boulders and the occasional shower of smaller stones did come down on them from the obscurity above, but these were scanty enough to do little damage. Undoubtedly up there men were too busy fighting for their lives to concern themselves with the stone-rolling tactics. Sometimes, indeed, a body it was that came hurtling down — and these were not always MacDougalls. The Battle of Brander was being fought up on Cruachan, not in the pass.

There were two more barricades to negotiate. But the first was deserted and the second but half-heartedly held, the defenders not unnaturally conceiving the situation to be desperate. For now the sounds of fighting could be heard directly ahead, and low as the track level, presumably from the western mouth of the pass. The MacDougalls were looking as anxiously back as forward.

The smoke was beginning to thin. Sore-eyed, Bruce led his force cautiously on.

That, in fact, for the main body, was the last of the fighting. Presently they could sense the fierce sides of the defile to be drawing back, opening, even though they could not actually see it. Then, where the track bent, to cross a spidery timber bridge over a sudden narrowing of the river, they came across many bodies, dead and wounded. The marks of axes on the bridge timbers told the story. Some of the casualties were MacDonald islesmen — the crews of Angus Og's galleys. They had saved the bridge, anyway.

Soon after, with an abruptness that was startling, and painful to streaming eyes, Bruce strode out of the mirk and constriction, into sunlight again and wide, colourful vistas. Blinking, bemused, he and his stared around them.

They had passed the wide belt of burned heather hillside, which now stretched upwards, to their right, in blackened, smouldering ruination, the flames dying away as they reached the rocks of the defile proper. In front, the wide basin of Etive, with its glittering waters, opened out. Those waters were positively littered with shipping, galleys, some beached, some lying out, some manoeuvring, some apparently fleeing down-loch with others in pursuit. And along the south shore a running fight was proceeding westwards, most clearly at speed.

Bruce turned his aching gaze uphill and slightly backwards. Because of the still-smoking hillside it was impossible to see what went on up there; but men could be seen elsewhere, streaming away over the various western flanks of Cruachan in large numbers, scattered and without order. Douglas's people, had they been defeated, certainly would not have fled in that direction.

The King, breathing a long sigh, relaxed for the first time for hours. He sent young Irvine with a few hundred clansmen, to climb up there, to see if they were required. The rest he led on towards salt water, the smell of the tangle in their nostrils, instead of the sharp tang of smoke.

"Another battle fought — or not fought — in no heroic fashion, Thomas," he observed, to Randolph, who had been at his side throughout. "But, I think, a battle won. How say you, nephew?"

"Won, yes. But against Highlanders, Sire. Not against armoured chivalry."

"It was against the enemy! Are your notions of knightly warfare only to apply to southron lords and the like?"

"No, uncle. I have learned my lesson. But I remind you that one day you will have to fight *my* way. One day come to grips with the armoured might of England, in true embattled war."

"One day, yes. I know it. When I am ready — not before. When I have a united realm behind me. Or as united as I can make it. Until then we fight *my* way! However it shames you! With my wits."

"It shames me no longer. I see that your wits can do great things. And save many lives, thousands of lives. Any other, to take that pass, would have sacrificed thousands. On both sides."

"You see that, do you? Good." He turned. "And you, Sir Hugh? What do you see?"

Ross, the hostage, inclined his red head. "I see, my lord, that I would never wish to fight, nor pit my poor wits against, King Robert the Bruce!" The word king was slightly emphasised.

"Ha! So the tide turns, indeed! I am glad of it . . ."

Two days later, the mighty and ancient fortress of Dunstaffnage, on the point of its green peninsula jutting into the mouth of Loch Etive, capitulated — the celebrated castle which had once been the seat of the early royal line whose latest descendant now hammered at its doors, where the Stone of Destiny had been enshrined before it was taken to the capital of the newly united Scotland, at Scone. Alexander of Argyll, aged, white-haired, stumbling, came out alone, bareheaded, barefooted, to make at least superficially humble submission to the monarch — and was received with stern dignity, decision and no recriminations. But he did not produce his son and heir Ian Bacach, John the Lame, of Lorn, who had commanded at Brander — who had indeed commanded at Strathfillan, that bloody day two years before. He had slipped away, by night, in a small boat, from a postern gate. The lack of him took something of the shine out of the King's victory.

But it was nevertheless a great and sudden triumph, achieved in infinitely less time than might have been expected. Alexander MacDougall yielded up Dunstaffnage, ordered the dispersal of his clansmen, and swore future allegiance. His Comyn wife glared daggers at Bruce, but said no word, as they were banished, under Campbell guard, to the small and remote castle of Gylen, at the southernmost tip of the island of Kerrera.

There was great feasting and much Highland jubilation that night in the lofty stone halls of Dunstaffnage — for the castle had not yielded through any lack of provisioning, at least. And next day Angus Og, with a much augmented fleet of galleys, the largest probably that even he had ever commanded, sailed south down the Sea of the Hebrides for Galloway. He took with him James Douglas, and many another, as passengers.

The King, in a strange mood of reaction, almost sadness, turned his face eastwards, once more. For the first winter in a dozen years there would be approximate peace in the North.

Chapter Fifteen

If Robert Bruce has first turned his hand to stage-management, and what his brother called mummery, almost a year before at Aberdeen, for the setting of his first Privy Council, now, in the spring of 1309, he really went about the business with a will. While quite a number of his friends and supporters, as well as Edward, either disapproved of the entire proceedings as unsuitable, unnecessary and beneath the dignity of a monarch, or at least showed no enthusiasm, others again responded heartily, even gleefully. Of these the most useful and active were James Douglas, Gilbert Hay, Ranald MacRuarie, Bernard de Linton — and, strangely enough, Thomas Randolph. Also, of course, Christina of Garmoran, who had once again crossed Scotland to the east coast for the occasion.

The King had put as much thought and planning into the affair as into any of his military campaigns. For this was, in fact, no less a campaign than any, however different.

Bruce would have preferred to hold his first parliament at Scone, the ancient Celtic capital. But unfortunately the English still held Perth, near by, although two attempts had been made to dislodge them. Stirling and Edinburgh, with all the South-East, likewise were in enemy hands. But St. Andrews was the ecclesiastical metropolis of Scotland, and had been cleared of the invader. Moreover, the Church's share in what had been achieved for the freeing of Scotland fell to be recognised. So St. Andrews it was, thrusting out at the very tip of Fife into the North Sea.

The actual parliament was by way of being only the necessary excuse and setting for the entire programme. This was to be a show, a demonstration, a play-acting as Edward accused — but for a vastly greater audience than could ever crowd into the grey episcopal city by the sea. And St. Andrews was certainly crowded, that March, as never before.

It was a strange town, unlike any other in the land in that an actual majority of its population consisted of clerics and churchmen of one degree or another. Nowhere else was there such a concentration of abbeys, priories, monasteries, nunneries, churches, chapels, cells, shrines and colleges. While the huge cathedral, triple-towered and still a-building, dominated all architecturally, and the castle, which was the primate's palace, did so administratively, every street, square, wynd, lane and alley within the lofty enclosing walls was in fact a huddle of handsome ecclesiastical building, so cheek-by-jowl as to be bewildering, almost ridiculous, the close proximity tending to cancel out the frequently rival magnificence. Bruce, seeing St. Andrews for the first time, perceived something of how the extreme trait in the Scots character, and its fondness for religious and metaphysical argument, had led to this concentration; also, how it was that Lamberton, master of all this, had been able, through Balmyle, to continue to subsidise him so munificently — for here obviously was every indication of accumulated wealth such as even the nobility could only gape at with incredulous envy. The English had of course taken what they could, and done much damage to the city; but it was off the beaten track of invasion, and the churchmen were clearly much wilier at protecting their own than were the mere laity — and probably, so many of Edward's alien administrators being themselves clerics, had helped to save St. Andrews. At any rate, the King found here a city which seemed to belong almost to another world from that in which he had warred and campaigned for so long; and one with resources available to his hand, and for the moment freely granted — since it seemed that Master Bernard, who it transpired had succeeded Bishop Balmyle in the office of Official and Receiver, had a grip over central purse-strings much more effective than that of more highly-titled prelates.

The King, therefore, did not lack the wherewithal, the premises, or the personnel, to set his scene — for churchmen at this level were quite the finest organisers, showmen, pageant-masters and providers of good living. And they and theirs were here in abundance.

The session of parliament — to which all entitled to attend, throughout the realm, of whatever faction, had been summoned — was proclaimed to occupy the two days of the 16th and 17th March, with Lent ended — a matter of some importance in the circumstances. But the previous evening had been set aside for the more dramatic and significant if less constitutionally important events. These were to be staged in the largest available premises in the city, other than the cathedral, the Guest Hall of the Augustinian Priory, one of the greatest and richest monasteries in the land. The lead of its roof had been carried off by the late King Edward for his battering machines at the siege of Stirling, and other damage done, but temporary roofing had been improvised. To this huge hall, officially de-sanctified for the occasion by Bishop Balmyle, just returned from his consecration in Rome, the King made his way in splendid procession through the narrow crowded streets, from his quarters in one of the undamaged towers of the castle. He went on foot, beneath an elaborate purple-and-gold velvet canopy held above him on poles by four lords — Douglas, Hay, Campbell and Fleming — dressed at his most magnificent in cloth-of-gold and ruby trimmings, under the spectacular Lion Rampant tabard, a slender open gold circlet with strawberry-leaf points around his otherwise bare head. He was preceded by the cathedral choir of singing boys chanting sweet music; then by a covey of the fairest daughters of the nobility, dressed all in white and carrying garlands; and followed by no fewer than five bishops — Moray, Dunkeld, Brechin, Ross and Dunblane — and a great company of mitred abbots, priors, deans and the like, all in their most splendid vestments. Then came an almost more colourful cohort of Highland chiefs, chieftains and captains of clans, led by the Lord of the Isles, all in fullest Highland panoply, including Christina of Garmoran actually wearing a helmet and chain-mail for the occasion. An illustrious and unnumbered array of lords and knights, lairds and sheriffs and other notables, with their ladies, composed the central body of the procession; and the provost of the royal burgh, with the magistrates, brought up the rear, another contingent of choristers finishing things off. Happily the threatening rain forbore, although there was a frolicsome wind off the sea. More than 500 people took part in that procession — and all had to be got into the Priory Guest Hall, with sufficient space left centrally for what was to follow.

It took time for busy ushers, like clerical sheep-dogs, to marshal and arrange everybody approximately in position, while musicians played from the gallery and the King sat patiently on a throne — episcopal, but better than none — on the Prior's dais at the far end of the huge apartment, backed by his lords temporal and spiritual and a selection of the ladies. At length, at a sign from the door, trumpeters sounded a rousing fanfare, and Bruce rose to his feet.

"My lords and ladies, my friends, my people," he said, into the hush, "I greet you well, this fair and happy day, each and all. We have waited long for it, and many have died that it might dawn for us who remain — God rest and reward eternally all such. Few here do not mourn for some of these. As I do for three brothers, and friends beyond all counting." His strong voice quivered noticeably — and that was no play-acting. "With all my heart I mourn them. But likewise from my heart thank you all who have fought and survived to see this day."

There was a strange sound from the great company, that started as a mere murmur, swelled to a rumble, rose suddenly to a mighty shout of acclaim, and so continued until the King's hand rose to quell it.

"So I, and you, rejoice as well as mourn, and thank Almighty God," he went on, voice under control again. "But, though much has been attained, and we assemble here again in council and rule, as has not been in this realm for a dozen years, yet much is yet to be done. The invader still defiles parts of my realm and our land, lurks in many strong castles, and beyond our borders still turns malevolent eyes upon this kingdom. Today, my friends, is but a pause in the struggle."

The reaction now was a low muttering roar, like distant thunder.

"But at least we can now face our enemy squarely, eyes forward, like our swords. Not for ever glancing back over our shoulders. Hear you — I say enemy, not enemies! For that is the greatest joy and comfort of this day. Our enemy is now plain to discern. It is the English invader only, and no longer those of our own kin and people who were led astray, by error, offence or fear. That is past and done with. Today, my friends, the King of Scots is king of all Scots again — as has not been since the good Alexander died at Kinghorn cliff twenty-three years ago." That was something of an exaggeration, but perhaps permissible. "In token whereof I now call upon the Lord High Steward of this my realm to carry out his duty and service."

There was a ripple of exclamation at this, for James Stewart, the Hereditary High Steward, had of recent years been lying notably low on his island of Bute in the Clyde estuary. He had, of course, been one of the leaders of revolt against the old Edward once, but, an elderly man and no warrior ever, had sickened of war and come to terms with the English. He had used Bruce's stabbing of the Red Comyn at Dumfries as excuse to disassociate himself — as had many another — and had not attended the coronation at Scone although he had sent his surviving son Walter. His last service to the King had been surreptitious, provision of the secret vessel which had taken the fleeing Bruce from the Clyde to Dunaverty and the Hebridean interlude. The son of his brother John, who had fallen bravely at Falkirk fight, Sir Alexander of Bonkyl, had openly taken the English part thereafter, and in fact had been captured with Thomas Randolph, and since held prisoner.

A single blast of a trumpet cut short the murmuring, and a side door of the hall opened to admit two men, one old and one young. James, the fifth High Steward of Scotland, a tall, gaunt and gloomy man, dressed as usual all in black, but richly, had aged greatly of late. Always shambling and gangling of gait, he now moved forward stiffly, awkwardly, but with some dignity too, nothing hangdog about him. Nor was there any sign of guilt about his son Walter, a good-looking youth, arrayed in most handsome style and carrying himself proudly. If the concourse was looking for any kind of dramatic public humiliation, these two did not offer it.

The Stewarts advanced a few paces, bowed low to the throne, and then turned to look back.

"I, as Steward of His Grace's realm, summon William, Earl of Ross, and his household, to pay fealty to his liege lord, Robert, Kin of Scots," the old man called. He was not a good speaker for his tongue was too big for his mouth and he dribbled continuously. But the name he slobberingly enunciated was clear enough.

Now the comment in the thronged hall was not to be damped down. Everywhere men and women turned to stare, agog.

They had something to stare at. The man who led in the group of half a dozen was eye-catching by any standards. Of middle years, huge, ponderous, fierce-eyed and heavy-jowled, clad in a curious mixture of Highland and Lowland garb, decked with flashing jewellery, William son of William son of Farquhar Mac-an-Tagart, Earl of Ross, chief of his clan and hereditary Abbot of Applecross, stalked heavily forward, a target for all eyes — and for vituperation also, for all knew well the part he had played in handing over the Queen and the royal ladies, and in the death of the Earl of Atholl.

Ross paced on towards the dais, looking neither left nor right. Behind him came his two sons, Sir Hugh and Sir John, the former looking embarrassed, the latter scowling. Then three young women, the Ladies Isabella and Jean Ross, the former notably beautiful, and Sir John's wife, the Lady Margaret Comyn, daughter of the Earl of Buchan. The King was insisting on women being very much to the fore this day; and since Buchan had no son, the presence of this heiress daughter was important.

The Rosses mounted the dais, and after a reluctant pause, the huge Earl went down stiffly on one knee before the throne.

"My liege lord Robert," he said thickly, jerkily. "I, William of Ross, and my whole house, name and clan, do seek your royal pardon. For deeds past done. I acknowledge error and seek mercy.

As agreed at the settlement of Auldearn, six months past. And desire to be received into Your Grace's peace."

If the older man was tense and strained, Bruce, sitting before him, was no less so. Although he had planned it himself, this was one of the hardest things he had ever had to do. He saw, instead of the basically arrogant and only superficially humble face bowed before him, the reproachful loveliness of Elizabeth de Burgh and the childish innocence of his daughter Marjory. And seeing, he could have lashed out at those heavy features with the foot that tap-tapped so close to them. Hands gripping the arms of the bishop's throne so that the knuckles glistened whitely, he sought to control the surge of sheer elemental fury within him.

It was his brother Edward's denunciatory muttering at his back that saved him, ironically. He drew a deep breath.

"My lord of Ross — since you chose to conclude our truce by making submission to my representatives at Auldearn in October," he said levelly, "I have well considered the matter. I then, through others, accepted your subjection on terms I conceived to be generous. Those terms still stand. But now you would make closer bond and fullest allegiance. Do you, my lord, and your whole house, swear to serve me as your sovereign lord, and my heirs on the Throne of Scotland, well and faithfully until your life's end?"

"I do, Sire."

"Then, Earl of Ross, here is my royal hand. It is my pleasure to extend it to you." And might God forgive him that lie, for it was only with an actual physical effort that he managed to bring forward that hand! "That I do so is in no small measure due to the good offices and noble bearing of your son, Sir Hugh, while he was hostage for you."

The Earl took the hand between his own two, and kissed it briefly. He stood up, distasteful duty done.

His eldest son knelt, on both knees this time, and took the King's hand. "Your Grace's most leal knight and humble servant — if you will have me, Sire," he said.

"I will have you, Sir Hugh — never fear." The you was slightly emphasised.

His brother, Sir John Ross, dropped only one knee and made his fealty only sketchily. Bruce eyeing him closely, silent.

The ladies dipped in deep curtsy — but the King did not miss the smouldering hatred in the glance of the dark-eyed, plain-faced Margaret Comyn.

"My regrets that your father died," he told her formally. The Earl of Buchan had died in England at Yuletide, disgraced and dejected.

She made no acknowledgement, as the Rosses moved over to stand at the side of the dais.

At a sign from the throne, the trumpeter sounded once more, and the Steward again raised his peculiar voice.

"Sir Alexander Comyn, Sheriff of Inverness and Keeper of Urquhart, to pay homage to the King's Grace."

Buchan's brother, a fine-looking soldierly man, grey-haired but upright, came in at the side door and marched firmly up. His bow was vestigial but when he kneeled to take the King's hand he did so as firmly, frankly.

"Your Grace's true man, from henceforward," he said crisply. "You will not rue your royal generosity to me, at least."

"I never doubted it. Rise, Sir Alexander — and play my friend as stoutly as you played my enemy!"

"That I will, Sire."

The Steward's next announcement drew more gasps. "Alexander, son of Ewan, son of Duncan, son of Dougall, of Argyll. And his son, John of Lorn."

The old man who came in now, white-haired, thin and stooping, looked notably frail to be the puissant chief of MacDougall who for so long had terrorised the Highland West. He was simply clad in saffron tunic, a belt of gold the only symbol of his rank. No son John came behind him, but only his hard-faced and somewhat overdressed wife. Bruce knew well that Lame John was still in England, and defiant, but had chosen this way of emphasising the fact.

MacDougall kept his eyes lowered in front of the King — although his lady did not. "I come to make my peace with Your Highness," he said thinly. "I offer my allegiance."

"You give it, sir — *give* it! As is your simple duty." Bruce looked at this man who had hunted him and his over so much of the Highlands, his English enemies' most active and consistent supporter. "That allegiance is belated. But . . . you acknowledge your error now?"

"Aye."

"And your son and heir? John of Lorn?"

"I cannot speak for my son. I do not know his whereabouts, Were he with me, I have no doubt that he would say as I do."

"But he is not here, sir. Despite my summons. So, although I accept your fealty, and that of your name and clan, I hold you responsible for John MacDougall of Lorn. Until he submits himself to me, in duty and service, I must hold some part of your lands and castles forfeit to the Crown. What part is for parliament to determine. You understand?"

The old man did not look up, but nodded.

"Very well, sir. Here is my hand."

Bruce looked into the eyes of the woman behind, the sister of the man he had stabbed to death at Dumfries. He saw no relenting, no hint of forbearance. The Comyn women would never come to terms with him. Were women always more implacable than men? Or was it only in Scotland?

The MacDougalls moved over to join the Comyn and the Rosses, as the Steward proclaimed still another applicant for the King's peace and mercy — Sir John Stewart of Menteith, uncle and guardian of the child Earl of Menteith.

For the Lowlanders present — the majority of the company, that is — though not to Bruce's own entourage, the announcement of this name held more significance even than those of the Highland Rosses and MacDougalls, or of the northern Comyn. For this was perhaps the most telling recruit of all to Bruce's side, the most clear barometer of the prevailing climate within Scotland, a prince of time-servers not conquered in war but choosing of his own judgement to change sides. This was the man who had handed over Wallace to King Edward, and death, in 1305, as Sheriff of Dumbarton; who was Keeper of Dumbarton Castle, one of the keys of the kingdom, for the English interest; who had been given, in name, the allegedly forfeited earldom of Lennox by King Edward, and who until a few weeks before had been calling himself Earl thereof. That he should be here in St. Andrews this March day, with the true Lennox standing just behind the King, was not only dramatic but very eloquent of the situation.

For so expert a fence-sitter, Menteith was an unlikely type, nervous, tense, ill-at-ease always. He came hurrying towards the throne, a swarthy, slight, youngish man, with strained anxious expression and great eloquent Stewart eyes. Whatever he gained by his changes of allegiance, it did not seem to be satisfaction. He faltered and halted below the dais, more like a hunted stag than a powerful noble.

Bruce was contained to encourage him. "Come, Sir John," he said easily, the mockery behind his voice fairly well disguised. "It is good to see you. We have not met since that day in Stirling Castle when we heard of Sir William Wallace's death, I think? We are four years older — and wiser, perhaps?"

"To be sure, Sire — wiser," the other said, in a rush of what seemed like relief. "I thank you — wiser." He came up the steps. "I crave Your Grace's favour and indulgence. And that you will accept my regrets for past misjudgements."

"Misjudgements you call them, Sir John? Well, it may be that you are right. That all is a matter of judgement. And you judge, now, that my cause is worthy of your support?"

"I do, Sire. The support of all true men."

The snorting from behind the King was in chorus, though Edward led it.

"I am encouraged by that!" Bruce answered gravely. "I am sure that we all are. From so practised a judge."

Menteith dropped on his knees, holding out his arms for the monarch's. "You will accept me into your peace and company? And my ward, the Earl of Menteith? As you accepted the castle of Dumbarton from me?"

"A moment, sir. While I may judge such acceptance suitable, as King, there is another who is concerned, I think. My good and leal friend the Earl of Lennox." Bruce turned in his chair. "My lord Malcolm — how say you? Sir John Stewart has misjudged your interests, as well as mine! I seek your advice."

The kneeling man cast apprehensive glances around.

"My lord King," Lennox answered quietly, "I rest content that this man enters your peace. If you can stomach him. So be it he restores what is mine. I say receive him."

"As I do not!" Edward exploded.

The King ignored his brother. "I thank you, my lord. You are magnanimous. As a monarch must be also." He extended his hand, even though his lips curled a little in distaste. "Make your belated fealty, sir."

When the trumpeter blew another blast, Edward Bruce could contain his righteous indignation no longer.

"Brother! Sire!" he exclaimed, loud enough for all to hear. "Of a mercy, have done! No more, surely! No more forgiven traitors, received into your arms! Any more forsworn miscreants on this dais and there will be no room for honest men, I say!"

Frowning, Bruce cut through the murmur of support that arose from many around him. "Enough, my lord of Carrick. In the field your services are excelled by none. Within doors, they can be less valuable! A realm is not governed as by a charge of cavalry! Proceed, my lord Steward."

"Sir Robert de Keith, hereditary Knight Marischal of Scotland, to do homage to the King."

There was less stir over this announcement than there should have been — for the adherence to Bruce's cause of the stocky square-faced man of early middle-age, who came striding in, was of major importance, though not all perceived it. Keith had fought with Buchan and the Comyns in the old days of the Joint Guardianship, had been captured by the English in Galloway and imprisoned for four years. Released in 1304, he had been sent back to his own country, duly indoctrinated, as one of King Edward's four Deputy Wardens of Scotland. That he nevertheless was but little known by most of those present was perhaps an indication that he had served his new masters only modestly — indeed he had been relieved of his Wardenship before long. Now, voluntarily, he had taken this step. What was important to Bruce was not so much that he was by heredity the Knight Marischal of the Kingdom, but that he came from Lothian. Keith was a district in the north-western foothills of the Lammermuirs. All Lothian and the Merse of Berwickshire had from the first been completely under the thumb of the invaders; and still was. That so prominent and cautiously level-headed a Lothian man should have decided that this was the time to take an active part again, was encouraging. Others might be moved to do likewise.

Others already were, it seemed — for the next two applicants for the royal mercy were Sir Alexander Stewart of Bonkyl, the Steward's nephew, and Sir William Vipont of Langton, both from the Merse, and the latter an Englishman. Undoubtedly these submissions had the effect of turning men's eyes southwards.

A number of less important men came to make their peace. And if it was becoming a weariness to the great gathering, as well as an offence to those who thought like Edward, the King accepted them all patiently. So he had planned it, and so it was.

At length he rose to his feet. "My friends all," he said. "You have been patient, forbearing. Some may deem, like my brother, that *I* have been too forbearing, in this day's work. But if this realm is to regain its freedom, it is above all necessary that it should be united. Only so can we drive out the English from our borders, a more numerous people than we, and who act in unity. We have differences amongst ourselves, yes — but they are as nothing to our differences with the invaders who devour us. And who would keep us divided. For such is their policy, always. Therefore, it is my task, my duty, whatever my own feelings would have me do, to unite my people. Having taken the field against them, because I must, and shown my rebels who reigns in Scotland, I now must show that I am King of all Scots, not only those who supported me. This I have sought to do today. Some may accuse me of weakness. But is it weakness to know your enemy? I know my real enemy — and it is not my fellow-countrymen, my own subjects, even when they . . . misjudge!"

There was some applause then, some laughter, some murmurs.

"So be it, my lords and friends," he went on. "We have had sufficient of discourse and confrontation. And tomorrow, in parliament, we will have more — our bellyful of it! There is more to living than war and clash and wordy debate. For too long this land has been starved of mirth and gaiety, good cheer of body and mind. So now, to our due and overdue enjoyment! Thanks to my lord Prior of this great house, the refectory here is now set with meats and drink in abundance. For all are his guests, and mine. Let us regale and refresh ourselves, without stint. Let us make up for the many times when we have gone hungry and cold and in fear. And thereafter come back here, for masque and music, dancing and spectacle. Let us show all men that the Scots can laugh as well as fight, sing as well as suffer. And that, when this struggle is overpast, and my realm is free again, it will be a joyful, lightsome realm." He raised his hand high. "Enough, then — this audience is over!"

"God save the King!" Unexpectedly that cry came from the serious Sir Thomas Randolph. "God save our King, I say!"

In thunderous acclaim the entire concourse took up the refrain and so continued, until the Guest Hall rafters shook and showered down dust and cobwebs. To this clamant din, the King led the way out and across the cloisters to the monastery's refectory. On the way through the bowing, curtsying, shouting throng, he paused, beckoned, and offered his arm to the Lady Christina of Garmoran, and so proceeded.

* * *

Later, much later that evening, panting a little from his exertions in the wild Highland reel just finished — wherein not a few had had to drop out before the end, by reason of too much prior good cheer or sheer lack of staying-power — Robert Bruce shook his head at Christina MacRuarie smiling at his side.

"How you do it, I know not," he said, dabbing his moist brow. "You look cool as a . . . a water-lily, in one of your own Moidart lochans. Not even flushed. Yet you tripped that reel, as others before it, like any halfling laddie! Myself, I am more like a foundered horse! And look at the others . . .!"

"Perhaps I have drunk less deeply than some!" she suggested. "Than the King of Scots, even? Or it may be but that we women are differently made. Lighter of foot, as of head! With less weight to carry."

"Having eyes, and other parts, we all can see that you are differently made!" Bruce gave back, looking down with frankest admiration on the white bosom as frankly displayed. Christina was at her most handsome tonight, in a silken gown of black and gold, considerably more low-cut as to front than was the Lowland custom. "As to weight, I swear that you have more there to carry than have I!" And he brushed that swelling bosom lightly with his finger-tips as though only inadvertently in a gesture. "And, on my soul, it is only in your very difference that you display any sign of this crazed dancing, woman!"

She glanced down in turn. Admittedly her firm and pointed breasts were heaving slightly, and each stirring with its own individual motion in a rhythm intriguing as it was apparent. The jigging violence of the reel had rather disarranged the already somewhat precarious balance of her gown's bodice, so that on the left side fully half of the large and dark red-brown aureola was revealed at each quiet surge of breath.

"Does my . . . difference offend Your Grace?" she asked, making shift to adjust her dress, though by no means drastically.

"No, no. Let it be, Tina — let it be." He not exactly slurred his words, but spoke with a thickened intonation. He did not often use the diminutive of her name, either.

She looked at him sidelong, from beneath lowered lids, not coquettishly but thoughtfully. They had not slept together since that day in Aberdeen a year before, when Elizabeth de Burgh's letter had reached him from Yorkshire.

All around them the gaily-dressed crowd eddied and circled and swayed, laughing, calling, chattering — though some sprawled or lay on benches, even on the floor, overcome by too much or too sudden unaccustomed good cheer — while from the moment gentler music came from the gallery, and a hairy Muscovite with a pair of dancing bears paraded ponderously round the huge hall, the great shaggy brutes holding each other close, rubbing snouts, and occasionally pawing each other in obscene parody of human caressing. The smells of bear, sweating humanity, women's perfume, wine, lamp-oil, wood-smoke and horses — for one of the earlier masques had included white jennets bearing damsels representing the Graces — was heady indeed.

"What of a mercy have you as rod for our backs next?" the King demanded. "Any more of your mad Hielant cantrips and you will have all decent men on their backs! Like my lord of Crawford, there." He pointed to the recumbent Sir Alexander Lindsay near by, mouth open and snoring. "Even Angus Og and the MacGregor are far through with it! Worse than I am, i' faith!" James Douglas was in fact Master of Ceremonies tonight, but Christina had been largely responsible for compiling the programme.

"You have not done too much, Robert?" she asked, quickly concerned. "None intended that the King should dance all measures. You have been a sick man. You must not tax yourself . . ."

"Tush, woman — I am well enough. It is but your Highland

notions of dancing. A battlefield is kinder on the human frame, I vow, than your antic flings!"

"We of the Hebrides are of a lusty humour, perhaps," she conceded. 'Our blood not watered down with Sasunnach degeneracy! But, never fear — you shall have your wind back. There follows another masque, an allegory for the times. Demanding naught of you save open eyes . . ."

"Open eyes!" he took her up. "So long as certain eyes do not open too wide! In especial churchmen's eyes, in this house! Our Scots clerics are not inordinately nice, I think — but that last allegory of yours, whatever you named it, was scarce of monastic quality!"

"Save us, our Celtic churchmen would not have turned a hair at that! And your Master Bernard helped to devise it. Besides, most of the bishops and such-like are gone."

"But some are not. Nicholas Balmyle yonder. And David of Moray . . . though Davie, I swear, will shock hard! Did you see him dancing? Like a blackcock at a lek!"

"He is of good Celtic stock," she pointed out. "But . . . see you another of good Celtic stock, there. Of my own sex. And the fairest in this room, I judge. Have you noted, my lord King?"

He followed the direction of her glance, and nodded. "I have noted," he said shortly. "Edward was ever a lady's man. As you have reason to know, Tina."

"To be sure. But I can handle my good lord of Carrick. Can she? *Her* brother, I think, misdoubts it."

Over in a window alcove of the hall, hidden frequently by the circling throng, Edward Bruce had the beauteous Lady Isabella Ross, and was laying siege to her with the direct tactics and urgency which he used in the field — and apparently with some success. Clearly the contempt in which he held her menfolk was neither here nor there.

Bruce shrugged. "He is a man, is Edward — all man. And a grown man. In such matters I cannot harry him, as though a child. God forgive me, I harry him enough! And in this . . . in this he is not the only one, by the Rude!" That was true. In almost every corner and window-embrasure visible — and no doubt elsewhere likewise — similar activities were afoot. "Can you blame them? We have had little enough of this, for long years . . ."

"Far be it from me to blame any, in such matters. Your brother or other. You know that, Robert. But I think I see two who do!"

"Sir John Ross, maybe. That one is sour, and will bear watching, I agree. But not Sir Hugh, surely?"

"Not Sir Hugh, no. Hugh Ross has other concerns in mind! Has had, all evening!" And she nodded.

"Eh . . .?" He looked where she did, to see the Earl's eldest son, not huddling in any unseemly corner but nevertheless paying rapt attention to another personable young woman, and that the King's own youngest sister, Matilda Bruce. A mere child throughout most of the prolonged period of war, she had been sent for safety to the house of an aunt in deepest Galloway. Edward, after his recent successful campaign in that province, had brought her here to the Court, no longer a coltish gawky girl but a roving-eyed and attractive seventeen-year-old — and evidently one more problem for the King of Scots. "Aye," he said heavily. "So that is the way of it, now! It must be the spring, 'fore God!"

"Perhaps. But it is not the Lady Matilda and Sir Hugh that concerns me — for he is an honourable man, I think. Despite his father! But another lady, less fortunate. No gallant knight fondles Isabel de Strathbogie this night, you will perceive!"

Frowning, the King once more followed the percipient Christina's regard to where alone, neglected, the new Earl of Atholl's sister stood. The Earl himself was not present — for he was married to the Red Comyn's daughter and had taken the English side after Dumfries, remaining so even after his father's shameful hanging by King Edward. But his two sisters continued loyal. That they had turned up at St. Andrews was gratifying, for the earldom could raise many men — but perhaps more than loyalty had brought at least this Isabel. For Edward Bruce had been paying court to her for some time, off and on, as campaigning permitted. Now, it seemed, he had found alternative attraction.

"Would you have me play nurse to them?" he demanded.

"Not nurse. Midwife, perhaps!"

"What! You mean . . .?"

"Rumour has it that the Lady Isabel is with child. By your brother. She looks to be so, would you say? And he looks elsewhere."

"Damnation! You think it true? I had not heard of this. I knew they saw each other. But Edward plays with any woman. Here's a coil, then! Atholl's sister . . .!"

"A coil, yes. A woman is entitled to look heavy in more than body, earl's daughter or no! But when her lover shows his preference, before all, for the daughter of the man who betrayed her father to death, as Ross did old Atholl — then there could be trouble."

"M'mm. I will have a word with Edward on this. But not now. I cannot well reprimand him on such matter, in front of all. I will go speak with her. Though, God knows what I may say . . .!"

The King strolled over to the young woman, unhurriedly, exchanging a word or two with others on the way. He would not have noticed that she was pregnant for she was no sylph anyway, a strapping creature, high-coloured and comely enough but with no claims to beauty. She and her sister were notably good horsewomen, and many a hunt they had ridden with the Bruce brothers — for they were kin to the King in a sort of way, their mother having been elder sister to his own first wife, Isabel of Mar, after whom this girl was named.

"Will you dance the next measure with me, Isa?" he asked. "And save me having to trip another Highland reel with Christina MacRuarie! Or she will be the death of me!"

"I am not dancing, Sire," the other returned. "By your leave."

"No? You are the wise one, then! I should have said the same. I saw your sister dancing with Sir Gilbert."

"No doubt."

"Aye. I'ph'mm. You are well enough, Isa?"

"Well, yes. Over well, perhaps!"

"Eh?" Somewhat heavily he changed the subject. "Have you been at Kildrummy of late? We had good times there, did we not? It seems long ago. I have not seen it since . . . since the English took it. And Nigel with it." Strathbogie Castle was not far away from Kildrummy, at the junction of Bogie and Deveron, in Aberdeenshire.

"It is a sad ruin," she answered briefly.

"Yes. I will have to rebuild it. So much to do. They took young Donald of Mar south. To England. My nephew and your cousin. Have you heard aught of him?"

"If you mean, Sire, has my brother informed us of Donald, from England — then I say no. We have no truck nor communication with David. Do not reproach *us* with his treason!"

The King sighed a little. He had never thought of Isa Strathbogie as a prickly female. "I do not," he assured. "My lord of Atholl has a wife — and I murdered her father." Frequently he made himself use the word murder, lest he forget, a sort of penance. "Who am I to blame him? Blame is profitless, I have found, and men's passions not always subject to reason."

"Your Grace is magnanimous — as all do say today! Too magnanimous, *I* say! I am not! Towards my brother — or yours!" And she glared over towards Edward.

"M'mm. Well . . . Edward is Edward! You know him

"I know him! more to the point, he has known me! And seems to forget it. And with the assassin Ross's daughter, of all creatures! My poor slain father will turn in his English grave!"

Bruce shook his head wearily. "There is nothing in that, lass. A mere passing fancy..."

"And I a *past* fancy! Is that to be the way of it? We shall see! I promise you, we shall see..."

The King was grateful indeed for the sudden extraordinary noise which drowned his companion's bitter voice. It came from the minstrels' gallery. With the bears gone, the music had ceased, and now was succeeded by a high, wild moaning and whistling sound that rose and fell, rose and fell, for all the world like the gusting of a storm wind. Presumably fiddles and fifes, and the drones of bagpipes, were responsible. Then the splash-splash of water, slopped from pail to pail, was added. Everywhere talk died away.

At the foot of the hall the doors were thrown open, and the representation of a large ship moved in. It was handsomely made of painted canvas on a wooden frame, with three tall masts and sails. It held a crew of a dozen, who, although they actually walked on the floor, seemed to sit within. They wore breastplates and helmets, with the Leopards of England painted on them, and from the mastheads flew stiff banners, two red Crosses of St. George flanking another Plantagenet Leopard. They came in chanting, "Death to all Scots! Down with King Hob!"

King Hob was the English term of scorn for Robert Bruce.

This tableau produced the expected cries and groans of execration from the company, some of those who suffered most from liquor even advancing threateningly, fists raised.

Then, behind, emerged a smaller vessel, with only four occupants. These also were in armour, three with the white-on-blue Cross of St. Andrew painted on their breastplates, and the fourth, a handsome youth who stood amidships — indeed, none other than William Irvine of Drum, the royal armour-bearer — wearing the Lion Rampant and having a gold circlet round his brows. The supporting trio shouted "God save King Robert! Freedom or death!" while Irvine bowed graciously all round.

The loud applause that greeted this party was quickly drowned in violent shouting and war cries, as the larger craft swung cumbrously round and bore down on the smaller, its crew brandishing suddenly drawn swords.

A fierce and very noisy battle thereupon took place, a dozen against four, with much whacking and clashing of steel and the Scots taking some resounding knocks, the masts of their ship tending to come adrift realistically in the process — in fact, Irvine having to hold the mid-mast up. Sundry of the more excited spectators had to be restrained from forcibly joining in.

In the midst of this stirring if unequal contest a third vessel appeared on the scene, midway in size between the other two. This was skilfully represented as a galley, with a single mast, a great square sale on which was painted the device of three red lions on gold, and three oars pulling rhythmically on each side. Its crew wore Highland dress and bonnets, and its leader the eagles' feathers of a chief, with bunches of juniper as badge. Cheers shook the hall as the newcomers drove in towards the contestants.

But the cheers died away to shocked silence, and then changed to varied exclamations of wrath, jeering, abuse and laughter, as it became evident that the Highlanders were in fact attacking the Scots vessel, not the English. Only then it dawned on those sufficiently mentally alert at this hour of a gay night, that the red-and-gold colours, the juniper badge and the three lions device on the sail, were all the marks of the earldom of Ross; and that the leader with the eagles' feathers was a huge fat youth, made grotesquely fatter with pillows and the like.

Bruce, drawing a quick breath, looked over at Christina MacRuarie—who smiled back at him unconcernedly. This was her doing, for certain, her way of hitting back at Ross for many things, but in especial undoubtedly for the attack on her personal galley that October day some thirty months before, in the Hebridean Sea, when Bruce had first met her. This was her method of showing that while the King might overlook and forget slights and injuries, she and others did not. The realisation of it grew on all there, and the noise was deafening.

Not a little anxious now, Bruce glanced across to where he had last seen the Earl of Ross drinking at one of the side tables. He was still there, but now happily had fallen forward, head on arm, goblet spilt beside him. Nobody was thinking to rouse him, apparently, to view the spectacle, much as he might hear of it afterwards. His sons however were not thus spared. Sir Hugh, beside Bruce's young sister, looked discountenanced and unhappy; while Sir John, with his Comyn wife, fumed and spluttered. Farther over, Edward Bruce laughed loud and long, his arm still possessively round Ross's blushing daughter.

"Your Isleswoman has a nice wit, at least!" Isabel Strathbogie observed. "Pay heed to what she is telling you, Sire."

The King said nothing. A policy of statesmanlike forgiveness and unity might be well enough for the monarch, but it seemed to be less than popular with his subjects. How to impose it, then? Of all his close friends only Lennox supported it, and that scarcely wholeheartedly. And yet, was there any other way to face the greater menace, the English?

These thoughts were temporarily banished by still another disturbance at the door. Into the hall swept a fourth vessel, and this quite the most eye-catching of all, magnificent indeed. It was all white and gold, another galley, everything — sail, mast, hull, oars, hanging shields — dazzling white picked out in gold. The crew were all in white also — but any insipidity in this was banished by the fact that they were all young women. There were a score of them in the galley, all but one clad wholly in diaphanous snow-white lawn or cambric, of a clerical fineness of quality that was only made for high churchmen's surplices — indeed, these were all surplices, only a little adjusted — almost transparent. That the ladies wore nothing else beneath was swiftly apparent to delighted male and scandalised female eyes. The glow of pinkish flesh, with darker patches here and there, through the white, as well as the arms and legs more frankly bare, was the only failure, if such it could be called, in the white-and-gold harmony. Each girl bore a gold-painted wand in her hand.

The one exception to this unwarlike company was a splendidly built, laughing-eyed young female who stood alone on the raised poop of the galley, holding a golden arrow. She wore a handsome white-painted helmet above her cascade of corn-coloured hair, the wings on either side golden. A steel breastplate, also white, only partly hid her otherwise unclothed upper parts, and the very obvious fact that it had been designed to fit other than a particularly pronounced and rounded feminine form only enhanced effect. The back, save for the armour's straps, was wholly bare. A sort of brief skirt of chainmail, and tall riding-boots, both whitened, completed the costume — though leaving notable stretches of delectable thigh uncovered.

Needless to say this boatload aroused a masculine enthusiasm far outdoing even that for the stoutly-battling but sadly outclassed royal craft, the King himself cheering heartily.

"Hussies!" the Lady Isobel observed succinctly, at his side, to choke him off. After all, it *was* a monastery.

The galley of the nymphs, or whatever they were, bore down on the other embattled three — and now the wild storm music sank and dwindled to a gentle melody. Out from the canvas craft the maidens rose, to step over into the other vessels, lightly waving their wands before the receptive faces of the sword-whacking warriors, or at least those opposing the four heroes in the royal barge, now in dire danger of becoming a casualty indeed. The breastplated lady remained in the stern of her own galley, directing all with her arrow-like weapon. With remarkable speed and unanimity the Englishmen and the Rosses alike collapsed before this potent assault — not so remarkable perhaps in view of the closing in of all this unusually underclad femininity. In a disappointingly short time, in the circumstances, Scotia's rescue was accomplished and the heroic monarch was safe — though he still was landed with the task of keeping upright the swaying mid-mast and sail, to his evident embarrassment. At this stage the nymphs' leader vacated her poop and, stepping over into the Ross galley, poked her dart approximately into the stomach of the stout chieftain, in formally dramatic fashion, whereupon he sank away out of sight below the gunwale, clutching his middle and howling horribly. The music rose to a triumphant crescendo. Evidently this belated *coup de grâce* had some especial significance.

The resounding applause was cut short by Christina MacRuarie, who stepped out into mid-floor beside the victorious galley, hand raised.

"Hear me," she called, in her softly lilting Hebridean voice, into the eventual hush. "Hear me, all you most noble of Scotland's race, Highland and Lowland. And others!" Her pause was eloquent. "Here is the Princess Aoife, of Skye, mighty heroine, and mother of Cuchullin's son, come to the rescue of the King of Scots, with her train of pure maidens and her mystic *gaebolg*, the dart of justice and truth, from which there is no known protection so be that it is hurled over water. Thus the King's saving and sure support came from across the water, the Western Sea, as the seannachies of old have foretold. So long as King Robert remembers the true Celtic origin and honour of his kingdom, so long shall he triumph and his throne be glorious."

There was more applause, but some murmuring too from the non-Highland part of the assembly, which saw this all as rather too blatant a piece of propaganda for the barbarous Erse and Islesmen. As undoubtedly it was, of course, a flourish, but a warning too. Bruce recollected something of the saga of Aoife of Skye, the semi-mythological heroine of many a Highland camp-fire, Lady of the Sea, Princess of the North, mistress of the legendary Cuchullin after whom the Skye mountains were named, and mother of the beautiful but ill-fated Conlaoch, whose invincible belly-dart was only effective over water. Bruce glanced round to seek for the Lord of the Isles. Angus Og would have had a hand in this, to be sure.

Christina, helping down the voluptuous dart-wielder from the Ross galley, and beckoning young Irvine from the royal wreck — so that he had to dispose of his wretched mast to one of his colleagues — led the two principals across to present them to the King.

"Here is Marsala MacGregor of Glenkinglass, niece to the MacGregor," she introduced.

As the bold-eyed, high-coloured and excitingly-made girl sank in deepest curtsy before him, she might have been naked to the waist, as far as Bruce was concerned, her breastplate, by its very nature, weight and shape, being no protection to her in the least. Nor did the curtsy increase the efficacy of the chain-mail skirt. Clearing his throat, he leaned over to raise her up.

"Lady . . . Mistress . . . my dear," he said huskily, "I thank you. Indeed I do. We all do. You are most . . . superb! My felicitations. You are a credit to Clan Alpine, on my soul! A . . . joy to us all. I shall tell your uncle so." When she would have backed away, he held her arm and turned her, so that she stood by his side, flushed, radiant. The King was relieved to see that the Lady Isa had somehow removed herself.

He nodded to the young armour-bearer: "You wrought nobly, Willie," he acknowledged. "As who would not, knowing how you were to be delivered! You must act my tutor in some matters hereafter, I see!" He turned to Christina. "As for you, my Lady of Garmoran — I am beyond words! Your talents are such that we all are left speechless. Which, it may be, is as well! It is my hope that my lord Prior will so remain. Equally my lord of Ross! But . . . you have delighted our eyes and our . . . sensibilities. You and all those who have so ably entertained us. I thank you all." He found that he was clutching the MacGregor girl's arm, made to loose her, and then forbore. "All shall be rewarded, as is meet, I assure you!" And Tina MacRuarie could make what she would of that.

Sir John Ross, with his wife, turned and stalked from the hall, without any of the required bowing towards the monarch. It was difficult to say who led who.

Save for the King's captive, the galley-maidens fled for their lives and virtue, not only their late victims in hot pursuit.

The hour was late, and this obviously had been the highlight of the evening. There followed more music and dancing, and there was still cheer of more solid sort for all who desired it. But all was now by way of anticlimax. When the King decently could detain his fair prisoner no longer, and yielded her to Christina, he moved over for a word with Hugh Ross, to soothe susceptibilities and to ensure that the old Earl was got discreetly off to bed. He advised his young sister, in the by-going, that it was time that she too retired from the scene. He looked for Edward, but was too late for that active operator, who had already disappeared, and Isabella Ross with him.

Thereafter, commanding Gibbie Hay to see that all remaining guests obtained hospitality to their repletion, Bruce quietly slipped from the Guest Hall to make his way alone through the now deserted, night-bound streets to the Bishop's Castle and his own tower bedchamber. He was glad enough of the fresh North Sea air to clear a throbbing head.

It was William Irvine's duty, as page rather than armour-bearer, to attend at the King's chamber — but this night Willie would be otherwise preoccupied. After a word or two with the guard on duty, mounting the narrow corkscrew stair to his room at the tower-top, Bruce, at the door, paused, his nostrils catching the faintest whiff of woman's perfume. He smiled a little. He had a feeling that possibly Christina might seek him out, this night, for more than explanations. And, of a truth, he could do with a woman!

Entering the apartment, where a lamp was already lit and a fire burned brightly, the King was therefore not surprised to see the shadowy shape of a cloaked woman, back turned, over by the turret window. Small wonder the sentry downstairs had been rather more familiarly pawky than usual.

"Ha!" he said. "You should have allowed me to escort you here in person, my dear."

"Oh no, Sire. That would have been unseemly!" That was said with a giggle. And, though the voice was softly Highland, it was not Christina's.

"On my soul . . .!" Bruce stared, as the woman turned round. It was the MacGregor girl. She had discarded her helmet, but the long cloak, hanging open, revealed that she was still dressed approximately as before — if dressed is the word.

She sketched another curtsy. "I hope that I please Your Grace?" that was just slightly uneasy.

"Save us, girl — how did you get here?"

"The Lady Christina brought me."

"She did? And . . . where is she now?"

Again the giggle. "Gone, Sire. To her own chamber. In the Gatehouse. She said that she thought that she would not be required further! Tonight."

"So-o-o!" Plunging, his mind sought for reasons. Why had Christina done this? They had not bedded since Aberdeen. Because of the letter from Elizabeth. He had indeed bedded no woman since then. A long time. Could it be . . .? She sensed his need — that would demand no Highland second-sight! But had divined also that there was a bar between them in this matter, an obstruction to break down? And had chosen to break it down by means of a stranger, this MacGregor wench! A young lusty, compliant creature whom she could scarcely doubt had taken his eye, taken every man's eyes. Was that it? This Marsala was to prepare the way for Christina again. If he slept with her, could he deny the other his bed, once more?

It was the best that Bruce's somewhat bemused mind could do at this hour and with that piece of uncomplicated and quite distracting womanhood before him.

She had moved over to the fireside, and was holding out her hands to the blaze, though the room was warm enough, one booted foot on the raised fender — which meant that much of a white thigh and bent knee projected from the folds of the cloak, as well as the two bare arms. She smiled at him over her shoulder in simplest invitation, and shrugged the cloak a little, so that the cloth slipped further. Nothing could have been less subtle — or more effective.

Grinning, Bruce went over to her. "The Lady Christina is thoughtful and probably wise," he said. "We must not disappoint her! May I take your cloak? Marsala, is it not?"

She unfastened the clasp with alacrity, and stood revealed in her extraordinary but provocative costume. Her giggles were, in the circumstances, suitable, unexceptionable.

"You played your part well," he told her. "In the masque. But this heavy steel must irk your fair flesh sorely?"

"It does," she agreed, "I will be glad . . . to be quit of it!"

Nodding, he proceeded to unbuckle the strapping at her bare back — and found the contact with her soft, warm and firm skin set his fingers trembling; which, for a mature man, experienced and a monarch at that, was a sorry commentary on prolonged celibacy. Marsala MacGregor aided him.

The clumsy breastplate fell away to reveal breasts quite breathtaking in their shape and size. Too large, no doubt, in proportion to the rest of her, and likely in a few years to get quite out of hand and make her one of those top-heavy, quickly-ageing women. But that was no man's concern tonight. He found no fault as she turned towards him so that the thrusting points of her brushed his damnably quivering hands. It crossed his mind that she was better at this than he had been with Christina, earlier in the evening.

"You are . . . all delight," he said throatily. "This chain-mail? How is it secured . . .?"

She had anticipated him there, and at a little more than a touch from him the heavy if brief skirting fell to her feet with a satisfactorily solid crunch. Whatever may have been under it previously, there was nothing now save generous swelling womanhood, suitably framed and garnished.

Even as he looked down her white belly seemed to ripple and wave — or was that his own eyesight, affected by the liquor he had drunk? Or another symptom of his humiliating youth-like excitement and urgency?

She came close, to press all that undulating femininity against him, warm arms encircling his neck, red lips raised and open. The boots could wait. He would have picked her up in his arms and carried her to the bed, as the situation more or less prescribed — but the relics of sanity remained to him. She was after all a large creature, and would weigh more possibly than his dignity could survive. Moreover, he would be wise, almost certainly, to harbour his strength for his own immediate warfare. The priority now was to get some at least of his own splendid apparel off before the lower nature triumphed.

He strode for the bed, tugging off his magnificent tabard. She was not far behind, prepared to help in this also.

"It . . . has been long," he panted, warning her. "I am not perhaps . . . sufficiently a king tonight! Bear with me, girl. At first! And I will serve you . . . royally!"

"I am MacGregor," she answered simply. "And my race is royal!" It was her clan's motto.

For a moment he paused, to stare at her — but only for a moment.

Chapter Sixteen

Parliament was to open at noon, and the King to ride in state to the cathedral where it was to be held. About an hour earlier, dressing for the occasion and going over in a mind which had in its time felt fresher, more alert, the projected programme for the day, Bruce made frequent glances at and out of the window. The smirr of thin, cold rain off the North Sea, with which the morning had started, could spoil the procession. Not that this was so very important; yesterday had been the time for the play-acting, and today's business was on a different level, serious, formal, but vital. Nevertheless, the thought of a lot of wet, chilled men in that great cold church, sitting hour after hour in debate, was not one to which he could look forward. Perhaps he was a little testy this morning. Gibbie Hay and young Irvine certainly gave the impression that they thought so, tip-toeing about and keeping eyes averted. That could be guilty consciences, of course. He had slept less than usual last night, admittedly — but so probably had they, and for similar reasons.

A brief gleam of watery sun, coinciding with a commotion down in the castle courtyard below, took him to the window once more. A small party of cloaked men had ridden in under the Gatehouse arch, horses steaming. The visitors were now dismounting stiffly as from long riding. There was nothing unusual about this, with the quality of most of Scotland descending upon St. Andrews these days; but that they should come straight to this castle was perhaps significant. And something about one of the travellers caught the King's attention.

This man was tall, gaunt seeming and stooping a little, but strongly-built, and by the skirts of his habit below the folds of his long travelling-cloak, dressed in the style of a Benedictine friar. Nothing extraordinary about that. Yet, something about the man, even viewed from this tower-top angle . . .

Suddenly Robert Bruce emitted a cry of astonishment, and dropping the gold belt he was in the process of donning, and brushing past the surprised Sir Gilbert, he actually ran to the door, threw it open, and went down the winding turnpike stairs two or three steps at a time.

Out in the wet courtyard, past the startled guards, the King hurried towards the travellers, who were now moving in the direction of the main keep. "William!" he cried, "William, my friend! My lord Bishop — God is good!"

William Lamberton turned, stern and bony features lighting up. He came long-strided. He seemed about to drop on one stiff knee before the monarch, but at the last moment thought better of it and instead threw his arms wide and took the younger man into his embrace.

"Robert! Robert my liege, my son, my most dear friend — here is joy! So long, so long it has been. Three long years."

They clasped each other for a little, too overcome for coherent words.

Then they stood back and looked at each other — and the marks of those years were only too plain to see on both of them. Lamberton saw a lean, purposeful, strong man of a great natural dignity and almost alarming if unconscious authority, with keen distance-searching eyes — yet with a gleam of humour about them. Gone were the last traces of immaturity, the relics of youthful uncertainty and indecision. Here was a man in his prime, of body and of mind, but chiselled, tempered, almost graven in both as by a sculptor of fierce conviction. And Bruce saw a worn, lined and ravaged giant, old before his time — for Lamberton was but forty-six, with only eleven years between them — grey-haired, weary, but though bowed of frame most obviously not bowed in spirit.

The King had been demanding how came the other to St. Andrews this March morning, but struck by the Bishop's evident fatigue, took the older man's arm instead and led him towards his own tower. "You are tired. Come to my chamber. Eat and drink, while I dress. For this parliament. We can talk then . . ."

But Lamberton gave him some information even as they mounted the stairs. "I am tired, yes — for I have been in the saddle since dawn yesterday and rested but two hours in the night. But that is nothing in my joy in seeing Your Grace. It more than makes up for any weariness of the flesh. It will be the leaving you again, the *going* that will tax me sorely — not this coming."

"Leaving? Going? What do you mean?"

"Only that I have not long with you, Robert. A day and a night, no more. At this hour tomorrow I must be over Forth again and spurring for the Border."

"Dear God — not that! Here is foolish talk indeed . . ."

"Not so, Sire. For what I have left of honour is at stake. You see before you a man forsworn. I have broken my word, my parole. All for love of you, my friend. I gave King Edward my word that I would remain in England. Only on condition that I did not return to Scotland was I released from my prison. I seek to tell myself that this means only that I would not return to abide here — not that I could not visit. But that is merest casuistry. I was not to leave Edward's realm. He trusted me. And I have done so. I must return forthwith."

"But if the damage is done . . .?"

"Perhaps not. I came secretly. I am thought to be making a pilgrimage of the shrines of Saint Cuthbert, in Northumbria. For my sins! I left Hexham Priory at dawn yesterday, supposedly to make for a cell in the hills of Upper Tynedale. Instead, I hastened across the Border passes of Deadwater and the Note o' the Gate, into Teviotdale. And so here, by secret ways we both know well. If I can return by the same route, and at the same pace, I may reach the Abbey of Lanercost two days hence. Where I am expected. And be thought only to have been travelling amongst the remote hill shrines. There is a Pilgrim Road. This I pray for — so shameless a deceiver I have become!"

"But your men? Your companions?"

"Only one, my personal servant, came with me from Hexham.

In England I do not ride the land like a prince of the Church! The others I picked up at my Abbey of Melrose, in Tweeddale."

In Bruce's bedchamber, after Hay had paid his respects to the Bishop, and provided meat and drink, he and Irvine left King and Primate alone — with reminders of the procession's timing.

"This parole of yours is a sore burden upon you, my friend," Bruce said, after a little, as he watched the other eat. "I am not one for breaking faith, as you know. But this was no ordinary demand upon you. It was the only way that you might regain freedom from prison, yes. But you were unlawfully imprisoned. You went to the English, before Methven, as an emissary from me. To imprison such emissary was a dishonourable act. And to hold captive for years a consecrated bishop of Holy Church, Primate of Scotland, to prevent him from ministering to his people — this is doubly unlawful, against the laws of God and man. In such circumstances is your given word to be held to? Is it not your duty, to your people, to *me*, to return to Scotland, by any means possible? You owe no duty to Edward of Carnarvon."

"Think you I have not turned over and over in my mind all such thoughts, Sire? I had ample time to do so! It may be so, as regards my episcopal duty. But I have my personal honour to consider, surely? My given word, as a man. God forgive me, I have indeed broken it to be here at all. For that I might convince myself of excuse. A visit only. But to *stay* in Scotland there could be no excuse. From my own conscience. It is my conscience that I fear, Robert — not King Edward's wrath."

"Aye. I understand. Probably I would judge as you do."

"Besides, I believe that I may indeed serve you best, my liege lord, by returning to England. Here I am Primate, Bishop, and your Chancellor, yes. But others can perform these duties, or represent me in them. Can any other do what I am in a position to do, in England? Here is why, after long thought, I gave my word. That young man, Edward Plantagenet, has a liking for me. Why, I know not. As he has a hatred and suspicion of his own bishops, Beck in especial. They were all his father's creatures — and all to do with his father he hates. He sends me letters, messages, seeks my advice, summons me to wait on him. He is a strange man, weak yet wilful, stubborn. And I can influence him. Have already done so. And can learn much of what is planned, against you and Scotland. To inform you thereafter. God knows, I have no liking for the task, to act snake, deceiver, spy. But I *can* do it. And I tell myself that it is to the eventual benefit of England also — an end to oppression, invasion, peace with Scotland. Judas's code, perhaps? But . . .

I might achieve much. So my poor consience is torn two ways . . ."

"Yes. I see it. You may be right. Already you have sent me vital tidings. About Edward's wedding. This Piers Gaveston, and the nobles' resentment. You freed my hands, then, to deal with the North. That I can do with an ear, an eye and a voice at Edward's Court, there is no doubt. And you can . . . you can keep touch with my Elizabeth. Comfort her. That above all — although I should not say it! That above all." It came out in a rush. He had been urgent to ask about Elizabeth from the moment of their meeting.

"Yes, my son — yes. I know it. Elizabeth. God bless her! God bless you both. Being permitted to visit her is a great matter. I see her when I can. She is well. Brave. Proud in her sorrows. You chose wisely in your wife, Robert. Sinfully, I have ever begrudged Bishop Beck of Durham in that he wed you, not me."

"She is not misused? Maltreated? Humiliated?"

"No. She is not treated as a queen. But as the great Earl of Ulster's daughter she is respected. Young Edward does not love Ulster, his father's friend. But he does not vent his spleen on the daughter — save to keep her closely warded. A strange man, he has not his sire's savagery, but he hates almost as strongly. I think he hates the Scots little less than did Longshanks . . ."

"And his intentions, with Elizabeth? How long is he going to hold her captive?"

"That I know not. But I cannot raise false hopes for you, Sire. I would that I could say kinder. I think he will not release the Queen while ever you withstand him. Or your daughter. He uses them against you. Hoping your resolve will soften, your need and love for them bring you to terms. That is the English way . . ."

Bruce's groan was harsh.

Pityingly his friend eyed him. "It is an evil case. Here is dishonour indeed! But, at least, this Edward is less cruel. You heard that when I made representation to him, he ordered the release from their cages of your sister and the Countess of Buchan?"

"Yes. For that I am grateful. To you! Scarce to Edward, who kept them like cooped fowl for months after his father died. That any Christian prince could so act . . .! But — what is *my* duty, William? Towards my wife and daughter? I ask you — what is my true duty? I am a man, a husband and father, as well as a king. As *you* are a man as well as a bishop, as you have just said. I have set my throne before my wife. No — not my throne; my realm, my people. The freedom of Scotland before *her* freedom. And that of the child of my loins. And cursed myself for it every day of my life! What is my duty, man?"

"You know your duty, Robert. You have done it. And, I pray God, will continue to do it. You are King of Scots. I anointed you that day, at Scone. You are not as other men. This your burden you must carry, grievous as it is. All men know it. Elizabeth knows it, and would not have you fail in it. A king's is no mere title or honour, as is earl or knight. A king is wed to his people, first. You know it."

"I know it." Wearily the other nodded. "But, at times, I . . . I hope . . . weakly. That I might be spared this." Bruce straightened up. "But enough of this. You came because of today's parliament?"

"Yes. To support you in it. For I am still, in name, your Chancellor of the realm. And the Chancellor should conduct the business of a parliament, under the monarch's presidency. I cannot remain Chancellor — but at least I can support you at the opening of this, your first. This I had to do."

"It was kindly thought of. I am grateful. I had thought to use another acting-Chancellor. Nicholas Balmyle was formerly that. But now, as bishop, and administrator of your diocese as well as his own Dunblane, he is better as the realm's Treasurer. I had intended to appoint Master Bernard de Linton, my secretary, as acting-Chancellor. He is young, able, trustworthy, and of nimble mind. And loyal. Though of lowly rank. Shall I so appoint him, in your name, think you?"

"No, Sire. Not *acting*-Chancellor. Make him Chancellor of the Kingdom, in truth. An excellent choice. Better than Balmyle, indeed — who, though sound, has his limits. I wish to be relieved of this office. It is folly for me to remain in it, even in name. For too long there has indeed been no Chancellor. Give Bernard de Linton the seals of office. He will serve Scotland well."

"M'mmm. It is a big step, that. For one so humbly placed. There are those who will be envious. It is best to be a churchman, yes, a clerk and man of learning. But many others higher placed may demur. And since many must take instructions and even commands from the Chancellor, it would be unwise to offend such prelates. Taking instruction in *your* name, yes. But in the name of the Vicar of Mordington . . .!"

"True. Then we must use our wits. Between us, we can arrange it better, surely — King and Primate! Bernard is worthy of a promotion. It was on my suggestion that Nicholas Balmyle offered him for your service. He must be raised in rank." Lamberton permitted himself a wintry smile. "A mitred abbot? There is one abbey within my jurisdiction that is a thorn in my flesh — Arbroath! It is one of the richest in the land — yet Abbot John is for the English, as you well know. He cocks his mitre under the protection of the English garrison of Dundee! And refuses to pay his dues to my treasury here. See you how my mind works, Robert?"

"Ha! Appoint Master Bernard Abbot of Arbroath? In place of this John. One of the most senior abbacies in Scotland . . ."

"And let Master Bernard, who is an able chiel, and with his own ambitions no doubt, desire to get his hands on the revenues thereof, as well as the office! So, I think, we shall soon see notable efforts to oust the English from Arbroath and Dundee! To the benefit of all."

"Sakes, man — here is a ploy indeed!" Bruce chuckled. "Your wits have rusted nothing in your English prison, I vow! May I so announce to this parliament? The new Abbot of Arbroath to be Chancellor of the Kingdom, in your room? And Abbot John dismissed."

"When better to announce it, Sire? Although I had better have a word with Master Bernard first!"

"To be sure. I will send for him . . ."

* * *

So thereafter, when the King led the glittering mounted cavalcade through the rain-washed streets of the ecclesiastical metropolis, its own master, to the astonishment of all, rode at his side, clad in most magnificent episcopal canonicals hastily resurrected from secret storage for the occasion. If Lamerton's presence stole much of the limelight, in consequence, Bruce was the last to complain.

At the mighty cathedral, the largest in Scotland, all had been prepared with much care — though hardly for its own Bishop's presence. Certain damage had been caused by the English invaders but this was hidden behind evergreens and other decoration. The chancel-screens dividing the choir and high altar from the vast nave were further reinforced with more greenery and heraldic painted canvas, so as decently to shut off the holy parts from the rest. The nave itself, not normally seated, was now furnished with a great variety of chairs, benches, stools and forms, arranged in groupings and order to seat the varying degrees and status of the participating commissioners — and such was the scale of the place that there was still a large area at the west end available for onlookers. A dais had been erected at the chancel steps, for the throne, the Chancellor's table, the clerks' desks, and so on. Immediately below were seats for the great officers of state, and flanking them left and right were special stalls for the earls and bishops. Facing the dais were the three large groupings, already filled as the trumpets blared for the royal arrival — the estates of the Church, the barons and the burghs. Behind, the spectators' enclosure was packed. The lofty galleries of triforium and clerestories were today rivalling the splendour of such stained-glass windows as had not been smashed, in the kaleidoscopic colours of the ladies who thronged them.

Hidden choirs in the chancel sang anthems as the King of Arms and his heralds led in the King of Scots and his great entourage. Three men paced immediately behind him — James, the High Steward, Edward, Earl of Carrick, and William, Bishop of St. Andrews. Then, after an interval, came the Lords Spiritual — the Bishops of Dunkeld, Moray, Brechin, Ross and Dunblane. The earls followed — only Lennox and Ross, and the minors Sutherland and Menteith. Thereafter the Privy Council, followed by the provost and magistrates of the city.

At the dais the King halted, turned, and raised his hand — to some slight alarm on the part of the heralds, the masters of ceremonies, for this was unscheduled. When somebody had hushed the choirs to silence behind, the Bruce spoke.

"My lords spiritual and temporal, and all others here assembled — I require that the episcopal throne of this the prime diocese of my realm, be brought down from the sanctuary at the high altar, and placed near to my royal chair on this dais. For my well-beloved William, Lord Bishop of St. Andrews, Primate and Chancellor of this kingdom. Meanwhile, my lords — pray take your seats."

The gasp of surprise quickly grew into a chorus, a roar of cheering, as Lamberton stood, affected obviously, both nodding and shaking his grey head, and spreading helpless hands. In less orderly fashion than had been planned, the rest of the royal company moved to their places, guided by flurried heralds, while the gorgeously apparelled King of Arms sent scurrying servitors up into the chancel to carry down the Bishop's throne.

The King waited calmly throughout the commotion. Nobody else could sit down, of course.

At length, all were in their places, and with a certain amount of dislocation of decoration about the rude-screen, the massive chair with the high mitred back was manhandled down and on to the dais, men straining and panting with the weight of it. Bruce pointed exactly where it was to be placed, to the right and a little behind his own. Then taking the Primate's hand, he conducted him to it, with quite elaborate ceremonial. No one present had ever seen Lamberton look embarrassed, as now. As a tribute from sovereign to subject it was unique. It was also a highly significant gesture, creating a dramatic atmosphere, underlining the constitutional importance of the situation, and setting the scene and tone for the entire proceedings.

The King moved back to his own throne, stood for a few moments, and then sat. With a great sigh and much rustling and shuffling, the concourse took their seats and settled down.

The Scots regalia had been confiscated and taken south by King Edward in 1296, and never replaced. But after another flourish of trumpets, a gesture was made at representing these. Heralds brought up in succession Bruce's own long two-handed blade, as sword of state; a wand of office of the Silversmiths' Guild to serve as Sceptre; the golden spurs used at the coronation, and preserved jealously by the little Abbot of Scone; and the great and distinctly battle-worn Lion Rampant Standard. There was no Crown, other than the gold circlet the King already wore, and no Orb. These symbols should have been presented by the appropriate officers-of-state; but since only the Steward and the King of Arms were available, heralds brought them up, knelt before the monarch, holding the objects out for Bruce to touch, and then placing them on the Chancellor's table to the left.

This done, the King of Arms signed for another fanfare, and then called out, "I, High Seannachie of Scotland, declare this parliament and council of the kingdom and community of the Scottish realm, in the presence of the high and mighty Prince Robert, by God's grace King, with the three estates of that realm here assembled, to be duly constituted and in session. God save the King!"

After the bellowed response to this, which went on and on, Bruce raised hand again, remaining seated. "My lords and lieges here in session assembled—hear me, Robert. This day is a great day for this ancient kingdom, the most ancient of continuing subsistence in all of Christendom. It is the first parliament of my reign, the first for many bloody years. But more important still, it represents the resumption of rule and governance in this land, out of the blood-stained hands of the invader. Today, thanks to the courage and resolution, to the sacrifice and death of so many, and despite the error and folly of some, this Scotland stands a realm again. We are still invaded, our land defiled by the usurpers, still threatened by the might of England, Lothian and the South-East wholly occupied. But we are free men again, able to make our name and fame heard once more in the courts of Christendom. And especially in the court of the Plantagenet. To that end we must plan our strategies, muster our resources expend our energies, to the best of our abilities. Hence this parliament. Let us give thanks to God and His saints who have made it possible — especially the blessed Saint Andrew our patron, in this his city; nor forgetting the hallowed Saint Fillan, in whose especial care I have walked these many months. I, who sit upon a Celtic throne, the throne of one hundred monarchs, of Kenneth and Malcolm, Duncan and MacBeth, Canmore and David, and their predecessors and successors — I call upon two men to pray for God's blessing upon this assembly. The Dewar of the Coigreach, representative of the Abbots of Glendochart, in the Old Church, who gave me blessing when most I needed blessing. And Abbot Henry of Scone, who has served Scotland, and me, notably. I, the King, call these."

While from the benches of the clergy commissioners the small gnomelike person of Abbot Henry came forward briskly, a herald went to a vestry door opening from the south transept, to emerge again with the extraordinary hermit-like figure of the old Dewar, brought with some considerable difficulty from far Glen Dochart. It had been found impossible to part him from his rags, and he had blankly refused to don any of the Romish copes, chasubles or albs offered as a cover-up, plain or magnificent. However, the King had presented him with a fine black travelling-cloak, as a personal gift, and he had been persuaded to wear this, as showing suitable appreciation; and though the rags bulged out and showed very obviously beneath, at least the quite splendid and heavy gold-serpent belt of Celtic workmanship had been put on outside to hold the whole lot approximately together, looking strangely authoritative. Saint Fillan's famous crozier in hand, and venerable white locks and beard in tangled profusion, this eye-catching spectacle stumped over to the dais behind his superior-looking guide, scowling on all around — while the astonished murmur of much of the assembly grew and was shot through with widespread tittering.

Bruce stopped that promptly and effectively by rising from his throne and holding out his hand to the old man — an unprecedented mark of respect, which necessarily brought everyone else to their feet likewise, the noise and the scraping of chairs and forms drowning any remaining sniggers.

Abbot Henry, who was fortunately an unconventional cleric himself, and no formalist, as well as having a well-developed sense of fun, bowed to the Dewar, got no response, patted his shoulder nevertheless, and smiled genially.

The other raised his staff high, almost threateningly, and without waiting for any sign or cue, launched into a most vehement flood of Gaelic. Normally this is a liquid-sounding, misleading gentle-seeming language — but the Dewar of the Coigreach made it sound quite otherwise. Presumably what he was pronouncing was a prayer of blessing directed towards his Maker; but it sounded in fact more like a wholesale denunciation directed at the company present, delivered with quivering intensity. Fortunately it did not last long. Abruptly it ended, and as abruptly, without waiting to hear his Romish colleague's contribution, or making any acknowledgement to the monarch, the Dewar turned and stalked off as he had come.

Bruce kept a straight face throughout, and now inclined his head almost imperceptibly to the Abbot of Scone. His notion of bringing the Dewar here had been a gamble from the first. But despite this peculiar behaviour — which he had in fact anticipated — he was well enough satisfied. The gesture had been made. However comic or even unseemly might be the impact on the majority of Lowlanders present, on the Highlanders it would be otherwise. In two centuries the Romish Church had made only superficial headway in the West Highlands and Islands, and the ancient Celtic religious tradition still meant much, however inactive, latent. Bruce, above all, was concerned to rule a united kingdom, an idea almost totally abandoned since the Norman-French had come to Scotland. The Celic Church was a dead letter, of course, and could not be revived; but gestures such as this could greatly affect Highland sentiment.

Abbot Henry, a shrewd and practical man, saw what was required and, as the apparition disappeared into the vestry, staff thumping vigorously, made an equally brief but more conventional application for the Creator's blessing on their deliberations, and enduring mercies on the King, on the one Church, Holy, Catholic and Apostolic, and on all present, before bowing and returning to his place.

The monarchy, and all others, sat down with some relief.

"I now call upon the Chancellor to proceed with the business of this assembly," Bruce declared, in practical tones. "As is his duty and office."

Lamberton stood up. "Your Grace, my lords and commissioners," he said. "It is my great joy that I am able to be here for this great and memorable occasion. How I have achieved this, from ward in England, is not for me to explain to this parliament. Suffice it to say that I deemed it my prime duty to achieve this presence, at whatever cost — for two reasons. In order to support and acclaim our admired and heroic liege lord, King Robert, in his first parliament — without whom not only would there be no parliament but no Scotland today . . ." He waited until the storm of applause had spent itself. "And second, that I might decently and duly open this session, as Chancellor, and then resign the office to another more useful — as is right and proper. For I have to return to my ward in England tomorrow, and can therefore by no means serve in this important office further. His Grace needs an active Chancellor, not a paroled prisoner on foreign soil . . ."

There was an outbreak of groans and protest.

The Primate shook his head. "In this matter my mind is made up. The seals of office have been kept secure for me by my lord Bishop of Dunblane, during my captivity. For his good stewardship I thank him. Those seals and this office I now lay down before you all, for my successor." He paused. "Before I sit, I have one announcement to make, not as Chancellor but as Bishop. I hereby declare that I, for good and sufficient reason, have demoted and excluded the Abbot John of Arbroath, not here present, from the rule and supervision of that my great house; and have appointed Master Bernard de Linton, Vicar of Mordington, Official of this diocese and secretary to His Grace, to be Lord Abbot of Arbroath in his stead."

Lamberton sat down, to a stir of excitement.

Bruce spoke into it. "We receive my lord Bishop's resignation with regret but understanding. It is necessary that this realm, as this parliament, should have a Chancellor forthwith. I therefore here and now appoint Master Bernard, mitred Abbot of Arbroath, as Chancellor of the Kingdom, and require him to take up the seals of office, and to conduct the business of this assembly."

In absolute silence de Linton rose from his humble clerk's desk, walked to the Chancellor's table, bowed deeply to the King, less deeply to the Primate, touched the seals, and sat down.

There was no doubt about the sensation produced. For a young and unknown cleric to be appointed first minister of government was without precedent, however notable his suddenly enhanced rank. It was normal, though not automatic, that a cleric should be Chancellor, since few of the nobility were sufficiently learned in letters and Latin, the language of international correspondence, to cope with the duties. But there were many present who would have coveted the office, with all its influence — bishops, abbots, priors, of great seniority. Even Lennox himself, a scholar, Bruce suspected. But the King knew what he wanted from his Chancellor — and all recognised that this must be the monarch's personal choice. There were no formal protests, therefore, however much muttering.

"My lord Abbot — proceed."

Linton rose. "May it please Your Grace — first there are matters arising out of the recent wars, campaigns and truces. Certain matters fall within the authority of Your Grace's Privy Council.

But others require the decision of parliament. First, sentences of forefeiture. Such sentences have been passed against certain your subjects, and it is now desired that they be rescinded. Where these subjects hold the rank of earl or the office of sheriff, it is necessary for parliament to make the decision. To this rank and standing belong William, Earl of Ross, and Sheriff thereof; Alexander, Lord of Argyll and Lorn, and Sheriff thereof; and Sir Alexander Comyn, knight, Sheriff of Inverness. All now under sentence of forfeiture for rising in arms again the King's Grace. The Privy Council now requests that these forefeitures of lands and office be annulled. With the exception of certain lands within the Lordship of Lorn which shall continue in forfeiture. Is it agreed?"

Promptly, and on his cue, the Earl of Lennox rose. "My lord Chancellor — I so move, in the case of the Earl of Ross."

"And I in the case of the Lord of Argyll and Lorn," the Lord of Douglas added.

"And I in the case of Sir Alexander Comyn, knight," Sir Robert Boyd, knight, confirmed.

"All duly moved, each by one of his own degree," Abbot Bernard acknowledged swiftly. "Is there any contrary motion?"

With it all so obviously cut and dried, and by the King's closest associates, it required a bold man to question it. But such bold man was present.

"I know the warmth of His Grace's heart — none better!" Edward Bruce said, rising. "But I for one doubt the wisdom of these remissions. Traitors seldom cease to be traitors because they are softly used! Mercy is good, but may be overdone. At least some part of these forfeitures should be retained, to ensure future ... loyalty!" He sat down.

All held breath, as the brothers eyed each other.

The King did not speak.

The new Chancellor cleared his throat, his voice less certain now. "My lord of Carrick — I am not clear. Do you oppose the motion? Or make amendment? Or but ... advise? In general ..."

Edward shrugged. "I leave that to you, sir. I am no clerk, no dabbler in words. I but speak my mind."

There was a ripple of undoubted approval and agreement over a sizeable proportion of the cathedral.

Bernard de Linton looked unhappily at the King.

Bruce, whose desire it was to intervene as little as might be, to have the day's proceedings appear as much as possible to be the true voice of Scotland, sighed — although not audibly. Indeed, his voice sounded easy, relaxed, as he came to the rescue of his embarrassed secretary.

"My lord of Carrick has made no counter-motion, nor yet an amendment, as I see it," he observed. "He but speaks his mind as he says. He also says, wisely, that he leaves the interpretation of his words to you, my Lord Chancellor. I advise, therefore, that you proceed."

'H'rmm. Yes, Sire. Is . . . is there any contrary motion, then?"

Edward frowned. "If so you must have it. Yes — I oppose the motion."

Almost with relief, since his own way at least was now clear before him, the new Abbot nodded. "The motion for remission of forfeiture stands proposed and opposed. Does any wish to speak further? Before vote is taken?"

There was a considerable pause, as all saw crisis, decision, yawning before them thus early in the day. Many indubitably felt as did Edward about the King's policy of forgiveness, of working with his recent enemies — for the Scots are not notably a compromising or forgiving people. Indeed, despite all the previous day's stagecraft and drama in the Prior's Guest Hall, and despite the comprehensive nature of the next two days' parliamentary programme, this issue was the basic one behind all. Could Robert Bruce do what none other had achieved, succeed where even Wallace had failed, and lead a united Scotland? Or must he merely be the dominant head of the strongest faction, keeping the others down? A vote now would count heads with a vengeance. For and against the King's policy. The King could not fail to note, and would certainly remember.

It was Lamberton who, unexpectedly, broke the tense silence. "My lord Chancellor," he said, "may I, who have attended many parliaments, make bold to advise you in this? That all be done in order. You say that this was a motion of the Privy Council, which now asks for the homologation of parliament? Very well. May I enquire — was my lord of Carrick present at that Privy Council?"

"He was, my lord Bishop."

"And did he move, by vote, against the decision to put this proposal before parliament?"

Linton blinked. "No . . . no, I think not. He argued against the policy of remissions, yes. But not . . . no, there was no vote taken."

"Then, my lord Chancellor, I see your duty as clear. This being a Privy Council motion, no member of that Privy Council may move against it, unless he has first given prior notice. By the rules of procedure you should rule that my lord of Carrick's contrary motion is out of order, and so falls."

Into the hubbub of exclamation the younger man banged his Chancellor's gavel, with waxing confidence. "I thank your lordship. I do so rule. Is there any further contrary motion? Which in this case can be put forward only by other than a Privy Councillor? No? Then, I declare the motion carried. Without necessity of vote. And the said forfeitures remitted. And move to the next business."

Few present, probably, were any less relieved than the Chancellor sounded.

'Item. Notice of forfeiture passed upon the following, unless they return forthwith to the King's peace. Or if they be outwith the country, they send written testimony, duly witnessed, of intention so to do. The Earl of Atholl — in England. The Earl of Angus — in English-held Dundee. The Earl of Dunbar — in Lothian. The Earl of Fife — in England. The Earl of Strathearn — whereabouts unknown. Sir Ingram de Umfraville, former Guardian of this realm, brother to the said Earl of Angus, Sheriff of Angus — fugitive in Galloway. Sir Alexander, Lord of Abernethy, English-appointed Warden between Forth and the Mounth — fugitive in Galloway. Others in like case but of lesser rank, not the concern of this parliament. All these to be received back into their liege lord's service, without any grievous penalty, if so be they submit. Otherwise, forfeiture of all lands and office. This also a Privy Council motion. Any contrary?"

There was silence, not only because this was obviously part and parcel of the former motion, with the same dangers; but in alarmed recognition of the power and significance of that resounding list. Five great earls, no less, still to be beaten down or won over. And a former Guardian.

While Linton had been reading this dire list, the King beckoned to young Irvine who stood behind the throne. "My advice to the Chancellor to move now to appointments," he said.

On receipt of the page's message, the Abbot was nodding when there was an intervention.

"Wait you, wait you!" That was the Lord of the Isles, from the barons' benches. "I do not, as of the Privy Council, oppose the motion — although, God knows I do not approve of receiving to our bosoms traitors, when they so choose to come! I but ask a question. Why is the Earl of Buchan's name not included in this list of ill fame? He whose treason is worst of all. And whose office of Constable should be placed on other and honourable shoulders."

Cheers greeted that.

"The Earl of Buchan's name has been deleted, my lord. The Bishop of St. Andrews has informed His Grace this day that my lord of Buchan, High Constable of Scotland, is dead. He died in England last month, rejected by King Edward as by King Robert."

This news produced the inevitable buzz of comment and speculation. Linton took the opportunity to look enquiringly at the monarch — who shook his head.

Banging the gavel again, the Chancellor won silence. "Appointments," he said. "Certain offices, lands and titles are vacant, as result of the passing of time and the casualties of war. All are in the appointment of the King, but some fall to be confirmed by parliament. Item. Edward, Earl of Carrick to be Lord of Galloway, and Sheriff thereof. Also keeper of all the royal castles therein, with the revenues thereof."

Edward rose, bowed briefly to his brother, and sat down.

Bruce raised his hand. "This is to redeem a promise made to my lord by the shore of Loch Tulla six months past," he said. "I promised him Galloway, the greatest single lordship in Scotland, if so be he would win it back to my peace. This he has done, most notably. His autumn campaign in Galloway was bold, able, skilful. He was not gentle — but sternness was required in that province. He was most ably assisted, in especial by my lord of the Isles and my lord of Douglas. But his was the command, and I know of no other commander in this Scotland who could have done as he did, with the numbers at his command. In one battle he used but fifty to defeat fifteen hundreds. I am grateful. I believe parliament should be also. Is the grant confirmed?"

There was no doubt about that. Loud and long resounded the acclaim. Edward was popular, his very impulsiveness an acceptable fault — which often coincided with the mood of the majority. Probably most considered the King to be too hard on him. Some said — perhaps Edward himself the source of it — that Robert resented that it was Edward who survived, when Nigel, his favourite, had been taken, with Alex and Thomas. Now, the King's tribute was applauded mightily. Men saw it as an olive branch. Edward grinned, shrugged, and examined his finger-nails, clearly embarrassed. Olive branches were not really in his line.

At a sign from the throne, the Chancellor proceeded. "Item. By the death of the Earl of Buchan, without male heir, the office of High Constable of the realm is vacant. Parliament's approval of the appointment thereto of Sir Gilbert Hay, Lord of Erroll."

Here was surprise. All expected a new Constable to be appointed, but few could have anticipated that it would be Hay — certainly not that modest individual himself, who looked quite dumbfounded.

The King spoke. "Sir Gilbert has served me with loyalty and devotion unmatched, my cause and my person. I know of none better suited for the important office of High Constable. Is it confirmed?"

There was no storm of agreement; but nor was there any voiced objection. As in a dream, Gibbie was beckoned forward by the King of Arms and invested with the sword of state from the table, as indication that henceforward he alone was permitted to wear a sword indoors in the presence of the monarch. As High Constable it was his duty to protect the King at all times. Carrying the weapon he went to sit in the special stalls for the great officers-of-state, beside the Steward and the King of Arms.

"Item. Office of Lord High Admiral," Linton went on. "Approval desired that it be removed from the Earl of Dunbar, forfeit, and appointed to the Lord Angus, son of Angus, son of Donald, son of Ranald, son of Somerled, of the Isles."

Tumult broke out. There were cries of delight from the Highlanders, and cries of shock and disapproval from many Lowlanders. None were objecting that Dunbar be deprived; but that so important a position be given to a barbarian Islesman was more than many could stomach.

"Sire!" James the Steward rose to his feet, gobbling. "This is not well done. My lord of the Isles is an able warrior. His services are namely. But ... it is not suitable! His power belongs only to his own seas and coasts. The far Western Sea. All the other coasts of this realm require the protection of the High Admiral ..."

Coldly the King interrupted him. "Address yourself, my lord, to the Chancellor."

Put out, the Steward floundered. "I ... ah ... yes, Sire. I ... I move reconsideration."

"Aye! Aye!" came from various parts of the cathedral with opposing shouts elsewhere.

"My lord Chancellor!" James Douglas rose as the Steward sat down. "I ask — who has any shipping, not captured by the English, to defend our eastern coasts? Has my lord Steward? Has any other? Save Angus of the Isles. He displayed what his galleys could do, in Galloway. That campaign would not yet have been won, without his great fleets of galleys. Would the Steward appoint another to captain the Lord of the Isles' galleys? Would he? *Could* he? Yet those galleys alone can protect our shores. I say to the Steward — it is he who should reconsider!"

There was quiet, whilst men digested that. Then James Stewart half rose. 'Motion withdrawn," he mumbled.

"If there is no other contrary motion, the appointment stands confirmed," Linton said. He waited. "Angus, Lord of the Isles, to be Lord High Admiral of Scotland."

Into the Highland jubilation and Lowland dejection he went on: "Item. The office of Warden of the Middle and West Marches is vacant. Likewise that of Sheriff of Teviotdale. His Grace proposes therefore Sir James, Lord of Douglas. To which he would add the Keepership of the royal Forest of Ettrick, with the revenues thereof."

This time there was no opposition, despite the youthfulness of the nomineee for such vital responsibilities. There was no doubt, of course, that his jurisdictions would have to be fought for; and although potentially the revenues of the vast Ettrick Forest area were enormous, it would be some time, in the circumstances, before they made of Douglas a rich man.

Thereafter, a list of further sheriffships, including that of Argyll to Sir Neil Campbell, and Ayr to Boyd, as well as other titles and appointments, went through almost automatically — although for Sir Thomas Randolph to be Sheriff of Moray, formerly a Comyn appointment, raised some eyebrows.

Bruce was thankful when this important but controversial part of the proceedings was over. It had, on the whole, gone better than he had feared.

The lords spiritual had sat patiently, if with some expressions of pious disapproval, through all this. Now Nicholas Balmyle rose.

"My lord Chancellor," he said, managing to make the new and lofty title of his late assistant and protégé sound slightly ridiculous. "I have declaration to pronounce on behalf of the bishops, abbots, priors and others of the clergy duly constituted in the realm, relative to the position, state and title of our Lord Robert the King. We have drawn up and written a full and sufficient investigation into the claim of Bruce, Lord of Annandale, known as the Competitor, to the throne of this kingdom; which writings, here under my hand, are of too great length here to read. But I make summary. That in the competition for the vacant throne before King Edward in 1291, that prince wrongously adjudged Sir John Baliol to be made King of Scots, when the Lord of Annandale had better title. That the disasters that have befallen this realm are in consequence. That the grandson of the rightful Competitor, having recovered and restored the kingdom, is now most undoubtedly our liege lord in right as in fact. And that any oppression to King Robert hereafter, by means of documents written or sealed in the past, such as were effected by irresistible force and violence, are null and void. We, the clergy of Scotland, therefore do proclaim the Lord Robert as of right the true successor of the ancient and unbroken line of our chronicled kings, and none other."

A little mystified by this statement of the evident, this gilding of the lily, most commissioners applauded politely. They were the more surprised, therefore, when, immediately the Bishop sat down, Lennox rose, also with a paper.

"My lord Chancellor — we, the earls, lords, barons and nobility of Scotland, do likewise make full and detailed affirmation that King Robert is the true and nearest heir of King Alexander last deceased. And declare, with the estate of the clergy and the whole community of Scotland, that the grandfather of our Lord Robert ought to have succeeded the King Alexander, and none other. This paper, signed and sealed, as witness."

"I thank you, my lords." Bruce, not making too much of this, inclined his head towards the speakers. "To further business."

"Item. Letter addressed outwardly to Robert, Earl of Carrick; and inwardly to Robert, King of Scots, from Philip, King of France. Received ten days past by the hand of one Oliver de Roches, ambassador, after travel by safe conduct through the realm of England. Wherefore the outer superscription. His Grace of France recounts his special love for King Robert. Reminds the said Robert of the ancient alliance between their realms, which he would see renewed. Declares that he has besought King Edward that there should be truce and peace between England and Scotland hereafter, promising his utmost efforts to that end. Promises further his representations with His Holiness of Rome regarding the position of King John Baliol. And does request and invite our Lord Robert to engage and join with him in a crusade against the Infidel in holy places. This parliament to consider reply to His Grace of France."

Men stared at each other, uncertain whether to applaud, to laugh, or to decry. Was the Frenchman mad? A crusade! At his time! A renewal of the alliance, after the French had so shamefully broken it? Peace with England, with the English still occupying part of Scotland? Reply – how could parliament reply?

Bruce enlightened them. "My lords, my friends — here is a matter of great import. More than might seem. And to our encouragement. The King of France sees Scotland, and my cause, as worthy of consideration, possibly support. As he did not, before. He writes to me — but the reply must come from parliament. Since only so will he, and others, know that it is not just Robert Bruce who speaks, but the whole community of the Scots. The matters his Most Christian Majesty raises are of varying worth — and folly! That we should be asked to consider a crusade is almost beyond belief. But His Majesty is concerned to earn that title of Christian. Moreover, to earn the Pope's approval — since they have been at odds for long. I suggest that parliament replies that we shall gladly join with him in such crusade, not only myself but many in my kingdom, when the last Englishman is expelled from Scotland, and we have good assurance that they will not come back . . .!'

Despite the sin of interrupting the King, loud cheering drowned his voice.

"As to the rest, I advise this parliament in its wisdom to agree that our ancient alliance be in fact renewed — since it is only against the English that it has any meaning. That we send ambassadors to France so to do. Also, to ask for French aid in men and moneys for our warfare. I think that Philip will not grant this. But it may serve to make him the more inclined to use influence with the Pope to recognise my kingship and right. This we greatly require. Without it the nations of Christendom will be loth to accord us our due. His Holiness, to my sorrow, scarcely loves me! Perhaps he has right. But he recognises John Baliol as King of Scots still. This is folly also — but such is the Vatican policy. Hence the declarations of the clergy and nobility just pronounced — for which I am grateful. These are scarce necessary for ourselves, who know the truth. But for King Philip and the Pontiff, that they may be informed."

Men nodded sagely to each other, lest any thought that they had not understood.

"Such reply to the King of France must be carefully considered. I suggest, my lord Chancellor, that you, with your clerks, and any other's aid you require, draw up such letter, for presentation and consideration at tomorrow's session. So that the rest of us, who have sat here sufficiently long for one day, may now betake ourselves elsewhere!" He paused. "If all so agree?"

Relievedly men rose, shouted, stamped and waved approval. Parliaments were all very well, but could go on for too long. Into the hubbub Linton, gavel banging, declared the session adjourned until noon next day. All commissioners, with their ladies, to partake of the hospitality of the provost and magistrates of this royal burgh and city of St. Andrews . . .

* * *

That night, after an evening spent together, when Bruce left Lamberton's chamber in the main keep of the castle, earlier than he might have done — in order that the older man should have opportunity for a good sleep, in view of his dawn start on the testing journey back to England — he called in at the Gatehouse

Tower on his way across the courtyard. In its upper room, allocated to the Lady Christina of Garmoran, he found only that lady's buxom Highland tire-woman in possession — although a scurrying just before his entry gave him the impression that someone less than light-footed might just possibly be hiding behind the arras in a dark corner. Christina herself, it seemed, had not yet returned from whichever of the many entertainments she was decorating, and with which St. Andrews was catering for its flood of distinguished visitors, that night.

"When your lady comes, tell her that I was grateful for her provision and forethought last night," he instructed the somewhat confused and costume-rectifying abigail, grave-faced. "She was very kind, and I have not had opportunity to thank her, this busy day. But if so be it she is not over-weary when she does come in, and she would have my poor thanks in person — then tell her that my door in the Sea Tower will not be locked! You have it?"

Blinking, biting her lip, and smiling all in one, the other dipped low.

PART THREE

Chapter Seventeen

"Another hour," Bruce said. "We will give them another hour. Lest they are wakeful. And it will be darker." He looked up, sniffing the night breeze of the heather hills. "It will rain, I think. So much the better."

The Lord High Constable of Scotland turned to look in the other direction altogether, not westwards over the dark water to the darker castle on its tiny island, but behind them, south by east, towards the loch-head a couple of miles away, where red pinpoints of light marked the camp-fires of their enemies, their other enemies.

"I do not like it," he said. "We could be trapped here, all too easily. It is a bad position. If Atholl were to attack while we were assailing the castle, nothing could save us."

"Why should he do so? He has waited there four days. He awaits reinforcements, clearly. They have not come. He is young and inexperienced. He will not risk a night attack, I think. But, if he does, our scouts will warn us."

"Atholl may be young — but he will have experienced English captains with him, Sire," the third of the trio by the waterside put in — Sir Robert Keith, Marischal of Scotland. "If they had the least inkling that we would assault the castle tonight, they would advise him to advance. And they will have scouts on these hillsides, no less than we."

"I do not doubt it, Sir Robert. But why should they think it might be tonight? You have been here ten days and ten nights, and made no move. Why tonight?"

"They will have seen that *we* have arrived, Sire," Gilbert Hay pointed out. "They may not know that it is you, the King. But they know Sir Robert has been reinforced — though only by a small company. But they may look for action, therefore. I do not like it, Sire. We are less than their numbers. To risk yourself thus — the King! For this? A small unimportant place like Loch Doon . . ."

"Not so unimportant, Gibbie — to me!" the King said quietly. "This castle, though small, is a fist shaken in my face! Here in my own Carrick — or Edward's Carrick! From here, my good-brother

Christopher Seton was treacherously taken to his shameful death at Dumfries. And on this island, 500 years ago, died my ancestor King Alpin of Dalriada, father of the great Kenneth who united our realm — as I seek to reunite it now. I will have no Englishmen defiling Loch Doon Castle, I tell you."

His two companions were silent at that tone of voice. Nevertheless they were right — and Bruce knew it well. It was a kind of folly for the King of Scots to be here, in a dangerous position amongst the wild hills on the Carrick-Galloway border, with only a small force, besieging a strategically unimportant English-held fortalice. All over Southern Scotland, this summer and autumn of 1310, small or moderately-sized forces were besieging small and medium strongholds — not the great fortresses, such as Berwick, Roxburgh, Edinburgh and Stirling, for the Scots were almost wholly without the siege engines and trained sappers required to reduce such strengths. But the decision to drive the English out of the scores of lesser castles had been taken: Edward Bruce was investing Buittle in Galloway, Douglas was at Bothwell, Campbell at Livingstone, Boyd at Cavers, Fleming at Selkirk, Lennox at Kirkintillock, and so on. The situation at large, on a national scale, was as awkward and incipiently dangerous as here at Loch Doon, with the loyal forces so grievously scattered. But it was something that had to be done, sooner or later – and this time of alleged truce was as good a time as any. The uneasy and purely tactical truce, engineered by the French King, between England and Scotland, had been in force for nearly a year — but latterly King Edward had broken it by sending shipping to reinforce and supply his garrisons at Dundee, Perth and Banff, as well as commanding general musters to arms in England. Two could play that game. Hence this campaign of the castles.

Sir Robert Keith, the Marischal, as yet untried in the King's service, had been given the Loch Doon assignment, with a mere 200 men. He would have been left to deal with it on his own, undoubtedly, had it not been for the arrival on the scene of David de Strathbogie, Earl of Atholl. The birth of a bastard daughter to his sister, deserted by Edward Bruce, had so enraged this proud young man that nothing would do but that he must at once take the field actively. From being merely a high-born exile in England, he became a man with a mission — to wipe out this affront to his name and fame. The English gleefully had given him a following assessed at 400, and truce or none he had marched north from Carlisle. Presumably Edward himself, besieging Buittle Castle deeper in Galloway, was too ambitious a match for Atholl's first sally; at any rate, he had made for this, the next nearest siege, and taken up a threatening position at the head of Loch Doon — but so far had not dared an attack.

The King had been holding justice eyres in Kyle and Carrick, based on his own house of Turnberry, only twenty miles away, when he heard of this situation. Instead of finding reinforcements for Keith from elsewhere, he had come himself, with Hay and a mere bodyguard of two-score men-at-arms. Now he had to justify it . . .

Superficially that was not difficult — for he knew the castle on Loch Doon as few did. Though an ancient strength, renewed and restored by the Baliols during the period when they controlled the Galloway lordship, it had been incorporated in the Carrick earldom and used by Bruce's father mainly as a hunting-lodge. As boys, the Bruce brothers had spent happy days here amongst the cradling mountains, with the giants of Merrick, Cairnsmore and Corserine all close by. If anybody could discover a weakness in that castle, the King could — for twice he himself had had it repaired from ruin and the effects of siege, the second time, but a year before.

Loch Doon was six miles long, but very narrow, and the island with the castle lay some 300 yards off the east shore at the south end — where it was in a position to dominate the drove road through the high passes from the Ayrshire lowlands south to those of the Galloway Cree, its sole strategic purpose. In the early days, after the Turnberry landing, when Bruce had lurked in this country, he had deliberately avoided the ruined loch-bound castle as refuge, preferring as so much less obvious his spider-cave five miles to the north, away from the road.

Like so many island castles, this one had an under-water causeway out to it, cunningly twisted. Keith had been told about this, but an early night attempt to progress along it unseen had resulted in a sad reversal and loss — for the English had cut a large gap in the hidden stone pavement some two-thirds of the way out, and within arrow-shot of the walls. Not unnaturally the Marischal was wary of a second such adventure.

Back at the camp, where all fires had been damped down, so that no movement would be visible from the island, their hour almost up, Bruce made his final dispositions, taking over entirely from Keith. He arranged that the force should be split, one party taking up position at the head of the causeway; the other placed to guard the south flank from possible attack by Atholl. Then he had the men gather round him closely, so that he could speak to the shadowy ranks without having to raise his voice. A thin rain had begun to fall.

"I want a score of good men," he said. "Only men who can swim a little. And who are not afraid of cold water! No small men, see you. Who offers?"

Out of all the murmuring, questioning and humorous comment, little more than a dozen stepped forward. There were no Islesmen or Highlanders in Keith's force, and the ability or need to swim was not a Lowland priority.

"I hope none may have to swim, in the end. But your lives may depend on it, nevertheless," the King went on. He counted. "Fourteen. It will serve. Now — off with your clothes. Then, ashes from the fires, to rub on your faces and shoulders. Bodies will show white, even on a dark night." As he spoke, he was unbuckling his own sword-belt and beginning to draw off his chain-mail tunic.

"Sire — not you!" Hay exclaimed, shocked. "Not the King . . . in the water! Naked . . ."

"Tush, man — am I the King because of my clothes? It must be I who lead, since only I know what I would effect. Moreover, I do not ask others to do what I will not myself do. You know that." All men indeed did know that. It was one of the secrets of Bruce's success, in his kind of warfare, with his kind of people. The Scots character was always such as responded best not to clear orders and discipline but to personal leadership and close contact, where there was affection and involvement with the men. As soldiers they had never excelled at siege-warfare, any more than in great impersonal battles, for this very reason.

So, presently, a very odd-looking and inadequate-seeming party of warriors made their awkward bare-footed way along the pebble-and-sand beach northwards for about 200 yards, to where a fair-sized burn flowed in from the steeply-rising flank of the hugely looming hill behind them. Completely naked save for belts and cords to tie weapons to their persons, they were daubed with wood-ash which made them so much less visible in the mirk. As well as their weapons they carried rope-ladders fitted with grappling-irons, and single knotted ropes with hooks attached.

Immediately below the shallows at the mouth of the burn, Bruce halted and formed up his people in single file. "Keep close behind me, and follow exactly as I go," he directed. "As I mind it, we should not have to swim. I was a laddie when last I did this. But I do not think aught will have changed. The burn will still bring down much silt and stones, and the flow of the loch is still northwards. There is a spit of this silt reaching out and bending down-loch, towards the castle. Perhaps that is how the island was made. The water gets much deeper than the causeway. But not over our heads, I think. It has been a dry summer. I used to be able to walk it as a lad . . ."

He paused, as a fifteenth naked and besmeared volunteer came hobbling up, and had to peer close to discover any identification.

"Ha, my lord High Constable!" he whispered. "You also? Man, your costume fair becomes you! Would that the Lady Annabel could see you now! Come, then — and slowly, silently. Pray that we do not have to swim — for that might give us away. And pray that the sentries watch best the front and the causeway."

Carrying a coiled rope with hook over his shoulder, and a cut hazel-stick in his hand, the King waded in — and gasped a little despite himself at the chill of the water. Even though it was only early September, the loch lay nearly a thousand feet above the sea, and was fed from giants 3,000 feet high.

Gingerly, carefully feeling his way at each step with both stick and toes, he edged out into the loch, Gilbert Hay immediately behind and the party following close. Bruce had toyed with the idea of having Keith stage some sort of demonstration at the causeway-head, or at the camp itself, to distract the watch's attention; but had decided against it as likely perhaps to rouse more of the castle's defenders. Better that all should seem quietly normal, and the beseigers' camp asleep.

Quite quickly the water deepened to waist height — where its chill made maximum impact. Thereafter the depth increased only imperceptibly until it was halfway up the men's chests. This gradualness did not imply a smooth and easy advance, however; continually Bruce came across uneven stretches, holes, or stumbled over boulders, waterlogged tree-trunks or other hazards. Fortunately the shoal or spit was fairly broad, and keeping to its crown was the least of the problem.

Bruce could not recollect just where the thing tended to bend northwards, with the main current of the loch — which was more like a widening of a river, with the Gala Lane entering at the head, near by, and the River Doon emptying at the foot. But some 200 yards out, slantwise from the shore, it became obvious that they were curving round. The castle loomed about another 150 yards ahead.

This second leg was the most testing — for from the direction of progress it looked as though the spit might have changed course during the years and be going to miss the islet by quite a margin, to the west. Also, at every step, Bruce feared a shouted challenge from the castle battlements. The men behind him seemed to be making an unconscionable splashing, and moreover puffing like stranded whales. It was now raining heavily. He had never been so thankful for cold, driving rain.

But at length he was under the lee of the island. He was brought to a stop, almost within stick-reaching distance of the bank, by deeper water. There seemed to be some sort of channel circling the isle itself. Taking a long breath he gently but strongly launched himself forward with a swimming motion. But almost at once his feet touched bottom again — sorely indeed — with the water only up to his chin. From there he could clamber carefully out on to dry land, with the dark masonry of the castle's outer bailey rising directly above him.

He whispered to Hay to stand aside and warn each man of the ditch-like channel, as he came up. And he held out his stick for each to grasp as he came over.

It took only a few moments — although with some alarming splashing — for the entire party to join him below the walls, unchallenged.

There was no need for any instructions now. Each man knew his task. They spread out along the few feet between water and masonry. At the signal of a pebble thrown into the water at each end, they went to work.

Their task was in essence entirely simple – but not necessarily easy to perform, and quietly, nevertheless. It was to throw those rope-ladders and single climbing ropes upwards sufficiently high for them to go over the walling and their hooks and grapnels to catch in the crevices and fissures of the masonry beyond, and so to hold. This was elementary siege-procedure, and all had practised it many times, even if they had not actually taken part in previous such assaults. For all that, hooks and prongs could not be guaranteed to catch and hold fast. And the noise of all that metal clattering on the stonework sounded like a carillon of cracked bells ringing to rouse even the dead.

Bruce's own hook caught at the second throw. Dirk between his teeth, jutting his bare feet against the walling, he walked up hand over hand, foot over foot, counterpoised between knotted rope and stone. Getting over the wallhead was the difficulty, where rope and stone came together. He barked his knuckles, but managed to hoist himself bodily, bare stomach on the coping, and uncaring of the scraping on tender flesh, vaulted legs over and on to the parapet-walk.

One or two figures were there — but they were naked, and therefore his own men whose ropes had held first throw. Bruce sighed with relief. The most dangerous moment was past, when defenders might have unhooked the ropes and sent the attackers crashing down. There was as yet no sign of any defenders.

"Gibbie!" he said, in a whisper — for though the ash had been washed off their bodies, faces were still daubed and it was almost impossible to identify individuals. Hay, in fact, was almost at his side. "Take half. Round that side. The gatehouse. I take this. Quiet as you may."

They split up. The castle consisted of a central square keep, surrounded by this high perimeter wall with its parapet-walk on top, with subsidiary lean-to buildings within the courtyard. At the far side of the perimeter, or outer bailey, nearest the shore and facing the unseen causeway, was the entrance, an arched pend with iron grille gate piercing the small gatehouse-tower which contained the watch-chamber and guardroom. In castles this was always the base from which sentry-duty was taken. The naked attackers now stealthily approached it from two sides, swords and dirks in hand.

This was a comparatively small fortalice, and was unlikely to have a garrison of more than perhaps thirty men. So no large number were to be expected on night-guard at any one time, and the sixteen assailants had no fears of being unable to deal with them effectively. The danger was that the dealing might be insufficiently swift and silent, so that the rest of the castle might be warned before the main keep could be reached.

In the event, when Bruce reached the gatehouse-tower, it was to find its door, opening on to the parapet-walk at this side, shut. It faced east, and there was an east wind, so this would be for the guard's comfort. Holding up a hand to halt his party, he put his ear to the planking, to listen.

What he heard was a gasping, choking noise, the crash of an upset form, and then a single high cry, swiftly cut off. Almost immediately, from down in the courtyard somewhere a dog barked twice, with yelping enquiry. Bruce cursed and threw open the door.

By the flickering firelight within he saw that Hay was already in control, the small warm chamber crowded with unclothed men. The men with clothes, three of them, lay twitching on the floor.

"Quick!" Bruce said, "Down to the courtyard. That hound . . ."

A voice called out thinly from higher — a Northern English voice. "What's to do, down there? What was that, Tom?"

Frowning, Bruce took a chance. That had come from the keep parapet — so there was another guard up there. "Tom burned himself. His hand," he called, trying to sound as English as the others, and hoping the muffling of his voice from indoors would help. "A burn only. The fire." He even produced a hollow laugh.

The man above still called down enquiries, but less concernedly. He must be ignored. The King gestured urgently towards the turnpike stairway. The dog had not barked again.

Down they all streamed, into the entrance pend. Across the courtyard, the keep door stood ajar. Detaching three men to look to the buildings in the yard, stables and the like, and to silence the dog if need be, he led the others at a rush across the paving-stones for the other door.

The basement of the keep contained arms, food and storage; but within the springing of its stone vault would be a timber sleeping-loft for men-at-arms. Racing on silent bare feet up the main stair, Bruce signed to Hay, at the first door, to deal with that loft. He himself took only three men, and hurried on.

The Hall, on the first main floor, was empty, a dying fire on the great hearth. But two deer-hounds lay thereat, now sitting up at the arrival of intruders, growling deeply in their throats. Bruce pulled the door shut — but not before the hounds began to bay. He dashed on upstairs.

On the next floor would be the master's chamber, the keeper of the castle's quarters. As he reached the door it was thrown open from within, and dimly seen, a man stood there, pulling on a bed-robe, a woman's querulous voice sounding behind. Bruce felled him with a single great flat-sided blow of his sword. The woman began to scream. Motioning his three companions higher, he rushed into the dark room, made for the bed by ear rather than sight, groped hands on a naked squirming woman until he found her open mouth, and shut it.

"Silence!" he ordered. "More noise from you, and you die! You understand? Die! Bide quiet here, and no harm will come to you."

He left her, choking and gasping and whimpering, but otherwise quiet.

There was only the one room to each floor. Above he found two of his trio coming out of the chamber, wiping their dirks and going in higher. Inside sounded more female cries and sobs. Silence was pointless now. He demanded information, in the darkness.

"Two dead ..." he was answered grimly, and, after a brief pause, "Three now, by God! These bawling doxies! Dirty bitches!"

"Leave them. Come higher ..."

But they were not required higher. Men were coming bounding up the stairs, naked men, shouting that all was over below. Leaving the remaining two storeys, and the guard on the keep's parapet-walk, to them, Bruce went down.

Hay had not had to kill more than a few of the sleepers in the main dormitory-loft. Now, in the light of a smoky lantern, he had about a dozen sleep-bemused or terrified prisoners, staring at the demon-like naked apparitions with the dripping swords.

Loch Doon Castle was taken, a bedlam of shouting, moaning men, screaming, weeping women, barking dogs and stamping, uneasy horses.

"Neatly done," Bruce commended briefly. "Now—lights, And let us find some clothes, a mercy's sake! And get word to Keith . . ."

They found a timber pontoon contrivance laid along the entrance pend and weighted with stones, obviously an underwater gangway to bridge the gap cut in the causeway. Forcing at dagger-point sundry of their prisoners who clearly knew how this contraption worked, to manhandle it out into position, shouts from the victors soon brought Sir Robert Keith, and others, on horseback, out over the causeway, from the camp. The Marischal was suitably impressed by the swift and effective capture of the strength which had defied his 200 for ten days; but he was otherwise preoccupied also.

"A messenger has arrived, Sire," he said to Bruce, now in the bed-robe of the knightly but unfortunate English captain. "From Turnberry. He came soon after you were gone. From England. From Bishop Lamberton. The English invade. They are over the Border, in strength. King Edward at their head . . ."

Before the words were out, Bruce had grabbed the nearest horse, pulled himself into the saddle, and went clattering out through the pend and splashing into the dark waters above the causeway, robe flapping.

* * *

Before the misty dawn, the King and the Marischal's force, leaving only a small garrison in the captured castle, were on their way northwards through the sleeping hills for Turnberry, riding as fast as the night would permit. The Earl of Atholl would have a pretty puzzle to unravel in the morning.

Bruce learned from Lamberton's courier, another friar who had been searching for him for two days, that the truce was indeed broken with a vengeance. He had known that Edward of Carnarvon was mustering troops—but that strange, unpredictable man had done the same before and then failed to use the assembled host, to the fury and despair of his nobles. Indeed, latterly his lords had been ignoring his summonses. Now, it appeared, he had acted with unusual haste and vigour, and made a sudden dash northwards from York—possibly to impress his notorious favourite, Piers Gaveston, Earl of Cornwall, who was with him. Bishop Lamberton was actually with him also, taken along as an adviser apparently. The Primate had managed to send off this friar from Alnwick, five days before. Berwick should have been reached by the army, of about 75,000, two days later. The Earls of Gloucester and Surrey, with the Lords Percy and Clifford, were with King Edward. Lamberton believed the English to be heading across Scotland for Glasgow, before going on to relieve beleaguered Dundee.

At Turnberry, Bruce sent out couriers in all directions, to his so scattered captains. All present operations were to be suspended immediately. Most groups were to rejoin him with all speed. There was to be no large-scale confrontation with the main English army. Harassing of flanks, rear and lines of support might be engaged in, but all the major effort was to be concentrated on laying waste the land in front of the advancing invaders, denying them supplies and shelter. Any stand to be made would be made at or near Stirling; but that was for the future.

Scouting parties were, of course, sent off south-eastwards to ascertain the enemy progress. Because of the delay with the news, they could be expected by now to be well into Scotland. From Berwick, if they were in fact making for Glasgow — as was reasonable, so that they could relieve besieged Bothwell and Kirkintilloch also — they would almost certainly move diagonally across country by Roxburgh, following the Tweed up through Melrose and the Forest to Peebles, and then over the mouth of Tweedsmuir and the high spine of Southern Scotland, to the upper Clyde valley. There was not much that could be done to devastate the land before and through the Ettrick Forest — where there was little to devastate indeed — so that Bruce's main attention must be to the grim, heart-rending business of destruction of the fair Clyde valley and its surroundings — Douglas country. He had done it before, more than once, and he could do it again — but it went even more sorely against the grain, this harsh and wholesale eviction and impoverishment of his own people. But it was the only way that he could eventually halt the mighty invader, since he refused utterly to risk all in a great battle — which was what the English wanted, with their preponderant power in numbers, heavy cavalry and hosts of archers. But a huge army of scores of thousands had to live largely on the country it passed through, and inevitably eventually ground to a halt if it could not gain food for its men and, above all, forage for its horses.

Keith was sent off, therefore, with a small contingent, to do what he could by way of delaying tactics in the Forest area, while Bruce headed for upper Clydesdale, calling for men from all quarters to aid in the terrible work. Once it was confirmed that King Edward was to come this way, across the watershed, they would start. And he called a council-of-war at Cadzow for five days hence.

Joined by Douglas, the King was at Lanark with just over a thousand men, when a messenger from Keith confirmed that the English were coming indeed. Roxburgh, Melrose, Selkirk and

Peebles were ablaze, and, on the fringes at least, the Forest was beginning to hang with dead men.

So the order was reluctantly given, and the great burning of fertile Clydesdale began, and Douglasdale with it, James Douglas acceding. The people were dispossessed and herded into the hills; all houses great and small, all barns, mills and other buildings, even churches, unroofed; all grain, hay and standing crops burned — and where the latter would not burn, trampled and flattened and wasted methodically; all bridges were demolished and fords made impassable; river banks and mill-lades were breached, pastures flooded, wells fouled with the carcases of all stock which could not be herded away. Inexorable, Bruce drove his man-made desert north by west, on a vast ten-mile-wide front. It took him back over the years to 1299, when he had first ravaged this same country, though in the other direction. And still they were fighting for Scotland's very existence. Eleven years! How long, oh Lord — how long?

Those days the King was bad company indeed, a savagely-fierce unapproachable man, black-browed, bleak-eyed, as he burned the realm he had dedicated his life to saving, made homeless the people he had vowed to protect. Even Gilbert Hay and James Douglas kept their distance, warily.

Lanark itself was soon overtaken into the pattern of desolation and left a blazing pyre. The council-of-war was put forward two days and called now for Rutherglen.

Edward Bruce arrived, the next day, from Galloway with 400 cavalry and the word that 1,500 foot was coming on, by forced marches, behind him. He brought more bad news. Another English force had crossed Solway from Carlisle, under the Earl of Richmond, and was ravaging and slaying its way up their own Annandale and Randolph's Nithsdale. As angry a man as his brother, if in a different, hotter fashion, he asked, demanded, permission to take the main force and give battle in the passes of Moffat and Dalveen and Enterkin — and was curtly refused.

Lennox was the last to arrive, from besieging Kirkintiloch — for Angus Og and most of the other Highlanders were meantime back in their own territories. The Earl was sadly depressed. Were they back where they had started, after all the years of bloodshed and sorrow? For once he got only short shrift from his friend.

The council at Rutherglen was a sorry one, difficult, rancorous, with disillusion heavy upon all. Edward led a strong group in a mood of hot defiance, urging attack, attack. If they had to go down, let them go down fighting, like men — not running, savaging their own people. Campbell urged a retiral forthwith to Stirling, there to stand to the end, at the narrow waist of Scotland, abandoning all the South as hopeless but making a stronghold of the North. Reluctantly Lennox, Boyd and Douglas agreed. But Bruce was sternly adamant that they continue to drive their slow way north-westwards. They could by no means defeat the Plantagenet — but they could starve and sicken him. And this Edward would sicken more quickly than his sire. Abandon the South to him and he would install his armies in Glasgow and Edinburgh, if necessary for the winter, supply them by sea, and so be in a state to marshal his fullest force against the crossing at Stirling when he was ready. That way lay ultimate disaster — whereas his brother's way was to make disaster immediate.

Timeously, during the council, another courier arrived from Lamberton, forwarded by Keith from Biggar. It was to report that King Edward was now aiming, after relieving Bothwell, not at Glasgow but towards the sea — or at least, the mouth of the Clyde, in the Inverkip-Renfrew area. John MacDougall of Lorn had been sent to Dublin to collect and captain a fleet of shipping and Irish galleys from the Anglo-Irish there, with their mercenaries, and to sail up the Clyde with them. On the Renfrew coast he would make contact with the King, and ferry over the main English force to Dumbarton and the Lennox, so that it could then turn east, bypassing Stirling, and make direct for Perth and Dundee, avoiding the natural bastion of the Forth and Clyde and intervening wilderness of the Flanders Moss. Thereafter, John of Lorn would take his fleet north-west into the Hebrides, to win back his father's Argyll and to deal with the Lord of the Isles.

Much shaken, the council listened to these tidings — which of course made nonsense of much that had gone before. But it only confirmed Bruce in his determination to wear down the English before ever they reached the sea. The devastation policy would go on. In addition, wrecking parties would make for all the Clyde ports and havens, from Carrick northwards, to destroy and make unusable all harbour facilities, so that, on the west coast at least, the invaders could import no supplies. And he would send swift Highland messengers north, by sea, to warn Angus Og, and to urge him to assemble all his galley strength to sail south and cope with Lame John MacDougall.

Even Edward Bruce was silent now.

* * *

Edward of England never crossed the Clyde estuary. By the time that, in late October, his huge army reached the Renfrew coast, hungry, angry, soiled, frustrated and almost mutinous, the King had lost all taste for so inglorious an adventure — and Piers Gaveston with him. John of Lorn had not yet put in an appearance; the weather was bad, and there was famine in the land. Moreover Bruce was apparently prepared to burn all Glasgow and the West before him indefinitely. In petulant rage, he ordered a retreat by Linlithgow and Lothian, to Berwick, where they would winter. He did not trouble to try to inform John MacDougall.

That resentful man found Angus Og waiting for him at the mouth of the Firth of Clyde, and there was a great sea battle. It would be difficult to say who won — but MacDougall it was who broke off, and limped southwards, to vent his spleen on the Isle of Man for want of better target.

One more breathing-space gained — but at a price that could not continue to be paid.

Chapter Eighteen

"These larks, I swear, must be traitor birds!" James Douglas cried, gazing up into the pale cold blue of the early April sky, laughing. "Hear how they shout for joy. They cheer us on."

"I say they are Scots larks, blown south by some storm," Gilbert Hay declared. "No English fowl could sing so sweet and true."

"Sweet, perhaps." It was Thomas Randolph who took him up. "But true? Who are we to talk of Scots being true! I think the English are truer than we."

"Well may *you* say so!" Campbell accused quickly.

"He means but that they breed the fewer traitors, I think," Hugh Ross said, coming to the aid of his friend. These two had grown close since that day on Loch Ness-side three years before.

"You should know — both of you!"

"Peace, dolts!" the King said, but easily, almost automatically — for this was a perennial dissension. "Every man in this host will depend on every other for his life, from here on. So who should talk of traitors? Gibbie is right. These are Scots larks, strayed a little. Like ourselves! Perhaps we should sing like them, now — lest we cannot sing hereafter!"

That brought them back to reality. They had, hitherto, been almost too carefree this sunny morning, blithe as any larks, apt to sing indeed, in a fashion highly unsuitable for great officers of state, sheriffs and the like. It was high time to adopt a more sober mood — though surely not a bickering, carping one.

In their lighter travelling armour, under colourful heraldic surcoats, very fine, they sat their steaming mounts and looked back from the higher ground as the last files of their little army splashed across the ford of Esk near Kirkandrews. It was not in fact an army, but a hand-picked, tight-knit striking force of a thousand men, with a high proportion of them young knights, lairdlings or the sons thereof, superbly mounted, finely accoutred and armed. Here was indeed the cream of Southern Scotland — or such part of it as supported King Robert — selected thus for more reasons than one.

They stood, now, on the soil of England. It was five years since Bruce had last done that — and, as it happened, it was exactly here, at this remote and little-used ford that he had then crossed the Border, though then in the other direction, fleeing from Edward Longshanks' fury, a day or two before he had slain the Red Comyn. Now he was back, a king himself, and with a gallant if hard-hitting company.

It was against all his normal and cherished policy, a reversal to the old more brash Robert Bruce — or so it seemed. Yet he alone had decided upon it, and of a set purpose, just as he had carefully selected the men to take with him. This, in its own way, was in fact almost as much of a play-acting and demonstration as had been his St. Andrews parliament. Morale demanded that the risk be taken — the frustrated, angry morale of his own eager young captains and leaders, the knightly class, whom he had held back from battle during all the English invasion in the autumn and turned baleful incendiary instead; and the sagging, uneasy morale of the Northern English, whose men made up the bulk of King Edward's army, still kicking its heels at Berwick after the idle winter. That army had waited for this spring for campaigning weather again, when the passes would be free of snow, the rivers crossable, the bogs somewhat drier. Bruce had determined to move first, taking an enormous but calculated risk: The larks at least commended him.

They rode on through the gradually rising empty grassy moors, scarcely high enough by Scots standards to be called hills, into Cumberland. Deliberately Bruce had chosen this lonely unfrequented route. One thousand men, however disciplined, are not transported through the countryside without attracting notice, and at this stage he desired the minimum of attention.

As well as the route, he had chosen his destination with great care. It must be remote enough to receive no warning of approach, far enough into England to be significant, yet large or important enough to cause considerable heart-burning amongst the English.

There should also be secondary targets in the area. Moreover, for preference, it should belong to Robert Clifford — or some of it! He had a long score to settle with the Lord of Brougham. The valleys of the Irthing and the upper South Tyne fulfilled all these requirements in general, and the Gillsland area in particular.

By noon, the long, fast-moving column was almost twenty miles deep into England, heading east, and leaving behind the empty moors for lower ground. They had passed one or two remote villages, inevitably, as well as shepherds' houses and granges; but they had left them all severely alone, and their occupants were not such as were likely to hastily send off messengers to Berwick, or even Carlisle. Crossing Bolton Fell they had had to negotiate a great drove of cattle, being herded south to Brampton market — and the drovers would assuredly tell what they had seen; but fortunately such herds moved very slowly over rough country, and by the time the drovers might give the news, it should not matter.

They came to the summit of Banks Fell, the last long rolling ridge before the Vale of Irthing, and from the shelter of scrub woodland surveyed the scene. It all looked notably fat and fertile, prosperous and peaceful, with flocks and herds grazing far and near, fresh green everywhere with patches of new tilth showing brown, many farms and granges and hamlets scattered wide, and in the centre the sizeable town of Gillsland, grey-walled and red-roofed, sending its blue chimney-smoke into the clear air. A little to the east rose the warm yellow masonry, tall and fair, of Irthing Priory, amongst spreading gardens and orchards. Yet it was in the other direction, westwards, that Bruce's own glance kept turning. Some three miles away, taller, handsomer, more splendid walls soared, amidst its own larger township — Lanercost Abbey itself. Lanercost, where the old Edward had so long made his headquarters for the subjugation of Scotland, and from which he had set out on his last journey of hatred, to die at Solway cursing Bruce.

"A-a-aye!" the King breathed. "There is Lanercost, where my ruin, Scotland's ruin, was plotted. And here," he pointed closer at hand, "Here is my lord Clifford's domain of Gillsland, with his priory of Irthing." Sir Robert had recently been created a Lord of Parliament. "He has burned Annandale of the Bruces four times. And your Nithsdale twice, Thomas. I promised him a reckoning, once. This is not it, since he is not here. But it could be a first payment! For both of them."

The rumbling growl from those who could hear his words was a frightening thing. There was an involuntary surge forward of urgent horsemen.

"Wait, you!" the King commanded. "This is to be done heedfully. *My* way. I will have no unnecessary slaughter, no women ravished, no bairns savaged, no men hanging from trees. If any there be, others of *you* will hang with them, before we leave! Wallace made three mistakes. To fight at Falkirk. To trust a Halyburton. And to fail to keep his men under good control when he raided into England. So that he created here not fear and panic and a refusal to invade Scotland again, but a burning hatred, the more set on vengeance. It is not for that we are here, see you. We have not come for vengeance either — although, God knows, I could wish we had! We are here for set purposes. To create alarm and unrest in the English camp at Berwick, so that they do not march north into Scotland. To show the rest of the North of England what is like to happen to them if they continue to provide men for the Scottish wars. And last, to gain treasure." He smiled slightly. "I will not deny that it displeasures me nothing that it is my lord Clifford's lands, and those of the Abbey of Lanercost, that we work our purpose on!" And as an afterthought, he added, "I said treasure. Only such treasure as may be carried conveniently. None must lumber themselves with booty. All else is to be destroyed. And, I charge you — such treasure is not for your pouches, my friends! But for my Lord Treasurer's coffers. That our warfare may be maintained."

Men chuckled at that, and a better temper for the business was engendered.

Bruce went on to make his dispositions. At this stage, the force would split. He would take half, to Lanercost. Douglas would lead the rest down to Gillsland itself, and Irthing Priory. They had not unlimited time. But seven hours until sunset. By which all this valley must be destroyed, and themselves over into the next and greater valley southwards — the upper South Tyne. There, seven miles beyond, lay the market town of Haltwhistle, as well as the castles of Bellister, Featherstone, Unthank and Blenkinsopp. Fleeing men from Gillsland would carry the tale of the herShip of Irthing to these. They must not be given time to muster and prepare. Haltwhistle, therefore, must be taken before dark, and the castles isolated. Four hours only for the sack of Gillsland and Lanercost, and all on their swift way to Tyne. Was it understood?

"What of English forces from the garrison at Carlisle, Sire?" Campbell asked. "It cannot be more than a dozen miles from here. And Brampton nearer. There will be a garrison there?"

"Carlisle is too far to menace us before nightfall. And Brampton will not hold sufficient men to endanger us. That danger will come tomorrow. Today's is that Haltwhistle and the Tyne will gain warning before we reach them."

"Sire," Randolph put in. "I know this land. I was here, at Lanercost, with King Edward." Not all men would have admitted that, there and then. "There is a way through from Irthing to Tyne. Through the hills. A pass, by way of the Tipalt Burn. A small company could hold it, near where the Roman Wall crosses. And so prevent any flight of folk to the Tyne and Haltwhistle. A score of men sent there forthwith would not be wasted. Going round by Thirlwall Common."

Bruce looked at his nephew thoughtfully. "Well said," he nodded. "You have the sort of head on your shoulders that I need, Thomas. So be it. Yourself take them and place them." He raised his hand. "Come, then — enough of words. Now we act, Gibbie — 500 men for me ..."

So the two squadrons parted to turn, one west, one east, round the north base of Banks Fell, hidden from the unsuspecting Irthing valley.

The dual attack was indeed a complete surprise. As far as Lanercost was concerned, it was not even an attack. Bruce's party, emerging from the high ground behind the great Hadrian's Wall, had only a mile to cover in sight of the splendid Abbey, and their breakneck speed gave the Abbot's guard no time to assemble or even arm. Dispersing three-quarters of his force to deal with the large township of secular and domestic buildings surrounding the establishment, the King, with perhaps a hundred men, dashed up to the Abbey gatehouse, swept aside the dumbfounded porters, and rode into the precincts, calling loudly for the Abbot and Chapter. His men did not wait for any such formalities.

When the flustered and appalled cleric, a heavy moon-faced elderly man, was brought less than gently before the King, still sitting his horse in the wide courtyard, he was given no opportunity for protest, lamentation or plea.

"My lord Abbot — I am Robert of Scotland," he was told briskly. "Your abbey has in the past given much comfort to my enemies. Here was plotted my ruin, my death, my kingdom's devastation. The time has come for payment. I do not make war on Holy Church, unlike the Kings of England. But your treasure ought to be in heaven, rather than in your vaults! The late Edward, in gratitude, gave you much gold and silver and jewel, I understand. Plate, chalices, ewers, censers, lamps and the like. Much of it stolen from Scotland. I require it. All, mark you — all. And quickly."

"But ... but ... my lord! This is sacrilege!"

"It is war, sir. And retribution. Though not on the Church. On you. You have grown rich on the spoils of Scotland."

"I . . . I will not, may not, do it. You will not rob God's house? I will give you nothing, my lord."

"Address me as King, Englishman! And if God's house spills over with stolen treasure, should I respect it? I care not, priest, whether you give or I take. But all in this house is mine now. Choose you whether to deliver it up decently, or have my men pull your abbey apart to get it."

The banging and crashing and shouting that sounded from all around did not fail to underline his point. And looking up, the Abbot's pale prominent eyes widened as he saw the black smoke clouds begin to rise up from behind the precinct walls.

"You already . . . burn! Destroy!" he cried.

"Only barns, mills, gardens, my lord Abbot. Nothing sacred! Nothing that a man of God should set store by. But—your gold, now. Silver. Jewellery. Decide quickly, sir priest."

"Yes, yes. To be sure, my lord . . . Majesty. If you will spare the Abbey . . ."

"As your kings have not done in Scotland! In a hundred miles from my borders I have scarce an abbey, a priory or even a church with a roof to it! With doors to which abbots and monks have not been crucified! But . . . Sir Hugh. See that no chapels are damaged, no altars misused, no priests hurt. Sir Gilbert—go with my lord Abbot and take delivery of his treasure. All of it. And be not long about it." Abruptly Bruce reined his horse around and rode to supervise the destruction outside.

In ninety minutes the greatest, fairest establishment north of Durham was transformed utterly. The sacred buildings themselves remained entire, undamaged. But all else was smoking ruin, broken masonry, burning wood, trampled grain and garden and orchard, and the littered steaming carcases of slaughtered beasts. The Scots had had ample practice in the efficient spoiling of lands, their own lands; now they spoiled their enemies' with a will. In ever widening circles the devastation grew, until even the sun was obscured by the vast rolling pall of smoke which covered the valley of Irthing. Then Bruce, concerned with timing, and the fact that that smoke would be seen from Brampton, and far farther, called a halt. Detailing a score of men, under a young knight, to parcel up all the rich haul of the Abbey's treasure in emptied wool-sacks, and take it on a train of captured pack-horses quickly and secretly back to Scotland, he assembled his now smoke-blackened followers and headed off up the wide vale towards Gillsland without any leave-taking, abandoning Lanercost to its lamentations.

"At least they are alive, to wail!" he commented grimly to the somewhat doubtful Hugh Ross.

It was a westerly wind, and they rode, coughing, in the shroud of their own smoke that poured and billowed eastwards. But very quickly they were into still newer, thicker smoke, ruddy with fires and alive with fleeing folk, stumbling cursing men, sobbing women and wailing children, the sad exodus from blazing Gillsland, stricken to further abject terror and despair at the sight of this new looming host of grim horsemen.

Bruce found Campbell in charge at Gillsland, with Douglas superintending the spoliation of Irthing Priory a mile or so farther up the valley. The comprehensive burning, choking smoke clouds made all a chaotic nightmare, but Sir Neil declared that he thought there was not a single building left unburned in the town, or in a two-mile radius around. Catching and slaying the cattle had been the biggest problem. There had been no opposition worth mentioning.

Anxious about this vast pall of smoke being seen and interpreted from the Tyne valley five miles to the south-east, even above the hills between, the King ordered the trumpets to blow for disengagement and assembly. They rode southwards, out of the reeking, ravaged valley, almost an hour earlier than hoped for.

Now their route lay through the defile of the Tipalt Burn described by Randolph. The actual narrows of this comprised only the central mile or two; and well before this was reached the invaders found themselves having to plough through an unhappy flood of returning refugees streaming back northwards in renewed panic. Randolph's holding operation had served its purpose. When Bruce in due course picked up the little company strongly entrenched in the gullet of the pass, it was to be assured that no single messenger or escaper had got through to warn the Vale of Tyne — by this route, at least.

They were trotting through the final mile of the defile when, rounding a bend of its narrow floor beside the brawling burn, they came face to face with a mounted party of perhaps fifty, riding in the opposite direction. Bruce had not put out his usual scouting advance-guard on this occasion, no serious challenge being looked for, and as such would only be apt to offer prior intimation of something unusual happening. So this confrontation was a surprise to both sides.

However equal the surprise, reaction of course was quite otherwise, with so few facing so many — even though they would not see a quarter of them. Besides, these were not knights and men-at-arms, but looked like farmers and burghers on horseback. Almost certainly they represented a posse of Haltwhistle citizens hurrying to see what the great bank of smoke signified. At any rate, they behaved with commendable unanimity and expedition now, disciplined or not. With a great scrabbling, rearing and sidling of struggling mounts, they pulled round and went plunging off whence they had come, each jostling to be foremost.

"After them, Jamie!" Bruce commanded. "With our first ten files. Quickly! Head them off from the town. They must not warn."

Almost before the words were out, Douglas was spurring ahead, yelling to the front ranks of their company to follow. Pushing past the King's group, all but unseating some of them indeed, eager riders galloped in pursuit.

Bruce increased the pace of the entire host to a canter.

When they emerged, almost at right angles, into the open green vale, wider than that of Irthing, it was to see the better-mounted Scots dispersing the fleeing burghers left and right, like wolves amongst sheep, far ahead. The town of Haltwhistle showed grey beyond, its roofs and spires catching the glow of the sinking sun.

Ignoring the nearby castle of Blenkinsopp meantime. Bruce led his host directly and at fullest speed for the town, hooves drumming an earth-shaking, terrifying first intimation.

If many of the Scots were grievously disappointed at the lack of opposition they met, at the sheer anticlimax of the whole affair, the King was not. This was what he had planned and hoped for. By the time that they reached the first houses, the streets were quite deserted, no single face peered from door or window — although a few horses still stood tethered here and there. The host swept clatteringly through the town without meeting more than yelping dogs, squealing pigs and squawking poultry. It was not a large place, though larger than Gillsland; but it had a big and important church in its centre, with collegiate buildings attached. This church was a major reason for Bruce's presence here — for, oddly enough, it belonged to the See of Aberdeen, with considerable property in the town and surrounding country, a relic of happier days when the English were friends, and thus had been almost a detached part of Scotland. Holy Church was powerful and international, and Haltwhistle Church represented a useful excuse for the Scots incursion when the inevitable Papal fulminations began — for of course the Bishop of Aberdeen had been deprived of its due revenues for many a long year. Bruce, therefore, turned back for this church, to make it his base and headquarters, sending for the Vicar. Meanwhile he placed contingents of his men to dominate every street, lane and alley, with strong pickets to patrol the entire perimeter. But he gave strict instructions that there was to be no assault, pillage or burning here.

The terrified Vicar, when he was routed out of hiding and brought before the King, was assured that since Haltwhistle was as good as a Scots town, its people need fear nothing — so long as they co-operated and behaved discreetly. He was required to furnish a list of all Aberdeen property in the area; and then to go, under escort, and bring the principal citizens to Bruce, for their instructions.

So in due course these alarmed worthies were assembled to learn their fate — and could scarcely believe their ears. Haltwhistle would not be burned. Nobody would be hanged, beaten, ravished or otherwise molested. No hostages would be taken. The town would be treated as would a Scots town. The King of Scots and his force would occupy it for a few days — but they would pay for their keep and lodgings. Obedience and co-operation, that was all that was required. That, and the collection of the overdue and accumulated revenues for the Bishop of Aberdeen, which the King would take back to Scotland, as was suitable and lawful. For the rest, peace and goodwill. Only, the least hint of treachery, of attempts to communicate with other towns or areas, and there would be immediate and dire punishment, with no mercy shown. Was that understood?

There were no arguments, no questions.

That night the King, and most of his people, slept warm and comfortable, with minor detachments out guarding the approaches to the town, by the Tipalt Burn and both reaches of Tyne, while others kept careful watch on the small local castles. Bruce had chosen carefully in this, as in all else; Haltwhistle, placed as it was, was as good as a citadel for them.

* * *

Sunrise saw the Scots trotting in disciplined ranks down the broadening Tyne valley, leaving a small garrison, under Randolph, in Haltwhistle, with scouts carefully placed all around. The villages of Melkridge, Henshaw, Bardon Mill and Chesterwood went up in flames behind them, and by noon they were at the small town of Haydon Bridge, important strategically. There was a modest castle here, to guard the vital bridge over Tyne, but the word of the Scots advance had preceded them down the river and they found the castle abandoned, and town almost so. With the provisions of the whole missing community to sustain them, the invaders made their midday meal here. They moved on again in two sections, north and south of the river, under Douglas and the King respectively. They were seldom out of sight.

Newborough, Fourstones, Elrington and Wharmley fell to them, with many farms, mills and lesser places, without a sword drawn. All the vale behind was now hidden under a pall of smoke. The large town of Hexham, with its great and famous Priory, lay ahead, where North Tyne came in to join South.

Bruce had drawn up his contingent at West Boat, where there was a ferry by which Douglas came across to join him and receive orders, when scouts came to inform that a party under a white flag was riding out from Hexham. The King ordered the newcomers to be brought into his presence.

The white-flag party consisted of the magistrates and chief citizens of the town, looking very alarmed; and the Prior of Hexham looking magnificent, with even a silken canopy held over his head by four mounted acolytes on milk-white jennets, the stuff richly embroidered with a gold saltire on azure. Hexham had been a bishopric once, and its foundation in 674 by Saint Wilfred made it one of the most ancient and venerable fanes in all England. Undoubtedly the present incumbent was not disposed to forget it. Ignoring the genuflecting magistrates, Bruce addressed himself to the still-mounted prelate.

"You must be the Lord Prior of Hexham, sir, come to meet me. I thank you for your courtesy," he said gravely. "How may I serve you?"

Surprised, the other, a purple-faced, sagging-jowled man of strong features and intolerant eye, drew a much-beringed hand over his thin-lipped mouth. "If you would serve us, my lord — then come and accept of our hospitality, you and yours," he answered stiffly. "But spare our city." And he waved his plump hand towards the ominous smoke-clouds.

"Your hospitality it will be my pleasure to accept. But as to sparing your city, Sir Prior — tell me why I should?"

"Because it is a city of Holy Church. An ecclesiastical jurisdiction of great age and sanctity. As is all the country around — all Church land, Hexhamshire. Sacred to the blessed Saint Wilfred whom God loves, my lord."

"Sire!" James Douglas barked, at the Prior.

"Eh . . .?"

"I said, Sire. Not my lord. Address His Grace as befits a king, sirrah. And get down from that horse."

After a moment or two, the other slowly dismounted, frowning. He did not speak.

It was Bruce who inclined his head, not the other. "I have heard of Hexham Priory's fame, of course," he said. "Its greatness. And all this goodly land is yours also? This Hexhamshire? How far does it extend, my lord?"

"All around you. You have been on my land these last miles Since Allen River. Church lands. Hexhamshire comprises 50,000 acres."

The King looked approvingly around him. "A goodly heritage indeed," he nodded. "Rich. Fertile. How much had you in mind, my lord?"

The other opened his mouth, and shut it again, purple deeper.

"Come, sir. You must have some notion of your city's worth? And your 50,000 acres of Hexhamshire? You, and these others, came expressly to me. Came with a proposal to put to me, I think? How much? Out with it!" That last was snapped in a very different tone of voice from heretofore.

The Prior blinked rapidly. "I . . . we would be prepared to make some small . . . tribute, Majesty," he conceded guardedly. "A token of . . . of goodwill."

"A token, yes. In order that your town and country be not destroyed. How much, man?"

"What can I say, Sire?" The clerical voice held a note that might almost have been anguish now. "I am but a poor priest entrusted with the pastoral care and oversight of God's flock in this place . . ."

"Your town, shire and treasure. How much?" And when the other only compressed already thin lips, Bruce jabbed a finger towards the chief of the magistrates. "You, then — how much?"

That was more than the Prior could in any way allow. "We have some few cattle," he jerked. "Wool. Grain. Forage . . ."

"And silver," Bruce added.

"But little, Sire. We are not rich in moneys . . ."

"Tush, man — the rings on your hand alone do belie you! Your cattle and grain and forage I will accept. Such as I require. But to save your town and lands, you will pay me 2,000 merks in silver. Forthwith. Is it agreed?"

A stricken moan issued from the cleric's lips. "You cannot . . . you cannot mean it, Sire! Not 2,000! It is not possible. It would beggar us. Indeed, I do not have so much . . ."

"Then find it, sir. Sell your rings, perhaps? Or do you prefer that Hexham goes up in flames? Like Gillsland and others?"

"No! No, Sire — no!" came from the magistrates, in a wailing chorus.

"On payment of 2,000 silver merks, Englishmen, or £1,300, if so you prefer it," Bruce went on sternly, "I shall sign you a decree declaring that the town of Hexham, with Hexhamshire, be free from all further tribute of reparation for English damage done in Scotland for the space of one year from this date. The Prior of Hexham to remain hostage in my hands until such payment is made. Agree to this now, or I command immediate advance upon your town, without mercy. Is it so agreed?"

"Yes, yes," the townsmen cried. All eyes were on the Prior.

Slowly, expressionlessly, that man inclined his head.

"Very well. Then we shall accompany you back to your Priory, my lord," the King nodded. "As your guests, to receive your hospitality, as offered. Hexham is safe ... for a year. Come, to horse ..."

As they rode towards the town, Douglas, at the King's side, shook his head. "I mislike this chaffering with the enemy, Sire," he said. "We came to punish, not to barter and deal! To cause the English army at Berwick to look back over its shoulder ..."

"Spoken like my good brother Edward!" Bruce asserted, smiling. Edward had advisedly been left behind in Scotland to prosecute the siege of the English in Perth. He would have fitted but uncomfortably into this highly delicate campaign. "How do *you* know what we came to do, Jamie? We came to upset the Berwick army, without fighting it, yes. But much more. And that, I swear, is already achieved — or will be when the tidings reach them. Think you burning and hership the only way to cause the English alarm? It is their confidence, their pride, I would undermine. And this day's work will do that even better than yesterday's. Though yesterday's was necessary for today's."

"You mean ... you planned this, Sire?"

"Say that I hoped for it. This Prior has served me better than he knows. Better than just by filling my purse! He leads the way for others to follow. Others will be prepared to do what the proud Prior of Hexham did not balk at — to buy their safety. For the moment! All over the North of England, let us hope."

"But ... you could have had the wealth of Hexham — all of it — by but drawing your sword! Why this temporising ...?"

"Do you not see it, Jamie? I warrant Thomas Randolph would have understood! He has a head on his shoulders for more than swordery. See you — my realm is direly impoverished. The governance of a kingdom requires much money. My treasury is empty, and I can by no means fill it from Scotland. If I burned Hexham today and took its treasure — that would be all I would win from it. This way, I have given it assurance for a year, for 2,000 merks. Think you that next year it will not think perhaps to buy more safety, instead of fighting? And others like it? Another 2,000,

Riches breed caution, James — and the English North has grown rich on the spoil of Scotland. We shall see to it that all hear of Hexham's bargain. There are many, many towns and abbeys and priories in these parts. After my burning of Gillsland, as was necessary, and sparing Haltwhistle and Hexham, I swear others will seek to make similar bargains. We shall, of course, burn here and there, to remind all! Hereafter, by constant raiding over the Border, I intend to see that Cumberland and Northumberland — aye, and even Durham and York — pay their taxes to King Robert rather than King Edward! Think you this will not trouble the English at Berwick — or at least, their leaders — as much as a few more towns ablaze?"

Douglas was speechless.

Hexham was situated at a most vital junction of ways and roads and rivers. In every direction valleys and routes radiated. Even as the crow flew, however, it was sixty and more miles to Berwick. They had four days, Bruce reckoned. And with the sort of men he had brought, a great deal could be achieved in four days, from a centre like Hexham. That very evening he split up his force into two hundreds, under eager captains, and next morning sent them forth, strictly commanded, wolves amongst scattered sheep — but careful, calculating, persuasive wolves, who intended to come back this way again and again, seeking sheep's fleeces rather than their blood.

Then he rode back to Haltwhistle, where all would rendezvous four days hence — unless, somehow, a major English attack developed sooner. From Haltwhistle he could keep a general's eye on Carlisle and the south-west — and could be back through empty hills to the Border in two or three hours.

Glory could wait on another occasion.

Chapter Nineteen

The King wiped the rain off his reddened, weather-beaten, deeply-lined face, and cursed the blustering showers — even though it was April and the season for such; two Aprils since his first English raid. It was not the discomfort that concerned him, for he was now so inured to discomfort as scarcely to notice it. What worried him was the effect of all this wind on the sea, and therefore on the ships he was riding to join — or, at least, on the stomachs of the men behind him who would sail in those open galleys. Seasick warriors were any commander's nightmare. Lowering his head into the wet south-westerly gusts he kicked his stumbling horse up the last soggy-peat-pocked, outcrop-strewn rise of the long heather ridge, muttering profanities.

The tinkle of laughter at his elbow was mocking, challenging and affectionate in one. Christina MacRuarie, as befitted a Hebridean, cared nothing for wind or rain.

"You are getting old, Robert!" she accused. "Near to forty, and beginning to cherish your comforts. Of which, to be sure, I am one! A chair by the ingle — I swear that is what you are dreaming of!"

"A chair anywhere, woman!" he growled. "Anything but this saddle. I am never out of it. Dear God — I rule Scotland from the back of a horse! From over the Border to Inverness. From St. Andrews to the Forest. From Galloway to Argyll. Year in, year out, I live in the saddle. I vow my rump is so calloused that I shall never sit aught else in comfort!"

"It does not incommode you in bed, at least!" she asserted. "Nor, it seems, in scaling walls! And sitting on judgement-seats and in parliaments!"

"And I so old a man!"

"Never heed. Soon you will be standing on a galley's poop, concerned only for your belly, not your bottom! If Angus Og has waited for you at Dumbarton!"

"He will be waiting. I am none so late. Four days? Five?"

"Angus is not the most patient of mortals. And would have preferred to sail for Man direct, without calling into Clyde. He told me so himself, at Inverness. He says he could, and should, reduce the Isle of Man to obedience, of himself, without the King of Scots' aid!"

"No doubt — and so claim Man as *his* thereafter! As part of the Sudreys, the South Isles. No — Angus is my good friend — but he must learn who is master in Scotland. Man is part of my realm, and must remain so — not part of the Lordship of the Isles."

At last they had reached the summit of the long lateral ridge of Rednock, last outpost of the Highlands, and were able to look out over the vast trough of the Forth, and all the wide waterlogged vacances of the Flanders Moss. Below, the isle-dotted Loch of Menteith gloomed leaden under the scudding rain clouds, and to the west the tall hills of Loch Lomond and the Lennox were part-shrouded by drifting curtains. But eastwards there was a break in the overcast, and, in the slanting yellow afternoon sunlight fifteen miles away, Stirling rose proudly out of the level plain, castle crowning its soaring rock in a golden blaze.

The sight, sun notwithstanding, did nothing to sweeten Bruce's temper. Indeed, he turned abruptly away from it, in his saddle, to look back over the long straggling columns of his host, which seemed to extend quite a lot of the way back to Perth.

"Keith!" he jerked, to the group immediately behind him. "Sir Robert — you are Marischal of this realm, are you not? Look there! I warrant it is time that you did some marshalling! Call you that a royal progress? More like a flock of straying sheep! See you to it, sir!"

"Yes, Sire." Keith, without demur, wheeled round his mount and went cantering back, others with him. When the King was in this frame of mind, such reaction was the only wise one.

Christina, of them all, chose otherwise, as often. "Stirling!" she cried. "Stirling Castle, there, arrogantly lording it over all. The key to Scotland! When will the King of Scots do to Stirling what he had just done to Perth?"

"God's sake, woman — Stirling is like no other fortress in the kingdom! Even Edinburgh," Bruce flung back, rising to her taunt. "It cannot be taken by surprise, or battery, nor any device. Only starvation can take it — or treachery. Besides, it is Stirling, the *place*, that is the key to Scotland — not Stirling Castle. Wallace won Stirling Brig fight, while yet the English were secure in the castle. I have no time to spend on that hold."

"Yet you spent four days in Perth. At risk of Angus Og's patience!"

"Days! *Months* it would take. Five months I would require, to take Stirling Castle. I have more to do, by the Rude!"

She laughed. "Your brother told me once that he could crack that nut quickly enough — if you would let him try!"

"Edward! Edward speaks loud. He tried to take *Perth* — but did not!"

Christina smiled, with her woman's guile. This would bring the King out of his black mood. Set brother against brother, and there would be no more glooming, at least.

Not that Bruce had any immediate cause for gloom. His recent capture of the town of Perth had been a brilliant feat, and all his own. Many, including his brother, had tried, these past years, to reduce the Tayside city, but all had failed. The late King Edward had fortified it as only he knew how, as the strategic centre in the Southern Highlands. Sir Andrew Fraser had been the last to take its siege in hand; and on his way south for his parliament in Inverness, Bruce had come this way to see how matters moved. Matters had not been moving at all, and on the second night the King in person had led an assault, first by swimming the Tay in spate, and then the outer moat; then by scaling the outer rampart by rope-ladder and grappling-hooks, at this, the least well-guarded flank, to swim the second moat and thereafter gain the parapet of the inner bailey, from whence he could storm one of the gates from the inside, open it, and let in the flood of more conventional attackers. So, after nine long years, Perth was in Scots hands again; and only Dundee remained English-occupied north of Forth. Two more days Bruce had spent in the town thereafter, setting things to right — and hanging the Scots traitors who had aided the English and mistreated their fellow-citizens during the occupation. The English he had allowed to go to their ships in the Tay, and sail for home. It was, however, those hanging Scots, decorating the captured walls, who had sent the King on his way in this black temper — for though Robert Bruce could be ruthless and inexorable where sternness was called for, such measures always left him a prey to conscience.

Frowning still, but no longer sullen, Bruce led the way down the south-facing slopes into the Carse of Forth, to turn west along it for Gartmore and Drymen.

Next day they found the Lord of the Isles' great galley fleet awaiting them in the Clyde at Dumbarton — though with Angus Og himself away hawking with the MacGregor on Loch Lomondside, and his Islesmen setting a scandalised area by the ears. Embarkation had to delayed for another day. It was the King's turn to wait patiently.

This expedition against the Isle of Man had been decided upon at the recent Inverness parliament — for two reasons other than the simple fact that it was an integral part of the Scots realm presently occupied by the English. Firstly, Edward of Carnarvon had granted it in gift to his favourite, Piers Gaveston — and Gaveston was now beheaded, a piece of judicial murder by the Earls of Lancaster and Warwick as much deplored in Scotland, where the favourite's demoralising effect on King Edward was appreciated, as it was gleefully acclaimed by the English nobility; therefore there would for the moment be a hiatus in the control of Man. And secondly, John of Lorn, whom Edward had made his Admiral of the Western Seas, was using the island as a base, and interfering with the Scots lines of communication with Ireland, important for the supply of grain, arms, horses and other sinews of war. There was also the advantage, of course, that any such attack on Man might have the useful by-product of distracting the enemy from full-scale invasion of Scotland this coming campaigning season.

They sailed from Dumbarton, still in squally conditions. Bruce embarked some hundreds of his own force but sent the majority eastwards to aid Douglas, who was engaged in punitive raiding into English-held Lothian. This expedition was something of a waste of his cavalry, admittedly, since the horses had to be left behind; but the Isles lordship had always been interested in winning the Isle of Man for itself, and it was important that the King and his own troops should be to the fore in any taking of the place. Angus was a sound ally and friend — if less sound a subject — but he was no more immortal than the rest of them, and a successor in the Lordship of the Isles, holding Man, could be a thorn in the flesh. Yet, of course, Bruce could nowise assail it without Angus's galleys.

They made an uncomfortable voyage of it down the Firth and along the Ayrshire and Galloway coasts. Half a dozen of the Garmoran galleys were included in the fleet — hence Christina's presence, the only woman in the expedition — and the King sailed in her own vessel. Fortunately he was an excellent sailor; a sick monarch and commander would have cut a sorry figure amongst those Islesmen. There was considerable discussion as to whether these gales would give any tactical advantage. They would certainly make any attack on Man unexpected; and they would be likely to keep John MacDougall stormbound — but whether at Man itself or in any English or Irish ports, remained to be seen.

As to that, the King hoped to gain some prior information. For the fleet was going to make a call up the Solway Firth *en route*, to where Edward Bruce was at present besieging Dumfries and Caerlaverock. Here he hoped to get the latest news from England, and to pick up some further reinforcements for the expedition — however much of a waste of time Angus Og declared it.

It was a relief to turn into the shallow, sheltered waters of the Solway, and thereafter into the narrow Nith estuary. They found the English flag still flying defiantly from Caerlaverock Castle and then, six miles farther up, at Dumfries. They also found Edward to be absent, with the siege of Dumfries maintained by Sir Robert Boyd, and that of Caerlaverock by Sir Thomas Randolph.

Edward, it seemed, was off raiding in Cumberland across the Solway sands. Word had recently been brought back from England that the Scots commissioners, sent secretly to collect the annual dues from subscribing towns, abbeys and the like, had this year met with trouble. In fact, more than trouble — annihilation. They had reached Hexham-on-Tyne, with some of the moneys collected, and there, instead of receiving the third of the Prior's payments-for-safety, they had been hanged, and their treasure confiscated. That proud churchman had presumably decided that he might spare himself further expense. Only one or two of the Scots party had escaped, to win back to Dumfries with the tale of it. Edward

Bruce, being the man he was, had promptly mounted a fierce sally into the flat lands west of Carlisle.

The King's anger was cold where his brother's had been hot. Dumfries had a bad effect on him anyway — the scene of his slaying of John Comyn nine years earlier, even though also of his assumption of the crown. He had shunned the place, since. Even now he would not sleep in the armed camp which surrounded the walled town, but removed himself the few miles back to Caerlaverock, and Randolph's camp. Here he detached himself from all, to pace alone, well outwith arrow-shot of the magnificent fortress in the marshes. It was a time not for wrath so much as hard decision.

He had made up his mind before he slept that night. Major changes of programme were called for.

The next morning brought the need for still further and quite unanticipated decision. Boyd himself rode in from Dumfries, bringing with him a young man, square, stocky, richly-dressed but uneasy of eye and manner.

"Sire," Boyd declared, "here is one, MacDouall. Fergus, son to Sir Dugald MacDouall . . . of whom you know!"

There, in the tented encampment, Bruce stared, his breath catching in his throat at the identification of this son of his hated enemy, of the man who had given up his brothers to shameful death. He did not trust himself to speak. Those around him were suddenly silent quite.

"He comes under a flag of truce, Sire. From his father in yonder Dumfries Castle. He would . . . treat with you, he says!"

"Treat! That blood-stained traitor's son? God's mercy . . .!"

"Treat, my lord King," the young man reiterated, tense-voiced. "In my father's name."

"Hang him!" Angus Og advised succinctly. "Also in his father's name! As you will treat the other — not treat *with* him!"

Many around the King growled their agreement.

"No! No — hear me, Sire," the MacDouall cried. "You cannot so do. I came under flag of truce. By all the laws of war you cannot do it . . ."

"Did your father observe the laws of war, wretch, when he took his liege lord's brothers prisoner, and then sent them to their deaths?" That was Gilbert Hay.

"That . . . that was long ago. When I was but a child. And my father could not know. That King Edward would slay them. It was Edward's orders. My father recognised Edward as King — not you, Sire. Still he does — the new Edward. He is King Edward's governor of Dumfries and Warden of the West March . . ."

Bruce held up a hand that trembled slightly, for silence. "Well?" he grated. "Say what you have to say."

"Yes, Sire. My father sends me to say that if you will promise him, and his garrison, their lives and liberty, he will yield Dumfries. To you."

"So-o-o! That is it? And he thinks that I will grant him such terms?"

"Your Grace's clemency is known."

"Aye!" Angus Og snorted. "And there you have it. Any traitor and dastard in this land now conceives himself to be safe! That he will not have to pay for his sins. You have let off too many rogues, Sir King. That is what your clemency means now!"

Even Christina joined in the chorus of declamation. "Your Grace will perceive that MacDouall did not offer to treat with the Earl of Carrick! Who has been besieging him these many weeks. Only when you come, and he is gone, does this man seek these terms. Because he knows your brother would have none of him! Save hanging on a rope!"

All knew that to be the truth, Bruce better than any. Yet he turned and paced away some distance, to stand staring over towards the strange shield-shaped castle that rose out of its complicated system of morass and water-barrier, unseeing. Once again he was fighting, fighting one of his own dire battles with himself, the King fighting the man. Dugald MacDouall, the treacherous Gallovidian he had sworn a great oath to kill, the man for whose blood that of his young brothers cried out. He had spared those other two, whom he had likewise vowed to slay — William of Ross and Alexander MacDougall. Spared and accepted to his peace, his very company, after all they had done. Must he do the same with this, this third especial offender? Was this sacrifice demanded of him, also . . .?

He turned back to the waiting company, set-faced. "MacDouall," he said, expressionlessly. "Go back to your father. Tell him that he may march out of Dumfries, he and his, with my safe-conduct. To England. This day. Tell him — for I will by no means see him — that he will be wise to bide in England hereafter. For if he sets foot in my realm again, I will take him and hang him. You understand?"

The other's response was lost in the uproar of the Scots leaders' disbelief, wrath and reproach. The King signed to Boyd to take the young man away.

"My lord Constable," he snapped, to Gilbert Hay, "you will go, in my name, to receive the surrender of Dumfries. You will ensure the safety of the garrison, and see them sent on their way to the

Border. Let there be no mistake, see you." He paused, to run his eye sobrely over the critical ranks of his friends. "You all blame me, I see. You all name me fool, or worse. Think that I forget the blood of my brothers and my friends. Do not deny it — I see it on every face. Thank you God, then, that you are none of you the King! That you can afford to judge scoundrels on their merits — where *I* must judge causes, results, policies, the realm's best weal. How easy your judgement! How difficult mine."

"You will win few to your cause by sparing MacDouall," Angus Og declared. "You will not win *his* allegiance. He will continue to fight against you, hating you no less for your gentleness."

"Gentleness, man!" Bruce's bark of laughter had no mirth in it. "Think you there was any gentleness in that decision? Or in my heart? You know me little, it seems, still. I spared MacDouall because it was the price to pay for Dumfries. With Dumfries ours we can starve this Caerlaverock. It will soon fall. But by no other means. And Buittle thereafter. The last English stronghold in Galloway. This is of greater worth than my vengeance on MacDouall. And I have not the men, nor the time now, to spare in further prolonged siegery. You have heard what has happened at Hexham and the Tyne. Let that remain unpunished, and all that we have done in the North of England will fall. All others will follow the Prior of Hexham's lead. For two years we have milked Cumberland and Northumberland, to our great gain. And kept the English from winning any great army from their North. We have won silver we direly needed. And time, precious time. All that will be sacrificed if I do not immediately deal with Hexham and Tynedale and the rest. My brother saw it, dimly, and went raiding yonder, in anger. I cross the Border otherwise, not in angry raiding but of set policy. Although my anger may have some play also, I think! And I need these men who have wasted their time, and mine, at Dumfries and Caerlaverock."

There was question on every face, now.

"You change your course then, Sire?"

"You do not sail for Man?" That was Angus Og, almost hopefully.

"I do not. I have other work to do." Bruce straightened up. "Now — leave me, my friends. For I have much thinking to do, first. We shall have a council later. Gibbie — off with you to Dumfries . . ."

That evening Hay rode back, with Boyd and most of the besieging host, to announce that all had proceeded smoothly at Dumfries. MacDouall and his garrison had marched out just after midday, and were now well on their way over the Border, under escort. Sir Robert Fleming was acting as governor of the town.

Bruce sent a trumpeter and herald to announce these facts, across the sunset-stained waters, to Caerlaverock Castle — whose present captain, it transpired, was no other than David de Strathbogie, the offended Earl of Atholl.

The council called for that night was more than usually formal, and deliberately so. It was not so much a council as an audience. The King was not seeking advice, but giving decisions. But he commenced proceedings, in Randolph's tented pavilion, with some ceremony.

"It is my royal will and good pleasure," he announced, "to honour in especial at this time two lords in whom I repose much trust and confidence. Step forward Angus MacDonald of the Isles, Lord High Admiral of my realm; and Sir Thomas Randolph, Lord of Nithsdale, my sister's son."

Surprised, and eyeing each other a little askance, the pair came forward.

"My lord Angus — your service and leal devotion is of the greatest importance to my cause. There has been dispute in the past between you and your brother, Alexander of Islay, now in Ireland, who has not supported me and has given aid and comfort to my enemies, in especial the MacDougalls. Your desire to reunite within your Lordship that part of your ancestor Somerled's heritage now dispersed to other descendants, is known to me. Therefore it is my will that hereafter Islay and Tiree be forfeited by your brother Alexander, and bestowed upon yourself. Also that the former MacDougall lands of Duror and Glencoe, and the Isle of Mull, likewise be so bestowed. And that the former Comyn territory of Lochaber be included in your Lordship. Thus it becomes the greatest in territory in all my realm. In return, apart from your continued loyal friendship and aid, I but require that you provide and build for me a royal castle at Tarbert, between Knapdale and Kintyre, for my use and garrison."

There was a pregnant silence in that tent, as everyone, not only Angus Og, weighed the King's words, and probed their significance. That this was a highly important pronouncement went without saying, infinitely more vital than any mere appointment such as the High Admiralship, which could be revoked at the royal will. Once the Lord of the Isles occupied and possessed these extra vast territories, dispossession would be wellnigh impossible. Yet Tarbert, that tiny isthmus of land between Loch Fyne and the Western Sea, was in fact the essential key to any attempt to bring control to bear on the Sudreys — that is, the isles and mainland coasts south of the Ardnamurchan peninsula, to which the territories mentioned belonged — clear evidence that the King intended to retain at least some hold on the area. And, as it happened, the Isle of Man was always reckoned to be a detached but important part of the Sudreys. And the Isle of Man had not been mentioned.

Angus Og took the careful part, and inclined his head, without committing his thanks, or his doubts, to words.

Bruce went on. "Sir Thomas Randolph — after previous error, mistaken but honourable, you have proved yourself most loyal, reliable and able. Your judgement I have found valuable. As my near kin, it is right and fitting that you should be ranked other than as a simple knight. It is therefore my royal pleasure that you shall be raised to the station of an earl of this realm."

The other did not hide his surprise, as he bowed low.

"One earldom stands vacant, with the forfeiture and death, without male heir, of the late Buchan. I cannot conceive that you would wish to bear that dishonoured title. But there is another ancient earldom, of the Celtic polity to which you belong, vacant since the death of Earl Angus over a century ago — that of Moray. Ancient, honourable and great. The lands of that earldom have in the main been acquired by the House of Comyn, and are now at my disposal by forfeiture. Lands from the Spey to the Ness, including much of Buchan; and west to the borders of Lochaber, including the great Lordship of Badenoch. I believe that you are the man to control those wide and important lands well and ably, recognising their consequence to my kingdom and rule." He paused, unbuckling his own golden earl's belt. "I do now, therefore, name and appoint, invest and belt you, Earl of Moray." And stooping, the King clasped the golden girdle about his nephew's — and erstwhile enemy's — waist.

The acclaim from the company was polite rather than enthusiastic — for the stiffish Randolph was scarcely popular, though Gibbie Hay and Hugh Ross had become his close friends. Also few there failed to notice that the new earl's lands marched with Angus Og's new Lochaber on the west, and the Earl of Ross's territories on the north. In other words, the King was inserting both a buffer between these traditional enemies, and his own watchdog into the Highland provinces.

Randolph was obviously overwhelmed by this totally unexpected honour and promotion. He shook his head helplessly.

But Bruce was not yet finished. He stepped back, and dropping the ceremonial tone, spoke more briskly. "Furthermore, my lord of Moray, you may make shift to add to your possessions! I go to

Tynedale, not the Isle of Man. You shall go there in my stead, with my Lord of the Isles. Commanding my land forces, as he commands the sea. And if you can win Man back from the enemy, it is yours."

There was a great sigh from the company, as all was now clear. Man was to be prevented from becoming a conquest of Angus Og's, and he was given much else, less strategically dangerous, instead. The vital Sudreys were to be divided. It was seen why Randolph had been chosen for this venture, and created earl so suddenly — so that the Lord of the Isles could neither refuse to co-operate, nor insist on being in command over one of lesser rank. As King's nephew, and an earl, Randolph's position would be safeguarded, and offence by Angus Og be made difficult.

It was apparent that the monarch had indeed been thinking, and to considerable effect.

Thereafter, Bruce went on to deal with matters tactical and organisational, in businesslike fashion, so that the atmosphere lost much of its tension and drama. Christina MacRuarie looked cynical — but then she often did.

The two expeditions would part company next day.

During the night, Edward Bruce took the opportunity to slip back across the Solway sands, at low tide and in darkness. He came on from Dumfries to rouse his brother, full of news, question, advice and demands.

The King, who did not relish Edward's headstrong presence in either expedition, informed him that he was taking most of his brother's men to Tynedale; but that he wanted him to go north, forthwith, and set up the inevitably prolonged sieges of Stirling Castle and Dundee. Edward was not enthusiastic, pointing out the wearisome and static nature of the tasks — to have pointed out to him in return that means might be found, as at Perth, to expedite that procedure. The other was, understandably, a little hipped over Perth's fall — as he was about the Dumfries terms and surrender, after he had done all the work. He could hardly refuse the remit — but he took the opportunity to strike a blow for a concern of his own. Without actually framing it as a bargain, he indicated that he would tackle the task more enthusiastically if Robert would agree, as had been suggested on a number of occasions, to have him officially adopted as heir to the throne.

The King was careful, as in the past, not to commit himself. He would consider it — but his daughter's interests must not be overlooked, even though she was a captive in England . . .

Edward's vigorous exposition on the follies of having a reigning queen on the throne of battling Scotland — especially a young and absentee one — kept the King from his sleep for considerably longer.

* * *

So, while a somewhat disgruntled Earl of Carrick headed north, and a not entirely contented Lord of the Isles took the new Earl of Moray and a great fleet south-west to the Isle of Man, the King of Scots personally led a light cavalry force of some 1,500 south-east into England, by the same route as before. And this time he pulled no punches. Ignoring the Vale of Irthing, which had not yet recovered from the assault of two years earlier, he made straight down Tyne, spreading fire and destruction. Hexham was of course his especial target; and after cutting down the still hanging bodies of his commissioners, he destroyed the town entirely — save for the Priory itself, which he left undamaged, although he appropriated all its silver and treasure that he could find. It seemed that Prior Thomas de Fenwick had been replaced by a younger man, one Robert de Whelpington, with instructions from Archbishop Greenfield of York to have no more truck with the Scots.

Bruce decided that the Archbishop required instruction also.

Setting up his base at Corbridge, downstream from Hexham, he subjected the South Tyne area to a systematic devastation such as even Wallace's 1297 invasion had not equalled. Then, with no major opposition materialising, he drove on south-wards, not so much burning and harrying now as making demonstration and demanding tribute, payment for relief, and at high rates — and getting it. On to the very gates of Newcastle they pressed. But finding that strongly walled city too tough a nut to crack quickly, they by-passed it, assailing the Teame valley instead, with rich reward. Then on to Durham itself.

They were now nearly a hundred miles deep into England, and Bruce was growing a little anxious. His scouts gave him no intimation of any large enemy force being mustered against them; but if any were being raised in the west, he could be all too easily cut off from home. He decided that Durham — or at least, Hartlepool, where he had family lands whose revenues had long been denied him — was as far as he dared go on this occasion; York must wait. And, woefully, his wife Elizabeth, seventy miles farther than York, must wait also.

Bishop Kellew of Durham, successor to the late and unlamented Beck, was away at a parliament in the south, and his great castle on its rock safe from all but prolonged siege. But the rich city itself was vulnerable; and after some part of it was reduced to ashes, its chief citizens were urgent to persuade Bruce to accept an immediate 2,000 merks, with promises of a total of £5,000, and hostages to ensure payment. With the humiliating rider that they must agree to provide free ingress and egress through the County Palatine whenever the King of Scots chose to invade England, Bruce accepted their terms for one year's protection. The fact that it was the Prince-Bishop's land, and largely his money also, was the best of it.

The King turned for home not dissatisfied, the Scots Treasury in a better state, by a total of nearly £40,000, than it had been for many a year, the county authorities of Northumberland, Cumberland and Westmorland each having agreed to pay £2,000 over and above their constituent places, for a year's peace.

The Scots reached the Border area without interception; but Bruce's luck changed nevertheless, and the last stages of that ride were something of a personal nightmare. Sickness struck him, of the same variety that he had suffered at Inverurie six years before, brought on no doubt by the same causes — lack of rest and proper feeding, plus the hard and insanitary conditions of continuous campaigning. Once again fever, vomiting, skin-rash and intolerable itch was his lot, with ever-increasing weakness. But now he had to continue to ride.

Possibly his sickness was basically responsible for the second misfortune. His advance party was attacked and badly cut up by a company out from the Carlisle garrison, in the Haltwhistle area; and just because the King was only too well aware of the hindrance he had become to his people, he agreed to fierce demands for retaliation on the fortress of Carlisle itself, to which he probably never would have listened in less fevered state. In the event, the typical secret night attack was repulsed with serious losses, a barking dog alarming the guards, and the main garrison rallying swiftly. It was a sobered and reduced company which recrossed the Border line at length, with their semi-delirious monarch demanding to be taken to Jamie Douglas's camp at the siege of Roxburgh Castle.

Bruce was not aware of his arrival at Roxburgh, where Teviot joined Tweed; nor of the loving care he received *en route* or at Douglas's hands. And only dimly aware of the hot summer weeks that followed, while he lay helpless, and of the succession of his friends who came sorrowfully from far and near to visit him. At some stage he realised that Christina MacRuarie was back, nursing him, but did not know that it was for Elizabeth de Burgh that he constantly moaned and cried — with whom sometimes he believed that he gripped in his arms — thereby twisting a sharp knife in the Highlandwoman's heart.

Strangely enough, it was his brother again who really set him on the road to recovery, a recovery of the spirit primarily, rather than of the body. For in August Edward came in triumph to Roxburgh, thinking to cheer the King into health by the tale of his successes. Dundee had fallen at last, he announced. And Stirling would be theirs within the year.

Robert, on his sick-bed, required a little while to take this in, and Edward expiated on his tactics at Dundee and what he had done to the English and the traitors therein. But it was not on this that his brother's mind fixed.

"Stirling . . .?" he said thinly. "You said . . . Stirling will be ours? Within a year. How can you be so sure?"

"Because I have come to terms with the captain, Sir Philip Moubray. If it is not relieved within the year, he yields Stirling to me. Moubray — he who struck you down at Methven fight . . ."

"You gave him a year! To be relieved? And . . . and raised the siege? You did that?"

"Yes. So we win Stirling cheaply. I have his written word . . ."

"Cheap!" However weak the King's voice, it was intense enough. "You are a fool, Edward! A bigger fool than even I judged!"

"But . . . do you not understand? We are spared a long and wasteful siege. Such as you are ever against. Who will relieve Moubray? My men are freed — and are now investing Linlithgow. Then it will be Edinburgh's turn . . ."

"Edward — what did our sire endow you with, for wits?" his brother demanded. "You have given your plighted word? That Moubray has a year unassailed?"

"To be sure. Why not? Do you hate Moubray so much? Because he unhorsed you once! I say you should have hated MacDouall more, who slew our brothers! Yet he you gave honourable terms to . . ."

"God's mercy — listen to me, Edward! You have ensured the invasion of our country. On a scale we have not seen since Falkirk. Stirling is the key to Scotland, as all do know. The English cannot, I say, ignore this. Cannot fail to come to the relief of Stirling. Once that is yielded, they have lost this long war. Moubray knows that, if you do not. And now you have committed my honour, with your own. Given Edward of Carnarvon a year . . ."

"*You* have been giving English towns a year's truce. For money!"

The King, whose strength was ebbing, ignored that. "King Edward is now released from his foolish passion for his catamite, Gaveston. The English are no longer divided over that, for and against the King. His lords are spurring him to action against us, after all his folly and sloth. He is a weakling, but he has hard men round him. Men who will now control him. This of Stirling will give them what they need — a challenge. A challenge with a set time. To relieve Moubray and the key to Scotland. Edward will seek to redeem his name and fame. I see it all. All over England trumpets will blow . . ."

Robert Bruce's voice died away.

Chapter Twenty

Robert Bruce was right. All England saw that year's bargain at Stirling as a challenge and a rallying-cry, not to be ignored. Strangely, Bruce's own raids over the Border, with all their attendant blackmail, seemed to have little effect on opinion in the far south; but the Stirling ultimatum was different. England's name, fame and honour were at stake. That winter of 1313–14, plans were laid for the greatest invasion of Scotland ever mounted. Not only was Stirling to be relieved, and dramatically, but the whole wretched country was to be ground into the dust, once and for all. By spring the trumpets were sounding indeed, for muster from one end of England to the other. King Edward set his invasion for Easter.

Bishop Lamberton arrived back in Scotland, finally, for good or ill, to celebrate that Eastertide in his own land, parole broken — since no one seemed interested in it any longer, anyway. He brought word that the invasion had been postponed until late May, when there would be more grass to feed the hundreds of thousands of horses involved — always a major problem.

So, by late May, the Bruce, almost himself again, though thin, had reluctantly taken up his position just south of Stirling. A head-on confrontation with the embattled might of England was still the last thing that he desired; but now there was no alternative, unless he was prepared to abandon all but the Highlands to the enemy. The waist of Scotland had to be held.

The English would, of course, seek to relieve the castle. But that was not the vital matter. It was the crossing of the Forth at the narrow slip of firm land between the vast morasses of the Flanders Moss and the widening firth, that mattered — Stirling Bridge, as ever the key.

The enemy must approach that key crossing east-about or west-about; round Stirling Rock, castle and town, by the flat links of the Carse, boggy and broken by burns, runnels, ditches; or west by the scattered woodlands and hillocks of the former royal hunting park, really only an extension of the great forest of the Tor Wood. One, or both, of these. There was no alternative.

So, as his forces assembled from all over the land, Bruce applied his wits to the task of turning this entire approach area into a maze of traps. It was not difficult in the low-lying Carse, for the flats were already waterlogged and pitted with holes. It was the causeways and banks and dykes through it on which they had to concentrate, and, as mud-slaistered as his men, the King spent long May days cutting, digging, undermining and covering over, so that to the untutored eye the place appeared as before — but was not.

The inland higher ground was a much more difficult proposition. The scattered woodland would admittedly tend to break up enemy heavy cavalry formations; but the whole area was too widespread and open for defensive works. Only at one point was there any opportunity to improve on nature. All this upland of knowes and hollows was drained by small burns south-eastwards into a major stream, the Bannock Burn, which cut a deepish ravine for itself down to the windings of the Carse flats. The road from the south crossed this stream, just above the edge of the low ground, and there was no other convenient crossing near by. The ground on either side of this crossing was open, so there was no opportunity for ambush; anyway, a huge army cannot be ambushed. But some distance beyond the crossing, the road forked, one prong following the flats, the direct route to the town and Stirling Bridge; the other striking off to the left, and upwards, across King Alexander's New Park, round the west side of the Rock and so along the south lip of the Flanders Moss. If the English decided on a west-about approach, they were bound to take this road. And before it actually climbed to enter the wooded area, there was a wide grassy level entry — indeed, it was known as The Entry, especially constructed for deer-driving. The Entry was flat and nearly half a mile wide to the south, but narrowing-in like a funnel to a mere fifty or so yards on either side of the road.

Here Bruce got to work, using the same ideas that he had developed at the Battle of Loudoun Hill — and hoped that it would not again be Pembroke who led the English. Deep lateral trenches were dug at irregular intervals across that triangle of green, with stakes in their foot, and all carefully covered with woven brushwood and then grassy turfs brought from areas out of sight. The wooded flanks were honeycombed with individual pits, and the glades sown with spiked iron caltrops. It was all done on a vast scale, ten times that of Loudoun Hill, with thousands of men working, Bruce and some of his lords amongst the others, like labourers;

even bishops and abbots might be seen leading trains of pack-horses laden with turf and brush. All men, great and small, knew that Scotland's continued existence was in the balance.

And still the English did not come. Large numbers had assembled at Wark, on the south side of Tweed, spies informed — but the main armies delayed. To some extent, Bruce was grateful for more time — Angus Og, after capturing Man, had returned to his Hebrides, and dispersed his host. Summoned again urgently, he had not yet put in an appearance. It was possible that he might be sulking. But in another respect, this delay was a problem, for the camouflage over his pits and trenches tended to dry up a day or two after it was cut, and constant replacement was necessary. Bruce even had squads of men watering the turfs, like monks in a garden.

Then, in mid-June, word reached the King that the invasion had indeed started. The English had crossed Tweed with an incalculable host, its baggage-train alone extending for twenty miles. King Edward was leading in person, with the High Constable, the Earl of Hereford, and the Earl of Gloucester as deputies. Rumour had it that there were no fewer than ninety-three other English barons and lords present, with their levies, not to mention great contingents from Wales, France, Brittany, Guienne and the Low Countries. There were said to be twenty-three Anglo-Irish chiefs under the Earl of Ulster, Bruce's own father-in-law. Total numbers were impossible to ascertain, accounts varying from 70,000 to 200,000. Not that such figures were really significant. None knew better than Bruce that the true worth of any army depended not on sheer size — since this could only add to the problems of commissariat and mobility — but on its spirit, leadership and composition. It was that composition he demanded of his informants now; above all, what were the numbers of heavy armoured cavalry, and of longbowmen — the two vital arms in which Scotland was weakest.

Reports were now flowing in to the Scottish camp below the frowning battlements of Stirling, in a steady stream. The English were advancing, not by Berwick and the coast, but up Tweeddale and Lauderdale. They comprised ten distinct divisions, with Hereford's and Gloucester's in the van. Cavalry might number 40,000 or 50,000, but the heavy armoured chivalry, the knightly host, would be perhaps a tenth of that. Archers could be put at 7,000. Infantry was without number.

These figures, although still vague, were daunting. In a set battle, as this must be, the heavy chivalry were all-important — that is, knights and their like in full armour, mounted on destriers also fully armoured. Since the men's full armour weighed up to 100 pounds, and the beasts' five times that, only the most powerful horses could carry it for any length of time. Inevitably these were slow — but they were almost impervious to any assault save of their own kind. And of such Bruce would be hard put to it to raise 100; Scotland just did not breed such horses. Of light horse, moss-troopers and the like — hobelars, the English called them — he had perhaps 4,000; but against armoured chivalry these were of little avail, however splendid at mobile warfare. As to archers, he did not have 500, and no longbowmen.

And still no sign of Angus Og and the Islesmen — though it was known that they were on their way.

Bruce drew up his army in four main divisions, facing east so as to cover both possible approaches. The van, of picked infantry, with their long pikes for forming schiltroms, he put under his nephew Moray, as a sufficiently sober and steady man not to lose his head in the face of overwhelming odds. Edward, of course, wanted this place of honour; but his brother just did not dare risk it, with all at stake. Edward's brilliance was as a dashing commander of light cavalry, not the spearhead of a static and defensive host. He gave him instead half of the light horse, to hold the right flank, based on the line of the Bannock Burn. The other half was for Douglas, on the left — although nominally commanded by the High Steward; old James Stewart had recently died, and young Walter was now the Steward, a notable youth but inexperienced. Bruce himself commanded the main body, not exactly in the rear but somewhat back on the higher ground, where he could survey all, and especially the approaches to The Entry. Randolph's van was based on St. Ninian's Kirk, a strategic site above the Carse route.

It was Saturday, the Eve of the Vigil of St. John the Baptist, the 22nd of June — midsummer. Spies declared the English van to be at Falkirk, only ten miles away — though its rearguard and baggage was still rumbling through Edinburgh twenty-five miles to the south-east.

There was little sleep that night, and at four a.m. of a misty dawn, trumpets in the Scots host called men to Mass. There had to be, of course, many services — but there was an ample sufficiency of clergy, armed and armoured, to provide them. William Lamberton himself celebrated for the King's company. He sternly prescribed only bread and water for the day's substinence, as the Vigil required — poor fare as it was on which to fight a vital battle but he knew his fellow-countrymen, and the streak of fanaticism in them.

Bruce was still concerned to have detailed news of his enemy's numbers and quality, assessed not just by spies but by experienced commanders. He sent out a swift-riding vadette under Douglas and Keith the Marischal, to gain him the information he needed, risky as this was.

Then, as they stood to arms, the King reviewed his whole force, riding round the divisions, alone, on a small and wiry grey garron. He was clad in light chain-mail, under a gorgeous heraldic surcoat of the red Lion Rampant on gold, and on his helmet was a leathern crest of a demi-lion, ringed by a high crown. His review took a long time, with so many to exchange a word with — for surely never had a king and commander known personally so many of his host, veteran warriors with whom he had fought almost continuously for seventeen long years. Always concerned with the personal touch, today, which might well be the last for him as for them, he desired his identification with all to be complete. Besides, this uneasy waiting period had to be got over.

As he went his rounds, however, Bruce looked all too often back over his shoulder, westwards. Had he misjudged one man, in all these — Angus Og MacDonald?

Then back through the secret glades of the Tor Wood came Douglas and Keith, grave-faced. They had risked much, got very close to the enemy, and spoken with many scouts who dogged the English columns. And what they had seen and heard obviously had affected them direly.

"The van is not far off, Sire," Douglas reported, panting. "Indeed, it should be in sight at any time. The main host covers all the plain between the Sauchie Ford and Falkirk. And far beyond. I have never seen the like. As far as eye can see . . ."

"Sir James," the King interrupted him harshly. "Of course you have never seen the like! I did not send you out to tell me that. Such stories we have been listening to for days. I want facts. Firm details. Have you brought me none?"

Flushing, the younger man swallowed. "Yes, Sire. The van is of medium cavalry, under Gloucester and Hereford — about 6,000. It is said that there is bad blood between these, for though Hereford is High Constable of England, their King has appointed his nephew Gloucester, although but twenty-four, to be Constable for this battle. They have 500 mounted Welsh archers . . ."

"Pembroke? He does not ride with the van?"

"No — not Pembroke. But Clifford does . . ."

"Ha — Clifford! Clifford came too late for Loudoun Hill!"

"Pembroke, under King Edward, commands the main chivalry, Your Grace," Keith put in. "Three or four thousand strong, of barded destriers, a terrible sight."

"Only if they have ground they may fight on, sir!" Bruce snapped. "An armoured knight on a destrier, in a bog or a pit, is no terrible sight!"

His informants said nothing.

"It is my aim to make this an infantry, not a cavalry battle, God willing," the King went on. "Where is the English infantry?"

"Well back, Sire, I fear . . . the enemy will it otherwise. They will have it a cavalry battle."

"So much the better — so long as *I* choose the ground! It is all-important, therefore, that this day be fought where I want it. You understand? This day — and all days to come — depends on it. And, for the sweet Christ's sake — lift your visages! Smile, my friends! Men are watching you. Would you lose all, before we begin? I am fighting this battle with the land, and men's spirits. Have you naught of cheer for me to tell them?"

James Douglas blinked. "They are tired. The English are tired at least. Yesterday they rode over twenty miles. They have hurried. Men and horses are exhausted, they do say — in this hot dry weather. They can have slept little last night — and you burned all Falkirk's food and forage . . ."

"Aye — so be it. Order the trumpets to blow. I will address my folk."

"Angus, Sire? The Lord of the Isles? He has not come . . .?"

"No."

Edward Bruce had come up. "Did you really expect him, Douglas? I did not! The Islesman has ever fought for his own hand. And when it suited him. Now, at the pinch, why should he come?"

"He is on his way. That we know, my lord . . ."

"On his way! But will he arrive? In time? I think not. If we win — then, yes, he was on his way! And if we lose, he remains unscathed. And returns to his Isles faster than he came! That, I swear, is the MacDonald."

"And you, I swear, are wrong, my lord of Carrick!" Bruce exclaimed. "And even were you right — say nothing of it now, I charge you. This day depends on faith. Faith in God, in me, and in each other. Let no word or look or act destroy that faith."

When the trumpets had brought together a great part of the host, from its various positions, Bruce rode out alone on his grey pony, to westwards of them, so that his voice would carry from the slightly higher ground and on the westerly breeze.

"My friends," he cried, arm raised, when quiet was gained. "Today we put all to the test. Today Scotland stands or falls. And not only Scotland, but right, freedom and faith. If we fail today, these fall, with Scotland. Let none mistake. Today is fate hammered out on the anvil, hammered into shape."

There was a deathly silence at these grave words.

He went on. "But mark you, today we are the *hammer*, not the iron! And the land, our land, is the anvil. The iron is the arrogant invading English host, which once more desecrates our land. But this time, friends, is the last. This time, we shall hammer and bend and mould that great unwieldy host until it is fit—yes, and glad—only to be tossed into yonder pools and pows of the Carse, to cool its heat and hurt! This, God willing, we shall do. For it is a host as tired as it is great. Empty of belly, for it has outmarched its baggage train. At enmity within itself, out of envy and suspicion. And ill-led by a King whom men despise, and a Constable who has never fought a battle."

That aroused suitable spirited reaction, however exaggerated.

"We are otherwise. Few in numbers, yes—but united. We are rested, and if we fast, do so of our choice. Best of all, we know each other, have fought together over these long years. We are fighting men all. We know every inch of the ground. And our all is at stake. We win, or die."

Men cheered now, if a little grimly.

"I say, my friends, we win or die. The issue is simple as that. Therefore, I would have to command this day only those prepared to make the choice—to win, or die. Any who, losing would still live, I give fullest leave now to go. While there is yet time. I say this in good faith, and mocking none, deceiving none. Some may not be prepared to die, today, and for this cause. To all such, I say—go now. Any who have no heart in the business or qualms of spirit, it is best should leave us. Even should it be half our numbers. It is better for the rest..."

The King got no further. The snarling growl that rose from the packed ranks was angry, menacing, almost ferocious. If there was any movement, it was an edging forward.

Bruce was satisfied. He raised his hand again for quiet.

As he waited for it, and before he could speak, another sound than growling men reached all their ears. Thin, high, on the westerly breeze, came the wail of bagpipes at a distance.

Every head turned, to stare, the King's included—and, being higher than the rest, Bruce was able to see, curving round the base of the great Rock, north-westwards, the glitter of arms in the sun, and the waving of many banners.

"Thank God!" he breathed. "Thank God!" He raised his voice, to shout. "The Isles, my friends—the Isles! They come! They come! Angus of the Isles comes — in time. Constant was my faith in him — and justified!"

In the uproar that followed, Douglas it was who spurred out to the King's side, to grab his arm and point in exactly the opposite direction. There, eastwards, sunlight glittered on more arms and banners, more, vastly more. Rounding the shoulder of the land behind the township of Auchterbannock, where the road, the ancient Roman Road of Antonine, drove its causewayed course above the marshlands of Forth, came the English van. Calling for trumpets, Bruce commanded the swift dispersal to positions.

There was now no more waiting and talk. Deputing Campbell to welcome Angus Og, and to attach his force meantime to the main rearward, the King himself took the 300 or so light cavalry allotted to the main body, Carrick and Annandale mosstroopers, and rode with them at fullest speed south-westwards and into the cover of the scattered tree-dotted flanks of the Tor Wood. Hidden therein he swung eastwards, down through the twisting hollows of the broom-grown knowes, until they came out into the open level ground, the little grassy plain between the Bannock Burn and the mouth of The Entry to the New Park, with the road running through it. With the enemy not yet in sight from here, he and his men dismounted and seemed to take their ease in the sun. They were bait, royal bait, for the trap.

They had not long to wait. From here they could see the houses of the Milton of Bannock, where the road crossed the Bannock Burn; and here, presently, the English van began to appear, advancing cautiously, only two miles from Stirling and with some at least of the Scots army in view.

Bruce waited, himself hidden, fretting in the face of that daunting threat, until a considerable portion of the enemy cavalry was across the burn, and not only in full view but less than half a mile away. Then he ran out from cover towards his own scattered men, Irvine bearing a small version of the Lion Rampant banner behind him. Waving and shouting, as though in some panic, he got his 300 mounted, but slowly, awkwardly, and into some sort of order, seemingly just aware of the English approach. About one-third of the party he then sent streaming off, north-westwards into The Entry, along a line that would seem haphazard but was in fact carefully avoiding the hidden transverse trenches and lateral pits. The others he kept milling around, as though uncertain or waiting for stragglers.

To some degree the stratagem worked — but only partially. The apparently panic-stricken and retreating Scots did entice the English, but only a small portion of the van. One or two squadrons of cavalry, numbering about 400 riders, detached themselves from the mass and came spurring forward at speed.

Bruce cursed. This was of no use to him; no use in springing his elaborate trap for a few hundred, and so reveal it for all the rest. Swiftly he had to re-assess his position.

The lame-duck procedure would not serve now. But if they were instead to stand and fight, or seem to, the main van might be coaxed to come to the rescue of its spearhead. Unfortunately he had sent fully 100 of his men away in obvious flight already, which left him with only about half the numbers that were descending upon them. If he could get his detached hundred back...

Bruce sent a single rider after them, and then waved his 200 into two squadrons, to advance towards the now charging enemy at a trot, leaving a gap in the centre. Two-to-one was rather better odds than the day would average, after all.

"That banner?" he jerked, to Irvine, as he rode out, a little in front of the rest, into the gap. "That is the cotised bend between six lions, white on blue, of Bohun, is it not? Hereford. The High Constable. But... he would never lead so small a band."

"There are three mullets in chief, Sire. A second son, perhaps. But, Your Grace — this is folly! To hazard yourself thus. To give battle. On... on a garron! Unarmed! If you were to fall, now, all is lost before it is begun...!"

"Never fear, Willie! This is scarce giving battle. We but coax and draw and cozen. And this garron can outrun the heavier English beasts. And I am not unarmed." He drew out a light battle-axe from its socket at his saddle. "Hereford has no son. That must be his nephew, Sir Henry de Bohun. See — get back to the others. Tell them to wheel and sidestep. A mêlée. No true battle, but a mêlée. Go — quickly."

The enemy were less than 300 yards away now, their knightly leader and his esquire with the banner somewhat in front — a young man by his manner of riding. Pray that he was inexperienced.

Bruce was still moving forward, at a slow trot, vigilant, calculating. This must be timed to a nicety...

Then, suddenly, unexpectedly, the entire situation changed. That young knight had sharp eyes, it seemed, quick wits, and a lofty ambition. Even at 200 yards he must have spotted the gold crown that circled the King's basinet — the sun would be gleaming on it. Clearly his shouts rang out.

"The Bruce! It is the Bruce! Himself!" Then he was turning in his saddle, waving back his ranks. "He is mine! Mine! Back! Back, I say!" And couching his long lance, he stooped low, digging in his golden spurs. "A Bohun! A Bohun!" he yelled, as he thundered forward, alone.

Bruce caught his breath, taken by surprise. Here was a fix! Folly indeed. For both of them. To dodge and wheel and bolt now, before this open challenge to single combat, was inconceivable for the King of Scots. Yet he was undermounted and under-armed, without lance or even sword — these left with his heavy charger up on the hill. He had only this light battle-axe and a dirk. Yet he had no choice but to stand — or be for ever shamed. Irvine had been right. If he fell now, all was lost. This — this was worthy of his brother Edward!

There were only moments for racing thoughts. Grimly the King reminded himself that he was the veteran, the man of experience, his nerve tried in a hundred frays. He had other advantages — a more nimble horse, and a notable reputation with the battle-axe.

He altered nothing, therefore, as the other hurtled down on him. He did not draw aside, crouch, or even change his mount's quiet trot. Above all, he did not pull up — for a horse can much more swiftly answer the rein and knee when already in movement, than when halted.

It might so well have been a tournament, under the afternoon sun — save that one jouster had no lance. Now only a few yards separated them, and eye looked into hot eye. Brucc made his only disposition. Suddenly he tossed the battle-axe from his right hand to his left.

The Bohun saw it, and in the split seconds left to him, adjusted accordingly. It could only mean that his opponent was going to pull to his right, to the left of himself, and so any blow would have to be left-handed. He therefore swung his lance just a few degrees to his own left.

With only feet to spare, Bruce jerked and kicked his garron to the left, not the right, directly across the front of the galloping charger, causing it to veer and peck. In almost the same movement he flung his axe back into his right hand.

Only by bare inches was a collision avoided. But the lance-tip, swinging round wildly at the last moment to the other side, did not come within a foot of Bruce's shoulder. And as the other plunged past, bent low over his couched lance, the King rose higher in his stirrups, reaching up, and brought down that battle-axe right on the crown of the Bohun's crested helm, with all the violent strength of a mighty spring released.

With the deep crunching of shorn steel and bone both, the gleaming blade drove down and down, splitting the head open, in spouting blood, to the very breastbone and gorget, where it was jerked to such an abrupt stop that the wooden shaft snapped off in its wielder's hand. Charger and reeling, ghastly rider careered on until Bohun fell with a resounding crash.

The victor, his garron still trotting forward, was left with a foot or so of splintered timber and a wrist and arm numb with the shock. He had scarcely realised the power of that right arm, recent sickness or none.

The enemy line was still halted, under Bohun's esquire, so swiftly left leaderless. There were shouts from behind Bruce as his 200, ignoring previous commands, surged forward for the King.

The uncertainty, now, of Bohun's line, still 250 yards away, and stationary, was very evident, hesitating whether to resume the spoiled charge, stand still, or retire. Their doubts could only have been advanced by activity behind as well as in front. Trumpets sounded from the main English van, and some part of it at least began to move forward. At the same time, renewed shouting from still farther in front heralded the return to the fray of the 100 lame ducks. Bohun's esquire did what any sensible man would have done — nothing. He waited.

Bruce again was faced with decision. It would be suicide to confront the entire English van, with his 300. But by turning back, he still might be able to lead the enemy into his pits . . .

Then there was a new development, intimated by new trumpet-blowing from the right flank, from the Tor Wood. Down through the glades came Edward Bruce, to the rescue of his brother, with some 500 horse. The King almost wept. Everything was forcing him into battle, the wrong battle. Yet he could scarcely blame Edward.

It was with relief, therefore, that he perceived that only a small proportion of the English van was in fact advancing to the aid of the Bohun company — even though they did so under the ken-speckle banner of Gloucester himself. Hereford, the veteran, was holding the main host back. Those trenches and pits were still to be unused.

With Edward now charging down on the right, there could be no real choice for the King. He had to go forward, into the attack — and hope that it could indeed be a limited engagement. All would depend on Hereford.

Caught up by his own 300 now, Bruce rode straight for Bohun's waiting line, useless axe-shaft in hand. With a crash they met, and, since the English were in only two ranks, plunged through, on impetus rather than fighting, and little of casualties on either side. There was Gloucester, with perhaps another 500, not far ahead.

That Earl was a young man, barely twenty-four, and though

gallant, unused to battle. Seeing the King of Scots unhalted in his advance directly in front, and a new and large force charging down on his left flank, he did not panic, but sought to change his dispositions — not easy in a headlong cavalry attack. While retaining half his men to confront the King, he sought to swing the other half round to face Edward Bruce's assault. It was not entirely successful as a manoeuvre — and his whole force lost vital speed.

In the event, the result was complete chaos, on both sides, with mounted men crashing into each other, milling, falling, and no coherence or control anywhere, the sort of battle commanders suffer in nightmares. Gloucester himself was one of the first to be unhorsed. But any advantage was with the Scots, since they retained the impetus. In a whirling impenetrable mêlée, the clash moved south-eastwards. The English were not in fact defeated — but it looked as though they were.

In the confusion, two trends in the leaders' thinking had their inevitable effect on the struggle. Bruce did not want to get drawn within striking distance of Hereford's main van; and Gloucester desired to get back to that same van. As a consequence, both sides tended, almost imperceptibly, to draw back. Only Edward Bruce would have reversed the process — but his brother reached his side, and made his wishes known in no uncertain tones. He in fact ordered Edward's trumpeter to sound the retiral.

Whether Gloucester, shaken and remounted on a riderless beast, realised this is not to be known. But he was only too glad to be able to lead his own people in detaching themselves from the disorderly embroilment. In groups and batches and handfuls the English disengaged and streamed back towards their main body.

The Bruces found themselves masters of the field, such as it was. Edward would have pursued farther but the King was adamant.

"Back, Edward," he cried. "Back to your own position on the hill. As do I. God is good — but if Hereford attacks now . . .! Quickly, or we may have won a bicker and lost a battle!"

So the two Scots companies separated, and turned to ride back whence they had come, leaving the shambles behind. Sir Henry de Bohun was not alone, after all, on the trampled grass.

Avoiding the unused trenches, pits and caltrops, Bruce headed for the high ground. Hay, Campbell and Boyd, from the main rearward, came riding to meet the King's party, in highly doubtful frame of mind, not knowing whether to cheer or weep, to praise or rail. The grizzled Boyd was most certain, and outspoken.

"Sire," he accused, "you hazarded all! It was ill done. If you had fallen there, in that fool's ploy, Scotland would have gone down. Yon was a laddie's victory — not a king's."

"I know it, Robert my friend," Bruce admitted. "But my hand was something forced. You must bear with me. See — I have spoiled a good axe! Can anyone find me another?"

"Who was the Englishman, Sire?" Hay asked. "In the first fray. We saw it all, but could not tell the arms."

"Henry Bohun, I think — nephew to Hereford. Would you have had me run from him, in single combat? Before two armies?"

There was no answer to that, of course — save for the roaring cheer of the Scots massed ranks as their King rode up. That first blood of the battle may have been folly, bad generalship — but there was no doubt as to what it did for the Scots morale.

* * *

"Those are Clifford's colours," the King declared. "I know them all too well! Where is he going?"

"He takes the Carse road," Gibbie said. "Hereford will have sent him forward, as scout, to see if they may win round by the north and east, to Stirling Bridge. By the flats . . ."

"That is no scouting party. There are 700 or 800 there. And they have left the Carse road. They are heading farther out, in the marshes. Picking their way. Medium cavalry again."

"They must have a guide," Campbell suggested. "From Bannock, belike. Who knows the marshes."

"A guide, yes. But more than that, I swear. One who knows more than the marshes. Our traps and defences! Someone from Stirling Castle, perhaps. Who has watched us cutting and digging the Carse causeways. From the castle they could see all that we did. Someone may have won out, and reached Hereford. And now leads Clifford northwards through the outer marshes, by divers ways."

The King was back, with his rearward leaders, on the vantage knoll where he had spent the first part of the day, the rest of the Scots host returned to their allotted positions. The great English van was still stationary, cautious, around the Milton of Bannock, holding the burn-crossing. Obviously Hereford was awaiting the arrival of the main invading army under King Edward and Pembroke, which must have been far behind. But meantime he had despatched this powerful cavalry force under Clifford, to probe a way north-abouts to Stirling Bridge.

Angus Og, weary and yawning — for he had marched all yesterday, all night, and most of this day, after having had to fight a sea-battle with John of Lorn and the English fleet at the mouth of Clyde — pointed.

"These Carse marshes — who knows them well? Can the English

win round to Stirling, by the shore? The tidelands? If so, we must retire, behind the Rock. By the west. Or be cut off."

"Myself I know them well enough," Bruce answered. "Clifford can go another mile or so, twisting and turning. Then he will reach the Pelstream Burn, flowing into the Bannock. It is wide, with soft mud banks. Tidal there, a mile inland. They cannot cross that. They must turn inland also. There is no ford or crossing place until they reach the road again. That bridge we have demolished. But there is a ford there. And they will have avoided all our traps."

"We cannot halt them, then?"

"We must — God aiding! That is why Moray is posted at St. Ninian's Kirk, with our van. He is just above that reach of the Carse. Can see it all from there. But ... I never thought to see cavalry take the soft road through the marshes. Foot, perhaps — not horse. So Moray has only foot ..."

"Then send these, your own cavalry, to aid him."

"I dare not, Angus. Not yet. This may be but a ruse, to draw off our cavalry. That will never be the main battle, in those swamps and pows. So long as Hereford and Gloucester stand there, with the main van, I dare not detach my cavalry. Any of it. There are still 5,000 enemy cavalry waiting below us, in their van. My nephew must make do with his foot. Pray he uses them well ..."

"Sire!" Hay exclaimed, gulping. "Look there! He comes — my lord of Moray! Himself." And he pointed north-eastwards.

"Christ God in Heaven!" the King swore. "Has he taken leave of his wits, as well as his men?" Cursing, he left them, spurring.

"Sire — I have word for you," Randolph called, as they neared. "Ill word. We could be in trouble. I fear the English will know of the Carse traps ..."

"Damnation, man!" his uncle cried. "The more reason you be not here! What madness is this ...?"

"I had to see you. We must change our plans. I could not send another. One of the Carse fowlers came to me. He saw three men slipping through the marshlands, southwards. After midday. Secretly. One he swears was Sir Philip Moubray himself. From the castle. If it is he, he will know all. Our dispositions. Traps."

Bruce actually grabbed his nephew's arm. "Quiet, man! And look! See you there!"

Moray had cut across through the hillocks from St. Ninians, a mile away. For the first time, staring, he saw Clifford's force out on the low ground. "Merciful saints!" he groaned. "Already! And Cavalry ...!"

"Aye, cavalry. And you are here! Get back, man. Quickly!"

"But — here is what I came to say, Sire. This makes it more than ever vital. We must change plans. If we cannot hold the Carse road, you can be cut off. Your main host. We must retire on Stirling Bridge . . ."

"There is neither time nor the men to change our plans now, sir. Retire from our strong position, in face of the enemy ready to move, and we are lost. Better that we *be* cut off, I say — since if lose we die here. But, by the Rude — we have not lost the Carse road yet! Get you back, my lord of Moray, to your post. A rose has fallen from your chaplet, today! But you may pick it up again, yet! You have time, still. Get you down, with your foot, into those marshes, and halt me Clifford. At all costs. He must not cross the Pelstream ford. A schiltrom, this side of it . . ."

Without waiting for the rest, or another word, Moray went.

Bruce sent a runner to Douglas, on the left flank, to be ready to go to the assistance of Moray. But only if need be, and with only half his cavalry. Leave the Steward with the rest, in case the English main attack developed meantime.

Anxiously the King and his colleagues returned to the vantage-point, to watch.

Presently they saw Clifford's cavalry reach the south bank of the Pelstream Burn near its junction with the Bannock, and then turn westwards, inland, following it. No cavalry — nor foot either — could cross that mud-lined, mud-bottomed, tidal stream. If Moubray was leading them, he must have told them so.

The Pelstream meandered across the flats in serpentine coils, and Clifford's hundreds made slow work of following its sodden, sedge-lined banks. But even so, not slow enough for Robert Bruce, grudging them every step. He groaned at the thought of all their barriers and ditches avoided.

They could see the tip of St. Ninian's Kirk's tower from here, but Moray's force was not in view. Time — it was always timing that counted. Could they be in time? And would Hereford wait?

The first hint of action the watchers gained was from the enemy. Clifford had halted, facing almost due west now. Then his long straggling column began to fan out and form into some sort of line abreast over the marshy ground, no longer following the burn's edge. It was clear that they had seen something the King's group could not see.

"Moray must be down!" Bruce exclaimed. "The English prepare to attack."

Then the Scots began to appear, from the dead ground at the foot of St. Ninian's hill, just where the Pelstream Burn passed out of view, banners brave amongst them, but looking a rabble nevertheless. They were this side of the burn.

"What chance have they?" Hay demanded. 'Foot against cavalry. They must be ridden down . . ."

"They have a chance. If Moray holds them tight. Remember Wallace at Falkirk. The schiltroms held. The English cannot charge strongly in bog . . ."

This last was very obvious, even from more than a mile off. Distant trumpets shrilled, and in some sort of extended order, Clifford's cavalry began to advance again. But it was no charge, and no true line could be kept.

The Scots could be seen to be forming, now, into a single great square, based on the Pelstream ford. So their backs were secure, at least; only three sides might be attacked. The bristle of their long spears, thrust out like a hedgehog's spikes, could not be seen from this distance — but they could be visualised. Moray's and Hugh Ross's standards flew above the eight-packed ranks.

It was a strange battle to watch, so remote, so slow-motion. Like the cumbrous waves of a heavy tide, the cavalry lapped and swirled and seethed around the rock of the packed spearmen, unable to gain sufficient space or hard ground for the charging impetus they required, while the Scots had to adopt a purely defensive role. Moray was the right man for that, however. If anyone could hold those dense ranks tight, disciplined, unyielding either to panic or the temptation to rush out and break position, he could.

Bruce's glance often turned in the other direction, south-east instead of north-east. The main English van remained stationary, neither sending further reinforcement for Clifford nor itself moving out along the road towards the high-ground Scots positions. Either there was division in policy amongst the commanders, or the orders to await the arrival of the King and Pembroke, with the heavy chivalry, were paramount.

How long the struggle at the Pelstream Burn lasted, none could have told — but it seemed endless. Had Clifford had archers, all would have been otherwise of course; but lacking them, it was almost stalemate. At one stage, admittedly, it seemed as though the English were achieving a break-in, the schiltrom sagging in front until, at least from a distance, it appeared nearly divided. The watchers fretted helplessly — and then perceived a division of cavalry spurring over the higher ground, this side of St. Ninians, Douglas's well-known banner at their head. But Douglas halted there, on the lip of the descent, and waited, inactive but yet a threat. He could see the position better, and presumably decided that Moray did not actually require his intervention. He was obeying Bruce's commands to the letter.

Presently it was apparent that the English advantage was indeed not sustained, and the schiltrom restored to its proper shape. And gradually a new element in the battle became evident; a great bank of fallen horseflesh, dead and dying, was building up in front of the ranks of spearmen, helping to protect the Scots. No doubt there were fallen men amongst the beasts, but inevitably it was the horses that took the brunt of the punishment from that savage frieze of pikes, rather than their mail-clad riders.

This grim barrier of their own slain obviously became an increasing obstacle to the enemy. Still they continued to attack, but noticeably the pace flagged, intervals lengthened.

"Clifford is held!" the King declared, at length. "He cannot break Moray, and cannot cross the burn. He must turn back. Praise God — that fight is ours also!"

Soon it was apparent that Clifford perceived the fact as clearly as Bruce. A trumpet sounded the recall, out there on the flats, and the English cavalry, having lost perhaps a third of their number, drew off. Reforming, they turned heavily to ride back whence they had come. The sound of throaty cheering came echoing across the Carse — and everywhere re-echoed along the Scots positions.

"Whatever the result of the greater battle, there we have seen something men will wonder at for long," Bruce told his companions. "I have not heard, in all the story of war, where infantry have defeated a greater force of mailed cavalry in the open field. If Moray does naught else, he has had his hour, I say!"

"But by your contriving and devising, Sire," Hay pointed out.

The King shook his head. "Moray's glory is not thereby lessened."

Some time later, with the sun already sinking behind the Highland Line to the north-west, Moray, with Hugh Ross, was summoned to the monarch's presence, to receive a very different welcome from the last.

"Your chaplet is secure again, my lord," Bruce said, holding out his hand. "Would that I might add to it. But I am in no position to do so, this day — since my own wears none so well, as you will hear! But I thank you, and yours, in the name of all. Had you failed, and Clifford won behind us to Stirling and the bridge, we could I think, have but prayed that we might die bravely tomorrow, all of us. We may so have to do, for the main battle is still to be fought. But our rear is secure and our spirit high — thanks to you."

"I but obeyed Your Grace's orders," his nephew said, flushing. "For the rest, I have not even blooded my sword! Sir Hugh also. All was done by my stout spearmen."

"Very well so. It is as it should be. You have proved better commanders than I, today. We shall see if I can do better tomorrow!"

"Tomorrow, Sire?" James Douglas had come up, to add his tribute to Randolph, whom he had so chivalrously refrained from aiding lest any of his glory be diluted. "There are still two hours of daylight. And a midsummer night . . ."

"See there, Jamie," Bruce said, pointing. "King Edward has come, at last, with his main force. There will be no attack tonight, I swear. The English have much talking to do! Having waited so long, Hereford will not attack now that the King is here. And Edward will be in no state, after long marching, to throw in his army just arrived. At this hour. We have tonight."

The Scots stood to their arms for another hour and more, nevertheless, as ever more of the vast array of power and might came into view. It was a tremendous, a terrifying sight — although scarcely so for Bruce himself, whose commander's eye was inevitably taken up with the problems and logistics of it all. That enormous mass of men and beasts crowding in over the Bannock Burn, and stretching far out of sight beyond — where were they to be put? That night? The terrain just would not hold them.

Presently the King burst out with a mighty and wondering oath. The English van, so long stationary, had started to move again — but not now in battle array, or towards the foe. They were moving down into the Carse, slowly, in troops and squadrons and columns, picking their way amongst the pools and pows, the runnels and ditches, spreading out over the wide marshlands. On and on they went, and on and on others came after them, to appropriate any and every island and patch of firm ground, to settle and camp for the night. Down into that great triangle of waterlogged plain, rimmed by the Bannock Burn, the River Forth and the escarpment of St. Ninians, went the flower of England's chivalry and score after score of thousands of her manhood, in an unending stream.

Almost speechless, Robert Bruce shook his head. "Dear God," he muttered, "I would not . . . I would not have believed it. The folly of it!"

"They have little choice," Douglas said. "And is it so ill a choice? It will be uncomfortable, yes. But there is water for all their horse, at least. And the men, though scattered, are safe there from any night assault from us. Their flanks protected by the burn and the Forth . . ."

Bruce stared at him with a strange look in his narrowed eyes. "You think so? Pray God, then, that they stay there! Pray God, I say! And now — call me a council. We shall eat while we have it. Every commander here to this knoll . . ."

Chapter Twenty-one

There was little of darkness that June night, and little sleep in it for Robert Bruce at least. Despite the pleas of his friends that he should rest, much of it he passed in restless pacing, anxious eyes ever turned eastwards, down to where the myriad fires of the English host pinpointed the dusk and made the floor of the Carse like the reflection of a star-strewn sky.

The King was, for that stark period, a prey to doubts and dreads. He was that, indeed, a deal more often than even his closest colleagues knew, and always had been. In a few hours he might well be dead, along with so many others. But it was not that thought which unmanned him, but the fear that what he had fought for so terribly for seventeen long years might well be thrown away in one brief day. All along, he had had that dread, and so had resolutely refused to hazard his all in any great fixed battle. That evening, during the council-of-war, he could have been persuaded, even yet, to give up all and withdraw, under cover of night, far to the west, to Lennox perhaps, as that Earl had suggested, and the skirts of the Highland hills, where no English army could follow, so that at least total disaster was avoided. He had been tired, of course, as he was tired now — yet could not rest.

Oddly, almost as strong a fear in his mind was of a reverse sort. Fear that the English would perceive how dangerous was their present position, and move out of it, to the attack, before he could take advantage of their mistake. Attack — there was the crux of the matter. The enemy position in that marshland was fair enough as a resting place, if inconveniently waterlogged. At least it could not be outflanked. It was only a trap if the host had to fight therein, an armoured and horsed host. It was no place for fighting, and undoubtedly the English had only gone there to bivouac. But if they could be brought to battle there . . .! Which meant attack, early attack. By the Scots. But only if the Scots left their strong defensive positions, with their clear line of retreat westwards. Only thus could the potentialities of the carseland be exploited. Was this folly upon folly?

So Bruce paced the dew-drenched turf of his green knoll, and fought in his mind and spirit and will his own Battle of Bannockburn that night. Yet, at the back of it all, he knew what he was going to do, and his greatest fear was that the enemy would be aroused and on the move, out of the trap, before he could spring it.

When he could restrain himself no longer, soon after three o'clock of the Monday morning, the King had all others roused from their rest — but quietly and not by any blowing of bugles. Then, in the dove-grey, pre-sunrise light, Maurice, Abbot of Inchaffray, celebrated High Mass before the coughing, yawning shadowy host, and, aided by the other clergy, great and small, went round the serried ranks with the Sacrament.

As, thereafter, they all partook of a more material but still austere refreshment, Bruce addressed them sternly, but confidently, swallowing his own fears, telling them what he, and Scotland, expected of them this day, the birthday of John the Baptist, and of how it was to be achieved — with the help of the said saint, also Saint Andrew of Scotland and the martyr Saint Thomas. And not least, their own abiding belief in freedom. Where he led them today there could be no turning back, for him or for any. Holy Church had blessed them. And the Chancellor, the Abbot Bernard, would carry the sacred Brecbennoch of Saint Columba before them in the fray. As would the Dewar of the Main carry Saint Fillan's arm-bone. For himself, he here and now proclaimed full pardon for all and every offence committed against the Crown to all who fought that day, and relief from every tax or duty of any who fell in the battle. Let the victories of the day before hearten them — but also let them remember that today the veterans Pembroke and Ulster were with King Edward, and they must look for firmer command. Therefore, the Scots would strike first — and God be with them, and surprise likewise!

With a minimum of noise, no shouting or trumpeting, the Scots army then marshalled itself into its four great divisions under the same commanders as before — only this time, all the cavalry was put under the command of Sir Robert Keith the Marischal, to take the extreme left wing, nearest Stirling; and the non-fighting clergy, with the porters, grooms and other non-combatants, sent, with the baggage and pack-horses, to a green ridge north of St. Ninians, where they might watch and wait.

With the sunrise just beginning to stain the eastern sky in their faces, the silent advance commenced.

They gradually moved into line abreast, Edward Bruce's division this time in the place of honour on the extreme right, and very slightly ahead; then Moray; the Douglas and Walter the Steward; then the King with the largest number, including the Islesmen under Angus Og. Keith and the cavalry, farther left still, held back meantime. Bruce, only chain-mail again under his vivid surcoat, marched with the rest, Irvine leading his grey pony. Where he was going was no place for chargers — as he hoped he might have opportunity to prove to Edward of Carnarvon.

At every pace of the misty, mile-long, downhill march, the King listened with ears stretched for the sound he dreaded — English bugles blowing — and heard none.

At length, on the very lip of the Carse, the light growing and the night mists dispersing, the English outposts became aware of the untimely and outrageous Scots advance, and everywhere trumpets began to shrill.

"I swear King Edward must have had a better night than I!" Bruce commented to Angus Og, feeling better already with the prospect of action at last. "Now, let us give him a busy day!"

When Bruce had told his own trumpeter to make the first, short flourish of the day, he stepped forward, with Abbot Bernard and the Brecbennoch reliquary, a little in front, and sank to his knees. And behind him, while fiercest excitement and bustle, not to say panic, seethed in the roused and far-scattered English camp, the Scots ranks knelt in their thousands, and a ragged but heartfelt rendering of the Lord's Prayer rose amongst the shouting larks above the Carse of Stirling.

"Your prince is become much concerned with God, these days. For an excommunicate!" the Lord of the Isles murmured, to Lennox, as the droning prayer ascended. "Is it for his own soul? Or to encourage the faint-hearted? Or perhaps to please the flock of priests it is our misfortune to have with us?" The new Pope Clement had, unfortunately, been persuaded to renew the excommunication.

"I think that anathema weighs on his mind," the Earl said. "As does his recurring sickness. But — he will fight none the less well for it. As must we, to survive this day."

" 'Fore God — let us but commence it, Malcolm man!"

Rising from his knees, Robert Bruce slowly drew his great two-handed sword, and raised it high above his head. Then, swiftly, dramatically, he brought it down — but with explosive effort and every ounce of the strength of his powerful wrists, arrested the descent of its five-foot length so that it held sure, steady, pointing directly at the enemy's centre. No words were needed now. With a roar that drowned all the trumpet-calls, their own and the enemy's, the long Scots line surged forward.

The tactical situation was simple, astonishingly so considering the large numbers of men involved. The huge English army was penned in an enormous trap of level, pool-pitted and ditch-crossed swamp, with islands of firm ground, hemmed in on three sides by the Bannock Burn, the River Forth and the Pelstream Burn. The fourth side, to the west, where the ground lifted to the New Park escarpment, was now barred by the half-mile-long line of advancing Scots.

It was no charge, of course, even of infantry — the ground precluded that. Cut up with runnels and stanks and sumps draining into larger canals and ditches, it was terrain to be hopped and picked and sidled over, even by nimble men. For cavalry it was practically impassable, save by circuitous routes.

The English, of course, were not idle while this wholly unexpected attack on so broad a front was being mounted. Swiftly they were rallying, forming up into their troops, squadrons and companies. Already there was a distinct drift of mounted men southwards towards the entrance point to the carseland of the night before. Then the drift turned to something more definite as the cavalry of the English extreme left, bivouacked nearest to the Milton of Bannock, achieved some sort of formation and began to hasten to gain and hold that vital bridgehead. First to enter, the night before, it was Gloucester's section of the van. Yesterday's misfortunes had not quenched the young Earl's eagerness. His great banner well to the fore, his trumpets braying, he was going to be first into action again.

But another and equally impatiently active earl was intent on gaining the same bridgehead — Edward, Earl of Carrick. For this very reason Bruce had given his brother the extreme right today. Leaping, bounding, even using their long pike-shafts as vaulting-poles across the pows and ditches, the Scots foot raced for the bridge.

Gloucester's cavalry was grievously hampered by the terrain, though it was better here than elsewhere, as the English had pulled off the doors and roof-timbers of every building in the Milton and around to form little gangways and bridges across the ditches. But even so the horsemen had to twist, go slowly and most often in many single files. As a result, though a few reached the bridge first, they were isolated, and went down before the charge of the thrusting pikemen. By the time that Gloucester himself reached the scene, Edward Bruce had roughly formed his men into two schiltroms, side by side, at the bridge. There was no room, firm ground, for the English to pause and marshal their horsed ranks. Oncoming riders pushed earlier arrivals forward. Undoubtedly Gloucester would have formed up for a less piecemeal attack if he could; but like Clifford the day before the lack of firm ground gave no opportunity. He and his men plunged at and circled the schiltroms disjointedly.

Gallantly impetuous yet, and an example to his men, the Earl plunged into the narrow gap between the schiltroms, hoping no doubt further to divide them. None of his people followed him therein, not even his standard-bearer. With a wild yell the pikemen of the inner sides of both formations broke and surged towards each other, spears and dirks jabbing. Gloucester's horse went down, and its rider disappeared under the press.

Edward Bruce yelled also, not to kill, to save the Earl as prisoner, for his great ransom; but it was too late. Gilbert de Clare, nephew of King Edward and kinsman of the Bruces also, was dead, in the first minutes of the battle.

Unhappily his scattered cavalry drew back into the marsh's safety.

All of this was not, of course, evident to the rest of the advancing Scots line; but that their right had had the best of it was clear, and greatly enheartened many. Bruce himself, though cheered, was otherwise preoccupied. As well as having to pick an awkward way for himself, like the others, across the shocking terrain that he had chosen to fight on, his primary concern at this stage was the menace of the English bowmen. Properly handled they could yet end everything. The enemy might in heavy cavalry he believed he had neutralised, by fighting here; but the archers . . .?

Bowmen, to be of real advantage in any battle, had to be massed, preferably on a flank and if possible on ground somewhat higher than the rest, where they could see, and enfilade the enemy without endangering their own ranks. The previous night Bruce had recognised all too clearly where, in this situation, the archers should be placed. Indeed, there was little choice. Well to the north-west of the English position, on their extreme right not far from where Moray had fought Clifford at the Pelstream ford, was an isolated hogback of slightly rising ground amongst the marsh. Here the bowmen could stand secure and do maximum damage. But, in fact, no archers stood there this morning; instead heavy cavalry occupied this key position, excellent for weighty horses admittedly, but quite useless tactically in that they could not move from it without plunging into soft bog again. There the pride of England's chivalry was safe, but unserviceable. It had been the first magnet for Bruce's glance, when the mists cleared. Surely if Edward Plantagenet had not the wits to see it, Pembroke or Ulster should have done.

Now, amongst all that wild upheaval in the Carse, one double movement at least was clear, definite. The heavy chivalry at last was being moved south, out of the precious island, and from behind, nearer the Forth where the enormous numbers of English infantry had been allotted the softest ground of all, the archers were being marched out north-westwards. Somebody had recovered his wits.

Bruce himself, leading the left and most northerly of the Scots divisions, was most nearly opposite this danger point. But there was much of grievously waterlogged ground between. That was why he had given Keith the cavalry, and sent them still farther to the north. They could sweep down from the escarpment, cross the Pelstream ford, and reach the edge of that raised island via that burn's south bank — the way Clifford had come.

Bruce shouted to his trumpeter to sound the special call that would set Keith moving. It would be a race between light cavalry with a difficult mile to cover, and bowmen on foot, ploughing their way not only through marsh but through the confusion of their own moving and marshalling cavalry, with half that distance to go.

The King could do nothing more about that meantime. Because of the lie of the land, he had the widest stretch of carse to cover before making contact with the enemy. He could only continue his slow advance.

Moray, away to the right and nearest Edward Bruce, had already made contact, and, formed up into two schiltroms also, was creeping forward behind his frieze of long pikes. Douglas in similar formation would soon be doing the same. This was the chosen strategy and pattern of attack. In close hedgehog formation the Scots line was to move slowly but inexorably forward, whatever the state of the ground, pivoting on Edward Bruce at the Milton bridge, eventually one long line of no fewer than nine mobile schiltroms — for the King's own was to form into three — pushing back and compressing the enemy into the Forth. Such was the crazily ambitious design.

The English, admittedly, were in an appalling situation tactically as well as strategically. In essence they were a cavalry army, and their cavalry was all to the front. But to bring it to bear successfully on the advancing Scots, its commanders required space for marshalling and manoeuvre and firm ground to gain any impetus. Here and there, of course, there were better stretches, patches of solid footing, drained re-entrants. And here the knightly chivalry did well — although nothing like a real charge could be mounted. But though half a mile of front might sound a lot, in any modest battle, for the vast English numbers it was wickedly narrow. The enormous majority even of their cavalry could not be brought to bear on the Scots. As for the infantry, hidden behind all this, it might as well not have been there. Not at first, at any rate. Its time might come.

Bruce, with only 200 yards or so between him and the first of the milling enemy, paused to form into three schiltroms under Angus Og, Gilbert Hay and Neil Campbell. He remained with Angus in the centre. But while this went on, standing in mud up to the knees, his glance was ever turning northwards. Keith's horse were streaming across the Pelstream Burn with a bare 600 yards to go. The first of the bowmen had reached their stance, but only in twos and threes. They would all know the result of that race in a few minutes. And, if Keith lost it, his liege lord and many another might well be dead men in as brief minutes thereafter, skewered by the dreaded English cloth-yard shafts.

They moved on, stumbling, floundering, wading, cursing, in the mire, all the knights' fine surcoats and emblazoned shields now mud-covered, anonymous. The great Lion Rampant Standard of Scotland itself was blackened with slime, borne by Sir Nicol Scrymgeour, son of Wallace's faithful Alexander, whom Bruce had knighted only that morning, along with young Irvine and not a few others. On their right Douglas and the Steward's schiltroms were already engaged, but still moving forward by fits and starts, a sorry-looking crew of mud-plastered bog-trotters, but a-bristle with forward-pointed, jabbing pikes that no horsemen had yet penetrated.

Then the King's division were into the fray. Bruce had sheathed his great sword in exchange for a battle-axe, much handier in close fighting. Not that he had opportunity to wield it. The front ranks had to be pike-bearers, with their long spears outthrust. So long as they remained upright, those behind could only contribute moral and vocal support. Even the last was difficult for lurching, ploutering, bemired men needing all their breath.

Some of the English knights and chivalry, infuriated at the uselessness of their horses in this swamp, had dismounted and were fighting on foot, using their lances as spears. These presented the most serious threat. But the majority of the quality, the lordly ones, were so encumbered with heavy plate armour, weighing up to a hundredweight, that they could scarcely walk on firm ground, much less fight in a bog. Most therefore remained in the saddle — at least until their frightened and mud-fettered chargers were speared under them, and they crashed helplessly.

It was not a battle, in truth — only a vast, horrible and unimaginable chaos of mud and blood and screaming frustration. On both sides, but inevitably much the more so with the English, horse-and-armour-encumbered and lacking any true formation or plan of action. If battle it was, it was men against clutching, engulfing bog, the land of Scotland given its own chance to fight.

In all the excitement and confusion, it was some time before Bruce realised that they were not being showered with arrows. He could not pause in this undignified plunging amidst other jostling bodies, but he did make darting glances to the left. And there, on the higher ground, he could see Keith's banner flying bravely, and horsemen hacking and swiping at fleeing archers in every direction. The King's sigh of relief was only metaphorical, but very genuine.

He knew now that this battle could indeed be won.

But that, of course, was only a future possibility, however heartening. Meantime there was only bog to cover and English to kill, by the thousand, the ten thousand. That June Monday of 1314, hell had come to the Carse of Stirling, hell for all men, almost as much for the Scots as for their foes.

In fact, it was the Scots who grew exhausted first, since on them fell the greatest and most sustained exertions. And there were so many English to confront, to beat down, to drive before them, but still to cope with. Endless hosts and legions of men, penned in and therefore unable to escape, to be fought. There was no limit to it, no relief for flesh and blood on that terrible plain, hour after bloody hour.

At some stage Bruce realised, from his own state, that the said flesh and blood could not indeed stand much more. His men were dropping now, not so much from wounds as from exhaustion, stumbling into runnels and pools and just not rising again. The nine schiltroms now represented a barely recognisable line; in fact few were recognisable as even schiltroms any more. It was long since there had been any shouting and slogan-crying; only the involuntary screaming of agonised men and injured horses. And not half, perhaps not a third of the English host was accounted for. The vast mass of it was still there before them, ever more tightly compressed in its dreadful trap. Dying, yes — but dying so very slowly, selling its life so very dearly. This could not go on.

Yet — and here was the deepest hell of it — there could be no letup. The Scots could not, dare not, stop and go back, content with their partial victory. Still outnumbered fantastically, if they turned now, with all that quaking bog to cover again, they could and would be overwhelmed in disaster. There were still scores of thousands of the enemy who had not yet had opportunity to strike a blow, had barely moved, were fresh, unblooded. Give the demoralised cavalry a chance to get out of the way, and the untouched infantry behind could swarm forward to ultimate victory.

Bruce racked his tired, benumbed brain for what was to be done. He was still the commander, the only man in all this tortured plain who could still influence other men, by his decision, to any effective action — since the English leadership seemed to be completely at a discount. He had long since given up looking for King Edward, or Pembroke, or Ulster his own father-in-law. He was just one man struggling painfully on, in all-enveloping mud, amongst other weary men. What could he do?

If he halted the entire forward movement, however sluggish now, by trumpet call? What then? Exhausted men would sink, practically into torpor. He would never get them started again. The English would be given time to rally. At the very least, they would see opportunity to cut their way through, to escape. And on firm land again, those untouched thousands would recover.

What else? For once, Robert Bruce's mind, so fertile for stratagem, produced no alternative to this treadmill of horror.

Then, strangely, the matter was taken out of his drooping hands. Distant trumpets and thin high cheering, from far behind, turned some heavy heads, the King's included. There, coming rushing down the escarpment from the New Park, was a new host, horse and foot, banners flying. From nearly a mile away it could not be seen that its leader was a gaunt stooping bishop, William Lamberton, on a palfrey; that its cavalry were priests and grooms on packhorses; that its infantry were porters and cooks and old men, even women, with staves and meat-choppers and carving-knives; its banners blankets and plaids tied to tent-poles. On it came, out of hiding amongst the knowes, a new and vociferous host, with no hint of exhaustion about it.

In that moment the Battle of Bannockburn was finally won. Appalled, the English commanders saw their enemy reinforced, and accepted it as the last straw. King Edward had esteemed the battle lost long before. He was no coward, however poor a monarch, and had been agitating, not how to save himself but how to extricate any large number of his people from this trap. But now even the veterans Pembroke and Ulster urged immediate flight — and when the King would have turned his horse instinctively southwards, towards their entry to that place of disaster, Pembroke it was who grabbed the royal arm and practically pulled his monarch off his massive destrier. Unseating squires and heralds from lighter, faster horses, the two Earls got the King mounted again, and were off with him, northwards. They had learned from Clifford of the north-about route to Stirling by the Pelstream ford, and rightly guessed that it was unlikely to be guarded now. A score or so of determined, cruelly-spurring men, they left that stricken field while yet most men stared unbelieving at the baggage-train army.

Quickly, of course, the English command's flight was perceived, and swiftly men reacted. The Scots, suddenly reinvigorated, yelled their triumph and surged forward. The English decided that it was every man for himself, and acted accordingly.

Abruptly, then, the battle was over, although the fighting was not. That was to go on for hours yet, as men tried to hack or race or swim their way to freedom, and died in the process, thousands upon thousands of men, so that the very River Forth was choked with bodies. Not all died, of course, but a great many did, singly, in groups and in large companies that stood and sold their lives dearly — for there was a mighty backlog of old scores to pay off, and ordinary soldiers and men-at-arms were not worth taking prisoner. Lords and knights and gentry, of course, were different; their ransoms would set up many for life.

It was not much past noon, in fact, when King Edward fled the field; but King Robert was still there when the sun was sinking, still seeking to command, to control, to bring order if not mercy out of utter shambles and chaos. He had, indeed, exerted some major control from the beginning, detaching Douglas and sending him and Keith, with some part of the cavalry, in hot pursuit of King Edward and his fleeing nobility, round Stirling Rock. Then he set up some sort of headquarters on the green mound from which the archers had been dislodged, and from there endeavoured to bring order out of bedlam, fatigued as he was. And there, presently, William Lamberton came to him, and they gripped hands in silent, eloquent thankfulness, hearts too full for words, tears in their eyes for all to see, neither ashamed.

They were there still, as the sun sank, the Bishop superintending the treatment of wounded, Bruce, swaying on his feet, directing, directing, with all his commanders out supervising the clearance of that desperate field, halting massacres, shepherding prisoners, receiving belated surrenders, collecting and separating the dead, garnering and protecting booty — all this, when a party approached under Gilbert Hay. He brought a number of bodies borne on shields and hurdles, and beside one of these limped a tall, smooth-faced man in middle years whose magnificence was only partly hidden by the universal mud and dried slime.

"Here is one, Sire, who claims you owe him much," Hay said. "It may be that he speaks false — for also he claims to be Earl of Gloucester. Whereas here is the true Gloucester!" And he gestured to one of the corpses.

"Robert Bruce knows who I am," the prisoner declared, with dignity. "And if I know *him*, he will not forget."

"Aye — Monthermer! My lord — it is a long time. Twelve years, no less," Bruce said, and held out his hand. "I have not forgot.

Here are changed days — but had it not been for you, I would not have lived, I believe, to fight this day. My lord High Constable — this is the Earl Ralph de Monthermer, who held the earldom of Gloucester during his stepson's minority. He once served me more than well."

This was, indeed, the man who had sent Bruce the spurs and the shilling, that night in London in 1302, as hint to flee, when the Comyn had betrayed him to King Edward and he was to be arrested the next morning; the man who was Edward Longshanks' son-in-law, having married Edward's daughter, after her widowing from the de Clare Earl of Gloucester, Bruce's cousin, and so had been given the earldom until the child heir should reach man's estate. And that child heir it was who now lay, pierced by a score of Scots pikes, there beside his stepfather.

Bruce went to look down at the dead, once-handsome young man, his second cousin whom he had never met in the flesh, and shook his head. "Gilbert," he said, sighing. "Gilbert de Clare. At least you died nobly."

"Aye. He leaves this sorry field in better state than do most of us!" the older man said. "God knows, I could wish myself in Gilbert's place. Here, for the rest of us, was shame on shame."

"The fortunes of war, friend. Do not blame yourself. At least you did not run! With your brother-in-law!"

"I was not with him, the King, at the end. I took command of Gilbert's men, when he fell. But . . . Edward, the King — he is a fool! And has shamed us all this day. Yet, he could not stay to be captured, Robert. The King. You must see it. His ransom — his ransom would have bought all Scotland's freedom!"

Strangely, levelly, the tired Bruce looked at Monthermer, and then nodded. "Scotland's freedom is bought, I think!" he said softly. "Not by a king's ransom, but by the courage and blood and sacrifice of her people. Remember it!" Then he smiled, however slightly. "But you, Ralph — you are now my guest. You shall be treated as such. No ransom is required of you. I pay my debts — all of them! My lord Constable — have the Earl Ralph conducted to the Abbey of Cambuskenneth, to the Abbot's good keeping. And bestow the body of Earl Gilbert, my cousin, in his chapel. I will come there anon . . ."

But Hay had another body to show his monarch, covered by a cloak. Wordlessly twitching back the cloth, he revealed the dead but still arrogant face of Robert, Lord Clifford.

"Clifford!" Bruce cried, chokingly. "Robert Clifford, 'fore God!" And then more quietly, "Aye — before God, at last! May He . . . have mercy . . . on his soul! May he . . . rest in peace."

The King had made many merciful pronouncements of late. But this was as hard a sentence to say as any he had ever enunciated.

He turned blindly away, as William Lamberton gripped his arm.

Chapter Twenty-two

In the refectory of the Abbey of Cambuskenneth, almost islanded in a great bend of the Forth only a mile or so north of the battlefield, Robert Bruce played a new role, armour, weapons and the panoply of war for once cast aside. He sat at a table, with the Abbot Bernard, his Chancellor, and other clerks who yesterday had been soldiers, and was flanked by other tables manned by monks and priests, even of high degree — any who could write and figure on paper. And all around them men came and went, bringing, stacking, piling high, arranging, documenting the greatest treasure Scotland had ever seen. When the King of England went to war, it seemed, he did so in style — and in his haste to be gone, he had left his style behind. Cambuskenneth had become a counting-house.

Gold and silver vessels and plate, personal jewellery, gem-studded ceremonial weapons, crosses, orders and the like, gold-worked clothing, saddle-cloths, standards and banners, rich harness, was the last of it — even though there were over 200 pairs of knights' golden spurs alone. It was the armour, helmets and shields, much of it gold- and silver-enriched, captured or cast away by fleeing men, that half-filled the hall. King Edward's own shield, even his royal seal, lay on the table at Bruce's elbow.

The King yawned nevertheless. He was not much of an accountant — although none recognised better what this wealth meant to bankrupt, war-ravaged, all but starving Scotland. He had in fact slept no more that night than the nights before — though on this occasion he had been conducting a knight's vigil, in the Abbey chapel, over the body of Gilbert de Clare, of Gloucester, his cousin, a vigil and personal thanksgiving combined. Few, indeed, had slept much anywhere in Scotland that night, save for the drunken — the bells had seen to that. Every bell in the land had been ringing since nightfall — and not all were so mellow and harmonious as the great carillon of Cambuskenneth which even yet kept the warm noontide air throbbing around them. The jangle from nearby Stirling's host of belfries across the river was head-splitting, nerve-shattering, and dearly the King would have liked to command its cessation — but did not.

"I calculate the treasure already listed now at worth no less than £200,000, Sire," Bernard de Linton mentioned, pen pausing for a moment.

"Aye. No doubt," the King conceded. "Very good. A great sum. But — this is not a cattle-mart! Do you have me here to price and sum . . .?" He yawned cavernously.

"Your Grace," the Abbot said severely. "Here is new life for your kingdom. Yesterday we shed sweat and blood. Here is life's blood of a different sort. But a sort that the realm must have."

"I know it, friend. Know also that to you, as Chancellor, this is all-important. But for myself, I am more concerned to hear the figures of our losses yesterday, which still you do not find for me."

"It takes time, Sire. Until the Lord Edward comes back. And Sir James, with the Marischal. And Sir Neil, and the others, pursuing the enemy. We cannot know for sure. Even bodies counted are no sure token. For who can tell a Scots corpse from an English, sunk in mire? Stripped. Drowned in Forth. But — comfort Your Grace — we believe that our losses are small, as against those of the English. In dead. Even in wounded. Of these, they say there are more men injured by their own splintered pike-staffs than by enemy steel. Of knights we do know numbers. But three are dead. Sir William, younger son of the Earl of Ross. Sir William de Vipont. And Sir William Airth. Only these, though more are wounded. Against already counted thirty-five English barons and nobles, over 200 knights and 700 esquires and gentry. Dead. So great a victory is scarce believable . . ."

There was an interruption. A small party of Islesmen came into the hall, pushing before them a white-haired elderly man dressed only in blood-stained silken shirt and breeches, his fine features lined with pain and fatigue. Yet this man, though roughly handled, still clutched a sword to him, determinedly though not aggressively. After a word with the guard at the door, the little pary was permitted to approach the King.

"Lord," their spokesman said, in the soft Gaelic, "this man we have but now found. In a bush. He says that he will yield his sword to none but you. He said we could kill him before he gave it up. Almost we did . . ."

"Enough of this heathen gibberish!" the old man interrupted strongly, for so frail-seeming a captive. "I am Marmaduke Tweng. Will Your Majesty accept my sword?"

"Ha! Sir Marmaduke!" Bruce actually rose to his feet. "I greet you, sir. Yours is a name all men would honour. You are hurt?"

"Honour . . .?" the other demanded. "Is there honour for any Englishman hereafter? Our honour is fled! Better that it was trampled in yonder mire!"

"Not so, sir. Honourable men do not lose their honour so easily. Because others forget theirs. Yours is safe, I say. It came intact from Stirling once before!"

Sir Marmaduke Tweng was, in fact, one of the very few notable Englishmen who had come out of Wallace's campaigns, especially the Battle of Stirling Bridge, seventeen years before, with name unsullied — even though he had held Stirling Castle against the Scots for long years thereafter. Wallace had said that if there were but a few more Twengs in England, Scotland would never win her freedom.

"Aye — this foul corner of Scots mire has been the curse on me! I say, the curse of me." He had to shout, above the clamour of the bells. "King Robert — will you accept my sword?"

"That I will not, Sir Marmaduke! Keep your sword. No man wears one more worthily. You are no prisoner. So you pay no ransom." Bruce turned to the Chancellor. "Give these MacDonalds something for their trouble. A gold spur perhaps. And let them go. You, Sir Marmaduke, may not have lost your honour or your sword — but you have lost much, I see. Blood, it seems — and armour, helmet, mount, shield, seal? See you — take what you will from here." He waved a hand at all the stacked booty. "And choose you a horse. Moreover, show yourself to my physicians. You are my honoured guest until you leave this Scotland."

The older man's voice quavered now, and was barely to be heard above the bells. "You are kind. Noble. There speaks a king indeed!" He coughed, to hide his emotion. "Would . . . would we had such a king, in England. May I . . . kiss your Majesty's hand?" He raised his white head. "One matter more, Sire — of your patience. I have a friend. Sir Edmund de Mauley. Lord Seneschal of England. Do you know . . .?"

"I fear he lies in the chapel crypt, here, sir. With . . . others. He at least did not flee."

"And . . . and my cousin? Sir William, Lord of Higham? The Lord Marshal of Ireland?"

"He also, Sir Marmaduke. Their honour is safe."

"For that I thank God . . ."

A disturbance turned all eyes. A gorgeously-clad figure in splendid surcoat and gold-inlaid armour was being carried in on a cot-house door, a great eight-pointed cross picked out in rubies on his breast, one who had escaped the mud — but not the blood. Gilbert Hay escorted the body in.

"Sire — I know not who this is. None know. They found him beneath a heap of slain. But the cross, of St. John. Of Rhodes. A stranger knight. But important, I think . . ."

"Important, yes." That was Tweng, strongly. "*I* know who that is. He was with the King. But turned back when the King fled. Saying it was not his custom to flee. *He* would not run. Not he who is named the third greatest knight in Christendom!"

"Dear God!" Bruce exclaimed. "You mean . . .?"

"Aye, you should know — since you yourself are called the second such, Sir Robert! The first is the Emperor Henry of Luxemburg. And this, Sir Giles d'Argentin, was the third. God rest his noble soul!"

"Amen!" the King said. "D'Argentin! The Crusader. Name me not in the same breath with this man, sir. A man whose harness I am scarcely worthy to unloose! One day, I had hoped — do hope — myself to carry my sword against the Infidel. He, d'Argentin, would have been my choice as leader. Sweet Christ — what a loss is here! Had I but known his presence . . ."

"What could you have done, Sire . . .?"

Hay's words were drowned in the clatter of hooves and clank of armour outside. A new and larger party came stamping into the refectory, to bow, the Earl of Moray leading.

Bruce sighed, and shook his head. "Well, nephew?" he said, but scarcely welcomingly.

"Stirling Castle has surrendered, Sire," Randolph declared. "Your standard now flies over it, at last. Here is Sir Philip Moubray, the governor."

"Ha — Moubray!" Bruce stared at the narrow-faced, prematurely grey, youngish man, one of his principal enemies. "Moubray, who has cost me dear indeed. He gives me back my principal fortress? And himself! What shall I do with him, nephew?"

"Hang him, Sire!" Hay asserted, briefly.

"I asked my lord of Moray, Gibbie. Let him answer, for he is his prisoner, it seems."

"Your Grace," Randolph said slowly. "I would urge you to do with him as you did with me."

"You would? He is a traitor, my lord."

"As was I."

"You were my own kin."

"You seek my mercy on him, then?"

"I do. Two nights ago you praised my stand. At the Pelstream. Offered me reward. Now I ask it. This man's life. He was my friend once. He is a valiant knight. He would not have cost you so dear were he not. You have need of such still, I think."

"M'mmm. Sir Philip — how say you? It was on Methven field last we met, was it not?"

"Yes, Sire." The prisoner came forward, and fell on his knees. "I struck you from your horse. Sought to capture you. I have never failed to be your foe."

"Why?"

"I believed your cause wrong. And Comyn's right."

"And now?"

"I do not beg for my life, Sire. But if you choose to grant it, I will serve you faithfully until its end."

Bruce took a turn away, and looked down at the dead face of Sir Giles d'Argentin. "So be it, Sir Philip," he said. "Too many brave men have died, to no advantage. Live, then — and serve me as well as you served my enemies." And he gave him his hand to kiss.

When the King sat down again, the Abbot Bernard spoke as low-voiced as was practical, in the bells' clamour. "You are over-generous, Sire," he complained. "Needlessly so. Mercy is good. But . . . Sir Marmaduke Tweng is a rich man. He could well have paid a great ransom. And this Sir Philip Moubray has great lands. In Lothian. They should be forfeit. Your Treasury needs all such, with a whole realm to build anew."

"It will take more than siller to build it anew, Master Bernard! All this accounting and inventory is turning you huckster. Let us not become merchants, in this our deliverance. Forbye, we have plenty. Plenty for ransom, have we not? What did you say? Thirty-five lords and barons? 200 knights . . .?"

"No, no, Sire — that was the numbers slain. Captured, and for ransom, there are but twenty-two lords. Though some 500 of knightly rank."

"Mercy on us — and you grudge me Sir Marmaduke!"

"Yesterday Your Grace freed the Earl Ralph. He would have brought a mighty ransom. I but remind you not to be too kind in your triumph, too gentle . . ."

"Gentle! Save us — do you really esteem me so gentle, man? My brother Edward once named me that, I mind. But you are a wiser man, I thought! I am nothing gentle. I but choose my victims! Some, I swear, will not find me kind, nor gentle, hereafter."

The next visitors to Cambuskenneth Abbey proved the King's words, despite all their nobility. For this was a noble band indeed, brought in by Edward Bruce and Robert Boyd, weary with long riding, all of them, but proud still.

"These I have brought from Bothwell Castle, in Lanarkshire," Edward announced, without ceremony. "Fleeing, they took refuge there. But that place's governor, one Gilbertson, decided to turn his coat. He delivered them all into my hands, in return for his own life." He paused, grinning. "Henry de Bohun, Earl of Hereford, Lord High Constable of England. Robert de Umfraville, Earl of Angus. Sir Ingram de Umfraville, former Guardian of this realm. Maurice, Lord Berkeley. John, Lord Segrave. Hugh, Lord Despenser. John, Lord Ferrers. John, Lord Rich. Edmund, Lord Abergavenny. Sir Anthony de Lucy. Aye — and a troop of lesser men outside."

"So-o-o! Here is the cream in the pitcher!" This time Bruce did not rise to his feet. "Save for the illustrious dead, here is England's pride and glory! With . . . some leavening of my own! I thank you, my lord of Carrick. And Sir Robert Boyd. You have done notably well. You have not heard how James Douglas fares? Chasing the Plantagenet? And Pembroke? And my good-sire?"

"Pembroke left them behind Stirling," Edward reported. "There he halted, they say, to rally his own fleeing Welsh marchmen and archers. He has over 1,000 of them. He is marching them to Carlisle. In good order. Too many for me to hunt, with my sixty horse. Besides, I had another game!"

"Aye. Aymer de Valence plays the man, at last! But — the King? Ulster?"

"Douglas will never catch them. They have better horses and near an hour's start. We heard that they had not drawn rein by Linlithgow! And they were still passing their own baggage-train heading north! They will be in Berwick, by this."

"A pity. I would have welcomed a word with my good-sire. About his daughter!" Bruce looked for the first time directly at the galaxy of stiff-necked if wary-eyed English lords — for the Umfraville brothers, though they held the Scots earldom of Angus, through marriage, were English in all else. "My lords," he said, "I have been accused this day of being over-kind, over-gentle. Insufficiently a huckster, a merchant! You are all King Edward's men — the old Edward. He trained you, as he sought to train me. You know how he would have acted, had he sat here today!"

There was absolute silence. All knew only too well what their master, Edward the Hammer of the Scots, would have done.

"He slew my brothers, as prisoners — three of them. Hanged, drawn and quartered. And my good-brother, Seton. And innumerable of my friends. Wallace he butchered unspeakably. *Your* King hanged his prisoners, my lords — and the earls he hanged highest of all! Tell me why should not I do the same with you?"

"*We* are not rebels, sir," Hereford said, coldly.

"Ha! Not rebels, no. You still say *we* were?" And when none answered that, Bruce went on tensely. "I would you *had* been rebels. I would have honoured you more. One rebel I have freely pardoned. Moubray! You are not rebels — you are cowards! Dastards! Your late liege lord Edward Longshanks would not have lifted a single finger to save you, this day. You know it. He would have forsworn you all. He, from being a noble knight, grew to become a savage, a brute-beast! But he was never a coward. Never would he have fled a field leaving scores of thousands who still could fight. As did his son. And as did you, my lords!"

"I pray you — spare us your strictures, sir," the Lord Berkeley requested with heavy patience. "We are your prisoners, and there's an end to it. Do your worst — but no preaching. From a brigand, a rebel! Of a mercy!"

Bruce motioned to his brother, and the other Scots, for patience. "You are courageous with your tongue, at least! Or is it mere proud English insolence? You are my prisoners, yes. And a brigand would hang you, out of hand. Would he not?"

"I think not. A brigand, impoverished and beggarly, would sell us! As you will do. For as high a price as he could gain! Never fear, Robert Bruce — we will pay our ransoms!"

Fists tight clenched, the King looked at the row of cold, arrogant, all but bored-seeming faces. Urgently he sought to control his temper. "Sir Marmaduke Tweng — who stayed to fight — named me the second knight in Christendom. You name me rebel and brigand. Which is it to be, my lords? How do you elect to be treated? By the knight? Or by the brigand? Choose now, and make no complaint hereafter."

"What matters it? The leopard does not change its spots."

"Nor the jackal become lion because it dons a king's robe!" That was Ferrers.

"Sire — you have won a battle. You will not stain it with dishonour?" That was Ingram de Umfraville, the former Guardian, who, with his brother, was in somewhat different case from the others, being, in theory at least, Scots citizens — and therefore *ipso facto* themselves rebels.

"So be it," Bruce said. "I shall disappoint none of you, my lords. You shall all go into the deepest pits of Stirling Castle. Each alone. You shall not hang — not yet! Bread and water shall be your diet — lest you grow contented with your chains. And there you will lie until your ransoms are paid. A brigand, I will sell you for a high price, as you say!"

"And your price, sir? What is it?" That was Hereford, the Constable. "We are not paupers. We will pay your price, in gold or silver, never fear. How much?"

"Gold and silver? Aye, that too. But I will have more than gold and silver, my lords." Bruce leaned forward, speaking slowly, carefully. "I will have what is mine restored to me, first. And you have much that is mine, in your England. My wife. My daughter. My sisters. The Countess of Buchan. My friends a-many. Held prisoner for long years. Shut away. In cells and cages. Grown old in your foul prisons. I have waited long for this. You cannot give me back my dead brothers. But every one of these shall be returned forthwith. My Queen first of all. Before any one of you see the light of another day from your deep pits. The surest messengers and fleetest horses are yours, to send for them, this very day. And if they do not come, within six weeks — no, a month — then you die. All of you. Die as my brothers died, as Wallace died, hanged, disembowelled and your entrails burned before your eyes! You understand . . ."

Without waiting, without daring to wait for an answer, the King of Scots rose, his heavy chair thrust back to fall with a crash, and turning, strode from the refectory without a backward glance, lest any should see the tears that streamed from his eyes.

Outside in the Abbey garden, as the bells clanged their joyful paeans across the marshes, Robert Bruce stared away and away southwards, blinking.

"Elizabeth!" he whispered. "Elizabeth, my heart . . .!"

Book Three

THE PRICE OF THE KING'S PEACE

For

ANDREW HADDON

who, too late, pointed out to me that the English monarchs only became majestic from Henry the Eighth's time, an eminence to which their merely gracious Scots counterparts never aspired.

PRINCIPAL CHARACTERS

In Order of Appearance

ROBERT BRUCE, KING OF SCOTS; Three weeks after Bannockburn.

SIR JAMES DOUGLAS: "The Good Sir James", Lord of Douglas. Friend of Bruce.

LADY ELIZABETH DE BURGH, the QUEEN: Wife of Robert the First, and daughter of the Earl of Ulster.

SIR GILBERT HAY: Lord of Erroll, High Constable of Scotland. Friend of Bruce.

SIR NEIL CAMPBELL OF LOCHAWE: Chief of Clan Campbell.

LADY MARY BRUCE: third sister of the King.

SIR HUGH ROSS: elder son of the Earl of Ross.

LADY MATILDA BRUCE: youngest sister of the King.

SIR THOMAS RANDOLPH, EARL OF MORAY: the King's nephew by a half-sister.

SIR EDWARD BRUCE, EARL OF CARRICK: the King's only surviving brother.

ANGUS OG MACDONALD: Lord of the Isles and self-styled Prince.

CHRISTINA MACRUARIE, LADY OF GARMORAN: Chieftainess of branch of Clan Donald; widow of brother of late Earl of Mar.

SIR HUMPHREY DE BOHUN, EARL OF HEREFORD: Lord High Constable of England.

SIR WILLIAM IRVINE OF DRUM: the King's Armour-bearer.

LADY CHRISTIAN BRUCE: the King's second sister, widow of Earl of Mar, and of Sir Christopher Seton.

LADY MARJORY BRUCE: the King's daughter, by Isobel of Mar.

LADY ISABEL MACDUFF, COUNTESS OF BUCHAN: sister of the Earl of Fife, and widow of the Comyn Earl of Buchan.

WILLIAM LAMBERTON, BISHOP OF ST. ANDREWS: Primate. Friend of Bruce.

MALCOLM, EARL OF LENNOX: Great Celtic noble, and friend of Bruce.

WILLIAM, EARL OF ROSS: Chief of Clan Ross, betrayer of the Queen.

BERNARD DE LINTON, ABBOT OF ARBROATH: Chancellor of Scotland.

Sir Alexander Comyn: brother of Buchan, Sheriff of Inverness.

Walter Stewart: 6th Hereditary High Steward of Scotland, the Queen's cousin.

Master Robert de Whelpington, Prior of Hexham: prominent English cleric.

Patrick, Earl of Dunbar and March: great Scots noble, formerly on the English side.

Sir Alexander Fraser: High Chamberlain of Scotland.

Sir Robert Fleming: Lord of Biggar; Bruce supporter.

Malcolm MacGregor of Glenorchy: Chief of Clan Alpine.

Sir Robert Boyd of Noddsdale: veteran Bruce supporter.

John MacDougall the Lame, Lord of Lorn: son of the Chief of MacDougall, Lord of Argyll.

Robert Stewart: infant son of Marjory Bruce and Walter Stewart; to be King Robert the Second.

Sir William de Soulis: Lord of Liddesdale; Hereditary Butler; friend of Edward Bruce.

Sir Colin Campbell: son and heir of Sir Neil. Stepson of Mary Bruce.

O'Neil, King of Tyrone: Irish prince.

MacCarthy, King of Desmond: Irish prince.

Master Adam de Newton: Prior of Berwick.

Sir Alexander Seton: Seneschal of Scotland.

David de Moray, Bishop of Moray: Uncle of patriot, Andrew Moray.

Dewar of the Coigreach: Hereditary Keeper of St. Fillan's staff.

Dewar of the Main: Hereditary Keeper of St. Fillan's left armbone.

Maurice, Abbot of Inchaffray: friend of Bruce, later Bishop of Aberdeen.

Sir David de Brechin: nephew of Bruce by another step-sister.

Sir Ingram de Umfraville: uncle of Earl of Angus: one-time Guardian.

John of Brittany, Earl of Richmond: English commander; nephew of Edward the First.

Sieur Henri de Sully: Grand Butler of France.

Sir Andrew Harcla, Earl of Carlisle: English commander.

David Bruce: infant son of the King. Later King David the Second.

Sir Henry Percy, Lord of Northumberland: son of Bruce's late foe, of same name.

PART ONE

Chapter One

Robert Bruce chewed at his lip — partly to hold back hot words. Already he had all but bitten the head off not only this wretched Englishman, but off his own good friends James Douglas and Gilbert Hay. Which was quite uncalled for and deplorable, he well knew. He kicked gold-spurred heels into his magnificent horse's flanks — there was a plethora of both magnificent horses and golden spurs in Scotland, since Bannockburn — to urge his mount a little way forward, ahead of his companions, where at least he might be spared their inanities.

And immediately, of course, the others spurred after him.

"That ridge ahead, Sire," Sir Roger Northburgh said, gesturing. "It will make a good viewpoint. We may see something from there."

"Good God, man — think you I need to be told that!" the King burst out. "Need I schooling from you that ridges provide viewpoints?"

Abashed, offended, the Englishman closed his lips tightly and stared straight ahead of him at the rolling Cumbrian foothill landscape, southwards.

Sir James, Lord of Douglas, thirty-one and looking younger, with the dark, almost gentle good looks which so strikingly belied his reputation, coughed. "Shall we ride ahead, Your Grace? Prospect . . . ?'

"No!" That was a bark, vehement as it was unkind. Bruce kicked his horse again, from a fast trot to a canter. And promptly, inevitably, the ivory-headed if splendidly dressed group of his close companions did the same, to keep up, unable to understand when a man desired to be alone with his thoughts. Even the King of Scots was entitled to that, on occasion, was he not?

Behind them, at a short distance, the heavily armed and armoured force of some 200 knights and men-at-arms urged their more burdened mounts to maintain approximately the same position, and the entire brilliant company pounded and clanked its way up the long tussocky whin-dotted braeside of Banks Fell, which flanked the fertile Vale of Irthing in North Cumberland. It was almost two years since Bruce had last climbed this ridge, and with a sword in his hand. Gibbie Hay, Lord High Constable of Scotland, had been there too, though Jamie Douglas, as Warden of the West and Middle Marches, had been otherwise engaged.

On the gentle crest of the hill — although it was not what the Scots would call a hill, at all — the King reined up behind the same scatter of wind-blown, stunted ash trees which had shielded them from observation last time. There was no need for such hiding today — but old habits died hard, and this was the automatic reaction of that man on any skyline. He peered down into the fair wide dale beyond, narrow-eyed.

"There they are!" Northburgh exclaimed, pointing. "Down by the river. Beyond that farmstead, this side of the Roman wall . . ."

"I have eyes, sir," the King snapped. A pulse was throbbing where his hard lean jaw-line met his temple.

It was absurd, of course, but the warrior King of Scots was nervous. The veteran of seventeen long years of savage war; the leader of more forlorn hopes than he, or any man, could count; the man whom Christendom had called its second-greatest knight, and now was calling its first; the victor of Bannockburn but three weeks previously — this paladin was nervous, agitated, as any callow youth, and, aware of it, irritable, despising himself. Yet, nevertheless, that throbbing pulse was beating out a very different tattoo in his mind and heart, a fierce exultation such as he had never known at Bannockburn or before.

"Sire — the trumpeter?" Hay suggested. "A flourish? They are little more than a mile away. They would hear . . ."

"No! No trumpeting. Think you we are bairns at play?"

"I will go down, Sire. To prepare them," Northburgh said. "To acquaint them of your royal presence . . ."

"You will not, sir. You, nor any. I go alone."

"But, Your Majesty — it is not fitting. And these are my people. I left them only to find you, to bring you to them. It is my responsibility, until, until . . ."

"Quiet, man! Of a mercy! Wait you here — all of you. This is *my* concern." And kicking his mount into action again, Robert Bruce spurred on alone down the south-facing slope, a brilliant figure in blazing gold and scarlet.

Now there was no holding back, no restraint. In this, at least, he could allow his pent-up emotions release. Beating his beast's rump with clenched fist, he drove headlong down through the slanting grassland and scattered hawthorns, turfs flying from drumming hooves.

The company ahead was not so large as that he had left; but it was a sizeable party nevertheless, of perhaps 100 men-at-arms, steel-girt, led by three or four gaily-clad leaders. No more than Scotland, Northern England was not a place where travellers might safely go less than well protected, in that first quarter of the fourteenth century.

When he was yet perhaps a quarter-mile from the oncoming party a rider left the group at its head, and came fast to meet him, long flaxen hair escaping from a fillet to fly in the wind.

As they neared, Bruce suddenly altered course somewhat. There was a clump of thorn trees a little way to the right. That man was still preoccupied with cover. The other rider followed suit at once.

The man reached the slight shelter of the scrub thorn first, and reining up abruptly, jumped down, so that he was standing wide-legged, tense-faced, waiting, when the woman rode in. She drew up a few yards from him, panting a little, and so sat, staring.

For long moments they gazed speechless, hungrily searching each other's faces with an intensity that was painful; the medium tall, wide-shouldered but lean man, with the ruggedly stern features and fiercely keen blue eyes; and the achingly fair woman, superbly mature in person, her facial lines at once delicate and strong, her beauty proud yet gentled with the lines of sorrow and adversity. So they stared, utterly lost in each other, until the woman slowly reached out her hands to him.

"My dear! My dear!" she managed to enunciate, chokingly.

He ran to her then, stumbling amongst the fallen cattle-barked thorn boughs, and threw himself against her flank, arms reaching up to her waist, face buried against her thigh, shoulders heaving under the gorgeous Lion Rampant tabard, emotion released at last in scalding tears.

Tears had never come readily to Elizabeth de Burgh. Often she had wished that they might. Now she stooped to kiss that bent head, her trembling fingers running through his thick wavy auburn hair. It was the sight of the few strands of silver in that thatch which caught her throat and let her weep.

"Oh, Robert, my heart!" she cried. "The sin of it! The sin of it!"

He looked up, wet-cheeked. "Forgive me, lass. I am sorry. It is joy, not sin. Not tears. Dear God — at last!"

Then she was down beside him, on the grass, in a single lissome movement that blotted out the years for Robert Bruce. Always she had been a magnificent horsewoman. They came into each other's arms.

They had only moments, of course. Then the English party came jingling up, and though they halted at the edge of the hawthorn clump, its trees were small and scattered and privacy was gone. Sighing, the man released her.

"Care nothing," she whispered. "We have the rest of our lives, my love." She drew back just a little. "Wait, you."

"I have waited . . . eight years . . . for this!'

"Two thousand, nine hundred and twenty-seven days!" she amended, nodding.

"And yet — you are more beautiful than even I remembered you. Or ever knew you."

"My sorrow, my Lord King — your sight must be failing you!" she got out a little unsteadily, smiling through her tears.

They took stock of each other a little longer, wordless, before the Queen turned and gestured towards the waiting horsemen.

"Here is Sir William de Hotham, who has been my . . . my host these many months. And who, with Sir Roger Northburgh, has conducted me to Your Grace safely and without delay."

The handsome elderly Englishman inclined his grey head. "You are kind, lady. I but did my duty."

"Duty can be done in more ways than one, Sir William."

"I have ever sought to do mine fairly, lady. Without fear or favour," the other gave back stiffly, a little warily.

"Lady . . .?" Bruce barked. "You are addressing a queen, sir. Do you address Edward of Carnarvon's wife as lady? Do you?" The transformation in the King was quite dramatic.

"Er . . . no, sir. No."

"And do you sit your horse, sirrah, when in your own monarch's presence, and he standing? Get down, man!"

As Hotham hastily dismounted, and his three stylishly-dressed companions with him, Elizabeth looked thoughtfully at her husband, and saw anew what eight years had done for him. The sheer authority of the man was almost frightening. She said nothing.

Belatedly Hotham doffed his velvet cap, for good measure. "Your . . . Your Majesty's pardon," he muttered.

"I understand that you, none of you, have ever acknowledged Her Grace's royal style. In all her years in England. You will do so now, sir, before you take leave of her."

"We had our commands, Sire. From King Edward. The late King . . ."

"Aye. Well, you have different commands now. Make your proper duty to Her Grace, sir — and be gone!"

Frowning, the Englishman came forward and sank on one stiff

knee before Elizabeth. He took her hand, to kiss it, though sketchily. "Your Majesty," he muttered.

"We say Grace in Scotland!" Bruce said harshly.

"Your ... Your Grace's servant," the older man amended, unhappily.

"Yes, Sir William," the Queen acknowledged quietly. "You may rise."

As the other Englishmen came to follow their leader's example, Bruce asked, coldly formal, "Has Your Grace any matter you would wish to raise before I let these go? These, your late gaolers? Any matter for which you would have them held personally accountable?"

The woman looked from one to the other, and shook her fair head. "No, Sire. The times of my complaint are past and done with. Better forgotten. Go, Sir William — without ill will. There has been enough of that, God knows!"

It was Bruce's turn to eye his wife keenly. That had been said mildly, almost gently — and Elizabeth de Burgh, whatever else, had never been a markedly mild or gentle woman. What had the years done to *her*, other than enhance her beauty?

"You may go," he said to Hotham, with a brief gesture of dismissal. "Come, my dear." And he held out a hand to aid the Queen into her saddle again.

As the others bowed low, expressionless, the King vaulted on to his own horse with notable agility for a man of forty, and without a backward glance at them, led his wife at a quiet trot northwards.

Some way up the hill Bruce, spurring close, reached out a hand to squeeze her arm, unspeaking.

They smiled, and continued to ride closer together, and more slowly.

At the crest of the ridge a long line of bare-headed men awaited them, on foot, Douglas, Hay and Northburgh in the centre. As the pair drew near, two trumpeters sounded a long and stirring fanfare that went echoing over and around all the soft green hills. The trio in the centre came pacing forward. But still a dozen yards from the royal couple, Sir James Douglas could no longer restrain himself. Abandoning the dignified pacing, he broke into a run, and flung himself onwards to the Queen's side. He reached up for her hand, and at the same time sought to fall on his knee. This being something of a physical impossibility because of the height of her horse, he had to content himself with an odd bent-kneed posture while he clutched and kissed her fingers.

"Your Grace! Your Grace! Dear my lady!" he cried. "God be

thanked for this! It has been so long, so very long. Here is joy, indeed . . ."

"Jamie! Dear Jamie — my good friend! My true knight still!" Elizabeth said a little unsteadily. "I might have known that you would come to meet me. And . . . and looking scarce a day older, I vow!"

"A laddie still," the Bruce's voice commented quietly, deeply. "But, by his deeds, a man!"

"I have heard of the deeds of Sir James Douglas, never fear," the Queen agreed. "All England has! The Black Douglas has been a name to tremble at these past years." Smiling, she released her hand from the younger man's eager grip. But she gave his own a little stroke in the process, that brought a flush of gladness to those almost delicate boyish features which so many men feared, as she turned to Gilbert Hay.

That man, ever quiet, a little hesitant of speech, retiring save in the face of the enemy, took that hand silently. But his grey eyes, upturned to hers, were full.

"Sir Gilbert — Gibbie Hay, my friend! You also. Another paladin! Renowned Lord High Constable of Scotland, no less! My two most fond and favoured knights. I thank you — in the name of sweet Jesu I thank you both. Not to have . . . forgot me!"

"Forgot!" Hay all but choked. "Did you think . . .?"

"No, no, friend. But it has been so long. And you with so much else to consider than an Irishwoman captive in a far land . . ."

"You might well have believed yourself forgot!" Bruce interrupted, almost harshly. "That in eight long years these paladins, your husband and your so leal knights, could not come for you! Could not, in all their warfare and victory, lead an expedition into England to release their Queen! God knows, we thought of it, talked of it, enough! Sought to plan it. But . . ."

"My dear — how could you! Think you I did not know it was impossible? I am a soldier's daughter, you will recollect."

"And yet — you must have hoped, lass? I swear you did. Even *I* did that! Deceived myself. When we won as far south as Durham two years ago . . ."

"I knew. I knew it could not be. Even then. To get so far as Durham was a wonder. And a terrible hazard. How it warmed my heart to know you so near. If more than a hundred miles be near!"

"If they had not held Your Grace so far to the south," Douglas said. "On the Humber. All great Yorkshire in between. A populous land, of great lords, great castles, large cities. Northumberland,

Cumberland, even Durham itself — these are different. But great Yorkshire to cross. We would never have won back to Scotland."

"Do not vex yourselves," Elizabeth pleaded. "All this I knew. As did the English! That is why they placed me there. Just beyond your reach. Yet sufficiently near to Scotland to tempt you. So that perchance you might attempt a rescue — and be trapped. That is why I was not sent to London, to the Tower, like Marjory. Is it not so, Sir Roger?"

Northburgh, the English hostage knight, prisoner at Bannockburn and sent south by the Earl of Hereford, England's High Constable, and the vast company of captured lords, to effect this part of the exchange, shrugged. "His Majesty scarcely takes *me* into his royal confidence, Madam," he said.

"This William Lamberton told us," the King acceded. "But even so . . ." He sighed. "I was sore tempted, many times. But — I was a king. Not just a husband. With a realm, a people, to free. Not just a wife!" That was said hardly, deliberately. "You understand?"

"I understand," she agreed quietly, but as firmly as he. "I heard you swear your coronation oaths, you will mind. As I swore mine."

"Aye. Well, then — enough of this. It is fifteen miles to the Border. Thirty yet before Annan, where we lie tonight. Time we rode." He turned. "You, Sir Roger Northburgh — you have other duties to perform. A-many. My daughter. My sisters. The Countess of Buchan. Bishop Wishart of Glasgow. All these captives to bring to me, before your lords at Stirling go free. See you to it. And quickly."

The Englishman bowed and took his leave, to ride on alone downhill towards Hotham's waiting company.

To ringing cheers and acclaim the royal group rode up to the main body of the Scots, the most lovely Queen bowing and smiling. When the remaining knights and captains had been presented and had kissed the Queen's hand, many of them renowned veterans of savage warfare, and all of whom had sought eagerly for the honour of making up this escort, impatient to be off, the King signed to a trumpeter.

With the bugle-notes neighing, the whole company turned to face Scotland. And biting her lips, Elizabeth de Burgh looked back over her shoulder for a last look at the land which had held her captive for what should have been the best years of her life and the productive years of her marriage.

* * *

In the much-battered redstone castle of Annan that night, Robert Bruce, waiting with such patience as he could muster for the hour when he could decently announce his own and his wife's retiral from the convivial but maddeningly protracted scene was unexpectedly involved in another reunion. The clatter of many hooves in the courtyard below intimated the arrival of another party, thus late in the evening. And a little later, two figures appeared in the doorway of the Great Hall, weary, travel-worn but glad-eyed — a man and a woman.

Had it not been for the fact that the dark, saturnine man was Sir Neil Campbell of Lochawe, chief of his clan, whom he had sent to collect her, the King would scarcely have recognised the woman as one of his own sisters. Eight years had dealt a deal more drastically with the appearance of the Lady Mary Bruce than with that of the Queen. He had last seen her, a plump, laughing tomboy of a girl of seventeen, in the woods of Strathfillan, after the rout of Dail Righ; now he saw a haggard, thin, great-eyed woman of fine but ravaged features, obviously desperately tired and leaning on her escort's arm.

"Dear God!" her brother breathed, rising.

All others rose, likewise, in that crowded hall. But though it was the monarch who moved towards the pair at the door, his wife outpaced him.

"Mary!" the Queen cried, and ran to the other woman, arms outstretched, all formalities abandoned.

The two women were embracing, murmuring incoherencies, as Bruce came up. He glanced at the Highlander, brows raised.

"The accursed English!" Campbell all but snarled. He was ever a man of strong feelings and few words.

"Mary, lass!" the King said. "What . . . what have they done to you!"

"Robert! Robert!" His sister turned to him, still clutching Elizabeth. "Praise God! I never thought . . . to see you . . . again."

"Praise! *Praise*, you say?" her brother barked. And then softened his voice and forced a smile. "Aye, praises be, lass. Welcome home, Mary."

"Home, yes." Her voice cracked and broke on the simple word, and with them she was in his arms, sobbing. "Home, Robert! But where . . . where is Nigel? And Alex? And Tom?"

He swallowed, and found no words. Annan Castle was indeed home to Mary Bruce. Here, third daughter of the fifth Robert Bruce, Lord of Annandale, she had been brought up, and when, with endless invasion and terror come to Scotland, her Celtic mother having died, her rather feckless Norman-Scots father exiled to die in England, and her three older brothers away at the wars, she had kept house for her two youngers brothers, Alexander and Thomas, a gay and youthful establishment despite the constant alarms, assaults and intermittent flights to safety elsewhere. Now she was back to where she could see, just across Solway, where those two young men had been hanged and disembowelled by Edward of England, following all too exactly in the footsteps of the third brother, Nigel a year or so before.

They led Mary Bruce to the table between them, as she sought to staunch and dry her tears – and it was notable how close Neil Campbell stayed to her, gently taking her travelling-cloak. While his sister recovered herself, the King questioned his friend.

"You had no trouble, Neil? No challenge to your mission?"

"None, Sire. Since Bannockburn, a hundred of them run from a couple of Scots! Our hostage, Heron, was well known in Newcastle, and made his own and his lord's needs very clear! Henry Percy himself delivered the Lady Mary into our hand. And . . . as God is my witness, I near cut him down there and then at the sight of her!"

"Aye. Well I can credit it! They . . . they still ill-used her?"

Mary Bruce herself answered that, having pulled herself together with a major effort. "No. No, I was no longer ill-used. After . . . after Roxburgh, they shut me up in the Gilbertine nunnery at Newcastle. I was kept alone. By myself. For near four years there. But treated not unkindly. The sisters were not harsh. After Roxburgh it was . . . a kind of heaven!"

All that company, listening keenly, was silent. None would dare ask this gaunt woman of twenty-five years of the fifth of her life which she had passed at English-captured Roxburgh Castle near the Border. There, on the late King Edward's command, she had been immured in an open cage of wood and iron, day and night, summer and winter, hanging over the outer walls of the castle, like a wild animal for all to see and mock — as also had the young Countess of Buchan at nearby Berwick Castle. How these two women had survived such appalling and long-continued savagery, none knew — and could by no means ask, yet awhile.

Neil Campbell growled in his throat.

"God be thanked, all that is now past, Mary," the Queen said. "We can start anew. A new life. Prayers answered. At last. Free again. As is Scotland. Thanks to . . . thanks to . . ." She looked at the sternly-frowning man who was husband and brother.

That frown, so permanently there these last long, terrible years, faded momentarily to a smile of great warmth, almost sweetness, strange in that rugged face, the blue eyes gleaming — for Robert Bruce had been a gay and laughing character once, whom not only his enemies had labelled irresponsible. "Thanks to every man in this hall," he finished for her. "And so many others. Living and dead. I have been blessed in my friends."

The deep murmur from all around was no mere polite and courtly acknowledgement of a royal compliment. There was not a real courtier present — and the Bruce did not pay compliments.

"God be thanked indeed," Mary agreed. "I grow hoarse thanking Him, and all saints. But . . . Christian?" she asked, after her elder sister. "And little Matilda? And Edward? Aye, and your poor Marjory, Robert? How is it with them?"

"Edward you will meet in Stirling. He is well. And, it seems, contemplating marriage at last! Of all women, to Ross's daughter, Isabella. The man who betrayed you to the English, at Tain!" A shrug, and another brief smile. "Pray God she may tame him somewhat! Maltida is well also — and none so little now. Indeed, she looks for happiness already — and towards that same family, strangely. To Sir Hugh Ross. Who has proved a better man than his father! Christian and Marjory are still in England, prisoner — but likewise to be exchanged for these English lords at Stirling. Of whom we have a-plenty! I have sent for them. But they are held further south . . ."

Although it was not long before Elizabeth led her sister-in-law away to see her bedded, it was a deal later that, at last, the King could take his wife's arm and withdraw in becoming fashion from the bowing, excited company. Wordless, they climbed the winding turnpike stair together. In the lofty but modest tower chamber which had been his bedroom as a boy, the King closed the door behind him with a sigh, though of something other than relief.

"By the Rude — to be alone!" he said. "It is easier, I swear, to lead an army, to win a battle, than to gain a little solitude! For one who wears a crown. Always others there, thronging."

"That has scarcely been *my* burden, Robert," she observed.

"Ah — forgive me, my dear. Of course. You have been kept solitary. Fool that I am! Years alone . . ."

"Years, yes. So that now, Robert, you will understand — I am a little . . . strange. In company."

"To be sure. I should have thought of it, lass. But now, at last, we are alone. That is by with. The company. Care for nothing . . .'

"I will try. But the company I spoke of is not just those . . . others, I fear. You must be patient with me, my heart."

"You mean . . .? That I — I *myself* trouble you? You find me . . . find me other than you did?"

"Dear Mary-Mother — no! Oh, Robert bear with me. I am become a weak and foolish woman . . ."

"That, I vow, you are not! Weak you never were. Or of us two, the fool! Do not fear, Elizabeth. I shall not trouble you . . ."

"Oh, Robert — hear me. What have I said? It is nothing so. This, I think, is the most happy day of all my life! It is but that . . . eight years is a long time. With no man near my bed. Scarce a man to speak to, but some sour gaoler. Or a priest. And, on occasion, William Lamberton. My dear, I have longed for this night. And yet dreaded it. Lest . . . lest I fail you, in some measure. No longer please you."

He went to grip her arm. "Save us — is this Elizabeth de Burgh! Is this the woman I took, yon time, by Linlithgow Loch? Aye, and who took me! And the hundreds of times thereafter, through years of marriage?"

"I was younger then, my dear. And . . . and a nun since! Whereas you — you will have had women a-many."

That was a statement and no question. Nevertheless it gave the man pause. Still holding her, he eyed her from under down-drawn brows. "Tell me, Elizabeth — what do you desire?" he asked. "Believe me, it shall be as you say."

"You are kind. And I a fool, as I said. It is only this, Robert — woo me a little, this night. As though . . . as though I was a virgin. Your bride. Though I was no virgin when you wed me, to be sure! A little patience, my love. Of your mercy."

"Mercy!" he repeated. "You do not know what you say, lass. I it is who should ask for mercy. Of you. Since I have been no monk! Have known other women. Have failed you . . ."

"Do not say it, Robert. Let us have no talk of failure. Lest I seem to fail you now."

"Foolish one indeed! How could Elizabeth de Burgh fail Robert Bruce! You love me still?"

"I do love you. Not still, but more than ever I dreamed possible. And want you — want you with all my heart. Only — only this body I am afraid of, a little . . ."

He took her arm in his arms, then, and ran a gentle but strong and knowledgeable hand over her comprehensively, from the smooth crown of her flaxen head, down the tall white column of neck, over the rich, bounteous swell of bosom, down to the long flanks of hip and thigh, and felt her quiver as comprehensively to his touch.

"This body," he said, deep-voiced, "need not be feared for, I warrant! Now, or ever. It is the most splendid, the most challenging, that any man could ever have under his hand. Under his whole person! What ails you at it, woman?"

"I do not know." She sounded, and felt to his touch, breathless. "Only lack of use, it may be. And years. I am thirty-five, Robert. And feel . . . more!"

"Now? Do you feel so old, this moment? With my hands on you?"

"No-o-o. But . . ."

He stopped her mouth with his own. And after only a second or two, her lips parted.

Even as they kissed, his hands were busy with her gown, probing, loosening, sure hands, confident as they were unhurried, masterful but yet coaxing.

Soon her bodice slipped down, to uncover white shoulders. He left her mouth, to plunge his lips down into the noble curves of those magnificent breasts, urgent but tender.

She moaned a little, but neither urged him on nor held him back.

He had to hold himself back, indeed, with a stern curb; but sought that no hint of it should evidence itself, even though his breathing deepened. As the rest of her gown fell to the floor, he stooped and scooped her up in his arms, and carried her to the bed. She was no light armful — but that would serve to account for his disturbed breathing.

"There," he panted. "Lie you there . . . and let me tell you how beautiful you are."

"As well the lamp is low!" she got out. But she stroked his face.

"That is the second time this day that you have impugned my eyesight. Do you think *me* so old? At forty, woman?"

"I think you . . . besotted. With love, it must be!"

"So be it. I shall recount my love's loveliness. Here and now. She is tall, see you — tall, and proudly made, comely of feature and of form." Pressing her back on the bed, he ran a discerning finger down from head to toe. "Her hair is heavy as spun and shining gold, and has the colour of ripest corn." He lifted a long coil of it and kissed it, running its strands through his lips. "Her skin is honey and cream admixed, yet softer than either and firmer than both." He laid his rough cheek against her smooth one. "Her face is fine-wrought yet strong, clean-cut yet so fair as to break a man's heart. And her lips — ah, her lips are kind and warm and wide and open to all delight!" He covered her mouth with his, and sank his tongue to hers.

When she could speak, breathlessly, she gasped, "Since when... has Robert Bruce... turned poet!"

"No poet," he assured. "All this I have but rehearsed. On my bed so many nights. In camp and cave and heather. Going over every inch and line and joy of you. In my mind. So that I am expert. As thus." He touched the tall column of her neck. "Her throat is smoothest marble, but alive, warm, strong. Her shoulders are whitely proud, turned to perfection. As for her breasts, they are all heaven in their twin loveliness, rich and round and rose-tipped, bold, beautiful, frank and firm." He was moulding and caressing, thumbing, stimulating the awakening, rising nipples. "But — save us, the tongue of man should be better employed than parading mere words for such delights!" And he closed his lips to better effect on fair, throbbing, thrusting flesh.

Whatever sweet confusion he aroused in that superb bosom, Bruce was all too aware now that his own arousal was all too potent, and time running out. He dared not linger, then, as he would, and as the woman's reaction invited. Biting his own lip rather than her swelling flesh, he raised his head, hand drawing down the linen shift that still part-clothed her, spread fingers smoothing.

"Her belly is polished ivory. With a central well of sheer enchantment. Her bush a golden thicket of happy entanglement guarding the valley of... of paradise. In sweet delay."

But he did not delay there, a man all but in extremity. His touch on the soft insides of her thighs, he got out, "Thighs... thighs satin-smooth... long... long... smooth..." He smothered the rest against her breast, wordless, tense, no longer stroking.

"Robert, my dear," she whispered. "Have done, my heart. Yield you. Yield. Do not distress yourself. Come — yield now, Robert."

But whether she had thought of it or not, that was a man to whom the word yield had become, above all others, anathema. Whatever else, he was no yielder. Now the very sound of it seemed to give him new strength and control. Between clenched teeth he found more words.

"You are ... altogether beautiful. Desirable ... beyond all telling. A woman fairer than any... that man could dream of."

"Oh, my love! My love!" she breathed. "I pray you — do not wait. Do not withold. For *my* sake. Not yours! Quickly. Come — come into my love, Robert. Mine! Mine!"

"Is it true? Not for me? You do not cozen me? True that you *want* me?"

"Yes, yes. Quickly..."

He held back no longer from entry to her warm embrace. Yet still, even on the delirious tide of satisfaction, achievement, triumph, he did hold back, in some degree controlled himself with fierce effort, sought to contain himself, determined as ever he had been in all his struggling, that Elizabeth should know fulfilment at last. This he could do, must do, owed to her . . .

When at last, with a strangled cry, she reached her woman's climax, it was nevertheless not a moment too soon for Robert Bruce, as, thankfully, he let nature take its thwarted course. He had seldom fought a more determined fight. It was indeed sheer thankfulness, not any masculine triumph with which he let himself sink into the damned-back surging tide.

It was the taste of salt tears on his lips against her hot cheek which presently revealed to his returning awareness that Elizabeth was in fact quietly weeping.

"What now?" he mumbled. "Tears? Surely not. Why so, lass . . . ?"

"Tears — but only of joy, Robert. I thank you — oh, I thank you. Dear heart — you have made me whole again. My brave, true, kind knight — you have rescued me indeed! Lifted my fears from me. I was afraid that . . . that never again would I know this joy, this oneness with you. That the empty years had made me less than woman . . ."

"I' faith — if you are less than woman, then I am less than half a man!" he exclaimed. "A callow boy, no more! Who could not handle a full woman. Have mercy on me, lass!"

"I shall make up to you that sore trial, Robert. I shall . . ."

"You shall indeed. But give me a little time — just a little time! Have mercy on my forty years!"

"Sleep, then . . ."

"Sleep, no! I have had nights a-plenty for sleeping. To have all this splendour beside me in my bed, and to sleep — that would be sacrilege, no less! I can still . . . appreciate, woman, even when . . . a little spent!" And his hands began to prove his words once more.

Her chuckle was warm and throaty, and all Elizabeth de Burgh again.

After a while, out of the desultory talk and enriched silences, she spoke, without any change in tone or stress. "Christina MacRuarie?" she asked. "Tell me of her."

The man drew a long breath, and on his part at least, tension came back. "You know of her?"

"Think you that was a name of which my gaolers would leave me unaware?"

He moistened his lips. "Christina of Garmoran was — is — my friend. My good friend."

"Friend, yes. And lover?"

"Friend, I said. Lover only in so far as she gave me her body. From time to time."

"That was friendly, to be sure. And could conceivably be more than that!"

"Could be, but was not, Elizabeth That I assure you." He raised himself on an elbow, to address her. "See you, lass — only you I love." That was urgent. "Only you I *have* loved. That I swear."

"Yes, Robert — I believe you, I know you love me. Have given full proof of it. But she? How is it with the Isleswoman? When a woman gives herself, not once but many times, over years — then more than friendship is there, I think! Do not mistake me. I am lying here, in your arms, and joying to be so. Fresh from your loving. Not here playing the jealous wife. God knows I have no right to that role, even if I thought to play it. Which I do not. But — I would know what I have to face, in this. Will my husband's friend Christina be *my* friend? Or my enemy?" This was very clearly still the old Elizabeth de Burgh.

He shook his head. "Your friend also, I do believe. But, if she is not — if she becomes your enemy — then she becomes mine also. That I promise you. But why should she be your enemy?"

"When a woman loves a man, she will fight for him. Husband or other. Does this woman love you, Robert?"

He frowned. "No. Not as you mean love. As *we* mean it. We have never spoken of love, Christina and I. When . . . when she first came to me, at Castle Tioram, after we had rescued her from the Rossmen. When she came, she said that I had need of a woman. A woman, not a lover. That, being deprived, I was showing it. Less than the man I should have been — therefore less the king also. I came to accept that as true. And . . . and she could lend me many Highland broadswords, as well as her body!"

"Aye — that is one way into a man's bed! But it could also be the way to his heart. Was she content with the bed, think you?"

"I believe so. *I* was, at least. She was a woman of experience. Widow of Gartnait of Mar's brother. Your own age, or older. Proud. Hot of temper. A fighter . . ."

"As Elizabeth de Burgh once was! And as beautiful?"

"No. By no means. Different in all ways. But kind. When I needed kindness. And you not there. She said . . . she said that one day you would thank her. For me. That you would want a man returned to you. Not a half-man. Or an ailing cripple . . ."

"She said that, did she! I see. I think I have something of the measure of your Christina now! The Lady of Garmoran. And shall deal with her accordingly!" She gave a little laugh. "But, in this she was right, at least. It is a man that I have returned to — no half-man. I can feel it now!"

"Aye — enough of Christina! And enough of talk ..."

And now Robert Bruce did not have to hold back. Nor yet to coax and gentle. Elizabeth, it seemed, was thus abruptly herself again, vehement, zestful, far from passive. Joyfully, the man proceeded to lose himself in her returning passion.

In time, drowsily, he spoke. "What ails you at, Elizabeth de Burgh? Myself, I find no fault. Now you it is who makes *me* feel my years!"

"Years ... ?" she said. "What then are years? Time? In these last minutes you have given me more of true time and being than in all those lost eight years. I have begun to live again, my Robert ..."

Chapter Two

Stirling so throbbed with life and activity as to all but burst its bounds. The great castle on top of the towering rock; the grey, red-roofed town that clustered and clung round all the folds and skirts of that rock; and the handsome Abbey of Cambuskenneth with all the spread of conventual and domestic buildings that filled the wide near-island in the coiling, shining Forth below both — all were so full that lords and ladies roosted in attics, knights and lairds were thankful to share cot-houses, and bishops and mitred abbots must perforce occupy holy men's bare cells and the like which they had long since thought to have outgrown. Even the host of English prisoners from Bannockburn still unransomed, were packed and herded still more tightly into deeper pits and prisons, even dovecots, that their vacated accommodation might house their captors. Scarcely within living memory had the royal court of Scotland taken up full residence in this its so royal and ancient citadel — though King John Baliol had held a hurried and furtive convention here in 1295. That August of 1314, Stirling was the centre and heart of Scotland in more than geography, after being an enemy-held canker for eighteen years.

The atmosphere quivered, as it were, with more than just the numbers and the noise and the August warmth. There was a great sense of celebration, of relief, of achievement, in the air. After all these years of outright war, invasion, and usurping tyranny and terror, the land was free again, with no single English garrison remaining. After almost thirty years of weak rule, near anarchy, or foreign domination, Scotland had a strong king again, a firm hand at the helm. There was a vast amount to be done, a whole nation to build up from the ruination and savagery of the past; but the way seemed reasonably clear ahead, the task their own to handle or mis-handle. Six weeks after one of the greatest and most significant battles of history, this was the celebration of victory.

Strangely enough, it was with the victor himself, and those closest to him, that this attitude of celebration was least evident. For Robert Bruce realised as did few others that, substantial and seemingly overwhelming as was that victory, it was in fact inconclusive, partial, even dangerously illusory. A round had been won in this tourney, that was all. And there were still all too many in Scotland, and of the ruling class, who wished him less than well, and bided their time.

Nevertheless, it was right to celebrate, even wise, so long as the hazards were not lost sight of or minimised. This programme indeed was all of the King's own devising. But he hoped that even in its festive activities the lesson might be brought home in some measure — that the enemy was bloodied but unbowed.

The afternoon's tournament and games could be made fairly apt to his purpose. The theme and background was still warlike, competitive, challenging. And deliberately Bruce had made it more so by freeing, temporarily and on parole, not a few of the English prisoners, to take part. Some of the most renowned knights in Christendom had fallen captive at Bannockburn. The victor would use them, not to make any sort of Roman holiday, but to remind his own people that the foe was still potent, a force to be reckoned with.

The huge tilting-yard that lay just below and to the east of the castle proper, on a broad terrace of the rock, was the scene of the day's major activities. The English garrison had long used it for horse-lines and even cattle-courts, for the maintenance and provisioning of some hundreds of men. Bruce had had it cleared and cleaned up, and great quantities of dried peat brought from the nearby Flanders Moss to carpet it thickly. Lists had been enclosed, a great railed-off jousting-ground and arena, surrounded by hoardings and tiered timber seating, with a handsome royal box and gallery, the whole brilliant with colourful heraldic achievements and decoration, standards, flags and banners flying everywhere, by the hundred. Gaily-hued and striped tented pavilions had been set up, as undressing and arming rooms, and all around saints' shrines, and the booths and stalls of pedlars, chapmen, hucksters and entertainers proliferated. The clamour was deafening — minstrels played, merchants proclaimed their wares, mendicant friars touted supposed relics, children screamed, dogs barked and horses whinnied, all against the roars of acclaim, advice or disgust of the watchers towards the contestants in the arena.

Robert Bruce loved it all, for this was the heady, rousing clamour of peace, not war, something which had not been heard for long in this land. Up on the royal dais beneath the huge Lion Rampant standard of Scotland, where he stood beside the ornate throne, he gazed round on it all with satisfaction, if tempered with a kind of caution.

That the Bruce's place was to stand beside the single throne, today, not to sit in it, was because this was Elizabeth's day. In that throne she sat, radiant, Queen of the Tournament as well as the realm's queen. Dressed all in white and gold, golden circlet around her heavy flaxen hair, she looked regal, supremely lovely and supremely happy — and the man at her side as often glanced down at her for his satisfaction as at the stirring scene and activities, proud to pay her his own tribute. Occasionally she reached over to touch his arm lightly, and their eyes would meet.

As well that the Queen's beauty was thus supreme and quietly assured this day; for she was surrounded by beauty and good looks which might have proved a sore embarrassment to one less well endowed than Elizabeth de Burgh. A goodly selection of the fairest in the land were present today, and a surprising number seemed to have managed to insert themselves into the royal gallery. Moreover, all had somehow contrived to dress themselves, after long deprivement, in the height and extreme of fashion, so that the enclosure was a blaze of colour and pulchritude, with the women for once rivalling their knightly escorts, whose brilliant heraldic surcoats and coat-armour was so apt to steal any such scene.

Nevertheless it required all this beauty and colour to counter and balance the all but overpowering loveliness of the scene and setting itself. Surely nowhere could such an occasion have been so spectacularly placed as here, high on the flank of Stirling Rock. For this, the very key to Scotland, was also one of that most scenic land's most dramatic viewpoints, where the Highlands abruptly met the Lowlands, where the great estuary of the Forth became a river, where the noble vistas spread far and wide before the constrictions of the mountains. This terrace above the teeming town was so drenched in light and colour and vivid, challenging scene, as almost to be painful to contemplate. From the silver serpent of the Forth, coiling through the level carselands, to the thrusting green heights of the Ochils; from the vast rolling canopy of the Tor Wood to the village-strong shores of the Lothian coast; from the grassy glades of the royal hunting-park to the loch-strewn infinities of the Flanders Moss — all against the tremendous ramparts of the blue-shadow-splashed giants of the Highland Line, the eye of even the least perceptive was all too apt to be distracted from the small doings of men, however positive and spectacular.

A spectacle of some compulsion was indeed proceeding in the great arena. It was the final round in a prolonged contest between teams of wrestlers, four men to a team, each put forward by some great lord or other. Bruce himself had fielded a group from his own bodyguard – to see them soundly defeated in the second heat. Now, in this final round, the eight men who struggled there, all but naked save for the distinctively coloured drawers, represented, of all things, the Abbey of Inchaffray and the English prisoners. Egged on, implored and berated by their panting and gesticulating if non-playing captains, the Abbot Maurice and Sir Anthony de Lucy, the mighty but wearying musclemen were obviously nearing the limit of their efforts, their greased and shining bodies now so slippery and sweat-soaked as to prevent all gripping. Two pairs were already reduced to a merely formal and slow-motion pawing.

"Poor men — they are done, quite," Elizabeth declared. "There is no sport left in this. As Queen of the Tourney is it not in my right to call a halt? To declare the contest over and each side equal? And so spare us all more of this?"

"It is in your right and power indeed, my dear – if you would have both sides decrying you! Most of this assembly, indeed!" her husband told her, smiling. "Halt them now, and both sides will conceive themselves stripped of the laurels. And some of the crowd saying that you chose to spare the English, others that you chose to spare Holy Church! Either way, *you* lose! But have it your own way, lass — you are mistress here, today."

"Here is foolishness . . ." she said. But did not interfere.

Sir Hugh Ross, son and heir of the Earl thereof, who had once been Bruce's deadly foe, came up with the Lady Matilda, the King's youngest sister, a pair now all but inseparable.

"Your Grace," he put, to the Queen, "the English grow over-sure, I vow! They claim that they have as good as won this wrestling bout. And now they challenge us to a jousting. One, or many.

Single combat, or massed fight. They would try to wipe out the shame of Bannockburn, I think. Have I Your Grace's permission to break a lance with their challenger?"

"Mine, Sir Hugh?" The Queen looked doubtful. "Must I so decide?" She glanced over at her husband. When the English prisoners actually started to initiate challenges, it was perhaps time to pause and consider.

Bruce took over. "Who is this bold challenger, Hugh?"

"There were many in it. But the spokesman, the true challenger, was Sir John, the Lord Segrave."

"Segrave! That man!" The Lord Segrave was a senior English captain, brother to one Sir Nicholas who had once been as good as Bruce's gaoler. He had been Edward the First's Lieutenant in Scotland in 1303 when Comyn and Simon Fraser had ambushed the English army at Roslin, and he had barely escaped with his life — to make Scotland pay for his fright thereafter, to some tune. He was therefore one of the most important captives of the late rout. This might well pose a problem. To refuse the challenge of an eminent veteran could look unsavoury, playing safe; on the other hand, for Scotland to be beaten in so notable an encounter, in one single combat fight, would be unfortunate. And Hugh Ross, although a sound wartime fighter, was untried in the tourney. Yet the King could by no means put it to this eager young man that he might not be of the calibre required.

Matilda Bruce, now twenty-one and full of spirit, sensed her brother's doubts. "Let him fight, Sire," she pleaded. "He will carry my glove to victory!"

"Much good that will do him!" To allow him time for thought, the King turned to his nephew, Thomas, Earl of Moray, who stood behind, and who was friendly with Ross. "How think you, Thomas? You know Segrave. You worked with him, once. His was a hated name, when he lorded it here. Is he one whose challenge we should accept?" He could hardly ask Moray outright whether he thought Ross fit and able to do battle with the Englishman; but his nephew would not wish to see his friend bested too easily. The Earl had sided with the English for a while, against his uncle, and probably knew both possible contestants better than any other man there. Thomas Randolph was a tall, dark, splendidly handsome young man, possibly the best-looking man in Scotland, despite his serious expression and noble brow. It was strange that he was not more popular; he was one of the heroes of Bannockburn — but he lacked humour, and was too patently upright for many lesser mortals. Bruce had come to esteem him highly.

"He is a stark fighter, and a hard man to best, Sire. And sore over our victory, I think. Sorer than some. But he will fight fairly."

"M'mmm. Hugh — do you think . . .?" The King was interrupted by a shouting from all around, mixed with laughter. Down in the arena the wrestling seemed to have come to an end at last, with three of the brawny fighters in various recumbent attitudes, the victors either sitting upon them or otherwise expressing exhausted triumph. The last pair were down on their knees, growling at each other like angry dogs — but doing no more than growl, in the interests of economy. The scene was comic rather than dramatic, but the laughter was occasioned mainly by the fact that one of the victors was seen to have had his scarlet drawers torn right off him in the proceedings and was now standing, reeling, and grinning sheepishly, stark naked but notably well endowed, while the English knight, Sir Anthony de Lucy, had grabbed the said scarlet rags for want of better banner, to wave in exultation. It did not demand great arithmetical prowess to establish that, despite this misfortune, the red pants team had won, with two of the prostrate bodies blue, one kneeling, and only one Scot on his feet.

A trumpet fanfare preceded the Master of Ceremonies' declaration that England had won the wrestling match. The winning team should proceed to the royal gallery to receive the congratulations of the Queen of the Games.

While not a few Scots were consoling each other to the effect that wrestling had never been really a Scottish speciality, as it was in England, and some of the ladies were giggling wondering whether the winning team would in fact present themselves up here in the precise state of undress they were in at the moment, Hugh Ross reiterated his request to the King.

"You cannot deny me the joust now, Sire!" he exclaimed. "To reject the English challenge now would seem as though we feared another defeat."

"Aye. . No doubt." Bruce shrugged. "Very well. But, Hugh — arrange it with Segrave that there be more bouts than just the one. Lest all stand or fall by the one throw." That seemed to be the best that he could do in the circumstances.

De Lucy and the four grinning, panting and strongly-smelling champions — one with a towel of sorts hastily wrapped round his middle, to the manifest disappointment of some of the company — were conducted to the royal box, where they bobbed bows to the Queen and King and were presented with red roses by Elizabeth. They were receiving suitable praise and admitting that the conditions of their captivity had at least not emasculated them, when another trumpet neighed imperious summons from down in the lists, drawing all eyes.

Two mounted men had ridden out into the centre of the arena, a gorgeously tabarded herald wearing red and gold arms quartered with red and silver, and lowering a trumpet; and a magnificent figure in shining black gold-inlaid armour part-covered by a colourful surcoat of heraldically-embroidered linen and carrying in the bend of one arm a great jousting helm sprouting ostrich plumes. This eye-catching personage, bare-headed, dark-haired and smiling from a narrow tense hatchet face, sat on an enormous destrier or warhorse, also black-armoured and with flapping mantling of the same colours as the herald.

The King drew a deep breath.

"The most noble, puissant and renowned Sir Edward Bruce, Lord of Galloway and Earl of Carrick!" the herald cried, into the hush his trumpet had achieved.

The black knight raised his steel gauntleted arm. "I, Edward of Carrick, hereby declare," he shouted in ringing tones, "that the English are thinking to try their skill, in tourney if not in war! I do hereby challenge to single combat any soever they may put up. Hear you, English – I challenge your best!"

Hugh Ross's spluttered curse resounded in the pause thereafter.

Bruce drew a hand over his mouth and chin, uncertain whether to curse also or be relieved. Probably his brother, more experienced, would make a better showing than young Ross. And now the challenge came from the Scots, as was more suitable. But the thing raised other problems. None so lofty as the King's brother ought to be involved — it gave such contest altogether too great a prominence. Edward had not sought the Queen's permission, as he ought to have done — yet to forbid him now, before all, would be an intolerable affront, and to one of the most popular figures in the realm, a bad start for the so-long-absent Queen's new image. Moreover, his supercession would be bound to give great offence to Ross — where offence could well be done without, for he was heir to one of the greatest earldoms in the land, and already Edward was in bad odour in that quarter, having recently abandoned the Lady Isabella Ross after getting her with child – as he had indeed previously abandoned the Lady Isabel de Strathbogie, Atholl's sister, thereby throwing that powerful earl into the English arms. The Earl of Carrick was a brilliant commander of light cavalry, and courageous to a fault — but he gave his elder brother more headaches than he relieved.

"Sire — I sought this first!" Ross was protesting. "I told Segrave that I would fight him. If I gained your permission . . ."

"My lord of Carrick has not named Segrave," the King pointed out.

"But it was he who challenged . . ."

A new stir heralded the appearance of another figure, only partially armoured, who strode out into the arena, waving arms for silence. "I, John, Lord Segrave, accept the Earl of Carrick's challenge," he shouted. "He, or Sir Hugh the Ross, or any other. By lance, sword, mace or axe. To the fall, or *à l'outrance*!"

"A plague on him!" Ross growled. "Hear that?"

"Not *à l'outrance*!" Elizabeth exclaimed. "Not that. No killing. Has there not been enough of death?"

"I agree," her husband said, grimly. "My brother and I do not always see eye to eye. But I am not prepared to lose him yet! Nor am I prepared to forfeit Segrave's ransom! They must be told so."

"But, Sire . . .!" Ross objected. "Do you rule against me?"

"I have no choice, lad. Can you not see it? To deny my brother, now, in front of all, is inconceivable. He does amiss in this but he is still the second man in this kingdom. I am sorry."

Matilda made a most unsuitable face at the monarch.

The Master of Ceremonies, after some brief instruction, made loud announcement that the Queen of the Tourney graciously permitted, despite improper procedure, that the Earl of Carrick and the Lord Seagrave ride a joust together, Sir Hugh Ross having nobly yielded a prior right. The joust to be for a fall, an unseating only, and no *à l'outrance*. There would be no fighting to the death at this tournament. Let the champions prepare themselves, and might the best man win.

In the interval of waiting, and while sundry presentations were being made to the royal pair, a new sound above all the cheerful clamour caught Bruce's ear — the thin high squealing of bagpipes. In a flash he was transported back to that day six weeks before, when, in so very different circumstances but only a mile or so away from here, he had listened for and relievedly heard that same sound coming from the west round Stirling Rock. He raised his head.

"Hear that!" he cried. "It is Angus, for a wager! The Lord of the Isles arrived to greet you."

"Scarcely to greet *me*, I think," Elizabeth said. "From all accounts your Angus of the Isles rates women but lowly! It will be your Council he comes for — to make sure that his peculiar interests do not go by default!"

A great Council of State had been called for two days hence, to plot and steer the nation's course in the new circumstances. A parliament would have been better—but a parliament constitutionally required forty days' notice of calling, and Scotland had matters to settle which could not wait for six weeks.

"He will not rate *you* lowly, I swear! Or he ceases to be my friend," her husband declared dutifully.

She smiled. "Am I then to be kind to him? Generous? Aloof? Proud? Or cautious?'

"Be but yourself, lass—and you will have Angus in the cup of your hands in short minutes! He is very much a man, and so the more in danger from you!"

"I wonder! But I am agog to meet this Hebridean paladin who denies you his due fealty while accepting your friendship! This rebel whom you have made your Lord High Admiral."

"Angus Og is no rebel, Elizabeth. He but reserves his position as an independent Prince of the Isles. For which who am I to blame him? I have suffered sufficiently from would-be Lords Paramount of *my* realm! I owe Angus more than I can ever say. Without his great fleet of war-galleys we could not have freed Scotland. He gave us control of our seas, when none other could."

Now everywhere the throng was making way for the newcomers—who obviously accepted all passage and deference as their right. And if the company had been colourful before, it was doubly so now. For the piper-escorted party which came stalking up was so vivid in every respect as to bemuse the eye. About twenty strong—for Angus MacDonald, though a strangely modest man in his person, never moved abroad without his own court of chieftains, captains, seannachies, musicians and the like—these all were clad in saffrons and tartans and piebald calfskin jerkins, bristling with arms, glittering with barbaric jewellery, their heads mainly covered with the great ceremonial helmets that bespoke the Scandinavian background superimposed on their Celtic blood, outdated casques which sprouted at each side either curling bull's horns or whole erne's pinions, symbols that these were the representatives of a Norse sea-kingdom and no integral part of the Scottish realm.

Most of this alarming company were huge, raw-boned, rangy men, affecting long hair, only rudimentary beards, but lengthy down-curving moustaches reaching to the chin, which imparted a notably cruel and savage impression. But he who strode a pace in front was quite otherwise, a stocky man in his late thirties, dark, almost swarthy, but of open features, clean-shaven, and dressed most simply in a long saffron kilted tunic gathered at the waist by a heavy belt of massive gold links, from which hung a jewelled ceremonial dirk. Bareheaded and otherwise unarmed, he scarcely looked one of the boldest and most ruthless warriors Scotland had ever thrown up, a man whose name spread terror round every coast of England, Wales and Ireland—and not a few of Scotland's own, also.

"Angus!" The King went forward, hands outstretched, to greet him. "So again you come to Stirling! To my joy, if not this time my rescue! Greetings, friend. And to all your company, friends all. Come—here is my lady-wife. Elizabeth—this is Angus, son of Angus, son of Donald, Lord of the Isles and Lord High Admiral."

"The Lord Angus is known to me, as to all Christendom, by repute," the Queen said gravely. "King Edward kept me far from his coasts, I vow, lest the Lord of the Isles should come to rescue me!"

The other considered that, and the speaker, unhurriedly for a few moments, before inclining his dark head. He reached out to take her hand and kiss it.

"Would that had been my lot, lady," he said, then, equally gravely, and despite all the fierceness of his entourage, the West Highland voice was soft and gentle.

She smiled. "So do I! Though, mind, I am Ulster's daughter. And we in Ulster have not always had cause to welcome the Black Galley of the Isles!"

"Had I known of you, lady, you would not have remained in Ulster long, Richard de Burgh's daughter or none!"

"Save us!" Bruce exclaimed. "If that's the way of it, then I needs must keep an eye on my queen, now!"

The Islesman gestured, to include every male present. "That would be the act of a wise man, my Lord King," he agreed. "And no trial, at all!"

"As Queen of this Tournament, I give Your Grace leave to depart," Elizabeth mentioned. "I am sure that something requires your royal attention somewhere! My Lord Angus and I have matters to discuss."

Bruce was about to reply, in kind, when the words faded from his lips as he perceived who was standing amongst the press of Angus's men, a tall striking-looking woman, raven-haired, handsome, dressed none so differently from the others, in saffron tunic, short skirt and soft doeskin thigh-high riding boots.

Elizabeth, noting his expression and following his glance, spoke silkily. "You have a lady in your train, my Lord Angus. Not your wife?"

With a look shot at the King, that man shook his head. "No, lady — my cousin. The Lady Christina MacRuarie of Garmoran, chief of that name."

"I have heard of the Lady Christina also," the Queen said quietly. "Acquaint us, sir."

Bruce recovered himself. "*My* privilege," he said. "Christina — welcome back to my Court. You greatly grace it. Elizabeth, my dear — this is she of whom I have told you."

The two women eyed each other, while all around held their breaths and wondered what this totally unexpected confrontation might portend.

Elizabeth held out her hand. "His Grace's friends are my friends," she said. "I have heard that we both owe much to the Lady Christina."

The Isleswoman came forward to dip a deep curtsy. "Your Grace is kind as you are fair," she said. "As His Grace told us all. But even he could not say how kind, how fair! Accept my duty and esteem, Madam."

It was an odd speech from a female subject, but the Queen found no fault with it. Raising her up, she searched the other's dark eyes with her blue ones. "Yes," she murmured softly, slowly, "I understand much. Now."

"I came unbidden. Believing it my duty. To pay my respects to you, the Queen. Believing that I perhaps owed it to you."

"Yes. I am glad that you came."

Bruce endeavoured to disguise his sigh of relief. "I also am glad, Christina. Angus — present your company to Her Grace . . ."

Soon the trumpets drew all eyes to the lists again, as the two mounted champions came trotting out from either end, to meet in the centre, turn their beasts side by side to face the royal enclosure, and to raise their pennoned lances high. Understandably the Lord Segrave was less splendidly turned out than Edward Bruce, and his charger, though fine, was less heavy; on the other hand it would probably be the more nimble. After bowing formally to each other, they turned and trotted back each to his base, where esquires waited with spare lances, equipment, towels and the like.

"Your brother looks sure of himself, Sir King," Angus Og MacDonald declared. He was no friend to Edward, who despised Highlanders and was not at pains to disguise the fact.

"Edward is always sure of himself!" Bruce grunted. "Would I had his single mind. Or yours, Angus!"

"You are sufficiently well with your own," the other returned. "My lord of Carrick's sureness of mind is that of a captain, not a prince." He did not comment on his own.

"Yet, my friend, that is one of the important matters before this Council," the King said, low-voiced. "Edward is determined that he be appointed, formally and before all, heir to my throne. I cannot longer withhold it, I think."

"So much the worse for that throne, then. And your kingdom."

"What choice have I? Placed as she is, could Scotland survive with a young woman as monarch?"

"A regency? To rule in your daughter's name. Your brother not Regent, but one of a joint regency."

"This land has had its bellyfull of joint Guardianship. It will not serve, Angus. Jealousy, intriguing for power, a divided realm. And think you Edward would be content to be one of two or three? He is a man who must dominate, or be kept under by a strong hand. Whose hand would be strong enough, in Scotland, to dominate the Queen's uncle? He would rule, whatever his title. I fear my daughter would live happier with Edward king than with Edward regent. And, my sorrow, there is now no other heir to the throne."

"*Dia* — you talk as though you were a man dying!"

"No — not quite that. But... I am not the man I was, Angus..."

The single bugle-blast interrupted him, as the two knights below drove forward into action. It would be dramatic and telling to say that they hurtled forward at full gallop. But great destriers do not go in for galloping, especially when burdened with many hundredweights of their own armour-plating, to say nothing of their riders'. A heavy lumbering canter is as much as they can rise to — and even that takes a little time to achieve.

But at least they thundered towards each other, the ground positively shaking at the weighty hoof-beats. Lances levelled, the visors of their helmets closed, the contestants urged tons of steel and flesh on a collision course. In this sort of fighting there was little room for finesse; iron nerve, almost equally iron muscles, superb horsemanship and split-second timing — these were the prerequisites. And no weakness towards claustrophobia.

Since all might well end with the first headlong encounter, neither wasted any time on feints and gestures. Straight for each other they pounded, eyes busy behind the visors' slits. The least movement, change of position or attitude, cock of the head even, could give some indication of the vital information — just where the lance-point would be aimed — and great heraldic-designed shields over left arms were ready to react.

They met with a splintering crash which made even seasoned watchers wince. It seemed impossible that either of the mounts, or riders, could survive that impact. The horses struck at a slight angle, but near enough head-on to bring them both to an immediate standstill. But split-seconds before that the lance-tips had crossed — and in that instant both men rose in their stirrups for better control and avoiding action, altering the pitch of the said lances. Edward's, shrewdly aimed, struck home full at the other's breast — but by that time the Englishman had his shield up. It took the blow solidly, and the lance's timber shaft snapped clean in two, with the force of it. Segrave's own point, in the clash, missed the Scot's shoulder by a hair's breadth.

For strange moments time seemed to stand still, the tableau motionless. The two combatants were almost in each other's arms, Segrave thrown forward by the impetus and sudden halt of his mount and the failure of his lance to contact more than air. Carrick's position was different. The impact of his lance tended to throw him back, but his charger's abrupt stoppage countered this. Standing in his stirrups as he was, almost he was unseated, to fall sideways. But he was held upright, for the moment, by the pressure on his right leg, held between the two horses. So, poised, they glared into each other's visors, while the panting horses scrabbled great hooves to retain a footing. Then, recovering equilibrium and control simultaneously, they broke apart and went circling ponderously away.

A great corporate sigh rose from the crowd.

"What now?" Elizabeth demanded, breathlessly. "Edward had the best of that. Yet now he has no lance. While Segrave has. What now?"

"It is the fortune of the tourney," Bruce told her. "It has left the choice with the Englishman. He can ride Edward down — if he may! Edward will not run from him, that is certain! Four-foot sword against nine-foot lance! Or he may be chivalrous and allow Edward to collect a second lance."

Segrave did neither. Raising his undamaged lance, he cast it from him. Then he drew his sword, and waved it at his opponent invitingly.

"Ah — that is noble!" the Queen cried. "He rejects his advantage."

"Noble!" Hugh Ross exclaimed disgustedly. "No nobility there. He perceives that the Lord Edward is better than he with the lance, that is all. No point in allowing him another lance. So he will try the sword."

"That may very well be so," Bruce acceded.

Edward had drawn his own sword, and now the champions circled each other warily, while the watchers yelled encouragement or advice. Then Edward took the initiative and, holding his blade straight out before him like another lance, spurred directly for the other.

Segrave stood his ground until the other was almost upon him. Then he jerked his mount away to the right, the wrong side for the Scot's sword, and slashed his own in a sideways swipe as Edward swept past him. This was the classic move, and the other had anticipated it. By standing up and leaning as far to his own right as he could, he avoided that blow by inches. Thereafter he immediately pulled his destrier's head round viciously, hard round to the left and still round, sending the great brute rearing up and pawing the air, until it was completely turned and at the other's back. The Englishman perceived his danger, and spurred away — but just in time. Edward's blade struck a glancing blow, expending most of its force on the great wooden saddle behind the other. Segrave's slightly lighter horse enabled him to draw away.

"Another point to Edward!" the King cried. "That was featly done."

It was Segrave's turn to surprise them. He had only ridden away some twenty yards when abruptly he reined his mount directly round in its tracks, with more pawing of the air. His opponent was unprepared for this, and could not get his heavy charger out of the way in time. He took, in consequence, a heavy blow partly on his shoulder — fortunately not the sword-arm — and partly on his shield, before the other was carried past, and reeled in his saddle.

Everywhere Englishmen shouted hoarsely.

Their champion was quick to exploit his advantage. Swiftly he reined round once more, to drive in whilst the other was part numbed by the blow.

Edward, with only the briefest of seconds to take avoiding action, did not do so. Instead, he spurred to meet the challenge, canted over to his left side in pain as he was. And just before the attack was upon him, with a major effort he wrenched back his destrier's head with almost unbelievable savagery and at enormous cost to himself, so that he swayed dizzily in the saddle with the shock of it. The horse rose high on its hind legs, squealing its fright and hurt, great shaggy forelegs lashing directly in the face of the other charging animal.

Somehow the Scot managed to retain his seat, or rather his

stance, for he was standing upright. The other mount, faced with those weaving iron-shod hooves only inches from its face, flung itself aside as abruptly, almost falling over in the process. Segrave was all but thrown, his aimed sword jerked aside as he sought to save himself. And leaning far forward and over, Edward brought down his own brand in a mighty sledgehammer, pile-driving stroke, rough, ungainly but irresistible, which smashed flat-sided across the other's neck, shoulder and chest, and literally lifted him out of his saddle.

Segrave toppled, steel-clad limbs flailing, and crashed to the soft peat with a crunch which drew gasps from all around. He lay still.

After the moment or two of shock, the entire castle precincts rang with shouted acclaim, admiration, and groans. Edward, looking very unsteady, and still obviously twisted with pain, spared no glance at his victim, but raising his sword high towards the Queen, turned his snorting steed and walked it ponderously back to his own base.

Segrave's esquires ran out to the aid of their fallen champion.

"Your realm's credit was safe with your brother, this time, my Lord Robert," Angus Og observed. "It was a notable bout."

"Aye. Edward lacks nothing in courage. And daring. Even skill of sorts. It is judgement he lacks."

"He judged well enough there, did he not?" Elizabeth asked. I think you are too hard on Edward, Robert."

"Perhaps. Many, I know, think so. Women, in especial! Though some have been known to change their minds!"

"Too hard or not, the Lord Edward will never change," Christina MacRuarie put in. "Men must accept him as he is, I say. And women rejoice — and watch their virtue!"

The Queen considered her. "I think some women may be a match for even Edward Bruce!" she said, smiling a little.

They exchanged appreciative glances.

Presently, Edward himself arrived, shoulder still hunched a little, bare-headed now, but grinning, debonair. In his mid-thirties, he was dark, slenderly built, a much slighter man than was his brother, but tense as a coiled spring. Handsome in a sardonic fashion, he had a roving eye, a wide twisted mouth and a pugnacious jaw. But there was no doubt but that he was a Bruce.

"Bravely done, Edward!" Elizabeth greeted him. "You fought well."

"I fought to win," he told her briefly. "And now I come to claim my reward. From the Queen of these games."

"Far be it from me to withhold it, sir. What do you seek? A white rose? Or a red? A glove? A ring from my finger, perhaps? Or a pearl from my ear?"

"None of these," he declared. "I seek and I crave a kiss. A queen's kiss! And pray it be none too sisterly!" And he cast a fleeting glance at his brother.

"Why, my lord — that you shall have! And with my pleasure!"

He stepped forward, to stoop — even though he grimaced at the pain of it — and planted a smacking kiss full on her lips. Then, his good arm circling her to press her close for another and longer embrace, he drew back – but only for a little, preparatory to a third assault. The Queen's hand went up to take the lobe of his ear between thumb and forefinger, and to nip it hard, so that he yelped — without however any change of her own expression.

"Greedy, sir!" she said. "Would you shame me in front of my liege lord? And yours?"

"If needs be!" he asserted, caressing his ear. "But, save us — I'd prefer to do it more privately! Yours is the choice, woman!"

"Has a husband no say in such matters?" the King asked, but mildly.

"As that of the Queen of your realm, brother. Today this Elizabeth is Queen of the Tourney, and not troubled with a husband!"

"I am never troubled with my husband," the woman observed. "My trouble is to see sufficient of him!"

"Were I your husband, you would see sufficient of me, I vow!"

"Too much, perhaps, my brave lord! Like some other ladies say!" That was also a woman's voice, but different, softer, more sibilant.

Edward Bruce's head jerked up, to stare. "You! You here again! The Isleswoman! I' faith — here's a pickle! Christina of Garmoran come back to . . . confront us! What now?"

His brother frowned. "Christina's presence is welcome. As always," he said shortly.

"As always . . .? Ooh, aye!" Edward looked back at Elizabeth assessingly.

"Welcome," she nodded. "The more so, that she will perhaps help to keep such as the Earl of Carrick in their place!"

"Ha . . .!" Edward got no further. A trumpet blast heralded another announcement.

"The most noble the Earl of Hereford, Lord High Constable of England, craves the Queen's leave to speak."

Surprised, the occupants of the royal gallery looked at each other.

"Bohun! What does *he* want?" Bruce asked. But he nodded to Elizabeth. "We cannot withhold permission to the Constable."

At Elizabeth's wave of acceptance, another voice called. "I, Humphrey de Bohun, Earl of Hereford, do require satisfaction. Robert de Bruce, lately Earl of Carrick, who calls himself King of Scots, did fight and slay my nephew, Sir Humphrey de Bohun, Knight, before the past battle. For the honour of my name and house, I Humphrey do hereby challenge the said Robert to single combat as fought with my kinsman that day."

"A plague on the man — hear that!" Edward exclaimed, into the buzz of comment and astonishment. "A wretched prisoner — challenging the King! Insolent!"

Everywhere the shouts and growls of the Scots showed that they agreed with this judgement.

"Robert — you will not do this?" the Queen asked.

"You are not afraid for me, my dear?"

"Afraid, no. But . . ."

"Your Grace — Sire!" a voice called from some way off. "Allow *me*. That I meet Hereford's challenge." It was Gilbert Hay. "As Constable of Scotland, let me deal with this Englishman."

Bruce frowned. If the other English challenger had presented a problem, how much more did this. Had it been any other than Bohun who made it, there would have been little of difficulty — he would have rejected it out of hand. As King, he could do that without loss of reputation. Indeed, he would have felt almost bound to do so. But the Earl of Hereford was in a special category. As Lord High Constable of England he ranked next to King Edward himself. His capture, fleeing from Bannockburn, must have been a bitter blow indeed. Taken in the field would have been bad enough, but, like his monarch and so many other great lords, he had bolted before the end, and had been pursued and captured as far away as Bothwell, on his flight to England. Now he would be concerned to wipe out that stain. But, more than this, before the battle proper he had seen his nephew cut down in single combat with Bruce, and however much he might have wished to avenge that rash young man there and then, had in fact, despite overwhelming superiority in numbers and arms, withheld — as probably was no less than his duty as a responsible commander. But here too he must have felt his honour to have suffered. Now he required to make a gesture. And Bruce felt some sympathy.

The King waved a negative hand to Hay. "*My* concern," he said.

"You are not going to oblige this presumptuous captive?" Angus Og exclaimed. "You!"

"It is customary at a tourney, when one side has lost a bout, to allow them opportunity to redeem themselves, should they so challenge."

"Aye — but not the King."

"It was I who slew young Humphrey de Bohun. Besides, it was my brother who put down Segrave. Think you Segrave's superior should fight with my brother's junior?"

"And if you fall . . .?"

"Then Hereford will have proved himself the better man!" Bruce raised his hand. "I accept my lord of Hereford's challenge," he cried. "What weapon does he choose?"

Clear and cold the answer came from below. "You slew my nephew with a battle-axe. So be it. I choose the axe!"

"No!" As clear, ringing, came this denial. "No — I will not have it!" Elizabeth cried, rising from her throne. "I said there will be no killing. As Queen of this tournament, I forbid it! There will be no axes, I say."

Her husband smoothed hand over mouth and chin.

"As Your Majesty wishes," the challenger acceded thinly. "The mace, then. Will that serve?"

Bruce nodded. "The mace, yes." He turned to his wife. "Blunt enough, my dear?"

She bit her lip, saying nothing.

A hand touching her shoulder, and pressing, the King turned and strode off, calling for his armour-bearer, young Sir William Irvine, knighted after Bannockburn.

When at length the monarch rode out into the lists, clad now in splendid armour and with the Lion Rampant vivid scarlet on his yellow surcoat and horse-trappings, it was seen that he had chosen no destrier as mount, but the same grey light garron which he had ridden that day when he had fought Hereford's nephew. It lacked height and weight but its wiry nimbleness and sureness of foot were the assets he coveted today. Men noted the fact. De Bohun, given choice of the vast pool of captured horseflesh, had selected a mighty black charger — which might well have been his own.

Making their bows to the Queen, Bruce looked almost laughably lowly, under-horsed, by comparison, but none there thought to smile, even Edward. The King spoke to Hereford, voice hollow inside his jousting helm.

"My lord — why did you choose the axe? When I am accounted a master with it?"

"For that very reason," the other returned curtly. "And because, with the axe, you killed my nephew."

"He died honourably, in fair fight. No call for you to risk your life, proving your house's honour."

"You will allow me, sir, to be custodian of my own honour."

"Aye. But to choose the axe there, means that you meant to kill. Or be killed. And your ransom near paid. Why?"

"Need I account for my actions to you, sir. A rebel?"

"Ha! So it is still the same! You have learned nothing, my lord? The bitter English pride! I am sorry for you . . ."

Abruptly the other wheeled his charger round, and rode back to his base.

However blunt an instrument, the mace required considerable skill for effective use in mounted warfare. Like the axe, it was short in haft, but its knobbly head was heavier, and in consequence, less well-balanced. It was therefore notably short in range and hard on the wrist, and against armour demanded very shrewd placing.

At the trumpet's imperious signal, the two contestants rode at each other, a seemingly ill-matched pair. Bruce having to restrain his lighter mount. Hereford, with superior height, and therefore reach, but a horse which would tire more quickly, was out for a quick decision. He wasted no time on preliminary skirmishing, but drove straight at the other.

Bruce knew that he would be expected to dodge and use his agility. He therefore waited until the other was all but on him; then, as the Earl raised his mace high, ready to smash it down on whichever side his foe decided to veer, he jerked his pony right round in what was almost a full half-circle, under the very nose of the black charger. He achieved it with only bare inches to spare, and went trotting off a yard or so in front of the lumbering destrier whose rider was leaning forward over its neck, flailing furiously but quite ineffectually, the King not even turning his head to look back.

Oddly enough, this manoeuvre, which might have looked like the craven shirking of an encounter, did not; rather it gave the impression of cocky and quite insolent confidence.

The great shout of laughter from all around — which was partly what Bruce was playing for — revealed the appreciation of at least a majority of the company.

It was easy to keep just the right distance ahead of the challenger. The King kept it up for just long enough to make it clear that he was in command of the situation. Then, spurring, he cantered away for seventy yards or so, before flinging his beast round once more and sending it headlong towards the other.

This time Hereford was more wary however angry. He slowed

his destrier somewhat, and standing in his stirrups, mace swinging, waited for Bruce to make the move.

The other did not disappoint him now. Straight as an arrow he came, at full canter, almost a gallop. As the distance closed, at that speed it was clear that he could by no means repeat the previous manoeuvre and draw up. Hereford was poised, ready.

The King drove in. At the very last moment he achieved the unexpected in two ways. The first was not so very unusual; he twitched his mount's head so that it bore down on the enemy's left side, not his right, thereby spoiling the reach and stroke of both of them, since the maces were in their right hands. The second was altogether more dramatic; instead of standing, to gain height, he flung himself forward, almost flat along his garron's outstretched neck, and so lying low, half-turned to his left, shield up to take the other's mace-blow.

The Englishman's was a botched stroke, inevitably. He was too high, and his weapon on the wrong side — and in heavy armour a man does not twist and bend with any great suppleness. Only a glancing blow struck the swift-moving shield, and then they were past. Bruce slamming in an unhandy sideways swipe over his horse's ears in the by-going, more as a gesture than anything. It contacted Hereford's leg-armour — but only just.

Again the laughter rose in great waves. This was clowning rather than true jousting, deliberately making a fool of England's High Constable.

If anyone doubted this interpretation of the King's purpose, they did not do so for long. He proceeded to make circles round his less nimble opponent, without ever coming close enough for a blow. Time and again the Earl had almost opportunity to use his superior height and range, and then was denied it. More than once, as the other swept past, he heard Hereford shouting wrathfully within his helm for him to stand and fight like a man.

Even the crowd grew a little tired of this, and offered some positive advice to both contestants.

Bruce had not come into the arena to fight in this way. But the Englishman's arrogant words, his insolent naming of him as a rebel, demanded different treatment from sporting gallantry and knightly behaviour. He fell to be humiliated rather than just defeated.

So Hereford was made angry, resentful, outraged — and tired. Tired as his heavy war-horse was already growing tired. And then, in one of his innumerable darts-in and drawings-off, Bruce did not draw off. Instead he swung round hard in a tight circle, his garron rearing, almost walking on hind hooves, to come down immediately at the rear of the other beast, all but pawing its back. And before either horse or rider could twist round, Bruce rose this time in his stirrups and stretching his fullest reach, smashed down his mace between Hereford's armoured shoulder-blades. The Earl pitched forward, toppled from his seat, and fell in clanking ruin.

Without any of the usual flourishes and bows towards the royal box, or any acknowledgements of the crowd's applause, the King turned and trotted out of the arena.

Armour discarded, with Irvine, he made his way back to the gallery, rather shortly rejecting the plaudits of those he passed. Sir Gilbert Hay came to meet him.

"Let that teach overbearing Englishery to challenge the King of Scots, Sire!" he exclaimed. "Here was pretty fighting."

"That was not fighting, man!" Bruce snapped. "Mummery, play-acting, call it what you will — but it was not fighting. He required a lesson, that is all."

"Nevertheless, it was notably well done."

"You think so? I do not."

Mounting to the royal enclosure, the King paused in his steps. The gallery was a deal more crowded than when he had left it. And markedly quiet, silent. He stared.

A new party had obviously arrived in the interim, dusty and travel-stained, half of them women. All looked towards him, and none spoke.

He recognised his sister Christian. She was older, of course, with grey in her hair — but hadn't they all? She was smiling, and though drably dressed, still looked remarkably unlike a nun despite all her years shut up in an English nunnery.

"Christian!" he cried. "Praises be — here's joy! For a wonder! Welcome! Welcome home." And he started forward.

Her smile fading, and the jerk of her head to one side, gave him pause. He glanced quickly towards where she had indicated. A young woman stood beside Elizabeth, thin, anxious, shrinking almost, great-eyed. Two great tears were trickling down the Queen's cheeks.

"Sweet Christ-God!" Bruce gasped, and stood, for once utterly at a loss.

None there could find words to help the moment past. And Christian and Edward Bruce, at least, were seldom at a loss for words.

It could only be Marjory, his own daughter. His only child. And he had not known her. He had welcomed his sister, but not his child. But . . . how could he have known? He had thought of her always as last he had seen her, a child of eleven. His mind knew that she would have grown up, in eight years; but his inner eye had still looked for the child he knew. Not that he knew her very well. In all her nineteen years he would not have totalled three passed in her company, more was the pity. But this sad, pallid, ravaged and unhealthy-looking young woman — this to be Marjory Bruce, the chubby child he once had discovered to be a poppet . . .

She was gnawing her lip, her huge eyes never leaving his face. Not realising himself how stern was Robert Bruce's face now, in repose, they confronted each other.

It was Elizabeth's open hand, upraised and held out, that saved him.

"Marjory! Marjory, lass!" he cried chokingly, and strode towards her, arms wide.

At the last moment, stumbling, features working sorely, she ran into that embrace, coughing.

"Girl, girl!" he got out, clasping her frail shaking body. "Lassie — my own daughter! Dear God, Marjory — together again! At last. Och, och, lass — all's well now. It's all by with. You are safe. Safe again."

A young-old bedraggled waif, the Princess of Scotland wept on her father's splendid shoulder, wordless.

Elizabeth came to them. Her quiet strength helped them both. They managed to master their painful emotion.

"Here is another you should greet, Robert," Christian said. "Who crowned you once!"

Again Bruce would not have known that the emaciated, raw-boned, hard-faced woman who waited there was Isabel MacDuff, Countess of Buchan, the sonsy girl-wife of his late enemy Buchan, who had played truant to place the gold circlet on his brow at Scone, at his coronation, as was the MacDuff privilege. The years in the cage on Berwick walls had left their indelible mark. Unlike Mary Bruce she had toughened to it, coarsened, become a lean, stringy woman of whipcord and iron, instead of the eager, high-coloured laughing girl.

As she dipped a stiff curtsy, he raised her up, taking both her hands. "Isa," he jerked. "What can I say? What words are there? To greet you. To welcome you back. What words are there for what lies between us?"

"None, Sire," she answered, level-voiced. "Words are by with. Only deeds will serve now. As ever. Deeds."

He eyed her a little askance, at her tone of voice. "Aye, deeds. It has to be deeds, in the end. It took . . . too long, Isa."

"Aye, But there is still time."

"For what, mean you?"

"Vengeance," she said. "I want vengeance."

"M'mm. To be sure. Some vengeance you have had already, I think . . ."

'Not sufficient."

"No. Perhaps not, Isa. But — we have had more to do than just seek vengeance." He turned, gesturing. "At least I have been humbling one of their arrogant lords, their Constable . . ."

"That is not how the English humble their prisoners!" the Countess said thinly.

"No. No — I am sorry." He moved back to his daughter's side. "You will be tired, lass. With your long journey. This is no place for you — a tournament! No place for any of you. Come — we will go in. We are very grand, in Stirling Castle now! Elizabeth, my dear?"

"I shall stay, Robert. A little longer. Queen it here. Many would be disappointed if we both leave now. Go you. With Marjory. I will come later."

"My thanks." Holding his daughter's arm, he looked at the other returned prisoners, set-faced. "Thomas!" he called. "Where is my lord of Moray? Ah, Thomas — those English lords. The captives. I will not have them near me, now. Hereford and the rest. Send them away. Ransom paid or no. I would be quit of them. Before I am constrained to use them as they have used these! You understand? Off back to England with them."

"But — much of the money is as yet unpaid, Sire. The return of these *your* captives was but to be Hereford's ransom. The rest . . ."

"Money! Think you I care for their money? Now! Seeing my daughter . . .! Get them away, I say. Before I further stain my honour and do them the mischief they deserve. See to it, my lord."

"Is this the King of Scots' vengeance?" Isabel MacDuff demanded.

"It is the King of Scots' royal command!" he returned. And then, more kindly. "We shall pay our debts otherwise, Isa. Never fear. Come you, now, Marjory . . ."

Chapter Three

The vast Council Chamber of Stirling Castle, true seat of government of the realm, was fuller than it had been for many a year. It was the first Privy Council that Bruce had held here — the first full Council that he had ever held, many as he had attended, one even in this great hall, summoned by John of Brittany, Edward the First's nephew and Governor of Scotland, to hear, amongst other things, the ghastly details of William Wallace's death at Smithfield, London. A number then present were here again now, and, like the King himself, must have been very much aware of the shadow of that great and noble man whom the Plantagenet had butchered in his insensate hate, and who had contributed so much to make such Council as this possible.

Not all there, however, would have the man Wallace at the backs of their minds. Indeed, not all present were inclined to look upon today's as at all any sort of celebratory occasion; but rather as a making the best of a bad job. For this was the first Council of a united Scotland — and the Scotland which had fought the English for so long had been far from united. Whether it was so now, for that matter, remained to be seen: though the monarch had done all in his power to make it so — more in fact than most of his close associates, of the mass of the people even, deemed either prudent or right. The unity of the kingdom was almost entirely Bruce's own conception; just as the idea of patriotism, the love of Scotland as an entity, a nation, for its own sake, had been almost solely Wallace's. If the ancient realm now stood free, and facing the future with at least a semblance of confidence and unity, it was the work of these two very different men with their differing visions.

It had never been easy, any part of the forging of those visions into reality. And it was not easy now. Since other men, through whom it all fell to be achieved, saw the visions only dimly or not at all. The clash of outlook, temperament, interest and will was unending. The Scots were ever a race of inveterate individualists and hair-splitters. With men such as the Earl of Ross, Sir Alexander Comyn, Alexander MacDougall of Argyll and Sir John Stewart of Menteith — all of whom had fought against Bruce, seated round a table with such as Edward Bruce, the Earl of Lennox, the Lord of the Isles, Sir James Douglas and Sir Neil Campbell, it required a strong hand to control them. But a great deal more than merely a strong hand.

"Do I have it aright?" Angus of the Isles was demanding. "Edward of England, despite his defeat, refuses a treaty of peace on all terms? Or just the terms we offer?"

"On all terms, my lord." Bishop William Lamberton of St. Andrews, Primate of Scotland, had just returned from a brief embassage to London. "He still names us rebels. His Grace an imposter, and will consider no treaty. I did what I could to persuade him, and his Council, but to no purpose. To my sorrow."

"The war, then, goes on?"

"In name, yes. Since they will not make peace."

"Our terms were easy, generous," Lennox said.

"Too generous!" Campbell jerked. "I said we should have invaded England after the battle — not sought to treat. Given them no rest. We had the advantage."

"We still have," the King pointed out, from the head of the long table. "Nothing is lost. But . . . I had hoped that they would have learned their lesson."

"The English never learn," old, blind Bishop Wishart of Glasgow said.

"Any more than do we!"

"What do we do now, then?" Hay the Constable asked.

"Muster to arms — what else?" Edward Bruce declared strongly. "Do what we should have done six weeks ago — invade. In this, at least, I am with the Campbell." He and Sir Neil had never been friends.

"Aye! Aye!" Many there undoubtedly agreed with this course.

But some did not. "It is peace we need, not war," Lennox insisted. Essentially a gentle man, it was his misfortune to have been born one of the great Celtic earls of Scotland; and so, willy-nilly, a leader in war. "The English may be too proud to treat with us. But they are nevertheless sore smitten, and cannot be looking for war. Meantime. They need peace. But, I say, *we* need it more!"

"I agree with Malcolm of Lennox," the Earl of Ross, his fellow Celt put in, a huge man, with something of the appearance of an elderly and moulting lion. "Our land is in disorder. We have had enough of fighting."

"Hear who speaks, who fought nothing!" That was Angus Og MacDonald. The Highlands were no more united than were the Lowlands — and Ross and the Isles had been at feud for centuries.

"If it is fighting you want, Islesman — I am ready to oblige you, whatever! And gladly . . .!"

"My lords," Bruce intervened patiently. "May I remind you that we are here discussing the English peace treaty. Our terms are rejected. They were honest terms — not hard. Merely that the English should renounce all their false claims of suzerainty over Scotland, assumed by the present king's father. And that they recognise myself as lawful king here. This, in their pride, they will not do. We are still their rebels! So peace is not yet, whatever we may wish.

So we plan anew. I seek your advice, my lords. That only."

None there was abashed by any implied reproof, being Scots.

"How does my lord of St. Andrews gauge the English mind in this matter?" Sir James Douglas asked. "The English Council, rather than King Edward? Since they sway him greatly. Is it only pride and spleen? Or do they intend more war?"

Lamberton shrugged wide but bent shoulders. Like so many men there, he was aged before his time, only in his mid-forties but looking a score of years older, his strong features lined and worn. The years of war and captivity had left their marks — and the Church was far from spared.

"Who can tell? With the English. As a people they are assured of their superiority over all others. Nothing will change them. Now they are struck in their pride — which is their weakest part. Galled by their defeat, who knows what they will do."

"But that very defeat! Surely it must give them pause?"

"Pause perhaps — but little more, I fear. If England was governed from York, I'd say we should have peace. But from London . . .!"

"Why say you so?"

"Because the South is too far from Scotland and their warfare. Shielded from war and its pains, the Southrons are the arrogant ones. Their armies are mainly of Northerners or Welshmen, or mercenaries. With these they will fight to the last! The southern lords are beyond all in pride. And they are rich — we here cannot conceive of their riches. And there are so many of them . . ."

"Here's a sorry tale, i' faith!" Edward broke in. "Must we sit here and bemoan our lot? We, the victors! We beat them, did we not? And shall do so again. Enough of such talk. I say, muster and march!"

"What my lord Bishop says is wise," the King declared, the more sternly in that it was his brother whom he contraverted. "I, who also know the English south, take his meaning. He says, in fact, that the English will not make peace until their southlands suffer. How to make them suffer, then? Here is our problem."

"How can we reach them, Sire? They are safe from us," Douglas said.

"Directly, yes. But there may be other ways."

"What has Your Grace in mind?" the warrior Bishop of Moray asked.

"Not outright war. But enough to make them fear war. And its hurt. To *them*. On more sides than one. The French threat, again, We are still in treaty with France. There is a new king there, now that Philip the Fair is dead. Louis is weak, perhaps, and may not act — but he mislikes Edward of England and grudges him his French possessions. He could be persuaded to threaten, if no more, I think. Across the Channel."

"Little that will serve us!" Angus Og commented. Although one of Bruce's most formidable and valuable supporters, he always required to assert his cherished status as a semi-independent princeling, and frequently chose to do so by way of criticism and by never using the normal honorifics of the other's kingship, to imply fealty.

"Ay, my lord — of itself. But taken with other measures. As, let us say, your own! How far south, on the English coasts, would my Lord of the Isles venture his galleys?"

"Ah — now you talk good sense, Sir King! My wolfhounds will raid right to the Channel, to the Isles of Scilly, if need be. There is naught on the seas to stop them!"

"The English have many stout ships, friend."

"Stout, it may be — but slow. They have no galleys. My galleys are faster than any other ships that sail the seas."

"So be it. You will go teach the proud Southrons what war means! Raiding their coasts. My lord of Ross has galleys also — as I know to my cost! He can serve their east coast, while you the west and south."

The two chiefs glared at each other.

"At the same time, there should be raiding all along the North of England. That is easy. But one fast-moving strong column to drive south. Its flanks and retreat covered by others. To strike fear — nothing more. Deep into the soft Midlands. As far as may be, and return safely. How far, think you, it might win?"

"London!" James Douglas exclaimed, amidst laughter. "*I* will frighten London for you, Sire!"

"Scarce that, Jamie! But, moving fast enough, you could win far, I believe. Well below Yorkshire."

"Far further than that . . ."

There was much spirited agreement now.

But Lennox was doubtful. "This is war, Sire. Will it not but provoke retaliation? It is peace we need, I say, not such prolonging of the war."

"To be sure, my friend. It is for peace I plan this. For permanent peace. Not merely a pause in the fighting. Somehow we must win that peace treaty out of the English — or Scotland will never be able to use her freedom, to gain the benefits of her long struggle. We must make them desire such treaty. I think we shall not do it if *we* do nothing. So we must strike fast now, whilst they are still licking their wounds. Not full invasion. That would cost us too dear. Especially at harvest time. We need this year's harvest indeed. But sufficient to alarm them, down there in their south. How say you, my lord Primate?"

Lamberton, his most trusted friend and councillor, former Chancellor of the realm, raised his brows. "It is worth the trial, Sire."

"You say no more than that?"

"I do not know, Sire. It would have to be done at once. Before representatives could be sent to the French. If there was something else that we might do . . ."

"Ireland," Edward Bruce said shortly. "Threaten them from Ireland, instead of France."

"You mean . . .?"

"I mean use Ireland. The Irish hate their English oppressors near as much as do we. They have risen against the English many times, always they are doing so. Invade, and they will rise again. Together we shall drive the English into the sea! Then, from the South of Ireland, we shall offer a threat that will make the English tremble in their beds!"

There was much acclaim and support for this bold programme and for the dashing Earl of Carrick. It was not a new idea, of course. Bruce and his associates had often discussed it in the past, as a means of reducing the pressure on Scotland. This was but a fresh aspect of its possibilities.

"That would entail a major campaign, brother," the King objected. "Much time. Many men. Too great an undertaking . . ."

"Not so. Give me but 5,000 men and I will win Ireland for you. and quickly. Our own Galloway, Carrick and Annandale men, and some chivalry. Have the MacDonald put us over the water in his galleys, before he goes raiding."

"I say this is folly, my lord," his nephew Thomas Randolph, Earl of Moray, contended, the most level-headed as well as the most handsome young man in the kingdom. "A new war. Across sea. This would be a mighty adventure. But is it what we would have today? To win Ireland could take years. A sink for men and ships. When we require swift results . . ."

"I tell you—give me but 5,000. Less. And I will have an Irish host facing the South of England in but weeks."

"There is sense in this," Angus Og asserted. It was not often that the Lord of the Isles and the Earl of Carrick agreed. "At such invasion, Ulster would rise, you may be sure."

Bruce smoothed hand over mouth. Angus and Edward made a formidable coalition: and the Islesman knew Ireland better than any there, since it was in Ulster that he was apt to earn his living, with his broadswords and galley-fleets hired for the interminable clan wars.

"Ulster is not Ireland," he mentioned. "The south is very different. And it is the south which would count, in this. Besides, brother — you it is who I would look to lead this dash deep down into England." This, in fact, had by no means been the King's intention, for Edward was far too rash a commander to entrust happily with so disciplined a thrust as this must be; but the command would undoubtedly appeal to him — that went without saying — and would probably wean him away from his Irish ambitions.

The other looked thoughtful.

"This we can do, then," the monarch went on. "At no great upset to our realm. The Irish adventure can wait. My brother of Carrick, and Sir James, Lord of Douglas, to make the dash for the south, my Lord of Moray at their backs to guard their flanks and retreat. Sir Gilbert, the High Constable, and Sir Neil Campbell of Lochawe, with Sir Robert Keith, the Marischal, to command more general and shallow raiding into the English North. While the Lord of the Isles, Lord High Admiral, and the Earl of Ross, harry the coasts southwards. Is it agreed?"

"At least it could be noised abroad, in the North of England, that the French are like to invade across the Channel," Lamberton suggested. "No harm in that — and it would add to alarm. Soon reach London's ears."

"When do we ride, Sire?" Douglas asked.

"So soon as we can muster the men."

"Numbers?" Edward jerked.

"For your company? How many do you want? To make a swift, tight, manageable force? Strong, but not too large."

"Six hundred. Well mounted."

"Very well. And you, Thomas?"

"More, Sire. Since I will require to divide, flanks and rear. And hold a corridor secure. Two thousand."

"Yes. As I would have said, myself. So be it."

There was excitement in the great chamber now, men stirring in their seats. Bruce had to call for silence. "My lord Chancellor," he said, "the next business?"

At a parliament the Chancellor acted as chairman, with the monarch merely present in a presidential capacity; but a Privy Council was the King's own meeting, and the Chancellor only acted as secretary. Bernard de Linton, Abbot of Arbroath, was young for such an appointment, young even to be an abbot; but he had one of the shrewdest brains in the kingdom, and Bruce had never regretted his choice of him, even though it had offended more senior clerics who coveted the position of first minister. A long-headed, lantern-jawed man, with hair receding and smouldering dark eyes, he sat at the King's left hand.

"My lord of Carrick's claim to be appointed heir to the throne, Your Grace," he said, tonelessly.

The stir round the table now was different, with new elements in it, discomfort, some resentment, as well as tension. All eyes were on the two brothers.

"Ah, yes," the King nodded. "This matter has been raised before. But without decision. You would speak to it, my lord?"

Edward cleared his throat. "You all know the position," he said abruptly. "This rejection of our peace treaty makes it the more urgent. The King is no longer young. He has these bouts of sickness. And war is still our lot. The succession must be assured — and he has only a daughter. The Lady Marjory has now returned to us. We all esteem her well. But she would make no monarch for Scotland — any can see that. This realm requires a king, and a strong king — not a weakly lassie as queen. In peace as in war. None can gainsay that. As next male heir, I say that, for the good of the realm, the succession should be settled on myself. Herewith." He ended as abruptly as he had begun.

"You have heard, my lords. The situation is known to you all. I shall value your advice."

"Your Grace, it is not for us to decide this matter," David, Bishop of Moray objected. "Only a parliament may change the succession. With your royal approval."

"True. But a parliament will need guidance. I believe the next parliament would approve the decision of this Council."

"If, as God forbid, our liege lord was to be taken from us," Lamberton observed, "would not a strong regent serve the Queen and the realm almost as well as a strong king?"

"No!" Edward barked. "There is a world of difference."

"Admittedly, my lord. But that difference need not be to the hurt of the realm. Or to the hurt of an already much-wronged young woman!"

"Aye! Aye!" That evoked considerable agreement.

"She may marry. What then? How would the Queen's husband esteem a regent over them? There would be factions, divisions, parties. This kingdom is sufficiently divided. I say only a king's strong hand can unite it."

"With all respect to the Earl of Carrick," James Douglas said, "I hold that it is wrong, shameful, even to consider this change. The throne is the Lady Marjory's birthright — unless a son be born to His Grace. What right has any, save God, to take it from her?"

"Well spoken, Sir James!" Hay supported.

"Nevertheless, it could be the kindest course," Sir Alexander Comyn, Sheriff of Inverness, pointed out reasonably, an elderly grave-faced man. "The princess might well be the happier. Would the position of a young and inexperienced queen be so enviable? This kingdom will not be a sure and settled one for many a year. Let us hope King Robert is spared to see it so. But, if not, how would it be for the Lady Marjory? Even with a strong regent. She might thank you to be spared the crown, I think."

Men considered that, thoughtfully.

"Surely, above all, the desires of two persons require to be considered in this," the Earl of Moray put in. "Those of the lady herself, and of His Grace. Lacking that knowledge, how may we decide?" He looked at his other uncle.

Thus appealed to, the King sighed. "It is a hard matter. My personal desires, my love and affection for my daughter, my duty to the realm — all are here at odds. My daughter has suffered terribly. I would now deny her nothing. And yet — could her hand steer this realm? As to her wishes, it is too soon to have put it to her. For my own desire, then I would say — if she marries and bears a son, I would wish that one day he wore my crown."

A murmur of understanding and sympathy greeted that.

"It could be so," Edward took him up. "The Act of Succession passed at a parliament could be so written. Myself as king. The Lady Marjory's son, if such should be, thereafter king."

"And if *you* had a son, brother?" The King did not add the adjective 'lawful', there, as he was tempted to do — for Edward had indeed recently had a son by the Lady Isabella Ross, whom he had omitted to marry. The wronged lady's father's snarling noises from down the table made the point for him, however.

"*My* son would, by decree, take second place to hers."

Many looked at him doubtfully, wondering how likely any of them were to see such a thing happening.

"Let us leave it so, then," the King suggested. "I will ask my daughter her wishes. Consider this matter well, my lords, before the next parliament. Remembering that all must be decided for the best weal of this realm which we have fought so long to free and save." He drew a long breath. "Is there other business, my lord Abbot?"

"Only this of the awards, appointments and grants of lands, following upon the recent victory, Sire. The forfeited lands and positions available for distribution," the Chancellor said. "A long list."

"Ah, yes. Long, indeed. As is only fit and proper, since so many fall to be rewarded. But, happily, it is all set down, is it not? But requires reading over. My will in this matter. Do so, my lord, for this Council's approval — and let us be out of here, this warm summer day . . ."

* * *

That evening, in his private quarters of the castle, Bruce broached the matter with his daughter.

"As my only child, lass, you have all along been heir to Scotland's throne," he told her. "Now that you are a woman grown, and home again — how do you esteem it? How do you feel?"

"Feel? I feel no different than ever I have felt, Sire. I pray that I may never have to be queen."

"M'mmm. Why, my dear?"

"You would be . . . dead."

"Aye. But death comes to us all, one day. It may be a long while yet. But, in that day, you should be queen."

"Unless I die before you!"

"Marjory!" Elizabeth protested. "Such a thing to say, at your age! Not yet twenty years. At the beginning of your life."

"Many a time I wished myself dead. In London Tower," the girl said. Hollow-cheeked, pale, she looked a sad creature.

"But that is all past now, my dear. You must try to forget it."

"Yes. I am sorry. But it is not easy. To forget. So long . . ."

"To be sure, lass," her father said. "We know. We will do all in our power to help. But meantime you are heir to Scotland."

"Must I be so? Could it not be . . . another, Sire?"

"Is that your wish? Your considered wish? And . . . must you Sire me, girl? Can you not name me Father?"

"Yes. Yes — I am sorry."

"No, no. But — I would take it more kindly, lass. Now, this of the throne. All it means. Have you thought well on it?"

"I do not know. All that it means. Save that I have no wish to rule a nation."

"What *do* you wish for, Marjory?"

"Only . . . I think . . . to be left . . . in peace."

He sighed, and looked at Elizabeth, who spoke. "How can she know, Robert? Think you for her. She has been home only two days. If you can name this home. She has had no home, ever. No father, no mother. A captive for eight of her nineteen years. Long years held solitary, confined in London Tower. None permitted to speak with her. Then in a nunnery, alone again. Shut away from the world. If *I* near lost my reason, I, a grown woman, how would she, a child, fare? How can she tell you what she will wish, as heir to the throne?"

"To be sure, yes . . ."

"I had time and enough to think of it, Madam," the girl said. "This I do know — that I have no wish to rule. Is there no other? Must it be I?"

"Aye. Your uncle. Edward would have it, if he could. But yours is the right."

"Let him have it. I want nothing of it."

"It is less simple than that, girl. Edward, I think, would make but a poor king for Scotland. He acts first and thinks after."

"My dear — must we talk of this? Now? As though you were as good as dead!" Elizabeth protested. "You are but forty. Twenty years hence, perhaps, such might be needful. Not now."

"With a realm at war, see you, the succession is important. And we are still at war, more's the pity. Edward demands a decision. The matter will come before the next parliament. It is necessary that I know my mind, in this. And Marjory's."

The great-eyed girl looked from one to the other. "You . . . you could yet have a son, could you not?"

Her father drew a long breath. "That is in God's hands, lass."

Elizabeth spoke quietly. "It is our prayer, Marjory. But it seems less than likely. At my age. When no children came before. I fear that I am . . . barren!" What it cost Ulster's magnificent daughter to make that declaration, Bruce could only guess at.

"Say it not, my dear!" he exclaimed. "One so strong, so fine, so lusty as you! Here is nonsense. We have been parted long. But there is time yet."

"Perhaps. But I think we should not cozen ourselves. The chance of a prince is small. From me."

Her stepdaughter bit her lip. "Then . . . do you mean . . . would you have me . . . to marry? To beget a prince?"

Bruce cleared his throat. "That would be best. Advisable. A blessing for all. But — we would not push you. Into marriage. There is time."

"I do not wish to marry."

"Perhaps not. Yet. But, in time. It is expected. In your position. You know that."

"Who?" she demanded, baldly.

"Eh? Save us, Marjory — not so fast! You could have your choice. Of almost any unwed man in this land! Always remembering that he should be of a quality and name to father an heir to the throne. To choose one of lesser estate and fame could cause jealousies, offence, you understand . . ."

"I am not like to choose any," she said.

"You may change your mind, my dear," the Queen observed gently. "Once young men come wooing you!"

"Who would come wooing *me*?"

"Plenty, lass!" her father told her grimly. "But not all for the right reason. To be husband of the reigning queen, father of the king-to-be, many would be ambitious."

Distastefully Marjory Bruce screwed up her features. "I would have none of them. Find another monarch, Sire. Father. I am sorry. If not my Lord of Carrick, some other."

Exasperatedly Bruce gazed at her. "See you, girl — there is more to life, for a king's daughter, than saying you do not want this and you will not have that!"

"I am sorry . . ."

"And for all saints' sake, do not keep saying that you are sorry for everything! You are a Bruce . . .!"

"Robert," Elizabeth intervened, "the hour is late. We are all tired. Another time. This great matter of the succession need not be settled tonight?"

"No. That is true. Time enough . . ."

Later that night, Bruce and Elizabeth lay in each other's arms in the sweet exhaustion of love.

"By the Rude," the man murmured, running a caressing hand over the rich satisfactions of her person, "what ails us that we cannot make a child, sweeting? Between us. Our flesh is as one, if ever man's and woman's was. Is it so much to ask? That we achieve a son? A thing any scullion and kitchen-wench can do, with all the ease in the world! What ails us? When a son would banish so many of our troubles."

"Nothing ails *you*, my dear. That is proven! Other women have not failed you in this respect!" That was true. More than one of the ladies with whom he had consoled his manhood during those long years had produced sons which they proudly claimed were the King's.

He shrugged. "Is it that we are not suited, then? Each to each? 'Fore God — I *feel* suited to you, woman! As to none other."

"It is a strange thing. *I* could not feel more truly a woman, and giving."

"Giving, yes. None give as you do. Nor take! Bless you."
"Giving. Taking. But not making!"
"At least, the giving and taking is no burden, no hard task, lass!"
"Ah, no. No! The trying is joy! Joy!"
"Joy, aye. Then, shall we try once more, my love? Try . . .?"
"With all my heart!"

Chapter Four

It was surely as strange a sight as those quiet, green, south-facing Cheviot valleys had ever witnessed. As far back as eye could see, along the narrow winding floor of Upper Redesdale, was a dazzling mass of colour and stir in the mellow autumn sunlight of an October early afternoon. The place was in fact packed full of men and horses, richly caparisoned, armour gleaming, painted shields, heraldic surcoats and trappings, banners by the hundred. Women too added to the colour — for although the men greatly predominated, and mostly wore breastplates of steel or shirts of chain-mail, they were none of them in full heavy armour. At the head of this so strangely located and holiday-minded host, facing into the wider reaches where the Rede suddenly opened out of its hill-bound constrictions just north of Otterburn, and Lower Redesdale expanded into more populous territory, was still more colour and brilliance; for here the King and Queen and almost their entire Court waited and watched, while an impromptu archery contest proceeded. Bruce was anxious to encourage archery and bowmanship amongst his people — for it was an arm in which the Scots had always been weak, and had paid dearly for their weakness.

If this joining of green valleys was a strange place to be practising archery, it was a still stranger place to look for the royal Court of Scotland, fourteen miles into Northumberland, and facing south. Yet they had been here for a couple of hours already, and the long column, however vital and active seeming, was stationary.

Bruce himself, like most there, was not wholly preoccupied with the bows and arrows. His glance was apt to stray away southwards, down the widening vale ahead, eyes screwed up against the slanting yellow sunlight. And when he did not see what he wanted there, he tended to look over to where his daughter sat, drawing grass-stalks between her fingers. Marjory was never alone; yet somehow she gave the impression of being alone. Men eddied around her, young and not so young, the most gallant in the land. She was quietly civil towards them all and equally — but that was all. None received encouragement to linger.

Three months had done much for Marjory Bruce, physically. She has filled out not a little, the hollow cheeks and bent shoulders were largely gone. Indeed she was by no means unattractive. But the great eyes were still anxious, wary, her whole attitude tense, reserved. Men she obviously distrusted; women she kept at a distance. And she still had grievous coughing bouts.

"Walter is attentive," the Queen said, following the direction of her husband's gaze. "Of them all, he is the most . . . determined."

"And gaining little advantage, I fear!"

"Fear? Would you wish Walter success, then?"

"Why not? He is young. Honest. And looks well enough. I think he would be kind. And he is already kin. To you, at least." Walter Stewart was indeed Elizabeth's cousin, his father, James, the previous High Steward, having had to wife the Lady Eglidia de Burgh, the Earl of Ulster's sister.

"She shows no fondness for him."

"She shows no fondness for any! Is he ambitious, do you think?"

"To be more than Steward? Who knows. At least he is loyal, and always has been. And of as good blood as any in Scotland." She paused. "Keith, there. The Marischal. What of him? He also dances attendance."

"A sound man," Bruce acknowledged. "Sober. But older. And less illustrious of lineage. And was not always my friend. I would prefer young Walter."

"And Marjory? Which would *she* prefer?"

"Neither, it seems. None, indeed. I fear that if she is to marry, we will have to choose her husband for her. It is strange — the Bruces were ever a lusty race. The Mar blood it must be."

"Or the life she has had to lead. You must bear with her, Robert."

"Aye — but something must be contrived. I had hoped this adventure would have brought her out."

A shout of acclaim indicated that once again Sir Neil Campbell had won the archery by a clear lead; and none was louder in praise than the Lady Mary Bruce — nor more demonstrative in her whole-hearted kiss of approval. Her brother grinned.

"There is how Bruce women are apt to behave! Mary, God be thanked, has made a good recovery." It was certainly scarcely believable that the haggard, gaunt wreck of a woman of three months before could have been restored to this laughing, lively creature. Thin she still was, and was likely to remain; but vigour and the joy of life had returned.

"Mary would compound these last years, I think," Elizabeth said. "Will you let her wed Sir Neil, Robert?"

"To be sure. He is my very good friend. I have given him all Argyll, on the forfeiture of Lame John MacDougall of Lorn. Which makes him a very great lord. And a sound support of the crown in the Highland West. Such match pleases me well."

"I am glad. For they like each other assuredly, and will make a good couple. As, I hope, will Matilda and Sir Hugh. When he is at home!"

The King smiled a little. "Aye — Matilda is a born flirt. Young Hugh will have his hands full with that one. But she is not truly wanton, I think. At the test, she will be true."

"To be sure. And meanwhile, young Mentieth makes haste to test!" Hugh Ross was still away with his father and the Lord of the Isles, raiding in their galley fleets the English southern coasts. The Earl of Menteith, not yet of age but the more eager to play the man, was not letting the grass grow.

"No harm in that. My sisters can well look after themselves, the saints be praised!" And he jerked his head towards where Christian, Lady Seton, erstwhile Countess of Mar, held her own court of slightly older men. Christian had always been a woman who needed men about her, and her years of confinement in the nunnery must have taxed her hard. Now she was making up for lost time.

The Queen smiled. "I think, perhaps, it is some of your young men who need the taking care of! Sir Andrew Moray of Bothwell, for instance. How old would you say he was?"

"M'mm. His father, my friend, was slain at Stirling Bridge. That was in 1297 — seventeen years ago. That one was a boy of eight, then. That makes him twenty-five. Old enough to know his own mind! And to need no protection from me!"

"Christian is a year older than yourself, is she not? Forty-one!"

"What of it? There is much life in her yet. If only my daughter was as my sisters!"

On the fringe of the Lady Seton's group, a tall, serious but good-looking young man lingered, much junior to the others, the son of a hero, of the man who had done most to bring Bruce and Wallace together. His fascination with the King's elder sister was something of a joke at Court — but there was no doubt that Christian Bruce was not averse to Andrew Moray's attentions.

"And there is Isobel. In Norway. Is she of a like humour?" The eldest of the Bruce family was Queen of Norway.

"The good Lord knows! I have not seen her since I was a laddie. But she was beautiful — I remember that. The best looks of the family. And married very young. I have no doubt but that she sets the Court of Norway by the ears!" He sighed. "I wish that Isabel MacDuff could so find an interest in men. To take her mind off her hurt. She used to be spirited enough."

"Your Christina MacRuarie seems to have taken her under her raven wing! I wonder why?"

The Countess of Buchan, sour-looking, stern, did not so much avoid men as repel them. She had insisted on coming on this expedition, in her search for vengeance, that was all; Bruce would have left her behind, if he decently could, sympathetic as he was towards all that she had suffered in his cause. She was now sitting a little way apart, set-faced, eyes part-hooded, while Christina of Garmoran chatted to her.

"Christina is kind in more ways than one! I thought that you would have learned that, my dear. Clearly she feels for Isabel."

"Do not we all. But she will not be comforted . . ."

Shouts interrupted her, and turned all heads southwards. From the direction of Otterburn, banners, many banners, were showing above a low grassy ridge. More than rivers were joining in Redesdale that day.

As the heads of men and horses appeared, nodding plumes, gleaming lance-points and tossing manes, it could be seen that three great banners dominated all — those of Bruce, Douglas and Moray. The impression was of a triumphant host.

The King, with Lennox and Hay and a few other lords, strode out a little way to meet the newcomers. Cheering arose from both hosts.

James Douglas flung himself down from his horse, armour notwithstanding, and ran to fall on his knees before the monarch. "Sire," he cried, "Greetings! I rejoice to see you. Well met. Your message reached us at Simonburn. Last night. To our great good cheer."

"Aye, Jamie — it is good to have you back. And you, Thomas." His nephew, Moray, was not far behind Douglas. Edward Bruce remained in his saddle, grinning his mocking smile.

"What is this? Another tourney?" he exclaimed. "Have you brought all Scotland to meet us, Robert?"

"Call it a progress, brother. With a purpose. Has all gone well?"

Edward shrugged. "Well enough. It would have gone better had our nephew here not interfered."

"That is scarce fair, my lord!" Douglas protested. "The decision had to be Moray's."

"He was welcome to decide for his own force. Not mine."

"My decision could not but effect both forces, my lord," Moray conceded. "Yet it fell to me to make it. Mine was the responsibility."

"The command was mine . . ."

"My friends — I asked if all had gone well," the King cut in, only a little sharply. "I expected an answer not a dog-fight!"

"Your Grace's pardon," Douglas hastened to apologise. "It is a foolish bicker, no more. We won as far south as the Humber. Beverley and Holderness, on the east. Richmond on the west. Then my lord of Moray, keeping our rear, sent word that the Yorkshire lords were gathering men in great numbers, that he could not much longer promise to hold our rear secure. He said we must retire."

"Fleeing from shadows!" Edward scoffed. "I would have driven on. Cut my own way back and through, when I was ready. If Moray was so fearful, and must retire. But Douglas, on the east, played his game and turned back. I could not go on . . ."

"And by the Rude — why should you, man? At Beverley you were near 200 miles deep into England. More than half-way to London! Eighty miles further than ever before. That is magnificent, I say. Not a cause for quarrel! That you got so far was a wonder. And I thank you all."

"I would have reached the other Richmond. On the Thames!" Edward declared. "Even without this fine nephew of ours! Scared the Plantagenet out of his catamite's bed! But when Douglas deserted me . . ."

"My lord — you will take that word back!" Sir James cried. "On my oath, you will! I desert none. His Grace told me, before we started — told *you* that we were to be guided by Randolph, in our rear."

"I was given the authority in this . . ." Moray asserted.

"Not over me, Carrick, by God! You were not . . ."

"Silence!" the King cried, suddenly furious. "All of you. Not another word of this. It is unseemly. In my royal presence, and before all these. My lord Constable. And Sir Robert the Marischal. See that all are marshalled. Ready to move. The two hosts as one. Sir Neil Campbell to command the rearward. See you to it."

"Where go we now, Sire?" Edward demanded, unabashed.

"Down Redesdale to the North Tyne. And we burn Redesdale as we go — in the hope that we need not burn Tynedale."

"You make for Tynedale? With all this company? And intend to spare it? *We* spared nothing that we had time to burn!"

"Perhaps. But Tynedale is an ancient fief of the Scots crown. I go to resume suzerainty over it." He shrugged. "You were not pursued? No? Then, since you are good at burning, brother, will you aid with this business? Redesdale to be a balefire, to warn Northumbria that the King of Scots approaches!"

"As you will . . ."

So, as the royal cavalcade slowly made its colourful way southwards towards the great valley of the North Tyne, it did so down a corridor of fire and billowing smoke, a new and unwelcome experience for the ladies present — save perhaps for the Countess of Buchan who would fain have used a torch herself — however used to it were most of the men. In a belt some two miles wide, every manor and farm, every cot-house and barn and mill, went up in flames; all stacked grain and hay likewise, all cattle, horses and sheep driven off and sent herded back on the road to Scotland, with such booty as was readily transportable. All less mobile stock pigs, poultry and the like, was slaughtered and added to the flames. The unfortunate inhabitants themselves were not physically maltreated, unless they made actual resistance — which few indeed were unwise enough to attempt. Pathetic parties, groups of families, either fled apace into the hills, left and right, or stood afar off and watched their homes and livelihood devoured. Only churches were spared, and to these many of the refugees flocked, amid lamentations.

The Queen and her ladies had been brought up in a hard school, and did not complain. Indeed, they knew that they would have to put up with this, before they left Stirling. But they did not enjoy it, and were notably silent throughout. Fortunately the wind, from the south-west blew up the valley, largely carrying the smoke away from them.

"Unhappy Redesdale," Elizabeth said, "that it should lie north of Tynedale, and so be used as warning and example. When any other might have served."

"Aye, it is hard. But there is more than that to it," her husband told her. "Redesdale was paying its tribute. These last two years. To be spared our raiding. Like so many others. But at this last collection, they refused to pay. They fall to be taught another lesson."

"No doubt. But still, I say, poor Redesdale!" She glanced over her shoulder. "Robert — have pity on James Douglas," she urged, low-voiced. "He rides behind, there, a picture of woe. Edward, even Thomas Randolph, can take your strictures and be none the worse. But Sir James is otherwise. And surely he deserves well of you?"

"To be sure. But Jamie ought to know me better. We have been close for ten testing years. I could not berate my brother alone, before all. So I needs must seem to blame Douglas and Moray equally with him. They know that. But likewise, Jamie should have known not to persist with that bicker, as he did."

"He was so anxious to tell you all. How well they had done, how far they had won. And then, this!"

"Aye, Well . . ." Bruce half-turned in his saddle. "My Lord of Douglas to ride with the Queen and myself," he called clearly.

Eagerly the younger man spurred up. "I am sorry, Sire," he burst out. "It was ill done. I forgot myself. Your pardon, of a mercy! I shamefully forgot myself."

"The fault was scarcely yours, Jamie. But you know, better than most, that I cannot too openly chastise the second man in the kingdom, seem to take sides against my own brother. Even when it is clear that he is in the wrong. As here. Think no more of it. My sorrow that I had to speak as I did. When I so greatly esteem what you all achieved. You did very well. Better than I could have hoped. At what cost? In men, Jamie?"

"Very little, praise be. Scarce any, indeed. We fought no single battle, nor even a major skirmish. The English seem to have lost all spirit, since Bannockburn. A hundred will flee from two or three Scots. The terror of us went before us, melting the sinews of men. We burned so many towns that we lost all count. Their castles we could not spare time to assail; but manors we laid waste by the hundred. Most left abandoned before us. Surely we taught the English a sufficient lesson."

"Let us hope so. If it will but persuade King Edward to sign a peace treaty. Somehow he must be forced to it, if we are ever to build the Scotland we should have, the Scotland we have bought so dearly." The King shook his head. "That is why I make this progress to the Tyne. Something more that Edward Plantagenet cannot ignore. I go to assert my ancient overlordship over Tynedale. No King of England could accept that, I think, and still face his people. Either he must fight on again, or come to terms. And he is in no state to resume the war. Not for some time." Bruce paused. "These Yorkshire lords that Moray feared? How great a force did they assemble? And do they follow on, northwards?"

"They mustered a great host, yes. Many thousands. But of no great quality, and lacking in spirit. They did not attack us, either before or after we turned back — although our scouts told us that we passed within a few miles of their camp. They followed on after, but at a careful distance. How far, we could not tell, for our rearward lost touch with them. They are no danger, Sire — that I am certain."

"Good. I would prefer no battle with the ladies present . . ."

Lower Redesdale converged on the wider vale of the North Tyne near Bellingham, some ten miles down. Here, that evening, opposite the hamlet of Redesmouth, the Scots halted for the night, leaving a wide trail of complete devastation behind them. But no burning and ravage went on into Tynedale. Instead, many splendidly attired heralds and couriers, well escorted, were sent out, east and west, to make summons and proclamations.

The tented camp Bruce set up was deliberately magnificent, rivalling the tourney-ground cantonments of Stirling, with multi-hued pavilions, silken awnings, heraldic banners, and colours everywhere. In contrast to the grim business of burning and spoliation, a picnic and holiday atmosphere now prevailed, with feasting, music, even dancing on the greensward. Nevertheless pickets maintained a sharp watch around a wide perimeter — to the occasional discomfiture of sundry highly-placed love-makers and philanderers.

The King was in no hurry to move off, next day, to give his heralds — and the stern warning of burned Redesdale — time to make their maximum and widespread impact. It was noon before they started, and now a large company of mounted musicians led the way, dispensing sweet melodies. High officers of state, bishops and senior clergy, even three of the newly-arrived foreign ambassadors, from France, Norway and Hainault, came next, before the royal party, all clad in their most brilliant. The solid ranks of armour and men-at-arms kept well to the rear. The sun failed to shine, unfortunately, but at least it did not rain.

Five leisurely miles brought them to Wark, now only a village but formerly a place of some size and importance, chief messuage-place and administrative centre of one once-mighty Lordship and Honour of Tynedale. Here Bruce left most of the baggage and a substantial number of men, to erect a more permanent camp in the level and readily defendable haugh between the Wark and Dean Burns and the River North Tyne. Here they would return.

Another seven miles or so, by Chipchase, Simonburn, Humshaugh and Chollerford, brought them to Hexham, at the junction of the North and South Tyne. They met with no opposition — and if their reception by the country-folk was scarcely rapturous, at least some people did peer from windows and doorways and pend-mouths. Tynedale waited, tense, watchful – but it did wait.

At the famous and ancient ecclesiastical town of Hexham-on-Tyne, dominated by its great Priory, larger than many a proud abbey, it was Robert Bruce's turn to wait, outside the massive walls, while the Prior was summoned with the keys. It was not much more than a year since Bruce had last been here, and in a different mood, and Master Robert de Whelpington came in fear and trembling. But he was greeted genially.

"A good day to you, my lord Prior. I hope that I see you well? And your Priory and town prosperous?"

The cleric, a stocky, red-faced man, young for so eminent an office, swallowed. "Aye, Majesty. Or ... no, Majesty," he stammered. "Not ... not prosperous. No. Not that. In these hard times. We are poor. Much impoverished ..."

Bruce, glancing over the other's rich clothing and beringed fingers, smiled. "Come, come, Master Whelpington! Surely you mistake? This is one of the richest foundations in the North of England. Unless ... unless you are so sore hit by raising and equipping your steward and the men you sent to fight against me at Bannockburn! And paying their ransoms thereafter!"

The Prior positively gobbled. "No, no, Sire — not so! It was not me. It was my Lord Percy. My lord of Nothumberland. He it was. He insisted that we provide a troop of men. Under his banner. He is a hard man ..."

"I know Henry Percy passing well, Sir Prior. But also I know your Priory's banner and livery! I hold that banner, sir, a Saltire Or on Azure, captured amongst a thousand others. It lies at Stirling still. Perhaps I should have brought it back to you?" He shrugged. "But that is not my concern today. I am here on kindlier business. My herald would inform you, last night? I am come to lift the burden from your shoulders. The burden of Henry Percy and his like! You say that he is a hard man. Then, my friend, you may find me kinder! For I have come to resume this Honour and Lordship of Tynedale into the Scots crown. Percy is no longer your lord. I am. The King of Scots."

The Prior stared, biting his lip. But he risked no words.

"How say you, sir? Is not this good news? A king to protect you, not a robber lord who cares nothing for Holy Church!"

"Ah ... yes, Sire."

"Is that all you can say, my Lord Prior?"

"No, Sire. I . . . I am overwhelmed. It is too much for me. Give me time, Your Majesty . . ."

"Aye. But only until tomorrow. Tomorrow you, and all Tynedale, shall swear fealty to me. Not here. At Wark, the ancient seat of this lordship. You will see to it. You understand. You and yours. Meanwhile — my lord of Moray, take these keys. I place the town in your charge. See that my lord Prior, the magistrates, and all men of substance, present themselves before my royal presence at Wark by noon tomorrow, to take the oath of fealty. No excuses will be permitted. Bringing their tokens of service and allegiance. Detach sufficient men for this duty, nephew. The Prior will give you all aid. I will not enter Hexham today. When I do, I expect to be received fittingly. Bells ringing, streets garlanded, townfolk out and in their best. Is it understood? Very well. Let us return to Wark, Your Grace, my lords and ladies. We rest there hereafter."

With no further leave-taking of the unhappy Prior, the King led his great company round and back whence they had just come, northwards. He signed to the instrumentalists.

"Let us have music . . ." he called.

* * *

Back at Wark, the Scots settled in for a stay of days. The working-party had been busy erecting streets of tents, field-kitchens, horse-lines and watering-points, a tourney-ground, even a temporary market-place — since the existing one in the village was small and inadequate — on the level meadows to the south of the township. For a few days at least, little Wark was to become a worthy capital of the historic and once illustrious Honour and Liberty of Tynedale — in the interests of political strategy.

The Tynedale lordship was important from any point of view. For one thing, it comprised no fewer than thirty-eight manors, many of them rich ones, and included its own royal forest and numerous special and hereditary privileges. Its significance as a Scottish crown holding within the realm of England was self-evident. Alexander the Third, of blessed memory, had almost come to blows with the young King Edward the First over it, in 1277; and, as events turned out, it might have been better had he in fact done so, while he and Scotland were still strong, and his realm united, and Edward was not yet intolerably puffed up with grandeur and successful conquest in France, Wales and Ireland. As it was, to keep the peace and promote good relations, Alexander had consented, against better judgement, to do fealty to Edward for this ancient Scottish crown heritage, inherited from an ancestress, Matilda of Northumberland, wife of David the First and grand-niece of William the Conqueror. Alexander, needless to say, had drawn the line at going in person and kneeling before Edward to take the feudal oath of homage, and had actually sent Robert Bruce, Lord of Annandale, Bruce's grandfather, to do it for him — one of the few weak and unwise acts of a puissant monarch; though it falls to be remembered that Scotland and England were then on excellent neighbourly terms, with no bad blood between them. Edward Plantagenet changed all that. Consumed by his ever-growing lust for power and domination, he used this proxy act of homage for the Tyndale lordship, and other of Alexander's English estates, as excuse for the subsequent claim for overlordship over all Scotland. When Alexander fell to his untimely death over Kinghorn cliff, and his grandchild heiress, the Maid of Norway, died on her way to Scotland to take up her kingdom, Edward declared that he was suzerain of all Scotland, Lord Paramount, since the King of Scots had done homage to him, the King of England. The fact that the homage had been done only for lands in England, and that Alexander had proclaimed that Tynedale was a detached part of Scotland and therefore not a subject for homage anyway, was ignored. Edward used one of the greatest armies in Christendom to back up his claim. Tynedale, then, was one of the basic causes of the long and bloody Wars of Independence.

Bruce now planned to give a different twist to the screw.

That evening was passed in feasting, music and a torchlight and bonfire festival of dance and song, after the Highland fashion that Bruce had learned to appreciate during his campaigns in the North. Sundry of the local folk were constrained to attend, and treated kindly — to their manifest wonder and suspicion. Tynedale these last twenty years, was more used to being a battleground than a royal playground.

In the morning, happily, the sun shone. All forenoon, while a programme of horse- and foot-racing, wrestling and manly sporting contests proceeded, people kept arriving from all the castles, manors and villages of the lordship, doubtfully, reluctantly, in obedience to the imperious summons of heralds and messengers. All were courteously received by various officers of state, dined and looked after — but none were presented to the King and Queen, however lofty their status. The royal family kept their distance in a special elevated enclosure of silken awnings and banners which crowned a green mote-hill where once the timber castle of Wark had risen.

A carefully-calculated few minutes before noon, the Prior of Hexham arrived, in very different state from his yesterday's appearance. He came in full canonicals, under a resplendent cope, at the head of quite a lengthy procession, with singing choristers and men-at-arms, mounted on a white jennet and with a silken canopy of the Priory colours of blue and gold held over his head by four mounted acolytes. Holy Church had apparently decided that some display was in order.

The Church had dominated Tynedale, of course, since Alexander's day. On King Edward's unilateral assumption of suzerainty over Scotland, he had casually handed over this lordship to Anthony Beck, Bishop of Durham — whom he had promoted to that princely see from being one of his wardrobe clerks. And that bullet-headed militant clerk had naturally used Hexham, the ecclesiastical centre, rather than Wark, to control his new domain, ruling Tynedale through the Priors thereof, and with a rod of iron as he did all else. So, for twenty years, successive monkish incumbents had lorded it in the name of their episcopal master, as well as owning great Church lands of their own — and scarcely gained in local popularity in the process.

At midday exactly, a fanfare of trumpets gained silence for the herald King of Arms, who then called on all present to draw near, in orderly fashion, to the mote-hill, into the presence of the most puissant and mighty prince, by God's grace, Robert, King of Scots. Thereafter, himself proceeding half-way up the grassy mound, he declared:

"Hear me, King of Arms and Grand Seannachie of the realm of Scotland. In the name of His Grace, our liege lord Robert, I do now declare, affirm and pronounce that he, the said Lord Robert, hereby resumes and takes unto himself, this his Honour, Liberty and Lordship of Tynedale, justly and duly by his inheritance, edict and law, to have and to hold for all time coming as a royal patrimony and as an integral part of his realm of Scotland, as did his ancestors before him, and as is duly documented, signed and sealed in the Assize Roll of this the county of Northumberland of the year 1279, and otherwhere, acknowledging the said Lordship of Tynedale to be outside the Kingdom of England within the Kingdom of Scotland. Moreover, all grants, charters, detachments and privileges in the said Lordship, wrongously and unlawfully given by the Kings of England, Archbishops of York, Bishops of Durham, or any other whatsoever, of late years, are hereby cancelled, withdrawn, nullified; and only those grants, charters and privileges granted by the said gracious Lord Robert, King of Scots, his heirs and successors, shall stand and hold good for all time coming. In token whereof it is required that all occupiers, holders and tenants of lands, office and privileges in the said Honour, Liberty and Lordship of Tynedale do herewith come forward, in due order, and do homage for the same, as is just, lawful and proper, to the said Robert, as liege lord, taking the oath of fealty on their bended knees, renouncing all other. This in the name of Robert, King of Scots. God save the King!"

The flourish of trumpets that followed this peroration was drowned in the great shout of acclaim from thousands of Scots throats — if from few English.

"To present himself first before the King's Grace," the speaker went on, when the noise had abated, "I call upon Sir John de Bellingham, Hereditary Forester of the Royal Forest of Tynedale, to make homage."

After a little initial shuffling and delay, an elderly man came limping forward from the long file of Englishmen, to climb the mound, flanked by two Scots esquires. He bowed before the King, shook his head as though recognising that protest was pointless and sank down on stiff knees, holding out his hands. He did not once raise his head.

Bruce extended his own hands, palms together, for the other to take within his.

"Repeat the oath of fealty," the King of Arms commanded. "In these words. In the sight of God and all these present, I, John de Bellingham, knight, do acknowledge . . ."

"In the sight of God and all present," the older man mumbled, "I, John de Bellingham acknowledge . . ."

"Speak up, man! Do acknowledge the noble and mighty Robert, King of Scots, to be my liege lord . . ."

"I cannot, Sire!" the Englishman burst out. "I cannot take you as my liege lord. King Edward is my liege, and to him I have sworn my fealty."

"Silence, sirrah!" the herald barked. "Or do you wish to lose your lands and your liberty both?"

"One moment, my lord King of Arms," Bruce intervened. "Sir John — King Edward of England is indeed your liege lord in matters pertaining to the realm of England. This I do not gainsay. But for the lands you hold in Tynedale, pertaining to the realm of Scotland, *I* am your liege. You are at liberty to refuse fealty therefor; also for the office of Royal Forester of Tynedale, with all its rights and profits. But, if so, you lose the said lands and office forthwith, I promise you. Choose you, my friend."

The other moistened his lips and glanced up at last at the King, swiftly, briefly. He nodded, unspeaking, submitting.

"Proceed, King of Arms," Bruce murmured.

"Do acknowledge Robert King of Scots, to be my liege lord, for the lands of Bellingham and Henshaw, and for the office of Keeper of the said King's Forest of Tynedale, with all its pertinents and profits."

The knight muttered the required words.

"Speak plain, man. And say further—in pursuance of which oath, I do swear to uphold the said King Robert with all my strength against all and any who may hereafter hold contrary interests, so help me God!"

"... so help me God!" the other ended, unhappily.

"I accept your fair oath of fealty, Sir John, and rely upon your good support hereafter," the monarch acknowledged gravely. "Also I shall require account for your stewardship of my Forest of Tynedale over these years past, and payment of what is mine by right and law. See you to it. You may retire, and hereafter be my guest in the festivities that are to follow. Next, my lord?"

"I summon Sir Adam de Swinburne, Sheriff of Northumberland," the herald cried.

A big, florid, bull-like man came striding forward, by no means hanging his head. Handsomely clad in velvets and fur, he gave no impression of submission. He drew himself up before the King, and bowed briefly.

"I am prepared to offer a limited form of homage for my Tynedale lands, Sir King," he jerked. "As to yourself, as lord of these manors."

"On your knees, fellow!" the King of Arms rasped.

Bruce waited until the other was approximately and awkwardly down on one thick knee.

"It is not for you to offer anything, Sir Adam!" he said. "I *command*. Command fullest fealty and allegiance. If you choose not to yield it—why, I understand you have still large lands outside Tynedale. You may repair to them! And leave Tynedale to others."

"Sire—you would put a noose round my neck, in this! I am King Edward's sheriff of this county."

"Not I, my friend. *I* do not put a noose round any man's neck. You do, of yourself. Yours is the choice."

Swinburne cleared his throat. "Then ... I must accept. Under protest, Sire."

"No. *I* do not accept. I accept nothing under protest. You make the full oath freely, or none at all. Nor do I debate further with such as you, sir!"

Wordless, the other held out his open hands for the King's.

"Proceed, my lord King of Arms."

The next to be called up was one Sir William de Ros of Yolton, for the manor of Haltwhistle. A diffident and nervous youngish man, he made no fuss nor protest about the oath-taking, however much he stammered over the words. When he had hurried off, the herald asked whether he would now call the churchman.

"Not the Prior, no. Not yet. Master Whelpington, I think, will be none the worse of a little more waiting!"

Undoubtedly the Prior of Hexham would have expected to be the first to be summoned to the royal presence, however reluctant he might be to make any vows of fealty. The Church's holdings in the lordship were greater than any other, and its senior representative a power to be reckoned with.

A succession of smaller men were called out and made their obeisance and allegiance without demur, as a gabbled formality, only anxious to be back into a safe anonymity. Prior Whelpington fretted under his splendid awning.

At length the King of Arms pronounced his name and style. Frowning, he came forward, still under the canopy, although the acolytes were now, of course, on foot. The King raised a single eyebrow towards the herald, who promptly flicked a dismissive hand, and two of his minions stepped out in the Prior's path and peremptorily ordered the acolytes back. Less assuredly the cleric came on, alone.

"So, my lord Prior," Bruce greeted him, "do you find the sun trying?"

"The sun . . .?"

"Your canopy. I hope that you may subsist without it, at least while you take your vows of fealty."

"Your Majesty — I pray to be excused. Any taking of vows. It is not right and proper. That I should kneel before you. I am the representative of Holy Church, here in Tynedale. My allegiance is not to an earthly king . . ."

"It is not as representative of Holy Church that I summoned you here, Master Whelpington. It is as holder of large lands in this my lordship."

"But the lands are held by Holy Church, not of myself."

"To be sure. But if Holy Church elects to hold large lands and temporalities, collect rents, extort dues and service, and so to act the temporal lord, then Holy Church must pay the price. You are here to do feudal homage to me, as feudal lord and superior, for lands and privileges which the Church hold of me in feudal tenure. It is simple."

"But, Sire — the Church is different. It is not as these others. It is Christ's own Body. His divine substitute, here on earth."

"I do not recollect hearing that Christ was a holder of great lands and privileges when He was on earth, sir!"

"The Church is in the world, and so must act as in the world. It cannot be otherwise . . ."

"Precisely, Sir Priest! Therefore, in your wordly capacity as Steward of the Church's wordly gear, tenancies and lands, you will do homage for those that stem from my lordship, like every other worldy tenant. Unless, to be sure, you prefer to relinquish them. That course is open to you, and no oath-taking necessary."

The Prior twisted the glistening rings on his fingers. Then he jutted his plump chin, and stared at a point somewhere above the King's head. "I cannot swear fealty to you, Sire," he said in a strained voice. "It is impossible. You are . . . man excommunicate!"

Bruce said nothing for long moments. When he spoke, his voice was level. "You say that? You are bold, at least! Then, if you cannot render what is due to a man excommunicate, neither can you accept from him such lands, titles and tenancies. I must needs withdraw them therefore, for your sake and mine. And bestow them elsewhere. Others will be glad to have them. My lord King of Arms — how many manors of mine does the Priory of Hexham hold in fee? Not Church lands, but manors of which I am the superior?"

"Nine, Your Grace. Nine entire manors, besides rights of pasture, turf-cutting, millage, water and the like, over much other land."

"Aye. Then we shall find new vassals for all such, on the resignation of the Prior of Hexham. Let it be so proclaimed."

"No, Sire — no!" Whelpington cried. "I do not resign them. I cannot!"

"If you are not prepared to make fealty for them, you must." Bruce was suddenly stern, patience exhausted. "But enough of this, sirrah. It is not my habit to debate with vassals! You have my royal permission to retire."

"Majesty — of a mercy! Not that. I will do homage. Whatever you say." He plumped down on his knees. "My lord Bishop — and the Archbishop — they would be wrath. Exceedingly. If the lands were lost. I would be dismissed. Let me take the oath . . ."

"Very well, my lord Prior. I will overlook your ill-spoken words. On this occasion. But not again. Say on."

Not waiting for the herald's prompting, the cleric launched into the fealty formula, clutching the King's hand between sweating palms.

The entire distasteful business over, Bruce rose, wiping his hands. He turned to his wife and daughter who had sat throughout just behind his chair. "So much for the delights and majesty of kingship!" he said wryly. "A huckster, I have something to sell, and must needs drive a hard bargain! Men are scarce at their noblest when chaffering. I hope that you have been entertained, if not elevated?"

"Better this than swordery and bloodshed. Or burning," Elizabeth commented. "Think you this will bring Edward of Carnarvon to the conference table?"

"If it does not, nothing will!" He shrugged. "But that is the worst of it done with, God be praised! Now for better things — the tourney, games, feasting. Be gracious to these English now, my dear — but not too gracious! They must learn who is master here. And tomorrow we will enter Hexham . . ."

Chapter Five

Turnberry, in spring, was a fair place, all shouting larks and wheeling seabirds, great skies, spreading sandy machars, blue seas, white waves and magnificent vistas across the Firth to the soaring, jagged mountains of Arran. The castle itself, above the shore, was less daunting than many, a wide-courtyarded place of mellow stone with walls which, because of its low protective cliffs on three sides, did not require such lofty and prison-like masonry as was usual. It was Bruce's birthplace, chief seat of his mother's Carrick earldom, and his memories of it still tended to glow with the light and lustre of boyhood's carefree days — even though there were now apt to be occasional shadows from the grim night of massacre, eight years before, when he had returned here from his Hebridean exile, to make his first bloody assault on an English-held fortress of his mainland realm.

But, this breezy, bright morning of billowy white cloud galleons and the scent of clover, seaweed and raw red earth, the man's thoughts were concerned with the future, not the past, as he picked his way alone down over the rocks, sand-slides and crevices of the shore. It was good to be alone for a little; yet he frowned as he went. Elizabeth said that he frowned too much, these days . . .

He was seeking his daughter Marjory. Elizabeth said that she came down here, to the shore, a lot, to sit, also alone. With any other young woman of her years, status and looks, such withdrawals could be looked upon as far from unnatural — and the parallel absence of one or more young men could be looked for also. Not so with Marjory Bruce. If one thing was sure, it was that his only child *would* be alone, despite the plenitude of escorts who would have jumped at the opportuntity to accompany her.

He found her in a hollow of the broken cliff-face, dabbling her feet in a clear rock-pool, and gazing out across the sparkling Clyde estuary to the blue, shadow-slashed mountains. She withdrew and hid her white foot hastily at sight of her father. Bruce shook his head at that automatic, almost guilty gesture, but restrained his tongue.

"I used to know every inch of this shore," he told her, casually. "I played here, as a boy. And found it a deal more kindly kingdom than that I now cherish!"

"Yes," she said.

He sat down near her, and began to loosen his boots. "A pool, replenished by the tide, is a world in itself, is it not? A different order, of time, strength, beauty. A starfish for king! These winkles, in their shells, for knights and lairds in their castles. Clinging little limpets who cleave to their patch of stone, for the humble folk — for it is all they have. Scurrying, fearful creatures that hide in the waving forests of weed. Hunters or hunted? All conforming to some laws and order we know not of. Until some uncaring, heedless god puts in his great foot — so! And all seems changed. For a moment. And only seems so. For all is everlastingly the same." And he dabbled his bare foot in the cold water.

She did not comment, nor ventured her own foot back again.

"Each creature's world is, in the end, what he makes of it," he went on. "The heavy feet of fate disturb the surface, yes. But underneath, the inner life is our own. To make or to mar. I have marred much of mine. Shamefully, terribly marred. But I have made something, also."

"Yes."

"You lass, esteem this world but little, I think? And would make your own? Withdraw from the one, into the other. Is it not so?"

The inclination of her head was barely perceptible.

"That is well enough. As an escape, a refuge. But not as a world to live in, my dear. We must live in the world into which we were born. And make what of it we may."

"What are you seeking to tell me?" she asked then, level-voiced. "That I must do better? That I must laugh and sing and dance? That I must find all men a joy and a delight? And all women, too?"

"Scarce that, lass. I would but have you to understand that your life can still be full and rich. Rich, for you. That although you have suffered grievously, that time is past. You are young, and have most of your life to come. You can still make much of it. Being my daughter is not all trial and sorrow. You can have . . . almost anything that you ask for. Anything you may wish."

The look she turned briefly on him, then, shocked him.

He bit his lip. "Marjory — I know that, for my sake — or because you were my daughter — you suffered intolerable things. Were for years shut up, alone, first in that Tower of London, then in a nunnery. Kept alone, spoken to by none. God knows I do not, cannot, forget this. Part of the price I paid for this kingdom! But . . . you must seek to put the ill past from you. As I seek to do. As the Queen seeks to do. And your aunts. I have much to put behind me, sweet Christ! I, who murdered a man at Christ's own altar. Who have condemned three brothers, by my actions, to death most shameful — three brothers, and friends innumerable. The guilt of it comes to me, often. In the night, especially. But, see you, I do not, must not, dwell on it. *You* have no guilt; the guilt is mine. But the weight of woe is ever with you. You must put it from you, lass — I say, you must!"

Marjory only shook her head. "You do not understand," she whispered.

"Then tell me. Tell me, your father."

Helplessly she spread her hands. "How can I? It is not possible." Her eyelids drooped. "I wish that I had died. In the Tower. Almost I did. They wished that I would. As did I. But I did not die. It would have been better . . ."

"Dear God, girl — never say it! Not that."

"Why not. When I think it, know it. What is wrong with death?"

Almost he groaned, as helplessly he looked at her. "What . . . what have they done to you?" he said.

She made no answer.

Bruce fought down the rising tide of anger, frustration, apprehension. Determinedly he steadied his voice. "See you, daughter — I ask you to turn your mind to this matter. This matter of the realm. Of today's parliament. It is necessary that we speak of it. Now. I have tried to speak with you on it, so many times. But you would not. The succession. Today it will be decided. You are listening? Today's parliament must decide the matter."

"Is it not already decided?" she returned listlessly. "My Uncle Edward is to have the succession, is he not?"

"It is less simple than that, Marjory. Edward desires it, yes. And I hear must have it. Many will support him. But he will not make a good king. He is rash, headstrong — and his very rashness poses a further problem. For he is unmarried, and has no heir — however many bastards! He is, indeed, more like to die a sudden death than I am! The wonder is he has not already done so! Leaving none to succeed him. The succession could scarce be in worse hands."

She shook her head, as though deliberately disassociating herself from responsibility.

"Any Act of Succession, therefore, by parliament, must declare a second destination. Should the first heir to the throne die without lawful issue. It must, can only, be yourself, Marjory. After Edward. Whether you wish it or no. There is none other."

"What are you telling me, Sire?"

That word sire rankled. Bruce frowned. "This, girl. That the throne's succession is of the greatest importance for the realm. A continuing succession. If it is to be saved from internal war and misery, and the evils of rival factions fighting for the crown. It is my duty, as monarch, to ensure that succession to the best of my ability."

"Yes."

"Therefore, Marjory, since it seems that you will make no move in the matter, I intend to announce to this afternoon's parliament at Ayr that it is my decision to give your hand in marriage to Walter Stewart, High Steward of Scotland. And that, failing other heir of my own body, the succession, after Edward, shall devolve upon you, my daughter, and thereafter on any issue from such marriage." Robert Bruce did not realise how sternly, almost harshly, he had made that difficult pronouncement.

The young woman, after an initial catch of breath, made no comment whatsoever.

"You hear? Walter Stewart."

"Yes."

"Save us — have you nothing to say, girl? When your husband is named for you?"

"Only that I guessed it would be he."

"You did? How so?"

"From the way you spoke to him, these last months. Looked at him. Left us together."

"So! And what have you to say? Of Walter Stewart?"
"As well he, as other."
"Of a mercy! Is that all?"
"What would you have me to say?"
"At least, how he seems to you as a man, a husband. He is handsome, well-mannered — but no pretty boy. Younger than you, but able with a sword, sits a horse well, can wrestle. He is a great noble, with large lands, head of one of the most illustrious houses in my kingdom."
"Yes. So you would have him for your good-son. Have his child heir your throne."
"No! Or . . . i' faith, girl — you are sore to deal with! It is necessary that you wed. You know that. You could have your choice of any in the realm. But you would not. Would choose none. So I must needs choose for you. Walter Stewart asked for your hand. I know none better. Do you?"
"I have said, as well he as other. What more do you want from me? I shall obey you."
"From my daughter, my only child, I look for more than obedience."
"Your only child born in wedlock," she corrected.
His brows shot up. "Ha — does that gall you, then?"
"You must wish that it had been otherwise. That one or other of these had been my mother's child. And I had been born bastard. It would have spared us both much."
He stared at her nonplussed, at a loss. "I never wished you other than very well," he said. "As a child, I found you . . . a joy."
"When you *saw* me, came near me."
"I was fighting, girl! Fighting for this kingdom. For eighteen years I have been fighting."
"Yes," she nodded. "You have your kingdom."
Sighing, he began to pull on his boots. "I have my kingdom," he agreed heavily. He stood up. "Was I wrong to believe that I could have my daughter also?" When she made no response, he went on, "I go back to the castle. It is a dozen miles to Ayr, and we leave at noon. Do you attend the parliament?"
She shook her head. "Only if you command it."
"I command nothing of you, lass."
"Save that I marry. And produce you an heir."
He spread his hands in token of resignation, or possibly defeat, and left her sitting there.

* * *

The Ayr parliament of April 1315 had much to discuss besides the question of the succession. Foremost came the peace offensive, the great endeavour to bring the English to negotiate a firm and lasting peace, not just another temporary truce in this unending warfare; and part and parcel thereof, their recognition of Bruce's kingship and the essential and complete independence of his kingdom. This was elementary, basic to all settlement; yet strangely, though the English claim to overlordship, suzerainty, was only some twenty years old, and the product of one man's megalomania, this was the stumbling block holding up all agreement — despite Edward the Second's hatred for his late father and all his works.

But before this vital issue, there was a symbolic item to be staged, a mere ceremony but significant of much, in the Great Hall of Ayr Castle, the same slightly smoke-blackened hall, built by the English invaders, where once William Wallace had hanged the fatly obscene nude body of the sheriff, Arnulf, and his two chief henchmen, before burning all. This afternoon, Abbot Bernard of Arbroath, in his capacity of Chancellor of the realm and chairman of the assembly, after bowing to the King and opening the proceedings, called the name and style of the most noble Sir Patrick Cospatrick, 9th Earl of Dunbar and March.

There was a hush, as everywhere men eyed the side door which opened to reveal the slender, darkly handsome person of a proud-featured middle-aged man, splendidly attired. Looking neither right nor left, this newcomer strode firmly down the long aisle between the ranks of Scotland's great ones, unhesitant, straight for the dais, which he mounted, to bow before the throne.

"Your Grace, my lord Robert, I, Patrick of Dunbar, humbly crave leave to make my due homage to yourself as liege lord," he announced in clear, almost ringing tones.

Bruce, in his gorgeous scarlet and gold Lion Rampant tabard, permitted himself just the glimmer of a smile. There was nothing humble about the voice or attitude, nor in the level glance of those dark arrogant eyes. Nevertheless he inclined his head, graciously, as though well satisfied. "Welcome to my Court, Cousin," he said.

The fact of the matter was that this represented victory, undeniable victory. This man, perhaps the greatest in power of all Scotland's thirteen earls, and second only to the absent Fife in seniority, had been the most unswervingly of all on the English side. Which was scarcely to be wondered at, since his lands, such as were not in Northumberland and further south, were all in the Merse, the East Borders, in Berwickshire and Lothian, areas which had been wholly and consistently in English occupation, almost defenceless against invasion. This man's father, dying five years before, had fought boldly with the English on every major battlefield of the wars, from the very first, that of Dunbar itself. And the son it was who had aided Edward the Second to escape James Douglas and his other pursuers after Bannockburn by providing a boat to take him from Dunbar to Bamburgh. Now this confirmed Anglophile had decided that it was time to change sides. Nothing could more plainly underline the fact that he believed that Bruce's hold on Scotland was secure.

Taking the King's hands in his, the Earl repeated the oath of fealty as forthrightly as he had done all else. Bruce nodded.

"Your homage I receive gladly, Cousin," he said. "We shall let the past be past, for our mutual weal. And that of this realm. Your lands and estates are herewith returned to you." This was said more loudly than the rest, and was aimed at the ears of those who believed still that the King was over-kind and gentle to traitors. For Patrick of Dunbar could still indeed have represented much danger to Bruce's throne.

This was not only for geographical and strategic reasons, important as these were. It was what was in the Earl's veins that represented the greater menace. For his line was royal, descending directly—more directly than Bruce's own—from the ancient Celtic monarchs. The first of the line had been Malcolm, a grandson of Malcolm the Second, and the brother of Duncan the First whom MacBeth had murdered. The descent had been from father to son since then. Moreover, this same first Malcolm had married a granddaughter of Ethelred, King of England: while the 4th Earl had wed an illegitimate daughter of King William the Lion. In the great competition for the Scots crown, after the Maid of Norway's death, this man's father was one of the competitors. In the end he had thrown in his weight behind Bruce's grandfather's claim. But the fact remained that here was an alternative line to the Scots throne, which could be used against Bruce and his successors. This oath of fealty, pronounced before an entire parliament, was a major insurance against trouble.

As Dunbar stepped down from the dais and proceeded to the earl's benches, amidst mutterings from sundry present, led by Edward Bruce, the Chancellor raised his voice again.

"The matter of the recent negotiations at York relative to a peace between this realm and that of England. My lord William, Bishop of St. Andrews, who led His Grace's commissioners, to speak."

William Lamberton rose, at the head of the bishops' benches.

Last time he had sat in this castle of Ayr, he had been a hunted refugee, dressed in ragged, nondescript style, and hungry, seeking to persuade Robert Bruce to accept the Guardianship along with John Comyn. His great gaunt frame had a permanent stoop to it now.

"My lord Chancellor, we have little good to report. After the raids deep into England, and His Grace's resumption of the Tynedale lordship, King Edward was forced to take measures. He appointed Aymer de Valence, Earl of Pembroke, to be governor of all the North of England, between Trent and Tweed, wielding viceregal power and authority — a thing unprecendented in England while the monarch is himself in the country. But Pembroke, although a hard man and an able soldier, found both lords and people in no mood for fight. Or, let us say, in no mood to fight the Scots, since they were scarce loth to fight amongst themselves. Indeed, defeat in the field, at Bannockburn, and weak leadership, has brought the English to do what they have ever mocked the Scots for doing — fighting each other instead of the enemy! There was, and is, near to civil war in the North of England, with large bands, often led by lords and knights, harrying the land. Some even claim that they do so in the name of the King of Scots!"

There was some laughter and acclaim at this picture of their enemy's discomfiture, but Lamberton held up his hand sternly. "If this is of no credit to the English, nor is it of any benefit to us," he declared. "It but creates confusion, and distracts King Edward from the true issue — coming to terms with His Grace. He did go so far as to agree to talk with us. At York. On the subject of a peace. His Grace sent four commissioners, myself honoured to be one. We went to York, to treat with the English commissioners. And did so treat. For weeks. With little result. The English would not concede our terms. Even the most modest."

"How modest, my lord Bishop, were your terms?" the Earl of Dunbar and March asked, not aggressively but not diffidently either. Obviously he was going to be no cypher in the realm's affairs.

"Questions may be asked only through myself, my lord," Abbot Bernard reminded, but not objectionably.

"Entirely modest," Lamberton answered. "We demanded the recognition of this realm of Scotland as the indepedent kingdom which it always was; and that our Lord Robert was our lawful and rightful king. And, secondly, that the English troops be withdrawn from Berwick-on-Tweed, the only Scots fortress they still hold. This, and assurances of no further interference in the affairs of our realm. Sundry other small matters, but these were the main requirements. None can say that they are not modest. We could demand nothing less. Yet it is these that King Edward will not accept. The independence of Scotland, and the suzerainty of King Robert. He still claims to be Lord Paramount of Scotland, as did his father. Despite all. Despite defeat, raids, and His Grace's homage-taking in Tynedale."

"Then we must teach him otherwise!" Edward Bruce cried. "I have said all along that we were too gentle, too soft. The English understand only one argument — force. Naked steel. Show them that, and they will bargain. If I had but been allowed to drive on to London, last June . . .!"

There was a growl of approval from many throats.

"My lord Bishop — have you finished?" the Chancellor asked.

Lamberton nodded. "Save only to say that though we talked for weeks, we could move them nothing, in this. King Robert is a rebel, they said. The English have an arrogant assumption of authority that is beyond all debate. I do believe that they conceive it God-given! Certain subjects are not for discussion. One is that the Scots are an inferior people. As are the Welsh and the Irish. They cannot be other than subject. Possibly the French also. Save that there are more Frenchmen!" That the stern and statesmanlike Lamberton spoke so, was eloquent testimony of his frustration and helplessness.

Sir Neil Campbell, who with the Earl of Lennox and Bishop Balmyle of Dunblane had been Lamberton's fellow-commissioners, stood up. "My lord Chancellor," he said, "it is my belief that we but waste our time seeking this treaty of peace. The English have no intention of making such. And even if they signed some form of words, it would not be worth the paper on which it was written. They lick their wounds, yes — but only that they may be able to strike back. It is not peace they seek. One of their lords, at York, told me that, now that the former King John Baliol is dead, in France, King Edward is cherishing his son. In London. The English king, who hated the father, has taken the son into his personal care. For what purpose, think you?"

Bruce was struck anew by the sad change in his old friend and companion-in-arms — who was now his brother-in-law, having recently married the Princess Mary. Campbell, although still on the right side of forty, had grown thin and hollow-cheeked of late, a man fading before their eyes. Wags put it down to marriage with the over-sexed Mary — but Bruce knew that it had started even before Bannockburn. One of his original band, the King grieved for him sorely; also for his sister, who had surely suffered enough.

Lennox spoke up, amidst the exclamations at this revelation. "My good friend, the Lord of Lochawe, takes too gloomy a view. I say. This of Edward Baliol could be only a bargaining gesture. To win better terms by the threat. Such as we ourselves make, with the raids and the Tynedale progress. The English are sore troubled. They have lost much faith in themselves. All that has been done — the expedition of my lord of Carrick, the raids on their coasts of my lords of Ross and of the Isles, Your Grace's move in Tynedale — all this has indeed struck them hard. They are, perhaps, nearer to yielding than we think. Pembroke himself confided to me, at York, that King Edward scarce knew where to turn, he has so many problems. And he is unpopular with his people. He is blamed for the defeat at Bannockburn — although I think the fault was more Hereford's and Pembroke's own. I say, let us have patience. Keep up our present tactics. King Edward may be nearer breaking than we know."

"Patience!" Edward Bruce burst out, from almost the next seat on the earls' benches. "There speaks folly! Patience! Do nothing! And give the English time to recover. That way, we will have to fight another Bannockburn before long. By being patient! Campbell, for once, was right!" These two had never been friends. "Patience is no way to deal with the English. Only force do they heed. The harder you strike them, the more ready they are to talk. So, I say, let us strike them hard. And where they are weakest. In Ireland."

That gained a mixed reception, cheers and objections, both. The King frowned.

"Ireland is where we can do most damage with fewest men," his brother went on. "The Irish chiefs are ready to revolt. They have gallowglasses by the thousand. Properly captained, and with an armoured host of chivary to lead them, they could drive the English out of Ireland in weeks. Then astride the Irish south, we threaten the *English* south. Across their channel. The Welsh, too, would rise at that stage. They love the English no more than we, or the Irish do! Give me a few thousand men, and I will win Ireland for you!" Edward looked directly at his brother now.

All others, the Chancellor included, perforce did likewise.

The King took his time. This was serious, he recognised. Edward had long cherished the notion of invading Ireland. But to raise it, like this, in parliament, where he could demand a vote — and quite possibly command a majority from frustrated members — put the project into a different category. He knew that he, Robert Bruce, was against it; therefore Edward must be fairly sure of himself, sure of large support.

"My lord of Carrick's proposal is not new," he said. "It has been discussed many times. And always the decision has been against it. Because it must amount to a major campaign of war. It cannot be otherwise. And we have had more than sufficient of war. It is peace Scotland needs now, not more war."

"The King says that we need peace," Edward took him up promptly. "But my lord Bishop, and these others, tell us that the English will not make peace. Not yet. We must force them to it. We can do that only by making them choose peace rather than war. *I* would say that, while they are in defeat, at odds with each other, licking their wounds as the Campbell says, we should invade them. Invade England with all our power. Not just raids. I say that we could be hammering at the gates of London within a month! And then they would be praying on their knees for peace — their bended knees! But, if that is too great a venture for those of you who are so weary of warfare — then, I declare to you, this Irish venture should commend itself. My royal brother says that it would be a major campaign of war. Yes — but not for the *Scots*. Only for the Irish. All I need is a spearhead. A small force, to give them a lead. Five or six thousand men. Of these, I will take 3,000 of my own. From my Lordship of Galloway and earldom of Carrick. So I ask this parliament for a mere 2,000. To purchase an English peace for you. And, moreover, to make an ally of Ireland instead of an English province."

This was heady stuff, and for the victors of Bannockburn dangerously so. Bruce could sense how a large part of the assembly rose to it.

"Will my lord of Carrick tell us what makes him so sure that the Irish will rise in large numbers?" he asked, evenly. "The English have a strong grip. The Anglo-Irish lords are powerful, and notable fighters. They have had to be! Witness my own good-father, the Earl of Ulster. They will not be so easily broken."

"Ulster and many others are still in England. And the Irish chiefs will rise. O'Neill. O'Connor. O'Brien. Sorley McDonnell. Young MacQuillan. MacSweeney. Forty thousand men are committed, for the start. If we land before May is out. Twice that within two weeks of landing."

There was absolute silence in Ayr Castle hall now, at what Edward had said and what it implied. All eyes turned on the King.

The knuckles gleamed whitely on Bruce's clenched fists as he fought to control his hot temper. For long moments he did not risk words. When he did, they came jerkily, almost breathlessly.

"You ... have done this! Written to them? These Irish chiefs. Planned a campaign. With them. Gone so far. Won promise of support. Numbers of men. Without ... without my authority. Without so much as informing me! The King!"

Even Edward Bruce was abashed in some measure by his brother's obvious tight-chained fury. He spread his hands. "Not so, sire. I but sounded them. Sought opinions as to the chances of success. Made inquiries, as would any prudent man. Before I raised the issue here ..."

"Prudent man! By the living God ...!" In his extremity, Bruce gripped the arms of his throne with a force almost enough to wrench them apart. Somehow he managed to master himself. "Continue, my lord."

"Because there had been talk of this before. And no true decision. I deemed it right to make such inquiries. To bring to this parliament. So that you, and others, may judge aright. The worth of it. Surely that is no fault?"

"You named these chiefs as committed. To whom committed?"

His brother hesitated. "To myself. At this present. But to Your Grace, as King, when the matter is settled and the invasion begins."

"So! Meantime, they are committed to you, the Earl of Carrick! But great chiefs such as these do not commit themselves and their thousands to war without prior commitment being made to *them*. For the matter to get thus far, *you* also must be committed. How far?" That was a bark.

"I ... I have promised to go. With my own force. From Galloway and Carrick. Whatever you do. Before May is out." That admission came in a rush, but forcefully, defiantly, not conceding anything. And then, as the merest afterthought. "With Your Grace's permission."

So it was out. Plain to all men. The King's brother, the second man in the kingdom, entering into secret warlike negotiations with the leaders of a neighbouring realm. It could be called *lèse-majestié*. Even high treason. Or just plain, insolent contempt of any authority other than his own.

Bruce's every impulse was to hit back, to assert his own overriding authority, to show who was master in Scotland, brother or none. But the long hard years of self-discipline, of taking the long view, of thinking for the realm rather than for himself, triumphed.

A public break between himself and his brother could do untold damage — especially if indeed many supported Edward's project. Moreover, this was a parliament, not a council, convened to hear the will of the community of the realm rather than that of the monarch. And there was the matter of the succession, which was due to come up hereafter, and which any drastic break with Edward would throw into confusion.

When Bruce spoke, he had himself in hand. "It was not well done, my lord," he said severely. "The secrecy. This of committing yourself, without my knowledge and assent. For whatever reason. This is the King's business, and his only. But ... since the policy behind it affects the whole realm, I would hear the will of this parliament. How do you say, my lords?"

There was a long pause, with some shuffling of feet. Few there could fail to recognise the awkwardness of the situation; that an expression of approval for the Irish venture could be taken as a gesture against the monarch. Yet obviously, not a few were in fact in favour, even amongst the most loyal.

Well aware of their predicament, Bruce spoke again. "My friends — in a parliament, all should speak their minds. Their true minds. For the weal of the realm. It is your duty to give me guidance. Without fear or favour."

Lamberton rose. "I am against such adventure, Sire," he said. "Ireland could become a bleeding wound in Scotland's side. As it has been in England's. I say no."

From the nods of the six other bishops present, it was clear that the Lords Spiritual as a body were the Primate.

Edward's snort was eloquent of his contempt for all such.

"I also am against," the Earl of Lennox said.

"As am I," Patrick of Dunbar declared. "The English hold on Ireland is stronger than my lord of Carrick deems it."

"I believe it rash, to the point of foolhardiness," Randolph, Earl of Moray, said.

"That you would!" Edward exclaimed. "All of you!"

There was a shocked hush, at this discourtesy, and the King wondered whether his brother was going to destroy his own case. Then, unexpectedly, and out of due order, Neil Campbell spoke — although, not so much out of order as it seemed perhaps, for Sir Neil was now the King's kinsman by marriage, and moreover had been promised the earldom of Atholl, which was in process of forfeiture, David de Strathbogie being still sufficiently offended over his sister's betrayal to remain in England and in enmity.

"I do not often agree with my lord of Carrick," the Campbell declared. "But here I do. I believe invasion of Ireland will alarm the English more than anything else we may attempt, barring invasion of England itself. Possibly even more so. For the southern English care nothing for what goes on in their North, where we would be fighting. As we have seen. But many southern lords have great lands in Ireland. I say, let my lord of Carrick have his 2,000 men. It will not sorely hurt the realm. And may win us much."

The elderly Earl of Ross, who had seemed to be asleep throughout, suddenly raised his nodding leonine head. "I agree," he said briefly, and let it sink again.

Thus encouraged, others spoke up.

"So I think," Sir Alexander Fraser announced.

"As do I," Sir Robert Fleming nodded.

"It can do no harm," the Lord of Crawford said. "So long as we keep it to small numbers."

"I agree," Malcolm MacGregor, chief of his name, gestured, with the dramatic flourish with which he did all things.

"And I," the veteran Sir Robert Boyd of Noddsdale put in — and Bruce valued his decision more than most.

The King drew a hand over his mouth. These were the fighters, his late colleagues of desperate days, speaking now, men close to him by every bond men can forge between them, the loyalest of the loyal. Many of them, he knew, were no friends of Edward's, however much they might admire him as a brave man and noted leader of light cavalry. Yet they were supporting this Irish venture. Almost involuntarily he glanced across to where James Douglas and Gilbert Hay sat, on the benches of the great officers of state, Warden of the Marches and High Constable respectively. These two, closest of all . . .?

Jamie was looking unhappy. Seeing his friend and liege lord's gaze, he rose. "I . . . I say against," he jerked, and sat down.

"I also," Gibbie blurted, as briefly.

There were a few more, for and against, after that. But Bruce paid little attention now. He perceived how it was, and accepted that he must change his position. The discomfort on the faces of Douglas and Hay left him in no doubt. These two leal friends, whom he knew loved him beyond all telling, would not for anything on earth seem to take part against him; but he knew that were it not for that, they would have decided for the Irish project. So be it.

"My lords," he said, when there was a pause. "I am grateful for your advice and counsel. Your guidance. It is clear that there is much division on this matter, but that many whose opinion I value greatly do commend the Irish adventure. My lord Chancellor need not, I think, put it to the vote. Unless so my lord of Carrick demands. As is his right. I am agreeable that a limited expedition shall go to Ireland. I will double the numbers that my lord of Carrick raises from his own lands. He shall lead the project, as it seems, he has arranged. But my men, the realm's men, shall be under the command of my nephew, the Earl of Moray, whose ability, most certainly, will be of the utmost benefit to his uncle."

There was a great indrawing of breaths as all considered this. The monarch, Bruce the hero-king, had given in. But only so far. And he had appointed Moray, the level-headed and imperturbable Moray whom Edward hated, perhaps the one man within the kingdom who could cope with his fiery uncle, as watchdog.

Edward glared from his brother to his nephew, gulped, but nodded. "So be it," he repeated. "No vote."

The audible sigh of relief from all around was interrupted by the King himself. "One further matter, before I ask my lord Chancellor to proceed with the business. Five or six thousand men cannot be carried over to Ireland without a large fleet. My lord of Ross, who favours this venture, will no doubt lend his galleys. But that will not serve for half of it. There will be required my lord of the Isles' galley fleet."

That gave all pause — as it was meant to do. Angus Og was not present. On principle, he avoided parliaments, as his attendance might be construed as in some measure admitting that his lordship was a constituent part of Bruce's kingdom, a contradiction of his notional independence. And Angus Og cordially loathed the Earl of Carrick.

Edward looked put out. "Angus of the Isles will not refuse? Will not withhold his galleys?" That was a question rather than one of Edward's confident statements. "He is the Admiral. High Admiral of Scotland. He will do as you say."

"The galleys are his own, not the realm's. And Angus of the Isles is . . . Angus! If he disapproves of this venture . . .!" Bruce did not need to enlarge on that. "But I will speak with him."

The King paused, and all recognised that he remained the master. That he could prevent the expedition from sailing, if he would, without having to order it. He went on.

"There is another matter to be considered. In this. It was next on my lord Chancellor's list for discussion. But it has relevance now. Lame John MacDougall of Lorn, in rebellion, whom King Edward made his Admiral of the Western Sea, to harass us, has returned to the Hebrides. In force. So the Lord of the Isles sends me word. And urges a campaign against him. He by sea, myself by land. MacDougall has a large fleet. Part his own, part English, part Anglo-Irish. I need not tell you what he could do against any invasion fleet for Ireland, carrying thousands of men. Across the Irish Sea."

There was silence now. Even Edward looked thoughtful at the prospect.

"It would be better, then, if we dealt with Lame John first. Before my lord of Carrick's venture."

Edward Bruce was looking anxious. He shook his head. "No," he cried. "It must be in May. That was the agreement. With the chiefs. O'Neill in especial. Before their hay-harvest, he said, when the men return to their crofts. After the end of May it will be too late. I am committed to a May expedition."

"Then, my lord, I say that you should have thought more fully on how you were to carry your thousands to Ireland!" The King had his headstrong brother now. But scoring points off Edward was not Bruce's main concern. It was the maintenance of his own magnificent team of lieutenants and friends in harmony, as one of the most effective fighting units in all Christendom. Much was worth sacrificing for that. He shrugged.

"The safety of my own realm is paramount, and must come first," he went on. "I must deal with John MacDougall. But it may be that this can wait until, let us say, the end of June. I shall speak with the Lord of the Isles. I may be able to persuade him to come here to the South-West, in mid-May, a month from this. With his galleys. To carry the Irish expedition across. And then to return for the assault on MacDougall. This I will seek to do. Is it agreed?"

Heartfelt applause greeted this suggestion, this gesture, from all parts of the hall, so that Edward was constrained to join in. He was aware that he had been in some measure out-manoeuvred, made to look slightly foolish, and put in his brother's debt. But at least his project could go ahead.

"My lord Chancellor," the King turned. "My regrets that I have for so long obstructed your place and function. To the next business."

Bernard de Linton bowed. "I declare the matter of the Act of Succession to the Throne, to be decided by this parliament. It has long been His Grace's concern that in the event of his death, without a son, the succession should be secured, in proper fashion, for the due maintenance and good governance of the kingdom. Since Almighty God has seen fit, in His infinite wisdom, to deny His

Grace such lawful son, the King has hereby sought to make such provision, and now declares the matter for this parliament's acceptance, or otherwise." He paused.

"Hear, then. It is the King's wish and proposal that, in the event of his own death without a son being born to him in wedlock, his right noble and well-beloved brother Edward, Earl of Carrick and Lord of Galloway, does thereupon succeed to the throne as lawful King of Scots. And should the said Lord Edward die without lawful son, before or after, the said succession shall revert to His Grace the Lord Robert's daughter, the Lady Marjory, and any heirs to her body. Is this accepted and agreed?"

There was a mixed reception and little enthusiasm. Few there, even amongst those who most admired his dash and spirit, considered that Edward would make a satisfactory monarch. Yet the alternative was a spiritless girl who most clearly desired no part in kingship. A regency, to rule, while Marjory reigned, might have been better — except that the regent would have to be Edward, and if he was going to rule, he might as well be the King. And, if there was suggested a triumvirate of regents, say Moray and another, Edward would seek to dominate, inevitably; all the troubles of the old Guardianship days would be renewed. The assembly signified assent, that was all.

The Chancellor nodded. "It is the King's added proposal that in the Act to be drawn up to make this parliament's decision lawful and binding, it should be stated that, if the said Lord Edward, or the said Lady Marjory, should die leaving a male heir who is a minor, in that event the most noble Thomas, Earl of Moray, His Grace's sister's son, should administer the governance of the realm until such heir reached due age. Is this agreed?"

There was more general applause for this.

"Furthermore, and related to this matter, it is His Grace's royal pleasure and satisfaction to make known to his loyal lieges of all Estates here assembled, that he has decided to bestow the hand of his daughter, the said Lady Marjory, upon his leal and true councillor and friend, the noble Lord Walter, High Steward of Scotland. Which match he believes will well serve the realm and well please all those here present."

The shout of acclaim which greeted this announcement proved that belief true, at least. Everywhere men cheered. It had been feared that Marjory would never marry; and Walter Stewart was well liked, of good blood and sufficiently lofty in rank to satisfy all. Or nearly all. The young Earl of Mentieth looked glum, as did his uncle, Sir John Stewart. The Earl of Strathearn, though not quite so young, was unmarried and had had his eye on Marjory likewise; he did not look overjoyed. Nor, for that matter, did the Earl of Carrick himself. But such doubtful looks were confined to the earls' benches.

At the King's signal, Walter Stewart rose in his seat amongst the great officers of state, and bowed modestly, flushing a little. It was a notable moment for the House of Stewart.

Eyes rose to search the minstrels' gallery, on this occasion reserved for a few privileged lady spectators, in case the bride-to-be had slipped in to join her stepmother and aunts, there from the beginning. Such searchers were disappointed.

"What have you for us further, my lord Chancellor?" Bruce asked.

"Certain forfeitures, grants and appointments, Your Grace . . ."

The drama was over for the day — and men were only anxious to escape from the over-warm hall to discuss it all. The remainder of the programme was rattled through in record time.

After his formal retiral, the King summoned his brother to a small private room of the castle. There they faced each other alone.

"Edward," Bruce said shortly, "You will now give me such explanation as you may."

"Is any required?" the other demanded, equally brief. "I would have thought the matter sufficiently clear."

"I had hoped, for your sake, that there might be some reason, something I knew not of. To excuse you a little."

"I do not look for excuses," Edward returned. "You should know me better."

"I it was who sought excuses for *you*. For my brother."

"Then spare yourself, my good Robert! And me. I did what I did because it was the only way to force your agreement. To the Irish project. You would not have it, otherwise. I knew it to be the right course. To bring the English to heel. But you would have none of it. So I forced your hand. You will thank me, one day!"

"I do not thank you now. Think you I have not considered this Irish matter as deeply as you have done? And decided against it, with good reason. It is too dangerous. Its success depends on others than ourselves. There lies the greatest danger. That, and maintaining supplies by sea. Remember it. But – you have, as you intended, forced my hand. You have set up your judgement against mine, and acted in secret to enforce it, to constrain me. That is neither the action of a brother, nor yet of a loyal subject."

"Of a mercy, Robert — forget that you are a king, for a moment!

Remember that you are just your father's son, as am I — save that you happened to be born first! And *he* was a fool! We are not play-acting now, before your parliament or Court. Have I not as much right to do as I believe to be right, as have you?"

"I would remind you, brother, that you took your oath of fealty to me, as your liege lord."

The other snorted. "I did as much to Edward Plantagenet, once! As did you!"

"So! Loyalty means nothing to you? As brother *or* subject!"

"It means that I shall serve you, and the realm, to the best of my ability and my wits. As I have done. *My* ability. And *my* wits. And, for a while, in Ireland!"

"I see. So now we have it. I marvel that you dare to speak so. To me. Even you, Edward. When I could have you silenced so easily. Clapped in the pit of this castle, to wait until you learned your duty."

"Could — but will not. Will not, Robert! I know you too well. To do that you would require to be a different man from what you are. And a fool, into the bargain — which you are not. For many think more of me than you do!"

"I will not, no. You are right in that. I will let you go to Ireland. But . . . I will never trust you again, Edward. Remember it."

"Have you trusted me, for long? Setting your tame watchdogs on me — Thomas Randolph and the Douglas! Always watching me, holding me back. You have never trusted me, Robert."

"I have ever known you headstrong. Rash. And taken precautious. That is all. As was my duty."

"Duty . . .!"

"Edward — God help Scotland when you are King!"

Laughing suddenly, cheerfully, uninhibitedly, the other clapped his elder brother on the shoulder. "At least I will be a less solemn and sober monarch, man! You will see." And still laughing, he flung out of the little room.

Frowning perplexedly, Bruce stared after him.

Chapter Six

It was two months to the day later, and Ayr was the scene of a very different activity, the bustling excitement and noise of an army in embarkation. The entire town was like a disturbed ant-hill of armed men. But like the ant-hill, there was method, order, in the seething and at first glance aimless commotion. Angus Og MacDonald and his captains and clansmen were getting used to embarking armies.

His great galley fleet, one of the most significant weapons in Bruce's armoury, however independent its master claimed to be, covered not only all the harbour and jetty area but also the sand and shingle beaches for half a mile — for galleys were constructed for drawing up on the open strands of their home islands and sea-lochs. In their scores they lay, long lean greyhounds of the sea, high-prowed and high-pooped, low-waisted, banking twenty, forty, sixty oars, single masts with their great angled booms rising like a forest. These were the swiftest, most savage and dangerous ships in the world — and amongst the most comfortless to sail in.

So Edward Bruce's 6,000 had found, nearly a month before, when they had been ferried across the Irish Sea, from Ayr to Larne, in Ulster, in unseasonable weather, with MacDougall of Lorn's craft lurking hull-down to the north, afraid to attack while the Lord of the Isles was there in force. Angus had seen the invaders safely landed and consolidated, indeed win their first small battle against only moderate opposition at Carrickfergus, and then had returned here to Ayr, on the King's business.

The royal army now assembling, despite all the activity, was in fact a modest one, by kingly standards, although hand-picked. Most of the host for the Highland expedition had been gone for two weeks, horsed, by land, around the innumerable sea-lochs and estuaries between the Lowlands and Argyll. Bruce was transporting a bare 1,000 men by sea, and with a special objective.

There had been a great splitting up of forces and captains. As well as Moray, Bruce had sent Sir Robert Boyd, Sir William de Soulis, Sir Hugh Ross, Sir Philip Moubray and others, to back up Randolph as much as to support his brother. At home the Earl of Lennox, Neil Campbell and Alexander Fraser were commanding the main host marching north-west. James Douglas, Keith the Marischal, Robert Fleming and young Scrymgeour were to keep up a series of hit-and-run raids into England, and to collect the mail, or protection money therefrom, which had become an ever more important item of the Scots revenues. William Lamberton and Abbot Bernard would see to the rule and governance of the realm in the interim. While Bruce took his new son-in-law and Gilbert Hay with him in the galleys.

Walter Stewart had been married, three weeks before, to Marjory Bruce, amidst great pomp and ceremony. He was nowise averse, however, to this interruption of the honeymoon period; indeed, his father-in-law feared that he had been positively relieved. The bride showed no signs of distress, either.

They sailed on Midsummer's Day, a stirring sight, the Queen and her ladies waving them off in fine style, into the west. The King did not go in Angus Og's galley, as was usual, but in a command craft of his own. His thousand men were not evenly disposed over the fleet, but concentrated less than comfortably in a mere dozen vessels.

There was grumbling amongst the men at this overcrowding; even some recognition of danger, when the fleet should reach the open sea and the notorious hazards of rounding the Mull of Kintyre. For these galleys had very low freeboards, and moreover were already well filled with their own double crews, with two men to each oar and the spare team required to maintain high speeds and act as boarding crews. The largest were already carrying 250 Islesmen, without passengers — although none of Bruce's dozen craft were of that size.

It was not long, however, before all concerned perceived the reason for this crowding. Off the south tip of Arran, with a freshening breeze and the long Atlantic swell already beginning to make the overloaded craft pitch and roll alarmingly, the fleet split up, and into very unequal squadrons. Angus Og himself, with about thirty ships, continued on course for the open sea, south-westwards now. While the King's galley, with its tail of heavily-laden followers, swung off to starboard in a fully ninety-degree turn, to proceed due northwards up the narrow Kilbrandon Sound, between Arran and the eastern coast of long Kintyre.

Quickly the breakwater effect of Kintyre became apparent, and the ships gained speed and comfort both. The south-west breeze, funnelling round the Mull, now much aided them, bellying out the great single square sails, which each bore the proud undifferenced device of the Black Galley of the Isles. With the long oars sweeping rhythmically, to the squeal of rowlocks, and the gasping, unending chant of the crews, they thrashed up-Sound at a speed fast horses would have been unable to maintain, exhilarating, scarcely believable. The smell of sweat was almost overpowering, as strong men purged their bodies with vast exertions after the over-indulgences in the taverns, alehouses and brothels of Ayr.

By evening they had left Arran behind and were into the lower reaches of Loch Fyne, one of the longest sea-lochs in all Scotland. It probed for forty miles deep into the mountainous heart of Argyll. But the King's squadron was not going so far; not half-way in fact, to where, a mere dozen miles up, a small side-loch opened off to the west — East Loch Tarbert.

In June it is never really dark in Scotland, and the galleys drove on through the half-light confidently, even in these narrow, skerry-strewn waters. Before dawn they turned into the side loch.

It was only a mile long, and at its head was a settlement where a new stone castle was being built — Bruce's own, the result of an understanding with Angus of the Isles, who was also Lord of Kintyre. Below these unfinished walls the galleys moored.

But there was no rest for the crews or passengers. Immediately all were set to felling trees, in which the area was rich, choosing straight pines. Oatmeal and water, laced with strong Highland spirits, served for breakfast, eaten as men laboured.

By early forenoon all was ready. The logs, trimmed and smoothed, were in position on the shingle beach. Long ropes were run out from the first two ships, and hundreds of men attached themselves thereto, like trace-horses. Crews waded chest-deep into the water to push. Then the King's trumpets blew a long blast that set the echoes resounding through the enclosing hills.

As more than a thousand men took up the strain, and heaved mightily, the two vessels began to move forward, up out of the water like leviathans. Under the tall thrusting prows teams pushed the round logs to act as rollers, a team to each log, positioning them, guiding them beneath the keels, catching them as they came out below the sterns, and then picking them up and hurrying to the bows again. The galleys moved up the slope, heavily, but went on moving. Bruce led the way, encouraging the long lines of haulers, taking a hand frequently at the ropes himself.

He had remembered what the chief of MacGregor had told him, long ago when he was a hunted fugitive, how from time immemorial the proud Clan Alpine had been wont to drag their chiefly galleys across that other *tairbeart*, the narrow isthmus of land between Loch Long and Loch Lomond, from sea-water to fresh; and how King Hakon's son-in-law Magnus, King of Man, had heard of the device over fifty years ago, before the Battle of Largs, and had surprised the Scots by appearing without warning in the Clyde estuary, from the Hebridean Sea, by crossing this more westerly tarbert. For here also was only a mile-wide isthmus. Just over the intervening low ridge, *West* Loch Tarbert struck inland for ten miles from the Sound of Jura and the Western Sea.

The ascent was stiff for such heavy loads, and taxed all the muscle and determination. Then Bruce realised that, as so often of a summer morning, there was an onshore wind. This, sweeping down Loch Fyne's cold-water surface, blew on to the warmer land here from an easterly direction. Hurrying back to the leading galley, he yelled to the few men still on board to raise the great sail. It was worth trying, and could do no harm.

The moment that the sail began to open, the effect was felt by every man pulling and pushing. The wind seemed to take half the weight off the vessel. Speed increased dramatically. Quickly the other craft hoisted sail likewise. Everywhere men laughed and cheered, however breathlessly. Here would be a tale to tell, a great song to sing, something to twit Angus Og with — how the Lowland king sailed from Loch Fyne to Jura Sound!

They did not in fact sail all the way; for once the crest of the ridge was passed, the east wind died away, and any breeze there was came from the west. However, it was now downhill and easier going. In little more than two hours after leaving the East Loch, the first two vessels were dipping their forefeet into the West.

There was no triumphant pause in the men's Herculean exertions. Without delay, all but a few turned back, to repeat their performance.

They improved on their methods, their route and their expertise, but it was early evening nevertheless before all the galleys were safely into the West Loch, with men exhausted and tempers frayed. The King himself had been seeking to hide his fretfulness for hours. It had all taken longer than he had anticipated, and he was working within narrow time limits.

Whenever the last keel was in the water, and despite the grousing of tired and hungry men, he gave the order to sail. Down the long narrow loch they sped, in line astern, through the low Knapdale hills, into the eye of the westering sun.

In ten miles the wide waters of the Sound of Jura opened before them, ablaze with the sunset. Only a few miles ahead, to port, lay the small isle of Gigha, with beyond it all the long unbroken line made by the great islands of Jura and Islay, purple against the evening light.

Walter Stewart, who did not know the Hebrides well, standing beside the King on the high poop of the foremost galley, stared. "A goodly sight, Sire," he said. "Fair. But . . . where is John of Lorn?"

Bruce pointed southwards. "Between us and Angus Og, I think!" he said. "It is my prayer that he will learn the fact before long. And too late!"

MacDougall was, in fact, using the narrow seas of the Sound of Jura as a fortress area, guarding his own territory of Nether Lorn.

It was ideally suited for this purpose, skilfully used. A great funnel fifty miles long, a dozen miles wide at its base between Kintyre and Islay, it narrowed in to a mere couple of miles between the Craignish peninsula and the northern tip of Jura. By massing his fleet at the southern end, and stretching a boom across the narrows at Craignish, with guard ships, the rebel Lord of Lorn, whose mother was a Comyn, could turn this whole great area into an inland sea; and even though the islands to the west were Angus's, his ships of war could dominate all therein. Only the one alternative water access was available, the narrow gap lying between the north end of Jura and the next island of Scarbia. And this was the famous Sound of Corryvrechan, with its menacing whirlpools and tidal cauldrons, better guard than any boom of logs and chains.

Angus Og's information had been that MacDougall was using the Isle of Gigha as headquarters and base. On Gigha, therefore, the King's flotilla bore down.

As they approached the green, rock-bound and fairly low-lying isle, a mere five miles long and a quarter of that wide, all aboard the royal squadron, who were not working the sweeps, stood to arms. There was only the one effective landing-place of Gigha, the small shallow bay of Ardminish two-thirds of the way down the east side, and it could be seen that it was packed with shipping. But experienced eyes quickly discerned in the level beams of the setting sun, that these were not fighting ships, galleys, galleasses, carracks, sloops, but rather supply vessels, transports, shallops, and the like. As might be expected, the fighting force would be at sea, somewhere to the south, facing the threat of Angus Og's fleet.

"We leave this for later, Sire?" Gilbert Hay asked. "Go seek Lame John, while there is yet light?"

"I think not, Gibbie. It will be a clear night, never truly dark. John MacDougall can wait a little yet. I told Angus to give me until dawn tomorrow. Then to do as he would, lacking us. We will take this island, behind MacDougall. Give our force a taste of fight, to rouse and inspirit them. And these ships anchored there — we might put some of them to use. Aye — we will assault Gigha."

It was eloquent of the sense of complete security of whoever commanded on the island that no alarm was taken at their approach, no postures of defence made. Bruce had ordered his own galleys' sails to be furled, so that the black device painted thereon would not be visible from land, and they drove on under oars only. No doubt they would seem to be no more than a detachment of MacDougall's fleet returning to port for some reason. At any rate, as they beat round the little headland of Arminish Point, wary of the skerries, the twelve galleys encountered no sort of opposition. The newcomers were drawing in alongside the craft already ranked there, and armed men in their hundreds pouring over the side, before anybody on Gigha realised that there was an emergency.

As an armed assault the occupation of Gigha was laughable; but as a strategic exercise it could hardly have been more successful, or more speedy. There was a little fighting, but of so sporadic and minor a nature as scarcely to be worth the title. A few men were slain and some seriously injured, admittedly — but such casualties were mainly the work of angry islanders themselves, MacDonalds — for this was of course one more of Angus's many territories — who had suffered much at the hands of the invaders and were not slow to take this opportunity for revenge. Bruce had to clamp down swift and stern discipline, to prevent a general massacre. Nearly all the prisoners were English sailors and their Irish women camp-followers. He left a small garrison under Sir Donald Campbell, Sir Neil's brother, and sailed away before the islanders or his own people could organise the inevitable celebration. As it was, a lot of strong liquor came aboard the squadron with the returning warriors. They were not quite so cramped for space now, for Bruce ordered the addition of a number of the captured ships to their strength temporarily. There were murmurs at this, for these were slow non-fighting vessels, which could only be a weakening influence. But the King was adamant.

It was nearly midnight, and they drove southwards over a smooth, quiet translucent sea which looked like beaten pewter. Visibility was good for that hour, but provided little definition beyond a mile or so.

Bruce had few doubts as to where to look for John MacDougall. Just a few miles ahead, beyond the islet of Cara, the coast of Islay, to the west, became much littered with a host of outlying reefs, rocks and skerries, south of Ardmore Point; and thereafter swung away westwards towards the Oa, vastly widening the mouth of the funnel-shaped inland sea. The line for MacDougall's fleet to hold was obviously one stretched between these Islay skerries and Glencardoch Point on Kintyre. Patrolling a ten-mile belt, his vessels could act as an almost impassable barrier, giving each other mutual cover and support. Angus Og was bold, and probably had slightly the larger fleet; but he would be rash indeed to try to break through such a barrier head-on. He might succeed, but hardly without heavy losses; and even so would be apt to find not a few of his craft trapped thereafter in the Sounds of Gigha and Jura, facing unknown odds. Hence Bruce's manoeuvre.

Sure enough, look-outs from two or three leading vessels shouted almost simultaneously their sighting of ships ahead. The long low craft did not stand out very clearly against an uncertain horizon, and they were probably not more than two miles off.

"Many of them, Sir King," the MacDonald shipmaster of Bruce's galley reported, from some way up the mast-stay. "A great host of ships. Sails furled, mostly. Beating to and fro. But, if we can see them, they can see us better. The light is behind us."

That was true. Sunset in these latitudes is almost due north at midsummer, and it is the northern sky which remains lightest until sunrise. Bruce's squadron would probably have been visible to MacDougall for some time, and would inevitably be causing major astonishment and speculation.

"Aye. Then let us give them something to fret over. Trumpets to sound the signals for line abreast. And for the torches to be lit."

And so the trumpets neighed shrilly out over the summer sea, and their martial notes could not fail to be heard by the patrolling fleet. As the King's vessels moved up into a long line, red flame blossomed aboard each, as the pine-branch torches, contrived from selected material from the tree-trimming operations at East Loch Tarbert, were set alight.

Quickly the entire scene was transformed. The night, from being one of quiet luminous peace, became angry with the crimson murky flame of smoking pitch-pine. Hundreds of the torches flared, and stained sea and sky.

Bruce's reason for bringing along nearly a score of the anchored vessels from Ardminish Bay was now clear. He had almost trebled the size of his fleet, and this would be all too evident from the enemy's standpoint. Yet the half-light would prevent it from being apparent that these were not fighting ships. John MacDougall could not be other than a very alarmed man.

Bruce kept the trumpets blaring, a martial challenging din, as they drove down upon the patrolling squadrons on a two-mile-wide front.

Then the pinpoints of red light began to break out far to the south. One or two, wide-scattered, quickly multiplied into scores, winking, flickering, growing. Cheers rose from the King's ships. Angus Og was there, and responding.

MacDougall of Lorn was no craven; but nor had he the rash, headlong gallantry of, say, Edward Bruce. And his role here, anyway, was to harry the Scots' flanks, to seek to prevent major operations against England, not to fight pitched battles against odds. He could not know whose was this northern fleet; but clearly it was in league with Angus of the Isles. He had to accept that his present position was untenable, and took steps to alter it.

He had not much room for manoeuvre. The very strength of his former situation, in the narrows, was now its weakness. He had three choices. Either he sought to break through to the south, or to the north; or else tried to escape to the west, into the open Hebridean Sea.

That he chose the third was hardly to be wondered at. Angus's power he knew, and feared. What threatened from the north was a mystery — and therefore the more alarming. An escape round the west of Islay would give him the freedom of wide waters, and the possibility of communicating with his base of Gigha, from the north.

Bruce was far from blind to these alternatives. He himself would probably have chosen as did MacDougall, in similar circumstances — especially as the loom of the great island of Islay would provide a dark background against which shipping would not be readily visible.

The King was ready, therefore, for the first signs of a sustained westerly movement amongst the ships ahead. Swiftly he sent orders to his fast galleys to swing out of line to starboard at fullest speed, west by south, torches doused.

It became a race, a race which the King could not really win, clearly, since many of MacDougall's ships were already to the west of his own. Some inevitably would escape; but he might trap much of the centre and east of the enemy line.

The breeze was south-westerly, and of no use to either side. It was now a case of sheer muscle and determination, the oars lashing the water in a disciplined frenzy of urgent rhythm, the panting refrain abandoned now for the clanging beat of broadsword on metal-studded targe, faster and faster. Each galley surged ahead in a cloud of spray raised by its scores of oars.

Soon it was evident that at least some of Angus Og's ships were on the same mission, on an intercepting course. The three groups, or rather lines, of galleys, approximated to an arrowhead formation with an extra long point.

Inevitably, it was a short race, of only three or four miles, and for the last of them the leading ships were within hailing distance of each other — near enough for Bruce to try to pick out flags and banners, the sail devices being meantime hidden. There seemed to be two or three of the fleeing line wearing flags of various shapes and sizes.

"Which will be MacDougall's own?" the King demanded of his shipmaster.

"Who knows? Angus Og flies always a long whip-pennant at his masthead. But Ian Bacach . . .?"

"He will be proud to be the English king's Admiral of the West," Gilbert Hay suggested. "He will likely fly a large flag of that traitorous office, as well as his own banner of Lorn."

"Aye, you are right. Two large flags . . ."

The trouble was that there seemed to be two vessels wearing two large flags each, sailing close together. Perhaps King Edward appointed a deputy admiral to keep an eye on MacDougall? It would be typical English practice.

There was not much time for any decision. Ardmore Point of Islay looked very close, half-right, and the profusion of skerries and reefs would be closer still. Details were hard to distinguish in the half-light. Any action would have to be taken quickly now.

"Cut in between those two," the King jerked. "Can we do it? A last spurring of speed. Are they able? The rowers?"

"Clan Donald are always able! Most of all against MacDougall. Murtach — the pipes!"

So, with the bagpipes screaming and sobbing their high challenge and the oarsmen miraculously redoubling their huge efforts — aided undoubtedly by the High Steward of Scotland who went along the benches with a great flagon of the islanders' whisky, proffering each open, gasping mouth a swallow — the King's galley swung to port and hurled itself across the intervening quarter-mile of sea, at a steepening angle, to head in between the two fleeing beflagged craft in a burst of speed that had to be experienced to be believed.

Now it was possible to distinguish banners. Both ships ahead flew the Leopards of England; but, while that in front also flew a blue and white device of three boars' heads, two and one, the second flew also the emblem of a galley, not unlike Angus Og's own. Only this galley was on gold, not silver, and with dragon heads at stern and prow, and a cross at the masthead. It was the Galley of Lorn. The similarity was not so strange; for Clan Donald and Clan Dougall were descended from brothers, Ranald and Dougall, sons of the mighty Somerled. The fact made their descendants only the more bitter rivals, especially as Dougall had been the elder brother.

There was no need for Bruce's command to turn in. The MacDonald skipper was already steering a collision course, and every man not at the oars, save those who had grabbed grapnels and ropes, had swords, dirks, or axes in hand. The piper, Murtach, blew his lustiest.

The oarsmen on both vessels were equally expert. They kept up their deep driving strokes until the very last moment, when another second's delay would have meant rending chaos, the snapping of long shafts, men broken as well as oars. Up in the air the inner teams of each raised the sweeps, in a rippling progress. Then the two galleys crashed together.

Instants before that even, the grapnels were flying, with their snaking cables to warp the craft securely. Men were leaping, from the moment of impact.

Walter Stewart was one of the first over the side, sword held high.

Bruce touched Hay's arm. "After him, Gibbie. See that he comes to no harm. He is keen — but I do not want to lose a good-son so soon!"

The King himself waited, however contrary to inclination. Indeed, when at length he leapt, battle-axe in hand, he was one of the last to leave the galley. But he was able to jump straight on to the other vessel's high poop, from his own. And it was on that poop that John MacDougall was likely to be found.

This manoeuvre, although logical, had its own danger. For it ensured that the King stepped almost alone into the thick of the enemy leadership. Sir William Irvine, Bruce's armour-bearer, who never left his master's shoulder during active service, was close behind; but nearly all the others had already gone.

In consequence, Bruce found himself hotly engaged from the moment of jumping. Many of the poop's former occupants had already leapt down into the well of the ship to help repel the mass of the boarders; but half a dozen or so, of chiefly or knightly rank, extra to the shipmaster and helmsman, still remained. These, with one accord, hurled themselves on the royal intruder with eager swords.

Robert Bruce had fought on a galley poop before, and knew its hazards and limitations. Indeed it was on such a constricted, crowded, lofty and slippery platform that he had first made the acquaintance of Christina MacRuarie, amidst flashing steel. He had chosen the battle-axe now, deliberately — and he was a renowned master of that difficult weapon. Irvine, behind him, and lacking the experience, bore the conventional sword — and quickly learned his error.

In the confused mêlée which immediately followed, three swordsmen vied with each other to strike down the King — and thereby got not a little into each other's way. Two others circled, to get behind Bruce, and these Irvine made shift to deal with.

Bruce's shield jerked up to take the first clanging sword stroke. The second, a sideways swipe, he drove down and away with a blow of the axe. The third, impeded by the other two, was off-true and slightly short, merely scraping the King's chain-mail and achieving nothing. Seeing his opportunity, with the three men bunched together and for the moment off guard, Bruce hurled himself bodily at them, using shield as battering-ram. He sent them spinning like ninepins, their long swords a handicap. One crashed all his length, the battle-axe smashed down to fell another, and the third, a knight in full armour, went staggering backwards, retaining his feet on the heaving deck only with difficulty. After him Bruce plunged.

Behind, Will Irvine was discovering the disadvantages of a full-length sword in a confined space. Admittedly his two opponents were similarly handicapped; but even so he had not space to wield the weapon effectively. Bruce's lunge forward had left his back unprotected. Irvine had to keep close. After a couple of abortive thrusts in the general direction of the assailants, he fore-shortened his weapon by grasping it one-third of the way down the blade, and flung himself after his master, turning so that they were approximately back to back. Only just in time. As one sword came jabbing viciously, he beat down on it blindly with all his strength, using his weapon purely as a weight. Both swords clattered to the deck.

The hapless armour-bearer snatched out his dirk, all he had now to face the other two. "Sire! Sire!" he yelled. To give him his due, that was all warning and no cry for help.

Bruce, flinging himself after the staggering knight, had perceived as he did so that, in the limited space of the poop-deck, one of the men dodging aside to avoid the rush did so with a limp. Immediately the King changed direction. Lame John, for a wager!

It was at that moment that Irvine's cry sounded in his ear. Biting off a curse, he whirled round. He recognised the situation in a moment — one man driving in with a sword, another reaching for his dagger, and his armour-bearer swordless. He leapt for the first, leaving the other to Irvine.

The swordsman had to change his target and tactics hurriedly — and such slight hesitation was fatal in face of the Bruce with a battle-axe. The shorter-handled, more adaptable weapon, which was effective as a blunt instrument almost any way it might strike, greatly outclassed in speed and wieldiness the long, heavy sword which had to use point or cutting edge. A quick feint with the axe to the thigh area brought the sword sweeping down in a defensive stroke — and a still quicker and explosive upward jerk drove under the man's sword-arm. Though he was armoured in mail, the fierce impact of it cracked the shoulder-blade above with an audible snap. Limply the arm sagged and the sword fell. Bruce, who saw that one of his earlier toppled foes was now on his feet again, dirk in hand, did not waste more time on the shocked swordsman, only using his shield to give the man a violent if contemptuous push that sent him reeling back, while he swung the axe on the dirker. That unfortunate went down for the second time, and stayed down.

The King turned to find Irvine and his original opponent grappling, seeking to invalidate each other's daggers. He raised his axe once more — then, ever mindful of other men's *amour propre*, desisted. His armour-bearer would not thank him for a rescue in equal combat. Only brief seconds had elapsed, as he swung back on his former objectives.

Four men only remained before him now, clustered around the helmsman — the armoured knight, one who was almost certainly the shipmaster, and the limping individual.

"John MacDougall — submit you!" the King panted. "I, Bruce, demand it."

The Lord of Lorn did not lack courage, but he had been lame from birth and so inhibited from personal armed prowess. He did not fling himself forward, therefore, to contest that challenge, but jerked a word to the others. The knight moved out, but warily. Then the shipmaster, quick as a flash, drew a dirk and flung it, spinning through the air.

It was a wicked, accurate throw, with only two or three yards to cover, and had Bruce not been wearing a chain-mail jerkin he would have been transfixed. As it was, striking him on the chest with considerable force, the weapon's impact made him catch his breathing, and he knew a burning pain. But, axe swinging, he came on. And now he was angry.

Almost casually he brushed aside the less than enthusiastic knight, keeping his eye on the skipper — for a man who could throw one knife could throw another.

"John MacDougall," he cried again, "I am waiting."

There was no reply.

The shipmaster had something else in his hand now. It looked like a spike rather than another dirk. MacDougall also held a sword, but looked not in a posture to use it.

"Lord of Lorn," the King barked, "do you wish to live? Or die? Choose quickly." Seeming to look only at the chief, now but a pace or two in front of him, all his attention was nevertheless concentrated on the shipmaster.

"On my ship, *I* command, Sir King!" the other threw back, in his sibilant West Highland voice, so misleadingly gentle.

Then Irvine was at Bruce's side, and sword in hand again. "Let me deal with this dog!" he gasped.

Even as the shipmaster hesitated between targets, Bruce leapt. It was a violent sideways jump, like the release of a coiled spring. And it was at the captain, not at Lame John, that he leapt. Before the other's arm could adjust to a jabbing instead of a throwing position, the King's axe smashed down. The man dropped like a slaughtered stirk.

The helmsman had a dirk, but seemed doubtful about using it — as who would blame him. Bruce gestured his reddened axe round at the chief.

"You are my prisoner, MacDougall. Yield you!"

For answer, the other made use of his sword, at last, in a savage despairing poke.

Bruce eluded it with ease, and slapped down the flat of the axe on the outstretched sword-arm — which broke like a dead stick. The man squealed with pain.

"Fool!" his monarch told him, breathlessly. "You are fool . . . as well as traitor! I could have slain you. Tell me why . . . I should not . . . even now?"

Nursing his arm, and gritting his teeth, MacDougall found no words.

Walter Stewart came bounding up the poop-steps now, Hay following. "The ship is ours! The ship is ours!" he cried excitedly. "We have them. Have you seen MacDougall?"

His father-in-law smiled. "He is here. I fear that he has hurt himself a little. We must ensure his comfort, now. His close comfort, see you!"

All resistance in this galley was soon over. Bruce took stock of the wider scene. Pairs of ships seemed to be fighting it out over a wide area of water, and in the half-light it was almost impossible to decide which side had the advantage. The only clue was that few vessels seemed now to be heading westwards. Some of the enemy had undoubtedly escaped past Islay. But with the Lord of the Isles' fleet now fully engaged, it seemed improbable that many more would do so. There was no sign of the beflagged galley which had formerly been so close.

"It is enough," the King decided. "Leave the rest to Angus. He would have it so, I swear. Gibbie — find means to find him a message that I have this Lord of Lorn. Walter — have our foolish friend back to our own galley. He is almost the last of my rebels. Will — see that this craft is taken back to Gigha. Find sufficient rowers. And the wounded seen to. I return there, hereafter. Now, Sir Knight — your name? An Englishman, I think . . .?"

Chapter Seven

The sudden and unexpectedly swift collapse of the MacDougall-English naval threat left Bruce, for once in his career, almost at a loose end — and in quite the most beautiful part of his kingdom, in high summer and fine weather. All his affairs elsewhere were under control, in the short term, with his disturbing brother away in Ireland, Douglas keeping the English North on the hop, Lamberton and the other churchmen in firm and effective control of the kingdom's essential governance. There was a certain amount of mopping-up and example-making to be done in the Clan Dougall lands, but there was more than sufficient men to see to that. A unique holiday spirit seemed to develop in Argyll and its adjacent isles. Instead of returning forthwith to Ayr or Stirling, therefore, the King decided to send for Elizabeth and the Court to join him in a Hebridean idyll.

Such an expedition, of course, would take a little while to mount, if he knew anything about women folk, and their ideas and priorities. While he waited, Bruce thought up an interim and more personal design. It was only some seventy or eighty miles north from Gigha, as the crow flies, to Moidart and Castle Tioram, beyond the Ardnamurchan peninsula. He felt that perhaps he owed a visit to Christina MacRuarie — owed it to himself, as well as her. So, one early July morning of blue skies, high fleecy clouds and sparkling waters, a single galley flying no banners, royal or otherwise, slipped out of Ardminish Bay northwards up the amethyst, green and azure Sound of Jura. It left behind the High Steward of Scotland, the High Constable of Scotland, and the Lord High Admiral of Scotland, to see to affairs in Argyll. Surely that should be sufficient.

By the narrows of Craignish, boom now removed, the Isles of the Sea, the Ross of Mull and fabled Iona, the ship threaded the colour-stained Hebridean Sea in as joyous and carefree a voyage as this essentially lonely man had ever known. He decided that he must bring Elizabeth to see Iona, and the tombs of his Celtic ancestors, the semi-legendary royal line of which he was the heir. Meantime, he had other business.

On he sailed, by pillared Staffa and the Treshnish Isles, up between long Coll and the Cailleach Point of huge Mull, with the thrusting promontory of Ardnamurchan, the most westerly point of the mainland of the British Isles, seeming to bar the way ahead. Then, beyond its white-fanged snout, with all the spectacular loveliness of the jagged mountains of Rhum, Eigg, Muck and the saw-toothed Black Cuillin of Skye, opening before them, they swung in eastwards to a great bay, lined with silver cockle-shell sands, towards the wooded narrow jaws of Loch Moidart. And there, on a rocky half-tide islet in the green throat of the loch, the mighty Castle Tioram rose, aglow with the westering sun, seat of the MacRuaries, the children of Rory or Roderick, another of great Somerled's sons.

Here the dark and fiery Lady Christina ruled supreme. A dozen of her own galleys and birlinns rode at anchor in the loch.

The King's unheralded arrival created less stir at Castle Tioram than it would have done at most houses. Christina treated it as a perfectly normal development, and with no Court or strangers to consider, behaved towards Bruce as she might have done to a brother—and a younger brother at that. He had spent weeks in this castle when his fortunes were at their lowest ebb, and none were likely to forget.

But after a great meal, with music and saga-telling in the Highland fashion, in the Great Hall, Christina took her guest up to the castle battlements, to watch the blazing spectacle of the sunset over the isle-strewn sea. Eyeing the ever-changing wonder of it, she spoke her mind.

"I think you will not come seeking my bed tonight, Robert," she said. "Not now. Why, then, have you come to Moidart? You do not need men. Nor ships. Nor, I scarce think, counsel. What brings you?"

"Think you I must only come to you needing something. Tina?"

"It is the way of men."

"You think less than highly of us, if you say so."

"I am not a girl, Robert. I was wed at fifteen, near twenty years ago, and widowed three years later. I have had much experience of men."

"You have had much experience of *me*, lass. Yet you still believe I must only come to you in my need?"

"I will tell you that when you tell me why you have come."

"Could I not have come for love of you, Tina?"

"So it *is* my body? My bed?"

"I have not said so. But ... if I did come knocking at your door — would you accept me? Tonight?"

"Have I ever turned you away, Robert?"

"Not yet."

"Nor would I." She looked at him, in that strange painted light. "Yet you will not come, I think. Now that you have your Elizabeth. I believe I know my Robert Bruce! That is not why you have come."

"No," he admitted. "That is true. Although . . . I am tempted! But, nor is it true that I came seeking your aid, your help."

"Why, then?"

"What I said, woman. I came for love of you," he insisted. "Can you not conceive that a man can see a woman as a friend? Not only desire her body? Even when her body is desirable indeed. I came as a friend, Tina. Is it so strange? You are my very good friend. Have been for long years. Is that not sufficient reason to come visiting you?"

She reached out to touch his arm. "Robert — I believe that you mean it. That you do not cozen me!"

"Why should I cozen you? You, of all women. You, who have cherished me, nursed me, sailed with me, fought with me ..."

"And lain with you! There is the heart of the matter, Robert. A man and a woman who have lain together can never be ... just friends. It is not possible."

"You say so? I do not see why not. They but know each other the better. You are no less my friend, Tina, that we have bedded together."

"No less, but more. Different. Otherwise."

"As you will. Whatever you say, I have come to Castle Tioram kindly affectioned. I never might speak with you fairly, at the Court. Speak as now. Alone, for any time. To thank you for how you were kind with Elizabeth. When you could well have been other. For much patience. Understanding. And you not a patient woman, as I know well! So I came. From Gigha. In friendship."

She smiled, now. "Then I thank you. From my heart. You are a strange man, Robert Bruce. But you are very welcome to Castle Tioram. Whatsoever your reason for coming. And you keep your own chamber, this night?"

"God aiding me, woman!"

"Oh, and I shall aid you also, never fear! With a locked door, no less!"

He looked a trifle put out. "No need for that. You may trust me, I think. And no need to sound . . . so keen!"

"You would have me temptress, Sire?"

"No-o-o. But you can still be friendly, Tina." It was his turn to reach out a hand. "A chaste kiss now, would harm none . . ."

"I do not give chaste kisses, friend! I am Christina of Garmoran! One way, or the other. Mind it, sirrah!"

"Why are women ever so difficult?" he demanded, of the last rays of the sunset.

"Women are women," she returned. "Not half-creatures. Not Isleswomen, at least! Come you, and I will show you to your lonely chamber."

He grinned. "Elizabeth, I think, would scarce believe this . . . !"

* * *

Five days of hunting, hawking, fishing and sailing at Castle Tioram, and much refreshed—and still his own man—Bruce sailed south again. He would have taken Christina with him, to Gigha, but she declared that it would look a deal better if she appeared, a day or two later, in her own vessel.

In the event, Christina and the Queen arrived at Gigha on the same day. Elizabeth was enchanted with all she saw, falling in love with the Hebrides at first sight. Even Marjory appeared to be less abstracted and withdrawn than usual—although Walter Stewart took credit for that.

Gigha was much too crowded now, and a move was made to Angus Og's "capital" of Finlaggan, on Islay, where, on islands in the freshwater loch of that name, he had a large castle, chapel, hall of assembly, and burial-place. This was the seat of government of the Isles lordship, princedom, or as it still called itself, kingdom — and Angus was at pains to demonstrate to his visitors something of the princely state he still maintained. He called a Council of Sixteen, consisting of four thanes, four Armins or sub-thanes, four great freeholders or lesser lords, and four knights; these, advised and guided by a large number of people whose right it was — judges, seannachies, chiefs, the Bishop of the Isles and seven senior priests, plus numerous hereditary officers such as MacEachern the sword-maker; MacArthur the piper, MacKinnon the bow-maker, and MacPhie the recorder, sat at stone tables round a central flat rock on which sat Angus himself. All this on the not very large Council Island, and in the open air, so that the place was already overcrowded before the distinguished visitors got a foothold. The proceedings were formal and merely ceremonial, a strange admixture of the purely Celtic and the Norse.

Thereafter, however, in his own house, Angus played host in truly princely and utterly ungrudging fashion, almost to the exhaustion of his guests. Every conceivable aspect and speciality of the Hebridean scene was exploited, and day after day of brilliant sunshine and colour was succeeded by night after night of feasting, dancing, music and story-telling. Practically every major island of both the Inner and Outer Hebrides was visited — and under the Lord of the Isles' protection the holiday-makers were safe from the attentions of even the most notoriously piratical chieftains, like MacNeil of Barra, MacMath of Lochalsh and MacLeod of the Lewes. Iona was the favourite with the ladies; and Staffa, with its caverns and halls like cathedrals of the sea, a close second. So taken was Marjory Bruce with Iona that she insisted on being left on that sacred isle of the sainted Columba, with or without her husband. Certainly it was beautiful, its white sands a dream, and its little abbey a gem; but the King feared that his death-preoccupied daughter was perhaps morbidly concerned with the serried tombs of her royal ancestors — allegedly no less than forty-eight kings of Scotland, eight Norse, six Irish and even an Englishman, Ecgfrid, King of Northumbria, lay here. Nevertheless, at least she had found an interest in something. Walter and she were left to work it out.

Nearly four weeks of this pleasant lotus-eating existence had passed, when one sultry August day the peace of it was shattered. A small fast galley arrived at Islay from the south, an Irish one this time, one of O'Neil's. It brought Thomas Randolph, Earl of Moray.

Moray was an able, clear-headed, unexcitable man, the last to raise hares or scares. That he should have left his command to come all this way was indicative of some major development. Bruce, about to set out on a deer-driving expedition on neighbouring Jura, drew his nephew aside when he had raised him from knee-bent hand-kissing.

"Well?" he demanded.

"Less than well, Sire."

"Is it defeat? Disaster?"

"Not that. Not yet . . ."

"What, then? My brother — is he well?"

"Well, yes. Very well . . ."

"Then why are you here, man?"

"I was sent. The Lord Edward sent me. Commanded me to come."

"You went to Ireland, Thomas, under *my* command. Not Edward's."

"Aye, Sire. But — in Ireland *he* commands. Commands all. He is master there. Much the master. And Your Grace is far away."

Keenly Bruce eyed his nephew. "This is not like you, Thomas," he said. "I sent you, as the one man whom my brother might not over-awe and browbeat. To curb and restrain him, should need be. And I put all but Edward's own levies, from Galloway and Carrick, under your command. Yet you let him send you back?"

Calmly the other nodded. "All true, Sire. But I come not only because my uncle sent me. I came because I believed it best. That you should know what transpires. With the Lord Edward."

"M'mmm. Very well, Thomas. Say on."

"It grieves me, Sire, to speak so. Of my uncle and your brother. To seem the tale-bearer. But I believe the Lord Edward works against your interests, not for them. Always he was headstrong, going his own way. But this is different. Now he seeks power. In Ireland. Rather than to defeat the English. And no longer talks of the threat to the English South. Or of forcing a peace treaty. Now he talks of uniting Ireland."

Bruce, well aware of all the eyes that watched them closely, and the minds that would be wondering, putting their own construction on secret converse and grave faces, mustered a sudden laugh, and slipped an arm around his nephew's shoulder.

"Come, Thomas — you ever were a sober fellow!" he exclaimed, loud enough for many to hear. "Here's little cause for gloom. So it ever was. Come — tell me of the campaigning. How far south you have won . . ." And he linked the arm now through the younger man's, and led him away along Finlaggan's loch shore.

"Your Grace is pleased to laugh," Moray said stiffly. "But there is little laughter in Ireland, I promise you . . . !"

"Tush, man — that was for these others." The King's voice was lowered again. "It will serve our purposes nothing to have men construing trouble. And women turning it into catastrophe. Now — apart from this of Edward, what of the campaign? What of our arms?"

Moray shrugged. "As to soldiering, we have done well enough. But at a price. We have won many battles and lost none. In Ulster at least the Irish have risen well in our cause. O'Neil, O'Connor,

MacSweeney are never out of the Lord Edward's presence. We overran the provinces of Antrim, Down, Armagh and Louth, even Kildare and Meath. We defeated many English captains and magnates, and many of the Anglo-Irish lords. But at Dundalk, in Louth, we turned back, instead of pressing on. Back to Ulster to Connor, in Antrim. From whence I came here, on my uncle's command."

"Back to Antrim? Giving up all that you had won in the south? Why?"

"Well may you ask, Sire. As did I! But it was the Lord Edward's decision. And he commands not only his own troops, but all the Irish also. Moreover, most of our Scots knights look to him, rather than to me. Even those supposedly under my command."

The King looked thoughtful indeed. "But this is not like Edward," he objected. "Edward was ever for pressing on, not for turning back. There must have been a reason. You were winning — yet he retreated?"

"There was a reason, yes — but not sufficient. Not sufficient for *me*, let alone my headstrong uncle! There is famine in Ireland, see you. Living off the country is hard indeed. Our men were hungry, our horses weak, many dying. There is disease also. We have lost more men from sickness than from battle. Even so, better to have pressed on — for the famine is less grievous the further south you go, the country ahead less devastated than that we had already fought over. We could have taken Dublin, where the English have much food stored. We were but thirty miles from it, and the English there in panic. Said to be fleeing southwards. But — we turned back."

"And Edward's reason? His proclaimed reason? He must have had one."

"To consolidate Ulster, he said. To make the North a secure base for further drives southward. To gain reinforcements. More men. That is why I am sent here — that, and to get rid of me, I think! To seek more men from Your Grace."

"God's mercy! I told him. Three thousand only I would give him. *Lend* him. Said before parliament. No more. Less than three months past. And now he sends for more? Knowing my mind full well. Yet . . . you say the Irish have risen well? In Ulster, at least. What needs be with more men, then?"

"He uses the Scots as his spearhead. Always. As would any commander. Our men, trained in the long wars against the English. The Irish gallowglasses are brave, good fighters. But they lack discipline, one clan at feud with another. They are less than reliable,

And they fight on foot. It is our light cavalry that ever leads. And so suffers most."

"Our losses *have* been heavy, then?"

"Not heavy, as war is reckoned. For what was gained. Half the men you sent are no longer effective. Either from battle, sickness or hunger. Horses worse."

"I see. But, still — you have not given me reason for Edward, of all men, to retire. From Dundalk to Antrim. When he was winning."

"That is why I consented to be sent home, Sire. I believe that the Lord Edward — and O'Neil and O'Connor with him — is winning Ulster for himself. Is more concerned in setting up a government for Ulster than for forcing the English to a treaty. He is summoning all chiefs and landholders, appointing officers and sheriffs, acting viceroy rather than commander."

Bruce shook his head. "*You*, Thomas, I could have conceived might act so. You — but not Edward. So — he now waits, for you to return with more men from me?"

"I do not know if *that* is why he waits, Sire."

"What mean you?"

"Perhaps he does not expect you to send him more men, in truth. Or me to return!"

"Ha! You think that?"

"I do not know. It may be so. Or I may be wrong. Certainly he *wants* more Scots light cavalry. But whether he truly expects it, knowing Your Grace's mind, I know not. Any more than I know his true purpose in Ireland."

For long moments the King was silent. At length, he spoke thoughtfully. "My brother is not a devious man. He ever prefers to act, rather than to plan. I conceive, Thomas, that you may be attributing to him something of your own mind and mettle. Seeing deeper into this than does he. You would not act so without careful intention and purpose. With Edward it could be otherwise. He could be merely gathering strength for a greater, stronger thrust to the south. And making sure of a secure base behind him, in truth."

"It could be. I know it. So I have told myself many times. And yet — somehow, he has changed. He acts the governor, not the commander. For weeks I have been ill at ease. It came to me that I must tell you. I could not tell you all this in a letter. Nor by the lips of any messenger. Even my own lips falter over it. Perhaps I did wrongly to come, Sire — to leave Ireland. But . . ."

"No, Thomas — not wrong. You knew that I trusted you, relied on your judgement. It was right to come to me. But this is *all* a matter of judgement, is it not? Of interpretation. Of one man's mind, by another and very different man."

"Your Grace thinks me in error, then? In my judgement. Such as it is!"

"I do not know. You have been with Edward, close, these last months. Heard him, seen him. But I *know* him better than you do. Have known him since a child, grown up with him. And he has never been . . . devious."

"Save before the Ayr Parliament. When he admitted to secret correspondence with these Irish chiefs."

"True. True. That was not very like Edward, either," Bruce shrugged. "It is difficult. What would you advise that I do, nephew?"

Without hesitation the other answered, "Send me back. With more men. Enough men, under my close command, to ensure that my uncle heeds my voice! With orders, strict orders, for me to prosecute the war southwards. With all speed."

Impulsively the older man clapped the other's shoulder. "I' faith, lad — we may on occasion differ in judgement! But our minds think alike when it comes to strategy! That was my own design. You shall go back. And I shall send with you more men of substance. Lords, committed to *your* support. Now that we have disposed of MacDougall, men and captains are available. So be it, Thomas — you shall return to Ireland with another 2,000 men . . ."

They turned back.

That finished holiday-making for Robert Bruce. In two days, most of his company were on their way southwards, leaving the painted paradise of the Hebrides to its own colourful folk. There was work to do elsewhere.

Chapter Eight

Elizabeth de Burgh stood beside the great bed, rocking the tiny red-faced morsel in her arms as it snuffled and wheezed and whimpered. Softly she crooned to it, her voice alive with the aching longing of the childless woman. But her eyes never left the white, grey-streaked, strained face on the pillow below.

She had stood there for half an hour now, in the tower-room of Turnberry Castle, waiting, a prey to so many and conflicting emotions. The physicians, midwives and other serving-women she had long since banished from the chamber. Only the Queen herself, her stepdaughter and the new-born infant remained in the tapestry-hung, over-heated apartment, with the flickering firelight and the smell of sweat, blood and human extremity.

Marjory Bruce's breathing was quick and shallow, her lips blue, her closed eyelids dark. For long she had lain so, unmoving save for the light uneven breathing. Since the afterbirth indeed. It was nearly three o'clock of a wild March night, and the waves boomed hollowly beneath Turnberry's cliffs, seeming to shake the very castle.

The Queen's patience was inexhaustible, her cradling and whispering continuous.

Without a flicker of warning the heavy eyelids opened and the dark eyes stared up, deep, remote, expressionless, unwinking.

Elizabeth held the baby out, and so that those eyes could see it.

They changed neither in direction nor in their lack of expression.

"All is well," the older woman said quietly.

The other closed her eyes again.

There was another long interval, silent save for the muted thunder of the waves, and the creak of the dying log-fire as the embers settled deeper in the glowing ash.

When the girl opened her eyes again, the Queen was still there, and in the same position and attitude. Once more she held out the child.

After a while, and without turning her glance on the infant, the blue lips moved, almost imperceptibly.

Elizabeth leant closer, to hear.

"It is . . . complete?" the faint words whispered. "Sound? No . . . monster?"

"It is a fine boy. Small, but perfect. See. A boy. An heir. And well. You have done so very well, my dear."

There was the tiniest shake of her head.

"It is true. All is well, Marjory. Look — see for yourself."

Still the girl did not look at the child.

"Shall I put him here? Beside you. In your arm?"

"No." That was certain, at least. She turned her head away, and the eyelids closed again.

Elizabeth bit her lip, and sighed, but waited still.

Presently, seemingly out of great depths, the other spoke, her voice little more than a breath. "A boy. He . . . will be . . . glad. As am I. Now . . . I can die . . . in peace."

The older woman gasped, with the shock "Ah, no, child — no!"

she said. "Do not speak so. All is well, now. You will see. You will soon be well again. And so very happy."

There was no least response from the bed.

"Hear me, Marjory," the Queen persisted, strangely uncertain for that assured and beautiful woman. "You should rejoice, not talk of dying. Now that you have something to live for. A child. A man-child." And as an afterthought, "And a husband. This fine boy — he needs his mother."

Silence.

"He is yours. All yours. An heir, yes — but also a part of yourself. To cherish and nurture. To watch grow into a man. To love and guard and guide. A man-child . . ." The older woman's voice broke. "Oh, God!" she said.

She might not have spoken.

The Queen began to pace up and down the room, still holding the baby. Every now and again she came to stare down at the ashen face, so still, so death-like. And each time it was with a stoun at the heart. For here was the shadow of death indeed, called for, besought, and approaching near. Elizabeth de Burgh could feel its chill hand, there in that overwarm chamber.

Her fears were not all fancy, an overwrought imagination born of weariness, distress and the small hours of the morning — just as Marjory Bruce's talk of death was not just the near-hysteria of a young woman new out of the ordeal of childbirth. For it had been a bad birth, a terrible birth, with the child six weeks premature added to a breach presentation. It had gone on for fourteen evil hours, and Marjory, never robust nor inspirited, had screamed and begged for death. Grievously torn and with internal haemorrhage, she had lost a great deal of blood — was probably still bleeding under all the physicians' bindings, for they had been unable to staunch the flow, try as they would. Death was no figure of speech in that apartment. And the girl had no wish to live.

Bruce and Walter Stewart had been sent for immediately after Marjory's fall from the horse which had touched off this emergency. She ought not to have been riding, of course; but she had all her family's stubbornness, and found a horse's saddle one means of attaining the solitariness which she seemed to crave. If anything could be called fortunate about the entire unhappy business, it was that she had been thrown not far from the castle, and her fall seen from a cot-house; otherwise she might well have been dead by now.

The King and her husband, as it happened, were not so very far away as they might have been, since they were soldiering again — besieging Carlisle, some ninety miles away, at the request of James Douglas, who was finding its English garrison a thorn in the flesh for his campaigning over the Border. Carlisle and Berwick were now the only enemy-held fortresses north of Yorkshire. Walter, if not the King, would almost certainly leave all and come hot-foot the moment the news reached him; but even the fastest and best-founded horses would take many hours to cover 180 miles across the Border hills and mosses. A galley would have been quicker — but not in these March equinoxial gales. Riding all through the night as they probably would, they could scarcely be at Turnberry before daylight.

Elizabeth was intensely weary, anxious and at a loss. She had never left that bedside since the younger woman had been carried to it, still in her disarranged riding attire. But she would not, could not, abandon her vigil. She would not even lay down the child. Endlessly, patiently, she walked and watched, hushed and murmured.

The long desperate hours passed. On the bed, Marjory Bruce did not stir, scarcely seemed to breathe.

How many inspections of that slight, motionless figure the Queen had made she did not know, when she noticed the single gleaming tear-drop on the pallid cheek. The sight of it moved her almost intolerably. It was long since Marjory had been seen to weep. Hers had been a dry-eyed ordeal and agony. Elizabeth sank down on her knees beside the bed, child still in her arms, and sank her head on the soiled coverlet. Almost she beat it there.

"Oh, lassie, lassie!" she cried brokenly. "How they have hurt you! Injured you. Men! Men, with their evil passions, their blind pride, their selfish folly! They have spared you nothing! Nothing!"

Long she crouched there, the baby part-supported by the bed. Perhaps, in time, she dozed a little. For when she became aware again it was with a jerk. The tear-drop was gone, evaporated. But the eyes were open. So was the mouth, slightly.

She stared, as her mind grappled with what her eyes told her — the ashen pallor waxen now, the dark glance fixed, glazed, the parted lips stiff. And looking, she knew, and a great convulsive sob burst from her. She clutched the morsel of humanity in her arms almost to suffocation.

After the first onslaught had worn off, Elizabeth's impulse was to run for the others, the physicians, midwives, courtiers, anyone to take the burden from her shoulders, the burden of what she alone now knew. But she told herself that was folly. Marjory was dead, undoubtedly. No one would bring her to life again. And, for herself, she wanted no strangers intruding on her grief.

She closed those glazing eyes, but otherwise did not handle the body. For a while she could not bring herself to lay down the baby, moaning over it in an extravagance of sorrow for the motherless mite, saying to it what she could not say to Marjory Bruce. But at length she placed it in the handsome cradle Stewart had had made before he went to the wars. Then she went and sat, crouched, gazing into the smouldering fire. She tried to pray for the departed, but could not. Her mind sank away into a grey vacancy of regret and fatigue.

It was thus that Robert Bruce and Walter Stewart found her when, between five and six in the morning, they came storming into that fetid chamber out of the blustering night, covered with mire and the spume of foundered horses, urgent, vehement, demanding, sweeping aside the servitors and others who cowered outside.

The hush and atmosphere of that room, with the drawn, almost blank face that the Queen turned to them, hit them like a mace-stroke. Each halted, drawing quick breaths.

There was no other sound but the snuffling from the cradle.

The men reacted differently. Stewart strode straight to the cradle. Bruce, after a long look at his wife's strained and warning face, went to the bed.

For long moments he stood staring down, fists clenching. Then a great shuddering groan racked him. "Dead!" he cried. "Dead! Oh, God, oh, Christ-God — dead!" And he raised those clenched fists high, up above his head, towards the ceiling, beyond, towards heaven itself, and shook them in a raging paroxysm of grief terrible to behold.

Elizabeth came to him then, to reach out a tentative hand to him. Walter Stewart came, faltering-stepped, gulping, looking askance at the bed, his normally ruddy face suddenly pale.

Bruce saw neither of them. "I am accursed! Accursed!" he ground out, from between clenched teeth. "All that is mine, rejected of God! Now my daughter, my only child. Dead. Slain. Slain by myself! Who forced her to marriage! One more. One more to pay the price of my sin. My brothers. My kin. My friends. Now, my daughter." He gazed around him wildly, although he saw none of them. "Why these? Why not myself? God, in Your heaven — why not myself?"

"Not your sin, Robert," the Queen said, level-voiced. "If this was for the sin of any, it was Edward Plantagenet's sin. Who ruined her young life in hatred and vengeance. Vengeance on you. Here was the sin."

"*I* defiled God's altar, woman! *I* slew John Comyn, in passion, in the holy place. I, excommunicate, who presumed to this unhappy throne, with a murderer's hands. *I* desired an heir from my own loins. I, not Edward Plantagenet. I slew my daughter as truly as I slew the Red Comyn!"

The woman shook her head, but attempted no further comfort. Her weariness and pain were such that she drooped as she stood, the proud de Burgh.

Walter Stewart turned and strode to the window without a word. He stood blindly staring out into the darkness, his face working. He had not so much as touched the bed.

The King's wide shoulders seemed to sag and droop, likewise. He sank forward on to the bed, arms outstretched over that still, slight body. "Marjory! Marjory!" he whispered. "Can you forgive me? Where you are now. Can you forgive? The father who brought you to this? Can you, girl? Of your mercy!"

Silence returned to that chamber, save for the child's little noises.

At length, heavily, Bruce rose, and looking round him as though a stranger there, paced across to his son-in-law who still stood at the window like a statue.

"I am sorry, lad," he said. He laid a hand on the other's shoulder. "Sorry. It may be that I need your forgiveness also. I ask it of you." Though his voice quivered, all was quiet and sane again.

The High Steward of Scotland shook his fair head, helplessly. "Have I ... Your Grace's permission ... to retire?" he got out. And without waiting for an answer, turned and hurried from the room.

Bruce looked over to his wife by the fire. "How was it?" he asked, evenly. "How did she die?"

Slowly, carefully, Elizabeth told him the grievous tale of it. But she spared him not a little.

He heard her out, silent. But he asked no questions. Indeed, he scarcely seemed to listen, his mind plumbing depths of solitary despair.

Finishing, she took his hand and led him over to the cradle. "A boy," she told him. "A boy, perfectly formed. A fine boy. And well. Your ... grandson."

For long he looked down at the shrivelled, red-faced little creature.

"Aye," he said, at length. "This ... this is all! All for this. This puny scrap is destiny! The destiny for which I have fought and schemed and struggled. For which countless men have died. For which a realm waits. The destiny for which my brother seeks to conquer Ireland, MacDougall languishes in Dumbarton's dungeon, Douglas hammers Durham city and I besiege Carlisle. For this handful of wrinkled flesh!"

Elizabeth opened her lips to speak, but could not. She busied herself instead with smoothing the baby's coverings, and sought to still her quivering mouth. "Carlisle?" she got out, aside. "Is it well, there? The siege? Does all go well? Sending for you was no hurt? That you should leave . . .?"

"No. It mattered nothing. I was gaining nothing. This siege is a folly. Carlisle will not fall. It is too strong. Its walls and towers. Without siege-engines we can do nothing. We sought to make a sow, to take us close to undermine the walling. But it sank into the earth made soft by these rains. Too heavy. They indeed have better machines than have we. Their governor, Harcla, can snap his fingers at us. I should never have begun it. But I promised Douglas. The least I could do, when he was hazarding all, deep in England. To protect his rear. But I will raise it now. End it. Assail Berwick instead, where we have more chance . . ." His voice tailed away, and the soldier was quickly superseded by the man again. "But what matters Carlisle! Or Berwick either. With what this room portends. Destiny is here, not in Carlisle. Here is the prize! That! And here the price paid!" Bitterly he said it.

She shook her head, and took his arm. "Your grandson," she reminded. "And motherless. Helpless."

"Aye." Nodding, he stooped then, to reach out and pick up the closely bundled infant. "So be it. This, then, is my heir. Scotland's heir. One day this will wear my crown!"

"Perhaps," the Queen said, strangle-voiced. "Perhaps not, Robert."

"If God has any mercy for me, he will. Is it too much to hope? You say that he is well-made? Healthy?"

She moistened her lips. "He is a fine boy, yes. But still, he may not wear your crown. Who knows? For I . . . I am pregnant, Robert! At last. At my age! Sweet Jesu — I am pregnant . . .!" Her voice broke.

For moments he could not so much as speak, lips parted. Then, "Dear God of all the saints," the man gasped. "Christ, Son of the Father — pregnant! You! It is true?"

Dumbly she nodded.

"You are sure? Not some false sign? Some cozening of the body . . . ?"

"No. It is sure. Oh, Robert . . .!"

Hurriedly but gently, then, he laid his grandson back in the cradle, and turned to take his wife in his arms. "My dear, my dear!" he said. "Here is wonder. Here is miracle. Here, here . . ." He wagged his head. "Lord Jesu, woman — what are we? What are we I say? The playthings of God? Playthings, no more . . .!"

"Say it not, Robert — say it not!" she urged, chokingly. She turned her face and buried it in his chest, clutching him convulsively, half-sobbing, half-laughing.

Chapter Nine

Two months later, almost reluctantly, the King was besieging Berwick-on-Tweed instead of Carlisle. He was against siegery, on principle. Being almost wholly devoid of the necessary engines for the business — mangonels, trebuchets, ballista, rams, sows and the like — where fortresses could not be successfully assaulted, stormed or infiltrated, or their water-supplies cut, he was left with the wearisome business of starving them out. And this was quite foreign to Bruce's vigorous, not to say impatient nature. The siege-maker has to have special qualities — and this man just did not have them.

But pressure to invest Berwick had been strong. It was the only Scots soil still in enemy possession, and as such a standing reproach, a denial of their limited victory. Moreover, it had usually been the headquarters of the English administration over Scotland, and for it still to be in Edward's grasp was galling in the extreme. Now that MacDougall was put down, this assault was the only action the King could take, within his own realm, to hasten Edward's acceptance of the peace treaty. Also James Douglas, Warden of the Marches, saw Berwick as a perpetual challenge to his authority, and claimed that he could not go raiding deep into England with any peace of mind leaving this occupied stronghold, which could be reinforced by sea, behind him. Douglas, of course, had a sort of vested interest in Berwick. Here his father had been governor, in 1296, had gallantly withstood Edward the First's siege throughout the terrible sack of Berwick town, had been tricked into terms by the English, and then shamefully betrayed and sent walking in chains, like a performing bear, down through England to imprisonment in the Tower. James was concerned to avenge his father.

He was, in fact, the moving spirit in this siege, the King, though present, being less than well. Since his daughter's death he had been moody, at odds with himself and others, dispirited for so purposeful a nature. It was not that he was actually and recognisably ill. He went about, if somewhat lethargically, and indeed denied that there was anything wrong with him. But those close to him knew well that he was not himself, and veterans like Gilbert Hay and Lennox claimed that they recognised the same symptoms that had laid him low at Inverurie in 1307, and at Roxburgh in 1313 — though, they admitted, with much less virulence. Certainly Bruce itched a great deal, his skin hot and dry, and of an evening was apt to be flushed with a slight fever. Elizabeth, who had little objection to camp-life and had accompanied her husband to Berwick, was anxious — but Bruce was not a man to fuss over and she had to content herself with small ministrations and watchfulness.

This was the situation one evening of late May when the burly, grizzled and tough Sir Robert Boyd of Noddsdale was ushered into the royal presence, from long travelling. He found the King and Queen, with Lennox, Hay and Douglas, in the vicarage of Mordington a mile or two north-west of the walled town, which had been Bernard de Linton's pastoral charge before he became royal secretary, Abbot of Arbroath and Chancellor of the realm. It was a small house for so illustrious a company, and plainly plenished, but the nearest stone and slated residence left intact near the beleaguered citadel.

"Welcome, Sir Robert," Bruce greeted him. "Here's an unexpected pleasure. Have you fallen out with my brother? Or have you come to aid us in this plaguey siege? You have the soundest head for such matters in my kingdom, I vow." News of late from Ireland had been good, and he had no reason to anticipate ill tidings.

"Your siege I know not of, Sire," the other returned. "I came at the command of my lord of Moray. And in haste. To outpace another. From your royal brother. Another courier, from the Lord Edward. My lord of Moray conceived that you should have warning."

"Warning of what, man? Not defeat? Only a week past we had word of victories, progress . . ."

"No defeat, no. Quite otherwise. The Lord Edward has assumed the crown. Has been enthroned King of Ireland."

"Wh-a-t!" Not only Bruce but all other men in the room were on their feet at this bald announcement.

"King, no less. Crowned and installed. At Dundalk. Ten days past. King."

"But . . . great God — how came this? Is it some mummery? Some foolish play-acting?"

"Not so, Sire. It was a true coronation. He was solemnly led to the throne by O'Neil, King of Tyrone. And supported by many sub-kings and chiefs. All assenting. Crowned High King of All Ireland."

"It is scarce believable. My brother. To do this . . ."

"Only Edward would do it!" Elizabeth said. "Only he would conceive it possible. The bold Edward!"

"Bold, woman! This is . . . more than boldness. This is folly, beyond all. Treason indeed — highest treason."

"You say so? How can it be treason, Robert? Against you? You are not king in Ireland."

"Do you not see? Edward went to Ireland as my lieutenant and representative. Leading an army of my subjects. On a campaign to advance the interests of my realm of Scotland. Now, he has thrown all that to the winds. He has made himself a monarch, and therefore no subject of mine. He thus rejects both my authority and my interests. The campaign to win a peace treaty."

"But may not this but aid in it? In bringing the English to treat? If he unites Ireland, as its king . . ."

"Save us — *you* should know the English better! This will end all possibility of a treaty. For us to defeat their minions, in a rebellion. To drive many of their captains out of Ireland — that might have served our purpose. But to set up Edward as King of All Ireland — that is no mere rebellion. That is the greatest challenge to England's might and pride. For to them Ireland is a province. They will, and must, treat this as fullest war. To the death. They will now muster all their power, to keep Ireland. And because this new king is my brother, with Scots troops aiding him, they will conceive me as behind him. And refuse to make any peace treaty. With this one stroke Edward has destroyed all we have worked for, since Bannockburn."

There was silence in that room for a little, as all considered the implications.

"Why? Why did he do it?" Bruce went on. "He is rash, yes. But this is not the result of a sudden whim. This he must have planned."

Boyd coughed. "My lord of Moray believes that he intended this, before ever he went to Ireland. That he had O'Neil's, and the others', offers of the throne, secretly, all along. That this was the real reason for the Irish adventure — not the English treaty. So my lord said, to tell Your Grace."

"Aye. I can see it now. Was I blind? How could I tell that he, my own flesh and blood, could so intend?"

"Edward was ever ambitious," the Queen reminded. "Chafed under authority. Yours or other."

"He was not content to be named as heir to your throne," Lennox put in. "He required a throne *now*!"

"Once I heard him say that there was not room in Scotland for both Bruces!" Douglas added.

"He said that . . .?"

"Aye, Sire. I did not tell you. But he said it."

"He thought me hard on him, yes. But was I so? He seldom obeyed my orders. Chose his own way. But there can only be one king in a realm, one master, not two. I' faith, I learned that lesson sufficiently in the Guardianships!"

"So now he has gone to be king in a realm of his own, Robert," Elizabeth said soothingly. "Is that so ill, in the end? For you? At least Edward cannot now afflict you by his disobedience and resentment. As King of Ireland he will no longer trouble you. And will be a sore thorn in the English flesh."

"Your Grace's pardon," Boyd interjected heavily, "but I fear that it is less simple than that. The Lord Edward sends a courier, Sir William de Soulis, the Butler, to inform His Grace of all this. And to seek more men. Aid. Money. Food. Horses."

"Mother of God — he does?" Bruce cried. "After this, he turns round and seeks my help!" The King actually barked a harsh laugh. "Edward! Edward would! Save us — that is my brother, to be sure!"

"What will you do, Sire?" Hay asked.

"What *can* I do?" Bruce took a pace or two back and forth. "The deed is done. I cannot undo that. I can refuse him aid. Recall all Scots forces from Ireland. Leave him to his Irish. That, yes." He paused. "But . . . will it serve me any advantage? Serve Scotland's cause? Good, or ill?"

"You will not further support him, Sire!" Douglas exclaimed. "Now! After this . . .?"

"Let me think, Jamie — let me think, a mercy's sake. I *must* think, even if Edward does not! Poor Ireland, with an unthinking king!" He looked up. "Sir Robert — how does my nephew say? My lord of Moray? His judgement in matters of state I ever esteem. Did he reveal his mind to you?"

"He did not make so bold as to send advice, Your Grace," Boyd answered carefully. "But he did say that, though you would be angry, wrathful, he did not believe that you would break with the

Lord Edward. That though your cause suffers set-back in this, all may not be loss. That you may still use him, and the Irish, to your advantage."

"Aye. So I begin to think also. He is a long-headed wight is Thomas! And how think yourself, man? Your counsel also I value."

"Since you ask, Sire — I say likewise. Send him support. Possibly but little. But promise more later, on condition that he moves south forthwith against the English, with all speed and strength. Before they can learn of this, and send reinforcement from England. Since you cannot unmake this king, use him while you may. It will not bring about your peace treaty. But it could weaken your enemies. Which is always profitable."

"There speaks good sense. I thank you, friend." Bruce smiled grimly. "Was that why you came so fast? From Ireland. To reach me first. So that I should not, in my wrath, say what could not be unsaid? Refuse all support? And so, in haste, injure my cause?"

The other looked uncomfortable. "Not so, Sire," he said gruffly. "Or . . . but little. I came swiftly that you should have the tidings from your own friends. The more so in that I mislike William de Soulis!"

"Ah. Very well, Sir Robert. I thank you, whatever your reasons. Now, refreshment . . ."

* * *

So Bruce was well prepared when, two days later, Sir William de Soulis, Lord of Liddesdale and Hereditary Butler to the King of Scots, nephew of the late Guardian, came riding into the camp outside the walls of Berwick with quite an imposing cavalcade, all under a great banner bearing the three golden crowns of Tara, on blue — a device not seen in Scotland for centuries.

The King received him in a grassy hollow at a bend of Tweed. But however ready he was for the other's mission, he was scarcely prepared for his manner and style.

"Greetings, Sire!" the newcomer called, after the considerable trumpet flourish. "I, William de Soulis, Lord of Liddesdale in the Kingdom of Scotland, and Earl of Dundalk in the Kingdom of Ireland, bring greeting and God-speed from the mighty, puissant and gracious Lord Edward, by God's grace High King of All Ireland, to the illustrious Lord Robert, King of Scots. Hail!"

Bruce blinked. "All that?" he wondered. "Between brothers, Sir William, is that not . . . too much?"

It was the other's turn to blink. But he was a suave and quick-witted man, handsome, florid, courtly and not easily put out. "Your Grace has heard?" he wondered. "Heard that His Grace your royal brother is now King of Ireland?"

"Aye, friend — I have heard. Though not that he had started to make earls so soon!"

De Soulis bowed. "My poor worth over-valued," he agreed smoothly. "But the greetings I bring are none the less hearty. I bring them with love and esteem."

"I would esteem them more, sir, if they were offered in more seemly fashion. I am not used to receiving greetings from seated subjects, while I stand!"

Hastily de Soulis dismounted, and his entourage with him. "Your Grace's pardon. I was conveying greetings from one monarch to another. As envoy."

"Sir William, on Scottish soil you are the servant of one monarch only. Lord of Liddesdale — nothing else. Save my household butler! Remember it!"

"Yes, Sire. To be sure. I crave pardon."

"As you ought, sir. Now — deliver my brother's message. But as *my* subject."

"H'mm. As you will. His Grace of Ireland sends royal greetings and fraternal affection. He informs you that he has accepted and assumed the crown of All Ireland, duly offered and presented by O'Neil, King of Tyrone, with the Kings of Munster, Leinster, Meath and Thomond, and other sub-kings and lords of that realm duly assembled. For the welfare of that kingdom, the better prosecution of the war with England, and for the good alliance and support of your realm. To such end His Grace offers a treaty of alliance between both equal realms, of mutual support and aid of all kinds, against all and soever. This in love and esteem. God save the King!"

"Indeed! Which king?" Bruce observed mildly. And when the other did not answer, went on. "Why did my royal brother not inform me of such assumption of this throne?"

"Inform, Your Grace? But surely . . . surely you knew? That it was possible. Mooted. Long since. Surely you knew that?"

The King eyed the other searchingly. De Soulis seemed genuinely surprised. It was quite possible, quite in keeping, that Edward might not have informed even his closest associates that he had not told his brother of his monarchial ambitions and secret moves. In which case it might be wisest to let de Soulis remain in ignorance of the fact.

"I should have been informed of the impending coronation," he said carefully. "Who knows, I might have wished to grace it by my presence!"

De Soulis shook his head. "That His Grace did not confide in me. No doubt there was an urgency, Sire. No time. It would have taken many weeks to bring Your Grace to Dundalk."

"No doubt." Bruce let it go. "Well, Sir William," he went on, as though terminating the audience, "you have brought your tidings and my brother's greetings. For which I thank you. I now must needs consider my reply, for you to take back to Ireland."

"But, Sire — there is more." The other looked concerned.

"Ah."

"Yes. In return for this proposed alliance of the two kingdoms, this aid in your war against England, His Grace requires aid also. He requires trained cavalry, with the horses. Arms. Money. Also provisions — for there is famine in Ireland. He requires these from Scotland . . ."

"Requires, sir? *Requires!*"

"Requests, Your Grace. In exchange for Ireland's adherence to your cause."

"So! May I remind you, Sir William, that my brother went to Ireland as my lieutenant. To prosecute the war. To force a treaty from England. He took 6,000 of my subjects — mine, not his. And I have since sent more, with the Earl of Moray. Thus far, I have done the paying, provided all. With little result. Save, it seems, to win a throne for my brother! At my charge. Yet now he *requires* more from me, men and money. In exchange for *his* support! Here seems to me to be strange bargaining, sir!"

"Matters have much changed, Sire, since our expedition left Scotland."

"Seemingly! But not of my will. I still expect my brother's fullest support in this warfare, without any talk of exchange."

"I would remind Your Grace that Ireland is an independent kingdom . . ."

"Ireland is today a conquered province of England. I have had sufficient travail and sorrow in freeing Scotland from a like state, not to take on the reconquest of Ireland! If such is my brother's design, he must needs find Irishmen to do it. Or other allies. My Scots forces are there solely to win a treaty of peace from Edward of Carnarvon."

There was silence while de Soulis digested that.

"Then — you will not send aid to the Lord Edward? To His Grace?"

"I have not said so. But any that I send will go on *my* terms. Not as part of any bargain. They will be sent to the Earl of Moray, under his command. And he will take orders from myself. You understand? All Scots forces will he command, as my lieutenant — since my brother is no more that. And a full offensive southwards will be mounted forthwith. Before the English hear of this and send reinforcement. This is my decision. You will inform my brother."

The other bowed. "And . . . and how many men will I inform His Grace that you will send? Under these conditions."

"One thousand within the week. Light horse. More later, and when I hear that these are being used to good purpose. With silver. And food."

"His Grace hoped for many more than a thousand."

"His Grace will have to earn them, then! He has set back my hopes of a peace treaty, set back Scotland's full recovery, by years. As the price of his crown. This you will tell him. You have it? Then, I declare this audience ended, Sir William. You may retire . . ."

Chapter Ten

Bruce, typically, had chosen his own way to counter incipient sickness and debility. He had always claimed that it was the Earl of Buchan's imminent threat, and the subsequent vigorous action of the Battle of Barra, which he had risen from his sick-bed at Inverurie to fight, which had cured him that first time. So, in midsummer of 1316, he had impatiently shaken himself, left the weary siege of Berwick to underlings, and exorcised his ill humours of body and mind by setting off personally, with James Douglas, Walter Stewart and a large, fast-moving force, on a massive, deep-penetration raid into England.

And, surprisingly, it had worked. In the saddle, at the head of an armed host in enemy territory, the hero-king became himself once more.

Now in the golden days of early October, they were on their way home again, a little weary but flushed with success, and with almost an embarrassment of booty and prisoners to delay them. And Bruce was in no mood for a leisurely progress through the English North, however subservient its people. For the Queen's time was due towards the end of the month, and the King was agog, eager, to be back for this momentous event. Also to be with Elizabeth in what could only be an anxious time. A first child, at her age, was bound to be less than easy; and Bruce's first wife, as well as his daughter, had died in child-birth. Moreover, he had delayed a little longer than he had intended, in the south, due to the concomitants of unprecedented success.

They had won as far south as Richmond, again, without major opposition — and even to Bruce it had seemed strange for a King of Scots to be ranging at large so deep into the green heart of England without let or hindrance, entering cities, receiving addresses of reluctant welcome and even more reluctant tribute and treasure. Richmond itself, protected by its great castle, had been almost too reluctant, and had been all but committed to the flames before the unhappy magistrates realised that the castle would not, could not, save them, and had painfully paid up the promptly increased demands. Thereafter a certain amount of organised resistance in the West Riding had required that an example be made, and the Scots had swept through that fair land with fire and sword before, concerned about the time factor and the long journey home burdened with so much booty, Bruce had sent one more letter to an apparently unconcerned London urging an immediate treaty of peace. Perhaps he had waited rather too long for the answer which did not come. Quite unable to understand Edward of Carnarvon's ideas as to ruling a kingdom, it had been the Scots' turn for reluctance as the order for retiral was given.

So it was that, in a mellow autumn noonday, hazy sun, turning bracken and reddening leaves, the long, long, winding column of chivalry, armed might, highly-placed prisoners for ransom, and laden pack-horses by the thousand, had crossed Liddel Water north of Carlisle and was nearing the subsequent crossing of Esk on the line for Annandale, when another and scarcely less impressive, though smaller cavalcade came into sight ahead, over the green Border hills. No great noble or officer of state left in Scotland was likely to travel the land in such style, especially on apparent road to England, and the tremor of excitement ran through the royal host.

When the sound of music and singing reached them on the still air, wonder grew. Admittedly great prelates sometimes travelled the country so with their choirs, acolytes and relics; but this was not Lamberton's and certainly not Abbot Bernard's style, and old Robert Wishart of Glasgow was practically on his death-bed.

Then somebody perceived the preponderance of dark blue about the host of banners, and from that it did not take long to discern the three golden crowns on the greatest.

"By the Rude — another embassage from Ireland!" the King cried. "What will it be this time? More men required? More money? More royal greetings?"

"Sire — is that not the Earl of Moray's banner?" Douglas asked. "Near the front. It is his colours — red and ermine."

"Not under the Irish standard, surely! Not Thomas . . .!"

Then suddenly, as they drew closer, many about the King recognised something about the head-high, shoulder-back carriage of the slender figure in black armour that rode in the forefront of the oncoming brilliant company.

"It is Edward himself!" Walter Stewart exclaimed. "My lord of Carrick. This . . . this king!"

"Aye," Bruce said.

Men stared at each other doubtfully.

The King drew rein. "Let us await His Grace," he said carefully.

To a vigorous fanfare of Irish trumpets they met there on the open side of one of their own Annandale hills. Edward drew up a yard or two away, the others falling back from the two principals. He raised a steel-gauntleted hand.

"Hail, brother!" he said.

Robert smiled a little "Well met, Edward," he nodded. "Here is surprise."

"Yes. I greet you. Greet you in the name of all Ireland."

"Indeed? William de Soulis did that also, if I mind aright. What does it mean, Edward?"

Somewhat taken aback, the other cleared his throat. "It means . . . it means that it is not only as a brother that I greet you now, Robert. But as a monarch. Another king. One realm greeting another. That much, does it not?"

"I do not know. Tell me how much it means. From one to whom words, professions, compacts, mean but little, it seems!"

Edward flushed under his magnificent crested helm. "I was never one for splitting hairs, no," he agreed. "Bartering words. I prefer to act, brother. I find it more profitable."

"Profitable," Bruce nodded. "There we have it, yes. You have an aptitude for profit, Edward!"

His brother frowned. "I do not know what you are at, man. Do not talk in riddles. I could never abide you in such mood. But . . . I had expected warmer welcome than this. After so long a parting. See you — here is no way for kin to meet, after so many months."

"Aye — perhaps I am too sober. You must bear with me. But . . . I cannot forget that at our last leave-taking you promised leal service as my lieutenant and representative, Edward. And then abused my trust. Used my forces for your own ends."

"Not so. What I did was for the benefit of your realm as well as of Ireland. To further the fight against the English. But, i' faith — I have not come all this way to listen to your strictures, Robert! To be hectored by you. I have had enough of that in the past, by God! I would remind you that matters have changed since our last meeting. That although I am still your brother, I am no longer your subject! We are equals, now — equals, do you hear? Monarchs, both. I beg you not to forget it!" That was hot.

As Edward grew the hotter, so Robert became the cooler. "That is exactly the issue, the point I make," he said. "You left here my subject, my sworn servant, owing me and my realm allegiance. And you return quite otherwise. Disclaiming all allegiance, claiming equality. And to win this equality, and throw off your allegiance, you used my power, my name, my trust. Without my knowledge or consent. Knowing that I would not have given it . . ."

"There you have it! Knowing that you would not have given it! Here is the heart of the matter. This thing had to be done lacking your consent, or it would not have been done at all. *You* must ever be master. *You* command. You would never have agreed to have me a king, so that you could no longer command me. I know you, man! You are a notable captain, but you cannot abide that others should rival you. I know you — therefore I acted as I did."

Bruce shook his head. "By each and every word you speak, you prove that you do *not* know me, brother though you are! Neither know nor understand. Nor ever have, I think. I was against the Irish adventure from the start, because it would be like to draw away my strength, Scots power seeping away into the Irish bogs. How much worse that you should become King of that sorry country. With a kingdom to make and unite and hold together and defend. As well as forcing the English to a needless challenge. You must see it?"

"It was to challenge the English that I went to Ireland, was it not? With your agreement."

"To harass, to worry, to hinder. Not to force major war upon them. Think you the King of England can stomach a King of Ireland?"

"I know not, nor care. What is more to the point — it seems that the King of Scots cannot stomach it either."

And Edward Bruce reined round his splendid mount and rode back to his own party in most evident and high dudgeon. All around, men looked askance.

His brother sighed, and beckoned forward the Earl of Moray, to his side.

"So, Thomas, you are returned. With good reason, I have no doubt. I am glad to see you — I am indeed. Yours has been a thankless task, I think?"

"Thankless, Sire. And fruitless, I fear. I have done what I could — but that is little. My uncle now is gone quite beyond me. Only you can affect him now."

"I! Sweet Mary — that seems less than likely! I, of all men, he resents most."

"Yet you, of all men, he requires, Sire. He thinks to need no others. But your goodwill and aid he must have. Else, I swear, he would not be here today!"

"So he come a-begging, Thomas? Despite all?"

"Yes. Or, he would rather say, a-bargaining, I think."

"And chooses a strange tone to bargain in!"

"Aye. But he will change his tone. If he must. Give him time. He has not travelled these hundreds of miles just to bicker with you."

"M'mmm. Perhaps you are right. And *you* would have me ... bargain?"

"I believe so, yes. That is why I have come with him. There are reasons."

Moray was proved right about Edward changing his tone, there and then, for now the other was calling back.

"Brother — whither? Where do you make for, Annan? Lochmaben?" He sounded himself again.

"Lochmaben tonight," Bruce answered.

"Then I shall press on. We have been long on the road. I will await you at Lochmaben. And hope for better talking!" And in fine style he swept off, under his forest of banners, whence he had come — although minus Moray.

"His Grace is recovered," that man said dryly. "As he needs must, if he is to gain what he requires from you. He has brought two sub-kings with him, and dare not fail."

"You say so? And what does he want, Thomas?"

"He wants 10,000 men, 100 heavy chivalry and 500 bowmen. He wants Angus of the Isles' galleys. He wants silver enough to pay his Irish host. Also knights and trained captains, veterans, as many as he can win."

Bruce eyed the other for long moments, thoughtfully. "Jesu Son of God and Mary!" he said. "Would he have my crown also?" He gestured to Moray to remount, and turning in the saddle, almost absently waved on the vast column that had ground to a halt behind him.

"Of my brother," he went on. "I am now prepared to believe anything. Anything under heaven! But you, nephew — did I misunderstand? Or did it seem that you would have me listen to these . . . these rantings? Could that be Thomas Randolph?"

"Aye, Sire. It is my belief that you should heed and consider well. You cannot grant him all that he asks, to be sure. But some consent may be to your advantage. Indeed, I see you left with scant choice. The English must now, I think, attempt the re-conquest of Ireland. Nothing less will serve. So, either you hinder them, or you do not. If you do not, the country will fall to them like a ripe plum. I know it. I have made it my business to know it. Your brother is king in name only. Less king than were you at the start — for you at least were of the blood, had been Guardian, and had fought long for the realm. My uncle has none of that. The Irish people know him not, nor care. He is a magnificent captain of light cavalry, but no general. With no notion of statecraft. He has won many small victories, but consolidated nothing. These Irish kinglets and chiefs hate each other. They fight together all the time, like our Highland clans. They made him High King only to spite others — who therefore love him the less. And to gain *your* aid, against the English. That is why he must win that aid, now. Without it, his kingdom will fall fast. Even faster than it was raised up."

"And you think that should concern me?"

"Aye, Sire, I do. For if the English win a swift and easy campaign in Ireland, you — and Scotland — will suffer. That is sure. Now they are down, licking their wounds, out of faith in themselves and their leaders. But give them a quick and easy conquest of Ireland — as it would be, God knows — and there will be no holding them. They will be up again. And the English, sure of themselves, resurgent, are hard to beat. *You* know that. And there are still ten times as many of them as of us."

Bruce was looking at the younger man sidelong. "My sister bore a son indeed!" he observed. "What has ailed me from doing the same?"

Moray flushed a little. "If I have learned anything of affairs and rule, I have learned it of you, Sire."

"But your wits are your own, lad."

"You take my point, then?"

"I perceive that there is much in what you say, yes. That will require much thought."

"So long as you do not dismiss the Lord Edward's requests out of hand. As they would seem to deserve. And then have to face a triumphant England, in Ireland! Victorious and but fourteen miles from the coast of Galloway!"

"Aye. But what of consuming away my power? The very real danger of wasting my strength in Ireland? Always this is what I have feared in the Irish adventure. Of draining my Scots forces into the bottomless bogs. Already I have sent many thousands. To what end? How many remain? Ill-led, misused, they are squandered. I make no criticism of you, Thomas, who are only their commander in name. I have well understood your difficulties. That it was not for you to devise campaigns and teach your uncle how to fight a war."

"Sire — it is all true. You say that you fear to waste more men, to squander your strength. There is one sure way to avoid that, to make certain that your forces are used to best advantage. Go with them. Come back to Ireland with us!"

"Eh . . .?" Bruce frowned.

"Do you not see? This could answer all. With you there, my uncle could no longer delay, hold back, and use your forces for his own ends. With your sure hand on the helm, the galley of war would sail straight. Moreover, Angus of the Isles would work with you, where he would not with the Lord Edward."

"But, man — you are asking me to engage in full-scale war. Across the seas. The thing I have ever been most against."

"Not full-scale war, no. Not for you. Not for Scotland. For the Irish, perhaps. But for you, only a campaign. Which you can leave when you will, commit such forces as you will. It is your *presence* that is required. That could change all."

"The English are already pouring new forces into Ireland. In the south. You know that? We learned it in Yorkshire."

"No. But I did not doubt but that they would. They must. That is why I say that they will overrun all Ireland, and swiftly. If *you* do not stop them. And if they do, you will have to try to stop them, one day. Somewhere. Better to do it on Irish soil, with mainly Irish levies. Is it not so?"

"I will have to consider this," Bruce said slowly. "Here is a great matter."

"That is all I ask," the younger man acceded. "That you think on it . . ."

Not a great deal of that thinking was done that day, or night.

For just before they reached Lochmaben in mid-Annandale, an urgent courier caught up with them, with the news from Turnberry that the Queen's labour had started, at least two weeks early. In a cursing flurry of alarm, Bruce abandoned all else, and leaving the supervision of his army, guests and prisoners to others, spurred off on the sixty-mile road to the Ayrshire coast. On this occasion Walter Stewart stayed behind, but Douglas and Moray, hastily yelling orders and instructions, flung themselves after their liege lord.

They were hard put to it to catch up. The King rode like a madman, taking shocking risks, savaging his horse. If the blight and doom which seemed to hang over his life — or, at least, the lives of those near and dear to him — was to strike again, if he was to fail Elizabeth as, he told himself, he had failed so many, then Scotland truly would have to look for a new king!

Far into the night they rode, through the shadowy hills, with mounts stumbling now, flagging, snorting with every pounding beat of their hooves. Bruce pounded his own mind as relentlessly. What had he done? What had he done? Elizabeth! Elizabeth! A little light-headed, perhaps, he was beginning to confuse this night with that he had ridden seven months before. And the horror grew on him.

When at last he thundered over the drawbridge timbers at Turnberry, the watch shouted down at him from the gatehouse-parapet. But he did not pause. He flung on through the outer bailey to the inner, vaguely aware of all the lights ablaze. It was one of the grooms who ran to catch his steaming, blown mount as he leapt down who shouted after him.

"You have a bairn, my lord King! A bairn. A wee lassie!"

Bruce hardly took it in, as he ran clanking into the keep and up the winding turnpike stairs.

It was not the same room, at least. He knew that it would be their own chamber, up at parapet-level, indeed the apartment in which he had been born. Outside, on the small landing, was the usual group of whispering servants, who fell back at the sight of the frowning, mud-stained monarch. A courtier hurriedly threw open the door.

There was the sound of a child crying — but it came from a little turret chamber off, where lay Robert Stewart, Marjory's child, whom meantime the Queen was bringing up almost as her own.

He strode across to the great bed, and as he came Elizabeth's corn-coloured head, damp a little with sweat, turned. She smiled up at him. It was a good, honest smile, though tired.

"Thank God! Thank the good God!" he gasped. "Elizabeth, lass — praises be! You are well? Dear heart — you are well?"

"Well, yes, Robert. Weary a little, that is all. I am sorry. Sorry that I came before my time. That I brought you hastening. After . . . after . . ."

"I feared, lass. I feared. Greatly."

"I know what you would fear. But you need not have done. You wed a great strong Ulsterwoman, Robert!" She looked down at the infant that slept within the crook of her arm, so like that other wrinkled entity whom he had stared down at in March, and who now cried fitfully in the turret. "I should not say it, my dear. It is unfair to this moppet, who has come to us after so long. Is she not a joy? And so like you, Robert! The same frown! The same haughty disdain of mouth! I should not say it — but I am sorry that I have not given you the son you sought."

"I care no whit! So long as you are well. Nothing else concerns me . . ."

"No — you must not speak so," she chided. "It is not true. Not kind. This little one is a great concern. Part of you, and part of me. The Princess of Scotland. It has taken me long, long to produce her! I will not have her spurned. Least of all by her sire! Take her, Robert — for she is yours. More so than that boy in there, that you dote on! Take her."

"As you will." He lifted up the baby, gingerly, in his arms, steel-clad and spattered with horse's spume as they were. He peered into the tight-closed tiny face. "Another Bruce," he said, gravely. "Dear God — what have You in store for this one!"

"Enough of that!" Elizabeth exclaimed, with surprising strength and at her most imperious. "Such talk I will not have. I am a mother now — and no mere queen! We will have no talk of fate or curse or doom. This is our daughter, not any pawn of fate. Mind it, Robert Bruce!"

He smiled, then, and almost involuntarily jogged the infant up and down. "We shall call her Matilda," he said.

"Matilda? Why, of a mercy? Why Matilda?"

"Because she *is* Matilda — that is why."

"I had thought to call her Bridget. A good Ulster name. Celtic, too . . ."

"Matilda," he insisted. "Just look at her. She could be no other."

"I am her mother. Surely I have some say . . ."

"And I am the King! My word is law. Hear you that, Matilda Bruce? Remember it!" Stooping he laid her gently down within

Elizabeth's arm again. "Care for her well, woman. She is the King's daughter." And the hand that replaced the child brushed lingeringly over the mother's cheek and brow and hair.

"Oh, Robert," she whispered. "I am so very happy."

He nodded, wordless.

PART TWO

Chapter Eleven

It took some six weeks to mount the great expedition, in especial to convince Angus Og to bring his galleys south for a winter campaign. Bruce himself was well aware that he was violating his instincts, not only in going campaigning at this time of year, but in involving himself in the entire Irish project. But he accepted that what Moray had said was true; the dangers of doing nothing were greater than the risks he now ran. And this was the only time when he could contemplate leaving Scotland, when winter snows and floods sealed the Border passes and made any large-scale attack from England out of the question. He was assured that it seldom snowed in Ireland, and though it rained not a little, winter was often the dryest period. Indeed it seemed that it was apt to be a favourite campaigning time in Ireland, once the harvest was ingathered. He must be back, whatever happened, by late spring. So he assured Elizabeth.

So they assembled and embarked at Loch Ryan, in Galloway, in late November — the same place where Thomas and Alexander Bruce had landed ten years before in their ill-fated attempt to aid their brother's re-conquest of Scotland, an attempt which ended in their betrayal and their shameful executions. Angus of the Isles had landed them, and, however reluctantly, once again he was co-operating; but only because Bruce himself was going on the expedition. He certainly would not have done it for Edward. For he was not just acting the transporter, this time; he was taking part with his friend, if not his monarch, and a thousand of his Islesmen with him. Indeed, most of the transporting was being done otherwise, in a vast and heterogeneous fleet of slower vessels drawn from all the South-West, under the pirate captain, Thomas Don — for the narrow, fast, proud galleys were hardly suitable for the carrying of great numbers of horses and fodder and stores.

It was not all just what Edward had asked for, of course. There was a considerable array of knights and captains, yes; some heavy chivalry, some bowmen, and much light cavalry; in all perhaps 7,000. Also many spare horses, largely captured from England, grain, forage and money. All went under King Robert's personal command. Edward indeed was not present, having returned to Ireland weeks before, with his court of kinglets and chiefs, and in a very uncertain frame of mind. He was getting men and aid — but scarcely as he had visualised. Although he could hardly object to his brother's attendance he was obviously less than overjoyed. But at least it had all had already had one excellent result; for Edward, put out and concerned to prove his prowess, had managed to reduce the important English base at Carrickfergus, which had long been a thorn in Ulster's side, in a great flurry of activity on his return. Oddly enough, though Ireland's new monarch would have been the last to admit it, he had to thank his brother's father-in-law mainly for this. Richard de Burgh, Earl of Ulster, sent home by Edward of England to take command of the military side of the reconquest of Ireland, had made a peculiar start by diverting the convoy of ships sent to Drogheda, farther south, for the relief of Carrickfergus, using their stores and arms to ransom his own kinsman, William Burke, or de Burgh, captured by Turlough O'Brien, King of Thomond. Apart altogether from the consequent fall of Carrickfergus, a most strategic port on the north side of Belfast Lough, in Antrim, all this added a hopeful flavour to the venture, the hope of divided loyalties amongst the English and the Anglo-Irish.

Bruce was leaving James Douglas behind, with Walter Stewart, to see to the protection of Scotland, while William Lamberton, Bernard de Linton and the other clerics looked to its administration. Jamie would dearly have liked to accompany them — and Bruce to have had him. But there was no one on whom he could rely so completely in matters military — save Thomas Randolph, who had already returned to Ireland with Edward. Moreover the Douglas had become a legend in the North of England, by his brilliant and unending raiding, so that fathers used his name as a warning for unruly children, and mothers hushed their offspring to sleep with assurances that the Black Douglas would not get them. The young idealist of a dozen years before had become worth an army in himself.

Douglas, then, and the Steward, with the Queen and her ladies, were there at Loch Ryan to see the expedition sail. Elizabeth herself would have accompanied them had it been possible; not only had she a taste for camp-following, but Ulster, after all, was her home, and she had brothers and sisters there. Bruce's intended programme was not one into which a woman with a new-born babe would fit, however tough; and with her father a leader of the enemy, complications would be likely.

Actual sailing was held up, in the end, by the non-arrival of Sir Neil Campbell and his contingent from Argyll. These had by no means the furthest to come, and there was some wonder at this, for Campbell, although in poor health, was not the man to be behindhand in any adventure. When, at length, with the King ordering no further delay and the Campbells to follow on their own later, the famed black and gold gyronny-of-eight banner did appear on the scene, it was at the mast-head of a single galley, not a squadron, coming from the north. And the man who stepped ashore at Stranraer and came hastening to Bruce was not Sir Neil but his son by a mother long since dead, Colin Campbell, a young man in his early twenties, darkly handsome.

"My sorrow, Sire, that I come late," he cried. "But I needs must bury my father!"

"Bury ...? By the Rude — do you mean ...? Mean that Neil Campbell ... is dead?"

"Dead, yes. He died the day after Your Grace's summons arrived at Innischonnel. The Lady Mary, your sister, found him. In the water. At the edge of the loch."

"Drowned! Neil Campbell drowned? I'll not believe it! I have seen him swim a hundred lochs and rivers ..."

"Not drowned, Sire. He had fallen there. Dead where he fell. Alone. He was a sick man. Had been failing ..."

"Dear God — Neil! Neil, my friend." Bruce was shaken, and showed it. Not all had loved the Campbell chief, an abrupt, secretive man of few graces, tending to be quarrelsome — who yet had captured Mary Bruce's heart thus late in their lives. But he was a mighty warrior, loyal to a fault, and the King loved him well. One of the original little band of heroes who had shared their lord's trials and perils when he was a hunted fugitive, who indeed had saved them all time and again by his hillman's skill in the desperate Highland days after Strathfillan, he had become the first to die. A thousand dangers, battles, ambushes, treacheries, he had survived — to die thus on the edge of his own Highland loch, a done man. The shock to Bruce, his friend, was partly for himself; for they were of a like age, both in their forty-third year, and the cold hand of the Reaper, in clutching one, momentarily brushed the other's heart also. In that instant the King felt old.

But he pulled himself together, as he must ever do, and put on the stern calm face of the monarch. "I am sorry, my friend," he said. "Beyond telling. Sorry for you and for my sister. Especially for her, who has suffered too much already. Some, it seems, are fated to suffer more than their share in this life. In the next, it may be, they will have their recompense. As for you, you are your father's son. And he ever lived with death, as any knight of mine must. Duly ready to entertain him. Neil Campbell was a noble knight, and many times held my life in his strong hands. Not for you to grieve him. Only to emulate."

"That is my humble prayer, Highness. That I may serve you as he did. To that end I would come with you on this sally to Ireland. In whatever lowly office."

"And so you shall. But in no lowly office, sir. You are a Highland chieftain now, head of a great clan. And an earl's son, in all but the name. I had intended to belt your father Earl of Atholl, in room of my kinsman, David de Strathbogie, traitor. The good Neil is gone to higher honour than I might give him. But to provide for his wife and my sister, I shall appoint her Countess thereof, and endow her with the lands of the earldom. As for you, friend — kneel you!"

And drawing his sword, Bruce there and then knighted the surprised young man, tapping him on both shoulders with the flat of the great blade which had shed so much blood for Scotland. "Arise, Sir Colin. Be thou a good and true knight until thy life's end!"

There was murmured acclaim, and appreciation of a right royal gesture. But some undoubtedly perceived that it was also a shrewd move indeed, binding one more great earldom closer to the crown, as the King had done with Moray and Ross, and territorially isolating the hostile earldoms of Angus and Fife by putting Atholl in the care of the Campbells — but only in the care. The Lady Mary was known to be pregnant, and the earldom was for her, not for her stepson. Elizabeth at least recognised a king's mind at work over a man's heart.

They sailed later, on a calm grey day of leaden seas and chill airs. The galleys took most of the men, leaving the great fleet of assorted slower craft to transport the horses, stores, armour and fodder. It was not a long voyage, with the coasts of Scotland and Ireland only some twenty-five miles apart at this point; but with Carrickfergus to reach, half-way up Belfast Lough, it would be more like a forty-mile sail from Loch Ryan. The Lord of the Isles had scouting galleys out, for there was always the possibility of attack by English ships, but so far there had been no alarms.

In one of Angus Og's sixty-oar greyhounds, Bruce could have dashed across the North Channel of the Irish Sea in three or four hours. But he stayed with his heterogeneous armada, which was soon scattered far and wide over the waters, with impatient scornful galleys circling and herding slow craft, like sheep-dogs, in their efforts to maintain some semblance of order, unity and a protective screen. Fortunately no enemy ships put in an appearance; but it was an uncomfortable interlude for the Scots leadership. And it was cold for everybody but the galley oarsmen.

Edward Bruce, who had an eye for appearances, had sent a squadron to meet them at the mouth of the Lough, under Donal O'Neil, King of Tyrone, no fewer than four of the vessels being packed with musicians and singers; so that the foremost Scots ships went heading up-lough thereafter to the sound of spirited Irish melodies — to the disgust of Angus Og, who considered this an insult and a travesty. Carrickfergus drew near, its lofty, high-set, English-built castle dominating the narrow streets of a walled sea-port town.

But when Bruce landed, with the streets and alleys decked with bunting and evergreens, he discovered that little or no arrangements had been made for reception and dispositions of the Scots forces. A resounding committee of welcome was very flattering to himself, but no other provision seemed to have been made for the disembarkation and housing of 7,000 men and almost twice that number of horses. The town was already full to bursting point with the wild followers of Irish kinglets, chiefs and clerics, and the harbour and even the approaches thereto crammed with shipping. Bruce's veterans swore feelingly. Fortunately, as the King was refusing to proceed with the welcoming magnates up to the citadel for the official ceremonies, without first being assured of the proper reception of his army, a harassed Moray made an appearance, with the suggestion that the main mass of the Scots should not disembark here at all, but sail up the lough a further four miles or so, to a level area of meadow and greensward, at White Abbey, where there was space, water and wood for fuel.

Unceremoniously Bruce returned to his ship, leaving his high-sounding escort standing at a loss, and sailed on, to see to the due installation of his troops in the spreading demesne of White Abbey — much to the outrage of its Anglo-Irish abbot.

As a consequence, it was well after dark before the King came back to Carrickfergus, with his lieutenants, through the crazy confusion of shipping that packed the lough, to meet a much reduced and very agitated committee of magnificos, now including de Soulis the Butler. By them he was hastily conveyed, in torchlight procession, through the network of lanes and alleys where pigs, poultry and children got in the way, towards the great castle on its rocky terrace, which Edward was making his capital.

If that proud man was put out by the prolonged delay and implied rejection of his welcome, he did not permit it to divert him.

Everywhere around the castle torches turned night into day, bonfires blazed and coloured lights flared. Every tower and turret was stance for a beacon. Probably his display gained in impressiveness thereby, even if choking smoke was the inevitable concomitant. Music resounded, by no means all of it harmonising.

The wide forecourt of the castle had been turned into a great amphitheatre, lined by thousands, while in the centre, jugglers, tumblers, bear-leaders and other entertainers performed by the light of the flames, all to the strains of pipers and minstrels and drummers. Through this the visitors were conducted in procession, O'Neil pointing out this and that. Across the drawbridge into the outer bailey, beyond the lofty curving curtain-walls, the scene was different. Here dancers in strange barbaric-seeming costumes paced and glided and circled to less lively melodies, while rank upon rank of personages stood, bowing low as the King's party passed. A great many of these appeared to be clergy, for Carrickfergus was a great ecclesiastical centre. Beyond the gatehouse, the inner bailey, narrower, was full to overflowing with chieftains, seannachies, knights and captains, drawn up in groups according to their rank and status. Then up the keep steps, past the yawning guardroom vaults and dungeons, and up into the Great Hall, a dazzlement of light and colour, where scores of young women all in white gyrated and dipped and postured to the gentle strumming of harps, with great beauty and dignity.

'The daughters of kings,' O'Neil observed confidentially. 'A hundred virgins."

Bruce doubted it, somehow. A lot of highly interested, roguish, not to say downright bold glances were emanating from the ladies; and his brother was not the man to neglect his opportunities in that direction. But he nodded gravely.

At the far end of the huge hall was the dais platform, here occupying almost a quarter of the total space. It was more crowded than the main floor. Massed to the right were standing rows of mitred bishops and abbots, with unmitred priors, deans, archdeacons and other prelates, all in most gorgeous robes. On the left were lords and officers of state of every degree and highly colourful variety of costume, from wolf-skins and embossed leather to silks, damasks and brocades. And in the centre, forming a horseshoe, were ten thrones, two of them empty. The arrangement of these chairs was almost symmetrical—but not quite. All were gilded and handsome, with crowns surmounting their high backs, four curving on one side and four on the other of two at the head of the horseshoe. These two, although placed side by side, were not quite a pair; one was of the same size and type as the other flanking eight, while its neighbour was not only larger, taller and more splendid, but was raised on a little platform of its own. On it Edward Bruce lounged, magnificently clad in cloth-of-gold and blue velvet, with a great cloak of royal purple fringed with fur and sparkling with jewels, flung negligently over one shoulder. The chair beside him was empty.

As the new arrivals came up, trumpeters set the rafters ringing with an elaborate fanfare which drowned and stopped all the competing music, and the dancers with it. In the silence that followed, O'Neil of Tyrone turned and bowed, wordless to Bruce, more deeply to Edward, and then stalked over to one of the empty thrones, on the right, and sat down.

Another trumpet-blast, and a resplendent herald stepped forward, to intone:

"The mighty O'Rourke, King of Meath, offers greeting to Robert, King of Scots."

A thick-set, grizzled man rose from one of the chairs and held a hand high, unspeaking.

Bruce inclined his head.

Another trumpet. "The illustrious MacMurrough, King of Leinster, offers greeting to Robert, King of Scots."

A giant of a man, but strangely bent to one side from some ancient wound, went through the same procedure.

"The high-born O'Brien, King of Munster, offers greeting to Robert, King of Scots."

A white-haired and bearded ancient, fine featured, serene, but frail, stood with difficulty and raised a quivering arm. Bruce knew him by repute as a sacker of monasteries and ruthless slayer of women and children, but bowed nevertheless.

The next, a kinsman, O'Brien, King of Thomond, was little more than a child, a pimply, fair-haired youth who scowled—perhaps with reason, for his father was alleged to have been boiled to death in a cauldron by the previous saintly-looking welcomer barely a year before.

"The puissant O'Carroll, King of Uriel." A slender dark elegant, who would have been supremely handsome but for a cast in one eye, made flourish of his salute, while Bruce decided that he would not trust him one yard.

The sixth to rise was the valiant MacCarthy, King of Desmond, a man almost as broad as he was high, with long arms which hung to his knees, said to have the strength of an ox. He, certainly, would be an excellent man to have at one's side.

The amiable, red-headed O'Neil, King of Tyrone, was next, and hurried through his performance with some embarrassment, barely rising from his seat.

Last rose O'Connor, King of Connaught, first among equals, who should have been High King—had the others been prepared to accept him. A studious, delicate-seeming man, he looked more of a scholar than a warrior. He alone did not raise his hand, but bowed towards Bruce, stiffly formal.

Then the trumpets sounded once more, louder and longer, and the herald took a deep breath.

"The serene, right royal and victorious Lord Edward, king of kings, by God's grace *Ard Righ*, High King of All Ireland, greets the Lord Robert, King of Scots, and welcomes him to this his realm and kingdom."

Edward broke the pattern. He did not stand up, or raise his hand, or even bow. "Come, brother," he said, conversationally. "You are late. I looked for you hours ago. Have you not some captain, some horse or baggage master, capable of settling your people into quarters?"

Bruce eyed this good-looking, awkward brother of his, biting back the hot words — as seemed to be ever necessary. "I came here to play the captain rather than the monarch, Edward," he said evenly. "I shall continue to do so."

"M'mm." The other considered that. He shrugged. "Come, anyway, Robert. It is good to see you, however ... delayed. All Ireland welcomes you. Come — sit here."

Bruce nodded, and moved unhurriedly up between the seated kings. He stood, looking down at his brother for a few moments before he sat down in the lesser throne. "You are content, now?" he said, smiling a little.

"Content?" Edward frowned. "How mean you — content?"

"Why — High King! So very high!"

"It is the style. The Celtic style."

"Aye. I seem to have been climbing, ever since I set foot on Irish soil! And now my neck suffers stretching!" The elder brother exaggerated the necessary upward-looking posture somewhat, from his lower chair.

The other ignored that. He clapped his hands. "The music. The dancing. Resume," he called. "You like my dancers, Robert?"

"They are very fair. And doubtless they do more than dance? But I might have esteemed them better as cooks! Or even scullions, brother! We have travelled far, and our bellies in more need of distraction than our eyes and ears!"

"You will be feasting in plenty, anon, never fear. Be patient. As I had to be, awaiting you! Much of my provision was spoiled. By the delay. My cooks are working to repair that delay. We would have eaten well, two hours ago, brother. Roasted peacocks. Breast of swan. Sucking boar seethed in malvoisie. Spiced salmon. Peppered lobster. Woodcock . . ."

"*We* would have eaten well, to be sure. But the men I brought — what of them? I found no provision made for them, cold, tired, hungry. This is the first day of December, Edward — winter is on us. Even in Ireland! To have them lie under the open sky . . . !"

"It is an army you have brought, is it not? Not a parcel of clerks or women! I' faith — in the past, our armies found their own meat and shelter well enough! Did they not?"

Curiously Bruce considered his brother. "*You* say that? You would have me turn my people loose on your land? To do their will? An army foraging! Is that the King of Ireland speaking?"

"From the man who burned half of Scotland, and more than once, you are becoming exceeding nice, I think!" the other gave back.

Robert drew a long breath. "Remember that, Edward, when your Abbot of White Abbey comes making complaint that I have misused his property!" he said grimly. "Now — what of the enemy? The English? Do they press heavily? How far south are your outposts? And where is my god-father, Ulster . . . ?"

Edward was not, in fact, eager to discuss the strategic position; but thereafter, and especially when presently they moved into the banqueting-hall, next to the kitchens across the courtyard, where he found the soldierly MacCarthy, King of Desmond, sitting at his right hand, Bruce did learn sufficient to give him a fair overall picture. Hostilities were at the moment more or less suspended, without there being any accepted truce, while both sides regrouped and drew on their strength — or so Edward described it. He had had to give up Dundalk — where the coronation had taken place — and their farthest south outposts were at Downpatrick and the line of the Quoile River, not thirty miles south of Belfast Lough. North of that was in their hands, although there were one or two Anglo-Irish lords holding out. The entire west side of the country was an unknown quantity, although some of the chiefs there believed to be in revolt. In fact, only Ulster was secure — and not all of that, it seemed. Edward might be King of All Ireland, but three-quarters of the country had yet to be convinced of it.

Not even all the Irish princes were on Edward's side. O'Hanlon,

MacMahon, Maguire and MacGoffey were known to be co-operating with the English meantime, as well as many lesser chieftains. Some would change sides at the first sign of success, no doubt; but the reverse might well apply with others presently accepted as loyal.

However, all the news was not of this calibre. The English leadership seemed to be having its own troubles. Nobody was very sure who was in command. Sir Edmund Butler, the Justiciar, over whom Edward and Moray had won a victory earlier, had been thereafter replaced, on orders from London, by Roger, Lord Mortimer. But at the same time, a tough and militant cleric, John de Hotham, Bishop of Ely, had been sent over as Chancellor of Ireland, and political overlord, and there was bad blood between him and Mortimer. The de Lacy brothers, important Anglo-Irish Lords of Meath, appeared to be offended at both of these appointments, and with their friends and allies were not exactly in revolt but were refusing to co-operate. Most uncertain of all was Richard de Burgh's position. As Earl of Ulster he was the greatest of the Anglo-Irish nobles — indeed the native Irish referred to the Anglo-Irish as the Race of Richard Burke — as well as the foremost commander in age as in seniority and in rank, of any in Ireland; and had more than once acted as commander-in-chief of Irish forces. But he was apparently now only to command in the north — although admittedly that was where the main fighting would be apt to be — and presumably under the authority of both the Bishop and Mortimer. The reason for this was difficult to fathom — although some suggested that it was because de Burgh had been Edward the First's great crony and comrade-in-arms, and Edward the Second, hating his late father and all his works, might not trust him, might even wish to humiliate him.

Whatever was behind it all, it seemed to Robert Bruce a situation which should be exploited, and swiftly. But it quickly became apparent that such was not his brother's opinion, nor that of most of those around him. Let the English squabble amongst themselves, was the reaction. Why interfere, when that would most probably just unite them? Let them grow weaker, while they themselves gathered their strength. Besides, here was no time for campaigning, before the Yuletide festivals were over. Ireland was a notably Christian, not to say, holy, country, the most pious in the western world. They must not offend religious feeling.

Bruce, aware of how much religious feeling his brother possessed, did not take this seriously at first. But as time wore on, he realised that it was no laughing matter. Edward was himself quite ruthless about religious susceptibilities, strong though they were; but he was using them as excuse for delay. He was not ready to move, and he found the peculiar Irish preoccupation with religious form, observance and display convenient to his purpose.

Certainly that of 1316–17 was the busiest, fullest Yuletide Bruce had ever experienced. Every day for weeks seemed to be a saint's day — the names of most of which the Scots had never so much as heard. Not that the consequent celebrations were in the main tiresomely sanctimonious, or even very recognisably sacredotal. Parades, pageantry, contests, feasting, singing and dancing, even horse-racing, were seemingly all part of the programme of worship, the clerics foremost in promoting all. The rain, which tended to fall daily, did nothing to damp down at least local pious spirits.

Bruce fretted but conformed. He could, of course, have taken matters into his own hands, and led his Scots force southwards independently. But that would have much offended the Irish, and involved lack of co-operation if not actual hostility on the part of the local populations through which they must pass, a serious matter. Irish politics being what they were, and the Church being so all-pervasive and influential, such a move would have been rash indeed.

Not that the period of waiting was wholly wasted. It gave time for Scots captains to get to know their Irish forces, as well as for more men to flood in from various parts of Ulster and the North. Time also for the integration of the army, and a certain amount of training — though this was scarcely popular. Bruce quickly realised that there was little that he could do to make a more unified force out of the Irish legions, neither themselves nor Edward being prepared to tolerate any such interference. He contented himself with picking out men for a light cavalry force — for which, since he was providing the horses and squadron commanders, they could hardly object. This he prevailed on MacCarthy of Desmond to captain, with Angus Og as liaison, who knew the Irish best from his many mercenary campaigns here. These made a dashing, swift-moving force — if only they could be relied upon to do as they were commanded. Working with the Scots, they would form the spearhead of the campaign.

In the end, it was not until the beginning of February, with rumours of de Burgh massing troops at Drogheda, that at long last a start was made from Carrickfergus — inevitably on the Day of the Blessed Brigit, Abbess of Kildare. There were, in fact, two distinct armies — Bruce's light cavalry host of Scots and selected

Irish, to the number of about 9,000; and the great composite mass of Irish gallowglasses, kerns and clansmen, stiffened with Scots veteran captains and some heavy chivalry, unnumbered but probably totalling some 40,000. One was fast, to conduct hard-hitting, swift-striking warfare of the sort Bruce had perfected; the other slow, cumbersome, to come along behind, consolidating, occupying, supplying. Edward, of course, should have commanded the second and main army — as he did in name; but he was a cavalry commander above all, and he insisted on riding with the first force. In fact, much of the time he was out in front with the advance guard, however unsuitable in a monarch. He had been reluctant to start — for he had wanted the Scots strength to stabilise his hold on his kingdom and defeat his internal enemies — but once committed, typically, he was all fire and energy.

As much to keep up with Edward as anything else, the cavalry army, after rounding the head of Belfast Lough, dashed the twenty-odd miles south to the limits of their occupied territory on the very first day. Bruce was uneasy at already leaving the main host so far behind — but was more uneasy still when he discovered that Edward's advance party, finding their welcome insufficiently enthusiastic, had burned the church at Bright, and already sacked the monastery of the walled cathedral town of Downpatrick, where they had proposed to spend the night. This in allegedly friendly country. Admittedly there had been some opposition at Greencastle, which had an Anglo-Irish de Courcy lord, and which Edward took with a flourish — but, after all the religious observance, this seemed to be an odd way to start a campaign. Edward had Irish backing, however, for his assertion that this was how wars were conducted in Ireland.

There being insufficient forage for the thousands of horses at Downpatrick, allegedly St. Patrick's burial-place, they moved two miles eastwards to the wide abbey-lands of Saul, flanking Strangford Lough, where St. Malachy had built the abbey on the site of the barn wherein St. Patrick held his first Christian service in Ireland, and where there was grass in plenty. There was no getting away from saints and sanctity in this country. Even the grass, it was alleged, would be the better for the horses, in these holy pastures — although this did not prevent Edward's men from treating the abbot and his monks less than gently. Bruce forbore criticism thus early. Assuming that Edward would remain with his main infantry army, he had underestimated the difficulties of a divided command, and this *was* his brother's country.

Next day they rode so fast and so far that there was little time for adventures on the way, and no real opposition showed itself. They were still near Ulster, of course, County Louth. Leaving unmolested the Knights Templar castle of Dundrum, they went by Castlewellan and Rathfryland, with the mountains of Mourne on their left, through Newry and Faughart until, at dusk, they came to Dundalk itself, the farthest south of Edward's penetrations hitherto, where he had been crowned. Ahead lay the English-dominated territories. They were exactly half-way to Dublin in two days.

The clash of will between the two brothers, which was bound to take place sooner or later, occurred soon after they left Dundalk, on a chill morning of wind and threatening rain. Beyond the ford of the Fane River, the road forked. Edward wanted to drive southeast, straight for Drogheda, the English seaport-base, twenty miles away, while still they held the initiative and at least partial surprise. Robert, ever against siegery and time-consuming attacks on fortresses, said no. They should make for Dublin itself, fifty miles on. That would be totally unexpected, whereas Drogheda might well already be expecting attack. Dublin was far too large to be defended in total, having long outgrown its walls. It was the capital, and ostensible seat of government. Capture of Dublin would rally the whole of Ireland.

It was not like Edward to reject anything so bold and vigorous as this. But having declared for Drogheda, his authority was at stake, and he evidently felt bound to insist.

"Drogheda first," he declared. "What good Dublin if Drogheda remains a threat at our backs?"

"Dublin is worth a dozen Droghedas, man. We will cut the line between the two. Then your Irish army of foot can move down to seal off Drogheda. That is not *our* task. Let them do it."

"No! It is fifty miles to Dublin. All the country will be roused before we get there. Surprise lost."

"Edward — you have the pig by the tail, not the snout! Do you not see? Drogheda is the English base — but Dublin is the government centre for all Ireland. None will expect us to make straight for it. At the speed we rode yesterday, we can be there before tomorrow's dusk. Think of it! Before Bishop Hotham and Mortimer can decide who commands what! Or my good-father Ulster can succour either!"

"*That* is why you will not attack Drogheda, I swear!" his brother cried. "You are afraid to meet Richard de Burgh! Or too nice! Your Elizabeth's sire. Well — I am not! We ride for Drogheda, I say."

"We do not, Edward," Bruce said, softly now. "Or if *you* do, we part company."

"You . . . you challenge my word? Mine? Here in Ireland, I'd remind you, *I* am king, not you!"

"King you may be, Edward—but I command all Scots forces. Not you. On these terms alone I brought them to Ireland. They follow *me*, in Ireland as in Scotland."

"So-o-o! This is your vaunted aid!"

"This is my aid, yes. Though I never vaunted it. Far from it. I would have preferred to stay in Scotland, where there is much to be done. But . . . I warned you. I came as a captain, and will continue to act as such."

Edward twisted in his saddle, a magnificent figure in his dazzling, gold-inlaid black armour and purple cloak, against his brother's somewhat rusty chain-mail, and stared at the group of senior commanders who rode just behind, and who could not fail to have heard this exchange—Moray, Gilbert Hay, Keith and Marischal, Fraser the Chamberlain, Angus of the Isles, de Soulis and MacCarthy of Desmond.

"Well?" he demanded. "Who, in Ireland, obeys the King of Ireland?"

De Soulis moistened his lips. "I do, Sire."

No one else spoke.

"And you, MacCarthy?"

"I must obey my liege lord," the King of Desmond said, all but growled. "Since I am vowed to it. But I agree with the Lord Robert. Go for Dublin, I say."

With a glare at the level-eyed, silent Scots, Edward faced the front again, and dug in his spurs savagely, to race ahead.

Bruce and the others made no attempt to catch up with him too soon. At least he took the road that forked towards Dublin, south-west.

Whatever else, Bruce had thereafter no cause for complaint about the speed at which they made for the capital. A horsed host of thousands travels at the pace of its slowest riders, not its fastest and there was no keeping up with Edward. But even so the main body had reached Slane, on the Boyne, half-way to Dublin, with dark falling, when Bruce called a halt. He had half expected the river-crossing to be held against them. Here was good grass, and meadow-land for camping, and nearby to the south was the fabled Hill of Tara, site of the ancient capital of Ireland and seat of the pagan kings. That day they had engaged in no fighting, assaulted no castles, by-passed all major towns. They were only twenty-five miles from Dublin, and on the edge of the Pale, level with Drogheda nine miles to the east. To have gone farther that night would have been folly. But of Edward there was no sign. Young O'Donnell, son of the King of Tyrconnel, was leading the advance party, with Sir Colin Campbell. Presumably his liege lord had taken over.

Bruce sent a fast rider after him, to inform that he had halted at Slane, in a good defensive position, holding the river's ford. A couple of hours later the courier was back, alone. He announced that His Grace of Ireland was at the small monastery of Skreen, on the side of the Hill of Tara, eight miles on, and entirely comfortable. He would stay where he was.

This would not do. Bruce recognised only too well the dangers of this sort of situation — especially with Richard de Burgh not so far away. Gulping down the last of his meal, dark as it was and raining thinly, he wrapped himself in his cloak, called Gilbert Hay to accompany him, left the army in the care of Moray and told the courier to turn again and lead him to Tara.

It was an unpleasant ride, over benighted, uneven country, with the streams funning full. Of Tara's renowned hill they saw only the dark loom as they circled its broken skirts, to come at length to the modest ecclesiastical establishment of Skreen, alleged to have risen on the site of the hermitage of St. Erck, in one of its southern folds. Here, the advance guard of 150 men lay at ease — and no sentry saw fit to challenge Bruce's little party. In the Prior's room — with no sign of the Prior — Edward lounged before a glowing peat fire, with the young Prince of Tyrconnel.

"So you have seen fit to honour us with your royal presence!" he greeted his brother. "Have you eaten? We do very well here."

"No doubt. But I did not come here to eat, Edward. I looked for you, and this forward squadron, at Slane. Not eight miles beyond!"

"Then you should have used your wits, Robert. Where else would the King of Ireland rest, in this corner of his dominions than on Tara's Hill?"

"It matters not where the King of Ireland rests the night! Nor the King of Scots, either," Bruce answered harshly. "What matters is where their army rests. And this small monastery on an open hillside, however notable, is not it."

"The army, you assure me, is your concern! So be it. Rest it where you will. For myself, I am very well here."

Robert bit his lip. He looked from O'Donnel to Hay, and then to the door. "Leave us, if you please," he told them. And when he and Edward were alone, moved to stand at the side of the fire, the steam rising from his cloak.

"Edward," he said heavily, "you know as well as do I that for a small advance column to camp in open enemy country, unscouted country, eight miles ahead of its main force, is folly. And when that small party contains the king of the land, proclaiming his presence and caring nothing for his safety — then that is worse than folly. You could be captured, easily — and where is your kingdom then? Held to a ransom that could spell the end of your ambitions. If the English did not first hang you as rebel!"

"Save us — more fraternal preachings! Spare me that, of a mercy!"

The other shook his head. "No — I did not come to preach, to berate you. To quarrel, Edward. The reverse, indeed. If you and I quarrel on this campaign, it will come to disaster. Nothing surer."

"For once we are in agreement, brother!" Edward conceded, jerking a laugh.

"Yes. Then we must come to terms in this foolish warfare."

"I am glad to hear it. But — whose terms? The King of Ireland's? Or the commander of his host's?"

His brother took a pace or two across the room. 'See you, Edward — it is not my purpose to belittle your position. To undercut your authority. As king. You believe that I cannot abide your being my equal, a monarch such as myself. That is not so. I am not such a fool. Your Irish kingship I respect. And am sustaining. And will continue to do. But I was against this whole Irish adventure. I was forced into it against my judgement. Yet it is in the main by *my* power and strength that it is being pursued. You know very well that as a united force to conquer Ireland, all your kinglets and princelings amount to so much wind — swelling names, resplendent titles, brave men enough, but hating each other and with no least notion of discipline. What is happening far behind us even now, in that great rabble of foot, God knows! I would have thought that would have been *your* task, to command and seek to unify."

"I believe you said that you did not come to berate and belittle!"

"Aye. My concern is that my Scots host is used to the best advantage. And for Scotland. To that end I retain full command. But that also serves your interests, Edward."

"On my territory *I* should command. It is intolerable that in his own realm a monarch should see his authority set aside by another whom he brought in to aid him. And that his own brother."

"Two men may not command a host. Nor a kingdom. Once before, I gave you that answer, you will mind! When I was sick, years back, and you proposed that you should share the Crown of Scotland with me! Both kings. I did not love you for that, I do admit! But it would not have served then. And it will not serve now. Committed to this campaign, *I* command."

"And I? What am I? A lackey, for you to order as you will? Great God — I have had enough of that in Scotland!"

"Not so. I have come here tonight with proposals. Either go back to your own great Irish host, and command that as you will — if it will obey you! Or stay with me and the Scots, as my equal in kingship but accepting my command as captain. Agree to be second in the command of the cavalry host."

"Second? When you have our precious nephew Moray, to your hand! And that barbarian Angus Og! And Hay, Keith, and the rest! Do you think that I am witless enough to believe that you may prefer me to any of these? You never have done!"

His brother opened his mouth for a hot reply, then closed it again. He looked instead into the red glow of the fire. "You do not remark on my first proposal? That you go back to your Irish host. So . . . hear what I propose here," he said levelly. "Now that we are like to meet with the enemy at any moment, with de Burgh only an hour or two's ride away, our present headlong riding will no longer serve. We must advance with a deal greater care — though still fast, if we are to surprise Dublin. And in different formation. No longer a small scouting force ahead, and then all the main host. Still we need scouts in front, flanking vedettes, and a rearward. But the main host should now be split into two. Say 3,000 and 6,000. Each to remain near the other for support, but some way apart, for safety, for easier handling in close country, for better observation of enemy forces. You understand? I offer you command for the first host. Of the 3,000."

The other stared. "You mean it? Command? Full command?"

"Full command, under my direction. I retain overall command. But within that, this host will be yours. Mainly MacCarthy's Irish horse, but with a stiffening of Scots. How say you?"

"Why? Why do you do this, Robert? Is it a trick . . .?"

"No trick. I offer it because we must come to terms, Edward. If this campaign is not to fail. It may be that I keep too much in my own hands, that I assign too little authority to others. I think not — but it may be so. I am willing to try this. For harmony and the sake of our cause."

Edward was on his feet now. "Under your direction I am in full command of this first cavalry force? Is that it? I will not have Moray, or the Islesman, or other of your friends, sitting on my heels? Frowning and reproving . . .?"

"No. Any Scots veterans that I give you will be lesser men. You will have full command. Only — I expect my directions to be obeyed, Edward. Or else we think again. Or we turn back, here and now — for me, all the way back to Scotland!"

His brother searched his face for a long moment, and then grinned. "Very well, Robert — we shall try it. Try again. On these terms. Here is my hand on it!"

They shook hands there before the Prior's peat fire. It was a long time since these two had made any such gesture.

"Now — to planning," Bruce said briskly, "MacCarthy says that there is much broken, forested country ahead. Mid-Meath. Between Trim and Dunshaughlin. My good-father has a manor and castle at Ratoath, in this part. And Trim is the de Lacys' most powerful castle. We do not know how they will jump . . ."

Chapter Twelve

It was just after noon next day that the first fruits of the royal brothers' rapprochement became apparent. Bruce, at the head of the main Scots force, now little more than 5,000 men, with detachments well out on the flanks and to the rear, was riding at a fast trot through scattered and broken woodland country south of Dunshaughlin, when young Sir Colin Campbell came galloping back from the forward host.

"His Grace of Ireland, Sire, sends me to inform you that he has captured a kern who declares that the Earl of Ulster is here. Here, not at Drogheda. At his own house ahead. This Ratoath, he names it . . ."

"De Burgh, here? In front? With how many men, Sir Colin? An army?"

"No, Your Grace. Not many, the man said."

"That sounds strange. He can scarce be ignorant that we are near. My brother — what does he do?"

"He rides for Ratoath, with all speed. To capture the Earl."

"He does? Aye, he would!" Bruce frowned. "I do not think that I like the smell of this! How far ahead is he?"

"Four miles. With another three to go to Ratoath, the kern said."

"And the country? What is it like? It is still wooded, close? As here?"

"Thicker, Sire. More hills. Rocks."

"M'mmm. This kern that you captured? How was he? Did you see him taken?"

"Yes. He was sitting at the roadside, watching us pass . . ."

"Watching! How many of the people here do that? They flee at the sound, much less the sight, of us! Was he armed?"

"No, Sire. Save with a cudgel. He seemed a simple countryman . . ."

Bruce turned to his close lieutenants. "How say you?" he demanded.

"It could be honest. Or it could be false. A trap," Angus Og said.

"I mislike the sound of it," Moray asserted.

"The Lord Edward has 3,000 men now," Gilbert Hay reminded. "It would require to be a large trap!"

"What do you fear, my lord King?" Campbell asked. "What is wrong?"

"Two matters smell wrong. One large, one small. Your Queen's father is no ordinary man, no mere Anglo-Irish baron. He is a warrior, and wily, a veteran trained by that great schemer, the late Edward Longshanks. He cannot but know of our advance. Last night we were only ten miles from Drogheda. If he is indeed in front of us now, is he the man to have left Drogheda with only a few men? For this Ratoath, directly in our path?"

"How do we know when he left Drogheda, Sire? He may have been at Ratoath for days," Hay pointed out. "We have had no sure news."

"Our flank vedettes to the east have sent us no warnings of any movement of men, from Drogheda or anywhere else," Sir Alexander Fraser put in.

"The Earl of Ulster is thought to be at odds with this Bishop and Mortimer," Angus added. "He acted strangely over the relief fleet for Carrickfergus. If they have superseded him as commander in Ireland, it may be that he does not seek to fight you now, but to talk. Parley with his good-son?"

Bruce drummed fingers on his saddle-bow. "It is possible. But . . . this other matter does not smell well, either. This of a knowledgeable kern, who waits to watch my brother's host go by. That metal does not ring true. Had de Burgh wished to parley with me, would he have done it thus? Sent a common kern to let slip that he was in the neighbourhood? However secret, he would have sent me a messenger of quality."

"The kern could still be just a kern, Your Grace. A villager of this Ratoath, who knows the Earl . . ."

"Could be — but may not be! I shall ride the easier when I am assured of it. Meantime, we shall hasten. Four miles is too great a gap, in this close country."

The King's face grew longer, his frown darker, as they drove on, at a canter now, into ever thicker and rougher country, with rocky bluffs, densely wooded and with flooded scrub-covered bottom land. This was the sort of territory in which a cavalry host was least effective, even light cavalry. If an attack was indeed to be made on them, this was the place for it. Yet, no word had come back from Edward that his force was meeting with any difficulties. And Bruce's own flanking scouts sent no warning of anything unusual.

When Colin Campbell at length announced that it was here that the kern had been taken, here that he himself had turned back with his message, his liege lord all but snapped his head off. They were passing through a small open glade with evil swamp on the left and a steeply rising bank on the right.

"Did MacCarthy, did any of the Irish, say what sort of a castle this of Ratoath is?" he interrupted. "I think it cannot be a great place, in this wretched country. I had never heard its name, never heard my wife speak of it."

"The Prince of Tyrconnel named it a small place, Sire. Scarce a castle at all, I think, as we Scots would say. A moated manor, rather . . ."

"Aye. I like this less and less . . ." Bruce chewed on his thoughts for a while. The swamp on the left was drying up somewhat, with more trees; but the bank on the right was growing ever steeper, taller, almost a cliff. Apart from famous death-traps like the Pass of Brander in Lorne, and Glen Trool in Galloway, he had seldom seen territory which he liked less, from a military point of view. He had reduced the pace to a slow trot now. Yet Edward's force had gone through here, only a short time before. There was no least sign of trouble, only recent horse-droppings.

He took a sudden decision. "Campbell," he ordered, "ride you forward, after my brother. Take a small party — a score. My salutations to His Grace — but request him to turn back. Forthwith. Whatever he is doing, besieging this Ratoath, or other. His host to return. To close up, until we are safely through this evil country. It may be little necessary — but we could meet disaster here. We should not be more than half a mile apart. Where each could cover the other. You have it? With my salutations, mind—but it is a firm command." And as the other, nodding, turned to collect his twenty or so men from the first files behind, the King added, "Do not be distracted, left or right, see you. You are not scouts. Ride fast. Press on to my brother. If you get hint of trouble, avoid it. I shall have others out, to scout, behind you."

"Do you but make siccar, Sire?" Fraser asked, as the little party clattered ahead. "Or have you more reason than we here perceive?"

"I smell danger, Sandy," the King answered that implied criticism. "It stinks in my nostrils. Do not ask me for better reason!"

The words were hardly out of his mouth when a scream from ahead, around a bend in the woodland track, was immediately followed by shouting, confused, urgent.

He dug in his spurs. They all did.

Hurtling round the bend, Bruce saw a scene as confused as the noise. One man lay spread-eagled on the road, an arrow transfixing his chest. Two horses were down, hooves lashing. Others were milling about, one with a long shaft clearly projecting from its haunch. Colin Campbell was seeking to marshal his men and lead them off to the left, off the track, down into the boggy woodland.

"Follow me!" he was shouting, "Follow me!"

Cursing furiously, Bruce drove his horse straight for the young knight, shaking a suddenly upraised fist.

Campbell saw him, and mistook the gesture. "I will get them!" he yelled and spurred on.

After him the King plunged, pushing aside two men-at-arms in the way. Coming up with the eager Highlander, he reached over and struck him a resounding buffet with his steel-gauntleted fist, that sent the other reeling in his saddle.

"Fool!" he cried. "Back! Back, I say! If your life means nothing to you, think of these others. *My* subjects! Back, man!"

Shaken, Campbell pulled up, staring as though his monarch had run mad.

"What were my last words? The last I spoke you?"

Appalled, the young man reined round, waving his men back now. "I . . . I am sorry, Sire. I did not think. Or . . . I thought otherwise. To save Your Grace. The next arrow might have struck *you* . . . !"

"When *last* I struck you a blow, man I said that you should be a true knight until your life's end!" Bruce panted turning back for the track. The heat was going out of his voice, however. "You were near your life's end there I swear! But a true knight obeys his liege lord's commands. Remember it I said turn aside for nothing."

Back at the halted column, Fraser called out. "You have a good nose, Sire! Even for so small a trouble."

"Small, Sandy? What mean you by small?"

"I count but eight arrows. There may be more in the bushes, missed their mark. But no large force would shoot so few."

"But they are English clothyard shafts, see you — not our short Irish or Scots bolts"

"Even so, Sire, but few. And now they have seen how large a force we are, they forbear."

Moray had men dismounted, awaiting his order to slip off into the trees. He looked at his uncle.

"Leave them, Thomas. They will not shoot against us again I think. Not here. Sandy is right — these must be a small party. But English, mark you. They made a mistake, opening up on Campbell's troop, not knowing that we followed so close. They will have fled now, deep into these fastnesses. Let them go. But — this is not all the danger that I smelt, by the Rude!"

"You think there are more, Sire?" Hay asked. "Yet they have let the Lord Edward's force go past, it seems . . ."

"To be sure there are more. And if my good-father is behind them, many more. A small band of archers would never have risked shooting at Campbell's score if they had not greater numbers near. Besides, what are a dozen English archers doing in such a place? That is not how these fight. They are part of a scouting patrol, I say, sent to watch. Their leader misjudged, that is all. But, if they were sent to watch this road, from these woods, then whoever sent them is expecting us! Yet he has let my brother past. You see the pattern? Remember we are likely dealing with Richard de Burgh, fox as much as lion! I would say that he is waiting for *me*. In ambush."

There was silence, as the leaders of the long column eyed the King.

"And the Lord Edward?" somebody asked.

"The Lord Edward no doubt goes on with a blithe heart! He is likely already besetting an empty Ratoath Castle, waiting for him as bait!"

"You conceive the Earl of Ulster as between us and Ratoath, between us and my uncle?" Moray asked.

"I would judge it likely."

"And we cannot get word to him?"

"We can try. Not along this road. By sending men on foot, back and up by the high ground, to the right. That way they may win through, unseen. Your Islesmen would be best, Angus. But it cannot be other than slow."

"And us? While they do it, dare we go on?" Fraser demanded. "Yet we cannot wait here. As ill a place to defend as any I have seen. And if we retire, will not de Burgh turn on the Lord Edward's force instead? From behind. Where he will think to be safe, with us at his back."

"We will not retire, no. Edward apart, I did not bring these thousands to Ireland to retire in the face of the first threat. But — I prefer that *I* choose the battle-ground, not my good-sire!"

"How can you do that? Placed as we are?" Angus Og said. "We dare not retire. There is no good ground to fight on for miles back, as we have seen. Since we cannot stay here, we can only go on, de Burgh or none!"

"Aye, my lord — you are right. But we go on warned. Warned, and dismounted. If there is to be fighting, in such country, I would do it afoot."

"Aye! Aye!"

"Is that best, Sire?" Hay wondered. "To throw away our speed. Should we not remain mounted, and charge our way through. Many as we are. Using our speed and weight . . ."

"No, my lord Constable — for that is what de Burgh would expect us to do. If that earl is indeed before us, he will have planned for that, the wrecking of a mounted host. So we go afoot. Horses, in these bogs, are useless. All horses, therefore, to be sent to the rear. Lest arrows get them. We need them hereafter, if we are to conquer Ireland! But not here and now. If Richard de Burgh is here. *If*, I say . . ." The King shrugged.

Metaphorically they all shrugged. It was all supposition, after all. Save for those clothyard shafts and the one dead man. There was nothing hypothetical about them.

With a certain amount of difficulty, and even some grumbling, along the line, the cavalry host there and then converted itself into an infantry host, passing the horses back. Bruce had the men close up into a much tighter and broader formation, as broad a front as the terrain would allow. Also, he insisted that all shields be carried, and on the left arms, not left with the horses — never a popular move with cavalrymen.

And so they moved on southwards, slowly now. And silently, with the command passed down for the maximum of quiet.

It made a strange progress through the early February afternoon, thousands of armed men all but tiptoeing, unspeaking, watchful, aware. Bruce had their relatively few archers up near the front. Never for a moment did any of them cease to scan the woodland ahead and to the left.

The King gave his instructions as they walked. "Thomas — our first warning may well be a hail of arrows. They will seek to pick off our leaders first. But if they have any wits, they will let us get well into their trap. Go you part way down the column. If we are attacked from the woodland, have all behind you, save for the horse guard, swing off the track. Down into the wood. A wide sweep, to take the archers in flank. And swiftly. Or we may not survive! You have it?"

"Aye, Sire. But you?"

"We will play the poltroons! We will throw ourselves down. As poor marks for arrows as may be. Covered by our shields. To give you and your men time to get in amongst them. Then we shall up and charge to your aid." He glanced upwards, half-right. "Pray for us that there are no rocks loose, up there!"

The bank above them was steep but mainly of earth and rough grass, with scrub clinging. Higher, perhaps 200 feet above, the slope eased back out of sight, and the lessened gradient permitted taller trees to grow.

"At least it is no place for archers," Moray commented. "They could not shoot down at that angle, without exposing themselves. And it is too steep for men to charge down."

"Aye — as for men to charge up! So long as it remains so. It pens us in, cramps us — but it does not threaten us greatly. Off with you, then, Thomas — and God go with you. If a bend of the track comes between us, three short blasts from my trumpeter means that we are attacked. One long blast, and you hasten directly forward to me. Gibbie — pass the word back. All men to fall flat if the arrows come, and so lie."

They had gone perhaps another half-mile when Colin Campbell spoke suddenly, low-voiced. 'I saw something, Sire. Movement. In the trees . . ."

"Where, man? Where?"

"Yonder. Near that white tree. The dead tree. Right of it." He pointed to an area about 250 yards away.

"Do not point, man. That could bring the arrows. Do you see aught . . .?"

No movement showed.

"It could be a deer. A boar. I have seen droppings," Angus Og said.

"Shall I go search?" Campbell demanded.

"No. That will serve nothing. Send a man back to Moray. Tell him of this. The place. For the rest, move on."

Now the sensation of tiptoeing, of walking on hot stones, was intensified. It would have been a clod-like dolt indeed who could have stalked on unconcerned. Stout warriors found themselves stooping a little, hunching their shoulders, seeking to shrink their persons behind shields and armour.

No attack developed.

Then, round a substantial bend in the road, there was a major change in the scenery. Temporarily the scattered woodland rolled back, to reveal a wide clearing, perhaps a quarter-mile across. Ahead was more forest, but the high bank on the right began gradually to break down and level off.

Bruce drew a long breath. "If I planned an assault, this is where I would choose," he said. "Before this bank ceases to wall us in. With a killing ground, open for archers. Yet cover all round for my forces. It . . ."

"Sire — see! A flash. A flash of light," the keen-eyed Campbell cried. "Ahead. Half-left . . ."

"I saw it," Hay confirmed. "'Sun on steel, for a wager!"

"Look — another! Farther over . . ."

"So be it." Bruce was all decision now, raising his battle-axe in his right hand and slamming it downwards twice. "Down!" he commanded. "Down!" And all along the line the cry was taken up, as men fell flat on their faces, shields jerking up to cover them. It was though a giant sickle mowed them down.

"Trumpeter — three blasts!" the King panted, as he himself went low.

Somewhat off-note and gaspingly, the trumpet neighed its warning from the mud of the track.

Results were immediate and quite fantastic. As though echoes had gone crazy, other trumpets and horns began to shout and yelp and ululate all around at some distance, in a shrill cacophony. There were urgent cries. And, within seconds, the first arrows began to hiss and twang and fall, raggedly admittedly, but in ever increasing numbers and accuracy.

It is safe to say that never before had Bruce's veterans had a like experience. To lie flat on the ground and allow oneself to be shot at, without any answering gesture, was beyond all belief frustrating, humiliating, as well as alarming. Yet none there failed to realise how much better off they were lying down than standing up. From 400 yards or so lying men make a very poor target, largely invisible as individuals. When there were thousands, as here, the arrows could scarcely fail to find them, but it had to be by dropping shots, not directly aimed. And it is quite the most difficult feat in archery to so direct an arrow, and by your bow-string pull so control its flight, that at a given exact distance it will change its upward course and curve down in a parabola so as to land at a steep angle on even a wide target. This is the science of ballistics, and although the English and Welsh bowmen were apt to be the best in the world, few could be expert at this. Moreover, by its very nature, anything such could only be contrived by effecting a slackening of velocity at the given point; which meant that unless the angle of fire was very high indeed, the fall of the shaft, by the time it reached its target, had lost more of its impetus.

As a consequence, though a great many arrows were shot, comparatively few landed amongst the recumbent Scots at an angle to do any damage; and of these most were of insufficient velocity to penetrate leather, much less armour and chain-mail. There were some deadly hits, some screaming — but for a major archery attack casualties were negligible.

Nevertheless it was not pleasant to lie there, pinned down, helpless. The waiting seemed endless. Not to be hitting back was the worst of it; but there was nothing that men could do in a prone position. The arrows continued to fall. They were tending to come in volleys now.

It was the volleying becoming ragged again, with the change in tenor and scale of the shouting from their hidden assailants, that gave the prostrate host some indication that at last this stage of their ordeal might be ending. The anger, threat and jeering in the chorus of hate was being affected by new notes that spoke of surprise, urgency, even alarm. Moray's people were beginning to concern the enemy's right flank.

It was possible thereafter for the Scots to trace the advance of their friends, unseen as they were. The archery became ever more erratic, and died away at the north. But presently the advance slowed, if not ceased altogether. It was obvious that fierce fighting was taking place in the swampy woodland. Bruce counted every second.

The arrows had not stopped their dropping shower altogether, but it was on a vastly lessened scale.

"Will," the King cried. "Now! Cover us." Sir William Irvine, Bruce's former armour-bearer, had been put in command of the six-score or so Scots bowmen.

These now, at Irvine's order, were the first to take the grievous step of rising from the prone. They rose each only on one knee, admittedly — and in this their shorter Scots bows aided them, lacking though they were in hitting-power. But it took a deal of courage for men to hoist themselves up, to make immediate targets of themselves. As swiftly as they might, their own arrows began to fly, practically unseen as *their* targets were. Some few never drew string before they fell back, pierced through.

Although they were shooting blind, even such attack would be alarming for men standing up behind six-foot-long bows just within the screen of bushes. The enemy fire slackened almost to nothing. It was more than Bruce had hoped for.

"Sound the advance!" he jerked. Then, as the trumpeter's unsteady notes rang out, he was the first to his feet. "Up!" he shouted. "Up! A Bruce! A Bruce!" Axe raised, shield held up before him, he leapt forward, down off the track and into the softer ground to the left.

He did not look back, nor did he have to. He did not have to shout for speed, either. No man there was going to linger, with even a few arrows in the air and some 300 yards of open ground to cover. Yelling, the Scots line rose and surged after him, while their own archers raised their bows to shoot above their heads, in their turn having to attempt dropping-shots.

By the noise, Moray's people had redoubled their efforts on hearing Bruce's advance trumpet-call.

What with the return archery, and the twin Scots assaults, the enemy clearly were thrown into considerable confusion. Their own surprise attack had proved no surprise, and the biters were being bitten. Some arrows did still come over at their suddenly mobile opponents — and now with a higher percentage of casualties; but they were no longer volleyed, or anything but individual and spasmodic efforts.

Bruce was fortunate, considering his prominence, foremost position, and the Lion Rampant of his surcoat and shield. Two shafts did strike that shield, harmlessly, and another ripped along his right forearm, tearing the surcoat's linen sleeve but failing to penetrate the chain-mail beneath. A fourth actually clanged on his helmet, knocking it slightly askew and setting his head ringing, but doing no damage. Then he was close enough to the trees for archers to be considering their own safety rather than throwing good arrows after bad.

Shouting the dreaded Bruce slogan, the Scots flung themselves into the wood, thankful to have covered the intervening open ground alive. It was no conventional woodland, tall trees being fairly wide-scattered; but there was a great deal of low scrub and bush, rising out of undrained boggy ground — difficult country to fight in. But almost certainly less difficult for the Scots than for their opponents, or many of them — English archers with six-foot bows and footmen with long pikes, both of which were of no help to passage through clutching undergrowth.

Immediately the struggle became indiscriminate, utterly confused, catch-as-catch can. There was no line, no distant prospects, no means of assessing numbers. Each man fought whom he could see — or tried to avoid fighting. And in this again the Scots had the advantage. For archers were precious, highly-skilled folk, and knew it — specialists with a clear-cut role. Not for them the cut-and-thrust of a hand-to-hand mêlée, in bogs and bushes, where their unwieldy bows and quivers of yard-long shafts got entangled in everything that grew. Their duty, most certainly, was to retire — and their protecting pikemen's duty to get them out of a dangerous position, not to engage in needless heroics.

So the mood was sensible retreat on the one hand, and angry advance on the other — a situation liable to develop predictably.

The Scots, however, chased their foes through the scrubland with more sound and fury than actual bloodshed, more shouts than blows, without even having any clear idea how many of them there were, or where their line was, if any. The enemy retiral was in roughly a southerly direction, which was as far as certainties went.

Presently these fleeing men became involved with others fleeing diagonally across their front, south-westwards, left or right. This must mean that Moray's advance was close on the left. In a very rough and ragged fashion the pursuit swung round also, so that all movement was approximately in the same direction.

A number of archers fell, and rather more pikemen. But it could by no means be called a slaughter. The King himself did not achieve a single victory, none waiting sufficiently long for him to get within axe-range.

Ploughing his way through clutching brambles, he found a panting Moray at his elbow.

"Too easy," that man gasped. "They flee . . . too easily."

"They are not the main body."

"They lead us to it?"

Bruce nodded. "If we let them."

"You suffered badly? With the archers?"

"No. Little. Thanks to you."

"De Burgh's position? Formation? His main body. How think you?"

"If he leads this host, they will be a-horse. In that, he is like my brother, a cavalryman. He would never demean himself to fight on foot! I judge him waiting somewhere that he may use his horse. Open firm ground in front of him. The bowmen sent to trap us. Pin us down. On that road. Against the cliff. He and his horse to finish us off. My guess, they must be massed to the south, and so that they can see some way down that road."

His nephew nodded. "He will not expect attack from this flank."

"He *would* not. He will now, with this rabble fleeing back on him."

"He will not know our strength."

"Not in here. But he will know our *total* strength. Less than 6,000. He will have watched Edward ride past, with 3,000 men. He can count, Thomas!"

The trees were thinning before them now and the brittle winter sunlight flooding the area beyond. Into this open space the fleeing archers were bolting, Scots at their heels.

Suddenly Bruce held up his hand, and barked a command to the trumpeter, "Sound the halt! Quickly, man!"

He could see, now, beyond the last of the trees. There, across another 300 yards or so of grassy clearing, were the solid, serried ranks of a great army drawn up, silent, waiting, menacing, horse and foot, banners, trappings, knightly chivalry, helmeted steel-girt infantry and Irish irregulars. Stretching right across the line of vision, each flank disappeared into trees again.

Even Moray jerked a shaken curse.

"So-o-o!" Bruce said. "My good-sire!" He pointed to where, near the centre, the great red-cross-on-gold standard of de Burgh stirred beside that of the Leopards of England.

"God save us there are tens of thousands there!" Hay, at their backs, exclaimed.

The King did not comment. "Have our bowmen forward," he ordered. "Now is their opportunity."

So, in a strange, unequal way, the situation was reversed. The Scots were in cover and the enemy stood as a vast target for archers in open ground. Unfortunately the bowmen were too few to take fullest advantage; nor were they so expert as their English counterparts — for archery in war had never been greatly practised in Scotland. But they did their best, and soon their shorter arrows were winging their way into the waiting host, scattered and few at first but ever increasing as men came scrambling out of the scrub. And no difficult dropping shooting was required here. Richard de

Burgh was no crawler on the ground; his ranks stood upright, or sat their mounts as knights should. The least expert or most breathless marksman could not miss.

However staunchly gallant — and well encased in steel — the Anglo-Irish knights might be, de Burgh's rank-and-file could not stand still and take this for long. Fairly quickly the massive line began to sag and fold and break, as men and horses went down screaming. Obviously the English leaders were seeking to rally and bring back into action their own disheartened archers.

"Will he charge us?" Moray demanded. "His chivalry?"

"Would you?"

The other bit his lip. "I . . . I do not know."

"Nor, I think, can he know. He cannot know how many bowmen we have. It is no lengthy charge — but in face of strong and direct shooting he must lose many. When he reaches here — what? In this scrub forest, heavy chivalry is useless. Horses hamstrung, and out of every bush our people leaping up to pull his knights out of the saddle. No — I think de Burgh will not charge with his chivalry yet. His foot, yes."

Angus Og came stumbling up, cursing the clutching brambles. 'A diversion? To turn their flank?" he suggested. "From the east. I could take my Islesmen . . .?"

"To be sure, friend. Good! To harry them, make them fear for their rear. But . . . I cannot afford you many. Their foot will rush us here, any moment. We are too few already. Three hundred, no more . . ."

Some English arrows were coming back at them now. And some of the Scots were running short of shafts. This could not continue.

"Where is the Lord Edward!" Hay cried, hotly.

None answered him.

"Keith is back with the horse," Bruce said. "Send back to him, Gibbie. Tell him I need a cavalry feint to the right. Along the road. The cliff levels off. To use that. Swing round their left flank. He has not many men, with the horses. But a few score would do. Not to sacrifice them. Only a gesture. To pin down their cavalry there . . ."

"I think their foot are preparing to rush us, Sire," Moray interrupted.

"Aye. Pray they don't send in too many for us, at once! Sir Colin — gather men with horns, trumpets. Send them over into the woodland to the left. To scatter. And blow. Sound as though we have a host marshalling there. Continue to blow. It may trouble de Burgh . . ."

The expected charge of the enemy foot erupted — and the Scots bowmen had but few arrows left for them. It made a terrifying sight, with thousands coming. Bruce drew back his line deeper into the wood, to allow the scrub and trees to fight for them, break up the impetus. In a way it paralleled their own first charge from the road — save that they had been charging archers, specialists with a high assessment of their own skins. These would meet a less careful reception.

In yelling fury the enemy foot hit the tangled woodland, pikemen, sworders and dirk-wielding Irish kerns — and the last were the most effective. Utter chaos resulted, in seconds, and continued, a crashing, slashing, cursing, stumbling frenzy, wherein all sense of lines and fronts disappeared and men fought perforce as individuals and little groups — when they could fight at all. Pikes were proved useless, indeed a handicap, and abandoned, long swords being only a little better. Battle-axes, maces, dirks and knives were the weapons that counted — and here the Scots were better equipped and versed.

For once Bruce could partially forget his allotted role of the calm, detached general who stood back and directed. The man was, in fact, a fighter of fierce and terrible effectiveness, especially with his favourite weapon the battle-axe. Seldom indeed in these last years had he had opportunity to indulge this savage prowess. Now he could and did. Tireless, shrewd, wickedly skilful, he wielded the dripping, slippery axe, and left a trail of felled men behind him.

Time had little relevance in these circumstances, and how long it was before a slackening in the fury of the struggle indicated to the King that this particular stage of the battle was ending, there was no knowing. His personal awareness had been of consistent victory, but as to how his cause had gone, he had only a vague impression. Now he perceived that not only was he, and other Scots, still in sight of the southern edge of the wood, but that they were in fact edging still nearer to it. Which could only mean that the enemy, in general, was retiring.

Presently it became obvious to all, and the retiral turned into headlong retreat, as men turned and ran from those damnable thickets for the open ground and freedom from probing, thrusting steel. The Scots retained possession of the wood.

Breathlessly Bruce took stock, wiping blood-stained hands on torn surcoat. Horn and trumpet-calls were still sounding from the east. Peering out of the trees, he could see that there was considerable stir on the right wing of the enemy host across the clearing. Angus Og's diversion, plus all the horn-blowing, was evidently preoccupying them there. The Marischal's projected thrust on the other flank could hardly have developed yet; but something had kept the main body of the mounted men inactive and in their place.

"How now, Sire?" Alexander Fraser asked, mopping blood from his jaw. "These are dealt with. But how do we deal with the mounted host?"

"We do not. We leave them to try to deal with us. Are you hurt, Sandy?"

"A thrown dirk. A graze only." He shrugged. "It is stalemate, then? They cannot risk to charge their heavy chivalry into this wood. And we cannot attack them."

"Scarce that, yet. They have still many foot. They will try again."

"If only the others would come back. In their rear. The Lord Edward..."

"Forget the Lord Edward's host — as *I* have done!" That was harsh.

In the breathing-space they regrouped, assessed casualties. On the whole they had got off lightly, so far. The fallen enemy lay thick around them, and not all were dead, by any means — but this was scarcely the time to tend them. Men grumbled, but more at the clutching brambles and thorns than at their hurts.

It could be seen that some proportion of the English cavalry was dismounting. And there was more marshalling of foot.

"Another assault. This time stiffened by armed knights and cavalry on foot. Slower, but harder to bring down," the King said.

"Archers forward, Sire?" Fraser asked. "Few arrows left."

"No. Hold them back. Then, move into position behind the attack. A few shafts at de Burgh, then. To keep him from moving in his mounted host in support. More value in that."

Trumpets blaring, men yelling, the second assault began, though inevitably it came much more slowly. With no arrows aimed at them, many men must have been grimly relieved. But the leaders seemed wary, too.

This time, save for the hundred or so archers, who remained hidden, Bruce withdrew his men before the long enemy line. The deeper into the wood's entanglements, the more broken those ranks must become. But he detached groups under Sir Robert Boyd and

Sir Hugh Ross, right and left, to seek to work round behind, both to upset the advance and to support the bowmen.

This battle, as it developed, held a less feverish note. Men were tiring, as well as wary. Towards the end of a hard-fought day, men who have managed to preserve their lives thus far tend to have a growing interest in prolonging them further. This applies to both sides. Moreover, the heavily armoured dismounted chivalry added a new dimension. There could be nothing feverish about their fighting, nor their movement amongst the undergrowth. But they were very hard to lay low. This, indeed, became a ding-dong struggle, dour, hard-hitting, but lacking the fervour of heretofore.

Bruce, well aware of it, recognised its dangers for the side with the smaller numbers. He racked his tired wits and splitting head, even as he fought, for some livener, some new factor — and could think of nothing. That insidious word stalemate had got into his mind. Damn Sandy Fraser for pronouncing it! But the situation did indeed seem to have become almost static, unsusceptible to successful manoeuvre.

Who would have prevailed in the end it would have been hard to forecast. But, no thanks to Bruce, or any Scots plan, a new factor did arise. Angus Og and his Islesmen got tired of making gestures and shadow-fighting, isolated on the main enemy's east flank — as fiery Gaels would — and came back to their comrades for some real fighting. They picked up most of the hornblowers in the process, who likewise had become disillusioned. But entry into a wildly confused battle in dense woodland is a dangerous operation, with friend and foe inextricably mixed and not always easily identifiable.

The Lord of the Isles, therefore, had his 300 come in dramatically, vigorously chanting their wild Hebridean slogans, shouting for Clan Donald, and identifying themselves with great success, while trumpets and horns blew varying versions of the Scots advance. Certainly it sounded an infinitely greater influx than any mere 300. Moreover, and perhaps most telling of all, the newcomers sounded fresh, enthusiastic and vehemently aggressive.

Almost everywhere the enemy foot wavered a little.

When the majority of the Highlanders, left with Bruce, heard their fellows' stirring arrival, they raised their own similar yells and slogans, in welcome. This could not but affect the rest of the Scots around them. Everywhere the shouts and challenge arose, with an inevitable if temporary increase in the tempo of the fighting.

It was too much for a foe already weary and lacking confidence.

There was no wholesale giving up or retreat; but from that moment the second assault on the wood was lost. The drift back southwards began.

Nothing spreads faster than the aura of defeat. Soon it became almost a rout. Angus Og's fire-eaters were, in fact, balked of their fine fighting.

The Scots leadership, at least, had no regrets. Panting, thankful, they watched the tide ebb. It was not always that they blessed Angus of the Isles.

Whether it was the ignominous return of his second attack, a cavalry engagement which seemed to be developing on his left flank — where Keith the Marischal was at last making his gesture — or merely the accumulated disappointments of a long day, Richard de Burgh suddenly seemed to have had enough. He was not so young as once, of course — now in his mid-sixties — and no doubt the stalemate was even more apparent to him than to his son-in-law. At any rate, to the surprise of the Scots, trumpets began to sound purposefully across the clearing — and these were clearly not for any further advance or attack. There was a marshalling of a screen of light cavalry behind which the main body could retire in good order. Riders went spurring off, right and left, no doubt to order the break-off of hostilities on the flanks. Without haste, with discipline and dignity, the Earl of Ulster turned and left the field in a south-easterly direction. He was no panic-monger, just a realist.

From the woodland the Scots jeered — but none sought more actively to speed the enemy retiral.

Heavily Bruce leaned against a tree. "Praises be to God!" he said. "But . . . what was that? A victory? Or a defeat? Or . . . a great folly? A waste?"

"A victory, surely, Sire," Colin Campbell averred elatedly. "Since we retain possession of the field."

The King looked around him. "The field! Such trophy, lad, for such battle — if you may call it that. Which ought not to have been fought."

"Your Grace is weary, dispirited," Fraser declared. "It is a great victory, by any counting. An English knight we have captured, one Cosby, says that the Earl had 40,000 men."

"Dear God — 40,000? I'll not believe it! Half that, perhaps . . ."

"There were great numbers in the trees to the east. Foot. That you never saw," Angus Og put in. "Mostly these Irish kerns. None too eager to fight for the English, I think."

"Aye. My good-sire no doubt had his problems. And his own doubts. His supersession must injure him. Divided interests. I could conceive that he loves *me* even better than he does Edward of Carnarvon! Or this Bishop!"

There was much to do, with the wounded and the dead of both sides to attend to. Even though the Scots had got off comparatively lightly, considering what might have been their fate, they were not less than severely mauled. And the enemy wounded was legion. The aftermath of battle was, in its way, as taxing, and a deal more distressing, than the fighting. However fierce a warrior, Bruce himself was ever affected by suffering. Not a few, even of his close colleagues, considered him soft, unsuitably weak, in this.

It was some time, therefore, before he moved back to the road, and then on to the open space where de Burgh had waited for them, and when there was sufficient firm ground to set up camp for the night — for the early winter dusk was beginning to fall. It was hardly likely that there would be another attack, in the circumstances, but scouts and pickets were sent out all around.

It was one of these who presently returned to announce the approach of His Grace of Ireland's host, from further south.

Edward rode up in style and flourish, as always. And in some haughty reproach. "I hear that you have had some fighting, brother!" he called. "A victory, of sorts. Over de Burgh. Need you have kept it to yourself? Might you not have deigned to share the honour with me? It is my territory. I have thought that we were to share more equally, henceforth?"

Bruce drew a hand slowly over set features. "You conceive *me* at fault, Edward?" he asked, as his Scots lieutenants growled in their throats.

"Would not any man of honour? You must always retain any glory for yourself. We were beleaguering Ratoath Castle, de Burgh's house. Believing him within."

His brother turned away while he mastered his tongue. "I fear that there was little of glory to share in this," he said stiffly. "Or honour. It was an unnecessary battle. We were in fact ambushed. And yet, we had 3,000 men as advance guard! To protect us from ambush!"

The other drew up in his saddle. " 'Fore God — you are not seeking to lay blame on *me*? For your fault!"

"Fault, man! If there is fault in this, where lies it? In the main host, which rode into a trap? Or in its forward guard, which rode blithely through that trap, unknowing, with no flanking scouts —

since such must have discovered a great army there. Some say as many as 40,000, lying close in wait."

Edward stared. "Forty thousand . . .!" he said.

"Myself, I do not believe it was so many. A prisoner says it. But even half as many — what difference?"

"They . . . they must have moved in after we passed."

"To be sure. But since they were largely foot, and we followed you within the hour, they cannot have been far off. I think, brother, that I am entitled to better advance guarding than that!"

"I sent you word, did I not? That the peasant said de Burgh was here, at Ratoath. Not at Drogheda."

"With a small number of men, only! No thanks to you that I did not believe that tale."

"If he lied, am I to blame? At least, I informed you . . ."

"Aye." Wearily Robert shrugged. His head was aching, had been since cessation of battle had given him time to recognise it — no doubt the effect of the arrow on his helm. "You informed me. Of that. But . . . let us have done, Edward. It is past . . ."

"You still were at fault in not sending *me* word. Informing me. Of this battle. That I might have my part . . ."

"Christ God!" Bruce burst out. "Are you crazed, man? What think you it was? A tourney? Young Campbell I did send, before the assault began. But he was himself ambushed. Well you know the advance's duty to spy for and protect its rear. In this also you failed . . ."

With a muffled oath, but no other leave-taking, the King of All Ireland wheeled his charger round and plunged off, waving his colleagues after him, to their great confusion.

That night the two hosts camped a good mile apart. The royal brothers were wider apart than that.

Chapter Thirteen

The battle of Ratoath may have been one which should never have been fought, but it proved to be a highly significant turning point, materially affecting more than merely those taking part. Although that was not immediately apparent.

It changed the course of the Scots' campaign in Ireland. Bruce's force had to halt in its drive on Dublin, to lick its wounds and reorganise, and the vital element of surprise was eliminated. Then Richard de Burgh had the trouble which so often follows defeat in the field, having to face near-mutiny from lieutenants and allies who alleged mismanagement and half-heartedness. He retired on Dublin, not Drogheda, presumably with the intention of strengthening the capital's defence. But with unanticipated results. Instead of being welcomed as reinforcement and comfort, he was in fact arrested and warded in Dublin Castle by Sir Robert Nottingham, the mayor, presumably on the orders of Bishop Hotham, the Chancellor, charged with dereliction of duty and succouring the enemy. The Scots did not learn this until later. But they did know that his thousands were now in the city.

Scouts brought back even more significant news, militarily speaking. The citizens, under this Nottingham, had risen to the defence of their town, with spirit. They were abandoning areas which had grown up outside the old walls, and these suburbs, being mainly of timber, had been set on fire, to offer no cover for the attackers. They had even pulled down the great church of St. Saviour's, to use its stones to repair breaches in the said walls, and to extend the defences of the quays, so that reinforcements might come in. Indeed, they had demolished the bridge across the Liffey. If these energetic measures were typical of the determination of the Dubliners, then a new situation had arisen.

While Bruce reorganised and sought news and reports, his brother, hot for action to redeem his name, made a brilliant assault on Castleknock, only eight miles from the city, using MacCarthy's Irish horse. He was successful enough to capture Tyrrel, lord thereof, and burned the town, church and district, sending its smoke billowing up within sight of the Dubliners. This was the sort of swift, individual operation at which Edward excelled. It was questionable, however, whether it did more than stiffen the Dublin people in their determination to resist.

The royal brothers were now on coolest terms, for all to perceive. It could not go on thus.

The third night after the Ratoath battle, Bruce rode with Moray and Angus Og to Edward's camp at Castleknock—where they were kept waiting a considerable time until Edward received them in the castle hall. Robert was primed to set and deadly patience.

"Brother," he declared, when at last they confronted each other. "I have come for a decision. It is time that we took it. High time."

The other looked wary and hostile in one. "Decision? How mean you?"

"Decide how and where we go, now. For no longer is it sound strategy to assail Dublin."

"What! You mean . . .? You resile? From Dublin? Now, before it. You shirk it . . . ?"

'Call it that if you will. Only by surprise could we have taken it. With our numbers. Ratoath meant that there was no surprise. The city is to be held, and vigorously. To attempt to besiege it would be folly. And give time for our enemies to bring great numbers against us, from all over Ireland. I will not hazard my Scots in such case. A swift-moving cavalry force is not for siegery—as you well know."

"I' faith—*you* it was who must take Dublin! Not Drogheda. Against my wishes . . ."

"That situation has changed. Vastly. We must change strategy accordingly."

"*We* must! I'd mind you who reigns here. Not *Robert* Bruce!"

The other ignored that. "We have three choices. We can turn back to Ulster—but that would look like defeat, and gain us nothing. We can move around Dublin and proceed towards the south—but this leaves the enemy in force between us and our base in Ulster. And the south-east is where the English are strong. Or we can turn west. All the West of Ireland is open to us, save Limerick. There the English are least strong, and your Irish princelings rule. Two-thirds of the land. How say you?"

Edward gnawed his lip, his dilemma obvious. Clearly the last was the best course. But as clearly it was his brother's course.

"I do not say any," he jerked. "I will not be thrown choice of this or that. By you!"

Robert shrugged. "It is not I who offer the choice. I only put it in words. It is there. The facts are there. Only the decision is ours. Have you better choice, Edward?"

"If you fail me over Dublin, the capital . . .!" Edward looked away.

"There is famine in the West, my lord King," MacCarthy of Desmond, one of those who stood behind Edward, pointed out.

"I know it friend. But we have a saying in Scotland that hungry men are angry men. They will rise the more readily against the English. And Englishmen are notable for their great eating! I think the hunger will bear more heavily on their people than on ours. Have you better course?"

"No. Save for the famine, it is the best. We could win the whole West."

"If we could have surprised Dublin I would have preferred to move south and east. With a possible sea descent upon Wales. That was formerly my aim. But that is not possible now, with the enemy well warned. The West alone offers opportunity to us, in this pass."

"You are set to go West. Then go alone!" Edward snapped.

They eyed each other.

"Your Grace of Ireland — you would not split the host!" Moray put in.

"Ask that of your uncle!"

"And you? What will you do?" Robert asked.

"I want Dublin. My capital."

"No doubt. But how to win it, and it embattled against us, with a few thousand men?"

"Not a few thousand. I have a great army of foot at my back. Have you forgot? An army that will grow greater."

"I have not forgot it. Nor the pace at which it moves! Nor that it wars in itself. And lacks a commander! It will take two weeks to reach Dublin — if it ever does. By then, the English will have 100,000 in the city."

"And I will have more! I will call all Ireland to Tara. To Tara's Hill, the true heart of this land. They will rally to me there, their King."

Speechless, Robert regarded him, the cynical realist, the hard-bitten cavalry leader. Could a crown do this to a man?

"My lord King — you will not wait here, idle, for weeks?" MacCarthy said.

"Idle, man? Think you I am an idler? By the Mass — I will not be idle! While I wait I shall raise my standard on Tara. But I shall do much more."

All men looked from one monarch to the other.

"Very well then, brother," Bruce said at length. "This is the parting of the roads. I have had my bellyful of waiting, at Carrickfergus. I brought these thousands of picked men for swift warfare. I move west."

"As you will. Better thus, perhaps . . ."

So, two days later, the Scots host turned its face from Dublin and trotted off to the west, without ceremony or formal leave-taking. It would be debatable which brother heaved the deeper sigh of relief. Bruce left Angus Og and his Islesmen with Edward, since that man did not want to go too far from his ships; moreover he understood the Irish best.

They forded the Liffey at Leixlip, the Salmon Leap, and then moved south-west to Naas, in Kildare, meeting no resistance, riding free. Almost a holiday atmosphere prevailed, after the strains and stresses of the last weeks. To be on their own, responsible only to themselves, with the clouds of disagreement and suspicion removed, was as good as a tonic.

Not that it was anything in the nature of a joyride, from the first. At every township they passed, King Edward of All Ireland was proclaimed, and local lords and chiefs urged not only to declare their allegiance but to take or send contingents to Tara forthwith, lest their loyalty be doubted. They took the castles and manors of a number of Anglo-Irish barons who failed to declare their adherence to Edward Bruce, but wasted no time on besieging strong points. Their scouts and flanking pickets fought a number of skirmishes; but the main force was never engaged.

Bruce by no means allowed either this easy progress or the holiday atmosphere to put him off his guard for a moment, to distract him from a commander's duty. He was there, basically, to cause the maximum of concern and difficulty to the English occupying forces; secondly to give armed support to his brother's throne. Both with as little loss to Scotland as might be. To that end he was seeking to draw the English and their allies away from the Pale, and from Eastern Ireland generally, into the native and wilder West where they would be infinitely more vulnerable. But that he was taking risks he knew well, especially in the essential matter of sustenance. Six thousand men and their horses require a lot of food and forage, and in an impoverished and war-ravaged country, such was hard to come by.

So, as they went, Bruce was more concerned with collecting and transporting feeding-stuffs than with actual fighting, at this stage. The area was not actually famine-stricken, but the warnings were that it would get worse as they proceeded westwards. Wherever opposition developed, therefore, they made the people pay, not in blood and treasure but in cattle, horses, grain, meal and hay. And where there was no convenient opposition, supplies were bought from the local population at fair prices — for it was no part of the Scots' intention to antagonise those disposed to be friendly. Herding cattle along with them would have delayed their advance greatly, so beasts were slaughtered, and evening camp-fires were as much for smoking and salting meat for the future as for cooking the day's meal. It was only a very rough-and-ready curative process, but it would serve for men whose standards were not too nice. The season of the year helped, though not really cold as Scots knew cold. Long and ever-growing strings of packhorses followed the host, laden with food for man and beast. This supply-train was not allowed to straggle, and was carefully protected.

From Naas, the seat of MacMurrough, King of Leinster, they

went by Castledermot in Carlow to Callen in Kilkenny, de Clare country — where, however, the de Clares remained discreetly out of sight. And ever the face of the land changed. There was no great deal of tillage in the Irish countryside at best, and grain was correspondingly scarce. Gradually even what there was died away. But not only this. The rich grasslands and pastures for which this land was famous were now dwindling also, and moorland, bogs, peat-moss, rushes and outcropping stone became ever more dominant. There were green oases in it all, but the terrain was becoming ever barer. Yet it was not an empty country. There were people in plenty, living in miserable cabins and huts of turf and reeds. The castles and manors and abbeys grew fewer, the townships smaller, the churches less ambitious. Yet it was probably true to say that the population increased as the living conditions deteriorated. And everywhere hunger increased until it became the very taint on the air. From being a faint shadow it became a threat and then an all-pervading aura, a condition of life.

The Scots host's supply-train began to shrink.

There was no problem in recruiting the Irish for Edward's cause, now. The difficulty, indeed, was to prevent thousands from joining Bruce's own company, with immediately available food as added attraction. He had to struggle now to keep down his numbers. This was Munster, where the ancient O'Brien ruled, and he was known to support Edward. But only mounted men were of any use to Bruce — and horses seemed this year to be for eating, in Munster, rather than riding. He found it hard, nevertheless, to reject and drive off hungry men. And, willy-nilly, his train grew. And slowed in consequence.

All this time Bruce saw nothing of the real enemy. But they heard of them, frequently. Sir Edmund Butler, the former commander in Ireland, who had susperseded de Burgh, and then himself been superseded by the Lord Mortimer, was still in effective control in Kilkenny, with, it was said, 30,000 men. Hence Bruce's drive in this direction. An interesting report said that the de Clare brothers had joined him there — and the de Clares, related to the English Earls of Gloucester, and therefore distantly to Bruce himself, were amongst the most powerful and influential of the Anglo-Irish nobility known to be highly resentful over the present English demotion of their kind.

Bruce pondered this circumstance not a little. Mortimer himself was said to be on the move, from the east, with a large English force, part of it no doubt de Burgh's late army. De Burgh was said to be still languishing in prison in Dublin Castle; although how rigorous was his captivity would be hard to say, for it was rumoured that the city mob had broken into the castle and slain eleven members of the Earl's staff — which indicated less than solitary confinement.

Out of all this varied information Bruce made what plans he could. He conceived the disgruntled Butler to be the weakest link in the chain. He would concentrate on him, if possible before Mortimer could effect any link-up.

Then, at Callan, only ten miles from Kilkenny, and Butler, chance took a hand. One of the Scots patrols captured an Anglo-Irish knight named de Largie, with a small escort, who turned out to be a courier from Mortimer to Butler. Brought to Bruce he was civilly treated, but his despatches carefully unsealed and perused. He proved to be carrying a peremptory message, in unflattering terms. The Englishman told the Anglo-Irish noble that he was coming south-west to take over his army when he had dealt with the presumptuous Scots rebel Edward Bruce and his Ulstermen; but meanwhile Butler was to hold his hand, do nothing without further orders, and to have no truck with de Clare, who was under suspicion.

Reading this, Robert Bruce slapped his knee and barked a laugh. "The English!" he cried. "Will they never change? Never learn? The blind arrogance of them! This, from a newly appointed commander to the man he succeeds, a man of twice his own years and of prouder lineage!" He tossed the letter across to Moray. "Read it, Thomas — and then have Will Irvine to fasten this seal down as though it has never been tampered with. He has nimble fingers. Then give the letter back to de Largie, and let him go on his way to Kilkenny — with my regrets for having interfered between a courier and his duty!"

"Aye, Sire — to be sure. This will gravely offend Sir Edmund Butler. And the Lord de Clare. Who is his friend, indeed his kinsman, I think. But — what then?"

"Then, Thomas, I too shall write a letter. To Butler. At once. To follow this de Largie in, say, two hours. That should give Butler time to digest the one and be ready for the other! A much more civil letter."

"Saying, Sire?"

"Saying that I regret an honourable man's adherence to the wrong side. That I find him, and his people, an obstruction on my road to Limerick. That I suggest our differences would best be resolved, in true knightly fashion, before Kilkenny two days hence. Say, noon. In honest armed combat, knight to knight, host against host, myself against himself. A challenge, Thomas — the gauntlet thrown down. From the King of Scots. How think you Butler will answer that?"

Moray looked thoughtful. "I do not know."

"How would you yourself, man? In like case. After receiving that insolent letter from Mortimer?"

"I think ... I think that I would remove myself. Make shift to some other place. Quietly. If I had opportunity."

"Precisely. As would I! That is why I have given him two days. We shall see. Aye — and Thomas, before you let de Largie go, see that he believes us to have more horse than we do. Say, 10,000 ...!"

Butler and de Clare did, in fact, rather better than Moray's suggested reaction, even though they did not commit themselves to pen and ink. The very next morning they disbanded their entire army, ordered its component parts to return to their homes, and then themselves quietly disappeared. Whichever way they went, they did not go to meet the Lord Mortimer.

The Scots army was astonished — even if their liege lord was slightly less so. It was as good as a great victory, and bloodless. The fact that Butler had been having enormous difficulties in feeding his host no doubt contributed.

The way clear before them, Bruce pressed on westwards.

They came to famed Cashel, in Tipperary, with its cathedral, round tower and abbey, one of the most holy places in a holy land, a rock rising from an extensive plain. Here was also the palace of the Munster kings; but O'Brien was presumably with Edward, and no supplies were forthcoming from either his servants or the monks. The army moved on towards Limerick and the Shannon, with the Western Sea beginning to draw them.

Now, with the elimination of Butler's host, and Bruce's fame spreading, everywhere the Irish rose in support, and in their thousands, their tens of thousands. As day followed day, they came flocking to Bruce's banner, and paid little heed to his instructions to head eastwards to join their own monarch at Tara and Dublin. Instead they attached themselves to the Scots, and came west with them — or at least, travelled behind, an embarrassment and a delay. Yet it was their country and their cause, and Bruce was not the man ruthlessly to spurn and drive them away. Especially as they were almost all hungry and he was known to have food.

Unfortunately he had far from enough food for all, and inevitably there was trouble. Moreover the Irish clans were even more quarrelsome than the Scots variety, and internecine battles of real violence were an almost daily occurrence. Worst of all, these unwanted cohorts raided and pillaged wherever they went, in typical clan-war fashion, not only in the names of their chiefs and sub-kings but in the name of the King of Scots also.

All this was outside Bruce's calculations, and he blamed himself for not having foreseen it. But regrets and recriminations aside, this could not be allowed to go on. Most evidently it was possible to be bogged down in Ireland in more ways than one.

It was, therefore, a vast and sprawling horde, quite unlike any army with which Robert Bruce had ever been connected, which at last reached the Shannon at Castleconnel, a few miles north of Limerick, on the 10th of March, the Feast of St. Bronach. Limerick was the greatest city of the West, the third largest in Ireland, and, with its port, had all along been the Scots objective. It was a fortress-town set on an island in the wide river, and was thought to be fairly strongly garrisoned — but by Anglo-Irish and pro-English Irish under O'Hanlon and MacMahon. Butler's, and de Clare's, disaffection might well have spread here. If it could be taken, the whole of the West ought to fall like a ripe plum.

But a welter of reports reached Bruce concurrently with his arrival at Castleconnel. The most immediate informed that, only a few days earlier, a large English fleet had sailed up the Shannon to reinforce and stiffen the garrison of Limerick. And to feed it, which was more vital still. The second was from the east, from Angus Og, whom Bruce had left with Edward, declaring that Mortimer had trapped the Ulster host in a bend of the Liffey near Naas, with a vastly superior army, and though the position had its own strength, protected by river and marshes, the situation was serious. Edward would never bring himself to ask his brother for aid in it, but he, Angus Og, could and did. He urged King Robert to turn back from the West, and take Mortimer in the rear, to their mutual advantage. But quickly — for the Ulster force had insufficient supplies to hold out for long.

The third report was from O'Connor, the studious King of Connaught, from Athlone, announcing that famine was making terrible inroads in the areas to the north and west, with plague in its wake, and advising Bruce strongly against making any advance meantime into those parts.

These tidings set the King urgently to think.

That same night he was given still further cause for cogitation. Early in the morning there was a great disturbance of shouts and screaming and the clash of arms, at the north part of the camp. The King rose immediately, to learn from the captain of the guard that it was not truly an attack or even one of the typical inter-Irish affrays. It was an assault, yes — but with a difference. The Irish this time were not fighting amongst themselves. The assault was against the Scots lines — not the men, but the horses. They had been driving the beasts off and slaughtering them, there and then, for food.

"How many?" the King rapped out. "How many gone?"

"I fear, Sire, that they may have taken some 200. There were thousands of them, crazy with hunger. The Irish . . ."

Bruce looked from the speaker to Moray and Gilbert Hay, who had joined him. "This, then, is the end of the road, my friends," he said heavily. "Once this has started, it will continue. Starvation is the enemy we cannot fight, and win. Our horses are vital to us. Without them we are lost. I have misjudged. Tomorrow, we turn back."

They nodded, silent.

So next day, to the consternation, reproach, even fury of most of the Irish chieftains — though not all — the Scots disengaged themselves. It had to be ruthlessly done, in the end, and Bruce did not enjoy doing it. But he had made a mistake, and this was part of the price he had to pay. His first duty undoubtedly was to his own people. They rode away fast from Castleconnel, eastwards, leaving Limerick and its investment to the great, quarrelling Irish host. They turned their backs on the enemy, and rode. Robert Bruce who had never done such a thing in his life, was not a man any dared speak to for some time thereafter. It was St. Patrick's Day.

They continued to ride fast, for day after day, eating up the miles — for that was almost all there was to eat. No laggards needed to be reminded that it was a race against time, against growing hunger, especially against the failing strength of the horses — for forage for beasts was as scarce as food for their riders. There were two schools of thought about this — one said that they should not press the animals, use them lightly, so as to cherish their flagging powers; the other that they should drive on at their hardest while any strength remained. The King inclined to the second course, especially in present circumstances, with the Ulster army to relieve if at all possible.

Avoiding all entanglements, fighting and delay, they were at Kells, half-way across the land, by the third night. But this pace could not be kept up, all knew. At least they were facing east — and by contrast with the famine-stricken West, in their hunger-dominated minds they recollected the East as a land of plenty.

Next day another courier caught up with them, about ten miles north of Kilkenny, from Angus of the Isles. He informed that the pressure was off the Ulster force. Mortimer, who appeared to be a quarrelsome man, had fallen out with Sir Robert Nottingham, Mayor of Dublin — and presumably with Nottingham's superior, the Chancellor, Bishop Hotham — for he had now taken sides with de Burgh, and was demanding the earl's release from Dublin Castle, Hotham's headquarters. This having been refused, he had abandoned his assault on Edward's force and marched on Dublin instead. None knew now what went on in the city, and who prevailed.

"My brother scarce needs me to aid him in this Ireland! Or any other," Bruce commented. "These Englishmen that Edward of Carnarvon sends over are all the aid he needs! What does His Grace of Ireland do now, then?"

"He marches, Sire. Northwards. For Ulster. For Dundalk and Carrickfergus."

The King stared. "You mean that he retires? Not just changes position? Retires hot-foot for Ulster?"

"Aye, Sire."

"But why? I sent word that we were returning to his aid. And what of his great host of Irish foot? The host that was marching south?"

"It is said that they are dispersed, Your Grace."

"Dispersed! I' faith — what mean you? Dispersed?"

The messenger shrugged. "That is all that I know. My lord of the Isles said dispersed. The talk is that they quarrelled amongst themselves. The Irish kings. And so broke up. Before Drogheda. But I know not . . ."

"Save us all — if this is how wars are fought in Ireland! It is beyond all belief. Are they all crazed in this island?"

"When men are in doubt for what they fight, this could be the position," Moray suggested. "We, in Scotland, knew for what we fought. Believed in it. Here it is otherwise. And in such case men tend to fight for their own hands. Or not fight at all."

"On my word, you are a sage, Thomas!" the King cried, ruefully but not really unkindly. "But no doubt you have the rights of it. As usual! But — what of us? For what, for whom are *we* to fight? Now? Tell me, you who are so often right, nephew! Tell me. On my soul, I think that we should go home to Scotland! And as fast as we may. What do we here, in the middle of Ireland?"

The heartfelt acclaim of all who could hear the King's voice was interrupted by the Earl of Moray.

"You say that I am right — so often right. But I was not right that day in Annandale. When I came to you, with the Lord

Edward. I it was who urged Your Grace to lead this campaign in Ireland. In person. Lest the English win a swift and easy victory. Against *your* judgement. I believed it to be the wise course. I much blame myself now . . ."

"We can all misjudge, Thomas. Ireland has confounded more hopes than yours. Or mine. It is a strange land, where no cause ever truly triumphs, I do believe. The English are finding it so, equally. I fear my brother is likely to discover the same. But that is his concern, not ours. Dear God — I could wish that Scotland seemed less far away . . .!" That was strange talk from Robert Bruce.

In the days that followed, as March turned to April, that wish of the King's became a litany with them all, a refrain often on their lips and never absent from their hearts, as the road home stretched out and seemed to grow the longer. They were forced to turn partly west again, in their travelling north, for the English had now partly reinforced the Pale, and mid-East Ireland was something of an armed camp. The point of fighting battles seemed highly debatable in the present circumstances; certainly the Scots were past the stage of looking for trouble — their empty bellies saw to that. The central counties of Leix, Offaly, Westmeath and Cavan which they were forced to cross, were good lands ruined, pastures neglected and covered with reeds and rushes, peat-bog spreading far and wide, lakes and tarns and swamps everywhere. These were the lands of the O'Farnells, O'Molloys, O'Regans, O'Mores and MacGeoghegans, and these tribes had been far too long fighting the English and each other to care for their land. All was in the fiercest grip of famine. Two nights after the Scots turned north-west from Kilkenny, they started to kill their starving horses. It was a grim but significant milestone on their way.

Thereafter, each day inevitably they covered fewer miles, and more slowly. The magnificent light cavalry host of the warrior King of Scots, one of the most renowned and potent striking forces in all Christendom, was no longer magnificent, scarcely even any longer cavalry. It had become a horde of hungry, silent, scowling men, dragging themselves northwards with only a dogged determination not to leave their prominent bones here in an alien land. It was perhaps as well that the enemy seemed no more inclined to fight than they were. Starvation may not make for peace and goodwill, but it certainly limits war.

At Rahan, on the 10th of April, they heard that Mortimer, with de Burgh's men, if not de Burgh himself, was as good as sacking Dublin, and that the savaged citzenry were wishing that they had opened their gates to the King of Scots. Widespread civil war appeared to be breaking out between the English and the Anglo-Irish. These, at least, were apt to have enough food in their stomachs to sustain the effort.

But even this news was insufficient, now, to distract Bruce and his people from their course. It did mean, however, that they could probably risk moving further to the east in their northwards march. They turned to cross the bare uplands of Westmeath, towards Trim, and, they hoped, fatter lands.

But now the concomitants of under-nourishment were taking their toll. Sickness and disease were growing rife, and men were dying in increasing numbers. Horses also, so that starving cavalrymen were now concerned to eat their mounts while still they represented sustenance. Only the sick rode, any more, and not all of them.

For Bruce to maintain a degree of discipline in his host, in the circumstances, was no small feat — especially as he was now a sick man himself, His old trouble of fever, vomiting and itching skin had come back — and on an empty stomach vomiting bore especially hard. Nevertheless he sought vehemently to retain his hold both on himself and on his men, to keep it a unified and manageable force, to uphold the morale of all. He had seldom had a more testing task. That he succeeded was in no small measure thanks to the sheer love his hardened veterans bore him, a love which let them accept from this man what no other, king or none, dared have posed.

They reached Trim on the 19th of April. Here they were only a few miles from Tara, Slane and Navan, a countryside they knew, with the new season's pasture beginning to sprout for their remaining horses, and a certain amount of food still available for men — at a price. And the Ulster border was only thirty miles away.

Perhaps the Bruce brothers were not so very different in all respects. Robert was not entirely free from the same damnable pride that made Edward so awkward a man to deal with. Here, at Trim of the de Clares, near the Ulster border, when he ascertained that there was little of real scarcity, that cattle and fodder were to be had for good Scots silver, and that no enemy concentrations seemed to be taking any special interest in them, he ordained a halt. A major halt, not of hours' but of days' duration, a full week of resting, eating and recuperation, followed by some modest raiding and spoliation in the Boyne valley, wherein men regained a considerable degree of strength, vitality and self-respect, and the horses became less like walking skeletons.

As a consequence when, on the last day of April, 1317, the Scots force crossed back into Ulster, with the bells of Dundalk and Carlingford celebrating the Day of the Blessed St. Ninny, it was as a dignified, disciplined if depleted body of men, at least half of them mounted, carrying along with them a number of highly-placed Anglo-Irish prisoners for hostage and ransom, with sundry enemy banners and standards displayed beneath their own. Also there was quite a sizeable herd of cattle driven along behind, as thoughtful contribution, gesture and parting-gift for his brother, even if these cost Bruce the last of his money to purchase. He was still less than well, but he would die rather than turn up at Edward's court looking like anything but a victor with largesse and to spare. He had brought a starving, disease-ridden army right across a famine-stricken, pestilence-devastated Ireland, from south-west to north-east, over 200 miles, mainly on foot — but that must not be obvious to any at Carrickfergus. He was still The Bruce, the First Knight of Christendom — God help him! Highheaded then, the Scots marched round Belfast Lough, conquerers, and even found breath to blow fanfares of trumpets to announce their coming. But, previously and privily, the King had sent messengers ahead to the Lord of the Isles, to have his galleys ready, if possible, for an immediate embarkation.

For this, and various other reasons, the final meeting of the royal brothers went off a deal better than it might have done. Edward did not wish to make explanations as to why he had hastened north and left his brother's flank entirely unprotected. Nor what had happened to his great resounding Irish host of foot. And Robert was determined not to reveal that he was sick and weary and indeed, for that man, dejected, at odds with himself, and preoccupied with his failure in this wretched campaign. They forebore mutual recrimination, for once.

On the 2nd of May, Festival of St. Begha, Bruce and about 4,000 men took to Angus Og's galleys, and sailed away from Ireland. Of the rest, those that were not filling nameless and hastily-dug graves across the length and breadth of the land, had elected to stay behind, accepting Edward's offers of large lands, titles, even knighthoods, for continuing and experienced armed support. Bruce put no hindrance in their way — but found it strange that any should so wish, after the experiences of these last months. Though such failure to understand, he told himself, was a sure sign of advancing years. Once, might he not have seen the thing differently?

For himself, all Robert Bruce looked for now was the sight of

Scotland's hill-girt shores. And then the soft arms of Elizabeth de Burgh.

He still shivered and vomited and itched, however hard he sought to hide all three.

Chapter Fourteen

As they had done three years before on the high ground above Lanercost and the Vale of Irthing, after much longer parting, the two of them spurred urgently ahead of their respective parties, alone, to meet together this time on the heather moorland above Ballantrae where Ayrshire merged with Galloway, the King of Scots and his Queen. Eager-eyed, calling, they rode — but as they drew close, Elizabeth's face fell a little if the man's did not. But only momentary was her hesitation. Then they were in each other's arms, mounted as they were, the lean, haggard, sweat-smelling man, and the splendid, statuesque yet voluptuous woman, clutching, kissing, gasping broken, incoherent phrases.

"Robert! Robert, my love — God be praised that He gives you back to me! Bless you! But . . . oh, Robert — you are thin! Wasted. Drawn, You are sick, I swear! Mary-Mother — what have they done to you . . .?"

"Tush, my dear, my sweeting — it is nothing! We are none of us fat, see you! Ireland is scarce a fattening land. But, you — you make up for us, by the Rude!" He held her away for a moment, the better to see her. "I' faith, you bloom, woman! You burgeon! You . . . you fill my arms most adequately!" And he reverted to their embrace.

He squeezed a strangled laugh out of her. "Lacking this riding-cloak, you would see me burgeoning indeed! Swelling. Fruiting, no less! I am quite gross . . ."

"You mean . . .? Fruiting? You mean . . .?"

"Aye, Robert — that is what I mean! Once more. I am six months gone. Now I have started, my dear, I swear there will be no stopping me!"

"Dear God — here's joy! Here's wonder! Another child. And you did not send me word . . ."

"Time enough for that. As *you* did not tell me that you had been sick! But you have. I can see it, trace it on you . . ."

"Smell it, be like!" he jerked. "But that is by with, now. Nothing. What of Matilda? The child? Is she well? Come, lass — here come the others. Greet them. But briefly. And then let us ride on together, alone. There is so much to say . . ." He looked past her shoulder. "Is that Walter?"

"Walter, yes. He has been acting the son to me. And I mother to both his child and my own. That is, between distinguishing himself, with Jamie Douglas. They have been doing great things on the Border."

"Aye. I will speak with him . . ."

When, presently, they were riding on northwards together, to Turnberry, and Bruce had treated his wife to a very foreshortened and carefully expurgated account of the Irish adventure, at length she interrupted him.

"Robert — what you are telling me scarce makes sense, unless there is a deal more to it than you say. You have starved and suffered grievously, have you not? The campaign little less than a disaster?"

He grimaced. "You could say so."

"That fault was not yours, I swear!"

"Whose, then? Who do I blame? Mine was the decision to go. I commanded. I it was who urged the move south from Carrickfergus, out of Ulster. I believe Edward would have been feasting there still, had I let him! It was I who changed, and refused to assail Dublin. I who elected to make for the West. If none of it was successful, who should I blame? *I* misjudged. And when a king misjudges, lesser men suffer."

"But the famine . . ."

"I knew of the famine. And thought that I had its measure! In that I misjudged also."

"And Edward? You have scarce mentioned Edward. What of the King of Ireland?"

"Edward . . . is Edward!"

"He failed you, did he not? Is that not the truth of it? The gallant, dashing Edward failed you?"

"He would tell you, belike, that I failed *him*!"

She shook her fair head. "Robert, my heart — I am a woman. But not, I hope, a fool! And I know you, know that it is not in you to fail anyone. Know also that you blame yourself too much. A strange thing for so potent a man. But I shall learn the truth of all this. From Thomas. From Sir Gilbert. They will not deceive me . . ."

Bruce changed the subject. "What is this of James Douglas? And Walter? On the Border. He is still besieging Berwick?"

"Yes. After a fashion. The siege of Berwick continues. But Jamie is seldom there. King Edward, *English* Edward, hearing that you were gone, called a great muster of his armies, at Newcastle, to come and raise the siege and to punish Scotland. Save us — we were all prepared to send for you to come home, Robert. William Lamberton had the letter written. Then we heard that Edward himself had failed to come. To Newcastle and his host. All awaited him there, but he stayed in London. This second Edward is a strange man."

"He blows hot and cold. Unlike his sire, who blew only hot!"

"Perhaps. At any rate, when still he came not, the Earl of Lancaster, whom he had made lieutenant of the venture, would have no more of it. He dispersed the great army, saying that those who wished to relieve Berwick and punish the Scots could do so, and merrily. For himself, he was going home to his lady! And so we breathed again."

"This is none so different from Ireland!" Bruce observed.

"I would not have thought it. But, in the English array were some hardier spirits. Notably the young Earl of Arundel. And some Gascon knights the Plantagenet had brought over to fight for him. These were not be put off from winning booty. So fragments of the great host came north — though most, they say, followed Lancaster's lead. It was not a great invasion, but savage and scattered raiding across the Border."

"And Jamie dealt with it to his satisfaction?"

"Ask Walter. Walter was there with him, much of the time. Let him tell you himself."

Bruce turned in his saddle to call his son-in-law forward.

That young man, modestly disclaiming any major prowess, attributed all to the lord of Douglas — whom he obviously hero-worshipped. He described how the Earl of Arundel had come first, with Sir Thomas de Richemont and many thousands, crossing the Cheviots at the Carter Bar. And how Douglas and he had ambushed them, by Jed Water, at Lintalee, making a narrow passage even narrower by plaiting and lacing together the scrub birch-trees so that scarcely even a rabbit could have got through, much less a cavalry force, ill-led. The slaughter had been enormous. Douglas killing de Richemont with his own dagger — though Arundel had escaped. Later a strong party of Edward's Gascon knights forded the Tweed at Coldstream, and were raiding and burning in the Merse and Teviotdale, when Douglas slipped down out of Ettrick Forest and waylaid them as they returned towards England, sated with booty, wine and women. Most of the invaders died there, at Skaithmuir, including Raymond de Calhau, Piers Gaveston's nephew, whom King Edward had made Governor of Berwick. Douglas said it was the hottest encounter he had ever known. On another occasion, near to Berwick itself, Sir Robert Neville of Raby, the Peacock of the North, with a strong squadron of English North Country knights, was routed. Douglas himself slaying Neville. These were only a few of the victories.

"Bless him — Jamie was ever my best pupil!" the King said. "But — what of defeats, Walter? Even Douglas cannot have *all* victories!"

"None, Sire. Save that we have not yet taken Berwick."

"Aye, Berwick is a hard fist to unclench. One of the hardest in the two kingdoms. It can be supplied by sea, and is protected also by the town and its walls. If a besieger is prepared to sack the town first, and slay its people — as was Edward Longshanks — then perchance he may win Berwick Castle. That I am not."

"There was another victory — but not of Jamie's winning," the Queen put in. "Despairing of getting past the Douglas, an expedition from Yorkshire, from the Humber, came by sea. They sailed up Forth, and landed at Inverkeithing, in Fife. The Sheriff of Fife made but feeble resistance, it is said, and the Englishmen drove them towards Dunfermline. But the good Master William Sinclair, Bishop of Dunkeld — he that is brother to my lord of Roslin — was at his manor of Auchtertool. Perceiving disaster, he grasped the Sheriff's spear from him, shouting shame, and with sixty of his own servants rode back to charge the enemy. It was more than the Fifers could stomach, and with or without their master, they followed on. The Yorkshiremen were driven back to the sea, with 500 dead it is said, and more were drowned in their boats. And the good Bishop none the worse!"

"They do say the Bishop told the MacDuff that Your Grace would do well to hack the spurs from off his heels!" the Steward added. "And cried that all who loved their lord and country should follow him."

"Ha! We must cherish my lord of Dunkeld — a cleric after my own heart. And, I think, find a new sheriff for Fife. A case of poor master, poor man — for though the Earl of Fife has been returned to my peace for two years now, with all his lands returned to him despite his former treachery, he still loves me not. Alas for MacDuff! We must consult William Lamberton on this . . ."

"I sent a messenger to him so soon as I heard of your coming," the Queen said. "If I know my lord, it will not be long before he is at Turnberry."

Bruce gazed around him as he rode, sniffing the scents of heather dust, pine resin, opening bracken and raw red earth, laced with the overall tang of the sea — which was for him the smell of springtime in Scotland. He would not have disclosed how glad he was to be back in his own land, how inexpressibly dear and sweet that land was for him. He had scarcely realised, until now, just how much it meant to him, the very growing, enduring land itself, not only the idea that was Scotland and its people — a land which, God knew, he had paid enough for, to call his own. If Ireland had taught him how much his own land, the actual soil of Scotland, meant to him, then perhaps Ireland was not all loss.

As ever, thereafter, Robert Bruce found the waiting until he could be alone with Elizabeth frustrating, almost intolerable. But he was the King, not his own man; not even, in this his wife's. At Turnberry Castle innumerable men waited to see him, officers of state, secretaries, ambassadors, churchmen, courtiers, kinsmen, deputations. A banquet had been hastily conjured up for the returned, tired and hungry warriors, and entertainment thereafter. Through it all the man forced himself to patient endurance, even apparent appreciation. At his side, Elizabeth watched him and understood. Occasionally she touched his wrist, his forearm, with gentle pressure — and grieved to feel him so thin.

At last, up in their own tower-chamber, at parapet-level, with the door closed behind them and the half-light of the May night about them, he held her in his arms for long, just held her, not speaking, not even kissing, gripping her splendid rounded body to him, face buried in her plenteous flaxen hair. Quiescent she waited.

Weary, strained, jangled as to nerves and emotions as he was, the desire rose in him. Smiling, she responded, aiding his suddenly eager fingers to unfasten and drop her gown, her shift; then, feverishly now, to throw off his own attire.

The great bed received them. Their urgency had become mutual.

When the fierce first passion was spent, and the man at least lay back, exhausted, Elizabeth raised herself on one elbow, to consider him, running light searching fingers over his hot, but not sweating person. And as he jerked and shivered uncontrollably, involuntarily pushing her hand away, she sat up.

"Robert!" she said. "What is this? You are burning hot. Your skin. I can feel it. And rough. Broken. What is this?"

"Only my old trouble, lass. You know of it. This itching . . ."

"But this is worse. Harsher." She peered, in the dim half-light, trying to inspect him. Then she jumped up and hurried, wholly naked as she was, to an aumbry near the door, where was kept a lamp and flint and tinder. Lighting it, she came back to him.

"Hold it up," he instructed. "No — to yourself, not to me. That I may see. I' faith, woman — you are magnificent!"

"And you are not! Robert — you are patched red! Patched like an old hide. Great marks. Rough. Flaking. My dear, my dear! And so thin, so desperately thin. Oh, my love — what has become of you?"

"Nothing that your presence and your fine feeding will not cure," he asserted strongly. "I have been in the saddle for months, lass. Eating poorly. And living less cleanly than I would. Give me time . . ."

"No! This is more than that. More than you say. Here is no mere chafing of the skin: No simple dryness. You are sick, Robert. Sick."

He was silent.

"This is worse than it has ever been, is it not?" she demanded, holding the lamp close. "Even the time you told me of. At Inverurie. And at Melrose. I think it was less harsh, less angry than this, was it not? It is a scurvy!"

"It is only the skin. I was more ill then. Weaker, more fevered. It is but this skin affliction that is worse. Nothing of grievous hurt."

"How can you say that? This of the skin is like to be but the outer sign of inner sickness. The scum that rises to the surface of a pond speaks but of foulness beneath. This ailing of your skin keeps returning. When you are weak, weary, low in body. I do not like it, my dear . . ."

"And think you I do!" he burst out abruptly, harshly, surprising even himself.

Biting her lip, she eyed him. "You are concerned, Robert. Concerned for yourself. I can tell. Of yourself, you fear. Fear some worse sickness, do you not? I know you . . ."

"Have I said a word? You dream it all, woman!"

"Perhaps. Perhaps. At least, I can anoint it. Comfort you. With some salve. Did not Christina MacRuarie have some salve that greatly soothed? We must send to her. But, meantime, I have only what we rub on the children, the babes, when their skin is chafed. It may help a little . . ."

"God's death! Think you balm for babes can wash away *this* soiling!" he cried, sitting upright. "As well feed me mother's milk from these breasts! I am soiled, woman — soiled! You will not wash it off with salve!"

"So-o-o!" she said slowly. "It is as I thought. You conceive yourself to be sicker than you say. You admit it, Robert? You fear it."

"Aye, I fear. I fear that my sins have caught me up!" His voice was tense now. "Fear that I am not to escape the price of murder, of presumption before God, of excommunication!"

She stared. "What . . . what do you mean?"

"Elizabeth." He gripped her with both his hands. "You do not think . . .? It is not . . .? It could not be . . . leprosy?"

She drew a quick, gulping breath, speechless, appalled.

"Sweet Christ — am I a leper!"

As still the woman did not answer, save to wag her head, he sank back on the bed. But not in despair. Suddenly he was less tense. It was out, at last. This ghastly secret dread, this spectre that had haunted him for so long. He had put a name to it now, said the dire words, shared the fearful weight of horror with another. He knew a kind of relaxation.

"No, Robert! No!" Elizabeth cried, when she could find words. "Not so. It is not true. Never think it. This is not leprosy. I swear it. You are wrong, wrong!"

"It . . . it is my daily prayer that I am. But I fear . . ." He paused. "It could be God's will. His punishment."

"No. You torture yourself. Just as you blame yourself too much. You punish *yourself*, Robert. For what was no fault. Or little. The death of a foresworn and dangerous traitor. The assumption of a crown that was yours by right both of blood and conquest. You punish yourself. God is less harsh, I vow!"

"Yet He punished full harshly others for less fault. For *my* fault. My brothers. My sisters. Marjory. Christopher Seton. Atholl. Isobel of Buchan. Your own self indeed . . ."

"Was that God? Or but the savagery of a man, a man crazed with hatred? Edward Longshanks is not God!" She shook her head. "Besides — this is not leprosy. The leper's skin is white, not red, is it not?"

"I believed so once, told myself so. But in a lazar-house at Cashel, in Tipperary, I saw two men with skins as red as mine. Saw them, forced myself to speak with them. I tell you, they itched as do I! Were fevered. One of them vomited. Not the other . . ."

"But were they lepers? You are sure?"

"They were in a leper-house. Believed themselves to be so. Tended by the Brothers of Saint Lazarus."

"That need mean little. Ignorance. The folly of neighbours. Have you spoken with a physician, Robert?"

"I have spoken with none. Until you. I . . . I dared not."

"And you were right, in that. I say you were right to speak of this fear to none. This is not to be spoken of. None must hear of it . . ."

"If I am unclean, my dear, shutting our eyes and ears to it will not cleanse me."

"Merciful Mary — you are *not* unclean! Oh, Robert, my heart — never say it, never think it! It is a folly, a sin! This is no more leprosy than is a rash of the fowl-pox, or the ruby-pox. Say nothing of it to any, Robert. Or all the world will have you leper by the next day, as good as dead and buried! Men shunning you. You, the King!"

"And yet I must know, lass. For certain. I cannot live with this sore secret, uncertain. I have done so for too long as it is, gnawing at my mind . . ."

"But I tell you it is not leprosy. That you are wrong . . ."

"Because you wish it so, Elizabeth. You are my wife, my other part. You cannot judge, I think, more truly than do I. I need another to tell me, another who loves me less. But who will not noise it abroad. With that I do agree. It must not be spoken of, until, until . . . God help me, until I am sure it is true! Or the rule of this my kingdom will become confusion impossible. A leper-king! Already dead under the law! Banished the presence of clean men. Who would succeed me? There is none. This also I have thought on, through the long nights, and over many a weary Irish mile. None must learn of this — until it is sure . . ."

"Myself, I would tell no man," Elizabeth said. "But if you must, ask William Lamberton. He is wise, knowledgeable — and discreet. He would be best."

"Ay — Lamberton. I will tell Lamberton. He should know, too, for he is my confessor, my spiritual adviser. He will tell me truly." The man paused, looking at her, surveying her, all her naked loveliness, and frowning. "Elizabeth," he went on, from stiff lips, as though forced to it. "And you? What of you, lass? If indeed I am a leper. What of you?"

"What of me, Robert? I am your wife."

"You . . . you could not remain so."

"I am your wife," she repeated. "Your other part, as you said but then. Said truly. For we are one."

"But . . . no, lass. I could not be. Tied to a leper. It is against the law, besides. You know it. All marriage ties are dissolved, the law declares. The leper is dead, in the eyes of the law. A leper may not cohabit with a clean woman . . ."

"Robert — be silent! How can you say such things? I wed you for better or for worse, did I not? Before the altar in Linlithgow did we say aught about leprosy? Besides, you are no leper, I tell you. But if you were, think you I would leave you? I, Elizabeth de Burgh!"

"My heart — heed you. Would you become a leper too? Already — already it may be too late! Already I may have given you this evil thing. Lying here with you tonight. I should not have done it, I was weak, wickedly selfish. By fouling this dear flesh . . .?"

"Mary-Mother — hear me! If you *are* leper, think you I would wish to be other? I waited eight years in English prisons — when I would not have cared whether I was leper or clean. Only waited for this, to be with you, *you,* once more. United with you. Your wife. Now, we are together — and I thank God daily. Think you that anything, anything under heaven, will part us now, save death itself? I, Elizabeth, am wife to Robert Bruce. I told you, on that island in Linlithgow Loch, that I would be a jealous wife. In this, more than in your casual taking of other women. Those whom God hath joined together let no man put asunder! No man, Robert Bruce — even you!"

"And the law of the land, woman?"

"You are the King. The law itself, and above the law. And even if you were not, I would say the same. God's law is above man's law, is it not?"

He sat up again, to take her in his arms. "My dear, my dear," he said.

Clean or unclean, they lay in each other's arms through that night, although there was no more of passionate coupling. Strangely, it was not long before the man slept, a sleep which he had been desperately needing. Hour after hour the woman lay at his side, staring up at the painted ceiling, an arm about his jerking, twitching troubled body. The cocks were crowing before her eyes closed.

* * *

The Primate, Bishop of St. Andrews, arrived there three days later, days in which a constant stream of visitors descended upon Turnberry, lords, sheriffs, councillors, officers, in great style or no style. William Lamberton came in a litter, not because it became his dignity, as did some clerics, with musicians and choirs of singing boys to mark their presence, but because he was now partly crippled with arthritis and found sitting a saddle almost as trying as walking. He had, in fact, walked the length and breadth of Scotland too much, in too much harsh weather, slept under too many dykes, suffered too much hunger, exhaustion, for even such a powerful frame as his; so much that now he, who was Wallace's friend before he was Bruce's, and whose service with both had brought pain and sorrow as their main reward, though not yet fifty, had to travel in a litter slung between pacing jennets — even though the pace, for jennets, was apt to be forced and uncomfortable. But if the great rawboned, lanky body somewhat failed the man, the spirit within, like the shrewd, searching, patient mind, did not.

Primate and King, in a corner of the parapet-walk that overhung the beach and the white lacework of the tide, sat on the rose-red, sun-warmed masonry and looked out across the sparkling waters to the dramatic skyline of Arran and the Highland hills behind Bute — that is, when they were not considering each other's appearance a little askance.

"It grieves me to see you so sore stricken in the joints, old friend," Bruce declared. "A hard burden for a doing man such as yourself. It should not have been for you to come all this way, from St. Andrews. Rather I should have come to you. I would — but Elizabeth had sent for you . . ."

"And think you I would have my liege lord waiting on me like some suppliant for a vicarage? I am not so far done that I cannot fulfil my duties, however halting my gait, Sire."

"We have a compact, do we not William, that you name me by my name when we are alone? Have you forgot?"

"Not forgot, Robert. It is a graciousness I treasure but can scarce bring myself to invoke. But at least I can still cross a few miles of Scotland to welcome home her monarch — even though I do it in a bed of sorts!" The hollow, lantern-jawed features creased to a smile. "Mind, I would be better pleased to come less far than to Turnberry and the Ayr coast. Not for my old bones' sake, but in that I believe you would be better seated nearer the centre of your realm, Robert. Where your people can see you and savour your royal presence. Now that you need not watch the Border like a hawk. And Galloway and the Isles likewise. No Kings of Scots have made Ayr, this Carrick, their chosen seat heretofore. You are not, surely, to be a warrior all your days, my friend? Dwelling in an eagle's nest of a fortress. A royal palace in a kinder place, amidst your people, at Stirling or Dunfermline or St. John's Town of Perth? Where you may put aside your well-worn armour and live more gently. Besides being nearer to your old done William Lamberton!" He looked at the other keenly. "I think that such time has come, Robert. That you *need* such easement."

The King frowned. "I would remind you that there is still no peace treaty with England. Nor is our campaign in Ireland like to bring it much nearer. They are still set on conquering Scotland."

"Set — but now in the dogged, obstinate English fashion. And a deal less sanguine of success."

"Perhaps. But — you have been on this matter to me before. I fear that I am in no state, no frame of mind and body, to start building palaces, to settle to this easement you speak of. That is not to be for Robert Bruce, I think."

"Frame of mind and *body*?" the other took him up quickly. "What mean you, friend?"

Bruce shook his head, actually fearful, afraid to put this matter to the test, afraid of the possible sentence that spelt doom, afraid even of the impact of his revelation on their cherished friendship. Holy Church was stern in its measures towards lepers, men rejected of God. He sidestepped, put off, weakly.

"I ailed somewhat, in Ireland. It is a hard country to campaign in. There was much famine. I have been . . . less than myself."

"Aye, Robert — I saw it with my first glance at you. And felt a stoun at my heart. Here is sorrow, pain, trouble for us all. For all Scotland. A plague on it that you ever went to that unhappy country. That my lord of Moray convinced you . . ."

"A plague, truly! But I went of my own will. We cannot blame Thomas. The failure of judgement was mine. And many have suffered for it. If *I* must suffer a little, it is but due." He faltered, at the sound of his own words. And then pulled himself together. "Forgive me, friend. I talk like a sickly woman, concerned with her health. When you, *you* sit before me, crippled and in pain, from hurts, wounds, privations, gained in my service. I crave pardon."

"Not so. I am bent, yes. I creak like an old door. But I am none so hard-used. I can still serve my time, serve my liege and his realm. I am still fit for my tasks. Although, God be thanked, my task, my true life's tasks, are near fulfilled now. I have been privileged in a small way to aid you in saving this realm. I have held the Church, in Scotland, free from domination. And I have near finished the rebuilding of the cathedral. At St. Andrews. Only months now, and it should be done. And very fine — even though I wickedly boast. A house to God's glory, which I believe Scotland may be proud to have raised in her prostration. Thanks to you who made it possible — as you made so much else. I make no complaints."

"You never did, man. But I am glad that your cathedral is near done. A noble work to have conceived, and concluded, while the realm was still fighting for its life. Only a man of your spirit, your faith, would have done it, could have done it. I rejoice for you, and with you, William."

"Bishop Arnold it was who conceived it, 150 years ago. I but finish his work. But, it is my hope, Sire, that you will come to St. Andrews and rejoice indeed with me, with all the Church, with half Scotland, to celebrate the work's completion. It will scarce be ready for St. Andrew's Day. But St. Rule's Day, perhaps. Next mid summer. God being willing, we will make a great jubilation, a solemn consecration. Not only to crown the long task, but to demonstrate to all, to all Christendom — and especially to His Holiness in Rome — that we are not just a small quarrelsome folk, as I fear he thinks us. Nor murderous rebels as King Edward seeks ever to teach him. But a proud and independent nation, concerned, even in our extremity, with God's work. We will invite embassages from far and near, Sire. From Rome — aye from England itself. We will make sure that they see a realm united and strong, which can turn its mind to other concerns than war. With a sovereign lord whose fame rests on more than winning battles . . ."

Bruce's finger-tips had begn to tap-tap on the stonework as the other propounded his great and politic conception. The frown had come down again.

"Do not build on it," he interrupted harshly. "Or, not on my presence thereat. A year hence. I may be . . . otherwhere!"

"Eh . . .? Not, not another campaign? You are in no state, Robert, for more soldiering, meantime. I swear it. Do not say that you contemplate more warfare?"

"Not warfare. The warfare I fear is different — a battle I am not like to win! If it is as I fear." He was gripping the stone now, knuckles white. "William — if I was a leper, I could scarce attend your celebration!" That was rapped out.

"A leper! Saints have mercy — what mean you by that?"

"What I say. I may be a leper. Unclean."

"Dear Saviour Christ! Sire — you do not mean this? You cozen me . . .?"

"I cozen none. But nor would I cozen myself. This sickness of mine — I fear that it may indeed be leprosy. Of a sort. I have feared something of this for years. But, in Ireland, I saw others. As myself. Lepers . . ."

"Robert — Your Grace's pardon. But this is folly. Beyond all belief!"

"Why? Think you kings must needs be spared the ailments of lesser mortals? Say you I *could* not take this evil? Because of my anointing, perhaps . . .?"

"No. But . . ."

"Hear me, man. Before you are so sure . . ." Voice subconsciously lowered, Bruce leaned forward to tell the other the reasons for the dread that nearly came between him and his sanity.

His first shock over, the Bishop heard him out without interrupting, however often he shook his grizzled head. When the other had finished, he reached out and took the King's hand to place and hold it between his own two palms, a gesture as eloquent as it was simple.

It was Bruce's turn to shake his head. "You are good, William. Kind. But your kindness will not serve," he rasped. "It is the truth I need, not kindness. I need to *know*. Know my fate." He withdrew that hand.

Lamberton was silent for a little. "You have spoken of this to a physician?" he asked, at length.

"No. I have spoken of it to none. Save Elizabeth. And now you."

"That at least is wise. Heed me, Robert — and say nothing to any. I am no physician. But I cannot believe that what you have told me truly signifies leprosy. A skin ailment, yes — but there are many. The true leper is much more wasted, stricken. His sores remain, they do not come and go. They grow worse. You have suffered this sickness, at times, for years. Ten years. That cannot be leprosy. When I took your royal hand between mine, Sire, it was not only in token of continuing fealty and love, whatever sickness you may have. It was that I do not, cannot conceive your person as unclean, not to be touched. I truly conceive your fears to be groundless."

"You do?" The sudden rise, the hope, in his voice, was not to be disguised.

"I do, as God is my witness. And I urge that you put it from your mind. Say naught to any. Even those closest."

"And physicians?"

"No, Robert, my friend. Not unless your sickness grows the worse. I do not believe that we may trust any man with so dire a secret. Physicians have tongues like other men. Someone would whisper. Then there would be talk — and talk become clamour. And once there was such clamour, the Church would be invoked. Its laws on lepers. However firm I stood out against it, some would demand that the Church acted as ordained. You still have our enemies. You know how this, of all ills, frightens men. Faced with leprosy, the worst in men comes out. You know what they would demand?"

"I know enough."

"I pray that you know enough, then, to say nothing. To any. For Holy Church could be invoked to declare you lawfully dead. To conduct funeral obsequies over your empty coffin. To declare your throne vacant. Your marriage dissolved. Masses to be said throughout the realm for the benefit of your soul, as departed this life. Your child declared orphan. You could be ejected by bell, book and candle from the haunts of men. Debarred from entering any city or town or village, save at certain seasons, and then only sounding a clapper before you, that folk might avoid you. You, Robert Bruce! Thus until your dying day. Which could be years later. Sweet Saviour — think of it, Robert! You, Scotland's deliverer, Scotland's hope. I would sooner that you cut out your tongue, and mine, than that you spoke of this to any!"

For long moments the King stared out across the sparkling water. "As you will," he said, at last.

Chapter Fifteen

Elizabeth de Burgh and William Lamberton made a notable confederacy, and they had their way with Robert Bruce. And not only in the matter of keeping secret the King's fear of leprosy. On the subject of making a new home for the royal family, the Queen added her voice to the Primate's. She had never been particularly attached to Turnberry and since Marjory's death there she had frequently wished to be gone. The place spoke to her too much of alarms, fears and hurried journeys. Moreover she agreed with Lamberton that the monarch should dwell near the centre of his kingdom, not on the outskirts. And setting up a new home might well be a useful distraction for a man with a dark shadow on his mind.

Bruce, of course, was not really an enthusiast for castle or palace building. Throughout his life he had been more concerned with pulling down such places, either as enemy-held or as constituting threats to his security. He was not disposed to start erecting some new and ambitious edifice, therefore, especially in present circumstances. But he acceded to the others' advice that a move should be made to a more central spot — not the least of his considerations being that Turnberry was really Edward's house now, the seat of the earldom of Carrick which he had granted to his brother — and it went against the grain to be beholden to Edward for anything. Of the other great Bruce castles, none were any more central than this. Moreover, Lochmaben was largely in ruins, since the last English withdrawal; Annan little better, and almost in England; and Buittle, in Galloway, was also Edward's, as Lord thereof. While Iverurie, up in Aberdeenshire, had been demolished early on by Edward Longshanks, and was as remote in the other direction as these South-West houses.

The obvious choice lay between Stirling and Dunfermline, royal palaces both — for Linlithgow had been destroyed, on Bruce's own commands, as too dangerous a place to permit near the strategic battleground of Stirling. It was that vital strategic situation which told against Stirling itself, in this issue. He would have gone to dwell there readily enough; but Elizabeth was set against it. She coveted as home no fortress skied on a rock overlooking half a dozen past battlefields — and who knew how many more to come? She wanted to wean her husband's mind away from war and strategy, in so far as this was practicable; and Stirling, with Bannockburn spread below, was scarcely the place to achieve it. With Lamberton's help, she influenced the King strongly in the direction of Dunfermline, therefore. After all, it had been the great Malcolm Canmore's capital, its abbey superseding Scone as the burial-place of the Scottish kings. Here were interred Malcolm and his beatified Queen Margaret, as well as their sons. Also the Kings Donald Bain, Eadgar, Alexander the First, David the First, Malcolm the Fourth and Alexander the Third. It was, next to Iona's remote isle, the most royal place in Scotland; moreover it was in Fife, the same county as Lamberton's St. Andrews. Elizabeth pointed out that the child in her womb might well be a son, the heir to Scotland. If it was, surely it was right that he should be born in this hoary cradle of the Scots monarchy?

So, with still nearly two months to go until the birth-date, the move was made, from Clyde to Forth, that midsummer of 1317, and the Court of Scotland came to settle in the modest grey palace above Pittendreich Glen, overlooking the widening Firth of Forth, with the ancient climbing town of Dunfermline in a horseshoe behind, and the great abbey towering close by. Edward the First had burned all on his departure therefrom in 1304; but less thoroughly than was his wont, and the churchmen had been busily repairing it, the abbey especially. Much more remained to be done at the palace, but there was still more habitable accommodation than there had been in Turnberry's fortified towers. The King and Queen moved into the Abbot's quarters while their own apartments were being made ready for them; and the Court settled itself to roost where it could. It was thirty-one years since last this had been the seat of government, when Alexander the Third had ridden away that stormy evening towards St. Andrews, to fall over the fatal cliff at Kinghorn.

Despite her condition, Elizabeth was in her woman's element. She had been married, and Queen of Scotland, for fifteen years, and at last she had a home which she might call her own. She busied herself from morn till night in supervising, planning, furnishing. She deliberately involved her husband in the business much more than was absolutely necessary, or considered suitable by many, Lamberton aiding and abetting. And Bruce, after a little initial resistance, became interested, even moderately enthusiastic, finding small challenges, problems, decisions on a domestic scale new to him. His physical betterment was evident, undeniable, his preoccupation with himself fading.

The sudden, slightly premature accouchement and, after only four hours of comparatively light labour, birth of a second princess, was only marginally a disappointment. There was heartfelt relief too, not only in that Elizabeth, at her age, had had no difficulties of delivery; but that the child was perfect, small but entirely healthy, lovely. It had been Bruce's second, secret dread, from the moment of learning that his wife was pregnant again, that the child would be affected in some way by his feared disease, sickly, handicapped, even a monster. That she was not so engendered so great a joy and comfort that her sex seemed scarcely a major matter.

They called her Margaret, after the sainted queen who had made Dunfermline her home two and a half centuries before.

Bruce was busy at more than domestic matters. There was so much to be done, in the rule and governance of his realm, so much that had been neglected, not only during the Irish campaign but during the long years of war. He was not a man for idling and inactivity, however much his wife might urge a period of recuperation, and he threw himself into the business of civil administration with a will, almost as though in an effort to wear himself out with work. Dunfermline buzzed like a bee's bike disturbed, the old grey town on the ridge above the Forth fuller of folk, of clamour and colour, than it had ever been. Bernard de Linton, who perhaps had thought that the return of the monarch would lift some of the burden of administration from his shoulders, as Chancellor, instead had to find a deputy Abbot for Arbroath and come to take up residence at Dunfermline, there to labour harder than ever.

Bruce required his churchmen's help and advice for more than mere civil administration and the day-to-day running of the kingdom. After his military rebuffs in the Borders and at Donibristle, in Fife nearby, Edward of England, far from conceding the desired peace treaty, had turned to Rome for aid in his warfare against Bruce and Scotland. And the present Pope had found it convenient to pay heed. He was attempting to organise a crusade against the Turks, and desired the adherence of England. Scotland he appeared to consider as not worth including in the matter. He proceeded, therefore, at Edward's request, to fulminate against Scotland in general and Robert Bruce in particular. He ordained a compulsory two-year truce between the two countries, and addressed a Bill to the King of England and to "Robert Bruce who carried himself as King of Scotland". He also commanded that the Scots immediately stopped besieging the English in Berwick-on-Tweed — an unusual provision in a papal bull. And he sent two cardinals to present his commands — a subtle move.

Bruce had lived under the papal frown for years. But this new assault was serious, in that it specifically denied him recognition as true king before all the princes of Christendom, so implying that he was not a person with whom any Christian ruler could properly conclude any agreement or treaty. Not only would England, therefore, be sustained in its reluctance to enter into a peace treaty, but other and more friendly nations were also thus inhibited from establishing and maintaining relations. Scotland was to be a pariah amongst the peoples.

This was all a great blow, of course, not only to Bruce but to Lamberton the Primate, who had anointed him King and consistently supported him — as well as to all the other clerics of the realm. They were loath to rebel openly against the authority of the Holy See, from whom they drew their own spiritual authority. A policy of pressure and counter-intrigue at Rome, allied to a masterly inactivity at home, was their obvious recourse; but the former took time, and much money, to arrange intrigues at Rome as elsewhere being largely a matter of massive bribery. And this device of sending the two cardinals was a notably skilful move, since these Princes of the Church outranked Lamberton. They were heading for Scotland via London — where they collogued with King Edward — and Durham, where Lewis de Beaumont was about to be consecrated and installed Prince-Bishop of the Palatinate.

At a Privy Council at Dunfermline in September, Lamberton strongly contended that they must do all in their power to keep the cardinals out of Scotland for against their rank and authority, his own authority must yield and go down.

"How can we keep them out?" the King demanded. "They have announced to the world that they are coming. You would not have me to use force against the representatives of Holy Church? *Such* representatives!"

"Not force, no. But a little guile perhaps," the Bishop suggested. "Prevail upon them to send, in the first instance, envoys, nuncios, of lesser rank. To prepare their way. Men whom I, as Primate here, can outspeak. So that I may seek to teach them their lesson, to take back to their masters."

"Aye, but how is that to be done, my lord?" Bishop Sinclair of Dunkeld, the hero of Donibristle, asked. "How to make these cardinals send nuncios? They are already at Durham for this Beaumont enthroning. What will halt them now?"

"We, the bishops of Scotland, could send them a message of welcome, my friend. Greetings to our illustrious brothers in Christ. But at the same time urge that they delay a little." He glanced at the King. "Say that we are uncertain as to how our liege lord Robert might receive their eminences. In view of the unkind, and we are sure incorrect, accounts that have reached Scotland. As to the Holy Father's pontifications. Until these are put right, these misunderstandings cleared, we urge discretion. We are concerned that the Holy Father's lofty emissaries be received with the respect and honour due to their high office. So we advise that they send nuncios to prepare the way."

"Ha — guile indeed!" Lennox said. "And these envoys? How would you serve them, my lord Bishop?"

"Indifferently. Confusedly. Send them back to Durham in greater doubt than heretofore. As to their masters' reception in Scotland. But with an invitation for the cardinals to attend the celebrations at the consecration of my cathedral at St. Andrews next year. So that there is no hint of unwelcome. From Holy Church."

"I do not fully see the wherefore of this," the King observed.

"Time we need, Sire. Time for representations to Rome. Time for our friends there to serve our cause. Time to gather gold. Aye, time for Berwick to fall, if possible, so that this Bull is outdated. All this, and more. We must buy time. This device is to buy it."

Sinclair intervened. "If they agree to nuncios, then let us teach these a lesson. To pass on to their principals. If they travel north from Durham they must pass through Northumberland. You, Sire, have resumed the Lordship of Tynedale, and much of Northumberland now pays you fealty. Yet men still consider it to be in England. Some of Your Grace's Northumbrian lieges could surely be prevailed upon to waylay these nuncios before they reach Scotland. To somewhat mishandle them, rob them even — delay them, certainly. In England. So that the blame lies at England's door, not ours! That might help the cardinals to love the English less!"

Bruce actually slapped the table. "There's my Bishop!" he exclaimed.

"Better, Sire," Abbot Bernard added. "They could be relieved of their letters to you. These opened privily, the seals unbroken. Scanned and copied. Then handed back, but their contents sent to Your Grace hot-foot. So you would know before the nuncios arrived what their terms were. And be prepared to receive them aptly."

Grinning for the first time in months, Bruce looked at the Primate. That man inclined his grizzled head — as much perhaps in satisfaction at his friend's improved spirits as at the programme proposed.

"It behoves us, since the realm's safety is at stake, to play with such cards as we hold," he acceded.

"Spoken like a churchman!" the Earl of Dunbar and March declared, with sarcasm.

"Even churchmen may have their small diversions, my lord. So long as they do not cheat thereat!"

The Earl frowned.

"Save me from ever having to differ from the Lords Spiritual!" Walter the High Steward said fervently — and none of the Lords Temporal present thought to say otherwise.

It was a full six weeks later, therefore, before two indignant and unhappy clerics, in shabby, borrowed habits and high dudgeon, presented themselves at Dunfermline and the Court of the King of Scots — the Bishop of Corbeil and Monseigneur d'Aumery. They were civilly received — but not by the King — and kept kicking their heels for some considerable time before an audience could be arranged. Meantime, however, they were lent rich clothing, and given much sympathy over their dire experiences and shameful treatment at the hands of the North Country English. It seemed that when, with a splendid retinue, the nuncios were half-way through Northumberland, en route for Berwick, they had been rudely and savagely set upon by lawless hordes, at Rushyford, and despite their protestations and claims to sanctity, had been seized, insulted, stripped of their fine raiment, and carried off prisoner to the rude castle of one of these ruffians, by name Gilbert de Middleton, at Mitford. There they were thrown into dungeons, their baggage stolen, even the sealed letters they carried. They had been held in this horrid and distressing state for some considerable time, until eventually they were freed, but only the said letters given back to them. Since when, suffering grievous discomfort and privations, they had made their difficult way hence, to fulfil their charge and duty.

When Bruce found time formally to receive these ill-used and outraged envoys of Holy Church, he was courteous and sympathetic, seeking sad details and shaking his head. When at last they graduated from complaints to the object of their visit, and read the open letter that constituted their credentials, he still listened to them with attention — even though the tenor of their delivery was hardly flattering towards an independent monarch, and their references to the cardinals' requirements less than tactful. It was only when the Bishop moved forward actually to hand the sealed envelope to him that Bruce's expression changed to the stern.

"I rejoice in His Holiness's interest and care for my realm," he declared. "And I have, myself, long desired a firm and lasting peace with the kingdom of England. In this, we are agreed. But" — he tapped the sealed letter — "I fear that I cannot accept and open this letter. I see that it is addressed to 'The Lord Robert Bruce, Governor of Scotland'. It seems, my lord, that this is not for me!"

The nuncios blinked, and exchanged hasty glances.

"But . . . we do assure you that it is," the Bishop asserted. "The cardinals themselves gave it into my hand. For delivery to yourself."

"Then the fault, I concede, lies not with you, my friends, but with those who sent you. I cannot open, or reply, to a letter which is not addressed to me as King. It says but 'Lord Robert Bruce, Governor'. Amongst my subjects there are many bearing the name of Robert Bruce, who share with the rest of my barons in the government of the kingdom of Scotland. This letter may possibly be addressed to any of them!"

"No! Not — it is not so. It is to you, sir . . . my lord . . ."

Bruce frowned. "Do you deny me the witness of my own eyes? The words are here written. But, enough. I have heard what you have had to say, permitted you to read aloud the open letter. To these, since they refused me my title of King, I will give no answer. Nor will I by any means suffer your sealed letter to be opened in my presence. Take it back to those who gave it."

"My lord—Your Excellency!" the Bishop protested, in agitation. "I ... We regret if this letter is not addressed to your liking." But it is not for our holy mother the Church either to do or to say anything, during ... during the dependence of a controversy, which might, might prejudice the right of either of the parties. You understand ...?"

"So!" Bruce cut him short. "You acknowledge the controversy, and the rights of parties? *Two* parties! Both parties. Yet, in your open letter of introduction did you not read out more than once the style of Edward, King of England? Did you not? If, then, my spiritual father the Pope, and my holy mother the Church profess themselves unwilling to create a prejudice against my opponent by giving me the title of King, I am at a loss to see why they have thought proper to prejudice *my* cause by withdrawing that title from me. During—how did you say it? During the dependence of the controversy! All my subjects call me King. By that title do other kings and royal princes address me. My friends—if you had presented a letter addressed such as is this to any other kings, you would, I swear, have received a still rougher answer! You have mine—and less than roughly! For I do not fail to respect your calling and authority, and I entertain all reverence for the Holy See. Say so, when you return this unopened letter to your masters."

Monseigneur d'Aumery sought to retrieve something from the wreck. "Your Excellency—at least will you accept this two-year truce. His Holiness requires? Command a temporary cessation of hostilities?"

Bruce shrugged. "To that I can by no means assent without the advice of my parliament. Aye, and while the English spoil the property of my subjects and invade my realm. My friends—convey my respects and good wishes to those who sent you. You have my permission to retire."

William Lamberton led the chagrined nuncios away.

The crestfallen emissaries had hardly left for the South before Bruce prepared to follow them, for at least some of the way. The surreptitiously-opened papal Bull had revealed that one of the specific demands was that the siege of Berwick should be raised forthwith. Actual and public disobedience to the Pontiff's express commands was to be avoided if at all possible. Therefore it behoved the Scots to get Berwick safely out of the arena of controversy before the Bull was officially broadcast, if by any means this could be effected. James Douglas had been besieging the place off and on, the last Scots territory in English hands, for well over a year — but it was a most difficult task, the castle surrounded by its powerfully-walled town, both of which could be supplied and reinforced by sea. Against siegery, in principle, as he was, Bruce decided on an all-out effort to reduce the place before the cardinals could trumpet forth their rejected Bull, from Durham.

On this occasion he did not intend to rely wholly on military threats, encirclement, starvation, and the like. A little guile might conceivably help. He sent a royal proclamation before him, which was to be conveyed somehow to the citizens of Berwick, by writings smuggled into the town by any means possible.

A few days later, he set out in person for the Border.

Siege warfare had never been really mastered in Scotland, by more than Robert Bruce — like military archery — for this was a concomitant of *aggressive* war, the conquering of other nations' fortresses, and hitherto the Scots had had no such ambitions. But in Ireland Bruce had had opportunity to confer with Sir Hugh de Lacy, Anglo-Irish baron, who had served extensively in foreign wars and engaged in much siegery. His advice and guidance, on proper engines and methods for the business, Bruce had sought and obtained. As a consequence he now had ideas to put into practice.

Much solid and mature hardwood was required for the construction of adequate engines and rams, and the neighbourhood of Berwick itself was not rich in old woodland. But the Earl of Dunbar and March, lord of this area, knew of some good oak forest at Aldcambus, on the north flanks of Coldingham Moor, near Cockburnspath, about a dozen miles north of the Tweed. Here the royal party repaired, to cut timber and build siege-machinery — and give time for the royal proclamation, perhaps, to make some impact in beleaguered Berwick. It was nearly Yuletide, and no time for this sort of thing; but time was of the essence, with those cardinals liable to sound off any day.

The cardinals in fact did make their presence — and their indignation — felt rather sooner than Bruce had bargained for; but fortunately in a less damaging fashion, at this stage, than might have been. They sent another intermediary, bearing a very stern open letter, plus verbal messages, to Bruce, with many threats should these be ignored; also they included once again the unopened papal Bull, to present. But this time they chose a Scot to do the presenting, one Adam de Newton, Prior of the Minorite Friars of Berwick, a former colleague and superior of Bernard de Linton when Vicar of Mordington. In some fear and trembling, this unfortunate cleric was brought north by James Douglas himself, to Aldcambus, after having sought a safe-conduct. Prudently, perhaps, he had left behind in Berwick both the Bull and the open letters, still inadequately addressed as they were, in the shrewd belief that the verbal messages would be more than ample to deliver, in the first instance.

Prior Adam's fears as to a dire confrontation with his monarch did not materialise. Bruce in fact would not see him. In his joyful reunion with Douglas, the King wholly ignored the cleric. It was their first meeting since Ireland, for Douglas had been away on one of his periodic deep punitive raids into England at the time of the royal return. Their delight in each other's company only increased with the years and their long partings. An arm around his friend's shoulder, Bruce led him away along a woodland path amongst the rustling fallen leaves — and only as an afterthought, signed to Sir Alexander Seton, now the Seneschal, to take the Prior in hand.

Douglas was somewhat concerned at the King's appearance, although this was a great deal improved from what it had been a few months before. The younger man himself was beginning to show the signs of continual campaigning and command, the lines and bearing of authority, confidence, decision, implicit in his slender person and darkly handsome features. They had much to say to each other.

At length Bruce got round to questioning the other about the Prior.

"He brings fulminations and threats against you from these insolent cardinals, Sire," Douglas informed. "The man himself, is leal enough, I think. He is in much fear — as he should be, by God! When I heard something of his mission, myself I near hung him up from the nearest tree! But he declares that he had no option but to obey these arrogant Princes of Holy Church, as he names them. They are his superiors, his masters. They sent for him, to Durham, and he could not refuse their command. But at least he left their letters in Berwick meantime, wisely deeming his life of greater value than them! One, he told me, is addressed to Robert Bruce, calling himself Kings of Scots!"

"Ha — *calling* himself! They learn but slowly, these Romish eminences!" Bruce shrugged. "I expected no better. So he comes with only verbal threats and pontifications?"

"Aye — but I believe they are strong enough! The man trembles at the thought of delivering them to Your Grace."

"Then we shall spare him that ordeal, Jamie. It is best that I do not see this priest. Do not hear these threats and fulminations. We shall get Seton to deal with him. Now — what of Berwick . . .?"

With Seton acting as go-between, the Prior's message was soon interpreted — interpretation rather than declaration being involved, the envoy being inhibited from speaking out, and Seton outraged that open threats should be made against his liege lord. Simply, the message was this — that unless an immediate two-year truce was concluded, all raiding against England stopped, and all English hostages and prisoners freed, the whole people of Scotland, as well as The Bruce personally, would be declared excommunicate, and the wrath of God and the castigation of Holy Church would descend upon a contumacious and disobedient nation. There did not seem to be any concessions required of the English.

"Sweet Christ — can they do this?" Douglas exclaimed, when they heard the terms. "Excommunicate a whole people? What of Bishop Lamberton? What of *all* the Scots bishops and clergy?"

"I fear that they can do it — in name at least," the King said. "If the Pope is Christ's Vicar on earth, he can withdraw Christ's holy sacrament. Whether he *should*, whether God accepts such harsh judgements, such sweeping condemnation of innocent folk, is not for me to say — I, who have lived under excommunication from Rome these many years."

"Aye, Sire — and is that not sufficient answer to this folly? You survive such censure passing well! Why not lesser men?"

The King bit his lip, and said nothing.

Seton nodded. "Who cares for these monkish cursings?"

"I do, Sir Alexander — I do!" Bruce answered tightly. "As must you. As must all. You and I may be prepared to defy the Holy See, in this. But that cannot be expected of all the people. Their faith in God is precious, and the Pope God's mouthpiece. *We* may say that his mis-speaks — but others will be less bold. Moreover, this cannot but weaken the authority of Lamberton. It is a grievous matter."

"What then can we do?"

"God knows — save seek to make time. To delay decision. As I have been doing. So far, this is but a threat. We must seek to keep it only that. For so long as we may. Until we can make this Pope think anew . . ."

Both men looked at him blankly, at a loss.

"We can start by sending Prior Adam back to Berwick. For his papers, his letters. We will see that he is delayed. When he finds us again, with them, there will be more delay. We — or *you* — will find them to be wrongly addressed, so that we must debate and consider. Whether to receive them. Then send him, and them, back all the way to Durham. For amendment of superscription. Unopened. Once he is safely out of Scotland, evil men could again waylay the Church's representative — godless men caring nothing for the true religion! Rob him, shamefully destroying the letters, even this Pope's Bull. How say you — without that Bull, can these cardinals act? Make final denunciation? When the Bull has not been read by or to me? Or made known to the people?"

"I' faith — I would say not!"

"Here's a ploy, by the Mass!"

"No ploy, Sir Alexander. It is no game, I promise you. It is deadly earnest. Much may depend on it . . ."

Prior de Newton was detained at Aldcambus two days, and then sent back for his documents — but not before Seton wormed out of him much about the state of Berwick, the people's morale, the unpopularity of the harsh and overbearing governor of the town, Sir John de Witham, and what bad terms he was on with Sir Roger Horsley, governor of the castle. All of which Bruce heard with interest.

But that same evening there were tidings of even more immediate interest. A messenger came from Moray, who latterly had been aiding Douglas with the siege, to the effect that one Peter de Spalding, who claimed to be a kinsman of Sir Robert Keith, the Marischal, in view of the royal proclamation of mercy and in pursuit of a full pardon for past adherence to the English, was prepared to open a section of the town walling adjacent to the Cow Port, to King Robert's forces one night — he apparently being one of the captains thereof.

Keith, summoned, admitted that he had a cousin of sorts a merchant in Berwick, by name Spalding, although he had not heard of him for many a year.

This was news indeed — although there were many who smelled a trap, and the treachery on the wrong foot. But Bruce, with the need to capture this fortress urgent, was prepared to take the chance that it was a genuine offer. He sent Douglas back to the town's outskirts forthwith, with orders to contact this Spalding somehow. He himself would wind up this siege-engine building, and come on with the main force next day.

* * *

The following night, in sleet-laced rain driven by a salt wind of the North Sea, the King rode down the south-facing slope of the Lamberton ridge. The town of Berwick-on-Tweed lay unseen below and before him — for lamp-oil would be scarce in the beleaguered town and no lights showed, although it was not yet midnight. The land ahead, indeed, seemed darker than the sea; an indefinable belt of wan glimmer stretched all along their left flank somewhere, the phosphorescence of breaking combers on an ironbound coast.

It was not an army that Bruce led down the long slow hillside; merely a motley company of lords, knights and men-at-arms, with the carpenters, wrights and smiths who had been constructing the siege-engines. These unwieldy, lumbering machines, dragged by oxen, their axle-trees screaming, their timbers creaking, had greatly delayed the royal progress that day; but they were much more important, in this context, than any thousands of men, and the high-born warriors had just had to summon their patience. Getting the things across the bog and innumerable streams of Coldinghame Moor, for instance, had been a desperate, mud-slaister of a business. Proud lords would have left it to others more suitable for the task, and hurried on to Berwick; but that was not Robert Bruce's way. It had taken them fourteen hours to cover the dozen miles.

They were past Halidon Hill, the last prominence on the long green ridge, and were dropping to the farmstead of Camphill, only a mile from the north-western walls of the town, when suddenly lights began to appear ahead of them, lights that flared and blazed and sank, then blazed again, and at some distance. An indescribable noise also came to them on the south-east wind, rising and falling likewise, but different from the distant thunder of the tide.

"Save us — have they started?" Gilbert Hay cried, at the King's side. "Jamie has not waited for us — for Your Grace?"

"Jamie is in command at Berwick," Bruce reminded. "Yet I would have thought that he would have delayed until I came."

"It may not be the assault. Just some disturbance in the town," Sir Hugh Ross suggested.

"I think not. Those are torches and fires. And at the far side of the town, where this Cow Port lies. Douglas has struck. Come — leave these engines. Irvine will bring them on." And he spurred his mount forward.

A courier met them as the hillside levelled off to the town meadows. "My lord King!" he shouted. "Word from my lord of Douglas. The assault is on. We are into Berwick. Over the walls . . ."

"I have eyes and ears, man! What are Douglas's tidings?"

"These, Sire. That my lord of Dunbar would not wait. Would not abide your royal coming. He and his were stationed to the east of the Cow Port. He must have given the signal. To those within. The three lights, two and one. Without word to my lords of Douglas and Moray, he advanced. Scaled the walls and over. With ease. And so on in."

"Curse the arrogant fool!" the King exclaimed. But it was himself he cursed, in fact; himself others would criticise. For in his efforts to hold together his warring, jealous nobles, he had allowed the Earl of Dunbar and March a command under Douglas. It was, after all, Dunbar's country, his earldom, and he could raise thousands of men hereabouts, in the Merse — *had* raised them, in the past, for the English. Here was opportunity to redeem himself. Instead — this! He was, of course, senior in rank and status to Douglas — although the latter was Warden of the Marches. Even senior to Moray, ranking only second to Fife in the hierarchy of Scotland's great earls, as descendant of Kenneth MacAlpin and the true Celtic line.

As others growled and muttered around him, Bruce rapped out, "And Douglas? And Moray? What of them?"

"With Earl Patrick into the town, my lord needs must follow. Or lose the surprise, lose all. He said to tell Your Grace. My lord of Moray took the left flank, the west. The walls were not defended, not there . . ."

"Aye. This Spalding, then, was honest in his treachery! Enough, then. Lead us down to this part . . ."

The uproar from the town was much louder now, the flames ever growing, heightening, buildings evidently afire. The area of battle was spreading, at least.

They reached the walls in the vicinity of the Cow Port. That great gate was still closed; but scores of scaling ropes and ladders hung from the parapets — and, unlike most siege-scalings, no layer of bodies lay inert at the foot. In the flickering light of the fires, Bruce was one of the first to clamber up.

The scene that met their eyes was dramatic as it was chaotic. All this part of the town was already ablaze, the sea-wind fanning the flames and causing them to leap the narrow lanes and vennels. Against the red and ochre glare, and amidst the rolling smoke-clouds, black figures were silhouetted, running, darting, wrestling, falling. Frequently steel flashed, reflecting the fires. Shouts and fierce laughter, screams and wails, penetrated the roar of the conflagration. Hell had come to Berwick that night!

Frowning, the King eyed it all. This was not as it should be.

Berwick was a Scots town, its greatest seaport, an important part of his realm however grievously it had been forced to co-operate with the enemy. Seventeen thousand had been massacred here by Edward Longshanks, in 1296, as an example to other Scots — hence perhaps the subsequent co-operation. It was no part of the King of Scots' policy to emulate.

"Find me Dunbar. Also Douglas," he ordered his companions. "And command this slaughter to cease. Our enemies are in Berwick Castle, not in this town. Quickly. I shall stand here."

Douglas was first found. He came running, eyes streaming, features blackened with soot. "Thank God you are come, Sire!" he cried, panting. "I can do nothing with the man Dunbar. Earl Patrick. Nor can Thomas. He will have the whole town ablaze. His men are sparing none. They heed no word of mine . . ."

"I have sent for him. This slaughter of citizenry must be stopped. But — the castle, Jamie? What of the castle?"

"Thomas watches it. He holds the Castlegate. That before all else. They have not sought to break out. Into the town. Horsley's garrison. As yet."

"As well! And the other? This Witham? The town governor?"

"I have him. Captured. Drunken, and bedded with a whore. The town is mainly in our hands. A few pockets of Englishry still hold out, but not many. Mainly by the harbour. But, see you, our men are much scattered. Or Dunbar's men are. If there was a sally in force from the castle, and Moray could not hold it, all might yet be lost."

"I know it. Get your men gathered together, Jamie. How many have you?"

"Near 600. Moray has half that."

"And Dunbar?"

"Who knows? Perhaps 1,500."

"Aye. Well, leave Dunbar to me. Gather your men, and reinforce Thomas at the Castlegate. At all cost we must contain Horsley. He has the name of a fighter. And keep the remnants of Witham's force from reaching the castle likewise."

The King waited on the high wall, above the holocaust, where he could be found, while Douglas made off again, to dodge and double, threading his way to avoid the burning streets.

Hay brought the Earl of Dunbar and March to his monarch at length — as High Constable of Scotland his authority was undisputable.

"My lord," Bruce snapped, at once, "I am much displeased. Who gave you leave to burn this my town of Berwick?"

"Your Grace's town of Berwick is a nest of adders that should be smoked out," the other returned coolly. "That I do."

"Douglas commanded here, in my name, as Warden of the Marches. His orders were to spare the town. He has been besieging Berwick for a year — Berwick Castle. As you know well. At any time he could have contrived that the town should burn. Such was not my will. You knew it, my lord. Yet you have chosen to do this. You will tell me why, anon. Meantime, you will halt this folly, this carnage, immediately. Have your men withdrawn. All burning, and slaying of the citizenry to cease. You understand?"

"If you wish Berwick Castle to fall, Sire, you will think again," the Earl declared thinly. "This town protects it like a breastplate. I remove that breastplate for you."

"Silence, sir! Do you debate my commands with me, the King?" Bruce cried. "My lord Constable — see that the Earl of Dunbar calls off his men forthwith. No further delay. Have them assemble at the Salt-market. There is room there."

Bowing stiffly, the Cospatrick was led off.

But it was not so simple as that. Dunbar, it proved, had but little hold over his irregular force of Mersemen, many of whom had old scores to pay in Berwick town. Men inflamed with passion, liquor and rapine were not to be restrained, controlled, assembled, now scattered wide as they were. They continued to run riot, roaming where they would. In his efforts to bring them to heel, the King had to order the detachment of large numbers of Douglas's and Moray's veterans, thus greatly endangering the entire venture. Bruce made his own way through the inferno to the narrow, climbing Castlegate, which rose steeply from the town to the frowning fortress which dominated all from its rocky eminence high above the Tweed. If Sir Roger Horsley and his large garrison chose to clear this Castlegate with volleys of missiles flung from their great slings and mangonels — as they could readily do — and then sallied out in force, the depleted Scots force could by no means hold them. As cork for this bottle, Bruce knew his stopping-power to be quite inadequate.

That Horsley continued to hold his hand was surprising.

All that grim night the situation remained unresolved, with a confusion of fighting in narrow flame-lit streets, as much between Douglas's veterans and Dunbar's local levies as between Scots and English. Yet no break-out was attempted from the castle, no stones and projectiles were hurled down the Castlegate — which even in semi-darkness could not have failed to be effective, so narrow was the gullet. Bruce stood through the long hours, in the throat of the ascent, with a mere handful of men — although trumpet calls could have brought at least a hundred or two others fairly swiftly. Lights shone up at the citadel, but no stir of movement — that same castle where exactly twenty years before Edward Plantagenet had so deliberately humiliated him before Elizabeth, before all, at the Ragman Roll signing.

A chill grey dawn brought no immediate easement, for though the fighting and burning was tailing off, through weariness and satiety rather than any major imposition of discipline, the danger from the castle was heightened, since Horsley could now see how comparatively few he had to deal with; and missile-fire — and worse, arrows — could now be used accurately. But still no sally developed. Gradually Bruce began to breathe more freely. For some reason Horsley did not commit himself. To help matters along, the King ordered much blowing of trumpets from various parts of the smoking town, much unfurling and parading of standards. And he sent an impressive deputation, under the High Constable and the Warden of the Marches, to within hailing distance of the fortress gatehouse, to demand the immediate surrender of this Scots citadel to the King of Scots in person, offering honourable terms and safe conduct for the garrison to Durham. Also he hanged a couple of score of Dunbar's looters and rapers, from beams made to project from Castlegate windows — as much to impress the garrion as to enforce his authority and punish the men, on the principle that any commander who could so afford to deal with his own troops must be very sure of his own strength. The Earl of Dunbar was constrained to officiate at these hangings, for sufficient reason; also it allowed the King to give it out that it was punishment for indiscipline against the Earl's own orders, a face-saving device that was important if this powerful noble was not to be totally estranged and thrown back hereafter into the English arms.

By midday, although there was no response from the fortress to the surrender demand, Bruce was satisfied that there was not now likely to be any break-out. Even with his siege-machines, however, he could not effectively assault the citadel, so secure was its position. But at least it was now cut off from the harbour, as from the town, and from reinforcement and supply by sea and land. Giving orders for such salvage and aid operations as were possible in the unhappy town, the weary and hollow-eyed monarch allowed himself to be persuaded to take a few hours' rest on the late Governor Witham's bed.

Prior Adam de Newton arrived back in Berwick that same morning, having been unaccountably delayed *en route*. His Minorite priory had been spared the flames, and his precious letters and Bull were intact. Wisely he decided that the moment was scarcely ripe for any attempt at presenting them to his difficult liege lord. First things probably came first, and there was ample for priests to do in Berwick-on-Tweed for the moment. The lords Cardinal would surely understand.

* * *

It was not long before Sir Roger Horsley recognised realities, saw that if he had been going to attempt any counter-measures, he had left them too late, and decided to accept the terms of honourable surrender. It said something for the Scots King's reputation, as a man who kept his word, that the Englishmen were prepared to trust to it; for at the last siege of Berwick, Edward of England had likewise offered honourable terms to the Scots castle garrison, after the capture and massacre of the town; and when Douglas's father Sir William, the governor, had submitted on those terms, the Plantagenet had laughed aloud, put him in chains, and sent him to walk, thus, with common jailers, all the way to London, for imprisonment in the Tower—thereby creating more than one deadly enemy. His son, grim-faced, watched the English garrison ride out from the castle and town, swords retained and flags flying, a few days after the fall of Berwick, on their way to Durham; but he made no protest.

Berwick was a tremendous prize, in more than the mere cleansing of the last inch of Scots soil from the invader. It was one of the most renowned fortresses in the two kingdoms, and its loss a damaging blow to English morale. It dominated the Border, and all of Northumberland right to Newcastle. It gave the Scots a first-class seaport. And it endowed them with a mighty collection of warlike engines collected here, springalds, cranes, sows, ballista and the like, such as they had never had before. Above all, of course, Berwick's restoration to Scotland, before the Papal edict anent it had been made public, invalidated the said edict—which was Robert Bruce's urgent preoccupation meantime, in this strange contest of wits with the Holy See.

Ever a believer in striking while the iron was hot, and in order further to demonstrate to the Papal envoys that they were backing a losing side, Bruce sent for his son-in-law, the Steward, to come south with as large a mounted force as he could quickly raise. This, with Douglas's own Border contingent, was to form one of the swift, hard-hitting raiding columns beloved of the King, to stage one more deep penetration of England, for the cardinals' benefit mainly. Douglas and Moray would lead it—for though Bruce dearly would have liked to do so in person, he could not fail to recognise that in his present state of health this would be foolhardy and might endanger more than the operation itself. Walter Stewart would take over the governorship of Berwick meantime.

On learning of these preparations, Master Adam de Newton summoned up his courage and once again presented himself at the King's door, this time complete with his letters and Bull. Sir Alexander Seton received him, as before, turning the sealed letters over in his hands.

"To whom are these sent, Master Prior?" he asked, as though coming new to the whole matter.

"To the King, sir. To King Robert."

"It does not say so. You have failed to address them properly, I fear."

"That was not for me to do, Sir Alexander. I am but the bearer. I cannot change the superscriptions. Nevertheless, they are written to the King, and none other."

"We have but your word for it, man. And you admit that you are but the bearer. I cannot take these to His Grace. All must be in the proper form, for King Robert. It is as much as my neck is worth!"

"But, sir—this is of vital import. This is the voice of Holy Church. From the Holy Father himself."

"The more necessary that it is properly directed and addressed. Take it back, Master Prior. Take it to those who gave it to you."

"I dare not . . ."

"You dare not do other, Sir Priest! It is the King's command. How think you he will look on one of his own subjects who contests his royal decision? In favour of a stranger's?"

"These . . . these are Princes of the Church. The spokesmen of Holy See. They will be very wroth . . ."

"More wroth than The Bruce, angry?"

The other swallowed. "I dare not counter them. They could unpriest me. Their patience is ended."

"Is it so? I wonder? For the man Witham, whose house this was, tells us that King Edward much consoles Their Eminences in their waiting at Durham, in many ways! In especial, he has conferred pensions upon them. Pensions for their lives. Why, think you?"

The Prior shook his head, wordless.

"Go then, Master Newton — and bring back your letters properly inscribed. His Grace will then read them. He does not reject the letters of His Holiness. Only requires that in so important a matter there should be no mistake." Seton shrugged. "If he wrote a letter and sent it to the Bishop John, calling himself Pontiff, at Rome? How then? Would the Pope receive it?"

"I know not. It is not for me to say. But . . . something other is." He drew himself up, as with a physical bracing. "Other than these letters to deliver, I have a second duty. A message to proclaim. To all. A verbal message, Sir Alexander. I have delayed too long in proclaiming it. If King Robert will not hear it, his subjects shall."

He turned. Quite a crowd of citizenry and soldiers had collected, as at any development around the King's house. The Prior raised his hand.

"Hear me, good people — in the name of His Holiness the Blessed John, Pontiff and Vicar of Christ. His Holiness blesses you all. He desires and decrees that a truce of two years' duration is now in force. Between the peoples of Scotland and England, their rulers and councils. In this evil warfare which has shed so much blood, and defiled the fair face of Christendom. His Holiness decrees that none soever, be he named Robert Bruce or other, shall raise hand or sword against the English, from now on, for the space of two years. Nor any at his behest or command . . ."

Newton had been raising his voice as he went on, to counter the murmuring of the crowd. But he got no further than this. The murmur rose to a great and angry shout. The mob surged forward, gesticulating furiously.

With difficulty Seton extricated the alarmed Prior from the outraged crowd, pulled him inside the house and slammed the door. Then he hustled him through the building, past the kitchen premises, and so to its backdoor courtyard, and there ejected him into a lane.

"Off with you Sir Prior, before worse befall you," he said. "Happily, I did not rightly hear your message — which may well have been treasonable, I do very much fear! Thank you your saints that I did not. To Durham with you — and come back better instructed. Quickly — before they find you! See — you have dropped your Bull . . .!"

Master Adam's troubles were far from over, even though he did manage to escape amongst the warren-like burned-out streets of Berwick. Only a few days later, as King Robert rode south-westwards a little way with Douglas and Moray, on the start of their punitive raid into England, news was brought him that the unfortunate Prior had fallen into the hands of more broken men, some way to the south, in the region of Belford, presumably Northumbrians. Heathenish scoundrels, anyway. He had been most roughly used, his servants beaten, and all he had possessed taken from him, even his very clothing, so that he was left to continue his journey to Durham on foot, barefoot, and completely naked — a latter-day martyr, no less.

Gravely the King listened to these shameful tidings, and desisted from making anxious enquiries about the safety of the Prior's precious documents.

Bruce parted from his friends on the banks of the Till near Etal, to turn back for the ford at Coldstream and his return to Dunfermline.

"Go where you will — but take no greater risks than you must," he told them. "This is no invasion, see you, but only a demonstration. Take heed — for I need you both. More than you know. And do not be gone too long."

"How far shall we press, Sire? How far south?" Moray asked.

"I care not — so long as you press south of Durham! I would like to see my lords Cardinal make for London. In a hurry! But not *you* see you! No probing for London, this time. Yorkshire will serve very well. If you seemed to move in eastwards somewhat, once past Durham, so much the better."

Douglas smiled. "Your Grace does not wish a captive Prince of Holy Church?"

"God forbid . . .!"

Chapter Sixteen

St. Andrews had known many stirring occasions in the past, not least Bruce's first real parliament nine years before, after he had completed his conquest of the Highland area, the Rosses and the MacDougalls. But this outdid all. Indeed it was probably Scotland's greatest spectacle and celebration ever, to date, both church and state combining to make it so, each with good reason. William Lamberton was as anxious as his monarch that far-away Rome should hear of this glittering event, be aware of the splendid edifice erected to God's glory and Holy Church's pride, in the ecclesiastical metropolis of Scotland, and to perceive that this far northern kingdom was no rude, impoverished wilderness, inhabited by semi-barbarians, but one of the most ancient, vigorous and cultured nations of Christendom and a strong buttress of Christ's Church. He had even invited the Pope's two representatives, from London, to be present for the occasion — after carefully ascertaining that they had already departed for France, on their way back to Rome, in high dudgeon, following upon their undignified scuttle south from Durham.

Bruce, while equally concerned over this aspect of the business, had further reasons of his own for making the most of events. He, the warrior-king, was at pains now to build up an image of a monarch of peace and prosperity, the father of his people, not just their shield and sword, the patron of things beautiful and enduring — above all, the founder of a dynasty. And his dynasty, obviously, was going to need every support and buttress it could possibly claim. This was his constant preoccupation, these days. Therefore, as well as out of gratitude and love for his friend, he had given Lamberton every available aid and encouragement in the lengthy, at times seemingly hopeless, task of completing the mighty and magnificent cathedral of St. Andrews; and now flung himself wholeheartedly into helping to make the opening and consecrating thereof an occasion which men would speak of for centuries.

To this end all Scotland had come to the grey city in the East Neuk of Fife, at the tip of the promontory between Forth and Tay — or all therein who were of any note, or conceived themselves so to be, apart from the vast numbers who were not. The royal summons had been clear and emphatic. The King had even had Lamberton hold up the celebrations until Douglas and Moray could get back from their successful and extended demonstration sweep of Northern England — and they had had to return from as far away as Skipton in Craven, and Scarborough. Now they were back, triumphant, with no losses to speak of and legendary exploits for their men to boast — as well as vast trains of booty, which had much delayed them, innumerable illustrious and valuable hostages for ransom, and indeed a magnificent collection of church plate, gold and silver vessels, fonts, crucifixes, chalices, lamps, candlesticks and the like, jewelled vestments, and other treasure, as votive offerings for the newly-completed cathedral. Lamberton received this largesse, the cream of apparently no less than eighty minsters, churches, abbeys and monasteries, in Yorkshire and Durham, somewhat doubtfully — and wondered what sort of letters were speeding from Archbishop William Melton of York to the Vatican. But at least all this was probably better installed in the sanctified premises of St. Andrews than decorating rude barons' halls or melted down for money.

Even Walter Steward had taken brief leave of absence for a couple of days from his onerous duties as governor of Berwick-on-Tweed, in order to attend. The King had insisted on this; for one of the secondary objectives of this whole affair was to bring before the people the infant Robert Stewart, Walter's son and Bruce's grandson, second heir to the throne and, in view of Edward Bruce's Irish preoccupations, of growing significance. The boy was now two and a half, a fine, sturdy, laughing child, seeming wholly to take after his very normal father – though Marjory Bruce had been a laughing normal child, indeed a poppet, once.

So, on a day of blustery wind and sunshine and showers, all rainwashed colour and contrasts, at noon two great processions set out into the crowded streets, the King's from the great Augustinian Priory, which he was making his headquarters meantime, and the Primate's from the episcopal castle. At the head of the first, behind a large company of musicians playing stirring airs, Bruce walked, splendid in cloth-of-gold and scarlet beneath the Lion Rampant tabard studded with jewels, bareheaded save for the simple circlet of gold with which he had been crowned at Scone when Scotland could not rise to better. But to compensate, Elizabeth who paced at his side, regal in purple and silver, wore a magnificent crown on her yellow hair, flashing with gems and pearls, especially made for the occasion.

Immediately behind stalked a distinctly embarrassed High Steward, leading his grinning, skipping son at his right hand, and the toddling Princess Matilda at his left — a thing that he would have died rather than be seen doing, for anyone else than his beloved father-in-law who, however, had been smilingly adamant on Elizabeth's advising. And she had been right, for the crowds went wild with delight at the spectacle. Thereafter a nun all in white carried the infant Princess Margaret in her arms.

Next came the heroes, Douglas and Moray, in gold-inlaid half-armour, bearing in the crooks of their right arms gold-plated and engraved jousting helms, plumed with their respective colours — although these latter were only recent replacements of English lord's crests. Sir Gilbert Hay, the High Constable, whose duty and privilege it was always to be close to the monarch, walked with them.

These were followed by the King's sisters and their husbands — Christian, with Sir Andrew Moray of Bothwell, son of the hero of Stirling Bridge, her third spouse and a deal younger than her still highly attractive self; Mary, now Countess of Atholl in her own right, and wed to Sir Alexander Fraser, the Chamberlain; and Matilda, with Sir Hugh Ross.

Alone, after them, grim, sour-faced and clad in little better than rags, for all the world like a witch, hirpled the Countess of Buchan, eyed askance by all yet condemned by none, a woman who had paid a more terrible price than most for that day's celebrations.

The man who, after a noticeable space, stalked next, handsome narrow head held high, weakly chin out-thrust, tongue ever moistening lips, was MacDuff himself, the Countess Isabel's brother—although she would by no means recognise his presence—Earl of Fife and senior magnate of the land, heir of a line older than the dynasty, making his first public appearance since his belated change of allegiance—and unsure of his reception. He led the Earls of Scotland, as was his right—although some of that splendid group would have voted to see him beheaded. But his presence, along with that of many another ex-traitor, represented not only victory for Bruce but the continuity and wholeness of his kingdom. The King's pardon embraced all. Only Mar was missing, Bruce's own nephew and Christian's son, who still preferred Edward of England's service, and was said to love that strange man. The Lord of the Isles strode, a little apart, inevitably.

Sir Alexander Seton, in the scarlet robe of Seneschal and King of Arms, led the resounding company of the lords and barons, with the colourfully-garbed Highland chiefs carefully mixed amongst them—for the King was concerned, as ever, to heal this grievous dichotomy between the Highland and Lowland polities—however much not a few of the proud Scoto-Norman barons resented being coupled with Erse-speaking barbarians with touchy tempers.

There followed the almost unnumbered host of the knights and lairds and sheriffs, the lesser officers of state, the captains and chieftains, far enough behind to have their own band of musicians. Many of these were the veterans of twenty years of grim warfare, hard-bitten, tough, the most seasoned fighting men in all Christendom, with no traitors here. If Robert Bruce could have followed his own choice, it was with these that he would have marched, for it was on their broad shoulders that his throne rested. He had much ado keeping such out of the way of Fife, Menteith and their like. He was at pains to remind them that a kingdom, a realm, was not all composed of heroes and patriots.

Long before all this resplendent throng could emerge from the Priory, the King at its head had met the even more resplendent procession of the clergy, from the episcopal castle. Here was magnificence on an awe-inspiring, dazzling scale, with robes and copes and dalmatics, chasubles and tunicles, stoles, mitres, pastoral staffs and enshrined relics, in every colour under the sun, ablaze with jewels, coruscating, scintillating. Even Bruce was shaken at the magnitude and quality of this splendour, of its wealth and riches. Where had all this been hoarded away, hidden, during the long years of war and want? Certainly the Church had been his most faithful and generous supporter — but it seemed that it had been better able to afford that help than he had realised. Today, Holy Church had come into its own, and something of the accumulated wealth of the centuries was revealed — no doubt deliberately, as part of the lesson to be spelt out.

Even the Primate himself, who usually affected the plainest of garb, was magnificent in brocaded purple velvet, stiff with gold wire and rubies, his fingers sparkling with diamond rings, as, from his litter, he raised them to bless the genuflecting crowds. The King scarcely recognised his worn and shrewdly humorous friend. Behind him paced every bishop in Scotland — if in reality Master John Lindsay could be called Bishop of Glasgow. Bruce, and the Scottish clergy headed by the Primate, had appointed him to succeed old Bishop Wishart, who had died two years previously. But the Pope had refused to confirm; indeed had appointed an English Dominican, one John of Egglescliffe, who, though duly consecrated at the Vatican, had never dared to show his face in Scotland. Amongst all these splendid clerics was the odd shambling figure of the timeless Dewar of the Coigreach, from Strathfillan, wild-looking as ever, hobbling with the aid of St. Fillan's Staff; and, now looking middle-aged, stocky and ill at ease, the Dewar of the Main. Thereafter, Bernard de Linton, Chancellor and Abbot of Arbroath, led the cohort of abbots, mitred and otherwise, priors, deans, archdeacons, prependaries and canons, such as Bruce had not fully realised even existed. When it came to making a demonstration, it seemed, Holy Church required lessons from none.

Fortunately the approach to the cathedral was broad, spacious, and the two processions could proceed side by side without confusion — although the King silenced his musicians in favour of the choir of one hundred singing boys, which preceded the prelates with chanted anthems of heart-breaking sweetness and purity.

Vast, lofty, massive, but perfectly proportioned, the mighty building reared before them, its huge central tower soaring over 200 feet, its steep roofs rivalling its spires, turrets and flying buttresses in their aspiration towards heaven. Cruciform in shape, 350 feet long by 160 feet wide at the transepts, of developing design from Romanesque to first-pointed Gothic, illustrating the 160 years of its building, it was the largest single edifice in the kingdom, and made all the other fourteen churches of the ecclesiastical metropolis look puny, dwarfed.

As they drew near, the great carillon of bells, brought at major expense from the Low Countries, rang out in joyous pealing harmony, vibrant, resonant but clear. And quickly, skilfully, the choir changed and spaced its singing and rhythm so that it blended and fitted into the bells' clangour in extraordinary fashion, something which must have demanded long practice and unlikely patience on the part of impatient boys. To this accompaniment the two processions branched apart again, to enter the mighty building by different doors, the clerics by the chancel to the east, the King's party by the great arched main entrance, deeply recessed and with triumphant wealth of mouldings.

Within, all was calm, hushed, even the filing in of large numbers of not very silent people seeming to create but little stir in the vast quiet of the towering forest of stone. Quite daunting indeed was the effect of it all, the richly ornamented arches crossing and recrossing to seeming infinity above the double rows of stately pillars, the soaring clerestory with triple rows of pointed and mullioned windows above, richly stained, with the brilliant hues of tempera paintings on the walling, lightening any claustrophobic effect of tremendous, overwhelming masonry. From mighty nave, built to hold 3,000, by transepts, choir and chancel to the High Altar, the place combined sheer beauty and strength with transcendent size, to an extraordinary effectiveness. Even David, Bishop of Moray, had to admit that it outdid his own beloved cathedral of Elgin, which hitherto had been called the glory of the kingdom.

The boys had not ceased to sing, and were now climbing winding turnpike stairs within slit-windowed pillars, from which their anthem came in strange, unearthly fashion, to join the ranks of older choristers and musicians who were already installed up there in the three lofty galleries which surmounted the clerestory, with open arcading inwards. To their harmonies, now reinforced by soft instrumental music, Bruce and Elizabeth made their way slowly up through the centre of the nave, to climb the choir and chancel steps to their thrones, set on the right side; while the bishops and senior clergy all but filled the rest of the chancel. Lamberton himself, leaning heavily on his golden pastoral staff, and supported by his acolytes, limped directly to the High Altar. It was ablaze with candles, their flames diffused by the rolling clouds of incense.

It took little under an hour to fill that tremendous place—

although even so it presented no appearance of fullness, so noble were the proportions. Then, as at last the bells ceased their pealing, and in shattering contrast to the sweetly melodious chanting maintained all this time, suddenly the Te Deum crashed out, in splendour, with trumpets, horns, shawms, tambours, cymbals and men's voices, rich, deep, quivering with power. The Service of Thanksgiving, Dedication and Consecration began.

Bruce shook the tears roughly from his eyes. And not for the first time, his wife pretended not to notice. If emotion was an essential part of Robert Bruce, she was prepared to thank God for it.

The praise, prayers, singing and sonorous Latinities had given place to the Primate's address — for it was that, rather than any sermon — when the King's attention was distracted by some small commotion nearby, where a side-door opened from the dormitory, so that the canons might slip in to perform their midnight services. Two newcomers had entered there, no canons but notably richly dressed gallants, though obviously travel-stained. One was already beginning to move towards the throne, when Sir Alexander Seton hurried to halt him. The whispers of altercation could be plainly heard, through the Primate's richly harsh voice speaking on in strange power to be issuing from so gaunt and racked a body.

Bruce frowned — the more so as he suddenly recognised one of the intruders to be Sir William de Soulis, Hereditary Butler of Scotland, Irish Earl of Dundalk.

Sir Alexander, as High Seneschal and Herald King, was clearly urging the visitors to wait, to turn back — but de Soulis would have none of it. All but pushing Seton aside, he shouldered his way round him and came striding towards the King. All around, the ranks of the nobles seethed and stirred.

Bruce, for his friend Lamberton's sake, at this the climax of his career, was not going to allow any unseemly disturbance to break out. With an imperious hand he flicked Seton and the others back, and beckoned de Soulis on — but his brow was black.

The Lord of Liddesdale dropped on one knee at the side of the throne, and reached for the King's hand — but it was snatched away from him.

"Your Grace — hear me!" he exclaimed.

"Hush, man! Quiet!" the monarch jerked, below his breath. "How dare you!"

"Sire — you must listen. I pray you. It is your brother. His Grace, the Lord Edward. His Grace of Ireland. He . . . he is dead."

The King stared, suddenly still, rigid. Elizabeth's hand slipped over to find his wrist, to hold it.

All anywhere near could see that the King had received shattering news. Lamberton himself could not but see it; be very much aware of the interruption; yet he prevailed, in that most difficult of tasks, to keep his voice steady and even and to continue with his celebratory discourse seemingly undisturbed.

"Sire," de Soulis whispered. "You heard? King Edward, your royal brother is killed. Fallen in battle. At Dundalk. A great slaughter. Eight days ago . . ."

"Dear God — dead! Edward dead!"

"Aye, Sire. It was a sore battle. The English, under the Lord John Bermingham, were advancing on Ulster. His Grace moved to meet them. We camped at Tagher, near Dundalk. His Grace would hear nothing but that we attack the enemy — though they were ten to one. He . . . he was one of the first to fall."

"You have brought his body home?"

"Alas, no, Sire. The English — they took it. Dead. They beheaded him. Quartered the body. Sent it as spectacle to four parts of Ireland. The head to be sent to Edward of England . . .!"

"A-a-a-ah!" That strangled sound was not so much a groan as a snarl. And loud enough for many to hear. Even Lamberton paused for a moment in his delivery, brows raised towards the King.

But that last intimation of English savagery had made Robert Bruce himself again, the warrior he had always been rather than the gentler monarch and father of his people he now sought to be. The iron came back into his features, and he raised his head. He caught the Primate's eye, and gave a brief shake of his head to the latter's enquiry, sitting back in his throne, a clear indication that Lamberton should proceed. Still low-voiced, he said to de Soulis:

"Very well, Sir William. I thank you. Of this more anon. You may retire!"

"But, Sire — there is more . . ."

"Later, sir."

It was the other's turn to frown, as he rose, bowed stiffly, and backed away.

The celebrations continued, as planned.

Later, the long service over, and when the processions had wound their colourful way back to their respective bases, a great banquet, masque and dancing was arranged for the evening — more than one indeed, for all walks of men and women. Bruce cancelled none of it. But he did call a hurried Privy Council, for the hour or so intervening, in the refectory of the Augustinian Priory.

It was a larger Council than usual, for practically every member entitled to be present was already in the city. Sir William de Soulis himself was present, in his capacity of Lord of Liddesdale, if not Butler of Scotland.

"My lords," the King said, without preamble, when all were seated, Lamberton himself the last to hobble in. "I grieve to upset this great and auspicious day's doings, and to inconvenience you all thus. But you should know what tidings the Lord of Liddesdale has brought me. Some may already have heard. And to give me your counsel as to the necessary decisions. My brother, the Lord Edward, Earl of Carrick and latterly King of Ireland, is dead. My . . . my brother, the last of four. All slain. By the English. At least he died honourably. On the field of battle. Yet he was dishonoured in his death, in that the enemy's spleen triumphed, even so. They dismembered his body. Cut it up — as they did the others. To exhibit as trophies. Despatched throughout Ireland. His head sent to England. Such, my lords — such are they with whom His Holiness of Rome makes cause! These to whom he would have us submit!"

In the hubbub that followed the King waited set-faced. Then he banged on the refectory table.

"My lords — may I remind you that this is a Council, not a wives' gossip!" he declared, with a harshness that had not been heard in his voice for long. "My lord Edward's death I shall mourn, in my own way. We were not close. We much disagreed. But we were brothers. But — that is my business. Not this Council's. What is, is twofold, and to be considered herewith. The Lord Edward was appointed by parliament first heir to my throne. It therefore becomes necessary for parliament to appoint anew. For my bodily health is not of the best, and I need remind none that the succession is all-important." He caught Lamberton's eye, and the older man shook his head almost imperceptibly.

"So this Privy Council must guide parliament in the matter. A parliament to be called as soon as may be possible. As you know, forty days' notice is required. But effective decision cannot wait so long. So decide, my lords." He paused. "Secondly — there is to decide what to do about the Scots forces still remaining in Ireland. They are not so many, but still some thousands . . ."

"Sire," de Soulis interrupted — and men, however distinguished in blood or position, did not interrupt their sovereign. "They are fewer than that. Fewer than you think. For they were all at this battle. The spearhead of the King's army. Two thousand and more. Few now are alive. Of any degree, noble or simple."

Every eye stared at him.

"All are dead. My cousin, Sir John de Soulis. Sir Philip de Moubray, Sir John Stewart of Jedburgh, my lord Steward's cousin, Sir Fergus of Ardrossan. Ramsay of Auchterhouse . . ."

"Christ's mercy! All these — my good friends! How came they all to die, man? Here must have been utter folly!"

"The English were strong in cavalry. They were commanded by the Lord John Bermingham. With many notable captains. Sir Miles Verdon, Sir Hugh Tripton, Sir John Maupas. He it was who slew the King. I, and others, urged that we should retire. But His Grace must attack. They outnumbered us ten to one. The Irish levies fled. The King fell, early. The Scots would not flee. They died there, around their King."

"A-a-aye! God rest their souls! The brave ones. My men. But — the waste! The folly of it. Men who had fought with me on a score of fields. To die so!"

"They died honourably, Sire. Choosing death with their monarch."

"No, sir. Not their monarch. Their leader, perhaps their friend. But the Lord Edward was not their monarch. These were subjects of *mine*. I say that here was waste and folly. As was all the Irish adventure. But — what matter? They died. And you, sir, did not!"

"Eh . . .?" De Soulis blinked, and flushed. "What means Your Grace?"

"What I say. These, you said, chose death with the Lord Edward. *You* did not, it seems, Sir William!"

"By God's good providence I was preservd. Unhorsed in a charge. Stunned. Led off the field by my esquire. And so preserved. I seem to mind Your Grace in similar case at Methven!"

"That is true. I stand rebuked. My claim is that these stout friends of mine, old friends — their deaths were waste, folly. You say not — yet you were less foolish. I commend your wisdom in this, at least!"

"Your Grace is not doubting my courage? My honour?"

"Your courage — no, sir. Your honour — who knows? It is a chancy commodity, honour! It is concerned with more than battles, Sir William. You have been privy to much that was against my interests — you, my Butler. You ever supported my brother in his Irish follies — against my known wishes. You worked against my lord of Moray, my lieutenant, sent to Ireland to guide my brother.

Your courage I do not doubt, sir — but let us leave honour out of this!"

De Soulis had half risen from his bench, glaring. It was most plain how these two men disliked each other.

"Sire — I do protest!" he exclaimed. "You wrong me, in more than in my honour. Without cause. Moreover, you miscall me. I would remind you that I am a peer of the realm of Ireland. Earl of Dundalk. I would request that you style me so!"

"Sir William de Soulis," Bruce grated, "in this realm of Scotland, you are Lord of Liddesdale — by my good favour. You are Hereditary Butler — by my good favour. These, and nothing else. You have not surrendered your Scots citizenship. Or not to me. For Irish. Or you would not be sitting at this Council. Do you wish to do so?" That was rapped out.

The other sat back, biting his lip. He had great lands in Liddesdale and the South-West March. And his new Irish lands were already overrun by the English. "No, Sire," he said, thickly.

"Very well. Remember it. Remember also that at my Privy Council I expect to receive counsel. Not bickering and disrespect. In this realm no man trades words with the monarch — save in a privy chamber. Now — let us proceed, my lords. It seems that there is little that may be done anent bringing back of the Scots force from Ireland. Though what can be done, must. Therefore, our immediate concern is this of the succession."

"My good liege lord," Lamberton said, at once, "I speak for all when I say that we all do most deeply grieve for you in the loss of your royal brother. This, the last of your brothers. He was a brave man, and a mighty fighter. As are all of your race. He was perhaps over-bold. But who here will judge him, in that? Is it Your Grace's wish that this night's feasting and masque be set aside, in mourning? For the heir to your throne?"

"I think not, my lord," Bruce answered. "I know — or knew — my brother, passing well, whatever our differences. His failings were those of a high spirit and a light heart. He would never wish this great day's celebrations to be curtailed — he who would most have found them to his taste. Nor do I believe it right. This day we celebrate not only the completion of a large work in God's name and to His Glory, but the final freeing of this realm from the invader. After the fourth part of a century, no enemy English foot defiles our soil. To this end Edward Bruce laboured, fought and suffered as much as did Robert. As have done so many. All here — or most! Therefore, since this day will not come again, let there be no damping of its joy. So Edward would say — of that

I am sure. And all those, our friends, who died with Edward. So say I. Let all proceed. Now — to this sore matter of the succession."

"Lord King." Again it was William Lamberton who spoke. "I think it no such sore matter — by Your Grace's leave. All sorrow that your royal health has in some measure suffered the price of a score of years of war and privation. But it is none so ill that we must conceive the appointment of a successor to your throne to be of urgency. God willing, you will reign over us for long years yet. I pray you not to conceive otherwise."

Again the two men's eyes met, sharing their grim secret, as all around men cried acclaim and agreement.

"You have much recovered, Sir King, since your return from Ireland. Do not tell me that Robert Bruce has become fearful for his body, like some old woman — for I'll not believe it!" Only Angus Og would have dared to speak thus to the monarch, even with a smile, the independent Prince of the Isles.

"His Grace was more sick than you know, my lord," Moray declared stiffly. "Even though he was concerned to hide it from all."

Bruce glanced quickly at his nephew. He was a keen and observant man. Could he possibly know? Have guessed?

"I am less young than once I was," he said, shortly. "Sickness that in a younger man might be thrown off, might serve me less lightly now. I desire the succession to be settled."

There was a pause. Then Gilbert Hay spoke.

"Is there indeed any choice, Sire? Lacking a son from your own loins — which, pray God, may still be — there is only your grandson, the child Robert Stewart. No other of the royal line survives. Since the Lord Edward had no lawful issue."

The old Earl of Ross was not asleep after all. He cleared his throat, and looked at his son, Sir Hugh. Edward Bruce had indeed a son, by their daughter and sister, the Lady Isabella Ross — only he had omitted to wed her. As he had omitted to wed that other, the Lady Isabel de Strathbogie, the forfeited Earl of Atholl's sister, to the realm's cost. Neither of the Rosses spoke.

"There is surely more choice than this?" James Douglas pointed out. "Your Grace has two fine daughters. Although the realm has never had a queen-regnant — save for she who died at Orkney, the little Maid of Norway who never ascended the throne — is there aught to make such Queen impossible? Other realms have had such monarchs. Must Scotland be different?"

There was a muttering round that table, from many. Clearly it was an unpopular suggestion — although it was like loyal and devoted Jamie Douglas to have made it, for his liege's sake. And Elizabeth's.

When none actually raised voice to speak against it, Douglas reiterated, "I say is there aught against it? In fact? Other than prejudice? If, as God forbid, we should have a child as monarch, does it matter so greatly if the child is a female? Either would require sound guardians, regents. Does the law of this land say otherwise? I know little of these matters, of rights and laws of succession. My lord Primate — can you tell us?"

Lamberton spread his hands. "It is scarcely a matter of law or right, Sir James. I see it as a matter of choice. Two concerns bear on our decision — or, on parliament's, for we only do advise parliament on this issue. One concern is what is best for the realm. The other is His Grace's own desires. I agree that, as an infant, a princess might serve as well as a prince. But infants grow apace. And in a nation which must ever fight for its survival, a Queen would serve less well, I fear. And there comes the thorny question of marriage, and a new male strain to the dynasty. Too many would seek to supply it! A realm with a young Queen to marry, could be endangered, a bone of contention for dogs to fight over."

"There are dogs a-plenty to fight for this bone, it seems — Queen or none!"

"My lords," Bruce intervened. "I have thought much on this matter, in the past. I believe there is a side to it which we must needs consider. It may be as my lord Bishop says, that the succession is not a matter of right, of law. But I think that there is guidance, at least. Consider. My style and title is not as that of the King of England. Or the King of France. Or of Norway. I am, for better or worse, the King of Scots. Not the King of Scotland. Here is more than the mere form of words. It is so because of our ancient Celtic polity. From which this crown descends. Never forget it, when you think of Highlands and Lowlands. It was the Celtic support, which saved me, and the realm, at our lowest fortunes." And the King glanced over at the Lord of the Isles, Sir Colin Campbell, and other Highland chiefs present.

"In that language," he went on, "I am *Ard Righ. Ard Righ nan Albannach*, High King of the Scots. As in the Irish polity — also Celtic. And if High King, or King of Kings, there must be lower kings. In Ireland they so call themselves. Here, this has not been our custom. Save in the Isles. And in Man. The great Earls of Scotland were our lesser kings — the Seven Earls. But now more.

All the land was divided between these. The *Ard Righ* was appointed by them, his line sustained by them. But, unlike the monarchs of other lands, the *land* of Scotland was not the High King's. It was, and is, that of the lesser kings, or earls, who support him. As an Earl himself, he has his own lands — but as King, no. So he is not King of Scotland, but of Scots. The people of the land, not the land itself."

Men nodded. "It is both the strength and the weakness of your throne, Sire," Bishop Moray said.

"Perhaps. But all this you know. It bears, however, on this of the succession. Our kingship is different — as you say, in some matters weaker than others. The *Ard Righ,* if he rests on the support of his earls, and other lords, must be their choice, their representative. Hence this Council; hence parliament's decision. And if this is our ancient custom, then it follows that the succession is one of *choice,* within the royal line. And where there is doubt, as here, the choice should be such as the lesser kings would select to be their strong right arm. Therefore, I say, it should be of a man, a male, a prince, where possible. As it ever has been hitherto."

There was a murmur of agreement.

"Spoken like a Bruce, Sire!" Malcolm, Earl of Lennox declared — as one of the original Seven Earls. "Your grandsire said the same. When Alexander, of blessed memory, lost his son and there was no heir. Save the princess in Norway. Your grandsire claimed to be named heir. Until a prince might be born. King Alexander acceding."

Bruce nodded. "So be it. We nominate to parliament, to be held so soon as may be, the child Robert Stewart, son to the High Steward, as first heir to the throne."

"Lacking a son to Your Grace," David of Moray put in. "But with regents. Good regents. Governors. Two. Other, my lord Steward, than yourself. I mean no disrespect. But this is necessary."

"I say the same, my lord Bishop," Walter Stewart agreed readily.

"What two better than my nephew, Thomas of Moray? And the good Sir James Douglas?" the King said. "In their strong hands Scotland would be safe."

Approval for that was fairly general — although inevitably some frowned or looked blank.

De Soulis spoke again. "And, Sire — what if the child Robert Stewart dies? Bairns are fragile stuff on which to build a kingdom! What then?"

Men, who had sat back, thankful for the business to be over, turned frowning faces on the Butler, annoyed that the thing should be further dragged out.

"The boy is lusty. That can wait," Angus Og jerked.

"Have you other suggestion, my lord of Liddesdale?" Bruce asked level-voiced.

"I would but remind this Council, Sire, that there are more strings to the royal lute, in Scotland, than that of Bruce. If male heir is to be found."

There were not a few indrawn breaths, at that.

"So Edward Longshanks took pains to show, at the Competition. In 1292," the King acknowledged grimly. "Do you wish another such contest for the throne?"

"By God — no!"

"A mercy — not that!"

"Better a Queen than that!"

"Are you crazy-mad, man . . .?"

When de Soulis could make himself heard above the outcry, florid features empurpled, he said, "I made no such suggestion. I but reminded the Council of a fact. If a man to rule Scotland is vital, there are men to consider. With the blood-royal in their veins."

"Comyns . . .?"

"Traitors!"

"Who, man — who?"

Bruce raised his hand. "We shall not forget it, Sir William," he assured, carefully.

Others were less calm, restive, scowling, eyeing each other.

"I move that we proceed to the next business, Sire," Lamberton said.

"Is there more business, my lord Primate?"

"It may scarcely be Council business. But it is of interest to all here, and should be made known throughout the realm. The two Cardinals, before they left England, I am informed, made pronouncement of excommunication against Your Grace, and against all who supported you. This latter, I say, was not within their power to do, without my knowledge and agreement. *I* represent Holy Church in this realm. And I support Your Grace to the full. No Cardinal, or other than the Pontiff himself, can excommunicate me, as Primate. Or over-rule me within my province. Therefore this pronunciamento is faulty. Faulty in one respect, faulty in all. It is to be ignored. These are my instructions, as Primate."

Bruce actually smiled. "I thank you, my lord Bishop. We all do, I vow. Not only that you remove such great weight from our souls.

But that you end this Council on a light note. All shall hear of this. I thank you all, my lords, for your attendance and your advice. Let us now resume our celebrations. And mourn the Lord Edward, in our private chambers, anon . . ."

Chapter Seventeen

Robert Bruce wondered how many times he had sat thus, in the saddle, at the head of a company of grim-faced armed men, great or small, and gazed southwards across the Borderline into England. How often they had looked, dreading what would sooner or later bear down on them from over there, the great enemy hosts, intent on the annihilation of Scotland. Lately, of course, it had been rather the other way, and it would be the folk over there, south of Tweed, Esk or Solway, who must dread and quake when the smaller but faster lines of steel appeared on the Scottish slopes. How much longer, he asked himself? How long before proud, stubborn men, in York and London and Rome, would accept hard facts, recognise his kingship, and come to a peace conference? How much longer before he could lay down his sword?

Not that July night of 1319, at any rate. It was still the unsheathed sword. The only question was in which direction to wield it. Along the gentle ridge of Paxton, above Tweed, only five miles west of Berwick, they waited, the great Scots cavalry host, stretched out along the escarpment behind Bruce for a full mile, ten thousand armed and horsed men, silent, menacing, the largest raiding-force that he had ever mounted. Waited for James Douglas, as the grey summer night settled on land and sea.

They had moved south through Lothian and the Lammermuirs and into the Merse, by quiet, little-known passes, by Garvald and Spartleton Edge and Cranshaws. At Edrom, Jamie had left them, four hours earlier, and raced ahead with half a dozen of his own mosstroopers. None knew Berwick and vicinity, nowadays, so well as the Douglas. He had spies and informants scattered all around the area. Jamie would gain the information they required, if anybody could. He had promised to bring tidings to the King, here at Paxton, by an hour before midnight. He was almost an hour late. Ten thousand men fretted and fidgeted.

"Shall I take a troop? To seek him?" the Earl of Moray asked, at his uncle's elbow. "I know many of the places where he would go. To gain news . . ."

"I think Jamie would scarce thank you, Thomas!" Bruce answered. "To play nurse. Give him time."

"He should have taken more men," Gilbert Hay, at the other side, declared. "He should be less rash. More careful of himself."

"Less rash? Gibbie, we are getting old when we talk so! James Douglas remains young at heart."

"So did my uncle, the Lord Edward!" Moray murmured.

"No, Thomas. I said young of heart. Not young of head! Jamie's head is not so young. He will not take undue risks. And sound tidings we must have."

"You fear the King of England may have learned cunning, with the years?" Fraser the Chamberlain asked.

"No, Sandy. Edward of Carnarvon will never learn cunning. It is the loyalty, or otherwise, of his lords, that concerns me. Notably one — Lancaster. That man's behaviour, of royal birth and five Earls in one as he is, could change all at this juncture. I must know his dispositions."

Edward of England, stung by the loss of Berwick, the repeated Scots raids deep into his kingdom, and the Cardinals' failed mission, had not proceeded to a peace-treaty, but had raised a new army and marched north to retake Berwick-on-Tweed, summoning all his northern vassals to support him there. But his unpopularity was as great as ever, as even in the days of Piers Gaveston — for he had elevated new favourites, the Despensers. The northern lords looked towards Lancaster as their leader. If Lancaster came to join his monarch before Berwick, as commanded, then the Scots host, tough and potent as it was, would look puny.

"Lancaster hates King Edward — all men know," Fraser was saying, when the drumming of hooves silenced him. All heads turned in an easterly direction.

It was Douglas and his half-dozen, lathered in horse-spume.

"My sorrow that I have kept you waiting, Sire," he exclaimed, panting. "But the English have got two great rings around the town. Earthworks. A double circumvallum. Thick with men. Winning through these is no light matter. It took time . . ."

"Double earthworks? That bespeaks many men."

"Many, yes. Too many. Lancaster is come. He has joined the King. With unnumbered thousands. He came but yesterday."

"A curse on it! I had hoped . . ." Bruce frowned. "Did you learn anything of numbers, Jamie?"

"Not that I could rely on. The King may have brought some 20,000. But Lancaster and the northern lords have many more."

"And you say that they have dug these trenches and banks. All round the town?"

"Save at the harbour, yes. The King's force did that. He has brought a host of foreigners, Low Country men, versed in siege war. With many great and strange engines and devices, I am told. He intends to have Berwick again. At all costs. The Steward must be sleeping but poorly!"

"Perhaps. But I am more concerned for ourselves than for Walter! Our own attack. These trenches and earthworks may have been dug to encircle the town. But equally, they will protect the besiegers against ourselves. To assail the English dug into these, their spearmen and archers, with our smaller force — and that cavalry — would be folly. That way lies disaster."

"So fear I. With Lancaster's host on the flank. To sweep us up," Douglas agreed. "We cannot do this by assault, Sire."

"What, then?" Hay demanded. "Must we sit and besiege the besiegers? Call for more men?"

"The English could call up more men more readily than could we," Moray pointed out. "There are more of them nearer at hand."

"They have brought a fleet of ships, with their siege engines, into the harbour," Douglas went on. "These also are a danger."

"I much fear ..." Moray was saying, when the King cut him short.

"Fear nothing, Thomas," he said. "This is not the way. I have not come so far to throw my people into hopeless slaughter. As it would be. No — we adopt the other project. We seek to draw King Edward off, since he is too strongly placed for us to fight. Or *you* do. For this will take too long for me to be away from Dunfermline. You and Jamie will take the road south, once more."

To none did Bruce have to explain why he wanted to get back to Dunfermline quickly. The Queen was pregnant again, and nearing her time. The King was on edge, for more reasons than he would admit. This time it might be a son. But Elizabeth was getting past normal child-bearing age. And what effect might his sickness have on any issue now . . .?

Douglas nodded. "Gladly. How far south this time?"

"York, I think, will serve."

"Would not further serve better, Sire? To draw King Edward after us?" Douglas suggested. "The nearer to London we win, the better. The South will lie unprotected, with his armies here."

"Perhaps. But York should suffice, I think. I have word that

Edward's Queen, Isabella, is presently there. He left her at York when he marched north."

"Ha! You mean . . .?"

"I mean that, unlike the English, I do not usually make war against women. But this lady, taken into your custody for a little — or even the threat thereof — would, I believe, fetch Edward south promptly, and shorten the siege of Berwick more swiftly than any other means."

James Douglas slapped his saddle-bow gleefully. But Moray shook his upright handsome head.

"I do not like it, Sire," he said.

"Of course you do not like it, Thomas! It conflicts with your honour— well known to us all! But it could, nevertheless, save many lives. Thousands, it may be. Perhaps this city itself."

"It was *your* honour, Sire, that I was considering — not my own," his nephew answered stiffly. "This they would hold to your blame. Not mine. Or the Douglas's."

"I could thole it! Jamie — I fear this must be your especial task, then. Unless you also scruple?"

"It shall be my delight. I have heard that the lady is . . . generous!"

"Aye. That is why I jalouse that her husband will hasten south when he hears! But, on your return, remember Lancaster. He may seek to cut you off." The King paused. "There is another matter that might bear on this. William Lamberton tells me that Archbishop Melton is now holding some great gathering of his priests at York — synod, convocation, chapter, I know not what. Churchmen have much sway with Edward. This may also help to bring him south."

"We shall attend on their deliberations, with pleasure!" Douglas nodded, grinning.

"How many men do we take?" Moray asked, rather emphasising the pronoun.

"Take all. I will go with you as far as my lordship of Tynedale. To Wark Castle. It is important that I treat it as part of my realm of Scotland. Receive fealties and homage, conduct an assize, show my writ to run there, as monarch. Something to bargain with, when I bring Edward to the peace-table. From there, I shall return to Dunfermline. And expect you both to rejoin me within the month."

"So soon, Sire . . .?"

"So soon. I want Walter Stewart relieved quickly — since the English have these especial siege-engines. He may not be able to withstand them. So what you do must be done swiftly, or it may be to no profit. It is not a campaign that I send you on, but a single stroke. You are not going south to fight battles, only to draw Edward of Carnarvon away from Berwick. I am weary of bloodshed — even English blood. I want these thousands of stout lads back, my friends. Is that understood?"

The great mounted force moved on, quietly, down to the ford of Tweed.

* * *

Two weeks and a day later, again at midnight, in the bedroom which had been Queen Margaret's above the plunging ravine of Pittendreich, where her four fine sons had been born, all to be Kings of Scots, her descendant watched his wife in labour, and suffered each pang with her. He would not leave the chamber though she urged him to, and cursed the physicians and midwives as bungling incompetents. Emotionally wrought up, he equally cursed his own uselessness — and possibly, by his sheer helpless invalidity may have somewhat aided Elizabeth by distracting her from her pains.

When, after a moderately short labour, the child was born, a boy, and dead, Bruce was a stricken man. He left the bedchamber at last, set-faced, and went to lock himself into his own room.

Something had told him that this would be the son on which he had set his heart. Head in hands now, he crouched at the window, staring out into the blue night. Accursed, excommunicate, rejected of God, the refrain beat in his brain. And behind it all the still more ominous word, leper, leper . . .

It was that word which presently sent him hurrying back to his wife's chamber. It was not to Elizabeth's side that he went, however, but to the cot where the pathetic bundle lay inert, silent. Snatching up his son, he tore off the blood-soaked wrappings and carried the tiny, wrinkled, naked body over to a lamp, there to peer and examine.

From the great bed Elizabeth raised her voice, tired, husky. "What . . . what do you, Robert? I am sorry, sorry, my love. Again I have failed you. But — why torture yourself so?"

"I look . . . to see . . . if the finger of God . . . is on him also!" her husband grated. "The mark of my sin! To see if . . . if there is . . ."

"Hush Robert!" Despite her weakness and the sweat that started from her brow, Elizabeth de Burgh sat up. "Say it not, I charge you!" That was as good as a command. She looked warningly towards the women who still remained in the room. And as he paid no heed, and went on muttering, she deliberately swept down a goblet of wine which stood untasted on a table beside her bed. It fell with a crash.

That startled him. He transferred his stare to herself. Then curtly he dismissed the women, and laying the child down came to her side.

"I am sorry, lass," he said, his voice sane again. "Forgive me." He took her hand.

"Robert — you must watch your words," she chided, sinking back on her pillow. "You might have let out, before all, your fear, your *wicked* fear!" For that strong woman, there was near-hysteria in her voice. "It is not so, I tell you. This has become a madness with you. Let the evil word once fall from your lips, into the ears of others, and hell itself will engulf Scotland. Hell, I tell you!"

"Hell, perchance, is here already!" he answered grimly. Then he shook his head. "But I will not say the word, Elizabeth my heart. Content you. God forgive me — if He has any forgiveness for such as Robert Bruce — I will act this out, keep silent. And thereby, it may be, further burden my soul. With others smitten, perhaps, from me."

"No! No, my dear — it cannot be so. Do not rack yourself so. If you were indeed . . . unclean, would not I now be so also? I, who share your very bed? Could I have escaped? And are others like to be smitten when I, your wife, am not? I tell you and tell you — your sickness is not what you fear. It is but a scurvy, an affliction of the skin, or some such. It cannot be the evil thing. You have been better these past months. Much better . . ."

"The redness is still there. I still sweat . . ."

"Yes. But in yourself you are stronger. More as you were. Think you I do not watch you? You cannot deny that you are better. Could it be so if it was what you dread?"

"I do not know. I am no physician. But those that I saw in Ireland were just as am I." He looked towards the cot. "And the child was born dead." Flatly, tonelessly, he said it.

"And are not other children born dead, Robert, and their sires in good health? Your own sister Mary bore one such. And my brother Richard. Oh, my dear — I am sorry, sorry for this death. Your son. *Our* son. After so long." She was panting with exhaustion. "But there was no mark on the child? No flaw? Was there? The women said it."

"No," he admitted. "No mark."

"You must see that you are wrong, my dear. Our daughters — they are both well. Perfect. Fine children. Yet they both were born since you have had this sickness. I pray you, put it from you. This fear . . ." Her voice tailed off, and her eyes closed, wearily.

He looked down on those heavy-lidded, blue-circled eyes, with sudden great compassion, and kneeled there beside her bed. "Oh, lassie, lassie," he said. "Here I cark and lament — while you suffer. You are worn, done, my sweet, needing my help, my strength. And I but make moan! Forgive, Elizabeth . . ."

"I . . . I am not done, Robert," she whispered. "Not yet." Her hand came out to touch his hair. "I will give you a son, yet — God willing. A living son. You will see . . ."

* * *

James Douglas and Thomas of Moray failed to conform to orders by exactly one week — which was accounted for by the vast amount of booty they brought back with them from Yorkshire, which had delayed them. Apart from that, they could claim that the expedition had been a success, indeed a triumph — even though they had not managed to capture Queen Isabella.

"She escaped us by a single day," Douglas told his monarch, who had come out to meet his friends at the foot of the palace hill. "She was warned, and fled to Nottingham from York." He glanced sidelong. "I have not charged my lord Earl with sending the warning — but who knows!"

Moray was not much of a smiler, but he at least raised his eyebrows. "My lord of Douglas was inconsolable," he said. "Yet, from all accounts, he should thank me. The lady would have devoured him quite, so tender a morsel!"

Despite their differences of character and outlook, these two were good friends, and the most able and effective joint commanders in Christendom.

"Yet Berwick was saved?" Bruce said, an arm linked with each, as they climbed the hill. "Walter Stewart sent me word, ten days back, that the siege was raised and King Edward gone."

"Yes. Perhaps the Chapter was even more effective a draw than his Queen!" Douglas suggested.

"The Chapter . . .?"

"Aye, Sire — we have been keeping strange company since we parted from you. You mind the convocation you told us of? At York? We were constrained to take some part." Douglas chuckled. "We made debate with their spiritual lordships and eminences! They are naming it, we heard, the Chapter of Myton!"

"A plague on you, man!" the King cried. "Enough of this — or I will have you both clapped in the pit on charge of *lèse-majestié*! Out with it? What happened?"

"Heed him not, Uncle," Moray advised. "As I do not. He has been deranged since his disappointment over the English Queen! The matter is simple. King Edward having scoured the North of England for soldiers to take to Berwick, there were none left at York to oppose us. Save churchmen and their soft levies. The Archbishop, at least, did not flee, with the Queen. He is a man, that — if something of a fool in the matter of warfare! He raised a motley host of clerks — bishops, abbots, monks, priests, acolytes and the like, with their servants, and sallied out to contest our passage. At a place called Myton-on-Swale, east of Boroughbridge, they sought to give battle."

"William of Melton, did that? He chose to fight? Fight the two most redoubtable captains in these islands!"

"Aye, Sire — he might almost have been a *Scots* bishop!" Douglas put in. "Only, had he been so, he would have known better how to fight, I swear! His flock were as sheep to the slaughter."

"Save us — did you have to do it? Slaughter them?" It was at Moray that Bruce looked.

"We had little choice. There were great thousands of them — and more dangerous in their flight than in their fight! They streamed across a bridge, to our side of the river — and then quickly decided that they were better back on their own side. Some of our people had set some stacks of hay afire, and the smoke confused them . . ."

"You would have thought that priests would have been at home in smoke, incense!" the irrepressible Douglas asserted. "Naught would do but that they all should be back across the river. The bridge would not take them — since I held it — so they must needs swim! In future, clerks should learn to swim!"

"I think you make more of this than you ought, Jamie?" the King said. "Is it your conscience troubling you?"

"Conscience, Sire? Why, we were picking them out on our lancepoints! Never have I seen such urge to the water. Nor such panic. The Gaderene Swine were not to be compared with the priests of York! More drowned than died in fight — but more still died of fright, I do believe! Of stopped clerkly hearts! It was a sight to be seen. And — we loaded a thousand horses with their spoil. It seems that they thought to fight more with golden crucifixes and croziers than with swords!"

The Queen, almost recovered, met them at the palace entrance.

"Welcome back, my heroes!" she greeted. "I have missed you both. As has His Grace. Did all go well?"

"Your heroes have been distinguishing themselves by slaying priests. Not one, or two, but a host, it seems. A shameful massacre. God knows what they were at!"

"We spared all we could," Douglas protested. "They died like flies in a frost. There was no stopping them."

Bruce shook his head over his friends. "How many? How many died?"

Douglas glanced over at Moray. "Four thousand," he admitted.

"Dear Christ-God!"

"Not all priests and the like," the other hastened to assert. "The mayor and burgesses of York were there likewise. And their trainbands."

"Fit foes for Douglas and Moray!"

"There were more than 20,000 of them, Sire. What could we do . . .?"

"We restrained our men as best we could," Moray put in. "But the confusion caused by the panic of so many was worse than anything I have ever seen."

"Did many great ones fall? Bishops, abbots and the like?"

"Some were wounded. Many roughly handled. But I do not think that many died," Douglas said. "They were the nimblest at escaping, first back across the bridge. We captured the Bishop of Ely—but he ransomed himself quickly and most generously, having a high opinion of his own worth!"

"Aye. You may smile, Jamie. But we are in bad enough odour with the Holy See, as it is. How think you the Pope will look on this? How will it be recounted to him? Not as panic and folly, but as a terrible and sacrilegious slaughter by the godless and rebellious Scots. The cry will ascend to heaven itself! For a year and more I have been at pains to fend off the Vatican's assaults and anathemas. Yet to preserve a face of respect and worship of Christ's Vicar. And now . . .!"

"His Holiness may perhaps be placated," Elizabeth put in, "by a display of the King of Scots' generosity and liberality towards Holy Church. Not Holy Church in Scotland or in England, but in Rome! Laying up treasure in heaven is, I am sure, his prime concern. But treasure on earth has its value also! You gained great spoil from this clerical host, you say, Sir James? Why not send part of it to His Holiness? As token of your humble faith and loyal worship?"

Moray swallowed, the King stroked his chin, and Douglas burst into laughter.

"By the Mass," he cried, "Your Grace has the rights of it! Here's a ploy! A selection of crosses, croziers and reliquaries — even Saint Etheldreda's thigh-bone! What more apt? Better than handing all over to Master Lamberton!"

"I do not like it," Moray objected. "It smacks of blasphemy, of irreverence . . ."

"Tush, man — leave such to the priests," Bruce told him. "It is their business, smelling out the like. It might serve — it might well serve. At least to give us time. Bless you, my dear! We will reinforce our envoys at Rome with a train-load of treasure-on-earth from Yorkshire. But I think not Ely's bone. To be of value, that must be named — and might prove a bone of contention indeed, an embarrassment. Even to His Holiness. But — come, my heart. You should be seated. You are not wholly yourself yet. You must preserve your strength . . ."

The two younger men hastened to apologise, to offer arms, to all but carry the Queen indoors between them.

"I am sorry, Sire. About the child," Douglas said, over his shoulder. "It was a sore blow. A prince at last — and then . . ."

"God's will be done," Moray said.

It was Elizabeth who answered, not Bruce. "We shall test God's will again," she declared. "Let us pray, with greater success."

There was a pause. Then Bruce rather abruptly changed the subject.

"Lancaster did not intercept you, on your road home?" he asked.

"Not Lancaster, no. King Edward himself sought to do so — but we eluded him by striking westwards. Across the hills," Moray answered. "Saddled as we were with booty and prisoners, we were in no state to meet him. Besides, we had Your Grace's command."

"I am glad that you remembered it. Even belatedly!"

Hurriedly Douglas spoke up. "Lancaster was not there, Sire. Prisoners told us that he had quarrelled with King Edward. When the news of our raiding southwards, and our defeat of the Archbishop's host, reached Berwick, there was trouble in the King's camp. Lancaster had words with him. Probably he would have had him march south with him. Or continue the siege alone. Whatever the cause, he marched off to the south-west, to his own territories, taking near half the force with him. But he gave *us* no trouble."

"Aye. There is a lesson there, for any monarch!" Bruce nodded grimly. "Too great and powerful a noble. Of the king's own blood. On such, a realm may founder. You note it, Earl of Moray and Lord of Nithsdale?"

His nephew looked shocked. "*Me*, Uncle? You do not suggest ...? I am your loyalist servant ..."

Bruce laid a hand on the other's arm. "I know it, Thomas. I but cozen you. Nevertheless, you heard de Soulis, at that last Council. There are other strings to the Scots lute than Bruce, he said. It behoves us not to forget ..."

Chapter Eighteen

It was to be doubted whether the old Dewar of the Coigreach fully understood the honour that was being done him. Certainly he did not appreciate it. But then, he was a very ancient man, now, and had always been difficult; though far from senile, he was distinctly set in his strange ways, and found anything new deplorable. His next junior, the Dewar of the Main, probably had not the wits fully to grasp the significance of the occasion; but at least he approved of his fine new clothes, and the handsome croft of land he had been granted further down the glen. He was cheerful now, if a little drunk, and indeed adopting a definitely superior if not patronising attitude to the other three Dewars of Saint Fillan, custodians of the Mazer, the Bell and the somewhat mysterious *Fearg*—which, being wholly encased in silver was of unstated composition but the greater worth. These three had done nothing to aid Bruce in his hour of need, preferring to follow their chief, Patrick MacNab of that ilk, Hereditary Abbot of Glendochart, who was a kinsman of MacDougall of Lorn, and so pro-Comyn and anti-Bruce. The King had forfeited MacNab, after Bannockburn, and given his barony to Sir Alexander Menzies of Weem, a loyal supporter. However, the three junior Dewars, hereditary custodians of the other relics of St. Fillan, were in a different case. Humble enough men of the hills, however significant their office in the old Celtic polity, it was unthinkable that the Abbey of Glendochart should be reconstituted without their presence—or, at least, the presence of their relics, from which of course they were by no means to be parted. So there they were, hanging about in a wary and somewhat suspicious group, scarcely prepared to believe that they all had been forgiven and indeed granted crofts likewise, for the maintenance of their office, out of the former MacNab lands — for they were now dignified as prebendaries or canons of the restored Abbey.

For that was what was being done this blowy spring day of sun and shower of the year 1320; reconstituting the ancient Culdee Abbey of Glendochart. It had taken nearly six years to see this fulfilment of Bruce's vow, taken before Bannockburn, that if he had the victory that vital day, he would renew this renowned shrine of the Celtic Church. Building such a place, comparatively modest an ecclesiastical establishment as it was, in such a remote Highland glen, had been slow and difficult, especially with so much else on the King's mind. At Bannockburn, the Dewar of the Main had carried his relic, the saint's arm-bone in its silver reliquary, ever close to Bruce and so in the thickest of the battle. The King, excommunicated by Rome but blessed in despite by the strange representatives of the former Celtic Church, was now showing his gratitude.

Although the Culdee Church was long gone as an entity — Queen Margaret had seen to that, in her burning zeal for Rome — the memory of it and its practices and attitudes was by no means lost, especially in the Highlands, where it was an undying influence. After all, it had flourished for 700 years, and as late as 1272 it had retained an establishment at St. Brides, Abernethy, the old capital. Therefore, this restoration was not wholly an anachronism, however much the Romish clerics felt bound to frown on it. Glendochart could not now be a Culdee establishment in fact, of course, since no such persuasion existed any more, even in Ireland. But Bruce had done the best he could, setting the Abbey up as part of the Augustinian Order, the nearest in attitude and sympathies to the Celtic ideas of worship. Moreover he was placing it under the general supervision of Abbot Maurice of Inchaffray, now Bishop of Aberdeen nominally, but not confirmed by the Pope, a fighting cleric of similar spirit — who indeed had been the young Dewar's mentor at Bannockburn, fighting and praying as lustily.

So, in the same green glen of Strathfillan, under the towering and still snow-capped giants of Ben More and Stobinian, where fourteen years before the fugitives had worshipped in the cabin-like chapel, and then gone out to their defeat at Dalrigh at the hands of MacDougall, the King and Queen now with a great company, splendid but almost wholly secular, watched Abbot Maurice consecrate the new chapel and bless the new and simply-pleasing whitewashed conventual buildings; supported by the five Dewars, however out of place and uneasy they seemed. All was done in the open air — for three good reasons; the new place of worship would not hold one-tenth of the company; the Celtic Church had always been very partial to the open air, caring little for buildings; and this would tend to prevent any embarrassment to such clerics as were present and who might lack Maurice of Inchaffray's rugged independence of spirit. Most, of course, had diplomatically been engaged otherwise this March day. Even Bishop David of Moray, who had been one of those present fourteen years before — although even then he had refused to enter the chapel — found it reasonable to absent himself.

The fact was that this was wholly Bruce's affair, and he was glad enough to excuse the Romish clergy. In essence, it was but a way of saying thank-you to the strange creature who had blessed him when no other would or could — perhaps saving his reason at the same time — and who later had equally saved his life by getting him across Loch Lomond when trapped by his foes. He owed a lot to the Dewar of the Coigreach and his Saint Fillan. The fact that the saint's Gaelic name was *Faolain an Lobhar*, Fillan the Leper, was very much to the point — though some doubted if this was the same Fillan.

So a highly unorthodox consecration service was followed by an outdoor celebration of the Eucharist, dispensing both elements to all who would partake, in the old Celtic fashion, using fistula to suck up the wine. Thereafter a banquet was spread there beside the rushing peat-brown river beneath the mountains. The people of Strathfillan, Glen Dochart, Glen Falloch and other surrounding valleys, were there to watch and participate, along with the more splendid folk of the Court and nobility. Even Patrick MacNab himself was there, from the rump of his lands up on Tayside, forgiven but by no means restored; for he was still Hereditary Abbot of Glendochart, to the Highlanders. And there was the MacGregor, too, Chief of the Children of the Mist, who had surprised all by re-appearing from Ireland, after being presumed dead at Dundalk, lame now but very much alive, and more fiercely proud than ever.

It was on this scene of *al fresco* feasting, after the ceremonies, that another abbot appeared, Bernard of Arbroath, Chancellor of the realm. De Linton was fattening up nicely with the years and responsibility, as was entirely suitable for so important a prelate; but the eager brown eyes were still those of the young vicar who had acted Bruce's chaplain and secretary on many a rough and bloody campaign.

"You have timed your arrival nicely, i' faith," the king greeted him smiling. "All the sacrileges and barbarous rites are now safely past. Yet you are not too late to partake of the provender! Holy Church may now unbend!"

The Abbot coughed. "I fear not, Sire," he said, low-voiced. "Holy Church is scarcely unbending yet! From further afield than Abroath. Or St. Andrews. That is why I am here now. May I have Your Grace's private ear?"

Head ashake, the King took him aside.

"A nuncio has arrived at Dunfermline, Sire. Unannounced. From Rome. Or, at least, from Avignon. From His Holiness, personally. He landed at Dysart, and the first we knew, he was chapping at your palace door, in Dunfermline. No Cardinal this, but a papal secretary. Bearing no letter addressed, or mis-addressed, to any. Carrying instead an open paper, a pronunciamento signed and sealed by Pope John, declaring that he is there to speak with the voice of the Supreme Pontiff."

"M'mmm. So Pope John learns cunning! We have taught him this, at least!"

"We have taught him only the *need* for cunning, Sire. Nothing else. For the nuncio is directed to pronounce, from the Cathedral of St. Andrews, the excommunication not only of your royal person, but of all and sundry who support you, clergy as well as lay. Not only so, but my lords Bishop of St. Andrews, Dunkeld, Aberdeen and Moray, are especially cited as excommunicate. It is, therefore, the entire realm which he is to declare excommunicate. Without question or delay. In the name of the Vicar of Christ and God's Vice-regent."

"The bishops! The whole realm! Surely not?"

"The whole realm, Sire."

"But, 'fore God — this is impossible! The clergy, too? They are part of the realm, yes. But can it be so? It means *you*, man! You support me. It means every priest. And Lamberton. By the Rude, he cannot excommunicate Lamberton! The Primate. This cannot be."

"The nuncio is specific. There is no mistake. The Scottish realm *is* excommunicate, in its entirety, since it supports Your Grace. Already is, since the anathema was pronounced at Rome before the nuncio left. He is but to acquaint us. Not only so, but His Holiness has commanded the Archbishop of York, and the Bishops of London and Carlisle, to repeat the excommunication on every Sabbath and saint's day throughout the year. Against every man, woman and child, clergy and laity, of this people. Until, as he says, we submit and put ourselves under the proper rule and governance of King Edward of England, as Lord Paramount of Scotland."

King stared at Chancellor, for once at a loss. "The folly of it!" he cried. "The wicked, purblind folly! Here is heresy, surely? To pronounce such sentence. Even for the Pope. He cannot do it."

"He has done it, Sire. And who may declare that the Holy Father himself commits heresy? Not you. Nor I. Nor any man. Since the Pope it is who rules what is heresy and what is not."

"But to excommunicate, to cut off the sacraments from a whole nation. Including its bishops and priests. For the sins of one man. Or what he claims are sins, in his ignorance. Ignorance — that is what it is. Are we to be at the mercy of one man's blind ignorance? The eternal souls of a whole nation endangered because this Frenchman in Avignon does not know the truth? Believes English lies. Are we, man? Are we?"

De Linton spread his hands helplessly. "The Pope, ignorant or other, is still the Pope, the voice of Christ on earth . . ."

"You say that? This is blasphemy, man! Would you make Christ-God a liar also? Make him speak lies, trumpet forth the falsehoods of men? Watch *your* words, I charge you!" the King cried, his voice shaking.

Robert Bruce, in anger, was a terrifying sight. De Linton actually backed away. All around, eyes watched the pair anxiously, not knowing the trouble but concerned.

The King took fierce grip of himself, turning to pace a few steps away and back. "What says Lamberton to this?" he demanded thickly, at last.

The other could barely find words. "I . . . I do not know, Sire. I sent word to him. As I came here, to tell Your Grace. The nuncio — the nuncio himself was for St. Andrews. When he discovered you absent. I know not what my lord Bishop will say . . ."

"William Lamberton will not take kindly to being excommunicate! Dear God — have you considered what this means, my lord Abbot? It means that neither he, nor you, nor any priest who supports me — and that should be every priest in this land — may give or receive the sacraments! Does it not? If you are excommunicate yourselves, you are, indeed, no longer priests. You are no longer Abbot of Arbroath. Lamberton no longer Bishop of St. Andrews, or Primate of Scotland. Save us — the thing is beyond all in madness!"

"Such thoughts have not escaped me, Sire. I have had ample time to think of them, riding here from Dunfermline." De Linton was recovering.

"M'mm. No doubt. Forgive me, my friend, if I spoke you too harshly. But — what are we to do?"

"We can only do the one thing, Sire. Labour to change the Pope's mind. So that he withdraws this anathema."

"At least, you do not suggest obeying him! Submitting, as humbled rebels, to the English."

The other drew himself up. "Did you think that I would, my lord King? I, or any?"

"No, Bernard — I did not. But changing the Pope's mind will be a sore task, I fear. And long. He is set against us. Our envoys to Avignon have not moved him. Nor our treasure, sent in October. Although he has not sent it back! What else can we do?"

"I was thinking, as I rode here. Of more than the consequences, Sire. We could send him a letter. Not your Grace — for that he would reject. But the whole community of the realm of Scotland. A letter from the nation. Signed by all who have any authority in this kingdom . . ."

"A letter? Is he going to heed a letter, at this pass? A piece of paper? You know how we treated *his* letters!"

"This would be more than a letter, Sire. A statement of a people. A declaration. The signed declaration of a nation. His Holiness could scarce ignore such. Not if it was signed and sealed by hundreds, great and small. You said that he had acted in ignorance. That the Pope was ignorant of the true facts of our independence as an ancient realm. Let us inform him, then. Let us dispel his ignorance, declare the truth of our history and our polity. That we have never been subject to the English, or any other in Christendom. That we love freedom above all things, and will submit to none. Though we would be friends with all."

Bruce eyed the younger man, in his eagerness, keenly. "Think you he would read it? Heed it? Where silver-voiced envoys, and silver in treasure have failed?"

"I believe that he might. Pope Boniface heeded the letter of the English barons against us, in 1301. This would be better, greater, the voice of a people. If the names of a whole realm subscribe it. Never before has there been such a letter, I think. From so many. His Holiness could not but heed it."

Bruce shrugged. "I am less sanguine, I fear. But it is worth the attempt. It can do no harm. And I can think of nothing else we may do. But . . . how shall we get men to subscribe it? This will be difficult. If we could hold a parliament . . . But there is no time for that. Since a parliament requires forty days of warning. We cannot wait. Yet a Privy Council would not serve, I think."

"No. It must be greater than that. Councils are of picked men. Our enemies would say that such men are creatures of Your Grace. To be of value, this must stand for all your realm. Not just Your Grace's friends. A Convention? Would not that serve? Not a parliament, but a Convention of the Estates. A meeting. Call such forthwith, Sire. And if we do not have sufficient attending, we can have others to sign elsewhere. In their homes, if need be."

"Aye, a Convention. You have it. And for another matter also. I need something of the sort. Too many lords and chiefs are coming to blows over who has what lands in this realm. During the years of war, many have won or taken themselves lands. Many of one faction or the other. Those who held them formerly dispute. There is much bad blood. Even here, this morning in Glen Dochart, Sir Alexander Menzies and the MacGregor, both my friends, all but had their swords drawn. Over a mere parcel of land in Glen Falloch. A Convention called to settle such matters. An assize of lands, before judges. All holders of disputed land to show by what title they hold them. Then, when they are assembled — this letter. They will come — for lands! There is nothing like a little soil and rock to bring men out of their chimney-corners! See that this matter is made known, my lord Chancellor."

"Gladly, Sire. It is well thought on. It is excellent reason for calling a Convention. So we shall have no lack of signatories."

"Draw up some such letter for all to sign, then, my friend. Word it so that the Pope learns how well-established and ancient is our kingdom, how long our line of kings. How ever we have been independent. And how freedom is our very life. That above all. For if freedom fall, all falls. Say that no power on earth shall make us subservient to the English — and the powers of heaven would not try! Say that if I, the King, were to countenance any such subservience, the realm would drive me from its throne. To my proper deserts. Tell the Pope that, Bernard. Write it down. And then bring it all to me, that I may approve it. And to Lamberton also. His is a wise head."

"With all my heart, Sire. And this Convention? Where shall it be held? And when?"

"So soon as may be. So soon as messengers can carry the word. We must not delay — or the country will be in a turmoil. Unless your priests will reject the Pope's anathema, and dispense Mass as before. Will they?"

Abbot Bernard looked unhappy. "Not . . . not on their own authority, Sire. That would be apostasy indeed. Not to be countenanced. But . . . it is not for me to decide. I am but an abbot. This is for the Primate."

"The excommunicated Primate! Yes, it is Lamberton's business. I must see him quickly. But the need for haste, in the matter of the Convention, is the more evident. Seven days? Ten? Can it be done?"

"It must, Sire. And where?"

"Not at Dunfermline. Nor yet at St. Andrews. I do not wish to meet this nuncio. Yourself avoid him — since he claims to speak with the Pope's voice. I have promised to attend young Scrymgeour's marriage, at Dundee, on St. Ambrose's Day. That is eight days from now. Make it there, at Dundee."

"My abbey of Arbroath, Sire, is nearby. Accept the hospitality of my house for this meeting. It is larger than any in Dundee."

"Ah, yes, my princely abbot! So it is. Next to Dunfermline, the greatest abbey in the land. So be it. Call the Convention for Arbroath, the day following St. Ambrose's Day, the day after the wedding . . ." The King paused, blinking. "Dear God!" he said, "Can there *be* any such wedding? Lamberton was to officiate. But if he is excommunicate? If you all are excommunicate? Must we stop marrying now? And burying? As well as Mass?"

Abbot Bernard wagged his head, lost in consternation.

* * *

William Lamberton was made of sterner stuff, ecclesiastically, than Bernard de Linton. Or perhaps it was but that he had more experience of churchmen's politics. At any rate, he celebrated young Scrymgeour's nuptials as planned, before a great and splendid if somewhat uneasy congregation. But he did more. After the bride and groom had passed out of the Church of St. Mary, Nethergate, for the banquet to be held in the Greyfriars Monastery, the Primate, with the royal permission, asked the congregation to remain a little longer. And there, from his throne, in full canonicals, he read out a curious announcement, his harsh voice resonant with great authority.

The pronunciamento of the Papal Nuncio from the Cathedral of St. Andrews no doubt had been heard by all, he said. He himself had listened to it sadly. But as senior bishop and Primate of this realm, it was his simple duty to advise his flock on the situation. He had consulted with other bishops, and now made declaration that, while he, and the whole Scottish Church, was in most filial obedience to the Holy See in all things, there was, at this present time, some dispute as to the position and validity of its present incumbent. His Eminence the former Monsignor Jacques d'Euse, hitherto Archbishop of Avignon, and these past three years styled Pope John the Twenty-second.

After a sort of corporate gasp, not a sound was heard from that huge company, every eye fixed in an apprehensive fascination on the bent wreck of a man up there beside the High Altar.

The dispute was on two grounds, Lamberton proceeded. One, that being forced by French might to dwell in Avignon, not in Rome, the said John was indeed under the pressure and influence of the King of France, who at this time was in alliance with the King of England. And so unable properly to exercise due rule and justice within Holy Church. And two, that he had himself been declared heretic by certain authorities for maintaining the doctrine that the blessed do not in fact enjoy the vision of God until their resurrection, contrary to the teachings of the fathers. Until these doubts and disputes were resolved therefore, he personally, William, Primate of Scotland, could not accept any sentences of excommunication, or other assaults upon his spiritual authority, not specifically promulgated by the College of Cardinals in full consistory court — which he learned from the Papal Nuncio aforementioned had not been done.

The long sigh of breath exhaled was like a wind over a heather hillside, as the company perceived relief, remission, at least a temporary lifting of the dark shadow which had come to loom over their lives.

It was inconceivable, in the circumstances, that church government and worship of God should be allowed to break down, Lamberton rasped, at his sternest. In consequence he required all bishops, priests and deacons, all abbots, priors, friars and monks, all who owed obedience to himself in this Province of Holy Church in Scotland, to continue steadfast in their said offices, to perform their full duties, and to ignore all utterances and commands from other ecclesiastical authorities than himself. On *his* head, heart and conscience, rested the full responsibility. And so, let all go forth, in God's peace, from that place.

They all went forth indeed, but hardly in God's peace.

That night, after the feasting at Dundee, Bruce, Elizabeth and the Primate sat together alone in the abbot's study of the vast Abbey of Arbroath, over a well-doing fire of logs, grateful for the warmth after the long ride in the face of a chill wind off the North Sea. They waited while Abbot Bernard went to fetch the papers of his draft of the projected letter to the Pope. It was their first opportunity for private talk that day.

"How dear did that announcement in St. Mary's cost you this day, old friend?" the King asked. "It was as brave a deed as any I have known. Braver than any done on a field of battle. To take upon yourself, your own shoulders, the entire burden of this rejection of the Pope's commands and anathema. To accept the responsibility for a whole nation's disobedience to the Holy See, to the head of the Church you represent. This was truly great, truly noble William. I know of no other who would have dared it."

"Noble is scarce the word I would use, Robert my liege," Lamberton said, shaking his grey head. "What I did was expedient, lacking in scruple, cynical, maybe. But not noble."

"Yet you perhaps jeopardised your own soul to do it. For the nation. That is, if you believe what you profess."

"Aye — and there's the rub! Do I, William Lamberton, believe what I profess? Sometimes, I confess to you, my friends, I do wonder! I fear that I have become but a wavering leader of this flock."

"Wavering? After today? I would I had more such waverers!"

"Wavering in what I believe, and should teach others, Robert. Which is no state for a bishop to be in. The older I grow, I find, the less of accepted doctrine I truly respect. Save for the faith of Christ crucified. And the all-embracing love of God."

"Is that not enough?" Elizabeth asked quietly.

"For you, perhaps. For most. But — for me? For the Primate? The foremost representative of the One, Holy, Catholic and Apostolic Church, in this land? The fount of doctrine, the source of dogma? I would not have our nuncio, or indeed any priest anywhere, to hear me say it!"

"Perhaps you do not altogether accept the doctrine of a papal infallibility!" Bruce observed gravely. "Even if the said Pope is truly Pope."

The other looked into the fire, as gravely. "Would my liege lord have me to burn as an heretic? To deny so essential, so vital, a doctrine!"

"Deny nothing, then. But . . . I think you do *not* indeed consider that you have placed your immortal soul in jeopardy, by this day's work?"

"My soul, I fear, has been in jeopardy all my days! For my many sins. But such faith as I cling to assures me that Christ's sacrifice and God's infinity mercy are sufficient to save it, nevertheless." Lamberton raised his head. "But, see you — this of the Pope's position. I but prevaricated, quibbled, there at Dundee. God forgive me. This Pope is truly Pope — of that there is no real doubt. His residence at Avignon is by his own choice, not by *force majeure*. Even though the Curia does not like it. And he is said now to be much less hot on his doctrine of resurrected bliss. Moreover, such would not invalidate his appointment, whatever Philip de Valois may say. No — I but used subterfuge, used these things to gain time, to soothe anxieties, to enable the rule and charge of the Church in this land to continue. To have accepted the papal ban would have meant the breakdown, not only of the Church, but of all Christ's work, in Scotland. Therefore I did what I did. But there is no substance in my doubts as to His Holinesss' authority — as many of the clergy at least must know. And the College of Cardinals will endorse Pope John's anathema — nothing is more sure. Unless we can change their minds. And his. We have but gained a breathing space."

"A costly breathing space for you, William — which we must use to good advantage. This of the letter — de Linton's letter. The declaration, from all the realm. You think well of it?"

"Well, indeed — very well. So be it that it says the right things. And is signed by the right people."

"The *right* people? Not all the people? That is, the people who have any rule and authority in the realm?"

"That as a principle, yes. But in fact we must be careful. To give His Holiness no excuse to ignore it. By including signatures which he must reject."

"*Must* reject?"

"Must, yes. He may have no relations with an excommunicate. Therefore excommunicate's signature on such letter could be held to invalidate it, I fear. He has, in a fashion, excommunicated the entire nation. But that is different, a mere form. Those who have been excommunicated by name — these should not sign. Your royal self. Myself. The Bishops of Moray and Dunkeld and Aberdeen. These, I fear, he could reject as offensive, in the present circumstance. And therefore claim that he could not read or accept the letter."

"I had never thought to sign it," Bruce said. "Since it is from my subjects, not myself. But you? If you and the other senior bishops do not sign, it could be claimed that there was division amongst the clergy. That the most important might not be in favour of what was written."

"True. I think, therefore, that *no* clergy should sign. Let it be a letter from the temporality of Scotland. It might have the more force. Seem less of a disobedience to the Church's supreme Pontiff. See you — the clergy have already sent a manifesto to the Vatican, on the subject of Your Grace's right to the crown. From Dundee. In 1309. Asserting Scots independence. This new declaration would come better from the laity. It could be couched in stronger terms than would be seemly for the clergy to use towards their Pontiff!"

"That is true . . ."

Abbot Bernard came back with a great sheaf of paper. "I fear that there is overmuch writing here, Your Graces," he apologised "A great plethora of words. But there is so much to be said. So many matters to cover. I have written and scored and written again. Many times. I cannot make it shorter, with all said. Your Grace, and my lord Bishop, may do better than my poor efforts . . ."

He spread his papers out on the table, and lit a second lamp. "Here is the start:

"To the most Holy Father in Christ our Lord, the Lord John, by Divine Providence, of the Holy Roman and Catholic Church Supreme Pontiff, his humble and devoted sons and servants, the earls, bishops, barons, abbots, priors, priests, freeholders and whole community of the Kingdom of Scotland, send all manner of filial reverence with devout kisses of your blessed feet . . ."

"Not servants, my friends—not servants," Bruce intervened. "Sons, perhaps. Sons in God. But I will not have my good Scots subjects servants to any. Not even to myself! And is it necessary to kiss the man's feet? If the Lord Christ Himself was content to *wash* others' feet, I do not see why we should kiss the Pope's."

"In letters to the Pontiff it is the customary style," Lamberton said. "No doubt it is fulsome, unsuitable. But this he expects. And it costs us little—since the signatories will never have to do it!" And, as the King shrugged acceptance, "But this of bishops and priests, my good Bernard. His Grace and I have come to decision that this letter should not seem to come from the clergy at all. Only the temporality. To avoid sundry pitfalls. It will lose nothing thereby, and be the less rebellious towards His Holiness. And after your devoted sons, I would leave space for the names of the signatories. Rather than have all signed and sealed at the end only. It must needs be a long letter, as you say. Therefore, to ensure that His Holiness reads it, he should know from the start the quality of the signatories."

"As you will, my lord . . ."

The Queen spoke. "But, my friends—do you forget? If it is not the priests and clergy who sign, then most of the barons and lairds will not be able to sign, at all! Since they cannot write. Only make marks and append their seals."

Bruce smiled. "Trust a woman to see the thing clearly!" he commended. "It is true. In the main it will not be signatures we send. But names, written by clerks. With their seals. The more reason, then, to have the names at the start. But, proceed, my lord Chancellor."

"Yes. I then recite something of the history of our race, as recounted by the books and chronicles of ancient writers. How our nation came out of Scythia and through the Mediterranean Sea, by Spain, to Ireland. And thence 1,200 years after the outgoing of the people of Israel, acquired for themselves the land of the Picts and Britons in Dalriada, naming it Scotland, from their one-time princess. And how, from then, we have had 113 kings . . ."

"Save us — have we indeed? So many?"

De Linton coughed. "So the chroniclers and seannachies have it, Sire. And who am I to disprove it? Since it is our concern to convince His Holiness of the ancient establishment and continuing independence of our realm. Do you wish this altered?"

"No, no. By no means. The more the better. Save that most of them must have been heathens!"

"Aye, Sire — I have considered that. I put it thus:

". . . 113 of their own royal stock, no stranger intervening, have reigned, whose nobility and merits, if they were not clear otherwise, yet shine out plainly enough from this that the Kings of Kings even our Lord Jesus Christ, after his passion and resurrection, called them, though situated at the uttermost parts of the earth, almost the first to His most holy faith, nor would have them confirmed in this faith by any one less than His first Apostle, although in rank second or third . . ."

The Abbot paused. "I walk warily here — for, of course, His Holiness occupies the throne of St. Peter . . ."

"Very wise, Bernard," Lamberton nodded, straight-faced. "Precedence is most important!"

"Yes, my lord. So I say:

". . . to wit, Andrew the most meek brother of St. Peter, whom He would have always preside over them as their Patron. Moreover the most holy fathers, your predecessors, considering these things with anxious mind, endowed the said kingdom and people, with many favours and very many privileges. So that our nation,

under their protection, has hitherto continued free and peaceful, until that prince, the mighty King of the English, Edward the father of him who now is, under the semblance of a friend and ally, in most unfriendlywise harassed our kingdom, then without a head, and unaccustomed to wars and attacks . . ."

"I would put in there that we were guiltless of offence towards Edward," the Primate said. "That it be clear that the English invasion was wholly one of aggression by Edward."

"To be sure. So:

"The injuries, slaughters, and deeds of violence, plunderings, burnings, imprisonments of prelates, firing of monasteries, spoliations and murders of men of religion . . ."

Abbot Bernard looked apologetic. "You understand, Sire, why I stress that Christ's Church suffered so greatly? It must be made clear to His Holiness that the English are the enemies of the Church, not its friends."

"The point does not escape me, friend. But—I think that we might leave all this of history to yourself. Let us on to the point of today."

"I come to that now, Sire. To where Your Grace comes into it. I say:

"From these evils innumerable, by the help of Him who, after wounding, heals and restores to health, we were freed by our most gallant Prince, King and Lord, our Lord Robert who, to rescue his people and heritage from the hands of their enemies, like another Maccabaeus or Joshua, endured toil and weariness, hunger and danger, with cheerful mind . . ."

"I swear we could dispense with that . . .!"

"No, Robert," Elizabeth declared. "That must go in. It is no more than the truth. My Maccabaeus! My Joshua!"

"M'mmm. Proceed then, my friend."

"Him also the Divine Providence and, according to our laws and customs which we will maintain even to the death, the succession of right and the due consent and assent of us all, have made our Prince and King; to whom, we, for the defence of our liberty, are bound, and are determined in all things to adhere. But, if he were to desist from what he has begun . . ."

The Chancellor's voice tailed away, as he swallowed, and looked up apprehensively.

"Well, man? Go on. What will you do if I desist in my duty? I told you to make it clear that the freedom of the realm is above all things precious. Be not mealy-mouthed in this."

"Aye, Sire. But it sounds ill, coming from your most leal servant. I put it so:

"If he were to desist from what he has begun, wishing to subject us or our kingdom to the King of England or the English, we would immediately endeavour to expel him as our enemy, and the subverter of his own rights and ours. And make another our king who should be able to defend us."

Appalled, de Linton looked at his liege lord.

"Bravo! Well said, my lord Abbot! This is simplest truth. Look not so like a dog expecting a whipping, man! If this letter is to mean anything, it must declare without a doubt that the Scots make their own masters, and that freedom is all."

"That is what I say next, Sire:

"For, so long as a hundred of us remain alive, we never will in any degree be subject to the dominion of the English. Since it is not for glory, riches or honours we fight, but for liberty alone, which no good man loses but with his life."

There was a brief silence in that lamp-lit room, as the words burned themselves into their consciousness. Then Bruce actually rose from his seat, and put his hand on de Linton's shoulder.

"I thank you, Bernard, for those words," he said, his voice thick. "No man spoke nobler, or truer. Here indeed is the message which we declare. Not only to this Pope, but to all Christendom, to all men everywhere. I thank you. And I thank God that I chose you to write this letter!"

"Amen," Lamberton added, simply.

Quite overcome, the younger man shook his head.

"Abbot Bernard," Elizabeth said gently. "You make me wish that I was born a Scot, I vow!"

Bruce cleared his throat. "After that, my friend, the rest cannot but suffer descent, decreasement. Read no more. But tell us the sense of what remains."

"There is still much, Sire. Perhaps too much. For I am wordy, I fear. But we have to make our needs and requests clear. I therefore beseech His Holiness, who must be no respecter of persons, to admonish and exhort the King of England to desire no more than his own, and to leave us in peace. I say that it derogates from His Holiness himself if any part of the Church suffers eclipse or scandal — as does this part, in Scotland, through English avarice and lust for power. And I urge, Sire, that he, His Holiness, rather stir up the Princes of Christendom to better warfare than attacking their weaker Christian brethren, by leading a great crusade against the heathen, for the succour of the Holy Land — to which, if the English will leave us in peace, we will adhere with our whole strength. And the King of England also be able to aid the better, for not warring with us!"

"Splendid! Excellent!" Bruce cried. "Here is shrewd work, indeed. Is that not sharp steel, William? Your Pope can scarce deny that — since he has declared such crusade to be his aim and ambition. Master Bernard has him there!"

"It is a notable thrust, yes. I say I served Your Grace well when I recommended this young man to be your secretary. Is this your closing note, Bernard?"

"Not quite, my lord Bishop. I . . . I have made very bold in this letter, already. Regarding His Grace. But this was on his own royal command. I make very bold again. If your lordship thinks too bold, I will score it through. But . . . in the name of this people and nation I have seen fit to rebuke His Holiness. Is this apostasy?"

"I shall tell you, friend, when I hear it. But, to my mind, His Holiness could perhaps do with some rebuke! What say you?"

"I finish by declaring that . . . where is it? Here it is:

"that if trusting too much the reports of the English, Your Holiness do not give to this implicit belief, and abstain from favouring them, to our confusion, then the loss of life, the ruin of souls, and other evils that will follow, will we believe be laid to your charge by the Most High!"

He looked up. "Is it . . . is it too much?"

The King slapped the table-top, making the heap of papers jump. "By God, it is not! Apostasy, or what you name it, it may be. But it is true, and just, and requires to be said. You are a bold priest, Bernard de Linton — but praise the saints for it! Let it stand."

Lamberton nodded. "Never before have I heard a cleric, even Abbot of Arbroath, charge the Supreme Pontiff with the ruin of souls!" he observed. "But it is not before time for Pope John, I think. I almost wish that I was signing this declaration after all!"

"I say that it makes a most splendid end to a splendid letter," the Queen added. "You are a priest after a de Burgh's heart!"

The King pushed the papers away. "Better than anything I could have asked for," he said. "But, now — how best to gain the necessary superscriptions and seals? After tomorrow's Convention, my lord Chancellor, I will have you to read aloud this letter to the assembled company. I will declare that its every word meets with my approval. And you, my lord Primate — will you say likewise? Then, I will ask if any present makes objection to any of it. Not this word or that, or we should spend the day at it. But with its sense and purpose. I cannot believe that any will speak contrary. Then I shall ask that all who will put their names to it, affix their seals. It will take time, so many. But your clerks will see to that. No clergy, but all earls, lords, barons and freeholders, in their due order."

"All, Sire? Surely not all?" de Linton protested. "You would not wish certain names on this letter, I think? Those of traitors. Men who have worked against you . . ."

"There you are wrong, my friend. This is a letter from the realm of Scotland. The whole realm. Therefore all of any degree must subscribe to it, friends or unfriends. If it is headed, as it should be, by Duncan MacDuff, Earl of Fife, premier earl and noble of this land, whom all know is no supporter of mine, so much the more effective a letter it is. Is it not so?"

"Indeed it is," the Bishop agreed. "I have no doubt but that His Holiness at Avignon knows well enough who are Your Grace's unfriends. Yet, I think, the said unfriends will not refuse their names tomorrow! That would be next to proclaiming their continuing treason and treachery. Moreover, not only will this test their new-found loyalty, but it will serve as a chain to bind them to Your Grace hereafter. Their seals and superscriptions on this great document. Do you not see it?"

"Ah, yes. Yes — you old fox! This I had not thought on. But it is so. Only — this letter will go to Avignon. To the Pope. So I will not hold those seals and superscriptions."

"Then there must be two copies. Sire. One to be sent, and one to hold in your Chancery. Both subscribed and sealed. Bernard — you must needs have your clerks work on it. Two copies. All night, if need be. For tomorrow's meeting. Busy pens, indeed — but it must be."

De Linton nodded. "Myself, I shall check each word, my lord."

The Queen smiled. "Poor Abbot Bernard!" she said. "I fear that he will get but little sleep this night."

"The Chancellor has spent harder nights than this will be, in my service," Bruce said. "Till tomorrow, then, my good friends."

* * *

Strangely, it was not the subscribing and sealing of the famous Declaration of Arbroath which went partly agley that next day, the 6th of April, but the superficially unimportant preliminary. Bruce had conceived rightly that a summons to show title to all lands held, would be an excellent, almost foolproof means of ensuring a full attendance at his meeting, since land-holding was the vital concern of all; but he had not foreseen the reaction to its inquisition and assize on land-titles. In the great refectory of Arbroath Abbey, when de Linton, as Chancellor, made formal announcement in the King's name that all who held land of the Crown in this realm of Scotland should now show by what right and title they held it, for the good will and better administration of the kingdom, he was answered by a great shout, and the shrill scream of steel. All over the hall swords were whipped out and held high, while their owners cried aloud that it was by these, their swords, that they held their lands — good and sufficient title.

Bruce half-rose in his throne, set-faced. Behind him his great officers of state clapped hands to their own sword-hilts, glaring, astonished. Appalled, Abbot Bernard turned to look at the King.

Although the sword-barers were fairly numerous, and scattered about the hall, they did not in fact represent more than a quarter of those present, it could be seen after a moment's scanning. Some indeed were quick to sheathe their weapons again, when they perceived the frowns of the majority. Those who persisted with the naked steel and shouting were mainly younger men, hot-heads. But not all. There were some notable and more mature figures amongst them.

Sinking back in his chair, though his brows were black, Bruce gestured to de Linton to hold his peace, and then turned, to nod to Sir Gilbert Hay, at his other side.

That man, Lord High Constable of Scotland, was nothing loth. His hands had been itching on his hilt. With a sweep he now drew his own great brand, and held it out straight before him, menacingly.

"Hear you!" he cried. "I, Gilbert, Great Constable of this realm, alone may carry a naked sword in the presence of our liege lord the King. All others who do so can be held guilty of *lèse-majesté*, even treason! Put back your steel, every man. In the name of the King!" For so modest and normally quiet a warrior, Gibbie Hay's voice sounded almost like thunder.

None disobeyed. But one spoke back — Sir William de Soulis, Lord of Liddesdale, recently appointed Governor of Berwick in place of the Steward. This had been one of Bruce's innumerable attempts to create unity and harmony in his realm — for de Soulis held that he should be Warden of the Marches, instead of Douglas, since Liddesdale formed part of the Borderline while Douglasdale did not; moreover, as Hereditary Butler and distantly of the blood-royal, he was senior in rank as in age.

"His Grace the King has no reason to fear *these* swords, my lord Constable!" he called. "All have been drawn in his service times a-many. Which is more than can be said of some of those present! But they are good, just and sufficient title to the lands which we hold, nevertheless, gained by the sword and held by the sword. As, indeed, is His Grace's kingdom!"

There was a breath-held silence at such bold words, until Hay answered.

"That is as may be, Sir William. But you know well, as do all here, that it is not lawful, indeed is a notable offence, to draw sword in the presence of the monarch, unless commanded to do so. Only the Constable may do so, for His Grace's protection. Must I protect His Grace from *you* sir?"

"That will not be necessary, Sir Gilbert. As, equally, all well know," the other returned coolly.

"Sir William is right, nevertheless, Sire," another voice spoke up — and a significant one. For this was Sir David de Brechin, the King's own nephew, like Moray, by another half-sister, a daughter of the Countess of Carrick and the Lord of Kilconquhar. He was a highly popular individual, winsomely handsome, champion at games and tourneys, and sometimes styled the Flower of Chivalry. "By sword we took lands from the King's enemies, while fighting in his cause. Should other title, mere papers, be required of us?"

"Aye, Sire," still another cried, "and why is our title to such lands being now questioned? From those who have shed their blood for you!" That was Sir Gilbert Malherbe of Dunipace, who, indeed, had shed no blood of his own.

"Is it to take these lands back from us, to give to highly-placed traitors who now surround Your Grace's throne?" Brechin shouted.

Uproar shook the abbey refectory.

Bruce, who preferred as far as possible to leave the conduct of such meetings to the officers concerned, and not to interfere, nevertheless raised his hand towards the Chancellor.

"Since you have addressed *me,* Nephew, with my lord Chancellor's acceptance I shall answer you," he said calmly — however inwardly he raged. "This assize into title is necessary, for the common weal of this my kingdom. The holding of much land is in dispute, claimed by more than one liege or vassal, fought over, to the disturbance of my peace. Marches between lands and estates are often undefined. Tenants know not to whom to pay their rents. Some are paying twice over, threatened by these same swords you shamefully brandished! *My* subjects, whom I, the King, am sworn to protect. As I shall. Loyal barons of mine are at each other's throats over handfuls of acres of ground, brave fighters acting like hucksters! To the troubling and weakening of this realm, and the harassing of my judges. This must not continue. The purpose of this Convention is not to take land from any. That will be for parliament to decide, if it is necessary. It is but to establish who can show best right and title to what. I will not have my lieges snarling over my land like curs over a bone!" He paused, gazing round him sternly. "Nor will I hear talk of traitors in my royal presence — for past trespasses which I, in parliament, have forgiven and wiped clean. Understand it — or bear my most sore displeasure."

There was a long silence. Even though the King had not raised his voice, and spoken almost conversationally, none there failed to recognise the steely grip on the royal temper, and what it could mean should that grip weaken. As Robert Bruce grew older, his anger was demonstrated less and less; but it was sensed the more alarmingly beneath his self-imposed restraint. And was the more terrifying. These were brave men, fighters who had spoken; but they would have been foolhardy so indeed had they pressed their case further, there and then.

"So be it," Bruce nodded, sitting back. "Sir Gilbert — overlook the drawn swords this once, if you please. Let all proceed in order. My lord Chancellor — continue."

Moistening his lips, Abbot Bernard went on to outline the procedure whereby every landholder would present himself, in due order, before the earl and sheriff of whatever earldom and county his lands were situate, with his proofs; and all who might dispute such claims should likewise so present themselves. All in different chambers of the abbey. Clerks would take due and proper note of all. Where dispute still prevailed, and the claimants could not accept the earl's or sheriff's ruling, appeal could be made to judges appointed by the crown. And in final instance, if such was necessary, to the King himself. Such decisions and judgements to be laid before a parliament to be called for later in the year, at Scone, where was the Moot-hill of the Scots realm, traditional scene of landed exchange, tenure and grantage. This by order of the King's Grace.

This businesslike statement had the effect, as intended, of calming tempers and damping down histrionics. There would undoubtedly be much debate and many hot words in the various abbey apartments thereafter; but meantime, and in the presence of the monarch, order prevailed.

As de Linton, finished, looked towards the throne, Bruce raised his hand again, to still the murmur of talk.

"My lords, my friends, my comrades all," he said, in a different tone. "Before you disperse about this business, there is another matter which requires your attention. A matter of great import. As all know, our neighbours of England, whom we have given cause to heed our love of liberty and freedom, have turned in their extremity to the Pope for aid in their assault on our realm. Unfortunately His Holiness, insufficiently informed as to our history, our ancient kingdom and our independence, has believed the lies told him by King Edward, and . . ."

His voice was drowned in the growl of men, a menacing sound.

"Hear me, my friends. His Holiness, I say, believing these things against us, has pronounced his anathema against us, as a people and nation. I say, hear me! Your turn comes. While my lord Bishop of St. Andrews makes due and proper enquiry as to the present Pope's appointment and authority, it is nevertheless necessary that he should be fully informed of the truth as to Scotland's state. Therefore the Chancellor has drawn up a letter, a declaration, to send to His Holiness. It is long, but resounding. And I, and the Primate, have heard and agree every word. Now it is for you to hear it. And, if you agree, to append your names and seals. All of you. For this letter is from *you,* the temporality of this kingdom, to inform the Pope of who you are and what you are, and who you have freely chosen as your king. But, above all, what you will pay for liberty, freedom, the freedom to live your lives according to your own land's laws and customs, and to choose your own rule and governance . . ."

The crash of acclaim and applause and feet-stamping shook the abbey, and continued.

Bruce gave them their head.

"My friends," he went on, at length, smiling a little, "I perceive our temper agrees. We demand to be allowed to belabour each other — but woe to him who seeks to belabour *us* from outside the realm! This we have sufficiently demonstrated. Now it is your turn to enlighten, to declare. My lord Chancellor will read out this letter. Heed it well. Each word has been well chosen. It is my hope but not my command — never my command — that all here will subscribe to it. That it may go as a united declaration from this Scottish nation, since you, in your persons, represent all the people of the kingdom. But if you wish not to subscribe, to lend your names to it, you must not do so. If our vaunted freedom means anything, then each is free *not* to agree. No steps will be taken against any who abstain. This on my royal word. My lord Chancellor — pray read your letter."

Never, undoubtedly, had so many hardened warriors and men of action listened to so long a composition and with such close attention. But after a few snarls at kissing the Pope's feet and suchlike, there was a notable and complete silence. That is, until the item about expelling even the King himself, should he fail to uphold Scotland's liberty, was reached, when there was a considerable commotion, exchange of comment, staring at the throne, and nodding of solemn heads; and when that dealing with their willingness to die for freedom came up, and the refectory throbbed with vehement chorused assent. The final indictment of the Pope himself, should he ignore all this, raised not a few eyebrows, but the majority swallowed it without objection, some with glee. At the end, a positive storm of affirmation broke out, and maintained. For a non-letter-writing and not very literate company, the enthusiasm for this lengthy epistle was extraordinary.

Exchanging glances with Lamberton, Bruce at last raised hand. "Who, then, will lend his name and seal to this letter?"

A forest of hands shot up, many with fists clenched, and a roar of "I will! I will!" resounded.

"Those of contrary mind, to declare it."

No single arm or voice was lifted.

"It is well. Very well. The clerks will take names, and instruct in the business of sealing. Two copies. To work, my friends. This convention stands adjourned . . ."

Chapter Nineteen

Egged on by Elizabeth, the King was planning both a new house and a ship. He was less than keen on either, to tell the truth, but the Queen was urgent and persuasive. She was anxious to have his mind occupied with forward-looking projects, plans assuming that there were many long years of active life ahead of him yet. For the fact was that, when the pressures of national emergency and immediate crisis of one sort or another lessened, as now, and Bruce had time to brood, his attitude to the future tended to become dark and cloudy. Indeed, whether it was the need for action which kept his recurrent sickness at bay, or the lack of it which made of his mental state more apt breeding-ground for the distemper of body, such times as he was not occupied with vigorous activities and urgent demands on his attention, his illness regularly grew worse. Not merely in the mind. The red itch spread in ever larger patches on his skin, vomiting and shivering became more frequent and violent, and the accompanying lassitude and weakness grew. It was Elizabeth's concern, therefore, to keep her husband involved in activity — since it was equally true that, the more demanding the problems, the more was required of him, the less evident became his bodily troubles. She could not engineer crises of state; but at least she could try to entangle him in domestic preoccupations.

She used the fact that Bruce had never really taken kindly to Dunfermline — although she herself liked it well. Brought up amongst hills, by the more colourful Western Sea, he found Fife too green and tame for his liking. Moreover, the older he grew, the more Celtic in sympathy he became, his mother's strain getting the upper hand. And Fife, like Lothian, was scarcely Celtic in its aura. He could hardly be said to pine for the Celtic West; but undoubtedly his preferences lay there. Shrewdly, therefore, Elizabeth fostered them.

He should build a new house. Not another great castle — since his policy still was rather to demolish all such, in case they might be used against him — but a comfortable house to live in, graciously, by the Western Sea, where he could look out over the colourful skerry-strewn, weed-hung bays and sounds rimmed by blue mountains, where he could hunt and fish and hawk, and talk with the seannachies and bards and story-tellers of the Celtic environment. She was at pains not to make this programme seem like that for an ageing man — for he was, in fact, still not forty-seven years old. So she stressed the activities which could conveniently be carried on from such a base — the sailing amongst the Western Isles and Highland coasts in especial, for it was one of Bruce's great dreams to fully integrate his Highland and Lowland divisions within the realm. He should have a special ship built, large enough to carry him and a small court — including herself — in reasonable comfort; yet small enough and suitably designed to wheel across the narrow isthmuses and tarberts with which that seaboard abounded. In it he could sail all the Hebridean seas he loved, keep in closer touch with Angus of the Isles and other island chiefs — even with Christina MacRuarie. She was cunning, was Elizabeth de Burgh.

Because he was still the monarch, however, such western domicile of delight could not be too far away from the core and centre of his kingdom, the Stirling-Scone-St. Andrews triangle. At need, he must be able to travel quickly thence, and others from there reach him readily. Therefore, with mountain passes, rushing rivers, winter snows and the like to consider, the nearest Highland seaboard was indicated. Bute, his son-in-law the Steward's island home in the Firth of Clyde, was thought of, and its Rothesay Castle was in better state than most; but actually to be confined to an island was risky, and the King could be storm-bound at some most inconvenient moment. Nearby, however, on the northern mainland shore of Clyde, looking towards the mountains of Cowal, Gareloch and the Kyles of Bute, might serve. This was Lennox territory — and his old friend Earl Malcolm eager to co-operate.

So, this July evening, four men sat on the platform roof of one of the flanking-towers of Dunfermline Palace, overlooking the deep, steep, tree-filled ravine of the Pittendreich Burn, as the sun sank over the Stirlingshire hills far to the west, and discussed designs for house and ship both — Angus of the Isles, greying now, Malcolm of Lennox, and Walter Stewart, with the King. The house, it had been decided, was to be Cardross near Dumbarton, where the royal fortress, of which Lennox was Hereditary Keeper, could protect it; for it was to be no stone castle or stronghold, but a rambling, pleasant manor-house, perhaps within a far-flung stone wall of enceinte. Bruce had always had a nostalgic fondness for Christina MacRuarie's house of this sort, at Moidart, and was seeking to have the new building modelled on such, Lennox and Walter Stewart suggesting modifications and improvements. Angus Og was not interested in houses, only in ships, and was impatiently, indeed scornfully, pressing claim for a design of his own.

The caphouse door opened, and the Queen came out. The men rose from their benches, Stewart and Lennox each seeking her approval for suggestions of their own. But, smiling briefly, she shook her head, and looked at her husband.

"Sire, we have a visitor," she said. "A lady. The Countess of Strathearn."

"That woman! What of it, my dear? I do not greatly like her. Whatever she wants, she may wait a little."

"I think that you should see her, nevertheless," Elizabeth said. "And . . . not here."

At the gravity of her voice, the King eyed her quickly, and nodded. "Very well. Await me, friends . . ."

Going down the twisting turnpike stair of the tower, Elizabeth spoke. "Robert — I fear that there is trouble. Sore trouble. If what Joanna of Strathearn says is true. She comes from Berwick-on-Tweed. And talks of treason. A plot. Against you, my heart. Against your life."

"Joanna of Strathearn in a plot? That empty-head! I'll not believe it! None would trust her with a part in a masque . . .!" He paused. "From Berwick, you say?"

"Yes. Hotfoot, she declares."

"M'mmm. De Soulis! I heard that she had become his mistress."

"She was more ambitious, I think! See — I have her in my own chamber . . ."

The Countess, a somewhat over-ripe and vapidly pretty woman in her late thirties, of slightly royal birth, only child of the late and weakly Malise, Earl of Strathearn, who had been so notable a weathercock during the late wars and died seven years before, was pacing the floor in evident agitation. She dipped a perfunctory curtsey, and burst forth without preamble.

"Your Grace — you are in danger of your life. Of your life, I say! From a wicked, evil man. He plans to slay you. William de Soulis. To slay you, and seize your throne. He is a monster! You must move against him. With all speed. Take him. Hang him, the forsworn wretch! Rack him! No fate is too bad for him. He must die, I say . . .!"

"You may be right. But calm yourself, Lady Joanna," Bruce interpolated. "Do not distress yourself so. I swear matters cannot be quite so ill as you fear . . ."

"They are, I tell you — they are! He is a devil, a satyr! A betrayer. A betrayer of . . . of . . . of Your Grace, Sire. His King." That last fell distinctly flat.

"And of you, I think? Which is perhaps more greatly to the point!"

She bit her lip. "He . . . he plans to slay you, Sire. And then to mount your throne. It is the truth. I swear it. By all the saints of God!"

"Then he is a bigger fool than I esteemed him!" Bruce snorted.

"Fool he is, yes. But scoundrel more. Lying wretch! Ingrate . . .!"

"How can this be?" Elizabeth asked, more to halt the other woman's humiliating vituperation than for information. "What claim can William de Soulis have to the throne?"

Bruce answered her. "His grandsire, Sir Nicholas de Soulis of Liddesdale, was one of the original fourteen competitors for the crown, in 1291. Before Edward. He claimed in the right of his maternal grandmother, Marjory, bastard daughter of King Alexander the Second, married to Alan the Durward. All knew her as bastard — but the Durward sought to have her legitimated. And when he failed, claimed her as legitimate daughter of King William the Lion, Alexander's own father! On such claim, de Soulis made his stand, saying, in consequence, that he was indeed nearer to the main royal stem than either Bruce or Baliol! But he could produce no proof or papers of legitimation. And all agreed, besides — save himself — that no child born bastard, even though legitimated later, could in fact heir or transmit the crown."

"He says that is not true. William de Soulis says," the Countess declared, impatient of any diversion of interest from herself. "He says that is but the invention of others. He says that once Your Grace is dead, men will be glad to have him as King, rather than any puling infant."

"Then he little knows his fellows!" Bruce commented grimly. "What support does he expect to gain? Who will rally to such a cause?"

"Already many do. He has much support."

"I'll not believe it! Name me names, woman!"

"For one, your nephew, Sir David de Brechin."

"Dear God — no! Not he. He would never so betray me. My own kin. He is headstrong, but loyal . . ."

"Then why, Sire, has he been accepting a pension from King Edward these last years? If he is so loyal!" Her face contorted. "As has the precious Sir William!"

Bruce stared. "Not that! I cannot accept that . . ."

"I have seen it. How, think you, can your Butler, Governor of

Berwick, pay 360 esquires, in his own livery, to ride in his train? As he does today. Not on the rents of Liddesdale, I vow!"

Shaken, the King looked at his wife. "De Soulis — of him I could believe it. But not my own nephew . . ."

"And why not?" Shrilly the Countess spilled out her hate. "Many another is in the plot. Why not he? You have, it seems, offended many. By your assize of lands. There is Sir Gilbert de Malherbe. Sir John de Logie, Sir Eustace de Maxwell, Sir Walter de Barclay, as well. Aye, and Sir Patrick Graham likewise . . ."

"Sweet Jesu! That these, my own lieges, men I myself have knighted, every one, should turn against me! For the sake of a few miserable acres of land."

"Sir William has promised them great things. In his kingdom. Great estates and high office. As he promised me . . ." The Countess caught her breath, and her words, blinking rapidly, as though that had slipped out unawares.

"Ah, yes, Lady Joanna? And what did Sir William promise *you*?"

The woman looked from one to the other, uncertainly. "Marriage, Sire," she said, at length, almost defiantly.

"Marriage, heh? So — you were to be the Queen!"

"I, I never approved this plotting, Your Grace. I swear it."

"Of course you did not! Yet you would have married the Lord of Liddesdale, in despite of it?"

"We . . . we have been close. In . . . in an association. For many months. Since he returned from Ireland."

"And you are no longer?"

"He is a deceiver, I tell you! A miscreant! He has become embroiled with a chit of a girl. Daughter of some mere Northumberland squire! All paps and calves eyes! But she has him cozened and bewitched, the fool. Naught will do but that he weds *her*. A man old enough to be her grandsire . . ."

"So this squire's daughter is to be Queen in Scotland!"

"Not if I may prevent it, by the saints!" That was almost a whisper.

"Do not distress yourself, lady! I think the chances are but small. Sir William will have to dispose of Robert Bruce first!"

"But you are to be slain, Sire. It is all plotted. He says that the Pope has accepted your letter. The great letter of Arbroath. And has agreed to recall his excommunication and to urge a peace upon the English. He is sending a messenger, an envoy — I mind not what they call them — to Berwick. To have a truce signed, preparatory to peace. Before yourself and the King of England . . ."

"I' faith — de Soulis is well informed! I myself but learned of this a week past. The coming of this nuncio."

"He learned it from the King of England, Sire. I told you, he serves England. On your way to Berwick, for this, you will be attacked and slain. In the Pease Dean, where the hills come down to the sea. It is all arranged for. Men chosen . . ."

"Robert — the shame of it! The foul and filthy shame!" Elizabeth exclaimed, coming to grasp his arm. "Oh, my dear — that men, your own men like these, should be so vile!"

"Aye. Shame, indeed. De Soulis never loved me. He was ever my brother's man, not mine. But these others — David Brechin, Logie, Maxwell, Barclay, Graham — Graham whose father died gallantly fighting the English at Dunbar!" The King shook his head. "What is this evil of treachery, this canker that ever and anon grows in the heart of this people?" He drew himself up and pointed at the Countess. "And you, madam! You say this was all plotted. For long. You must have known of it, in part. The grasp for the throne. To be so advanced, it must have been plotted for long. Yet only now do you come to me! Because – because you are no longer to be the Queen! This is the worth of *your* loyalty?"

Joanna of Strathearn shook her head, wordless.

"Very well. Is there aught else that I should know, woman? No? Then you have my permision to retire. Go. I shall not thank you for what you have done, I think! Remain meantime in this house. But — keep out of my sight! Now — I want Walter Stewart . . ."

When the Steward came pounding down the stairs, Bruce was calm, specific, but harsh.

"Walter — there is a plot against my life and crown. William de Soulis. At Berwick. I want him. I want him taken, forthwith and brought in custody. For trial. This parliament called for Scone, on the 4th of August. Twelve days hence. I want him there, to stand trial, before all. And not only he. I want David Brechin, John Logie, Walter Barclay, Eustace Maxwell, Patrick Graham, and so many others as are in their fell company. A large party. Therefore you will need many men. Go to Douglas, Warden of the Marches. At Roxburgh. Berwick is his responsibility, de Soulis governor under him. He will aid you. It is understood?"

"By the Mass — a plot! Against Your Grace? I will not believe it, cannot conceive it . . ."

"You are not asked to believe it, man! But do as I command. Forthwith. You have the names? Soulis, Brechin, Logie, Barclay, Maxwell, Graham. And all such others as may be implicated. I want all such before parliament at Scone, twelve days hence. But be discreet about it, Walter. I do not want any to get word that their schemes are known, and escape over the Border into England. See to it..."

* * *

And so there was another great assembly in the refectory of another great abbey, in slightly smaller hall if more ancient, Scone of the Moot-hill and the Stone of Destiny, dynastic heart of Scotland, on the 4th of August 1320. Again it was hugely attended, since this parliament was to hear, consider and pronounce upon the holdings and titles of lands in dispute. But before this judging, another was thrust unexpectedly upon the delegates.

Trial before parliament was quite a normal procedure, for treason, where the accused could be assured of a fair hearing and not be at the mercy of the Crown — although sentence on any condemned was usually left to the Crown. The King presided, but he seldom took any active part in the proceedings, content to leave all to his officers. The accused spoke for themselves and could attempt to sway the assembly as best they might.

On this occasion those in charge were distinctly surprised that there was little or no attempt by the prisoners to excuse themselves, or even to seek support and sympathy. All the principals to the plot had been captured and were present, save for one who had been implicated later, and then had been found to be seriously ill at his own house of Methven, not far away — the same Sir Roger Moubray who had betrayed Bruce at the Battle of Methven soon after his coronation. Also the Countess of Strathearn was not present; her attendance would have been off-putting and unsuitable; and fortunately, her evidence was not necessary.

The fact was, William de Soulis had confessed readily enough to the entire indictment. He was ever a fiercely proud man, and found it beneath his dignity, once things had gone unredeemably wrong, to deny, argue or plead. Throughout the hearing at Scone he kept a lordly silence. The others in some measure took their cue from him, as leader — although Sir Gilbert de Malherbe, Lord of Dunipace, always a shifty character, broke down after a bit and disgraced the knightly code, shouting and beseeching wildly, to the distaste and embarrassment of all present, his co-defendants in particular. David de Brechin, around whom most interest centred, as the King's nephew and because of the esteem in which he was held for gallantry on Crusade as on games-field and tourney-ground, contended briefly that he had taken no part in the conspiracy; but admitted that he had known of it and had taken no steps to controvert it. There was some sympathy for a fine and handsome young man led astray — until it was revealed that he had in fact been in English pay for years, whereupon all turned against him and his fate was sealed. Maxwell, Barclay and Graham all strenuously denied any involvement in the plot. All they admitted was that they were friends of de Soulis, and had been approached, in some fashion, to take part in a protest against the King's policy on the assize of lands; but none knew of any plan to kill or replace the monarch. De Logie, and a Liddesdale esquire named Richard Broun, who was said to have acted as principal go-between, maintained only a rigid silence.

So, much more quickly than might have been expected, the thing was over. Maxwell, Barclay and Graham were acquitted. The rest, including the absent Moubray, were found guilty, and worthy of death, the accepted penalty for high treason, and turned over formally to the King, for sentence at his pleasure. Then, relievedly, the parliament moved to the next business.

This was an announcement by the Chancellor of the reported comparatively favourable reaction of the Pope to the Declaration of Arbroath, and the proposed truce with England. Men heard the first with satisfaction, but the second with doubts. Truces were of little interest to the Scots, since they were so regularly and wantonly broken. But the withdrawal of the papal anathema was something different, a major success and an augury for the future.

They passed on to the vexed and prolonged business of land titles and tenures. Many had come prepared to fight the entire policy; but the conspiracy against the King, shaking all, had the effect of deflating the opposition. The difficult and controversial business went through with the minimum of trouble and delay. By such extraneous influence did a major land reform go through.

Later, with time unexpectedly to spare, Bruce called a Privy Council, to aid him decide on the sentences to be imposed. The decision had to be his own, however.

By common consent, all waited for William Lamberton, the senior of the Lords Spiritual, to answer the King's question first.

He shook his head. "In sorrow I must say it, Sire. But for the weal of the realm, and the security of our nation, there can be but one due decision. All should die. Mercy is godly — but for a people embattled, treachery, the hazarding of all that we have fought for and gained by infinite bloodshed and pain, is too great a danger for mercy. Here is evil, which must be stamped upon before it poisons the realm."

Most present nodded agreement.

"My lord Earl of Fife?"

The thin-faced, uneasy-eyed Duncan MacDuff, premier noble of the land, who had consistently taken the English side in all the troubles, and not even lifted a hand to save his sister when she hung for years in her cage on Berwick Castle's walls, shrugged stooping shoulders. "Who am I to disagree?" he said.

Men noted that answer.

"Does any say otherwise?"

Sir Ingram de Umfraville, one-time Guardian of the realm, uncle of the absent Earl of Angus, English by birth and always anti-Bruce and pro-Comyn — but an honest man enough — spoke.

"Mercy may be too costly, Sire — but discretion should not be. Must all these be treated alike? De Soulis should die. De Malherbe and de Logie likewise. And the man Broun. But David de Brechin, your kinsman and my friend — he is in different case. A younger man, and an ornament to your kingdom. Beloved of many, honoured by the Holy See for his crusading zeal. He was in grievous error in not making report of this wicked plot. But he refused to take part in it. He might well, in the end, have used his guilty knowledge to save Your Grace. He is not to be judged as the others. Banish him your realm for a time, Sire. But do not hang him."

"I hold with Sir Ingram," Patrick, Earl of Dunbar and March said.

"As I do not!" Douglas asserted. "He has been receiving English gold. A paid traitor."

"It was not for that he was tried, Sir James."

"Hang all, and be done," the Lord of the Isles advised briefly.

Bruce turned to his other nephew, Thomas Randolph. "My lord of Moray — your guidance in this? You are of like kinship to me as is Sir David. And you also once embraced other cause to mine. This man is your cousin. What say you?"

Moray took long seconds to answer. When he looked up his noble features were drawn. He spoke almost in a whisper. "What he did is unforgivable. He contemplated the murder of his liege lord, of his own blood, the man who had forgiven him his error. He it was who, by every law of God and man should have come and made known this wickedness to Your Grace — not that woman in her bitterness. Those nearest the throne bear the greater responsibility to support it. I cannot say other than that my cousin should die."

There was silence for a little.

The King broke it. "Very well, my lords. I thank you for your counsel. But the decision remains mine. Mine only. If I decide ill, I take the blame — not you. I speak, *must* speak — and think — for the realm. Not myself. I have decided. Sir William de Soulis should die. But because he is of the royal descent, one of the few who are, for the realm's sake it should not be said that the King took the life of a rival to his throne. Many would so claim. I sentence him therefore to perpetual imprisonment. I can do no other. In this I do him no kindness. He will not thank me. Nor would any here. Better a quick death than to rot in a cell in Dumbarton Castle. That proud man will suffer the more. This, for the realm's sake."

Gravely men nodded. None questioned.

"His paramour, the Countess of Strathearn, was content that I should be slain so long as she was to be de Soulis' Queen. Only when supplanted did she turn. Not for my sake, or the realm's, but to spite her betrayer. It is not suitable to execute a woman. Or to cast her in a cell. She shall be banished the kingdom. For the rest of her life."

All approved.

"De Malherbe, de Logie, and this Richard Broun, have nothing in their favour. They are proven traitors who plotted my death only for gain. De Soulis at least believed he had a right to my throne. These would have plunged Scotland into war, internal war — and English domination thereafter, to be sure — for their own gain. They die. They shall be hanged. As for Roger de Moubray, I will not hang a dying man — as they say he is. Let him be."

Again there was no dissentient voice.

Then Bruce leaned forward and spoke differently. "David de Brechin, my sister's son. Here is a stab at the heart! He chose to support Comyn, not me. He refused to attend my coronation. He fought against me at Inverurie. But these could be forgiven. Others did as much, and more. But . . . he signed your letter at Arbroath, a solemn declaration. While yet he was in receipt of English gold. Now, within weeks, this! He is the fruit of my mother's tree, a fair and goodly fruit to be seem — but rotten at the core. When I condemn others to the gallows, should I spare him?"

There was not a word spoken, although Umfraville nodded head.

"I cannot, my lords. I will not. David de Brechin hangs with the others. It is my royal decision." The King's jaw was set, his lined and craggy face like granite.

Umfraville leapt to his feet. "It is not right! Unfair!" he cried. "You must not do it, Sire! Stain your honour so. Will you, the First

Knight of Christendom, hang the Flower of Chivalry? And let de Soulis live! Here is shame . . .!"

"Shame, yes, Sir Ingram. Shame that the Flower of Chivalry is cankered in the bud! Shame to spare him because he is my own kin."

"I esteemed you greater than this. Robert Bruce! I have fought against you, yes. But I ever esteemed you noble. This young man is my friend . . ."

"As all know but too well, man!" That was Fraser, the Chamberlain, with a coarse laugh.

Umfraville, spare, grey, but flushed, ignored him, and the murmurs of others. "If you do this wicked thing, Sire — I shall leave your kingdom. Leave this Scotland. I have chosen to dwell in for thirty years. Wipe the dust of it from my feet. For ever!"

Curiously, compassionately, Bruce eyed the strange man. "That I shall regret, Sir Ingram. You must do what you will. But you have great estates in Northumberland. Go to them. Like your nephew, Angus. None will hinder you. But this alters nothing. Sit, sir — or leave my Council table. My decision stands. The matter is closed. Now, to this of the proposed truce . . ."

PART THREE

CHAPTER TWENTY

ON a slow rise of ground above the wide, sluggish River Ribble, to the north-east of the town, and so clear of the billowing smoke-clouds, Robert Bruce, in mud-spattered, travel-stained armour, sat his horse and watched Preston-in-Amounderness burn. The sight gave him not even a grim satisfaction; Wallace's burning of the Barns of Ayr, and the times without number when he himself had been forced to set afire his own Scots towns, villages and countryside, to deny their food, shelter and comfort to the invading English, had left him with a revulsion against the sight of blazing towns and fleeing, unhappy citizenry. Nevertheless, this deed was necessary — or so he assured himself — if Edward of Carnarvon was to be dissuaded from his new invasion of Scotland; just as burned Lancaster behind them had been necessary.

If the King of Scots did not display any satisfaction, most of those around him certainly did. And with some reason. For the burning of Preston and Lancaster was only the culmination of the most brilliant piece of raid-warfare yet to be demonstrated against the stubborn English who would not come to the peace-table. Never had there been anything like this, even under Douglas at his most inspired, the hardened veterans averred — and led by the King himself, indeed entirely planned by him. This should prove, if anything could, that there was no truth in the rumours of a sore sickness that was said to be eating into the Bruce and debilitating him. If this campaign was the work of a sick and failing man, then pray the gods of war for more of the sort, they said!

The plunder had been phenomenal — this area was rich, and had never before been ravaged, the County Palatine, Furness, Amounderness, almost down to the Welsh marches. For all that, they were not weighed down, as so often, and dangerously, with booty; for Angus Og's galley-fleet had kept them company, offshore, and now lay in the Ribble estuary nearby, laden with treasure, hostages and prisoners for ransom. They had had to fight nothing like a pitched battle throughout — Bruce had seen to that; but such skirmishes as had developed, they had won with ease. This was coolly planned, strategic warfare, with a vengeance, and no mere rough raiding.

Preston's smoke was intended to blow eastwards indeed, right across the Pennines, to York itself, where King Edward was mustering hugely; and to Teesdale, where Douglas and Moray waited, left in dangerous isolation when Thomas, Earl of Lancaster's revolt collapsed at Boroughbridge, yet reluctant to retire on Scotland while they might yet menace Edward's flank and hinder his advance.

For the entire strategic and military situation had changed, these past three months of 1322. It had all come about by what might seem utterly irrelevant happenings. King Edward's new favourite, Sir Hugh le Despenser, had finally become so obnoxiously arrogant and greedy that many of the old aristocracy had been driven to take arms against him and his father, led by Thomas, Earl of Lancaster, and the same Humphrey de Bohun, Earl of Pembroke, who had played a less than glorious part at Bannockburn. In this civil warfare, Lancaster, who was of English royal blood and had an eye on his unpopular cousin's throne, got in touch with the King of Scots, seeking his support, with promises of peace and friendship when he won the crown. Bruce, who neither admired nor trusted traitors, however much he had been forced to work with them, did not rate Lancaster's chances highly; but it suited his tactics meantime to fish in troubled waters, and the moment the Pope's two-year truce expired, he sent Douglas, Moray and the Steward south, not so much to aid the revolt as to take advantage of King Edward's pre-occupation — always with the objective of bringing that obtinate weakling to a peace-treaty at last.

After Hereford had won a victory over the Despensers on the Welsh marches, he marched north to effect a junction with Lancaster, in Yorkshire. Now it was outright rebellion against their King. Edward mustered a loyalist army at York, and was fortunate indeed in that Sir Andrew Harcla, recently made Earl of Carlisle, decided to switch his allegiance. Harcla was a fine soldier if an unreliable man, and had hitherto worked in co-operation with Lancaster, his patron. In March, he moved south with the levies of Cumberland and Westmorland, caught the rebel army by surprise and in the rear, at Boroughbridge, where they were penned against the River Ure with the King's forces in front, and defeated them entirely, with great slaughter. Hereford was slain in the battle, and Lancaster captured, with many other lords. For once, thereafter, Edward acted decisively. Lancaster and the others were summarily beheaded — Lancaster, who had slain Piers Gaveston.

Douglas, Moray and the Steward, operating independently in

Cleveland, to the north, with a force of about 4,000 only, found themselves in a potentially dangerous position.

The King of England, for his part, suddenly was in a stronger position than any he had known since Bannockburn, at the head of an enormous and victorious army, with the defeated rebels anxious to flock to his banner and prove their new loyalty, and his main internal oposition discomfited, the Despensers carrying all before them. Out of the blue Edward announced that he would proceed north, to punish the rebellious Scots at last and wipe out the stain of Bannockburn.

In this abruptly transformed and unexpected situation, Bruce flung aside all his preoccupations, and acted with his old dash and verve. He sent couriers to order Douglas and the others to remain as a threat to the English host on the north-east, but to retire discreetly before it; he himself would make shift to pose another threat on the west. Fortunately Angus Og's fleet was mobilised, indeed at its old game of raiding the Antrim coast. Bruce sent urgent pleas to his friend for help, and offered vastly richer pickings on the North-West coast of England than anything he could gain in Ireland. Himself, with a hastily-raised light cavalry force of about 8,000, raced south by west.

West indeed they had raced, in a fashion never before attempted, Bruce using knowledge gained as a youth in wildfowling expeditions on the Solway marshes and coasts. At low tide, the great shallow West Coast estuaries, in North England as well as South Scotland, all but dried out; and the King now risked a great series of gamble with sea and tides. Avoiding all the normal and necessarily slow routes by the Border passes and the Cumberland mountains, he had led his galloping horsemen splashing across the successive daunting shallows of the Solway estuary, then south round the West Cumberland coastline by Silloth, Workington and Whitehaven, across the estuarine sands of the Esk, at Ravenglass, and the Duddon at Millom, into Furness. Then on over the levels of Leven-mouth near Ulverston and so into Cartmel, finally thundering over the Kent-bank sands of wide Morecambe Bay and down upon Lancaster itself. By taking enormous risks with racing tides, quicksands and mud-banks, and the fording of innumerable channels, by the most skilful calculations of tidal-timing, the Scots force had descended, totally without warning and at an almost unbelievable speed, upon an area in the heart of England thought to be entirely immune, more than one hundred miles south of Carlisle — and, at Preston, slightly south even of York. All this in the course of a few hectic days.

So now Preston burned and Robert Bruce watched it, sitting like a hunched eagle in his saddle. He hoped that he had come as far as need be, that Edward would take fright at this brazen intrusion on his right flank, and would call off the declared invasion of Scotland. With any true soldier and sound commander, he could have wagered on it; but this Edward Plantagenet was none such, an unpredictable law unto himself. Before the Scots the land lay soft, green and open to the Mersey — the late Lancaster's territories, lordless now and in confusion. There was nothing to stop Bruce between here and Wales. But he had not come south for such conquest. He awaited couriers from Douglas. He had indeed been waiting for three days, since Lancaster burned. Preston was as much a filling in of time as added warning for King Edward.

"There are rich towns on the Mersey, Sire," Sir Alexander Fraser, his sister Mary's husband, suggested hopefully.

The King said nothing.

"Give me but a thousand men and I will burn them all for you, my liege!" That was Sir Andrew Moray, his sister Christian's latest spouse, fiercer fire-eater than his father.

"No."

His third brother-in-law, Sir Hugh Ross, Matilda's husband, was more diplomatic. "If we turned east here, Sire, and made for the passes between Ribble and Aire, and so into mid-Yorkshire, we would meet Douglas's messengers, and also save our time."

"To no advantage," the King replied. "Our purpose is to make Edward of Carnarvon call off his plans to invade Scotland. That only. We shall do it better by remaining a threat of unknown strength here in his West. The nearer we move to him, the more like he is to learn our true numbers. He has ten times our forces, man. We wait here until we hear from Douglas. The further south we drive, the greater danger of being cut off. Remember that we are dealing with Harcla now — a shrewd and able captain. If Edward heeds Harcla, we must needs watch our every step."

"An upsprung Cumberland squire!" the Chamberlain snorted. "I do not see the Despensers touching their caps to *him*!"

"He fought Boroughbridge as I fought Bannockburn — and won. With like tactics. The Despensers lost *their* battle. Even Edward Plantagenet must heed Harcla now. As I do. We wait."

They had to wait until early evening of that day, in fact, before the looked-for couriers arrived, exhausted, on foundered horses, having had to ride half as far again as contemplated. This was because Douglas, Moray and the Steward were now far further north than Cleveland, they explained. They were retiring steadily towards Scotland. For King Edward was not to be distracted. Against Harcla's advice, it was said — against even the Despensers' advice — he was determined on his invasion of Scotland, the more so in that the rebel Bruce was not there to stop him. He and his main force were marching north with all speed, by the east route, Douglas retiring before him, as commanded.

"And Harcla?" Bruce demanded. "What of Harcla?"

"Harcla is sent, with 20,000 men, back to the West, Sire. Through the dales and the passes, by Wensley and Dee. To ensure that Your Grace does not get back to Scotland."

"So-o-o!" The King beat a mailed fist on his saddle. "The fool — the purblind fool!" he exclaimed. "And myself as great a fool! To have believed that Edward of England would ever act as a man with wits in his head! I have wasted my time and strength on a royal dolt! You — how far north was King Edward when you left Douglas?"

"Near Darlington, Sire . . ."

"Then he is sixty or seventy miles nearer Berwick-on-Tweed than am I! With Harcla between us. See you how a misjudgement of one man's temper may endanger an entire kingdom!" That was thrown at his companions. But Bruce's glance was not on them. It was turned westwards towards the sunset and the sea. "How far ebbed is yonder tide?" he demanded, in a different voice.

"You mean . . . you mean . . .?" Ross asked.

"I mean, Hugh, that we go now. Go as we came. But faster. Much faster!"

"But . . . the ships, Sire? MacDonald's ships . . .?"

"We cannot load 8,000 men and their horses on Angus's galleys, man. And I shall need every man and every horse, in Scotland. I mean to meet Edward Plantagenet when he crosses my march! So we ride. Day and night. Across the sands again. Even if we must swim for it! Sound the trumpets, I say . . .!"

* * *

Time may indeed be made to seem to wait for a sufficiently determined man; but the tides will do so for none, even kings — as another had found out before Bruce. The Scots did indeed cross the Border slightly before King Edward did, having avoided Harcla by keeping to the sea, practically *in* the sea, all the way. But they crossed Solway, whereas Edward crossed Tweed, the one a hard day's riding south-west of the other, and some eighty miles apart.

In consequence, although Douglas and the others gallantly

sought to delay the English host all through the Merse, they could do little against twenty times their number. It was *only* some slight delay that they achieved, before the Lammermuir Hills passes, where a comparative few could hold up a legion. This Douglas did, Moray and the Steward hurrying on ahead to try to raise a defensive army at Stirling. But such delay could be only brief, inevitably. Numbers told, and Douglas had to fall back amongst the round green hills, to burn Lothian before the invaders, buying time for his monarch and friend.

Bruce and his desperately weary host — or most of it — arrived at Stirling two days after Moray and the Steward. Drawn and gaunt with fatigue as he was, the King was by no means exhausted, nevertheless; indeed he seemed able now to draw on some hidden and scarcely believable fund of nervous energy, setting an almost impossible example to his lieutenants. Gulping down food and wine as he questioned Moray and others in Stirling Castle, he was rapping out orders the moment the tactical position began to become clear.

The situation he uncovered was thus: Lothian was ablaze, and much of Edinburgh with it — this at Scots hands. Already the English advance-parties were in the city, with the main body pushing forward in the Haddington–Gladsmuir–Tranent area, a vast horde of over 100,000. A large English fleet had sailed up the Forth, and was now at Leith, the port of Edinburgh. Douglas, who had contested every pass of the Lammermuirs, had now fallen back, via the Moorfoot and Pentland Hills, organising the burning of all grain, food and forage stocks in the low ground as he went, and the fouling of wells. King Edward had travelled far and fast — for so huge a force — and therefore had far outdistanced his heavy baggage-trains. Food for man and beast was now his great, his only problem.

"Scarcely his only problem, Thomas," Bruce said. "He has still to cross Forth. It has stopped better soldiers than he!"

"Those ships, Sire. At Leith. The word is that they are transports. Not food ships. Little food is being landed from them — desperately as it is needed. It seems that they have been sent to ferry the army across the estuary. The English will not be coming up here, to cross Stirling Bridge. Or not all of them. Two prongs, it may be. One on either side of Forth."

"Then we must prepare to receive them. In Fife, and here. How many men have you gathered?"

"All too few, as yet, Sire. A general muster is ordered — but it will take time. There are some 5,000 here. Lennox has 2,000 on the way. Sinclair, Bishop of Dunkeld is raising Strathearn. Menteith is marching. MacGregor and the nearer Highland clans are coming. And no doubt Bishop Lamberton is raising Fife — since its Earl is not like to!"

"Aye. Then you will command here, Thomas. Hold Stirling and the bridge. I will take Fife. You will send on to me the forces as they come in. We do not know where Edward will choose to land, if he crosses Forth. But I cannot think that he will use wide crossings, with so many to transport. Moreover he will wish to take my seat of Dunfermline — that you may be sure. He will not cross east of Aberdour, I think. I will base myself midway between there and Stirling. At the port of Culross — that would be best. From there I could quickly come to your aid, if need be. Or strike east along the Fife coast. Or even cross to the south shore, in small boats, to get in the English rear, should there be opportunity. And it is but a few miles from Dunfermline. Keep your 5,000 here, and have all other sent there."

"How long, think you, have we?"

"Not long — if it was I who commanded. Only days. But with Edward of Carnarvon — who knows? Th English must be desperate for food. Because of the speed of their advance, and the land burned before them. Waiting in Edinburgh will serve them nothing. Unless they have more ships coming north, with provision and fodder. Their strategy is to attack us quickly, while they are strong and we are not. So we must use what forces we have — and thank God for every day He grants us for more aid to come up. I sent commands to Galloway, Annandale and Carrick, to muster, as we came up. Many thousands will come from these — but not within a week."

"Walter Stewart has ridden on, Sire. To Dunfermline. To be with the Queen and the Court. To have all ready to flee northwards. We did not know how long Your Grace would be . . ."

"That is well. But we wili not have them to flee yet awhile, let us hope. This English army is great in numbers. But I cannot think that it is great in much else! It has been too swiftly put together. Insufficiently ordered. And I cannot believe it better led than that which failed at Bannockburn — for it has even less able commanders. Edward and young Despenser are babes in warfare! Had Harcla been in command, I would have been more fearful."

"The Despensers do not love Harcla, it is said. And King Edward does not trust him."

"For that the good Lord be praised! But — enough of this. I ride for Culross. My lord Chamberlain — I want messengers sent to every Fife burgh and provost, every village in South and East Fife. All shipping, boats and fishing-craft to be sent up-Forth to Culross. And fires to be lit everywhere along the shore. Inland also. Great fires, with much smoke. Burn straw, thatch, brushwood — what they will. So that from Edinburgh and the Lothian coast it will seem as though all Fife is being burned, as Lothian has been. That there will be no food for the hungry English there! It may discourage Edward from his sailing. Aye — but tell the Fifers to be ready to fire the food and forage in truth, if and when the enemy sails. But meantime, let the smoke serve . . ."

* * *

August 1322 was wet and cold and windy. In it, East Scotland smoked, while still King Edward sat in Holyrood Abbey, at Edinburgh, and did not move. Every chill, rain-soaked day of it the Scots forces grew in numbers and preparedness, at Stirling and Culross. Probing English sallies were made south and west, into Ettrick Forest's outskirts and North Clydesdale, in especial — but these were in search of cattle, sheep, even deer, and grain and hay, sustenance for 100,000 hungry men, and rather fewer hungry horses, since the latter were now being eaten. The Scots' grim joke was that the invaders were settled down to wait for this year's harvest.

It was no secret in Edinburgh — and therefore to Bruce's innumerable spies therein — that Edward was in fact waiting for a provisioning fleet to sail up from the Humber. A wiser commander would surely have organised this somewhat earlier.

When Bruce heard the reason for the English delay, he sent immediate word to his Lord High Admiral, Angus Og, now recruiting legions of Islesmen, amongst the Hebrides, to send to the aid of his friend. The King's request — he never sent commands to the Lord of the Isles — was that he cease these activities forthwith, and drive with his galleys, with all their famed speed, up and round the north coasts of Scotland, through the Pentland Firth, and so down the eastern seaboard, to intercept Edward's victualling fleet if at all possible. How many days it would take these wolves of the sea to make the difficult 500-mile circuit depended on the winds and tides, as well as on strong men's sinews. But the MacGregor himself an expert on galleys, come limping from Loch Lomondside with his Children of the Mist, declared that *he* could do it in five days and nights of even winter seas. Though MacDonalds, of course, were not MacGregors . . .!"

Be that as it may, on the 10th of August a single long, low galley came racing up Forth from the open sea, its great square sail painted with the black Galley of the Isles, its double-banked oars raising a curtain of spray on either side. On board was young John of Islay, Angus's son and heir, little more than a boy, but splendid in antique Viking-style winged-helm and golden chain-mail. He announced that his father's full strength, in ships, now lay in the Tay estuary, hidden, with scouting craft as far south as Berwick and the Farnes. There had been no sign of any English fleet — save what they had glimpsed, in passing, in Leith harbour. Did the Lord Robert want that routed out, and sunk?

Laughing, in his relief and satisfaction, Bruce declined this particular service meantime, and knighted the young man there and then.

By the third week in August there was still no sign of the victualling fleet. The cold, wet and unseasonable northerly winds continued, and the Islesmen's protracted vigil must have been a sore one. Presumably it was the said contrary winds which delayed the English ships — or else treachery at home, from whence rumours of new revolts of rebellious barons came daily. King Edward ventured neither upon the Forth nor along its Lothian shores, westwards. The tales from famine-stricken Edinburgh were harrowing.

Bruce had now some 25,000 men assembled, the majority at Culross, some 8,000 at Stirling. He had even sent a couple of thousand Highlanders south to reinforce Douglas in the Forest, from which that stalwart was assailing the English lines of communication and preventing food-trains and cattle-herds from winning northwards through the hills.

On the 2nd of September, Holyrood Abbey went up in flames, and a valedictory slaughter took place in unhappy Edinburgh. It was the equally unhappy Plantagenet's leave-taking. He turned his petulant and haggard face to the south, and led — if that is the word — his now semi-mutinous host homewards. Knowing too well the burned and smoking desert of East Lothian and the Merse, they took the hill road this time, by Soutra and Lauderdale and the eastern skirts of the Forest — but found neither food nor comfort there, for now Douglas gave them no rest. Out-of-hand, unruly, the English were easy prey for that hardened scourge of their kind. He and his slew and slew, but seemed to make only little impact on the vast, sprawling, starving thousands. There was nothing like a battle, nor even a standing fight. The nearest to anything of the sort was when Douglas came rushing to the rescue of Melrose Abbey, that lovely fane where Leader joined Tweed — but not before most of the rose-red buildings were ablaze and Abbot William Peebles and many of his monks crucified or otherwise shamefully slaughtered.

It was a disorganised and demoralised rabble, of barely half the numbers that had gone north, which crossed the Border on the 5th and 6th of September, the King and the Despensers spurring far ahead. Northumberland thereafter wilted and cringed under the infamous influx. Douglas followed on, direly busy.

It did not seem so long since Elizabeth de Burgh had been concocting activities to keep her husband's mind off himself. Now, despite her pleas that he hold back, rest awhile, himself was not to be considered. The words sickness and leprosy had not passed his lips in months. He saw opportunity wide before him, and was not the man to fail to take it. He had an unblooded army standing impatient, and an enemy in hopeless rout and confusion, their land defenceless. He sent some mounted reinforcements for the busy Douglas; besought Angus Og to continue down the English east coast with his ships; and, saying good-bye to his protesting Queen, left Lamberton, Lennox and Abbot Bernard in charge of his kingdom and set off with Moray and Walter Stewart for England once more, with a picked force of 20,000 light cavalry and Highlanders.

The iron was hot, he said. He would forge a lasting peace out of it, for Scotland, if it was the last thing he did.

* * *

It was early October before Bruce and Douglas joined forces. They met deep in the North Riding of Yorkshire, indeed just three miles from Northallerton, on the same hill where, nearly two centuries earlier, the King's ancestor, David the First, had suffered resounding defeat at the Battle of the Standard. Bruce had come, more slowly this time — for now his host was an army, even though a small one, and no mere swift raiding force — once more by the tidal sand of Solway and Cumberland, since he had no wish, at this stage, to try conclusions with Harcla, sulking at Carlisle. Then, hearing that King Edward was in the neighbourhood of York again, and joined by his doleful cousin John of Brittany, Earl of Richmond, with a new English army from the south, the Scots had turned eastwards through the Pennine passes, warily — for here they could, indeed should have been ambushed. But they encountered no opposition, and proceeding down Wensleydale towards the lowlands of Swale and Ouse, they saw once again the familiar sight of burning towns, villages and farmsteads in the plain below, and recognised that Douglas was there before them.

So presently summoned from blazing Northallerton, the now saturnine Sir James came cantering up to meet his liege lord on the Hill of the Standard, their first encounter in eight months.

"Jamie, Jamie—what an executioner, what a brand of destruction, I have made of the gentle chivalrous youth once I knighted!" Bruce said, clasping the other to him. "Wherever I go, I hear tell of you. Every prisoner brought before me whispers dread of the Black Douglas! My courtly friend has become the very Angel of Death!"

"Only to the King's enemies," the younger man said. "And until such time as these proud and stubborn English acknowledge your kingship, and my right to be ruled by none other."

"Aye. It is eight long years since Bannockburn, and still they will not learn their lesson. Nor ever will while Edward lives, I think. Strange that so weak a man should, in this, be as obstinate as was his strong father. So different, yet both equally blinded with hatred and the lust to dominate other than their own. When they have so much. To the terrible cost of their own, as well as of ourselves." Sombrely, Bruce looked around him at the fair but burning plain of Swale.

"Harcla, Sire? What word of Harcla?"

"None. He has not emerged from Carlisle. He is holed up in that fortress like a fox in a cairn. Thomas, here, thinks that he sulks. That Edward preferred the Despensers to command the Scots venture, rather than himself. He now will teach his silly liege a lesson!"

"He is a strange man," Moray said. "Able, but no more to be trusted by friend than by foe."

"So I have sent him a message," the King went on. "Offering my lord of Carlisle . . . an accommodation. To Thomas's much disapproval!"

"I say that there is no good to come of dealing with traitors," his nephew averred. "He was Lancaster's feudal vassal, yet betrayed him. Effected his death. Now he withholds his service from his king. Why should *you* trust him?"

"I do not. I would but instil in his treacherous but nimble mind that it might pay him better not to offend both the King of Scots and the King of England at the same time! So that he does not seek to interpose his Cumberland army between us and Scotland. For such accommodation I am prepared to treat even with such traitor. You are still too nice, Thomas—after all these years and bloodshed. Unlike Jamie here, who has learned my lesson all too well! Praise your God that you are not King!"

"I do, Sire — I do!"

"So speaks Saint Thomas!" Douglas laughed, but affectionately. "Praise, I say, the other saints that his niceness does not extend to his sword-hand! I have missed you of late, friend."

Moray nodded in stiff embarrassment, and found no words.

Bruce looked from one to the other of his two most brilliant captains, and most valued lieutenants. "What news have you for me of Edward, Jamie?" he asked. "And this of John of Brittany, that soured fish! Where are they?"

"Yonder, Sire!" Douglas pointed south by east. "Not far off. I have kept on King Edward's heels ever since Melrose. Never more than a score of miles behind him and his rabble. We are less than that, here. They say he bides at Rievaulx Abbey. Just behind those Hambleton Hills. Beyond the plain. Fifteen miles."

"A-a-ah!" Bruce gazed narrow-eyed at the smoke-hazed line of low green hills. "So near? Only two hours' riding. Edward Plantagenet so near." He looked thoughtful.

"Aye, Sire — but Richmond is in the way. The Lord John of Brittany. He occupies a strong position on the hill ridge."

"How many?"

"His own force, some 20,000. The remainder of the King's army — who knows? And local levies . . ."

"But not all up on this ridge?"

"No. Richmond holds the ridge, watching us. Or watching *me* hitherto. He has sat up there these three days, and seen me burn this Vale of Mowbray. Not ventured down, although many times my numbers. Therefore, I think, he but holds a line, behind which King Edward may rebuild his broken host. At Rievaulx in the Rye valley. He is but giving the King time."

"Can we turn his flank? Richmond's? Reach the King's horde behind. Without taking the ridge. I do not know this country."

"I think not. Northwards, these Hambleton Hills run into the Cleveland Hills. Where I campaigned before Boroughbridge. No route through for an army. South are more hills, to Ampleforth. Not high, but steep escarpments, easily defended. Between, there is but the one gap, by Scawton and Helmsley, to the Rye. But my scouts declare it strongly defended."

"M'mm. We are well used to mightier hills than these. We have thousands of Highlandmen. It ought not to be so difficult . . ."

"What would you, Sire?" Moray asked. "A battle? Or just a stratagem?"

"I never fight battles, Thomas, unless I must. If we can gain our ends without a battle, that is best. Edward Plantagenet is but a few miles away. It is not likely that he, nor Richmond, yet knows that I am here. Jamie, yes — but not ourselves. If we struck swiftly, we might surprise Edward. Who knows, even capture him!"

"*Capture* the King!"

"It might be the quickest way to win our peace-treaty!"

"God in heaven — here's a ploy!" Douglas cried. "Could we do it, Sire?"

"Who knows? But we could try. Only, it would have to be done swiftly. Today. By tomorrow's dawn Edward will know that there is more than Douglas on his heels. He will flee southwards, I swear. We have but four hours of light — and, not knowing the country, we cannot here fight well in the dark." Bruce was peering across the three-mile-wide Vale of Mowbray, south-eastwards. "Is that not a break in the escarpment? Yonder, south of that village. Beyond the knoll. A stream comes down there, for a wager. From the high ground."

"I see it, yes," Douglas nodded. "It drives up towards the ridge. Shallowy. A steep, dead-end valley, I'd say. You think . . . ?"

"It is wooded in the lower parts, I'd say. A plague on all your smoke, Jamie! I cannot see clear."

"As neither can Richmond see clearly over here, Sire! To perceive your coming."

"True. How far north of your gap through to Rievaulx is this break? This corrie? How far north of the defended pass by the place you named?"

"The Scawton Moor and Helmsley gap. But a couple of miles, I'd say. Less, it may be."

"Good. Richmond, then, sits up on the ridge facing us, with this Scawton gap on his left. If an attack was mounted up the smaller valley, the corrie, directly on to his escarpment — what would be the result?"

"Massacre, I'd say, for the attackers!" Walter Stewart put in from behind, grimly.

"Only if the attack was pressed home. To the end."

"Ah! A diversion only?" Douglas said.

"More than that. A true attack. But in stages. And for special purpose. What result, I say? If Richmond believed it the *main*, the only attack?"

"I' faith — I see! He would withdraw his men out of the Scawton gap, to aid him and protect his flanks. I see it . . ."

"Only if he believed his flanks threatened," Moray interposed.

"And if he was sure that there would be no secondary assault, through the gap. By a larger force."

"As you say, Thomas. But if he does not know that there *is* a larger force — my force — in this vale? And Douglas, whom he knows of, attacks with his full strength up this corrie? And nimble Highlandmen climb both flanks of the corrie, north and south? And are seen so to do. What then?".

"It might serve . . ."

"There looks to be much woodland over there. If my main force was hidden in those woods. With scouts out to watch the Scawton gap. Then, if Richmond withdraws his people from it, I rush down and through with my cavalry, we are into the Rye valley behind him, cutting him off from the king. And Rievaulx is at our mercy."

"Sweet Mary-Mother — a joy! A delight!" Douglas slapped his thigh.

"Scarce a joy for you, in that shallow valley, under Richmond's nose! Acting bait for this trap. And only possible if Richmond does not know Your Grace is here," the cautious Moray pointed out. "How can we cross an army to the shelter of those woods, over the open plain, without being seen? Which would ruin all."

"Jamie has already shown us. His smoke. Even now it obscures the view. It is a west wind. If there was greatly more smoke, if Jamie set his torchmen to fire everything that would burn down there, all along the vale — hay, straw, reeds, thatch, brush, scrub — then this would roll towards Richmond's escarpment, to the east, and he would see nothing of what went on below. If done skilfully."

"He would guess that an attack was being mounted . . ."

"To be sure. But it would be *Douglas's* attack. And when Douglas appeared indeed in this corrie below him, it would all fit well enough. He would have no reason to fear that another and much larger host was still lying below, in the woodland."

Moray had to admit that this was so.

"Now, then. Time is our enemy," Bruce declared. "Only four or five short hours, to do so much. But tomorrow it will be too late. I fear we will be fighting in the dark, this night. You have it, Jamie? Yours is the heavy weight of this task. You can have so many more men as you need. Richmond may charge down on you. It may be sore fighting, there in the bed of the corrie — although then, the Highlandmen on the heights could come down on his flanks. Are you content?"

"Content," Douglas nodded. "It is a ploy after my own heart.

Save that it will not be I who rides to capture King Edward! That I would wish to see."

"That we none of us may see. Now — to work. The fires first . . ."

"Sire — you do not need me, in this," Moray said. "Your permission, I pray, to ride with Sir James?"

The King looked quizzically at his nephew. "You consider his to be the dangerous part, and needs must share it?"

The other shrugged. "I am like to see more fighting with him than with Your Grace, I think!"

Wryly Bruce grimaced. "How true, Thomas — if scarce your most courtly speech! Go, lad — go, both of you. With my blessing. I will see you, I hope, at Rievaulx . . ."

* * *

Two hours later Bruce stood within the shelter of the last of the trees, and gazed eastwards, upwards, blinking away tears from smoke-reddened eyes. Visibility was still not good — although the billowing smoke-clouds had thinned greatly now — and the smarting did not help. All around him men were sniffing and coughing, and horses snorting and blowing through inflamed nostrils.

The viewpoint was as good as any they would get; yet it was markedly inadequate to see what went on up in the upper corrie of that southern spur of the Hambleton Hills. Indeed the King could see only the tail-end of Douglas's force disappearing, for this hanging valley of the escarpment mounted in steps, and from his lowly position in the wide skirts of it, he could not see into the upper section. Though above and beyond it, the ridge itself was clear enough — or as clear as the smoke-haze allowed. Wide as it was down here, half a mile at least, up there it tailed away into a fairly narrow but shallowing gut, flanked by lofty and prominent green shoulders. At least he could see what went on up on these, where swarms of Highland clansmen climbed quite openly, their drawn broadswords glinting in the westering sunlight.

But that was the least of the glinting. Along the escarpment edge itself, just about a mile away, the afternoon was ablaze with flashing steel, reflecting from armour, helmets, lances, swords, maces, battle-axes. The Earl of Richmond's splendid southron host was drawn up there, in full view on the skyline, stretching as far as eye could see, from here, under a forest of banners, pennons and spears. It made a magnificent and daunting sight. Yet it was with satisfaction that Bruce eyed this part of the picture — for this was what he had visualised and planned for. What did make him anxious was not all that glinting steel and martial chivalry, but how many archers Richmond might have, and where, and what he might do with them. Archers were the great imponderable. Used to pick off those Highlandmen on the open shoulders, they could be enormously damaging to the entire strategy. And if the English chose to use such on Douglas's packed host in the corrie below, once they came within effective range, there could be a terrible slaughter. Bruce was gambling that this they would not do — not out of chivalry but out of a different kind of knightly pride. It was apt to be only up-jumped men like Harcla who would allow base-born archers to steal the day when high-born knights stood by. In near-defeat or serious crisis it would be different. But this should look like neither.

Bruce had his thousands of light cavalry hidden in the scattered woodland which clothed all these hillfoot skirts. Two miles to the south, still in the foothills, a small detachment under Walter Stewart were as well hidden on a wooded knoll at the western end of the road through the pass-like gap in the hill, which led over the Scawton Moor to Helmsley. From here they could see if and when the forces holding the gap were withdrawn.

The King rather envied Douglas and Moray. He too would have preferred to be riding up that corrie, even though in full view of the enemy and with the risk of unanswerable archery attack from above. It would at least be action, better than waiting here, a prey to the misgivings of the commander who plans a battle and then must leave its carrying out to others — and who may see all his visions and forecasts made nonsense of by events. Not that he feared greatly for his friends; he had sent them into a dangerous situation, admittedly — but they were as well able to look after themselves therein as any men living. And, because he knew John, Earl of Richmond, he did not believe that the worst would happen.

John of Brittany had been Edward the First's nephew, and one-time Lieutenant of Scotland, in 1305, the year of Wallace's death. Even then he was a sombre, gloomy man, prematurely grey. Seventeen years later he was not likely to have become any more fiery or apt to take risks. No fool, but over-cautious, conservative, he was the sort of man who could be relied on to do the obvious, conventional thing; and if he erred in doing so, it would be on the side of delay, of prudence, of circumspection. Nor would he allow in others the rashness he himself abhorred — for he was inordinately conscious of his rank. But he was no craven, and of a bull-like stubbornness of purpose. Taking all this into account, Bruce had planned the day.

He was jerked out of his introspection by the thin high ululation of trumpets blowing up there on the summit ridge, many trumpets, the first peremptory bugling taken up by others right and left along the escarpment. And before these had died away, the entire centre of the steel-clad line seemed to buckle and bend. Instead of a line, a front, it became slowly a moving wide V, as deliberately, without any excited charging, the English mounted chivalry surged forward and over the lip of the escarpment of Roulston Scar, and on down the steep slope, in perfect order. As far as could be discerned from below, not a single arrow had preceded them.

"There rides a confident commander!" Hugh Ross commented, at the King's side. "As well he might be. He has all the advantage. Height. Ground. And four times the number of men. Can Douglas hold him, think you, Sire?"

"Would I have sent him up there if I did not believe so, man?" Bruce snapped. "Use your wits!"

Abashed, Ross bit his lip, silent.

The King relented, more on edge than he hoped to appear. "See you, Hugh — that narrow place hems in Douglas, yes. But it also prevents Richmond from deploying, from bringing his superior force to bear. There is just no room on the floor of the corrie for large numbers. The very ground will force Douglas into a long schiltrom formation, a hedgehog of spears. The English will only be able to attack in any strength at the head of the formation. If they swing round the sides, they will be on steep and difficult ground. And Douglas will retire, slowly. My orders were that he retires down the corrie, drawing Richmond after him. The further the better."

"It will be strange fighting for the Douglas!"

"Jamie's turn will come." Bruce turned. "Young Campbell there. Colin — your turn now. Off with you! And Ranald MacRuarie. God speed — and watch for their bowmen."

Nothing loth, the two young Highland chiefs, impatient this last half-hour, raced off, dismounted and in opposite directions. Right and left, but half a mile apart, their two large groups of clansmen waited, as eager as themselves.

For a little there was nothing to be seen from the King's position, not only in new developments but in the main cockpit of the corrie. For now the leading ranks of the English chivalry were low enough therein to be hidden, as were Douglas's men. Only to be seen were the new and seemingly endless rank of advancing steel-clad horsemen, coming over the skyline and down the slope — a daunting enough sight. Detachments of enemy infantry were now striking out along the shoulders of both flanking hillsides, to engage the Highlanders already up there. These, their part largely played, were falling back somewhat.

Dependent on their ears now, the King and those around him fretted. It was galling indeed not to be able to see the drama up in the corrie. But at least something of the noise of it came down to them, the shouts and screams, the clash of steel, the whinnying of horses, the trumpeting.

Sir Alexander Fraser, the Chamberlain, an impatient man, stamped about on the fallen leaves of the wood, cursing their inactivity — until Bruce, rounding on him, outcursed him into muttering quiet.

Gilbert Hay, the Constable, touched the King's arm, and pointed upwards to the left. "Stones," he said briefly.

High on the northern of the flanking shoulders, the English infantry, spreading quickly along in the wake of the retiring Highlanders, were beginning to prise loose stones and rocks, large and small, and send them hurtling down into the gut of corrie.

Bruce nodded.

"Campbell and MacRuarie should have been off earlier," Fraser growled.

"How could they, man? Seen from up there too early, and Richmond might never have moved. He had to be committed to the descent before I dared send them. Douglas will have to thole the stones meantime. Besides — so long as they roll stones down, it must mean that Richmond is not seeking to attack Douglas's flanks. Or the rocks would hit their own men, first."

With that doubtful consolation they had to be content. They waited.

Presently, again it was Hay who pointed. This time downwards, not up. He pointed at the stream which ran close by, and which came tumbling out of the corrie. It was running red.

None commented.

At last, when inactive watching and waiting and listening had become almost insupportable, there was a diversion. On the same northern shoulder of hill, Campbell's clansmen came into view, from the far side, in their hundreds, running and leaping and yelling over the skyline — to the obvious alarm of the stone-rollers. Quickly a new infantry battle developed up on the high ground.

"Thank God for that!" Fraser jerked.

It was less easy to see to the top of the right-hand and southern shoulder, from here; but within minutes noise was coming from up there also. Presumably there was less available loose stone there, for the fighting seemed to be taking place on the crest of the hill, as Christina MacRuarie's nephew attacked.

Now trumpets were blowing again, up on the main escarpment, in a crescendo, as the English rear saw a new and utterly unanticipated menace developing. Bruce sighed his relief.

The trumpeting continued. Somebody in command was in major alarm — Richmond himself perhaps, if he had not ventured down into the corrie personally. Thereafter a novel feature could be discerned in the confused picture — a distinct trend of some few horsemen spurring *uphill* out of the corrie again, back to the escarpment, against the stream, as it were — although this itself was now slackening notably. Recalled captains, undoubtedly.

"There!" Bruce cried. "There is what I looked for, schemed for! They are confused now. Where have these new Highlandmen come from! More than ever Douglas had, in the vale. We have them in doubt." He turned. "Willie Irvine — now!" he ordered, playing his last card in this game of bluff. "Up there, to Douglas's aid!"

Thankful for action at last, Irvine, the former royal armour-bearer, led his 300 mounted men out of the cover of the woodland, straight uphill towards the corrie, at the canter, yelling as they went. They had been sitting their horses amongst the trees all this time, for this moment. Their own three trumpets brayed their lustiest, to draw attention to themselves.

The braying was more than echoed from above, as this surprising cavalry reinforcement for Douglas appeared on the scene. Indeed the English buglers sounded almost hysterical.

"Pray that is sounding in the Scawton gap," Gibbie Hay said.

"If it is not, what then?" Fraser demanded.

"Then we move up to rescue Jamie Douglas," the King answered. "And say farewell to any chance of capturing Edward Planagenet. But — wait you. Learn what it is to be a King, Sandy! Who commands — and then waits.'

Even Bruce's apparently steely resolve was wilting before, at last, a young Stewart esquire came crashing his horse through the woodland glades, shouting for the King.

"Sire!" he called, "Sire — word from the Lord Walter! The enemy are riding out of the gap. Back to the east and north. Up the hill. In force. They leave, he says — they leave. They draw out, towards yonder fight, up there . . ."

"All the saints be praised! My lords — to horse! Our's the opportunity now . . . !"

The change from frustrating idleness to hectic movement was crazily dramatic. The entire woodland burst into feverish activity, and in only moments the King was leading the way in a headlong dash by thousands, due southwards along the foothills. Avoiding the thicker cover now, since it delayed them, he accepted the certainty that they would be seen from above, for only a mere haze of smoke remained caught by the trees, and led out by the higher and open braesides. Speed was everything — speed, allied to the effect of appalled surprise and confusion above.

They had almost two miles to cover, and did so in a wild, strung-out gallop, more like an enormous deer-hunt than a disciplined cavalry advance, Bruce caring nothing. Never had the shaggy, sure-footed garrons of the Scottish hills better demonstrated their qualities.

Just before they reached the knoll where the Stewart had lain hidden and watching, with his 200, another messenger met them. The Lord Walter had ridden on, up the Scawton road, he reported. To take it and hold it, at all costs. Not many of the enemy had appeared to remain . . .

Without so much as drawing rein, Bruce swung his mount round, eastwards, into the gap.

For those enthusiasts demanding more militant action than mere hard riding, there was disappointment in that shallow groove through the escarpment and the moorland behind — no pass by Scots standards. Obviously, by the horse-droppings, the still burning fires, and abandoned material such as cooking-pots and horse-blankets, quite a large force had been guarding it, and presumably settling down for the night, not anticipating any large-scale assault so late in the October day. Their withdrawal had been sudden, and any numbers left must have been small, for only one or two bodies of men and horses lay scattered along the roadway, indicative of a running fight, a mere chase on the part of Walter Stewart's 200. There was nothing here for the King's force to do, save ride after, at speed.

As they went, however, Bruce's glance was apt to be as much pre-occupied with the rising ground to his left, as to the front. His host's emergence from hiding, in force, could not fail to have been observed; and Richmond, or whoever was now in command on the escarpment, must surely recognize the extreme danger to his left flank. He was almost certain to send the former gap-stoppers hastening back, and with reinforcements. It was a race, then.

The little water shed between Swale and Rye was only three miles wide, with the hamlet of Scawton at the far end. Over it the King's force streamed, no impediment developing from the left flank. Where the land began to drop, from tussocky moorland to the gentler levels of the Rye, less wide a vale than Mowbray but very fair, Walter Stewart waited. Wordless he pointed northwards.

Behind the escarpment, the Hambleton Hills sank much less dramatically, in rolling green waves of downland, to the riverside. Stretched along these, over a wide front, a large cavalry host was in process of advancing southwards, at right angles to the valley, its ranks less than a mile off. Bruce looked from it, eastwards, across the levels, to where, about three miles further, the mellow stone buildings of the great Abbey of Rievaulx stood out clear amongst copses, orchards and gardens. A sigh escaped him.

"I must attend to these others, Walter," he called, reining up only partially. "I had hoped ..." He shrugged. "I fear that Edward will be warned. He is fleet of foot! Go you, and try to take him. Take another 200, 300, of swift riders. Enough to grip him, if he is not gone. You understand? To Rievaulx. If he is gone, do not pursue too far. In darkness, you could run into trouble. Myself, I have work to do here!"

"Aye, Sire — I will bring King Edward, if it may be done."

The King waved his son-in-law off, and turned to his brothers-in-law and Hay. "Three divisions," he barked. "Quickly. Each to make arrowhead. And all three in another arrowhead. Sandy — the right. Hugh, the left. Gibbie, with myself in the centre. You wanted fighting! Quickly, I say. No marshalling. Work into formation as we advance. We will teach these Southrons how we fight in Scotland!"

It was all, necessarily, a very hurried and rough-and-ready division and forming up. But these men were, in the main, hardened veterans, and their captains amongst the most experienced cavalry commanders alive. Moreover, they all knew the Bruce's methods, and had complete confidence in his leadership. In only a brief minute or two, out of seemingly hopeless, streaming confusion, two distinct divisions appeared in the still turning Scots host, divisions which grew wider. It would be foolish to assert that the three resultant groupings approximated to any recognisable shape or order, or even were roughly equal in numbers; 15,000 mounted men cannot be so readily marshalled. But at least the advance uphill, northwards, began in triple formation, the centre foremost, and gradually its composite arrowheads began to form.

That they had time to do so was the measure of their foe's uncertainty and indecision. They should, of course, have been swept down upon at once, the English using their advantage of height and impetus, though probably not numbers. But this did not happen. It might be that there was in fact no overall and accepted commander up there, if Richmond and his chief captain were over in the corrie dealing with Douglas and Moray. These people would be mainly the formation which had been recalled from the Scawton gap, and then hastily turned back again, with, probably, the rearguard left up on the escarpment — a hurriedly patched-up company. Moreover, they were strung out in a wide line abreast, covering a lot of the downland country, a sensible formation enough for an assault on an enemy threading a long pass through hills; but unmanageable as to unified command, and hopeless for dealing with a tight-wedged charge aimed at one point.

And it was such that Bruce was mounting. An uphill charge is almost a contradiction in terms; but the slopes at this side of the hill were comparatively gentle, and the Scots' garrons bred to the hills. Gradually, from a fast trot, the King, at the very apex of the central arrowhead, lashed his own mount into a heavy canter — and none behind him were prepared to allow their middle-aged and allegedly sick monarch to outdo them. Gilbert Hay and young Scrymgeour, now standard-bearer, with the great Lion Rampant banner of Scotland held high, vied with each other to be closest to the King, so near that their knees rubbed his at each side. "A Bruce! A Bruce!" the famous, dreaded slogan rose from thousands of panting throats, as men savaged their beasts forward and up.

It was hardly to be wondered at that the English line lost its momentum, indeed faltered, and those who found themselves in the unenviable position of facing directly the spearhead of the charge took thought as to how to be elsewhere. Efforts were being made to concentrate, to draw in the spreading horns of the long line; but obviously this could not be done in time.

In the event, Bruce was not even involved in a clash, did not so much as swing his battle-axe. The enemy flung themselves aside right and left, to avoid the dire impact — and the Scots point was through. The ever-broadening wedge behind thereafter inevitably created its own effect. Sliced in two, the English front was rolled up on each side, without any real fighting developing, outmanoeuvred rather than defeated.

Fraser and Ross did not require their liege lord's urgent trumpet-signals to tell them their duty. As with one accord they wheeled their respective commands around, outwards, east and west, to double back on the confused halves of the enemy front which was thus abruptly no front. Now they would have their bellyfuls of fighting — but it would be a great number of close-range, hand-to-hand tulzies rather than any practical battle. Bruce had seen to that.

The King himself, with his 5,000 rode directly on, content to leave that matter to his lieutenants. Before him now was approximately a mile of slightly rising ground lifting to the escarpment, and thereon only scattered groups of infantry, spearmen, archers and a few horsemen and wounded men come up from the battle in the corrie — nothing that even a genius of a commander could whip up into a coherent and effective force in a few minutes. The spearmen could form themselves into one or two hedgehogs, schiltroms, and the archers could do some damage before they were overwhelmed; but they could by no means halt or break the charging mass of light cavalry.

That infantry, nevertheless, earned any renown available to Richmond's force that evening. Some, but only a few, fled. Most formed up to face this dire and unanticipated threat, in tight groups — it would be too much to name them schiltroms — and stood their ground nobly until ridden down in the rush of pounding horses and yelling men. There were no very large numbers of bowmen, but these acquitted themselves well — and almost all such Scots casualties as fell were the victims of these. But they had no backing and there was no unified command. Gilbert Hay lost a horse shot under him, and was in dire danger of being trampled to death by his own oncoming followers. The standard-bearer took an arrow in his shoulder, but his chain-mail and the padded leather doublet he wore beneath saved him from serious hurt. Bruce himself was untouched. They plunged on and past the scattered and heroic infantry, leaving them for the rear ranks to deal with.

And now, in front, was only the escarpment edge and empty air. Bruce indeed saw himself in real danger of being forced right over the lip of it by the charging press of so many behind, and yelled to his personal trumpeter to sound the halt. Only just in time the pressure relaxed, as the arrowhead's flanks swung outwards, amidst savage reining in of pawing, rearing, slithering, colliding horses.

And there, lining the edge, the Scots sat their panting, snorting, steaming mounts, and stared down into the already shadow-filled cauldron of the corrie, at the quite extraordinary sight of a separate and quite self-contained battle, a tight-packed struggle, concentrated by the shape and dimensions of that hollow of the Roulston Scar, where in a huge U-shaped conformation Richmond assailed Douglas's elongated schiltrom, 15,000 men locked in a death-struggle — or as many of such as could get to grips with each other, which was no large proportion at any one time. Some subsidiary activity was still going on along the flanking shoulders, distinct smaller battles of Highlanders and English infantry.

Bruce did not plunge down that slope to the rescue, as all impulse dictated. Instead, he called orders to be passed along for every trumpeter, and bugler in his host to sound the Rally, and to keep on sounding it. Ragged and scarcely recognisable as such, the call began to blare out, along the escarpment edge, and went on, gaining in power, coherence and authority.

The effect down in the corrie was quite electrical, almost comic. Suddenly the contestants therein seemed to become the merest puppets, toys that abruptly ceased to be manipulated. As with one accord, friend and foe left off belabouring each other to pause, to stare upwards.

Douglas and his Scots recovered first, since they were the less surprised. Raising a tremendous, spontaneous shout of triumph, they renewed their efforts with redoubled vigour and entire confidence. Their tight-pressed ranks surged outwards. There was little corresponding renewal of the conflict on the English side. Their fate was writ altogether too clear.

In fact, the battle ended there and then. So obvious was it that they were trapped between the upper and nether millstones that, whatever Richmond himself might decide, his people unanimously recognised complete and ineluctable defeat. Escape was the only recourse now, all perceived.

But that corrie was a difficult place to escape from, hemmed in steeply on all sides save the west and lowermost. On either flank the mass of the enemy, as with one accord, sought to stream away westwards, around the Scots. Douglas saw it, and ordered his men to press still further right and left, well up the enclosing braesides, to stop the escape routes. And Bruce despatched contingents slantwise down both shoulders of hill, to aid in the business. Men still got past, but only individually and in small groups.

Otherwise everything was over, to all intents and purposes. Fighting died away, save for isolated incidents. At the head of the corrie, the Lord John of Brittany, Earl of Richmond, sourly yielded his sword to James Douglas, his lieutenants with him. Or such as remained on their feet.

Not a few had died, and died bravely, with their men. Fully a score of knights lay amongst the slain, there in the gut of the hanging valley, for it had been a fierce and prolonged struggle. Douglas's own casualties were not light.

He and Moray, the latter slightly wounded, his sword-arm roughly supported in a sling made by his golden earl's belt, brought their prisoners slowly up the steep slope, to present to their monarch, who had sat motionless in the saddle from the time of his arrival at the escarpment edge.

"A notable victory, Sire!" Douglas cried. "Hard smiting — until you came. As stark a tulzie as I have known since Bannockburn. But — it all fell out as you judged. I have here the swords of sundry lords, for Your Grace."

"Aye, Jamie — a notable victory. And all yours. You have borne the brunt — as I said you would, lad. And you, Thomas. Myself, I have not struck a single blow! Has it cost you dear, Jamie?"

"Dear enough, Sire. For this fight. But, if all is won elsewhere, a great victory — then the cost is light indeed. Our fallen are not yet counted — but I would say 500 perhaps. With many more but lightly wounded. As my good lord here."

Moray grimaced. "A pike-thrust meant for another! Nothing more honourable. What of King Edward, Sire?"

Bruce shrugged. "Walter went seeking him. In haste. But, I fear that he would be warned, in time to flee. He did not come to aid his cousin, at least!" And he looked at Richmond at last where that thin and tall individual, dressed all in black armour, stood in sullen and depressed silence, with sundry other notables. "I cannot congratulate you on your liege, my lord!"

The other inclined his long, grey head stiffly, and said nothing. He looked an old man, although in fact only a couple of years senior to Bruce.

"It is many years since we met," the King went on. "That day you gave us the tidings, at Stirling, of what your then King did to *his* prisoners! Sir William Wallace in especial. You considered it well done, then, I mind."

"A rebel, he died a rebel's death," John of Brittany said, almost primly.

'And do you, sir, expect better treatment?"

"I am no rebel, my lord of Carrick."

"So! You still hold to that folly, man!" Bruce shook his head. "Are you wise, think you? If I am but Earl of Carrick, and a rebel to your English King — then may not you, and these, expect the treatment a rebel would mete out? To hang you all from the nearest trees! Whereas, were you prisoner of the King of Scots, you might look to receive more courtly treatment! How say you?"

Richmond, in fact, did not say anything to that.

The King turned from him. "And these others, Jamie?"

"This is the Sieur Henri de Sully, Grand Butler of France, Your Grace. And these behind him are French knights also."

"Indeed. And what do Frenchmen fighting for a monarch who will not fight for himself? In a strange land?"

De Sully, a florid, powerfully-built man in splendid armour gold inlaid, bowed low. "We but visit, on our liege lord's command his sister, the Queen Isabella, Sire. The King of England being our host, we must needs fight for him when he is beset."

Bruce nodded. "True, sir. That is our knightly code. Your master, the King of France, is I hope my good friend. I accept therefore, that you are present in this battle not from enmity to myself. I think that I can serve him, and you, better than does His Grace of England! Remain you with my Court awhile, my friends. Come back with me to Scotland. Not as prisoners but as honoured guests. And I will send you home to France, in due course, wiser men! How say you?"

To a man the Frenchmen expressed entire satisfaction with this sudden turn in their fortunes.

James Douglas presented the other prominent captives. "This is Sir Ralph Cobham, Sire — called by some the best knight in England. He led the English van down upon us. And fought bravely."

"Then we welcome him to our company. I have known of Sir Ralph. Make his stay with us comfortable, Sir James. And this?"

"Sir Thomas de Uhtred, Keeper of the Castle of Pickering. He cost us dear, but fought nobly."

"Such knights are an honour to encounter. My lord of Moray — see well to Sir Thomas's relief, I pray you. Like yourself, he has taken some hurt. But — hold my lord of Richmond close I charge you — since he esteems himself in rebel hands! The rest I will speak with anon. Now — to see to our own hurts . . ."

The Scots set up camp down where the corrie joined the woodland, where was shelter, fuel and water. And there, hours later, Walter the High Steward came to the King, riding out of the darkness into the firelight. Save for his Steward esquires, he was alone.

"Too late, Walter?" the King said. "I feared it. Edward of Carnarvon has as long legs as his father, but uses them a deal differently!"

"He was not long gone, Sire. From Rievaulx. Departed in much haste. His meal left on the Abbot's table! All his guard not yet gone. These we cut down — but got out of one that the King had fled for Bridlington. To take a ship to London. Fifty miles. We took that road after him, by Helmsley and Nunnington, ten miles and more. Near to Malton. But he had fresh horses and we had not. And in the darkness, not knowing the land, we took the wrong road at Slingsby. So, in obedience to your royal command I turned back. I am sorry, Sire. I know that your heart was set on this. That all was planned to this end . . ."

"With any other King but Edward, you would have been successful, Walter, I swear! Never heed — none would have done better against this fleet-foot monarch, who yet calls himself Lord Paramount of Scotland!"

"At least I have brought Your Grace something," the younger man said. He drew from within his steel breastplate a golden casket, shaped like a double saucer, richly jewelled and engraved. "A token, Sire. The Privy Seal of England, no less! Left behind, in its keeper's, Sir Hugh Despenser's haste!"

"Dear God! Their Privy Seal of the realm! Abandoned in craven haste? What shame is here! Humiliation. Save us — this day Edward Longshanks must be birling in his grave at Westminster!"

"More than that, Sire. We captured great treasure in gold, silver and jewels. Rich rainment, the King's own clothing. His tabard, with the Leopards of England. Horse-trappings and harness. We have a hundred horse-loads of rich spoil."

"Aye." That, strangely, was almost a sigh, as Bruce looked round in the firelight at all his lords and knights and captains, the Frenchmen also, and other knightly prisoners — although not Richmond himself, who was being kept rigorously apart, out of the King's circle. "You hear, my friends? This day a great and proud realm eats dust! This day is sorer in proud England's story than was Bannockburn. The day of Byland Ridge — as they tell me is the name of this hill — will go down in a people's annals as the very depth of shame. Because of the unreasoning hate, the stubborn pride and the craven hearts of those who led her. Bannockburn was grievous defeat followed by shameful flight, but all honour was not lost. Today, beaten deep in the heart of his own country, by lesser numbers of those he elects to call rebels, yet without himself raising a hand to strike back, or aid his fighting subjects, the King of England flees in abject fear, leaving even his Privy Seal behind. From this, his name and repute can never recover, I say. But I grieve not for this craven fool, Edward. I grieve for England, the greatest realm in Christendom, laid low for its lord's dastard fault. Mind it, my friends — mind it. The Battle of Byland, that was indeed no true battle, is not England's shame, but Edward's. Mind it, lest you come to crow overloud! And mind, too, how ill served may be even the greatest realm by its leaders — lest Scotland be ever likewise! Mind this day, I say."

There was silence around the great fire, as men heeded those words, and the stern tones in which they were spoken.

Then Fraser spoke up. "So? Do we drive on to London then, Sire? There will be little to halt us, I vow!"

"No, Sandy, we do not! Have you not learned yet? The conquest of another's realm is a hateful thing, a shame on the conqueror as on the vanquished. I am not here for conquest. I am here for one purpose only — to force a peace treaty, lasting peace, between the realms of Scotland and England. That only. What we have achieved today may serve. Pray God it will. But setting all the English South afire and in arms, in largest war, as it would be, would breed only hate, bitterness, needless bloodshed. And probably defeat — for be it never forgotten that they are ten times more numerous than are we. No, friends — *I* turn face for Scotland tomorrow. Although some of you may remain here in Yorkshire a little longer. To recoup the cost of burned Edinburgh, Lothian and the Merse! From these rich, undamaged towns. As is but fair. Tax-gatherers, my friends — that is your role, now, not conquerors! And, who knows — you may teach the proud English a sharper lesson thereby . . .!"

Chapter Twenty-One

It was long since Bruce had visited his castle of Lochmaben, in Annandale. Nor would he have chosen to visit it now, in early January 1323 — for this was no time to be travelling across Scotland, with snow on the hills and the passes choked. Moreover, the Yuletide celebrations were not yet over. Again, Lochmaben was still largely in ruins, and inadequate shelter for a winter visit — for the King, holding to his policy of having as few castles as possible for invaders and traitors to occupy against him, had never repaired it after its last battering by the English. However, Sir Andrew Harcla, Earl of Carlisle, had sent most urgent word, via Bishop Lamberton whom he had known, requesting a secret meeting with the King of Scots, and so soon as might be, at some spot which the Englishman could reach from Carlisle in a day's riding; and Bruce, intrigued, preferred to have the meeting sooner rather than later, for Elizabeth was, beyond all expectation, pregnant again, with delivery expected in only six or seven weeks. He was not going to risk being absent from his wife's side in the event of any premature birth. So he had settled for this early date of the new year, and at Lochmaben, remote and ruinous, as a suitably secure venue. There were not many men the King would have travelled so far to meet — but Andrew Harcla of Carlisle, in present circumstances, was one.

The new Earl was already waiting, in the castle's former brew-house, the only building still intact, when Bruce, with Moray and Douglas and a small escort, clattered into the grass-grown court-yard on the green peninsula of the loch. Beating their arms against their sides, to warm their frozen fingers, they stamped into the brew-house, where Lochmaben's keeper, Bruce's own illegitimate son by his second cousin, Christian of Carrick, entertained the Englishman with meats and wine before a roaring fire of logs.

The King embraced this other Robert Bruce briefly, a young man of whom he was not particularly fond, and who seemed to take after his late Uncle Edward rather than his father, fruit of the enthusiastic and comprehensive hospitality shown to the fugitive monarch at Newton-of-Ayr eighteen years before, but whom he dutifully cherished, as it were from a distance.

"Ha, Rob — so you are growing a beard already! On my soul, they start younger each year! To make me feel the older, i' faith!" he greeted. "How is your lady-mother, lad?"

"Well, Sire — and sends greetings. And hopes that Your Grace will honour her house at Newton hereafter. But, Sire — yourself? You look but poorly. Thin. Is the sickness back again?"

Douglas coughed hurriedly.

Moray looked away. "This will be my lord of Carlisle, I think, Your Grace," he said.

"Ah, yes." The King turned, smoothing the quick frown from his brow. "My lord — your forgiveness that we are late. The snow blocked the pass by Beattock, and we must needs make circuit by Moffat. You would have little difficulty, coming up Annandale?"

"None, Sire. And I crave your royal pardon and patience in bringing you so far. But the matter is vital, and my position . . . difficult."

Andrew Harcla was a short, stocky, powerfully-built man of early middle-age, plain, heavy-featured, jerky of manner and without obvious graces, not unlike one of his own Cumberland bulls. But his small darting eyes were notably lively, and shrewd.

Bruce inclined his head. "That I understand, my lord. I came, since it was the best soldier in England today who besought me."

"I thank Your Majesty. More's the pity, I think, that I need not to be very able, and yet that! For these are sorry days for England."

"I do not deny it. And what would you with the King of Scots?"

The Englishman looked at Bruce's companions. "Your Majesty will understand how delicate is my situation, how secret is my visit. And how for your royal ear alone are my words."

The King shook his head. "My son, here, will leave us. But these — no. My nephew of Moray is now as my right hand in the governance of this my realm, since my lord Bishop of St. Andrews, to whom you sent your letter, is sore stricken, bedbound. Anything that you have to say to me, he should hear. And my good friend Sir James of Douglas is Warden of the Marches. Any matter which concerns the Border — and surely this must — is within his bailiewick. These remain, sir."

The other shrugged. "As you will." But he waited until the young man had left the brewhouse before continuing. "My head could fall, for what I say now, Sire. I beg you, and these, to mind it well. It could be called treason. My very presence here. Yet I am no traitor."

"That we will judge when we hear you, my lord. Yet, it comes to my mind that you once betrayed the Earl of Lancaster!"

Harcla set a heavy jaw. "I prefer that you use another word, Your Highness!" he said thickly.

'Perhaps. Let it be. What is your urgent matter, then?"

The Englishman took a deep breath. "This, Sire. Because of the follies, failures and misgovernance of King Edward and his friends the Despensers, England is in sore straits, and in a state of revolt. Not yet open revolt, but near it. The country has never been so mismanaged and disgraced. Your own defeat of the King at Byland, and his shameful flight, has lost him all support. Especially in the North. The North, I say, has had enough of Edward of Carnarvon!"

"So! And you are King Edward's commander in the North!"

"The better to know the temper there. The better to take steps to improve the position."

"*You* take steps?"

"Yes, Sire. I, and those who think as I do. Which is the greater part of the lords and barons of the North. We know well that Your Majesty has long sought a peace treaty and recognition of your sovereignty and independence. We would undertake to urge this course upon King Edward by every means in our power — and such means are not little. And if he will not listen, then to ally ourselves with Your Majesty against him!"

Bruce stared at the man. "Ally . . .! You?"

"Aye, Sire. I, and others. Many others."

"You would turn your coats? Turn traitors. Against your own realm?"

"Not traitors. Not against our own realm. Only against Edward, who cannot and will not preserve us, our land, people and goods. He is incapable of defending the North of England — nor does he care to do so. For years, Sire, you and yours — these same lords of Douglas and Moray, indeed — have raided and devastated and held to ransom our entire North. As far south as York. Has the King of England ever sought to aid us? Never! He has invaded Scotland — but that was for his own pride and glory, not our help. We have pleaded with him for what should be our right, the right of any part of the kingdom — protection, aid, governance. And received none. So, we say, it were better that the North of England came under the King of Scots' protection than his enmity! We are too far from London, Sire. And once, Scotland reached as far as Lancaster . . ."

"You are proposing that I annexe the North of England — with your help, man?"

"I am. If King Edward will not heed our last demand for a peace treaty."

Bruce looked at Douglas and Moray, at something of a loss. They appeared only astonished, and offered him no guidance.

"How much of substance is there here?" he demanded. "I do not doubt your serious intent, my lord — or you would not have come here at the risk of your head. But — how much of backing have you? Few can know of your move — or King Edward's spies would know of it also, by this!"

"I know the temper of the North, Sire. I am Governor. And I am no fancy fool sent up from the South. I am a Cumbrian. See you, the North has been in a ferment for years. The Earl of Lancaster knew it. But he acted foolishly, and too soon. Nevertheless, his execution grievously offended the North, where so many were his vassals. I heard cheers for Edward's defeat at Byland in Carlisle's streets! Northumberland is ready to revolt — for they have been harder hit by the Scots raiding than have Cumberland and Westmorland. Indeed, many there believe that Your Highness intends to annexe Northumberland to Scotland anyway. After your claim to Tynedale. That it is in your realm."

"There could be a grain of truth in that," the King admitted. "I *have* considered it. And I will so do — if it will bring King Edward to his senses and the peace-tables."

"It is my belief that it would fail to do so. Even this. Never was a king so set in his folly. I say, Sire, that you will have to reckon without Edward of Carnarvon! He will not negotiate with you, because to do so he must recognise you as King of Scots, equal with himself, and independent. This he will never do. All the defeats and raids since Bannockburn have not brought him to it. Annexation of Northumberland to your realm in itself will not do so either. Other steps Your Majesty must take. You will only gain your peace treaty with another king on England's throne!"

"M'mmm." Bruce took a pace or two over the flagged floor of the brewhouse, in a quandary. In his heart, he knew that this man was probably right. Yet it went against the grain, against all his instincts, for himself, a king, to plot with a traitorous subject to bring down another king. Not that such qualms had ever affected Edward or his father. He swung on Moray.

"How think you, Thomas?" he demanded, to gain time for decision. "Is there to be no peace while King Edward reigns?"

"It is now nine years since Bannockburn, Sire. And you have done all that man can do to gain a treaty. In this I fear my lord of Carlisle is right. King Edward will not change now. Yet both realms need peace above all things. It seems that other means must be used to bring it about. Has my lord firm suggestions?" Recognising his uncle's difficult position, Moray asked the question himself.

Harcla responded without hesitation. "I have, my lord. I propose that King Robert should give me firm terms to lay before King Edward. If he rejects them — then we make armed revolt in the North, assisted by the Scots, to have the King deposed and his son appointed in his place, with a regency. On understanding and agreement that the first act of the new sovereign would be the conclusion of a treaty of peace with Scotland, accepting the independence of that realm and the authority of King Robert."

"Firm terms, you say. From King Robert. What terms have you in mind?"

"Fair and honourable terms. Which King Edward, were he honourable, could accept. More important, which an English parliament could accept. Each realm to maintain its own king, laws and customs, unthreatened by the other. Each to promote and advance the common advantage of the other. All English claims on Scotland to be withdrawn, and all Scots claims on England. Arbiters to be appointed, of equal number and rank on both sides, to settle all differences between the realms, and subjects of the realms."

"These are fair conditions, sir," Bruce acknowledged. "But scarce inducements! There is nothing here to *induce* King Edward to agree."

"I do not believe that anything will so induce him!" the other returned. "Whatever terms you send, he will reject, I think. But these would commend themselves to a parliament. And give the lords and barons of England good cause to unite against the King, when he refused. Which is important."

"Yet inducement there should be, surely," Moray said. "To make it *possible* for King Edward to accept."

Harcla shrugged. "Anything such must come from you, the Scots."

"Long I have sought for, fought for this treaty," Bruce said slowly. "Therefore I would give much to see it concluded. For my people's sake, who need peace. I have thought much on it. I would agree that one of my daughters should wed King Edward's heir, now some ten years of age. And I would make some payment in gold in reparation. For injury done to the realm of England these last years, some generous payment. If such would aid in the acceptance of these terms."

Douglas stared. "*Pay* the English . . .!" he exclaimed.

"King Edward is said to be short of moneys. All his treasure gone on his favourites. He might listen to the chink of gold, where other persuasion fails."

"Very well, Sire. Such generous offers I will make to the King. But still I fear he will not heed, and we shall require to take to arms."

"It may be so. But, see you, I will not now commence a war against the might of England. It is peace I seek, not large war. Revolt by Edward's lords is one matter. Invasion by my Scots host is another."

"Not war for you, Sire. Only support, we seek. No greater force than you have sent raiding into England times unnumbered. With captains such as these to lead that support!" Harcla nodded towards Moray and Douglas. "For I do not deny that England is short of able captains. However many great lords she has!" And the new Earl sniffed his contempt of all such.

"That is true, at least. But — these lords? How many would rise against the King?"

"Many. Most, indeed. Those whose stomachs King Edward has not turned, the Despensers have . . .!"

"Names, man — names!'

"The King's own brother, for one — the Earl of Kent. The Earl of Norfolk. The Lord Berkeley. The bishops of Ely, Lincoln and Hereford. The Earl of Leicester, who is my lord of Lancaster's heir ..."

"Kent would turn against his own brother?"

"He is hot against the King. The Despensers slight him. And not only he. The Queen herself, I think, would not be sorry to see her husband deposed and her son king. Her lover, young Mortimer, is one of those strongest for revolt — and he does nothing that displeases Her Majesty."

"So-o-o! England is in sorry state, I see!" Bruce looked at the stocky man shrewdly. "And you, my lord? What will be *your* place in the new kingdom?"

Harcla was nothing if not frank. "In the said revolt, I command. For none of these others is fit to lead an army. And when we win, I expect to be one of the regents of the young King."

"You do! You fly a high hawk, my lord — for one who but a year or so past was but a Cumberland squire!"

"My hawk has strong wings, Sire."

They eyed each other like wary dogs. Then Bruce inclined his head.

"Very well, my lord. We shall have a compact. I have a clerk out there, who shall write us the terms you are to put before King Edward. For the rest, if he refuses, it is between ourselves. On the day that you rise, with major force, a Scots cavalry host of 5,000 will join you, under my lord of Douglas. To remain under his command. You understand? I will have no Englishman commanding my Scots subjects. And, before then, I want proofs of your support, in more than in the North."

"That Your Majesty shall have. In abundance. I thank you. Give me but six months, and you shall have your peace treaty ..."

* * *

Two of those months were passed before the King heard more of Andrew Harcla. And, when he heard, Bruce was in little state to pay fullest heed, in a turmoil of emotion, agitation, joy, concern, inextricably mixed. For the very night before, or in fact the same dawn, Elizabeth had given birth, at Dunfermline, to a son — a living and perfect son. But the birth was a dreadful one, lasting over twelve hours and almost killing a woman too old for normal childbearing. That the Queen survived the desperate night was indeed something of a miracle — just as the production of a hale male child at last, after twenty-one years of marriage, was a miracle.

So now all Scotland rejoiced in that an undoubted heir to the throne was born, and the bells that had celebrated Bannockburn now pealed and clanged and jangled as endlessly. But Bruce himself sat, a prey to anxiety, fears, self-blame — indeed could have wished the child unborn that his Elizabeth should have been spared this. For she was more than exhausted. She was direly weak, her features woefully waxen and drawn, her eyes dark-circled. She had lost great quantities of blood. She had lain, only part conscious, all that March day, whilst Dunfermline throbbed to the joyful clangour of the bells, and the King watched her every shallow breath. So he had sat hour after hour — and fiercely repelled any who sought to intervene, console, consult or otherwise distract.

It was a brave man, therefore, who entered that bedchamber above the Pittendreich Glen that late afternoon, unbidden — but then, this *was* a notably brave man, as all Christendom acknowledged whatever else it might say of him. James Douglas, come from the Borders, stood with his back to the door and looked at his friends.

Hollow-eyed, hunched, the King stared at him dully for long moments after he had recognised who was there — for he had not slept in forty hours, and was all but dazed. He did not offer a single word of greeting.

"I . . . I have heard all, Sire," Douglas said, low-voiced. "An heir. And Her Grace in sore state. But — God is good. He will aid Her Grace."

"Is He? Will He? What makes you so sure, James Douglas?" That was said thickly, in a monotone.

"Because He gave the Queen a notable spirit, Sire. That is why. It is that spirit will save her."

It was not the King who answered. Just audible, from the bed came the whispered word, "Jamie!"

Douglas came forward, then, and Bruce sat up. It was the first word Elizabeth had spoken, for hours.

She did not say more. But before her heavy-lidded eyes closed again, she mustered a tiny smile for them both. It lifted the King's heart.

"Oh, lassie! Lassie!" he said brokenly.

She raised the long white fingers of her left hand in brief acknowledgement, and his own rough and calloused hand reached out to grip and grasp.

So these three remained, silent.

At length, when it was clear that the Queen slept, Bruce spoke softly. "An heir for Scotland was not worth this, Jamie."

The other made no comment.

"But it was not this that brought you from Roxburgh Castle, I think," the King went on. "Word of it could not have reached you in time."

"No, Sire. It was other."

"Grave tidings? To come yourself, not send messenger?"

"Harcla, Earl of Carlisle, is dead. Tortured, half-hanged and disembowelled, after the Plantagenet fashion! There will be no revolt, Sire."

Bruce looked at the other heavily. "So Edward was not . . . agreeable!" he said. "Harcla went to him, with the terms?"

"Yes. And King Edward esteemed it high treason. To have approached Your Grace, without his royal authority. No subject of his will have truck with rebels, he said! He dealt so with Harcla, as a warning to others."

The King drew a hand wearily over his brow. "How above all stubborn can be your weak and stupid man! Shall we never see peace, because of this royal fool? What of all the others, the great lords who were to support the revolt? Are these all taken also?"

"No. Harcla went alone to the King — and was requited thus. Your Grace will wonder at how I had the news. It came from Umfraville. Sir Ingram himself brought me word, at Roxburgh."

"Umfraville! So we have not heard the last of that strange man. He ventured into Scotland again?"

"Aye, Sire. His Northumberland lands march with yours at Tynedale, as you know — none so far from the Border. He was not ill-pleased at Harcla's death, esteeming him up-jumped traitor. But he is for a peace treaty between the realms, nevertheless. He says that he believes King Edward to be nearer to it than ever before. That he, Umfraville, seeks to prevail with the King to conclude such . . ."

"Ha! He would regain those great lost lands of his, in Scotland, if he might!"

"It may be so. But, whatever his reasons, he is working for a peace treaty. And is hopeful — despite Harcla's execution. Harcla died, he says, not because he favoured a peace, but because he chose to negotiate without his master's authority. Umfraville said to tell Your Grace that if you sent an embassage to King Edward to discuss terms, it might be favourably received. He suggested

Bishop Lamberton, since King Edward had a liking for him once. I told him Lamberton was too sick a man to travel . . ."

'Aye. It is as much as he may do to come to Dunfermline. But — this of an embassage. Will Edward receive an embassage from rebels, as he names us? I think not. Has Umfraville forgotten this?"

"No. He says that the embassage must not seem to be that. Just travellers on their way to another land. France, or the Low Countries, perhaps. Who could call at London in passing. And see the King privily. Through Umfraville himself. He has Edward's ear, he says . . ."

"That would be difficult. Whom could I send, that I could trust in this, whom Edward would not take and slay out-of-hand? In his stupid arrogance and hate. William Lamberton would have served, yes. But you, or Moray, or Hay — such he would never tolerate. He has put prices on all your heads. We deal with no reasonable man."

"Some other cleric, Sire? Whom he would scarce slay . . .?"

Bruce looked at his sleeping wife thoughtfully. "Umfraville believes there to be hope in this? True hope of Edward's acceptance?"

"He says so. The King is alarmed at the enmity of his nobles. So he made example of Harcla. But he would wish the Scottish entanglement over, the better to deal with these others."

"Aye. Then I have thought of a way. David, Bishop of Moray, has long sought to go to France. It has been his desire to found a college there. In Paris. For Scots. A cherished project. I will send him, with the Sieur de Sully, Grand Butler of France, and the other French knights taken at Byland. Time they went home. Edward will give them safe-conduct, since they were captured fighting for him. On the way to France they will call to pay their respects to the King, in London. And carry with them such terms as I can offer." He nodded. "Harcla was too ambitious, too fast. But it may be that he did not die in vain . . ."

The Queen stirred, and opened her eyes. Both men sat forward. But, after another faint flicker of a smile, she closed her eyes again. Her breathing deepened a little.

"In that smile is your hope, Sire," Douglas said gently. "Her Grace is of all women both finest and fairest."

Bruce looked at the younger man keenly. "Of all women . . .? *I* say so, yes. But you, Jamie? You have never wed, my friend. You have never given your heart to another?"

"Given long years ago, Sire. To one man — yourself. And to one woman — who lies there. And smiles!" Douglas rose. "Have I Your Grace's permission to retire? I have travelled far and fast . . ."

* * *

Some eight weeks later, with the broom abloom and the first cuckoos calling hauntingly in Pittendreich Glen, and with the Queen on her feet again, although pale and frail, only a shadow of her former proud womanhood, but the new Prince David thriving lustily, Bishop David Murray of Moray sent word back to Scotland, not from London but from York, where King Edward had returned. He and de Sully had been received by the King, in Umfraville's company. Edward would not hear any terms from him, the Bishop, whom he declared to be both rebel and excommunicate. But he had been prepared to listen to de Sully, as a Frenchman and man of honour. Sully had announced the Scots terms. Later, the King had summoned only Sully to his presence, and told him that he favoured peace and could accept all save two of the Scots proposals. But these two were the basic independence of Scotland; and the kingship of Robert Bruce. These he could never accept. Therefore there could be no peace treaty, since the King of England could never sit down at such table with rebels. But, for the sake of peace, he was prepared to accept a prolonged truce — with the Leader of the Scots people, not the King of Scots, of which there was and could be none. He suggested a truce of thirteen years. He was prepared to send commissioners to sign such a truce at Berwick, on intimation that the Leader of the Scots people would meet them to endorse it.

"God in His heaven!" Bruce groaned to his wife, as this was declared to them. "The man is crazed! Run wholly mad. Will nothing teach him, nothing open his eyes? Must two whole realms remain for ever at war because of one man's insensate vanity? His own kingdom falling about his ears, and all he can think of is to deny me the name of mine!"

"It is beyond all·in folly, yes," Elizabeth agreed. "But — this of a truce? Why thirteen years?"

"God knows! The man is deranged. In one *half* of thirteen years all could be changed. *Will* be changed. Neither he nor I alive, it may be! How can a man deal with such as this . . .?"

"His Grace of England says that he will send his commissioners to Berwick, Sire. Next month," Bishop David's courier went on. "To sign the terms of the truce. With Your Grace . . ."

"Not with my Grace! Only with the rebel leader of rebellious Scots! As though I would sign anything on those terms. The crass fool! Small wonder that his lords are in near revolt, that England is riven and prostrate. With such a monarch . . .!"

"And yet, my heart, is the case so ill?" the Queen put in, gently. "Edward's pride is all that is left to him, empty, profitless pride. So he assails yours. Withholds all, for a couple of words, king and kingdom. Yet gives all nevertheless, in fact . . ."

"Gives all? What do you mean? He denies all. This treaty of peace — without it, I can never build up Scotland to what the realm should be, must be. All our treasure and strength is wasted in maintaining armed men, ever and again having to burn our own country in the face of invaders, living in our armour, horses saddled, our trading ships attacked on the seas. Near on thirty years of war! Scotland needs peace . . ."

"Yes, Robert — peace. But, see you — you blame Edward for flinching at a word. Your kingship, the realm's independent name. But are you not in danger of a like fault, my dear? This word treaty? What is but a word? It is not the treaty that is important, but the peace. The peace that Scotland needs. And what is a thirteen-year truce, but peace? Bannockburn was but twelve years ago. So long a truce is as good as a peace, is it not? Since it is the peace you want not the treaty, let not *your* pride deny it, Robert."

Biting his lip, the man stared at her.

"Moreover," she pressed him, "Edward's folly will not permit that he reigns for thirteen years. Or three, I think! Why wait for the peace which may follow, when you can have it now? Peace, whether in the form of truce or treaty, is the same, is it not? Both can be broken, or kept. I say, Robert — go to Berwick, and sign this truce. You will be none the less king."

"It may be that you are right . . ."

Chapter Twenty-Two

Elizabeth de Burgh smiled into the early afternoon sunshine, at the picture they presented, the man and the two boys, the stocky, sturdy ten-year-old and the toddler of not yet three, walking up from the shore together hand in hand, with the ribs of Robert's fine new ship in the foreground, and as background all the weed-hung skerries and headlands of the Clyde estuary and the heart-catching, colour-stained loveliness of the Western mountains. It was a fair and satisfying scene — but there was pain as well as pride and love and satisfaction in the woman's smile. For the man who held the children's hands walked with a clumsiness that was far different from his accustomed sure stride, and held himself with a stiffness that was almost the posture of age — although he was in fact but fifty-three. These last years his legs had been tending to swell; and although she had not said anything, Elizabeth feared the dropsy. The long years of stress, privation, hard-lying and irregular eating, were telling on Robert Bruce.

But it was not only the sight of the man that affected her. The two boys, uncle and nephew as they were, brought a lump to her throat at times. The good God only knew what trials lay in store for those two. Their two-year-old David was the child of ageing parents, like to be a king long before man's estate — no desirable fate. And Robert was an orphan now, Walter Stewart having died suddenly, unaccountably, five months before, at the age of thirty-three, leaving this ten-year-old boy High Steward of Scotland.

Bernard de Linton, at the Queen's side on the grassy terrace before the house, did not see the trio quite as did she. "A fair picture, Your Grace," he commented. "The King and his heirs. The succession assured. Concerned with the things of peace, not war. These ships. It is well."

"Well, yes." Elizabeth agreed, whatever her personal reservations. "I do not know who wins most delight from this ship-building — the princes or His Grace! Or, indeed, my lord of the Isles! They are all children together, in this, I do declare. I hear nothing but talk of ships and shipping, of keels and bulwarks and draughts, of beams and timbering and cordage, from morn till night. Cardross, I vow, is no place for a woman, my lord Abbot — unless she be a Hebridean woman perhaps!" She said that with a smile.

The Chancellor coughed, wondering whether the Queen was indeed referring to the Lady Christina MacRuarie of Garmoran. He did not concede, as he might have done, that Cardross was no place from which to rule Scotland, either; and that he, the Chancellor, had to spend an unconscionable part of his time traipsing between Dunfermline and here, or Arboath and here, or Scone and here — less than suitable employment for a mitred abbot and chief minister of the kingdom. His unannounced arrival, this sunny afternoon, from Dunfermline, was only one of many such occasions when events demanded that he should see the monarch personally rather than just send messengers and clerks, with papers for scrutiny, signing and affixment of the Privy Seal. Abbot Bernard was a patient and shrewd man, if inclining towards pomposity in a small way with the years.

"Your Grace mislikes this new house?" he asked.

"No. I like it very well. As a house. It is more comfortable than all the great stone castles. But I have scarce my liege lord's passion for the sea, these islands and mountains. Nor indeed for his Highlandmen! They are well enough — but I cannot think that they conceive women to have any place in God's world, and theirs! Other than in their beds, to be sure!"

The Chancellor coughed again, rather disapprovingly for so stalwart a fighter. Where women were concerned, de Linton was slightly prim — and Elizabeth seldom failed to tease him, although mildly.

The two royal daughters, Matilda and Margaret, came running, laughing and shouting aloud, from the braes of Carman Hill behind the house, where they were tending to run wild, these days, with the herd-boys and milkmaids — unsuitable upbringing for princesses, but in tune with the King's frame of mind. After the tragedy of Marjory, Bruce had vowed that no other child for whom he had responsibility should have his or her youth spoiled, and young freedom denied, for any trammels of state and trappings of royal position. About this he was adamant. All too soon the demands and coils of their high estate would entangle his offspring. Meanwhile, let them have their fill of freedom, and learn to know their fellows, of all ranks and classes — especially these Highlanders. It rejoiced the King's heart that both girls, and Robert, already spoke the Highland Gaelic as well as they did French. Elizabeth was less sure that this was the way to train princesses — but her own strength was not what it had been, for she had never fully recovered from David's birth, and she tended to assert herself less.

"We need cakes. Cakes. And wine," Matilda cried, now aged ten, and an eager tomboy, all arms and legs. "It is a wedding-feast. A great feast. Up in the sheep-stall yonder. I am marrying Seumas. Am I not lucky? He is the best! We are going to have seven children. All boys. Seumas says we will not have any girls. Seumas says we must have cakes and wine. He would rather have *uisge-beatha*, but . . . wine will do. I said we would not get *uisge-beatha* . . ."

"You did not! *I* said it," Margaret, a year younger, and slighter, prettier, objected. "I said we would not get wine either. Only milk . . ."

"Milk is of no good for a wedding, silly! Only wine will serve, Seumas says . . ."

"I am marrying Ranald," Margaret revealed, but with less pride than her sister's announcement. Seumas Colquhoun was the head shepherd's son, while Ranald was Angus of the Isles' second.

"Ranald is not so strong as Seumas . . ."

"Hush you, hush you, shameless ones!" the Queen told them. "Can you not perceive that you outrage my lord Abbot? Make your reverences to him — and then be gone. Or your sire will hear you. Here he comes. Tell Mistress Kate in the kitchens that you may have oaten cakes, and a little watered wine. Watered, mind you! Now — off with you . . ."

"Ha, Bernard — I never know whether to rejoice to see you, for your own sake, or to fear for what brings you!" the King exclaimed, as he came up. His voice was strong as ever, at least. "Welcome to Cardross, whatever. These ones have been down with me inspecting the new trading galliot we build. They declare that she is too heavy and will surely sink. How think you?"

"I know not a galliot from a gallimash, Sire. I prefer God's good firm land . . ."

"Like Her Grace. I grieve for you both! Well — where have you ridden from today, my friend? Dunfermline?"

"Aye, Sire. With news. Grave news. Yet — perhaps none so ill. For us. For Your Grace. Concerning . . . concerning His Grace of England." The Abbot glanced down at the small boys, warningly.

"Edward, heh? I have never heard good news from that quarter, alack! Rob — take Davie. Go with the girls, there."

"I would rather stay with you, Sire," the Lord High Steward of Scotland objected. "The girls care only for that sheepleader Seumas Colquhoun!"

"Tush, man — you will not be outdone by a Colquhoun! Away with you both. And do not let the bold Seumas blood your nose again!"

The Chancellor looked after the small and reluctantly departing backs. "King Edward is dead, Sire. And . . . evilly!"

Bruce caught and held his breath, his eyes narrowing. He did not speak.

"Dead, Abbot Bernard? The King?" Elizabeth whispered. "Edward of Carnarvon dead! You are sure?"

"Yes, Madam — dead. Slain. And beyond all evilly. And the Despensers, father and son, likewise. All dead. England has a new king — Edward the Third. And a new ruler — the man Roger Mortimer!"

"Mortimer? That puppy! The Frenchwoman's paramour!" Bruce frowned. "Edward Plantagenet was a fool, and grievous thorn in my flesh. I cannot weep for him. But . . . may he rest in

God's peace, now. Like his dire father. How came he to die, Bernard?"

It was the Queen's turn to be glanced at by the hesitant Chancellor. "I think perhaps, Sire — alone?" he suggested. "It makes ill telling . . ."

"I am no blushing maid, my lord Abbot. And Ulster's daughter!" Elizabeth reminded. "Say on."

De Linton inclined his head. "Queen Isabella returned from France. Where she has dwelt these last years, away from the King. She brought a French force, under the man Mortimer. And the Count of Hainault. Henry, the new Earl of Lancaster, and the Earl of Norfolk, the Marshal, and others, joined her. The standard of revolt was raised against the King. And swiftly all was over. He did not fight any better against his wife and Mortimer than against ourselves, Sire! He fled to Wales, making for Ireland. He surrendered to their army, and was immediately deposed. And Edward the Third, aged fourteen years, declared in his stead."

"But was not killed? Deposed? Yet you say he is dead?"

"Aye. Murdered. Thereafter. Most terribly. By Mortimer's creatures. They . . . they thrust a red-hot iron up into his vitals. By the back passage. That he should die without evident wound. Secretly. But one boasted of it. And then confessed . . ." The Abbot's voice tailed away.

"Sweet Christ Jesu!" Shaken indeed, Bruce looked at his wife. "That men . . . should be . . . so vile! 'Fore God — Edward! Their King! To die so! He was young, yet . . .?"

"But forty-three, Sire. But old in folly and misadventure . . ."

There was an interruption. Malcolm, Earl of Lennox, an elderly man now, put in an appearance. He came over from nearby Dumbarton almost every day to see his friend and liege. Always a hater of violence, told the grim tidings, he was greatly upset.

"What is it that is in these English?" he demanded. "This savagery, butchery? That they break into. To speak with, they are like ourselves. More careful, indeed. But scratch their fine skins, and they are thus beneath!" Pure Celt himself, he paused, a little alarmed at what he had said, remembering that Bruce, at least on his father's side, was of the same basic stock as most of the English nobility; and Elizabeth was wholly so.

"Mortimer is from the Welsh marches, is he not?" The King shrugged. "I know not, Malcolm, what makes them so. We Scots have sins enough. But . . ."

"It is conviction, straight from God, that they are superior!" the Queen said quietly. "Always, they are assured that they are superior, right. There is no question. Therefore others must be wrong. And if wrong, inferior. All men are inferior to the English. They do not require to say it, even think it — they *know* it! And inferior creatures are lesser men, scarcely men at all! They cannot conceive themselves in place of such — and so can inflict these terrible savageries on others. For they cannot feel it in themselves, being otherwise. Being a different creation, superior, English!"

The men looked somewhat askance at the sudden unexpected vehemence of that outpouring. It was not often that Elizabeth de Burgh revealed something of the hurt and battened-down hatred which long years of imprisonment and scorning had bred in her.

Her husband changed the subject. "So what now?" he asked. "How shall these tidings affect us in Scotland? The new King is little more than a child. *He* will not refuse to sit at a peace-table with me, I think! But those who control him? His mother is a vixen, an evil woman. And this Mortimer an insolent popinjay. There will be a regency. Is there word of its members, Bernard?"

"Only that Henry, Earl of Lancaster, is chiefest, Sire."

"A weak man. Weaker than his brother Thomas, whom God rest. I' faith — they could have done with Harcla, now! So much the better for us. The old Lancaster was always of a mind to talk with us. He was kin to me, far out. His brother may think the same. We may yet win our peace treaty."

"Pray that it is better kept than the thirteen-year truce, then!" Lennox exclaimed. "I swear that meant little enough to Edward. First he brought young Edward Baliol to his Court, to set up as a puppet-king for Scotland! Within months of signing the truce! He seized our ships on the sea. Commanded the warding in prison of all Scots in England . . ."

"Aye — it has been a travesty of peace," the King agreed. "Two years of pin-pricks . . ."

"Yet it has given you breathing-space," Elizabeth insisted. "Time to think of other things than war. Trade, see you — and shipbuilding! There has been no invasion, no major raiding. I say that it was worth the signing. As says Thomas — my lord of Moray. And he has the wisest head in this land, I think."

"It may be so," Bruce allowed. "But what now? The truce was made with Edward the Second. It does not bind his successor. It is now at an end. I want no more truces, but a true peace. An embassage to the new regents . . .?"

"I think not, Sire — not first," the Chancellor advised. "It would smack of too great eagerness, perhaps. On the part of rebels! Better some less open move first, lest we be rejected, to our hurt. Do as Your Grace did with the Frenchman, de Sully. Send an embassage travelling to France. Or to the Pope. If to the Pope then such cannot be denied a safe-conduct by the English. Then, in passage, it could sound out Lancaster and the others privily . . ."

"Aye — that would be wiser, Bernard. You are right. Moreover, a treaty with France would be easier to forge than with England! But since the King of France's sister now controls the King of England, the one could well aid the other! Since the Pope now recognises me as king — since our great letter, and Moray's visit to him — if he could be prevailed upon to urge on the King of France, and the new King of England, to recognise my kingship, the thing might be achieved. An embassage therefore, first to the Pope, and then to France. Moray again?"

"Assuredly, Sire. Send my lord of Moray — since it seems the Pope liked him well. But we require more than this peace treaty. We require that his offence against the Church in Scotland be lifted by His Holiness. It still remains, and is a grave inconvenience, if naught else! For it means, as you know, that new appointments within the Church, new bishops and abbots and the like, cannot be approved from Rome. And so do not carry full weight. Send a churchman also, therefore, to convince His Holiness of our true obedience and duty."

"M'mmm. Obedience and duty! Words I like not, my lord Abbot!"

"Yet in matters ecclesiastical we must use them, Your Grace," the other declared. "Since only in obedience to the Pontiff do we gain full authority for our offices in the Church."

"Very well, Bernard. Whom shall we send? Yourself?"

"No, Sire — not me. I am still in His Holiness's disfavour. As is my lord of St. Andrews. It must be one who did not defy him. In 1318."

"But you all did, man. All the bishops and senior clergy."

"Then it must be a younger man. Yet in high office. Send my lord's Archdeacon, Sire. James Bene. Archdeacon of St. Andrews. He is young, but sound, and no fool. The best of the new men. My lord's right hand . . ."

"Very well. So be it. Moray and Master Bene shall go. To the Pope, and then to King Charles of France. But by London. Send for a safe-conduct for them, from the new King Edward. We shall sound out this new rule in England . . ."

* * *

"You are not the only one to make a vow, Robert," the Queen said, one day the following spring when the King, confined to the house of Cardross with badly swollen legs, was bewailing many things but in especial that he was never likely now to lead that Crusade which the Pope was so anxious to sponsor, and which he had vowed to make that time in the Galloway cave when the spider had inspired him to his duty. "I also made a vow, once. And And of late I have been minded to fulfil it."

"You? A vow? A woman, on a Crusade? That I'll not believe . . .!"

"Not a Crusade, no. But still a vow. And a pilgrimage. Is it so strange? Cannot a woman, in her extremity, also call upon God and His saints for especial aid? And promise to make some reparation should her call be heard, her requirement granted?"

"No doubt but you are right, lass. It is but that vows seem scarce a woman's part. But then, Elizabeth de Burgh is no common woman! When did you make this vow? And on what terms? What pilgrimage do you speak of?"

"I made it all those years ago, at St. Duthac's sanctuary, at Tain. Before the altar. When William, Earl of Ross betrayed us to the English. When all was at its blackest, after the defeats of Methven and Strathfillan, the fall of Kildrummy, you a hunted fugitive and Nigel captured — then I vowed that if God, hearing perhaps the intercessions of your Celtic Saint Duthac, would one day grant me a safe return to my husband's arms and make me the mother of his children, then I would make a pilgrimage of thankfulness to this far northern shrine. It has been on my conscience that I have never done it — and I grow neither younger nor stronger for journeying. I think the time has come to fulfil my vow, Robert — if you will give me leave?" She did not add that, since Duthac had proved effective once, she might well seek to enlist his aid a second time, for the same husband, whose physical state was now much concerning her. She had never taken his leprosy fears too much to heart; but this trouble with his leg-swellings and breathlessness worried her greatly.

Not a little touched by her revelation, Bruce put an arm around his wife's shoulders. "My dear — you never told me. We would have gone together."

"When have you had time, opportunity — or latterly the strength — to spare for such lengthy pilgrimage into the Highland North? With the saving and governance of this kingdom on your shoulders? Moreover, this was for myself alone. I would not, will not, be taken on such errand by you, Robert. You understand?"

"Aye, lass. As you will. And you think to go now?"

"Soon. Now that I may leave little David. And you all. The snows are melting in the passes. With May blooming, and the cuckoos calling, I shall go. A woman's oblation."

"Yet you must not go alone. That I will not have. You are the Queen. If I may not go with you, another shall. Whom will you have?"

"I would choose James Douglas. But since I know this to be impossible, I would have Gilbert Hay. He has ever loved me, in his quiet way. And makes undemanding companion."

"No—I could not spare Jamie. I but await Thomas's return from France, to send them both south once more. On their old ploys! Deep raiding into England. You know it. This cannot wait. But Gibbie you may have."

Elizabeth nodded. They were back to that—Scotland and England at war. The Queen-Mother, Mortimer, and the Regency Council had at first unilaterally confirmed the thirteen-year truce, to the Scots' surprise; but latterly it had become clear that this was merely a convenience to gain time to assemble their strength against Scotland. Spies informed that secret orders had gone out all over England for a May muster at Newcastle, where Count John of Hainault, the noted commander—to whose niece the young King had recently become betrothed—was to command with his fine force of heavy Flemish horse. Bruce intended to strike first, as of yore, with another of the Douglas-Moray swift cavalry drives, as dissuasion. But it was depressing to have to return to such tactics.

When Elizabeth went off about her own affairs, Robert Bruce smiled a little, to himself. He was not quite so moribund and immobile as she seemed to think him—even though horse-riding nowadays did tend to make him breathless and his heart to beat irregularly. He was damned if he was going to be carried about in a litter, yet—but there were other methods of transport. The new trading galliot he and Angus Og had been building, to be the first of a trading fleet, was all but finished. It would be a good opportunity to test its qualities out, while Elizabeth was elsewhere—for nothing was surer than that she would insist that he was not in a fit state to go sailing. He loved her dearly—but he was not going to be coddled. And he had been wanting to go to Ireland again, for some time, to Antrim, where the Irish chiefs and kinglets were once more wishing to enter into a league for the expulsion of the English. Since his brother Edward's death he had consistently refused to consider any suggestion that he should assume the highly theoretical and nominal High Kingship of All Ireland; but he was not against using his undoubted influence with the Irish to bring pressure on the new English régime, parallel with the Douglas-Moray expedition.

Once Elizabeth was safely off on her pilgrimage, he would go sailing.

* * *

The Queen gone, the galliot's trials satisfactory, the Irish agreement usefully concluded, and Bruce tired but not displeased with his physical state, the galliot returned up the Clyde estuary in late August, that year of 1327, escorted by a squadron of Angus Og's galleys. Thomas, Earl of Moray, himself was waiting for his uncle on the jetty at Cardross.

Moray had stirring tidings to relate. Douglas and he had twisted the English leopard's tail, with a vengeance. Not content with raiding and making diversionary gestures deep into England, they had had a confrontation with the young King Edward himself; indeed they had sought to capture him, and Douglas had been within yards of succeeding, the youthful monarch's personal chaplain being slain in the skirmish. They had defeated a forward force of the main enemy army at Cockdale, in Durham. Then slipped over the high moorland to Weardale, forcing the cumbrous English array to make a great and tiring detour in wet weather with rivers in spate, on terrain where the Hainaulters' heavy cavalry was bogged down. At Stanhope, a hunting-park of the Bishop of Durham, they had taken up a strong position on the hillside, for all to see, and waited, leading the enemy to believe that they would do battle there — despite the enormous difference in size of the respective forces. Presuming that a full-scale confrontation must develop the next day, the English leaders had camped for the night on the low ground. This was when Douglas had tried his audacious night raid, for a capture. They had collected many prisoners, including courtiers, before the camp was roused — though the King unfortunately escaped. And thereafter, since they had never intended to do set battle with a host ten times their size, in enemy country, they slipped away northwards in the darkness, and returned to Scotland forthwith. Douglas was now back on the Border, and he, Moray, had come for further orders.

"I' faith, Thomas — here is excellent news!" Bruce cried, his limp weariness forgotten. "On my soul, you make a pretty pair of brigands! That youth begins his reign with a notable indignity, indeed. Like his father! Perhaps it will teach his advisers that the Scots would make better friends than foes! With my Irish arrangements, just completed, I swear they will have to come to the conclusion that a peace treaty is the only way in which they will win respite in their own realm!"

Moray coughed. "Unfortunately, Sire — it may prove otherwise. As I said, we captured prisoners close to the King. One, a Thomas Rokeby, esquire to King Edward, declared that it was common knowledge that Your Grace was dying! And that the English need not trouble — that once you were gone the rebel Scots would soon come to heel, with no need for any treaty . . ."

"By the Rude — they think that! So I am dying, am I? 'Fore God, I will teach them otherwise!" The King's eyes blazed with all their old fire.

"We told Rokeby so, Sire — and let him go free, to convey the facts to his King. But — I doubt if he will be believed. Or even believed us."

"Then we will show them, beyond a peradventure! Hear you that, Angus my friend? I am dying. The English have only to wait! So — they will learn differently, and swiftly! By two days from this I will be on English soil, by God! And we shall see who dies . . . !"

Robert Bruce was as good as his oath — however much it cost him, in bodily fatigue, pain in his legs and at his heart, and such exhaustion that he had to be propped up in his saddle by esquires, one on either side of his horse. Nevertheless, two days later and ninety weary horseback miles south-eastwards, he led James Douglas and Moray and their host over the Coldstream ford of Tweed, and on to besiege the Bishop of Durham's castle at Norham. Also he sent lieutenants to invest Warkworth Castle, and even the Percy stronghold of Alnwick, while others went further south still, and west, to waste Northumberland — saving always Tynedale — North Durham, Cumberland and Westmorland. Even though Bruce conducted this warfare largely from a tent under Norham's walls, the King of Scots' presence was made abundantly clear to all the North of England. He sent heralds to announce to the King of England, wherever he should be found, the Earl of Lancaster, the Archbishop of York and the Bishop of Durham, that he, the King of Scots, intended to annexe the county of Northumberland to the realm of Scotland forthwith.

It was in these circumstances, on a mellow autumn day of October, that Sir Henry Percy of Alnwick, Lord of Northumberland, with Sir William de Denham, of the English Chancery, came riding under a white flag to the Scots camp at Norham — an unhappy and nervous delegation. This was Bruce's first meeting with the son of his old enemy — for the previous Henry Percy had died the same year as Bannockburn. He was, in fact, very much a replica of his father, tall, thin, foxy of face and prematurely stooping, balding. Eyeing him, Bruce knew a little disappointment. This man was not worth his vengeance. He had dressed himself in full armour to meet the envoys. It mattered not, after all; but he was glad that his swollen legs were hidden beneath the steel, uncomfortable as it was.

The Englishmen brought a request for a peace treaty, from King Edward and his regents. They wanted to know King Robert's terms.

"Have you writing to show me, my lord?" Bruce barked at Percy. "From your liege lord?"

The other nodded. He handed over a sealed missive, addressed to the Lord Robert, King of Scots.

The sigh that escaped from the Bruce was eloquent as it was long. He had waited and worked for thirteen years for that simple superscription.

The day following, the envoys were sent away with the Scots terms. They comprised six points — and were more favourable, generous indeed, than even Moray advised. Nothing must stop a settlement now. The points were: (1) That the King of England, and parliament, must acknowledge that King Robert and his heirs for all time coming should rule the independent kingdom of Scotland, without rendering any service or homage to any. (2) That the King of Scots' son and heir, the Prince David, should have for betrothed bride the King of England's young sister, Princess Joanna of the Tower. (3) That no subjects of the King of England should hold lands in Scotland; nor subjects of the King of Scots hold lands in England. (4) That King Robert and his heirs should lend military aid, if requested, against all save the French, with whom Scotland was already in alliance; likewise English aid should be available to the Scots, if required. (5) That the King of Scots would pay the sum of £20,000 within three years, as reparation for damage done to the kingdom of England. (6) That the King of England should use all powers to persuade the papal curia to repeal the sentence of excommunication against King Robert and his Council and subjects. And this forthwith.

If the King of England would confirm these terms, under the Great Seal of England, King Robert would send his commissioners to Newcastle, to negotiate the peace. And promptly.

Bruce had himself hoisted into the saddle again, and turned his horse's head for home.

They had not long crossed the ford of Tweed when a small party, riding hard, came galloping across the green levels of the Merse, to meet them. The King perceived that it was his Lord High Constable, Gilbert Hay, and reined up. And at his friend's grim, unhappy features, the royal heart missed another beat.

Pulling up before him, Hay flung himself down, knelt, looked up, opened his mouth to speak — and said no word.

"Well, Gibbie — well? You are back, from your travels. How is the Queen?"

Hay moistened his lips, and dropped his glance again. Still he knelt.

The scene swam before the King's eyes. "Out with it, man! She is not sick? In trouble . . . ?"

"Sire . . . my good lord! Oh, my friend, my liege — the Queen . . . she is dead! Dead!" Hay's voice broke completely. He rose, turning away, stumbling, blinded by his tears.

For long moments there was silence. After a stricken pause, Moray and Douglas urged their horses close, to support the King's person. He waved them back.

As from a great distance he spoke, levelly, evenly, his voice steady. "Speak on, Sir Gilbert," he said, staring straight ahead of him.

The Constable made two or three false starts, the King waiting patiently. At length, mumbling disjointedly, he got it out. The Queen had made her pilgrimage to Tain successfully, although it had taxed her strength sorely, the weather so ill, the rivers all in spate. But returning, at Cullen in Banffshire, near Sir Alexander Comyn's house, whilst fording a flooded stream, her horse had slipped and thrown her. She had fallen on rocks, in the water, and grievously injured herself. Within. An issue of blood, which would not staunch. She said that it was from her womb; after the prince's birth it had never fully recovered. They had carried her, wet and cold, to the nearest house. From thence to the Comyn's castle of Cullen. But nothing could aid her. The bleeding from her woman's parts, would not staunch. She died there, calm, composed, kind, a Queen to the end, sending warm messages of love and devotion to her lord, her children, her friends . . .

Gilbert Hay, once started, was jerking and mumbling on. But he had lost his main audience. Robert Bruce had set his horse in motion, and was riding slowly away, head up, straight of back, jaws sternly clenched. Some yards on, without turning, he called back, and strongly.

"See kindly to Sir Gilbert," he said.

Chapter Twenty-Three

The King was stubborn. He would not be carried in a litter. Against all advice, he rode all the way from Cardross to Edinburgh, although by slow stages — and gained some small satisfaction to set against the pain, discomfort and exhaustion when, at Cramond near the city, he caught up with the train of Bishop Lamberton, himself lying in a litter, after crossing the ferry from Fife. Riding alongside his old friend's equipage the few remaining miles, he was perversely pleased to be upright in his saddle and so able to condescend to the other — however shocked he was by the wasted and emaciated state of the Primate.

Nevertheless, Bruce had to take to his bed on arrival at the Abbey of Holyrood, at Edinburgh, since he could by then by no means stand on his feet. This was a humiliation, and perhaps deserved; for not only was all the world coming to Edinburgh these March days of 1328, but the city had organised a great pageant and demonstration for the King and his guests — anxious no doubt to establish its loyalty in the end. Not that Bruce cared overmuch about disappointing the fathers and citizens — for Edinburgh was a place he had never loved, always looking on it as almost an English city, which had taken sides against him more often than for him; but it must emphasise to all that the King was a sick man, when the pageantry had to take place without his presence, with Moray and young Prince David deputising for the monarch — for he flatly refused to view the proceedings from a litter, as the Primate did, rain nonetheless.

His infirmity could not but be obvious to the Englishmen also, of course — although he kept them from his room, and only appeared before them on occasion, and briefly, fully clad and making an almost pugnacious attempt to appear fit and hearty.

To all intents, it was a parliament, on the Scots side, Bruce having summoned everyone of standing in the kingdom, to witness this consummation of a life's work. The terms of the treaty had been thrashed out at York; but despite objections by the English, Bruce had insisted that the actual signing should be done in his realm. There were a few outstanding details to be settled, but it was entirely evident that nothing now would hold up the ratification. It was to be the Treaty of Edinburgh, not of Newcastle or of York, or anywhere else — whatever the English chose to call it thereafter.

King Edward had sent up a resounding team of commissioners, headed by Henry de Burghersh, Bishop of Lincoln, a most able prelate and Lord High Chancellor of England. He was supported by the Bishop of Norwich, Sir Geoffrey le Scrope, the Chief Justice, and de la Zouche, Lord of Ashby, along with Sir Henry Percy again. It was noteworthy that both Percy and Ashby formerly held large lands in Scotland. Some trading was obviously envisaged.

Bruce was glad to leave the wrangling over details to others — although he and Lamberton were kept informed of every point, and maintained their fingers grimly on the pulse of the negotiations. The main difficulty was the matter of the betrothal of Prince David and the Princess Joanna of the Tower — or at least, the date of such marriage contract. The English renunciation, as they called it, of all claims of sovereignty over Scotland, was dependent on this marriage, it seemed. And David Bruce would not reach the age of fourteen, legal age for consent to actual marriage, until 1338, ten years hence. Much might happen in ten years — and the King of France was already suggesting that David Bruce would be better married to a French princess. Mere promises were insufficient for the English, on this score — since they, if any did, knew the worth of mere promises. It was not until Bruce offered the enormous and quite unobtainable sum of £100,000 to be paid by the Scots if by 1338 David was *not* married to Joanna, that this matter was settled. Money always spoke loud, in the South.

A second point of difficulty was the matter of military aid, in alliance. The situation if France attacked England was thrashed out. It was eventually agreed that if their French allies drew Scotland into war, the English would be free to make war in return, without infringing the treaty. The Irish position was equally troublesome. In an effort to get the Scots to agree that they would not aid any Irish rebellion, the English commissioners offered the return to Scotland of the Black Rood of St. Margaret and the Stone of Destiny, stolen by Edward the First from Scone in 1296. This, needless to say, was a grave embarrassment, since the true Stone had never left the Scone area, but had been kept in secret at various places thereabout. Evidently the Hammer of the Scots had kept to himself his undoubted knowledge that his Stone was false, and the English fully accepted it as genuine. Bruce certainly did not want Edward's lump of Scone sandstone back; but nor was this the time to reveal the presence of the authentic original, he decided. He had plans for the Stone of the Scone. So the Scots showed no interest in this offer, and instead obtained a promise that if anyone in Man or the Hebrides made war against the King of Scots, the English should not aid them. This matter had rankled in Bruce's mind ever since Lame John MacDougall of Lorn had been made English Admiral of the West, and had had to be driven out of Man by Angus Og and Moray.

At length, all was settled, and the great ceremony of the signing took place in the refectory of Holyrood Abbey, crowded as it had never been before. For this occasion Bruce was fully dressed in his most splendid cloth-of-gold, under the jewelled Lion Rampant tabard of Scotland — even though he sat on his day-bed, and could raise and rest his swollen legs thereon when necessary. Lamberton was also present, in his litter. And if these two seemed, by their obvious physical disability, to lend an atmosphere of invalidism and infirmity, there at least was nothing of senility or weakness about it, as their eyes, speech and bearing made abundantly clear. For these two, head of State and Church in Scotland, were indeed the most mentally alive and determined men in all that great company. Beside them, Percy was a drooping, hesitant ineffectual, Bishop Burghersh an anxious fat man eager to be elsewhere, and le Scrope a stiff, parchment-faced lawyer, niggling over words.

Before the actual signing, the English Lord Chancellor was to read out the Declaration of King Edward, written at York and to be incorporated in the treaty as preamble. As he was about to begin, Bruce intervened.

"My lord Bishop and Chancellor," he said, "it seems to me meet and suitable that your liege lord's pronouncement should be read by Sir Henry, my lord of Northumberland. His father was, to our cost, Lieutenant and Governor in Scotland, once! All knew him well, had to heed his voice! Let us be privileged to hear his son's, on this occasion, if you please."

And so it was that the son of the man who had hectored, lectured, reproved, deceived and harried the Bruce on so many occasions through the years, had to read aloud the words which were the justification and coping-stone of the hero-king's thirty years of striving and suffering, indeed of his entire career. That he did so in an undignified and scarcely intelligible gabble, was neither here nor there.

"Whereas we, and some of our predecessors, Kings of England, have attempted to gain rights of rule, lordship or superiority over the Kingdom of Scotland, and terrible hardships have long afflicted the realms of England and Scotland through the wars fought on this account; and bearing in mind the bloodshed, slaughter, atrocities, destruction of churches, and innumerable evils from which the inhabitants of both realms have suffered over and over again because of these wars; and having regard also to the good things in which both realms might abound to their mutual advantage if joined in stability of perpetual peace, and thus more effectually made secure, within and beyond their borders, against the harmful attempts of violent men to rebel or make way; we will and concede for us and all our heirs and successors, by the common counsel, assent and consent of the prelates, magnates, earls and barons and communities of our realm in our parliament that the Kingdom of Scotland, shall remain for ever separate in all respects from the Kingdom of England, in its entirety, free and in peace, without any kind of subjection, servitude, claim or demand, with its rightful boundaries as they were held and preserved in the times of Alexander of good memory King of Scotland last deceased, to the magnificent prince, the Lord Robert, by God's grace illustrious King of Scots, our ally and very dear friend, and to his heirs and successors.

EDWARD REX"

There was no cheering, no exclamation, no spoken comment at all, in that great chamber, as those words tailed away into a long and pregnant silence. All men considered them, on both sides, and the price paid for their pronouncement, and held their peace.

Robert Bruce took up the quill in a hand that trembled very slightly.

* * *

On an impulse, Edinburgh emptying of the distinguished company, the King did not return direct on the uncomfortable horseback journey all the way to Cardross, but instead accompanied William Lamberton by sea from Leith to St. Andrews — this on the Primate's quite casual mention that he would not survive the transport by road in a horse-litter; and when the King remonstrated that this was no way to talk, the Bishop as factually announced that he would be dead within the month anyway. In the circumstances, the King remained with his friend.

Lamberton was too exhausted during the journey to talk at any length. But, in his own room of St. Andrew's Castle the day following, he was strong enough to speak with Bruce — and eager to do so. They had much to discuss. The Primate was particularly concerned about the future governance of the Church in Scotland, a matter that was now urgent. He advised that, much as he valued most of them, none of the present Bishops should be elevated to the Primacy. Not even the good Bernard, Abbot of Arbroath — who might well be given the bishopric of Man and the Sudreys, just become vacant. But the national leadership of the Church demanded a strong, sure and experienced hand. His own was about to be removed, and he urged the appointment of his Archdeacon of St. Andrews, the vigorous James Bene, who had so distinguished himself as diplomat and negotiator in Moray's French and papal embassages, and who had in fact been administering the metropolitan see for long. The canons of St. Andrews had faith in him, and would elect him. With the King's support he would serve Church and realm well . . .

"Yes, yes, my friend," Bruce agreed, concerned that the other should not tire himself thus. "He it shall be, never fear. But there is no such haste. Leave it now . . ."

"There is so much to say, Sire. Haste indeed. For my time is short."

"You mean . . . ? You in truth meant what you said at Edinburgh, William? That you do not expect to live out the month?"

"To be sure," the other said, his voice weak, but only his voice. "My fear has been that I should not last thus long, to speak with you."

"That is grievous hearing, my old friend."

"Why grievous, Robert? *I* grieve not, I promise you. I am more than ready to go. I am much blest. My work is done — all I have lived for. To few is so much granted. Scotland free. Your royal state recognised by all Christendom. Your succession assured. The Church here sound, in fair order, sure of its place, united. And this great cathedral completed." Gaspingly he enunciated these satisfactions.

Bruce nodded, understandingly.

"Life should mean achievement, in great things and small," the other went on, picking his slow words. "Without achievement, life is merest existence, of neither virtue nor relish. *You* know it well, Robert. I shall achieve nothing more here. Beyond — I believe that I shall. If the good God will find work for me in His greater purpose. I pray that He will. I long to be at it — not a bed-bound hulk here. Do you understand?"

The King nodded again. "That I do, my friend. Indeed, you

could be speaking from my own heart, from my own mind, For . . . such is my wish also."

For long these two colleagues and comrades considered each other.

"I thought that it might be so," Lamberton acknowledged quietly. "I am the happier in going. Happy for you, that such is your spirit. For here is joy, Robert. Although you have longer to wait for it than I."

"Not so much longer, I think."

"No? Have you more reason to say that, Robert? You believe your days here short? This is not the matter of the leprosy again?"

"No. It is strange. The leprosy — all these years I have lived with it. And kept it close. That none should know. At your behest. And Elizabeth's. I believed that it would kill me. But, no. It was not to be. That was the finger of God, only — not the sword of God! Now I have the dropsy. Have had it near two years. It strikes surer, deeper. At my heart. I have had many warnings. One day, soon I think, I shall receive my last. Perhaps before you do, old friend. But — I pray not before I am ready — or have *made* ready. *My* work is not fully done, I fear — but most of it is. Like you, I have no desire to linger, as less than myself. And like you, I hope to do better, hence."

They considered the future, in silence.

"You do not fear death, William," the King went on presently, not a question but a statement. "That I see — and rejoice in it."

"No, I do not fear it. Nor should any true man. Only those who have striven for nothing, buried their Lord's talent. The dying itself may be unpleasant — but let us hope, short. Being dead — that foolish word we use — that must be otherwise. An excellence. Fulfilment."

"You rate it so high as that? Excellence?"

"I do. For it is part of God's ordained progress and purpose with men. God's, not men's. And all such is excellent." The other raised an open hand, frail but eloquent. "What has God been doing with us this while, Robert, think you? In all our joys and sorrows, our achievements and defeats? What, but building — making *us* build. As I built that cathedral. Stone by stone, building our character. Heart, mind, will, understanding — aye, and compassion, above all. These things we have been attaining unto. Their fullest flowering in us. The body is as nothing, compared with these. All our years, these have been building up, for better or for worse. Now, they are at their height. Think you the All Highest ordained it thus for nothing? The patient moulding, ours and His, the secret strivings of the heart, this edifice that is our life's essence. Just to cast it away, discarded, unused, spurned, like a child's bauble? In all His creation, this is the height of His achievement — not the tides of the oceans, the lands, the sun, moon and stars. Man, at the summit of his earthly character — which is when he dies. Here is God's achievement — and man's, in His image. Purpose and order are in all His works — that is plain to all. Should, then, the greatest work of all be purposeless?"

This urgent profession, declaration, whispered but intense, had taken much out of the Primate, so that he lay back, panting, eyes closed.

Much moved, Bruce waited.

"This is fulfilment, therefore," Lamberton resumed, after a long interval. "God has given us reason. To use. If we cannot see this, we are fools. Failures. We move on, to *use* what has here been built up — of this I have no doubt. And, Robert — I would be about it! About it, man!"

The King gripped the other's thin hand. "Then, I rejoice," he said, deep-voiced. "With you. No mourning, William. I have never heard greater sense spoken. For you, then, all is well. You go on, joyfully. Prepared. But — *you* have not murder on your conscience, my friend! What of me? I murdered Comyn, at God's own altar. What of me?" There was intensity there also.

"What of you, then, Robert? Are you different from other men — save in that you have had greater testing? That was sin, yes — although the man deserved to die if ever man did. But it is repented sin. And paid for a thousand times in the years since. I say, without that sin, and the need to expiate it, who knows — would Robert Bruce ever have achieved what he has done? For a whole nation? Would this character you have built up be so sure, so sharp and tempered a sword for God's use in His purpose hereafter? I think not."

"I would that *I* could be so sure of God's forgiveness!"

"Then use your wits, Robert! Use them. God is purpose, order, power. But, forget it not — love, also. Else where comes love? Love, the force which drives all else. Love is compassion, understanding. If *you* can forgive — and you have forgiven many, too many for your nobles — then do you deny it to God? Dare you?"

"No-o-o . . ."

This time the Bishop's eyes remained shut for long; and thinking he slept, Bruce lay back, thinking, thinking.

But then the weak-strong voice spoke on, as though there had been no pause. "If life has taught me anything, Robert, it is that love is of all things great, powerful, eternal, the very sword of God. Not weak, soft, pap — as some would have it! Love is God, therefore it is eternal. Cannot die — God's, or yours, or mine. Here is the greatest comfort in all creation. Love cannot die with the body. It must go on, since it is eternal. See you what this means, my friend?"

"I think I do, yes. Elizabeth . . . !"

"Aye, your Elizabeth. She is loving you still. As you love her. Scorning, straddling this hurdle we call the grave! And not only she. Your Marjory. Your brothers. All those who have loved you, to the death. Whom you mourned for, unneeding. And I, who have loved you also — I take it with me. But its chain will link us still. And God's love, of which it is a part, will see that it grows and burgeons. In the fuller life to which we are headed. This . . . this is what I had to say to you, Robert Bruce. Thank God . . . He has left me time . . . to say it."

Those last words were barely distinguishable, spoken beneath the shallow breath, yet with a certainty to them that spoke of strength not weakness — William Lamberton's last service to his two masters.

Bruce remained beside the bed for some time thereafter, but there was no more talk. Once the dying man moved his lips, but no words came; a faint smile, that was all. They were content. When, presently, the other closed his eyes, the King pressed his hand for the last time, and walked slowly from that room, leaving his friend to the hush of the waves far below, and the seabirds' crying.

Chapter Twenty-Four

"Gibbie," the King said, a little thickly, "it is time. There is not long now. Bring me these three. And thus. Thomas Randolph. Angus of the Isles. And James Douglas. These three only do I wish to see, now. And, man — of a mercy, lighten your face! Have you vowed never to smile again? Here is nothing so ill. Another pilgrimage, and a lighter one — that is all. Less wearisome than that we have just completed. William Lamberton taught me how to die, a year ago. Now, get me my nephew Thomas — and not on tiptoe, 'fore God!"

Bruce's voice was surprisingly strong, however thick, and as vehement as ever — when he could speak — even though scarcely any of the rest of him could move. When, at times, overwhelming pain at his heart blacked out all things for him, he knew fear — not fear of the next step, but that it should come upon him before his tongue could enunciate what still had to be said. This had been Lamberton's fear, and then final relief — time to give his message to his friend.

So, while Hay fetched Moray, Bruce lay in the great room of Cardross, bathed in the bright June sunshine, and prayed that the roaring blackness would hold off sufficiently long, and that nothing should tie and hamper his tongue. He was the King. Pray God he could remain the King to the end — until he became just another new pilgrim . . .

Moray came quickly, with the Constable — for none of them was far away. All knew the end was near; indeed most of his friends had not expected their liege lord to survive the long pilgrimage to St. Ninian's shrine at Whithorn, at the tip of Galloway, and back, the astonishing epic itinerary of a dying man, out of which none had been able to dissuade him, litter-borne indeed as it had had to be.

"It is Thomas, Sir," his nephew said.

"I am not blind, man!" his uncle asserted. "Not yet. Come close. Do not go, Gibbie — you shall listen to this also. As witness. Thomas — hear me. You have good shoulders. You will require them. On them I now place my burden. Of rule and governance in this land. I leave a bairn as king — a child of five. An ill thing. For a dozen years, God willing, the rule of Scotland must be yours, in his name. You are regent, with James Douglas as co-regent. But yourself chiefest. Jamie is the greatest fighter — but yours is the wisest head. I have instructed Bernard de Linton, and signed all that is necessary. You understand? From this day, Thomas, this hour, you take up my burden."

"This day, Sire . . . ?"

"This day. The gate stands wide for me. I will not hold back now, I think. Not of *my* will. But, be that as it may, from now, Scotland is in your strong hands. I thank God for them. You know my mind, what I would have for my son and his realm. See you to it."

"That I will. You may rely on me. And . . . I thank your Grace. For all things. But, above all, for your faith in me. I, who betrayed you once . . ."

"You never betrayed me, Thomas. Only set too high a standard, to which I could not aspire — and feared to betray yourself. Since you learned that kings, and yourself, are but men, and men are finite, you have served me better than any. Now the decisions are no longer mine, but yours."

"It will be my endeavour to make them as you would, Sire . . ."

"No! Not that. You have a better head than I, in some matters. And a stout heart. Make your own decisions now. And for my son. They will often enough be hard decisions, and men will not love you for them. You will have a King's work to do, yet not be a King. I do not envy you your task, Thomas."

"I take it up willingly, proudly, Sire."

"Aye. Only, remember this, Thomas. All men have not your stature, your integrity of spirit. Be merciful. Particularly towards a fatherless and motherless laddie, who sits in a lonely throne — God knows how lonely! That alone I counsel you — be less unbending. Much proud uprightness, such as yours, must be swallowed for a realm's unity. I learned it, and so must you. That — and trust not the English. In matters of statecraft. However fair-seeming. Now — let us say God-speed. For my time runs out . . ."

Moray knelt by the great bed, to take and kiss his uncle's swollen, stiff hand. "Your servant, now and for ever," he said simply, and stood.

"Aye, lad. See, Gibbie — here is a man who knows how death is to be treated! No moping and long faces. No tiptoes! Now — Angus. Farewell, Thomas . . ."

The Lord of the Isles came in, greying but still the stocky, assured figure on which Bruce had always relied so heavily. He eyed his friend with his accustomed calm and practical gaze, his reserve innate even yet.

"I said that foolish pilgrimage would kill you," he observed dispassionately.

"It was meant to, man! Think you I, Robert Bruce, would rust away, like an old sword in a sheath? Besides, I had to see Carrick and Annandale and Galloway again. Before I moved on. But — here, Angus. And listen well." The King's voice was urgent, now, as in haste.

"I listen . . . Sire," the other said, coming close.

"Ha! You say it! You have never said that word until now, man! Long years I have waited for it — from the Prince of the Isles!"

Angus smiled grimly. "I can afford it — now! Can I not, Your Grace?"

"Aye — Angus Og, as ever! You do not change. But thank you, nevertheless, my friend. Now, heed. Moray I leave as regent. With Douglas. This you knew of. You do not love him, I know. But, for my sake, give him your sure support. For my son's sake. This I charge you, if our friendship means aught. He will need all your strength. The English will not be long in showing their teeth, treaty or none. When I am gone, they will be at Scotland's throat once more. Edward and his regency are cherishing this Edward Baliol, at their Court. Not for nothing, you may be sure. A child of five years, on my throne, and they will not delay in recollecting past wrongs and humiliations. Moray is going to require your strong right arm — and your galleys, Angus!"

"I shall not fail your son," the other assured quietly.

"That is what I desired to hear, my friend. I thank you. But — there is something else. The Stone. The true Stone of Destiny, at Scone. Baliol knows of it, if the English do not — that their stone is false. His father was crowned on the true Stone. I prophesy that it will be Edward Baliol's ambition and desire to be likewise! And the English are grooming him for some great role, nothing more sure. Pray God Moray can keep him, and them, at bay. But, if he comes, I want that Stone hence. That he, and the like, may never sit thereon. Take it, Angus — take it. After my son's coronation. Take it to your Isles, where none shall be able to follow it. And keep it safe, on some fair island. Until one of my line, or whoever is true King of Scots, requires it again for coronation. Will you do this for me, old friend?"

"It is as good as done."

"Praise be! Then — farewell, Islesman! Your isles were my sanctuary once, your stout arm my strength, your Celtic folk my saving. You have my thanks. And, Angus — when you sail next by Loch Moidart, carry my last salutation to Christina MacRuarie. I owe her much — not the least of my debt to the Isles. Now, go, my friend — and send me Jamie."

For the first and last time in his life, Angus, Lord of the Isles, knelt and kissed another man's hand.

"Quickly, Jamie — quickly!" the King muttered, to himself.

That darkly graceful man, still youthful-seeming, did not keep him waiting. He came in almost at a run, went straight to the bedside, and dropped on his knees, reaching for the King's hand. Obviously he had been waiting at the door, in a fever, for this moment.

"My dear liege! My beloved lord!" he cried. "Tell me that it is not true! That this is . . . this is . . ." His voice broke.

"Jamie, Jamie — this is not you! The Black Douglas! He they frighten bairns with!" Bruce said, seeking a smile. "Have I not taught you better than this — you, my especial pupil! This is not the end."

"You mean . . .?"

"I mean that I but take a new road. The road your Queen took. And my brothers, my daughter, Lamberton, my friends. *Your* friends. So many of them. Do you grudge me this? Now that this gross body has failed me?"

The other shook his head, wordless.

"Come. You are as bad as Gibbie Hay, Jamie! Thomas and Angus Og knew better, I vow! What mumble you there?"

"I but pray, Sire, that I may follow you . . . along that road. And soon! As I have always done . . ."

"That you will do, most assuredly!" Bruce agreed. "How soon — who knows? That is in God's hands. But, the same God willing, I will be looking back for you. I . . . I . . ." The thick voice choked to silence.

"Sire! Sire!" Douglas started up, eyes wide. Gilbert Hay moved in, at the other side.

As from far, far away, in a few moments, the King's voice returned.

"Are you there, Jamie? You are . . . still with me? Give me your hand. It is not, not this time, I think. Not yet."

"Dear God — are you in pain, Sire? Great pain . . .?"

"No. Little pain. It is the darkness. The waters. A great darkness of waters. Roaring loud. Little pain."

Distracted, helpless, his two friends watched him.

"Ha — I see you again, now. Both of you. The tide ebbs a little. Look not so affrighted, Jamie. And you, Gibbie. Who ever was afraid of dark water, save bairns? We, who have faced together the worst that men can do to men, a thousand times? Here is naught for hurt. Only — time. Time is short. Hear then, Jamie. I have a vow unfulfilled. You know of it. I made promise once, in a Galloway cave. That, given my kingdom, given peace, my cause won, I would draw my sword again. And go against the Infidel. Who defies God's holy places. A Crusade. I swore it there . . ."

"But how could you do it, Sire? How fulfil it? You have had to fight and battle, always. Until this last year . . ."

"Wheesht, man — wheesht! Let *me* talk — for I have not long. *You* have time enough! You, Jamie, must be my lieutenant in this, as so often. Warden of my March. *You* shall ride for me against the Saracen. Fulfil my vow. This I charge you. When I go hence, so soon as I am on my way, take this useless body. Cut out my heart, from within it. Part of it was ever yours. Cut it out, and place it in a casket. And take it with you. Against the Infidel. Wherever he may best be struck. We shall go crusading together . . . after all. You understand?"

Douglas's lips moved, but no words came.

"It is my ... my royal command, Jamie — my last, here. My body you shall place beside Elizabeth. Under the fair tomb I had made for her in Paris. In Dunfermline Abbey. Side by side lay us, in that place. But ... my heart goes on to war! In God's cause, this time. And in your company. Close company, Jamie. You have it?"

The other could only nod.

"It is well, then. God be thanked — all now is done. I want for nothing. The tide may come again, when it will. I am ready. Bide with me, Jamie. Gibbie — fetch the children. My son, my daughters, young Robert. For but a moment — then away with them. Here is no place for bairns. I would but bid them ... good day. Jamie and you ... will bide ... thereafter. To see me on my way my good way ..."

Postscript

Sir James Douglas raised steel-gauntleted hand to shade his narrowed eyes against the glaring Mediterranean sun, under the upraised visor of his great war-helm.

"I fear that I have led you but ill, my friends," he said. "These Moors have outwitted us. They think, and fight, differently from the English, I perceive! Too late I perceive it. It seems that I have led you into a trap. Were the wits here which belonged with this royal heart, it would have been different. Forgive me."

His companions, at the head of the small Scots host, protested as with one voice.

"Who could tell that they had these numbers hidden in this hellish valley?" Sir Alexander Fraser, the Chamberlain said.

"The Castilians are at fault, not you," Hugh Ross averred — Earl of Ross these last two years, since his father's death. "They declared these valleys clear."

"Your strategy is still right, my lord," young Sir Andrew Moray of Bothwell, the third of Bruce's sisters' husbands, declared stoutly. "Were there fewer, as we believed, we still needs must cut our way through them."

"Aye — there you have it, friends. We cannot turn back, with these on our flanks, and the great canyon to cross. This cliff-girt valley will not let us climb out. We can only go forward, southwards — and cut our way through. Despite odds. King Alfonso will not come to our aid — that is sure!" Douglas shrugged, under his armour. "Arrowhead formation, then, my lords — the formation *he* loved well! Bruce's wedge! We will drive his wedge through them, and teach the Saracen how the Bruce fought! Pass the word — Bruce's wedge!"

He raised his hand again, and drew over head and helm the silver chain and casket that hung before him and never left his person, day or night.

The trumpets shrilled their commands, and the 500 mounted Scots of the Northern Division of the army of Alfonso the Eleventh of Castile and Leon, hemmed in in the bare, baking, hostile Spanish valley of Tebas de Ardales, reined and sidled and prepared to marshal themselves into the driving spearhead formation which their late monarch had perfected, and which, given sufficient impetus, was the hardest man-made force on earth to halt. Far ahead, half a mile at least, the vast host of the main Moorish cavalry completely blocked the widening mouth of the dry valley, southwards towards the open plain; while to east and west the rocky heights of the sierra were lined by the serried ranks of the Infidel foot, stretched as far as eye could see on either side.

Douglas, at the apex of the wedge, rose in his stirrups. "God, Saint Andrew and Saint Bride be with us, now, my friends." He raised the chained casket high. "And the Bruce!" With a snap he shut his helm's visor. "Come!"

Out of seeming chaos the great arrow-head developed and took shape. Heedfully Douglas gave it time, restraining his own and the other leaders' impatience to attain swiftly the necessary momentum. Fortunately they had that half-mile — and as fortunately, the Moors did not ride to meet them, content to wait in solid phalanx for the impact of this suicidal charge of 500 against 5,000.

Half-way, peering behind him in the saddle, and cursing the helmet which so restricted his view, Douglas was approximately satisfied. He dug in his spurs, and gestured to his personal trumpeter. Jerkily but unmistakable, the Full Charge call rang out.

They had just the time and space to achieve the outright gallop. Thundering on the dry, sun-baked ground, they bore down on the waiting palisade of mounted spearmen and curved-sword warriors, some of the fiercest cavalry in the world, and crashed headlong into them like a battering-ram. But crashed at only one point in the long front, a point where only two or three dark fighters would not have been human had they not wilted somewhat, reined aside, drawn back.

With a resounding crash, the screaming of men and horses, and a lance-tip glancing harmlessly off shield and armoured shoulder, Douglas was through the first and second lines, thrust and driven on by the hurtling weight behind. Ignoring the waving swords of the enemy, attempting no swordery of his own, he swung the chained heart round and round in windmill fashion, right and left, and beat and beat with his other clenched fist at his mount's flank, through the splendid heraldic trappings, to keep up the impetus. Impetus, momentum, thrust — that was all, that was everything.

"A Bruce! A Bruce!" he shouted, as he rode, and all behind him cried the same.

Their tight-packed formation in the bottleneck of the valley was both the Mohammedans' weakness and strength. They presented an almost solid barrier to the Scots drive, however much individuals in the way sought to draw clear — but could not. On the other hand, they were so close ranked, drawn up to oppose the conventional cavalry attack on a wide front, line behind line, that they had no room for manoeuvre, to bring their weapons to bear; and, of course, because of the narrow-fronted penetration by the wedge, not one in a score of the enemy could be in contact with their swift-moving assailants.

So long as it remained swift-moving. There was the difficulty, the danger. Strive as Douglas and the Scots leaders would, their speed fell, the press too thick. And as their pace slackened, so increased their vulnerability. Sundry blows of lance and scimitar set Douglas reeling in his saddle — yet he scarcely noticed them. All his attention was concentrated on the way ahead, forcing the wedge through.

And there *was* a way ahead, space, a thinning of the tight-packed host. That was ever more apparent. If they could win through to it . . .

Their fine gallop reduced now to a mere lumbering, stumbling trot, Douglas broke through into the open, Fraser and Ross close at his flanks, still the head of the arrow, however misshapen it was behind. But now the impetus was gone. And immediately in front, not seventy yards off, was not another rearguard line but a single large group of white-robed Saracen notables, emirs, imams, the enemy high command, under a great Crescent banner. Beyond was practically empty plain.

The dark chiefs did not hesitate. With a mighty shout they spurred forward to the assault.

Douglas knew a strange, fierce exultation. This, then, was the end. The way was open for escape — but not for Douglas. With the enemy leaders before him, not for Douglas to waver or dodge or bolt. He stood in his stirrups, dizzy from the blows he had received, and drew his great sword at last. But with his left hand. His right still swung the chained heart. Higher he raised it, and plunged forward, at a canter now, to meet the foe.

"Lead on, brave heart!" he cried. "As ever — was your wont. Douglas follows! Or else dies! A Douglas! A Douglas!" And with all his strength, he hurled the glistening silver casket and its chain before him into the midst of the Saracens, just before they closed on him.

He went down, horse beneath him, under a hail of lance and sword thrusts. The arrow-head was disintegrated. But the mass of the Scots were through. In their hundreds they swept out of the great mêlée, and down upon the Moslem leadership. In the chaos of those final moments, with their own people milling and streaming past, Ross, Fraser and Sir William Keith of Galston reined round and back, smiting, to where Douglas lay. Keith, an enormous man, leapt down, while his companions, now joined by others, circled and caracoled and slashed protectively. Keith grasped the slighter and limp body in the black armour, and with a mighty effort hoisted it right on to the front of his own saddle. Beneath the body lay the gleaming casket-heart. Grabbing this also, he clambered up behind the Douglas.

"A Bruce! A Bruce!" they all cried, as they spurred after the others, out into the open plain.

The good Sir James left his last battlefield, following in his liege lord's road.

NIGEL TRANTER

THE YOUNG MONTROSE

James Graham – the brilliant young Marquis of Montrose.

One man alone could not change the course of history. But James Graham was determined to try. A gallant soldier, talented leader and compelling personality, his fame has echoed down the centuries. For the young Marquis of Montrose was to give his utmost in the service of his beloved monarch.

The first of two magnificent novels about THE MARQUIS OF MONTROSE.

HODDER & STOUGHTON PAPERBACKS

NIGEL TRANTER

MONTROSE: THE CAPTAIN GENERAL

The Marquis of Montrose – mainstay of the Stewart cause.

Montrose was the most loyal servant any king had ever had. In the darkest days of the Civil War he risked all in the fight to save his king.

His only reward was royal betrayal. Unwavering on his loyalty, he returned from dreary exile to fight for another king, only to experience the final betrayal of the hangman's noose.

HODDER AND STOUGHTON PAPERBACKS

NIGEL TRANTER

TRUE THOMAS

Thomas Learmonth of Ercildoune, Thomas the Rhymer as he came to be called, was one of the strangest figures in Scottish history. A poet and a visionary, his extraordinary gift of prophecy has echoed through the centuries. This is his story – set against the canvas of the wild and rugged times of Alexander III, when the sword ruled over all and the treachery of the powerful earls had never been greater.

The story of True Thomas is a vivid tale of adventure, brutality and romance, in which for the very first time this treasured character of Scottish history springs from legend into life.

HODDER AND STOUGHTON PAPERBACKS

NIGEL TRANTER

MARGARET THE QUEEN

Against a vivid backcloth of violence, treachery, invasion and conflicting faiths, here is the story of the mild and saintly Margaret of Scotland.

Read how a young refugee Saxon princess, twenty-four years old when she arrived north of the Border, rose to the throne of Scotland and tamed her wild and warlike people. How singlehanded she changed that nation's destiny, and won their lasting love.

NIGEL TRANTER

ROUGH WOOING

The young James, King of Scots is a beleaguered man.

Still grief-stricken at the untimely death of his queen, Madeleine, he is without an heir. Both he and his throne are vulnerable. All round him he sees conspiracies. Some may lie in his imagination but all too many are real, for there are many who would supplant him or control him.

Even his own mother, Margaret Tudor, plots against him. But then she is the sister of the English King Henry VIII who sprawls like a bloated spider south of the border, his greedy eyes ever on the realm of Scotland, hungry to bring it within his grasp.

The young king's advisors, the two Davids, Beaton and Lindsay, have preserved him so far but the threats to James and his country seem to grow by the year . . .

HODDER AND STOUGHTON PAPERBACKS

NIGEL TRANTER

LORD IN WAITING

In 1460, when clan feuds were rife, and the threat of English invasion was ever-present, James the Third, one of Scotland's weakest monarchs, came to the throne.

Before long, John, Lord of Douglas, a born leader and a man of conscience and vision, found himself wishing that James' wise and strong-minded sister Princess Mary had succeeded in her brother's place.

A fact compounded by the feeble king's habit of ignoring high-born nobles, and succumbing instead to the influence of the astrologer and alchemist William Sheves, Archdeacon of St Andrews, who was one of the cleverest and most unscrupulous individuals in Scotland's history.

HODDER & STOUGHTON PAPERBACKS